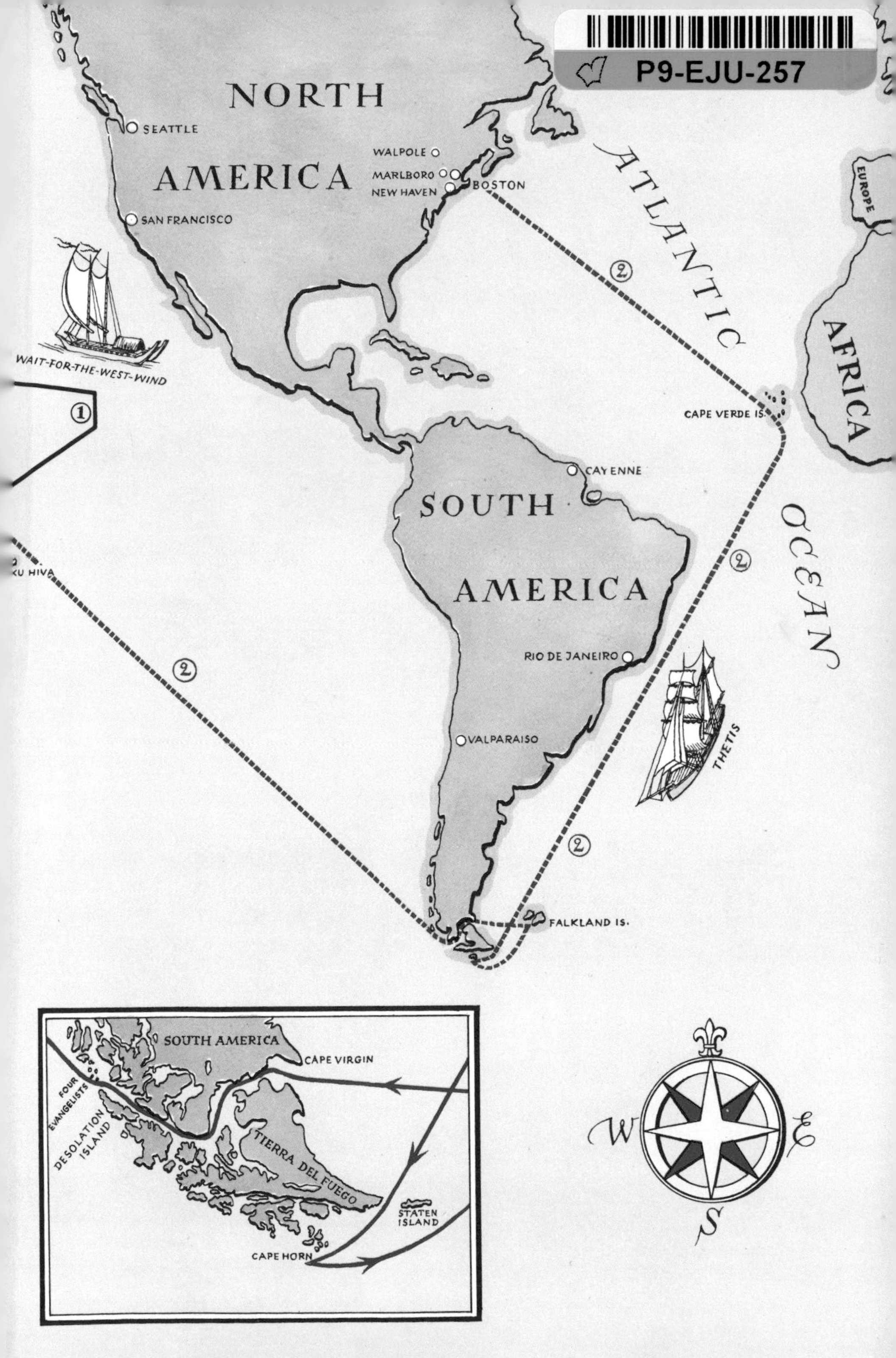
NORTH AMERICA
SEATTLE
SAN FRANCISCO
WALPOLE
MARLBORO
NEW HAVEN
BOSTON
ATLANTIC OCEAN
EUROPE
AFRICA
WAIT-FOR-THE-WEST-WIND
①
②
CAPE VERDE IS.
CAYENNE
SOUTH AMERICA
KU HIVA
RIO DE JANEIRO
VALPARAISO
THETIS
FALKLAND IS.
SOUTH AMERICA
CAPE VIRGIN
FOUR EVANGELISTS
DESOLATION ISLAND
TIERRA DEL FUEGO
STATEN ISLAND
CAPE HORN
W
E
S

Hawaii

BY JAMES A. MICHENER

Tales of the South Pacific
The Fires of Spring
Return to Paradise
The Voice of Asia
The Bridges at Toko-ri
Sayonara
The Floating World
The Bridge at Andau

WITH A. GROVE DAY
Rascals in Paradise

Hawaii

James A. Michener

RANDOM HOUSE · NEW YORK

Published in New York by Random House, Inc., and simultaneously in Toronto, Canada, by Random House of Canada, Limited.
Library of Congress Catalog Card Number: 59–10815
Manufactured in the United States of America

To

All the peoples who came to Hawaii

This is a novel. It is true to the spirit and history of Hawaii, but the characters, the families, the institutions and most of the events are imaginary—except that the English schoolteacher Uliassutai Karakoram Blake is founded upon a historical person who accomplished much in Hawaii.

Contents

I

From the Boundless Deep

MILLIONS UPON MILLIONS of years ago, when the continents were already formed and the principal features of the earth had been decided, there existed, then as now, one aspect of the world that dwarfed all others. It was a mighty ocean, resting uneasily to the east of the largest continent, a restless ever-changing, gigantic body of water that would later be described as pacific.

Over its brooding surface immense winds swept back and forth, whipping the waters into towering waves that crashed down upon the world's seacoasts, tearing away rocks and eroding the land. In its dark bosom, strange life was beginning to form, minute at first, then gradually of a structure now lost even to memory. Upon its farthest reaches birds with enormous wings came to rest, and then flew on.

Agitated by a moon stronger then than now, immense tides ripped across this tremendous ocean, keeping it in a state of torment. Since no great amounts of sand had yet been built, the waters where they reached shore were universally dark, black as night and fearful.

Scores of millions of years before man had risen from the shores of the ocean to perceive its grandeur and to venture forth upon its turbulent waves, this eternal sea existed, larger than any other of the earth's features, vaster than the sister oceans combined, wild, terrifying in its immensity and imperative in its universal role.

How utterly vast it was! How its surges modified the very balance of the earth! How completely lonely it was, hidden in the darkness of night or burning in the dazzling power of a younger sun than ours.

At recurring intervals the ocean grew cold. Ice piled up along its extremities, and so pulled vast amounts of water from the sea, so that the wandering shoreline of the continents sometimes jutted miles farther out than before. Then, for a hundred thousand years, the ceaseless ocean would tear at the exposed shelf of the continents, grinding rocks into sand and incubating new life.

Later, the fantastic accumulations of ice would melt, setting cold waters free to join the heaving ocean, and the coasts of the continents would lie submerged. Now the restless energy of the sea deposited upon the ocean bed layers of silt and skeletons and salt. For a million years the ocean would build soil, and then the ice would return; the waters would draw away; and the land would lie exposed. Winds from the north and south would howl across the empty seas and lash stupendous waves upon the shattering shore. Thus the ocean continued its alternate building and tearing down.

Master of life, guardian of the shorelines, regulator of temperatures and heaving sculptor of mountains, the great ocean existed.

Millions upon millions of years before man had risen upon earth, the central areas of this tremendous ocean were empty, and where famous islands now exist nothing rose above the rolling waves. Of course, crude forms of life sometimes moved through the deep, but for the most part the central ocean was marked only by enormous waves that arose at the command of moon and wind. Dark, dark, they swept the surface of the empty sea, falling only upon themselves terrible and puissant and lonely.

Then one day, at the bottom of the deep ocean, along a line running two thousand miles from northwest to southeast, a rupture appeared in the basalt rock that formed the ocean's bed. Some great fracture of the earth's basic structure had occurred, and from it began to ooze a white-hot, liquid rock. As it escaped from its internal prison, it came into contact with the ocean's wet and heavy body. Instantly, the rock exploded, sending aloft through the 19,000 feet of ocean that pressed down upon it columns of released steam.

Upward, upward, for nearly four miles they climbed, those agitated bubbles of air, until at last upon the surface of the sea they broke loose and formed a cloud. In that instant, the ocean signaled that a new island was building. In time it might grow to become an infinitesimal speck of land that would mark the great central void. No human beings then existed to celebrate the event. Perhaps some weird and vanished flying thing spied the escaping steam and swooped down to inspect it; more likely the roots of this future island were born in darkness and great waves and brooding nothingness.

For nearly forty million years, an extent of time so vast that it is meaningless, only the ocean knew that an island was building in its bosom, for no land had yet appeared above the surface of the sea. For nearly forty million years, from that extensive rupture in the ocean floor, small amounts of liquid rock seeped out, each forcing its way up through what had escaped before, each contributing some small portion to the accumulation that was building on the floor of the sea. Sometimes a thousand years, or ten thousand, would silently pass before any new eruption of material would take place. At other times gigantic pressures would accumulate beneath the rupture and with unimaginable violence rush through the existing apertures, throwing clouds of steam miles above the surface of the ocean. Waves would be generated which would circle the globe and crash upon themselves as they collided twelve thousand miles away. Such an explosion, indescribable in its fury, might in the end raise the height of the subocean island a foot.

But for the most part, the slow constant seepage of molten rock was not violently dramatic. Layer upon layer of the earth's vital core would creep out, hiss horribly at the cold sea water, and then slide down the sides of the little mountains that were forming. Building was most sure when the liquid rock did not explode into minute ashy fragments, but cascaded viscously down the sides of the mountains, for this bound together what had gone before, and established a base for what was to come.

How long ago this building took place, how infinitely long ago! For nearly forty million years the first island struggled in the bosom of the sea, endeavoring to be born as observable land. For nearly forty million submerged years its subterranean volcano hissed and coughed and belched and spewed forth rock, but it remained nevertheless hidden beneath the dark waters of the restless sea, to whom it was an insignificant irritation, a small climbing pretentious thing of no consequence.

And then one day, at the northwest end of the subocean rupture, an eruption of liquid rock occurred that was different from any others that had preceded. It threw forth the same kind of rock, with the same violence, and through the same vents in the earth's core. But this time what was thrown forth reached the surface of the sea. There was a tremendous explosion as the liquid rock struck water and air together. Clouds of steam rose miles into the air. Ash fell hissing upon the heaving waves. Detonations shattered the air for a moment and then echoed away in the immensity of the empty wastes.

But rock had at last been deposited above the surface of the sea. An island—visible were there but eyes to see, tangible were there fingers to feel—had risen from the deep.

The human mind, looking back upon this event—particularly if the owner of the mind has once stepped upon that island—is likely to accord it more significance than it merits. Land was finally born, yes. The forty million years of effort were finally crowned by the emergence of a pile of rocks no larger than a man's body, that is true. But the event was actually of no lasting significance, for in the long history of the ocean many such piles had momentarily broken the surface and then subsided, forbidden and forgotten. The only thing significant about the initial appearance of this first island along the slanting crack was the fact that it held on and grew. Stubbornly, inch by painful inch, it grew. In fact, it was the uncertainty and agony of its growth that were significant.

The chance emergence of the island was nothing. Remember this. Its emergence was nothing. But its persistence and patient accumulation of stature were everything. Only by relentless effort did it establish its right to exist. For the first ten thousand years after its tentative emergence, the little pile of rock in the dead, vast center of the sea fluctuated between life and death like a thing struck by evil. Sometimes molten lava would rise through the internal channels and erupt from a vent only a few inches above the waves. Tons upon tons of material would gush forth and hiss madly as it fell back into the ocean. Some, fortunately, would cling to the newborn island, building it sturdily many feet into the air, and in that time it might seem as if the island were indeed secure.

Then from the south, where storms breed in the senseless deep, a mighty wave would form and rush across the world. Its coming would be visible from afar, and in gigantic, tumbling, whistling, screaming power it would fall upon the little accumulation of rocks and pass madly on.

For the next ten thousand years there would be no visible island, yet under the waves, always ready to spring back to life, there would rest this huge mountain tip, rising 19,000 feet from the floor of the ocean, and when a new series of volcanic thrusts tore through the vents, the mountain would patiently build itself aloft for another try. Exploding, hissing, and spewing forth ash, the great mountain would writhe in convulsions. It would pierce the waves. Its island would be born again.

This was the restless surge of the universe, the violence of birth, the cold tearing away of death; and yet how promising was this interplay of forces as an island struggled to be born, vanishing in agony, then soaring aloft in triumph. You men who will come later to inhabit these islands, remember the agony of arrival, the rising and the fall, the nothingness of the sea when storms throw down the rock, the triumph of the mountain when new rocks are lifted aloft.

For a million years the island hung in this precarious balance, a child of violence; but finally, after incredibly patient accumulation, it was established. Now each new lava flow had a solid base upon which to build, and inch by inch the debris agglutinated until the island could be seen by birds from long distances. It was indeed land, habitable had there been existing men, with shelters for boats, had there been boats, and with rocks that could have been used for building homes and temples. It was now, in the real sense of the word, an island, taking its rightful place in the center of the great ocean.

But before life could prosper on this island, soil was needed, and as yet none existed. When molten lava burst upon the air it generally exploded into ash, but sometimes it ran as a viscous fluid down the sides of mountains, constructing extensive sheets of flat rock. In either case, the action of wind and rain and cooling nights began to pulverize the newly born lava, decomposing it into soil. When enough had accumulated, the island was ready.

The first living forms to arrive were inconspicuous, indeed almost invisible, lichens and low types of moss. They were borne by the sea and by winds that howled back and forth across the oceans. With a tenacity equal to that of the island itself these fragments of life established themselves, and as they grew they broke down more rocks and built more soil.

At this time there existed, on the distant continents visited by the ocean, a well-established plant and animal society composed of trees and lumbering animals and insects. Some of these forms were already well adapted for life on the new island, but were prevented from taking residence by two thousand miles of open ocean.

Consequently, there began an appalling struggle. Life, long before man's emergence, stood poised on distant shores, pressing to make new exploratory journeys like those that had already populated the existing earth with plants and animals. But against these urgent forms stood more than two thousand miles of turbulent ocean, storm-ridden, salty, and implacable.

The first sentient animals to reach the island were of course fish, for they permeated the ocean, coming and going as they wished. But they could not be said to be a part of the island. The first nonoceanic animal to visit was a bird. It came, probably, from the north on an exploratory mission in search of food. It landed on the still-warm rocks, found nothing edible, and flew on, perhaps to perish in the southern seas.

A thousand years passed, and no other birds arrived. One day a coconut was swept ashore by a violent storm. It had been kept afloat on the bosom of the sea by its buoyant husk, traveling more than three thousand miles from the southwest, a marvel of persistence. But when it landed, it found no soil along the shore and only salt water, so it perished, but its husk and shell helped form soil for those that would come later.

The years passed. The sun swept through its majestic cycles. The moon waxed and waned, and tides rushed back and forth across the surface of the world. Ice crept down from the north, and for ten thousand years covered the islands, its weight and power breaking down rocks and forming earth.

The years passed, the empty, endless, significant years. And then one day another bird arrived on the island, also seeking food. This time it found a few dead fish along the shore. As if in gratitude, it emptied its bowels on the waiting earth and evacuated a tiny seed which it had eaten on some remote island. The seed germinated and grew. Thus, after the passage of eons of time, growing life had established itself on the rocky island.

Now the passage of time becomes incomprehensible. Between the arrival of the first, unproductive bird, and the second bearing in its bowels the vital seed, more than twenty thousand years had elapsed. In another twenty thousand years a second bit of life arrived, a female insect, fertilized on some distant island on the night before a tremendous storm. Caught up in the vast winds that howled from the south, she was borne aloft to the height of ten thousand feet and driven northward for more than two thousand miles to be dropped at last upon this new and remote island, where she gave birth. Insects had arrived.

The years passed. Other birds arrived, but they bore no seeds. Other insects were blown ashore, but they were not females, or if they were, not pregnant. But once every twenty or thirty thousand years—a period longer than that of historic man—some one bit of life would reach the island, by accident; and by accident it would establish itself. In this hit-or-miss way, over a period of time that the mind can barely digest, life populated the island.

One of the most significant days in the history of the island came when a bird staggered in from some land far to the southwest, bearing in its tangled feathers the seed of a tree. Perched upon a rock, the bird pecked at the seed until it fell away, and in the course of time a tree grew. Thirty thousand years passed, and by some accident equally absurd, another tree arrived, and after a million years of chances, after five million years of storms and birds and drifting sea-soaked logs bearing snails and borers, the island had a forest with flowers and birds and insects.

Nothing, nothing that ever existed on this island reached it easily. The rocks themselves were forced up fiery chimneys through miles of ocean. They burst in horrible agony onto the surface of the earth. The lichens that arrived came borne by storms. The birds limped in on deadened wings. Insects came only when accompanied by hurricanes, and even trees arrived in the dark belly of some wandering bird, or precariously perched upon the feathers of a thigh.

Timelessly, relentlessly, in storm and hunger and hurricane the island was given life, and this life was sustained only by constant new volcanic eruptions that spewed forth new lava that could be broken down into life-sustaining soil. In violence the island lived, and in violence a great beauty was born.

The shores of the island, weathered by the sea, were stupendous cliffs that caught the evening sun and glowed like serrated pillars of gold. The mountains were tall and jagged, their lower levels clothed in dark green trees, their upper pinnacles shod in ice, while the calm bays in which the grandeur of the mountains was reflected were deeply cut into the shore. Valleys and sweet plains, waterfalls and rivers, glades where lovers would have walked and confluences where towns could have been built, the lovely island had all these accouterments, these alluring invitations to civilization.

But no man ever saw them, and the tempting glades entertained no lovers, for the island had risen to its beauty long, long before the age of man; and at the moment of its greatest perfection it began to die. In violence it had been born; in violence it would die.

There was a sudden shudder of the earth, a slipping and a sliding, and when the readjustment was ended, covering a period of thousands of years, the island had sunk some twelve hundred feet lower into the ocean, and ice nevermore formed upon its crests. The volcanoes stopped, and no new lava poured forth to create new soil to replace that which had sunk into the sea. For a million years winds howled at the hills, the ocean gnawed away at the ramparts. Year by year the island withered and grew less. It began to shred away, to shatter and to fall back into the ocean from which it had sprung.

A million years passed, and then a million more, and the island which had grown so patiently at the northwest tip of the great crack in the ocean floor slowly, slowly vanished. The birds that had fed upon its hills went elsewhere, bearing in their bowels new seeds. From its shore fertilized insects were storm-blown to other islands, and life went on. Once every twenty or thirty thousand years some fragment of nature escaped from this island, and life went on.

But as the island subsided, a different form of life sprang into increased activity. In the warm, clear, nutritious waters that surrounded the shores, coral polyps began to flourish. and slowly they left behind them as they died their tiny calciferous skeletons, a few feet below the surface of the sea. In a thousand years they built a submerged ring around the island. In a thousand more they added to its form, and as the eons passed, these tiny coral animals built a reef.

Ice melted in the north, and the coral animals were drowned in vast weights of unexpected water. The seas changed temperature and the animals died. Torrents of rain poured down from island hills and silted up the shoreline, strangling the tiny coral. Or new ice caps formed far to the north and south, pulling water away from the dying island. Then the coral were exposed and died at once.

Always, like everything to do with this island, throughout its entire history, the coral lived precariously, poised between catastrophes. But in the breathing space available, the coral built. And so it was that this tiny animal, this child of cataclysm, built a new island to replace the old as it gradually wore itself away and sank into the sea.

How terrible this passage of life and death! How meaningless that an island that had been born of such force and violence, that had been so fair upon the bosom of the great ocean, so loved of birds, so rich in trees, so willing to entertain man, should he ever arrive . . . how wasteful it was that this island should have grown in agony and died in equal agony before ever a human eye had seen its majesty.

Across a million years, down more than ten million years it existed silently in the unknown sea and then died, leaving only a fringe of coral where sea birds rest and where gigantic seals of the changing ocean play. Ceaseless life and death, endless expenditure of beauty and capacity, tireless ebb and flow and rising and subsidence of the ocean. Night comes and the burning day, and the island waits, and no man arrives. The days perish and the nights, and the aching beauty of lush valleys and waterfalls vanishes, and no man will ever see them. All that remains is a coral reef, a calcium wreath on the surface of the great sea that had given the island life, a memorial erected by the skeletons of a billion billion billion little animals.

While this first island was rising to prominence and dying back to nothingness, other would-be islands, stretching away to the southeast, were also struggling to attain brief existence followed by certain death. Some started their cycle within the same million years as did the first. Others lagged. The latest would not puncture the surface of the sea until the first was well into its death throes, so that at any moment from the time the first island began to die, man, had he then existed, could have witnessed in this two-thousand-mile chain of islands every sequential step in the process of life and death. Like an undulating wave of the sea itself, the rocky islands rose and fell; but whereas the cycle of an ocean wave is apt to be a few minutes at the most, the cycle of the rising and falling of these islands was of the nature of sixty million years.

Each island, at any given moment of time, existed certainly and securely within that cycle: it was either rising toward birth and significance, or it was perishing. I do not mean that man, had he been able to witness the cycle, could have identified which part of the cycle a given island was in; there must have been periods of millions of years when no one could have ascertained that condition. But the impersonal, molten center of the earth knew, for it was sending that island no new supplies of lava. The waiting sea knew, for it could feel the cliffs falling into its arms a little more easily. And the coral polyps knew, because they sensed that it was now time to start erecting a memorial to this island which would soon be dead . . . that is, within twenty or thirty million years.

Endless cycle, endless birth and death, endless becoming and disappearing. Once the terrifying volcanic explosions cease, the island is already doomed. Peace and calm seas and the arrival of birds bearing seeds are pleasant to experience, but the residence of beauty is surely nominated for destruction. A sŏng at night of insects, the gentle splash of surf against the sand, and a new ice age is beginning which will freeze out all life. Limitless cycle, endless change.

TOWARD THE END of the master cycle, when the western islands were dying and the eastern were abuilding, a new volcano pushed its cone above the surface of the ocean, and in a series of titanic explosions erupted enough molten rock to establish securely a new island, which after eons of time would be designated by men as the capital island of the group. Its subsequent volcanic history was memorable in that its habitable land resulted from the wedding of two separate chains of volcanoes.

After the parent volcano had succeeded in establishing an island, its mighty flanks produced many subsidiary vents through which lava poured; whereupon a greater volcano, separated from the first by miles of ocean, sprang into being and erected its own majestic construction, marked by an equal chain of events.

For eons of time the two massive volcano systems stood in the sea in fiery competition, and then, inevitably, the first began to die back, its fires extinguished, while the second continued to pour millions of tons of lava down its own steep flanks. Hissing, exploding, crackling, the rocks fell into the sea in boundless accumulations, building the later volcano ever more solidly, ever more thickly at its base on the remote floor of the ocean.

In time, sinking lava from the second master builder began to creep across the feet of the first, and then to climb its sides and finally to throw itself across the exposed lava flows that had constituted the earlier island. Now the void in the sea that had separated the two was filled, and they became one. Locked in fiery arms, joined by intertwining ejaculations of molten rock, the two volcanoes stood in matrimony, their union a single fruitful and growing island.

Its soil was later made from dozens of smaller volcanoes that erupted for a few hundred thousand years, then passed into death and silence. One exploded in dazzling glory and left a crater looking like a punch bowl. Another, at the very edge of the island, from where it could control the sea approaches, left as its memory a gaunt headland shaped like a diamond.

When the island was well formed—and what a heavenly, sweet, enchanting island it was—some force of nature, almost as if by subtle plan, hid in its bowels a wealth of incalculable richness. It could not be diamonds, because the island was 250,000,000 years too young to have acquired the carboniferous plant growth that produced diamonds. It could not be either oil or coal, for the same reason. It wasn't gold, for neither the age nor the conditions required for the building of that metal were present on this island. It was none of these commonly accepted treasures, but it was a greater.

The volcanic basalt from which the island was built was porous, and when the tremendous storms which swept the ocean struck the island, the waters they disgorged ran partly out to sea in surface rivers, seeped partly into the heart of the island. Billions of tons of water thus crept down into the secret reservoirs of the island.

They did not stay there, of course, for since the rock was porous, there were avenues that led back out to sea, and in time the water was lost. But if any animal—a man perhaps—could penetrate the rocks, he could intercept the water and put it to his use, for the entire island was a catchment; the entire core of the island was permeated with life-giving water.

But that was not the special treasure of this particular island, for a man could bore into almost any porous rock on any island, and catch some water. Here, on this island, there was to be an extra treasure, and the way it was deposited was something of a miracle.

When the ice came and went, causing the great ocean to rise, when the island itself sank slowly and then rebuilt with new lava—when these titanic convolutions were in progress, the south shore of the island was alternately exposed to sunlight or buried fathoms deep in ocean. When the first condition prevailed, the exposed shore was cut by mountain streams which threw their debris across the plain, depositing there claylike soils and minute fragments of lava. Sometimes the sea would wash in bits of animal calcium, or a thundering storm would rip away a cliff face and throw its remnants over the shore. Bit by bit, over a hundred thousand years at a time, the shore accumulated its debris.

Then, when next the ocean rose, it would press down heavily upon this shelving land, which would lie for ages, submerged under tons of dark, green water. But while the great brutal ocean thus pressed down hydraulically, it at the same time acted as a life-giving agent, for through its shimmering waves filtered silt and dead bodies and water-logged fragments of trees and sand. All these things, the gifts both of land and sea, the immense weight of ocean would bind together until they united to form rock.

Cataclysmically the island would rise from the sea to collect new fragments washed down from the hills, then sink beneath the waves to accumulate new deposits of life-building slime. But whenever the monstrous ocean would beat down heavily upon the shore for ten thousand years at a time, new rock was formed, an impermeable shield that sloped down from the lower foothills and extended well out to sea. It was a cap rock, imprisoning in a gigantic underground reservoir all that lay beneath it.

What lay trapped below, of course, was water. Secretly, far beneath the visible surface of the island, imprisoned by this watertight cap of rock, lay the purest, sweetest, most copious water in all the lands that bordered upon or existed in the great ocean. It lay there under vast pressure, so that it was not only available, should a man deduce its secret hiding, but it was ready to leap forth twenty or thirty or forty feet into the air, and engulf with life-giving sweetness any man who could penetrate the imprisoning rock and set it free. It waited, an almost inexhaustible supply of water to sustain life. It waited, a universe of water hidden beneath the cap rock. It waited.

The adventurous plants and insects that had reached the earliest northwest island had plenty of time in which to make their way to the newer lands as the latter rose to life. It might take a million years for a given grass to complete its journey down the chain. But there was no hurry. Slowly, with a patience that is difficult to comprehend, trees and vines and crawling things crept down the islands, while in other parts of the world a new and more powerful animal was rising and preparing himself for his invasion of the islands.

Before the two-volcanoed island with its trapped treasure of water had finished growing, man had developed in distant areas. Before the last island had assumed its dominant shape, men had erected in Egypt both mighty monuments and a stable form of government. Men could already write and record their memories.

While volcanoes still played along the chain, China developed a sophisticated system of thought and Japan codified art principles that would later enrich the world. While the islands were taking their final form, Jesus spoke in Jerusalem and Muhammad came from the blazing deserts with a new vision of heaven, but no men knew the heaven that awaited them on these islands.

For these lands were the youngest part of the earth's vast visible surface. They were new. They were raw. They were empty. They were waiting. Books which we still read today were written before these islands were known to anyone except the birds of passage. Songs which we still sing were composed and recorded while these islands remained vacant. The Bible had been compiled, and the Koran.

Raw, empty, youthful islands, sleeping in the sun and whipped by rain, they waited.

Since, when they were finally discovered, they were destined to be widely hailed as paradises, it is proper to study them carefully in their last, waiting moments, those sad, sweet, overpowering days before the first canoes reached them.

They were beautiful, that is true. Their wooded mountains were a joy. Their cool waterfalls, existing in the thousands, were spectacular. Their cliffs, where the restless ocean had eroded away the edges of great mountains, dropped thousands of feet clear into the sea, and birds nested on the vertical stones. Rivers were fruitful. The shores of the islands were white and waves that washed them were crystal-blue. At night the stars were close, great brilliant dots of fire fixing forever the location of the islands and forming majestic pathways for the moon and sun.

How beautiful these islands were! How shot through with harmony and peace! How the mind lingers on their pristine grandeur, a grandeur that nothing so far devised could permanently destroy. If paradise consists solely of beauty, then these islands were the fairest paradise that man ever invaded, for the land and sea were beautiful, and the climate was congenial.

But if the concept of paradise includes also the ability to sustain life, then these islands, as they waited in the time of Jesus and Muhammad, were far from heavenly. They contained almost no food. Of all the things that grew on their magnificent hillsides, nothing could be relied upon to sustain life adequately. There were a few pandanus trees whose spare and bitter fruits could be chewed for minimum existence. There were a few tree ferns whose cores were just barely edible, a few roots. There were fish if they could be caught and birds if they could be trapped. But there was nothing else.

Few more inhospitable major islands have ever existed than this group. Here are the things they did not have: no chickens, or pigs, or cattle, or edible dogs; no bananas, no taro, no sweet potatoes, no breadfruit; no pineapple, or sugar, or guava, or gourds, or melons, or mangoes, no fruit of any kind; no palms for making sugar; no food. The islands did not even have that one essential, that miraculous sustainer of tropical life, the coconut. Some had drifted to the shores, but in salty soil along the beaches they could not grow.

Any man who came to the islands would, if he wanted to live, have to bring with him all food. If he were wise, he would also bring most of the materials required for building a civilized society, since the islands had no bamboo for decorating a home, no candlenuts for lamps, no mulberry bark for making tapa. Nor were there any conspicuous flowers: neither frangipani, nor hibiscus, nor bright croton, nor colorful orchids. Instead of these joy-giving, life-sustaining plants there was a hidden tree, useless except that its wood when dried yielded a persistent perfume, and this was the tree of death, the sandalwood tree. Of itself, it was neither poisonous nor cruel, but the uses to which it would be put on these islands would make it a permanent blight.

The soil of the islands was not particularly good. It was not rich and black like the soil which Russian peasants were already farming, nor loamy and productive like that known to the Dakota and Iowa tribes of Indians. It was red and of a sandlike consistency, apparently rich in iron because it had been formed of decomposed basalt, but lacking in other essentials. If a farmer could add to this soil the missing minerals and supply it with adequate water, it had the capacity to produce enormously. But of itself it was not much, for the minerals were absent, and so was the water.

Tremendous quantities of rain did fall on the islands, but it fell in an unproductive manner. From the northeast, trade winds blew constantly, pushing ahead of them low clouds pregnant with sweet water. But along the northeast shores of each island high cliffs rose, and mountains, and these reached up and knocked the water out of the clouds, so that it fell in cascades where it could not be used and never reached the southwest plains where the red soil was. Of the flat lands that could be tilled, fully three fourths were in effect deserts. If one could capture the wasted water that ran useless down the steep mountainsides and back out to sea, bringing it through the mountains and onto the flat lands, then crops could be grown. Or if one could discover the secret reservoirs waiting in the kidneys of the islands, one would have ample water and more than ample food. But until this was accomplished, men who lived on these islands would never have enough water or enough food.

And so these beautiful, inhospitable islands waited for some breed of men to invade them with food and courage and determination. The best that could be said of the islands, as they waited, was that they held no poisonous snakes, no fevers, no mosquitoes, no disfiguring diseases, and no plagues.

There was one additional aspect that must be remembered. Of all the growing things that existed in these islands at the time of Jesus, ninety-five out of every hundred grew nowhere else in the world. These islands were unique, alone, apart, off the main stream of life, a secluded backwater of nature . . . or, if you prefer, an authentic natural paradise where each growing thing had its opportunity to develop in its own unique way, according to the dictates and limitations of its own abilities.

I spoke of that adventurous bird that brought the first seed in its bowels. It was a grass seed, perhaps, one whose brothers and sisters, if the term may be used of grasses, stayed behind on their original islands, where they developed as the family had always done for millions of generations. On those original islands the grass maintained its standard characteristics and threw forth no venturesome modifications; or, if such mutations were offered, the stronger normal stock quickly submerged them, and the dead average was preserved.

But on the new islands the grass, left alone in beauty and sun and rain, became a different grass, unique and adapted to these islands. When men looked at such grass, millions of years later, they would be able to discern that it was a grass, and that it had come from the original stock still existing elsewhere; but they would also see that it was nevertheless a new grass, with new qualities, new vitality, and new promise.

Did an insect from one of the huge continents reach these islands? If so, here he became a different insect, his legs longer or his nose more adapted to boring. Birds, flowers, worms, trees and snails . . . all developed unique forms and qualities in these islands.

There was then, as there is now, no place known on earth that even began to compete with these islands in their capacity to encourage natural life to develop freely and radically up to its own best potential. More than nine out of ten things that grew here, grew nowhere else on earth.

Why this should have been so remains a mystery. Perhaps a fortunate combination of rainfall, climate, sunlight and soil accounted for this miracle. Perhaps eons of time in which diverse growing things were left alone to work out their own best destinies was the explanation. Perhaps the fact that when a grass reached here it had to stand upon its own capacities and could not be refertilized by grasses of the same kind from the parent stock, perhaps that is the explanation. But whatever the reason, the fact remains: in these islands new breeds developed, and they prospered, and they grew strong, and they multiplied. For these islands were a crucible of exploration and development.

And so, with these capacities, the islands waited. Jesus died on a cross, and they waited. England was settled by mixed and powerful races, and the islands waited for their own settlers. Mighty kings ruled in India, and in China and in Japan, while the islands waited.

Inhospitable in fact, a paradise in potential, with almost no food available, but with enormous riches waiting to be developed, the islands waited. Volcanoes, still building the ramparts with fresh flows of lava, hung lanterns in the sky so that if a man and his canoe were lost on the great dark bosom of the sea, wandering fitfully this way and that, he might spot the incandescent glow of the under side of a distant cloud, and thus find a fiery star to steer by.

Large gannets and smaller terns skimmed across the waters leading to land, while frigate birds drew sharp and sure navigation lines from the turbulent ocean wastes right to the heart of the islands, where they nested. If a man in a canoe could spot a frigate bird, its cleft tail cutting the wind, he could be sure that land lay in the direction toward which the bird had flown at dusk.

These beautiful islands, waiting in the sun and storm, how much they seemed like beautiful women waiting for their men to come home at dusk, waiting with open arms and warm bodies and consolation. All that would be accomplished in these islands, as in these women, would be generated solely by the will and puissance of some man. I think the islands always knew this.

Therefore, men of Polynesia and Boston and China and Mount Fuji and the barrios of the Philippines, do not come to these islands empty-handed, or craven in spirit, or afraid to starve. There is no food here. In these islands there is no certainty. Bring your own food, your own gods, your own flowers and fruits and concepts. For if you come without resources to these islands you will perish.

But if you come with growing things, and good foods and better ideas, if you come with gods that will sustain you, and if you are willing to work until the swimming head and the aching arms can stand no more, then you can gain entrance to this miraculous crucible where the units of nature are free to develop according to their own capacities and desires.

On these harsh terms the islands waited.

II

From the Sun-Swept Lagoon

I HAVE SAID that the islands along the rupture in the ocean floor were not a paradise, but twenty-four hundred miles almost due south there did exist an island which merited that description. It lay northwest of Tahiti, already populated with a powerful, sophisticated people, and only a few miles from the island of Havaiki, the political and religious capital of the area.

It was Bora Bora, and it rose from the sea in sharp cliffs and mighty pinnacles of rock. It contained deep-set bays and tree-rimmed shores of glistening sand. It was so beautiful that it seemed impossible that it had arisen by chance; gods must have formed it and placed the bays just so, an illusion which was enhanced by the fact that around the entire island was hung a protecting necklace of coral on which wild ocean waves broke in high fury, trying vainly to leap inside the placid green lagoon, where fish flourished in abundant numbers. It was an island of rare beauty—wild, impetuous, lovely Bora Bora.

Early one morning, while in Paris the sons of Charlemagne quarreled among themselves as to how their late father's empire should be ruled, a swift single-hulled outrigger canoe, sped along by sturdy paddlers and a triangular sail, swept across the open ocean leading from Havaiki and sought the solitary entrance to the lagoon of Bora Bora, on whose shores a lookout followed the progress of the urgent canoe with dread.

He saw the steersman signal his sailors to drop sail, and as they complied he watched the canoe pivot deftly in high swells that sought to crash it upon the reef. But with enviable skill the steersman rode with the swells and headed his canoe toward the perilous opening in the coral wall.

"Now!" he shouted, and his paddlers worked feverishly, standing the canoe off from the rocks and speeding it into the channel. There was a rush of water, a rising of huge waves, and a swift passionate surge of canoe and flashing paddles through the gap.

"Rest!" the steersman called quietly, in audible relief. Gratified with his minor triumph, he looked for approval to the canoe's solitary passenger, a tall gaunt man with deep-set eyes, a black beard, and long thin hands in which he clutched a staff carved with the figures of gods. But the passenger offered no commendation, for he was lost in the contemplation of certain mighty processes which he had helped set in motion. He stared through the steersman, past the paddlers and onto the towering central rock that marked the heights of Bora Bora.

It was from a point part way up the slopes of this rugged mountain that the lookout now rushed down steep paths leading to the king's residence, shouting as he went, "The High Priest is returning!" The instinctive dread which the lookout felt was transmitted in his cry, and women who heard the message drew closer to their men and looked at them with new affection across dark, palm-thatched huts.

Although the agitated lookout delivered his frightening message to the general community, he was actually speeding to alert one man, and now as he darted along in the shade of breadfruit trees and palms, he kept whispering to himself, "Gods of Bora Bora, speed my feet! Don't let me be late!"

Dashing up to a grass house larger than its neighbors, the lookout fell to the ground, shouting, "The High Priest is in the lagoon!" From the grassy interior a tall, brown-skinned young man, courtier to the king, poked a sleepy head and asked in some alarm, "Already?"

"He has passed the reef," the lookout warned.

"Why didn't you . . ." In great agitation the young man grabbed a ceremonial tapa robe made from pounded bark, and without waiting to adjust it properly went running toward the palace crying, "The High Priest approaches!" He hurried past other courtiers like himself and right into the royal presence, where he prostrated himself on the soft pandanus matting that covered the earthen floor, announcing with urgency, "The august one is about to land."

The man to whom these agitated words were addressed was a handsome, large-headed man of thirty-three whose close-cropped hair showed gray at the temples, and whose unusually wide-spaced eyes were grave with wisdom. If he experienced the same dread at the High Priest's return as did his underlings, he masked it; but the tall young courtier nevertheless observed that his master moved with unaccustomed alacrity to the treasure room, where he donned an ankle-length robe of light brown tapa bark, throwing about his left shoulder and around his waist a precious cordon made of yellow feathers, his badge of authority. He then adjusted his feather-and-shell helmet, while around his neck he placed a chain of shark's teeth. At this appropriate moment the tall courtier issued a signal, and drums along the shore began to throb in royal rhythms.

"We go to honor the High Priest," the king announced gravely, waiting while an impressive train of tanned warriors, naked to the waist and wrapped in brown tapa, formed behind him. Almost against his will, the king found himself urging his men, "Hurry, hurry! We must not be tardy," for although everyone acknowledged that he was supreme on Bora Bora, he had found it prudent never to be wanting in courtesies to the spiritual ruler of the island, especially since the attributes and requirements of the new god, Oro, were not yet clearly known. The king's father had underestimated the power of the new deity, and during a solemn convocation in the temple of Oro, his high priest had suddenly pointed at him as one failing in reverence, and the king's brains had been clubbed in, his body dragged away as the next human sacrifice to red Oro, the all-powerful, the uniter of the islands.

But in spite of the king's care, when the royal procession left the palace the tall young courtier had to warn, "The august one already approaches the landing!" whereupon the king and all his retinue began to run, holding onto their various badges as they did. The king, aware of the ridiculous sight he presented, yet unwilling through fear to go more slowly, glared at the tall courtier whose information had been delivered late, and the aide, who was having difficulty keeping his tapa cloth straight as he ran, began to sweat and prayed beneath his breath, "If there is to be a convocation, O gods of Bora Bora spare me!"

The king stumbled on in the hot morning sun, angry, muttering, damaged in pride. But he did reach the landing place a few moments before the canoe, and although he could not have known it at the time, his sweaty embarrassment helped rather than hurt, for from the outrigger the High Priest noticed with satisfaction the king's discomfort and for a moment allowed a smile to creep toward his lips. But it was quickly suppressed, and the priest resumed his aloof study of the mountain peak.

Gently, the steersman brought his canoe to rest, careful lest any untoward accident draw the priest's attention, for the paddlers knew what message the religious man was bringing from the temple of Oro, and on this day it behooved all men to be careful. When the canoe was secured, the High Priest disembarked with imperial dignity, his white-bark cape with its fringe of dog's teeth shining against his long, black hair.

He was a powerful symbol of Oro as he moved with his god-carved staff to meet the king, genuflecting slightly as if to indicate that he acknowledged the latter's supremacy. Then, recovering his posture, he waited grimly while King Tamatoa, the supposed ruler, bowed low and held a subservient position long enough to impress all witnesses with the fact that power had somehow been mysteriously transferred from his hands into those of the priest. Then the king spoke.

"Oh, blessed of the gods!" King Tamatoa began. "What is the wish of Oro?"

The pressing crowd, handsome men and fine women, naked to the waist and dark-eyed, held its breath in apprehension, which the High Priest sensed and relished. He waited, while soft winds from the green lagoon tugged at palms that lined the shore and made the dark green leaves of breadfruit sway. Then he spoke solemnly: "There will be a convocation!" No one gasped, lest he draw fatal attention to himself.

The High Priest continued: "A new temple is to be erected in Tahiti and we shall convene to consecrate the god who is to live in that temple." He paused, and visible fear crept over the faces of his listeners. Even King Tamatoa himself, who could with reasonable assurance count on being spared, felt his knees weaken while he waited for the dread details that completed any announcement of a general interisland convocation at Oro's temple.

But the High Priest also waited, appreciating that the longer his terror continued, the more effective it would be in impressing the sometimes recalcitrant Bora Borans with the temper and might of their new god. On this day he would maneuver the king himself into asking the fatal questions.

Flies that had been feeding on dead fish along the lagoon shore now turned their attention to the bare backs of the waiting crowd, but no man moved lest in the next dreadful moments he become conspicuous. The king waited. The priest waited. Finally in a hushed voice Tamatoa asked, "When is the convocation?"

"Tomorrow!" the High Priest said sternly, and his news was instantly interpreted as he had intended. Thought the king: "If the convocation is to be tomorrow, it must have been decided upon ten days ago! Else how could the news reach Tahiti in time for their canoe to return to Havaiki tomorrow? Our High Priest must have been in secret consultation with the priests of Oro during all those ten days."

The flies stung perspiring backs, but no man moved, awaiting the next ominous question. Finally Tamatoa asked, "How many men for Oro?"

"Eight," the priest replied, impersonally. Placing his staff before him, causing watchers in the muted crowd to fall back, the gaunt dark man in shimmering white robes moved off toward his temple, but when it appeared that he had finished with the crowd he suddenly whirled about, made a terrifying sound in his throat, and thrust his staff directly at the steersman who had brought him into the safety of the lagoon.

"And this one shall be first!" he screamed.

"No! No!" the steersman pleaded, falling to his knees on the sand.

Implacably, the great gaunt priest towered over him, pointing at him with the staff. "When the seas were upon us," he intoned mournfully, "this one prayed not to Oro for salvation but to Tane."

"Oh, no!" the sailor pleaded.

"I watched his lips," the priest said with awful finality. Attendants from the temple gathered up the quaking steersman and hauled him off, for his legs, surrendering to terror, could not be forced to work.

"And you!" the dreadful voice cried again, thrusting his staff at an unsuspecting watcher. "In the temple of Oro, on the holy day, your head nodded. You shall be second." Once more the attendants closed in on the culprit, dragging him away, but gently lest Oro be offered as a human sacrifice a man who was bruised or in any way imperfect.

Solemnly the High Priest withdrew and King Tamatoa was left with the miserable task of nominating the six additional human sacrifices. He asked, "Where is my aide?" and from a spot toward the rear of the crowd, where he had hoped to remain unnoticed, the tall and trembling courtier stepped forth.

"Why was I late in greeting the sacred one?" the king demanded.

"The lookout stumbled. It was he who was tardy," the aide explained.

From the rear of the crowd a woman's voice inadvertently blurted, "No, that is not true!" But the woman's husband, a small man of no on which the local temple sat, and where the priests were dedica eight doomed men to Oro, he spoke without the animal anger th possessed him during the ceremonies.

"I'm not afraid of the convocation, Marama," he said firmly.

"I am afraid for you," his wife replied.

"Look at our canoe!" he digressed, pointing to a long shed near th temple, under which a mammoth twin-hulled canoe rested. "You wouldn't want anyone else to guide that, would you?" he teased.

Marama, whose priestly father had selected the sacred logs for the craft, needed no reminder of its importance, so she contented herself with pointing out: "Mato from the north can guide the canoe."

Then Teroro divulged his real reason for attending the dangerous convocation: "My brother may need my help."

"King Tamatoa will have many protectors," Marama replied.

"Without me events could go badly," Teroro stubbornly insisted, and wise Marama, whose name meant the moon, all-seeing and compassionate, recognized his mood and retreated to a different argument.

She said, "Teroro, it is you mainly that the High Priest suspects of being disloyal to his red god Oro."

"No more than the others," Teroro growled.

"But you're the one who shows your disbelief," she argued.

"Sometimes I can't hide it," the young chief admitted.

Furtively, Marama looked about to see if any spy had crept upon them, for the High Priest had his men in all places, but today there was none, and with her feet in the lagoon she resumed her careful reasoning. "You must promise me," she insisted, "that if you do go to Oro's temple, you will pray only to Oro, think only of Oro. Remember how the steersman's lips were read."

"I've been to three convocations at Havaiki," Teroro assured her. "I know the dangers."

"But not this special danger," his wife pleaded.

"What is different?" he asked.

Again Marama looked about her and again she saw nothing, so she spoke: "Haven't you wondered why the High Priest spent ten extra days at Havaiki?"

"I suppose he was preparing for the convocation."

"No. That must have been decided many days earlier. To permit canoes from Tahiti and Moorea to return to Havaiki by tomorrow. Last year a woman from Havaiki confided to me that the priests there consider our High Priest the ablest of all, and they plan to promote him to some position of prominence."

"I wish they would," Teroro grumbled. "Get him off this island."

"But they wouldn't dare make him paramount priest so long as his own island is not completely won over."

As Marama talked, her husband began to pick up a thread of importance, which often occurred when the wise, moon-faced woman spoke, marked intelligence, was dragged before the king, where he shook like a torn banana leaf, and the king surveyed him with disgust. "He shall be third," the king commanded.

"Oh, please, no!" the lookout protested. "I ran true. But when I reached the palace," and he pointed to the aide, "he was asleep."

The king recalled his earlier impatience with the young courtier and announced peremptorily: "He shall be fourth. The rest shall be taken from the slaves." With this he strode back to the palace, while the lookout and the tall courtier, already pinioned by the priests, stood in limp amazement, appalled by the catastrophe in which each had so accidentally involved the other.

As the frightened crowd dispersed, each congratulating himself that for this convocation he had escaped the insatiable hunger of Oro, a young chief clothed in golden tapa, which indicated that he was of the royal family, stood bitter and silent in the shade of a breadfruit tree. He had not hidden himself through fear, for he was taller than most, better muscled than any, and marked by a lean, insolent courage that no man could mistake. He had remained apart because he hated the High Priest, despised the new god Oro, and was revolted by the incessant demand for human sacrifice.

The High Priest, of course, had immediately detected the young chief's absence from the welcoming throng, a breach of conformity which so enraged him that during the most solemn part of the ceremony his penetrating gaze had flashed this way and that, searching for the young man. Finally the priest had found him, lounging insolently under the breadfruit tree, and the two men had exchanged long, defiant stares that had been broken only when a golden-skinned young woman with flowing hair that held banana blossoms tugged at her husband's arm, forcing him to drop his eyes.

Now, with the ceremony ended, the stately wife was pleading: "Teroro, you must not go to the convocation."

"Who else can command our canoe?" he asked impatiently.

"Is a canoe so important?"

Her husband looked at her in amazement. "Important? What could there be more important?"

"Your life," she said simply. "Wise navigators do not sail when the clouds are ominous."

He dismissed her fears and strode disconsolately to a fallen log that projected into the lagoon. Falling angrily upon it, he dipped his brown feet into the silvery waters, and kicked them viciously as if he hated even the sea; but soon his placid wife, lovely in the fragrance of banana blossoms, came and sat beside him, and when her feet splashed in the cool green waters, it was as if a child were playing, and soon her husband forgot his anger. Even when he stared across to the small promontory and he leaned forward on the log to listen. She continued: "It seems to me that the High Priest will have to do everything possible in this convocation to prove to the priests of Havaiki that he is more devoted to Oro than they."

"In order to make himself eligible for promotion?" Teroro asked.

"He must."

"What do you think he will do?" Teroro asked.

Marama hesitated to utter the words, and at that moment an unexpected wind blew across the lagoon and threw small waves at her feet. She drew her toes from the lagoon and dried them with her hands, still not speaking, so Teroro continued her thought: "You think that to impress others, the High Priest will sacrifice the king?"

"No," Marama corrected. "It is your feet he will place upon the rainbow."

Teroro reached up and tugged at the tip of a breadfruit leaf and asked thoughtfully, "Will the killing then stop?"

"No," his wife replied gravely, "it will go on until all of your friends have left the lagoon. Only then will Bora Bora be safe for Oro."

"Men like Mato and Pa?"

"They are doomed," Marama said.

"But you think not the king?"

"No," the queenly young woman reasoned. "Your brother is well loved by the kings of Tahiti and Moorea, and such a bold step might turn not only those kings but people in general against the new god."

"But offering me to Oro would be permitted?" Teroro pursued.

"Yes. Kings are always willing to believe the worst of younger brothers."

Teroro turned on the log to study his beautiful wife and thought to himself: "I don't appreciate her good sense. She's a lot like her father." Aloud he said, "I hadn't reasoned it out the way you have, Marama. All I knew was that this time there was special danger."

"It is because you, the brother of the king, still worship Tane."

"Only in my heart do I do that."

"But if I can read your heart," Marama said, "so can the priests."

Teroro's comment on this was forestalled by an agitated messenger, his arm banded by a circle of yellow feathers to indicate that he belonged to the king. "We have been looking for you," he told Teroro.

"I've been studying the canoe," the young chief growled.

"The king wants you."

Teroro rose from the log, banged his feet on the grass to knock away the water, and nodded an impersonal farewell to his wife. Following the messenger, he reported to the palace, a large, low building held up by coconut-tree pillars, each carved with figures of gods and highly polished so that white flecks in the wood gleamed. The roof consisted of plaited palm fronds, and there were no floors or windows or side walls, just rolled-up lengths of matting which could be dropped for either secrecy or protection from rain. The principal room contained many signs of royalty: feather gods, carved shark's teeth, and huge Tridacna shells from the south. The building had two beautiful features: it overlooked the lagoon, on whose outer reef high clouds of spray broke constantly; and all parts of the structure were held together by thin, strong strands of golden brown sennit, the marvelous island rope woven from fibers that filled the husks of coconuts. Nearly two miles of it had been used in construction; wherever one piece of timber touched another, pliant golden sennit held the parts together. A man could sit in a room tied with sennit and revel in its intricate patterns the way a navigator studies stars at night or a child tirelessly watches waves on sand.

Beneath the sennit-tied roof sat King Tamatoa, his big broad face deeply perturbed. "Why has a convocation been called?" he asked peremptorily. Then, as if fearing the answer, he quickly dismissed all who might be spies. Drawing closer on the tightly woven mat that formed the floor, he placed his two hands on his knees and asked, "What does it mean?"

Teroro, who did not see things quickly himself, was not above reciting his wife's analyses as his own, and now explained, "It looks to me as if our High Priest must be seeking promotion to the temple in Havaiki, but in order to be eligible he has to do something dramatic." He paused ominously.

"Like what?" the king asked.

"Like eliminating the last signs of Tane worship in Bora Bora. Like sacrificing you . . . at the height of the convocation."

"I'm fearful of just such a plot," Tamatoa confessed. "If he waits till we're in convocation, he could suddenly point at me the way they pointed at our father, and . . ." The troubled king made a slashing swipe at his brother's head, adding dolefully, "And my murder would be sanctified because Oro had ordained it."

"More likely the High Priest," Teroro corrected.

Tamatoa hesitated, as if probing his younger brother's mind, and then added petulantly, "And my death would go unavenged."

Self-pity was so alien to Tamatoa, whose warlike capacities and prudent leadership had kept little Bora Bora free from invasion by its larger neighbors, that Teroro suspected his brother of laying some kind of trap, so the younger man fought down his inclination to confess his own plans for the convocation and observed idly, "The canoe will be launched at noon."

"Will it be ready by sunset?" the king asked.

"It will, but I hope you won't be on it."

"I am determined to go to this convocation," Tamatoa replied.

"Only evil can befall you," Teroro insisted.

The king rose from his mats and walked disconsolately to the palace entrance, from which he could see the majestic cliffs of Bora Bora and the sun-swept lagoon. "On this island," he said with deep emotion, "I grew in joy. I have always walked in the shadow of those cliffs, and with those waves clutching at my ankles. I've seen the other islands, and the bays of Moorea are lovely. The crown at Tahiti is good to see, and the long beaches of Havaiki. But our island is man's heaven on earth. If I must be sacrificed to bring this island into harmony with new gods, then I will be sacrificed."

The images evoked by Tamatoa's memories of the Bora Bora of their youth accomplished what his guile had been unable to do, and Teroro cried, "Brother, do not go to Havaiki!"

"Why not?" Tamatoa asked, flashing around and moving back to the mats.

"Because your departure to the gods will not save Bora Bora."

"Why not?" Tamatoa demanded, thrusting his face close to Teroro's.

"Because when the club falls, I shall kill the High Priest. I will rage through all Havaiki and destroy it. Then the other islands will destroy us."

"As I thought!" the king cried sharply. "You have a plan to riot. Oh, Teroro, it will accomplish nothing. You cannot go to the convocation."

"I will be there," Teroro muttered stubbornly.

The king stood grave in the morning shadows and pointed his right forefinger at Teroro. "I forbid you to leave Bora Bora."

At this moment the warrior-king Tamatoa, burly and serious-faced, was a symbol of overpowering authority to his younger brother, and the projecting finger almost made Teroro tremble; for although he wanted to grasp his brother by that finger, and then by his hand, and finally by his strong arm and thus pull him down onto the mats for an honest conversation, the young chief could never have brought himself to touch the king, because he knew that the king was the instrumentality whereby the gods delivered mana—the spiritual sanctification of the heavens—to Bora Bora, and even to touch a king or pass upon his shadow was to drain away some of that mana and thus imperil not only the king but the entire society.

Yet Teroro's desire for words with his brother was so great that he prostrated himself on the matting, crept on his belly to him, and pressed his face close to the king's feet, whispering, "Sit with me, brother, and let us talk." And while the flies droned in morning heat, the two men talked.

They were a handsome pair, separated in age by six years, for a sister had been born between, and each was aware of the special bond that linked him to the other, for as boys their wrists had been opened one solemn day, and each had drunk the blood of the other. Their father, dead as a sacrifice to Oro, had named his first son Tamatoa, the Warrior; and then when a younger brother was born the family had reasoned: "How fortunate! When Tamatoa becomes king he will have his brother to serve him as high priest." And the younger child had been named Teroro, the Brain—the intelligent one, the man who can divine complex things quickly. But so far he had not proved his name to be appropriate.

Tamatoa, of course, had developed into a classical island warrior, rugged, big-boned and grave. Like his dedicated ancestors he had defended Bora Bora against all cabals and concentrations. Six times in his reign of nine years he had been called to beat back invaders from powerful Havaiki, so that the sudden supremacy of that island's new god, Oro, was especially galling; the ancient enemy seemed about to conquer by guile what it had never been able to take by force. Teroro, on the other hand, had not lived up to his name, and showed no signs of becoming a priest. Tall and wiry, with a handsome thin face, he loved brawling, had an impetuous temper and was slow to grasp abstract ideas. But his greatest failing was that he could not memorize genealogies or sacred chants. His love was navigation and the challenge of unknown seas. Already he had driven his canoe to distant Nuku Hiva, while a run down to Tahiti was familiar play.

"I am afraid it is for you the gods will send the rainbow," Tamatoa whispered.

"We have stood against them in the past, we can do so again."

"In the past they had canoes and spears. Now they have plans and plots. I don't feel hopeful."

"Are you afraid?" Teroro asked bluntly.

"Yes," the king confessed. "New ideas are afoot, and I can't seem to grasp them. How has the High Priest succeeded in manipulating our people so successfully?"

"New gods are popular, I suppose," Teroro hazarded. "When our people see many sacrifices they know the gods listen. It makes the island seem safer."

The king studied his brother for a moment, then asked cautiously, "Would it not be possible for you to accept their new god?"

"Impossible," Teroro said flatly. "I was born with the blessing of Tane. My father died defending Tane, and his father before him. I will never consider another god."

The king breathed deeply and said, "Those are my thoughts, too. But I am afraid the High Priest will destroy us, Teroro."

"How can he?" the impetuous young warrior demanded.

"By tricks, by plans, by clever ideas."

"I'll trick him!" Teroro cried in frustration. Slashing his hand across his knee he muttered, "I'll trick his head into a mass of coconut jelly."

"That's why you mustn't attend this convocation," Tamatoa said.

Teroro stood humbly before the king, yet spoke stubbornly: "Beloved brother, that is why I must go." Then, rising, he moved about the palace mats and said prophetically, "The High Priest will not destroy us. If we go down, he goes down with us. The whole island goes down. Brother, I swore to our father that I would protect you. I'm going to the convocation, to protect you. But I will give you my promise not to riot unless they strike you."

"They won't strike me, Teroro. They'll strike you."

"They had better strike with the speed of a hungry shark," Teroro laughed, and with this he walked out into the glorious high noon of Bora Bora, when the sun blazed overhead and filtered through palm fronds and breadfruit leaves, making soft patterns in the dust. Naked children called back and forth in their games, and fishermen hauled their canoes onto the beach. The soporific haze of noon, compounded of sunlight and dust, was upon the island, and all things were beautiful. How restful this moment was, when the sun hung for a moment in midheaven, casting no shadows; flies droned and old women slept.

Through the beautiful and dusty heat Teroro moved slowly to where the great ceremonial canoe of Bora Bora rested, and as he went he called, "Into the water! Into the water!"

From various grass houses along the lagoon, men appeared, drowsily wrapping themselves in tapa and swallowing the last bits of coconut. "Send for the priests to bless our canoe," Teroro called, and soon four holy men arrived, pleasure on their faces, for among all the functions of this island, there was nothing that exceeded in common joy the returning of the ceremonial canoe to its natural element. Palm fronds that had enclosed the seaward end of the long shed were taken down, and the twin hulls of the immense canoe were edged carefully toward the water. Then a rare old priest named Tupuna, his long white hair piled on his head and stuck with skewers, separated his beard, and with his eyes on the lagoon and on the open sea beyond, cried:

"Ta'aroa, god of the dark and sweeping sea,
Ta'aroa, master of tempest and gentle calm,
Ta'aroa, protector of men with vision of the reef,
Ta'aroa, take *Wait-for-the-West-Wind* to thy bosom,
Take it to Havaiki and to Moorea and to Nuku Hiva,
To the Black Shining Road of Ta'aroa,
To the Black Shining Road of Tane.
To the Road of the Spider,
To the Much-traveled Road of Ta'aroa.
God of the dark and sweeping sea,
Accept as thy gift, this canoe."

In silence and in spiritual exaltation, Teroro pulled away the last prop that bound his glorious canoe to land, and slowly it began to taste the lagoon, to dip its high-tiered stern into the gentle waves, and finally to ride upon the bosom of Ta'aroa, which was its home.

The young chiefs who would paddle the canoe that night now leaped into the two hulls and adjusted the movable seats that slid back and forth along the dugout sections. Teroro, grabbing his personal god-carved paddle, gave the canoe a mighty shove that sent it far into the lagoon, with him trailing his feet aft in the green waters. "Hoist sail!" he cried. "We'll test the wind." And when a noonday breeze dropped down from the cliff, it caught the sail and began to move the great double-hulled canoe, and men paddled briskly, and soon with lightning speed *Wait-for-the-West-Wind* hurtled across its home lagoon.

It flew like a special albatross, just dipping into the waves. It went like the wind-caught leaf of a breadfruit tree, skimming the waters. It went like a young woman hurrying to meet her lover, like the essence of the god Ta'aroa majestically inspecting the ramparts of his ocean. It sped like the spirit of a warrior killed in battle, on its swift journey to the everlasting halls of Tane. And it flashed across the lagoon like what it was: a miraculous, slim, double-hulled craft of Bora Bora, the swiftest ship the world at that time had ever known, capable of doing thirty knots in bursts, ten knots for days at a time, hour after hour; a huge, massive craft seventy-nine feet long, with a tiered stern twenty-two feet high and a solid platform slung across the hulls on which forty men or the statues of forty gods could ride, with pigs and pandanus and water stowed safely in the hidden innards.

"Wait for the west wind," the men who built the canoe had advised, "for it blows strong and sure from the heart of the hurricane." The north wind cannot be depended upon, and the east wind is no treasure, for it blows constantly, and the south wind brings nothing but irritating minor storms, never those that shake the earth, not storms that last for weeks at a time and which can be counted upon to drive a canoe to the farthest points of earth. Wait for the west wind! It blows from the heart of the hurricane. It is a wind to match this great canoe.

On this day, it was an ordinary eastern wind. Some of the world's sailors might even have counted it a considerable breeze, but to Bora Borans who longed for the westerly gale that could carry them even to distant Nuku Hiva, the day's wind was really nothing. But it did bear a hint of invitation, and so on the spur of the moment Teroro cried, "Through the reef!"

Wait-for-the-West-Wind was already doing better than fifteen knots, and a prudent navigator usually took his craft through this perilous reef at slowest speed, but on this sun-swept day Teroro shot his precious craft directly at the small opening that marked the dividing line between the placid green waters of the lagoon and the thundering blue ocean which pounded outside.

The canoe seemed to anticipate the impending crash of giant waves, for it tensed in the wind, cut a little deeper into the lagoon, and leaped toward the passageway through the reef. For an instant the crew could glimpse cruel fingers of gray coral clutching at the defiant craft, but this danger was quickly forgotten, for ahead loomed the towering waves.

With a song crying from its sail, with vigor to match that of the young chiefs who manned it, the swift canoe shot into the combers, lost its nose in a great gray-blue wave, then rose triumphantly onto the crest and sped away into the very center of the wind and the rousing waves and vast blue sea of Ta'aroa.

"What a canoe!" Teroro exulted, the spray whipping his black hair about his face.

It was with special exhilaration that the thirty paddlers tasted the last moments of freedom with which Teroro had provided them, for each man knew that at nightfall he would embark upon a different journey: solemn, joyless, with the constant threat of death impending. In their imagination they could see the altar where the blood would be. They could visualize the dreadful sacrificial clubs. But worse, each man knew positively that when *Wait-for-the-West-Wind* touched Havaiki's shore at dawn tomorrow one of today's crew would be struck down forever.

So in the day's bright sunlight, with spume about them and the sound of sea birds, they experienced momentary joy as they drove their swift canoe, champion of the islands, with the assurance that only competent men ever know. To their wishes the canoe responded; to their efforts it leaped forward; and now as they turned it in the free and joyous ocean, it responded as they willed, exactly to the inch as they intended, and found once more the opening through the reef, and came at last to shore. How competently these island men had built and mastered their canoe; how securely it obeyed their will.

BY NIGHTFALL *Wait-for-the-West-Wind* had assumed a much different aspect. The upswept sterns were decorated with flowers and pennants of yellow tapa. The permanent platform which held the two hulls together was covered with polished planks. At the forward end stood an ultra-sacred grass-thatched temple, toward which a solemn procession of priests in sacerdotal attire now moved in dread silence.

The High Priest, clad in white and with a fringe of shark's teeth about his ankles, a skullcap of red feathers on his black hair, proceeded to the grass temple and paused, at which all Bora Borans, king and slave alike, fell to the ground and hid their faces, for what was about to occur was too sacred for even a king to behold.

The feather-figured statue of Oro himself, woven of sennit and with sea shells as eyes, was about to be placed inside the temple for its journey to Havaiki. From his white robes the High Priest produced a wrapping of ti leaves, which hid the god, and holding the bundle high above him, he prayed in terrifying voice, then kneeled and placed the god inside the temple. He moved back, struck the canoe with his staff and cried, "*Wait-for-the-West-Wind,* take thy god safely to Havaiki!"

The prostrate crowd rose, no man speaking, and the paddlers assumed the positions they had held earlier that day. Next the seers of the island, old men of wisdom, stepped onto the polished platform wearing solemn brown tapa and skullcaps edged with dog's teeth. Some carried gourds with which to divine portents, while others studied the dying sun for auguries which they shared with no one.

Teroro, robed in yellow and wearing a warrior's helmet of feathers and shark's teeth, took his place in the prow, while the king, in precious yellow robes which covered his ankles, stood amidships. Silence resumed, and the High Priest announced that he was ready to accept the sacrifices.

Servants of Oro came forth with palm fronds which they spread in careful patterns, aft of the temple, and on these were laid strange gifts: a large fish from the lagoon, a shark caught at sea, a turtle taken on a special island, and a pig that had from birth been dedicated to Oro. These four dead sacrifices were not placed side by side, but about eighteen inches apart, and were promptly covered with additional palms.

Now, at the last moment, priests led forth the eight human sacrifices, and the people of Bora Bora, in awful silence, watched their neighbors depart for the last time. They saw the steersman who had been trapped praying to the old god Tane. And the man who had dozed in the temple. And the tardy lookout, and the sleepy young courtier. With grief the citizens watched them go. They were followed by four slaves, those unspeakable, untouchable things, known even in life as foul corpses.

As the intended victims were shoved aboard, the wife of one of the slaves, if a slave's woman could be so dignified, uttered a piercing scream. "Auwe! Auwe!" she lamented, reciting that heart-tearing word of the islands that has always been reserved for moments of supreme anguish.

Her outcry was such an appalling breach of discipline, especially on the part of a slave, that all in the canoe shivered with apprehension at such an evil omen. Teroro thought: "Now our island is truly disgraced. The king will surely be sacrificed." King Tamatoa thought: "The High Priest will have a right to be outraged. My brother is doomed." The thirty paddlers thought: "They may have to sacrifice two of us tomorrow."

The High Priest thought nothing. He was too astonished by this infraction of the tabu to do anything but point his staff at the offending woman, whereupon four priests grabbed her, rushed her to the lagoon, and pinioned her head under water. But with demonic strength the slave broke loose from their grasp, got her head free, and wailed prophetically: "Auwe! Auwe, Bora Bora!"

A priest struck her in the face with a rock, and when she staggered backward, two other priests leaped upon her and held her under the water until she died. But this did not compensate for the broken tabu, and the High Priest cried, "Whose woman was she?" Someone pointed to one of the slaves in the canoe, and the High Priest nodded slightly.

Swiftly, from the rear of the platform a burly priest, custodian of this job for many years, stepped forward and with a mighty swing of a knobbed war club crushed the skull of the unsuspecting slave. The body slumped, but before its blood could stain the canoe, it was pitched headfirst into the lagoon, where the swimming priests gathered it up as a sacrifice for their local altar. Automatically, from the shore, a substitute slave was whisked aboard, and amid such disasters and ominous portents, *Wait-for-the-West-Wind* headed out to sea. This time, as if sharing the guilt that had settled upon the passengers, the canoe did not spring lightly toward the reef but moved reluctantly, so that by the time the stars had risen for Teroro to steer by, *Wait-for-the-West-Wind* had covered only a small portion of its gloomy journey to the temple of Oro on the island of Havaiki.

Toward dawn, when the constellation which astronomers in other parts of the world had long since named the Lion was rising in the east, the seers whose responsibility it was to determine such things, sagely agreed that the time was near. The High Priest was consulted, and he confirmed the fact that the red-tipped hour of dawn, sacred to Oro, was at hand. He nodded, and a huge, slack-headed drum was struck in slow rhythm, sending its cry far out to sea.

The rest of the world was silent. Even the lapping waves and birds who customarily cried at dawn were supposed to cease their murmuring at the approach of dread Oro. There was only the drum, until, as night paled and red streamers rose in the east, Teroro caught the sound of another drum, and then a third, far in the distance. The canoes, still invisible to one another, were beginning to assemble for the solemn procession into the channel of Havaiki. Now the drums increased their beat, until a vast throbbing was set up—hammering, hammering—and the red dawn increased, and over the silent sea one could begin to spot tall sails and mournful pennants hanging in the breezeless air. The High Priest moved his hands faster, and the drummers speeded their beat, and the paddlers began to move the canoe, always in silence, toward the gathering place, and as the red sun burst from its pit in the horizon, eleven canoes, brilliant in color and sacrificial gifts, stood forth and formed two majestic lines, each headed for the temple of Oro; but as they moved and as Teroro studied them carefully, he concluded with satisfaction: "No one has a canoe like ours."

The drums abruptly stopped, and the High Priest began an agitated chant, into the middle of which a terrifying, inhuman sound intruded: it was the frenzied beating of a very long, small-headed drum which gave an anguished cry, and as it rose to its climax, the High Priest screamed, and the burly executioner swung his studded club and crushed the head of the tall young courtier who had slept when he should have been awake.

Reverently, priestly attendants caught the corpse while others removed the palms that had covered the earlier sacrifices: the fish, the shark, the turtle and the pig. It now became obvious why spaces eighteen inches wide had been left between these offerings, for into the first gaping slot was carefully fitted the dead body of the courtier.

The chanting resumed and the dreadful drum began a new lament for the feckless lookout. The club fell with great fury, and the body was tenderly slipped in between the shark and the turtle. Three more times the frenzied little drum was beaten, and in the red light of dawn the awful club crashed down upon some head, so that when day commenced, the fore part of the platform was filled with Bora Bora's diocesan statue of Oro, wrapped in ti leaves and wreathed in golden feathers, surveying the five fresh human sacrifices that lay interspersed with the fish, the shark, the turtle and the pig. Each of the other ten canoes, their wild drums wailing, had offered identical sacrifices, and all now moved the last half mile to the temple.

The travelers in *Wait-for-the-West-Wind* had varied thoughts as they approached the sacred landing, but on one thing all agreed: it was reasonable for a god to require special sacrifices on days of particular solemnity, and as for the customary four slaves, no one was concerned about their deaths, especially since one of their congregation had broken a tabu so shamelessly. Slaves were ordained for sacrifice.

The High Priest reasoned, in these last minutes, that considering Bora Bora's stupid persistence in allegiance to Tane the more sacrifices made to Oro the better, particularly when one of them happened to be yesterday's steersman, a man notoriously dedicated to Tane. "Weed them out, root and branch," he muttered to himself. He did not consider the five men so far sacrificed an unusual number, nor did he think that the four more who were marked for sure death, nor the slave and his wife, nor the chance ones that would be killed at the convocation itself exceeded a reasonable limit. Oro was a powerful god. He had accomplished what no other god before him had attained: the consolidation of all the islands; it was only appropriate that he be honored. Prayers, respect and observance of tabus had always been accorded all gods, but a master god like Oro merited supreme sacrifices like sharks and men. Far from feeling that a quota of nine was excessive, he was already dreaming of the time when Bora Bora could invade some outward island and return with thirty or forty captives to be offered up at one sublime ceremonial. "We must impress the islands," he mused.

King Tamatoa's thoughts were different. To be sure, he felt no regret or responsibility for the death of his tardy lookout and his one-time courtier. They had failed, and death was customarily the penalty for failure. Nor could he lament in any way the four foul corpses; slaves were born to be sacrificed, but he was personally ashamed that one of his slaves had been so weak as to cry out merely because her man was being taken to Oro. Tamatoa looked upon a reasonable number of sacrifices as the simplest way of obtaining a steady flow of mana, but he nevertheless felt considerable uneasiness over the fact that the total of sacrifices for any given convocation had now been established as nine, plus more perhaps according to the chances of the day. Bora Bora was not a large island. Its men were numbered, and if in the past they had maintained their freedom it was because of their superior courage. The king wondered: "Is this sudden conversion to Oro a device by the wise men of Havaiki whereby they can depopulate my island and thus accomplish by guile what they have always been unable to do by battle?" He was deeply perplexed by a further haunting possibility: "Do you suppose the priests at Havaiki are teasing our High Priest along with promises of promotion only until such time as he has disposed of Teroro and me?" Then, for the first time he expressed in words his real perplexity: "It is very difficult to be king when the gods are changing."

Teroro saw things more simply. He was outraged. His thoughts were forthright and purposeful. The death of slaves he could condone, for that was the law of the world, on every island. But to execute for trivial reasons the best fighters on Bora Bora, merely to appease a new god, was obviously wrong and disastrous. "Look at the body of Terupe, lying there between the shark and the turtle! He was the best steersman I ever had. And the High Priest knew it. And Tapoa, useless beside the shark. He was wise and would have made a good counselor." Teroro was so furious that he did not trust himself to look either at his brother or at the High Priest, lest he uncover his thoughts. Instead, he contented himself with staring ahead at the impressive canoes and listening to the mournful drums, speaking of death. He thought: "Unless we settle the High Priest now, these drums are the requiem of Bora Bora." He saw clearly that the death of eight or ten more key warriors would lay the island open to assault. "I'll work out a plan," he swore to himself.

The minor priests looked with some satisfaction upon the sacrifices already consummated and those about to occur. With the advent of Oro, each priest had faced an inner struggle: "Shall I go over to the new god, or shall I remain faithful to Tane?" It was gratifying to know that one had chosen the winner. The priests acknowledged that there remained some dissidence in the island, but they had observed that after each convocation, adherence to Tane weakened. "Sacrifices help us attract the attention of Oro," they rationalized, "and then he sends us mana." Their conclusions were influenced perhaps by the fact that as priests they could be reasonably sure that they would not be sacrificed to obtain mana; their role in the upcoming ceremonies was simple and known: to hoist the sacrifices into place, to eat the sacrificial roast pig, also the boiled bananas, the baked taro and the salted fish. And when the convocation ended, they had to throw the human bodies into the sacred pit. There was an exhilaration about Oro that other gods did not have, and they felt gratified that they had been among the first to join his side.

The thirty rowers had only one thought: "Will it be I?"

And the three remaining slaves had no thoughts . . . none, that is, that would have been remotely comprehensible to the non-slaves in the canoe; for curiously, these three men, even though each had known from birth that he was doomed, had exactly the same fears, the same sick feeling beneath their hearts, and the same unaccustomed sweat in their armpits as did the men who were not slaves. But this would never have been believed.

The palpitations of the slaves did not continue long, for on the instant that Teroro touched his canoe onto the beach of Havaiki, the burly priest flashed his brutal club and killed first one, then two, then three. Their bodies were pitched onto the runway up which the canoe was to be drawn, and soon every passenger who had come in the canoe, even the king and the High Priest, bent himself to the hallowed task of hauling the mighty craft ashore and onto a small plateau where it would be consecrated for the coming year.

At the precise moment when the canoe came to rest, the High Priest whirled in the morning sunlight and dipped his staff toward one of Teroro's most trusted companions, and before the man could move, the awful club descended and his skull was cleft in two. His body was strung from the stern to stand guard during the ceremonial days. The surviving crewmen, aghast at the rank of the man who had been slain, tried in deepest shame to prevent the thought that rose to their hearts: "It was not I."

The convocation was planned to last three days, during which no sound but the problems of priests should be heard. Assemblies took place in an extensive, roofless rock temple perched on a magnificent plateau overlooking the ocean across which the participating canoes had come. It was a low, sprawling edifice paved with blocks of black lava, from which even blades of grass had been swept. At one end an inner temple, thatched with palm, had been constructed, and in it reposed the ark which housed the holy of holies, the ultimate statue of Oro.

The exposure of this source-god, the essential being of Oro himself, was so solemn an undertaking that not even kings or their brothers could witness the ceremony; they were excluded during the first august meeting when Oro was taken from his ark.

There were, however, witnesses. From each canoe the five human sacrifices had been hauled to the temple, plus five from Havaiki itself, and had been stacked in a pile for Oro's approval. When through his highest priest Oro granted assent—the priest-as-man thinking: "It's impressive, seeing so many bodies at once. Proves the islands are beginning to demonstrate their love for Oro"—lesser priests stepped forward and engaged in one of the convocation's most solemn rituals.

With long bone needles, threaded with golden sennit, they pierced the left eardrum of each corpse, thrust the needle on through the dead brain, and jerked the sennit out through the right ear. Then, fashioning a long loop, they strung each of the sixty corpses onto trees surrounding the temple, and for the succeeding hours these sacrificial men were free to gaze with dead eyes upon what not even kings could witness.

Tamatoa was required to sit apart with his brother kings, absolutely silent for seven hours, for spies supervised the kings to note any who failed in just homage to Oro; but in truth this was not necessary, for the twelve kings appreciated that their divinity derived from some august ultimate source beyond themselves, and their reservoirs of mana required constant replenishment through sacrifice and prayer. The world itself, in terrified silence, now paid reverence as mana flowed into both island statues and island kings.

The temple grounds were not entirely silent, and had this fact been ascertained by spies, those who were secretly breaking the tabu would have been instantly sacrificed; but Teroro knew this, and for his hushed conversations with his twenty-nine remaining crewmen he had chosen a remote glade ringed by palms.

"Are we willing to speak with frankness?" he asked.

"What risk do we run?" a fiery young chief named Mato asked. "If we talk they will kill us. If we remain silent . . ." He bashed his fist into his hand. "Let's talk."

"Why should so many of our men be given to Oro?" another asked.

Teroro listened to the complaints and then said, "I have been willing to run the risk of getting you here, because it doesn't matter whether there's a spy among us or not." He stared at each of his men and continued: "If one of you is a spy, inform the High Priest, because that will scare him from carrying out what I think is his plan. If no one betrays us, we're even better off."

"What is your plan?" Mato, from the north side of Bora Bora, asked.

Teroro held a small length of sennit, which he twisted and untwisted, saying slowly, "I think the High Priest intends to offer our king as a supreme sacrifice to Oro. He wants to impress the other priests with his control over Bora Bora. But he's got to give the signal himself, because if he kills by stealth, where would be his political advantage? So we must watch the High Priest constantly."

The young chiefs sat silent, because whatever Teroro divulged as his plan was bound to involve maximum danger. Then a lesser noble pointed out: "It isn't today we have to worry about."

"That's right," Teroro agreed. "Today they're occupied." And he indicated the ghastly circle of dead men dancing in trees.

"But what about the general meeting tomorrow?"

Teroro untwisted the sennit and nodded judiciously. "If I were the High Priest," he said, "with his plans, I'd strike tomorrow."

Mato was in reckless mood, for during an awful moment that morning he had felt sure that the High Priest was going to nominate him as the skull-split guardian of the canoe. He said sternly, "I think that if the priest even begins to point at Tamatoa, we must surround the king and fight our way to the canoe."

"I think exactly the same thing," Teroro said abruptly.

There was a long silence as the other twenty-eight men contemplated what such a bold step involved, but before any could turn away in cowardice Teroro threw down the sennit and spoke rapidly: "To succeed we must insure three things. First, we must somehow move our canoe to the top of the hill so that we can rush it into the water without cutting down our speed."

"I'll take care of that," Hiro the steersman promised.

"How?"

"I don't know."

Teroro liked his honest answer but nevertheless pushed his face to within a few inches of the steersman's. "You know that if the canoe is not in position, we will all die?"

"I do," the young chief said grimly.

"Next," Teroro said, "we must have two very determined men sitting on the rocks at the temple exit."

Brash Mato cried, "I'm one, and I want Pa for the other."

A wiry shark-faced man with no chin, Pa, the Fortress, stepped forward and announced: "I'm the other."

"You may not escape," Teroro warned them.

"We'll escape," Mato swore. "Men of Havaiki have never . . ."

"The third requirement," Teroro said impatiently, "is that each of the rest of us be prepared to kill instantly anyone who moves toward Tamatoa."

"We know the executioners," Pa growled.

"And once we make a move, we must sweep Tamatoa up and with an unbroken rush get him to the canoe." He paused and then added softly, "It sounds dangerous, but once we are seaborne, *Wait-for-the-West-Wind* will be our safeguard."

"They will never catch us," the steersman promised.

"And if they did, what could they do?" Mato boasted, and as the men talked it was apparent that all wished they were in the certainty of the canoe and not in the temple grounds of Oro, which were alien and unknown.

"This will be the signal," Teroro said. "You will watch me, and the moment I move to defend the king, the steersman must dash for the canoe and you men must see that he gets through the exit."

"Who will disarm the executioner?" Mato asked.

"I will," Teroro said coldly. Then, to inspire his men, he boasted, "No club will fall tomorrow swifter than my arm."

The men appreciated this assurance, but Mato killed their ardor by stating, "There is one grave fault in this plan."

"What?" Teroro asked.

"Yesterday, before we sailed, Marama took me aside and said, 'My husband is sure that the High Priest plans to kill the king. But I am certain that Teroro himself is the target.' I think your wife is right. What do we do if she is?"

Teroro could not reply. He could see only his patient, worried wife moving among the men, enlisting their promises to protect him. He looked at the ground, recovered the sennit he had been twisting, and placed it in his belt. It was shark-faced Pa who spoke. "Marama spoke to me, too," he said, "and our duty is clear. If they strike at the king, everything goes as planned. But if they strike at Teroro, you, Mato, with your men save the king and I with mine will rescue Teroro."

"I am not the important one," Teroro said honestly.

"To us you are," his men replied, and they proceeded with their plans.

But there was a mind at work that night much keener than either Mato's or Pa's, and it belonged to the High Priest. During the most solemn part of the convocation he had been thinking, and when great Oro was returned to the ark, the High Priest called his assistants to him, and they sat cross-legged in a shadowy corner of the great temple, with the bodies of men dancing above them in the night air.

"Have you noticed anything today?" he began.

"Only that you are right," a young priest reported. "Teroro is our mortal enemy."

"What makes you say that?"

"As you directed, I studied him constantly. Four separate times I caught him struggling against the will of Oro, terrible be the name."

"When?"

"Principally, when the king's courtier was slain. He drew back, markedly."

"I thought so, too," the High Priest agreed.

"And when one of his crew was sacrificed to guard the canoe."

"He did?"

"And it seemed to me that when it came time for Teroro to lead the king away from the temple, while we came in, he acted joyously rather than in sorrow."

"We thought so, too," several priests chorused.

"But what confirms it is that this afternoon Teroro must have held some kind of meeting with his men."

"Is that correct?" the High Priest snapped.

"I can't be sure, because as you know, I had to leave him when we entered the temple, but immediately after Oro was returned to the ark, I slipped out to check on our men."

"What did you find?"

"Nothing. They had vanished."

"How could they?" the High Priest demanded.

"I don't know, but they had vanished."

"Was the king with them?"

"No," the spy reported. "He sat properly with the other kings."

"Can we be sure that Teroro held a meeting? If we were sure . . ."

"I searched everywhere," the young spy insisted, "and in my own heart I am sure."

For a long time the High Priest contemplated this unwelcome news, fingering his staff and driving it into the ground. Finally he mused: "If we could be certain that a meeting was held, we could eliminate the entire canoe. We would . . ." But when he weighed all consequences he apparently decided against this, for he suddenly turned to his burly executioner and said softly, "Tomorrow I don't want you at any time to stand either near the king or near Teroro. Keep completely away. You, Rere-ao," and he addressed his spy, "are you as swift of club as you once were?"

"I am."

"You are to place yourself inconspicuously so that at an instant's signal you can kill Teroro. You are to watch him constantly. If he makes even the slightest move. Anything . . ."

"Do I wait for a signal from you?" Rere-ao asked.

"No, but as you strike I will point at him, and his dead body will be sacred to Oro."

The High Priest moved on to discuss their roles with others, but he soon returned to Rere-ao and asked, "You understand? You don't wait for a signal. You kill him if he moves."

"I understand."

The High Priest concluded his meeting with a long prayer to Oro, at the end of which he told his men, "One way or another, tomorrow will see Bora Bora finally delivered to Oro. The old gods are dead. Oro lives."

His assistant priests breathed deeply with excitement, for their struggle to implant their new god on the backs of Tane and Ta'aroa had not been easy, and for several months they had longed for some positive event of magnitude to assure them that they had won. Their leader, sensing this desire for the spectacular, cautioned them: "There are many roads to ultimate victory, my brothers. Oro has many paths by which he can travel to triumph. Tomorrow one of them will result in his final capture of Bora Bora, but you must not anticipate which one. That is up to Oro."

With this the High Priest folded his hands, took off his skullcap, and inclined his head toward the inner sanctuary of Oro. His fellow priests did likewise, and in the deep silence of the night, dimly lit by distant fires and the glow of shimmering stars, the holy men prayed to their all-powerful god. It was a solemn moment at the end of an exciting day, a moment sweet and meaningful, with the essence of immortality hovering above the assembly, the sacrifices in place, great Oro brooding over his faithful, and all the world subdued in silent reverence to him. At such a moment, with the greatness of Oro pulsing in the night and throbbing in the veins more powerfully than the beat of a drum, it was incomprehensible to the priests that anyone should cling to old gods when the new deity was so powerful, so rational and so benevolent.

Next morning Hiro the steersman was up early, and with a sharp rock hidden in tapa he slashed several of the sennit strands that bound *Wait-for-the-West-Wind* together, shuddering with regret as he did so, then burying the rock and hurrying to the priest in charge of the canoe's welfare to announce: "We must have scraped coral."

The priest hurried to the canoe, which rested under the surveillance of the dead crewman lashed to the stern, and studied the broken sennit. "It can be mended with fresh cord," he said, hoping to get the accident repaired before the High Priest blamed him for it.

"Yes," the crewman agreed, "and we ought to do it while we are all under the protection of Oro."

Such sentiment charmed the priest, and he was therefore receptive when Hiro suggested, "Wouldn't it be easier to drag the canoe out here, where the sun can tighten the new sennit?" And they edged the canoe into the exact position Teroro required.

"Will the mending take long?" the priest asked.

"No," Hiro assured him. "I mustn't miss the convocation of Oro."

"You must not," the priest agreed, recalling the High Priest's assurances of the night before that on this day Oro would consolidate his victory over Bora Bora, and it seemed a good omen that Hiro, one of Teroro's prominent supporters, had thus voluntarily signified his affection for Oro.

The convocation began with a startling scene, so that all who later reviewed the day agreed that it had been doomed from the beginning, although at the time that was not apparent, since the priests had quickly converted an error into a blessing. The assembly had seated itself on rocks stretching out from the main altar, and the first two pigs were being disemboweled when a boy of seven came running into the temple, crying for his father who sat near the altar.

"Father!" the lost little child shouted.

The man, a lesser chief of Havaiki, looked in horror at the approach of his son, for the boy had committed so vast a sin that no excuse could pardon it. No woman, or child, or animal had ever strayed into the temple, and the father's arms trembled as he gathered the handsome little fellow to his heart.

"I was looking for you, Father," the lost child whimpered.

In austere silence the priests at the altar, their sacrifices to Oro interrupted, stared at the offending child. His father, aware of the tabu his family had broken, rose haltingly with the boy still in his arms. Suddenly, in an act of total dedication, he thrust his son toward the altar, the child's hair falling over his father's strong left arm.

With anguished but unfaltering conviction the man spoke: "Take this child and sacrifice him to Oro! For the consecration of the temple has been broken by him, the thread of our union with Oro has been entangled. He is my son. I begat him. But I do not weep in losing him, for he has outraged Oro."

At first the priests ignored the man and left him standing with the boy in his arms while with haughty indifference they finished slaughtering the pigs. Then, with fresh blood for Oro on their hands, two priests picked up a pair of stout bamboo rods. Holding one pair of ends rigidly together, they opened the others and formed a giant pincers which they deftly dropped over the child's head, one bamboo catching him at the nape of the neck, the other across the throat. With remorseless force they closed the pincers and held the little boy aloft until he strangled. Then, with one swift slash, the High Priest laid open the child's stomach and ripped out the entrails, placing the body reverently on the highest altar, between the pigs.

"This father does well," the priest droned. "All do well who honor Oro. Great Oro, bringer of peace."

The incident unnerved Teroro, because he recognized it as an omen for this faithful day, but how to interpret it was beyond him, and for a moment in his perplexity he forgot his brother whom he had come to protect. "What could such an omen signify?" he asked stubbornly, but no answer was forthcoming, so he breathed deeply and attended to his business; yet when he looked across the temple square toward the steersman Hiro, to check the man's position, he came upon a second omen which had to be interpreted as ominous: the present steersman sat directly under the swaying body of the earlier steersman who had been killed at the whim of the High Priest, and the corpse's distended belly, already disintegrating in the tropical heat, hung heavy over Teroro's accomplice.

In confusion Teroro dismissed all omens and watched first the High Priest and then the king, for he was totally resolved to defy Oro, even if it had to be done in the very seat of the red god's omnipotence. But he was not prepared for the High Priest's strategy, for while Teroro was anticipating an entirely different tactic, the priest suddenly whirled and pointed his staff at one of the least offensive members of Teroro's crew, and one of the finest warriors.

"He ate of the sacred pig of Oro!" the accuser shouted, but the young chief did not know why he died, for the burly executioner had anticipated the charge and had already crushed the man's skull.

Priests from other islands, gratified that Oro was being protected from apostasy, chanted: "All-powerful is Oro, the peace-giver, Oro of the united islands."

As they continued their droning, Teroro sat stunned. The young chief had been his special friend, an unassuming warrior who could not possibly have eaten sacred pig. Why had he been sacrificed? Teroro could not focus upon the problem. He had a fine plan to protect King Tamatoa, and he knew that if he himself were menaced, Mato would save him. But he had not foreseen the High Priest's clever assault upon lesser members of the Bora Bora community.

In dismay Teroro looked at the steersman, who stared with equal dismay at him. No answer was available there, so Teroro tried to catch the eyes of Mato and Pa, at the exit, but they were obsessed by the altar, where the body of their companion now lay. The other members of Teroro's plot were equally stunned, and in mounting confusion their leader stared at the polished rocks which formed the platform on which they had convened.

Of the Bora Bora contingent, only one man saw clearly in these awful moments. Tamatoa, like many successful kings, was gifted not with marked intellectual ability but with a powerful, stolid insight; and he realized that the High Priest had determined not to assassinate Tamatoa and his brother, but to drive them from the islands by irresistible pressure, constantly applied. "He will avoid a direct confrontation," the king reasoned. "There will be no battle. Patiently and with cunning he will alienate and terrify my people, and we will have to go."

Tamatoa was confirmed in his analysis when the High Priest whirled his staff of death at another member of Teroro's crew, and the terrible club of death descended once more. Sick at heart, King Tamatoa looked at his younger brother and saw Teroro befuddled and distraught. The king thought: "He probably had some grandiose plan to save my life today, and probably the High Priest had spies who told him the whole plot. Poor young man."

In his compassion, the king kept his eyes fixed on his brother until, bedazed, the latter looked up. Almost imperceptibly the older man shook his head, cautioning his brother not to act, not in any way. Teroro, catching the message, sat numb in fury.

It was at this moment, in the sacred temple of Oro, with the bodies of his finest men dangling before him and strewn upon the altar, that King Tamatoa whispered in his heart: "Oro, you have triumphed. You are the ultimate god, and I am powerless to oppose you." When he had said these words of contrition, a great peace came over him and he saw, as if in a revealing vision, how foolish he had been to combat the will of the inevitable. New gods were being born, and new gods conquer; but what Tamatoa did not realize was that the contentment of soul which his confession induced was merely the prerequisite for a decision toward which he had been fumbling for some months, but from which he had always hitherto retreated. Now that he had accepted the obvious—that Oro had conquered—the next obvious conclusion was easy to reach, and in the stillness of the morning Tamatoa said the fatal words for the first time, and in uttering them an enormous burden was lifted from his heart: "We will depart from Bora Bora and leave it to you, Oro. We will go upon the sea and find other islands where we can worship our own gods."

During the rest of the convocation, King Tamatoa did not confide his decision to anyone, not even to Teroro. In fact, he avoided his hot-headed younger brother, but he did summon Mato, to whom he spoke harshly: "I hold you responsible for my brother's life, Mato. If he has plots afoot, I am sure you are part of them. He must not die, even if you have to tie him to the canoe. He must not die. I need him now more than ever."

So when Teroro convened his bewildered companions to dream up some new fantasy, Mato spoke first: "We must go back to Bora Bora and plan our revenge."

"We'll go back and work out a plan," shark-faced Pa seconded.

With the decision taken from his hands Teroro could only mutter, "We will have revenge! That we will have!" and thinking only of some utter destruction and disaster, he bided his time.

WHEN A CONVOCATION ended, the priests wisely withdrew and encouraged the population to release its tensions in a wild, spontaneous celebration that sometimes lasted for three days. Now women were free to join their men, and musicians crowded the night with echoes. Beautiful girls, flashing bits of brown radiance dressed in skirts of aromatic leaves, swept into the mad hula of Havaiki and danced provocatively before the visitors of other islands, as if to challenge: "Do the women of Tahiti have soft breasts like ours? Can they move their knees to music the way we can?"

One spectator watched the dances and muttered to himself, "May the women of Havaiki be damned." Teroro would take no part in the celebration. Neither the magic hammering of the excited drums, nor the sweet voices of older women chanting love songs, nor the beauty of the girls enticed him to join the dancers. When special beauties, their bodies illuminated by palm-frond torches and etched in smoke from the fires where pigs roasted, danced past him in direct invitation, he would look at the ground and mutter to himself, "I will destroy this island. I will kill every priest of Oro. I will desolate . . ."

His men could not maintain such powerful resolve. One by one the young chiefs threw aside their spears, wiped their hands on their bare chests and leaped into the dancing circle, shouting and entering into the wild gyrations of the Havaiki hula. When they had driven themselves into an ecstasy, they would leap high into the air, slap their thighs and prance for a moment before their equally frenzied partners. Then each would pause, look at the other, and break into laughter, whereupon the girl would unconcernedly start to walk idly toward the shadows, her partner following with equal unconcern until at the last they gave a cry and rushed together to the seclusion of some protected glade.

As they disappeared, old women in the chanting circle were free to shout encouragement, usually of the grossest kind, at which the general audience roared with approval.

"He'll be tired before she is!" one old woman predicted.

"Show him what Havaiki's famous for, Rere," another screamed.

"Don't let him stop till he begs for mercy," the first added.

"Auwe!" another cried. "Make the moon hide its face for shame!"

"Remember what I taught you, Rere!" the first chanter shouted. "Don't make him do all the work."

When the advice became almost unbearably clinical, the general audience collapsed into gales of merriment, the music halted, and everyone rolled about the earth in animal joy. What delight the wildness of sex brought with it. Then the tiniest drum—no more than eight inches of hollowed-out branch beaten with a wand—would begin a wild, high rhythm that could almost compel a man to dance, and larger drums would pick it up, and soon some other of Teroro's men would begin dancing with a dark Havaiki girl, and they too would go into the shadows accompanied by ribald advice from the lusty old women, for an island hula was meaningless unless at its climactic moment a man and woman so desired each other that they were propelled explosively into fulfillment.

Teroro alone was not captured by the mystery and joy of this night. He did not even look up when the leading heckler shouted, "I always thought there was something wrong with the men of Bora Bora. Tetua, dance over there and tell me if he's capable!" A marvelous young girl of fifteen danced almost on Teroro's toes, flashing her body very close to his. When he ignored her, she ran laughing into the middle of the fire-rimmed circle and shouted, "He can't do!"

The old woman cackled above the drums, "I keep wondering how they have babies on Bora Bora. Men from Havaiki must swim over at night!"

At this sally Teroro had to look up, and against his will he had to smile at the raucous old woman, for islanders loved wit and liked to acknowledge it, even when directed against themselves. The old chanter, seeing that she had pierced Teroro's indifference, cried passionately, "Auwe! If I were only twenty years younger, I'd explain to you what men were made for!" When the crowd roared she shouted, "I can even yet!" And she started an outrageous hula, moving toward Teroro with her white hair dancing in the night and the memory of great sexual feats animating her hips. She was prepared to make a great fool of Teroro, but at this moment a famous chief of Havaiki, fat Tatai who guarded the temple, appeared and said quietly, "We would like you to eat with us, Teroro." And he led the young chief away from the fires, but not away from the old woman's biting tongue, for as the two men disappeared she screamed, "Oh, now I understand. It's men he likes."

Fat Tatai laughed and said, "Only death will silence that one's tongue." He led Teroro to the outskirts of the village, where his imposing family grounds had for centuries been enclosed on three sides by a rock wall head-high, the fourth side free to open on the ocean. As he entered the enclosure, Teroro saw dimly eight or nine grass houses and he could identify each: the main sleeping hall, the women's hall, the women's cook house, and the separate houses for each of Tatai's favorite wives.

It was to the men's area that fat Tatai took his guest, and there, in moonlight and to the music of waves, the feast was spread.

Teroro had barely finished licking burnt pig fat from his fingers when to the west of the compound a tiny drum, beaten frantically with a length of wood, began its persuasive chatter, followed by the steadier throbbing of several big drums as the musicians entered. "I wonder why Tatai bothered to set such a feast for me?" Teroro mused, pushing away the food. He wandered to a group seated by a fire and watched casually the figures that began to materialize from the night's soft shadows. They were the women of the Havaiki chiefs, and in tones less raucous than Teroro had recently heard in the village square, they began the haunting strains of old island love songs, and the bitterness went out of his heart:

"When the rolling surf
And the rising moon
And the swaying palm
And the high white bird
And the lazy fish
All speak of love,
I cry in the night:
Where are you, love?"

It was to the strains of this languorous island song that Teroro saw approaching him, in the gentle rhythms of a chief's hula, a slim, wiry-hipped girl of fourteen with midnight-black hair that fell to her knees. She swayed delicately, her dark eyes fixed on the ground, but when the plaintive old song ended, she raised her right finger about two inches from the fall of her ti-leaf skirt, shimmering in the flares, and indicated a swifter beat, which the drums initiated.

Now she danced on her toes, her knees and elbows out in an excitingly awkward position, with the fronds of her ti-leaf skirt whirling about her handsome legs. In this dance she allowed her face to show, and it was remarkably beautiful, and she brought it close to Teroro's, her full young breasts almost brushing his hands.

Against his will Teroro gazed back at her dark eyes and for a moment was inspired to leap to his feet and join her in the dance; but he felt that he must ignore Havaiki women, since he would one day destroy this evil place. He felt no burning sexual desire, for on Bora Bora he had always been allowed almost any girl he wanted; like all young chiefs, at puberty he had been handed over to an older woman who had instructed him long and intimately in the proper behavior of men and what pleases women, and it was this preceptor who had selected his first four partners. Later, after long consultations with a genealogist, the instructress had decided that moon-faced Marama was the girl he must marry. "She will fit you appropriately in all ways," the older woman had decided, and she was right. His subsequent girls Teroro had picked for himself, and sex had been as natural to him as swimming, so that now he was constrained to ignore the dancing girl before him, except that when he saw the look of intense disappointment on her face he felt ashamed, and against his better judgment, looked at her and smiled. And in that instant he saw her framed against palm trees, with long black tresses glistening in the fires, and on some surging impulse he leaped to his feet, whirled into the dancing area and positioned himself before her, swinging his body in the frenzied postures of the even more erotic Bora Bora hula.

Now the beautiful young girl acted as if she had never seen her new partner before. Dancing impersonally, her eyes far away, she led the drums to faster rhythms until in mounting fire her entire body quivered and a soft glow of perspiration reflected from every angle of her golden brown skin. She bent her knees and danced close to the ground. Then, in the most characteristic passage of the Havaiki hula, she spread her knees as if entertaining a man in love, whereupon the drums retarded their beat to allow her movements to become slow and madly provocative. She closed her dark eyes and held her head far back. With one hand she caught the ends of her hair and passed them between her teeth.

Over her a savagely aroused Teroro danced until with a fiery leap he sprang high into the air, descending with his toes not inches from hers. He now bent his body, spreading his knees, and for at least a minute the two bronzed bodies swayed until a woman shouted, "Auwe!" and the drums rose to new violence and the dancers entered upon the final wild gyrations.

Then, magically, everything stopped. There was dead silence, and the young girl, walking slowly like a sea goddess come ashore, moved demurely toward the shadows that marked the sleeping areas of the compound. When she had vanished, Teroro with maximum indifference stooped to throw a driftwood brand into the fire. Then tardily, like a boy summoned to a temple, he started edging toward the shadows, but this was too much for one of the chief's women, and she called in a wild, penetrating voice, "Take your skirt off, Tehani, I can't make you another."

He found her waiting for him in the far corner of the compound, before a small house which her family had reserved for her on her thirteenth birthday, for island parents encouraged their daughters to experiment with many young men and to learn the ways of love, since potential husbands did not like to marry any girl who had not already proved that she could bear children.

"This is my house," she said simply.

"What is your name?"

"I am Tehani, Chief Tatai's daughter."

"Tehani," Teroro interpreted. "The little darling."

The girl laughed nervously and replied, "My mother was beautiful." With a swift passage of his arm about her hair-hidden waist, Teroro swept Tehani into the air and carried her into her house. Happily, she twisted her long tresses about his face and pressed her lips to his. When he had placed her on the soft pandanus mats she pulled away her skirt of ti leaves and said, "It was my mother who warned me not to tear the skirt." And she pulled Teroro onto her and wrapped her arms about him, twisted and sought him, pressing him ever more strongly to her. But later, as he lay in the starlight that drifted in through the doorway, he swore to himself: "I will destroy this compound . . . this whole island."

But in the morning, after he had eaten in the men's house, where his adventure with Tehani occasioned no comment, he returned to the girl's secluded house, and after a while the two lovers began idly toying with the famous Havaiki slapping game, wherein to an ancient chant each gently tapped the other's finger tips, then shoulders, then sides, then thighs; as the game progressed the slaps grew in intensity, until perversely they dropped away to the tenderest of caresses, so that a gesture which started as a quick slap might end as a long embrace. At last Tehani lingered so gently over one slap, that Teroro caught her skirt and pulled it from her. Completely naked, she continued the game, chanting a few haphazard bars and attempting a few more desultory slaps, now grown breathless and passionate, until with a cry of soft triumph she surrendered the game and rolled into Teroro's arms, pushing him back onto the matting.

Later she whispered, "This is the way we fight on Havaiki." When Teroro laughed she asked, "Can girls of Bora Bora fight with their men like this?" Teroro was not pleased with the question, and although Tehani sensed his irritation she nevertheless pursued: "Is it true that on tiny Bora Bora you still pray to Tane?" The manner in which she pronounced *tiny* and *Tane* betrayed the contempt with which people of her island had always regarded Bora Bora.

Teroro did not rise to the insult. With studied courtesy he said, "We pray to Oro, which is why, even though we are so small, we invariably defeat Havaiki in war."

Tehani blushed at the memory of her island's humiliations and asked, "Did you wonder why my father came for you last night? And why I danced for you?"

"I thought about it. It looked planned."

"And why I brought you here?"

"At first love-making a man sometimes wonders," Teroro said. "At the second he no longer bothers."

"And at the third," Tehani whispered, "he decides to stay with this girl . . . to make his home here . . . to become a man of Havaiki."

Teroro pulled away and said, "For a warrior there is only one home, Bora Bora."

It was an ancient island custom that high-born women could seek their husbands, and Tehani now did so. "I plead with you, Teroro. Stay here with me."

"If you want to be my wife," he said, "you'll have to come to my island."

"You already have a first wife there, Teroro. Live here, and I will be your first wife."

The young chief held the girl off and studied her marvelous face. "Why do you ask this, Tehani? You could have any man on Havaiki."

The girl hesitated, then decided to speak the truth. "Your island is doomed, Teroro. You must escape. Come here. Be loyal to Oro. We can have a good life."

"Has your father suggested this?"

"Yes."

"What evil is he planning?"

"I dare not say," she answered. Taking Teroro's hands, she knelt before him and pleaded softly, "I have shown you how sweet Havaiki could be because I want to save your life. Here you can become a powerful chief. My father has many lands, and Oro is generous to warriors like you."

"I belong to Bora Bora," Teroro said with passionate conviction. "I will never lcave that island," and he started for the canoe, but pleading Tehani caught him by the legs, and he stayed with her that second night, so that on the next morning when the conch shells told of departure, he was reluctant to go.

"There are no women like you on Bora Bora," he confessed.

"Stay here with me," she pleaded.

At this moment he was almost tempted into confiding to her the revenge he had been formulating in his mind, but he fought back the impulse and said, "If I ever did come back to Havaiki, you would be my woman. A man could enjoy you."

"Come soon, Teroro, for Bora Bora is doomed."

Certainly, when the eleven visiting canoes departed the temple and stood out to sea, each breaking off from the column for its own destination, it seemed that the days of Bora Bora's greatness had vanished, for it was a dispirited group that occupied *Wait-for-the-West-Wind*. King Tamatoa acknowledged that in the game of power at the temple, he had permanently lost. All strength now lay with the High Priest, and abandonment of the island to Oro was the only sensible course. Teroro, surveying his depleted ranks, brooded on revenge, but had to recognize that the priest had outwitted him and had stricken down enough of his men to demoralize the rest. The crewmen sensed that their chiefs were disorganized and that ultimate power now lay with the High Priest, but they did not know by what political contrivances the power would be transferred; while the junior priests were so excited by the obvious victory of Oro that they had volunteered, while still on Havaiki, to assassinate both Tamatoa and Teroro and thus to settle the island's problems once and for all.

To their surprise, the High Priest had not assented to this; in fact, he had condemned his overeager assistants and had reasoned: "If we dispose of the king and his brother in this manner, the people will lament their passing and might even rise against us, but if we continue as we have been doing, then the people themselves will discover that their king is powerless against the wishes of Oro, and they will either force him to Oro's will, or they will desert him."

"But what if the king is obstinate?" an old priest had asked, recalling the record of Tamatoa's father, against whom Havaiki, Tahiti and Moorea had united in war, fruitlessly.

The High Priest had looked up at the sacrifices dangling in the moonlight and had observed: "Tamatoa may remain obstinate, but his people won't. Have you been watching how his men are even now confused and bitter? Where is Teroro, their leader, right now? Idling in the hut of Tehani!"

The old priest, not certain that Tamatoa would abdicate, had argued: "Whom shall we select to rule Bora Bora if we do depose the king?"

The High Priest had hoped that this question would not be raised, because he did not wish to stand forth among his followers as the originator of a plan that had indeed been devised by the generality of priests, so he had equivocated and said, "Oro has chosen a successor."

"Who?" the old man had pressed.

"Oro has chosen Tehani's father, the great chief Tatai."

There had been a long silence as the enormity of this decision struck the priests, for they were Bora Bora bred, and what was proposed was nothing less than the submission of their island to the ruling house of Havaiki, a thing never accomplished in the past by siege or war or contrivance. The High Priest had known that this intelligence must at first be repugnant, so before anyone could speak, he had added, "It is Oro who has chosen Tatai."

The invocation of Oro's name among men who had only recently staked their lives on this god, effectively halted comment, and the High Priest had continued: "That is why Tatai has urged his daughter Tehani to become the wife of Teroro. He will move to Havaiki and take with him most of his vigorous supporters, and they will soon become swallowed up among the men of Havaiki. Tatai, when he becomes king of Bora Bora, has agreed to leave his wives behind and to marry our women. In this way, Oro will be supreme." He had not added that when this was accomplished, he hoped to move his own headquarters to the great temple at Havaiki, and that at such time he would take along with him those Bora Bora subordinates who most heartily supported his master plan. But none of his listeners required to be told this, and with these exciting thoughts coursing through their minds the holy men returned to Bora Bora.

The twenty-seven surviving crewmen had few coherent thoughts. They had watched, helpless, while their original number was decimated by the power of Oro, and they had shared their leaders' confusion. Contrary to what the High Priest believed, they were gratified rather than disturbed by the fact that Teroro had spent his time with Tehani, for Mato had spread the news that Teroro must be got back to Bora Bora alive. They suspected that King Tamatoa had some solid plan of revenge, and they hoped to be a part of it. But beyond animal revenge they could not see.

There was one emotion which all in the boat shared, for at the end of the day, just before entering the home lagoon, the travelers saw the sun sink toward the west, throwing rich golden lights upon their magic island, and each man, no matter what his plots, instinctively felt: "This is the beautiful island. This is the land upon which the gods have spent particular care."

For to see Bora Bora at the end of a journey, with sunset upon the peaks, with dark night drifting in upon the valleys, and with sea birds winging homeward; to see the red line of sunset climbing the mountain faces until the top was reached, and darkness, and to cry, "Hold! Hold! Let it remain day until I touch the shore!" and to catch within the lagoon the sounds of children at play and the echoes of home, while outside the reef the ocean roared—to have known Bora Bora at such a moment was to have known beauty.

It was with enhanced regret, therefore, that King Tamatoa led his brother to the palace and bade him recline on the pandanus mats, whereupon the king carefully lowered the matting walls, and when he was thus protected from spies, lay down facing Teroro. Secretly and in a low voice he delivered the striking words: "I have decided that we must leave Bora Bora."

Teroro was stunned. He had never even contemplated such a retreat, for he still did not appreciate the untenable position into which he and his brother had been maneuvered. "Why should we leave?" he gasped.

"There is no place for us here any longer."

"We can fight! We can kill . . ."

"Whom shall we fight? The people? The other islands?"

"We could . . ."

"We can do nothing, Teroro."

"But where can we go?"

"To the north."

This simple phrase carried implications that were difficult for Teroro to digest, and as the idea climbed from one level of his consciousness to another he could only repeat his brother's startling words. "To the north?" He recalled that other canoes had left for the north centuries before, legendary canoes which had never returned. There existed, however, a mysterious old chant which purported to give sailing directions to a distant land that lay under the Seven Little Eyes, the holy constellation whose rising launched the new year, and some said that this chant implied that at least one of the legendary canoes must have returned, and words from the chant came to his mind:

Sail to the Seven Little Eyes,
To the land guarded by Little Eyes.

But as soon as he spoke the words he grew angry, for they conjured up a picture of him fleeing Bora Bora.

"Why should we go?" he blustered.

"Don't take refuge in empty words, Teroro," the king snapped impatiently. "When you sailed to Nuku Hiva, did you find any certain knowledge of any of the canoes that have sailed to the north?"

"No."

"I understand there's an old sailing chant."

"No one knows for sure where it came from."

"What does it say?"

"If I remember, it says to sail until you come to land that lies under the Seven Little Eyes."

"How many days?"

"Some men say thirty, some say fifty."

"Teroro, if we decided to sail with the next big storm that brings us a west wind, how many people could we carry on our canoe?"

"Would they let us take *Wait-for-the-West-Wind?*"

"If not, we would have to fight for it."

"Good!" Teroro grunted, for now he could begin to see specific action.

"How many men?" Tamatoa pressed.

"About sixty."

"And all supplies?"

"Everything."

"And a house for our gods?"

"Yes."

The brothers lay on the matting with their faces at arm's length apart, whispering, and finally Tamatoa asked, "Who should join us?"

Teroro quickly rattled off the names of many warriors: "Hiro, Mato, Pa . . ."

"We aren't going to battle," Tamatoa corrected. "We are going to the north . . . forever."

In the hushed room the word overcame Teroro. "Leave Bora Bora forever?" He leaped to his feet and cried, "We'll kill the High Priest tonight!"

Tamatoa grabbed him by one leg and hauled him down to the matting. "We are concerned with a great voyage, not revenge."

But Teroro cried, "At the convocation I and my men were ready to fight all the islands if anyone touched you, Tamatoa. We would have strewn the temple with bodies. We feel the same way now."

Tamatoa smiled and said, "But the High Priest outsmarted you, didn't he?"

Teroro pressed his fingers into a tight knot and mumbled, "How did it happen? Our plan was so good."

"Oro has triumphed," the king said sadly. "We had better take our gods and go."

Teroro growled, "I should like to be set free on Havaiki one night before we go. They'd never put out the fires."

"Is there anyone on Bora Bora who knows the directions north?"

"Our uncle. It was Tupuna who taught them to me."

"Is he loyal to Oro?" Tamatoa asked.

"Yes, but I think he is also loyal to you."

"Impossible," Tamatoa objected.

"For wise old men like Tupuna, many things are possible," Teroro laughed. "Do you want me to call him?"

"Wait. Won't he be in session with the others?"

"They don't pay much attention to him," Teroro explained. "They suspect he's loyal to you."

"We wouldn't dare take so long a voyage without a priest," Tamatoa said gravely. "To be alone on the ocean for fifty days . . ."

"I would want a priest along," Teroro agreed. "Who would read the omens?" And he sent a messenger to fetch old Tupuna.

In the interim the brothers resumed their positions and their planning. "Can we gather all we need?" the king asked.

"We can get spears and helmets . . ."

"Brother!" Tamatoa cried impatiently. "For the last time, we are not going forth on some adventure. What I mean is can you get breadfruit shoots that will survive? Seed coconuts? Bred sows? And some good eating dogs? We would need a thousand fishhooks and two thousand lengths of sennit. Can you get those things?"

"I'll get them," Teroro said.

"Keep thinking about whom we shall take with us."

Again Teroro rattled off the easy names and again the king interrupted: "Find a man who can make knives, one who can strip pandanus, a good fishhook man."

"Well, if we take sixty men it ought to be easy . . ."

"I've been counting the spaces in my mind," Tamatoa reflected. "We can take only thirty-seven men, six slaves, and fifteen women."

"Women," Teroro gasped.

"Suppose the land to the north is empty," Tamatoa mused. "Suppose there are no women. We would watch our friends set their feet upon the rainbow, one by one, and each man as he left would be forever irreplaceable. There would be no children."

"Will you take a wife?" Teroro asked.

"I will take none of my present wives," the king replied. "I'll take Natabu, so that we can have royal children."

"I'll take Marama."

The king hesitated, then took his brother by the hands. "Marama may not go," he said gravely. "We will take only women who can bear children."

"I would not want to go without Marama," the younger man said. "She is my wisdom."

"I am sorry, brother," the king said with complete finality. "Only women who can bear children."

"Then I won't go," Teroro said flatly.

"I need you," the king replied. "Don't you know any young girl to take?" Before Teroro could reply, the flaps parted and his uncle, old Tupuna of the white topknot and the flowing beard, came into the palace. He was nearly seventy, a remarkable age in the islands, where a man of thirty-three like the king was already an elder, so he spoke with exceptional authority.

"I come to my brother's sons," he said gravely, taking a seat on the matting near them. "I come to my own children."

The king studied the old man carefully, and then said in a low voice, "Uncle, we place our safety in your hands."

In a striking voice mellowed by years and wisdom Tupuna said, "You're planning to leave Bora Bora and want me to join you."

The brothers gasped and looked about lest any spies should have lingered, but the old man reassured them. "All the priests know you're planning to leave," he said benevolently. "We've just been discussing it."

"But we didn't know ourselves until we entered this room an hour ago," Teroro protested.

"It's the only sensible thing to do," Tupuna pointed out.

"Will you join us?" Tamatoa asked directly.

"Yes. I told the priests I was loyal to Oro, but I could not let my family depart without an intercessor with the gods."

"We couldn't go without you," Teroro said.

"Will they let us take *Wait-for-the-West-Wind?*" the king asked.

"Yes," the old man replied. "I pleaded for that in particular, because when I was younger I helped consecrate the trees that built this canoe. I shall be happy to have it my grave."

"Your grave?" Teroro asked. "I expect to reach land! Somewhere!"

"All men who set forth in canoes expect to reach land," the old man laughed indulgently. "But of all who leave, none ever return."

"Teroro just told me that you knew sailing directions," the king protested. "Somebody must have returned."

"There are sailing directions," the old priest admitted. "But where did they come from? Are they a dream? They tell us only to sail to land guarded by the Seven Little Eyes. Perhaps the chant refers only to the dream of all men that there must be a better land somewhere."

"Then we know nothing about this journey?" Tamatoa interrupted.

"Nothing," Tupuna replied. Then he corrected himself. "We do know one thing. It's better than staying here."

There was silence, and then Teroro surprised the king by asking, "Have they agreed to let us take our gods, Tane and Ta'aroa?"

"Yes," the old man said.

"I am glad," Teroro said. "When a man gets right down to the ocean's edge . . . when he is really starting on a voyage like this . . ."

He did not finish, but Tupuna spoke for him. He said, in a deep prophetic voice, "Are there people where we go? No one knows. Are there fair women? No one knows. Will we find coconuts and taro and breadfruit and fat pigs? Will we even find land? All that we know, sons of my brother, sons of my heart, is that if we are in the hands of the gods, even if we perish on the great ocean, we will not die unnoticed."

"And we know one thing more," the king added. "If we stay here we shall slowly, one by one, be sacrificed, and all our family and all our friends. Oro has ordained it. He has triumphed."

"May I tell the High Priest that? It will make our departure easier."

In complete humbleness of spirit, King Tamatoa replied, "You may tell him."

At this moment there came from the beach a sound which thrilled the three plotters, converting them at once from mature men into the children that they essentially were; and as each heard the exciting message, his eyes widened with joy and he threw off whatever badges of position he might have been wearing and ran toward the palace door, looking out into the starry darkness with the same pulsating thrill he had known as a boy.

For there along the waterfront, in the midnight hour, the citizens of Bora Bora, without king or priest, had assembled with drums and nose flutes for a night of wild merriment. The apprehensions of the convocation were ended and childish revelry was again in command. Therefore, with only the rank of commoners, Tamatoa, Tupuna and Teroro hurried eagerly to the beach. A raucous old woman was yelling, as they came, "Let me show you how our great helmsman Hiro steers a canoe!" And in superb mimicry she became not an old woman with few teeth, but a malicious lampoon of young Hiro steering his canoe; in a dozen ways she caught his mannerisms: the way he looked out to sea, and his swagger; but what she steered was not the canoe's tiller but the make-believe male genitals of another old woman who was playing the part of the canoe. When the steering was done, the first woman screamed, "He's very smart, Hiro!"

The crowd bellowed, particularly when they saw Teroro applauding the vicious mimicry of his helmsman. "I'll bet she really could steer a canoe!" he shouted.

"You'd be surprised at what I could do!" the lascivious old woman replied. But the crowd left her antics and started to applaud as blunt Malo, from the other side of the island, suddenly wrapped a bit of yellow tapa about his shoulders and made believe he was fat Tatai of Havaiki, executing ridiculous steps to the music and lampooning that chief's pompous ways. To the great joy of the assembly, King Tamatoa nimbly leaped into the smoky arena and took his place beside Malo, and both imitated Tatai, each more foolishly than his competitor, until at last it was difficult to say which was Malo and which the king. The foolish little dance ended with Tamatoa sitting exhausted in the dust, laughing madly as if he had no cares.

Again the crowd looked toward a new clown, for shark-faced Pa had grabbed a leaf-skirt and was crying in a shrill high voice, "Call me Tehani!" And he pirouetted grotesquely but with uncanny skill, evoking the Havaiki girl, until Teroro asked himself, "How could he have seen her dance?" But his preoccupation with Pa was broken when he saw his own wife, Marama, leap into the dance in hilarious burlesque of her husband. "It's Teroro!" the crowd applauded as the skilled woman ridiculed her man, gently and with love, but also with keenest perception. As she danced Teroro wondered: "Who told her about Tehani?"

Marama and the shark-faced man were the night's success. Pa was so ugly and his features so preposterous that he could make them seem like those of any man; and he could be both gentle, as in his mimicry of Tehani, and savage, as in his next burlesque of the High Priest. With a bit of black tapa for a wig and a breadfruit branch for a staff, Pa gyrated furiously in demented manner, whirling about and pointing his stick at first one islander and then another. As he did so, Marama, dancing behind with a feather bag, played the burly executioner, clubbing down one victim after another. Finally, in mock frenzy, the crazy dancer Pa gyrated directly up to King Tamatoa and pointed his stick at him, whereupon Marama rushed along, swung her feather bag, and brought it within an inch of the king's face. The victim fell as if his skull had been crushed, and lay in the sand, laughing, laughing.

As the long wild night progressed, every item of island life was brought under ridicule, with chinless Pa as the ringleader. He possessed what islanders loved: a child's sense of fairy tale, and to watch his amazing pointed face move from one characterization to the next was endless joy. Toward dawn, when the fears and repressions of the past weeks were dissipated, a group of old women approached King Tamatoa and began pleading with him, obviously seeking some special boon for the people, until at last he gave assent, whereupon the delegation's leader leaped withered-legged into the center of the crowd, screaming the good news: "Our great king says tonight we play the gourd game!" With hushed excitement the men and women separated into facing groups as King Tamatoa ceremoniously tossed toward the men a feathered gourd which glistened in the firelight. A chief reached out and caught it, danced a few ritual steps, then pitched it in a high, shimmering arc toward the eager women. A young girl who had long lusted after this man leaped into the air, snatched the gourd and dashed with it to the man who had thrown it. Clutching him by the waist, she rushed him passionately into the shadows, while the feathered gourd flew back and forth, determining the sleeping partners for that wild night.

Teroro, although he had the island to choose from, elected his own wife, Marama, the penetrating clown, and as they lay quietly in the gray-and-silver dawn, with the timeless waves of the lagoon once more established over the night's loud revelry, Teroro confided, "Tamatoa has decided to leave the islands."

"I suspected he had reached some grave decision," Marama said. "He was so eager to laugh."

"What I don't understand is, the High Priest has agreed to let Tupuna join us. And also to let us take *Wait-for-the-West-Wind*."

Marama explained: "He's wise. He knows that islanders like to avoid direct conflicts that humiliate others. It's good procedure."

Her words were so in conflict with his plans for revenge that he asked, "What about the humiliation we suffered at Havaiki? Would you forget that, too?"

"I would," she said firmly. "When we're safe on some other island we can afford to forget Havaiki."

He started to explain that she would not be going on the voyage, but he could find no words to do so gracefully; in cowardice he fell asleep, but after a while he half-woke and mumbled, "You were very funny tonight, Marama. You were really wonderful."

WHEN THE DECISION to depart from Bora Bora was whispered from one village to the next, the island became a curious place, because no one admitted officially that the king was leaving. The High Priest continued to pay public deference to Tamatoa, and old Tupuna officiated at daily prayers to Oro. Young chiefs who had determined to join the expedition embraced wives who were obviously going to be left behind; but under this surface of indifference, all were preoccupied with one job: loading a canoe for an unknown voyage.

Particular care was given to food supplies. It was relatively easy to prepare food that was to be consumed on the voyage; it was dried in the sun and compacted into small bundles tied with ti leaves. What required special thought was the selection of roots and saplings for a new land. Experts sought taro roots that would produce the gray-blue tuber which made the best poi, and coconuts that came from the strongest trees, and breadfruit that did not grow too high but which did produce big heads rich in starch and glutinous sap. White-haired Tupuna spent three days selecting chickens that would yield meat and dogs that would bake well, for he constantly reminded his charges that they were heading for land that might be very spare, indeed.

Then came the day when departure could no longer be politely masked, for with a saw made from a large sea shell, Teroro boldly cut eleven feet from each of the canoe's high sterns. "We cannot risk such high adornment on a long trip," he explained.

"Auwe!" cried men and women along the shore. "The great canoe of Bora Bora is being desecrated." Gently Teroro handed down the god-carved sterns, and priests bore them to the temple. The crowd watched while he used dried shark's skin to smooth the ends of the truncated stern, and he kept his back to the watchers as he worked, for he was praying, *"Wait-for-the-West-Wind,* forgive me for this mutilation," and out of his humiliation at having to cut down his own canoe, an obsessive rage was generated which was to make his departure from Bora Bora an event ever to be remembered in the islands.

His rage increased when he left his deformed canoe and went to his own hut, where he threw himself on the floor and hammered the pandanus mats. Marama came to sit with him and assured him: "When we have found a new home we will find big trees and we can make new pillars for our canoe."

"No! They'll remain as they are! A signal of our shame."

"You talk like a boy," the placid-faced woman chided.

"When I was a boy," he corrected, "if anyone insulted me, I beat him on the head. But now I'm a man, and Havaiki insults me without risks."

"Teroro," his wife pleaded. "Look at it sensibly. What has Havaiki really done? They've invented a new god, and the world seems to prefer him. They haven't . . ."

Teroro grasped his wife by the arm. "Haven't you heard the whispers?" he asked bitterly. "When Tamatoa goes, who is to be the new king? Fat Tatai of Havaiki."

Marama gasped. "Have they gone so far?" she asked.

"Yes!" Teroro snapped. "And do you know what they had the insolence to do? They proposed that I desert my brother and leave Bora Bora. I was to marry Tatai's daughter . . . trade places with him!"

"Why didn't you tell me this?"

"It was only now that I figured it out," he replied sheepishly. And as always, when he felt humiliated, he decided upon a plan of swift action. "Marama," he said hurriedly, "go across the mountain and assemble all who have agreed to paddle the canoe."

"What are you planning?" she asked suspiciously.

"To take *West Wind* for a trial, on the ocean. To see if the new stern works. Tell anyone who asks, that's what we're doing. But whisper to each man that he must also bring his best war club."

"No, Teroro!"

"Do you want us to creep away, unavenged?"

"Yes. There's no dishonor in that."

"Not for a woman, perhaps," Teroro said.

Marama considered what was involved, the possibility of death and the chance that Havaiki might send canoes in retaliation, thus ending escape to the north, but after she had considered for a long time she said, "Since men are what they are, Teroro, you ought not to go unavenged. May the gods protect you."

So, toward midafternoon two days before the intended departure for Nuku Hiva, and while a good wind blew from the west, promising a later storm of some dimensions, thirty determined paddlers, plus the steersman Hiro and the navigator Teroro, set forth from Bora Bora to test their canoe. It moved sedately across the light green waters of the lagoon and stoutly into the dark waters of the outer ocean, already whipped by the wind into sturdy waves. The canoe moved back and forth in speed tests, then hoisted sail and darted into a long leg down wind. When it had left the lee of the island Teroro asked, "Are we agreed?"

"We are," Mato said, pulling his war club into position.

"To Havaiki!" Teroro shouted to the steersman, and *West Wind* tore into the waves and its paddlers strained as darkness fell over the impartial sea.

For generations out of mind Bora Bora had been known among the islands as the land of the muffled paddles, for since it was the smallest of the major islands, its men were required to practice added caution. Now, with the dying moon not yet risen, they paused to wrap their paddle handles in tapa, so that they could creep silently, leaving barely a ripple on the sea, toward the hallowed landing of Oro, where only a few weeks before they had been so deeply humiliated.

Gently, gently, the double canoe was beached before any outlook spotted it, and thirty resolute men, leaving two to guard the canoe, slipped into the night toward the village where fat Tatai, the intended king of Bora Bora, slept. The avengers had almost reached the village when a dog barked, causing a woman to cry, "Who's stealing breadfruit?" She sounded an alarm, but before effective action could be taken, Teroro and his men had fallen upon the village and were seeking out all who had insulted them, and most particularly fat Tatai, the nominated king.

It was Teroro who led the avengers to Tatai's compound. There he and shark-faced Pa swept into the main hut, smashing and crashing all they encountered. A girl's voice, soft and petulant, whispered, "He is not here, Teroro!"

Then she screamed in pain, for Pa's great club struck her, and from the floor she whimpered, "He is not here."

Pa was about to crush her skull when Teroro pulled him away and with his left hand dragged her to safety. From a flare set ablaze by the frugal woman who was determined to protect her breadfruit, Teroro saw that Tehani was naked except for a hastily grabbed skirt which she held before her, and he rediscovered her spectacular beauty. From a distance came his brother's voice: "Don't you know any young girl?" and on the impulse of the moment he brought Tehani's face to his and rasped, "Will you go north with me?"

"Yes."

"Are you hurt?"

"My shoulder."

"Broken?"

"No."

"Wait for me at the canoe." He thrust her toward the shore and then caught her again, muttering, "We have come to kill your father. Do you still want to go?"

"I'll wait at the canoe," she said.

Now he heard Mato shout, "We've found him!"

"Save him for me," Teroro pleaded, swinging his club, but when he reached the prostrate figure of Tatai he saw that Pa had already killed him. Grabbing a handful of thatch from a roof he spread it about the dead man's head. "The new king of Bora Bora!" he cried derisively.

"To the canoe!" the steersman shouted.

"Not before we destroy this place!" Teroro cried, and grabbing from the woman's hand the brand by which she was inspecting her breadfruit, he swept it along the thatch of a nearby house; the rising wind ripped the flames along, and soon the sacred channel of Oro and the environs of his temple were ablaze. In this light, the men of Bora Bora retreated.

At the canoe a battle raged, only prompt reinforcement saved the craft, for one of the guardians was already dead and the other was badly wounded. As the Bora Borans drove back the attackers and leaped into the truncated canoe, Tehani ran from a clump of palms, crying, "Teroro! Teroro!"

"Traitor!" the defeated Havaiki warriors cried, already inventing an explanation that would excuse their defeat. They launched their spears and in their frustration would have killed her, except that Teroro left the canoe, leaped into the surf, and ran back to rescue her.

"We are in danger!" the steersman warned, standing the canoe out into the channel.

But Teroro continued running until he intercepted the girl and swept her into his arms. Then, dodging spears, he dashed for the beach and into the surf. He might not have made the canoe, except that Mato dived into the channel and took the girl, whose shoulder was so damaged that she could not swim. Together they lifted her into the canoe and set their course for Bora Bora, but before they had left the shadow of Havaiki, Teroro said to the girl, "We found your father."

She replied, "I know."

The return trip was one of intense excitement, marked by psychological relief at having struck a blow at Havaiki and at the just punishment of a stranger who had presumed to rule Bora Bora. And there was the ironic joy of knowing that before Havaiki could retaliate—if indeed they ever dared try—all involved would be on the open sea, far from Bora Bora.

But above all, there was great animal joy in realizing that during the strike at Havaiki, the promised storm had actually formed and that it now blew with real force, for although the unexpected strength of the westerly made the journey back to Bora Bora difficult, it also meant that the one essential requirement for a long journey to the north was at hand.

"This storm will blow for days!" Teroro assured his men.

At daybreak it became possible to turn and run before the wind safely into the lagoon, and as they reached its protection Teroro drilled his men in the story they must tell: "We took *West Wind* for a trial. The storm came up. We saw we couldn't get back. So we laid over in the channel at Havaiki." He repeated the sequence and added, "In this storm no one from Havaiki would dare come here with the true story."

"What about the girl?" Pa asked.

Everyone looked at Tehani, huddling wet in the hull, and it was immediately apparent, especially to Tehani, that the simplest solution to the difficulty she presented would be to knock her on the head and throw her into the storm. Pa was ready to do this, but Teroro stopped him.

"She's my girl," he said bluntly. "We'll take her to my house."

"She'll betray us."

"She won't. We'll say that while we were in the channel I went ashore to get her for the journey north."

"Do you intend taking her?" Mato asked.

"Yes. She's my girl."

"What about your wife Marama?"

"She can't bear children. She can't go."

"This one will betray us!" Pa warned.

Teroro reached down into the hull and pulled Tehani to her feet. Thrusting his face into hers he said, "Until we leave Bora Bora you will speak to no one about this night. No one."

"I understand," she said, sinking back into the canoe.

"It is you I will take north," Teroro promised her.

As the canoe neared shore, Mato cried, "What a storm! We went all the way to Havaiki."

Of all the listeners, only Marama knew the full significance of this statement: that some great revenge had been carried out. Swiftly she counted the canoe and saw that the young chief Tami had been lost. "Where is Tami?" she called.

"He was lost reefing sail in the storm," Pa lied.

A man called, "Why did you go all the way to Havaiki?"

Pa answered, "Teroro went to fetch the girl he will take north with him."

From the bottom of the hull, where she had lain hidden, Tehani slowly rose, and it was in this way, with the west wind of the storm beating in her face, that Marama learned she would not be accompanying Teroro to the north. No sound escaped her lips. She stood in the wind with both hands pressed against her sides, her hair whipping about her shoulders, her great placid face, handsome as a moon on the thirteenth night, staring at the stranger in the canoe.

She thought: "A man is dead. Some dreadful event has occurred that will contaminate the islands for years. Brave stupid men like my husband have gained their revenge, for what it matters. And a young stranger takes my place in the canoe." Patiently she studied the newcomer and thought: "She is beautiful and her body is well formed. Perhaps she can have children. Perhaps it's better." But then she looked at Teroro, and her heart broke.

Hiding her tears she turned to go home, but her degradation was not completed, for her husband called, "Marama!" She returned to the canoe and he said, "Take Tehani home," and Marama reached down and took the girl's hand and led her home.

In its second night the storm rose to an intensity that quite precluded any departure on the day planned, and as the winds howled, those responsible for the voyage had a few last hours free for dreaming. The visions of Teroro were agitated, and toward dawn he saw two women standing by *West Wind,* and the canoe had no mast on which to hang its sail. He awoke in fright, shook his head vigorously, and realized that the two women were merely Marama and Tehani and their standing by the canoe signified only that each wanted to go north with him, so he wakened Marama, explaining, "The king will allow only one woman to go, Marama, and he insisted that I take a younger."

"I understand," she said dully.

"It isn't that I've grown tired of you," he whispered.

"Tupuna explained," she replied.

"You understand how it is?" he pleaded.

"I understand that I have given you no children."

"You've been a good wife, Marama, but the king . . ."

He fell asleep, but before the birds had wakened, he dreamed again and saw his canoe with no mast, and this time the two women spoke, Marama in a deep voice crying, "I am Tane!" and Tehani singing in a lilting voice, "I am Ta'aroa!"

Teroro woke trembling and cried, "Why should the gods speak to me on such a night?" And for a long time he tried to decipher the dream, for he knew that before a voyage each dream meant something, but he could not find the key. So he rose in the gray light of dawn, while winds howled and drove rain across the island, and hurried, almost naked, to the hut of old Tupuna.

"What did such a dream mean?" he pleaded.

"Did the voices sound like those of gods?" the bearded old man queried.

"No, they were women's voices, and yet Tane's was deep as it should be, and Ta'aroa's was high and piercing like his voice in a storm."

The old priest sat gathering his wisdom and listened to the roaring wind that must take them on their way. Finally he announced: "It is very clear, Teroro. Tane and Ta'aroa speak most forcefully when they speak in the wind. You must obey them."

"What do they want me to do?"

"There was no mast in your dream canoe, and no sail?"

"None."

"Then it's simple. The gods wish you to take down your single mast and to raise instead two masts, one in each hull."

It was such an obvious explanation that Teroro laughed. "I've seen canoes like that. One came to Nuku Hiva from the south."

"It's natural," Tupuna explained. "When Tane, who rules the land, and Ta'aroa, who rules the sea, speak to a navigator in unison, they must be referring to the element that they rule together, the wind. They want you to erect two sails so that you can catch the wind better."

"I will do so," Teroro said, and forthwith he called his men together, and even though departure could not be far off, he ripped down the mast, found a matching tree, and erected one in the right hull, which he named Tane, and the other in the left, which he called Ta'aroa. Then he lashed each with sennit shrouds, so that by nightfall a man could climb to the top of either and not tear it loose. It would have been unthinkable for a navigator not to obey the gods.

On the third night of the storm it was the king's turn to dream, and he witnessed a fearful sight: two planets in the western sky at sunset, fighting with the sun and pushing it from the sky, whereupon one moved anxiously east and west, while the other roamed north and south. This dream was so ominous that the king summoned his uncle immediately and lay facing him in dead of night, imploring counsel.

"Does it mean that we are doomed?" Tamatoa asked in distress.

"Which of the wandering stars went searching east and west?" Tupuna inquired.

"The great star of evening."

"And they were both searching?"

"Like a dog combing the beach or a woman seeking a lost tapa."

"This is not a good omen," Tupuna said gravely.

"Could it mean . . ." the king began, but the concept was too foreboding to be put into words.

"Failure?" Tupuna asked bluntly. "You think it means that our canoe will wander north and south, east and west, until we perish?"

"Yes," Tamatoa answered weakly.

"It cannot mean that," Tupuna said consolingly, "for Tane and Ta'aroa themselves spoke to Teroro last night, and he governs the canoe."

The king was not relieved, for he confided: "My other thought is just as bad."

"What is it?" the old man asked.

"I wonder if the two stars do not represent Tane and Ta'aroa, and the thing they are looking for is Oro. I wonder if they acknowledge Oro as supreme and do not want to go in our canoe unless he goes along?" He dropped his head and muttered, "Uncle, I am sick with fear that we are doing something wrong."

"No," Tupuna assured him, "I've studied every omen. There is no indication of failure. Remember that Tane and Ta'aroa brought us significant advice, the need for two masts. Would they trifle with us?"

"But these searching stars?"

"I'll confess, not a good omen. But I am sure that all it means is that in some manner your preparation for the voyage is incomplete. You have forgotten some vital thing."

"What shall I do?"

"You must unpack everything and then repack it, and when you have accomplished this, you will know what oversight has displeased the gods."

And so, on the third day of the storm, King Tamatoa did an unprecedented thing: he threw open his tabu palace to the boat's crew, and they assembled, on mats which the day before it would have been death to touch, each item that was to go north, and before the king's careful eye they unwrapped and repacked their treasures.

"Have we our tools?" Tamatoa inquired, and his men brought forth the basalt stones used for cooking, and the sand. They produced bundles of sticks, some hard, some pithy, for making fire. Fishlines of sennit, fishhooks of pearl, nets and spears for sharks, all were in order. There were bluish-green adzes, stone chisels, pounders for crushing taro and others for making cloth. Some chiefs produced digging sticks, harder than many stones and covered with mana from long use in planting taro. There were gourds and calabashes and cups for cooking. Men hauled in bows and arrows, and slingshots with pouches of special stones. There was a long pole with sticky gum for catching birds, a conch shell for calling to prayer, and four heavy stones to serve as sea anchors. The women who had been designated to go, proudly presented fine mats, tight in structure and waterproof. There were bailers to keep the canoe dry, paddles to speed it forward, and extra mats to use as sails. During the passage of a thousand years these wandering island people had, without the assistance of any metal or clay, perfected an intricate civilization and its tools. In one double canoe they were now ready to establish that culture on a distant island. The king was satisfied.

"Have we cared for the plants and animals?" he next inquired. Tenderly, the farmers from the group unwrapped the seed-things that would, in time, sustain life in new lands. Taro corms were kept dry and twisted inside pandanus leaves until such time as they could be plunged into soft, wet mud for a new harvest. Banana shoots, on which the voyagers must depend for quick crops, were wrapped in damp leaves and kept cool, while choice coconuts, their eyes unopened, had to be kept dry lest they launch their shoots. Sugar cane, which all loved, had been cut into joints and was kept alive inside dark bundles made of leaves.

"Where is the breadfruit?" Tamatoa asked, and four men dragged onto the mat large bundles swathed in leaves and mud. These contained the breadfruit shoots, most delicate of the cargo, whose fruit was so loved by the islanders. When the shoots lay exposed, the king called for his uncle to bless them anew, and the group prayed for their safe transit.

Men now hauled two squealing sows into the palace. "Have they been bred?" the king asked.

"To our best boar," the men replied, hauling into the august presence an ugly, protesting beast, followed by two bred bitch dogs and a male, two chickens and a rooster.

"Have we feed for these animals?" the king inquired, and he was shown bags of dried coconut, mashed sweet potatoes and dried fish. "Place these living things before me, and their food," Tamatoa commanded, and when the assemblage was completed he cried in terrifying voice, "These are tabu! These are tabu! These are tabu!"

In solemn chant the witnesses repeated, "These are tabu!" Then Tupuna blessed them with long prayers of fertility, ending with his own warning: "These are tabu!" It was not just a word that was being used; it was a divine inhibition, and it signified that a man on this trip could see his woman die of starvation, but he could not hand her one morsel of the tabu food, nor eat any himself, for without this seed even those who did reach land would perish.

Teroro now brought in the rations: breadfruit partially dried and rolled into wads for fermentation; pandanus flour made by baking and grating the untasty fruit, just barely palatable but useful on long trips; dried sweet potatoes, shellfish, coconut meat, bonito hard as rock; more than eighty drinking coconuts; three dozen lengths of watertight bamboo filled with clear water. When the food was assembled all could see that it did not bulk large, and Tamatoa studied it with apprehension.

"Have we enough?" he asked.

"Our people have been starving themselves for weeks," Teroro replied. "We can live on nothing."

"And have they been drinking little?"

"Barely a cupful a day."

"Are your fishermen prepared to catch us extra food along the way?"

"They have prayed to Ta'aroa. There will be fish."

"Then let us bless this food," Tamatoa said, and Tupuna recited the long chant which dedicated these rations to the gods. He hoped that the deities would allow his companions to eat the food while searching for a new land, and if it was found, the gods would be rewarded with an endless supply of pigs.

"Let us check the canoe," the king said, and he led his subjects into the storm, where they went over each portion of *Wait-for-the-West-Wind.* The two hulls were not made from single hollowed-out trees, but were built up by butting together three separate sections, each about twenty-five feet long. This meant that the canoe had to be tied together at the joints, and it was here that Bora Bora's skill with sennit showed itself to greatest advantage, for the huge canoe was as rigid as if carved from a single log, yet it was composed of many pieces, lashed intricately together, and it was these joints that the king now inspected. They leaked, of course, and without constant bailing the canoe would sink, but they did not leak much. The strakes which formed the sides of the two hulls were also lashed on, and were also nearly watertight. The two halves of the canoe were held together, about four feet apart, by eleven stout beams that passed through the inside wall of each hull, and were again bound by powerful sennit, while to them was lashed the long, solid platform upon which the passengers and the gods would ride. This left, in each hull, a narrow space between the edge of the platform and the outer edge of the hull, where the paddlers sat on small movable seats which they shifted back and forth until they found a place amid the cargo where their feet could reach the bottom of the hull.

"The canoe is fine," Teroro assured his brother, and the crowd waited in silence while the two brothers and their uncle studied the storm. Finally Tamatoa said, "If the omens are good, we will leave tomorrow at dusk. We must be at sea when the stars rise."

When the others had gone, Tamatoa led Tupuna back to the palace and sat disconsolately upon the matting. "What have we overlooked?" he fretted.

"I saw nothing missing," the old man said.

"Have we forgotten some vital thing, Tupuna?"

"Nothing that is apparent."

"What does it mean?" the king cried in deep perplexity. "I have tried so desperately to arrange this correctly. Where have I failed?"

His uncle said quietly, "I noticed that as we inspected the goods, when we were through, each man tied his bundles up a little more tightly. At the canoe they fastened the sennit just a bit more strongly. Perhaps that is what the gods wanted us not to forget. The last effort that insures success."

"You think it could have been that?" Tamatoa asked eagerly.

"It's been a long day," Tupuna evaded. "Let us all dream one more night, and if the omens are good, that must have been the meaning."

So on the fourth night of the storm all men who would make the voyage assembled at the temple according to ancient custom, there to acquire their last flow of mana and to sleep in terror, awaiting the omens that would lay bare the future. Once more Teroro dreamed of his canoe, and again Marama called that she was Tane and again Tehani was Ta'aroa, and just before he wakened, each woman was transformed into a mast, so that the omen was obviously hopeful. Teroro was so pleased that he risked a powerful tabu and crept out of the temple and went to the bed of Marama, lying with her for the last time and assuring her that it was only the king's command that kept him from taking her, and in the last stormy darkness, she wept. He consoled her by taking from his pouch the length of sennit that he had picked up at the temple in Havaiki, and taking Marama out into the storm, he upturned a large rock and carefully placed the sennit under it. "When I have gone for a year, turn the rock aside and you'll know whether I survived," for if the sennit still lay clean and straight, the canoe had reached land; but if it were twisted . . .

King Tamatoa woke from his dream and beat his matting with fists of joy, for incredible as it seemed, he had seen the Seven Little Eyes. He had seen them! They had actually hung over Bora Bora and moved off with the canoe. "Oh, blessed Tane!" the king cried in ecstasy. And for the rest of the night he did not sleep, but stood in the doorway of the temple surveying the storm, with the rain in his face, and in those solemn hours he knew an abiding content: "Our boat is well loaded. We have good men. My brother knows the sea and my uncle knows the chants. On this day we shall set forth."

But the dream that actually launched the voyage occurred in the hut of old Tupuna, for he saw in dream-spun heavens a rainbow standing directly in the path the canoe must take, and a worse omen than this there could not have been, but as he watched, Tane and Ta'aroa lifted the rainbow and placed it abaft the canoe, where it shone brilliantly on the waters. The omen was so auspicious, evil changing to positive good by the action of gods, that the old man did not even wake to record his dream. In the morning he was suffused with delight and told the king, "Some wonderfully good thing took place last night. I forget what it was, but we will sail tonight."

He went directly to the altar and took down the final precious essentials for the journey: one stone was black and white with flecks of yellow, and round, the size of a fist—it was Tane; the other stone was long and thin and greenish—it was Ta'aroa, god of the oceans on whom they must now depend. Tupuna wrapped each in a small cloth made of yellow feathers, and bearing his deities, he went to the canoe. In a small grass hut erected on the platform just abaft the masts, he placed Tane toward the right mast and Ta'aroa toward the left. The canoe could now be loaded.

Aft of the gods' house the platform provided an open space which Tupuna would occupy during the entire voyage, tending the deities. Behind him was sleeping space for those members of the crew who were not paddling, and behind them a large grass hut for the twelve women who had been chosen to accompany the crew. Aft of them sat Natabu, silent and sacred, the wife of Tamatoa, accompanied by red-eyed Teura, the wife of Tupuna and seer of the voyage; it was her duty to read omens. At the rear of the house, alone, sat Tamatoa beside a small doorway leading aft, from which he could watch the stars and check the steersman. The captaincy of the canoe lay with Teroro, who stood farthest forward with Tehani at his side; but the actual life and death of this bold adventure rested with the king. Only he could say turn or stay.

As the stormy day progressed it seemed inconceivable that any sensible man would venture outside the reef, but all knew that only in such a westerly gale could a canoe go forth with much chance of success, so when the winds kept strong, so did the hearts of the voyagers. They spent the day in prayer and in stowing the canoe. The slaves, the animals and the heavier bundles went into the left-hand hull, whose lead paddler would be Mato, upon whom the beat and rhythm would depend. Into the right-hand went the food, the trees and the extra mats. This would be headed by Pa. At the rear of this hull, cornerwise from Mato, the steersman Hiro would stand.

The afternoon wore on and the crew said good-bye to wives they could not take, and to their children. Teroro went for the last time to see grave Marama in the little house where they had been so happy. She was dressed in her finest tapa, yards and yards of it about her handsome body, and her hair was marked with flowers.

"Guide the canoe well, Teroro," she said softly. "I shall pray for you."

"You will always be in my heart," he promised.

"No," she corrected. "When you are gone you must forget me. It would not be fair to Tehani."

"You are my wisdom, Marama," he said sorrowfully. "When I see things clearly it is always because you showed me the way. I need you so much."

"Be quiet, Teroro," she said, and as they sat on the matting for the last time she tried to share with him all the things she had forgotten to tell him. "Never go against the counsel of Mato. He sometimes seems stupid because he comes from the north side of the island, but trust him. If you get into a fight, rely on Pa. I like Pa. The man you prefer is Hiro. He's fun, but can you trust him in an emergency? Listen to your uncle Tupuna. His teeth are yellow with wisdom. And, Teroro, never again go on a journey of simple vengeance."

"Would you have had us depart in shame?" he countered.

"Well," she admitted, "one can never defeat Havaiki enough." She caught her breath and confided, "It would have been unbearable to have a Havaiki man for king." Then she added quickly, "But mere revenge, especially when the king does not give consent. That must be past."

For the last time she talked with her man, and as the time came when he was forced to go she thought: "There is so much more he needs to know." When he took his first step toward the door she fell on the matting and kissed his ankles, and heard him say haltingly, "Marama, when we sail, please don't come on shore. I could not bear it," at which she rose full height and cried sharply, "Me! Stay hidden indoors when my canoe is leaving? It is my canoe. I am the spirit of the sails and the strength of the paddlers. I will take you to land, Teroro, for I am the canoe."

And when the men climbed aboard *Wait-for-the-West-Wind,* Marama, with her beautiful hair in the storm, guided them with her spirit and blessed them, and said to young Tehani, "Take care of our husband. Fill him with love." But at the last minute she was thrust aside by a most unexpected arrival. It was the High Priest, come down to the launching with a long retinue of assistants, and he went to the canoe and cried, "Great Oro bids you safe journey!"

Grabbing hold of the bowsprit, he stepped aboard, clutching the mast Tane as he did so. Kneeling before the gods' house, he pushed aside the grass door and deposited inside a sanctified statue of Oro, made of sacred sennit woven with his own hands and clothed in feathers. In haunting voice he cried into the storm, "Great Oro, bless this canoe!" And as he stepped ashore, Teroro saw that a smile of enormous relief had come upon the face of his new wife, Tehani. She had been willing to go upon the seas with strange gods, but now that Oro was with her, she knew the journey would succeed.

And so the double canoe, *Wait-for-the-West-Wind,* loaded and creaking with king and slave, with contradictory gods and pigs, with hope and fear, set forth upon the unknown. At the prow stood Teroro, ill-named the wise one, but at this fateful moment he was wise enough not to look back at Bora Bora, for that would have been not only an evil omen, but folly as well, for he would have seen Marama, and that sight he could not have borne.

When *West Wind* reached the reef, and stood for a moment in its last stretch of easily navigable water, all in the canoe experienced a moment of awful dread, for outside the coral barrier roared the storm on slashing waves and tremendous deeps. Just for an instant Mato, lead paddle on the left, whispered, "Great Tane! Such waves!" But with prodigious force he led the paddlers into a swift rhythm that bore them directly into the heart of the storm. The canoe rose high in the sea, teetered a moment with its shrouds whistling, then ripped down, down into the valley of the waves. Spray dashed across all heads and the two halves seemed as if they must tear apart. Pigs squealed in terror and dogs barked, while in the flooded grass house women thought: "This is death."

But instantly the powerful canoe cut into the waves, found itself, and rode high onto the crest of the ocean, away from Bora Bora of the muffled paddles, away from the comforting lagoon and onto the highway that led to nothingness.

IN SUCH WEATHER King Tamatoa led his people into exile. They did not go in triumph or with banners flying; they fled at night, with no drums beating. They did not leave with riches and in panoply; they were rudely elbowed off their island with only enough food to sustain them precariously. Had they been more clever, they would have held their homeland; but they were not and they were forced to go. Had they perceived the deeper nature of gods, they would never have fallen prey to a savage deity who tormented them; but they were stubborn rather than wise, and the false god expelled them.

Later ages would depict these men as all-wise and heroic, great venturers seeking bright new lands; but such myths would be in error, for no man leaves where he is and seeks a distant place unless he is in some respect a failure; but having failed in one location and having been ejected, it is possible that in the next he will be a little wiser.

There was, however, one overriding characteristic that marked these defeated people as they swept into the storm: they did have courage. Only if they had been craven could they have swallowed their humiliation and remained on Bora Bora; this they would not do. It is true that they fled into the dusk, but each man carried as his most prized possession his own personal god of courage. For Teroro it was the mighty albatross that winged its way over distant seas. For King Tamatoa it was the wind that spoke to him in tempests. For Tupuna it was the spirit of the lagoon that brought fish. And for his ancient bleary-eyed wife, Teura, the keeper of omens, it was a god so powerful that she scarcely dared mention its name. But it followed her in the ocean, her great and sweet and powerful deity, her courage in the unknown.

When they had reached, more swiftly than ever before, a point off the north coast of Havaiki, Teroro crawled over to where Mato paddled and said, "I am going to speak with the king about our feeling. Promise me that you will support me."

"I promise," Mato said.

"Even if it means death?"

"Even then."

Precariously, Teroro made his way aft to consult with his brother, laying bare a wish that startled the king: "I cannot sail with Oro in this canoe. Let us throw him into the ocean."

"A god!"

"I cannot sail with him."

Tamatoa summoned old Tupuna, who struggled aft with difficulty and sat with the brothers. "Teroro wants to throw Oro into the ocean," Tamatoa explained.

The thought was even more repulsive to the old man than it had been to the king, and he warned in powerful voice that such a thing had never been done. But Teroro was adamant: "We have suffered enough from Oro. My men cannot sail this canoe with such a burden."

"If we were on land . . ." Tupuna protested.

"No!" the king said firmly. "It is impossible."

But Teroro would not surrender. He shouted forward for Mato, who soon appeared. Tamatoa was grave and said, "Teroro wants to throw the god Oro into the ocean."

"It must not be done!" Tupuna warned.

"Let Mato speak!" Teroro demanded.

"Teroro is right," the stocky warrior said. "We have known only terror from this red god, deep, humiliating terror."

"But he is a god!" Tupuna protested.

"We must not carry such poison to a new land," Mato insisted.

Tupuna warned: "If you do such a thing, the winds will tear this canoe apart. The ocean will open to its depth and swallow us. Seaweed will grow in our hair."

"I would rather be dead," Mato shouted back, "than to install Oro in a new land."

At this point Teroro faced Tupuna and cried, "You say Oro will punish us? I say this to Oro." And he flung his head back, howling into the wind, "Oro, by your sacred pig, by your length of banana shoot, by the bodies of all men sacrificed to you, I condemn you and declare you nothing. I curse you and revile you and cast excrement in your face. Now strike me down. If you control the storm, raise your bloodstained hands and strike me down."

He stood motionless as the others listened in horror, waiting. When nothing happened he fell to his knees and whispered, just loud enough for the others to hear, "But, gentle Tane, if you guide this canoe, and powerful Ta'aroa, if you control this storm, forgive me for what I have just said. Forgive me especially for what I am about to do. But I cannot go forward with Oro as a passenger in this canoe."

He rose like a man in a dream, bowed low to his brother, and made dutiful obeisance to the priest. "Forgive me," he said in a choking voice. "If in the next moment we are swept to death, forgive me."

He stumbled forward in the storm, but when he reached the gods' house itself he was powerless to open the rain-sodden door. Inherited fear of gods, plus what he remembered of his early training when it was hoped he would become a priest, rendered him incapable of action and he returned to the rear. "I cannot act without your approval, brother," he confessed. "You are my king."

Tamatoa cried, "We shall be lost if we destroy a god."

Teroro fell on the platform and clutched his brother's feet. "Command me to destroy this evil thing."

"Don't do it, Tamatoa!" his uncle warned.

In this moment of indecision, when the ultimate values of the canoe were laid open on the stormy deck, it was tough Mato who acted. He shouted, "King Tamatoa, if we take Oro with us, when you land you kill more people to show him gratitude, just in case it was he who brought us there. And once started, we will kill more, and more. You, Tupuna, you love gods, but we must save you from the temptation of growing to love this one!"

And he rushed to the gods' house, uncovered the sennit-and-feather form of the avenging god and raised it high into the storm. "Go back to Havaiki where you came from!" he shouted. "We don't want you. You've eaten our men. You've driven us from the home of our ancestors. Go away!" And with a vast sweep of his arm, Mato threw the god far out to sea.

But winds caught at the feathers and for an awful moment held the god aloft, so that it kept pace with the canoe. "Auwe!" shrieked the priest. "Auwe! See, Oro follows us!"

King Tamatoa, perceiving this miracle, fell to the platform in prayer, but Teroro, awakened from his indecision, grabbed a spear and with fury launched it at the god. It missed, but the shaft brushed the feathers and deflected the deity into the turbulent deep. Calmly, he turned to the prostrate king and said, "I have killed the god. You may do with me as you wish."

"Go to your post," the king mumbled, stricken with fear.

As Teroro moved forward upon the canoe whose burden of terror he had helped diminish, he felt his craft sweep into the storm with new vigor; the stays sang a sweeter song; and he could see from their smiles that his men were assured. But when he passed the gods' house and recalled how powerless he had been at the vital moment, he looked across to where Mato sat, stubbornly paddling to keep the canoe right with the storm, and he wanted to clasp the man in brotherhood, but only Mato's shoulders were free, and no man would dare touch another's shoulders, for they were reserved for the personal god to perch on when he inspired a man with courage; so Teroro merely whispered into the storm, "You were the brave one, Mato," and the sturdy paddler replied, "The canoe feels lighter."

When Teroro recovered his post he found Tehani, the daughter of Oro, weeping. He knelt beside her and said, "You must try to forgive me, Tehani. I killed your father and now I have killed your god." He took her by the hands and swore: "I will never offend you again." The dazzling girl, storm upon her face, looked up. She was bereft of the very foundations of her being, and although she tried to speak she could say nothing; but from then on Teroro treated her with extra kindness.

It was at this moment, when the captains of the canoe were most agitated, that Tane and Ta'aroa conspired to present them with an omen that erased from all hearts memories of what had just happened. The rain came heavily for about fifteen minutes, followed by strong winds that blew clouds scudding ahead in darkness until the clouds parted and the fine stars of heaven were momentarily revealed.

Then it was that the wisdom of Tupuna in setting forth at dusk on the new day of the month became apparent, for there, rising in the eastern sky and with no bright moon in competition, sparkled the Seven Little Eyes. It was their first twilight appearance of the year, their reassuring return which proved that the world would continue for at least twelve more months. With what extraordinary joy the voyagers greeted the Little Eyes. From the grass house women came forth and filled their hearts with comfort. Those crew members who had to keep the canoe headed with the wind found new resilience in their tired muscles, and Teroro knew that he was on course.

Then, the miracle vouchsafed, Tane drew the clouds once more across the heavens and the storm continued, but contentment beyond measure settled upon the canoe, for it was at last apparent that the company moved in accordance with divine laws. How sweet the roar of the wind that bore them on, how consoling the motion of the waves that carried them into the unknown; how appropriate the world, how well ordered and secure the heavens. On the canoe, that daring and insignificant bundle of wood lashed together by sennit and men's wills, all hearts were deep in peace, and the onwardness of their journey sang contentedly in all parts of the craft, so that when old Tupuna crawled back to his watching point abaft the gods' house, he called softly to Teroro ahead, "The king is content. The omen proves that Oro was caught by Ta'aroa and conveyed safely to Havaiki. All is well." And the canoe moved on.

The most critical part of any twenty-four-hour period came in the half hour just before dawn, for unless the navigator could catch a glimpse of some known star and thus check course he would have to proceed through an entire day with only the unreliable sun to steer by; for while it was true that master astronomers like Teroro and Tupuna could follow each movement of the sun and take from it their heading, they could not use it to determine their latitude. For that they depended upon the stars; their sailing directions reminded them which stars culminated over which islands, and to pass the last moments of night without seeing any constellations was not only an omen of bad luck in the future, it was also proof of present difficulty, which, if it persisted for several days, might develop into catastrophe.

For example, after their first fleeting glimpse of the Seven Little Eyes, Teroro and his uncle had waited anxiously for Three-in-a-Row, which other astronomers then living in distant deserts had already named Orion's Belt, for the sailing directions said that these stars hung over Nuku Hiva, their replenishment point. But Three-in-a-Row had not appeared during the night watch and Teroro had been unable to determine his latitude. Now the conspicuous stars were setting without having been seen, and the navigator was worried.

He had, however, observed on earlier trips that it was a peculiarity of his ocean that in the last few minutes of morning twilight, some star, as if determined to aid mariners, pushed clouds aside and showed itself, and he thought there was still time for this to happen.

"Three-in-a-Row will appear there," Tupuna announced confidently, but Teroro wondered if the night's strong wind might not have blown the canoe rather farther north than his uncle suspected.

"Maybe they will be closer to that cloud," Teroro suggested.

The difference of opinion was not to be resolved, for clouds continued to streak out of the west to meet the sun rising on the other side of the ocean. On this day dawn was neither inspiring nor refreshing, for the sun straggled reluctantly up behind many layers of cloud, half illuminated the ocean with dull gray and proved to the voyagers that they did not know where they were.

Teroro and Tupuna, having accomplished all they could, fell into immediate sleep in the stormy daylight; and it was then that the latter's wife, wizened, red-eyed old Teura, paid for her passage. She climbed out of the grass house, splattered sea water over her wrinkled face, rubbed her bleary eyes, threw her head back and started studying the omens. In nearly two thirds of a century of living with the gods, she had unraveled many of their tricky ways. Now she watched how Ta'aroa moved the waves, how the spume rose, how the tips fell away and in what manner they tumbled back into the troughs. She marked the color of the sea and the construction of the basic swells that underlay the more conspicuous waves.

At midmorning she saw a land bird, possibly from Bora Bora itself, winging its way out to sea, and from its flight she was able to determine the bird's estimate of how long the storm would continue, and it confirmed her own. A bit of bark, washed out to sea days before from Havaiki, was of particular interest to the old woman, for it proved that the ocean had a northerly set, which was not apparent from the wind, which blew more toward the northeast.

But most of all the rheumy-eyed old seer studied the sun, for although it was well masked behind layers of cloud, her practiced eye could mark its motion. "Star men like Tupuna and Teroro don't think much of the sun," she snorted, but when she placed her observations of its course beside the deductions she had made from earlier omens she concluded: "Those men don't know where they are! We're far to the north of our course!"

But what Teura particularly appreciated were those unexpected messages from the gods which meant so much to the knowing. For example, an albatross, not large and of no possible importance as food, happened to fly past the canoe and she saw with gratification that he kept to the left, or Ta'aroa's side, and since the albatross was known to be a creature of that god's, this was a refreshing omen; but when the bird insisted upon returning to the canoe, also from the left side, and finally perched on the mast of Ta'aroa, the coincidence could no longer be termed an omen. It was a definite message that the god of the oceans had personally sent to an old woman who had long honored him, and Teura looked at the sea with new love, and sang:

"O, Ta'aroa, god of the boundless deep,
Ta'aroa of the mighty waves
And the troughs that lead down to blackness,
We place our canoe in your hands,
In your hands we place our lives."

Contentedly, the old woman gathered her many omens, and they were all good. The men of her canoe might be lost, and the stars remain hidden, and the storm continue, but Ta'aroa was with them and all was well.

In the late afternoon, Tupuna and Teroro, before resuming their duties, came aft to find out from Teura where they were, and she advised them that they rode much farther north than even Teroro had suspected.

"No," the men reasoned. "We've been to Nuku Hiva. Directions don't call for a turn yet."

"Head for the pit from which Three-in-a-Row climbs," she warned with stubborn finality, "or you'll miss Nuku Hiva."

"You wait till the stars come out," Teroro challenged. "You'll see we're on course."

Teura would not argue. For her any problem was simple: either the gods spoke or they didn't, and if they did, it was useless to try to explain to someone else how the message was delivered. "We are far to the north," she snapped. "Turn."

"But how can we know?" Teroro pleaded.

"The gods said so," she muttered and went to bed.

When she was gone, the two men reviewed her various omens, but the only one upon which they were willing to place much reliance was the albatross. "You can't have a much better omen than an albatross," Tupuna reasoned.

"If Ta'aroa is with us," Teroro concluded, "we must be on the right course."

From the grass house old Teura stuck out her head and snapped, "I've noticed that Ta'aroa stays with a canoe only as long as its men keep it on course. Turn."

That night it could not be proved that Teura was either right or wrong, for no stars appeared, neither in the darkness of midnight nor in the anxious dawn, and Teroro steered solely by running directly before the wind, with only a small section of sail out, trusting that the storm was steady and not blowing in circles.

On the third starless night, when the canoe could have been in real danger, Teroro reached a major decision. While consulting with Tupuna he said, "We've got to believe that the storm is blowing true."

"Arrival of the albatross is best proof of that," Tupuna pointed out.

"Then I think we'd better take full advantage of it."

"You intend hoisting the sails to the peak?"

"Yes. If it is the gods who are sending us, we ought to go forward as fast as we can."

When they presented their proposal to King Tamatoa, he showed his disturbance over the lack of stars and pointed out that the night crew's estimate of position did not jibe with that of the old woman, but he also appreciated the good sense of his brother's proposal. "I am much impressed by that albatross," Tamatoa reasoned. "Teura confided one fact to me that she didn't tell you. When the bird came back the second time to land on the mast of Ta'aroa, it landed with its left foot extended."

The astronomers whistled, for this was a most propitious omen, since it confirmed the leftness of the bird's intentions and its peculiar inclination toward the mast of Ta'aroa. "I can only conclude," the king reasoned, "that Ta'aroa, for some reason of his own, has sent us this unusual storm. I agree with Teroro. Hoist the sails."

So Teroro sent Mato and Pa up the masts, and in complete darkness, while the canoe was already speeding forward into deep swells, the two young chiefs lashed fast the sturdy matting sails and with shouts of accomplishment slid down and began to play out the sails until they trapped the wind and whipped the canoe forward. Through the rest of the night and into the third disappointing dawn the canoe raced ahead on a course no man knew, for King Tamatoa realized that there came a time on any voyage when a man and his canoe had to trust the gods and to run forward, satisfied that the sails had been well set and the course adhered to whenever possible; but when all precautions failed to disclose known marks, it was obligatory to ride the storm.

At daylight, gnawed by uncertainty, the men went to sleep and old Teura came forth to gather omens. A white-bellied petrel wheeled in the sky but said nothing. Fishermen forward caught bonito, which helped conserve food but told nothing about position, and several fine squalls deposited calabashes full of sweet water trapped by the sails.

At noon when Teura advised the king that things were going well, he shrewdly asked, "Any omens of position?"

"None," she replied.

"How is the ocean running?"

"No signs of land, no islands ahead, the storm will blow for five more days." In such brief report she summed up two thousand years of study by her ancestors, and had she been required to explain why she knew that there was no land ahead, she would have been unable to do so. But there was none, and of this she was absolutely certain.

"Has the albatross returned?" the king asked anxiously.

"No omens," she repeated.

It was now seven days since the storm had risen on the night of Bora Bora's revenge against Havaiki, and three complete days that the canoe had been at sea, but true to Teura's prediction and to the amazement of all, the gale continued, and when the evening watch took over, Teura and the king wondered if the sails should not be lowered, for there were not going to be any stars that night, either. But in the consultation Teroro said, "I am convinced we are going forward," and since there was no one with superior knowledge to contradict him, Tamatoa asked, "You are willing to keep the sails aloft tonight?"

"We must," Teroro said. And through that starless night and into the starless dawn, he ran with the storm, insisting upon this because of his canoe's name. More than a century ago a wise man had named the predecessor of the predecessor of this canoe *Wait-for-the-West-Wind* because he had found that when Bora Borans went forth driven by the western hurricane, they went well. And until the stars had a chance to prove the contrary, Teroro was willing to abide by this ancient wisdom.

He was somewhat shaken however on the fifth night when Tupuna crept up to the prow and whispered, "I have never known a storm from the west to blow so long. We are entering the ninth night. It surely must have veered."

There was a long pause in the darkness and Teroro looked down at the slim body of his wife, curled against the mast. He wondered what she would say to this problem, but she was not like Marama; she had no ideas. So he wrestled with the alternatives alone and felt irritated when Tupuna pressed him: "Can you recall a constant wind of such duration?"

"No," Teroro snapped, and the two men parted.

But toward dawn of the fifth day, when it seemed probable that no stars would show, Tupuna became frightened: "We must drop the sails. We don't know where we are."

He insisted upon a conference with the king and Teura, which produced three voices against Teroro, for it was obvious that the canoe was lost and that to persevere blindly without some confirmation from the stars would be folly. But Teroro could not accept this reasoning.

"Of course we're lost," he confessed. "But Ta'aroa sent his bird to us in the storm, didn't he?"

"Yes," they had to agree.

"This isn't an ordinary storm," he argued. "This is an unheard-of gale sent to the canoe of Bora Bora. From the oldest days, what has been the name of our canoe?"

"But we are lost!" the king reasoned.

"We were lost from the moment we set forth," Teroro cried.

"No!" Tamatoa cried, refusing to be enticed by his brother's rhetoric. "We were headed for Nuku Hiva. For fresh water and new supplies."

"And to listen once more to the sailing chants," Tupuna added cautiously.

"We must lie to," the king announced firmly. "Then, when we catch a glimpse of Three-in-a-Row, we will know where Nuku Hiva is."

It was under this pressure that Teroro broached his bold plan. He spoke quietly and without gestures, saying, "I am not lost, brother, because I am riding with the desires of Ta'aroa. I am heading with a great storm, and I am content to ride that storm."

"Do you know how to get to Nuku Hiva?"

Teroro looked at each of his companions and replied, "If we are concerned only with Nuku Hiva, I am lost. If we are going to Nuku Hiva only to get additional food and water, I am lost. But in all sense, brother, do we need to go to Nuku Hiva?"

He waited for these strong words to sink into the hearts of his seafaring companions, and he saw that he had used words they understood. Before anyone could speak he added, "What is there for us in Nuku Hiva? To get water we have to fight with those who live there, and some of us will be killed. Do we need water? To get food we must take great risks, and if we are captured, we are cooked alive and eaten. Do we need food? Hasn't Ta'aroa sent us fresh fish in abundance? Have we not disciplined ourselves as men have never done before so that each eats only a shred each day? Brother Tamatoa, if the storm is with us, what extra things do we need?"

Tamatoa resisted his brother's eloquence and asked, "Then you are lost. You can't take us to Nuku Hiva?"

"I cannot take you to Nuku Hiva, but I can take you to the north."

As if in support of his bold plan, a sudden force of wind ripped across the waves and spilled into the sails, whipping the canoe along in a burst of speed. Spray leaped, and dawn, still blotting out the stars and all certain knowledge, came upon the men of Bora Bora.

"We are alone on the sea," Teroro said solemnly. "We are engaged in a special voyage, and if it takes us past Nuku Hiva, then I say good, for we are doubtless being sped by the gods on some great mission. Brother, I beg you, let us keep the sails aloft."

The king would not present this dangerous request to the opinion of the group, for he knew that the old people, Tupuna and Teura, would insist upon caution, and he suspected that perhaps now was a time when caution was not required. Weighing all possibilities, he sided with his brother and said, "We should get some sleep."

So for two more nights, the sixth and seventh of the voyage, the canoe sped on, safe in the mighty arms of Ta'aroa, and in those somber, critical days, all eyes were kept on the left mast, for it was obvious that not the man Teroro but the god Ta'aroa was in command of this canoe. And then, on the late afternoon of the seventh day, red-eyed Teura spotted an omen. On the left side of the canoe came five dolphin, a propitious number in itself, followed by an albatross of some size. The creatures of Ta'aroa had come to celebrate the deliverance of this canoe from the storm, but before Teura could alert her companions to this fine intelligence, an event of transcendent importance occurred. A shark appeared not far from the canoe and followed it lazily for a moment, trying to catch Teura's attention, and when she saw it her heart cried with joy, for this great blue beast of the sea had long been her personal god; and now, while the others were blind with their work, it swam along the left side of the canoe, its blue head above the waves.

"Are you lost, Teura?" it inquired softly.

"Yes, Mano," she replied, "we are lost."

"Are you searching for Nuku Hiva?" the shark asked.

"Yes. I have said that it was . . ."

"You will not see Nuku Hiva," the great blue shark advised. "It is far to the south."

"What shall we do, Mano?"

"Tonight there will be stars, Teura," the shark whispered. "All the stars that you require."

In perfect contentment the old woman closed her tired red eyes. "I have waited for you for many days," she said softly. "But I did not feel completely lost, Mano, for I knew you must be watching us."

"I've been following," the shark said. "Your men were brave, Teura, to keep the sails aloft like that."

Teura opened her eyes and smiled at the shark. "I am ashamed to tell you that I argued against it."

"We all make mistakes," the blue beast said, "but you are on the right course. You'll see when the stars come out." And with this consoling assurance, he turned away from the canoe.

"There's a shark out there!" a sailor cried. "Is that a good omen, Teura?"

"Tamatoa," the old woman said quietly, "tonight there will be stars." And as she spoke two land birds with brown-tipped wings flew purposefully toward the south and Tamatoa saw them and asked, "Does that mean that our land is far to the south?"

"We shall never see it, Tamatoa, for we are safe on a new heading."

"Are you sure?"

"You will see when the stars come out."

With what excited apprehension Tupuna and Teroro waited for the dusk. They knew that when the Seven Little Eyes peeked above the eastern horizon, the canoe's course would be apparent; and when Three-in-a-Row appeared, they could deduce where Nuku Hiva lay. With what apprehension they waited.

Exactly as Teura had predicted, toward dusk the clouds disappeared and the evening sun came out. As it sank, a tremendous exhilaration filled the canoe, for trailing the sun was the bright star of evening, visible even in twilight and soon accompanied by a second wandering star of great brilliance, and like the two gods on whom the canoe depended, the stars marched grandly toward the rim of the ocean and vanished in their appointed pits of heaven.

On the platform old Tupuna called all passengers to silence as he threw back his white head and intoned a prayer: "Oh, Tane, in our preoccupation with the storm of your brother Ta'aroa we have not thought of you as often as we should. Forgive us, benevolent Tane, for we have been fighting to stay alive. Now that the heavens are restored to remind us of your all-seeing kindness, we implore you to look with favor upon us. Great Tane, light the heavens that we may see. Great Tane, show us the way." And all prayed to Tane and felt his benevolence descend upon them from the nearer heavens.

Then, as darkness deepened over the still heaving ocean, and as the winds died momentarily from the gallant outstretched sails, the stars began to appear; first the mighty golden stars of the south, those warm familiar beacons that showed the way to Tahiti, followed by the cold blue stars of the north, scintillating in their accustomed places and competing with the quarter moon. As each star took its position, its friends in the canoe greeted it with cries of recognition, and an assurance that had been absent for many days returned.

The critical stars had not yet risen, so that in spite of their joy, men could not suppress the questions that often assailed voyagers: "What if we have sailed away from heavens we knew? What if the Little Eyes do not rise here?" Then slowly and uncertainly, for they were not brilliant stars, the sacred group arose, precisely where it should have been, climbing up out of its appropriate pit.

"The Little Eyes are still with us!" Tupuna shouted, and the king raised his head to offer a prayer to the guardians of the world, the core around which the heavens were built.

The astronomers then met to read the signs, and they concluded that the storm had blown fairly steadily from the west, but apparently there had been, as Teura had guessed, a definite drift of the sea northward, for the Little Eyes were going to culminate much higher in the heavens than would be proper were the canoe on course to Nuku Hiva; but to say specifically how serious the drift had been, the navigators would have to wait until Three-in-a-Row appeared, which would not be for another two hours.

So the three plotters waited, and when Three-in-a-Row was well up into the heavens it became self-evident that the canoe was far, far north of the course to Nuku Hiva and was thus committed to an unknown ocean with no opportunity to replenish stores. It was therefore a solemn group that went aft to report to the king: "The storm has carried us even more swiftly than Teroro imagined."

The king's face showed his distress. "Are we lost?"

Uncle Tupuna replied, "We are far from Nuku Hiva and will see no land we know."

"Then we are lost?" the king pressed.

"No, nephew, we are not," Tupuna said carefully. "It is true that we have been carried into far regions, but they are not off our course. We seek lands which lie beneath the Seven Little Eyes, and we are nearer to them tonight than we had a right to expect. If we do not eat too much . . ."

Even though Tamatoa had given permission to keep the sails aloft, and even though he had known that the canoe thus ran the risk of missing Nuku Hiva, he had nevertheless hoped that they would stumble upon that known island, and perhaps find it congenial, and possibly establish homes there. Now he was committed to the greater journey, and he was fearful.

"We could still alter course and find Nuku Hiva," he suggested.

Teroro remained silent and allowed old Tupuna to carry the argument: "No, we are well on our way."

"But to where?"

Tupuna repeated the only chant he had ever memorized for sailing to the north. In effect it said: "Keep the canoe headed with the storm until the winds cease completely. Then turn into the dead sea where bones rot with heat and no wind blows. Paddle to the new star, and when winds strike from the east, ride with them westward until land beneath the Seven Little Eyes is found."

The king, himself an adequate astronomer, pointed due north and asked, "Then the lands we seek are there?"

"Yes," Tupuna agreed.

"But we go this way?" and he pointed eastward, where the winds of the dying storm were driving them.

"Yes."

The course seemed so improbable, to head for a promised land by fleeing it, that the king cried, "Can we be sure that this is the way?"

"No," the old man confessed, "we cannot be sure."

"Then why . . ."

"Because the only knowledge we have says that this is the way to do it."

The king, ever mindful of the fact that fifty-seven people were in his care, grasped Tupuna by the shoulders and asked bluntly, "What do you honestly think about the land that is supposed to be under the Little Eyes?"

The old man replied, "I think that many canoes have left these waters, some blown by storms, others like us in exile, and no man has ever returned. Whether these canoes reached land or not, we do not know. But some man, with a vision of what might be, composed that chant."

"Then we are sailing with a dream for our guide?" Tamatoa asked.

"Yes," the priest answered.

Gloom was not allowed to capture the canoe, for the reappearance of the stars had excited the paddlers and the women, so that even while the astronomers were consulting, shark-faced Pa had handed his paddle to another and had grabbed a length of tapa which he had wrapped around his shoulders, masking his head. Now imitating a very fat man, he pranced up and down the platform, shouting, "Who am I?"

"He's the headless king of Bora Bora!" Mato cried.

"Look at fat Tatai coming to be our king, with his head knocked off!"

In wild burlesque, Pa ridiculed the coronation of the headless would-be king. Paddlers stopped and began to beat rhythms on the canoe, and a woman produced a little drum with a high, almost metallic sound, and the night's revelry was launched.

"What is this new dance?" Tamatoa inquired.

"I've never seen it before," Tupuna replied.

"Do you know what he's doing?" the king asked Teroro.

"Yes," the younger man said hesitantly. "Pa is . . . Well, Tamatoa, some of us heard that fat Tatai was to be king after we left . . . and . . ."

Tamatoa looked at the headless dancer and asked, "So you sneaked over to Havaiki . . . some of you . . ."

"Yes."

"And now Tatai has no head."

"Well . . . yes. You see, we felt . . ."

"You could have ruined the entire voyage, couldn't you?"

"We could have, but we figured that Tatai's village wouldn't come over to Bora Bora very soon . . ."

"Why not?"

"Well, when we left there wasn't any village."

In the light of the quarter moon King Tamatoa looked at his daring young brother, and there was much that he would have said, but the sound of ancient drumming stifled his logical thoughts, and with a stirring leap he whirled forward to where Pa was dancing and entered into the ritual dance of the kings of Bora Bora. Like a boy, he gestured and postured and told forgotten stories, until toward the end he grabbed Pa's tapa and threw it over his head and did the now popular dance of the headless king from Havaiki. When the drums had reached a crescendo he threw off the tapa, stood very straight in the night wind, and exulted: "We did not go like cowards! I, the king, was afraid to strike at those evil worms, those faces of excrement, those vile and awful dead fish of the stinking lagoon. I was afraid to endanger the coming voyage. But Pa here was not afraid. And Mato was not afraid. And my brother . . ." In gratitude Tamatoa looked aft to where Teroro stood in darkness. The king did not finish his sentence. With demonic energy he leaped into a dance of victory, shouting, "I dance in honor of brave men! Let's have the celebration you were denied!" And he ordered extra rations of food to be broken out, and more drums, and all the water anyone wanted.

Like children careless of the dawn, they reveled through the night, got drunk on laughter, and feasted on food that should have been conserved. It was a wild, wonderful night of victory, and each half hour someone shouted, "Pa! Do the dance of the headless king!" Then, one by one, in savage triumph, they rose and screamed classic island insults at the vanquished.

"Havaiki is the strong scent of spoiled meat!"

"The worthless trash of Havaiki take pleasure in their shame."

"Fat Tatai trembles in fear. The hair on his head trembles. He crawls away and hides like a hen in a secret place."

"The warriors of Havaiki are the froth of water, boys playing with mud balls."

Teroro, succumbing to the excitement, shouted, "Fat Tatai is a sneaking little dog, excrement of excrement." But as his voice shrieked in the wind, he happened to look forward to where beautiful Tehani huddled against the masts, weeping as her father was reviled. Then he also saw Mato, from the left hull, touch the girl's hand.

Mato said, "This is the way of victory. You must forgive us." From the rear new voices rose with foul invective, and the drums beat on.

In the rainy dawn, of course, King Tamatoa took gloomy stock of what the celebration had cost and for a moment he thought: "We are children. We discover we're lost and half an hour later we eat enough food for a week." Contritely, he issued stringent orders that what had been wasted must be made up by austere rationing. "Even though we have plenty of water," he warned, "each must drink only a cupful a day."

So, with the remnants of the tempest at their back and with victory in their hearts, the voyagers sailed eastward for the ninth night, and the tenth, and the fifteenth. Their swift canoe, fleetest large craft that ever up to then had plied the oceans of the world, averaged two hundred miles a day, better than eight miles an hour, day after day. They sailed more than halfway to the lands where Aztecs were building mighty temples, and well onto the approaches of the northern land where Cheyennes and Apaches built nothing. In the direction they were then headed they could encounter no land until they struck the continent itself; but before that happened they would have perished of thirst and starvation in the doldrums. Nevertheless, they carried on, according to Teroro's plan. There was fear each dawn when the sun rose; there was momentary joy each night when the stars reappeared to tell their progress; for day was the enemy, crowded with uncertainty and the hourly acknowledgment of their forlorn position; but night was consolation and the spiritual assurance of known stars, and the waxing of the fat moon through its many stages, and the soft cries of birds at dusk. How tremendous an experience this was, at the end of a long day which had provided only the unstable sun, to watch the return of night and to discover, there in the west where the sun went down, the evening star and its wandering companion, and out of the vastness to see the Little Eyes come peeping with their message: "You are coming closer to the land we guard." How marvelous, how marvelous the night!

AS THE CANOE REACHED EASTWARD and the storm abated, the daily routine became more settled. Each dawn the six slaves stopped bailing and cleaned out the canoe, while farmers moved among the animals and fed them, giving the pigs and dogs fish caught in the early hours, plus some mashed sweet potatoes and fresh water trapped in the sails. The chickens got dried coconut and a fish to pick at, but if they lagged in eating, a slim, dark object darted out from among the freight and grabbed the food away, unseen by the slaves, for as on all such trips, some rats had stowed aboard, and if the voyage turned out badly, they would be the last to die . . . would indeed sustain themselves for many drifting days on those who had already perished.

After the women in the grass hut had wakened, the female slaves would move inside, throw out the slops and do the other necessary chores. Particularly, they kept clean that corner of the hut which had been cut off by lengths of tapa and reserved for those women who were experiencing their monthly sickness, for it was a tabu entailing death for there to be any communication between men and women at such time.

In general, however, the tabus which were rigidly enforced on land had to be suspended aboard a crowded canoe. For example, had any of the rowers while ashore come as near the king as all now were, or had they stepped upon his shadow, or even the shadow of his cape, they would have been killed instantly, but in the canoe the tabu was suspended, and sometimes when the king moved, men actually touched him. They recoiled as if doomed, but he ignored the insult.

The tabus which centered upon eating were also held in abeyance, for there was no one aboard of sufficient status to prepare the king's food as custom required; nor had the keeper of the king's toilet pot come on the journey, so that a slave, terrified at the task, had to throw into the sea the kingly bowel movements, rather than follow the required custom of burying them secretly in a sacred grove, lest enemies find them and with evil spells conjure the king to death.

Women upon such a trip did not fare well. Obviously, the food had to be reserved for men who did the hard work of paddling. The pigs and dogs also had to be kept alive to stock the new land, which left little for the women. That was why, at every opportunity, they set fishing lines and tended them carefully. The first fish they caught went to the king and Teroro, the next to Tupuna and his old wife, the next four to the paddlers, the seventh and eighth to the pigs, the ninth to the dogs, the tenth to the chickens and the rats. If there were more, the women could eat.

With great niggardliness, the prepared foods were doled out, a piece at a time, but when they were distributed, how good they tasted. A man would get his stick of hard and sour breadfruit, and as he chewed on it he would recall the wasteful feasts he had once held, when abundant breadfruit, fresh and sweet, had been thrown to animals. But the food that gave most pleasure, the master food of the islands, came when the king directed that one of the bamboo lengths of dried poi be opened, and then the rich purplish starch would be handed out, and as it grew sticky in the mouth, men would smile with pleasure.

But soon the poi was finished and the bundles of dried breadfruit diminished. Even the abundant rain ceased and King Tamatoa had to reduce his rations still further, until the crew were getting only two mouthfuls of solid food, two small portions of water. Women and slaves got half as much, so that unless the fishermen could land bonito, or trap water in the sails, all existed at the starvation level.

Early in the dry period the king and Teroro made one discovery, a tormenting and frustrating one made by all similar voyagers: when the tongue was parched and the body scorched with heat, when one's whole being craved only water, an unexpected squall often passed a mile to the left or right, dumping untold quantities of water upon the sea, just out of reach, but it was no use paddling furiously to overtake the squall, for by the time the canoe reached the spot where the rain had been falling, the squall had moved on, leaving all hands hotter and thirstier than before. Not even an expert navigator like Teroro could anticipate the vagaries of a rain squall and intercept it; all one could do was to plod patiently on, his lips burning with desire and his eyes aflame, trying to ignore the cascades of water that were being dumped out of reach; but one could also pray that if one did continue purposefully, in a seamanlike manner, sooner or later some squall would have to strike the canoe.

On a voyage such as this, sexual contact was expressly tabu, but this did not keep the king from gazing often at his stately wife Natabu; and old Tupuna saw to it that Teura got some of his food; and in the heat of day Tehani would dip a length of tapa into the sea, cool it, and press it over her husband's sleeping form. At night, when the stars were known and the course set, the navigator would often sit quietly beside the vivacious girl he had brought with him and talk with her of Havaiki, or of his youth on Bora Bora, and although she rarely had anything sensible to say in reply, the two did grow to respect and treasure each other.

But the most curious thoughts between men and women involved the twelve unassigned women and the thirty-four unattached men. Perhaps the word *unassigned* is not completely accurate to describe the women, because some of them in Bora Bora had been specific wives of individual men, but on such an expedition it was understood that upon landing, any such woman would accept as her additional husbands two or three of the men who had no wives, and no one considered this strange. So on the long voyage men with no women began cautiously to do two things: to form close friendships with men who had women, establishing a congenial group of three or four who would later share one woman as their common wife; or to study the unmarried women in an effort to decide which one could most satisfactorily be shared with one's group; so that before the voyage had consumed even fifteen days, groups had begun to crystallize, and without anything definite having been said, it was remarkably well understood that this woman and these three men would build a house for themselves and raise common children, or that that husband and wife would accept those two friends of the man into complete and intimate harmony, thus populating the new land. It was further understood that each woman, until she reached the age when children no longer came, would be kept continuously pregnant. The same, of course, was true of the sows and the bitches, for the major task of all was to populate an empty, new land.

On the eleventh night occurred an event which, in its emotional impact upon a people who lived by the stars, had no equal on this voyage. Even the abandonment of Oro had failed to generate the excitement caused by this phenomenon.

As the *West Wind* crept constantly northward it became obvious to the astronomers on board that they must lose, and forever, many old familiar stars which lay below what astronomers would later call the Southern Cross. It was with sorrow, and even occasionally with tears, that Tupuna would follow some particular star which as a boy he had loved, and watch it vanish into the perpetual pit of the sky from which stars no more rise. Whole constellations were washed into the sea, never to be seen again.

Although this was cause for regret, it did not occasion alarm, for the men of Bora Bora were exceptional astronomers. They had developed, from careful observation, a year of 365 days, and they had found that from time to time an extra day was required to keep the seasons aligned. Their ritual life was organized around a moon-month of twenty-nine and a half days, which is the easy way to build a calendar; but their year of twelve months was founded on the sun, which is the right way. They could predict with accuracy the new appearance and subsequent motion of the wandering stars, while the merest glimpse of the moon told them in what phase it stood, for each night of the moon-month bore its own special name, derived from the progress of the moon through its cycle. Men like Tupuna and Teroro even knew, by counting ahead six months, in what constellation the sun stood; so they were prepared, as they sailed north, to lose some of their familiar stars; conversely, they knew that they would come upon new stars, and it was with the joy of discovery that they identified the hitherto unseen stars of the north. But in all their wisdom, they were not prepared for what they discovered on the eleventh night.

Having set their course, they were surveying the northern heavens when the old man saw, bobbing above the waves, a new star, not of maximum brightness like the vast beacons of the south—for the voyagers found the northern stars rather disappointing in brilliance in comparison with theirs—but nevertheless an interesting newcomer.

"See how it lies in a direct line from the two stars in Bird-with-a-Long-Neck," Tupuna pointed out, referring to stars which others called the Big Dipper.

At first Teroro could not catch the bright star, for it danced up and down on the horizon, now visible above the waves, now lost. Then he saw it, a bright, clean, cold star, well marked in an empty space of the sky. Speaking as a navigator he said, "That would be a strong star to steer by . . . when it rises a little higher."

Tupuna observed, "We must watch carefully, the next few nights, to see which pit of heaven it goes into."

So on the twelfth night the two men studied the new guidepost, but as dawn appeared each was afraid to tell the other what he had seen, for each realized that he had stumbled upon an omen of such magnitude that it did not bear speaking of. Each keeping his own counsel, the two astronomers spent the last minutes of darkness watching the new star with an apprehension that bordered upon panic, and when daylight ended their vigil, they licked their dry lips and went to their beds knowing they would not sleep.

It was no more than midafternoon on the following day when the two men took their positions to study the heavens. "Stars won't be out for many hours," Tupuna said warily.

"I'm watching the sun," Teroro lied, and when Tehani brought him his water and stood smiling by the mast of Tane, her preoccupied husband did not bother to smile back, so she went aft with the women.

Swiftly, at six in the evening, and not lingeringly as at Bora Bora, the sun left the sky and the stars began to appear. There were the Seven Little Eyes, blessing the canoe, and later Three-in-a-Row, now well to the south, and the very bright stars of Tahiti; but what the men watched was only the strange new star. There it was, and for nine hours the two astronomers studied it, unwilling to come to the conclusion that was inescapable. But when they had triangulated the sky in every known way, when they had proved their frightening thesis beyond doubt, they were forced, each working by himself, to the terrifying conclusion.

It was Tupuna who put it into words: "The new star does not move."

"It is fixed," Teroro agreed.

The two men used these words in a new meaning; they had always spoken of the bright wandering stars that moved in and out of the constellations like beautiful girls at a dance; and they had contrasted these with the stars of fixed position; but they realized that in a grand sense the latter also moved, rising out of pits in the east and falling into the pits of the west. Some, who hurried around the Southern Cross, rose from one pit and quickly dropped into another, and there were even a few that never disappeared below the waves; but all moved through the heavens. The new star did not.

"We had better consult with the king," Tupuna advised, but when they went aft they found Tamatoa sleeping, and no man would dare waken another suddenly, lest the sleeper's spirit be out wandering and have no time to slip back in through the corner of the eye. A man without a spirit would go mad, but Tamatoa slept soundly and his uncle grew nervous, holding as he did the news of the ominous fixed star.

"Could you cough?" he asked Teroro. The navigator did, but with no results.

"What would let him know we are waiting?" Tupuna asked petulantly. He went outside the grass house, took a paddle and tapped the side of the canoe, whereupon the king, like any captain who hears a strange noise aboard his ship, rolled uneasily, cleared his throat and gave his wandering spirit ample time to climb back into his eye.

"What's happening?"

"An omen of terrible significance," Tupuna whispered. They showed Tamatoa the new star and said, "It does not move."

Anxiously, the three watched for an hour and then summoned old Teura, advising her: "Tane has set a star in the heavens which does not move. What can it signify?"

The old woman insisted upon an hour in which to study the phenomenon for herself, at the end of which she decided that the men were correct. The star did not move, but how should such an omen be read? She said, haltingly, "Tane is the keeper of the stars. If he has placed this miracle before us, it is because he wishes to speak to us."

"What is his message?" the king asked apprehensively.

"I have never seen such an omen," Teura parried.

"Could it mean that Tane has put a barrier, fixed and immovable, before us?" Tamatoa asked, for it was his responsibility to keep the voyage harmonious with the will of the gods. Others could afford to misinterpret omens, but not he.

"It would seem so," Teura said. "Else why would the star be set there, like a rock?"

Apprehension gripped them, for if Tane was against this voyage, all must perish. They could not go back now. "And yet," Tupuna recalled, "the chant says that when the west wind dies, we are to paddle across the sea of no wind toward the new star. Is this not the new star, fixed there for us to use?"

For many minutes the group discussed this hopeful concept and concluded that it might have merit. They decided, therefore, that this should be done: continue for the coming day along the course set by the westerly wind and consult again at dusk, weighing all omens. The four went to their appointed places and discharged their various tasks, but in the remaining moments of the night Teroro stood alone in the prow studying the new star, and gradually a new idea germinated in his brain, tentatively at first, like a drum beating in the far distance, and then with compelling intensity.

He began softly: "If this new star is fixed . . . Suppose it actually does hang there night after night and at all hours . . . Let's say that every star in the new heavens can be associated with it in known patterns . . ." He lost the thread of some compelling thought and started over again.

"If this star is immovable, it must hang at a known distance above the horizon . . . No, that's not right. What I mean is, for every island, this fixed star must hang at a known distance . . . Start with Tahiti. We know exactly what stars hang directly over Tahiti at each hour of the night for each night of the year. Now if this fixed star . . ."

Again he was unable to draw together the threads of his thought, but he sensed that some grand design of the gods was making itself manifest, so he wrapped one arm around the mast of Tane and concentrated his entire being upon the new star. "If it hangs there forever, then every island must stand in some relationship to it. Therefore, once you see how high that star is, you know exactly how far north or south you must sail in order to find your island. If you can see the star, you will know! You will know!"

Suddenly, and with dazzling clarity, Teroro saw an entirely new system of navigation based on Tane's gift, the fixed star, and he thought: "Life must be sweet indeed for sailors in these waters!" For he knew that northern sailors had what southerners did not: a star which could tell them, at a single glance, their latitude. "The heavens are fixed!" he cried to himself. "And I shall be free to move beneath them." He looked happily to the west where the Little Eyes blinked at him prior to dawn, and he whispered to them, "The new land you lead us to must be sweet indeed if it exists in such an ordered ocean beneath such an ordered sky."

And for the rest of the voyage, through the terrible days that lay ahead, Teroro alone, of all the canoe, knew no fear. He was sure. He was secure in his conviction that Tane would not have hung that fixed star where it was except for some high purpose, and he, Teroro, had divined that purpose. Up to now he had given no one cause to think that he merited his name, the Brain; certainly he could never be a knowledgeable priest like his uncle Tupuna, and that was a pity, for priests were needed. Nor had he wisdom in political counsels like his brother; but on this night he proved that he could do something that none of his companions could: he could look at the evidence planted in the universe and from it derive a new concept, and a greater thing than this no mind can accomplish. On what Teroro foresaw that night the navigation of the islands ahead would be built and their location in the ocean determined. In his joy of discovery Teroro wanted to sing, but he was not a poet.

Yet in his very moment of triumph, he experienced an emptiness that had been with him for many days and which apparently was not going to dissipate. When he finally grasped the significance of the fixed star, he wanted to discuss his concept with Marama, but she was absent and there was not much use talking about a thing like this with Tehani, for whereas Marama would have grasped the idea at once, beautiful little Tehani would have looked at the heavens and asked, "What star?" It was curious the way in which Marama's last cry persisted in Teroro's ears: "I am the canoe!" In a most strange way, she was, for she was the on-going spirit of the canoe; it was her grave face that Teroro often saw ahead of him on the waves, and when *Wait-for-the-West-Wind* in its swift flight overtook the vision in the waters, Marama smiled as the canoe swept past, and Teroro felt that all was well.

Into the arid heat of the doldrums they plunged. The sun beat upon them by day and the rainless stars mocked them at night. Now not even distant squalls passed with the tantalizing hope that rain might come. They knew it would not.

Teroro planned so that Mato and Pa, the two sturdiest paddlers, would not work at the same time; also, after an hour's stint in the right hull, which tore the muscles of the left shoulder, the paddlers would shift sides and wear out their right shoulders. At each shift six men would drop out and rest. But onward the canoe went, constantly.

From time to time the stronger women would take paddles, whereupon the shift was shortened to half an hour; while in the bottom of each hull the artisans and the slaves worked constantly baling the water that seeped in through the calked cracks where the pieces of log which formed the hull had been tied together.

It was ironic, and a fact remarked by all, that in the storm when fresh water was plentiful, the sails did most of the work, whereas now, when men sweated and strained endlessly with the paddles, there was no water. The king ordered it to be doled out in ever-decreasing portions, so that the harder the men worked, the less they had to drink.

The women, with scarcely any water, suffered miserably, while the slaves were near death. The farmers had an especially cruel task. Tenderly they would hold open the mouth of a pig and drop water inside to keep the animal alive, whereas they needed the fluid more than the animal; but the death of a farmer could be tolerated; the death of a pig would have been catastrophe.

Still the canoe bore on. At night Teroro, with his lips burning, would place on the platform near the prow a half coconut, filled with placid sea water, and in it he would catch the reflection of the fixed star, and by keeping this reflection constant in the cup, he maintained his course.

At daybreak, red-eyed Teura would sit in the blazing heat, her old body almost desiccated by the sun, and speculate upon the omens. Hour after hour she muttered, "What will bring rain?" The flight of birds might indicate where islands were, and water, but no birds flew. "Red clouds in patches in the eastern sky bring rain, for certain," she recalled, but there were no clouds. At night the moon was full, brilliant as a disk of polished Tridacna, but when she studied the moon she found no ring around it, no omen of storm. "If there were a wind," she muttered, "it might bring us to a storm," but there was no wind. Repeatedly she chanted: "Stand up, stand up, the big wave from Tahiti. Blow down, blow down, the great wind from Moorea." But in these new seas her invocations were powerless.

Day followed day of remorseless heat, worse than anyone in the canoe had ever previously experienced. On the seventeenth day one of the women died, and as her body was plunged into the perpetual care of Ta'aroa, god of the mysterious deep, the men who were to have been her husbands wept, and through the entire canoe there was a longing for rain and the cool valleys of Bora Bora, and it was not surprising that many began to deplore having come upon this voyage.

Hot nights were followed by blazing days, and the only thing that seemed to live in the canoe was the dancing new star as it leaped about in the coconut cup which Teroro studied; and then late one night as the navigator watched his star, he saw on the horizon, lighted by the moon, a breath of storm. It was small at first, and wavering, and Mato whispered, "Is that rain?"

At first Teroro would not reply, and then, with a mighty shout, he roared into the night, "Rain!"

The grass house emptied. The sleeping paddlers wakened and watched as a cloud obscured the moon. A wind rose, and a light capping of the sea could be seen in starlight. It must be a substantial storm, and not a passing squall. It was worth pursuing, and everyone began to paddle furiously. Those with no paddles used their hands, and even the king, distraught with hope, grabbed a bailing bucket from a slave and paddled with it.

How desperately they worked, and how tantalizingly the storm eluded them. Through the remaining portion of the night, the canoe sped on, its men collapsing with thirst and exhaustion, in pursuit of the storm. They did not catch it, and as the blazing day came upon them, driving the clouds back to the horizon, and then beyond, an awful misery settled upon the canoe. The paddlers, their strength exhausted in the fruitless quest, lay listless and allowed the sun to beat upon them. Teroro was of no use. Old Tupuna was near death, and the pigs wept protestingly in the waterless heat.

Only the king was active. Sitting cross-legged on his mat he prayed ceaselessly. "Great Tane, you have always been generous to us in the past," he cajoled. "You have given us taro and breadfruit in abundance. You brought our pigs to fatness and birds to our traps. I am grateful to you, Tane. I am loyal to you. I prefer you above all other gods." He continued in this way for many minutes, hot sweat upon his face, reminding the deity of their close and profitable relationships in the past. Then, from the depth of his despair, he pleaded: "Tane, bring us rain."

From a short distance forward, red-eyed Teura heard the king praying and crept back to him, but she brought him terror, not assurance, for she whispered, "The fault is mine, nephew."

"What have you done?" the king asked in spittle-dry tones.

"Two nights before we left Bora Bora I had a dream and I ignored it. A voice came to me crying, 'Teura, you have forgotten me.' "

"What?" the king rasped, catching his aunt's withered arm. "That was my dream."

"A voice crying, 'You have forgotten me!' Was that your dream, too?"

"No," the king replied in ashen tones. "Two stars, combing the heavens, looking for something I had forgotten to put into the canoe."

"Was that why you unpacked everything at the last?" Teura asked.

"Yes."

"And you discovered no lack?"

"Nothing." The two wise people, on whom the success of this voyage now depended, sat despondent. "What have we forgotten?" They could find no answer, but they knew, each now fortified with substantiation from the other, that this voyage was conducted under an evil omen. "What have we forgotten?" they pleaded.

In bleak despair they stared at each other and found no answer, so Teura, her eyes already inflamed from watching the merciless sun, went out to the lifeless platform and prayed for omens, and as she gave her whole being to this duty, the great blue shark came beside the canoe and whispered, "Are you afraid that you will die, Teura?"

"Not for myself," she replied calmly. "I'm an old woman. But my two nephews . . . Isn't there anything you can do for them, Mano?"

"You haven't been watching the horizon," the shark admonished.

"Where?"

"To the left."

And as she looked, she saw a cloud, and then a disturbance ruffling the ashen sea, and then the movement of a storm, and rain. "Oh, Mano," she whispered, afraid to believe. "Is the rain coming toward us?"

"Look, Teura," the great blue shark laughed.

"Once before it looked the same," she whispered.

"This time follow me," the blue beast cried, and with a shimmering leap he splashed into the sea, her personal god, her salvation.

With a wild scream she cried, "Rain! Rain!" And all rushed out from the house, and dead sleepers wakened to find a storm bearing down upon them.

"Rain!" they mumbled as it marched across the ocean nearer and nearer.

"It's coming!" Tamatoa shouted. "Our prayers are answered." But old Teura, laughing madly as the benign water struck her face, saw in the heart of the storm her own god, Mano, his blue fin cutting the waves.

Almost as if by command, the near-dying voyagers began to throw off their clothes, their tapa and their shells, until each stood naked in the divine storm, drinking it into their eyes and their blistering armpits and their parched mouths. The winds rose, and the rains increased, but the naked men and women of Bora Bora continued their revel in the slashing waves. The sails came down and the mast of Ta'aroa was almost carried away, and the dogs whined, but the men in the canoe swept the water into their mouths and embraced each other. Into the night the storm continued, and it seemed as if the sections of the canoe must break apart, but no one called for the storm to abate. They fought it and drank it and washed their aching bodies with it, and sailed into the heart of it, and toward morning, exhausted in sheer joy, they watched as the clouds parted and they saw that they were almost under the path of the Seven Little Eyes, and they knew that they must ride with the easterly wind that had brought the storm. Their destination lay somewhere to the west.

IT WAS A LONG leg to windward they took. For nearly two thousand miles they ran before the easterlies, covering most days more than a hundred and fifty miles. Now the fixed star remained at about the same height above the horizon, on their right, and they followed close to the path of Little Eyes. At sunset Teroro would tilt his coconut cup backward to catch the bright star that stood near Little Eyes as they rose in the east. Later, as the constellation which men in the deserts had named the Eagle sank into the west, he would steer by its bright star, shifting back and forth between it ahead and Little Eyes to the rear, thus keeping always on course.

It was on this long westward leg that King Tamatoa's earlier insistence on discipline preserved the voyage, for now food had run perilously low and for some perverse reason the numerous fish in these strange waters would not bite; Tupuna explained that it was because they lived under the influence of the fixed star and that the Bora Bora fishhooks had not been adjusted to this new consideration. Every woman and all men who were not paddling kept lines, long and short, in the sea, but to no avail.

There was a little coconut left and a small amount of breadfruit, but no taro. Even the pigs, absolutely essential to the success of the journey, were famishing. But in this extremity the thirty paddlers, who worked constantly, survived amazingly. Their stomachs had long since contracted into hard little fists, shrunk to nothing under tight belly muscles. Their strong shoulders, devoid of even a trace of fat after nearly a month's steady work, seemed able to generate energy from nothing. With neither food nor adequate water, the men sweated little; through sun-reddened eyes they constantly scanned the horizon for omens.

It was old Teura, however, who saw the first substantial sign; on the twenty-seventh morning she saw a small piece of driftwood, torn away from some distant tree, and Teroro avidly directed the canoe toward it. When it was pulled aboard it was found to contain four land worms, which were fed to the astonished chickens.

"It has been in the ocean less than ten days," Teura announced. Since the canoe could travel five or six times faster than a drifting branch, it seemed likely that land lay somewhere near; and old Teura entered into a period of intense concentration, clutching at omens and interpreting them hopefully by means of old prayers.

But *West Wind* was not to be saved by incantations. It was Mato, a trained sailor, who late one afternoon saw in the distance a flock of birds flying with determination on a set course westward. "There's land ahead. They're heading for it," he cried. Tupuna and Teroro agreed, and when, a few hours later, the stars rose, it was reassuring to see that the Seven Little Eyes confirmed that they were near the end of their journey.

"A few more days," Teroro announced hopefully.

And two days later, aching with hunger, Mato again spotted a bird, and this one was of special significance, for it was a gannet, poised seventy feet in the air; suddenly it raised its wings, dropped its head toward the waves, and plunged like a thrown rock deep into the ocean. It looked as if it must have split its skull on impact, but by some mysterious trick, it had not, and in a moment it flew aloft with a fish in its beak. Deftly it flipped the food into its gullet, then plunged again with head-splitting force.

"We are surely approaching land!" Mato cried. But many on the platform thought of the gannet not as a harbinger of land, but rather as a lucky bird that knew how to fish.

In the early morning of the twenty-ninth day a group of eleven long black birds with handsome cleft tails flew by on a foraging trip from their home island, which lay somewhere beyond the horizon, and Teroro noted with keen pleasure that their heading, reversed, was his, and while he watched he saw these intent birds come upon a group of diving gannets, and when those skilled fishers rose into the air with their catch, the fork-tailed birds swept down upon them, attacked them, and forced them to drop the fish, whereupon the foragers caught the morsels in mid-air and flew away. From their presence it could be deduced that land was not more than sixty miles distant, a fact which was confirmed when Teura and Tupuna, working together, detected in the waves of the sea a peculiar pattern which indicated that in the near distance the profound westerly set of the ocean was impounding upon a reef, which shot back echo waves that cut across the normal motion of the sea; but unfortunately a heavy bank of cloud obscured the western horizon, reaching even to the sea, and none could detect exactly where the island lay.

"Don't worry!" Teura reassured everyone. "When the clouds do lift, watch their undersides carefully. At sunset you'll see them turn green over the island. Reflections from the lagoon." And so convinced was Teura that they were approaching some small island like Bora Bora with a lagoon, that she chose the spot from which the wave echoes seemed to be generating and stared fixedly at it.

As she had hoped, toward dusk the clouds began to dissipate, and it was Teura who first saw the new island looming ahead. Gasping, she cried, "Oh, great Tane! What is it?"

"Look! Look!" shouted Teroro.

And there before them, rearing from the sea like an undreamed-of monster, rose a tremendous mountain more massive than they had ever imagined, crowned in strange white and soaring majestically into the evening sunset.

"What a land we have found!" Teroro whispered.

"It is the land of Tane!" King Tamatoa announced in a hushed whisper. "It reaches to heaven itself."

And all in the canoe, seeing this clean and wonderful mountain, fell silent and did it reverence, until Pa cried, "Look! It is smoking!" And as night fell, the last sight the men of Bora Bora had was of a gigantic mountain, hung in the heavens, sending fumes from its peak.

The vision haunted the voyagers, for they knew it must be an omen of some proportions, and in the quiet hours of the night old Teura dreamed and woke screaming. The king hurried to her side, and she whispered, "I know what it was we forgot."

She went aft with her nephew, to where no one could hear, and she confided: "The same dream returned. I heard this voice crying, 'You have forgotten me.' But this time I recognized the voice. We have left behind a goddess whom we should have brought."

King Tamatoa felt a sick quaking near his heart and asked, "What goddess?" for he knew that if a goddess felt insulted, there was no restriction on the steps she might take in exacting revenge; her capacity was limitless.

"It is the voice of Pere, the ancient goddess of Bora Bora," the old woman replied. "Tell me, nephew, when your wandering stars were searching the heavens, were they not attended by specks of fire?"

The king tried to recall his haunting premonitory dream and was able, with extraordinary clarity, to conjure it, and he agreed: "There were specks of fire. Among the northern stars."

They summoned Tupuna and told him the burden of his wife's dream, and he acknowledged that it must have been the goddess Pere who had wanted to come on the voyage, whereupon his nephew asked, "But who is Pere?"

"In ancient days on Bora Bora," the old man explained as the thin-horned curve of the dying moon rose in the east, "our island had mountains that smoked, and Pere was the goddess of flame who directed our lives. But the flame died away and we supposed that Pere had left us, and we no longer worshiped the red-colored rock that stood in the temple."

"I had forgotten Pere," Teura confessed. "Otherwise I would have recognized her voice. But tonight, seeing the smoking mountain, I remembered."

"And she is angry with us?" the king asked.

"Yes," Teura replied. "But Tane and Ta'aroa are with us, and they will protect us."

The old seers went back to their places, and the king was left alone, in the shadow of his new land now barely visible in the misty moonlight. He was disturbed that a man could take so much care to satisfy the gods, and that he could nevertheless fail. He could study the omens, bend his will to them, and live only at the gods' commands; but always some small thing intruded; an old woman fails to recognize the voice of a goddess and disaster impinges upon an entire venture. He knew the rock of Pere; it had been retained in the temple for no known reason, both its name and its properties forgotten; it was no longer even dressed in feathers. It would have been so simple to have brought that rock, but the facts had eluded him and now he felt at the mercy of a revengeful goddess who had been deeply insulted, the more so because she had taken the trouble to warn him. He beat his hands against the poles of the grass hut and cried, "Why can we never do anything right?"

If the king was perplexed by his arrival at the new land, there were other passengers who were terrified. In the rear of the left hull, the slaves huddled in darkness, whispering. The four men were telling the two women that they had loved them and that they hoped the women were pregnant and that they would bear children, even though those children would be slaves. They recalled the few good days they had known on Bora Bora, the memorable days when they had chanced upon one of the king's stray pigs and had eaten it surreptitiously, for to have done so openly would have meant immediate death, or the days when the high nobles were absent from the island and they had been free to breathe. In the fading darkness of the night, for a day of great terror was about to dawn, they whispered of love, of human affection and of lost hopes; for the four men knew that when the canoe landed, a temple would be built, and when the four corner post holes had been dug, deep and sound, one of them would be buried alive in each, so that his spirit would forever hold the temple securely aloft, and the doomed men could already feel the taste of earth in their nostrils; they could feel the pressure of the sacred post upon their vitals; and they knew death.

Their two women, soon to be abandoned, could taste worse punishment, for they had come to love these four men; they knew how gentle they were, how kind to children and how alert to the world's beauty. Soon, for no ascertainable reason, the men would be sacrificed, and then the women would live on the edge of their community, and if they were already pregnant, and if their children were sons, they would be thrown under the prows of canoes to bless the wood and to be torn in shreds by it. Then when they were not pregnant, on strange nights men of the crew, their faces masked, would rudely force their way into the slave compartments, lie with the women, and go away, for if it were known that a chief had had contact with a slave woman, he would be punished; but all had such contact. And when the children of these unions were born, they would be slaves; and if they grew to manhood, they would be ripped to pieces under canoes or hung about the altars of gods; and if they grew to comely womanhood, they would be ravished at night by men they never knew. And the cycle would go on through all eternity, for they were slaves.

In the early light of morning it became apparent that the smoking mountain and its supporting island lay much farther away than had at first been supposed, and a final day of hunger and work faced the paddlers; but the visible presence of their goal spurred the famished men so that by nightfall it was certain that next morning the long voyage would end. Through the last soft tropical night, with the luminous mountain ahead, the crew of the *West Wind* followed their rhythmic, steady beat.

As they approached the end of a trek nearly five thousand miles long, it is appropriate to compare what they had accomplished with what voyagers in other parts of the world were doing. In the Mediterranean, descendants of once-proud Phoenicians, who even in their moments of glory had rarely ventured out of sight of land, now coasted along established shores and occasionally, with what was counted bravery, actually cut across the trivial sea in voyages covering perhaps two hundred miles. In Portugal men were beginning to accumulate substantial bodies of information about the ocean, but to probe it they were not yet ready, and it would be six hundred more years before even near-at-hand islands like Madeira and the Azores would be found. Ships had coasted the shores of Africa, but it was known that crossing the equator and thus losing sight of the North Star meant boiling death, or falling off the edge of the world, or both.

On the other side of the earth, Chinese junks had coasted Asia and in the southern oceans had moved from one visible island to the next, terming the act heroism. From Arabia and India, merchants had undertaken considerable voyages, but never very far from established coasts, while in the undiscovered continents to the west of Europe, no men left the land.

Only in the north of Europe did the Vikings display enterprise even remotely comparable to that of the men of Bora Bora; but even they had not yet begun their long voyages, though they had at their disposal metals, large ships, woven sails, books and maps.

It was left to the men of the Pacific, men like cautious Tamatoa and energetic Teroro, to meet an ocean on its own terms and to conquer it. Lacking both metals and maps, sailing with only the stars and a few lengths of sennit, some dried taro and positive faith in their gods, these men accomplished miracles. It would be another seven centuries before an Italian navigator, sailing under the flag of Spain and fortified by all the appurtenances of an advanced community, would dare, in three large and commodious ships well nailed together, to set forth upon a voyage not quite so far and only half as dangerous.

At dawn Teroro brought his canoe close to land at the southeastern shore of the vast volcanic island that rose from the southeast end of the rupture in the ocean floor. When the shoreline became visible, the voyagers had many thoughts. Teroro reflected in some disappointment: "It's all rocks. Where are the coconuts? Where's the water?" Mato, who paddled in the hull nearest the land, thought: "No breadfruit." But King Tamatoa mused: "It is the land Tane brought us to. It must be good."

Only Tupuna appreciated the profound problems which the next few hours would bring. In trembling apprehension he thought: "The children of my brothers are about to step upon new land. Everything depends on the next minutes, for this island is obviously filled with strange gods, and we must do nothing to offend them. But will I be able to placate them all?"

So he moved with agitation about the canoe, endeavoring to arrange things so that the unknown gods would be offended as little as possible. "Don't pick up a single stone," he warned. "Don't break a branch or eat a shellfish." Then he went to the gods' house and called Pa to his side, handing him a square of flat stone. "You will follow me," he said, "because you are extremely brave." He adjusted the king's feather cape, handed Teroro a spear, and lifted into his own shaking hands the two gods, Tane and Ta'aroa.

"Now!" he cried, and the canoe touched land.

First to disembark was Tamatoa, and as soon as he had made one footprint in the sand, he stopped, kneeled down, and took that earth into his hands, bringing it to his lips, where he kissed it many times. "This is the land," he chanted gravely. "This is a man's home. This is good land to settle upon, a good land on which to have children. Here we shall bring our ancestors. Here we bring our gods."

Behind him, in the prow of the canoe, stood Tupuna, his face upraised. "Tane, we thank you for the safe voyage," he whispered. Then, in penetrating voice, he called, "You unknown gods! You brave and gentle gods who hold this island! You fine and generous gods of the smoking mountain! You forty gods, you forty thousand gods, you forty million gods! Allow us to land. Allow us to share your treasures, and we will honor you." He was about to step ashore with his own gods, but the idea of invading a new land was too overpowering, so he shouted once more, "Terrible, all-seeing gods, may I please land?"

He stepped upon the land, expecting some awful omen, but none came and he told Pa, "You may bring the rock of Bora Bora onto its new home," and the shark-faced warrior leaped ashore with the only lasting memorial of home: a square of rock. When he stood beside the king, Tupuna cried, "Now you, Teroro, with your spear."

But when it came time for Teroro to leave the canoe, he did not worry about new gods. He placed his two hands on the prow of *Wait-for-the-West-Wind* and whispered, as gently as if he were speaking to Marama, "Beautiful, lovely ship. Forgive me for cutting away your glory. You are the queen of the ocean." And he leaped ashore to guard his brother in the next fateful moments.

Tupuna left three warriors at the canoe to guard it, while the others strung out in line and formed the solemn procession that would invade the island. At the head of his nervous column marched Tupuna, and whenever he came to a large rock, he begged the god of that rock to let him pass. When he came to a grove of trees he cried, "God of these trees, we come in friendship."

They had gone only a short distance inland when a passing cloud dropped misty rain upon them, and Tupuna shouted, "We are received! The gods bless us. Quick! See where the rainbow ends!"

It was Pa, holding the stone of Bora Bora, who saw the arc come to earth, and Tupuna cried, "There will be our temple!" And he hurried to the spot, crying, "Any evil that is here, Tane, push it aside, for this is to be your temple!"

The foot of the rainbow had fallen on an inviting plateau overlooking the ocean, and Tamatoa said, "This is a good omen indeed." Then he and his white-bearded uncle began their search for a high male rock, for both knew that the earth itself was female, and therefore polluted, but that solid rocks of impermeable stone were male, and therefore uncontaminated, and after a long search he found a large protrusion of male rock coming erect out of fine reddish soil, and when Tupuna saw it he said, "A perfect site for an altar."

So Pa placed upon this male rock his slab of Bora Bora stone, and with this symbolic action the new island was occupied, for upon the flat stone Tupuna reverently placed the fine old gods Tane and Ta'aroa. Then he climbed back to the sea with a coconut cup which he filled with water, and this he sprinkled over the temple area, over the gods, and over every human being who had come in the canoe, flicking it into their faces with the long finger of his right hand. "Now let us purify ourselves," he said, leading every living thing into the ocean: king, warrior, pig, chicken and breadfruit bundle. In the cool sea the voyagers replenished themselves and a canny woman cried, as soon as the job was done, "Do you know what I stood on? Hundreds of shellfish!" And all who were purified fell back into waves and began routing out succulent shellfish. Prying the sweet snails loose, they popped them into their mouths and grinned.

When they were satiated, Tupuna announced, "Now we must design the temple," and the slaves began to tremble. The old man led everyone back to the plateau, and while they watched, he and Tamatoa laid out the four sacred corners of the temple, and large piles of rock were collected about deep holes which the farmers dug.

The king signaled his warriors to bury the four quaking slaves, but

Teroro prevented the sacrifice. Placing himself before the slaves, he pleaded: "Brother, let us not launch our new island by more killing."

Tamatoa, astonished, explained: "But the temple must be upheld!"

"Tane doesn't require that!" Teroro argued.

"But we have always done so."

"Isn't that why we left Havaiki and red Oro?"

"But that was Oro," the king rationalized. "This is Tane."

"Brother! I beg you! Don't start this killing!" Then, remembering how his best men had been sacrificed, he pleaded: "Ask the men!"

But this was not a question on which Tamatoa could take a vote. It concerned his relationship to the gods; perhaps the entire fortune of the voyage depended on these next few minutes. "Your words are ill timed," he said stubbornly.

Tupuna supported him, grumbling petulantly, "From the beginning of time, temples have been held up by men."

"Bury the slaves!" Tamatoa ordered.

But again Teroro spread his arms before them and cried, "Brother, don't do this thing!" Then an idea came to him and he pleaded, "If we must sacrifice to Tane, let us sacrifice the male pig."

For a moment the idea was appealing; all knew that Tane loved pig sacrifices more than any other. But Tupuna killed the suggestion. "We must keep the boar to breed more pigs," he said flatly, and all agreed.

But Teroro, impassioned by his desire to start the colony correctly, cried, "Wait! Long ago when we had no pigs, we gave Tane ulua, the man-of-the-sea!"

When Tamatoa looked at his uncle for confirmation, the old man nodded. "The gods are pleased with man-of-the-sea," he admitted.

"Give me half an hour," Teroro pleaded, and he took six of his best fishermen, and they waded onto the reef and cast their lines and Teroro prayed, "Ta'aroa, god of the sea and of the fish that live therein, send us ulua to save men's lives." And when they had caught eight, two for each corner, they returned to the plateau, and Tamatoa looked at the big handsome fish and said, "For three of the corners we will use the man-of-the-sea. But for the essential corner we will use a man."

"Please . . ." Teroro began, but the king roared in anger, "Silence! You are in command of the canoe, but I am in command of the temple. What would Tane say if we begrudged him his due?" So, in anxiety of spirit, Teroro left the scene, for he would not be partner to what was about to occur, and if the priest and the king conspired to kill him for his offense, he did not care. He sat on a distant rock and thought: "We flee an evil, but we bring it with us," and he knew bitterness.

When he was gone the king said to Mato, "Bury the fish," and they were placed in three of the holes. Then he directed: "Mato, bring us one of the slaves." And the warrior went to the six who huddled apart and said bluntly: "I am sent by the king to select one of you to be the spirit for the temple."

Although the slaves were gratified that only one had to die, they were anguished that the choice of that one was forced on them. Looking at one another, they asked, "Which of us shall go to die for our masters?" The six wept, and one who had a position of leadership finally pointed and said, "You, perhaps."

The man identified gasped and steeled himself for his ordeal. First he moved to the leader who had named him and rubbed noses with him, signifying that he went to his death with no hatred. Then he rubbed noses with the other two men, saying to each, "It is better that of the two of us I should die. Between you and me, good friend, it shall be I." But when he came to the second woman, whom he loved, and when he rubbed noses with her for the last mournful time, he could not speak, and he marched from her to the pit, where he was thrown in, with the stones crushed down upon him, and where earth was pounded about him and over him, and where in silence he met dark death.

When the consecration of the temple was completed, and when mana had again begun to flow from the gods into King Tamatoa, so that he could function as king, Tupuna organized his second expedition, and with all save four who guarded the canoe and the animals, he probed deeper into the unknown in search of food. It was not a productive journey, for there was almost no food available. They did come upon a fern whose inner core was just barely edible, and to the fern Tupuna said, "Oh, secret god of this sweet fern, we are hungry. Allow us to borrow your trunk, and we will leave the roots so that you will grow again."

They came upon a taller tree than any they had known in Bora Bora, and Pa observed: "One tree like that would build a house," so Tupuna reverently prayed, "Mighty tree, we need your wood to build a house. Please let us borrow your strength. See, I plant at your roots a rich ulua for you to eat, and when you are finished, may we come and use your wood?"

If they did not find food, they did come upon something almost as good: a cave well up from the reach of the sea, and dry. At its entrance Tupuna buried his last ulua and prayed: "Gods of this cave, please take away any dark things you have left hiding here. Allow me to sprinkle holy water that this place may be sanctified." Then he entered and called back: "This will be our home."

At this point there came a shout of laughter from the shore, where the pigs had been turned loose, and it was obvious that the old boar still had sea legs, for he would take a few steps, wait for the canoe to surge beneath him, adjust his legs to meet it, and then fall snout-first into the sand. Looking dazed, he would grunt loudly and adjust his wobbly legs for the next roll, only to fall on his face again. The watchers roared with glee and forgot the haunting uncertainties that perplexed them, for the infuriated hog brought them the therapy of laughter, so that when Tupuna cried, "Move everything to the cave!" they responded willingly, and in labor ignored the danger, threatening all of them, that in their new home there might be no food.

But when they got to the cave with their burdens, two farmers reported: "There are many birds on this island, good ones," and as if to prove this claim, overhead flew a line of terns, which ate clean fresh fish, so that when baked they tasted like delicious chicken and bonito, mixed. Tamatoa, looking at the terns, said, "Tane would never have brought us here if there were no food. It may not be the food we have known, but it's here. Our job is to find it."

Now, with the temple established and the gods at home, with the great canoe properly beached, and all treasures stowed in the cave, the hungry men who had completed this long voyage began to look at their women, and one by one the emaciated but handsome girls of the long black hair were led into the bushes and cherished, and strange multiple marriages were begun, and new life was launched on the island.

But of the women, the fairest could not find her man, for Teroro was brooding by the sea, reflecting on the sacrifice of the slave and its dark portent for the new homeland, so Tehani left the cave and walked down to the sea, crying in vain, "Teroro, Teroro!" until Mato, who so far had no woman of his own and who had sat close to Tehani all the way north, thus seeing her in many lights and appreciating her quality, heard her and ran through the woods until he could, as if by accident, encounter her along the shore. "Can't you find Teroro?" he asked casually.

"No."

"Perhaps he has important business," Mato suggested.

"Where?" Tehani asked.

"I don't know. Maybe . . ." He took Tehani's hand and tried to lead her back into the trees through which he had just run, but she pulled away.

"No!" she insisted. "I am a chief's daughter and a chief's wife."

"Are you Teroro's wife?" Mato chided.

"What do you mean?" she demanded, her long hair flashing across her delicate breasts as she turned her head sharply.

"I sat very near you on the trip, Tehani," Mato explained. "It didn't look to me as if Teroro thought of you as his wife."

"I was tabu," she explained.

"But thinking of you wasn't tabu," Mato said. "Teroro never thought of you, Tehani. I did."

He took her hand again, and this time she held on to the rugged young chief, because she knew that what he said was true. "I am very alone," she confessed.

"Do you know what I think, Tehani? I think you will never be Teroro's wife. I think he is hungry for his old wife Marama."

Since Tehani shared this suspicion, she experienced a moment of recognition and felt strongly drawn toward Mato and allowed him to pull her into the dark glade away from the shore, and to slip her leafy skirt from her, until in her nakedness she looked at him and realized how desperately she wanted this young man who did not reject her; and he, looking for the first time at her exquisite beauty, diminished though it had been by the voyage, felt a pang of sorrow that such a girl should have been given to a man who did not want her. Gathering her in his arms he whispered, "You are my woman, Tehani."

But when she actually felt his body against hers, and when she heard his words, she grew afraid, for she knew that she was not his woman, and she broke away and ran back to the beach, adjusting her skirt as she went. Before Mato could overtake her she saw Teroro and ran up to him, crying nervously, "You must make peace with your brother."

And she led her husband back along the ocean front, past where Mato stood bitterly watching her, and onto the plateau where King Tamatoa surveyed the rude temple. At first neither man spoke, but Teroro, looking over his brother's shoulder, could see the ominous stones resting on fresh earth. He was dismayed but said grudgingly, "This is an appropriate temple, brother. Later we will build a better." The king nodded, and it was then that Tehani of the long tresses and the flashing eyes led her bewildered husband into the darkness, knowing in her heart that it was another who should have accompanied her.

The sexual life of the king was much too important to be conducted in darkness and hidden glades, so on the next day, after the fishermen had brought in their first substantial catch and women had boiled their unpromising pandanus drupes, Tupuna announced that his wife Teura had ascertained that the time of the month was propitious and that their king, Tamatoa, would that afternoon lie with his wife Natabu. That grave and stately woman was then brought forth from beneath a tree, where she had been secluded, and a temporary shelter, made of cut saplings stuck into the ground and covered with the most consecrated tapas, was erected according to ancient custom.

When the tent was completed, sedate Natabu, who rarely spoke and who was, by a peculiar combination of omens and good circumstances, the most holy of all the voyagers, was blessed by Tupuna and led into the nuptial area and placed according to ancient custom upon the woven mats. The king was then blessed, and the entire company, including even the five slaves, surrounded the tapa house and chanted. Then, with the prayers and blessings of all the community, the king was taken to the sanctified house, placed inside by the priest, and hidden by the lowered tapa. At this point the prayers mounted in frenzy.

The woman with whom the king lay was his sister Natabu. It had been discovered anciently in the islands that for a king to breed a proper heir to the throne, one who would combine the finest lineage and the utmost sanctity, he must mate only with his full-blood sister, and although both Tamatoa and his sister Natabu might later take other spouses, their principal obligation was the production—under circumstances of the most intricate propriety, and under the surveillance of the entire community—of royal descendants.

"May the union be fruitful," old Teura chanted as her niece and nephew lay inside the tapa tent. "May it produce strong kings and princesses blessed with godlike blood." The crowd prayed: "May this union produce for us a king," and although they had prayed thus on occasion in the past, when the nuptial tent had been raised over Tamatoa in hopes of breeding an heir, they had never prayed with equal fervor, for it was apparent that in a strange land an heir of the most impeccable lineage was essential, for who else could represent them before the gods if Tamatoa died.

In the late afternoon, when the king and his sister left the rude tent, the eyes of the people followed them, and the chants continued, and all prayed that a good thing had been accomplished on that auspicious day.

When the nuptial tent was taken down and all omens pertaining to it examined, King Tamatoa faced another major obligation, for he was led by Tupuna to a field into which the farmers had diverted a small stream. This would become the taro bed upon which the community would depend for its basic food, and already the mud walls surrounding it imprisoned a foot of water, making the bottom of the field a deep, soft mass of mud. Standing at the edge, where the stream entered, Tamatoa cried, "May the mana of my body pass through my feet and bless this field!" Whereupon he stepped knee-deep into the muddy water and began trampling the bed. He was joined by Tupuna, Teroro, Mato and Pa, the men with most mana, and for hours they passed back and forth over every inch of the taro patch, hammering the mud into a watertight basin, sealing it with their mana. When they were done Tamatoa shouted, "May this bed be forever sealed. Now plant the taro!"

And according to customs more than two thousand years old, the people planted not only the taro, but the breadfruit and the bananas and the pandanus; but for no crop were they as fearful of failure as when they planted coconuts, for to a large extent their entire manner of life was intertwined with this extraordinary tree. When the nuts were young they gave delicious water; when old, a precious oil or a sweet milk. Palms from the coconut thatched many of the houses; hard shells formed cups and utensils, fibers from the husks yielded sennit. Timber from the trunk was used for building and for carving gods; the wiry fiber that grew in the crown was woven into fabric; ribs of the fronds when dried were suitable for starting fires, and sharper ribs, from the leaves, were used in making darts. But most of all, the coconut gave food, and the vocabulary of these people contained twenty-eight different names for the maturing stages of this marvelous nut; from the time when it contained a just-formed, jelly-like substance eaten with scoops by the old or ill to the day when it was a firm, sweet nut.

Therefore, when a coconut was planted, the people placed about the nut a baby octopus to hold the resulting tree erect and prayed: "May the king have done a good job this day."

When the crops were planted, a question arose as to what the island should be named, and the warriors, who knew little of omens, agreed that it ought properly to be called Bora Bora; but a great surprise was in store for them, for when Tupuna of the ancient mane heard the report he was outraged. "There is only one name for our island," he announced stubbornly.

"What?" the warriors asked.

"Havaiki," he replied.

The settlers were aghast at this suggestion and began to swear that the hated name Havaiki would never exist in their new-found refuge; and both King Tamatoa and Teroro agreed, but the old priest, his white beard long and blowing in the breeze, began the most ancient chant of his people, and no interruption of the king could stay him until he had explained, in words more precious than coconuts, for they summarized the race-experience of his people, and were its soul, who the settlers were: "In ancient times, when great Tane lay with a goddess, the people of the swift canoes were born. They lived then in Havaiki, but it was not the Havaiki we know. It was Havaiki-on-the-Great-Land, and from there King Tamatoa's father's father's father, back to forty generations, led his people in a canoe, and they went to Havaiki-Where-the-Animal-Is-Like-a-Man, and there they lived for many generations, until King Tamatoa's father's father's father, back to thirty generations, led his people in canoes to Havaiki-of-the-Green-Lagoon . . ." And in a wild soaring voice he recalled the search of his people, wandering from one land to another, always seeking an island where they would find peace and coconuts and fish. Always, wherever they landed with their burning hopes, they called their new home Havaiki, and if the new Havaiki treated them badly, it was appropriate that they set forth in search of a better, as their parents had done from time immemorial. Thus, in parables, he spoke of the migration of his ancestors from the interior of Asia, to the north coast of New Guinea, through the Samoan islands and out to distant Tahiti; later men, reconstructing the voyages, would discover more than a dozen Havaikis, but none closer to the ancient dream than the island about to be dedicated.

"For us there is only one name," the old man insisted in a burst of rhetoric. "Havaiki of the manifold riches, Havaiki of the brave canoes, Havaiki of strong gods, and courageous men and beautiful women, Havaiki of the dreams that led us across the endless oceans, Havaiki that has lived in our hearts for forty and fifty and sixty generations. This is the island of Havaiki!"

When he was finished, King Tamatoa, who had forgotten his own history, spoke solemnly: "This will be the island of Havaiki, and if you have evil memories of old Havaiki let it be remembered as Havaiki-of-

Red-Oro, but our land is Havaiki-of-the-North." So the island was named Havaiki, the last successor in a mighty chain.

It was only when Teroro, accompanied by Mato, Pa and three others, had sailed completely around Havaiki, requiring four days for the exploration, that the settlers appreciated what a magnificent island they had found. "There are two mountains, not one," Teroro explained, "and many cliffs, and birds of endless number. Rivers come down into the sea, and some of the bays are as inviting as Bora Bora's lagoon."

But it was blunt Pa who summed up what they had learned: "It looked to us as if we had picked our cave on the worst land in Havaiki." Gloomily, Mato agreed; but King Tamatoa and his aunt and uncle looked at the newly planted crops and at the temple and said stubbornly, "This is where we have established our home"; but Mato and Pa thought: "If anything should happen, we know where the good land is."

And then the forgotten one appeared. It was on a hot, dusty afternoon when Teroro had gone into the forest seeking birds, that he turned to avoid a tree and found a strange woman confronting him. She was handsome in figure, dressed in a fabric he had not seen before, and her hair, of a strange material that glistened in the sun, stood out like wild grass. She was of his race, yet she was not. With most mournful and condemning eyes she stared at Teroro until he felt his head swimming, but she did not speak. When, in unaccustomed fright, he started to run, she ran with him, and when he stopped, she stopped; but always when he paused, she stared at him in reproach. Finally, she departed in silence, whereupon Teroro regained some of his bravery and ran after her, but she had disappeared.

When he returned to the settlement, he was shivering, but for some reason which he could not explain he did not confide his experience to anyone; but sleep did not come to him that night, for he could see the deep-set, fanatic eyes of the woman staring at him in the darkness, so that on the next morning he took Mato aside and said, "I have found some birds. Let's go into the woods," and the two young chiefs moved through the trees, and Mato asked, "Where are the birds?" And suddenly the gaunt, distracted woman stood before them.

"Who is this?" Mato asked, astonished.

"She came to me yesterday. I think she wants to speak."

But the woman said nothing, content merely with admonishing the young men by her wild stare, so that Teroro said to his companion, "When we move, she will move with us." And certainly, when the warriors started walking under the trees, she walked with them, her garments disheveled and her strange hair glistening in the sun. Then, as they watched, she vanished.

"Where did she go?" Mato cried.

"Woman! Woman!" Teroro called, vainly.

The two young men consulted as to whether they should advise the others, and it was finally decided that they should, so they went first to old, red-eyed Teura and said, "In the trees we met a strange woman with different hair . . ."

Before they could finish, the old woman burst into a long wail, "Auwe, auwe! It is Pere! She has come to destroy us."

The old woman's husband hurried in and she announced: "They have seen Pere, of the burning fire!" And when the king arrived at the commotion she warned him: "The forgotten one has come to punish us."

"Auwe!" the king mourned, for he perhaps best of all understood the unforgivable error they had committed in abandoning a goddess who had warned them beforehand that she wished to accompany them, and he decided that the entire community must assemble at the temple to pray for respite from the goddess. But the prayer was not uttered, for at this moment the earth began to shake violently.

In a manner unknown to the strangers, the red earth of Havaiki rose and fell, twisted and heaved, and cracks appeared through the heart of the settlement, and pigs squealed. "Oh, Pere!" the king cried in terror. "Spare us!" And his prayer must have had power, for the trembling stopped, and the horrified voyagers huddled together to decipher this mighty omen.

They did not succeed, for a much greater was about to envelop them. From the mountain that reached high above their heads volumes of fire began to erupt, and rocks were thrown far into the air. Scattered ash fell back onto the earth and settled on the king's head and on the newly planted banana shoots. All day the fires continued, and into the night, so that the undersides of the clouds that hung over the islands shone red, as if even they were ablaze.

It was a night of terror, fearful in its strangeness and paralyzing in its power. The settlers gathered at the shore and hovered near *West Wind,* thinking that if the land caught fire, they might escape in it, and when the eruptions grew worse, Tupuna insisted that the king and Natabu, at least, be sent out to the safety of the sea, and it was because of this foresight that the colony was saved, for Teroro dispatched Hiro and Pa with the canoe, and when it was a mile out to sea, lighted by the blazing mountain, a great ocean wave sped toward shore, and if the canoe had not already reached the sea, its appropriate element, the onrushing wave would have destroyed it.

As it was, the water swept far inland, and tore down the temple and uprooted many of the crops. In its swirling return to the sea, it dragged with it one of the pigs, most of the bananas and old, red-eyed Teura. The goddess had warned her, but she had failed to interpret the dream correctly, so that when the turbulent sea reached far inland to grab her, twisting her this way and that, she was not afraid. Committing herself entirely to the gods, she whispered into the engulfing waves, "Great Ta'aroa, keeper of the sea, you have come for me and I am ready." As she was dragged across the reef, the green water rushing over her, she smiled and was relaxed, for she was certain that somewhere out beyond the coral she would encounter her personal god, Mano, the wild blue shark. "Mano!" she cried at last. "I am coming to talk with you!" And she was carried far from land.

When dawn rose, accompanied by new explosions of ash and flame, King Tamatoa studied his stricken community, and he could explain the ravages, especially the fallen temple, only by the fact that no slaves had been planted alive at three of the corners, but Teroro would not tolerate such reasoning.

"We are punished because we forgot our most ancient goddess, and because we built in the wrong place," he insisted.

How wrong the place was would now be proved, for Mato came running with the news that up on the side of the mountain a creeping wall of fire was slowly descending toward the settlement. A dozen men went back into the trees and climbed toward where Mato had pointed, and they saw a fearful thing: above them, and marching over all obstacles on its way to the sea, came a relentless wall of fiery rock and molten lava, turning over and over upon itself, devouring trees and rocks and valleys. Its ugly snout, thirty feet high, was not ablaze and seemed dead, until it struck a dried tree, whereupon flames leaped mysteriously into the air. At intervals long tongues of molten rock spurted through the ominously creeping front and spread out like water. It was obvious that crawling monster must soon devour the entire community.

"It will be upon us by tomorrow," the men calculated.

When he was satisfied with the news, King Tamatoa reacted without fear, for his brother's bold words had strengthened him. He commanded: "We will first pray for the old woman Teura," and he blessed her to the gods. When this was finished he said calmly, "All planted things will be dug up immediately and wrapped carefully, even if you must use your own clothes." Then he showed the slaves how to load the canoe, and when, at a distance of less than three miles, the molten lava began pouring over a low cliff, like a flaming waterfall, he studied it for a long time. Then he said, "We will stay ashore tonight and get all things ready. In the morning we will leave this place. Pa says he has found a promising land to the west."

Through the night the settlers worked, seeing one another in the dim flares of the volcano, and when dawn came they were ready to go. They had recovered much of their seed, and had saved their gods, their pigs and their canoe. With these they escaped, but when they were safe at sea, they saw the vast, fiery front of the lava break through onto their plateau, where it ate its way impersonally across all things. The temple site was burned away in a flash; the fields where crops had rested were gone; the taro patch was filled with fire; and the cave disappeared behind a wall of flame. From the plateau, the cascade of fire found a valley leading down into the sea, and after building its strength aloft, it plunged down this avenue and poured into the ocean. When it struck the water it hissed and groaned; it threw columns of steam into the air and exploded the waves; it sent noisy reports of its triumph and filled the sky with ash; and then, conquered by the patient and accommodating ocean, it fell silently into dark caverns, as it had been doing here for the past thirty million years.

The men of Havaiki, seeing for the first time the incredible fury of which their new land was capable, sat awestruck in their canoe and watched for a long time the cataclysm that had destroyed their home; but a gust of wind, stronger than the rest, carried down from the crest of the volcano a wisp of hair, spun by the breezes from the molten lava, and Teroro caught the hair and held it aloft, where the sun played on it, and he saw that it was the hair which the strange woman in the forest had worn, and he announced: "It was the goddess Pere. She came not to frighten us but to warn us. We did not understand."

His words gave the people in the canoe great hope, for if the goddess had thought enough of her erring people to warn them, she must retain some love for them; and all was not lost. The hair of Pere was given to the king as an omen, and he placed it upon the neck of the only remaining bred sow, because if this animal did not live and deliver her litter it would be as bad an omen as the volcano.

In this manner, but bearing only half the cargo with which they had arrived, and a bred sow clothed in Pere's hair, the voyagers started for a new home; and Pa and Mato had chosen wisely, for they led their companions around the southern tip of the island and up the western coast until they found fine land, with soil that could be tilled, and water, and it was here that the settlement of Havaiki began in earnest, with new fields and a new temple built without sacrifices. When the sow threw her litter, the king himself watched over the young pigs, and when the largest and strongest reached a size at which he could have been eaten—and mouths had begun to water for the taste of roast pig—the king and old Tupuna carried the pig reverently to the new temple and sacrificed it to Tane. From then on the community prospered.

WHEN THE SETTLEMENT was established, Tupuna took the steps which were to give it the characteristics which marked it permanently. He said one day to the king, "Soon I shall follow Teura, but before I go upon the rainbow, we ought to protect the life of our people. It is not good that men roam freely everywhere, and live without restraint."

Teroro, listening, argued: "We had too many restraints in Havaiki-of-Red-Oro. Here we ought to be free. I like our life the way it is."

"For a few months, perhaps," the priest argued. "But as the years pass, unless a community has fixed laws, and patterns which bind people into their appointed place, life is no good."

"But this is a new land," Teroro reasoned.

"It is in a new land that customs are most necessary," the priest warned, and the king supported him, and out of their discussions the tabus were established.

"Each man lives between an upper, which gives mana, and a lower, which drains mana from him," Tupuna explained in words that would never be forgotten. "Therefore a man must plead with the upper to send him mana and must protect himself from the lower, which steals mana from him. That is why no man should permit a slave to touch him, or to pass upon his shadow, or to see his food, for a slave can drain away a man's entire mana in an instant, for a slave has no mana.

"The way for a man to obtain mana is to obey his king, for it is the king alone who can bring us mana directly from the gods. Therefore no man may touch the king, or the garment of the king, or the shadow of the king, or in any way steal his mana. To break this tabu is death." Tupuna then enumerated more than five dozen additional tabus which protected the king in his suspension between the upper gods and the lower men: his spittle may not be touched; his excrement must be buried at night in a secret place; his food must be prepared only by chiefs; his reservoir of mana must be protected; he is tabu, he is tabu.

Men with mana required protection from defilement by women, who usually had none. Since men were of the light, and women of darkness; since men were outgoing and strong, and women intaking and weak; since men were clean and women impure; since it was nightly proved that even the strongest man could be slyly drained of his power by a clever woman, dreadful tabus were set about the latter. They must never eat with men, nor see men eating, nor touch food intended for men, on pain of death. Each month they must spend the moon-days locked up in a tiny room, on pain of death. They must eat none of the good foods required to keep men strong: no pig, no sweet fish, no coconuts, on pain of death. "And since the banana has obviously been created by the gods to represent man's fertility," Tupuna wailed, "no woman may even touch a banana, on pain of instant strangulation."

The days of the moon, the turning of the season and the planting of crops were all placed under tabu. So were laughing at improper moments, certain sex habits, the eating of certain fish and the ridicule of either gods or nobles. Tabu was the temple, tabu were the rock-gods, tabu was the hair of Pere, tabu was the growing coconut tree. At some seasons, even the ocean itself was tabu, on pain of death.

In this manner, and with the approval of the people, who wanted to be organized within established levels, the tabus were promulgated and patterns were developed whereby each man would know his level and none would transgress. What had been a free volcanic island, explosive with force, now became a rigidly determined island, and all men liked it better, for the unknown was made known.

It is not quite true to say that all men were content. One was not. Teroro, as the king's younger brother, was the logical man to become priest when old Tupuna died. He had inherited great sanctity and was growing into an able if not a clever man; there was no greater astronomer than he, and it was tacitly understood that he would in time become guardian of the tabus.

But he was far from the dedication required for this exacting job. Instead of the equanimity that marked the king, Teroro was torn with uncertainties, and they centered upon women. Day after day, when he wandered in the woods, he would come upon Pere, her shining hair disheveled and her eyes deep-sunk. She said nothing, but walked with him as a woman walks with a man she loves. Often, after her appearance, the volcano would erupt, but what lava flows there were, went down the other side of the mountain and did not endanger the growing settlement, where many pigs roamed, and chickens, and sweet, succulent dogs; for Tamatoa and Natabu had done their work well and had produced a son.

Only Teroro did not prosper; often he would turn the corner of a well-known footpath, and there would be silent Pere, hurt, condemnatory and yet speaking her love for her troubled young chief. Always, in the background of his mind, there was Pere.

Yet his real agony concerned not a shadowy goddess, but a substantial woman, and this was Marama, his wife whom he had abandoned in Bora Bora. He thought: "How wise of her to speak as she did on that last day!" For he could hear her voice as clear as it had been a year ago: "I am the canoe!" It seemed to him almost godlike wisdom on Marama's part to have used that idiom; for she was the canoe. Her placid face and sweet wisdom had been the continuing thread of his life; over all the waves and through the storms she had indeed been the canoe. And for the first time, here on remote Havaiki, Teroro began to understand how desperately a man can remember a strong, placid, wise woman whom he had known before. She was the symbol of earth, the movement of waves, the song at night. Hers was the weight that rested in memory; her words were recalled. He could see the movement of her skirts, and the way she wore her hair; once on Bora Bora when he had been sick she had washed his fever and he could recall her cool hands.

In consternation he remembered that on the canoe young Tehani had done the same; but it was different. He had never known with older Marama one fifth of the sexual excitement he had experienced with Tehani; and yet his mind was tormented by his wife. He would see her at night when he returned from his silent walks with Pere. In his dreams he would hear Marama speak. And whenever he saw *Wait-for-the-West-Wind,* that perfect canoe, he would see Marama, for she had said, "I am the canoe!" And she was.

It was in this mood that one morning he dashed from his thatched hut where Tehani slept and ran to Mato, at the fishing grounds. Grabbing the surprised chief by the hand he dragged him to the hut, and jerked Tehani to her feet. "She is your woman, Mato," he shouted with unnecessary force.

"Teroro!" the young girl cried.

"You are no longer my woman!" Teroro shouted. "I watched you on the canoe. Mato never took his eyes from you. All right, Mato, now she is yours." And he stalked from the scene.

That afternoon, in torment of spirit, he sought out his brother and said simply, "I shall go back to Bora Bora."

The king was not surprised, for he had been watching his brother and news of his rejection of Tehani had been discussed with old Tupuna, who had said that Teroro was ill in spirit. "Why will you go?" Tamatoa asked.

"I must bring Marama here," the younger man said. "We need more breadfruit, more dogs, everything. We need more people."

A council was held and all agreed that a trip south could prove helpful, especially if foodstuffs were brought back. "But who can be spared for such a long voyage?" Tupuna asked, and Teroro replied that he could sail *West Wind* to Bora Bora with only six men, if Pa and Hiro were two of them.

"I'll go," Mato insisted, but Teroro growled, "We have treated Tehani badly. You stay with her." And he would not take Mato, his greatest friend.

So the return trip was authorized, and the community began assembling its pitiful stores of spare food. This time there was no dried taro, no coconut, no breadfruit, no bamboo lengths to carry water. There were, fortunately, some bananas, but they did not dry and carry well. Dried fish there was in plenty, and on this the men would exist.

When the food was collected, Teroro divulged his plan. Drawing a rough pattern of the trip north, he pointed out that the canoe had sailed far east, then north, then far west. With a bold line in the sand he cut across this pattern and said, "We will sail directly south, and we will find the island."

"There will be no storm winds to aid you," Tupuna warned.

"We will ride with the currents," Teroro replied, "and we will paddle."

On the last day before departure, Teroro was sitting alone when one of the village women came to him and said plaintively, "On the return, if there is room in the canoe, will you please bring one thing for me?"

"What?" Teroro asked.

"A child," the woman said.

"Whose child?" he inquired.

"Any child," the woman replied, adding softly, "It is woeful to be in a land where there are no children."

It was impractical to bring a child so far, and Teroro said so, and dismissed the woman, but in a little while another came to him, saying, "Why should you bring pigs and breadfruit, Teroro? What our hearts ache for is children." And he sent her away.

But the women came again, and while they did not weep, there were tears in their throats as they spoke: "We are growing older, all of us. You and the king and Tupuna and all of us. There are babies, to be sure, but we need children."

"There are no children playing along the shore," another said. "Do you remember how they played in our lagoon?" And suddenly Teroro could see the lagoon at Bora Bora with hundreds of brown, naked children in the green waters, and he realized why Havaiki-of-the-North had seemed so barren.

"Please," the women pleaded, "bring us back some children."

Then, on the night of departure, for Teroro insisted upon leaving when the stars were visible, he confided to his brother: "I am not going solely for Marama. I am going to bring back the stone of Pere. I think an island should have not only men gods, but women, too."

On the long voyage south, while his men starved and grew parched in the doldrums, Teroro put together the rough chant that would be remembered in the islands for generations after his death and which served to guide subsequent canoes from Tahiti to the new Havaiki:

> Wait for the west wind, wait for the west wind!
> Then sail to Nuku Hiva of the dark bays
> To find the constant star.
> Hold to it, hold to it,
> Though the eyes grow dim with heat.
> Hold to it, hold to it,
> Till wild Ta'aroa sends the winds.
> Then speed to the clouds where Pere waits.
> Watch for her flames, the flames of Pere,
> Till great Tane brings the land,
> Brings Havaiki-of-the-North,
> Sleeping beneath the Little Eyes.

But when the chant was finished, Teroro realized with some dismay that finding the home islands was not going to be easy, and he missed them altogether at first, reaching all the way down to Tahiti before he discovered where he was. Then, beating his way back north, he found Havaiki-of-Red-Oro, and there at sea, in the gently rolling swells, the seven men held a council of war. Teroro posed the problem simple: "If we sail into Bora Bora without a plan, the High Priest, who must know about our attack on Oro, will command his men to kill us."

"We've got to risk it," Pa growled.

"We are very weak," Teroro pointed out.

"We can still fight," Pa insisted.

"There is a better way," Teroro argued, and with a newly developing sense of guile he reasoned: "Since we're not strong enough to fight the High Priest, we must outsmart him." And he suggested a way, but his men thought of other things when in the dawn they saw once more the pinnacles of Bora Bora and the wild cliffs dropping away to the lagoon.

Pa muttered, "We must have been insane to leave this place for Havaiki-of-the-North." And each man in the canoe acknowledged the fact that he had surrendered earth's paradise in exchange for a harsh new land.

As soon as *Wait-for-the-West-Wind* was spotted standing off the western entrance into the lagoon, the residents of its home port began to line the shores and shout with joy at the return of their people. It was this joy that Teroro counted upon to give him ten minutes' respite to develop his plan, because he believed that the islanders' spontaneous acceptance of the canoe would prevent the High Priest from ordering the crew's immediate death, and in that interval Teroro would have time to accomplish his mission.

As the canoe neared land he warned his men again: "I'll talk, but you must look pious."

And promptly the bow of the canoe struck land, he leaped ashore and cried, "We seek the High Priest!" and when that dignitary, older and more solemn, with flecks of white in his beard, approached, Teroro made deep obeisance and cried for all to hear, "We come as servants of Oro, seeking another god for our distant land. Bless us, august one, and send us another god."

The plea took the High Priest so by surprise, coming as it did even before any narration of the journey, that he was unable to mask his pleasure, and the staff with which he could have directed the sacrifice of the crew remained rooted in the ground, and he listened as Teroro spoke rapidly: "Under Oro we have prospered, august one, and our community grows. But life is difficult and we live scattered. That is why your servant old Tupuna requires additional gods. When we have borrowed them from you, we will depart."

The High Priest listened, and then stood aside as the new king of Bora Bora appeared, and Teroro saw with intense pleasure that the man was not from Havaiki, as planned, but from Bora Bora. "King," he cried, "forgive us for our midnight assault on Havaiki before our departure. We did this thing not to dishonor great Oro, but to prevent a Havaiki man from becoming king of Bora Bora. Forgive us." And Teroro was so weak, and so urgently in need of food and help, that he kneeled in the dust, and prostrated himself before the king, and then before the High Priest, and to his deep satisfaction he heard from the canoe the pious voice of Pa intoning: "Now let us go to the temple of Oro and give thanks for our safe voyage."

But as the men marched, Teroro caught sight of a woman at the edge of the crowd, a tall, solemn, patient woman with a face like a moon, and he thought no more of gods or kings or priests, for the woman was Marama, and solely by looking at each other, intently and with the love that consumes two thousand miles of ocean, she knew that he had come to take her with him, and while he prayed to a god whom he detested, she went to her grass house and started packing.

When the prayers were over he joined her there, and they sat in silence, profound communion passing between them, and she was both forgiving and consoling in the disappointing moments when they found him too exhausted with famine even to make love with her. She laughed softly and said, from the edge of the house, "See what happened on the last night we made love." And she took from a maid's arms a boy nearly a year old, with wide eyes and dark hair like his father's.

Teroro looked at his son, and at the wife he had left behind because she could bear no children, and in his embarrassment he began to laugh. Marama laughed too, and teased: "You looked so ridiculous out there, praying to Oro. And Pa putting on that long face! 'Now let us go to the temple of Oro!' It was a good idea, Teroro, but it wasn't necessary."

"What do you mean?"

"Haven't you noticed how much older the High Priest looks? He has been very badly treated."

"That's good news. How?"

"After all his scheming to banish you and Tamatoa, so that he could become the chief priest at Havaiki . . ."

"You mean, they were just using him? To subdue Bora Bora?"

"Yes. They had no intention of making him chief priest. After you killed your wife's father . . ."

"She's not my wife. I gave her to Mato."

Marama paused for a moment and looked at the floor. Quietly, she added, "The men of Havaiki tried to give us a new king, but we fought."

"Then why do you keep the High Priest?"

"We need a priest," she said simply. "Every island needs a priest." And they fell silent, listening to the soft waves of the lagoon, and after a long while Teroro said, "You must find a dozen women who will go with us. It's a hard journey." Then he added, "And this time we'll take some children with us." His voice brightened. "We'll take the little fellow."

"No," Marama said. "He's too young. We'll trade him for an older boy," and in the island tradition she went from house to house, until she found an eight-year-old boy she liked, and to his willing mother she gave her son. When Teroro saw the new boy, he liked him too, and after the child was sent away to wait for the canoe's departure, he took his wife in his arms and whispered, "You are the canoe of my life, Marama. In you I make my voyage."

At the consecration of the new idol of Oro, the High Priest insisted upon killing a slave, and Teroro hid his face in shame, for he and his men knew that once the reef was breasted, the idol would pitch into the sea, so that when the High Priest delivered the god to the becoming-priest Teroro, the latter took it gravely, not as an idol but as a symbol of the needless death of a man; and whether he or the crew liked the statue or not, it had somehow become a thing of sanctification, and Teroro treated it as such, for it spoke to him of blood. At the same time it reminded him of the difficulty which now faced him: he had to get the red-rock statue of the goddess Pere from the temple without exciting the High Priest's suspicion that that had been the real reason for the return. In secrecy he held council with Pa and Hiro to canvass the ways by which Pere might be kidnaped.

Pa suggested: "You fooled the priests with your talk of Oro. Fool them again."

"No," Teroro replied. "We were able to fool them about Oro because they wanted to believe. To mention a forgotten goddess like Pere would arouse their suspicions."

"Could we steal it?" Hiro proposed.

"Who knows where it is?" Teroro countered. They discussed other possibilities and agreed upon only one thing: to return to Havaiki-of-the-North without Pere would be insane, for since she had warned them once with such a disastrous wall of fire, the next time she would obliterate them altogether. It was then that Teroro proposed: "I shall talk with Marama. She is a very wise woman."

And it was Marama who devised the plan. "The island knows that you have come back for me," she pointed out, "and they recall that my ancestors were priests. When the women for our voyage have been gathered, two of us will go to the High Priest and tell him that we want to take one of the ancient Bora Bora gods with us."

"Will he allow it?" Teroro asked suspiciously.

"He is a priest of Oro," Marama pointed out, "but he is also a Bora Boran, and he will understand our love of this island."

It worked exactly as she planned, but when the time came for delivering the feather-draped red rock of Pere, the High Priest could not bring himself to place such treasure in the hands of a woman, insisting upon transferring the goddess directly to Teroro, and when the latter at last had the soul of Pere in his possession, the wild, passionate soul of the fire goddess, the mother of volcanoes, he wanted to shout in triumph, but instead he lay it aside as if it were only a woman's god, a whim of his wife's, and the High Priest thought the same.

The men were fattened and the food was packed. Twelve women were selected and put on starvation diets to prepare them for the voyage. King Tamatoa's favorite wife was included, for everyone agreed that since their king had produced with his sister a royal heir of greatest sanctity, he should be encouraged to import at least one woman he loved. For seed crops the crew emphasized pigs, bananas and breadfruit. "How we yearn for sweet breadfruit," they explained.

When all was ready, Teroro was startled to see Marama lugging toward the canoe a large bundle wrapped in leaves. "What's that?" he cried.

"Flowers," his wife replied.

"What do we want with flowers?" Teroro protested.

"I asked Pa and he said there were no flowers." Teroro looked at the other crew members, and they realized for the first time that Havaiki-of-the-North owned no natural blooms. Even so, the bundle seemed excessively large.

"You simply can't take that much, Marama," he protested.

"The gods like flowers," she replied. "Throw out one of the pigs."

The idea was so offensive that the crew would not consider it, but they did compromise on this: they would put back one of the smaller breadfruit, but they all considered Teroro's woman demented.

Then came the task, most joyous and exciting of all, of selecting the children. The men wanted to take only girls, while the women wished only boys, so that the compromise of half and half pleased no one but did have certain sense to commend it. The ten children selected ranged from four years old to twelve: dark-haired, deep-eyed, grinning, white-toothed children. Their very presence made the canoe lighter.

But when all had stepped aboard, Teroro was unaccountably depressed by the gravity of the task he had undertaken, and this time with no guile he went gravely to the High Priest and pleaded: "Bless our journey. Establish the tabus." And the High Priest arranged the gods on the side of the voyagers and cried in a high voice, touching the food for the animals, "This is tabu! This is tabu!" And when he had finished, the canoe somehow seemed safer, and it set forth for the long voyage north.

It had barely escaped from the lagoon when Pa, the shark-faced, went for the offensive statue of Oro, to throw it into the deep, but to his surprise Teroro restrained him and said, "It is a god! We will place it reverently on the shore of Havaiki-of-Red-Oro," and when he had led the canoe to that once-hated island, slipping ashore where no lookouts could intercept him, he placed Oro in a sheltered position among rocks, and built a palm-leaf canopy; and he was overcome with the awareness that never again would he see Havaiki, from which he had sprung, and while the canoe waited, he stood on the shore of the ancestral island and chanted the story of the brave, lost people of Havaiki-in-Asia, who had set out upon innumerable voyages, never to return. This was his land, his home, and he would know it no more.

Pa and his rugged crew were further surprised when it came time to set the course back to Havaiki-of-the-North. This time Teroro would not permit them to follow his earlier reckless path far out to sea; he required them to take the cautious route to Nuku Hiva, where in all prudence they replenished their stores, so that in the heart-baking doldrums they had adequate food and water, especially for the children, who suffered intensely in the heat, for try as they might, they could not make their stomachs into tight hard knots. They were hungry and they said so.

At last the stars of the Little Eyes were overhead, and the canoe turned joyously westward before the wind. Now Teroro conducted daily lessons for every man and boy aboard the canoe: "You know the island lies ahead. What signals will prove the fact?" And every male above the age of six became a navigator, and Marama, taking the place of old red-eyed Teura, became the seer, collecting omens; and one day a boy spotted a black fork-tailed bird attacking a gannet, who had caught a fish; and Teroro showed all how to read the wave echoes as they bounced back from unseen Havaiki; but the most solemn moment came when Marama, reading her clouds, saw fire upon them, and she knew that the goddess Pere had lighted a beacon for her voyagers, and it was to this cloud of fire that Teroro directed his canoe.

As the craft neared shore Teroro faced one last odious job, but he discharged it. Moving among the men and women he told each: "The children are no longer yours. They must be shared with those on shore, and each child shall have many mothers."

Immediately a wailing set up, for on the long voyage men and women in the canoe had grown inordinately attached to the children, and the wild young things had found mothers and fathers whom they liked. "He is more than my son!" a woman cried, holding to her breast a nine-year-old boy with a broken tooth.

"No," Teroro said firmly. "If it had not been for the women on shore, pleading for children, I would not have thought to bring any. They must have their share. It is only just."

So when the canoe landed, there was a moment of intense anguish as the women from shore, too long without the sound of children, hurried down and saw the boys standing awkwardly by the mast and the little girls holding onto men's hands. The women on shore could not see the new pigs or the promising breadfruit or the bananas. All they could see were the children, and when the first child stepped ashore, a woman ran frenziedly to him with food, but the child drew back.

It was in this manner that Teroro, bearing in his hands the rock of Pere, stepped ashore to become the compassionate and judicious priest of Havaiki, with his gentle wife Marama as associate and seer, and with the volcano goddess as his special mentor. The pigs and the breadfruit and the children increased. Marama's flowers burst into brilliance. And the island prospered.

III

From the Farm of Bitterness

A THOUSAND YEARS after the men of Bora Bora had completed their long voyage to the north, a thin, sallow-faced youth with stringy blond hair left an impoverished-looking farm near the village of Marlboro, in eastern Massachusetts, and enrolled as a freshman at Yale College in Connecticut. This was the more mysterious for two reasons: to look at the farm one would never suppose that its owners could afford to send any of their ten children to college; and, having decided to do so, the parents must have had deeply personal reasons for sending a son not to Harvard, which was only twenty-five miles away, but to Yale, which was more than a hundred miles to the south.

Gideon Hale, a gaunt man of forty-two who looked sixty, could explain each matter: "Our minister visited Harvard and he assures us the place has become a haven for Unitarians, deists and atheists. No son of mine shall be contaminated in such a den of iniquitousness." So seventeen-year-old Abner was packed off to Yale, which remained a haven for the honest if austere precepts of John Calvin as expressed in New England Congregationalism.

As for the money, gaunt Gideon explained: "We are practicing Christians adhering to the word of Calvin as preached by Theodore Beza in Geneva and by Jonathan Edwards in Boston. We do not believe in painting our barns in worldly displays of wealth, nor in painting our daughters to parade their concupiscence. We save our money and apply it to the betterment of our minds and the salvation of our souls. When my son Abner graduates a minister from Yale, he will glorify God by preaching the same message and exhibiting the same example. How did he get from this farm to divinity school? Because this family practices frugality and avoids worldly exhibit."

In his senior year at Yale, emaciated Abner Hale, whose parents did not allow him enough money to live on, experienced a spiritual enlightenment which changed his life, impelling him to unanticipated deeds and imperishable commitments. It was not what the early nineteenth century called "conversion," for Abner had undergone this phenomenon at eleven, while walking at dusk from the far fields to the milking shed. It was a wintry Marlboro night, and as he walked through the crackling stubble, frost on his breath, he heard a voice cry distinctly, "Abner Hale, are you saved?" He knew he was not, but when he replied, "No," the voice kept repeating the inquiry, and finally a light filled the meadow and a great shaking possessed him, and he stood in the fields transfixed, so that when his father came for him he burst into wild tears and begged: "Father, what must I do to be saved?" In Marlboro his conversion was held to be a minor miracle, and from that eleventh year his pious father had scrimped and borrowed and saved to send the predestined boy to divinity school.

What thin-faced Abner experienced at Yale was far different from conversion; it was spiritual illumination on a specific point and it arrived through a most unlikely person. A group of his worldly classmates, including his roommate, the young medical student John Whipple, who had once smoked and drunk, came by his room as he was writing a long report on "Church Discipline in the City of Geneva as Practiced by Theodore Beza."

"Come along to hear Keoki Kanakoa!" his rowdy classmates shouted.

"I'm working," Abner replied, and closed his door more tightly against temptation. He had come to the part of his paper in which Beza had begun to apply the teachings of Calvin to the general civil life of Geneva, and the manner in which this was done fascinated the young divinity student, for he wrote with some fervor: "Beza constantly faced the problem which all who govern must face: 'Do I govern for the welfare of man or for the glory of God?' Beza found it easy to give his answer, and although certain harshnesses which the world condemned did unavoidably occur in Geneva, so did the Kingdom of God on earth, and for once in the long history of civilization, an entire city lived according to the precepts of our Divine Father."

There was a rattling at his door and wiry John Whipple stuck his head in and called, "We're saving a seat for you, Abner. Seems everyone wants to hear Keoki Kanakoa."

"I am working," Abner replied the second time, and carefully he closed his door and returned to his lamp, by whose amber light he wrote painstakingly: "The Kingdom of God on earth is not easy to attain, for mere study of the Bible will not illuminate the way by which a government can acquire sanctity, for obviously if this were the case, thousands of governments that have now perished and which in their day attended to the Bible would have discovered the godly way. We know they have failed, and they have failed because they lacked a man of wisdom to show them. . . ." He bit his pen and thought of his father's long and gloomy battle with the town fathers of Marlboro. His father knew what the rule of God was, but the fathers were obstinate men and would not listen. It was no surprise either to Abner or to his father when the daughter of one of these perverse men discovered that she was going to have a baby out of wedlock, although just what this sin involved, Abner did not fully know.

"Abner!" a stentorian voice called from the hallway. "It is your duty to hear Keoki Kanakoa." The door was thrust open, revealing a chunky little professor in a waistcoat too tight and a stock too dirty. "In the interests of your soul you should hear the message of this remarkable young Christian." And the man came over to the desk, blew out the light, and dragged his reluctant pupil to the missionary lecture.

Abner found the seat which handsome John Whipple had saved for him, and the two young men, so unlike in all ways, waited for the chairs on the college platform to be occupied. At seven-thirty President Jeremiah Day, calm but glowing with spiritual fire, led to the farthest chair a brown-skinned, white-toothed, black-haired young giant in a tight-fitting suit. "It is my honor to present to the students of Yale College," President Day said simply, "one of the most powerful voices in the world today. For when Keoki Kanakoa, son of a ruler of Owhyhee speaks, he speaks to the conscience of the world; to you young men who have already committed yourselves to Christ's ministry, the voice of Keoki Kanakoa brings particular challenges."

At this, the young giant, standing about six feet five and weighing more than two hundred and fifty pounds, rose and graced his audience with a dazzling smile, after which he raised his hands like a minister and prayed: "May the good Lord bless what I am about to say. May He open all hearts to hear."

"He speaks better than I do," John Whipple whispered, but Abner was not amused, for he wished to be back at his books, feeling that he had come close to the heart of his essay on Theodore Beza when his professor insisted upon dragging him to the lecture by this barbarian from Owhyhee.

But when the brown-skinned giant launched into his message, not only Abner Hale but everyone else in the auditorium listened, for the engaging young savage told how he had run away from an idol-worshiping home, from polygamy, from immorality, from grossness and from bestiality to find the word of Jesus Christ. He recounted how, after landing from a whaling ship in Boston, he had tried to gain entrance to Harvard but had been laughed at, and how he had walked to Yale College and had met President Day in the street and had said to him, "I come seek Jesus." And the head of Yale had replied, "If you cannot find Him here, this college should be dissolved."

Keoki Kanakoa spoke for two hours. Sometimes his voice fell away to a whisper as he spoke of the evil darkness in which his beloved islands of Owhyhee festered. Again it rose like a thundering sea when he told the young men of Yale what they could do for Christ if they would only come to Owhyhee and circulate the word of God. But what had captured earlier audiences throughout New England, and what now completely absorbed the men of Yale, so that no one stirred even at the end of two hours, was Keoki's impassioned story of what it was like to live in Owhyhee without Christ. "When I was a boy," he began softly, in the fine English he had mastered in various church schools, "we worshiped dreadful gods like Ku, the god of battle. Ku demanded endless human sacrifices, and how did the priests find victims? Before a sacred day my father, the Governor of Maui, would tell his assistants, 'We require a man.' Before a battle he would announce, 'We require eight men,' and his assistants would then gather and say, 'Let's take Kakai. I am angry with him,' or perhaps, 'Now would be a good time to get rid of that one and take his lands.' And at night two conspirators would creep secretly from behind while a third would walk up boldly and say, 'Greetings, Kakai, how was the fishing?' and before he could reply . . ."

At this point giant Keoki had been coached by his missionary preceptors to pause dramatically, wait, then hold aloft in his enormous hands a lethal length of coconut-fiber rope. "While my father's agent smiled at the victim, one conspirator crept up and pinioned his arms. The other slipped this rope around his neck . . . . like this." And slowly he twisted his two great hands together, compressing the rope into a tight knot. Making a strangling noise in his throat, he allowed his big head to fall on his chest. After a pause, while his enormous frame seemed to burst from its ill-fitting American suit, he slowly raised his head and disclosed a face masked in pity. "We do not know Jesus," he said softly, as if his voice were coming from a sepulcher.

Then he swept into his peroration, his voice hammering like thunder and tears splashing down like rain, so that the terror of his youthful days became clearly visible throughout his body. "Young men of God!" he pleaded. "In my father's islands immortal souls go every night to everlasting hell because of you! You are to blame! You have not taken the word of Jesus Christ to my islands. We hunger for the word. We are thirsty for the word. We die for the word. Are you, in your indifference, going to keep the word from us forever? Is there no man here tonight who will rise up and say to me, 'Keoki Kanakoa, I will go with you to Owhyhee and save three hundred thousand souls for Jesus Christ'?"

The gigantic man paused. In deep and honest grief his voice broke. President Day poured him a glass of water, but he brushed it aside and called, through choking sobs, "Will no one go with me to save the souls of my people?" He sat down, quaking in his chair, a man shattered by the revelation of God's word, and after a while President Day led him away.

The impact of Keoki Kanakoa's missionary sermon struck the roommates Hale of divinity and Whipple of medicine with stunning force. They left the lecture hall in shocked silence, brooding upon the misery depicted by the Owhyheean. In their room they did not bother to relight the lamp, but went to bed in darkness, weighed down by the indifference with which Keoki had charged them. When the awfulness of this indifference finally penetrated his conscience, Abner began to weep—for he had grown up in an age of weeping—and after a while John asked, "What is it, Abner?" and the farm boy replied, "I cannot think of sleep, seeing in my mind those human souls destined for all eternity to everlasting hell." From the manner in which he spoke, it was evident that he had been watching each separate soul plunge into eternal fire, and the misery was more than he could bear.

Whipple said, "His final call keeps ringing in my ears. 'Who will go to Owhyhee with me?' " To this Abner Hale made no reply.

Long after midnight, when the young doctor could still hear his roommate sobbing, he rose, lit the lamp, and began dressing. At first Hale pretended not to know what was happening, but finally he whipped out of bed and caught Whipple by the arm. "What are you going to do, John?"

"I am going to Owhyhee," the handsome doctor replied. "I cannot waste my life here, indifferent to the plea of those islands."

"But where are you going now?" Hale asked.

"To President Day's. To offer myself to Christ."

There was a moment's hesitation while the doctor, fully dressed, and the minister, in nightgown, studied each other. It was broken when Abner asked, "Will you pray with me?"

"Yes," the doctor said, and he kneeled beside his bed.

Abner, at his, prayed: "Father Almighty, tonight we have heard Thy call. From the starry wastes of the sky Thy voice has come to us, from across the boundless deep where souls rot in evil. Unworthy as we are to serve Thee, wilt Thou nevertheless accept us as Thy servants?" He continued for several minutes, issuing a prayer to a distant, living, full-bodied, vengeful yet forgiving God. If at that moment he had been asked to describe the Being to Whom he prayed he would have said, "He is tall, rather thin, with black hair and penetrating eyes. He is very serious, marks every transgression, and demands all humans to follow His precepts. He is a stern but forgiving Father, a harsh but just disciplinarian." And he would have described Gideon Hale in exactly the same terms. If anyone, at the end of his summary, should have asked, "Does this Father ever smile?" the question would have astonished young Abner as one he had not yet considered, but upon careful reflection he would have answered, "He is compassionate, but He never smiles."

When the prayer was ended John Whipple asked, "Are you coming with me?"

"Yes, but shouldn't we wait till morning to speak with President Day?"

" 'Go ye into all the world, and preach the gospel to every creature,' " the young doctor quoted, and Hale, acknowledging the aptness of this admonition, dressed.

It was four-thirty when they knocked at President Day's door, and with no visible surprise he admitted them to his study, where he sat in coat and muffler hiding his nightgown. "I surmise that the Lord has spoken to you," he began gently.

"We are offering ourselves for Owhyhee," John Whipple explained.

"Have you considered this grave step?" Day asked.

"We have often discussed how we should spend our lives in God," Abner began, but he was taken by a fit of weeping, and his pale young features became red and his nose runny. President Day passed him a handkerchief.

"Some time ago we decided to dedicate our lives to God," Whipple said forcefully. "I stopped smoking. Abner wanted to go to Africa to rescue souls, but I thought I would work among the poor in New York. Tonight we realized where it was that we really wanted to go."

"This is not then the decision of the moment?" President Day pressed.

"Oh, no!" Abner assured him, sniffling. "My decision goes back to Reverend Thorn's sermon on Africa three years ago."

"And you, Mr. Whipple? I thought you wanted to be a doctor, not a missionary."

"I vacillated for a long time between medicine and seminary, President Day. I chose the former because I thought I could serve God in two capacities."

The president studied his two able students and asked, "Have you prayed on this grave problem?"

"We have," Abner replied.

"And what message did you receive?"

"That we should go to Owhyhee."

"Good," Day said with finality. "Tonight I was inspired to go myself. But my work remains here."

"What shall we do now?" Whipple asked, as spring dawn came over the campus.

"Return to your rooms, say nothing to anyone, and on Friday meet with the committee of the American Board of Commissioners for Foreign Missions."

"Will they be here so soon?" Abner gasped in obvious delight.

"Yes. They have found that they are often needed after Keoki Kanakoa speaks." But noticing the joy in the young men's faces he warned, "Reverend Thorn, the leader of the group, is most adroit in uncovering young men who are guided by emotion and not by true dedication to Christ. If yours is not a profound commitment strong enough to sustain you for a lifetime, don't waste the time of Eliphalet Thorn."

"We are committed," Abner said firmly, and the two young men bade their president good night.

On Friday, John and Abner peered from behind curtains as the committee from the American Board of Commissioners for Foreign Missions gravely marched into Yale to hold sessions with various young men whose imaginations had been captured by Keoki Kanakoa. "That's Reverend Thorn," Abner whispered as the leader appeared. He was a tall, thin man, in a frock coat that reached his ankles and a black beaver hat that stretched far in the opposite direction. He had bushy black eyebrows, a hooked nose and a forbidding chin. He looked like a judge, and the two young scholars were afraid.

But John Whipple's fear was misguided, for he had an easy time when he faced Eliphalet Thorn. The intense, gaunt face leaned forward, while the four lesser ministers listened, and Whipple heard the first kindly question: "Are you the son of Reverend Joshua Whipple, of western Connecticut?"

"I am," John replied.

"Has your father instructed you in the ways of piety?"

"He has." It was apparent that the committee recognized Whipple for what he was: a forthright, appealing, quick-witted young doctor from a God-fearing rural family.

"Have you experienced conversion?" Reverend Thorn asked quietly.

"When I was fifteen," John said, "I became much concerned about my future, and I vacillated between medicine and the clergy, and I chose the former because I was not certain in my heart that I understood God. I did not feel myself a pious youth, even though my father so reported me to the church. And then one day as I was trudging home from school I watched a whirling-broom of dust as it became larger and larger, and I am certain that I heard a voice say to me, 'Are you prepared to serve Me with your life?' and I said, 'Yes.' And I shook as I have never shaken before and the cloud of dust hovered about me for some time, but did not get into my nostrils. From that time on I have known God."

The five austere clergymen nodded approval, for this kind of sudden discovery of God had grown commonplace in New England, following the Great Awakening of 1740, and no man could guess how another would experience conversion, but Reverend Thorn bent his icy face forward and asked, "If you were originally confused, Mr. Whipple, between medicine and clergy, and if your confusion rose from the fact that you were not certain that you knew God, why, after God spoke directly to you, did you not change your decision and study for the ministry?"

"I was perplexed by this problem for a long time," Whipple confessed. "But I liked medicine and I concluded that as a doctor I could serve God in two capacities."

"That's an honest answer, Mr. Whipple. Return to your studies, and you will receive a letter from us within the week."

When John Whipple left the interview he was in a state of such exaltation that he neither looked at his roommate nor spoke to him. In fact, it was the most completely sublime moment in his life up to then and the one in which he felt closest to God. He had committed himself totally to God's work and he was certain that no power on earth could ever divert him from that commitment. Without speaking, he told his roommate that he had been accepted.

Abner Hale had an entirely different experience with the committee, for when he appeared with his ill-fitting suit, his stringy blond hair pasted down, his sallow face flushed and his pinched shoulders bending forward too eagerly, one of the more worldly of the ministers asked himself, "Oh, Lord, why dost Thou choose for Thy work such mangy men?"

"Are you converted?" Reverend Thorn asked impatiently.

"Yes," Abner said, but his explanation grew long-winded and turgid. He spent a good deal of time explaining just where the meadow was and how it lay in relation to the milking shed. But there was no doubt that he personally knew God.

"Why do you wish to serve as a missionary?" Reverend Thorn asked.

"Because ever since my conversion I have been determined to serve the Lord," Abner affirmed hastily, too eager to convince, and it was apparent to the other members of the committee that the young man was making a bad impression on Thorn, who was chairman because he had done work in Africa and knew the problems faced by missionaries. After a previous meeting with would-be missionaries from Williams College he had told his committeemen, "The type of man we must avoid is the unbalanced young gentleman who is so certain of his personal relationship with God that he refuses to accept his subordinate role in the mission community at large. If we can weed such excitable men out now, we will save the mission much expense in money and confusion later." It was apparent that he was about to do some weeding, for he interrupted Abner's flow of piety and pointed out: "I asked you why you wanted particularly to be a missionary. You haven't explained."

"I always wanted to serve God," Abner repeated, "but I did not know that I was called to the mission field until the night of August 14, 1818."

"What happened then?" Reverend Thorn asked impatiently.

"You spoke on Africa, at the Congregational Church of Marlboro, Massachusetts. I date my true awakening from that night." Eliphalet Thorn dropped his head and pinched his long nose, wondering what to ask next.

"What particularly did Reverend Thorn say that impressed you?" the worldly minister inquired waspishly.

"It is easy to answer that, sir, because ever since, his words have lived in my heart as an ideal. He spoke of the mission in Africa and said, 'We were as one family in Christ, each contributing his gifts, each dedicating himself to the common cause of saving souls.' From that night I started to train myself to become a member of such a family in Christ. I have learned to saw straight and to build, against the day when I was sent where there were no houses. I've taught myself to sew and to cook, and to keep accounts. From the time Reverend Thorn spoke I have never thought of myself only as a college student or as a seminary scholar. I have been in solemn training to become one humble member of a family sent to some far place to serve Christ."

The young man's statement was so unexpectedly contrite and so choked with the spirit of Christ's discipleship that even the worldly minister who had earlier classified Abner as mangy, which he decidedly was, awoke to his possibilities. "One of the members of the faculty," this minister said, gracefully concealing President Day's name, "has reported to us, Mr. Hale, that you are vain of your sanctity."

"I am," Abner confessed bluntly, "and I know I must fight against it, but none of my brothers or sisters are pious. Most of the young men here at Yale are not. From these comparisons I did acquire a sense of vanity. I said, 'The Lord has chosen me, but not those others.' I am ashamed that even my teachers saw this failing in me. But, sir, if you ask them again, I think you will find that they were speaking of me as I used to be. I have repeated over and over again the text, 'Every one that is proud in heart is an abomination to the Lord,' and I have taken it to heart."

Reverend Thorn was deeply impressed by the changes that seemed to have taken place in this young minister's character, for Abner's reference to August 14, 1818, awakened in the older man vivid reflections. He well remembered that meeting, for he had reported on it to his companions in Boston: "I spent the evening addressing a group in Marlboro, and I was distressed by the smug indifference of these well-stuffed farmers from their well-stuffed farms. I might as well have been preaching to their cattle, for all they understood of missionary zeal." Yet in that indifferent audience there had been one sallow-faced youth acquiring the dedication which now brought him before this committee. The coincidence was too great, Reverend Thorn thought, and on the sudden he saw Abner not merely as a stringy-haired, pasty-faced young man with obvious tendencies toward identifying himself with God, but as a heaven-sent answer to a most pressing problem within the Thorn family. So the leader of the committee of inquiry leaned far forward and asked, "Mr. Hale, are you married?"

"Oh, no, sir!" the young man replied with what could have been interpreted as distaste. "I have never sought the companionship . . ."

"Were you aware that the Board will send no minister abroad who is not married?"

"No, sir. I told you that I had learned to sew and cook . . ."

Reverend Thorn pressed his inquiry. "Do you perchance know some dedicated young female, someone who has experienced conversion, who has thought of going . . ."

"No, sir. I know no females."

Reverend Thorn appeared to sigh with relief and indicated that he had no further questions, but after the committee had advised Abner to wait at Yale for a week, pending their decision on his case, their leader made a slight correction: "It may take us longer than a week to discover our minds in your case, Mr. Hale. Don't become impatient." And after the young man had returned to his room, somewhat dazed by the complexity of the questions he had been asked, he found worse confusion, for his roommate reported how relatively simple his examination had been.

"They asked me a few questions about my faith," John Whipple recounted, "and then told me to get married as soon as the letter arrived next week."

"Whom will you marry?" Abner asked.

"My cousin, of course."

"But you've never spoken to her!"

"I will. Whom will you marry?"

"The committee treated me much differently," Abner confessed. "I really don't know what was in their minds."

A knock came at the door, and when Whipple answered it, towering Reverend Thorn, his Adam's apple dancing, said, "Will you please excuse us, Mr. Whipple?"

"Please sit down, sir," Abner stammered.

"I shall only be a moment," the gaunt reverend replied, and then with the directness for which he was noted, asked, "I wish to verify my report. I understand that if the Board nominates you for Hawaii, you know of no young female whom you could invite . . ."

Abner was appalled at the idea that his careful life's plan should be frustrated in the bud because he knew no girls, so he said quickly, "Reverend Thorn, if that's all that's going to keep me . . . Reverend, I know I could ask my father . . . He's a very strong judge of character, sir, and if he picked a girl . . ."

"Mr. Hale, please. I didn't say that you would be forbidden to go. I didn't even say that you could go in the first place. I merely asked you, 'If we select you, do you know some appropriate female whom you could marry . . . well, rather promptly?' And you said no. All right."

"But, Reverend Thorn, if you would give me only two weeks," Abner pleaded, near tears, "I know my father . . ."

"I am much impressed with your piety, Mr. Hale," the older man began, on an entirely new tack.

"Then there's a chance?"

"What I wanted to speak to you about, Abner," said the tall, stern man in as kindly a manner as he could command, "is the fact that my sister in Walpole happens to have a daughter . . ." He paused in some embarrassment, hoping that Abner would anticipate his message and make its full delivery unnecessary. But honest Abner, with his hair pasted flat over his temples, could not imagine why the forbidding missionary was speaking of his sister, or his sister's daughter, and he looked with disarming innocence at Reverend Thorn, waiting for him to proceed.

The tall missionary swallowed his Adam's apple several times and wiped his forehead. "So, if you know of no young female . . ." he began.

"I'm sure my father could find one," Abner interrupted.

"And if the Board selects you . . ." Eliphalet Thorn doggedly continued.

"I pray it will!" Abner cried.

"I was wondering if you would entertain it kindly if I were to speak to my niece on your behalf?" The tall reverend swallowed heavily and stared at the sallow young man.

Abner gaped, then blurted, "You mean that you would help me to find a wife? Your own niece?" He thrust his hand out eagerly and pumped Reverend Thorn's for almost a minute. "That would be more than I dare ask," he cried joyously. "Really, Reverend Thorn . . ."

Withdrawing his hand, the gaunt missionary interrupted the effusive flow and added, "Her name is Jerusha. Jerusha Bromley. She is a year older than you, but a most devout young woman."

The mention of a specific name, and attributing to that shadowy name a corporeal being with a given age, quite overcame Abner and he started to weep, but quickly he mastered himself and said, "Reverend Thorn, too much has been happening today. Could we pray?" And in the small room at Yale College the experienced missionary and the emotional boy stood with their heads raised to heaven as Abner prayed: "Dear gentle and supervising Lord, I am unable to comprehend all that has occurred today. I have talked with Thy missioners, and they have said that perhaps I may join them. One of Thy servants has volunteered to speak to a young female of his family on my behalf. Beloved and powerful God, if these things come to pass through Thine aid, I shall be Thy servant to the end of my days, and I shall carry Thy word to the farthest islands." He dropped his head in humility and Reverend Thorn breathed a husky "Amen."

"It will take about two weeks," he said as he left.

Tact was something Abner Hale would never have. "John Whipple said that he would know within a week," he reminded the committeeman.

"Your case is different," Thorn replied.

"Why?" Abner demanded.

Reverend Thorn wanted to blurt out the truth: "Because you're an offensive, undernourished, sallow-faced little prig, the kind that wrecks any mission to which he is attached. There's not a man on my committee that really thinks you ought to be sent overseas, but I have a niece who has got to get married one of these days. And maybe if I can talk to her before she sees you, possibly I can force her into marrying you. That, young man, is what requires two weeks." Instead, with the self-control he had acquired in Africa, the sagacious minister recovered quickly and offered what he considered a rather clever explanation: "You see, Mr. Hale, Dr. Whipple will be going to Owhyhee as missionary doctor. If we accept you, and if you can find a bride, you will be going as an ordained minister. That's why your case requires more careful investigation." The answer was so reasonable that Abner accepted it at once, and when John Whipple received his letter of acceptance and immediately dispatched both an acknowledgment to the Board in Boston and a proposal of marriage to his cousin in Hartford, Abner smugly smiled at his roommate's excitement, repeating over and over to himself the reassuring thought: "Anyone can be a missionary doctor. But to be a fully ordained minister requires careful investigation." But whenever he indulged in this vanity he invariably recalled his Biblical antidote and he recited this, too: "Every one that is proud in heart is an abomination to the Lord," after which he recalled the powerful word from Job: "Behold every one that is proud, and abase him. Look on every one that is proud, and bring him low." Thus his two natures warred.

REVEREND THORN, as soon as his interrogations at Yale College were completed, hurried back to Boston and caught the stage running out to Marlboro, Massachusetts, to make inquiries as to the character and prospects of Abner Hale. Even as the coach neared Marlboro, he felt his old distaste for the village returning. The smug white barns in the smug spring landscape bespoke generations of thrifty, cautious people, proud of their possessions and deaf to the teachings of the Lord. His earlier impressions were fortified when he found the townspeople as smug as the outlying barns.

The school principal reported, airily: "Abner Hale! Ah, yes! There are so many Hale children it's rather difficult to keep them separated in one's mind. Abner, stringy hair, no good in games, worse in math, but rather gifted in the verbal processes that mark the cultivated mind. An austere young man who never pared his nails. Had good teeth, though."

"Was he pious?" Thorn pressed.

"To a fault," the airy schoolteacher replied. Then, sensing that this could be construed by his visitor to be a slur against piety, he quickly added, "By that I mean he was inclined toward priggishness, which I hold to be a fault, for does not the Bible counsel us: 'Dead flies cause the ointment of the apothecary to send forth a stinking savor: so doth a little folly him that is in reputation for wisdom and honor'?" And he held his hands up and smiled ingratiatingly.

"Would he make a good missionary?" Thorn asked in some anger, for he had been unable to follow the Biblical citation.

"Ah, yes!" the teacher cried. "To plunge into the unknown. To carry the good Word to the heathen. Yes, I think Abner Hale . . . Do I have the right boy? He was Gideon Hale's oldest? Bad complexion . . . really, an unlovely child? Yes, that's the one. Oh, yes! He'd make a fine missionary. Likes odd places and being alone."

The local minister was no better, and Reverend Thorn, schooled in the hard fields of Africa, could quickly spot where Abner had learned to weep. The doddering old man wheezed: "Little Abner Hale! I remember the year he found the Lord. It was in his father's meadow, and he stood transfixed . . ."

"Would he make a good missionary?" Thorn interrupted.

"Missionary!" the old man snapped. "Why should he leave Marlboro? Why not come back here and take my place, where he could do some good? Somebody ought to send some missionaries to Marlboro. Atheism, Deism, Unitarianism, Quakerism. Pretty soon there won't be a decent follower of John Calvin in all New England. If you want my opinion, young man, and I can see by your red face that you don't, you oughtn't to be coming here seducing our young men to go to Ceylon and Brazil and such places. Let 'em stay here and do some missionary work. But I haven't answered your question. Abner Hale'd make a wonderful missionary. He's gentle yet obstinate in the right. He's hard-working yet poetic in his love of nature. He's pious and he respects his parents. He's much too good to be sent to Ceylon."

On the dusty walk to the Hale farm, Reverend Thorn just about decided to give up his complex plan of first convincing the Board that they ought to take Abner and then convincing his niece Jerusha that she should do the same. All he had so far heard about the boy confirmed his committee's suspicions that Abner was a difficult, opinionated young man who was bound to cause trouble wherever he went, but then the gaunt missionary came upon the home of Abner Hale, and his mind was quickly changed.

From the road a line of maples led along a narrow lane to a wandering New England farmhouse with barn attached. For nearly a hundred and fifty years the buildings had known no paint and now stood grayish brown in the New England sun, which instead of brightening what could have been a lovely grassed-in square served instead to underscore the bleakness of the buildings. It was, recalled Reverend Thorn, the kind of Christian house in which he had been raised, the archetype in which to produce true piety. He understood Abner better from having seen merely the harsh outlines of his home.

Gideon Hale, angular and hard, completed the picture. Wrapping his skinny left leg completely around his right, so that one ankle locked into the other, he put his guest at ease by saying, "If you take Abner for Owhyhee you aren't getting an unmixed blessing, Reverend Thorn. He's not an average boy. He's not too easy to handle, either. He was pretty reasonable until he found conversion. Then he was certain that it was he and not me that was to interpret God's will. But he has enormous character. If you saw his marks in the Marlboro School, you'd find he started out poor in figures. But have you seen what he accomplished at Yale College? Only the best. In many ways he's an indifferent boy, Reverend Thorn, but where the right is concerned he's a rock. All my children are."

At supper Eliphalet Thorn saw the kind of granite from which Abner had been hewn. The nine little Hales, with no dirt on their faces and dressed in the cheapest kind of homespun, filed dutifully in and sat at a table marked by spotless cleanliness and very little food. "We will say prayers," wiry, hawk-eyed Gideon announced, and all heads were bowed. One by one the nine children recited appropriate verses from the Bible, after which Mrs. Hale, an almost dead bundle of bones, mumbled briefly, "God bless this house," which was followed by a five-minute prayer from her husband. These preliminaries over, Hale said, "And now will our guest consent to bless us with a word of prayer?" And the scene was so reminiscent of his own childhood that Reverend Thorn launched into a ten-minute blessing in which he recalled the pious highlights of his youth in a Christian family.

After the meager meal Gideon Hale took his entire brood into the front room, where a particularly dank smell proved that no fire was ever wasted, and he proposed formal evening prayers. His wife and daughters led in a spirited version of "All hail the power of Jesus' name," after which Gideon and the boys sang a hymn quite popular at the time: "Oh, for a closer walk with God." When they came to the stirring verse about idols, Reverend Thorn joined in forcefully, for the words could almost serve as the dominant motive of his life:

"The dearest idol I have known,
Whate'er that idol be,
Help me to tear it from Thy throne,
And worship only Thee."

Prayers by Gideon and his oldest boy followed, then an invitation to the visitor to say a few words. Reverend Thorn spoke long and passionately of the influence a Christian home can have upon a young man, or, as he remembered his sisters and the strong women into which they grew, upon a young female. "It is from homes like this," he said, "that God picks those who are to carry forward His work on earth." And in the fullness of his talk he committed himself to sponsoring Abner Hale, for he knew then that while it must be granted that the young man was unpleasant now, in the future he was going to be a great and solid implement of the Lord.

When prayers were ended, and the children dismissed, the reverend asked Gideon for a sheet of paper on which to report to the Board. "Will it be a long letter?" Gideon asked anxiously.

"A short one," Eliphalet replied. "I have happy news to report."

Gideon, therefore, prudently tore his letter paper in half and handed his visitor one portion. "We waste nothing here," he explained, and as the tall missionary began his letter: "Brethren, I have visited the home of Abner Hale and have found that he comes from a family totally dedicated to God . . ." he happened to look at the narrow shelf where books were kept, and he saw with pleasure that they much resembled the books his family had collected—a battered copy of Euclid, Fox's *Book of Martyrs,* a speller of Noah Webster's, and a well-worn edition of John Bunyan standing beside a family Bible.

"I see with some pleasure," Reverend Thorn interrupted, "that this Christian family does not surrender to loose poetry and the novels which are becoming so popular in our land."

"This family is striving toward salvation," Gideon replied bleakly, and the thin-faced missionary finished the letter which would send Abner Hale to Owhyhee.

As Eliphalet Thorn stepped into the cool spring air, Mr. and Mrs. Hale accompanied him to the bright road that shimmered in moonlight. "If it were raining," Gideon said, "or if there were no moon, I'd saddle the horses . . ." Instead, he pointed the way to Marlboro with his powerful right arm. "It's not far," he assured his guest.

Reverend Thorn bade the couple good night and started off toward the dim lights of Marlboro, but after he had gone a short distance he stopped and turned to survey once more the bleak and arid home from which his protégé had come. The trees were in line; the fields were well trimmed; the cattle were fat. For the rest of the farm, one could see only penury, a complete lack of anything relating to beauty, and an austerity of purpose that was positively repellent, except that it so obviously called to the passer-by: "Here is a home that is dedicated to God." And as if to underline that fact, it was less than two hours after Reverend Thorn's departure that Abner Hale's oldest sister rushed weeping into her mother's room and stood trembling in the moonlight, crying, "Mother! Mother! I was lying awake thinking of the poor Africans about whom Reverend Thorn spoke tonight, and I began to shake, and I heard God's voice speaking directly to me."

"Did you have a sense of overwhelming sin?" her mother asked, slipping into a long coat which she used as a night wrap.

"Yes! I saw for the first time that I was hopelessly and utterly damned and that I had no escape."

"And you felt willing to surrender yourself totally to God?"

"It was as if a great hand were shaking me, violently, bringing me to my senses at last."

"Gideon!" the girl's mother cried in ecstasy. "Esther has been initiated into a sense of sin!"

The news was more pleasing than any other that Gideon Hale could have heard, and he cried, "Has she entered into a state of grace?"

"She has!" Mrs. Hale cried. "Oh, blessed Beulah Land, another sinner has found you!" And the three Hales knelt in the moonlight and gave ardent thanks to their bleak and forbidding Protector for having disclosed to still another member of their family the remorseless weight of sin under which mankind lives, the nearness of the inextinguishable fires to which ninety-nine out of every hundred human beings are forever and hopelessly committed, and the joyless, bitter path of salvation.

Within three days Reverend Thorn approached one of the most gracious villages ever to have developed in America: the tree-lined, white-clapboarded, well-gabled village of Walpole, near the Connecticut River in southwestern New Hampshire. It was a village to gladden the heart, for its glistening church steeple could be seen from afar, and the rolling hills that surrounded it were prosperous. It was to Walpole that Reverend Thorn's older sister Abigail had come when she had stubbornly insisted upon marrying the young Harvard lawyer, Charles Bromley, whose family had lived in Walpole for several generations.

Reverend Thorn had never approved of either the Bromleys or their village, for both bespoke good living rather than piety, and he rarely approached Walpole without a definite feeling that God must one day punish this sybaritic place, a conviction which deepened when he neared the Bromley home, a handsome, large, white three-storied house with many gables. He could hear, with some dismay, his sister playing English dances on the family organ. The dance terminated abruptly and a bright-faced, round-cheeked woman of forty rushed to the door, crying, "It's Eliphalet!" He, avoiding her kiss and looking about anxiously, was gratified to see that his niece Jerusha was not at home.

"Yes, she is!" Abigail corrected. "She's upstairs. Brooding. She's doing very poorly, but if you ask me, it's because she wants to. She refuses to get him out of her mind, and just when time is about to solve the problem, a letter reaches Boston from Canton or California, and she goes into a decline again."

"Have you thought of intercepting the letters?" Eliphalet asked.

"Charles would never permit that. He insists that any room which an individual holds within a house is that individual's castle. And foreign powers, even though they be corrupt, have an inalienable right of communicating with that castle."

Reverend Thorn was about to say he still could not understand why the Lord did not strike Charles Bromley dead, but since he had been wondering this for the past twenty-two years, and since the Lord stubbornly refused to do anything about it, he left his hackneyed observation unvoiced. What did gall him, however, was the fact that the Lord went out of his way to bless Bromley's various occupations.

"No," he said stiffly when his sister asked if he would stay with her. "I shall stop at the inn."

"Then why did you come so far?" Abigail asked.

"Because I have found an opportunity whereby your daughter may be saved."

"Jerusha?"

"Yes. Three times I have heard her say that she wanted to surrender her life to Jesus. To work wherever He sent her . . . as a missionary."

"Eliphalet!" his sister interrupted. "Those were the words of a young girl disappointed in love. When she spoke thus she hadn't heard from him for a year."

"It is in moments of disappointment that we speak our true thoughts," Thorn insisted.

"But Jerusha has everything she wants right here, Eliphalet."

"She wants God in her life, Abigail, and here she lacks that."

"Now, Eliphalet! Don't you dare . . ."

"Have you ever discussed with her the things she has told me?" Reverend Thorn pressed. "Have you had the courage?"

"All we know is that if she has recently received a letter from him, she's in heaven on earth and wants to get married as soon as he docks at New Bedford. But if six or seven months of silence have gone by, she swears she will become a missionary and serve in Africa . . . like her uncle."

"Let me speak to her now," Eliphalet proposed.

"No! She's in a fit of depression now and she'd agree to anything."

"Even, perhaps, to the salvation of her immortal soul?"

"Eliphalet! Don't talk like that. You know that Charles and I try to live good Christian lives . . ."

"Nobody could live a good Christian life in Walpole, New Hampshire," he muttered with disgust. "Vanity is all I see here. Look at this room! An organ not used for hymns. Novels. Books of lascivious poems. Money that should be going to missions going into ostentatious decoration. Abigail, a young Massachusetts man, dedicated to God, is about to sail as a missionary to Owhyhee. He has asked me to speak to you regarding Jerusha's hand."

Mrs. Bromley fell back in her damasked chair, then collected herself and called a servant. "Go fetch Mr. Bromley immediately," she ordered.

"I did not come here to talk to your husband," Eliphalet protested.

"It is my husband, not God, who is Jerusha's father," Abigail replied.

"Blasphemy!"

"No, love!"

The brother and sister sat in hateful silence until Charles Bromley, rotund, jovial, successful and overfed, came into the room. "Family fight?" he asked robustly.

"My brother Eliphalet . . ."

"I know who he is, dear. Just call him Phet." He laughed and added, "I've found in these matters that if you can get the litigants to start off on an informal basis it's so much better. If you call a man 'My brother Eliphalet,' why, out of self-respect you've almost got to wind up in court. What'r'ya up to, Phet?"

"A fine young man in the divinity school at Yale College is about to depart as a missionary to Owhyhee . . ."

"Where's Owhyhee?"

"Near Asia."

"Chinese?"

"No. Owhyheean."

"Never heard of it."

"And he was much impressed with what I had to say about my niece Jerusha."

"How did her name come up?" Bromley asked suspiciously.

"It's humiliating," Abigail sniffed. "Eliphalet's going around peddling our daughter. To get her married."

"I think it's very generous of him, Abby," Bromley exploded. "God knows I haven't had much success peddling her. One week she's in love with a sailor, whom she hasn't seen for three years. Abby, did that sailor ever even kiss her?"

"Charles!"

"And the next week she's in love with God and self-punishment on some distant island. Frankly, Phet, if you could find her a good husband I'd be obliged. I could then spend my efforts on her two sisters."

"The young man of whom I speak is Abner Hale," Thorn said stiffly. "Here's what his professors think of him. I visited his home . . ."

"Oh, Eliphalet!" his sister protested.

"In the guise of satisfying myself as to his Christian upbringing."

"And was it a good Christian home?" Bromley inquired.

"It was," Eliphalet replied. "In every respect."

Charles Bromley paced the handsomely decorated room for several moments and then said unexpectedly, "If you say it was a good Christian home, Phet, I'm sure it must have been horrible indeed. I can see young Abner Hale right now. Skinny, bad complexion, eyes ruined through too much study, sanctimonious, dirty fingernails, about six years retarded in all social graces. And yet, do you know, as I watch life go past here in Walpole, it's often those boys who in the long run turn out to be the best husbands."

In spite of himself, Reverend Thorn always admired the acuity of his brother-in-law's mind, so now he added what he had never intended saying: "Charles and Abigail, this young man is all the things Charles has just predicted. But he's also a dedicated man, extremely honest with himself, and one who is going to grow in grace. I wouldn't want him as a son-in-law now, but in ten years he'll be the best husband a woman could have."

"Is he as tall as Jerusha?" Abigail asked.

"Not quite, and he's a year younger."

Mrs. Bromley began to cry, but her gruff husband joshed her. "You know how it is, Phet! This sailor that Jerusha fell in love with . . . Some ridiculous dance here in Walpole . . . He's a cousin of the Lowells, I think . . . I've always thought it was her mother who fell most completely in love that night. These tall men with commanding eyes!" He patted his own rotund belly and coaxed his wife away from her tears.

"It amounts to this," Eliphalet said bluntly. "You have a daughter and I have a niece. We both love her very much. She's twenty-two, and she grows more confused each day. We must find her a husband. We must help her choose a way of life. I offer both."

"And I appreciate the offer," Charles said warmly. "God knows I've been helpless."

"Do you still wish to speak with her, Eliphalet?" Abigail asked, swayed by her husband's reactions.

"No, Abigail," her husband interrupted. "This is your problem, not Phet's."

"It is, isn't it?" Mrs. Bromley sniffed. "But what can I tell her about the young man?"

Eliphalet, having anticipated this, handed her a neatly written dossier on Abner Hale, including a minute description of the young minister, a transcript of his marks in college, an essay he had written on Church Discipline in Geneva, and a sketchy genealogy of the Gideon Hales of

Marlboro, descendants of Elisha Hale of Bucks, England. There was also a separate sheet which indicated that confidential letters could be addressed to John Whipple and President Day at Yale, to several Christian citizens at Marlboro, Massachusetts, and to Abner's sister Esther on the family farm. Abigail Bromley peeked first at the physical description: "Fine clear complexion but sallow; fine teeth."

Bad news she could have taken, but these hopeful comments collapsed her and she sobbed, "We don't even know where Owhyhee is." Then she accused her husband of lacking parental love: "Are you willing to send your daughter . . ."

"My dear," Charles said firmly, "the only thing I'm not willing to do is to abandon my child to fits of depression and religious mania in a small upstairs room. If she can find love and a rich life in Owhyhee, it's a damned sight better than she's doing in Walpole, New Hampshire. Now you go up and talk with her. I believe she's in a religious swing of the pendulum this month and she'll probably jump at the chance of marrying a minister and going to Owhyhee."

Therefore, as a result of Reverend Eliphalet Thorn's importunate trip to Marlboro and to Walpole, young Abner Hale, sweating the June days nervously at Yale, finally received his letter from Boston: "Dear Mr. Hale: As a result of careful inquiries conducted on our behalf by Reverend Eliphalet Thorn, the American Board of Commissioners for Foreign Missions is happy in the will of God to advise you that you have been chosen for mission duty in Hawaii. You and your wife will depart Boston on September first in the brig *Thetis.* Captain Janders." There was enclosed a printed list of some two hundred articles that venturing missionaries were urged to carry with them:

3 razors	1 parasol	1 nest Hingham boxes
1 compass	3 scissors	1 pair bellows
21 towels	4 mugs	3 stone jugs
1 washbasin	3 chambers	1 pair andirons
1 calash	1 lantern	1 crane and hooks . . .

There was also a much shorter letter which said simply: "You would be well advised to present yourself in late July at the home of Charles and Abigail Bromley in Walpole, New Hampshire, there to meet their daughter Jerusha, a Christian girl of twenty-two. It occurs to me that you may require some few necessities to make yourself additionally presentable for this important meeting, so I enclose herewith three dollars, which you need not repay me." This letter was signed: "Eliphalet Thorn, of the African Mission."

IN THESE YEARS of the early 1820's there were many young ministers destined for Hawaii who, absorbed in study, found no time to make the acquaintance of marriageable young women and who were unexpectedly faced with the positive necessity of getting married within the space of a few weeks, for the A.B.C.F.M. resolutely refused to send any unmarried man to the islands and advised all such who wished to labor there for the Lord to inquire of their friends to see if a suitable female might be found, and there is no record of failure. Of course, some young ministers were rejected by the first nominees of their friends, but sooner or later all found wives, "not because the young fellers was handsome, but because New England turns out so danged many old maids. Our best boys is all out to sea." There was much argument as to whether the decision of the A.B.C.F.M. to reject unmarried men stemmed from understanding of what errors men living alone might fall into; or from specific knowledge of what life in Hawaii was like, and it seems probable that the latter was the case, for many whalers had often returned to New Bedford and Nantucket, if they bothered to come home at all, with faraway tales of generous maidens, endless supplies of coconuts and thatched houses in magnificent valleys. In all seaports one could hear the sad refrain:

"I want to go back to Owhyhee,
Where the sea sings a soulful song,
Where the gals is kind and gentle,
And they don't know right from wrong!"

From listening to such songs the Board concluded that, conditions being what they were, it would be prudent to require even young men who lived in a state of grace to take their own converted women with them. More potent however was the conviction that women were the civilizing agents, the visual harbingers of Christian life. The A.B.C.F.M. therefore required females, not only to keep the young missionaries in line, but also because a devoted young wife was herself a missionary of the most persuasive kind. And so the young men scattered over New England, meeting shy, dedicated girls for the first time on Friday, proposing on Saturday, getting married after three Sundays had elapsed for banns, and departing for Hawaii immediately thereafter.

But none of these amorous odysseys was stranger than the one conducted by Abner Hale. When he left Yale in early July, duly ordained a minister in the Congregational Church, he was five feet four inches tall, weighed one hundred and thirty-six pounds, had a most sallow complexion, a somewhat stooped bearing, and stringy blond hair which he parted in the middle and pasted down with water, bear grease and tallow. He wore the black claw-hammer coat favored by ministers, had a skimpy cotton stock about his neck, and a new ten-inch-high beaver stovepipe hat which tapered inward about five inches above his head and then flared out to a considerable expanse of flatness on top. In his meager luggage, tied together in a box, he carried a small brush which he had been told to use in grooming his hat, and this was the one vanity of dress he allowed himself, for he reasoned that this hat, more than anything else, heralded him as a clergyman. His cowhide shoes, black with elastic webs, he ignored.

When the coach landed him at Marlboro, he stepped primly down, adjusted his tall hat, grabbed his box, and set out on foot for home. To his disappointment, no one in Marlboro bothered to congratulate him on having attained the ministry, for in his tall hat no one recognized him, and he reached the tree-lined lane leading to his home without having spoken to anyone, and there he stood in the hot dust, greeting, as he felt, for the last time, this bleak, unkindly home in which generations of Hales had been born, and it seemed to him so marked with love that he bowed his head and wept. He was standing in this manner when the younger children spotted him and led the whole family out to welcome him home.

They had barely assembled in the austere front room when Gideon Hale, brimming with pride at having a son who was ordained, suggested, "Abner, will you lead your first prayer in this house?" And Abner took as his text Leviticus 25:10, "And ye shall return every man unto his possession, and ye shall return every man unto his family," and poured forth a minor sermon. The family glowed, but when services were over, shy, gangling Esther took her brother aside and whispered, "The most wonderful thing has happened, Abner."

"Father told me, Esther. I am deeply pleased that you have entered into a state of grace."

"It would be vain of me to speak of that," the eager girl said, in blushes. "That wasn't what I meant."

"What then?"

"I have received a letter!"

"From whom?"

"From Walpole, New Hampshire."

It was now Abner's turn to blush, and although he did not wish to display unseemly interest he nevertheless had to ask, haltingly, "From . . ." But he could not bring himself to utter the name he had not yet spoken to anyone. It seemed to him so improbable that he should even know of Jerusha Bromley, let alone be on his way to propose to her, that he would not profane her name by mentioning it.

Esther Hale took her brother's two hands and assured him, "It is from one of the sweetest, most considerate, gentle and Christian young women in all New England. She called me sister and asked for my prayers and guidance."

"May I see the letter?" Abner asked.

"Oh! No! No!" Esther protested vigorously. "It was sent to me in confidence. Jerusha said . . . Isn't that a sweet name, Abner? It was Jotham's mother's name in Kings. She said that everything was happening so rapidly that she had to confide in a trustworthy friend. You would be amazed at the things she asked me."

"About what?" Abner asked.

"About you."

"What did you say?"

"I wrote a letter of eighteen pages, and although it was a secret letter between my sister and me . . ."

"Your sister?"

"Yes, Abner. I'm convinced from the manner of her letter that she intends marrying you." Esther smiled at her confused brother and added, "So although it was a secret letter, I made a copy of one of the eighteen pages."

"Why?"

"Because on that page I listed every single one of your faults, as a young woman would assess them, and in sisterly love, Abner, I would like to give you that important page."

"I would like to have it," Abner said weakly, and he took the finely composed page, with its flowing penmanship, to his room and read: "Dearest Jerusha, whom I hope one happy day to have the right of calling sister, thus far I have told you only of my brother's virtues. They are many and I have not exaggerated them, for as you can guess, living in close harmony in the bosom of a large and closely bonded family provides even the dullest intellect with ample opportunity to penetrate even the most secret recesses of another's mind and temperament. Against the day, therefore, when we may meet as true sisters, and desirous of having you judge me as having been completely honest with you in true Christian principle as enjoined by our Lord in Ephesians 4:25, 'Wherefore putting away lying, speak every man truth with his neighbor: for we are members one of another,' I must now advise you of the weaknesses of my devout and gentle brother. First, Jerusha, he is not skilled in pretty manners and will surely disappoint you if you seek them foremost in a husband. That he could learn to be more gracious I feel sure, and perhaps under your patient counsel he might one day become almost civilized, but I doubt it. He is rude and honest. He is thoughtless and forthright, and from having watched my mother deal with such a husband I know how trying it can be at times, but in all of my life I have not seen my father make much change, so I must conclude that this is something which women prize but which they rarely find. Second, he is thoughtless where women are concerned, for I have lived with him in closest intimacy for nineteen years, and I have shared his secrets and he mine, and never in that time has he thought to give me a present other than some useful object like a straight-edge or a journal. I am sure he does not know that flowers exist, even though our Lord saw to it that

His temple in Jerusalem was constructed of finest materials and sweet woods. In this also he is much like his father. Third, he is not a handsome young man and his habit of stooping makes him less so. He is not careful of his clothes, nor of his person, although he does wash his mouth frequently to avoid giving offense in that quarter. On any day in Marlboro I see young men who are more handsome than my brother, and I suppose that one day I shall marry one of them, but I have not the slightest hope that this handsomer man will have the list of favorable attributes which I have just enumerated. But I know you will often wish that Abner stood a little straighter, wore linen a little whiter, and had a more commanding presence. He will never have these graces and if you seek them primarily, you will be grievously disappointed. Finally, sister Jerusha, for I make bold to call you this in the most fervent hope that you will accept my brother, for the spirit of joy I find in your letter is one that Abner sorely needs, I must warn you that he is both grave and vain, and if he were not destined for the ministry these would be insufferable traits, but his gravity and vanity spring from the same cause. He feels that God has spoken to him personally, as indeed He has, and that this separates him from all other men. This is a most unpleasant trait in my brother, and I can now say so because God has spoken to me, too, and I judge from your letter that He has come to you, and I find neither in you nor in myself the vanity that mars my brother. I have found in God's presence a sweetness that I never knew before. It makes me gentler with my sisters, more understanding of my little brothers. I take more joy in feeding the chickens and churning the butter. If only Abner could surrender his vanity in the presence of the Lord, he would be a near-perfect husband for you, Jerusha. As it is, he is a good man, and if you should elect him, I pray that you will keep this letter with you and that you will find as the years pass that your unseen sister told you the truth."

There was another letter waiting at Marlboro. It came from Reverend Eliphalet Thorn and said simply: "While you're at your father's, work each day in the sun with your hat off. If Jerusha accepts you, I'll perform the ceremony."

So for two weeks Abner worked in the fields as he had as a boy, and in time he grew bronzed and the sallow skin under his deep-set eyes tightened, so that when it came time for him to say farewell to his large and loving family he was as close to being handsome as he would ever be, but the relaxation from grimness that his sister Esther had sought to encourage had not taken place. This was partly because the young minister had a presentiment that this was the very last time on earth that he would see these eleven people, this barn, that meadow where he had known conversion, this warm fellowship of a Christian family. He shook hands with his mother, for he was never much of an embracer, and then with his father, who suggested cautiously, "Since you're leaving, maybe I ought to hitch up the wagon."

He was obviously relieved when his son replied, "No, Father. It's a good day. I'll walk."

"I'd like to give you a little money to go away with, Abner," his father began, hesitantly.

"That's not necessary," Abner replied. "Reverend Thorn kindly sent me three dollars."

"That's what Esther told me," Gideon Hale replied. Thrusting out a well-worn hand, he said stiffly, "May the Lord go with you, son."

"May you continue to live in grace," Abner replied.

He then said good-bye to Esther and for the first time realized that she was growing into quite a fine young woman. He had a pang of regret and thought: "I ought to have known Esther better." But now it was too late, and he stood in a welter of confusion when she kissed him, thus paving the way for each of his other sisters to do the same.

"Good-bye," he said chokingly. "If we do not meet again here on earth, we shall surely reassemble at His feet in heaven. For we are heirs of God and joint heirs of Jesus Christ to an inheritance uncorrupted, undefiled and limitless and which fadeth not away." With this he sternly moved away from his bleak parents and their bleak home with its unpainted boards and unlovely windows. For the last time he walked down the lane, out into the dusty road, and on to Marlboro, where the coach picked him up for New Hampshire and an adventure which he dreaded.

Arrived at the Old Colony Inn at Walpole, Abner washed and took from his papers one that had been written by his sister. Numerous items were set forth, and numbered, the first being: "Upon arrival wash, brush yourself thoroughly, and have the messenger deliver this note to Mrs. Bromley: 'My dear Mrs. Bromley, May I have the pleasure of calling upon you this afternoon at three?' Then sign your name and the name of the inn, in case one of the family should deem fit to come to escort you in person."

The letter had scarcely been dispatched when Abner heard a hearty male voice crying, "You got a young fellow from Massachusetts staying here?" And before Abner had time to read his sister's careful instructions for the first visit, his door was burst open and he was greeted by a generously filled-out New Hampshire gentleman who laughed, "I'm Charles Bromley. You must be nervous as a colt."

"I am," Abner said.

"You look a lot browner and tougher than everybody said."

"Reverend Thorn told me to do some work in the fields."

"Do me a lot of good to do the same. What I came for, though, was to tell you that we won't hear of you waiting around this inn till three o'clock. Walk right across the common with me, and meet the family."

"It won't be an imposition?" Abner asked.

"Son!" Lawyer Bromley laughed. "We're as nervous as you are!" And he started to lead young Hale home, but on the spur of the moment stopped and called to the innkeeper, "What are the charges here?"

"Sixty cents a day."

"Hold the bill for me. These young ministers don't earn much money." He then took Abner out into the midsummer perfection of Walpole. There was the village church, glistening white in its pre-Revolutionary splendor, the massive houses, the giant elms, the marvelous green common with a fretwork bandstand in the middle where Charles Bromley often delivered patriotic addresses, and straight ahead the lawyer's residence from which Mrs. Bromley and her two younger daughters peered like spies.

"He's not as bad as they said!" Charity Bromley whispered to her sister.

"He's not very tall," Mercy sniffed. "He's more your size, Charity, than Jerusha's."

"Now be composed, girls," Mrs. Bromley commanded, and all sat primly in large chairs. The door was kicked open in Charles Bromley's familiar way, and a young man in black carrying a large stovepipe hat entered the room. He walked firmly across the carpeting, bowed to Mrs. Bromley, and said, "I am honored that you would invite me to your home." Then he looked at Charity, nineteen and pretty, with curls to her shoulders, and said with a tremendous blush and a deep bow, "I am especially pleased to make your acquaintance, Miss Bromley."

"She's not Jerusha!" young Mercy squealed, attacked by a furious set of giggles.

Mr. Bromley joined the laughter and said, "You know how girls dawdle, Abner. You've got sisters. You'll know Jerusha when she comes down. She's the pretty one."

Abner felt a wave of paralyzing embarrassment sweep over him. Then he became aware that Mrs. Bromley had addressed a question to him: "Do you have a sister Mercy's age? She's twelve."

"I have a brother twelve," he fumbled.

"Well, if you have a brother twelve," Mercy said brightly, "you can't very well have a sister twelve, too."

"Could be twins," Charity laughed.

"No twins," Abner explained precisely.

"So then he doesn't have a sister twelve!" Mercy triumphed.

"What Mrs. Bromley was going to say, Abner," explained Mr. Bromley, "was that if you did have a sister twelve, you'd understand why we sometimes would like to drown this little imp."

The idea startled Abner. He had never heard his parents say such a thing, even in jest. In fact, he had heard more joking in these first few minutes with the Bromleys than he had heard in his entire family life of twenty-one years. "Mercy looks like too fine a child to be drowned," he mumbled in what he took to be gallantry, and then he gaped, for coming down the stairs and into the room was Jerusha Bromley, twenty-two years old, slim, dark-eyed, dark-haired, perfect in feature and with gently dancing curls which framed her face, three on each side. She was exquisite in a frail starched dress of pink and white sprigged muslin, marked by a row of large pearl buttons, not flat as one found them in cheaper stores, but beautifully rounded on top and iridescent. They dropped in an unbroken line from her cameoed throat, over her striking bosom, down to her tiny waist and all the way to the hem of her dress, where three spaced bands of white bobbin lace completed the decoration. Abner, looking at her for the first time, choked. "She cannot be the sister they thought of for me," he thought. "She is so very lovely."

With firm step she came across the room and offered Abner her hand, saying in a low gentle voice, "The wisest thing I have done in my life was to write to Esther. I feel as if I already know you, Reverend Hale."

"His name's Abner!" Mercy cried, but Jerusha ignored her.

It was a long, hot, enchanting afternoon from one o'clock to six. Abner had never before encountered such wit and relaxed laughter, marred only by the fact that upon his dusty arrival at the inn he had drunk enormous quantities of water, so that from four o'clock on he needed more than anything else a chance to go to the privy, a predicament which had never before faced him and with which he was incapable of coping. Finally, Mr. Bromley said openly, "Just occurred to me, we've been keeping this young man talking for five hours. I'll bet he'd like to visit the outhouse." And he led the blushing young minister to the most enjoyable relief he had ever experienced.

At dinner Abner was aware that the entire Bromley family was watching his manners, but nevertheless he felt that he was conducting himself fairly well, a fact which gave him some pleasure, for although he thought it was stupid to judge a man by his manners, he suddenly realized that he wanted this pleasant family to think well of him.

"We were all watching to see if you took the cherry pits out of your mouth with your fingers," Mercy teased.

"We learned not to do that at college," Abner explained. "At home I used to spit them out." The family laughed so merrily that Abner discovered he had made a joke, which had not been his intention.

At eight Mr. Bromley asked if Abner would lead evening worship, and he did so, taking for his text one that Esther had selected, after much study, for the occasion, Genesis 23:4: "I am a stranger and a sojourner with you: give me a possession of a buryingplace with you, that I may bury my dead out of my sight." Charles Bromley found the passage excessively gloomy for a beginning preacher of twenty-one but he had to confess admiration for the adroitness with which Abner converted death into a glowing assurance of life. Abner, for his part, held that the manner in which Mrs. Bromley played the organ for hymns and the way in which her three daughters sang them were both unnecessarily ornate. But granting these differences, the service was a success.

Then Mr. Bromley said, "To bed, family! These youngsters must have much they want to discuss." And with a wide sweep of his arms he projected his brood upstairs.

When they were gone, Jerusha sat with her hands folded, looking at the stranger in her house, and said, "Reverend Hale, your sister told me so much about you that I feel no need for asking questions, but you must have many that perplex you."

"I have one that surpasses all others, Miss Bromley," he replied. "Do you have unshaken confidence in the Lord?"

"I do. More than my mother or father, more than my sisters. I don't know how this happened, but I do."

"I am pleased to hear that you are not a stranger to our Lord and Master," Abner sighed contentedly.

"Have you no other questions!" Jerusha asked.

Abner looked startled, as if to say, "What other questions are there?" But he asked, "Are you willing, then, to follow blindly His grand purpose of life, even if it takes you eighteen thousand miles away from home?"

"I am. Of that I am quite certain. For some years now I have had a calling. Of late it has grown most powerful."

"Do you know that Owhyhee is a pagan land, barbarous with evil?"

"One night I heard Keoki speak at church. He told us about the dark practices of his people."

"And you are nevertheless willing to go to Owhyhee?"

Jerusha sat extremely primly for several moments, fighting down her natural inclinations, but she could not do so, and finally she blurted, "Reverend Hale, you're not hiring me to go to Owhyhee! And you're not investigating me to see if I should be made a minister! You're supposed to be asking me if I want to marry you!"

From his chair some few feet away, Abner swallowed very hard. He was not surprised by Jerusha's outburst, for he was aware that he knew nothing of women, and perhaps this was the way they were expected to act. So he did not panic. Instead he looked at his hands and said, "You are so beautiful, Miss Bromley. You are so much more lovely than I had ever a right to expect, that I cannot even now comprehend that you might consent to marry me. I am astonished that you would bother with me, so I have been thinking that you must have some powerful call to the Lord. It seemed safe and reasonable for us to talk about that."

Jerusha left her chair, walked to Abner and kneeled on the floor so that she could look up into his eyes. "Are you saying that you're afraid to propose to me, Reverend Hale?"

"Yes. You are so much more beautiful than I expected."

"And you're thinking, 'Why isn't she already married?' "

"Yes."

"Reverend Hale, don't be embarrassed. All my family and friends ask the same question. The simple truth is, three years ago, before I came to know the Lord, I was in love with a New Bedford man who came here on a visit. He was everything you aren't, and immediately everyone in Walpole decided that he was a perfect husband for me. But he went away and in his absence . . ."

"You used God as a substitute?"

"Many think so."

"And now you wish to use me as a substitute, too?"

"I imagine that my mother and sister think so," Jerusha replied quietly. The moment of emotion having passed without Abner's even having touched her hands, she rose demurely and returned to her own chair.

"Yet my sister Esther thought that your letter was sincere," Abner reflected.

"And when she thought so," Jerusha said wryly, "she did her best to convince me to marry you. If Esther were here now . . ."

Aloofly, two strange lovers, like continents undiscovered, sat apart, with oceans of uncertainty between them, but as the unique day drew to an end, Jerusha found that Abner Hale really did believe on the Lord and that in his heart he was truly afraid to take a woman to wife who was not wholly committed to God; whereas Abner learned that it was unimportant whether Jerusha Bromley was in a state of grace or not; what counted was the fact that she was willing to remain an old maid forever unless marriage brought her the honest passion of which life was capable.

On these mutual discoveries the first interview ended, except at the door to the Bromley home Abner asked quietly, "May I be so bold as to grasp your hand tenderly before I go . . . as a token of my deep esteem for you?" And when he first touched the body of Jerusha Bromley, spinster of Walpole, in what was for him the most daring gesture of his young life, a surge of such power sped from her finger tips to his that he stood for a moment transfixed, then hurried in confusion across the sleeping common and to his inn.

Before eight the next morning all the kitchens of Walpole—at least all whose members attended the local church—knew of the precise state of the Hale-Bromley courtship, for little Mercy had been spying, and now she went from house to house relating breathlessly, "Well, he didn't really kiss her, because that would have been improper on a first visit, but he did take her hand in his, like in an English novel."

At eight-thirty Mercy and her sister Charity called at the inn and advised their possible brother-in-law that he was about to be spirited away on a family picnic, and he asked impulsively, "Is . . . Miss Bromley attending?" And Mercy replied, "Jerusha? Naturally. How else is she going to become engaged?" But Abner, foreseeing another day spent far from a privy, refused to eat any breakfast or drink either milk or water, so that by the time the picnic baskets were opened on a New Hampshire hill, he was famished and ate prodigiously, after which he and Jerusha went for a walk along a stream, and he asked, "How do you find it possible to leave such a lovely place?" And she replied cryptically, "Not all of those who followed Jesus were peasants."

He stopped by a bending tree and said, "I could not sleep last night, Miss Bromley, thinking that I managed badly in our conversation, but then it seemed that I hadn't managed so poorly after all, because as a result of our talking I came to know you and to appreciate your qualities. Any fool could see that you were beautiful, so there was no sense talking about that, but in other circumstances we might have said a great deal last night without having discovered as much as we did."

"What we found out," Jerusha replied, holding onto a branch, "is that we are both stubborn people, but that we both honor the Lord."

Standing more than six feet from her, he asked, "Would you be willing to go to Owhyhee . . . on those conditions?"

"I would, Reverend Hale."

He swallowed, scratched at the tree trunk and asked, "Does this mean we are engaged?"

"It does not," she said firmly, holding onto her branch and swinging back and forth provocatively.

"Why won't you marry me?" he asked in great confusion.

"Because you haven't asked me," she said stubbornly.

"But I said . . ."

"You said, 'Would you be willing to go to Owhyhee?' and I said, 'Yes.' But that certainly didn't mean I'd be willing to go all the way around Cape Horn to Owhyhee with a man who wasn't my husband."

"Oh, I never intended . . ." Abner crimsoned in dismay and tried to make several different apologies, with no success. Finally, he stopped and looked at the slim girl in the silky summer dress, swinging on the bough so that she seemed to be dancing, and without her teasing him more, he discovered what he should say. He left the tree trunk and kneeled in the dust beside the faltering stream. "Miss Bromley, will you marry me?" he asked.

"I will," she replied, adding nervously, "I was so afraid, Reverend Hale, that you were going to say, 'Will you marry me and go with me to Owhyhee?' That would have spoiled it all."

She held down her hands and helped him to his feet, expecting to be embraced, but he dusted his knees and said in a burst of real joy, "We must advise your parents." Smiling wryly, she agreed, and they went back to the picnic area, but Mr. and Mrs. Bromley were sound asleep. Mercy and her sister were not, and could guess what had happened, so Mercy asked, "Are you engaged?"

"Yes," Jerusha said.

"Has he kissed you?"

"Not yet."

"Abner! Kiss her!" the sisters cried, and in the hot sun of a late July day, Abner Hale kissed Jerusha Bromley for the first time. It wasn't much, as kisses go, and the audience was nervously distracting, but when it ended he amazed himself by grabbing first Charity and kissing her and then Mercy, and crying, "You're the dearest sisters in the whole world!" Then he sat down, dazed, and confessed, "I never kissed a girl before but now I've kissed three of them!"

Mercy awakened her parents, screaming, "They've done it!" And there were more deep greetings, after which Charity produced a piece of paper on which she had outlined numerous dates: "We can post the banns on Sunday, that's the fifth, and on Monday the twentieth you can get married."

Mercy cried, "We'll turn Daddy's office into a sewing room and the cloth we've bought can be made into dresses and sheets . . ."

"You've bought the cloth?" Abner asked.

"Yes," Charity confessed. "Three weeks ago Jerusha decided to marry you, after she read Esther's letter. She told us, 'We'll let him come to visit just in case his sister's a wicked little liar.' But we all knew she wasn't. Anyway, Daddy must have got fifteen different letters about you, and we knew."

"Did all of you read all the letters?" Abner asked in embarrassment.

"Of course!" Mercy cried. "And the part I liked best is where you learned to cook and sew and keep house . . . in case you became a missionary. I told Jerusha to marry you quick, because then she'd never have to do any work at all."

But that evening, as the two younger sisters took their new brother-in-law-to-be back to the inn so that he could wash up before supper, Mercy pointed to a large white house and said, "That's where the sailor came to visit. He was a very handsome man, although I was only nine at the time, so he may have seemed taller than he really was."

"What happened?" Abner asked cautiously, and he saw Charity pinch her sister's arm.

"Ouch! Charity's trying to make me keep still, Abner, but I thought somebody ought to tell you. He was much handsomer than you are, but not as nice."

"Jerusha would never have married him, anyway," Charity added.

"Why not?" Abner asked.

"It takes a certain type of girl to marry a sailor," Charity said.

"What type?"

"The Salem type. The New Bedford type. Women who are willing to have their husbands away for years at a time. Jerusha is not that kind of woman, Abner. She lives on affection. Do be sweet with her."

"I shall be," he said, and on the marriage morning, when Reverend Thorn arrived by coach from Boston to conduct the ceremonies for his niece, he found his young minister friend from Yale in a state of gentle hypnosis. "I can't believe that I am going to marry this angel," Abner exploded, eager for someone to talk with after the three weeks of sewing and parties and meeting friends. "Her sisters have been unbelievable. Eighteen women were at their home all last week making me clothes. I've never known . . ."

He showed the tall missionary six barrels of clothing made by the women of Walpole, books donated for the mission in Owhyhee, and crockery. "I have experienced an outpouring of the spirit in this town that I never knew existed," Abner confessed.

"My sister Abigail is a girl who always made friends quickly," Eliphalet Thorn admitted. "I am so glad that you and Jerusha have found each other in God. Now if you'll excuse me, I'll step along to the house to complete arrangements with Charles."

But as he left Abner's room, the innkeeper called him and said, "If you're heading for Bromley's, you can take along this letter which just came in the mail," and he handed the missionary several sheets of paper folded upon themselves to form an envelope, and it was from Canton, in China, and had been on the sea for many months to London and to Charleston in South Carolina and to New Bedford. It was addressed to Miss Jerusha Bromley, Walpole, New Hampshire, and was written in a strong, fine hand. Reverend Thorn studied the letter for a long time and rationalized: "What chance is there that the innkeeper will mention this letter before Jerusha leaves Walpole? Not very much, I should think. But there is still a chance, so I must not burn it. Besides, to do so would be a sin. But if I now honestly declare, 'Eliphalet Thorn, you are to deliver that letter to your niece, Jerusha Bromley,' my intentions will be clear. Then, if I tuck it deep inside my inner pocket, like this, it would be only logical for me to forget it. Three months hence I can post it to my sister with apologies. And with Jerusha already married, why would Abigail want to bother her daughter with such a letter? Abigail's no fool." So he hid the letter and said in a loud voice as he walked across the common, "I must give this letter to Jerusha immediately I see her."

That afternoon Abner Hale, twenty-one, married Jerusha Bromley, twenty-two, whom he had known two weeks and four days, and on the next morning the young couple, accompanied by fourteen barrels of missionary goods, set out for Boston and the hermaphrodite brig *Thetis,* 230 tons, bound for Owhyhee.

The mission party assembled for the first time on August 30, 1821, in a brick church on the Boston waterfront. When Abner and Jerusha entered, John Whipple saw them and gasped with surprise at the beauty of the young woman who stood hesitantly in a fawn-colored coat and a pale blue poke bonnet that neatly framed her dancing brown curls and flashing eyes.

"Amanda!" he whispered to his wife. "Look at Abner!"

"Is that Abner?" the tiny bride from Hartford asked. "You said . . ."

"Hello, Abner!" Whipple called softly. When the couples met, Whipple said, "This is my wife, Amanda."

"This is Mrs. Hale," Abner replied, and they proceeded to meet the other nine mission couples.

Of the eleven young men convened in the church, all were under the age of twenty-eight, and nine were less than twenty-four. One had been married for two years, another for almost a year. The remaining nine had been married much as Abner and Jerusha. Friends had dispatched hastily written word pictures of unmarried girls of known piety, and weddings had been abruptly arranged, usually on the first meeting between the young people. Of these nine hurried marriages, only John Whipple and his tiny cousin Amanda had known each other for more than four days before banns were announced. Of the remaining eight couples, six, when it came time to sail, had not yet relaxed sufficiently for husband and wife to call each other by their first names, and that included Reverend and Mrs. Hale.

Few pilgrims have ever set forth upon great adventure with clearer directions than those promulgated by the American Board of Commissioners for Foreign Missions in the little brick church. Tall, godlike Eliphalet Thorn, drawing upon his hard years in Africa, said bluntly, "Brothers, you are about to immerse yourselves in one of the most difficult of all ventures, mission work in a pagan land. You are severely admonished to abide by these rules. First, all property is to be held in common. You are a family, and as a family you will receive from us here in Boston regular supplies which belong to no man or woman, but to the family in general. If you who are farmers raise fruit and sell the surplus, the proceeds belong to the family. If you who are good seamstresses sew clothing and sell it to the sailors in Owhyhee, the returns belong to the family. You are a family in Christ, and it is as a family that you own your houses, your lands, your schools and your churches.

"Second, you are abjured from interfering in the government of the islands, for you must constantly repeat to yourselves the injunction of our Lord as found in Matthew: 'And they brought unto him a penny. And he saith unto them, Whose is this image and superscription? They say unto him, Caesar's. Then saith he unto them, Render therefore unto Caesar the things which are Caesar's; and unto God the things that are God's.' You are specifically abjured from participating in government. You are sent not to govern but to convert. You are directed to accomplish two divine missions: bring the heathen to the Lord and civilize him. How he governs himself is his concern. How he learns to know Christ and the alphabet is your concern, for remember that until he learns to read, he cannot know the Bible and God's redeeming word. Therefore, to speed this worthy end we are sending with you three full fonts of type, and you are to put into the language of Owhyhee the Holy Bible and such other learning as the Owhyheeans are capable of mastering. Provide them with a written language, and they will glorify the Lord.

"Third, there is an inborn inclination on the part of all New England men to trade, and I suspect from the natural abilities which I have found among you as I have studied your careers, that many of you would do conspicuously well in business, but you have been called to serve the Lord, and it is to this business that you must attend. You will receive no salary, and you are expected to earn none. Your sole job is to serve the Lord, and if you do this with all your ability, you will have no vain and idle time for business pursuits.

"Finally, you are to lift up the heathen step by step until he stands with you. Within the passage of years the schools you build must be taught by him, and before you leave the scene, the pulpits you erect and from which you deliver the word of God must be filled by him. You are setting forth to save immortal souls for the harvest of God."

After Reverend Thorn had taken up questions concerning medical practices to be followed, an elderly, white-haired minister who had worked in many parts of America and in Ceylon spoke briefly. "Brothers in God," he said simply, "you are not entering upon a limited mission. You are to aim at nothing less than the complete regeneration and salvation of a society. If children now die, they are to be saved. If minds are now ignorant, they are to be enlightened. If idols flourish, they are to be supplanted by the word of Jesus. And if a road is mired and useless, it is to be paved and made straight. If there is among you any man or woman with a hundred capacities, he will find in Owhyhee full outlet for all of them. Spend yourselves in Christ so that in later years it may be said of you, 'They came to a nation in darkness; they left it in light.' "

ON THE LAST DAY of August the mission family was introduced to the ship on which they would live during the six months required for the slow passage to Hawaii. Reverend Thorn led them from the brick church, where they had engaged in morning prayers, onto the dock where a large three-masted ship lay anchored while her cargo of whale oil was being unloaded.

"That's a substantial ship," Jerusha observed to some of the other women. "A person shouldn't get too seasick on that," she added hopefully.

"That's not the mission ship," Reverend Thorn corrected. "Yours lies ahead."

"Oh, no!" one of the women gasped as she saw the squat and ugly little brig *Thetis*. It looked scarcely large enough for a river boat.

"Are we sailing in that?" Abner asked shakenly of John Whipple.

"It says *Thetis,"* Whipple replied dourly.

The brig was almost the smallest two-master that could successfully round Cape Horn at the farthest tip of South America. It was seventy-nine feet long, twenty-four feet wide, and drew only a dozen feet when loaded. Jerusha, upon inspecting it more closely from the quay, confided to Amanda Whipple, "It looks as if it might sink if twenty-two missionaries step aboard."

"You're free to inspect the *Thetis,"* a rough voice called, and for the first time they met Captain Retire Janders, a rugged forty-year-old master with a circle of sandy beard that framed his clean-shaven face from one ear, down the jaw line, under the chin and up to the other ear, making him look like a ruddy-faced boy peering through a hedge.

As Reverend Thorn led his family aboard he introduced each couple formally to Captain Janders. "The captain has been instructed to look after you on this long and tedious voyage," Thorn explained. "But his first job is to run his ship."

"Thank you, Reverend," Captain Janders growled. "Sometimes folks don't understand that a brig at sea ain't like a farm in Massachusetts." He led the missionaries forward to where a hatch stood open, and deep in the bowels of the brig they could see their boxes and books and barrels. "It's impossible, absolutely and forever impossible for anybody to touch anything that's down in that hold before we get to Hawaii. So don't ask. You live with what you can store in your stateroom."

"Excuse me, Captain," young Whipple interrupted. "You pronounce the name of the islands Hawaii. We've been calling them Owhyhee. What is their accurate name?"

Captain Janders stopped, stared at Whipple and growled, "I like a man who wants to know facts. The name is Hawaii. Huh-va-eee. Accent on second syllable."

"Have you been to Hawaii?" Whipple asked, carefully accenting the name as it should be.

"You learn well, young man," Captain Janders grunted. "I've sure been to Hawaii."

"What's it like?"

The captain thought a long time and said, "It could use a few missionaries. Now this hatchway aft is where you come up and down from your quarters," and he led the twenty-two down a dark, steep and narrow flight of stairs so that each wife thought: "If the boat rolls I'll never be able to manage this."

They were little prepared for what Captain Janders now showed them. It was a gloomy, grimy, 'tween-decks area twenty feet long—less than the length of four grown men—and fifteen feet wide, out of which a substantial portion had been stolen for a rough table shaped in the form of a half-circle, through the middle of which rose the brig's mainmast. "Our public living area," Captain Janders explained. "It's a mite dark at present but when a stout storm comes along and rips away our sails, we'll take that extra suit from in front of the portholes, and things'll be a bit lighter."

The missionaries stared numbly at the minute quarters and Jerusha thought: "How can twenty-two people live and eat here for six months?" But the real astonishment came when Captain Janders kicked aside one of the canvas curtains that led from the public quarters into a sleeping area.

"This is one of the staterooms," Janders announced, and the missionaries crowded their heads into the doorway to see a cubicle built for dwarfs. Its floor space was exactly five feet ten inches long by five feet one inch wide. It had no windows and no possible ventilation. The wall facing the canvas was formed by the brig's port side and contained two boxed-in bunks, each twenty-seven inches wide, one atop the other. One of the side walls contained two similar boxed-in bunks.

"Does this mean . . ." Amanda Whipple stammered.

"Mean what, ma'am?" Captain Janders asked.

"That two couples share each stateroom?" Amanda blushed.

"No, ma'am. It means that four couples fit in here. One couple to one bunk."

Abner was stunned, but Jerusha, faced with a problem, moved immediately toward the Whipples, seeking them as stateroom partners, only to find that little Amanda was already telling the captain, "The Hales and the Whipples will take this room, plus any other two couples you wish to give us."

"You and you," the captain said, arbitrarily indicating the Hewletts and the Quigleys.

The others moved on to receive their assignments while the first four couples, knocking elbows as they stood, started making decisions which would organize their lives for the next six months. "I don't mind an upper bunk," Jerusha said gallantly. "Do you, Reverend Hale?"

"We'll take an upper," Abner agreed.

Immanuel Quigley, a small, agreeable man, said at once, "Jeptha and I will take an upper."

Practical Amanda suggested: "On the first day of each month those on top come down below. What's more important, the bunks along this wall seem longer than these. John, climb in." And when Whipple tried to stretch out, he found that whereas Amanda was right, and the bunks running along the wall of the ship were nine inches longer than the others, both were too short.

"Those who start with the shortest bunks," Amanda announced, "will switch to the longer ones on the first of each month. Agreed?"

And the eight missionaries formed their first compact, but long after it was forgotten, the one that Abner was about to suggest would mark the missionaries. Looking at the seven distressed faces in the little room he said, "Our quarters are not large and there will be many inconveniences, especially since four among us are females, but let us remember that we are indeed a family in Christ. Let us always call each other by true family names. I am Brother Hale and this is my wife, Sister Hale."

"I am Sister Amanda," the saucy little girl from Hartford promptly corrected, "and this is my husband, Brother John."

"Since we are only now met," Abner countered soberly, "I feel the more formal appellation to be the more correct." The Hewletts and Quigleys agreed, so Amanda bowed courteously.

"How's it look?" Captain Janders called, shoving his head through the canvas opening.

"Small," Amanda replied.

"Let me give one bit of advice, young fellow," Janders said, addressing Whipple. "Stow everything you possibly can right in here. Don't worry about having space to stand. Pile it bunk-high, because it's going to take us six months to get out there, and you'll be surprised how grateful you'll be to have things."

"Will we get seasick?" Jerusha asked querulously.

"Ma'am, two hours after we depart Boston we hit a rough sea. Then we hit the Gulf Stream, which is very rough. Then we hit the waters off the coast of Africa, which are rougher still. Finally, we test our brig against Cape Horn, and that's the roughest water in the world. Ma'am, what do you weigh now?"

"About a hundred and fifteen pounds," Jerusha replied nervously.

"Ma'am, you'll be so seasick in your little stateroom that by the time we round Cape Horn, you'll be lucky if you weigh ninety." There was a moment of apprehensive silence, and Abner, feeling a slight rocking of the ship, was afraid that he was going to start sooner than the rest, but the captain slapped him on the back and said reassuringly, "But after we round the Horn we hit the Pacific, and it's like a lake in summer. Then you'll eat and grow fat."

"How long before we get to the Pacific?" Abner asked weakly.

"About a hundred and fifteen days," Janders laughed. Then he added, "I'll send a boy in here with a screwdriver. Cleat your trunks to the deck. You don't want 'em sloshing about in a heavy sea."

When the missionaries saw the boy in their cramped stateroom, they were both amused and delighted, for he was so tall he had to bend over. "It's Keoki Kanakoa!" John Whipple cried. There were hearty greetings as the massive Hawaiian explained, "The American Board is sending me home to help Christianize my islands. I'm working for Captain Janders only because I like ships."

When the tiny cabin was finally packed, no floor was visible; there was no place to sit; there was only one solid layer of luggage upon the other, and four bunks so close together that the toes of one missionary couple were only eighteen inches away from the toes of the next pair.

Early on the morning of Saturday, September 1, in the year 1821, the mission family assembled on the wharf. Gaunt, God-stricken Reverend

Eliphalet Thorn conducted service, crying above the sounds of the port, "Brothers in Christ, I command you not to weep on this joyous day. Let the world see that you go forth in fullness of spirit, joyously to a great and triumphant duty. We who send you upon this mission to far lands do so in joy. You who go must evidence the same exaltation, for you go in the spirit of Jesus Christ. We will sing the mission song." And in a clear voice he started the anthem of those who venture to far islands:

"Go, spread a Saviour's fame:
And tell His matchless grace
To the most guilty and depraved
Of Adam's numerous race.

"We wish you in His name
The most divine success,
Assur'd that He Who sends you forth
Will your endeavors bless."

Reverend Thorn then spoke his final word of encouragement: "I have personally helped in the selection of each man in this group, and I am convinced that you will be adornments to the work of Jesus Christ. In storms you will not grow weary, in disappointments you will not question the ultimate triumph of your cause. Through your administration the souls of millions yet unborn will be saved from eternal hellfire. I can think of no better parting hymn than the one which sent me forth on such a mission some years ago:

'Go to many a tropic isle
On the bosom of the deep
Where the skies forever smile
And the blacks forever weep.'

You are to still that weeping."

Another minister issued a long prayer, not much to the point, and the service should have been ended on this high religious plane, with each of the twenty-two missionaries attentive to Reverend Thorn's injunction that they show no sadness, but the elderly wife of one of the supervising ministers, upon looking at the pretty young brides about to depart, and knowing that some would die in childbirth in Hawaii and others would waste away and others would lose their grip on reality because of back-breaking work and insufficient food, could not restrain her motherly emotions, and in a high piping voice she began one of the most truly Christ-like of all church hymns. Its old familiar strains were quickly picked up, and even Reverend Thorn, unable to anticipate what was about to happen, joined lustily in:

"Blest be the tie that binds
Our hearts in Christian love;
The fellowship of kindred minds
Is like to that above."

All went well in the first verse, and also in the second, but when the singers came to the succeeding thoughts, one after another began to choke, and at the end all the women in the audience were weeping:

"We share our mutual woes;
Our mutual burdens bear;
And often for each other flows
The sympathizing tear."

Reverend Thorn, his voice strong and clear to the end, thought ruefully, "Women ought not be permitted to attend leave-takings," for in the general sobbing that now overtook the congregation he witnessed the collapse of his plans for an orderly departure. Instead of triumphant testimony, the morning had become a sentimental shambles, the victory of common human love over black-coated respectability.

Nevertheless, and not by plan, the morning did end on a note of high religious emotion, for Jerusha Hale unexpectedly moved forward and in her fawn-colored coat and lively poke bonnet stood before Reverend Thorn, saying in a clear voice so that all could hear, "I speak to you not as my Uncle Eliphalet, nor as Reverend Thorn of Africa, but as an officer of the American Board of Commissioners for Foreign Missions. We place our futures in your hands. The eleven men here take no money with them, only those things required for life on a savage island. It would not be proper for me to take worldly wealth, either, and so I turn over to the Board the small inheritance I received from my loving aunt. It was to have been spent on my marriage, but I have married the work of the Lord." And she handed Reverend Thorn a packet containing more than eight hundred dollars.

Penniless, uninformed, ill at ease with their suddenly acquired partners, but strong in the Lord, the missionaries climbed aboard the brig *Thetis,* and Captain Janders cried, "Break out the sails!" and the tiny ship flung aloft her nine new sails and began moving slowly toward the open sea. Standing on the port side of the vessel, Abner Hale had the distinct premonition that he would never again see America, and he uttered a short prayer which invoked blessing for all those who lived on that bleak, ungenerous little farm in Marlboro, Massachusetts. If he had been asked at that solemn moment what mission he was setting forth upon he would have answered honestly, "To bring to the people of Hawaii the blessings that I enjoyed on that farm." It could never have occurred to him—as indeed it never did—that a better mission might be to bring to Hawaii the blessings that characterized the solid white home facing the village common in Walpole, New Hampshire, for although he had said nothing about this to anyone, he could not believe that the levity, the profane music, the novels and the deficiency in grace that marked the Bromley home were in any sense blessings. In fact, he rather felt that in bringing Jerusha onto the *Thetis* he was somehow saving her from herself.

She was now tugging at his arm and saying, "Reverend Hale, I think I'm going to be sick." And he took her below and placed her in one of the short berths, where she was to stay for most of the time during the first four months. Abner, to everyone's surprise, proved a good sailor, for although he constantly looked as if he were about to vomit, he ate ravenously and never did.

It was he, therefore, who led prayers, did the preaching, studied Hawaiian with Keoki Kanakoa, and frequently took care of eighteen or twenty seasick missionaries. Some of them came ungenerously to detest the wiry little man as he moved briskly among their sickbeds, assuring them that soon they would be up like him, eating pork, biscuit, gravy, anything. And yet grudgingly they had to admire his determination, particularly when Captain Janders began to rail against him.

Janders started with his first mate. "Mister Collins, you've got to keep that pipsqueak Hale out of the fo'c's'l."

"Is he bothering the men?"

"He's trying to convert 'em."

"Those monsters?"

"He's got his dirty little fangs into Cridland. I found the boy weeping last night and I asked him what was wrong, and he told me that Reverend Hale had convinced him that death and eternal hellfire were the lot of everyone on this ship who did not confess and join the church."

"Maybe he's right," Collins laughed.

"But in the meantime we have to run a ship."

"Have the men complained, sir?"

"No, that they haven't. Cridland says they sort of like to have the little squirt around. Makes them feel as if someone was interested in 'em."

"I'll tell him to stay clear of the men," Mister Collins promised.

Captain Janders knew precisely when the message was delivered, for two minutes later Reverend Hale, sputtering with rage, was 'tween decks, hammering on the half-circle table. "Do I understand, Captain Janders, that I have been ordered not to go into the fo'c's'l?"

"Not an order. A request."

"Then you were partner to this request?"

"I was."

"And you are consciously setting yourself athwart my efforts to save the souls of these forsaken men steeped in evil and abomination?"

"These are just good ordinary sailors, Reverend Hale, and I don't want 'em upset."

"Upset!" Reverend Hale beat the table more loudly, so that all the seasick missionaries could hear the argument, whether they wished to or not. "You call the conversion of an immortal soul to God's grace upsetting! Captain Janders, there are some aboard this brig who would profit from some upsetting, and I am not referring exclusively to those in the fo'c's'l." Thereafter, however, he stayed out of the men's cramped quarters forward, but he did lie in wait for them as they went about their duties, until Captain Janders had once more to call in the first mate. "Damn it, Mister Collins, now he's meddling with the men when they're trying to change sails. Warn him about it."

This led to further protests from the missionary, which Captain Janders patiently entertained. Finally Hale cried, "I don't believe you care, Captain Janders, whether you run a Christian ship or not. The men tell me that you issue rations of rum after a storm. That you never try to get them to take the pledge. Obviously, you try to impede me in every way possible."

"Reverend Hale," the captain pleaded, "I'm trying to get this ship to Hawaii. You seem to be trying to get it to Beulah Land."

"I am," Hale replied.

"The two ports are incompatible."

"Not in God's eyes, Captain Janders. You've forbidden me the fo'c's'l. Now you forbid me talk to the men on duty. Are you also going to forbid me the right to conduct Christian services on Sunday?"

"No, Reverend Hale, I aim to run a God-fearing ship, and when no ministers are aboard, I conduct services myself. Short ones. I'd be pleased to have you carry on for me. I'm in favor of church, at sea or ashore."

Later, when talking with the first mate, the captain asked, "Why do you suppose it is, Mister Collins, that with all these intelligent young men aboard, and with eleven damned attractive young women, it has to be Hale who is always well enough to eat with us? Why don't he get sick and his wife come to dinner?"

"Divine providence is sometimes malign, Captain Janders," the mate replied. But how malign, he was not to know until Reverend Hale preached his first Sunday sermon on the afterdeck. The *Thetis* rolled so sorely that no other missionary could appear above decks, but there stood Abner Hale, with a heavy Bible in his left hand, preaching into the winds.

"I have chosen for my text James, chapter 4, verse 8: 'Draw nigh to God, and He will draw nigh to you. Cleanse your hands, ye sinners; and purify your hearts, ye double minded.' " And he launched into one of the most violent attacks on the moral dangers faced by sailors that the crew had ever heard, for he charged that all who sailed before the mast were peculiarly tempted, that those who led them were apt to be insensitive brutes, that their employers who remained safe at home in Salem and Boston were determined to corrupt their vessels, and that every port they touched harbored instruments of evil that stay-at-home citizens could only dream of. Abner painted the men before him as the blackest, most evil and forlorn group of reprobates in Christendom, and the men loved it. Throughout his fiery sermon they nodded approvingly, and even Captain Janders and the first mate agreed that except in the part where Abner belabored them individually, he was close to the truth. But the result of his sermon was rather the opposite of what Abner had intended, for throughout the rest of the day the young sailors whom he wanted to reach most—for he felt that Janders and Collins were past saving—strutted with extra swagger as if in sudden realization of the fact that they "were among the evilest human beings known." They had suspected this for some time, and they derived positive pleasure from being told so by an expert. Only Cridland, a pathetic, undernourished boy with an overpowering sense of guilt, caught anything of Hale's message, and he appeared red-eyed and perplexed as Abner was about to go below, asking, "What must I do to be saved?" And from his question Abner knew that his sermon had been a success.

"You must pray. You must study the Bible. And you must try to save the souls of your mates in the fo'c's'l," Abner explained. He handed young Cridland his own Bible and said, "You may keep this tonight. I brought along eight seamen's Bibles, and I'll give you one at Sabbath service but it is only a loan from God to you. Only when you get some friend in the fo'c's'l to ask for his Bible, will you have started upon your true salvation."

At supper Captain Janders growled, "The mate says he saw your large Bible in the fo'c's'l, Reverend Hale. I thought it was understood that you were not to annoy the men down there any more."

"I have kept severely to my promise, Captain Janders, but since I am forbidden entrance into that pit of depravity, I feel sure that you will not object to my sending there, as my messenger better able to discharge my obligations than I myself, the holy word of God. If you wish to throw the Bible out of your ship, do so, Captain, and your name will become imperishable in the roll call of mariners."

"Please, Reverend Hale, don't preach sermons down here. I only asked if you had violated your agreement to stay out of the fo'c's'l."

"I have never violated an agreement," Abner cried. "Oh, I shall stay out! Never fear! But by next Sunday, Captain Janders, eight of my Bibles will be down there."

In spite of their arguments with the difficult missionary, both Captain Janders and Mister Collins were impressed by the fatherly way in which he tended his sick companions. Each dawn he went from one sickbed to another, collecting the night's slops, hauling them away and bringing fresh water to cleanse lips foul from vomiting. Before breakfast he visited each man and woman and read to them from the Bible. Men who wanted to shave were provided with hot water from the cook's galley, and women who required fresh linen could indicate to Abner which boxes were to be hauled out and opened. At mealtimes he took to each sick friend those portions of greasy food which had a chance of staying down in retching stomachs. He argued the captain into allowing him to cook up batches of oatmeal gruel for the women. And each evening, no matter how sick the missionaries were, they were hauled out of bed and made to attend divine worship conducted by Abner in the tiny, crowded cabin. If he saw that a man or woman could remain upright only with difficulty, he would conclude his prayer in half a minute and say, "The Lord has marked your presence, Joshua. You had better return to bed." Then, when the sick had mercifully departed, he would involve the others in long discussions, sermons, prayers, hymns. He was especially fond of one hymn which contained a verse which he held applicable to the *Thetis:*

He'll shield you with a wall of fire;
With flowing zeal your hearts inspire,
Bid raging winds their fury cease,
And hush the tempest into peace.

But after the eighth rendition of this hopeful assurance, John Whipple, barely able to stand, said shakily, "Abner, you keep singing that the tempest is going to subside, but it gets worse."

"When we reach Cape Verde, we reach fine weather for certain," Abner assured everyone, and as the creaking little ship plunged sickeningly on through the North Atlantic swells, he grew more cheerful and more helpful.

"He'd make a wonderful cook's helper," Captain Janders observed to the first mate one night.

"Have you stopped to think what this cabin area would be like without him," Mister Collins reflected. "Twenty-one sick missionaries on our hands."

It was therefore not surprising that long before the storm abated, Abner Hale was recognized by all on board as the unofficial father of the mission family. There were men who were older, and men who were wiser, but he was the one to whom all looked for aid and decision. So, when he announced on the fourth Saturday that the storm had sufficiently abated to hold next day's service topside, and that all who could possibly do so must attend, there was a general effort to drag bruised and smelling bodies back into some semblance of order.

In his own stateroom, Abner kneeled on boxes and assured the four sick women there that when Sunday came, he would do everything required to help them dress and climb topside to worship the Lord. Amanda Whipple agreed, as did the two others, and he laid out their things for them, but Jerusha, after trying to rise, subsided and whimpered, "I cannot even raise my hand, Reverend Hale."

"I will help you, Mrs. Hale. I have brought you some broth from the meat, and if you will drink this now, by morning you will be stronger."

Jerusha drank the greasy broth, and only with difficulty kept from throwing it back into the smelly stateroom. "I am so dreadfully ill," she insisted.

"In the morning you will be better," Abner assured her, and while she slept he went aloft under the first stars of the voyage. As he was standing by the starboard railing of the brig, two shadowy forms came to him and he heard Cridland say, "I've been talking all week with Mason, sir, and he wants a Bible."

Abner turned in the darkness and saw the indistinct form of a young sailor. "Do you wish to be saved?" he asked.

"I do," the boy replied.

"What has led you to this decision?" Abner asked.

"I've been listening to the older hands speak of a sailor's life ashore, and I'm afraid," the boy whined.

"You're a wise young man, Mason," Abner said. "The Lord has spoken and you have listened."

"No, sir, begging your pardon. It's been Cridland who's been speaking. He's made me see the error of my ways."

"Tomorrow after service, Mason, I'll hand you your Bible, when Cridland gets his. But it is only a loan from God to you. To keep it, you must get some friend in the fo'c's'l to acknowledge God and to ask for his Bible."

"Would you say a prayer for us, Reverend Hale?" Cridland begged.

"The Lord always provides wisdom for those who seek," Abner replied. And in the darkness he raised his head to the stars and prayed: "Lord, we are afloat on a great ocean in a little boat. The winds and the storms harass us, but we trust in Thee. Tonight we are only three praying to Thee: a young boy on his first voyage, a sailor who seeks guidance, and a beginning minister who has never had a pulpit of his own. Great Father in heaven, we are insignificant in Thine eyes, but guide us in Thy divine ways. For if we are only three tonight, later we shall be more, for Thy wisdom permeates all things and saves all souls."

He dismissed the two sailors and stood for a long time watching the stars and waiting till the midnight hour heralded the first Sabbath on which a substantial number of the missionaries could attend formal service. As the holy day crept across the meridian of night, Abner prayed that the Lord might make this day one of special significance. Then he went below and whispered to his unnerved wife, "My dearest companion, you would not believe what has happened. Tonight two sailors came voluntarily requesting evening prayers. The spirit of God is beginning to permeate this forsaken ship."

"That's wonderful, Reverend Hale," his wife whispered, lest they waken the three other couples who had been sick most of the evening.

"And tomorrow our family will celebrate its first holy service," Abner sighed. "But I forget. It's already Sunday. I studied where the tarpauling is to be hung. We're going to have a very handsome church, Mrs. Hale, on the bosom of the deep."

"I won't be able to go up the stairs, Reverend Hale, but I'll pray with you," she whispered.

"You'll be well enough," he assured her, and he crept into the short narrow berth beside her.

But in the morning she was no better, and the sight of little Amanda swaying back and forth on the piled boxes made her more ill, so that when Abner returned from checking all his charges he found his wife not dressing, but lying in bed pale and exhausted. "I'm awfully sorry, Reverend Hale," she sighed, "but I'll have to miss service this morning."

"Not at all," he protested cheerily. "I'll help you."

"But I'm sure I can't stand," she protested.

"Now, Mrs. Hale . . ." And he forcibly brought her slim legs down onto the boxes and caught her in his arms when she proved unable to maintain her balance. "Some breakfast will strengthen you. Then we'll have service. You'll see the sun. And you'll be fine."

In trying to get out of the little heaped-up stateroom she almost fainted, weakness and nausea combining to make her deathly ill, but again Abner helped her and maneuvered her through the canvas opening and on into the cramped and smelly cabin, where Keoki Kanakoa was spreading a breakfast consisting of cold suet beef, mashed beans and watery rice, left over from the night before. Jerusha closed her eyes when the sodden food was placed before her and kept them closed as Abner asked one of the older ministers to bless the day. Then Keoki prayed in Hawaiian, to familiarize the missionaries with the language, and the meal was begun.

Jerusha could manage a little hot tea and one bite of suet beef, but the clammy lard in the latter revolted her, and she rose to leave, but Abner's firm hand caught her wrist and she heard him saying, "A little longer, Mrs. Hale, and you'll conquer it." So she sat in agony as the cold lard slipped down into her stomach and nauseated her whole body.

"I'm going to be sick!" she whispered.

"No," he said insistently. "This is our first meal together. This is the Sabbath." And she fought her rising illness, with the smell of food and two dozen people crowding in upon her nostrils.

She was pale when the meal ended, and staggered toward her berth, but Abner refused to let her go, and with his strong hold on her arm, marched her up the stairs and onto the gently sloping deck, where a canvas had been hung to form a rude chapel. "Our first worship as a family," he announced proudly, but the entire family was not to participate, because one of the older ministers took one look at the slanting deck, rushed to the railing, relieved himself of his breakfast, and staggered white and gasping back to his berth. Abner stared at him as he left, interpreting the poor man's involuntary actions as a personal rejection of God. He was especially irritated because several of the sailors, who were idling the Sunday morning away by hanging on ropes to catch their first glimpse of the mission family, laughed openly as the distraught minister threw up his breakfast.

"There'll be more," one of the sailors predicted ominously, and his mates laughed.

Services were conducted by Abner, as the only one who was likely to be able to finish them, and the family, resting comfortably under canvas strung from the mainmast, sang as cheerfully as circumstances permitted, the fine old Sunday hymn of New England:

"Another six days' work is done,
Another Sabbath is begun;
Return, my soul, enjoy thy rest—
Improve the day thy God has blessed."

Abner then spoke at some length on various passages from Ephesians, chapter 3: " 'For this cause I bow my knees unto the Father of our Lord Jesus Christ, Of whom the whole family in heaven and earth is named, . . . That Christ may dwell in your hearts by faith; that ye . . . might be filled with all the fullness of God.' " He pointed out that the family of love within which they lived was open to all who were willing to confess their sins and work toward a state of grace. He was obviously preaching to two audiences: his brother missionaries, to remind them of the family within which they operated; and the eavesdropping sailors, tempting them to join this family of Christ; but his message to the latter was somewhat destroyed when Jerusha, experiencing a dreadful wave of nausea, tried to stagger to the railing, failed, fell on her knees and vomited over the deck.

"Watch out, lady!" a sailor called derisively, but Cridland and Mason, the two young men who were to get Bibles that day, quickly jumped forward, caught Jerusha by the arms and carried her below. Abner, infuriated at the disruption of his charge to the sailors, concluded his sermon in rather a jumble, and turned the prayer over to an associate. He was confused and angry, because he had arranged the entire service so that it would end dramatically with his presentation of the Bibles to Cridland and his friend, thus symbolically welcoming them into the Lord's family, but when the time had come to do this, those two were below decks, and Abner was painfully aware that his first major effort had ended like that of so many ministers: looking for a logical place to stop. Finally he had just quit.

When service ended, members of the family made a pretense of commending Abner for his sermon, but both the extenders of congratulations and the recipient knew that they were hollow. In an unruly fit of temper and disappointment, Abner started to go below, but he was met at the top of the hatchway by Cridland and Mason, who reported, "Your wife is very sick, sir."

"Thank you," he replied curtly.

"The minister who got sick first is helping her," Cridland said.

Abner started down but Mason stopped him and asked, "Have you our Bibles, sir?"

"Next week," Abner snapped, and was gone. But when he saw his wife, and how ashen white she was, he forgot his own problems and fetched water to wash her perspiring face.

"I'm sorry, my cherished partner," she said wanly. "I'll never make a sailor."

"We'll get you above decks just a few minutes each day," he said reassuringly, but even the thought of facing that slanting deck again brought back her nausea, and she said, "I'm going to weigh even less than Captain Janders predicted."

At noon, when the day's big meal was served, Janders saw with pleasure that seventeen of his passengers were at last able to eat. "On each trip," he observed, "as we approach Cape Verde, our sick ones get better."

"Shall we be stopping at the islands?" John Whipple asked.

"Yes, if weather permits." The news was so good that Abner rose from his pork-and-suet pudding and called into any staterooms where sick missionaries lay, "We'll soon be touching at Cape Verde. Then you can walk about on land and get fresh fruit."

"By the way, Reverend Hale," the captain added, "that was a good sermon you preached today. There is indeed a heritage that the Lord provides those who serve Him, and may we all come into it." The missionaries nodded their approval of this sentiment, whereupon Janders launched his harpoon: "Seems to me your message got a little tangled up at the end."

Since all knew this to be true, they looked at their plates and thought: "Our captain is a clever man." But Abner looked at him boldly and said, "I count a sermon a success if it contains one good Christian thought in it."

"I do too," Janders said heartily. "Yours had several."

"I hope we can all take them to mind," Abner said piously, but secretly he wished that services could have ended as planned. Then the ship would have heard a sermon.

After lunch Captain Janders invited the missionaries to tour the ship with him, and John Whipple asked, "I don't understand why, if we're bound west for Hawaii, we sail east almost to the coast of Africa."

"Mister Collins, break us out a chart!" And Janders showed the surprised missionaries how it was that ships wanting to double Cape Horn sailed from Boston on a heading which took them not south for the Horn but far to the east, almost to the coast of Africa. "It's so that when we finally turn south for the Horn, we can run in one straight line, down past Brazil and Argentine, straight on to Tierra del Fuego," Janders explained, and the chart made this clear.

"Are the Cape Verde islands pleasant?" Whipple asked.

"You watch! Some of our boys jump ship there on every trip. We'll be leaving Verde with a couple of Brava boys as replacements."

While the captain was explaining these things, Abner was on another part of the deck talking seriously with Cridland and Mason. "I did not give you your Bibles today because you did not earn them," he chided.

"But we had to take Mrs. Hale below decks," Cridland protested.

"The work of the Lord required you to be present topside," Abner said stubbornly.

"But she . . ."

"Others could have cared for her, Cridland. Next Sunday I shall give you your Bibles. I am going to preach from Psalms 26, verse 5: 'I have hated the congregation of evil doers; and will not sit with the wicked.' When I have finished my sermon, I shall hand each of you his Bible." Then he recalled what he had said earlier and, staring at Mason, asked, "But have you earned your Bible? I thought you were to have brought another soul to God."

"I am about to do so," Mason reported happily. "I have been reading the tracts you gave us to one of the older men. He had led an evil life, but last trip on a whaler he was swept overboard and was saved only by a miracle. Of late, he has been weeping very much and I shall keep talking with him. Perhaps by next Sabbath . . ."

"Good work, Mason," Abner replied, and although another might have thought it strange that the religious ardors of the two sailors were not dampened by their disappointment over the Bibles, particularly when their dereliction arose from their humane treatment of a woman, and she the wife of the minister himself, Abner Hale was not surprised. As he pointed out to the young men: "The Lord is a jealous master. You cannot approach Him at your determination. He tells you when you may come into His presence. And if you have been faithless in even small things, the Lord will wait until you have proved yourself worthy." For Abner knew that easy salvation was never appreciated; Cridland and Mason already treasured their forthcoming Bibles doubly because they had once failed to attain them.

If Abner's first Sunday sermon was something of a failure, his second was a stunning success, marred only by the fact that his wife Jerusha was unable to witness it. He had got her to breakfast, had forced a little cold pork and rice into her racked body, and had even carried her limply onto the deck, but one look at the wallowing waves put her stomach into gyrations, and she was hurriedly taken below by Amanda Whipple and Mrs. Quigley. The intellectual highlight of Abner's sermon came when he spent fifteen minutes on the congregation of evildoers that the devil had thrown together aboard the "hamferdite" brig *Thetis*. Like all the missionaries, he called it a hamferdite, not knowing exactly how to pronounce, spell or define the longer and more accurate word, since it was in none of the mission dictionaries. But according to Abner, few ships that had ever sailed the Atlantic knew such a congregation of evil, and his catalogue of what these sailors lounging idly on deck had perpetrated in their short and unspectacular lives was terrifying. The dramatic climax, of course, came when he announced to his startled missionaries and surprised ship's crew that God had been at work even in this den of vice and that three souls had already been saved, whereupon he produced Cridland, Mason and a beat-up old whaler with bad legs whose catalogue of sin actually surpassed Abner's conjectures. Some of the old man's friends, who had spent time ashore with him in Valparaiso, Canton and Honolulu, expected lightning to play upon the waves when he touched the Bible that Abner extended him. Captain Janders shuddered and said to his first mate, "Mark my words, Mister Collins, you'll be up there next week."

That Sunday the noonday meal was an unalloyed triumph. Captain Janders said it was one of the best sermons he had ever heard afloat, although he was satisfied that Reverend Hale must have been talking about some other ship, and Mister Collins confessed, "It's a strange phenomenon, but no matter what the ship, the closer it gets to Cape Horn, the more religious everyone becomes. It's as if all aboard sensed at last the futility of man in the face of God's awful power. I'm not sure that I would be even a moderately Christian man, which I hold myself to be, if I had never rounded Cape Horn." Captain Janders added, "I agree. No man by his own power could accomplish the transit we shall soon face."

No comment could have pleased Abner more, for like all the missionaries he had been contemplating with some dread the trial they would encounter as Cape Horn approached, and although it still lay eight weeks in the future, he felt that he would make no mistake in undertaking reasonable preparations. He therefore said, "I have observed, Captain Janders, that you spend your Sundays reading . . ." He found it difficult to say the word, and hesitated.

"Novels?" Janders asked.

"Yes. Profane books. I was wondering, Captain Janders, if you would entertain it kindly if I were to give you, from the mission stores, several books of a more appropriate and edifying nature?"

"Richardson and Smollett are edifying enough for me," Janders laughed.

"But when you have in your care some four dozen souls . . ."

"In those circumstances I rely on Bowditch and the Bible . . . in that order."

"Do I understand that you would not take it kindly . . ."

"I would not," Janders said stiffly.

"The mission family has decided," Abner said abruptly, having talked with no one of this project, "that starting with today we shall hold both morning and afternoon services on deck, weather permitting."

"Fine," Janders said. Then, always eager to keep the young minister off balance, he asked, "By the way, how's Mrs. Hale?"

"Poorly," Abner said.

"I should think you would spend some time with her," Janders suggested.

"I do," Abner snapped. "I pray with her morning and night."

"I meant, play games with her, or read her an interesting novel. Would you entertain it kindly if I were to offer you, from my own library, several novels of an entertaining nature?"

"We do not read novels," Abner retaliated. "Especially not on Sundays."

"In that case, when you do get around to seeing your wife, you can tell her that on Tuesday we'll land at Brava, and she can walk ashore. It'll do us all wonders."

Jerusha was elated by this news, and on Monday, when the calmer waters in the lee of Cape Verde were reached, she ventured on deck for an hour and the sun diminished her pallor. On Tuesday, when the islands were clearly in sight, she clung to the railing, praying for the moment when she could step ashore, but she was to be sorely disappointed, for a stiff breeze came up offshore, followed by heavy low clouds, and even before the *Thetis* began to roll in deep troughs, it became apparent that to beat into Brava would be too difficult a task, whereas to run before the mounting storm would carry the little brig so far on its westward heading that any attempt to recover Brava would be wasteful. Nevertheless, Jerusha stood in the rain, praying that some miracle would enable the ship to make land, and it was not until Captain Janders himself passed and said, "We're going to run before the wind, ma'am. There'll be no Brava," that she admitted sorry defeat. Then she discovered that she was very seasick, and began retching at the rail so that Janders shouted, "You, there! Take this poor woman below!"

It was a gloomy family that met that night in the swaying cabin for a supper of gruel and hard cheese. Half the missionaries were unable to leave their staterooms. The others wore bleak faces in recognition of the fact that a chance to step ashore had been missed, and that no other would present itself for many days. How lonely and mean the cabin seemed as the whale-oil lamp swung in the creaking night, as the latrine smelled up the fetid atmosphere, and as friends retched in new despair. Keoki, coming in with the food, said, "I would like to offer the evening prayer," and in rich Hawaiian he praised the open ocean as compared to land, for on the former one was required to know God, whereas on land there were many diversions. Therefore, reasoned Keoki, it was better this night to be on the *Thetis* than to be in Brava.

Of all the listeners, only Abner knew enough Hawaiian to piece together the message, and he thought it so felicitous that he interpreted it for the mission family, and then he surprised everyone by standing and uttering his first prayer in Hawaiian. It was halting, but it was the native tongue of the islands, and it helped acquaint God with the strange tongue in which this family was to work.

ON THE FORTY-FIFTH DAY of the voyage, Monday, October 15, the groaning *Thetis* crossed the equator in brilliant sunshine and on a glassy sea. The first victim was Reverend Hale. Since the day was hot, Captain Janders casually suggested at noon that his passengers ought to wear old clothes, and not too many of them. When he was satisfied that no one was wearing his best, he winked at Keoki, who passed a signal aloft.

"Oh, Reverend Hale!" a voice cried down the hatchway. "Cridland wants to see you!"

Abner hurried from table, grasped the handrail leading aloft, and swung up the narrow ladder. He had gone only a few yards forward when he was completely drenched in a bucket of sea water thrown down from the shrouds. He gasped, looked about in dismay, and felt his muscles contracting in useless fury. But before he could speak, Mister Collins winked at him and said, "We've crossed the equator! Call Whipple!" And Abner was so startled by the experience that he found himself calling, "Brother Whipple! Can you come?"

There was a movement at the hatchway as Whipple ran into a full bucket of water. "Equator!" Abner giggled.

John wiped himself off, then looked up into the shrouds where two sailors were dizzy with delight and reaching for fresh buckets. On the spur of the moment Whipple shouted, "Whales!" and stood back as several passengers from below came storming up the ladder and into their initiation. Soon the deck was choked with laughing missionaries, and Captain Janders announced that the crew would now initiate the sailors who had not yet crossed the line. But when one of the young men who had doused Whipple came up for his diet of gruel, whale oil, soap and grease, John shouted, "Oh, no! I'm to feed this one!" And to everyone's surprise he leaped into the middle of the fray, got himself roundly smeared with grease, and fed the laughing sailor, whereupon there was great hilarity and the captain ordered all hands an issue of rum, at which point the missionaries solemnly withdrew. An hour later Abner had visible proof of the horrors of ardent spirits, for Keoki Kanakoa begged him to come forward into the fo'c's'l, where the old whaler who had accepted the Bible had somehow collected six or eight extra rations of grog and was now cursing vehemently and bashing his head into a bulkhead. With some difficulty Abner got him into his foul bunk and sat consoling him. When the man was sober enough to speak coherently, Abner asked, "Where is your Bible?"

"In the box," the old whaler replied contritely.

"This one?"

"Yes." Primly, Abner opened the box, ignored the filth and disarray, and lifted out the Holy Book.

"Some men do not deserve Bibles," he said sternly, and left.

"Reverend! Reverend!" shouted the sailor. "Don't do that! Please!" But Abner was already far aft.

The strange day ended with a sight of incomparable beauty, for from the west, heading to the coast of Africa, came a tall ship with many sails, out of the sunset, and the *Thetis* spoke to her and lowered a longboat to greet the stranger, taking mail which could be returned to Boston; and as the longboat prepared to stand off, Captain Janders, in the stern, shouted, "Whipple! They might appreciate prayers!" And John swung down into the boat, and all aboard the *Thetis* watched as their men rowed into the sunset to visit the strange, tall ship, so beautiful in the dusk.

Jerusha was brought on deck, and although she tried to control herself, fell into tears at the sight of this curious meeting of two ships in the first shadows of night. "My beloved companion," she sighed, "it's the most beautiful thing I have ever seen. Look how the sunset rests on the waters. The sea is a mirror."

Amanda, not wishing to be alone at such a still moment, came to stand with the Hales and whispered, "It was almost unbearable, to see Brother Whipple rowing away like that. It's the first time we've been separated. He has been my dear companion and close friend. How lucky we are to be spending our first days of marriage like this."

But when the longboat returned to the *Thetis,* and when the tall ship had resumed its passage, with night upon it and the noiseless sea, Amanda saw that her husband sat in the prow biting his lip, while Captain Janders sat in the stern, riveted in hatred. Even the sailors, New England men all, were harshly silent, their mouths pursed into tight lines. Only Captain Janders spoke. "By God!" he cried. "At such moments I wish we were armed. I wish to Almighty God we had sent that damned foul thing to the bottom." In fury he threw a handful of letters at the missionaries' feet. "I would not entrust your letters to such a ship. A slaver."

Later, John Whipple reported to the missionaries: "It was horrible. They had not secured the chains below, and you could hear them swinging in the swell. It was a dark ship. Abner, would you pray?" And in the hot cabin, on their first night across the equator, the missionaries prayed and Abner said simply, "Where there is darkness, Lord, allow the light to shine. Where there is evil, substitute goodness. But let us not concern ourselves only with distant evil. Remind us always that our first responsibility is the evil that occurs within our immediate environs. Lord, help us not to be hypocrites. Help us to do Thy work day by day."

He was so moved by this chance brush with the slaver that he could not sleep and spent the night on deck, peering off into the direction of Africa, hoping that God would vouchsafe him a flash of light indicating that the blackbirder had exploded. Toward morning he was visited by Keoki Kanakoa, who said, "Reverend Hale, you worry so much about Africa. Did you not know that there are also slaves in Hawaii?"

"There are?" Abner asked in astonishment.

"Of course. On my father's island there are many slaves. We call them foul corpses, and they may touch nothing that we touch. They are kapu. Not long ago they were kept for the human sacrifices."

"Tell me all about them," the stunned young missionary said, and as Keoki explained the various rituals and kapus involving the foul corpses, Abner felt an impatient fury mounting in his throat, so that before Keoki finished he cried, "Keoki, when I get to Hawaii there will be no more slavery."

"It will be difficult," the giant Hawaiian warned.

"Keoki, you will eat with the foul corpses." He told none of the other missionaries of this resolve, not even Jerusha, but as dawn came he knew in his heart that that strange tall ship, that cruel Brazilian slaver, had been sent across his path at the equator for a purpose. "There will be no more slavery in Hawaii," he swore as the sun rose.

It was on the long, dreary run to Cape Horn, more than six thousand miles in almost a straight line, that the famous "missionary's disease" struck in earnest, so that long after seasickness was forgotten, missionary families would recall with embarrassment and discomfort the illness which really prostrated them.

They called it, in a blush of euphemism, biliousness, and day after day Jerusha would inquire cautiously, "Reverend Hale, do you still suffer from biliousness?"

He would reply, "Yes, my dear companion, I do."

Since all the other couples were conducting similar inquiries, with identical responses, the missionaries began to look with truly jaundiced eyes at their doctor, as if Brother Whipple ought by some miracle to be able to dispel the tormenting biliousness. He studied his authorities, especially the *Family Medical Book,* and prescribed various time-honored cures. "Two tablespoons of ipecac and rhubarb," he advised.

"Brother Whipple, I've been taking ipecac for weeks," a worried missionary reported. "No good."

"Have you tried two grains of calomel, Brother Hewlett?"

"It helps at the moment . . . but . . ."

"Then it'll have to be castor oil . . . and walking."

"I can't take castor oil, Brother Whipple."

"Then walk."

So the dreadfully constipated missionaries took ipecac and rhubarb and calomel and castor oil. But mostly they walked. After breakfast all who were able would stride purposefully up and down, up and down the cramped afterdeck, turning on the animal pens at one end, and the foremast at the other. Sometimes they walked for hours, trying to shame their recalcitrant intestines into action, but nothing really cured the biliousness.

The after quarters contained one latrine, unbearably foul, and if each missionary occupied it for only fifteen minutes at a time, which was not excessive in their condition, five and a half hours were automatically consumed, and the day was half spent with no time allocated for emergency cases on the part of those who in extreme desperation had taken a master dose of ipecac, rhubarb, calomel and castor oil, all together.

It therefore became necessary for Brother Whipple, with Captain Janders' amused consent and with able help from Keoki Kanakoa, to rig an unclosed improvised privy aft of the stern. At stated intervals all females would go below decks, and one minister after another would test his good fortune on the open seat, his hands wrapped desperately about the timbers Keoki had hammered into place, his pallid white bottom winking at the whales.

Day after day they walked. The boisterous sailors, whose bodies were kept functioning by the extraordinary amount of work they had to do, irreverently made bets as to which of the brothers would next try his luck on the precarious perch, and they referred to the constant walking as "the missionary waltz."

One day, in despair, poor, tied-up Abner demanded of Brother Whipple, "Why is it that God afflicts us so and docs nothing to thosc impious sailors."

"It's simple, Brother Hale," the doctor laughed. "We all got seasick and cleaned our lower quarters completely. Then we ate little and allowed it to compact itself. Lacking fruit and vegetables the compacting became harder. But most of all, we did no work. Sailors work, so God looks after their bellies."

Abner wasn't sure but what Brother Whipple had indulged in blasphemy, but he was too uncomfortable to argue, so he merely said, "I feel dreadful."

"Let me see your eyes," Whipple ordered, and when he saw the bleary yellow stains he said, "You are dreadful."

"What can I do?" Abner pleaded.

"Walk," Whipple commanded, and the missionary waltz resumed.

Brother Whipple took most of his walks at night, when the stars were out and when his interest in science could be freely indulged. His long discussions with the mates over astronomy came so to occupy his mind that he frequently absented himself from evening prayers, a dereliction which caused Abner to detail two brothers to investigate.

"We are a family, as you know, Brother Whipple," they said. "Our prayers are family prayers."

"I am sorry I was forgetful," Whipple apologized. "I'll attend prayers." But as soon as the first worshiper cried, "Amen!" the young doctor was up the hatch and talking astronomy.

"How does a mariner feel when he crosses the line and sees that the North Star has vanished?" he asked.

"Well," Mister Collins reflected, "no matter how well you know the southern stars, it's a wrench to see old reliable go down over the horizon."

From his work with the mates, Whipple learned to work Bowditch for both latitude and longitude, and occasionally his calculations coincided with those of Captain Janders, which led the latter to predict, "You'd make a better navigator than you ever will a missionary."

"We'll trap your soul yet," Whipple retorted. "If I could get Brother Hale up here . . ."

"Leave him where he is!" Janders urged.

Nevertheless, Captain Janders had to admit surprise at the success Abner was enjoying in converting the crew. He had five Bibles out and two more pending. Six men had been cajoled into signing temperance pledges, at which Janders growled, "Easiest thing in the world is to get sailors on board to become temperance. Trick is to do it in port."

The sailors appreciated Abner's curious gift of raising exactly those questions they had often pondered, so that even men who were not religious would stand about as he argued: "Suppose this voyage occupies four years. On the first week you are away, your mother dies. You don't hear about it. Now what is your relation to your mother during the next two hundred weeks? She is dead, yet you think of her as living. She is dead, yet she has the capacity to help you. Is it not possible that she is indeed living? In Jesus Christ?"

"I didn't think about it that way, Reverend," an unbeliever said. "But in another way I did. Suppose I'm married, and when I leave Boston my wife is . . . well . . . if you'll excuse me . . . expecting. Now I never see that baby for four years, but when I come home he looks like me, has my habits, and in some unknown way has come to love me."

"Only sometimes he don't look like you," the old whaler observed from his own experience. "What then?"

"Have you converted Captain Janders?" Cridland asked.

"No," Abner replied sorrowfully. " 'The fool hath said in his heart, There is no God.' "

"Wait a minute, Reverend!" an old hand corrected. "Cap'n believes. When you ain't aboard he conducts services."

"True believing requires that you submit your will entirely to God's," Abner explained. "Captain Janders will not confess that he lives in a state of abject sin."

"I don't classify him as no sinner," the old whaler reflected. "Not a proper, hard-working sinner, that is. Now you take a man like Cap'n Hoxworth of the whaler *Carthaginian* . . . I seen Cap'n Hoxworth get four naked Honolulu girls into his cabin at one time . . . Well, as a sinner, our cap'n just don't compare."

Nevertheless, Abner waged relentless campaigns against Captain Janders, particularly in the matter of novels, which the captain read ostentatiously immediately after each Sabbath sermon. "You will learn to call such books abominations," Abner mournfully predicted.

Janders fought back with irony: "You converting any more old whalers, Brother Hale?"

The question infuriated Abner, symbolizing as it did the world's pernicious habit of rejoicing over the downfall of sanctimonious men. Actually, he could have turned the tables on the captain, so far as the old whaler was concerned, for the man was agonizingly eager to win back his Bible before reaching Cape Horn. "Many's a sailor's been lost at the Horn, Reverend," he constantly pleaded. "Don't make me round the Horn without a Bible!"

But Abner had absorbed one fundamental lesson on this trip: the established church must not be maneuvered into a position of danger by the backsliding of fools who were never truly saved in the first place. It is such who have the greatest power to damage the church and they must be denied the opportunity of doing so. Frequently, on the long leg south Abner would sit on a trunk in his stateroom and analyze this case with his seven companions: "I was too prompt to accept this man . . . too eager for merely another number rather than for a secured soul. We must never repeat this foolish mistake in Hawaii."

And then, on the evening of November 24, just as Keoki placed on the half-moon table the Saturday night suet pudding, an unexpected gale from the southwest struck the *Thetis* port-side and threw her well onto her beam ends. Since the storm had come without warning, the after hatch had not been closed and torrents of cold gray water cascaded into the cabin. The lamp swung parallel to the decking. Food and chairs and missionaries were swept into a jumble and buried in new floods ripping down the hatchway. There were screams, and from the stateroom where Jerusha lay ghastly ill, Abner heard a plaintive cry, "Are we sinking?"

He stumbled to her and found her berth drenched with water, and everything in confusion. "We shall be safe," he said firmly. "God is with this ship."

They heard the hatchway being hammered into place and smelled the loss of air. Then the cook shouted, "Cape Horn is rushing out to meet us."

"Will the storm last long?" Brother Whipple inquired.

"Maybe four weeks," the cook replied, picking up the debris of his meal.

On Sunday, November 25, Abner ventured on deck to survey the damage, and reported breathlessly, "All the livestock was swept away. That first big wave almost capsized us." One by one the missionaries, those who were not confined to their bunks, viewed the storm and discovered what the cook meant when he said that Cape Horn had come to meet them. A cold, dismal fog enveloped the ship where the warm waters of the Atlantic met the icy wastes of the Antarctic, and the waves rose high in the gloom, falling away into icy depths.

"I'm fearfully cold," Jerusha told her husband, but there was nothing he could do. The little *Thetis* kept probing southward toward the Cape itself, and each day took her into colder waters. The thermometer stood at thirty-nine degrees, with no fires allowed on board. Bedding was wet from the dousing and all gear was molding in unaired boxes. Most of the time the hatchway was covered, so that no air swept into the dank confined cabin, and with no freedom for walking, griping biliousness overtook the missionaries.

On Tuesday, November 27, John Whipple hurried below with heartening news. "We can see Staten Island to port, so we must be approaching the Cape. The waves aren't as big as we feared." He led his companions aloft to view one of the bleakest, loneliest lands on earth, lying off the tip of the continent. Through partial mist its low treeless hills were visible, and Whipple said, "We are seeing it in summer. Imagine what it must be like in winter." But the missionaries were looking not at Staten Island, but rather at the terrifying waters that lay ahead.

There, at the southern tip of the habitable world, in a latitude of fifty-five degrees, the earth-girdling southern currents that thundered in from the lower Pacific crashed into the turbulent swells of the Atlantic, and the missionaries could see that the resulting waves were mountain-high and clothed with fog and fear. If a sailor were lucky enough to hit Staten Island with an easterly at his back, he could penetrate these monstrous waves with some hope of success, but when, as in late November of 1821, both the set of the Pacific and the bearing of its winds were from the west, there was slight chance of doubling the Cape.

But Captain Janders, face grim within the rim of sandy whiskers, was stubbornly determined to prosecute every chance. "I'll not be the captain who has to write in his log, 'Today abandoned hope of doubling Cape Horn and turned back across the Atlantic to try Cape Good Hope.' If you write that in your log, they never let you forget it. You're the Yankee who couldn't double the Cape." So he gambled that either the wind would veer to the east and blow him through, or that the Pacific swell would somehow abate and allow him to beat into the wind, no matter where it stood.

"I am convinced that one or the other will happen," Janders repeated doggedly. But on the evening of Thanksgiving Day he stumbled down into the cabin and said dourly, "If any of you missionaries have personal knowledge of God, I would appreciate your prayers now."

"Do the winds continue against us?" Abner asked.

"Never seen 'em so bad," Janders growled.

"Will we have to turn back?" one of the wives inquired.

"No, ma'am, we won't!" Janders said firmly. "There'll be no man say I tried the Cape and failed."

When he was gone back to the deck John Whipple said, "I see no fault in supporting him with our prayers."

"Nor do I, Brother Whipple," Jerusha said, and Dr. Whipple prayed: "Let us recall the reassuring words of Proverbs: 'I neither learned wisdom, nor have the knowledge of the holy. Who hath ascended up into the heavens, or descended? who hath gathered the wind in his fists? who hath bound the waters in a garment? who hath established all the ends of the earth? what is his name?' Brethren, we who stand at the ends of the earth, where the winds are gathered in God's fist against us, let us not forget that it is the just man whom God tries. The evil man passes and repasses this Cape with no concern, for he has already been tested. It is you and I who have not been tested. Let us pray that these winds abate in our favor, but if they do not, let us doubly rely upon the Lord."

By Saturday, December 1, the *Thetis* had spent seven full days negotiating a distance of one hundred and ten miles. During breaks in the storm, the forlorn missionaries had seen blunt and brutal Tierra del Fuego to the north and had retired to freezing berths, huddling together in fear and seasickness. The tempest from the west did not abate.

On Sunday, December 2, the *Thetis* turned due west to find a channel which would carry them north of Cape Horn itself, perched on an insignificant island to the south, but this day the waves from the Pacific were terrifying even to Captain Janders. Once, when the *Thetis* heeled far over onto her beam ends, he looked in dismay at Mister Collins, who was brave enough to say, "I've never sailed in a worse sea, Captain. We'd better run for it." In an instant Captain Janders swung his tiny brig about and sent her running before the violent storm, eastward past dangerous rocks, and within three hours, at the amazing speed of nearly thirty knots, the little *Thetis* lost all the westward progress she had acquired in eight days.

On December 3 Mister Collins asked the fatal question: "Shall we run across the Atlantic, sir, to Cape Good Hope?" and Captain Janders replied, "We shall not!" and he trimmed his sails once more for the westerlies that roared in upon the great Pacific swells. At noon of that day John Whipple reported startling news to the frightened and freezing missionaries: "I think we're right where we were eight days ago! I'm sure that's Staten Island to the south and the point of Tierra del Fuego to the north." His wife asked weakly, "You mean to say that we're being driven backward?" When her husband nodded, she said softly, "John, I have to fight so hard to stay in my berth that my elbows are bleeding. Do see how poor Sister Hale is." And when John looked, he saw that her elbows and knees were bleeding, too. But there was nothing anyone could do but lie in his cold, wet berth and fight the frantic rolling of the ship.

On December 4 the *Thetis* reached far to the south, so that the sun barely set at all, and night consisted only of a mysterious ashen haze, holding low upon the turbulent sea. And when it looked as if there might be better wind toward the Antarctic, Captain Janders tried his next trick. Running boldly on a tack that carried him away from the protecting island behind which mariners customarily doubled the Cape, he led his tiny brig into the waters of the Drake Passage, roughest in the world. It was a gallant move, but toward morning a vast Pacific accumulation swirling with sleet and snow swept down on the *Thetis,* lifted her high, and threw her sideways, so that water rushed into the terror-stricken cabin and filled the lower berths. "Abner! Abner!" bruised Jerusha screamed from the floor, forgetting his proper title. "We're drowning." He replied calmly, picking her up gently and moving her into John Whipple's upper bunk, "No, my beloved companion, God is with this ship. He will not abandon us." The terrifying shaking continued, accompanied by fresh torrents of water slopping aft from some ruptured forward area. "We cannot stand this!" a hysterical wife screamed. "God is with this ship," Abner quieted her, and in the weird darkness, with water about his ankles and the sobbing of those who thought they would soon be dead, he prayed in a strong voice and reminded the missionaries that they had come on this voyage to do God's work and it was notorious that God tested His chosen and that their way was never quick or easy. "We shall ride through this storm and see the pleasant valleys of Hawaii," he affirmed. Then he went to each freezing stateroom and helped lift luggage out of berths into which it had been swept. No attempt was made to serve meals, but when Captain Janders looked below and saw the work Abner was doing, he shouted to the cook, "Bring some cheese aft to these poor people." Abner asked, "Are we rounding the Cape?" and Janders replied, "Not yet, but we will be." However, toward six in the evening it became apparent that the night's waves were to be even more tumultuous, so he said at last to Mister Collins, "We'll run for it," and once more within less than an hour they lost all they had gained in two days.

On December 5 the wounded brig *Thetis,* coated with ice, was back at the Atlantic entrance to the waters that guarded the Cape, and there was no sign of either an easterly wind or an abated swell, so Captain Janders kept his ship tacking idly back and forth, waiting, and about ten o'clock at night it looked as if the big chance had come, for the wind seemed to veer. Crowding sail, the captain lashed his ship into the swells and for the remaining two hours of that gray day the *Thetis* chewed awkwardly into the heavy seas and apparently made some progress.

On December 6 the brig actually accomplished forty-eight miles into a snowstorm, bucking a sea as choppy and as sickening as any the missionaries had so far experienced. There was not the abstract terror of the ship on beam ends, but there was the constant rise and fall, wallow and recovery that made even inanimate objects like trunks and boxes creak in misery. The cold, intensified by the sleet and snow, grew worse, and wives huddled beneath wet blankets, shivering and convinced that death would be preferable to two more weeks of Cape Horn. But Brother Whipple reported heartily to all that at last the brig was making headway.

On Friday, December 7, the wind perversely returned to its former heading; the seas became more confused; and once again the *Thetis* stood on her beam ends. This time she came perilously close to foundering. Heavy trunks that had been cleated down tore loose and piled brutally into berths. Timbers creaked ominously as if they could bear no more, and the little brig fell sickeningly into a trough out of which it seemed it might not recover. "Oh, God! Let me die!" Jerusha prayed, for a trunk had her pinned against the bulkhead. Other women were crying, "Brother Hale! Can you move this box?" for they knew that he was the only missionary then capable of constructive work.

It was some minutes therefore before he got to Jerusha, and he found her wandering in speech. "Let me die, God. It wasn't Abner's fault. He was good to me, but let me die!" she whimpered. He pulled the trunk away and felt her limbs to see if they were broken, but as he did so, he heard her prayer for death. "What did you say?" he asked, appalled. "God, let me die!" she prayed blindly. With a violent slap he thrashed her on the cheeks and cried, "Mrs. Hale! You may not blaspheme!" He continued slapping her until she recovered her wits, and then he sat beside her and said, "I am afraid, too, my beloved companion. I am afraid we are going to drown. Oh!" And he braced himself for a wild ride down the hollow of a wave, and the shattering pause, and the groaning climb. "Do even you think we are lost?" Jerusha asked softly. "I am afraid," he said humbly, "but we must not blaspheme, even if we are deserted." She asked, "What did I say, dear husband?" He replied, "It's best forgotten. Mrs. Hale, will you pray?" And in the cold, dark 'tween-decks he coached her in what he thought would be their last prayer.

At that moment above decks, Captain Janders was shouting in fury, "Goddamnit, Mister Collins, we can't make it!"

"Shall we run for Good Hope, sir?"

"We shall not."

"We'll founder, sir," Collins warned.

"Turn around, and we'll lick our wounds in the Falklands," Janders replied.

"And then?"

"We'll go through the Strait of Magellan."

"Yes, sir."

SO THE HAMFERDITE BRIG *Thetis,* seventy-nine feet long, two hundred and thirty tons out of Boston, was finally turned away from Cape Horn, and on a northeast heading, which took advantage of the strong winds, it shot up to the Falkland Islands, which hung in the South Atlantic off the coast of Patagonia.

The Falklands were a group of rocky, wind-swept, treeless islands used by whalers—and those who could not double the Cape—for recuperation, and when the forbidding group hove into view on December 10 they seemed to the bruised missionaries like fragments of Beulah Land, and as soon as the *Thetis* had anchored in a rocky cove, all hastened to be among the first ashore. All through the brief, gray starless night John Whipple inspected the cold ground, and at dawn he hailed the brig with good news: "There are geese and ducks here and some small cormorants. Bring all the guns!" He organized a hunting party that was to provide the *Thetis* with fresh food for many weeks. Mister Collins led another group that found sweet water to replenish the barrels and stacks of driftwood that had reached the islands from the coast of Argentina.

"We'll keep fires going for ten days," he promised the missionaries. "We'll dry you out proper."

Wives decked the *Thetis* with laundry, since none had been done for more than a hundred days, but it was energetic Abner Hale, tramping to the highest spot of the island, who made the big discovery. There was another ship hugging one of the northern harbors, and he and two sailors ran down to it. It was a whaler just in from the Pacific, and before long its skipper and Captain Janders were comparing all the charts they had on the Magellan passage.

"It's a horrible passage," the whaler said, and he showed Captain Janders and Abner how the island of Tierra del Fuego, which they had tried to pass by the southern route, stood a narrow distance off the mainland of South America, so that the Strait of Magellan was actually the northern alternate route around Tierra del Fuego.

Nobody aboard either ship had ever penetrated the strait, but many recollected stories. "In 1578 Francis Drake made the passage in seventeen easy days," a historical expert recalled. "But in 1764 it took the Frenchman Bougainville fifty-two days. Record is two Spaniards who fought Magellan's route for a hundred and fifty days. But they finally made it."

"Why is it so difficult?" Abner asked.

"It isn't," the whaler explained. "Not until you reach the other end."

"Then what happens?" Abner pressed.

"See these rocks? The Four Evangelists? That's where ships perish."

"Why? Fog?"

"No. Westerlies from the Pacific pile up tremendous waves all along your exit from the passage. In trying to break out, you run upon the Evangels."

"You mean it's worse than where we just were?"

"The difference is this," the whaler explained. "If you try to double Cape Horn in adverse conditions, you might have fifty days of mountainous seas. It just can't be done. At the Four Evangelists the waves are worse than anything you've seen so far, but you can breast them in an afternoon . . . if you're lucky."

"Where is it precisely that so many ships go on the rocks?" Janders reviewed.

"Here on Desolation Island. It's not bad of itself, but when a ship thinks it's breasted the Evangelists, it often finds it can't maintain position. In panic it turns and runs, and Desolation grabs it. Fifty . . . hundred ships."

"Any survivors?" Mister Collins asked.

"On Desolation rocks?" the whaler countered.

"What is the trick?" Mister Collins pressed.

"Find yourself a good harbor toward the western end of Desolation. Go out every day for a month if necessary and try to breast the Evangelists. But always keep yourself in position so that when you see you've got to run back to harbor for the night, you'll be in command and not the waves."

"That's exactly as I understand it," Captain Janders agreed.

"Is this an easterly coming up?" Mister Collins asked hopefully. "Seems to me if we caught a reliable easterly we'd be in luck. It would push us right through the strait."

"There's an error!" the whaler snorted. "Because while it's true that an easterly will help you a little in the first part of the transit, by the time the wind has built up a sea at the western exit, it simply creates added confusion around the Four Evangelists. Then you really have hell."

"But even so, the waves can be penetrated?" Janders inquired.

"Yes. Dutchmen did it. So did the Spaniards. But remember, go out every day from Desolation and come back every night till you find the right sea. And you do the steering. Not the storm."

The whaler, sensing that Abner might be a minister, asked him if he would consent to conduct divine services as a guest, and this pleased the missionary very much, for he looked at Captain Janders as if to say, "Here's one sea captain who acknowledges God," but Janders could never willingly permit Abner complete triumph, so in snakelike tones he destroyed Hale's paradise by commenting, when the whaler went below to rouse the men, "He's probably run the vilest ship on the seas. Probably has crimes on his head no man could measure. Ask him what he did in Honolulu? Once these whalers get back around the Cape and near Boston, they all beg for one good prayer to wash away their accumulation of evil."

Nevertheless, a surly, husky lot of men and officers assembled for worship, and Abner flayed whatever crimes they had committed, with this text: "Leviticus 25, verse 41: 'And shall return unto his own family.' And upon returning, will his conscience return with him?" In impassioned words, heightened by Captain Janders' goading, he analyzed the condition of a man who had been away from both the home of the Lord and the home of his family for four years, the changes which had occurred both in him and in his home of which he could not be aware and the steps which must be taken to remedy those changes, if ill, and to capitalize upon them, if favorable. The whalers listened with astonishment as he laid bare their half-expressed thoughts, and at the end of the service three men asked if he would pray with them, and when the prayers were over, the captain said, "That was a powerful sermon, young man. I should like to give you a token of our ship's appreciation." And he surprised Abner by delivering to the *Thetis'* longboat a stalk of handsome green bananas. "They'll ripen and be good for many days," he said, "and the sickly ones will enjoy them."

"What are they?" Abner asked.

"Bananas, son. Good for constipation. Better get to like them, because they're the principal food in Hawaii." The whaler showed Abner how to peel one, took a big bite, and gave the stub to Abner. "Once you become familiar with 'em, they're real good." But Abner found the penetrating smell of the skin offensive, whereupon the whaler bellowed, "You damn well better get to like 'em, son, because that's what you'll be eatin' from now on."

"Were you in Hawaii?" Abner asked.

"Was I in Honolulu?" the whaler shouted. Then, recalling the sermon just concluded, he finished lamely, "We took a dozen whales south of there."

On Tuesday, December 18, after Captain Janders had copied all the charts that his fellow skipper could provide of the Magellan passage, and had compared them with his own, finding that no two placed any single island in the passage even close to where the others did, the *Thetis* weighed anchor and headed back for Tierra del Fuego, but this time to the northern end of the island, where it abutted onto South America, and where the forbidding passage discovered by Magellan waited sullenly. As its bleak headlands came into view on the morning of December 21, Captain Janders said to Mister Collins, "Take a good look at 'em. We're not comin' back this way." And with stubborn determination he plunged into the narrow strait which had defeated many vessels.

The missionaries were fascinated by the first days of the passage and they lined the rails staring first at South America and then at Tierra del

Fuego. These were the first days of summer, and once a band of natives clad only in skins was spotted. At night Abner saw the fires that had given the large island its name when Magellan first coasted, for in spite of the fact that all was bleak, it was also interesting.

The *Thetis,* aided by the easterly wind, sometimes made as much as thirty miles in a day, but more often about twenty were covered in slow and patient probing. After the first westward thrust was completed, the brig turned south, following the shoreline of Tierra del Fuego, and the days became somnolent, and there was scarcely any night at all. The missionaries sometimes slept on deck, wakening to enjoy any phenomenon that the night produced. When winds were adverse, as they often were, the *Thetis* would tie up and hunting parties would go ashore, so that for Christmas all hands had duck and thought how strange it was to be in these gray latitudes instead of in white New England. There was no seasickness now, but one passenger was growing to hate the Strait of Magellan as she had never hated any other water.

This was Jerusha Hale, for although her two major sicknesses had departed, another had taken their place, and it consisted of a violent desire to vomit each time her husband made her eat a banana. "I don't like the smell of the oil," she protested.

"I don't like it either, my dear," he explained patiently, "but if this is the food of the islands . . ."

"Let's wait till we get to the islands," she begged.

"No, if the Lord providentially sent us these bananas in the manner he did . . ."

"The other women don't have to eat them," she pleaded.

"The other women were not sent them by the direct will of God," he reasoned.

"Reverend Hale," she argued slowly, "I'm sure that when I get off this ship, where I've been sick so much, I'll be able to eat bananas. But here the oil in the skin reminds me . . . Husband, I'm going to be sick."

"No, Mrs. Hale!" he commanded. And twice a day he carefully peeled a banana, stuck half in his mouth, and said, against his own better judgment, "It's delicious." The other half he forcefully pushed into Jerusha's, watching her intently until she had swallowed it. The procedure was so obviously painful to the sickly girl that Amanda Whipple could not remain in her berth while it was being carried out, but what made it doubly nauseous was that Abner had strung the ripening bananas from the roof of their stateroom, and there they swung, back and forth, through every hour of the passage, and as they ripened they smelled.

At first Jerusha thought: "I'll watch the bunch grow smaller," but it showed no effect of her efforts to diminish it. Instead it grew larger, more aromatic, and swung closer to her face at night. "My dear husband," she pleaded, "indeed I shall be sick!" But he would place his hand firmly over her abdomen until the day's ration was swallowed, and he refused to allow her to be sick, and she obeyed.

After one such performance John Whipple asked, "Why do you like bananas so much, Brother Hale?"

"I don't," Abner said. "They make me sick, too."

"Then why do you eat them?"

"Because obviously the Lord intended me to eat them. How did I get them? As a result of having preached a sermon. I would be an ingrate if I did not eat them!"

"Do you believe in omens?" the young scientist asked.

"What do you mean?" Abner inquired.

"Superstitions? Omens?"

"Why do you ask that?"

"I was thinking. Keoki Kanakoa has been telling me about all the omens under which he used to live. When one of their canoes went out to sea, they had an old woman who did nothing but study omens. And if an albatross came, or a shark, that meant something . . . a god had sent them . . . you could learn what the god intended . . . if you could read the omen."

"What has that to do with me?" Abner asked.

"It seems to me, Brother Hale, that you're that way with the bananas. They were given to you, so they must have been sent by God. So if they were sent by God, they must be eaten."

"John, you're blaspheming!"

"Blaspheming or not, I'd throw those bananas overboard. They're making everybody sick."

"Overboard!"

"Yes, Reverend Hale," Jerusha interrupted. "Throw them overboard."

"This is intolerable!" Abner cried, storming onto the deck, from which he speedily returned to the stateroom. "If anyone touches those bananas! They were sent by God to instruct us in our new life. You and I, Mrs. Hale, are going to eat every one of those bananas. It is God's will." So as the *Thetis* crept agonizingly ahead, the bananas danced malodorously in the stateroom.

The brig had now left Tierra del Fuego and was amidst the hundreds of nameless islands that comprised the western half of the passage. The winds veered and the dreary days ran into dreary weeks and Captain Janders wrote repeatedly in his log: "Tuesday, January 15. Twenty-sixth day in the passage. Land close on both hands. Beat all day into adverse wind. Made 4 miles but toward sunset lost on every tack. Could find no hold for anchor on sloping shores. Ran back and moored where we anchored last night. But hope this westerly gale continues, for it will smooth out waters at 4 Evangels. Shore party shot fine geese and caught 2 pailsfl. sweet mussels."

Day followed day, yielding a progress of four miles or six or none. Men would tow the *Thetis* from anchorage out into the wind and gamble that they would sleep in the same spot that night. Two facts preyed increasingly on their minds. The land about them was so bleak that it could not possibly support life for long, especially if summer left, and it was leaving. And all thought: "If it is so difficult here, what will it be when we reach Desolation Island? And when we have reached there, what must the Four Evangelists be like?" It seemed that inch by painful inch they were approaching a great climax, and this was true.

On the thirty-second day of this desolate passage an easterly wind sprang up and whisked the little brig along the north shore of Desolation Island, a location made more terrible by the fact that sailors spotted the stern boards of some ship that had foundered on the rocks. The sea grew rougher, and eighteen of the missionaries found it advisable to stay below, where the smell of bananas added to their qualms. That night Jerusha declared that she could not, on pain of death, eat another banana, but Abner, having heard such protests before, gallantly ate his half, then forced the remainder into Jerusha's mouth. "You may not get sick," he commanded, holding her stomach in his control. But the ship lurched as the first fingers of the Pacific swell probed into the passage, and neither Jerusha nor Abner could dominate her retching, and she began to vomit.

"Mrs. Hale!" he shouted, clapping his other hand over her mouth, but the sickness continued until the berth was fouled. "You did that on purpose!" he muttered.

"Husband, I am so sick," she whimpered. The tone of her words impressed him, and tenderly he cleaned away the mess, making her as comfortable as possible.

"I'm not doing this to torment you, my dear companion," he argued. "God sent us these bananas. Look!" And he took down one of the yellow fruits, which he had grown to detest, and ate the entire thing.

"I'm going to be sick again!" she cried, and again he washed away the filth.

The next morning showed that the *Thetis* had run to the end of Desolation Island and had completed more than ninety-nine hundredths of the Magellan passage. All that remained was to effect the short dash past the Four Evangelists, four cruel and unpopulated rocks that guarded the western entrance to the strait. So at dawn on Tuesday, January 22, 1822, the little brig left the protection of Desolation Island to test the meeting ground of storms, the wave-racked confluence of the easterly moving Pacific and the westerly moving Atlantic, and as the whaling captain had predicted, the good winds that had accompanied the *Thetis* on her last days now accounted for a turbulence that no man aboard the ship had hitherto experienced.

Gigantic waves from the Pacific lashed in with terrifying force, apparently able to sweep all before them, but the choppier sea from the Atlantic rushed like a terrier into the thundering surf and tore it into a thousand separate oceans, each with its own current and direction. As his small craft approached this multiple maelstrom Captain Janders ordered, "All hands on deck lash yourselves to the ship," and lines were secured about waists and chests, and hand holds were quickly improvised, and the *Thetis,* all openings closed, plunged into the tremendous confusion.

For the first fifteen minutes the tiny brig was thrashed about as if the terriers of the sea had left off tormenting each other and had turned on her. She was lifted up and thrown down, ripped along on her port beams, then wallowed over and thrown backwards. She slipped and slid, and no man not tied to her decks could have survived aloft.

"Do you keep your eye upon the Evangelists, Mister Collins?" Captain Janders shouted above the fury.

"I do, sir."

"Can we take more seas, Mister Collins?"

"We cannot, sir."

"We'll turn and run."

"Mind the rocks, sir."

And the *Thetis,* whipping around, slashed into the violent seas coming from the Atlantic, and sped like a wounded sea animal back to Desolation Island. Below, the missionaries prayed. Not even the sick were able to remain in their berths, so violent the shaking and pitching had been.

Suddenly it was calm, and Captain Janders hid his little craft in a snug harbor whose shoreline was shaped like a fishhook. And each morning for the next week, Abner Hale, John Whipple, two other missionaries and four stout sailors rowed ashore with long ropes attached to the prow of the *Thetis.* Running around to the tip of the fishhook, they would strain and dig into the sand, pulling until the brig began to move. Slowly, slowly, they would tow it out to the entrance of the main passage, and then run back to the rowboat and overtake it.

And each day for a week the *Thetis* nosed its way carefully into the meeting ground of the oceans, tested them, tried, valiantly probed, and courted destruction. The turbulence was so majestic that there seemed no possibility of subduing it, and the sailors lashed to the masts wondered if the captain would turn and head back through the strait for Good Hope. But each evening Captain Janders swore, "Tomorrow we'll break the spell. Tomorrow we'll be free." In his log he wrote: "Tuesday, January 29. Tried again. Gigantic swells from Pacific clashing with choppy sea from Atlantic caused scenes of most frightful violence. Surges so high no ship could master them. Ran for same harbor."

On the thirtieth day of January the winds veered to the west, which in the long run was a good thing in that they would now stop supporting the Atlantic choppiness and turn to stabilizing the unhampered Pacific; but their immediate effect was to prohibit any further assault on the exit. Therefore, the *Thetis* remained tied to shore in her snug fishhook harbor while Captain Janders, Mister Collins, Abner and John Whipple climbed a small hill to survey the wild confluence of the oceans. They could not see the Four Evangelists, but they knew where they were, and as they studied the pattern of the giant waves, Abner said, "Have you thought, sir, that perhaps you are being held back by God's will?"

Captain Janders did not growl at the young man. "I am willing to consider anything, if only we can breast that damned mile of ocean."

"It occurred to me last night," Abner said, "that your insane refusal to dispose of your worldly novels has cursed this ship."

Mister Collins looked at the young minister with blank astonishment and was about to make an obscene expostulation when Janders silenced him. "What did you have in mind, Reverend Hale?"

"If we missionaries can pray, and if we can get this ship through the barrier, will you then dispose of your worldly literature, and as the captain of a ship that needs God, accept books from me?"

"I will," Janders said solemnly. And the four men, standing on a hill at the end of the world, entered into a compact, and when the missionaries were gone, Janders justified himself to his first mate: "I am determined to pass this point. I've never seen such seas as we encountered at Cape Horn. Now this. Call me superstitious if you will, but it's bad luck for a ship to carry a minister. We've got eleven of 'em. If they're the cause of the bad luck, maybe they can also be the cause of good luck. I'll try anything."

That night Abner assembled the missionaries and told them of the compact. "God has been holding this ship back to teach us a lesson," he assured them, "but our prayers will lift the curse." To John Whipple and others, this seemed like medievalism, and they would not pray, but the majority did, and at the end of the prayer Whipple asked if he might pray, too, and Abner assented. "Lord, strengthen the hands and the eyes of our mariners," Whipple prayed. "Abate the wind, lower the waves and let us pass."

"Amen," Captain Janders said.

After prayers, Abner visited Jerusha, still bedridden, and shared a banana with her. When she protested that it was this which was keeping her abed, he pleaded: "We are placing our destiny in the hands of God tonight. Please bear with me, beloved companion, and if we pass the barrier tomorrow, you will not have to eat any more bananas."

"Is that a sacred promise?" she asked.

"It is," he assured her. So she mastered her gorge, felt her husband's firm hand on her stomach, and ate.

At four o'clock in the morning the entire ship met for prayers, and after the missionaries had spoken long, Captain Janders prayed, "Lord, get us through."

It was not yet five when Abner and John rowed ashore with their six regular towing companions, and the small craft edged its way into the main channel, but when the rope men were hauled back on board, Abner announced: "This day I want to pray on deck."

"Lash yourself to the mast," Janders grunted. To Collins he said, "The waves are as big as ever, but the sea is steadier and we have a wind we can cut into."

"As good a day as we'll get," the mate calculated.

"We're away!" Janders cried, and the *Thetis* probed far out to sea, well south of the Four Evangelists and into the wildest part of the ocean.

These were the hours of decision. Two days ago the problem had been to ride with the helpful wind from the stern, trying to accumulate sufficient speed to penetrate the massive waves. Now the wind was full in the face, and the *Thetis* had to tack first north, then south, then north, trying always to gain a few hundred yards of purchase in the sea, so that on one great burst to the north the tiny brig would at last clear the Evangelists. The grave danger involved was that on the vital run to the north, the *Thetis* would not hold its advantage, but would be swept sideways by the waves, and onto the rocks, crashing in final and hopeless destruction.

The hours of early morning passed, and the *Thetis* made one fruitless tack after another. Often on her beam ends, she fought vainly for leverage against the sea, but Abner could feel her slipping away, back toward Desolation Island, away from the line of safety that would permit a long tack past the Four Evangelists.

The hours of midday came and went, and the little brig fought on. Now she gained a mile and entered a more turbulent part of the ocean, where the full and mighty Pacific lashed out at her, and the timbers creaked and the masts swayed and Abner watched the whiskered face of Captain Janders, peering ahead, calculating the wind.

At three in the afternoon the pounding became almost unbearable on deck, and all not lashed down would have been washed away by the gigantic seas, so that Abner prayed, "Dear God, care for those below. Let the air they breathe be sweet." And he could smell the foul air of the staterooms and pitied the missionaries.

At four o'clock, but with no fear of encroaching dusk, for the summer sun would not set till nearly ten, the position of the *Thetis* was perilous. For Captain Janders was required either to stand farther out to sea and thus surrender all hope of running safely back to Desolation Island, or to abandon this day's attempt. He was loath to do the latter, because he had got closer to position than ever before, so for some minutes in the height of the gale he pondered.

"There's only half a mile more of turbulence," he shouted to Mister Collins.

"Hardly that, sir."

"Do you keep your eye on the Evangelists?" Janders cried.

"I do, sir."

"How many points more to windward must we head to pass the rocks, Mister Collins?"

"Three, sir."

"Can we hold such a course?"

The question was an unfair one, and both Janders and Collins knew it, for the captain was trying to tempt his mate into making the ultimate life-or-death decision. Mister Collins looked doggedly ahead and said nothing.

"Can you ease her three points into the wind, Mister Collins?"

"That I can, sir!" And the creaking *Thetis* bit more directly into the storm.

"If we hold this tack, will we clear the rocks, Mister Collins?"

"Yes, sir. If we hold this tack."

The two men stood tensely, trying to detect any notice of the brig's slipping in the great troughs, but she held firm. A minute passed, then two, then three, and finally Captain Janders shouted to all topside, "We'll run for the rocks. Stand ready to cut yourselves loose and tend the ropes."

Rarely did a group of men sailing a ship face a more clear-cut problem. If the winds held, and the keel maintained its cut into the waves, this long tack would throw the *Thetis* just outside the Four Evangelists, and the penetration would have been accomplished, for on the southward tack the little ship could sail all night if necessary, until the last turbulence was cleared.

"Now's the time to pray, Reverend Hale," Janders shouted above the wind, and Abner, lashed to the mainmast at both the armpits and waist, prayed only that the present relationship of ship and ocean and wind be maintained.

Then came Mister Collins' calm warning: "She's slipping, sir."

"I feel her slipping, Mister Collins," Captain Janders replied, his stern face hiding his fear.

"Shall we raise the topsail a little more into the wind?"

"Raise her all the way, Mister Collins."

"She may carry away, sir, in this wind."

Captain Janders hesitated, studied the way in which his brig was losing purchase, and cried, "We've got to have that sail! If it holds, we'll make it. If it carries away, no matter. We were lost anyway." And he whipped around toward where his men were lashed, shouting directions that sent them hauling ropes which started the after topsail higher into the wind, where it could counteract the sideward set of the ocean. But as the men hauled, their lines caught in the top block, and the triangular topsail whipped dangerously in the wind, and the *Thetis* appeared doomed.

"You and you, clear the top block!" Janders shouted. And from the stormy deck, where they had been lashed to save themselves, Cridland and the old whaler cut themselves loose and grabbed for the ropes leading to the top of the mainmast.

They climbed like monkeys, four secure hands, four certain feet clinging to the ropes as the mast whipped back and forth in the freezing storm. Higher and higher they went, as their ship drifted toward the rocks. "May God protect them," Abner prayed, as they dangled far above his head.

The *Thetis* now entered a segment of the sea where the waves were of special violence, for they were rebounding from the Evangelists off to starboard, and as the little brig rolled from one beam end to the other, torn this way and that, the top of the mainmast, where the two sailors worked, slashed swiftly in great arcs of more than a hundred degrees. At the extremity of each swing the tall mast whipped sharply, whistling in the wind, as if determined to dislodge the men that annoyed its ropes. On one such desperate passage Cridland lost his cap, and in grabbing for it with his right hand, he seemed, as viewed from below, to have been swept away, and Abner screamed, "God save his soul!" But it was only his hat that was gone.

"Try the ropes again!" Captain Janders shouted.

"They don't pull clear yet," the second mate yelled above the storm.

"Are we drifting toward the rocks, Mister Collins?"

"We are, sir."

"Shall we send more men aloft?"

"Nothing any more can do," Collins replied.

So the two mariners stared ahead in the late afternoon storm, feeling the ship, praying. "Try the ropes again!" Janders cried, but again they failed to respond. Clasping his hands behind him, Janders took several deep breaths and said with resignation, "We've about eight more minutes, Mister Collins. This was a sane try."

At this point Abner forgot the navigators near him and focused only on the two sailors, who continued to fly through great sickening arcs of heaven. Freezing rain and howling winds were upon them; the violence of the pitching ship seemed concentrated at the point where they labored; and Abner recalled the plea of the old whaler: "I would not like to round Cape Horn without a Bible." And he began to pray for the salvation of these two brave men on whom the safety of the brig now rested. And as they flashed through the gray sky, riding high in the heart of the storm, his agonized prayers went with them.

"Try the ropes again!" Janders called at the expiry of two of his vital eight minutes, and this time the sailors shouted madly, and the ropes moved, and the after mainsail crept slowly up the swaying mast, and wind was mysteriously trapped in its triangular expanse, and the sliding shoreward stopped.

"I feel her steady on course," Janders shouted.

"She is steady on," Collins repeated.

"Will she clear the Evangels?" Janders checked.

"She will clear them," Collins replied dully, hiding the exultation his heart felt.

And as the last fearful moments passed, the little brig *Thetis* maintained her northward tack into the storm, until at last she neared the perilous rocks, and all on deck saw that she would pass them by a margin of dreadful precision.

"The Lord God of Hosts is with us!" Abner shouted in unministerial joy.

But Captain Janders did not hear, for he kept his eyes fixed ahead, refusing to look at the Evangelists. He was seeking the ocean area where it would be safe for him to swing the *Thetis* onto her new and final tack. Minutes passed, then a quarter of an hour, then a half hour, and still he kept his eyes monotonously fixed on the great, heaving ocean, until finally, in swift alteration, he heeled the brig over, and cut her back on a southward tack that would carry her through the last mountainous waves and down the final vile troughs. Then he shouted, "Bring the men down." And Cridland and the old whaler came down from their dizzy perch and found footing on the deck. "May God be praised," Abner mumbled.

Yet at this exact moment, when he was entitled to share in the ship's jubilation, Abner was grave, as if in a trance, thinking: "Two days ago when a comforting wind was at our back, we were unable to accomplish anything. But today, with the gale right in our faces, we were able to fight it." He studied the little brig to discover the secret whereby a New England ship could cut directly into the heart of a storm, combating the elements each inch of the way, and although he did not understand the technique Captain Janders had utilized, he understood the man, and all men, and himself. "How strange," he reflected in the howling wind, "that when the storm is in your face, you can fight it."

Later, when Captain Janders unleashed Abner, the mariner said, in a kind of daze, "I would not want to be the captain of whom it was said in Boston, 'He tried to round the Horn, but ran instead for Good Hope.' "

"No one will say that of you, Captain," Abner said proudly.

The hatches were broken open and Mister Collins shouted the good news to the missionaries: "We are safe!"

All below who could stand piled on deck, and in the cold wind Captain Janders said, "Reverend Hale, through God's grace we broke through. Will you pray?" But for the only time on the voyage, Abner was numbed into silence. His eyes were filled with tears and he could think only of Cridland and the whaler, whipping through distant space, working to save the ship, and of Captain Janders fighting the storm, so John Whipple read from the sweet thundering passages in the Psalms that sailors love:

"God is our refuge and strength, a very present help in trouble.

"Therefore will not we fear, though the earth be removed, and though the mountains be carried into the midst of the sea;

"Though the water thereof roar and be troubled, though the mountains shake with the swelling thereof. . . .

"The Lord of Hosts is with us; the God of Jacob is our refuge. . . .

"They that go down to the sea in ships, that do business in great waters;

"These see the works of the Lord, and His wonders in the deep.

"For He commandeth, and raiseth the stormy wind, which lifteth up the waves thereof.

"They mount up to the heaven, they go down again to the depths: their soul is melted because of trouble.

"They reel to and fro, and stagger like a drunken man, and are at their wit's end.

"Then they cry unto the Lord in their trouble, and he bringeth them out of their distresses.

"He maketh the storm a calm, so that the waves thereof are still.

"Then are they glad because they be quiet; so He bringeth them unto their desired haven.

"Oh that men would praise the Lord for His goodness."

It was then noticed that Captain Janders had disappeared during the reading, and he now climbed from the hatchway with an armful of books. "Yesterday I promised Reverend Hale that if his prayers could get us through this barrier, I would forsake my books for his. Richardson . . . Sterne . . . Smollett . . . Walpole." One by one he tossed them into the Pacific, already beginning to merit its name. Then he added, "From December 21 to January 31 we were forty-two days in these straits. I have never known such a passage, but we have made it safely. God be praised."

Abner's triumph was tempered by defeat, for as the missionaries were watching the worldly books disappear, they were attracted by the sight of Jerusha Hale climbing on deck followed by Keoki, who lugged the remnants of the bananas. Walking unsteadily past her husband, she found the railing of the ship and threw the bananas, one by one, far out to sea. That night she told her husband, in a berth already quieter, "You bullied me, Abner . . . No, I shall use your name from now, for to me you are Abner. You bullied me through your sin of overzealousness. Never in our life again will I submit to your bullying, Abner, for I am as good a judge of God's will as you, and God never intended a sick woman to eat so hatefully." When Abner showed his surprise at this ultimatum she softened it by adding the truth: "While you were away talking with the men tonight, Captain Janders said that at the worst part of the passage, he felt comforted that a man of your courage was with him. What is more important, Abner, is that I am comforted that a man of your courage and piety is with me." And she kissed him.

Before she could kiss him again, Keoki came to the cabin, saying, "Reverend Hale, the old whaler needs you. In the fo'c's'l."

"Is he drunk again?" Abner asked suspiciously.

"He needs you," the Hawaiian repeated, and he led Abner to where the rugged old man lay in his filthy bunk, mumbling.

"What is it?" Abner asked quietly.

"Can I have my Bible back, now?" the whaler asked.

"No. The church gave you a Bible once, and you defiled it. You brought scorn and ridicule on us all."

"Reverend Hale, you saw me in the ropes today. You know how I feared going aloft at Cape Horn . . . without a Bible, that is."

"No, the Lord is harsh with backsliders," Abner said sternly.

At this point Cridland, who had shared the perils with the old man, suggested, "Reverend Hale, suppose you didn't have to give him the Bible. Suppose I gave him mine. Would you then . . ."

"Give you another! Never! Cridland, the Lord has said, 'The backslider in heart shall be filled with his own ways.' It is these men, more than sinners, who damage the church."

"But, Reverend Hale, in the storm it was this man who saved us all. I tried to break the sail loose, but I couldn't. He did it all."

"It's true, Reverend," the old whaler confessed. "I saved the ship, and I want my Bible back."

"No," Abner said. "While you were aloft, I prayed for you. And I pray for you now. If you saved this ship, we all thank you gratefully. But run the risk of having the entire ship laugh at the church again? No. That I cannot do." And he stalked aft.

It was not until Saturday night that Abner noticed Jerusha without her Bible. He was conducting prayers and saw that his wife was reading from Sister Whipple's, so when they had returned to their quarters he asked quietly, "Where is your Bible, my dear wife?"

She replied, "I gave it to the old whaler."

"To the old . . . How did you hear of him?"

"Keoki came to me, weeping for the evil old man."

"And you sided with Keoki against your own husband . . . against the church?"

"No, Abner. I simply gave a brave old man a Bible."

"But, Mrs. Hale . . ."

"My name is Jerusha."

"But we discussed this in the cabin. How backsliders are the ones who do the church greatest damage."

"I didn't give my Bible to a backslider, Abner. I gave it to a man who was afraid. And if the Bible cannot dispel fear, then it is not the book we have been led to believe."

"But the position of the mission? The foundation of our church?"

"Abner," she said persuasively, "I'm sure that this old man will backslide again, and he may do us damage. But on Thursday night, when he climbed down from that mast, he was close to God. He saved my life, and yours. And the idea of God has no meaning for me unless at such times He is willing to meet even an evil old man with love."

"What do you mean, the idea of God?"

"Abner, do you think that God is a man who hides up there in the clouds?"

"I think that God hears every word you are saying, and I think He must be as perplexed as I am." But before he could continue his charges, Jerusha, with her liquid brown curls dancing beside her ears, kissed him once more, and they fell into their narrow bunk.

It was long after midnight when Abner Hale, troubled as never before, left his bunk and went on deck, where a few bright stars were strong enough to dominate the dim, gray Antarctic night. He was troubled, first because Jerusha had given the old man her Bible, against his orders as it were, but more because of his deep and growing appetite for his wife's consoling body. Three times on this trip major arguments with Jerusha had ended by her laughingly drawing him into the narrow bunk, across whose opening she lowered the curtains, and each time during the next dazzling half hour he had forgot God and the problems of God. All he knew was that Jerusha Bromley Hale was more exciting than the storm, more peaceful than the ocean at rest.

He was convinced that such surrender on his part must be evil. He had often listened, in the cramped stateroom, to John and Amanda Whipple whiling away the hours, and he had marked their sudden cessation of whispering, followed by strange noises and Amanda's curious, uncontrollable cries, and he had judged that this was what the church meant when it spoke of "sanctified joy." He had intended discussing this with Jerusha, but he had been ashamed to do so, for now and again his own great surges of "sanctified joy" had left him morally stunned. Anything so mysterious and powerful must be evil, and surely the Bible spoke frequently of women who tempted men, with disastrous results. So on the one hand, Abner's imperfect knowledge of life inclined him to think that as a minister he would be far better off with Jerusha not so close to him. She was too intoxicating, too instinct with "sanctified joy."

But as soon as he reached this confused yet understandable conclusion, he was faced with the undeniable fact, clear to even a fool, that for a minister to live without a wife was nothing but popery, and if there was one thing he wished with all his heart to avoid it was popish ways. "The great men of the Old Testament had wives," he reasoned, "and it is not until you reach St. Paul that you get such admonitions as, 'I say therefore to the unmarried . . . , It is good for them if they abide even as I. But if they cannot contain, let them marry: for it is better to marry than to burn.' What does such a passage signify?" he asked himself throughout the strange half-night.

He walked back and forth for several hours, and the night watch joked, "He really has to do the missionary waltz!" but being of simpler minds, and particularly of minds that had long ago settled this difficult problem of man and woman—"The reason Honolulu's the best port on earth is that in Honolulu the women climb aboard the ship already undressed and ready to work"—they would have been unable to comprehend his real perplexities.

"Do I love Jerusha too profoundly?" he asked the gray night. But whenever he came near concluding that he ought to love her less, he would think of her overwhelming loveliness and he would cry, "No! That is the Romish way!" and he would return to his dead center of confusion. Thus in the night hours he wrestled with his sweet, perplexing temptation.

Sunday rose brisk and clear, and for the first time on the voyage, the entire missionary family was able to attend topside service in the cold, bracing air which swept up from the Antarctic. Since it was to be an occasion of special celebration, the four wives in Abner's stateroom asked their husbands to move elsewhere while they helped one another dress.

For this thanksgiving day Jerusha modestly changed from the two-piece red flannel underwear she had been wearing for some weeks into a fresh set, over which she laced a stout corset held in position by a two-inch-wide busk of polished birch. Long hand-knitted black stockings were pinned to the bottom edge of the corset, and a corset cover, starched long ago in Walpole, was fitted into place, after which pantaloons, also starched, were drawn up. Thus properly founded, Jerusha now climbed into a woolen underpetticoat, a starched linen petticoat and finally a cambric petticoat, all lashed securely at the waist. A small bustle was added, over which a hooped broadcloth dress was hung, its alternate patterns of black and purple providing a properly subdued color.

Next Jerusha adjusted a paisley shawl about her shoulders, fitted a saucy poke bonnet about her pale face, slipped a knitted bag over her arm, tucked a handkerchief into one cuff of her dress, jammed her fingers first into silk mittens and then into woolen ones, and stood while Amanda Whipple held her coat for her. She was then ready for morning service, and after she had helped the other women into their coats, the four missionary wives climbed the hatchway ladder and appeared on deck.

NOW CAME THE DAYS of gold, the memorable days when the *Thetis* rolled gently in the sun, all canvas set, and dolphins chased flying fish that shone in iridescence as they leaped. The little brig was away on an unbroken leg of more than seven thousand miles from Cape Horn to Hawaii, and slowly the ugly cold of the south gave way to the increasing warmth of the north. The new stars of Tierra del Fuego began to disappear and the old familiar constellations of New England crept back into place. But most of all, the mission family became fused into a single organized and dedicated group. Some, who forgot how sick they had been and how Abner alone had kept the family functioning, protested at his assumption of leadership, and one sharp-tongued wife was heard to say, "You'd think he was the Lord's anointed," but her husband quieted her by remembering, "Someone had to make decisions . . . even in a family."

As the equator neared, the daily lessons organized by Abner became more meaningful, and many mornings were spent, after the missionary waltz had ended, with group sessions discussing Wayland's *Moral Philosophy* or Alexander's *Evidences of Christianity*. Keoki Kanakoa also gave lectures on the condition of the islanders, but when he cried, "In Hawaii women are forbidden on pain of strangulation from eating bananas!" his point was somewhat dulled by Jerusha, who whispered loudly, "I count that no great privation." But the most solemn moment in any session came when someone, usually a woman, intoned the first line of their most cherished hymn: " 'Blest be the tie that binds' "; for at such times the mission family was indeed bound together in a Christian brotherhood that few discover in this world.

With the Pacific more placid and daily walks more congenial, seasickness vanished and constipation diminished, but a strange new illness began to take their place. At the beginning of the day women passengers would often suddenly feel an overwhelming nausea attack them, and they would have to vomit, just as if the ship were rolling in its former manner. It soon became apparent to Dr. Whipple that of the eleven wives aboard the *Thetis,* at least seven and possibly nine were pregnant, and he was proud when his own wife became the first to acknowledge openly that she was, as she phrased it, "expecting a small messenger from heaven." Her handsome husband perplexed the missionaries by remarking cryptically, "It's not surprising. I've known her since she was seven."

Jerusha's pregnancy was one of the latest to be certified, but it was also the one which was most enjoyed by the mother, for she was almost unmissionary in her delight. "It is a great solace to me, Abner," she said, "to think that I am going to become a mother in a new land. It's beautifully symbolic . . . as if we were destined to accomplish great things in Hawaii." Abner, like the other husbands, was bewildered, for like them he knew practically nothing about having babies; and then a frightening discovery was made: of the eleven women aboard the *Thetis* not one had ever had a child, nor had any ever attended a birth. Neither had the men, excepting Dr. Whipple, and he suddenly became a most important man, breaking out his *Practical Handbook of Midwifery,* which everyone studied with care; and it was then that the first substantial shadow fell across the mission family, for women began to realize that when they reached Hawaii, Dr. Whipple would be assigned to one island and they would go to another, and when their time came, the mission's only doctor would be inaccessible, and birth would be given under primitive conditions with only such help as a wife's husband could muster. It was then that wives looked at their husbands with greater affection, knowing that upon these men depended the family safety; and in this way the cabin of the *Thetis* became a kind of obstetrical seminar, with Brother Whipple as instructor and his medical books as texts.

It was early one Sunday morning that the missionaries heard the first mate cry, "Whaler to starboard!" Jerusha and Amanda, experiencing morning dizziness, did not go on deck, but the other wives did and saw looming out of the morning mists a magnificent three-masted ship, all sails set and riding the waves majestically like a queen. Smoke from the oil pots had darkened her sails, proving her to be a whaler, and now one of her whaleboats was approaching the *Thetis*.

"What ship are you?" Mister Collins hailed.

"Bark *Carthaginian,* Captain Hoxworth, out of New Bedford. And you?"

"Brig *Thetis,* Captain Janders, out of Boston."

"We bring you mail to carry back to Hawaii," the whaler's mate explained, as he climbed deftly aboard. "And we'll take yours to New Bedford." Then, seeing the missionaries in their tall hats, he asked, "Are these men ministers?"

"Missionaries, for Hawaii," Captain Janders replied.

The whaler hesitated momentarily, then nodded deferentially and asked, "Would one or two of you come aboard and conduct Sabbath services for us. We haven't had any for months . . . really it would be years. We'll be home soon, and we'd like to remind ourselves . . ."

Abner, recalling his good work aboard the earlier whaler at the Falklands, quickly volunteered, and so did John Whipple, but principally because he wanted to see one of New England's great whaling ships at close hand. They were lowered into the whaleboat and started off, whereupon Abner as an afterthought shouted, "Tell our wives we'll be back after service."

At the *Carthaginian* the young missionaries were greeted handsomely. A tall, wiry, powerful man with a whaler's cap far back on his head shot out a big hand and cried in a deep, commanding voice, "I'm Rafer Hoxworth, out of New Bedford, and I'm mighty glad to see you good men coming aboard. We could use some prayers on this bark."

"Have you had a good trip?" Whipple asked.

"Whales are scarce," Hoxworth replied, cocking a long leg on the railing. "Our capacity is thirty-two hundred barrels, but we have only twenty-six hundred. Rather disappointing." Then he added, "But of course, we've already shipped twenty-two hundred barrels on ahead, so I don't think the owners will be unhappy."

"Have you been away from New Bedford long?"

"Coming four years," Hoxworth replied, rubbing his powerful chin. "That's a long time . . . a very long time."

"But the oil you have, plus what you sent home . . . does make it a good trip?" Whipple pursued.

"Oh, yes! Good enough so that our share will permit several of us to get married."

"Including you?" Whipple asked.

"Yes."

"Congratulations, Captain Hoxworth. Abner!" and he called his sallow-faced companion, who was already arguing salvation and temperance with some of the crew. "Abner! Captain Hoxworth's going to get married when he gets home."

The scrawny little missionary with the pale stringy hair looked up at the rugged whaler and said, "And after four years of doing whatever he wanted to in Honolulu, he now hopes to get back into Christian ways, and asks our assistance."

The big captain tensed his right fist and pressed his foot strongly into the railing, but kept his temper. To himself he muttered, "By God! These missionaries are all alike. All over the world. You try to meet them halfway . . ." And John Whipple thought: "Why can't Abner just accept the day's events as they transpire? If a whaler heading home desires a Sabbath service, why can't we simply have the service?"

Then Whipple heard Captain Hoxworth's booming voice break into laughter. "Yes, Reverend . . . What was the name? Hale. Yes, Reverend Hale, you're right. Us whalers hang our consciences on Cape Horn when we head west, and then pick 'em up three years later when we come back home. We'd kind of like to have you ready us up for the job of catching 'em as we glide past."

"Do you glide past Cape Horn?" Abner asked in some confusion.

"Certainly."

"How long did it take you to double Cape Horn coming out?" Abner continued.

"What was it?" Hoxworth asked one of the men, a scowling, evil-looking rascal with a long scar across his cheek. "Oh, you weren't with us. We picked that one up in Honolulu when our cooper jumped ship. You, Anderson! How long did it take us to double the Cape coming out?"

"Three days."

Abner gasped. "You mean you got around Cape Horn in three days?"

"It was like glass," Captain Hoxworth boomed. "And it'll be like glass for us when we go home. We run a lucky ship."

"That's the truth!" Anderson laughed. "If there's whales, we get 'em."

Abner stood perplexed in the sunlight, trying to rationalize the fact that an obscene whaler—for he was convinced that this was a hell ship—could double the Cape in three days whereas it had taken a group of missionaries almost eight weeks, and he concluded to himself, "The mysterious ways of the Lord with His appointed are beyond understanding."

"We'll pray aft," Captain Hoxworth announced, leading his men and the missionaries to an afterdeck that seemed as spacious as a village common compared to the cramped *Thetis*.

Abner whispered to Whipple, "You lead the singing and the prayers, and I'll give the sermon I gave on the other whaler," but just as the crew began singing, "Another six days' work is done," the lookout bellowed, "Thar she blows!" and the assembly disintegrated, some rushing for the whaleboats, some for glasses and some up the lower rigging.

Captain Hoxworth's deep-set eyes glistened as he spotted the blowing whales off beyond the *Thetis,* and he strode past the missionaries. "Get those boats away swiftly!" he boomed.

"Captain! Captain!" Abner protested. "We're having hymns!"

"Hymns hell!" Hoxworth shouted. "Them's whales!" Grabbing a horn, he shouted directions that sent the whaleboats far out to sea and watched with his glass as they closed in upon the mammoth sperm whales that were moving along in a colony of gigantic forms.

At this point John Whipple faced a major decision. He knew, for he was a missionary like Abner, that since this was the Sabbath he was bound not to participate in this desecration of catching whales; but he also knew as a scientist that he might never again have a chance of watching a crew fight a great sperm whale, so after a moment's indecision he handed Abner his tall hat and said, "I'm going up into the rigging." Abner protested, but in vain, and during the ensuing seven exciting hours, he stood glumly aft and refused steadfastly to look at the whaling operations.

Brother Whipple from his vantage point in the rigging saw the three whaleboats from the *Carthaginian,* each with sail aloft, a harpooner, a helmsman and four rowers, sweep down upon the massive whales.

"They're sparm!" Captain Hoxworth exulted. "Look at 'em!" and he passed Whipple a telescope. In the glass John spied the enormous beasts, wallowing in the sea and spouting a mixture of water and compressed air more than fifteen feet into the air.

"How many whales are there out there?" Whipple asked.

"Thirty?" Hoxworth suggested cautiously.

"How many will you try to take?"

"We'll be lucky if we get one. Sparm's smart whales."

Whipple watched the lead boat try to sneak up on a particularly large monster, but it moved aggravatingly off, so the mate directed his whaleboat onto a substitute, a huge gray-blue sperm that lazed along in the sun. Creeping up to it from the rear and on the right side, the mate maneuvered his prow deftly into the whale's long flank, and the harpooner, poised with left leg extended securely into the bottom of the boat, right cocked precariously against the gunwales, drew the harpoon back in his left hand and then flashed it with incredible might deep into the whale's resistant body.

At this first agonizing moment the great beast flipped out of the water, the harpoon lines trailing, and Whipple cried, "It's bigger than the *Thetis!*" For the men of the *Carthaginian* had hooked into a mammoth whale.

"It'll make eighty barrels!" a seaman cried.

"If we take him," Hoxworth cautioned. Grabbing the glass from

Whipple, he watched the manner in which the whale plunged in its first attempt to shake off its tormentors. "He's sounded," the captain reported ominously, waiting to see how the first mad dash of the monster would be handled by the crew.

Whipple could see the rope whirring out of the harpooner's tub, with a sailor poised ready with an ax to chop it free—thus losing the whale if trouble developed—and it seemed as if the leviathan must be probing the very bottom of the ocean, so much rope went out. The minutes passed, and there was no sign of the whale. The other two boats placed themselves out of the way, yet ready to assist if the whale surfaced near them.

Then, in an unexpected quarter, and not far from the *Carthaginian,* the whale surfaced. It came roaring up through the waves, twisted, turned, flapped its great flukes, then blew. A tower of red blood spurted high into the air, a monument of bubbling death, and poised there for a moment in the sunlight as if it were a pillar of red marble, falling back at last into the sea to make the waves crimson. Four more times the huge beast spouted its lungs' burden of blood. Hoxworth, noting the color, shouted, "He's well struck!"

Now came the most tense moment of the fight, for the anguished whale hesitated, and all knew that if it came out of this pause in the wrong direction it might stove the whaleboats, or crush them in its powerful underslung jaw, or even crash headfirst into the *Carthaginian* herself, sinking her within minutes, in the way many whalers had been lost. This time the whale ran true, and at a speed of thirty miles an hour, rushed through the open ocean, dragging the whaleboat along behind. Now the sail was furled and the four rowers sat with their oars aloft, while their mates aboard the *Carthaginian* shouted, "There goes the Nantucket sleigh ride!"

In this way six men in a little rowboat fought an enormous whale to death. The beast dived and paused, spouted blood and dived again. It ran for the open sea, and doubled back, but the harpoon worked deeper into its flank, and the rope remained taut. When the whale moved close to the boat, the oarsmen worked feverishly hauling in rope; but when the beast fled, they played it out again; and in this wild red game of take in and play out, the whale began to sense that it would be the loser.

Now a second whaleboat crept in, and its harpooner launched another cruel shaft of iron deep into the whale's forward quarter, and the chase was on again, this time with two whaleboats on the sleigh ride. Swiftly, they were hauled through the bloody sea, and swiftly their ropes were brought close in when the whale rested. Back and forth, up and down the leviathan fought, blood choking his lungs and beginning to paralyze his flukes.

"He's a monster, that one!" Captain Hoxworth said approvingly. "Pray God he doesn't catch one of the boats."

The minutes passed and then the quarter hours, and the whale fought on, bleeding profusely and seeking the safer depths; but always he had to surface, a great bull sperm whale in agony, until finally, after a last mighty surge through the red waves, he rolled over and was dead.

"Got him!" Captain Hoxworth shouted, as the third whaleboat moved in to attach its line to the second, and in this manner the three crews slowly began to tow the whale back to their mother ship. The *Carthaginian,* meanwhile, manipulated its sails so that it could move with equal caution toward the oncoming whale.

Aboard ship there was much activity. Along the starboard side a section of railing was lifted away, and a small platform was lowered six or eight feet above the surface of the sea. Men brought out razor-sharp blubber knives with twenty-foot handles. Others laboriously lugged huge iron hooks, each weighing almost as much as a man, into position for biting into the blubber and pulling it aboard. Where Abner was to have preached, the cook and his helper piled dry wood for firing the try-pots in which the whale oil would be rendered, while forward the scar-faced cooper supervised the opening of the hatch and the airing of barrels into which that blubber would be stowed that could not be immediately cooked. Just as these preparations were completed, with John Whipple noting each step in the process, and Abner Hale trying not to do so because all was being done on a Sunday, the whale was brought alongside and Whipple cried, "It's longer than the *Thetis,*" but Captain Hoxworth, who like all whalers never referred to the length of a whale, growled, "He'll make eighty, ninety barrels. A monster."

When the great sperm was lashed to the starboard side of the *Carthaginian,* and when the frail platform was adjusted, a black Brava sailor, from the Cape Verdes, nimbly leaped onto the whale's body and with a slashing knife tried to cut at the blubber so as to attach the giant hooks that were being lowered to him. Deft as he was, he could not make the enormous hooks fast, and when the *Carthaginian* took a sudden shift to windward, the Brava was struck in the chest by one of the swaying hooks and swept off the whale's flank and into the ocean, whereupon a dozen sleek sharks who had been following the blood stormed down upon him, but the men on the platform slashed and cut at the raiders and drove them off, so that the Brava climbed back on the whale, cursing in Portuguese, and this time, dripping in blood from whale and shark alike, he caught the brutal hooks into the blubber, and the unwinding was ready to begin. But before it could start, the whale's great head—twenty-six feet long and weighing tons—had to be cut away and fastened to the after end of the ship.

"You, Brava!" Captain Hoxworth shouted. "Tie this hook into the head!" And the sinewy black man leaped nimbly onto the whale's head, securing the hook, after which his mates with extra sharp knives on long poles sawed away the mammoth head.

When it drifted clear, they directed their knives to the body of the whale, slashing the thick blubbery skin in sloping spirals that started from where the head had been and ran down to the huge trail hanging limp in the sea. As the skilled workmen cut, they frequently paused for sport and slashed their deadly knives deep into some shark that had come to feed upon the carcass, and when the knife was withdrawn the shark would twist slightly, as if a bee had stung him, and continue feeding.

Now the men on the lines leading to heavy hooks began to haul, and slowly the whale rolled over and over upon itself while the blanket of blubber unpeeled in a huge spiral and was hauled aloft. When more than a dozen feet hung over the deck, one iron hook was cut free from the top and hooked into position lower down. Then the other was cut away and fastened beside the first, allowing the end of blubber to fall free upon the deck, where it was cut away, hacked into pieces, and thrust at first into the boiling try-pots, and when they were full, into the temporary barrels. Then the lines were hauled tight once more, and the thick blanket of blubber continued to unwind and swing aboard, as men on the swaying platform cut it free from the body of the slowly revolving whale.

At last the tail was reached, and in the final moments, before the monstrous carcass was set free for the sharks, the Brava leaped back onto it and cut away a dozen steaks of fresh whale meat. "Get some liver, too," a sailor shouted, but the Brava felt himself slipping toward the sharks, so he grabbed a line and swung himself back aboard the platform. With a final slash of their scimitar-like knives, the workmen cut the whale loose and he drifted away to the waiting sharks.

Next the giant head was cut into three sections and hauled aboard, where near-naked men scooped out of its vast case more than two dozen precious barrels full of spermaceti, which would be converted into candles and cosmetics.

At dusk, when the head sections, now empty of their treasure, had been dumped back into the sea where twelve hours before they had held a tiny brain which had steered the goliath through the waves, Captain Hoxworth shouted, "Through the generosity of the Lord, our prayers have been delayed. Let the try-pots tend themselves. We'll pray." And he assembled all hands onto the oily deck, but Abner Hale would not participate in the services, so John Whipple conducted both the prayers and the singing and delivered an inspired sermon on a passage from the 104th Psalm: "O Lord, how manifold are Thy works! . . . The earth is full of Thy riches. So is this great and wide sea, wherein are things creeping innumerable, both small and great beasts. There go the ships: there is that leviathan, whom Thou hast made to play therein. . . . The glory of the Lord shall endure for ever." In his peroration he preached quietly: "From the turbulent deep God has raised up leviathan. From the wastes of the ocean He has brought us His riches. But from the wastes of the human ocean, constantly He provides us with riches greater still, for the leviathan of man's spirit is immeasurable and its wealth is counted not in casks or spermaceti. It is counted in love, and decency, and faith. May we who have trapped the great whale trap in our own lives the greater leviathan of understanding."

Captain Hoxworth was visibly moved by Whipple's sermon and shouted, "Cook! Break out some good food, and we'll celebrate!"

"We ought to be getting back to the *Thetis,*" Abner warned.

"Forget the *Thetis!*" Hoxworth boomed. "We'll sleep here tonight." And he led the missionaries down into his quarters, and they were stunned. The cabin was spacious, with clean green cloth upon the table. The captain's retiring room was finished in fine mahogany and decorated with numerous examples of carved whale bone, while his sleeping quarters featured a commodious bed, furnished with clean linen and hung on gimbals, so that even though the *Carthaginian* rolled in a storm, its captain slept in a steady bed. Along the wall was slung a bookcase, filled with works on geography, history, the oceans and poetry. Compared to the mean and meager *Thetis,* this ship was luxurious.

And the food was good. Captain Hoxworth said, in a low strong voice that carried his magnetism through the cabin, "We fight hard for our whales. We never finish second best, and we eat well. This is a lucky ship, and, Reverend Whipple, at the conclusion of this voyage I'll own two thirds of her, and at the end of the next, she'll be mine."

"These are fine quarters," Whipple replied.

"I had the mahogany put in at Manila. You see, I'm bringing my wife aboard on the next trip." He laughed apologetically and explained, "When a captain does that, the crew calls the ship a 'Hen Frigate.' Some whalers won't ship aboard a 'Hen Frigate.' Others prefer it. Say the food and the medicine are apt to be better."

"Do captain's wives ever get seasick?" Whipple asked.

"A little, at first," Hoxworth boomed. "But on a bigger ship, like this, they get over it quickly."

"I'd like to see Amanda and Jerusha as captains' wives," Whipple laughed.

"Did you say Jerusha?" the captain asked.

"Yes. Jerusha Hale, Abner's wife."

"Excellent!" the big man cried. "It's Jerusha I'm marrying, too." And he reached out to grab Abner's small hand. "Where's yours from, Reverend Hale?"

"Walpole, New Hampshire," Abner replied, unhappy at mentioning his wife's name in a whaling cabin.

"Did you say Walpole?" Hoxworth asked.

"Yes."

Big Rafer Hoxworth kicked back his chair and grabbed Abner by the coat. "Is Jerusha Bromley aboard that brig out there?" he asked menacingly.

"Yes," Abner replied steadily.

"God Almighty!" Hoxworth cried, shoving Abner back into his chair.

"Anderson! Lower me a boat!" With fury clouding his face he grabbed his cap, jammed it on the back of his head, and stormed aloft. When Abner and John tried to follow he thrust them back into the cabin. "You wait here!" he thundered. "Mister Wilson!" he bellowed at his mate. "If these men try to leave this cabin, shoot 'em." And in a moment he was on the sea, driving his men toward the brig *Thetis*.

When he swung himself aboard, refusing to wait for a ladder, Captain Janders asked, "Where are the missionaries?" but Hoxworth, dark as the night, roared, "To hell with the missionaries. Where's Jerusha Bromley?" And he stormed down into the smelly cabin, shouting, "Jerusha! Jerusha!" When he found her sitting at the table he swept all the other missionaries together with his giant arms and roared, "Get out of here!" And when they were gone he took Jerusha's hands and asked, "Is what they tell me true?"

Jerusha, with an extra radiance now that she was both recovered from seasickness and in the first happy flush of pregnancy, drew back from the dynamic man who had wooed her four years ago. Hoxworth, seeing this, slammed his powerful fist onto the table and shouted, "Almighty God, what have you done?"

"I have gotten married," Jerusha said firmly and without panic.

"To that worm? To that miserable little . . ."

"To a wonderfully understanding man," she said, drawing herself against a small section of the wall that separated two stateroom doors.

"That goddamned puny . . ."

"Rafer, don't blaspheme."

"I'll blaspheme this whole goddamned stinking little ship to hell before I'll let you . . ."

"Rafer, you stayed away. You never said you would marry me . . ."

"Never said?" he roared, leaping over a fallen chair to grab her to him. "I wrote to you from Canton. I wrote to you from Oregon. I wrote from Honolulu. I told you that as soon as I landed in New Bedford we'd be married, and that you'd sail with me on my ship. It'll be my ship soon, Jerusha, and you're sailing with me."

"Rafer, I'm married. To a minister. Your letters never came."

"You can't be married!" he stormed. "It's me you love, and you know it." He crushed her to him and kissed her many times. "I can't let you go!"

"Rafer," she said quietly, pushing him away. "You must respect my condition."

The big captain fell back and looked at the girl he had been dreaming of for nearly four years. It is true that he had not, on that first wild acquaintance, asked her to marry him, but when the whales were good and his future known, he had written to her, three separate times, cautious lest any one letter not be delivered. Now she said that she was married . . . perhaps even pregnant. To a contemptible little worm with scraggly hair.

"I'll kill you first!" he screamed. "By God, Jerusha, you shall never remain married . . ." And he lunged at her with a chair.

"Abner!" she cried desperately, not knowing that he was absent, for she was certain that if he were aboard the *Thetis,* somehow he would rescue her. "Abner!" The chair crashed by her head and the wild sea captain was upon her, but before she fainted she saw Keoki and the old whaler leaping down into the cabin with hooks and clubs.

Later, the missionaries comforted her, saying, "We heard it all, Sister Hale, and we hoped not to intervene, for he was a madman and we trusted he would recover his senses."

"I had to club him, Mrs. Hale," Keoki apologized.

"Where is he now?"

"Captain Janders is taking him back to his ship," one of the wives explained.

"But where's Reverend Hale?" Jerusha cried in deep love and fear.

"He's on the other ship," Keoki explained.

"Captain Hoxworth will kill him!" Jerusha wailed, trying to get onto the deck.

"That's why Captain Janders went along," Keoki assured her. "With pistols."

But not even Captain Janders was able to protect Abner that night, for although Rafer Hoxworth quieted down on the cooling trip to the *Carthaginian,* and although he was a model of politeness to John Whipple, when he saw Abner, and how small he was and how wormy in manner, he lost control and leaped screaming at the little missionary, lifting him from the deck and rushing him to the railing of the ship, where the blubber had been taken aboard, and possibly because he slipped unexpectedly on grease, or possibly by intention, he raised Abner high into the night and flung him furiously into the dark waves.

"You'll not keep her!" he screamed insanely. "I'll come back to Honolulu and rip her from your arms. By God, I'll kill you, you miserable little worm."

While he was shouting, Captain Janders was desperately maneuvering his rowboat, warning his men, "After they cut a whale there's bound to be sharks." And the rowers saw dark forms gliding in the water, and one brushed Abner, so that he screamed with fear, "Sharks!"

From the dark deck of the *Carthaginian,* Captain Hoxworth roared, "Get him, sharks! Get him! He's over on this side. Here he is, sharks!" And he was raging thus when John Whipple reached into the vast Pacific and pulled his brother aboard.

"Did the sharks get you, Abner?" he whispered.

"They took my foot . . ."

"No! It's all right, Abner. A little blood, that's all."

"You mean my foot isn't . . ."

"It's all right, Abner," Whipple insisted.

"But I felt a shark . . ."

"Yes, one hit at you," Whipple said reassuringly, "but it only scraped the skin. See, these are your toes." And the last thing Abner could remember before he fainted was John Whipple pinching his toes and from a dark distance Rafer Hoxworth screaming futilely, "Get him, sharks! He's over there. Get the stinking little bastard and chew him up. Because if you don't kill him I'll have to."

That was the reason why Abner Hale, twenty-two years old and dressed in solemn black, with a beaver hat nearly as tall as he was, limped as he prepared to land at the port city of Lahaina on the island of Maui in Hawaii. The shark had not taken his foot, nor even his toes, but it had exposed the tendon and damaged it, and not even careful John Whipple could completely repair it.

THE ACTUAL LANDING of the missionaries was a confused affair, for when the *Thetis* drew into the famous wintering port of Lahaina, there was great commotion on shore, and the missionaries saw with horror that many handsome young women were throwing off their clothes and beginning to swim eagerly toward the little brig, which apparently they knew favorably from the past, but the attention of the ministers was quickly diverted from the swimmers to a fine canoe which, even though it started late, soon overtook the naked swimmers and drew up alongside the *Thetis*. It contained a man, a completely nude woman and four attractive girls, equally nude.

"We come back!" the man cried happily, boosting his women onto the little ship.

"No! No!" Keoki Kanakoa cried in a flood of embarrassment. "These are missionaries!"

"My girls good girls!" the father shouted reassuringly, shoving his handsome women aboard as he had done so often in the past. "Those girls swimming no good. Plenty sick."

"Heavenly Father!" Abner whispered to Brother Whipple. "Are they his own daughters?"

At this point two of the girls saw the old whaler who had saved the *Thetis* off the Four Evangelists, and apparently they remembered him kindly, for they ran across the deck, called him by name, and threw their arms about him, but he, seeing Jerusha Hale's dismay, tried to brush them away as a man keeps flies from his face when he is eating.

"Go back! Go back!" Keoki pleaded in Hawaiian, and gradually the four laughing daughters and their beautiful naked mother began to realize that on this ship, unlike all others, they were not wanted, and in some confusion they climbed back into the canoe, which their family had acquired by providing such services to passing ships. Sadly, the man of the house, his day's profits gone, paddled his employees back to Lahaina, and whenever he came to groups of girls swimming to the *Thetis* he called in bewilderment, "Turn back! No girls are wanted!" And the convoy of island beauties sadly returned to the shore and dressed.

Aboard the *Thetis,* Abner Hale, who had never before seen a naked woman, said dazedly to his brothers, "There's going to be a lot of work to do in Lahaina."

Now from the shore came out two other Hawaiians of sharply different character. Abner first saw them when a large canoe, with vassals standing at stern and prow bearing yellow-feathered staffs, became the center of an extraordinary commotion. Islanders moved about in agitation as among them appeared two of the most gigantic human beings Abner had so far seen.

"That's my father!" Keoki Kanakoa shouted to the missionaries, and by choice he came to stand with the Hales, repeating to Abner, "The tall man is my father, guardian of the king's estates."

"I thought he was King of Maui," Abner remarked with disappointment.

"I never said so," Keoki replied. "The people in Boston did. They thought it impressed the Americans."

"Who is the woman?" Jerusha inquired.

"My mother. She's the highest chief in the islands. When my father wants to ask her a question of state, he has to crawl into the room on his hands and knees. So do I." Along the railing the missionaries studied the enormous woman who half climbed, half relaxed as her subjects heaved her fantastic bulk into the canoe. Keoki's mother was six feet four inches tall, stately, long-haired, noble in every aspect, and weighed three hundred and twenty pounds. Her massive forearms were larger than the bodies of many men, while her gigantic middle, swathed in many layers of richly patterned tapa, seemed more like the trunk of some forest titan than of a human being. By her bulk alone it could be seen that she was a chief, but her most conspicuous features were her two splendid breasts, which hung in massive brown grandeur above the soft red and yellow tapa. The missionary men stared in wonder; the women gazed in awe.

"We call her the Alii Nui," Keoki whispered reverently, pronouncing the title Alee-ee. "It is from her that our mana flows."

Abner looked at his young Christian friend in amazement, as if some foul error had corrupted him. "It is from God and not from an alii nui that your spiritual consecration flows," he corrected.

The young Hawaiian blushed, and with attractive candor explained, "When you have lived a long time with one idea, you sometimes express better ideas in the same careless way."

Again Abner frowned, as if his labors with Keoki were being proved futile. "God isn't what you call a *better idea,* Keoki," he said firmly. "God is a superlative fact. He stands alone and brooks no comparisons. You don't worship God merely because He represents a better idea." Abner spoke contemptuously, but Keoki, with tears of considerable joy in his eyes, did not recognize that fact and accepted the words in love.

"I am sorry, Brother Hale," he said contritely. "I used the word thoughtlessly."

"I think it would be better, Keoki," Abner reflected, "if from now on you referred to me in the old way. Reverend Hale. Your people might not understand the title Brother."

Jerusha interrupted and asked, "Didn't we agree that we were to call one another Brother and Sister?"

"That was among ourselves, Mrs. Hale," Abner explained patiently.

"Isn't Keoki one of ourselves?" Jerusha pressed.

"I think the term *ourselves* refers principally to ordained ministers and their wives," Abner judged.

"When you have been ordained, Keoki, it'll be Brother Abner," Jerusha assured the young Hawaiian. "But even though you are not yet ordained, Keoki, I am your Sister Jerusha." And she stood beside him and said, "Your father and mother are handsome people."

With great dignity, and with yellow feathers on the staffs fluttering in the wind, the long canoe approached the *Thetis,* and for the first time the Hales saw the full majesty of Keoki's father. Not so large in bulk as the Alii Nui, he was nevertheless taller—six feet seven—and of striking presence. His hair was a mixture of black and gray. His brown face was cut by deep lines of thought and his expressive eyes shone out from beneath heavy brows. He was dressed in a cape of yellow feathers and a skirt of red tapa, but his most conspicuous ornament was a feathered helmet, close-fitting to the head but with a narrow crest of feathers that started at the nape of the neck, sweeping over the back of the head and reaching well in front of the forehead. By some mysterious trick of either history or the human mind, Kelolo, Guardian of the King's Estates, wore exactly the same kind of helmet as had Achilles, Ajax and Agamemnon, but because his people had never discovered metals, his was of feathers whereas theirs had been of iron.

Seeing his tall son on the deck of the *Thetis,* giant Kelolo deftly grabbed a rope as it was lowered to him, and with swift movements sprang from the canoe onto a footing along the starboard side of the *Thetis* and then adroitly onto the deck. Abner gasped.

"He must weigh nearly three hundred pounds!" he whispered to Jerusha, but she had now joined Keoki in tears, for the affectionate manner in which giant Kelolo and his long-absent son embraced, rubbed noses and wept reminded her of her own parents, and she held her lace handkerchief to her eyes.

Finally Keoki broke away and said, "Captain Janders! My father wishes to pay his respects," and the tough New England sea captain came aft to acknowledge the greeting. Kelolo, proud of having learned from earlier ships how properly to greet a westerner, thrust out his powerful right hand, and as Captain Janders took it, he saw tattooed from wrist to shoulder the awkward purple letters: "Tamehameha King."

"Can your father write in English?" Janders asked.

Keoki shook his head and spoke rapidly in Hawaiian. When Kelolo replied, the son said, "One of the Russians did this for my father. In 1819, when our great king Kamehameha died."

"Why did he spell it Tamehameha?" Janders asked.

"Our language is just now being written for the first time," Keoki explained. "The way you Americans have decided to spell it is neither right nor wrong. My father's name you spell Kelolo. It would be just as right to spell it Teroro."

"You mean the truth lies somewhere in between?" Janders asked.

Eagerly Keoki grasped the captain's hand and pumped it, as if the latter had said something which had suddenly illuminated a difficult problem. "Yes, Captain," the young man said happily. "In these matters the truth does lie somewhere in between."

The idea was repugnant to Abner, particularly since he had been increasingly worried about Keoki's apparent reversion to paganism as Hawaii neared. "There is always only one truth," the young missionary corrected.

Keoki willingly assented, explaining, "In matters of God, of course there is only one truth, Reverend Hale. But in spelling my father's name, there is no final truth. It lies between Kelolo and Teroro and is neither."

"Keoki," Abner said patiently, "a committee of missionaries, well versed in Greek, Hebrew and Latin studied in Honoruru for more than a year deciding how to spell Hawaiian names. They didn't act in haste or ignorance, and they decided that your father's name should be spelled Kelolo."

Thoughtlessly Keoki pointed out: "They also decided the town should be called Honolulu, but its real name is closer to Honoruru, as you said."

Abner flushed and was about to utter some sharp correction when Captain Janders rescued the moment by admiringly grasping Kelolo's tattooed arm and observing, "Tamehameha! A very great king. Alii Nui Nui!"

Kelolo, confused by the earlier argument, smiled broadly and returned the compliment. Patting the railing of the *Thetis* he said in Hawaiian, "This is a very fine ship. I shall buy this ship for Malama, the Alii Nui, and you, Captain Janders, shall be our captain."

When this was translated by Keoki, Captain Janders did not laugh, but looked steadily at Kelolo and nodded sagely. "Ask him how much sandalwood he can bring me for the ship?"

"I have been saving my sandalwood," Kelolo said cautiously. "There is much more in the mountains of Maui. I can get the sandalwood."

"Tell him that if he can get the sandalwood, I can get the ship."

When Kelolo heard the news he started to shake hands in the American manner, but cautiously Captain Janders held back. "Tell him that he does not get the *Thetis* until I have carried the sandalwood to Canton and brought back a load of Chinese goods, which shall be my property to sell."

"That is reasonable," Kelolo agreed, and once more he proudly held forth his hand to bind the bargain. This time Captain Janders grasped it, adding prudently, "Mister Collins, draw up an agreement in three copies. State that we will sell the *Thetis* for a full cargo of sandalwood now, plus an equal amount when we return from China." When the terms were translated, Kelolo solemnly agreed, whereupon Mister Collins whispered, "That's a hell of a lot of sandalwood."

Replied Janders, "This is a hell of a lot of ship. It's a fair deal."

While the towering chief was concluding the deal, Abner had an opportunity to study him closely, and his eye was attracted to the symbol of power that Kelolo wore about his brown neck. From a very thick, dark necklace, apparently woven of some tree fiber, dangled a curiously shaped chunk of ivory, about five inches long and an inch and a half wide, but what was remarkable was the manner in which, at the bottom, a lip flared out and up, so that the entire piece resembled an antique adz for shaping trees.

"What is it?" Abner whispered to Keoki.

"The mark of an alii," Keoki replied.

"What's it made of?"

"A whale's tooth."

"It must be heavy to wear," Abner suggested, whereupon Keoki took the missionary's hand and thrust it under the tooth, so that Abner could test the surprising weight.

"In the old days," Keoki laughed, "you would be killed for touching an alii." Then he added, "The weight doesn't bother him because the necklace of human hair supports it."

"Is that hair?" Abner gasped, and again Keoki passed his friend's hand over the woven necklace, which, Keoki explained, had been made of some two thousand separate braids of plaited hair, each braid having been woven from eighty individual pieces of hair. "The total length of hair," Abner began. "Well . . . it's impossible."

"And all from the heads of friends," Keoki said proudly.

Before Abner could comment on this barbarism a considerable commotion occurred at the side of the *Thetis* and the missionaries ran to witness an extraordinary performance. From the mainmast two stout ropes had been lowered over the canoe which still held Malama, the Alii Nui. The ends of the ropes were fastened to a rugged canvas sling that was customarily slipped under the bellies of horses and cows, hoisting them in this fashion onto the deck of the ship. Today, the canvas sling was being used as a giant cradle into which the men in the canoe gently placed their revered chief, crosswise, so that her feet and arms dangled over the edges of the canvas, which insured her stability, while her enormous chin rested on the hard rope binding which kept the canvas from tearing.

"Is she all settled?" Captain Janders asked solicitously.

"She's squared away," a sailor shouted.

"Don't drop her!" Janders warned. "Or we'll be massacred."

"Gently! Gently!" the men working the ropes chanted, and slowly the gigantic Alii Nui was swung aboard the *Thetis*. As her big dark eyes, ablaze with childish curiosity, reached the top of the railing, while her chin rested on the edge of the canvas and her body sprawled happily behind, she waved her right hand in a grand gesture of welcome and allowed her handsome features to break into a contented smile.

"Aloha! Aloha! Aloha!" she said repeatedly in a low, soft voice, her expressive eyes sweeping the row of black-frocked missionaries in their claw-hammer coats. But her warmest greeting was for the skinny yet attractive young women who stood sedately in the rear. It would have taken almost four Amanda Whipples to equal the bulk of this giant woman as she lay in the canvas sling. "Aloha! Aloha!" she kept crying in her musical voice as she swung over the women.

"For the love of God!" Janders shouted. "Take it easy now. Gently! Gently!" As the ropes were eased over the capstans, the canvas sling slowly dropped toward the deck. Instantly, Captain Janders, Kelolo and Keoki rushed forward to intercept the sling, lest the Alii Nui be bruised in landing, but her bulk was so ponderous that in spite of their efforts to hold the sling off the deck, it pressed its way resolutely down, forcing the men to their knees and finally to a sprawling position. Undisturbed, the noble woman rolled over on the canvas, found her footing, and rose to majestic height, her bundles of tapa making her seem even larger than she was. Quietly, she passed down the line of missionaries, greeting each with her musical "Aloha! Aloha!" But when she came to the storm-tossed women, whose voyage she could imagine and whose underweight she instantly perceived, she could not restrain herself and broke into tears. Gathering little Amanda Whipple to her great bosom she wept for some moments, then rubbed noses with her as if she were a daughter. Moving to each of the women in turn, she continued her weeping and smothered them in her boundless love.

"Aloha! Aloha!" she repeated. Then, facing the women and ignoring their husbands as she did her own, she spoke softly, and when her son interpreted the words, they said: "My adorable little children, you must think of me always as your mother. Before, the white men have sent us only sailors and shopkeepers and troublemakers. Never any women. But now you come, so we know that the intentions of the Americans must at last be good."

Malama, the Alii Nui, the most sacred, mana-filled human being on Maui, waited grandly while this greeting was being delivered, and when the missionary wives acknowledged it, she moved down the line again, rubbing noses with each of the women and repeating, "You are my daughter."

Then, overcome both by the emotion and the exertions of getting aboard the *Thetis,* Malama, her great moon-face sublime in new-found comfort, slowly unfastened the tapas that bound her great bulk. Handing the ends to her servants, she ordered them to walk away from her, while she unwound like a top until she stood completely naked except for a hair necklace from which dangled a single majestic whale's tooth. Scratching herself in gasping relief, she indicated that she would lie down, and chose the canvas sling as a likely place, but when she stretched out on her stomach the missionaries were appalled to see tattooed along the full length of her left ham the purple letters: "Tamehameha King Died 1819."

"Did the Russians do that, too?" Captain Janders asked.

"They must have," Keoki replied. He asked his mother about the memento, and she twisted her head to study it. Tears came into her eyes and Keoki explained. "She was the nineteenth wife of Kamehameha the Great."

Jerusha gasped, "Why she was no better than a concubine!"

"In many ways," Keoki continued, "Malama was the favorite of the king's last years. Of course, since she was the Alii Nui, she was entitled to other husbands as well."

"You mean she was married to your father . . . at the same time?" Abner asked suspiciously.

"Of course!" Keoki explained. "Kamehameha himself consented, because my father was her younger brother, and their marriage was essential."

"Throw some water on that woman!" Captain Janders shouted, for one of the missionary wives, overcome by Malama's nudity and marital complications, had fainted.

Keoki, sensing the reasons, went to his mother and whispered that she ought to cover herself, for Americans hated the sight of the human body, and the great sprawling woman assented. "Tell them," she said enthusiastically, "that henceforth I shall dress like them." But before Keoki could do this she quietly asked Captain Janders if he could provide her with some fire, and when a brazier was fetched she fed into its flames the tapas she had been wearing. When they were consumed she announced grandly: "Now I shall dress as the new women do."

"Who will make your dress?" Abner asked.

Imperiously, Malama pointed to Jerusha and Amanda and said, "You and you."

"Tell her you'd be happy to," Abner hastily whispered, and the two missionary women bowed and said, "We will make your dress, Malama, but we have not so much cloth, because you are a very big woman."

"Don't make her angry," Abner warned, but Malama's quick intelligence had caught the burden of Jerusha's meaning, and she laughed.

"In all your little dresses," she cried, indicating the mission women with a sweep of her mighty arm, "there is not enough cloth for my dress." And she signaled her servants to fetch bundles from the canoe, and before the startled eyes of the mission women, length after length of the choicest Chinese fabric was unrolled. Settling finally on a brilliant red and a handsome blue, she pointed to the housedress worn by Amanda Whipple and announced quietly, "When I return to shore, I shall be dressed like that."

Having given the command, she went to sleep, her naked bulk protected from flies by servants who swept her constantly with feathered wands. When she woke, Captain Janders inquired if she would like some ship's food, but she refused haughtily and ordered her servants to lift great calabashes of food from the canoe, so that while the mission wives perspired over the tentlike dress they were building, she reclined and feasted on gigantic portions of roast pig, breadfruit, baked dog, fish and three quarts of purple poi. Midway in the meal her attendants hammered her stomach in ancient massage rituals so that she could consume more, and during these interruptions she grunted happily as the food was manipulated into more comfortable positions inside her cavernous belly.

Keoki explained proudly, "The Alii Nui has to eat huge meals, five or six times a day, so that the common people will see from a distance that she is a great woman."

Into the evening the missionary women sewed while their husbands prayed that Malama would receive them well and allow them to lodge a mission at Lahaina; but the seamen of the *Thetis* prayed no less devoutly that soon both the missionaries and the fat woman would leave so that the girls waiting anxiously on shore could swim out to the brig and take up their accustomed work.

At ten the next morning the enormous red and blue dress was finished, and Malama accepted it without even bothering to thank the mission women, for she lived in a world in which all but she were servants. Like an awning protecting a New England store, the great dress was lowered into position over her dark head, while her streams of black hair were pulled outside and allowed to flow down her back. The buttons were fastened; adjustments were made at the waist, and the great Alii Nui jumped up and down several times to fit herself into the strange new uniform. Then she smiled broadly and said to her son, "Now I am a Christian woman!"

To the missionaries she said, "We have waited long for you to help us. We know that there is a better way of living, and we seek instruction from you. In Honolulu the first missionaries are already teaching our people to read and write. In Maui I shall be your first pupil." She counted on her fingers and announced firmly: "In one moon, mark this,

Keoki, I will write my name and send it to Honolulu . . . with a message."

It was a moment of profound decision, and all aboard the *Thetis* save one were impressed with the gravity of this powerful woman's determination; but Abner Hale perceived that Malama's decision, while notable in that an illiterate heathen of her own will sought instruction, was nevertheless a step in the wrong direction, so he moved before her and said quietly, "Malama, we do not bring you only the alphabet. We have not come here merely to teach you how to write your name. We bring you the word of God, and unless you accept this, nothing that you will ever write will be of significance."

When the words were translated to Malama her enormous moon-face betrayed no emotion. Forcefully she said, "We have our own gods. It is the words, the writing that we need."

"Writing without God is useless," Abner stubbornly reiterated, his little blond head coming scarcely to Malama's throat.

"We have been told," Malama answered with equal firmness, "that writing helps the entire world, but the white man's God helps only the white man."

"You have been told wrong," Abner insisted, thrusting his stubborn little face upward.

To everyone's surprise Malama did not reply to this but moved to face the women, asking, "Which one is the wife of this little man?"

"I am," Jerusha said proudly.

Malama was pleased, for she had observed how capably Jerusha managed the work of making the big dress, and she announced: "For the first moon, this one shall teach me how to read and write, and for the next, this one," indicating Abner, "shall teach me the new religion. If I find that these two new learnings are of equal importance, after two moons I shall advise you."

Nodding to the assembly, she went gravely to the canvas sling, commanding her servants to unbutton her dress and remove it. Then she ordered Jerusha to show her how to fold it, and in massive nakedness lay down crosswise upon the canvas, her feet dangling aft, her arms forward, with her chin resting upon the rope edging. The capstans groaned. The sailors hefted the ropes and swung them over the eaves, and Captain Janders shouted, "For Christ's sake, things are going well. Don't drop her now!"

Inch by inch the precious burden was lowered into the canoe until finally the Alii Nui was rolled off the canvas and helped into an upright position. Clutching the new dress to her cheek she cried in full voice, "You may now come ashore!" And as the ship's boats were lowered to convey the missionaries to their new home, they fell in line behind Malama's canoe, with its two standard-bearers fore and aft, its eager servants brushing away the flies, and with tall, naked Malama holding the dress close to her.

Prior to Malama's arbitrary choice of the Hales as her mentors, there had been some uncertainty as to which missionaries should be assigned to Maui and which to the other islands, but now it was apparent that the first choice, at least, had been made, and as the boats neared shore, Abner studied the intriguing settlement to which he was now committed. He saw one of the fairest villages in the Pacific, ancient Lahaina, capital of Hawaii, its shore marked by a fine coral strand upon which long waves broke in unceasing thunder, their tall crests breaking forward in dazzling whiteness. Where the surf finally ended, naked children played, their teeth gleaming in the sunlight.

Now for the first time Abner saw a coconut palm, the wonder of the tropics, bending into the wind on a slim resilient trunk and maintaining, no one knew how, its precarious foothold on the shore. Behind the palms were orderly fields reaching away to the hills, so that all of Lahaina looked like one vast, rich, flowering garden.

"Those darker trees are breadfruit," Keoki explained. "They feed us, but it's the stubby ones with the big heads that I used to miss in Boston . . . the kou trees with their wonderful shade for a hot land."

Jerusha joined them and said, "Seeing the gardens and the flowers, I think I am at last in Hawaii."

And Keoki replied proudly, "The garden you are looking at is my home. There where the little stream runs into the sea."

Abner and Jerusha tried to peer beneath the branches of the kou trees that lined the land he spoke of, but they could see little. "Are those grass houses?" Abner queried.

"Yes," Keoki explained. "Our compound holds nine or ten little houses. How beautiful it seems from the sea."

"What's the stone platform?" Abner asked.

"Where the gods rested," Keoki said simply.

In horror Abner stared at the impressive pile of rocks. He could see blood dripping from them and heathen rites. He mumbled a short prayer to himself, "God protect us from the evil of heathen ways," then asked in a whisper, "Is that where the sacrifices . . ."

"There?" Keoki laughed. "No, that's just for the family gods."

The boy's laugh infuriated Abner. It seemed strange to him that as long as Keoki remained in New England, lecturing to church audiences about the horrors of Hawaii, he had sound ideas regarding religion, but as soon as he approached his evil homeland, the edge of his conviction was blunted. "Keoki," Abner said solemnly, "all heathen idols are an abomination to the Lord."

Keoki wanted to cry, "But those aren't idols . . . not gods like Kane and Kanaloa," but as a well-trained Hawaiian he knew that he should not argue with a teacher, so he contented himself with saying quietly, "Those are the friendly little personal gods of my family. For example, sometimes the goddess Pele comes to talk with my father . . ." With some embarrassment he realized how strange this must sound, so he did not go on to explain that sharks also sometimes came along the shore to talk with Malama. "I don't think Reverend Hale would understand," he thought sadly to himself.

To hear a young man who hoped some day to become an ordained minister speak in defense of heathen practices was unbearable to Abner, and he turned away in silence, but this act seemed cowardice to him, so he returned to the young Hawaiian and said bluntly, "We shall have to remove the stone platform. In this world there is room either for God or for heathen idols. There cannot be room for both."

"You are right!" Keoki agreed heartily. "We have come to root out these old evils. But I am afraid that Kelolo will not permit us to remove the platform."

"Why not?" Abner asked coldly.

"Because he built it."

"Why?" Abner pressed.

"My family used to live on the big island, Hawaii. We had ruled there for countless generations. It was my father who came here to Maui . . . one of Kamehameha's most trusted generals. Kamehameha gave him most of Maui, and the first thing Kelolo did was to build the platform you saw. He insists that Pele, the volcano goddess, comes there to warn him."

"The platform will have to go. Pele is no more."

"The big brick building," Keoki interrupted, pointing to a rugged edifice rising at the end of the stunted pier that edged cautiously out to sea, "is Kamehameha's old palace. Behind it is the royal taro patch. Then, you see the road beyond? That's where the foreign sailors live. Your house will probably be erected there."

"Are there Europeans in the village?"

"Yes. Castaways, drunks. I worry about them much more than I do about my father's stone platform."

Abner ignored this thrust, for his eyes were now attracted by the most conspicuous feature of Lahaina. Behind the capital, rising in gentle yet persistent slopes, cut by magnificent valleys and reaching into dominant peaks, stood the mountains of Maui, majestic and close to the sea. Except for the ugly hills at Tierra del Fuego, Abner had never before seen mountains, and their conjunction with the sea made them memorable, so that he exclaimed, "These are the handiwork of the Lord! I will lift up mine eyes unto the hills!" And he was overcome by an urge to say a prayer of thanksgiving to a Lord who had created such beauty, so that when the little mission band stepped ashore for the first time on the beach at Lahaina, he convoked a meeting, smoothed out his claw-hammer coat, took off his beaver hat, and lifted his sallow face toward the mountains, praying: "Thou hast brought us through the storms and planted our feet upon a heathen land. Thou hast charged us with the will to bring these lost souls to Thy granary. We are unequal to the task, but we beseech Thee to give us Thy constant aid."

The missionaries then raised their voices in the hymn that had recently come to summarize such efforts around the world, "From Greenland's icy mountains," and when the surging second verse was reached, each sang as if it had been written with Hawaii alone in mind:

"What though the spicy breezes
Blow soft o'er Ceylon's isle,
Tho' every prospect pleases,
And only man is vile;
In vain with lavish kindness
The gifts of God are strown.
The heathen in his blindness
Bows down to wood and stone."

It was unfortunate that this was the first hymn to be sung in Lahaina, for it crystallized a fundamental error in Abner's thinking. As long as he lived he would visualize Lahaina as a place "where every prospect pleases, and only man is vile." He would perpetually think of the Hawaiian as both heathen and blind; and now, as the singing ended, Abner saw that he and his mission band were surrounded by a huge crowd of naked savages, and he was instinctively afraid, so that he and his friends huddled together for mutual protection.

Actually, no missionaries in history had so far visited a gentler or finer group of people than these Hawaiians. They were clean, free from repulsive tropical diseases, had fine teeth, good manners, a wild joy in living; and they had devised a well-organized society; but to Abner they were vile.

"Almighty God!" he prayed. "Help us to bring light to these cruel hearts. Give us the strength to strike down each heathen idol in this land where only man is vile."

Jerusha, however, was thinking: "Soon these people will be reading. We will teach them how to sew and to clothe themselves against the storm. Lord, keep us strong, for there is so much work to do."

The prayers were broken by the noise of men running up with a canoe, one that had never touched the sea, for it was carried aloft by ten huge men with poles on their shoulders. With ceremony they deposited it before Malama and she climbed in, for since the Hawaiians had not discovered the wheel they had no carriages. Standing aloft, Malama unfolded her new dress and ordered her servants to slip its enormous folds over her head. As it cascaded past her huge breasts and the tattooed shank with its memory of Kamehameha, the Alii Nui wiggled several times and felt the blue and red masterpiece fall into place. "Makai!

Makai!" squealed the women in the crowd, approving their Alii Nui in her new garb.

"From now on I shall dress like this!" she announced solemnly. "In one moon I am going to write a letter to Honolulu, because I have good teachers." Reaching down, she touched Abner and Jerusha, indicating that they must join her in the canoe. "This man is my teacher of religion, Makua Hale," she announced, and in Hawaiian style she called his name Halley, by which he was known thereafter. "And this is my teacher of words, Hale Wahine. Now we will build my teachers a house."

The bearers raised the canoe aloft, adjusted the poles to their shoulders, and at the head of a mighty procession containing feathered staffs, drums, court attendants and more than five thousand naked Hawaiians, the Hales set forth on their first magical journey through Lahaina, with Keoki trotting along beside the canoe, interpreting for his mother as she identified the subtle beauties of her island.

"We are now passing the royal taro patch," Keoki explained. "This little stream brings us our water. This field is a choice location, because it has so many fine trees, and this is where Malama says we are to build your house."

The bearers carried the Alii Nui to the four corners of the proposed dwelling, and at each she dropped a stone, whereupon servants began immediately to lay out a grass house, but before they had accomplished much, Malama grandly indicated that the procession must now move to her palace.

"This is the main road," Malama pointed out. "Toward the sea are the fine lands where the alii live. Toward the mountains are lands for the people. In this great park lives the king when he is in residence."

"What are all those little grass buildings . . . like dog houses?" Abner asked.

When his question was interpreted, Malama laughed vigorously and said, "Those are the people's houses!"

"They don't look big enough to live in," Abner argued.

"The common people don't live in them . . . not like the alii in their big house," Malama explained. "They keep their tapa in them . . . sleep in them if it rains."

"Where do they live the rest of the time?" Abner asked.

Spreading her huge arms grandiloquently to embrace the entire countryside, Malama replied, "They live under the trees, beside the rivers, in the valleys." And before Abner could reflect on this, the canoe came to a spacious and beautiful park, set off by a wall of coral blocks three feet high, inside of which stretched an extensive garden of flowers and fruit trees, interspersed with a dozen grass houses and one large pavilion looking out over the sea. It was to this building that Malama and the Hales were carried, and as the huge woman climbed out of the canoe, she announced: "This is my palace. You will always be welcome here."

She led the way into a cool spacious room outlined by woven grass walls, handsome wooden pillars and a narrow doorway which permitted a view of the sea. The floor was made of fine white pebbles covered by pandanus matting, upon which Malama with a gasp of relief threw herself, propping her big chin on her hands and stating firmly, "Now teach me to write!"

Jerusha, who could not even recall how she herself had been taught, sixteen remote years ago, stammered, "I am sorry, Malama, but we need pens and papers . . ."

Her protests were silenced by a voice as soft as polished bronze. "You will teach me to write," Malama commanded with terrifying majesty.

"Yes, Malama." Jerusha trembled. Looking about the room, she happened to see some long sticks with which Malama's women had been beating intricate designs onto tapa and beside them several small calabashes of dark dye. Taking one of the sticks and a length of tapa, she smeared out the word MALAMA. As the giant woman studied it, Jerusha explained, "That is your name."

When Keoki translated this, Malama rose and inspected the word from varying angles, repeating it proudly to herself. Grabbing the stick rudely, she splashed it in the dye and started to trace the cryptic symbols, sensing fully the magic they contained. With remarkable skill she reproduced the word exactly. "Malama!" she repeated a dozen times. Then she drew the word again and again. Suddenly she stopped and asked Keoki, "If I sent this word to Boston, would people there know that it was my word, Malama?"

"You could send it anywhere in the world and people would know that it was your word," her son assured her.

"I am learning to write!" the huge woman exulted. "Soon I shall send letters to all the world. The only difference between white men who rule everything and us Hawaiians is that white men can write. Now I shall write, too, and I will understand everything."

This error was too profound for Abner to tolerate, and he interjected, "I warned you once, Malama, that a woman can learn to write words, but they are nothing. Malama, I warn you again! Unless you learn the Commandments of the Lord, you have learned nothing."

The walls of the grass house were thick, and not much light entered the area where Malama stood with her length of stick, and in the shadows she seemed like the gigantic summary of all Hawaiians: powerful, resolute, courageous. Once on Hawaii in the days of her husband Kamehameha's war she had strangled a man much larger than the puny, sallow-faced individual who stood before her, and she was constrained now to brush him aside as her servants brushed away the flies, but she was impressed by his dogged insistence and by the power of his voice. More important, she suspected that he was right; the mere trick of writing was too easy; there must be additional hidden magic that enforced it; and she was about to listen to the little man with the limp, when he pointed his finger at her and shouted, "Malama, do not learn merely the outlines of the words. Learn also what they mean!" His manner was insufferable, and with a sweep of her immense right arm, thicker than his entire body, she knocked him off his feet. Returning to the tapa she wrote furiously, splashing her name across it.

"I can write my name!" she exulted, but even as she did so, Abner's persuasive words plagued her, and abruptly she threw down the stick and went to where he lay sprawled on the tapa. Kneeling beside him, she studied his face for a long time, then said softly, "I think you speak the truth, Makua Hale. Wait, Makua Hale. When I have learned to write, then I will come to you." Then she ignored him and in her silky voice commanded Jerusha: "Now teach me to write."

The lesson continued for three hours, until Jerusha grew faint and would have stopped. "No!" Malama commanded. "I have not much time to waste. Teach me to write!"

"I am growing dizzy in the heat," Jerusha protested.

"Fan her!" Malama ordered, and when the young woman indicated that she must halt, Malama pleaded: "Hale Wahine, while we waste time, men who can read and write are stealing our islands. I cannot wait. Please."

"Malama," Jerusha said weakly, "I am going to have a baby."

When Keoki explained the meaning of these words to Malama, the great Alii Nui underwent a transformation. Thrusting Abner from the large room, she ordered her servants to carry Jerusha to an area where more than fifty of the finest tapas had been piled to make a day bed. When the slim girl had been placed on the pile, Malama swiftly felt for her stomach and judged, "Not for many months," but without Keoki in the room she could not explain this conclusion to the white woman. She could see, however, that Jerusha was exhausted and she blamed herself for what had been a lack of consideration. Calling for water, she ordered Jerusha's white face bathed, and then lifted her in her arms, a mere child against her own huge bulk. Rocking back and forth, she nursed the tired mission woman to sleep, then placed her once more gently on the tapas. Rising quietly, she tiptoed to where Abner waited and asked in a whisper, "Can you also teach me to write?"

"Yes," Abner said.

"Teach me!" she commanded, and she kneeled beside the little New England missionary as he began logically, "To write my language requires twenty-six different letters, but you are fortunate, because to write your language requires only thirteen."

"Tell him to teach me the twenty-six!" she commanded Keoki.

"But to write Hawaiian you need only thirteen," Abner explained.

"Teach me the twenty-six!" she said softly. "It is to your countrymen that I wish to write."

"A, B, C," Abner began, continuing with the lesson until he, too, felt faint.

WHEN THE TIME CAME for the *Thetis* to depart, almost the entire population of Lahaina appeared to bid the ship farewell, and the foreshore was dark with naked bronzed bodies following each movement of the departing missionaries. At last the twenty who would go to other locations assembled at the small stone pier to sing their sweet blend of mournfulness and hope, "Blest be the tie that binds," and as their dedicated voices rose in unison, the watching Hawaiians could detect not only an inviting melody but a spirit of the new god of whom Abner Hale and their own Keoki Kanakoa had already begun to preach. When the hymn spoke of tears, the eyes obliged, and soon the vast congregation, led by the missionaries, was weeping.

In one respect the sorrow was not formal but real. When Abner and Jerusha watched John Whipple prepare to sail they could not mask their apprehension, for he was the only doctor in the islands, and with him absent, Jerusha knew that when her term of pregnancy was ended, the success of her childbirth would depend upon how well her youthful husband had mastered his book lessons. Whipple, sensing this concern, promised, "Sister Jerusha, I shall do everything possible to return to Maui to help you. But remember that on the other end of the island Brother Abraham and Sister Urania will be living, and since her time does not coincide with yours, perhaps you shall be able to visit by canoe and help each other."

"But you will try to come back?" Jerusha pleaded.

"I will do my best," Whipple swore.

Jerusha Hale and Urania Hewlett then sought out each other and shook hands solemnly: "When the time comes, we'll help each other." But they knew that they would be separated by miles of mountains and by treacherous seas.

Now the wailing increased, for from the shaded road that led southward to the homes of the alii, Malama's canoe advanced, borne on the shoulders of her men, and she, dressed in blue and red, wept more than any. Descending from her strange palanquin, she moved to each of the departing missionaries and said, "If elsewhere in the islands you find no home, come back to Lahaina, for you are my children." Then she kissed each in turn, and wept anew. But the gravity of the situation was somewhat marred by the fact that as the mission people rowed out to the *Thetis* they met, swimming back, more than a dozen naked girls, their long black hair trailing in the blue waters; and when they reached shore, each carrying a hand mirror—more precious here than silver in Amsterdam—or some lengths of ribbon or a hammer which they had stolen, Malama greeted them exactly as affectionately as she had the departing Christians.

And then, to the eastward where stout waves broke on the coral reef, thundering shoreward in long, undulant swells whose tips were spumed in white, the missionaries witnessed for the first time one of the mysteries of the islands. Tall men and women, graceful as gods, stood on narrow boards and by deftly moving their feet and the gravity of their bodies, directed the boards onto the upper slopes of the breaking waves, until at last they sped with frightening swiftness over the waters. And when the wave died on the coral beach, somehow the swimmer and his board subsided back into the water, as if each were a part of the Hawaiian sea.

"It's unbelievable!" Dr. Whipple cried. "The momentum creates the balance," he explained.

"Could a white man do that?" Amanda asked.

"Of course!" her husband replied, excited by the vicarious sense of speed and control created by the deft athletes.

"Could you do it?" Amanda pressed.

"I'm going to do it," John replied, "as soon as we get to Honolulu."

One of the older missionaries frowned at this intelligence, marking it down as one more proof of their doctor's essentially trivial attitude toward life, but his adverse opinion was not reported to his companions, because from a point forward of the *Thetis* a new board swept into view, and this one bore not a mere swimmer, but a nymph, a nude symbolization of all the pagan islands in the seven seas. She was a tall girl with sun-shot black hair streaming behind her in the wind. She was not grossly fat like her sisters but slim and supple, and as she stood naked on the board her handsome breasts and long firm legs seemed carved of brown marble, yet she was agile, too, for with exquisite skill she moved her knees and adjusted her shoulders so that her skimming board leaped faster than the others, while she rode it with a more secure grace. To the missionaries she was a terrifying vision, the personification of all they had come to conquer. Her nakedness was a challenge, her beauty a danger, her way of life an abomination and her existence an evil.

"Who is she?" Dr. Whipple whispered, in hushed amazement at her skill.

"Her name Noelani," proudly explained a Hawaiian who had shipped on whalers and who had mastered the barbarous pidgin of the seaports. "Wahine b'long Malama. Bimeby she gonna be Alii Nui." And as he spoke the wave subsided near the shore; the fleet rider and her board died away from vision and returned to the sea, yet even when the missionaries looked away they could see her provocative presence, the spirit of the pagan island, riding the waves, so that a blasphemous thought came to the mind of John Whipple. He was tempted to express it, but fought it down, knowing that none would understand his meaning, but at last he had to speak and in a whisper he observed to his tiny wife: "Apparently there are many who can walk upon the waters."

Amanda Whipple, a truly devout woman, heard these strange words and caught their full savor. At first she was afraid to look at her scientifically minded husband, for sometimes his thoughts were difficult to follow, but the implications of this blasphemous conclusion no one could escape, and at last she turned to look at John Whipple, thinking: "One person can never understand another." But instead of censuring the young doctor for his irregular thoughts she looked at him analytically for the first time. Coldly, dispassionately, carefully, she looked at this strange cousin who stood beside her in the hot Hawaiian sunlight, and when she was finished studying him, she loved him more than ever.

"I do not like such words, John," she admonished.

"I had to speak them," he replied.

"Do so, always, but only to me," she whispered.

"It will be very difficult to understand these islands," John reflected, and as he and his wife watched the sea, they noticed the nymph Noelani —the Mists of Heaven—paddling her board back out to the deeper ocean where the big waves formed. Kneeling on her polished plank, she bent over so that her breasts almost touched the board. Then, with powerful movements of her long arms, she swept her hands through the water and her conveyance shot through the waves faster than the missionary boat was being rowed. Her course brought her close to the *Thetis,* and as she passed, she smiled. Then, selecting a proper wave, she quickly maneuvered her board, and finding it properly oriented, rose on one knee. From the missionary boat John Whipple whispered to his wife, "Now she will walk upon the waters." And she did.

When the *Thetis* sailed, Abner and Jerusha, feeling dismally alone, had an opportunity to inspect the house in which their labors for the next years would be conducted. Its corner posts were stout trees from the mountains, but its sides and roof were of tied grass. The floor was pebbled and covered with pandanus, to be swept by a broom of rushes, but its windows were mere openings across which cloth from China had been hung. It was a squat, formless grass hut with no divisions into rooms. It had no bed, no chairs, no table, no closets, but it did have two considerable assets: at the rear, under a twisting hau tree, it had a spacious lanai—a detached porch—where the life of the mission would be conducted; and it had a front door built in the Dutch fashion so that the bottom half could remain closed, keeping people out, while the top was open, allowing their smiles and their words to enter.

It was into this house that Abner moved the furniture he had brought out from New England: a rickety bed with rope netting for its mattress; rusted trunks to serve as closets; a small kitchen table and two chairs and a rocker. Whatever clothes they might require in years to come they would get only through the charity of Christians in New England, who would forward barrels of cast-off garments to the mission center in Honolulu, and if Jerusha needed a new dress to replace her old one, some friend in Honolulu would pick through the leftovers and say, "This one ought to fit Sister Jerusha," but it never did. If Abner required a new saw with which to build even the minor decencies of living, he had to hope that some Christian somewhere would send him one. If Jerusha needed a cradle for her babies, she could get it only from charity. The Hales had no money, no income, no support other than the communal depository in Honolulu. Even if they were fevered to the point of death they could buy no medicine; they had to trust that Christians would keep replenished their little box of calomel, ipecac and bicarbonate.

Sometimes Jerusha, recalling either her cool, clean home in Walpole, its closets filled with dresses kept starched by servants, or the two homes that Captain Rafer Hoxworth had promised her in New Bedford and aboard his ship, understandably felt distressed by the grass hut in which she toiled, but she never allowed her feelings to be discovered by her husband and her letters home were uniformly cheerful. When the days were hottest and her work the hardest she would wait until evening and then write to her mother, or to Charity or Mercy, telling them of her alluring adventures, but with them, even though they were of her own family, she dealt only in superficialities; increasingly it would be to Abner's sister Esther, whom she had never met, that she would pour out the flood of deeper thoughts that swept over her. In one of her earliest letters, she wrote:

"My most Cherished Sister in God, Dear Esther. I have been strangely mournful these days, for sometimes the heat is unbearable in Lahaina, whose name I find means Merciless Sun, and no appellation could be more appropriate. Possibly these have been unduly difficult weeks, for Malama has pressed me endlessly to teach her, and although she cannot pay attention to lessons for more than an hour at a time, as soon as her interest flags she calls for her servants to massage her, and as they do, commands me to tell her a story, so I tell her of Mary and Esther and Ruth, but when I first spoke of Ruth's leaving her home to dwell in an alien land, I am afraid that tears fell, and Malama saw this and understood and drove the massaging women away and came to me and rubbed noses with me and said, 'I appreciate that you have come to live with us in a strange land.' Now whenever she wants a story she insists like a child that I tell her again of Ruth, and when I come to the part about the strange land, we both weep. She has never once thanked me for anything I have done for her, considering me only an additional servant, but I have grown to love her, and I have never known a woman to learn so fast.

"For some curious reason I have been impelled, these last few days, to talk with you, for I feel that of all the people I remember in America, your spirit is closest to my own, and I have wanted to tell you two things, my beloved sister in God. First, I thank you daily for having written to me as you did about your brother Abner. Each day that passes I find him a stronger man, a finer servant of God. He is gentle, patient, courageous and extremely wise. Sharing his burdens, in this new land which he is determined to resurrect, is a joy that I had never in America even dimly anticipated. Each day is a new challenge. Each night is a benediction to good work either started or completed. In my letters to you I have never spoken of love, but I think that now I know what love is, and my dearest wish for you is that some day you may find a Christian gentleman as worthy as your gentle brother. His limp is much improved, but I massage his muscles each night. To be more correct, I *used* to massage them, but lately a very plump Hawaiian woman who is known to be highly skilled in the lomilomi, the medicinal massage of the islands, insists upon doing the job for me. I can hear her now, a huge motherly woman announcing, 'Me come lomilomi little man.' I tell her repeatedly that she must refer to my partner and guide as 'Makua,' which means Father, but this she will not do.

"The second thought I would share with you is my growing sense of working directly under the will of God. At one time I did not know whether I had a true vocation for mission work or not, but as the weeks go past and as I see the transformation that we are accomplishing in these islands, I am doubly convinced that I have found for myself the one satisfying occupation on earth. I rejoice to see each new dawn, for there is work to do. At five o'clock in the morning, when I look out into our yard, I see it filled with patient, handsome brown faces. They are willing to remain there all day in hopes that I will teach them how to sew or talk with them about the Bible. Malama promises me that when *she* has learned to read and write, I can start to teach her people to do the same, but she will not allow any of them to master the tricks until she has done so. However, she has consented to this. In her afternoon lessons she allows her children and those of the other alii to listen, and I find that her beautiful daughter Noelani is almost as quick as Malama herself. My dear husband has great hopes for Noelani and feels certain that she will be our second Christian convert on the island, Malama of course being first. Darling Esther, can you, in your mind's eye, picture the intense wonder that comes over a pagan face when the clouds of heathenish evil and illiteracy are drawn away so that the pure light of God can shine into the seeking eyes? What I am trying to tell you, dearest sister, is that I find in my work a supreme happiness, and although what I am about to say may seem blasphemy—and I can say it to no other but my own dear sister—in these exciting fruitful days when I read the New Testament I feel that I am reading not about Philemon and the Corinthians but about Jerusha and the Hawaiians. I am one with those who labored for our Master, and I cannot convey even to my dear husband the abounding joy I have discovered in my grass shack and its daily circle of brown faces. Your Sister in God, Jerusha."

While Jerusha was teaching Malama, Abner was free to explore the village, and one day he noticed that all the men and many of the stronger women were absent from Lahaina, and he could not discover why. The alii were present, and in their large grass homes south of the royal taro patch they could be seen, moving about beneath the kou trees or going to the beach in order to ride their surfboards on the cresting waves. It was good to be an alii, for then one's job was merely to eat enormous calabashes of food so as to grow large, and to play at games, so as to be ready if war came. Year by year the alii grew greater and more skilled in games, waiting for a war that came no more.

But one of the alii was missing, for Kelolo had not been to visit the missionaries for some days. He had sent food and three planks out of which Abner had hacked shelving for rude closets, but he himself had not appeared, and this handicapped Abner, because only Kelolo could say where the church was to be built. Then, when the missionary had reached the height of impatience, he discovered that Kelolo was out at the edge of town, digging a deep, wide pit. Keoki was not present to translate when Abner found the excavation, and all Kelolo would say was, *"Thetis,"* measuring the deep pit with his arms extended.

Abner was still perplexed when he saw, staggering along the beach, a procession of more than two thousand men and women, the dust from their movements filling the sky. They were goaded along by royal lieutenants, and they were burdened heavily by bundles of logs cut into six-foot lengths and slung from their backs by vines. The yellowish wood was obviously precious, for if even a small piece fell, sharp-eyed lieutenants struck the careless carrier and directed trailing women to salvage the dropping, for this was sandalwood: aromatic as no other, choice in the markets of Asia, the life-blood of Hawaiian commerce, and the goal of all Americans. It was the treasure and the curse of Hawaii.

Deep in the forests the trees hid, less than thirty feet high and marked by pale green leaves. Years ago, before their worth was known, the trees had flourished even in the lowlands, but now all those of easy access were gone, chopped down by the alii for whom they were kapu. Kelolo, if he wanted the two shiploads that would pay Captain Janders for the *Thetis,* had to drive his servants high into the mountains and on into remote corners of the island. Now, as the heavily burdened men staggered to the pit, Abner understood. On that first day while he had been instructing Malama, Captain Janders had laid out a pit the exact size of the *Thetis'* hatch, and when the pit was filled with sandalwood twice over, the ship would be Kelolo's.

As the precious logs tumbled into the excavation, Kelolo's men jumped in and laid them close together, for Janders had insisted many times, "No air! No air!" and Abner realized that these men had been in the mountains for some days. He was therefore disturbed when Kelolo ordered them back into the forests immediately. Summoning Keoki, Abner argued: "Your father shouldn't take his men back at once. What will happen to the taro beds? Who will catch the fish?"

"They're his men," Keoki explained.

"Of course they are," Abner agreed. "But it's in Kelolo's own best interests that they be given a rest."

"When an alii smells sandalwood, the mind turns and thought departs," Keoki replied.

"I must see your father," Abner insisted.

"He won't want to see you now," Keoki warned. "His mind is concerned only with sandalwood."

Nevertheless, Abner donned his black claw-hammer, tall hat and best stock, his invariable uniform when delivering the word of the Lord. In the heat of the day he strode southward past the king's quarters and out to the cool kou trees and the great grass houses of Malama and her consort-brother. He heard his wife Jerusha instructing huge Malama in the writing of letters, American style, but he paid no attention, for he wished to see only Kelolo, and he found him playing in the surf.

The chief, seeing Abner's official uniform, and not wanting a lecture at this time, refused to come out of the water, so Abner had to pick his way gingerly along the sandy shore, shouting above the waves as they washed in. "Kelolo!" he cried like a prophet from the Old Testament. "You have broken every promise to me." Imitating his instructor's voice, Keoki repeated the words.

"Tell him to go away!" Kelolo grunted, splashing water into his big face and rolling about in deep pleasure.

"Kelolo! You have not set aside the land for the church."

"Oh, I'll give you land for the church . . . one of these days," the sybaritic nobleman shouted back.

"Today!" Abner demanded.

"When I finish with the sandalwood," Kelolo promised.

"Kelolo, it is not sensible to lead your men back into the forests right away."

The big man scratched his back on a coral head and growled, "You've got to get sandalwood when you can find it."

"It is wrong to demand so much of your men!"

"They're my men!" the chief insisted. "They'll go where I tell them to go."

"It is wrong, Kelolo, to hoard sandalwood when the taro patches and the fish ponds remain unattended."

"The taro will take care of itself," Kelolo said grimly, diving deep to be rid of the irritating voice.

"Where will he come up?" Abner asked.

"Over there," Keoki replied, and the missionary ran along the sand, holding onto his tall hat, so that when the chief surfaced, there was Abner staring at him.

"Kelolo, God says we must respect all who work."

"They're my men," the huge nobleman growled.

"And that platform," Abner continued. "It's not been taken down."

"Don't touch the platform!" Kelolo warned, but the missionary was disgusted with the chief's behavior and ran awkwardly across the sand to the offending platform of old gods and reached down to throw aside the rocks of which it was composed.

"No!" warned Keoki, but Abner would not listen, and began tossing the ancient stones into the sea. One rolled near Kelolo, and when he saw his own handiwork thus destroyed, he uttered a wild cry, leaped from the surf and dashed inland, grabbing the lame little missionary by his claw-hammer coat and throwing him violently to one side.

"Don't touch the rocks!" he roared.

Abner, stunned by the suddenness of the attack, rose unsteadily to his feet and studied the naked giant who guarded the platform. Recovering his hat, he placed it firmly on his head and moved resolutely toward the collection of rocks. "Kelolo," he said solemnly, "this is an evil place. You will not let me build a church but you hold onto your evil old gods. This is wrong." And with his right index finger extended as far as it would reach, he pointed directly at the chief. "It is hewa."

The naked warrior, hero of battles, was inspired to pick up this worrisome little man and crush him, but the solemnity of Abner's manner stopped him, and the two stood there under the kou trees, staring at each other, and finally Kelolo temporized: "Makua Hale. I promised you land for a church, but I must wait until my king sends word from Honolulu."

"Shall we tear down this evil place?" Abner asked quietly.

"No, Makua Hale," Kelolo said firmly. "This is my church in the old fashion. I will help you build your church in the new fashion."

Quietly Abner said, "When I stand beside these rocks, Kelolo, I can hear the voices of all the victims who were sacrificed here. It is an evil memory."

"It was not that kind of temple, Makua Hale," Kelolo said forcefully. "This was a temple of love and protection. I cannot surrender it."

Abner had the sense to bow to this decision, but he did so in a way that Kelolo never forgot. Lifting one of the stones reverently, the little missionary looked at it and said, "If you consider this a rock from a temple of mercy I can understand why you wish to preserve it. But I shall build a church that will truly be a temple of mercy, and you will see the difference. To your temple, Kelolo, only the strong alii could come. In my temple it will be the weak and the poor who will find mercy. And when you see the mercy that spreads out from my temple, Kelolo, believe me, you will come to this shore and throw every rock in this pile far out to sea." And Abner strode to the shore in as impressive a manner as his limp would allow, and at the edge of the sea he drew back his arm and pitched the solitary rock far into the waves. Then, holding his hat, he came back to Kelolo and said, "We will build my church."

The tall chieftain kept his promise. Wrapping his tapa about him, he marched through the hot sunlight to a fine piece of land north of the mission grounds, where he paced off a generous area and said, "You can build your church here."

"This is not enough land," Abner protested.

"Enough for one god," Kelolo replied.

"Your own temples have more land," Abner argued.

"But they also have more gods," Kelolo explained.

"My God is bigger than all the gods in Hawaii."

"How much land does he require?"

"He wants a church of this size," Abner insisted, and Kelolo was astonished.

But when the marking out was completed, he said, "Good. I will call the kahunas to determine how the church should be arranged."

Abner did not understand Keoki's translation and asked, "What's he going to do?"

"Call the kahunas," Keoki explained.

"What for?" Abner asked in astonishment.

"The kahunas have to decide where the door should be, where the people will sit," Keoki explained.

Kelolo, sensing Abner's repugnance, hurried to explain, "You must not build a church without permission from the kahunas."

Abner felt dizzy. Frequently since his arrival on Maui he had been confronted by positive confusion. Malama and Kelolo both eagerly wanted Christianity for their island, and each had given substantial signs of surrendering a good deal to the new religion, but repeatedly they indicated that they considered it not a new religion, not a truth that would shatter old ways and introduce salvation, but merely a better religion than the one they had. Once Kelolo had reasoned, "If Jesus Christ can give you big ships with many sails, and Kane gives us only canoes, Jesus Christ must be much better. He is welcome." Malama, impressed always with the power of the written word, had corrected her husband. "It is not ships that Jesus Christ brings. It is the mana there in the black box," she said, indicating the Bible. "When we learn to read what is in the box, we will know the secret of mana, and we too will be strong."

"Jesus does not bring either ships or books," Abner had patiently explained. "He brings light that illuminates the soul."

"We'll take the light, too," Kelolo had agreed, for he was tired of his smoky oil-nut candles when the white man's whale-oil lamps were so obviously superior.

"I do not mean that kind of light," Abner had started to say, but sometimes the Hawaiians were too much for him. Now, however, he was adamant. "No kahuna, no evil, heathenish priest is going to say how we shall build the church of God."

"But kahunas . . ." Kelolo began.

"No!" Abner shouted. "The door will be here. The steeple will be here." And he placed big stones at the critical orientations. When he was finished, Kelolo studied the intended building for a long time. He looked to the hills and beyond them to the mountains. He studied the pathway of the little stream and the distance to the sea, but mostly he studied the rise and fall of the land, as if it consisted of human hands waiting to receive the building which would soon rest within the palms.

Finally he shook his head sadly and said, "The kahunas won't like it."

"The kahunas will never enter it," Abner said stiffly.

"You'll keep out the kahunas!" Kelolo gasped.

"Of course. This is a church for those who obey Jehovah and keep his Commandments."

"But the kahunas are eager to join," Kelolo protested. "They all want to find what power it is your god has that enables his people to build boats and make new lights that are better than ours. Oh, you'll have no better people in your church than the kahunas!"

Again the dizziness—the crazy irrationality of Hawaii—attacked Abner and he explained slowly, "I have come with the Bible to wipe out the kahunas, their gods and their evil ways."

"But the kahunas love Jesus Christ," Kelolo cried. "He is so powerful. I love Jesus Christ!"

"But you are not a kahuna," Abner countered.

Slowly, Kelolo raised himself to his full austere height. "Makua Hale, I am the Kahuna Nui. My father was the Kahuna Nui, and his father, and his father all the way back to Bora Bora."

Abner was stunned by this intelligence, but he felt that the moment was critical and that he must not surrender his position. "I don't care if your great-grandfather Bora Bora was a kahuna . . ."

"Bora Bora is an island," Kelolo said proudly.

"I never heard of it."

Now Kelolo was astonished. "In Boston they did not teach you about . . ." He stopped, thought a moment, and then placed his right foot on the stone indicating the door to Abner's church. "Makua Hale, we are in the time when gods are changing. These are always difficult times. When I argue as a kahuna, I am not defending the old gods of Hawaii. They have already been defeated by your god. We all know that. But I am speaking as the kahuna who knows this land. I have often spoken with the spirits of Lahaina and I understand the hills. Makua Hale, believe me when I tell you that this door is wrong for this land."

"We will build the door here," Abner said resolutely.

Sadly, Kelolo studied the obstinate man who understood so little about churches, but he argued no more. "Now I will lead my men back to the sandalwood trees. When we have returned three times, I will direct them to build your church."

"Three times! Kelolo, the crops will be ruined by then."

"They are my men," the huge chief said stubbornly, and that evening he led two thousand of them back into the hills.

ON THE THIRTIETH DAY after the arrival of the missionaries at Lahaina, Malama, the Alii Nui, had her handmaidens clothe her in the new China silk dress that Jerusha Hale had sewed for her. She put on shoes for the first time—heavy sailor's shoes with the laces untied—and covered her wealth of long black hair with a wide-brimmed straw hat from Ceylon. Then she ordered her servants to lay new tapa with extra care, and when this was done she lay prone on the floor, directed the fanning to begin, and spread before her a sheet of white paper, an ink pot and a China quill. "Now I shall write!" she announced, and in a clean, disciplined hand she composed this letter in Hawaiian for her nephew in Honolulu:

"Liholiho King. My husband Kelolo is working hard. He is going to buy a ship. Aloha, Malama."

When this exacting task was completed, the huge woman heaved a sigh and pushed the letter toward Jerusha and Abner. Then women came in to lomilomi her, and she smiled proudly from the floor as Jerusha said, "I have never known a person to learn as fast as Malama." When Keoki translated this, his mother stopped smiling and brushed away the lomilomi women, saying, "Before long I shall write to the king of America . . . in your language . . . and I shall use all twenty-six letters."

"She'll do it!" Jerusha said proudly.

"Now, little daughter," Malama said, "you have taught me well. You must go home and rest. It is Makua Hale who shall teach me now." Dismissing Jerusha she rolled over on her belly again, propped her chin in her hands, stared at him intensely and commanded, "Tell me about your god."

Abner had long anticipated this holy moment, and he had constructed a patient, step-by-step explanation of his religion, and as he began to speak with Keoki's help, he sensed that the huge woman on the floor was passionately eager to know all that he knew, so he worked with special care, choosing each word exactly and consulting often with Keoki as to its translation into Hawaiian, for he knew that if he could win Malama to the side of God, he would automatically win all of Maui.

"God is a spirit," he said carefully.

"Can I ever see him?"

"No, Malama."

She pondered this for some moments and said, "Well, I could never see Kane, either." Then she added suspiciously, "But Kelolo has often seen his goddess, Pele of the volcanoes."

Abner had sworn to himself that he would not be led down by-paths. He was not here to argue against Kelolo's miserable assortment of superstitions. He was here to expound the true faith, and he knew from experience that once he started on Kelolo's gods he was apt to get tangled up in irrelevant arguments.

"God is a spirit, Malama," he repeated, "but He created everything."

"Did he create heaven?"

Abner had never confronted this problem, but he replied unhesitatingly, "Yes."

"Where is heaven?"

Abner was going to say that it is in the mind of God, but he took the easier course and replied, "Up there."

"Are you certain in your heart, Makua Hale, that your god is more powerful than Kane?"

"I cannot compare the two, Malama. And I cannot explain God to you if you insist upon comparing them. And don't call Him my God. He is absolute."

This made sense to Malama, for she had witnessed the white man's superior power and knew instinctively that his god must also be superior, and she was gratified to hear Abner proclaim the fact. On this principle she was ready to accept his teaching completely. "God is all-powerful," she said quietly. "Then why did he bring the sailors' pox to infect our girls? Why does he make so many Hawaiians die these days?"

"Sin is permitted by God, even though He is all-powerful, for it is sin that tests men and proves them in God's eyes." He paused, and Malama indicated to one of her many servants that they must keep the flies off the missionary, too, and soft feathers swept his neck and forehead. Although he appreciated the attention, he felt that Malama's instructions had been an interruption consciously commanded by the woman to provide time for her thinking, so he added gravely, looking directly at the chieftain, "If you continue in sin, you cannot know God." Pausing dramatically and bringing his face close to hers, he said with great force, preparing the way for the great decision that would later become inevitable, "Malama, to prove that you know God you must put away sin."

"Is it possible that the Alii Nui herself is sinful?" Malama asked, for her religion took care of this problem by postulating that the acts of the alii were the acts of gods.

But she was to discover that in Abner Hale's new religion the answer was strikingly different. Pointing his forefinger at the prone woman he said firmly, "All men on earth are totally depraved. We abide in sin. Our natures are permeated and corrupted in all parts of our being." He paused, then fell to his knees so that he would be closer to the Alii Nui, and added, "And because kings have greater power, their sin is greater. The Alii Nui is the most powerful woman in Maui. Therefore her sin is greater. Malama," he cried in the woeful, desperate voice of John Calvin, "we are all lost in sin!"

A child cried in one of the surrounding huts, and Malama asked, "Is that baby filled with sin, too?"

"From the moment that child was born . . . No, Malama, from the moment it was conceived, it was steeped in sin. It was drowned in mortal vice, horrible, perpetual, inescapable. That child is totally corrupt."

Malama pondered this and asked tentatively, "But if your god is all-powerful . . . ." Then she stopped, for she was willing to accept Abner's earlier answer. She thought aloud: "God has arranged sin to test us."

Abner smiled for the first time. "Yes. You understand."

"But what will happen, Makua Hale, to that baby if it is not rescued from sin?"

"It will be plunged into fire everlasting."

"What will happen to me, Makua Hale, if I am not saved from sin?"

"You will be plunged into fire everlasting." There was a pause in the grass house as Malama shifted her weight on the tapas. Rolling over on her right side, she leaned her jawbone on her right hand and motioned Abner to sit on the tapa near her.

"What is the fire like?" she asked quietly.

"It leaps about your feet. It tears at your eyeballs. It fills your nose. It burns incessantly, but you are constantly re-created so that it can burn you again. Its pain is horrible beyond imagining. Its . . ."

Malama interrupted, asking weakly, "Once I traveled with Kamehameha to the edge of a burning lava flow, and I stood with him when he sacrificed his hair to appease Pele. Are the fires worse than that?"

"Malama, they are much worse."

"And all the good Hawaiians who died before you came here, Makua Hale? Are they living in that perpetual fire?"

"They died in sin, Malama. They now live in that fire."

The huge woman gasped, took away her right elbow and allowed her head to fall onto the tapa. After a moment she asked, "My good uncle, Keawe-mauhili? Is he in the fire?"

"Yes, Malama, he is."

"Forever?"

"Forever."

"And my husband Kamehameha?"

"He is in the fire forever."

"And that baby, if it dies tonight?"

"It will live in the fire forever."

"And my husband Kelolo, who swears he will never accept your religion?"

"He will live in the fire forever."

"And I will never see him again?"

"Never."

The remorselessness of this doctrine overcame Malama, and for the first time she sensed the truly awful power of the new god, and why those who followed him were victorious in war and could invent cannon that swept away tribal villages. She fell to sobbing, "Auwe. Auwe!" and thought of her good uncle and her great king wasting in fires eternal, and her servants brought cool cloths to ease her, but she brushed them away and continued weeping and beating her huge breasts. Finally she asked, "Can those of us who are still alive be saved?"

This was the question that had once given Abner most trouble: "Can all be saved?" and it stunned him to hear it coming so precisely from the mouth of a heathen, for it was the touchstone of his religion, and he replied, "No, Malama, there are many whom God has predestined for eternal hellfire."

"You mean they are condemned even before they are born?"

"Yes."

"And there is no hope for them?"

"They are predestined to live in evil and to die into hellfire."

"Oh, oh!" Malama wept. "Do you mean that that little baby . . ."

"Perhaps."

"Even me, the Alii Nui?"

"Perhaps."

This awful concept struck Malama with great force. It seemed a lottery of life and death . . . a god throwing smoothed pebbles into a rock hole . . . and sometimes missing. But it was the god who missed, and not the pebble, for unless the god had wanted to, he need not have missed. With pebbles he was all-powerful.

Then Abner was speaking: "I must confess, Malama, that all who slide into evil do so by the divine will of God and that some men are destined from birth to certain fire, that His name may be glorified in heaven because of their destruction. It is a terrible decree, I do confess, but none can deny that God foresaw all things for all men before He created them. We live under His divine ordinance."

"How can I be saved?" Malama asked weakly.

Now Abner's face became radiant, and his infusion of spirit transferred itself to the weeping woman, and she began to feel in the grass house a consolation that would never depart. "When God foredoomed all men," Abner said forcefully, "His great compassion directed Him to send to us His only begotten son, and it is Jesus Christ who can save us, Malama. Jesus Christ can enter this house and lift you by the hand and lead you to cool waters. Jesus Christ can save us."

"Will Jesus save me?" Malama asked hopefully.

"He will!" Abner cried joyously, clasping her huge hands in his. "Malama, Jesus Christ will enter this room and save you."

"What must I do to be saved?"

"There are two things required, Malama. The first is easy. The second is difficult."

"What is the easy one?"

"You must go down on your knees before the Lord and acknowledge that you are totally corrupt, that you live in sin, and that there is no hope for you."

"I must confess those things?"

"Unless you do, you can never be saved." Now the little missionary became once more the stern teacher, for he withdrew his hands, moved away from the prone chieftain and pointed at her: "And you must not only say the words. You must believe them. You are corrupt, Malama. Evil, evil, evil."

"And what is the second task?"

"You must work to attain a state of grace."

"I don't know what grace is, Makua Hale."

"When you have honestly confessed your corruption, and when you plead for God's light, some day it will come to you."

"How will I recognize it?"

"You will know."

"And when I have found this . . . What is the word, Keoki?"

Her son explained again and she asked him, "Did you find grace?"

"Yes, Mother."

"Where?"

"On the stone pavement in front of Yale College."

"And was it a light, as Makua Hale says."

"It was like the heavens opening up," Keoki assured her.

"Will I find grace?"

"No one can say for sure, Mother, but I think you will, for you are a good woman."

Malama pondered this for some time, and then asked Abner, "What things have I been doing that are sinful?"

For a moment Abner was tempted to believe that this was the instant when he must excoriate the evil ways of the Alii Nui, but a more sober judgment prevailed and he restrained himself, saying, "Malama, you learned how to write in only thirty days. It was a miracle. Therefore I think you can perform the greater miracle that awaits."

Malama, loving praise and steeped in it since her first days as the Alii Nui, firmed her jaw and asked, "What is required?"

"Will you take a walk with me?"

"Where?"

"Through your land . . . through the land you rule."

Malama, exhilarated by her success in learning, agreed, and summoned her land canoe; but with all the able men in the mountains seeking sandalwood, there were none to man the carrying poles, and Abner raised his first disturbing question: "Why do you allow your workingmen to toil like slaves in the hills?"

"They're after sandalwood," Malama explained.

"For what?"

"For Kelolo's ship."

"Is the ruin of a beautiful island worth a ship?" Abner asked.

"What do you mean, Makua Hale?"

"I want you to walk with me, Malama, and see the fearful price Lahaina is paying for the sandalwood that Kelolo is seeking in the mountains." So Malama summoned her maids-in-waiting, and a procession was formed that would, in time, modify the history of Hawaii. The little missionary limped in front, accompanied by towering Keoki. Behind them marched gigantic Malama in a blue and red dress. On her right walked the handmaiden Kalani-kapuai-kala-ninui, five feet tall and two hundred and fifteen pounds, while on the left puffed Manono-kaua-kapu-kulani, five feet six inches and two hundred and eighty pounds. Side by side, the three alii women filled the road as Abner began his perambulatory sermon.

"A ship at this time, Malama, is merely a vanity. Look at the walls of the fish pond. Crumbling."

"What does it matter?" Malama asked.

"If the fish escape, the people will starve," Abner said.

"When the men come back . . . from the sandalwood . . ."

"The fish will be gone," Abner reported dolefully. "Malama, you and I will rebuild the fish pond." And he stepped into the mud, calling her after him. Quickly, she perceived what he was teaching and ordered her handmaidens to help, and the three huge women plunged into the fish pond, pulling the back hems of their new dresses forward and up between their legs like giant diapers. Giggling and telling obscene jokes which Abner could not understand—among themselves they called him "the little white cockroach"—the alii mended the breaks, and when they were finished, Abner hammered home his lesson: "The wise Alii Nui commands the fish ponds to be patrolled."

A little farther on he pointed to a grass house that had burned to the ground. "Four people died there, Malama. A wise Alii Nui would outlaw the use of tobacco."

"But the people like to smoke," Malama protested.

"And so you let them burn to death. Since I came to Lahaina, six of your people have burned to death. A wise Alii Nui . . ."

"Where are you taking me?" Malama interrupted.

"To a spot a little farther under the kou trees," Abner explained, and before long he had Malama and the women standing beside a small oblong of freshly dug earth, and she recognized it immediately for what it was. She preferred not to speak of this little plot of earth, but Abner said, "Beneath here lies a baby girl, Malama."

"I know," the Alii Nui said gently.

"The child was placed here by her own mother."

"Yes."

"Alive."

"I understand, Makua Hale."

"And while the child was still alive, the mother covered it with earth and stamped upon the earth until the little girl . . ."

"Please, Makua Hale. Please."

"A wise Alii Nui, one who sought grace, would order this evil to be stopped." Malama said nothing, and the procession marched on until it reached the spot where three sailors were buying whiskey from an Englishman, and on the arms of the sailors were the four pretty girls whose father had paddled them to the *Thetis* on its arrival. "These are the girls who will soon die of sailor's pox," Abner said mournfully. "A wise Alii Nui would outlaw whiskey and keep the girls from going to the ships."

They passed the taro patches, rank with weeds, and the little pier with bales of goods from China waiting in the sun and rain. No men were in the fishing boats. When the circuit was at last completed, the little missionary pointed at the platform of stones in Malama's own front yard and said, "Even at your door you harbor the evil old gods."

"That's Kelolo's temple," Malama said. "It does no harm."

At the mention of the absent chief, Abner knew that the ultimate moment had come, the one toward which he had been building. He asked Malama to dismiss her attendants, and when they were gone he led the huge chieftain and Keoki to a smooth spot under the kou trees, and when all were comfortably seated he said forcefully, "I have taken you on this walk, Malama, to show you that God appoints a woman His Alii Nui for a reason. He gives you great power so that you may produce great good. More is expected of you than of ordinary people."

This made much sense to Malama, for the tenets of her old religion were not markedly different . . . only the interpretation. If a man was an alii, he was expected to die in battle. A woman alii must appear noble and eat enormously so that she seemed bigger than she was. In all religions there were duties, but she was not prepared for the one which the little missionary was about to propose.

"You will never enter a state of grace, Malama," Abner said slowly, "so long as you commit one of the gravest sins in human history."

"What is that?" she asked.

Abner hesitated, and the concept he now had to discuss was so loathsome to him that he rose, drew back a few steps and pointed at the Alii Nui: "You have as your husband your own brother. You must send Kelolo away."

Malama was appalled at the suggestion. "Kelolo . . . why he . . ."

"He must go, Malama."

"But he is my favorite husband," she protested.

"This relationship is evil . . . it is forbidden by the Bible."

At this news a benign light of comprehension shone over Malama's face. "You mean it is kapu!" she asked brightly.

"It is not kapu," Abner insisted. "It is forbidden by God's law."

"That's what kapu means," Malama explained patiently. "Now I understand. All gods have kapu. You mustn't eat this fish, it is kapu. You mustn't sleep with a woman who is having her period, it is kapu. You mustn't . . ."

"Malama!" Abner thundered. "Being married to your brother is not kapu! It's not some idle superstition. It's a law of God."

"I know. I know. Not a little kapu like certain fish, but big kapu, like not entering a temple if you are unclean. All gods have big and little kapus. So Kelolo is a big kapu and he must go. I understand."

"You don't understand," Abner began, but Malama was so pleased with her comprehension of this aspect, at least, of the new god, that she was spurred to action, and she summoned her servants in a loud voice.

"Kelolo will not live in this house any more! He will live in that house!" And she indicated one of the compound quarters about twenty feet removed from his previous residence. The law promulgated, she beamed at Abner.

"That is not enough, Malama. He must move out of the compound altogether."

At this, Malama said something to Keoki which the young man was too embarrassed to translate, but Abner insisted, and Keoki, blushing, explained, "My mother says that she stopped sleeping with her four other husbands years ago and you need have no fear that she will misbehave . . ." Keoki stopped, for he did not have the words. "Anyway, she says that Kelolo is a kind man and she hopes he can stay within the compound."

Angrily, Abner stamped his foot and shouted, "No! This is an evil thing. Tell her it is the biggest kapu of all . . . Wait, don't use that word! Tell her merely that the Lord says specifically that Kelolo must move outside the compound."

Malama began to cry and said that Kelolo was more to her than either a husband or a brother and that . . . Abner interrupted and said simply, "Unless he moves, Malama, you will never be able to join the church."

She did not understand this and asked, "I will not be allowed inside the big new church Kelolo is going to build?"

"You may come inside," Abner said gently. "Even the worst sinner may come and listen. And you may sing, too. But you may never join the church . . . the way Keoki has joined."

Malama considered this for a long time, concluding brightly, "Very well. I'll sing and keep Kelolo."

"And when you die," Abner said, "you will burn in hell forever and ever."

Malama knew she was being maneuvered into a corner, so with tears in her big deep eyes she said to Keoki, using sly words that Abner would not be able to detect, "I do not want to burn in hell, so you must build Kelolo a small house outside the compound, but brush the path well so there are no leaves, and at night he can tiptoe back to my room and God will not hear him." Then, in a loud voice she announced: "Makua Hale, I am going to write a new letter."

When she was sprawled once more on the floor of her palace, she tore up the earlier message, bit her pen and wrote:

"Liholiho King. I have told Kelolo he must now sleep outside. He is buying a ship. I think it is a foolish thing to do. Your aunt, Malama."

She handed Abner the letter, and when he had read it she said, "Tomorrow and tomorrow and the day after that I want you to come here to talk with me about the duty of an alii nui. After one moon I shall find a state of grace."

"It cannot be done in that way, Malama."

"When can I find it?"

"Perhaps never."

"I will find it!" the great woman roared. "You will come here tomorrow and teach me how to find it."

"I cannot do that, Malama," Abner said resolutely.

"You . . . will . . . do . . . it!" she threatened.

"No man can find grace for another," Abner stubbornly insisted.

Malama leaped to her feet with strange agility and grabbed her little mentor by the shoulders "How shall I find grace?" she demanded.

"Do you really want to know, Malama?"

"Yes," she replied, shaking him as if he were a child. "Tell me!"

"Kneel down," he commanded, and he did so himself, showing her how to pray.

"What do I do now?" she whispered, turning her big eyes at him.

"Close your eyes. Make a temple of your hands and say, 'Jesus Christ, my master, teach me to be humble and to love Thee.' "

"What is humble?" Malama asked, her voice lower.

"Humble means that even the greatest alii nui in Maui is no more than a man who catches mullet from the fish pond," Abner explained.

"You mean that even the slave . . ."

"Malama," Abner said in ashen voice, overcome by his own perception of God's law, "it seems to me that right now the lowliest slave hauling sandalwood from the forest has a better chance of finding grace than you do."

"Why?" the kneeling woman begged.

"Because at any moment he may find God, for he has a humble spirit. But you are proud, and argumentative, and unwilling to humble yourself before the Lord."

"You are proud, too, Makua Hale," the huge woman argued. "Do you humble yourself before the Lord?"

"If He told me tomorrow to march into the waves until they overcame me, I would do so. I live for the Lord. I serve the Lord. The Lord is my light and my salvation."

"I understand," the Alii Nui said. "I will pray for humbleness." And when he left, she was still kneeling with her hands forming the steeple of a church.

For the next several days Abner did not see Malama, for serious riots were sweeping Lahaina, and with Kelolo and the men gone, only Abner was left to combat them. Trouble started when three whaling ships, in from the Off-Japan grounds, sent more than eighty men ashore on overdue leave. The first place they visited was Murphy's grog shop, and from there they branched out through Lahaina, fighting, debauching, and at last murdering. Emboldened by the lack of police to discipline them, they formed mobs and began sacking Hawaiian homes, searching for girls, and when they found any, they dragged them to the ships, not waiting to discover whether these were normal ships' girls or not, and in this way many faithful wives of men off on the sandalwood expedition were raped.

At last, Abner Hale put on his black claw-hammer, his best stock and his tall beaver hat, and went down to the pier. "Row me out to the whalers!" he commanded the useless old men who were lounging along the shore, and when he reached the first ship he found that the captain was gone, and at the second the captain was locked in his room with a girl and would not speak with the missionary, cursing him through the door, but at the third ship Abner found a captain who sat below drinking whiskey, and to him Abner said, "Your men are debauching Lahaina."

"That's what I brought 'em here fer," the captain said.

"They're raping our women, Captain."

"They always do, in Lahaina. The women like it."

"Last night there was murder," Abner continued.

"You catch the murderer and we'll hang him."

"But he could be one of your men."

"Probably was. Eight of my men deserve hangin'. I'd love to see 'em all swingin' from an arm."

"Captain, have you no sense of responsibility for what is going on ashore?"

"Look, Reverend," the captain said wearily, "for the last two nights I been ashore meself. Only reason I'm not there now is I'm too damned old . . . for three nights in a row, that is."

There was a great cry from ashore, and one of the grass houses went up in flames. From the captain's quarters Abner could see the blaze and it seemed near his home, and he was panicked for fear that Jerusha might be in danger. Pointing his finger at the captain he threatened: "Captain Jackson, of the *Bugle* out of Salem, I shall write to your church, Captain, and advise your minister of how one of his members conducts himself in Lahaina."

"By God!" the captain roared, pushing away his grog. "If you men tion my name in your letters . . ." He lunged at Abner, but was drunk and missed him, his huge bulk crashing into the wall.

"You cannot be two men, Captain," Abner said solemnly. "A beast in Lahaina and a saint in Salem. You must stop the rioting."

"I'll strangle your dirty little chicken neck!" Captain Jackson shouted, clutching for the missionary, who had no trouble evading him. "You get off this ship! Lahaina was a good port till you came along."

Ashore another house went up in flames, and as Abner reached the deck he could see four sailors chasing a girl who had thus been routed out for their sport. "May God forgive them," Abner prayed. "But with such leaders . . ." He swung himself down into his canoe and returned to shore, determined at least to protect Jerusha, lest the violence disturb her pregnancy, but before he could get to her, there was a new commotion, and now even the stragglers along the shore became excited, for three large sailors had been prowling about the back area of Malama's compound and had discovered her young daughter Noelani, and were now dragging her through the dusty streets until they could find a comfortable spot in which to rape her, and she was screaming in Hawaiian, while the sailors cursed in English.

A few old men, too weak to be with the sandalwooders, proved themselves loyal to their alii and tried to stop the rapists, but they were laughingly pushed aside, for in justice to the sailors they could not distinguish between an ordinary girl, with whom such conduct was customary, and an alii, with whom it was sacrilege. Other old men tried to intervene, but they also were bowled over with shocking jolts to the jaw, and the drunken sailors proceeded with their captive.

At this point Abner Hale limped up, holding onto his top hat, and he pointed his right hand in the faces of the sailors and cried, "Set loose that girl."

"Get out of the way, little man!" the sailors warned.

"I am a minister of God!" Abner warned them.

The first two sailors stopped at this, but the third swaggered up to the missionary and shouted, "In Lahaina there is no God."

Abner, who weighed only half of what the sailor did, impulsively slapped the man in the face. "God is watching you!" he said solemnly.

The slapped man quickly squared off, British fashion, to demolish Abner, whereupon the two other sailors released the girl and grabbed their partner, but when they saw fair Noelani run away, the most beautiful girl they had so far found, they became infuriated and started to strike and punch and kick at Abner. He was saved by Malama herself, for the great alii had seen the abduction of her daughter and had hurried up with what men and women she could command.

"It's the queen!" one of the sailors shouted, and as big Malama waded into the midst of the riot, the men withdrew from beating Abner and ran, cursing, to assemble their mates. Soon more than forty sailors, most of them drunk, crowded the dusty street and shouted imprecations at the missionary and the women who were protecting him. "Come over here, you coward!" they challenged, but whenever an especially bold one spoke, Malama went bravely to him and damned him in Hawaiian, so that after a while the sailors dispersed, and Abner saw with horror that from the shadows two ship's captains had watched the affair with approval.

"What kind of men are they?" he wondered, and when the mob had gone back to Murphy's grog shop and Malama was attending his bruises, he said quietly, in broken Hawaiian, "Do you see what happens when the men are away gathering sandalwood?"

"I see," Malama said. "I will send the women to the hills."

That night was one of terror, for the sailors, goaded by their captains, could find no girls, so they surrounded Abner's home and cursed him vilely till midnight. Then they burned another house and finally found three girls, whom they hauled off to the ship. At two in the morning, when the rioting was its worst, Abner said to Jerusha, "I will leave Keoki and the women here with you. I am going to speak with Pupali." And by a back route he scurried to the home of Pupali, the ardent canoeist whose occupation it was to paddle his own wife and four daughters to incoming whalers.

He sat on the floor with Pupali, no light showing, and asked in broken Hawaiian, "Why do you take your own daughters to these evil men?"

"I get cloth and sometimes even tobacco," Pupali explained.

"Don't you see that some day your daughters may die from the sailors' disease?" Abner pleaded.

"Some day everybody dies," Pupali rationalized.

"But is a little money worth this to you?" Abner argued.

"Men like girls," Pupali said truthfully.

"Do you feel no shame in selling your own wife to the sailors?"

"Her sister takes care of me," Pupali said contentedly.

"Are you proud when the sailors burn down the houses?" Abner pressed.

"They never burn my house," Pupali replied.

"How old is your prettiest daughter, Pupali?"

Abner could hear him suck in his breath in pride. "Iliki? She was born in the year of Keopuolani's illness."

"Fourteen, and probably already sick to death!"

"What do you expect? She's a woman."

On the spur of the moment Abner said, "I want you to give her to me, Pupali."

At last something was happening that the rough old man could understand. Smiling lasciviously he whispered, "You'll enjoy Iliki. All the men do. How much you give me for her?"

"I am taking her for God," Abner corrected.

"I know, but how much you give me?" Pupali pressed.

"I will clothe her and feed her and treat her as my daughter," Abner explained.

"You mean, you don't want . . ." Pupali shook his head. "Well, Makua Hale, you must be a good man." And when morning dawned, Abner, in the dust of riots, started his school for Hawaiian girls. His first pupil was Pupali's most beautiful daughter, Iliki, and when she appeared she wore only a thin slip about her hips and a silver chain around her neck, from which dangled a whale's tooth handsomely carved with these words:

Observe the truth; enough for man to know
Virtue alone is happiness below.

When the other island families saw what an advantage Pupali enjoyed by having his daughter as an observer within the missionary household, for she could report on the strangest occurrences, they offered their girls, too, which nullified Pupali's superiority, so that he countered by enrolling his other three daughters, and when the next whaling ship touched port, matters were different. Before, sailors had instructed the Lahaina girls in profanity in the steaming fo'c's'ls; now Jerusha taught them cooking and the Psalms in the mission garden, and her ablest pupil was Iliki, Ee-Lee-Kee, the Pelting Spray of Ocean.

ABNER WAS NOT PRESENT to congratulate Iliki on the August afternoon when she first wrote her name and carried it proudly to her father, for that morning had brought an exhausted messenger to Lahaina. He had run across the mountains from the other side of the island, blurting out so bizarre a story that Abner summoned Keoki to translate formally, and the young man said, "It is true! Abraham and Urania Hewlett have marched all the way from Hana, at the opposite end of Maui."

"Why didn't they take a canoe?" Abner asked, puzzled.

Keoki rapidly interrogated the gasping messenger and then looked blank as the man explained. "It's hard to believe," Keoki muttered. "Abraham and Urania set out yesterday morning at four o'clock in a double canoe, but at six o'clock the waves were so great that the canoe broke apart, so Abraham brought his wife ashore through the surf. Then they walked forty miles to Wailuku, where they are now."

"I thought that trail was impossible for women," Abner argued.

"It is. The worst on Maui. But Urania had to make it, because next month she is due to have her baby and they wanted to be with you."

"What can I . . ." Abner began in bewilderment.

"They are afraid she is dying," the messenger said.

"If she's dying . . ." Abner was sweating and nervous. "Well, how did she get to Wailuku?"

With gestures, the messenger explained, "The paddlers from the wrecked canoe tied vines under her arms and pulled her up the gullies. Then, when it came time to go down the other side, they grabbed the vines . . ."

Before the tired messenger could finish, Abner knelt in the dust and raised his hands. He could visualize Urania, a dull woman and frightened, undergoing this tremendous trip, and he prayed, "Dear Heavenly Father, save Thy servant, Sister Urania. In her hours of fear, save her."

The messenger interrupted and said, "Abraham Hewlett says you must bring your book and help him."

"The book?" Abner cried. "I thought . . ."

"They need you now," the messenger insisted. "Because when I left she seemed about to have the baby."

The idea of assisting at a birth appalled Abner, but he hurried out to the garden where Jerusha was teaching her girls, and from his frightened look she knew that some new island crisis had occurred, but she was not prepared when he said, "Sister Urania was trying to reach us for help, but she has had to stop in Wailuku." The Hales had never spoken of Urania's pregnancy, just as, for reasons of delicacy, they had never mentioned Jerusha's, trusting that by some miracle the baby would either be born without trouble or wait until Dr. Whipple happened along. Now, under the coconut trees, they had to acknowledge imminent facts.

"I will take Deland's *Midwifery* and do what I can," Abner said dully, but what he wanted to cry was: "I will be with you, Jerusha! By the will of God, I will see that your baby is well born."

And she replied, "You must help Sister Urania," but what she intended was: "I am afraid, and I wish my mother were here."

So the two young missionaries, each so desperately in love but lacking capacity to speak of it to the other, because they judged that Congregationalism would not approve, looked at each other in the noonday sunlight, and then looked away; but it was Abner who broke, for when they had gone inside to pack Deland it was he who could not control his hands, and the package fell awry and the crucial book fell onto the dusty floor, and when he kneeled to recover it he hid his face in his hands and sobbed, "Sister Urania, may God spare you!" But it was another name he longed to say.

The journey on foot from Lahaina to Wailuku, on the other side of Maui, took Abner and the messenger high into the mountains, and as they hiked over barren and rocky fields, with sweat pouring from them, they came upon a cloud of dust, and it was Kelolo and his lieutenants, driving their men down to the plains with a vast cargo of sandalwood. For an instant Abner was infuriated and admonished the chief: "While you cut sandalwood, your town diminishes." But before he heard Kelolo's justification—"These are my men. I do with them as I please." —he saw that many of the servants were carrying not sawed trunks from grown trees but saplings and roots grubbed out of the soil.

"Did you take even the new trees?" Abner asked in disgust.

"It is my sandalwood," Kelolo explained.

"You faithless servant," Abner cried and limped on.

When they reached the topmost ridge and could see the houses of Wailuku below, Abner paused to wipe away his sweat and thought: "If it is such hard work for us to climb this little hill, how could Urania have borne her journey?"

In the village of Wailuku they found out. When the canoe in which they were journeying broke up, Abraham had pushed and hauled his wife more than forty miles overland in an effort to join with the Hales at Lahaina, and this had precipitated her labor pains. Now they were bogged down in a trader's shack, helpless in panic.

It was a miracle that Urania, after such a trip, was still alive, but it was a greater miracle that Abraham had not thought to enlist the aid of Hawaiian midwives at his home mission, for they were some of the most highly skilled in the Pacific and within ten minutes would have diagnosed Urania's case as one of simple premature birth brought on by exhaustion. Had the Hewletts relied on them, they would have produced a clean birth and a healthy baby; but for the Hewletts to have accepted their aid would have meant admitting that a heathen, brown-skinned Hawaiian knew how to deliver a Christian white baby, and such an idea was unthinkable.

"I was sorely tempted to call in the local midwives," Brother Abraham confessed to Abner, when he ran up to meet the limping traveler, "but I was ever mindful of Jeremiah 10, verse 2: 'Thus saith the Lord, Learn not the way of the heathen.' So I have brought my wife to her own people."

Abner agreed that he had acted wisely, and for a moment the two young men congratulated themselves on their righteousness, but then Abner asked, "How is Sister Urania?"

At this question poor Brother Abraham was seized with a blush of respectability which made it almost impossible for him to say the words, but finally he blurted out: "She seems to have lost a great deal of her water."

In the growing dusk Abner looked sickly at his companion, then started feverishly unpacking his handbook. Thumbing it awkwardly he found a section titled "The Dry Delivery," and as he read it hurriedly, he became quite ill in the stomach, for the news was ominous, but when he looked up and saw how hopeless Brother Abraham was, he gritted his teeth and said boldly, "I should like to see Sister Urania."

Hewlett led him toward a low grass hut in which the Englishman who traded at Wailuku lived, but both the man and his wife were absent in Honolulu, and the house was surrounded by fifty or sixty natives, sitting on the ground and watching the amazing white men. Abner made his way through them, and with his medical book under his arm, went into the mean house to greet the frail woman with whom he had shared the tiny stateroom on the *Thetis*. "Good evening, Sister Urania," he said solemnly, and she replied bravely, "It is so consoling to meet again one with whom we journeyed on the small ship." And for a moment they spoke of happier days.

Then Abner asked, "Sister Urania, when did your . . ." He paused in acute embarrassment, and then finished with a rush: "Your labor pains, how long have they been occurring?"

"They started at six this morning," Urania said. Abner stared at her blankly, but his mind thought fiercely: "Oh, God! That was when she was climbing the last gullies!"

He mopped his forehead and said slowly, "That was twelve hours ago. Presumably then, Sister Urania, the child will be born at midnight." He consulted his watch: six hours to go.

Aching with embarrassment, he asked, "Your pains. Have they been frequent?"

"I don't think so," she replied.

"Excuse me," he said, and fumbled for his book of instructions, but the light was so bad that he could not read, and he directed Brother Abraham to fetch a kukuinut lamp, and by its flickering, wavering light he picked out the words that would guide him. "Have we a sheet of tapa?" he asked, and when one was found, he cut it into halves, twisted them to make ropes, knotted one end and tied the other to the foot of the bed. "You must pull on these knots, Sister Urania," he instructed her. "In a dry delivery you will be called upon for extra work."

Instantly he was sorry he had said these words, for Urania looked up in terror and asked, "Have I done something wrong?"

"No, Sister Urania," he assured her. "With God's help we shall do well."

Instinctively, she took his hand and whispered, "My cherished husband and I are so glad that you came." But when Abner, blushing like a child, wanted to examine her stomach, as the handbook directed, both he and the Hewletts thought it proper that she first cover herself with all of her personal clothing plus a stout sheet of tapa. Feeling through the several layers, Abner gravely announced: "There seems nothing awry."

But his head was snapped back by a sudden scream from the bed and an automatic tightening of the ropes. He hurried to the sputtering lamp and studied his watch. In four minutes another cry and another straining. Sweating, he leafed through his book and found reassuring news. Hurrying back to the bed, he announced happily: "Sister Urania, things are going well. Now time will work with us."

At this news Brother Abraham grew a ghastly white and it was obvious that he was going to be very sick, so Abner left the straining woman and ran to the door of the delivery room, crying in Hawaiian, "Somebody come in here and take care of Reverend Hewlett!" Two experienced midwives, who understood husbands, laughed hilariously and rescued the missionary, who was, as they had predicted in obscene asides to the gathering, conspicuously nauseated, but while the midwives comforted him other Hawaiians whispered, "Isn't this a strange way to do things? Our best midwives outside the hut caring for the husband, while a man who knows nothing is inside, caring for the mother."

"It's the way they do it in America," a listener explained.

Suddenly the midwives dropped Hewlett and listened acutely to Urania's cries, and it was sardonic that through the night these women, merely by listening, knew better what was occurring inside the hut than Abner, who was there with his book.

Hewlett, stabilized after his sickness, wiped his watery blue eyes and made his way back into the hut, demanding, "When will the child be born?"

"Brother Hewlett!" Abner cried in exasperation. "Unless you can make yourself to be of service, you will have to remain outside."

"When will the child be born?" the distraught man begged. Once more Abner went to the door and called for the midwives, who recovered Abraham and made him stay with them.

The pains now came at constant intervals, and Abner, checking his book constantly, found occasion to say, "Sister Urania, it does seem as if God were supervising us tonight."

"I am now in your hands, Brother Abner," the weak woman replied. "You must do with me as you require."

Later, Abner recalled that she had said these words with marked lassitude, and shortly thereafter he looked at her with horror and realized that she had not experienced a pain for some time and that she was still. Panic captured him, and he felt her wrists, but they seemed cold, and he ran to the door, shouting, "Brother Abraham! Come quickly!" And when the husband stumbled into the room, Abner reported, in a ghostly voice, "I fear she is dying."

Abraham Hewlett uttered a low sob and knelt at the bed, holding his wife's hand, and this unexpected movement caused Urania to shift her shoulders, and Abner in amazement cried, "Can she be sleeping?"

Outside, the midwives, listening intently, had already told the crowd, "She's sleeping. She'll probably stay that way for an hour or more. Then when she wakens, she'll begin all over again."

"Is it a good sign when a woman already in labor sleeps?" the crowd asked.

"No," said the midwives.

"Why not?" a man asked.

"It means she's weak," the woman said.

"What should they do . . . in there?" the man asked.

"They ought to be gathering herbs," the midwives explained.

"Why herbs?"

"To stop the bleeding, later on . . . since she is a weak woman."

Inside the shadowy house Abner and Abraham went frantically through their handbooks and could find nothing about sleeping at the eighteenth hour of delivery, and Abner began to experience an overpowering trembling and fear. "Somewhere in here there must be an explanation," he muttered, but his awkward fingers could not find it. "Brother Abraham, do you find anything?"

Then, mysteriously, the labor pains started again, rhythmically and in full force, but they gave Abner little help, for it was not Urania who was experiencing them, but her husband Abraham. It was pathetic to see the undernourished missionary grip at his stomach, following the exact course of a woman's pain, and for the third time Abner had to run to the door and beg the Hawaiians to take his assistant away. "And keep him away!" Abner snapped.

At two o'clock in the morning Urania Hewlett wakened and at five she had diminished her cycle of pain to intervals of a minute and half, whereupon the listening women outside predicted, "The birth will be soon." Abner, still fumbling with his book, his eyes bleary, came to the same conclusion, but his next half hour was one of special trial, for not knowing that Urania was undergoing a typical labor, he had leafed through the diagrams in the back of the book where unusual births were explained, with black-lettered titles, and he was possessed by one diagram: "Abnormal Birth: Shoulder and Arm Presentation." Turning rapidly to the associated text, he discovered how difficult his immediate task was going to be if he was, indeed, faced by such a presentation. It was therefore absolutely essential that he prepare for the actual birth, if only to anticipate an abnormality; but this he could not do, because Urania still lay swathed in bedclothes and tapa, and he could not in propriety either remove them himself or ask her to do so. So he went to the door, where streaks of morning light were beginning to penetrate the palm trees, and asked for Brother Abraham, who was sleeping. One of the midwives started toward the door, but Abner recoiled from her in honest horror, so Abraham was wakened and Abner said to him, "Brother Abraham, you must now undress your wife. The hour is at hand."

Abraham looked dumbly at his associate and started toward the bed, but his own labor pains returned with violence, and he had to flee the delivery room, but Abner's problem was solved by a vigorous movement on the bed, where Sister Urania, caught in the violence of birth, was kicking her clothes away and screaming for Abner to help her. Abner, swallowing like a schoolboy and shaking with embarrassment, approached the bed, and then strangely all of his uncertainty vanished, for he thought with boundless thanks to God: "That is surely the head. It is a normal presentation."

Outside, when the wail of the child was first heard, the two midwives said gravely, "He had better have the herbs ready."

Abner, preoccupied with the baby boy he held in his hands and with the nerve-racking job of cutting the cord and then tying it, summoned desperately every memory of his midwife's textbook and did a creditable job. Then he stood for a moment in the shadows, perplexed, holding the new child in his hands, and knowing not what to do, but finally he went out into the dawn and handed the child to a native woman, whom the Hawaiians had summoned twenty-four hours before, certain that she would be needed, and this woman placed the child to her breast.

The first midwife said: "He ought to be watching the mother."

The second replied: "I wonder if he is massaging her stomach to help her throw out the afterbirth."

And the first asked: "Do you suppose he would want these herbs?" And she indicated a brew that her people had used for two thousand years to stop bleeding.

But the second replied: "He would not want them."

Inside the shack Abner now feverishly thumbed his book, refreshing himself as to what he must do next. He cleaned the bed, washed the mother, listened to her breathing, and then saw with alarm that something was happening that the book did not tell about. "Brother Abraham!" he called in fear.

"What is it?" the sick husband replied.

"I am afraid she is bleeding more than she should."

Brother Abraham knew nothing, but he quickly looked through his book, and while the two well-intentioned missionaries tried vainly to catch the shreds of knowledge that would have saved a life, on the rude bed Sister Urania grew weaker and weaker. The long day's exertions and the long night's exhaustion were inexorably exacting their toll, and her face grew gray.

"She should not be sleeping so soundly," Abner cried in panic.

"What can we do?" Hewlett moaned. "Oh, God! Don't let her die now!"

Outside, the midwives said, "They ought to be massaging her stomach, but they seem to be talking, instead." And gradually over the large crowd of natives that had stayed through the night, crept the knowledge that the frail white woman was dying. The idea came upon them like the rays of the morning sun, sweeping down from the coconut palms, so that the Hawaiians, to whom birth was a mystical matter, were already weeping before the missionaries knew that Urania had bled to death.

Later, sitting exhausted under a kou tree, Abner said dully, "Brother Abraham, I did all I could to save your dear wife."

"It was the will of God," Hewlett mumbled.

"And yet," Abner cried, hammering the medical text with his fist, "there must have been something in here we didn't read."

"It was the will of God," Hewlett insisted.

The Hawaiians, watching, said, "How strangely the white men do things."

"They are so smart about reading and guns and their new god," an old woman observed, "that you'd expect them to have found a better way than this to birth a baby."

"What is most curious," pointed out another, "is that in America men do the work of women," but the old woman who had been most critical of the midwifery was first to acknowledge: "Even so, they make fine children."

After the burial of Urania—the first of many mission women to die in childbirth or from physical exhaustion due to overwork—Abner arranged with natives to care for Abraham Hewlett, his newborn son and the latter's wet nurse for the next two months until the difficult return journey to Hana at the tip of Maui was practical, and when these details were completed, Abner and the messenger climbed the hilly path to home; but they had not gone far when they heard a voice calling them, and it was Brother Abraham, pleading that they take his child with them.

"In Lahaina there will be people to care for the boy," he argued desperately.

"No," Abner refused. "It would be unnatural."

"What can I do with the boy?" Brother Abraham begged.

The question was abhorrent to Abner, who replied, "Why, Brother Abraham, you will care for him, and bring him up to be a strong man."

"I don't know about these things," Brother Abraham mumbled.

"Cease!" Abner cried sternly. "It is your duty to learn," and he turned the distracted missionary around and sent him back to Wailuku and the responsibility of his child. When the ungainly man had left, Abner remarked hotly to the messenger, who could not understand, "I think that if he had had courage, his wife need not have died. If he had kept her at Hana, and done the best he could, all would have been well. Sister Urania was killed by the long climb to Wailuku. And the poor thing, eight months with baby."

These thoughts drove him to the contemplation of his own wife, and he became afraid that news of Urania's death in childbirth might have an adverse effect upon her, so he devised an illogical plan for suppressing the news. He reasoned, more from hope than from common sense: "It will be some time before word of this bad business reaches Lahaina. I shall say nothing of it to my dear wife." He entered into a solemn compact with himself and even called God to witness, but when he reached home and saw the way in which Jerusha's six little curls fell beside her face, and the manner in which she leaned forward in eagerness to greet him after their first days of separation since marriage, his words were faithful to the pledge, but his actions could not be, and he looked at her with such love and apprehension that she knew instantly what had happened. "Sister Urania died," she cried.

"She did," Abner confessed. "But you will not, Jerusha." And for the first time he called her by her name.

She started to ask a question, but he grasped her harshly by her two wrists and looked hard into her brown eyes. "You will not die, Jerusha. I promise you by God's word that you will not die." He released her and sat on a box, holding his tired head in his hands, and said, half ashamed of what he was about to admit, "God protects us in the most mysterious ways, Jerusha, and although my thoughts may in some respects seem horrible, nevertheless they are true. I believe that God took me to the death of Sister Urania so that I would be prepared when your time came. Now I know what to do. I know what Brother Abraham should have done. Jerusha, I am prepared, and you will not die." He leaped to his feet and screamed, "You . . . will . . . not . . . die!"

More than anything else in life he wanted, at that moment, to sweep his wife into his arms and embrace her with kisses, wild bellowing kisses like the sounds of animals in the meadows at home, but he did not know how to do this, so all of his love expressed itself in this one profound resolve. "You will not die," he assured his wife, and from that moment on, no woman in a remote outpost, far from help, ever faced her last days of pregnancy with a sweeter resolution.

BUT IF ABNER thus found spiritual triumph in his missionary home, he encountered a fairly solid defeat at Malama's grass palace, for when he went to give the Alii Nui her day's lesson, he found that Kelolo had not moved to the new house built for him, but lived as usual with his wife. "This is an abomination!" Abner thundered.

The two huge lovers, well into their forties, listened in embarrassment as he explained again why God abhorred incest, but when he was finished, big Malama explained quietly, "I built the house for Kelolo outside the walls, and it is a good house, but he doesn't want to stay there alone." She began to cry and added, "He tried it for two nights while you were away, but when I thought of him sleeping alone, I didn't like it either, so on the third night I walked out to the gate and called, 'Kelolo, come inside where you belong.' And he came and it was all my fault. I am to blame, Makua Hale."

"You will never be a member of the church, Malama," Abner warned. "And when you die, you will suffer hellfire forever."

"Tell me about hellfire again, Makua Hale," Malama begged, for she desired to know exactly how much risk she was taking, and when Abner repeated his awful description of souls in eternal torment, Malama shivered and began asking specific questions while tears crept into her big eyes.

"You are sure that Kamehameha the king is in such fire."

"I am positive."

"Makua Hale, once a Catholic ship kapena came to Lahaina and spoke to me about God. Are Catholics in the fire too?"

"They are in the fire forever," Abner said with absolute conviction.

"And the same ship kapena told me about the people in India who have not heard of your god."

"Malama, don't speak of him as my God. He is God. He is the only God."

"But when the people of India die, do they go into the fire, too?"

"Yes."

"So that the only people who escape are those who join your church?"

"Yes."

Triumphantly, she turned to Kelolo and said, "You see how terrible the fire is. If you keep that platform out there, hanging onto old gods the way you do, you will live in everlasting fire."

"Ah, no!" Kelolo resisted stubbornly. "My gods will care for me. They will never let me burn, for they will take me to their heaven, where I will live beside Kane's water of life."

"He is a foolish man!" Malama reflected sadly. "He's going to burn and he doesn't know it."

"But, Malama," Abner pointed out, "if you continue to live with Kelolo in such horrible sin, you also will live in everlasting fire."

"Oh, no!" the big woman corrected. "I believe in God. I love Jesus Christ. I am not going to live in fire at all. I will keep Kelolo with me only until I begin to feel sick. We have agreed that before I die I will send him far away, and then I shall be saved."

Then Abner played his trump card. Pointing his finger at her, he boldly faced her and warned: "But it is your minister alone who can let you enter the church. Have you thought of that?"

Malama pondered this unexpected news and studied her tormentor. He was a foot shorter than she, less than half her age, and weighed about a third as much. Cautiously she probed: "And it will be you who judges whether I have been a good woman or not."

"I will be the judge," Abner assured her.

"And if I haven't been . . ."

"You will not be accepted into the church."

Malama reviewed this impasse for some time, looking first at Abner and then at Kelolo, until finally she asked briskly, "But maybe you won't be here at the time, Makua Hale. Maybe there will be some other minister."

"I will be here," Abner said firmly.

Malama studied this gloomy prospect, sighed in resignation, and then changed the subject abruptly. "Tell me, Makua Hale, what things must I do if I am to be a good Alii Nui for my people?"

And Abner launched into the work which would have great political consequence in Hawaii. At first only Malama and Kelolo attended his daily instruction, but gradually the lesser alii reported, and when King Liholiho or his regent-mother Kaahumanu were in residence, they too appeared, questioning, rejecting, pondering.

Constantly, Abner reiterated a few simple ideas. "There must be no slaves," he said.

"There are slaves in America," the alii countered.

"It is wrong in America, and it is wrong here. There must be no slaves."

"There are slaves in England," his listeners insisted.

"And in both America and England good men fight against slavery. Good men should do the same here." When his moral arguments bore no fruit, he resorted to exhortation, crying, "I was afloat on the ocean on my way to Hawaii, and we passed a ship at sundown, and it was a slave ship, and we could hear the chains clashing in the dismal holds. How would you like it, King Liholiho, if your hands were chained to a beam, and your back was cut with lashes, and the sweat poured down your face and blinded your eyes? How would you like that, King Liholiho?"

"I would not like it," the king replied.

"And the alii should see to it that no more babies are killed," Abner thundered.

Malama interrupted. "How should we greet captains from foreign warships when they come ashore at Lahaina?"

"All civilized nations," Abner explained, using a phrase that was especially cherished by the missionaries, "conduct formal relations with other civilized nations. The captain of a warship is the personal representative of the king of the nation whose flag he flies. When he comes ashore, you should fire a small cannon, and you should have four alii dressed in fine robes, wearing pants and shoes, and they should present themselves to the captain and say . . ."

There was no problem on which Abner was unprepared to give specific advice. This puny boy from the bleak farm at Marlboro, Massachusetts, had not in his youth foreseen that every book he read would one day be of value to him. He could recall whole passages about medical care in London, or the banking system in Antwerp. But most of all he remembered the studies he had conducted regarding the manner in which Calvin and Beza had governed Geneva, and it often seemed prophetic to him that each problem encountered by John Calvin in Switzerland now had to be faced by Abner Hale in Lahaina.

On money: "You should coin your own island money, and protect it against counterfeiters."

On wealth: "Money is not wealth, but the things you make and grow are. It is supreme folly for you to allow individual chiefs to trade away your precious sandalwood. And for any man to grub up the very roots of young trees is insane. The greatest wealth you have is your ability to service the whaling ships as they come into Lahaina and Honolulu. If the alii were wise, they would establish port dues for such ships and also tax each merchant who supplies the whalers."

On education: "The surest way to improve the people is to teach them to read."

On an army: "Every government needs a police force of some kind. I grant that if you had had a respectable army in Lahaina the whaling sailors would not have dared to riot. But I am afraid a large army such as you propose is ridiculous. You cannot fight France or Russia or America. You are too small. Do not waste your money on an army. But get a good police force. Build a jail."

On the good alii: "He is courageous. He protects the weak. He is honest with government money. He listens to advice. He dresses neatly and wears pants. He has only one wife. He does not get drunk. He helps his people as well as himself. He believes in God."

On Hawaii's greatest need: "Teach the people to read."

But often when he returned to the mission he would cry dejectedly, "Jerusha, I truly believe they didn't understand a word I said. We work and work and there is no improvement." Jerusha did not share his apprehensions, for in her school it was obvious that she was accomplishing miracles. She taught her women to sew, to cook better and to raise their own babies. "You must not give your children away!" she insisted. "It is against God's law." She was pleased when they nodded, but her greatest joy was young Iliki, who had once run off to the whalers but who could now recite the Psalms.

In teaching boys and men Keoki was indefatigable. He was both a devout Christian and a skilled instructor, so that his school was one of the best in the island group, but where he excelled was in his daily sermons, for he had the innate oratorical gift of the Hawaiian and exercised it in robust imagery and appropriate incident. So realistic was his description of the Flood that his listeners watched the sea out of the corners of their eyes, expecting engulfing waves to sweep in from Lahaina Roads.

But in long-range importance the most effective school was Abner's, where the alii studied, and his choice pupil was Malama's daughter, Noelani, whom he had rescued from the sailors. The girl was, by birth, entitled to be the next alii nui, for her blood strain was impeccable. Her parents were full brother and sister, each noble in his own right, so that she inherited the glory of numberless generations of Hawaiian greatness. She was clever and industrious, an ornament in any society. In a report to Honolulu, Abner said of her, "She is almost as good a student as her mother. She can read and write, speak English and do the easier sums. And I feel certain that she is dedicated to the way of God and will be one of our first full members of the church." When he told the girl this, she was radiant.

Teaching Malama was more difficult. The great alii was stubborn to a point of obstinacy. She required everything to be proved and she had that irritating quality which teachers deplore: she remembered what the instructor had said the day before, for after each visit she recalled the steps of his reasoning, so that when he reappeared she was able to present him with his own contradictions. Few classes in the history of education were more stubbornly hilarious than those which occurred when Abner tutored Malama alone. She would lie prone on her enormous belly, her round moonlike face propped on her hands, demanding, "Teach me the way to attain grace."

"I cannot do that," Abner invariably replied. "You have got to learn it for yourself."

What made the lessons difficult was not Malama's intellectual intransigence, which was pronounced, but her insistence upon answering all questions in broken English, which she quickly identified as God's chosen language, since the Bible was written in English, and since those who were dear to God conveyed their thoughts in that language. She was determined to learn English.

Abner, on his part, was equally insistent that the lessons be held in Hawaiian, for he saw that if he was to make progress in Christianizing the islands, he would have to speak in the native tongue. It was true that many of the Honolulu alii knew English, but it was not only to the alii that he intended speaking. Therefore, whenever Malama asked him a question in broken English, he replied in worse Hawaiian, and the lesson staggered on. For example, when he inveighed against eating dog, the conversation went like this:

"Dog good kau kau. You no like for what?" Malama asked.

"Poki pilau, pilau," Abner explained contemptuously.

"Pig every time sleep mud. You s'pose dog he make like that?"

"Kela mea, kela mea eat pua'a. Pua'a good. Poki bad."

If each had used his own natural tongue, conversation would have been simple, for each now understood the other's spoken language. But Malama stubbornly insisted that she be the first on Maui to speak English, while Abner was equally determined to preach his first sermon in the new church in flowing Hawaiian.

What irritated him most was that whenever he succeeded in backing big Malama into a logical corner, so that her next statement would have to be a confession of defeat, she would call for her maids to lomilomi her, and while they pounded her stomach, moving her enormous meals about, she would smile sweetly and say, "Go on! Go on!"

"So if civilized nations don't eat dogs, neither should Hawaiians," Abner would argue, and Malama would call sweetly for her maids to brush his face with feathers: "Kokua dis one man face. Fly too many on it, poor t'ing." And while Abner fought with the infuriating feathers his argument would die away.

But the two antagonists respected each other. Malama knew that the little missionary was fighting for no less than her entire soul. He would be content with no substitute, and he was an honest man whom she could trust. She also knew him to be a brave man who was willing to face any adversary, and she sensed that through her he intended to capture all of Maui. "That would not be a bad thing," she thought to herself. "Of all the white men who have come to Lahaina"—and she recalled the whalers, the traders, the military—"he is the only one who has brought more than he took away. After all, what is it he is trying to get me to do?" she reflected. "He wants me to stop sending the men into the forests for sandalwood. He wants me to build better fish ponds and to grow more taro. He wants me to protect the girls from the sailors, and to stop baby girls from being buried alive. Everything Makua Hale tells me is a good thing." Then she would pause and think of her kapu husband, Kelolo. "But I will not give up Kelolo until just before I am going to die." And so the warfare between Malama and Abner continued, but if a morning passed when duties kept him from the grass palace, Malama was uneasy, for her arguments with Abner were the best part of her day. She sensed that he was telling her the truth, and he was the first man who had ever done so.

When the time came for Jerusha's baby to be born she was faced by unwelcome news from Dr. Whipple: "I have been detained on Hawaii, where three mission wives are expecting babies, and it will be totally impossible for me to come to Lahaina. I am sure that Brother Abner will be able to handle the delivery capably, but nevertheless I beg your forgiveness. I am sorry." She grew afraid.

At one point she even went so far as to suggest: "Perhaps we should ask one of the local women to help us." But Abner was adamant and quoted Jeremiah: " 'Thus saith the Lord, Learn not the way of the heathen,' " and he pointed out how unlikely it was that a heathen woman, steeped in idols and vice, would know how to deliver a Christian baby, and Jerusha agreed. But this time stubborn little Abner had so memorized Deland's *Midwifery,* and Jerusha was finally so content to rely on him, that her boy was born without difficulty, and when Abner held the child for the first time he rather stolidly congratulated himself on having done such a good job of doctoring, but when the time came to place the boy in Jerusha's left arm and apply the infant's mouth to his wife's breast, the floods of emotion that he had so long imprisoned within his tight heart burst loose, and he fell onto the earth beside the bed and confessed, "My dearest companion, I love you more than I will ever be able to explain. I love you, Jerusha." And she, hearing these words of comfort in an alien land, the words she had so longed for, fed her child and was content.

"We will call the boy Micah," he announced at last.

"I had thought some sweeter name, perhaps David," she suggested.

"We will call him Micah," Abner replied.

"Is he strong?" she asked weakly.

"Strong in the goodness of the Lord," Abner assured her, and within two weeks she was teaching her classes again, a slim, radiant missionary woman sweating in a heavy woolen dress.

For one of the peculiarities of the missionaries was that they insisted upon living in tropical Hawaii exactly as if they were back home in bleak New England. They wore the same heavy clothing, did the same amount of tiring work, ate the same heavy meals whenever they could be obtained. In a land rich with Polynesian fruits, their greatest joy was to obtain from some passing ship a bag of dried apples, so that they could enjoy once more a thick, sweet apple pie. Wild cattle roamed the hills, but the missionaries preferred salt pork. There was an abundance of fish in the shallows, but they clung desperately to dried beef shipped out from Boston. Breadfruit they rarely touched, and coconuts were heathenish. In all his years on Maui, Abner Hale would never once do any of God's official work unless costumed in underwear, heavy woolen pants, long shirt, stock, vest, heavy claw-hammer coat and, if the meeting were outside, his big beaver hat. Jerusha dressed comparably.

But what was impossible to comprehend was the fact that each year, on the first of October, when the Hawaiian summer was hottest, mission families regularly climbed into heavy woolen underwear. They had followed this custom in Boston. They would follow it here. Nor did they ever find relief by swimming in the cool lagoon, for Bartholomew Parr's *London Medical Dictionary* specifically warned them: "NATATIO. Swimming is a laborious exercise, and should not be continued to exhaust the strength. It is not natural to man as to quadrupeds, for the motions of the latter in swimming are the same as in walking."

All these conventions resulted in one of the most serious breaches between the Hawaiians and the missionaries. The former, who loved to bathe and who rarely did even twenty minutes' work without sluicing themselves afterwards, found the missionaries not only dirty people but actually offensive in smell. Sometimes Malama, irritated by their sweaty odors, tried to suggest that Abner and Jerusha might like to swim on the fine kapu beach of the alii, but Abner rejected the invitation as if it had come from the devil.

So all the accumulated wisdom of the islanders was ignored by the mission families. Perspiring in unbelievably heavy clothing, eschewing the healthful foods that surrounded them, they stubbornly toiled and grew faint and lost their health and died. But in doing so, they converted a nation.

IN 1823, when the building of the church was two thirds completed, Kelolo approached Abner one evening with his final plea. "We can still change the entrance," he argued. "Then the evil spirits will be sure to keep away."

"God keeps evil from His churches," Abner replied coldly.

"Will you come with me to the grounds?" Kelolo begged.

"Everything has been arranged," Abner snapped.

"I want to show you a simple way . . ." Kelolo began.

"No!" Abner cried.

"Please," the tall chief insisted. "There is something you must know."

Against his better judgment, Abner threw down his pen and grudgingly walked in the night air to the church grounds, where a group of elderly men sat on their haunches, studying his church. "What are they doing?" Abner asked.

"They are my praying kahunas," Kelolo explained.

"No!" Abner protested, drawing back. "I do not want to argue with kahunas about a church of the Lord."

"These men love the Lord," Kelolo insisted. "Ask them. They know the catechism. They want the church to be built strong."

"Kelolo," Abner explained patiently, drawing near to the solemn kahunas, "I understand perfectly that in the old days these kahunas accomplished much that was good. But God does not require kahunas."

"Makua Hale," Kelolo pleaded, "we have come to you as friends who love this church. Please do not keep the door where it is. Every kahuna knows that that is wrong for the spirits of this location."

"God is the supreme spirit!" Abner argued, but since the night was pleasant, with a pale crescent moon in the west and occasional clouds sweeping in from the roads, he sat with the kahunas and talked with them about religion. He was surprised at how much of the Bible they knew, and at the skill with which they could accommodate it to their ancient beliefs. One old man explained, "We believe you are correct in what you say, Makua Hale. There is only one God, and we used to call Him Kane. There is a Holy Ghost, and we called Him Ku. There is Jesus Christ, and He is Lono. And there is the king of the underworld, and he is Kanaloa."

"God is not Kane," Abner reasoned, but the kahunas merely listened, and when it came time for them to speak they said, "Now when Kane, that is God, wishes a church to be built, he supervises it. He always did when we built our temples."

"God does not personally supervise the building of this church," Abner explained.

"Kane did."

"But God is not Kane," Abner patiently repeated.

The men nodded sagely and continued: "Now, since Kane is concerned about this church, and since we have always loved Kane, we thought it proper to advise you that this door . . ."

"The door will be where it now is," Abner explained, "because that is where the door to a church has always been. In Boston the door would be here. In London it would be here."

"But in Lahaina, Kane would not like it to be here," the kahunas argued.

"Kane is not God," Abner stubbornly repeated.

"We understand, Makua Hale," the kahunas politely agreed, "but since God and Kane are the same idea . . ."

"No," Abner insisted, "God and Kane are not the same."

"Of course," the kahunas agreed heartily, "their names are different, but we know that Kane would not like this door here."

"The door has to be here," Abner explained.

"If it is, Kane will destroy the church," the kahunas said sorrowfully.

"God does not go about destroying his own churches," Abner assured the men.

"But we know that Kane does, if they are built wrong, and since Kane and God mean the same thing . . ."

The solemn kahunas never lost their tempers with the stubborn little stranger who did not quite understand religion, so far as they could judge, and Abner had learned not to lose his, so the argument about the door lasted for several hours, until the moon had vanished from the west and only low dark clouds scudded across the mysterious and silent sky. With nothing agreed, but with the kahunas feeling very sorry for their misguided friend who insisted upon building a doomed church for Kane, the meeting broke up and Kelolo said, "After I bid the kahunas good night I will walk back home with you."

"I can find my way alone," Abner assured him.

"On a night like this . . ." Kelolo said speculatively, looking at the low clouds over the coconut palms, "it would be better, perhaps . . ." And he bade the kahunas a hasty farewell so that he could hurry down the dusty road and overtake the missionary, but they had progressed only a few hundred yards when Abner heard the kahunas walking behind them, and he said, "I don't want to argue with them any more," but when Kelolo turned to tell the kahunas so, he saw nothing. There were no kahunas. There were no walking men. There was only an ominous echo under the scudding clouds, and suddenly Kelolo grabbed Abner in a vise of death and muttered in horror, "It is the night marchers! Oh, God! We are lost!" And before Abner could protest, Kelolo had caught him about the waist and had swept him precipitately over a hedge and thrown him into a ditch, where foul water drenched him. When he tried to rise, Kelolo's mighty arm pinned him to the wet earth, and he could feel that the huge alii was trembling in terror.

"What is it?" Abner sputtered, but Kelolo's giant hand clasped his mouth, accidentally forcing grass and mud into his lips.

"It is the night marchers!" Kelolo whispered, his lips quivering in horror.

"Who are they?" Abner whispered back, pulling Kelolo's hand from his mouth.

"The great alii of the past." Kelolo trembled. "I am afraid they are coming for me."

"Ridiculous!" Abner grunted, trying to break free. But his captor held him pinioned in the ditch, and he could feel the awful tenseness of the big man's muscles. Kelolo was terrified.

"Why are they coming for you?" Abner whispered.

"No one knows," Kelolo replied, his teeth chattering. "Perhaps because I gave the land of Kane for your church."

With the greatest circumspection he lifted his huge head until it was even with the top of the hedge, looked for a moment up the dark path, and shuddered. "They are marching toward us!" he gasped. "Oh, Makua Hale, pray to your god for me. Pray! Pray!"

"Kelolo!" Abner grunted, smothered by the pressure on his chest. "There is nothing out there. When alii die they remain dead."

"They are marching," Kelolo whispered. And in the silence of the night, with only wind rustling through dead palm leaves, there was indeed a sound of feet. "I can see them coming past the church," Kelolo reported. "They carry torches and feathered staves. They wear their golden robes and feather helmets. Makua Hale, they are coming for me."

The giant alii pressed himself into the ditch, hiding Abner beneath his ample form, and the missionary could hear the man praying, "Oh, Pele, save me now; I am your child, Kelolo, and I do not want to die tonight."

The sound grew louder and Kelolo engaged in violent actions, almost smothering Abner, who mumbled, "What are you doing?"

"Undressing!" Kelolo grunted. "You cannot speak to the gods with clothes on." When he was completely naked he resumed praying in an agitated voice, but suddenly he grew calm and Abner heard him say, "The little man I am hiding is Makua Hale. He is a good man and he brings learning to my people. He doesn't know enough to throw off his clothes, so please excuse him." There was a long silence, after which Kelolo said, "I know the little man preaches against you, Woman of Whiteness, but even so he is a good man." There was another protracted silence, and then the sound of imminent feet, and Kelolo trembled as if a great wind tormented him and then he spoke: "Thank you, Pele, for having told the marchers I am your child."

The wind subsided. Only fitful sounds came from the topmost crowns of the coconut palms, and there was no echo of marching feet. It could have been the kahunas going home, Abner thought. It could have been a group of dogs. Or wind along the dusty footpath. Now there was no sound; the low scudding clouds were gone, and the stars shone.

"What was it?" Abner asked, as he wiped the mud from his mouth.

"They were marching to take me away," Kelolo explained.

"Whom were you speaking to?" Abner inquired, spitting the gravel from his teeth.

"Pele. Didn't you hear her tell the marchers that we were her children?"

Abner did not reply. He brushed the sand from his clothes and wondered how he would get the muddy portions of his clothing cleaned, and he was brushing his knees when Kelolo grabbed him and spun him around, demanding, "You did hear Pele, didn't you? When she protected you?"

"Did she mention my name?" Abner asked quietly.

"You heard her!" Kelolo cried. "Makua Hale, it is a very good sign when Pele protects a man. It means . . ." But his joy at having been saved from the revengeful night marchers was so great that he could not express his gratitude, either for her aid in saving him or for her unprecedented benevolence in protecting the little missionary. "You are my brother," Kelolo said passionately. "Now you see that it would have been foolish for me to have torn down my platform to the gods. Suppose Pele had not come to help us tonight!"

"Did you see the night marchers?" Abner pressed.

"I saw them," Kelolo replied.

"Did you see Pele?" the missionary continued.

"I often see her," Kelolo assured him. Then in a burst of passion he caught Abner by the hands and pleaded: "It is for these reasons, Makua Hale, that I beg you not to keep the door where it is."

"That door . . ." Abner began. But he did not bother to finish his sentence, and when he reached home and Jerusha cried, "Abner, what have you been doing?" he replied simply, "It was dark and I fell in a ditch." And the door was built where he intended.

Then, when it seemed as if the mission were gaining control of Lahaina, the whaler *John Goodpasture,* out of New Bedford, put in with a record tonnage of oil from the recently discovered Off-Japan whaling grounds, and Jerusha's school for girls was suddenly interrupted by the excited cry from the road: "Kelamoku! Too many sailors inside boat! Come right away here!"

Since the *John Goodpasture* was well and favorably known in Lahaina from previous visits, the intelligence created much excitement, especially among the four daughters of Pupali, who spent the next few minutes darting significant glances at one another. Finally, they rose as a team and marched out of class. When Jerusha tried to stop them, the oldest girl explained that their youngest sister felt ill: "Poor Iliki head all come sore," and amid loud giggles they disappeared.

At first Jerusha did not appreciate what had happened, but later when one of her students blurted out, "Kapena aloha Iliki. She swim ship, see kapena," it became obvious that the mission's moral teaching had been outraged, and Jerusha dismissed class. Wrapping a light shawl about her shoulders and placing her poke bonnet firmly on her brown locks, she marched down to the waterfront in time to see the four girls, largely naked, climbing eagerly aboard the *John Goodpasture,* where sailors who had known them before greeted them with cheers.

Running up to an elderly American sailor who was scrimshawing a whalebone beside Kamehameha's old brick palace, she cried, "Row me out to that boat!" But the sailor continued carving the whalebone and drawled, "Ma'am, it's best if you don't fight the laws of nature."

"But Iliki is only a child!" Jerusha protested.

"First law of the sea, ma'am. If they're big enough, they're old enough," and he looked out into the channel, where the girls' pleased squeals filled the air.

Appalled by this indifference, Jerusha ran over to an old Hawaiian woman who sat on a rock guarding the four mission dresses which the girls had discarded. "Aunty Mele," Jerusha pleaded, "how can we get those girls back?"

"You stop one time. Bimeby ship go," Aunty Mele assured her. "Wahine come back, same like always."

In frustration, Jerusha grabbed at the besmirched mission dresses, as if to take them home with her, away from the contaminated waterfront, but Aunty Mele held onto them grimly, saying, "Hale Wahine! Bimeby wahine come back, I make ready dress for dem." And like the good friend she was, she remained on the rock, holding the girls' apparel until such time as they might need it once more for resumption of their missionary lessons.

That night it was a gloomy mission household that reviewed the day's defeats. "I cannot understand these girls," Jerusha wept. "We give them the best of everything. Iliki in particular knows what good and evil are. Yet she runs off to the whaling ship."

"I brought the matter up with Malama," Abner reported in deep confusion, "and she said merely, 'The girl is not an alii. She can go to the ships if she likes.' So I asked Malama, 'Then why were you so angry when the three sailors tried to take Noelani to their ship.' And Malama replied, 'Noelani is kapu alii.' As if that explained everything."

"Abner, I shudder to think of the evil that flourishes in Lahaina," Jerusha replied. "When I left the waterfront, where nobody would do anything, I went into the town to ask for help, and at Murphy's grog shop I heard a concertina. And girls laughing. And I tried to go in to stop whatever was happening, and a man said, 'Don't go in there, Mrs. Hale.

The girls have no clothes on. They never do when the whalers are in port.' Abner! What is happening to this town?"

"For some time I have known it to be the modern Sodom and Gomorrah."

"What are we going to do about it?"

"I haven't decided," he replied.

"Well, I have," Jerusha said firmly. And that very night she marched down to Malama's palace and said in her able Hawaiian, "Alii Nui, we must stop the girls from going out to the whaling ships."

"Why?" Malama asked. "The girls go because they want to. No harm is done."

"But Iliki is a good girl," Jerusha insisted.

"What is a good girl?" Malama asked.

"Girls who do not swim out to ships," Jerusha replied simply.

"I think you missionaries want to stop all fun," Malama countered.

"Iliki is not engaging in fun," Jerusha argued. "She is engaging in death." And this Malama knew to be true.

"But she has always gone out to the ships," she said sadly.

"Iliki has an immortal soul," Jerusha said firmly. "Exactly as you and I."

"You mean to claim that Iliki . . . wahine i Pupali . . . like you or me?"

"Exactly like you, Malama. Exactly like me."

"I cannot believe it," Malama said. "She has always gone to the ships."

"It is our job to stop her. To stop all the girls."

Malama would do nothing that night, but on the next day she assembled the alii then in residence, and Reverend and Mrs. Hale presented their arguments, with Jerusha pleading: "You can tell a good town by the way it protects its babies and young girls. You can tell a good alii by the way in which he protects women. You are not good alii if you permit your own daughters to go out to the ships. In London the good alii try to stop such things. In Boston, too."

Kelolo contradicted this assertion by pointing out: "Kekau-ike-a-ole sailed on a whaler and he got to both London and Boston and he has often told us of how there were special houses filled with girls. Everywhere he went there were such houses."

"But the good alii in all cities try to control this vice," Jerusha argued bitterly.

It was Abner, however, who delivered the aching blow. "Do you know what happens if you alii of Lahaina permit your girls to be debauched in this way?" he asked ominously.

"What happens, Makua Hale?" Malama asked, for she trusted him.

"When the ships sail back home, the men laugh at Hawaii."

There was a long silence as this ugly accusation was digested, for the alii of Hawaii were proud people, desperately hungry for the world's approval. Finally, Malama asked cautiously, "Would the alii of Boston allow their girls to swim out to a Hawaiian ship?"

"Of course not," Kelolo snapped. "The water is too cold."

There was no laughter, for this was an honest observation, and Abner quickly added, "Kelolo is correct. The water in Boston is not so sweet and warm as here, but even if it were, no girls would be allowed to swim out to Hawaiian ships. The alii of Boston would be ashamed if that happened."

Malama asked quietly, "Do you think the sailors laugh at us, Makua Hale?"

"I know they do, Malama. Do you remember the whaler *Carthaginian* when it was here? I was aboard the *Carthaginian* on the whaling grounds, and the sailors were laughing about Honolulu."

"Ah, but Honolulu is known to be an evil place," Malama admitted. "That is why I will not live there. That's why the king keeps his capital here at Lahaina."

"And they laughed at Lahaina," Abner insisted.

"That is bad," Malama frowned. After a while she asked, "What should we do?"

Abner replied, "You should build a fort, by the roads, and each night at sunset a drum should beat, and any sailor who is ashore should then be arrested and kept in the fort till morning. And any girl who swims out to ships should be put in jail, too."

"Such laws are too harsh," Malama said, and she dismissed the meeting, but when the other alii had gone she took Jerusha aside and asked querulously, "Do you think the sailors laugh at us, because of the girls?"

"I laugh at you!" Jerusha said firmly. "To think of people debauching their own daughters!"

"But they are not alii," Malama insisted.

"You are the conscience of the people," Jerusha replied.

That night the Hales argued long as to whether the daughters of Pupali should be admitted back into the mission school, and Abner was for dismissing them permanently, but Jerusha held that they should be given another chance, and when the *John Goodpasture* left the roads, the four delinquent girls, dressed neatly in new dresses, came penitently back. The more Jerusha preached to them about the miserableness of their sin, the more heartily they agreed. But when, some weeks later, a child heralded the arrival of the whaler *Vashti* with the exciting cry, *"Vashti* iron hook fall now, plenty kelamoku," the four girls bolted again, and that night Abner insisted that the older three at least be expelled. They were, and since these were the years when whalers came to Lahaina with increasing frequency—seventeen were to arrive in 1824—the three older daughters of Pupali did a good business. They no longer had to go out to ships, for they became the dancers at Murphy's grog shop and kept little rooms aft of the small dance floor, where they were permitted to keep half of the coins they earned.

Iliki, the fairest of the daughters, was allowed to stay in the mission school, and under Jerusha's most careful guidance grew to understand the Bible and to forswear whaling ships. She was slim for a Hawaiian girl, with very long hair and flashing eyes. When she smiled, her handsome white teeth illuminated her face, and Jerusha could appreciate why it was that men wanted her. "When she is twenty," Jerusha said, "we will marry her to some Christian Hawaiian, and you mark my words, Abner, she'll be the best wife in the islands."

When Jerusha spoke thus, Abner was not listening, for he had erected for himself, out of rough ends of timber gathered here and there —for nothing in Lahaina was more precious than wood—a small table upon which papers were spread in seven or eight neat piles, each with a sea shell placed on it to preserve order. For he had begun, in co-operation with the other missionaries throughout the islands, the work which would be his most lasting contribution to Hawaii. He was translating the Bible into Hawaiian and sending his pages as they were finished to the printer in Honolulu, where they were being published a little at a time.

Nothing that Abner applied himself to in these years gave him greater pleasure, for he kept before him his Greek and Hebrew texts, Cornelius Schrevelius' *Greek–Latin Lexicon,* plus those versions of the Bible he had studied at Yale. He was happy, like a plowman who turns furrows in a field without stones, or a fisherman who sets his nets for known returns. Usually he worked with Keoki, laboring over every passage with the most minute attention, and as the years passed he reached those two books of the Bible which he cherished most. The first was Proverbs, which seemed to him a distillation of all the knowledge man could hope to know. It was especially appropriate for Hawaii, since its crystallizations were in simple language, easily understood and long remembered, and when he came to the glorious closing pages in which King Lemuel describes the ideal woman, his pen truly flew along the ruled pages, for it seemed to him that Lemuel spoke specifically of Jerusha Bromley: "Who can find a virtuous woman? For her price is far above rubies. The heart of her husband doth safely trust in her, so that he shall have no need of spoil. . . . She is like the merchants' ships; she bringeth her food from afar. . . . She stretcheth out her hand to the poor; yea, she reacheth forth her hands to the needy. . . . Strength and honor are her clothing; . . . Many daughters have done virtuously, but thou excellest them all."

When he finished translating Proverbs he left the last pages exposed, so that Jerusha might read them, and he was disappointed that she did not take notice of them, for she had learned not to interfere with his Biblical studies; so at last he was forced to hand her the pages of King Lemuel's conclusions, and she read them quietly, saying only, "A woman would do well to mark those pages." He was constrained to cry, "They were written about you, Jerusha!" but he said nothing, and put them along with the rest and forwarded them to Honolulu.

In the decades that were to follow, more than six committees would have occasion to polish this first translation of the Bible into Hawaiian, and in the portions contributed from the big island of Hawaii, or from Kauai, or Honolulu, the scholars frequently found understandable errors in translation or emphasis. But in the portions for which Abner Hale had been responsible, they rarely found an error. One expert, with degrees from both Yale and Harvard, said, "It was as if he had been in turn a Hebrew and a Greek and a Hawaiian." Abner did not hear this praise, for it came long after he was dead, but he reaped his full enjoyment from his great task when it came time to translate Ezekiel, for there was something about this strange book—a contrapuntal melody of the most banal observations and the most exalted personal revelations—that spoke directly to him and epitomized his life.

He loved the recurring passages in which Ezekiel, who must have been a rather boring man most of the time, laboriously set down the specific dates on which God spoke to him: "Now it came to pass in the thirtieth year, in the fourth month, in the fifth day . . . that the heavens were opened, and I saw visions of God. . . . The word of the Lord came expressly unto Ezekiel." The assurance with which Ezekiel spoke on all matters, and his confidence that the Lord personally directed him, gave Abner great consolation, and whenever he copied out Ezekiel's blunt statements of his correspondence with God, he felt that he, too, was participating in it: "In the sixth year, in the sixth month, in the fifth day . . . , as I sat in mine house, and the elders of Judah sat before me, . . . the hand of the Lord God fell there upon me." It was, to Abner Hale, clarity itself that the prophet Ezekiel, sitting in counsel with the elders of Judah, was markedly similar to the prophet Abner, sitting in counsel with the alii of Maui, and if the latter prophet sometimes spoke with an authority that the Hawaiians had difficulty in accepting, Abner felt that the elders of Judah must have had the same difficulty with the preachments of Ezekiel. Yet there it was in imperishable writing: "Again the word of the Lord came expressly unto me." A man required no greater authority than that.

IN 1825, Jerusha had a second baby, the saucy little girl Lucy, who was in later years to marry Abner Hewlett, whom her father had also delivered. As Keloło's big church neared completion, a serious problem confronted Abner, for he was determined above all things that when it was dedicated the Hawaiians who entered it must be dressed as proper Christians. "There will be no nakedness in this church," he announced. "There will be no wreaths of maile branches, with their distracting fragrance. Women will wear dresses. Men will wear pants."

But even as he promulgated the law, he wondered where enough cloth would be found to convert these heathens into Christians. The alii, with access to cargoes from China, were well taken care of. They had worn proper clothing from the first, and in recent months many visiting naval captains had been astonished by the gigantic and solemn noblemen who greeted them at the small stone pier. "They would do credit to the city of London," one Englishman reported to his superiors. "The men were dressed in black coats, proper trousers and yellow capes. The women wore strange but becoming dresses with a yoke at the neck, and an unbroken fall of expensive material from the tops of their bosoms to their ankles. When they moved, men and women alike seemed like gods, so straight and arrogant were they. They confided to me privately that a missionary from Boston had told them how to greet incoming ships properly, and if he has done as well with their souls as with their deportment he is to be commended, but this latter I doubt, for I have rarely seen so much open debauchery in any principal port as at Lahaina."

It was cloth for the poor people that worried Abner, and then from the coasts of China appeared his salvation. The hermaphrodite brig *Thetis* returned from its sandalwood expedition loaded with wares for sale in local markets. Captain Retire Janders, already committed to selling his ship to Kelolo, had determined to enter the trading business with a flourish and had gambled every farthing of his sandalwood sale in Canton on things he thought the Hawaiians might like. It was therefore an exciting moment when he opened his store next to Murphy's grog shop and started unloading the bales from China.

For men there were sturdy gabardine, shimmering silk shirts, knee-length black pants such as had been popular in France thirty years earlier, silk-ribbed stockings and shoes with fancy buckles. There were cigars from Manila, brandies from Paris, and one entire box filled with ready-made suits of which Captain Janders had told the Canton tailors, "Make each one big enough to hold three Chinese. These are for Hawaiians."

For the women the captain's lures were irresistible: bolts of fine brocades, lengths of satin, whole dresses made of velvet, yard upon yard of green and purple cloth, with boxes of lace edging. There were glittering beads, and bracelets and rings; fans for hot nights, and perfumes from the Spice Islands.

What the alii particularly prized, however, were the full-length mirrors, transshipped from France, and the massive mahogany furniture constructed in Canton from English patterns. Each noble family felt that it had to have a secretary, with two round rests for lamps and numerous pigeon holes for filing papers. The delicate china ware was also appreciated, especially that in blue and white, but more treasured than tableware were the gleaming white chamber pots, decorated with raised roses, etched in pink and blue and green.

And for the common people there were hundreds of bolts of turkey-red cloth, with some brown and white samples intermixed. It was this commodity that attracted Reverend Hale and led him to propose the strategy that laid the foundation for the Janders fortune.

"You have many bolts of good cloth here, Captain," Abner pointed out. "I have long dreamed of having my congregation properly clothed when the church opens. But the people have no money. Will you extend them credit?"

Captain Janders tugged at the rim of beard that still fringed his face and said, "Reverend Hale, long ago you taught me to revere the Bible. I have got to stand on Proverbs 22, verse 26: 'Be not thou one of them . . . that are sureties for debts.' Thus saith the Lord, and it's good enough for me. Cash! Cash! The rule of this establishment."

"I know that cash is a good rule," Abner began.

"The Lord's rule," Janders repeated.

Abner said: "But it doesn't have to be money cash, does it, Captain?"

Janders said: "Well . . . if something could be converted . . ."

Abner said: "A lot of whalers come into these roads, Captain. What do they need that my natives could supply?"

Janders countered: "Why are they your natives?"

Abner replied: "They belong to the church. What could they bring you?"

Janders mused: "Well, the whalers are always demanding tapa cloth for calking. And I could use a lot of olona twine."

Abner proposed: "If I could supply you with regular amounts of tapa and olona? Would you trade the cloth?"

So Janders sealed the deal which became one of the principal foundations of his fortune, for the explosion of whalers into Lahaina Roads was about to occur—42 in 1825; 31 in 1826—and when they arrived, Captain Retire Janders cannily waited to service them with products supplied by Reverend Hale's natives: tapa, olona, pigs, wild beef. At one point Kelolo protested: "Makua Hale, you used to fight with me when I took my men into the mountains for sandalwood. For me they worked only three weeks at a time. For you they work all the weeks." But Abner explained to the simple-minded man: "They do not work for me, Kelolo. They work for God." Nevertheless Kelolo insisted: "They still work all the time."

In one sense Abner did profit: he got each of his parishioners properly dressed for the opening of church, and on the Sunday when the sprawling edifice was consecrated, curious processions from miles around marched through the dust in their unaccustomed finery from Captain Janders' store. The alii, of course, made a respectable showing, the men in frock coats and black hats, the women in handsomely gored dresses made from rich, thick stuffs from Canton. But the common people, even though they had watched the alii shift from tapa breechclouts to London jackets, had not quite caught the niceties of western dress. Women seemed to have found the easier solution: prim high collars on tight-fitting yokes which encased the bosom and from which hung copious folds of cloth; long sleeves hiding the offensive nakedness of the wrists; this costume was the essence of practicality and ugliness, and that beautiful women should have submitted to it was incomprehensible. It was completed by a broad-brimmed hat of woven sugar-cane leaves, decorated with imitation flowers, for real ones were not allowed in church lest they exhibit vanity and distract the congregation.

Men faced more confusing problems, for each felt honor-bound to wear some one article from the Janders store, so that the first who entered the church after the alii wore a pair of shoes, a Bombay hat and nothing more. The second wore a man's shirt with his legs pushed through the sleeves and the collar tied around his waist with a strand of olona twine. When Abner saw these ridiculous worshipers he was inspired to send them back home, but they were so eager to enter the new church that he allowed them to do so.

The next pair were brothers to whom Janders had sold a complete Canton suit; one wore the coat and nothing else; his brother wore the pants and white gloves. Now a man came wearing a woman's dress, complete with a wreath of maile leaves about his head, and this time Abner was stern. "No flowers or pagan-smelling leaves in church," he commanded, tearing away the wreath and throwing it to the ground, whence the fragrance penetrated to the church. Some men wore only shirts with tails flapping over enormous brown buttocks, and some wore grass breechclouts and silk neckties, but in deference to the white man's God, who refused to share his mysteries with the naked, all wore something.

The interior of the church was impressive: a perfect rectangle with handsomely matted grass walls, an imposing stone pulpit, and not a shred of other furniture except one wooden bench for Jerusha and Captain Janders. The multitude, more than three thousand of them, spread individual pandanus mats on the pebbled floor and sat tailor fashion, elbow to elbow. Had Abner studied the climate for even a moment, he would have built his grass walls only a few feet high, leaving open space between them and the room so that air could circulate, but churches in New England were built foursquare, and so they were in Hawaii, with no air stirring and the congregation sweltering in the natural heat, plus the radiation of three thousand closely packed bodies.

The singing was magnificent: spontaneous, joyous, instinct with worship. The reading of the Scriptures by Keoki was impressive, and when Abner rose to deliver his two-hour sermon, the audience was thrilled to hear him speak in acceptable Hawaiian. He chose for his topic, Zephaniah 2, verse 11: "The Lord will be terrible unto them: for he will famish all the gods of the earth; and men shall worship him, every one from his place, even all the isles of the heathen."

It was a sermon almost ideally suited for the occasion. Phrase by phrase Abner interpreted Zephaniah's words. He defined the Lord and his powers, spending fifteen lyrical minutes in identifying the new god of the islands. It was a god of mercy and compassion that he expounded.

Then he described the terribleness of Jehovah when His anger was aroused, and he lingered over floods, pestilences, thunder and lightning, famines and the tortures of hell. To his surprise the Hawaiians nodded understandingly, and he heard Kelolo whispering to Malama, "The new god's just like Kane. Very difficult when he's mad."

Abner next turned to the specific gods of Lahaina whom the new God was determined to destroy. He specified Kane and Ku, Lono and Kanaloa, Pele and her attendants. "They shall perish," Abner shouted in Hawaiian, "both from Lahaina and from your hearts. If you try to hide these evil gods in your hearts, you will be destroyed, and you will burn in hell forever and ever."

After this he analyzed what the word *worship* meant, and here for the first time before the general public he expounded his view of the good society. "A man worships God," Abner said, "when he protects his women, when he does not kill girl babies, when he obeys the law." At one point he cried, "A man who grows better taro to share with his neighbors praises God." At another he came close to expounding pure New England doctrine when he suggested, "Look about you. Does this man have good land? God loves him. Does that man's canoe catch more fish? God loves that man. Work, work, work, and you will find that God loves you." Finally, with considerable courage, he stared directly at the alii and expostulated his concept of the good ruler, and the entire congregation, all but thirty of them commoners, heard a bold new concept of government. The sermon ended with one of the dramatic touches that Abner, like St. Paul before him, loved. He cried, "In the kingdom of God there is no higher and lower, there is no alii and slave. The lowliest man stands bright in the sweet gaze of God." And he summoned from the doorway, for the man would not otherwise have dared enter the edifice, a slave and he brought this slave to the pulpit area and put his arms about the man and cried, "You have previously called this man a foul corpse, one of the living dead. God calls him an immortal soul. I call him my brother. He is no longer a slave. He is your brother." And inspired by the awfulness of this iconoclastic moment, Abner leaned up and kissed the man on the cheek and made him sit on the ground, not far from Malama, the Alii Nui.

But the highlight of the dedication services came after a series of hymns led by Keoki, for Abner rose and announced, during the third hour of worship: "Entrance into the kingdom of God is not easy. Entrance into His church here on earth is not easy, either. But today we are going to allow two of your people to start their six months' trial period. If they prove good Christians, they will be admitted to the church." There was much excitement in the audience and open speculation as to who the chosen pair should be, but Abner stilled it by raising his hand and pointing to Keoki, tall, wiry and handsome.

"In Massachusetts your much loved alii, Keoki, was made a member of the church. He is the first Hawaiian to join. My dear good wife, whom you know as teacher, is also a member. So am I. So is Captain Janders. We four have met and have decided to test two others for membership. Mrs. Hale, will you rise and bring forth the first?"

Jerusha rose from her mat on the side, walked forward to the alii area, reached down and grasped the hand of the slave. In slow, careful Hawaiian she said, "This kanaka Kupa is known in all Lahaina as a saintly man. He shares his goods with others. He cares for children that have no parents." By her forceful enumeration of the man's extraordinary virtues, which were acknowledged by all, Jerusha made the consecration of the slave logical to the congregation. "In your hearts, people of Lahaina, you know that Kupa is a Christian man, and because you know him to be such, we are going to accept him into the church of God."

Abner took Kupa's hand and cried, "Kupa, are you prepared to love Jehovah?" The slave was so terrified by the experiences the missionaries were forcing upon him that he could only mumble, and Abner announced: "In six months you will no longer be Kupa the Foul Corpse. You will be Kamekona." And he gave the slave this treasured name, Solomon.

The audience was stunned, but before there could be any murmuring against the radical move, Abner said in his powerful and persuasive voice, "Keoki Kanakoa, rise and bring forth the second member of the church."

And it was with the greatest excitement and joy that Keoki rose, went to the alii area and reached down for his sister Noelani, the Mists of Heaven. That morning she was dressed in white, with a yellow feather lei about her head and white gloves on her capable hands. Her dark eyes were ablaze with sanctity and she moved as if God and not her brother had reached down to touch her. From a distance she heard the joyous acceptance of her nomination as the Hawaiians whispered, and then she was aware that Abner was addressing her: "You have been faithful to the Lord's ways. You have studied and learned to sew, for all women, alii and commoner alike, should know how to sew, for does not the Bible say of the virtuous woman, 'She seeketh wool, and flax, and worketh willingly with her hands.' But more than this, Noelani, you have been an inspiration to this island. In six months you will become a member of the church."

In her sweet resonant voice Noelani replied, "I shall make the learning and the law of Jehovah my guide," and Abner hid his irritation at the way these stubborn alii still insisted first upon the alphabet.

That night Malama summoned Abner, and when he was perched cross-legged on the tapa before her reclining bulk she said solemnly,

"For the first time today, Makua Hale, I understood what humility was. I saw, even though imperfectly, what a state of grace would be. Makua Hale, I have sent Kelolo to live in the other house. Tomorrow I am willing to lead a procession through the streets and announce the new laws for Maui. We must have a better way of living here. Will you have the laws ready for us to study at dawn tomorrow?"

"Today is the Sabbath," Abner said flatly. "I cannot work today."

"An island waits to be saved," Malama commanded. "Bring me the laws in the morning."

"I will," Abner surrendered.

And on his way home, he stopped at the new house outside the wall and said, "Kelolo, will you work with me tonight?" And the outcast husband agreed, and they gathered Keoki, too, and Noelani and went to the mission house.

"The laws must be simple," Abner said with a show of statesmanship. "Everyone must understand them and approve them in his heart. Kelolo, since you will be the man who will have to organize the police and enforce the laws, what do you think they should be?"

"The sailors cannot roam our streets at night," Kelolo said forcefully. "It is at night that they do their damage." So Lahaina's first and most contentious law was written into Abner's rudely folded book: "A drum will sound at sunset, at which signal all sailors must return to their ships on pain of instant arrest and incarceration in the Lahaina jail."

"The next law?" Abner asked.

"There must be no more killing of girl babies," Noelani suggested, and this became law.

"The next?"

"Should we stop the sale of alcohol altogether?" Jerusha asked.

"No," Kelolo argued. "The storekeepers have already paid for their supplies and they would be ruined."

"It is killing your people," Abner pointed out.

"I am afraid there would be riots if we stopped the sale," Kelolo warned.

"Could we stop the import of new supplies?" Jerusha proposed.

"French warships made us promise to drink lots of their alcohol each year," Kelolo pointed out.

"Could we forbid sales to Hawaiians?" Jerusha asked.

"French warships said we had to make the Hawaiians drink their alcohol, too," Kelolo explained, "but I think we should refuse to do so any longer."

Without ever insisting upon his own opinion, Abner extracted from his group a short, sensible body of law, but when it was finished he saw that one of the most typical of all Hawaiian problems had been overlooked. "We need one more law," he suggested.

"What?" Kelolo asked suspiciously, for he feared some action against kahunas and the old gods.

"The Lord says," Abner began in some embarrassment, "and all civilized nations agree . . ." He paused, ashamed to go on. After a moment's hesitation he blurted out: "There shall be no adultery."

Kelolo thought about this for a long time. "That would be a hard law to enforce," he reflected. "I wouldn't want to have to enforce that law . . . not in Lahaina."

To everyone's surprise, Abner said, "I agree, Kelolo. Perhaps we could not enforce it completely, but could we not get the people to understand that in a good society, adultery is not encouraged?"

"We could say something like that," Kelolo agreed, but then a look of considerable perplexity came over his features and he asked, "But which adultery are you talking about, Makua Hale?"

"What do you mean, which adultery?"

Kelolo, Keoki and Noelani sat in silence, and Abner thought they were being obstinate until he realized that each was thinking very seriously. In fact, he saw Kelolo's fingers moving and judged that the big alii was counting. "You see, Makua Hale," the tall nobleman said, "in Hawaii we have twenty-three different kinds of adultery."

"You what?" Abner gasped.

"And this would be our problem," Kelolo carefully explained. "If we said simply, 'There shall be no adultery,' without indicating which kind, everyone who heard would reason, 'They don't mean our kind of adultery. They mean the other twenty-two kinds.' But on the other hand, if we list all the twenty-three kinds, one after the other, somebody will surely say, 'We never heard of that kind before. Let's try it!' and things would be worse than before."

"What do you mean, twenty-three kinds?" Abner asked weakly.

"Well," Kelolo replied, from expert knowledge, "there is a married man and a married woman. That's one. Then there's the married man and the wife of his brother. That's two. Then the married man and the wife of his son. That's three. Then we have the married man and his own daughter. That's four."

"That's enough," Abner protested.

"It goes on through brothers and sisters, boys and their mothers, almost anything you could think of," Kelolo explained matter-of-factly. "As long as one of the pair is married, we call it adultery. So how can we stop it?" he asked, palms up. "If we name all twenty-three kinds we're going to have more trouble than we already have."

It was long after midnight and Abner sat chewing his pen. Like every religious leader in history, he knew that a good society started with a stable home, and that stable homes—either by design or accident—were usually founded on the disciplined sexual relationship of one man and one woman joined after due consideration of the world's accumulated judgment on such matters. It was not good for a man to marry his sister. It was not good for families to interbreed endlessly. It was not good for girls to be taken when they were too young. But how could this accumulated wisdom be summarized for the Hawaiians?

Finally, he came up with an answer so simple, so sweetly right, that generations of Hawaiians smiled every time they heard Abner Hale's profound directive. They smiled, because they understood exactly what he meant. It was a law that covered their experience on a tropical island, and of all the minor things Abner accomplished on Maui, this happy choice of words was most affectionately remembered among the people. For his final law read: "Thou shalt not sleep mischievously."

On Monday morning Abner presented his simple forthright laws to Malama, and she studied them. Two she threw out as too meddling in the lives of her people, but the rest she liked. Then she summoned her two maids-in-waiting, and the three enormous women, dressed in fine China silks and broad-brimmed hats, formed a procession which was headed by two drummers, two men sounding conch shells, four with feathered staves, Kelolo in charge of eight policemen, Keoki, Noelani and a brassy-voiced herald. Abner and Jerusha stayed away, for this was the work of Hawaiians for Hawaiians.

The drums began to beat, and when the conches sent their shrill blast through the kou trees, Malama and her two attendants started walking past the fish pond, along the dusty road beside the alii's houses, and into the center of town. Whenever more than a hundred people assembled, coming running from all sides, Malama would command the drums to cease and direct her herald to cry: "These are the laws of Maui. Thou shalt not kill! Thou shalt not steal! Thou shalt not sleep mischievously!"

The drums resumed, leaving people gasping in the morning sunlight. Fathers, who had been earning their poi by rowing their daughters out to the whalers, were stunned and some tried to argue with Kelolo, but he silenced them and marched on.

At the little pier Malama halted and had the bugle blown four times, assembling such sailors as were available at that hour. Two captains were present, and stood with their caps in their hands, listening to the astonishing news: "Sailors shall not roam the streets at night. Girls shall not swim out to the whaling ships."

"By God!" one of the captains muttered. "There'll be hell to pay for this."

"You'll find it was the missionary who did it," the other predicted.

"God help the missionary," said the first, running by a back way to Murphy's grog shop, but he had barely exploded the news when Malama and her two stout ladies hove majestically into view with the rumpled paper containing the new laws. This time, as the drums finished beating before Murphy's establishment, there were two special laws promulgated: "Girls shall no longer dance nude in Murphy's grog shop. From today no more alcohol may be sold to Hawaiians." The drums resumed beating. The bugles sounded, and Malama and her two enormous ladies-in-waiting retired. The laws had been handed down. It would now be Kelolo's job to enforce them.

That night there were riots. Sailors from several ships stormed through the town fighting with Kelolo's inadequate policemen. Girls were ripped away from their beds and hauled against their wills out to the ships. And toward midnight a body of some fifty sailors and Lahaina merchants gathered at the mission house and began cursing Abner Hale.

"He done the laws!" a sailor howled.

"He talked the fat lady into it!" another cried.

"Let's hang the little bastard!" a voice called, and cheers greeted the suggestion.

No immediate action was taken, but someone in the crowd started throwing rocks at the grass house, and occasionally one would ricochet into the room and fall harmlessly to the floor. "Let's burn his damned house down!" a voice screamed.

"We'll teach him to meddle in our affairs!"

"Come out here, you damned little worm!" a harsh voice called.

"Come out! Come out!" the crowd roared, but Abner kept huddled on the floor, protecting Jerusha and the two babies with his body lest the increasing storm of rocks find them.

The long night progressed with its vile insults, but toward morning the crowd dispersed, and as soon as the sun rose, Abner hurried to consult with Kelolo. "It was a bad night," the big alii said.

"I think tonight will be worse," Abner predicted.

"Should we discard the laws?" Kelolo asked.

"Never!" Abner snapped.

"I think we had better ask Malama," the tall chief suggested, but when they found her, townspeople were already there, bombarding her with their fears, and it was then that Abner realized what a tremendous woman she was. "Malama has spoken," she said sternly. "The words are law. I want you to assemble all the ships' captains in this room within an hour. Get them!"

When the Americans appeared, rough, rugged, good-looking veterans of the whaling grounds, she announced in English, "The law, me I gib you. More better you t'ink so, too."

"Ma'am," one of the captains interrupted. "We been comin' to Lahaina for a dozen years. We always had a good time here and behaved ourselves pretty well. I can't say what's goin' to happen now."

"I can say!" Malama cried in Hawaiian. "You are going to obey the laws."

"Our men got to have women," the captain protested.

"Do you riot in the streets of Boston?" Malama demanded.

"For women? Yes," the captain replied.

"And the police stop you, is that not right?" Malama pressed.

The captain wagged his forefinger and threatened, "Ma'am, no police on this pitiful island better try to stop my men."

"Our police will stop you!" Malama warned. Then she changed her tone and pleaded with the captains: "We are a small country, trying to grow up in the modern world. We have got to change our ways. It is not right that our girls should swim out to the ships. You know that. You have got to help us."

"Ma'am," one of the captains growled stubbornly, "there's gonna be trouble."

"Then there will be trouble," Malama said softly and sent the captains away.

Kelolo wanted to back down. Keoki was afraid there would be serious rioting, and Noelani counseled caution, but Malama was obdurate. She sent messengers to summon all the biggest men from the outward areas. She went in person to the new fort to see if its gates were strong, and she told Kelolo, "Tonight you must be ready to fight. The captains are right. There is going to be trouble."

But when her people had gone about their tasks, and when they could not spy upon her, she summoned Abner and asked him directly, "Are we doing the right thing?"

"You are," he assured her.

"And there will be trouble tonight?"

"Very bad trouble, I am afraid," he admitted.

"Then how can we be doing the right thing?" she pressed.

He told her of a dozen incidents in the Old Testament wherein men faced great adversaries in defense of God's way, and when he was through he asked her in a low voice, "Malama, do you not know in your heart that the laws you read were good?"

"They are part of my heart," she replied cryptically.

"Then they will prevail," Abner assured her.

Malama wanted to believe, but the cowardice of her other advisers had infected her, so now she towered above Abner, stared down at him and said, "Little mikanele," using the Hawaiian pronunciation of missionary, "tell me the truth. Are we doing the right thing?"

Abner closed his eyes, raised his head toward the grass roof, and cried in the voice that Ezekiel must have used when addressing the Jewish elders: "The islands of Hawaii will live under these laws, for they are the will of the Lord God Jehovah."

Assured, Malama turned to other matters and asked, "What will happen tonight?"

"They won't bother you, Malama, but I think they may try to burn my house. Can Jerusha and the children stay with you?"

"Of course, and you too."

"I'll be in the house," he said simply, and as he limped away, Malama loved her stubborn little mikanele.

That night the streets of Lahaina were a shambles. At dusk a drunken sea captain, in conjunction with Murphy, led a group of men to the fort and dared the policemen there to blow the conch shell. When the warning to sailors sounded, the mob grabbed every policeman in sight and threw them into the bay. Then they stormed back to Murphy's, where Pupali's three oldest daughters were dancing in the nude to wild shrieks of joy. As bottles were passed, sailors shouted, "Drink up. When this is done, the missionary says we can't have no more." The reiteration of this cry so maddened the mob that someone shouted, "Let's have done with that little pisser for all time." And they stormed into the street, heading for the mission house, but on the way someone proposed a better plan: "Why bother with him? Why not burn his goddamned church? It's made of grass!" And four men scurried through the night with torches, pitching them high onto the grass roofing. Soon the night breezes had whipped the flames across the top of the structure and had started them down the sides.

The great beacon thus lighted had consequences that the rioters had not foreseen, for the people who had worked upon this church had grown to love it as a symbol of their town, and now that it was ablaze, they rushed to save it. Quickly the area around the church was filled with sweating, silent, urgent men and women who beat at the walls to keep them from going up in flames, and by the incredible labors they performed that night, they saved more than half the walls, drenching them with water and beating at them with brooms and bare hands. The sailors, aghast at the bravery with which these illiterate islanders worked, withdrew and watched in wonder.

But when the people of Lahaina saw how little was left of their beloved church, where words of great hope had been preached to them, they became furious to the point of hysteria, and an islander cried, "Let us throw the sailors into jail!" The fire fighters greeted his challenge with cheers, and a wild manhunt was launched.

Wherever a sailor was spotted, three or four big natives crashed down upon him, often leaving him unconscious under some heavy woman who sat on him, banging his head while her men went off in search of others. Bo's'ns, captains, common sailors were treated alike, and any who resisted had their arms or jaws broken. When the assault was over, Kelolo sent official policemen around, searching for bodies which he pitched into the new jail. Then, with the foresight of a politician, he went personally among the piles of Americans and searched out all the captains, saying to each in his most fatherly voice, "Kapitani, I sorry inside me. We no see good, we t'ink you crew, we boom-boom good too much. No pilikia, I take care of you." And he took them to Murphy's and bought each man a drink, but as they pressed their broken lips to the glass, he was pleased to see how badly scarred they were.

At the next dusk, the conches sounded and a good many sailors climbed into boats and returned to their ships. Those that didn't were chased through the town, not by policemen, but by infuriated gangs of Hawaiians bent on thrashing them. But whenever a sailor was caught, some policeman was ready to rescue him, and by eight o'clock the jail was full. On the third night, most of the sailors who were caught ashore after curfew sought out the police, to whom they willingly gave themselves up, preferring that to the coursing mobs. And by the fourth night, order was restored in Lahaina. Kelolo's police were in command.

On the next day, Malama, at Kelolo's suggestion, summoned the whaling captains to her grass palace, where a feast had been spread. She greeted each bruised skipper with personal warmth and commiserated with him over the rude behavior of her people. She fed the captains well, offered them fine whiskey, and then proposed: "Our lovely church is burned. It was an accident, I am sure. Naturally, we want to rebuild it, and we will. But before we do, we want to do something for the fine Americans who come to Lahaina. Therefore we are going to build a little chapel for sailors. It will give them a place to read, and pray, and write letters home to their dear ones. Will you kind men set the example and give a few dollars for the chapel?" And by her daring charm she wheedled more than sixty dollars from the astonished captains, and another of Abner Hale's dreams, one that he had entertained since that day off the Four Evangelists when the sailors went swinging through the arcs of heaven, was realized: the Seamen's Chapel at Lahaina.

BY 1828 it seemed that Abner's world was at last beginning to be well organized. He had a rude desk and a whale-oil lamp by which he translated the Bible. He had three schools functioning with increasing success, and the day seemed not too far distant when Iliki, Pupali's youngest and loveliest daughter, would be married in church to one or the other of the established Hawaiian men who were trying with increasing regularity to peek into Jerusha's school. Captain Janders' return to Lahaina and his announced decision to settle down as a ship chandler, with his wife and children coming out from New Bedford, gave Abner a polished mind with whom he could conduct discussions; while the captain's happy knowledge that young Cridland, the devout sailor from the *Thetis,* was footloose in Honolulu, where the ship's company had been disbanded, encouraged Abner to direct a letter to the youth, asking him to throw in his lot with the Seamen's Chapel, so that Cridland was now employed there, giving guidance to the younger sailors who arrived in Lahaina on the rapidly increasing whaling fleet—45 whalers in 1828; 62 in 1829.

Malama was rapidly approaching a state of grace, so that it seemed assured that she would be accepted into the rebuilt church when it was dedicated, and there were really only two difficulties looming on the broad and lovely horizon at Lahaina. Abner had anticipated the first, for when it came time to rebuild the church, Kelolo announced that the kahunas wished to consult with Abner again, but he replied, "The door will stay where it was. All this talk in the community that the kahunas knew the church would be destroyed irritates me. Some drunken sailors burned it and that's that. Your local superstitions had nothing whatever to do with it."

"Makua Hale!" Kelolo protested gently. "We did not wish to speak about the door. We know your mind is made up, and we know that your church will always be unlucky. But there is nothing we can do about that."

"What did the kahunas want to see me about?" Abner asked suspiciously.

"Come to the church," Kelolo begged, and when Abner met with the wise old men they pointed to the two-third walls and the absent ceiling and made this proposal: "Makua Hale, it has occurred to us that the last church was very hot indeed, what with more than three thousand people huddled on the floor and no wind to cool them off."

"It was warm," Abner agreed.

"Would it not therefore be a wise thing if we did not build the destroyed walls any higher? Would it not be better, indeed, if we could pull them down even farther? Then we could erect high posts and raise the ceiling as it was before, so that when the church is finished, the winds will move across us and cool us as if we were on the shore."

It took some minutes for Abner to comprehend this radical suggestion and he tried to piece its various components together in his mind. "You mean, tear the present walls down to here?"

"Even lower, Makua Hale," the kahunas advised.

"Well . . ." Abner reflected. "Then raise the pillars as before?"

"Yes, and hang the ceiling from them, as before."

"But you wouldn't have any walls," Abner protested.

"The wind would move over us, and that would be better," the wise men explained.

"But there would be no walls. A man sitting here," and he squatted on the ground, "could look up and watch the sky."

"Would that be wrong?" Kelolo asked.

"But a church always has walls," Abner replied slowly. He thought of every church he had ever seen in New England. The very essence of a church was that it have four rugged, square walls and a steeple above them. Even the pictures he had seen of churches in foreign lands showed four walls, and those that did not were clearly popish, so he said firmly, "We will build the church as before."

"It will be very hot," Kelolo warned.

"A church must have walls," Abner said, and he left the wondering kahunas.

The second difficulty could not have been foreseen, at least not by Abner Hale. It concerned Keoki Kanakoa, whose school was accomplishing wonders in bringing Hawaiian boys from the Stone Age into the present. Half the sailors aboard the *Thetis,* as it plied from Lahaina to Honolulu on weekly trips, were young men trained by Keoki. The boys who worked at the mission printing press, publishing the Bible, were his boys, too. In community life he was a rugged, dependable tower of Christian strength, and his Bible readings in formal services were inspiring. It should not have been surprising therefore—but it was—when Keoki appeared in Abner's grass house one day and asked, "Reverend Hale, when can I hope to be ordained a full minister?"

Abner rested his pen and looked at the young man in astonishment. ' A minister?" he gasped.

"Yes, I was told at Yale that I must return to Hawaii and become a minister to my people."

"But you already work with them, Keoki," Abner explained.

"I believe I am ready to have a church of my own," Keoki suggested. "In some new part of the island where the people need God."

"But there can't be a church without a missionary, Keoki."

"Why not?" the handsome Hawaiian asked.

"Well . . ." Abner began. He threw down the pen. "I have no plans for ordaining Hawaiians," he said bluntly.

"Why not?" Keoki pressed.

"Well . . . It's never even been considered, Keoki," Abner explained. "You do excellent work in the school . . . of course . . . but a full-fledged minister? Oh, no! That would be ridiculous. Impossible."

"But I thought you missionaries came here to educate us . . . to get us ready to take care of ourselves."

"We did, Keoki!" Abner assured him. "You have heard me talk with your mother. I insist that she govern every aspect of the island. I touch nothing."

"You have been fine about that," Keoki acknowledged. "But the church is more important than the government."

"Exactly," Abner jumped. "The government could fail because of your mother's errors, and that would be no irremediable harm, but if the church failed because of your error . . . Well, Keoki, the damage could never be repaired."

"But how will you know whether I am strong enough to do God's work unless you test me?" Keoki pleaded.

"With the life of the church at stake, Keoki, we can take no chances."

"Does that mean that I can never become a minister? Here in my own land?"

Gravely, Abner leaned back in his chair and thought: "Somebody better tell him the facts." So he said coldly, "Would you have the strength, Keoki, to discipline your fellow Hawaiians as God requires? Would you seek out those who lead a lewd life and announce their names on Sunday? And track down those who drink? Would you dare to expel the alii who smokes? Could I trust you to use the right words in explaining the Bible? Or to refuse bribes when the alii want to join the church? Keoki, my dear son, you will never have the courage to be a true minister. For one thing, you are too young."

"I am older than you were when you became a minister," the Hawaiian pointed out.

"Yes, but I grew up in a Christian family. I was . . ."

"A white man?" Keoki asked bluntly.

"Yes," Abner replied with equal frankness. "Yes, Keoki, my ancestors fought for this church for a hundred years. From the day I was born I knew what a heavenly thing, what an inspired, divine thing the church was. You don't know yet, and we can't trust the church in your hands."

"You are saying very bitter things, Reverend Hale," Keoki replied. "Do you remember aboard the *Thetis,* when I gave the old whaler in the fo'c's'l the Bible, and how he brought ridicule on the Bible and on me and on God? That's what happens when we risk the welfare of the church in the wrong hands. You must wait, Keoki, until you have proved yourself."

"I have proved myself," Keoki said stubbornly. "I proved myself at Yale College, when I stood in the snow begging an education. I proved myself at Cornwall, where I was the top student in the mission school. And here in Lahaina I have protected you against the sailors. What more must I do to prove myself?"

"Those acts were your duty, Keoki. They qualified you for church membership. But to qualify for the ministry itself! Perhaps when you are an old, tested man. Not now." And he dismissed the arrogant young man.

He was rather startled when, in discussing these matters with Jerusha, she sided with Keoki, arguing, "Your commission, Abner, from the American Board that sent you here was to train up the Hawaiians so that they could organize and run their own churches."

"Organize them and run them, yes!" Abner instantly agreed. "Soon we will take in more members and institute a board of deacons. But to make a Hawaiian a minister! Jerusha, it would be complete folly. I couldn't tell poor Keoki, but he will never become a minister. Never."

"Why not?" Jerusha asked.

"He's a heathen. He's no more civilized than Pupali's daughters. One good hurricane, and he would lose all his veneer of civilization."

"But when we are gone, Abner, we shall have to turn the church over to Keoki and his fellows."

"We shall never go," Abner said with great solemnity. "This is our home, our church."

"You mean to stay here forever?" Jerusha asked.

"Yes. And when we die, the Board in Boston will send out others to take our places. Keoki running a church! Impossible!"

But Abner had acquired the habit of listening to his wife, and long after their discussion ended he brooded about what she had said, and at last he found a reasonable solution to the impasse over Keoki, and he summoned the young Hawaiian. "Keoki," he announced happily, "I have discovered a way whereby you can serve the church as you desire."

"You mean I can be ordained?" the young man cried joyfully.

"Not exactly," Abner replied, and he was so preoccupied with his satisfactory answer to Keoki's problem that he failed to observe how disappointed the latter was. "What I'm willing to do, Keoki, is to make you the luna of the church, the top deacon. You move among the Hawaiians and find out who is smoking. You check to see who has alcohol on his breath. Each week you hand me a list of people to be admonished from the pulpit, and you draw up the names of those to be expelled from church. At night you will creep quietly through Lahaina to let me know who is sleeping with another man's wife. I am willing to have you do these things for the church," Abner concluded happily. "How do you like that?"

Keoki stood silent, staring at the little missionary, and when the latter asked again for his response Keoki said bitterly, "I sought a way to serve my people, not to spy upon them." And he stalked from the mission, remaining in seclusion for many days.

If Jerusha and Keoki could not stand up to Abner's arguments against the Hawaiians, a visitor was about to descend on Lahaina who not only marshaled all of Jerusha's doubts and expressed them in vigorous English but who also brought along many of his own. It was Dr. Whipple, lean and brown from years of work on distant outposts, who came in one day on Kelolo's ship, the *Thetis*. He hurried immediately to the mission house and shouted, "Sister Jerusha, forgive me for not being here when you were pregnant. Good heavens! I forgot you have two children. And pregnant again!"

The years had mellowed Whipple and given him a strong no-nonsense vernacular. He had witnessed too much death—wives, children, black-frocked men who worked themselves to death—to bother any longer with the niceties of expression that had characterized the *Thetis*. "I had the same stateroom coming over. Only four other men in it with me, and I felt lonely. Sister Jerusha, how's the medicine box?" And he yanked the black box down and checked its contents against the new medicines he had lately received from Boston. "I'm giving you lots of ipecac," he advised. "We find it very good for children's fevers. And tonight you and Brother Abner and I are going to have a big dinner with Retire Janders in his new store. And because I was seasick on the damnable *Thetis* again, I'm going to have some whiskey. You'll be seasick too, when you go back to Honolulu."

"Are we required to go?" Abner asked, for like Jerusha he preferred to remain in Lahaina, finding Honolulu, at the yearly meeting of the missionaries, a dirty, dusty, ugly little collection of hovels.

"Yes," Dr. Whipple said sadly, "I'm afraid it's going to be a difficult meeting, this one."

"What's the matter?" Abner asked. "They going to discuss pay for the missionaries again? I explained my position last time, Brother John. I shall always be unalterably opposed to salaries for missionaries. We are here as God's servants and we require no pay. My mind will not change on this."

"That isn't the subject," Whipple broke in. "I don't agree with you on the salary question. I think we ought to be paid wages, but that's beside the point. We've all got to vote on the case of Brother Hewlett."

"Brother Abraham Hewlett!" Abner repeated. "I haven't heard from him since his baby was born. And he's on the same island with me. What is the question about Brother Abraham?"

"Haven't you heard?" Whipple asked in astonishment. "He's in trouble again."

"What's he done?" Abner asked.

"He's married a Hawaiian girl," Whipple said. There was a long, shocked silence in the grass house, during which the three missionaries stared at each other in amazement.

Finally, Abner took out his handkerchief and wiped his forehead. "You mean to say he's actually living with a native woman? A heathen?"

"Yes."

"And the meeting is to decide what to do about him?"

"Yes."

"There's nothing to decide," Abner said flatly. He went for his Bible and thumbed it for a moment, finding the text that applied to the case. "I think Ezekiel 23, verses 29 and 30, covers such behavior: 'And they shall deal with thee hatefully, and shall take away all thy labor, and shall leave thee naked and bare: and the nakedness of thy whoredoms shall be discovered, both thy lewdness and thy whoredoms. I will do these things unto thee, because thou hast gone a whoring after the heathen, and because thou art polluted with their idols.'" He closed the Bible.

"Are they determined in Honolulu to throw him out of the church?" Jerusha asked.

"Yes," Dr. Whipple said.

"What else could they do?" Abner demanded. "A Christian minister marrying a heathen. 'Gone a whoring after the heathen!' I do not want to go to Honolulu, but it seems my duty."

Dr. Whipple said, "Would you excuse us, Sister Jerusha, if we walk down to the pier?" And he led Abner along the lovely paths of Lahaina, under the gnarled hau trees and the palms. "You are fortunate to live here," Whipple reflected. "It's the best climate in Hawaii. Plenty of water. And that glorious view."

"What view?" Abner asked.

"Don't you come down here every night to see the best view in the islands?" Whipple asked astonished.

"I wasn't aware . . ."

"Look!" Whipple cried, as a kind of poetry took command of him, tired as he was from seeing so many bleak Hawaiian prospects. "To the west the handsome rounded hills of Lanai across a few miles of blue water. Have you ever seen gentler hills than those? Their verdure looks like velvet, thrown there by God. And to the north the clean-cut rugged mountains of Molokai. And over to the south the low hills of Kahoolawe. Wherever you look, mountains and valleys and blue sea. You lucky people of Lahaina! You exist in a nest of beauty. Tell me, do you ever see the whales that breed in the channel here?"

"I've never watched for any whales," Abner replied.

"A sailor told me, as I was cutting off his arm, that one night at Lahaina he saw a dozen whales with their babies, and he said that all his life he had been harpooning whales and had thought of them only as enormous, impersonal beasts so huge that the ocean was scarcely large enough to hold them. But when his arm was gangrenous and he knew that he was going to lose it, he, for the first time, observed whales as mothers and fathers, and they were playing with their babies in the Lahaina Roads, and he told me . . . Well, anyway, he won't be throwing a harpoon any more."

Abner was not listening. He was doing something he had not done before: he was looking at the physical setting in which his whaling town existed. To be sure, he had seen the hills behind the town, for he had walked over them, but he had not appreciated the glorious ocean roads: jeweled islands on every side, the deepest blue water, white sands and the constant scud of impressive clouds. He understood why the whaling ships were content to anchor here, for no storm could get at them. From all sides they were protected, and ashore they had Lahaina for water, and fresh meat and cool roads.

"This is rather attractive," Abner admitted.

"I was sorry to hear your view on Brother Hewlett," Dr. Whipple began when he had found a comfortable rock.

"It's not my view," Abner replied. "It's the Bible's. He went whoring after a heathen."

"Let's not use that old-style language," Whipple interrupted. "We're dealing with a human being in the year 1829. He isn't a strong human being and I never liked him much . . ."

"What do you mean, Brother John? Old-style language?"

"He wasn't whoring after heathens, Brother Abner . . . Do you mind if I quit this brother calling? Abner, this man Abraham Hewlett was left alone at Hana with a baby boy and not a damned thing to guide him in the care of that child."

"Brother John!" Abner exploded. "Please do not offend me with such language. And besides, Brother Abraham had as much . . ."

"And the Hawaiian girl wasn't a heathen. She was a fine, Christian girl . . . his best student . . . and I know, because I delivered her baby."

"She had a baby?" Abner asked in a whisper.

"Yes, a fine baby girl. She named her Amanda, after my wife."

"Was it . . ."

"I no longer count the months, Abner. They're married now and they seem very happy, and if there is any system of morality which requires a lonely man like Abraham Hewlett . . ."

"I hardly comprehend your words any longer, Brother John," Abner protested.

"I have buried so many people, cut off so many legs . . . Many of the things we used to worry about at Yale don't worry me any more, ancient roommate."

"But surely you would not allow a man like Brother Hewlett to remain in the church? With a heathen wife?"

"I wish you would stop using that word, Abner. She's not a heathen. If Amanda Whipple were to die tomorrow, I'd marry such a girl any day, and Amanda would want me to. She'd know at least that her children had a good mother."

"The others will not think as you do, Brother John."

"Immanuel Quigley does, I'm proud to say. And that's why I've come to Lahaina. We want you on our side. Don't drive poor Hewlett from his church."

"The Lord saith, 'Thou hast gone a whoring after the heathen.'" Dully, Abner closed the discussion, but in doing so he began to wonder about John Whipple. What the doctor said next erased the wonder and confirmed the doubt.

"I've been doing a great deal of speculation recently, Abner," he began. "Do you think we've done right in bursting into this island kingdom with our new ideas?"

"The word of God," Abner began, "is not a new idea."

"I accept that," Whipple apologized. "But the things that go with it? Did you know that when Captain Cook discovered these islands he estimated their population at four hundred thousand? That was fifty years ago. Today how many Hawaiians are there? Less than a hundred and thirty thousand. What happened to them?"

To Whipple's surprise, Abner was not particularly shocked by these figures, but asked casually, "Are your facts correct?"

"Captain Cook vouches for the first. I vouch for the second. Abner, have you ever seen measles strike a Hawaiian village? Don't. Ppppsssshhhh!" He made a sound like fire rushing through the grass walls of a house. "The entire village vanishes. For example, do you make your church members wear New England clothes?"

"I have only nine members," Abner explained.

"You mean that in this entire . . ." Dr. Whipple threw a pebble into the blue waters and watched a near-naked Hawaiian riding the surf onto the kapu beach. "On Sundays, for example, do you require a man like that one out there to wear New England clothes?"

"Of course. Doesn't the Bible specifically state, 'And thou shalt make them linen breeches to cover their nakedness'?"

"Do you ever listen to the hacking coughs that fill the church?"

"No."

"I do, and I'm terribly worried."

"What about?"

"I'm afraid that in another thirty years the Hawaiians will be not a hundred and thirty thousand but more likely thirty thousand. Out of all those who were here when we came, twelve out of thirteen will have been destroyed."

"Lahaina was never any bigger," Abner replied prosaically.

"Not the town, perhaps, but how about the valleys?" Whipple, as was his practice in touring the islands, called an old man to the seaside and asked in Hawaiian, "In that valley, did people used to live?"

"More t'ousand was stay before."

"How many live there now?"

"T'ree. Ikahi, ilua, ikulu. T'ree."

"In that valley over there, did people used to live?"

"More two t'ousand was stay before."

"How many live there now?"

"All dis fellow stay before, now make . . . die," the old man answered, and Whipple dismissed him.

"It's that way in all the valleys," he said gloomily. "I think the only thing that will save Hawaii is some radical move. There has got to be a big industry of some kind. Then we must bring in some strong, virile new people. Say from Java, or perhaps China. And let them marry with the Hawaiians. Maybe . . ."

"You seem beset with doubts," Abner marked.

"I am," Whipple confessed. "I am terribly afraid that what we are doing is not right. I am certain that we are sponsoring the spread of consumption and that these wonderful people are doomed. Unless we change things right away."

"We are not concerned with change," Abner said coldly. "Hawaiians are the children of Shem, and God has ordained that they shall perish from the earth. He has promised that their lands shall be occupied by your children and mine, Genesis 9, verse 27: 'God shall enlarge Japheth, and he shall dwell in the tents of Shem.' The Hawaiians are doomed, and in a hundred years they will have vanished from the earth."

Whipple was aghast, and asked, "How can you preach such a doctrine, Abner?"

"It is God's will. The Hawaiians are a deceitful and licentious people. Even though I have warned them, they continue to smoke, they circumcise their sons and abandon their daughters. They gamble and play games on Sunday, and for these sins God has ordained that they shall be stricken from the face of the earth. When they are gone, our children, as the Bible directs, shall inherit their tents."

"But if you believe this, Abner, why do you remain among them as missionary?"

"Because I love them. I want to bring them the consolation of the Lord, so that when they do vanish it will be to His love and not to eternal hellfire."

"I do not like such religion," Whipple said flatly, "and I do not aspire to their tents. There must be a better way. Abner, when we were students at Yale, the first tenet of our church was that each individual church should be a congregation unto itself. No bishops, no priests, no popes. Our very name bespoke that conviction. The Congregationalists. But what do we find here? A system of bishoprics! A solemn convocation to throw a poor, lonely man out of the ministry. In all these years you've allowed nine people to join your church as full members. Somewhere, Abner, we've gone wrong."

"It takes time to convert the heathen to true . . ."

"No!" Whipple protested. "They are not heathen! One of the most brilliant women I have ever met or read about was Kaahumanu. I understand you have one like her here on Maui, your Alii Nui. Heathen? The word doesn't mean anything to me any more. For example, have you admitted any of your so-called heathen to the ministry? Of course not."

Abner, finding the turn of Whipple's argument most distasteful, rose to go, but his old roommate grasped him by the hand and pleaded: "You have nothing more important to do today than talk with me, Abner. I find my soul wandering from its moorings, and I seek guidance. I had hoped that when you and Jerusha and Captain Janders and I sat down together, something of the spirit that animated us on the *Thetis* . . ." His voice trailed off, and after a while he confessed, "I am sick with God."

"What do you mean?" Abner asked quietly.

"The spirit of God fills my brain, but I am dissatisfied with the way we administer His word."

"You are speaking against the church, Brother John," Abner warned.

"I am, and I am glad that you said so, for I was ashamed to."

"It is the church that has brought us here, Brother John. It is only through the church that we build our accomplishments. Do you think I would dare to speak to the alii as I do if I were plain Abner Hale? But as the instrument of the church I can dare all things."

"Even wisdom?" Whipple inquired.

"What do you mean?"

"If your mind suddenly comprehended a new wisdom . . . some radical new concept of existence . . . well, could you as a servant of an all-powerful church dare to accept that new wisdom?"

"There is no new or old, Brother John. There is only the word of God, and it is revealed in the church, through the instrumentality of the Holy Bible. There can be no greater than that."

"No greater," Dr. Whipple agreed, "but there can be a different."

"I do not think so," Abner replied, and he wished to hear no more of this argument and left. But that night, in the warm fellowship of Captain Janders' excellent dinner, with good wine, and whiskey for the doctor, the old friends relaxed and Janders said, "Lahaina's becoming a first-rate city, thanks to Abner Hale's exertions."

"Who is that girl who's bringing in the dishes?" Abner asked, for her face seemed familiar, yet he did not recognize it.

Captain Janders blushed ever so slightly, in a way that Abner missed but which Dr. Whipple had seen often in the islands. "I understand you're bringing Mrs. Janders and the children out from Boston?" Whipple said by way of rescue.

"I am," Janders replied quickly.

"We need all the Christians we can get," Abner said heartily.

"Do you intend remaining here?" Whipple asked directly. "In Lahaina, that is?"

"It's the jewel of the Pacific," Janders replied. "I've seen all the towns, and this is best."

"You'll be in trade, I judge?"

"I see great opportunity for ships' chandlery here, Doctor."

"Do you suppose there is any way . . . it would be difficult I grant you . . . but do you suppose that if a man with good native connections could get some canoes at Hana . . . well, if he had some fine land there and energy, do you suppose he could grow things and sell them to you . . . for the whalers, that is?"

"You speaking of Abraham Hewlett?" Janders asked abruptly.

"Yes."

"If he could grow hogs . . . beef . . . I might buy 'em. He ever think of growing sugar? We could use a lot of sugar."

"I'll speak to him about sugar," Whipple said thoughtfully.

"You expect him to be giving up the church at Hana?" Janders inquired.

"Yes. I fear the Honolulu meeting is going to expel him."

Captain Janders sat very thoughtfully for some moments. He did not want to offend Reverend Hale, with whom he must live in intimacy, and yet he had always liked young John Whipple's honest approach to life. "Tell you what I'd be willing to do," he said slowly. "If Hewlett could get his stuff to me in the whaling season . . . on time and in good shape . . . well, I judge I could use everything he produces. But I want one thing he may not be willing to give."

"What's that?" Whipple asked.

"I hear his wife has claim to a nice piece of land at Hana, more than Abraham could possibly farm. Isn't he the scrawny fellow with big eyes that slept in your stateroom? He's the one I had in mind. I want him to enter into a contract with me so that I manage that land. I'll tell him what to grow and he won't ever have to worry about where his next meal's comin' from," Janders promised.

When it came time for the *Thetis* to carry the missionaries to Honolulu, Abner discovered the thrill that ugly memories yield when they have receded with their pain, for he was to bunk in his old stateroom and John Whipple would share it; but his pleasure was considerably dampened when a canoe arrived from the other end of Maui bearing the missionary Abraham Hewlett, his handsome little boy Abner, and his Hawaiian wife, Malia, the native pronunciation of Mary.

"Are they sailing with us?" Abner asked suspiciously.

"Of course. If we don't have them, we don't have a trial."

"Won't it be embarrassing if Hewlett's on the same ship with us?"

"Not for me. I'm voting for him."

"Do you think he'll be put in our stateroom?"

"He shared it with us once," Whipple replied.

The two missionaries looked with interest as Mrs. Hewlett, if anyone so dark could be given that name, came aboard the *Thetis*. She was taller than her husband, very broad-shouldered and grave of manner. She spoke to the little boy in a soft voice, and Abner whispered in disgust, "Is she talking to that child in Hawaiian?"

"Why not?" Dr. Whipple asked.

"My children are not allowed to speak a word of Hawaiian," Abner replied emphatically. " 'Learn not the way of the heathen!' the Bible directs us. Do your children speak Hawaiian?"

"Of course," Whipple replied with some impatience.

"That's very unwise!" Abner warned.

"We live in Hawaii. We work here. Probably my boys will go to school here."

"Mine won't," Abner said firmly.

"Where will you send them?" John asked with some interest, for he often discussed the matter with his wife.

"The Board will send them to New England. Then to Yale. But the important thing is that they never come into contact with Hawaiians." Dr. Whipple watched the Hewletts cross the deck and go down the hatchway aft, and the manner in which the Hawaiian woman watched over little Abner Hewlett proved that whereas she might have crept into the father's bed by some trick or other, she certainly loved the child.

"Boy's lucky," Whipple said. "He's got a good mother."

"She doesn't look the way I expected," Abner confessed.

"You expected a painted whore?" Whipple laughed. "Abner, once in a while you ought to look at the reality of life."

"How did she become a Christian?" Abner pondered.

"Abraham Hewlett took her into the church," Whipple explained.

There was a thoughtful pause, and then Abner asked, "But how could they have been married? I mean, if Hewlett was the only minister, who could have married them?"

"For the first year nobody did."

"You mean, they lived in sin?"

"And then I came along . . . on one of my regular trips. I was in a Russian ship."

"And you married a Christian minister to a heathen?" Abner asked, aghast.

"Yes. I'm probably going to be censured, too," Whipple said dryly. "And I have a suspicion in here," and he touched his heart, "that I won't accept the censure. I stand with St. Paul: 'It is better to marry than to burn.' Can anyone seriously doubt that Abraham is better off today than he was when you left him in Wailuku?"

The meeting in Honolulu went as expected. At first Abraham Hewlett made a sorry spectacle of himself, confessing that in marrying the Hawaiian girl Malia he had sinned against the decrees of God, thus bringing degradation upon both himself and the church. He begged forgiveness, asking the brethren to remember that he had been left alone with an infant boy; and at the recollection of his misery in those lonely days he wept. Later, when it was suggested that perhaps the sly Hawaiian woman had been responsible for his downfall, he recovered a portion of his dignity by avowing that he loved this gracious, tender girl and that it was he who had insisted upon the marriage, "and if the brethren think they dare imply censure of Malia, they are indeed mistaken."

The vote was an easily predicted condemnation and expulsion, only Whipple and Quigley speaking in defense. The meeting thought it best that the Hewletts leave the islands: "For your presence here would be a constant humiliation to the church. But it is recognized that it would be equally disgraceful for a Christian minister—an unfrocked one, that is—to return to America with a Hawaiian wife, for there are many in America who are eager to castigate missionaries, and your appearance among them would merely add ammunition to their blasphemies. It is therefore concluded that you and your family ought . . ."

At this point Abraham's tears were dried and he interrupted bluntly: "It is not within your province to advise me in these matters. I shall live where I wish."

"You will receive no sustenance from us," the meeting reminded him.

"I have entered into a compact to raise pigs and sugar cane for the whaling ships at Lahaina, and beyond this you are required to know nothing. But before I go I must point out that your mission is founded upon an impossible contradiction. You love the Hawaiians as potential Christians, but you despise them as people. I am proud to say that I have come to exactly the opposite conclusion, and it is therefore appropriate that I should be expelled from a mission where love is not."

Dr. Whipple thought that when the scrawny man with the big eyes finally left the judgment room, he departed with some dignity.

The meeting then turned to the doctor's case and condemned him for having married the pair, thus constituting himself, as one minister pointed out, "the agency, if not the cause, whereby our miserable brother from Hana fell into temptation and sin."

Dr. Whipple retorted, "I should rather have thought that I was the agency whereby he fell out of sin."

This sally, being both witty and cogent, furthered the case against the doctor, and all the missionaries except Quigley joined in a vote of censure. Whipple was reproved and advised to be more circumspect in the future. To Abner's surprise, his roommate accepted the condemnation and sat without even a look of resentment as the meeting turned to less weighty matters, including assignments of the mission family to new posts.

But when it came time for the *Thetis* to return to Lahaina, Abner was surprised to find Dr. Whipple, his wife Amanda, and their two boys ensconced in the stateroom. "I thought you were directed to go to Kauai," Abner remarked.

"Where I am directed to go and where I go are two vastly different matters," Whipple said easily, and Abner was relieved to notice that they had no luggage, so apparently they were on a short visit to one of the way islands, Molokai or Lanai. But when these ports were cleared, the Whipple family was still aboard, and at the pier in Lahaina, John grabbed Abner's hand and said, "Don't leave. I want you to witness exactly what happens. There's Jerusha. I'd like to have her come along, too, because I don't want contradictory reports circulated regarding what I'm about to do."

And with his wife and children in tow, he led the Hales to Captain Janders' store and said boldly, "Captain, I have come to throw myself on your mercy."

"What do you mean?" Janders asked suspiciously.

"You're doing a large business here, Captain, and with more whalers coming each year, you'll need a partner. I want to be that partner."

"You leaving the mission?"

"Yes, sir."

"Over the Hewlett affair?"

"Yes, sir. And others. I happen to believe that men who work should get a just salary." He tugged at his ill-fitting trousers, pointed at Amanda's dress and said, "I'm tired of going down to the mission grab bag in Honolulu to see what scraps the good people in Boston have sent us this year. I want to work for myself, get my own wage, and buy my own things."

"Does Amanda feel the same?" Captain Janders asked.

"She does."

"Do you, Amanda?"

"I love the Lord. I love to serve the Lord. But I also love an organized home, and in these matters I am with my husband."

"You got any money to put into the venture?" Janders asked warily.

"My family comes to you with absolutely nothing," the handsome dark-haired doctor, then twenty-nine, replied. "We have these clothes, picked from the rag bag, and that is all. I have no medicine, no tools, no luggage. Certainly I have no money. But I have a knowledge of these islands that no other man on earth has, and that's what I offer you."

"Do you speak the tongue?"

"Perfectly."

Janders thought a moment, then stuck out his rugged hand. "Son, you're my partner. On the *Thetis,* when you asked so many questions, I remarked you."

"I have only one request, Captain," Whipple said. "I want to borrow enough money . . . right now . . ."

"We'll fix you up with clothes and a place to live."

"Enough money to buy my own medical outfit. And anyone who wants medical advice from me can get it free. For I am a servant of the Lord, but I am determined to serve Him in my way, and not some other."

By the end of the week the Whipples had moved into a small grass shack, which Kelolo gave them along with a substantial square of land in return for medical care for Malama, whose exertions on behalf of the new laws had taxed her strength, and at the start of the next week the first of many signboards that were to become famous throughout Hawaii appeared on the dusty main streets of Lahaina: "Janders & Whipple."

ABNER'S DISTURBING EXPERIENCES in Honolulu, where both Abraham Hewlett and John Whipple had challenged the missionary board, confirmed his natural suspicion that there was inherent danger from too close relationships with the Hawaiian savages, and it was under the impetus of this fear that he built a high wall around his entire establishment, leaving an extra gate at the rear through which Jerusha could exit to her girls' classes, held in an open shed under the kou trees. Within the wall not a word of Hawaiian was spoken. No Hawaiian maid was allowed to enter unless she knew English, and if a deputation of villagers came to see Abner, he would carefully close the door leading to where his children were, and he would take the Hawaiians to what he called "the native room," where their voices could not be heard by the little ones.

"We must not learn the ways of the heathen!" Abner constantly warned his family, for what Abraham Hewlett had suggested in Honolulu regarding all missionaries was particularly true of Abner: he loved the Hawaiians, yet he despised them. He was therefore not in very good humor when Kelolo came to visit him one night, which forced him to close off the children's room, lest they hear Hawaiian being spoken.

"What is it you want?" he asked testily.

"In church the other day," Kelolo said in Hawaiian, "I listened to Keoki read that beautiful passage from the Bible in which this man begat that man, and the other man begat another man." The big chief's face was radiant with pleasant memory of the Biblical message which Hawaiians loved above all other. "The Begats," they called it among themselves.

Abner had long been curious about this partiality for the chapter in Chronicles, for he felt sure the Hawaiians could not understand it. "Why do you like that passage so much?" he probed.

Kelolo was embarrassed, and looked about to see if anyone was listening. Then he confessed somewhat sheepishly, "There is much in the Bible we do not understand. How could we? We don't know the many things the white man knows. But when we hear 'The Begats,' it is like music to our ears, Makua Hale, because it sounds just like our own family histories, and for once we can feel as if we, too, were part of the Bible."

"What do you mean, family histories?" Abner asked.

"That is what I came to see you about. I see you at work translating the Bible into my language, and we appreciate your hard work. Malama and I were wondering, if before she dies . . . No, Makua Hale, she is not well. We wondered if you would write down for us in English our family history. We are brother and sister, you know."

"I know," Abner mumbled.

"I am the last one who knows the family history," Kelolo said. "When Keoki should have been learning it, he was learning about God. Now he is too old to memorize the way I did when I was studying to be a kahuna."

Abner, a learned man, instantly saw the value of preserving old fables, and asked, "How does a family history sound, Kelolo?"

"I want you to write it as if Keoki were saying it. I am doing this for him, so that he will know who he is."

"How does it begin?" Abner pressed.

It was dark in the grass house, with only one feeble whale-oil lamp swaying with its retinue of shadows, when Kelolo, seated cross-legged on the floor, began: "I am Keoki, the son of Kelolo who came to Maui with Kamehameha the Great; who was the son of Kanakoa, the King of Kona; who was the son of Kanakoa, the King of Kona who sailed to Kauai; who was the son of Kelolo, the King of Kona who died in the volcano; who was the son of Kelolo, the King of Kona who stole Kekelaalii from Oahu; who was the son of . . ."

After Abner had listened for a while, his curiosity as a scholar overcame his initial boredom at this tedious and probably imaginary ritual. "How did you memorize this genealogy?" he asked.

"An alii who doesn't know his ancestry has no hope of position in Hawaii," Kelolo explained. "I spent three years memorizing every branch of my family. The kings of Kona are descended, you know, from the . . ."

"Are these genealogies real, or made up?" Abner asked bluntly.

Kelolo was amazed at the question. "Made up, Makua Hale? It is by these that we live. Why do you suppose Malama is the Alii Nui? Because she can trace her ancestry far back to the second canoe that brought our family to Hawaii. Her ancestor was the High Priestess Malama who came in that second canoe. My name goes back to the first canoe from Bora Bora, for my ancestor was the High Priest of that canoe, Kelolo."

Abner suppressed a smile as the illiterate chief before him tried to establish relations with some mythical event that must have occurred ten centuries before, if at all. He thought of his own family, in Marlboro. His mother knew when her ancestors reached Boston, but no one could recall when the Hales had got there, and here was a man who could not even write, claiming . . .

"You say you can remember the canoes in which your people came?"

"Of course! It was the same canoe on each trip."

"How can you remember that?" Abner demanded sharply.

"Our family has always known its name. It was the canoe *Wait-for-the-West-Wind*. It had Kelolo as navigator, Kanakoa as king, Pa at one paddle and Malo at the other. Kupuna was the astronomer and Kelolo's wife Kelani was aboard. The canoe was eighty feet long by your measures and the voyage took thirty days. We have always known these things about the canoe."

"You mean a little canoe like that one at the pier? How many people did you mention. Seven, eight? In a canoe like that?" Abner was contemptuous of the man.

"It was a double canoe, Makua Hale, and it carried not eight people but fifty-eight."

Abner was dumfounded, but once more his historical sense was excited, and he wished to know more about the myths of these strange people. "Where did the canoe come from?" he asked.

"From Bora Bora," Kelolo said.

"Oh, yes, you mentioned that name before. Where is it?"

"Near Tahiti," Kelolo said simply.

"Your people came in a canoe from Tahiti . . ." Abner dropped the question and said, "I suppose the family history ends there?"

"Oh, no!" Kelolo said proudly. "That is not even the halfway mark."

This was too much for Abner, and he stopped abruptly calling it a family history. He realized that he had got hold of one of the classic myths of the Hawaiian islands, and he said bluntly, "I'll copy it down for you, Kelolo. I would like to hear the story." He adjusted the swinging lamp, took fresh sheets of paper, and laid aside for some nights his Bible translation. "Now tell me very slowly," he said, "and don't leave out anything."

In the darkness Kelolo began to chant:

"The time of the birth of the tabu chief,
The time when the bold one first saw light,
At first dimly like the rising of the moon
In the season of the Little Eyes in the ancient past.
The great god Kane went into the goddess Wai'ololi
And the offspring of light were born, the bringers of men,
Akiaki who dragged the islands from the sea
And gentle La'ila'i who made the flowers and the birds,
And in the evening of the long day Akiaki knew his sister,
And the man was born, bringer of honor and war . . ."

And as Kelolo chanted the historic summary of his people the little room was filled with the clash of battle, the birth of gods, the abduction of beautiful women and the explosions of ancient volcanoes. Men in yellow capes, carrying spears, marched from one lava flow to another; queens fought for their children's rights and brave men perished in storms. In time Abner fell under the spell of the fabulous events, these made-up memories of a race, and when Kelolo and Malama and the canoe *Wait-for-the-West-Wind* made their second journey from Bora Bora to Hawaii the little missionary caught a momentary thrill of the vast ocean and its perils as Kelolo, sitting in the darkness, chanted what purported to be the song of directions for that imaginary voyage:

"Wait for the west wind, wait for the west wind,
Then sail to Nuku Hiva of the dark bays
To find the constant star.
Hold to it, hold to it
Though the eyes grow dim with heat."

But whenever Abner found his mind prepared to accept some small aspect of the narrative as true, ridiculous legendary events intruded, like Kelolo's account of how his ancestor in Bora Bora left for the trip north at the height of a hurricane, with waves forty feet high.

"Imagine a Hawaiian canoe even venturing out of port in a strong wind!" Abner laughed to Jerusha as he recounted some of the more fantastic passages in the history. "Just look! Right here we have more than forty generations of supposedly historic characters. Now if you allot twenty years to each generation, and that's conservative, Kelolo wants us to believe that his ancestors came here more than eight hundred years ago and then went back to get a second canoeload. Impossible!"

When Kelolo finished his genealogy—128 generations in all—Abner prudently made a copy of what he termed "this primitive and imaginary poem" and sent it to Yale College, where it formed the basis for most accounts of Hawaiian mythology; scholars appreciated in particular the detailed descriptions of the conflict between the Bora Bora god Kane and the Havaiki god Koro. Abner himself had slight regard for his work, and when he summoned Keoki to present the original he said condescendingly, "Your father claims it's a family history."

"It is," Keoki bristled.

"Now, Keoki! More than a hundred and twenty-five generations! Nobody can remember . . ."

"Kahunas can," Keoki said stubbornly.

"You sound as if you were defending the kahunas," Abner suggested.

"In the recitation of family histories, I am," Keoki replied.

"But this is ridiculous . . . mythology . . . fantasy." Abner slapped the manuscript with disdain.

"It is our book," Keoki said, clutching it to his bosom. "The Bible is your book, and these memories are our book."

"How dare you, a man who presumes to ask when he will be made a minister?"

"Why is it, Reverend Hale, that we must always laugh at our book, but always revere yours?"

"Because my Book, as you improperly call it, is the divine word of God, while yours is a bundle of myths."

"Are 'The Begats' any more true than the memories of the kahunas?" Keoki challenged.

"True?" Abner gasped, his temper rising with his astonishment. "One is the divinely revealed Word of the Lord. The other . . ." He paused in contempt and ended, "Good heavens, do you consider them equal?"

"I think there is much in the Old Testament that is merely the work of kahunas, nothing more," Keoki said firmly. Then, to repay Abner for his arrogance, he asked in confidence, "Tell me, Reverend Hale, don't you honestly think that Ezekiel was mostly kahuna?"

"You had better go," Abner snapped icily, but he felt some shame for having goaded the boy, so he put his arm about his shoulder and pointed to a canoe on the beach. "Keoki," he reasoned quietly, "surely you must know that a canoe like that could not carry fifty-eight people for thirty days . . . all the way from Tahiti."

Keoki moved so that he could see the broad, silvery passageway that lay between Lanai Island and Kahoolawe, leading south. "Reverend Hale, do you recall the name of that stretch of water?"

"Don't they call it Keala-i-kahiki?" Abner replied.

"And have you ever heard the name of that point at Kahoolawe?"

"No."

"It's likewise Keala-i-kahiki Point. What do you suppose Keala-i-kahiki means?"

"Well," Abner reflected. "*Ke* means *the; ala* means *road; i* means *to;* and I don't know what *kahiki* means."

"You know that what we call *k,* the people to the south call *t.* Now what does *kahiki* mean?"

Against his will, Abner formed the older word, of which *kahiki* was a late corruption. "Tahiti," he whispered. "The Way to Tahiti."

"Yes," Keoki said. "If you sail from Lahaina, pass through Keala-i-kahiki Strait and take your heading from Keala-i-kahiki Point, you will reach Tahiti. My ancestors often sailed that way. In canoes." And the proud young man was gone.

But Abner refused to accept such claims, and by consulting many Hawaiians he proved to his satisfaction that the word *kahiki* meant not Tahiti but any distant place, so he added his own note to the Yale manuscript: "Keala-i-kahiki may be translated as 'The Path to Far Places' or 'The Beyond.' " Then, as if to prove that Abner was right, the Hawaiian captain of Kelolo's ship *Thetis* got drunk, stayed in his cabin during a storm, and allowed his sturdy old veteran of many seas to climb upon the rocks off Lahaina, where it rotted through the years, a visible proof that Hawaiians could not even navigate in their own waters, let alone penetrate distant oceans.

IT WAS WHILE Abner was drafting a letter to Honolulu, advising the mission board that his assistant Keoki Kanakoa was behaving strangely, so that perhaps the board ought to consider Keoki's reassignment to some post of lesser importance, that the news was shouted through the still morning air that was to disrupt Lahaina for many days. Pupali's oldest daughter came screaming to Jerusha's school: "Iliki! Iliki! It has arrived! The *Carthaginian!*" And before the startled Jerusha could intercede, the bright-eyed beauty had leaped over the bench and dashed madly away with her sister. Together they swam out to the sleek whaler, with the dark sides and the white stripe running lengthwise, where naked and shimmering in the sunlight they were both gathered into the arms of the bark's tall captain and led below to his quarters, from which he shouted, "Mister Wilson, I don't want to be interrupted till tomorrow morning. Not even for food."

But he was interrupted. Kelolo dispatched three policemen to the *Carthaginian* under orders to drag Pupali's daughters off to jail, but when they climbed aboard the whaler, Mister Wilson met them on the afterdeck, shouting, "Get away! I'm warning you!"

"We come fetch wahines," the officers explained.

"You'll get broken jaws!" Mister Wilson threatened, whereupon one of the policemen shoved out his elbows, knocked the first mate aside and started for the after hatchway. Mister Wilson, thrown off balance for a moment, tried to lunge at the intruder, but another of the policemen grabbed him, which became the signal for a general scuffle, in which, because most of the men were ashore, the three rugged policemen appeared to be winning.

"What the hell's going on here?" came a roar from the lower deck, followed by a lithe form, tall and muscular, leaping up the ladder. Captain Hoxworth was dressed only in a pair of tight sailor's pants, and when he saw what was happening on his ship, he lowered his head, lunged at the first policeman and shouted, "Into the ocean with 'em!"

The agile officer saw Hoxworth coming, sidestepped with agility, and brought his right forearm viciously across the back of the captain's neck, sending him sprawling across the deck, where the New Englander cut his lower lip on his own teeth. Wiping the blood onto the back of his hand, Hoxworth glimpsed the red stain, and from his knees cried ominously, "All right!"

Rising slowly, testing his bare feet on the decking, Hoxworth moved cautiously toward the policeman who had pole-axed him. With a deceptive lunge to the right, followed by a snakelike twist to the left, Hoxworth brought his powerful right fist into the policeman's face. Then, with the Hawaiian's head momentarily snapped back, Hoxworth doubled up his own head and shoulders and drove into the man's stomach like a battering ram. The surprised policeman staggered backward and fell onto the deck, whereupon Hoxworth began kicking viciously at his face, but remembering, from the pain in his bare feet as they crashed into the man's head, that he wore no shoes, he quickly grabbed a belaying pin and started to thrash the fallen islander, thundering solid blows onto the man's head and crotch, until the policeman fainted. Still Hoxworth continued hammering him until sounds from other parts of the deck called him to activity there.

Brandishing his brutal pin, he whipped about to help Mister Wilson, who was having a bad time with a large policeman until Captain Hoxworth brought down with all the force in his bare arms the rugged belaying pin across the man's skull. The big islander fell instantly and Hoxworth instinctively kicked him in the face, then set off for the third officer, but this man, having witnessed Hoxworth's savage attacks upon his mates, prudently abandoned the battle and leaped into the bay. With a well-directed throw, Hoxworth spun the belaying pin through the air and caught the man in the face, cutting open a huge gash across his forehead. At once the man sank below the waves, leaving a patch of purple where he had gone down, and one of Hoxworth's sailors shouted, "He's drowning."

"Let the bastard drown!" Hoxworth shouted violently. "And let these swine join him." Alone he picked up the first unconscious victim, strained as the man's feet slowly cleared the railing, and then with a mighty heave tossed the policeman toward the general direction of the first, who had now dazedly regained the surface in time to help his battered and inert companion.

Now Hoxworth grabbed the feet of the third policeman and Mister

Wilson the hands, and with a one-two-three prepared to toss him overboard, but one of the man's hands was bloody, and on the three count, Mister Wilson lost his grip, so that when Hoxworth threw the legs mightily over the railing, the first mate failed to do so with the hands, and the policeman's face struck the wood with great force, breaking his jaw and cheekbones before he pitched into the bay. There he floated for a moment, then dropped slowly to the bottom, from which he was recovered a day later.

"I'm afraid he's drowned," Mister Wilson said apprehensively.

"Let him drown," Hoxworth growled, licking his damaged lip. Then, grabbing a horn, he shouted ashore, "Don't anybody try to board this ship . . . now or ever." Tossing the horn to his mate, he brushed off his sweating chest, stamped his bare feet to knock away the pain and growled at Mister Wilson, "I was disgusted with your performance."

"I stood them off, one after the other," the mate protested.

"You fought all right," Hoxworth admitted grudgingly, "but you had stout shoes on, and when I had the bastards down you didn't kick them in the face."

"It didn't occur to me . . ." Mister Wilson began apologetically.

Quickly, furiously, Captain Hoxworth grabbed his mate by the jacket. "When you fight a man aboard ship, and he knows he's licked, always kick him in the face. Because forever after, when he looks in a mirror, he'll have to remember. If you let him go without scarring him, sooner or later he begins to think: 'Hoxworth wasn't so dangerous. Next time I'll thrash him.' But if he constantly sees the memory of solid leather across his jawbone he can't fool himself." Seeing that his mate was shaken by this advice, he pushed him away and added coldly, "Keeping control of a ship is difficult duty, Mister Wilson, and until you nerve yourself to it, you'll never be a captain."

Abruptly, he swung himself down the after ladder, shouting, "This time I don't want to be disturbed." And he rejoined Pupali's daughters.

Ashore there was consternation. On the one hand, Kelolo was appalled that Americans would dare to kill one of his policemen in sight of the entire community, and he hurried to Malama to ask her what ought to be done. She was suffering from major ills and lay back on the floor, wheezing in the day's heat, but when she heard Kelolo's ominous report she called her attendants and with real effort rose and dressed. Then, with her two ladies-in-waiting, she went into the town, and after assembling all available policemen, she proceeded to the pier.

On the other hand, the various ships' captains who had been chafing futilely against the new laws saw in Hoxworth's bold action a chance to re-establish their control over Lahaina and to restore the good old days. Accordingly, they too assembled at the pier and passed the word to their men: "If they try to arrest Captain Hoxworth, we'll all fight." And as the sailors gathered, they armed themselves with stones and where possible with substantial clubs.

Malama pointed to the *Carthaginian* and said quietly, "Kelolo, arrest that captain."

Obediently, though with some apprehension, Kelolo adjusted his policeman's cap, picked three unwilling helpers, tested his two muskets, and set out for the whaler, but he had gone less than half the distance when Captain Hoxworth, alerted by Mister Wilson, rushed on deck with a brace of pistols and began firing madly at the rowboat.

"Don't you come a foot nearer!" he shouted, reloading and blazing away again. This time the bullets struck perilously close to the boat, and Kelolo did not have to order his men to cease rowing. They did so automatically, stared at the infuriated captain, then quickly retreated. To the surprise of all the watchers, and to the cheers of the sailors, Captain Hoxworth unexpectedly, perhaps even to himself, now swung barefooted over the side of the *Carthaginian,* one revolver in his left hand, one jammed into the belt of his trousers, and started rowing furiously ashore. The other sea captains formed a reception committee both to welcome and protect him. Before he had touched shore he was shouting, "Captain Henderson! Is that a cannon I see on the *Bay Tree?"*

"It is. I'm headin' for China."

"Got any balls?"

"I have."

Content, Hoxworth leaped ashore and strode up to Kelolo. Then seeing Malama in the background, he thrust the police chief aside and stormed over to the Alii Nui. "Ma'am!" he growled. "There's not goin' to be any more interference with the whalers in this port."

"The new laws have been announced," Malama said stoutly.

"The new laws be goddamned," Hoxworth stormed. The sailors cheered, so he left Malama abruptly and advised them, "Do any goddamned thing you like!"

The whaling captains applauded and one cried, "Can we bring whiskey ashore?"

"Whiskey, girls, any damned thing you want," Hoxworth roared. Then, seeing Kelolo's two assistants who carried the muskets, he rushed over, ripped the arms from them and fired twice into the air.

At this moment the crowd separated and onto the pier stepped Abner Hale, dressed formally in claw-hammer and top hat but still limping slightly from his old wound received at the hands of the blusterer who now threatened Lahaina's peace. Kelolo drew back, as did the bewildered policemen whose arms had been taken from them. "Good morning, Captain Hoxworth," Abner said.

The violent whaler stepped back, looked at the little missionary and laughed. "I threw this miserable little bastard to the sharks once. I'll do it again," he roared, and the captains, all of whom despised Abner as the author of the sumptuary laws, shouted encouragement.

"You will send the girl Iliki back to school," Abner said forcefully. The two men stared at each other for a long moment, and then almost unconsciously Captain Hoxworth's real intention in coming to Lahaina manifested itself. He wanted to see Jerusha Bromley. Desperately, driven by powerful memories and dreams of revenge, he wanted to see this brown-haired girl. He lowered his pistols, jammed them back into his pants, and said, "We can talk better at your house."

"Shall we bring the whiskey ashore?" one of the captains shouted.

"Of course!" Hoxworth snapped. "There are no laws."

"We'll meet at Murphy's!" the captains yelled.

"Where is your house?" Hoxworth asked.

"There," said Abner, pointing past the taro patch.

For a moment Captain Hoxworth stared aghast, and in his incredulity Abner perceived for the first time the really miserable hovel in which he and Jerusha lived. "Does Jerusha live there?" Hoxworth gasped, staring at the low grass roof, the rain-tattered walls and the Dutch doorway.

"Yes," Abner replied.

"Jesus Christ Almighty, man!" Hoxworth ejaculated. "What's the matter with you?" With huge strides the barefooted, bare-chested captain strode up the dusty road, kicked open the wooden gate in the high wall, and brushed into the grass house. Standing on the earthen floor he adjusted his eyes to the darkness, and finally saw, in the doorway that separated the children's quarters from Abner's study, the girl he had wanted to marry. He looked a long time, at the tired face, the hair not quite tended, the red hands. He saw the cast-off dress that did not fit, and the coarse shoes also second-hand, a size too large and scuffed from long years in the dust. Possibly because of the darkness, possibly because he did not wish to recognize such things, he did not see the persuasive radiance that shone from Jerusha's tired eyes nor did he sense the peace that encompassed her.

"My God, Jerusha! What has he done to you?" The harsh voice caused one of the children to whimper, and Jerusha left the doorway for a moment, but she soon returned and said, "Sit down, Captain Hoxworth."

"Where, for Christ's sake?" Hoxworth stormed, beside himself with anger and bitterness. "On a box? At a table like this?" With extreme violence he smashed at Abner's rickety table, sending the Bible translations into the wind. "Where could I sit down if I wanted to? Jerusha, do you call this a home?"

"No," the self-possessed woman replied, "I call this my temple."

The answer was so final, and implied so much, that Hoxworth set adrift his first fleet of compassionate thoughts and established in their place an overpowering desire to hurt Jerusha and her husband. Kicking at the fallen table he laughed, "So this is the senate from which the laws are handed down?"

"No," Abner said cautiously, recovering the fallen Bible, "this Book is."

"So you're going to rule Lahaina by the Ten Commandments?" Hoxworth asked with a hysterical laugh.

"As we rule ourselves," Abner replied.

Again Hoxworth kicked at the table, bruising his foot as he did so. "Does the Bible direct you to live like hogs? Does it say you have to work your wife like a slave?" Impulsively, he grabbed Jerusha's hand and held it aloft, as if he were selling her, but patiently she withdrew it and straightened her dress.

Her action infuriated Hoxworth and he backed away from the missionaries, lashing them horribly with insulting words, towering oaths and threats which he had the capacity to enforce. "All right, you goddamned sniveling little worms. You can pass the laws, but you can't make the fleet keep them. Reverend Hale, there's going to be women aboard those whalers by noon."

"The women will not be allowed to go," Abner said stubbornly.

"My men have been at sea for nine months," Hoxworth said. "And when they reach shore they're going to have women. All the goddamned black-assed Hawaiian women they want. Me. I always have two. One fat one and one skinny one."

"Will you go to the church, Jerusha?" Abner asked.

"She'll stay here!" Hoxworth shouted, grabbing her once more by the hand. "Let her hear how a real man lives." He had a consuming desire to abuse her mind with ugly pictures, to humiliate her. "Now when I get hold of a fat one and a skinny one, ma'am, I like to lock the door for about two days and I undress completely—that's why you find me only in pants; I was interrupted and had to kill a man—and when I'm undressed I like to throw myself back on the bed and say to the girls, 'All right, the first one of you who can . . .' " His explanation was halted by a stinging blow from Abner's open palm against his bruised lip.

He stopped in astonishment, then thrust out his big right arm and caught Abner by the wrist. Turning it until the missionary had to kneel in the dust of his own home, Hoxworth retained his hold on Jerusha and finished. "I tell the two girls that the first one who can make me get hard can climb aboard, and when she does the other one has to blow on me."

Jerusha kneeled in the dust beside her husband, and Rafer Hoxworth looked down with contempt at the two miserable creatures. "What're you doing, Jerusha?" he tormented. "Tending your little man?"

"I am praying for you," Jerusha said, in the dust. Impetuously, Hoxworth threw them both across the room and then stood over them, threateningly.

"There's a cannon aboard the *Bay Tree,* and by the guts of God, if there is any interference with the whaling fleet, I'll blow this house to pieces." He started for the open door but felt compelled to turn and laugh at the fallen missionaries. "You'll be interested to know that of all Pupali's daughters the young one, Iliki, is the best. Iliki . . . the Pelting Spray of the Sea! I started with Pupali's wife and worked my way right through his girls, but Iliki is my choice. And do you know why? Because you taught her such nice manners. Here at the mission. When she climbs on top of me she says, 'Please.' "

When he left, the two missionaries remained on their knees for some minutes, praying, and then Jerusha helped her husband rebuild the rickety table and collect his manuscript. Realizing that Captain Hoxworth meant his threats about the cannon, she took her two children over to Amanda Whipple's, but did not divulge the scenes that had taken place at the mission. Then she returned to Abner, desiring to be with him if further trouble developed.

It did. The general whaling fleet saw in Hoxworth's bold defiance a chance to abolish forever the restrictive laws, and they coursed through Lahaina tearing, raping and destroying. They drove policemen into hiding and then congregated at the new fort, where Kelolo and a last group of trusted subordinates were determined to make a stand.

"Rip down the fort!" sailors who had been jailed there shouted.

"Don't come any closer!" Kelolo warned. But before he took action, he climbed down from the frail ramparts and asked Malama what she thought he ought to do.

"What do you think is wisest?" Malama, breathing heavily, countered.

"I think we must defy them," Kelolo said gravely. "We have started good laws, and we must not surrender them now."

"I agree," Malama said, "but I do not want you to get hurt, my dear husband."

Kelolo smiled warmly at her use of this unexpected term, for he knew that she had been forbidden by the missionaries to use it in respect to him. "Do you feel better now?" he asked solicitously, as if he were a courtier and not a husband.

"I feel very ill, Kelolo. Do you think they will fire the cannon? I should not like to hear the noise of such a great gun."

"I think they will fire," Kelolo said. "And then they will be ashamed of themselves. And after a while they will stop."

"Do you think they will kill anyone?" Malama asked fearfully.

"Yes."

"Kelolo, I hope above all else that they do not kill you. There could be no finer husband than you have been to me." The enormous woman tried to find an easy position and then asked, "Did they harm the missionaries?"

"I don't know," Kelolo said.

"Isn't it strange?" Malama asked. "The little man spends so much time telling us how the Hawaiians ought to behave, but it is always his people who do the wrong things."

There was fighting at the gate and Kelolo was called away to make decisions. He told his men not to fire their few guns, lest a hopeless riot be initiated, but he did encourage them to use poles to push away the ribald attackers, so that from the *Bay Tree* Captain Hoxworth could see through his glass some of his own men from the *Carthaginian* being knocked off the walls, at which he grew agitated beyond control, and personally wheeled the cannon into position, ordering a charge to be fired. The forty-pound ball whistled high through the palm trees near the fort and he shouted, "Down twenty feet!"

The next ball crashed into the fort and threw bits of rock high into the air. The third ball struck the gate area and demolished it, so that hundreds of sailors were free to storm inside, where they elbowed Kelolo aside and threatened Malama.

"See that missionary house?" Hoxworth shouted, elated at his success with the cannon. "Up there to the left. Smash it."

Again the first ball was high, and Hoxworth danced barefooted with excitement as he directed the sights lowered. The fifth shot of the day tore completely through the mission house, as did the sixth and seventh. "By God," the captain screamed, "that'll end the laws!"

And then, as if he had been struck by some terrible unseen hand, he clasped his breast, cursed at the gunners and knocked them about like stones in a child's game. "Goddamn you!" he screamed. "What are you doing?" And leaping into the bay, he swam furiously ashore. Dripping wet he rushed past the breached fort, where sailors were abusing the chief of police and the fat woman, and onto the mission grounds, where the splintered wood from the shattered grass house appalled him. Bursting into the room he had visited only shortly before, he cried in anguish, "Jerusha! Are you hurt?"

He did not find her and started looking under the fallen beams—frail bits of wood hauled patiently from the mountains—and then from the inner room he heard sounds, and he smashed open the niggardly woven door and saw Jerusha and her husband praying in the dust of their destroyed home. "Oh, thank God!" he yelled with joy, grabbing Jerusha to his bare and salty body. She did not resist, but passively looked at him with horror which was heightened when she saw that her husband was approaching him with a broken knife.

"No!" she found strength to scream. "God will do it, Abner!" And with relief such as she had never known before in her life, not even when Abner alone and sweating had delivered her first baby, she saw her husband drop his arm. Quickly, Captain Hoxworth wheeled about, saw the knife, and smashed his fist into Abner's pale face. The little man doubled up and flew backwards against the grass wall and through its weakened portion. From inside the room he could hear his wife struggling with the sea captain. Before he could regain his feet he heard her screams and then the captain's cry of rage as she bit into the great salty hand. By the time he could get back into the room, brandishing a club, he saw Hoxworth standing at the front door, what was left of it, sucking his fiercely bitten hand. And then, as if nothing had happened, the huge sea captain said sorrowfully, "It is a dreadful place that your husband has brought you to, Jerusha. When did you last have a new dress?" He started to go, then added almost in tears, "Why is it that we always meet when you are pregnant . . . by this goddamned fool?"

The rioting continued for three more days, and girls who had been well along in Jerusha's school, standing midway between the savage and the civilized, reverted to the insane joy of sleeping, six and eight and ten at a time, in the hot fo'c's'ls of the whaling ships. Murphy's grog shop rollicked with songs. Old men who tried to keep sailors out of their homes were beaten up, and their daughters taken. And at the palace, tired, bewildered Malama ordered all women to the hills and found it increasingly difficult to breathe.

It was on the third day of the riots that she summoned Abner and asked with difficulty, "How did these things happen, my dear teacher?"

"We are all animals, Malama," he explained. "Only the laws of God keep us within the confines of decency."

"Why have your men not learned those laws?" Malama asked.

"Because Lahaina has itself been so long without the law. Wherever there is no law, men think they can do as they will."

"If your king knew about these days . . . the cannon and the burning of the houses . . . would he apologize?"

"He would be humiliated," Abner affirmed.

"Why is it that the Americans and the English and the French are so determined that we sell whiskey in our stores . . . and allow our girls to go to their ships?"

"It is because Hawaii has not yet established herself as a civilized nation," Abner explained.

"Are your men civilizing us?" Malama asked wearily. "By firing the cannon at us?"

"I am ashamed for our men," Abner said in despair.

This was the moment Malama had been waiting for, and after a long pause she said softly, "Now we are equal, Makua Hale."

"In what way?" Abner asked suspiciously.

"You have always told me that I could not achieve a state of grace without humility, without admitting to God that I am lost and totally evil. You would not accept me into your church because you claimed I was not humble. Makua Hale, I will tell you something. I wasn't humble. And you were right to keep me out of your church. But do you know why I could not be humble?"

"Why?" Abner asked carefully.

"Because you were not humble. Your ways were always right. Mine were always wrong. Your words were always white. Mine were black. You tried to make me speak Hawaiian because you wanted to learn Hawaiian, and I would not beg to join your church, because you spoke of humility but knew it not. Today, Makua Hale, with the fort destroyed and your home knocked down by your own people, we are equal. I am humble at last. I am unable to act without God's help. And for the first time I see before me a humble man."

The great huge woman began to weep, and after a moment she rose painfully to her knees, pushing aside her sorrowful attendants and making a prayer-temple of her hands. From that position she said in total contrition, "I am lost, Makua Hale, and I beg you to accept me into your church. I am going to die and I want to speak with God before I do."

From the *Bay Tree* some fools were firing the cannon again at the house of a man and wife who would not give them their daughter, and at the western end of town a building was ablaze. There was a dance under way at Murphy's, and three of Pupali's daughters were in Captain Hoxworth's cabin. It was under these conditions that Abner said, "We will baptize you into the church of God, Malama. We will do it on Sunday."

"We had better do it now," Malama suggested, and one of the waiting-women nodded, so Abner sent for Jerusha, Keoki, Noelani, Kelolo, Captain Janders and the Whipples. They came through the rioters, who jeered at Janders for not being a real sea captain and at the Whipples for being missionaries, but when Dr. Whipple saw Malama he was greatly concerned and said, "This woman is very ill," at which huge Kelolo began to sob.

It was a mournful crowd that formed a semicircle around Malama, who lay flat on the floor, wheezing painfully. The cannon sounded in the distance, and half a hundred hoodlums who had trailed the Whipples jeered outside the palace gates. Without a Bible, Abner recited from memory the closing passages of Proverbs, and the words had a special application to Malama, the Alii Nui: " 'Strength and honor are her clothing; and she shall rejoice in time to come. She openeth her mouth with wisdom; and in her tongue is the law of kindness. She looketh well to the ways of her household, and eateth not the bread of idleness.' "

Then he announced to the gathering: "Malama Kanakoa, daughter of the King of Kona, having entered into a state of grace, seeks baptism into the holy church of God. Is it your wish that she be accepted?"

Keoki spoke first, then Janders and the Whipples, but when it came time for Jerusha, who in the last days had appreciated for the first time the courage Malama had shown in governing Maui, she did not speak but bowed down and kissed the sick woman. "You are my daughter," Malama said weakly.

Abner interrupted and said, "Malama, you will now put aside your heathen name and take a Christian one. Which do you wish?"

A look of supreme joy came over the sick woman's massive face and she whispered, "I should like the name of that dear friend of whom Jerusha has often told me. My name will be Luka. Jerusha, will you tell me the story for the last time?"

And as if she were talking to her own children at dusk, Jerusha began once more the story of Ruth—Luka to the Hawaiians—and when she came to the part about the alien land she broke down and was unable to continue, so Malama concluded the story, adding, "May I like Luka find happiness in the new land to which I shall soon go."

After the baptism, Whipple suggested, "You'd better leave now. I have to examine Malama."

"I'll die with the old medicines, Doctor," Malama said simply, and she indicated to Kelolo that he must now bring in the kahunas.

"Are kahunas proper, when we have just . . ." Abner began, but Jerusha pulled him away, and the little procession marched back to the center of town, where Amanda Whipple suggested, "You had better stay with us, Jerusha and Abner."

"We will stay in our house," Jerusha said firmly, and when they were there, after the riotings had subsided and the ship captains were beginning to feel ashamed of themselves, for natives were whispering that sailors at the fort had killed Malama, or had caused her near-death, Captain Rafer Hoxworth, fully dressed, with polished cap and buttons, came up the pathway to the mission house, followed by five sailors with armloads of gifts.

Tucking his hat under his arm, as he had long ago been taught to do when addressing a lady, he said gruffly, "I apologize, ma'am. If I have broken anything I want to replace it. The other captains have contributed these chairs and this table . . ." He paused in some embarrassment and then added, "And I've gone among the ships and got this cloth. I trust you'll make yourself some decent . . . I mean some new dresses, ma'am." He bowed, placed his hat on his head, and left the mission grounds.

At first Abner was intent upon demolishing the furniture. "We'll burn it on the pier," he threatened, but Jerusha would not permit this.

"It has been sent to us as an act of retribution," she said firmly. "We have always needed chairs and a desk."

"Do you think that I could translate the Bible . . . on that desk?" Abner asked.

"Captain Hoxworth did not send it," Jerusha replied, and while her husband watched, she started arranging the chairs in the damaged room. "God has sent these things to the mission," she said, "and not to Abner and Jerusha Hale."

"I'll give the cloth to Malama's women," Abner insisted, and to this Jerusha agreed, but when he was gone, and the town was once more quiet, she sat in one of the new chairs at her new kitchen table and composed this letter:

"My dearest Sister Esther in God. You alone of all the people I know will have the grace to forgive me for what I am about to do. It is an act of vanity and one, under the circumstances of my life, truly unforgivable, but if it is sinful, it must rest on me alone, and I am powerless to avoid it. Dearest sister, do not smile at me and above all tell no one of my vanity.

"You have often asked me if there might be some small thing that you could send me, and I have always replied that God provided for my dear husband and me, and that is the truth. The mission board has sent us all that we require, but lately, as I grow older, I realize with some dismay that it has been many years since I have worn a dress that was made particularly for me. Quickly I must add that those which they send us from the charity barrels are good, and in fine style, but I find myself desiring just once more a dress of my own.

"I should like it to be russet in color, with either blue or red trimming, and I would be especially grateful to you if it could have the full round sleeves that seem to be in popular style today. I saw such a dress some years ago on a woman heading for Honolulu, and I thought it very becoming. But if the styles have changed substantially, and if there is now a fashion that I do not know of, I would rather wish you to follow the newer style. Hats I do not need, but if you could find it in your heart to send me a pair of gloves, with lace as in the old days, I should be most deeply appreciative.

"I do not need to tell you, dearest Esther, that I have no money wherewith to pay you for this extraordinary request, for I have not seen a dollar in over seven years and do not require to see any; and I appreciate that this is a vain and costly imposition to place upon a friend. But I pray that you will understand.

"I am not as stout as I used to be, and seem not to be as tall, so do not make the dress too large. I would judge from what your dear brother tells me that I am now about your size, but I do not want one of your dresses or anybody's. The cloth must be wholly new and mine. And may you find the charity in your heart to forgive me for this begging letter. Your sister, Jerusha."

When she went to Janders & Whipple's store to post the letter she discovered that the *Carthaginian* had sailed and that lovely Iliki, Pupali's youngest, had joined the captain. She felt sorrier for this than for anything that had happened in the past days, and she could not refrain from tears. "She was an adorable child," Jerusha said mournfully. "We shall not find another like her. Already I feel her departure as a great loss, for I had come to think of her as my own daughter. I do hope the world is good to Iliki." And she tried to dry her eyes, but the tears would not cease.

ONE OF THE LAST PUBLIC ACTS Malama performed was to climb into her land canoe, adjusting herself painfully on piles of tapa and directing her bearers to carry her through the damaged streets. Wherever she went she said simply, "The laws we gave are good laws. They must be obeyed." She stopped to encourage policemen, and at Murphy's grog shop again announced, in short gasps: "No more alcohol may be sold to Hawaiians. Girls must stop dancing here undressed." And the force of her words, coming as it did so soon after the riots, was four times what it had been before, and gradually Kelolo's policemen retrieved the control they had lost, and gained more besides. In her ludicrous canoe, followed by her two enormous ladies-in-waiting and the men with feathered staves, Malama became a figure of considerable dignity.

Both Abner and Jerusha noticed that on this strange canoe journey Malama's children, Keoki and Noelani, were drawn closely to her, and at the fort, where the largest congregation had assembled, Malama went so far as to announce: "I am going to die. My daughter Noelani will be the Alii Nui." There was no applause, but the citizens studied the handsome young girl with increased respect.

Abner now observed that the important kahunas of the island were gathering about Malama and arguing with her fervently, and he assumed that they were trying to cajole their renegade leader into abandoning her new religion, but this was not the case. The kahunas were satisfied with Christianity and were willing to acknowledge that its god was patently superior to their own, so prudence alone directed them to respect the potent newcomer; but they were also eager to overlook nothing in protecting their calm and massive alii in her last days, so as Abner prayed to Jehovah, they silently prayed to Kane. They massaged Malama with special care, sought traditional herbs to soothe her, and prepared favorite foods, on which she continued to gorge, feeling that only in this way had she any chance of recovering her strength. She ate four times a day, and sometimes five, and at a normal meal consumed a pound or two of roast pig, part of a dog, some baked fish, a substantial helping of breadfruit and not less than a quart of poi and oftentimes two or three, after which the lomilomi women would knead her stomach to spur her faltering digestion. Dr. Whipple stormed: "She's eating herself to death, but she started doing so when she was twenty. Such fantastic meals!"

When word reached the other islands that Malama, daughter of the King of Kona, was dying, the alii assembled, as they had at deathbeds for untold generations, and in after years whenever an American who had been in Lahaina at the time was asked for his most vivid impression of the island, he never referred to the cannonading but to this last mournful gathering of the alii: "They came from distant Kauai in ships and from Lanai in canoes. They came singly and in groups. Some came in western clothes, I recall, and some in yellow capes. But they all landed at our little pier, walked gravely past Kamehameha's old palace and eastward along the dusty road beneath the kou trees. I can see them now. What giants they were!"

Queen Kaahumanu, regent of the islands, came attended by Queens Liliha and Kinau, both of enormous girth. From Hawaii came Princess Kalani-o-mai-heu-ila, heavier by forty pounds than Malama, and from Honolulu, Kauikeaouli, the boy king. The great men of the islands were there: Paki and Boki and Hoapili and the leader called by westerners Billy Pitt; and Dr. Whipple, seeing them assemble, thought: "In one lifetime they lifted their islands from paganism to God, from the Stone Age to the modern. And to do so they had to fight off the Russians, the English, the French, the Germans and the Americans. Every time a civilized warship came to their islands it was to make them turn over girls for the sailors or rum to the natives." They were an amazing race, the old alii of Hawaii, and now as they gathered in formal panoply for the death of Luka Malama Kanakoa they seemed to be mourning for themselves.

Dr. Whipple observed to Abner: "They are like echoes of the great animals that once roamed the world and marched slowly to their death as changes overtook them."

"What animals?" Abner asked suspiciously.

"The monstrous ones before the ice ages," Whipple explained. "Some scientists think they vanished because they became too huge to be accommodated on the changing earth."

"I have no interest in such speculation," Abner replied.

In her grass palace Malama greeted each of the great old friends. "Aloha nui nui," she repeated constantly.

"Auwe, auwe!" they wept. "We have come to weep with our beloved sister."

When extreme pain in breathing attacked her, she bit her lower lip and gasped through the corners of her big mouth, resuming her smile as soon as the pain passed, while around her, in a vast semicircle, hunched the alii, whispering to themselves and praying.

Now Kelolo decided that it was time to move the woman he had loved so deeply onto the bed where she would die, so he sent his men to the hills to fetch bundles of fragrant leaves—api for protection against evil spirits, ti for healing, and mysterious maile whose penetrating aroma was the best loved—and when these leaves arrived, redolent and reminiscent of courtship days on Hawaii, Kelolo gently broke the back of each one so as to release its odor, and he arranged them in a formal pattern over the tapa blanket. Over this fragrant bed he placed a softly woven pandanus mat, and then a soft tapa, and over all a sheet of Cantonese silk embroidered with golden dragons. And whenever giant Malama moved on this bed, she caught the smell of maile.

Next, Kelolo went to the beach and had his fishermen procure fresh aholehole, which in the old custom of the islands he cooked himself. He grated coconuts and saw to the baking of breadfruit, and in her last days she ate not a morsel except from his fingers. In the long hours of the night it was he who waved the soft feathered wands to keep away the flies from the great sleeping body that he had loved so well, and he never approached her except on his hands and knees, for he wished to remind her that she was the Alii Nui, the one from whom his mana came. But what pleased her most was the morning, when Kelolo would leave her for a while and then come creeping back to her on his elbows, for his arms would be filled with red lehua blossoms and ginger and yellow hau. He brought them to her with dew still upon them, as he had done years ago, before the clashing battles of Kamehameha had interrupted their lives.

She died looking at Kelolo, seeing him as he had been in their youth, before strange gods and missionaries had intervened between them, but her last words reflected the new society which she had been instrumental in launching: "When I die no one must knock out his teeth. No one must blind his eye. There must be no furious lamenting. I shall be buried as a Christian." Then she summoned Kelolo and whispered to him for the last time, raising herself upon her elbow to do so, so that when she expired she fell backwards, a mighty surge of lifeless flesh, crushing the maile leaves.

Malama's wish was granted, and she was accorded a Christian burial in a cedar box on an island in the center of a marshy area where the alii had often gone on outings. Abner preached a moving graveside sermon, and the towering alii, standing beside the first Christian grave that many of them had ever seen, thought: "This is a better way to bury a woman than the old way," but the common people, not allowed onto the kapu island, stood on the shores of the river and wept piteously in the old fashion. None of them, however, knocked out their teeth or gouged their living eyeballs as they had done in the past when an alii nui died. Instead they watched in awe as the funeral procession formed: Makua Hale and his wife in front, intoning prayers for their beloved friend, followed by Captain Janders and Dr. Whipple and their wives. Then came the kahunas wreathed in maile and secretly muttering old heathen chants to themselves, followed by the towering alii, weeping in massive grief. Eight of the men, wearing yellow capes, carried poles on which was placed the cedar box. It was covered with maile and lehua blossoms and by a huge silken coverlet embroidered in purple dragons.

When the silent mourners reached the actual grave, the alii began to cry, "Auwe, auwe for our eldest sister." And the noise became so pitiful that Abner, attending to the Christian burial that was to expel heathen rituals, failed to observe that Kelolo, Keoki and Noelani did not approach the grave, but remained apart, conspiring with the major kahunas. What Kelolo confided was this: "When Malama whispered to me at her death she said, 'Let them bury me in the new way. It will help Hawaii. But when the missionary is finished, do not let my bones be found.'"

The plotters stared at each other gravely, and as Abner commenced his long prayer an old kahuna whispered, "It is right that we should respect the new religion, but it would be a shameful thing to the house of Kanakoa if her bones were found."

Another whispered, "When Kamehameha the Great died he gave those same instructions to Hoapili, and at night Hoapili crept away with his bones, and to this day no man knows where they are hidden. That is the way of an alii."

And while Abner pleaded, "Lord, take Thy daughter Malama!" the oldest kahuna whispered hoarsely to Kelolo, "Such a deathbed wish is binding above all others. You know what you must do."

At the grave the three missionary couples raised their harmonious voices in "Blest be the tie that binds," while each member of Kelolo's mysterious group whispered in turn, "It is your duty, Kelolo," but no such confirmation was really necessary, for from the moment Malama had whispered to her husband, he had realized what he must do. Therefore, when the singing at the graveside ended and Abner led the congregation in final prayer, Kelolo prayed: "Kane, guide us in the right way. Help us, help us." And the first Christian burial in Lahaina ended.

But as the funeral procession returned to the boats, Kelolo gently held his son's hand and whispered, "I would be happy, Keoki, if you would stay."

This was an invitation which the young man had anticipated, even though he had hoped to escape it. Now that it had come, he accepted and said, "I will help you." In this quiet manner, his appalling decision was made.

For some time he had sensed that a trap was closing about him, for he had been unable to hide from his father and the kahunas his bitter disappointment over Reverend Hale's refusal to accept him as a minister, a resentment which deepened when both Dr. Whipple and Abraham Hewlett quit the calling, proving that from the start they had had less dedication to God than he. The kahunas had whispered, "The missionaries will never allow a Hawaiian to join them." On the other hand, from the moment of his conversion in the snow outside Yale College, he had been totally committed to God and still stood willing to suffer the humiliation of seeing men with less vocation than he admitted to the ministry. He loved God, knew Him personally, spoke with Him at sunset. He was willing to devote his entire life to God's desires and he was ashamed of himself for having wondered, "Why should I remain faithful if the missionaries reject me because I am Hawaiian?"

In a curious way he had been content with his ambivalent position of loving God while hating His missionaries, for so long as he remained in that delicate balance he could escape making definite choices; but with the death of his great mother he had been subtly drawn by both Kelolo and the kahunas to a fundamental reconsideration of his beliefs. The cannonading of Lahaina and its debauch by Christian Americans had already pushed him to a stark question: "Is this new religion good for my people?" Now, on the evening of his mother's burial, as the pagan sun sank behind the fawn-colored hills of Lanai, lighting the sea roads with shimmering gold as it had in the days before Captain Cook, Keoki made his choice between the religions. "I will help you," he told his father.

When darkness fell, Kelolo, Keoki and two strong young kahunas proceeded to the fresh grave of their Alii Nui and carefully lifted aside the flower leis that covered it. Then they produced digging sticks which had been hidden earlier that day, and they uncovered the cedar box, pried away the top and reverently lifted out the black Bible that lay on top. Then they saw once more, wreathed in maile, their great alii. Gently they rolled the vast inert body onto a canvas sling and returned to repair the grave.

"You will cut the banana trunk," Kelolo directed, and Keoki went to the center of the island and cut down a leafy trunk which from time out of mind had represented man to the gods, and when he had a length as tall as Malama, he returned to the coffin, and it was placed inside, lest the Lord God Jehovah be angry, and the Bible was put in place, and the grave was resealed, with the flowered leis scattered upon it. Then the four strong men lifted the canvas and carried Malama to her true burial.

In darkest night they rowed to the shore where none could see them, then started a mournful march toward the hills of Maui. Toward morning they reached a secluded valley, where as soon as light came they dug a shallow grave and filled its bottom with porous rocks, upon which they placed banana leaves and ti. When all was ready, they tenderly put Malama into the grave, covering her with a sacred tapa and then with moist leaves and grass. Next they piled the grave high with such sticks as they could find, and lighted it. For three days they kept the fire slowly burning as the kahunas chanted:

"From the heat of living to the cool waters of Kane,
From the desires of earth to the cool waters of Kane,
From the burdens of desire to the cool retreats of Kane,
Gods of the many islands, gods of the distant seas,
Gods of the Little Eyes, gods of the stars and sun,
Take her."

On the fourth day Kelolo opened the grave whose burning heat had baked away Malama's flesh, and with a sharp knife he severed her head from her gigantic skeleton. Carefully scraping the skull to remove all desiccated fragments, he wrapped it in maile leaves, then in tapa and finally in a closely woven pandanus mat. For so long as he lived, this would be his perpetual treasure, and as he grew older, in the evenings he would unwrap his beloved's head and talk with her. He would recall that before the Christians came she had loved tobacco. He would light his pipe and when the smoke was good, he would blow it into her mouth, knowing that she would appreciate his thoughtfulness.

Next he cut away one of the huge thigh bones, and this he gave to Keoki both to scrape and to keep, and the young man proceeded with his ancient task as if voices from the past were calling him.

Now Kelolo cut off the other leg, and scraped the thigh bone for Noelani, the Alii Nui, so that she would always have with her some reminder of the source from whence came her greatness, and when these jobs were done, Kelolo gathered the remaining bones and embers and handed them to one of the kahunas who had brought with him a curious bag of sennit, so constructed that it looked like a woman, and into this receptacle Malama's final remains were put. The sennit bag was handed to Kelolo, and with it under his left arm and the wrapped head under his right, he started forth alone on his final pilgrimage.

He walked through the heat of day far up the valley from which the whistling winds sometimes came to strike Lahaina, over the saddle, along the crest of hills and on to a cave which he had discovered while gathering maile. Here he stopped and, crawling carefully inside, collected lava rocks with which he built a small platform. Here, safe from the corrupting earth, he deposited the last royal remains of his wife. Then, as in the old times, he prayed. When this was done he sat for more than an hour staring at the desolate and hidden pile of rocks.

"Oh, Kane!" he suddenly screamed, repeating the anguished shout until the cave echoed and until he became hysterical with grief. He threw himself against the platform, took a fragment of rock into his lips, ground it between his teeth until his whole body was racked with ugliness and despair. Beating the stones with his fists he screamed, "Malama, I cannot leave you. I cannot."

When he regained composure, he started a small fire beside the platform, then raved afresh as pungent smoke filled the cave. Grabbing a piece of bark he formed a tube which he held in the flames until it was ablaze, whereupon he jammed it against his cheek until he could feel the flesh burning in a small circle. Again and again he did this, seeking to scar his face so that all who saw him would know that he mourned the death of his alii.

Then, when the pain of burnt flesh was great, he grasped a pointed stick and jammed it between his two big front teeth. With a heavy rock he began to pound the opposite end, but his teeth were strong and would not break. In the quietness of the cave, with the smoke about him, he cursed his teeth and struck the stick with enormous force until he felt a horrible wrenching in his upper jaw. The bone had broken and the tooth dangled free. Clutching it with his fingers he jerked it loose and placed it upon the lava rocks, whereupon with demonic power he knocked its companion out with the stone itself, gashing his lips as he did so.

"Oh, Malama! Malama! Cherished of my heart, Malama!" In his misery he wept for some moments. Then with superhuman resolution he took the stick again and placed its dulled point next his nose and in the corner of his right eye. With a sudden inward thrust followed by a lateral pull, he scooped away his eye and threw it onto the grave. Then he fainted.

It was ten days before the powerful chief Kelolo Kanakoa reappeared in Lahaina. He came walking erect, proudly, but removed, as if he were still in contact with his gods. About his shoulders he wore a lei of maile leaves, its fragrance reminding him of his departed wife. His right eye socket, a horrible wound, was covered with morning-glory leaves, bound in place by olona and ti. His cheeks were scarred with ugly blisters and his lips, when closed, were thick with wounds; when opened they disclosed a lacerated jaw. He moved like a man set free from grief, a man who walked with love, and as he passed, his Hawaiian friends, knowing what he had done, stepped aside with respect; but his American friends stopped with horror, wondering how he could have borne so much.

It was important that he warn Reverend Hale, but when Jerusha saw him she screamed, but he was not offended, saying through lisping lips, "The whistling wind is coming. It always does at the death of an alii."

"What is the wind?" Jerusha asked, trying to compose herself, for she realized that he was speaking with great conviction.

"The whistling wind is coming," he repeated and stalked off, a man apart.

When Jerusha told her husband of the message, and of Kelolo's appearance, Abner held his head in his hands, lamenting, "These poor, bewildered people. Thank God we gave her a Christian burial." And Jerusha agreed, saying, "We should be grateful that Malama forbade heathen practices."

They grieved for obstinate Kelolo, and finally Jerusha asked, "What was the wind he spoke about?"

"One of his superstitions," Abner explained. "He's probably in a trance because of the horrible things he did to himself and is convinced that since an alii died, there will have to be some supernatural occurrence."

"Is the wind rising?" Jerusha asked.

"No more than usual," her husband replied, but as he spoke he heard a weird whistling coming down from the distant valleys that led to the crests of the hills where Malama, unknown to them, now lay.

"Abner," Jerusha insisted, "I do hear a whistling."

Her husband cocked his ear, then ran out into the dusty roadway. Dr. Whipple and Captain Janders were already listening to the ominous sound, while Hawaiians were running out of their houses and huddling under trees. "What is it?" Abner cried.

"Not like anything I ever heard," Janders replied, and the moaning whistle increased in pitch while high in the coconut palms dead branches began to tear loose. A Hawaiian sailor, who had swum in panic from one of the whalers, abandoning the ship to its fate, dashed by, wet and frightened and shouting in Hawaiian, "The whistling wind is upon us!"

"Should we go inside?" Abner asked hesitantly, but the same sailor yelled back over his shoulder, "No stay in house! Bimeby come plenty pilikia." And the three Americans remarked that the Hawaiians, who seemed to know what the wind could do, had abandoned their huts. Abner was already on his way to collect his children when Murphy, the saloonkeeper, rushed up and shouted, "This wind is a killer! Get out of your houses!" And while the three men scattered, the first important gust of wind struck Lahaina.

It bent the palm trees level, ripped off the roofs of several houses, then roared out to sea, where it threw great clouds of spume across the roads and tore away the masts of two whalers. During its destructive passage the whistling increased to an intense shriek and then subsided. Under the protection of a clump of kou trees Janders asked, "Where's the rain?"

None came, but the wind howled down from the mountains in new gusts, knocking down trees and throwing pigs into ditches. From the little stream before the mission house it picked up water, flinging it upon the trees, then passed out to sea, where it dashed three moored whalers together, staving in the sides of one and leaving it in perilous condition.

Still no rain came, but the winds increased, rising to even more furious levels than before, and now it became evident why the Hawaiians had left their homes, for one after another the little huts went flying through the air, crashing into the first solid object that intervened. "Will these trees hold?" Abner asked anxiously, but before anyone could assure him he saw a dark object hurtling through the air and cried, "The church!"

"It's the roof," Whipple shouted, astonished at what he saw. "It's the entire roof!" Majestically, the roof sailed over the town of Lahaina and plunged into the sea. "The walls are going down!" Whipple cried as the wind utterly destroyed the building.

But before Abner could lament his new loss, a woman shrieked, "The whaling boats are sinking!" And she was correct, for in the roads the demonic wind, still with no rain, had whipped up a sea that the rugged whalers could not survive. The unfortunate ones were those who were torn loose from their anchorages and dashed across the roads to the island of Lanai, on whose steep and rocky shores no rescue was possible. In that manner four ships and seventy men perished, and as they died, the Hawaiians of Lahaina mourned, "They are the sacrifices for the death of our Alii Nui."

Therefore, the sailors whose ships capsized off Lahaina would also have perished at the feet of the fatalistic Hawaiians had not Abner Hale limped among them, shouting, "Save those poor men! Save them!" But the Hawaiians repeated, "They are sacrifices!" until in frenzy Abner rushed up to one-eyed Kelolo, screaming above the storm, "Tell them, Kelolo! Tell them Malama does not require sacrifices! Tell them she died a Christian!"

There was a moment's hesitation during which the old man, weak from his vigil in the cave, looked out at the sickening sea. Then, throwing aside his tapa breechclout, he plunged into the waves and began fighting them for the bodies of sailors. Ashore Abner organized rescue parties which waded, tied together by ropes, onto the reef from which most of the water had been blown by the fantastic winds. At the end of each line swimmers like Kelolo battled the turbulent waters to haul foundering sailors across the jagged reef's edge, delivering them into the hands of rescuers. Without the work of Kelolo and Abner, the loss of American sailors would have been not seventy but nearly three hundred.

Toward the end of the struggle, Abner was limping about the reef, shouting encouragement, when he received from the hands of a swimmer the already dead body of a cabin boy, and he was overcome by the ceaseless tragedy of the sea and he started to pray: " 'They that go down to the sea in ships, that do business in great waters; These see the works of the Lord, and His wonders in the deep.' " But his prayer was halted when he looked into the violent storm and saw that the swimmer who had handed him the boy was Kelolo, who was shouting to the other Hawaiians, "Pray to Kanaloa for strength." And Abner could see that the swimmers were praying.

When the whistling wind subsided, Abner sat limply beneath the kou trees, watching Dr. Whipple treat the rescued sailors, and when the doctor came to him for a rest, Abner asked, "These things couldn't have had any connection with Malama's death, could they?" When Whipple made no reply, he continued, "John, you're a scientist." From the day Whipple left the mission, Abner had never again referred to him as Brother. "How do you explain such a wind? No rain? Coming not from the sea but from the mountains?"

Even while helping to rescue the whalers, Whipple had been perplexed by this problem and now suggested, "The mountains on the other side of our island must form a curious kind of funnel. I would judge there must be wide-open valleys up which the trade winds rush. When they roll over the tops of the mountains, the entire volume is compressed into this one narrow valley leading down into Lahaina."

"That wouldn't have anything to do with the death of an alii, would it?" Abner asked suspiciously.

"No. We can explain the wind as it roars down this side of the mountain. We know that's a force of nature. But of course," he added slyly, "it's entirely possible that the wind on the other side of the mountain blows only when an alii dies." Shrugging his shoulders he added, "And if that's the case, why you have just about what Kelolo claims."

Abner started to comment on this but instead changed the subject. "Tell me, John, how did you feel, at the very height of the storm, when you were on the reef rescuing the sailors . . . seeing the whalers that had so recently been tormenting us . . . well, seeing them destroyed by the Lord?" Dr. Whipple turned to study his companion, staring at him in disbelief, but Abner continued: "Didn't you feel that it was something like . . . well, I thought it was like the Egyptians at the Red Sea."

Whipple got up, disgusted, and called his wife, who was tending wounded sailors. "I don't think the alii sent the wind, and I don't think God sank the ships," he growled and left.

But he had not waited for Abner to develop the full meaning of his speculations, as they had matured on the coral reef, so Abner chased him and said, "What I wanted to ask, John, was this: 'At that moment of what I have called God's revenge for the cannonading, did you feel any actual sense of revenge against the sailors?' "

"No," Whipple said flatly. "All I thought was, 'I hope we can save the poor devils.' "

"I thought the same thing," Abner said frankly, "and I was astonished at myself."

"You're growing up," Whipple said sharply and left.

ONE UNEXPECTED BENEFIT came from the whistling wind that leveled much of Lahaina in 1829. When the damage was cleared away, Kelolo for the third time helped Abner rebuild his church, but this time the kahunas refused even to argue where the door should be. They put it where it should have been in the first place, where the local gods ordained, and the famous stone church they built that year stood for more than a century.

Now Lahaina, most beautiful of all Hawaiian towns, prospered as the national capital. The business center of the kingdom was Honolulu, to be sure, for foreigners preferred living near their consulates, but the alii had never liked Honolulu, finding it hot, cheerless and commonplace, so that even though it was true that the boy king and his regents had to spend more and more time there, he returned whenever possible to his true capital, Lahaina, and his women often remained in the cool grass houses under the kou trees even when he was called to the larger city.

Whaling vessels, their crews now better behaved, came to Lahaina in increasing numbers—78 would come in 1831, 82 in 1833—and because each stayed for about four weeks in the spring and four in the autumn, there were sometimes many tall-masted ships in the roads; and since the famous whistling wind of Lahaina blew only about twice a century, they rested in security within the charmed pocket of islands. The important thing to Janders & Whipple was that every whaler who came into the roads paid them a fee for something or other. Did the ship need firewood? J & W had it. Salt pork? Dr. Whipple found out how to salt down island hogs. Salt itself? J & W had a monopoly on the fine salt evaporated from the sea in flat lava-rock beds. Did a ship's captain insist upon fresh pork at sea? J & W could provide healthy live pigs and bundles of ti leaves for fodder on long trips. Sweet potatoes, oranges that had been introduced by Captain Cook, and fish dried by Dr. Whipple . . . J & W had them all. And if a ship required balls of olona twine, strongest in the world, or even cables woven of it, J & W controlled that monopoly, too.

It was John Whipple, however, who devised one of the simplest money-making schemes for the firm. When a whaler put in with an unwieldy amount of whale oil, not enough barrels to warrant sailing all the way home, but so many that there seemed no purpose in returning to the Off-Japan Banks, Whipple arranged for the captain to leave his entire cargo at Lahaina, under the care of J & W, who, when they had assembled half a dozen such cargoes, would argue some New England captain into running the entire lot back to New Bedford. In this way J & W made a profit on storing the barrels of oil, on shipping them, and on chartering the ship that did the work. It therefore seemed to Whipple that the next logical step ought to be for his firm to buy the odd lots of oil outright and to hold them on speculation.

Accordingly, he proposed that J & W acquire its own ships and take over the whale-oil business, but cautious Captain Janders, tugging at his red beard, was adamant. "Only one way to make money in this world," he judged. "My motto: 'Own nothing, control everything.' Own a batch of oil outright? Never! Because then you worry about the market. Let someone else own it. We'll handle it, and we'll make the better profit. But to own a ship. That is real madness. I've watched the tribulations of shipowners. They have to trust a rascally captain, a worse mate and a depraved crew. They've got to feed the lot, insure the vessel, live in anguish when there's a storm, and then share whatever profits there are with the crew."

"You bought the *Thetis,*" Whipple argued.

"Sure!" Janders agreed. "I bought her, but did you see how fast I sold her? On an earlier trip I had watched Kelolo's mouth watering for such a ship, and I knew I could turn a quick profit. Me operate a ship on my own responsibility? Never!" And he pointed to the rotting hulk that still hung on the reef. "Whenever you want to buy a ship, John, always remember the *Thetis.*"

Still Whipple was not satisfied, for he argued, "Somebody makes money on ships. I thought it might as well be us."

Janders agreed, in part, for he said, "I grant that properly handled a ship can make a little money, but if you and I learn how to manage the business and the lands right here, John, we'll make a fortune that will stagger the shipowners. Own nothing, control everything."

In the fields Captain Janders had determined to control, he was a master trader, sending meat to Oregon, picking up furs for Canton; sending hides to Valparaiso and tallow to California. He made a quick profit on each exchange and was always on hand when men were in trouble, for then money was free. Gradually, the whalers found that they could trust him with any transaction, and he became their agent. If a ship's captain wanted to risk the dying sandalwood trade, having heard that Captain Janders had made his fortune on it, J & W gladly accumulated the precious cargo and provided letters of introduction to the Canton merchants who would buy it. If another felt convinced that he could turn a handsome profit running fresh beef to Oregon, then ice to California, J & W would supply the live cattle, sending the crazy young cowboys of Lahaina up into the hills to lasso the wild animals that had been introduced into the islands by Captain Vancouver in 1794.

To win the good wishes of the mariners, J & W also provided many free services. If a sailor wanted to marry a native girl, there was no point in applying to Reverend Hale to conduct the ceremony, for he frowned on such alliances and invariably spent at least an hour praying with the sailor and pointing out that God had long ago warned against the sin of whoring after the heathen. Dr. Whipple, however, had been given the right by Kelolo to solemnize such marriages, and many families who were destined to live in Hawaiian history, producing the powerful half-caste politicians who organized the islands, sprang from marriages which started in the J & W store, where Reverend Whipple used Amanda, Captain Janders and his wife Luella as witnesses. Abner, of course, held that all participants in such marriages were living in whoredom, and he told them so.

J & W also served as mail drop for the fleet, and sometimes musty letters would lie in their bins for years before sailors came rolling up the wooden stairs and along the porch, shouting, "Any mail for me?" The wiry wanderer would sit in one of the J & W chairs and read of family affairs that had transpired forty months ago. Then he would ask John Whipple for a piece of paper, and the doctor would explain, "That building at the corner. It's a writing room for sailors, and if you ask for Mr. Cridland, he'll take care of everything."

Frequently, ship captains would transmit from the distant whaling grounds requests to J & W for a half-dozen replacements for their crews, to be picked up when the ship reached Lahaina. Captain Janders knew that whalers preferred stout Hawaiian boys, and he provided them at five dollars a head, but when none were available, he would visit Kelolo and tell the one-eyed, toothless police marshal, "Round up eight or ten deserters for next month," and Kelolo would move his men through the countryside, dragging in as worthless a lot of murderers, cowards, ship-jumpers, adulterers and hopeless drunks as any nation of the day could have provided. No American deserter could be so degenerate or worthless but that some kind Hawaiian family would give him refuge; they even fought the police to keep the murderers from arrest, but when the rogues were finally lodged in jail, Mr. Cridland, from the Seamen's Chapel, would move among them, explaining, "If you're taken back to America in chains, you'll be tried and sent to jail. But if you volunteer, you'll not only get wages but also escape trial." And with Abner's help, usually in the form of long prayers with the dissolute rogues, Cridland would whip the men into reasonable shape, and as soon as the shorthanded whaler hove into sight, Kelolo would release the imprisoned vagabonds, and Captain Janders would march them to the pier, where he would announce to the incoming captain: "A fine lot of men here for you to choose from!" And on every such recruitment J & W would make its small commission.

Other letters of more personal content sometimes arrived, and one day in 1831 Captain Janders sent Whipple through Lahaina, seeking the Hawaiian Pupali, for a letter awaited him from Valparaiso and it appeared to contain a substantial sum of money. When fat Pupali came to the store, Janders explained, "I no savvy, Pupali! One lettah for you, but."

"Me no savvy read," Pupali grinned.

"Okay. You lissen for me. I speak for you dis papah," Janders said.

"Alu, alu," Pupali nodded, his eyes bright with anticipation.

When Janders opened the Valparaiso letter, a handful of British pound notes fluttered to the floor, and Pupali jumped upon them, pinning them down one after another, like a man swatting cockroaches. "Pehea dis money? It b'long for me?" he grinned.

"We'll see," Janders said, pressing out the thin paper on which the letter was written. " 'To my good friend Pupali, of Lahaina,' " Janders began. "Well, at least the letter's for you. Now we'll see about the money," Janders announced, and fat Pupali laughed at the large circle that had now gathered at the startling news that one of their men had received a document from Valparaiso.

"Who's it from?" an onlooker asked, and Captain Janders carefully smoothed down and inspected the last few lines of the message. "It's from Captain Hoxworth!" he said with some surprise. At the name of the feared whaler, some of the Hawaiians drew back, for the memory of Hoxworth's cannonading was still vivid in their memories.

"Wha kine talk he make?" Pupali asked.

"I am sending you herewith, my long and trusted friend, the sum of forty-five pounds sterling, which is a goodly sum of money and which an English ship captain whom I bespoke off the Japan Coast gave me as a present when I gave him your daughter Iliki. He was a fine-looking man and promised to treat her well and said he would take her home with him to Bristol when his cruise was over. Since Bristol is on the other side of the world, you will probably not see Iliki again, but when I last saw her she was happy and in good health. I could not bring her back to Lahaina as I had made a full cargo off Japan and was sailing directly home, where a girl like Iliki would not be well received. Since I had to do something, it seemed to me better that I pass her along to a decent English captain than leave her in Valparaiso, where she would certainly get into trouble. I am sending you his entire gift, less five pounds which I gave Iliki for herself, because I think it good for a woman to have some money of her own in a strange country. I hope to see you again soon. Give my love to your wife and your other daughters. They are all good girls. Your trusted friend, Rafer Hoxworth."

It was the island consensus that Captain Hoxworth had behaved rather well in this matter, for all who knew Valparaiso and New England agreed that a girl like Iliki would not have prospered in either locale, and while it seemed likely that the English captain would pass her along to some other ship when the time came for him to return to Bristol, there was always the chance that he might grow fond of the lively girl and take her with him. Lahaina believed implicitly that the gift had indeed been fifty English pounds and that Captain Hoxworth had accounted honestly for all of it. His foresight in sequestering five pounds for the girl herself was widely praised, and carefree Pupali was suddenly looked upon as a wealthy man.

But the transaction was forcefully condemned by Reverend Hale, who, as soon as he heard of it, hurried to J & W to satisfy himself that the letter was authentic. He then sought out Pupali and charged in Hawaiian: "You cannot keep that money, Pupali. For a father to profit from the sale of his own daughter would be infamous."

"Is it a great kapu?" the fat Hawaiian asked, with his wife and three daughters at his elbows.

"A kapu so horrible that there is no word for it," Abner explained.

"But you just used a word for it," Pupali hopefully pointed out.

"I used several words," Abner snapped. "What I mean is that civilized languages are not required to have a single word because such an act . . ." He stopped in confusion and started over by stating flatly, "It is a horrible act, Pupali. You cannot keep that money."

"What shall I do with it?" Pupali asked.

"I think," Abner said after due reflection, "that you should turn it over to the church . . . absolve yourself of the sin of which you are now a part."

Pupali got the money, laid it out carefully and studied it. Then he shook his head negatively. "No," he reasoned, "if this money is as kapu as you say, isn't it better that it harm only me and not something as fine as your church?"

Abner coughed and explained, "It has always been the job of the church to correct the wrongs in any society, Pupali. If you give the money to a worthy cause, its kapu will be washed away."

"On the other hand," Pupali argued, "your fine church has already been destroyed twice because the spirits of the land were angry at the way you built it . . ."

"It was a fire and a wind," Abner corrected.

"And now if you make even your own god angry at the church, it would surely burn down again," Pupali reasoned triumphantly. "So I cannot let you run this risk, Makua Hale. I will keep the money." In fact, things had worked out so well for the shiftless man through the sale of Iliki, that he now started introducing his three other daughters to as many whaling captains as possible, but they had grown fat and careless and found no takers.

IN SPITE of many such defeats, these were good years for Abner and Jerusha. They now had four children, two boys and two girls, each apparently gifted with superior intelligence. Abner was disappointed that the young ones could not play with the Janders and Whipple children, but since both Mrs. Janders and Amanda stubbornly allowed their offspring not only to associate with Hawaiians but actually to speak that lascivious language, the Hale youngsters were kept rigidly alone within their walled garden. They appeared at church each Sunday, handsomely scrubbed, and often at twilight Abner would lead them to the waterfront, where they would study the marvelous islands that rimmed Lahaina Roads, and the clever children would play the game of "Spot the Whales!" in which at proper seasons of the year they would try to detect mother whales and their babies. The family came to enjoy these end-of-day respites as the finest part of the week, and much of the poetry of speech that marked the children derived from these hours when they watched the sunsets and the islands. In December the sun set almost over the middle of Lanai, as if it were a fireball going back to sleep in the dead volcano of that gracious island, but in June the great fiery sun sank off the coast of Molokai, rushing with crimson and orange streamers into the blue ocean. Then, with daylight fading, the children would listen for the talking owls and the gentle motion of the rising wind in the coconut palms.

What they loved best, however, was when their father pointed toward the rotting hulk of the *Thetis* and said, "I remember when your dear mother and I sailed from Boston in that brig." And he convinced the children that they belonged to three precious fraternities: "You are the children of God. All men are your brothers. And you are descended from the bravest group that ever came to Hawaii, the missionaries that sailed aboard the *Thetis.*" One night Micah whispered to his mother, "Father tells us that all men are brothers, but the ones who sailed on the *Thetis* are a little better than the others, aren't they?" And to the boy's surprise his mother said, "Your father is correct. The world holds no finer people than those who sailed aboard the *Thetis.*" But Micah noticed that year by year, in his father's stories of that fateful voyage, the waves got higher and the space in the little stateroom more cramped.

Jerusha found abiding joy in these days, for her nine years in Lahaina had taught her how to master life within a grass house. Her two great enemies were bedbugs and cockroaches, but scrupulous cleanliness controlled the first and meticulous care in wrapping every edible crumb in time dismayed the roaches so that they marched away to some more careless house. Even so, the grassy walls, lined though they were with smooth and fragrant pandanus matting, were convenient hiding places for all kinds of insects, and often at night one would roll over on his pallet and hear the squashing sound of some hard-shelled vermin being crushed. Nor could the dust from the pebbled floor ever be adequately controlled. But life was possible, and at times even palatable.

There was some talk between Amanda Whipple and Luella Janders that their patient sister Jerusha was killing herself in the damp grass shack, and together they sent a petition to the mission board in Honolulu begging for some lumber. "Our husbands have volunteered to build a decent house for this Christian and long-suffering woman, if you will but supply the timbers," they wrote. But since one of the signatories was Amanda Whipple, who was known to have encouraged her husband when he abandoned the mission, and since Whipple had twice been additionally censured for marrying American sailors to Hawaiian girls, the petition came to naught, and Jerusha continued to live and work inside the dark, damp grass shack.

Abner, had he known of Amanda's move, would have been outraged, for he stubbornly maintained his original conviction: "We have been sent here as the servants of God. Through gifts to the mission, He will provide for us as He deems best." It was, however, trying to Jerusha to see her four children clothed only in such remnants as the mission board could send her from the charity barrels, and she tried her health still further by constantly ripping apart gift clothing, smoothing out the larger pieces of cloth thus provided, and sewing them into new garments for her children. On one point, however, she was adamant: "We have got to have books for Micah. If you don't write to the Board demanding them, I shall have to." She was not above stopping whaling captains on the streets and begging them for any books which they might have done with and which her brilliant son could read. "I am trying to teach him all he requires for entrance into Yale," she explained. "But he reads so fast and understands so well . . ." In one way or another she got the books.

Each year Jerusha had had one moment of complete motherly happiness; it coincided with the arrival of the annual gift box from her parents in Walpole, New Hampshire. Each November they dispatched it, but she could never be certain when a ship's captain would knock on her Dutch door, saying, "We've a box for you, ma'am." How exciting it was to get that message, but how infinitely more exciting to see her family standing in a circle as Abner ripped away the top. There were dried apples, and spiced pears and hard dried beef. "These pants will be for Micah," Jerusha would say carefully, lingering over each item. "And this dress will fit Lucy. David can have this and Esther this." On the succeeding Sunday, at least, Jerusha could look back over her shoulder as her children marched to church in their new clothes, and she could be proud of them. She always allowed the box to stay in the house long after it was empty, and whenever she looked at it she could recall the cold winters of New Hampshire and the smell of cider.

A major reason why Abner would have found it impossible to accept aid from the Whipples was this: a phrase of John's kept running through his mind and seemed to him to summarize the apostasy into which his former roommate had fallen. At strange times Abner would hear ringing in his ears John's sharp pronouncement: "I don't think the alii sent the wind, and I don't think God sank the ships." The more he reflected on this the more contemptible it sounded. "In simple terms," Abner rationalized, "what he has done is to equate heathen idols of the alii with God himself. How appalling!" And increasingly he kept away from John Whipple, for without either man's being aware of the fact, as Whipple's financial fortunes grew, so did Abner Hale's deepening reliance upon the Lord; and since in Lahaina as elsewhere these lines of development are not parallel but are actually divergent, so that the distance between them increases, the two men grew not to comprehend each other.

Nevertheless, Whipple remained interested in Abner's welfare, and it was with both amazement and relief that he heard one day from a Salem captain, lately sailing from Boston, that a preposterous yet tantalizing thing was occurring on the wharves of that city. "Matter of fact, it's no doubt completed by now," the incredulous captain explained. "There was this man named Charles Bromley, out of New Hampshire, and he was building a complete two-storied wooden house right on the dock within spitting distance of the bay. No cellar, but everything complete, even to window cords. As soon as it was done, carpenters went over the entire thing with paint brushes and numbered every piece of wood in the house. Draftsmen drew pictures of everything, and indicated the numbers. Then what do you suppose happened?" the captain asked dramatically. "Damned if they didn't start knocking the whole house down and carrying it aboard this ship, plank by plank."

"What ship?" Whipple asked.

"*Carthaginian,* Captain Hoxworth, out of Bedford," the captain said.

"I would deeply appreciate it, Captain, if you'd keep this matter a secret," Whipple said.

"As a matter of fact," the man said, "the house is headed for these islands. Honolulu, probably. I was so fascinated I spoke to this fellow Bromley. He didn't want to talk but he did say that the idea was Captain Hoxworth's. The captain came to him and said that this mission family in Honolulu . . . living like swine . . . you know, grass house, bed-bugs, cockroaches. Why Bromley was building the house I didn't get clear."

"Will you promise me?" Whipple pleaded.

"Of course," the captain agreed.

"I assure you, Captain," Whipple said, "you will be protecting a wonderful woman from hurt if you will keep your mouth shut about this. And I shall, too."

Dr. Whipple's preoccupation with anything so minor as a new house was superseded when Abner became aware of mysterious events occurring in Lahaina without his being able to identify them; and since he considered himself arbiter of all that happened in the community, he was irritated to think that Hawaiians would wish to conduct important affairs behind his back. To the meeting in Honolulu he reported: "I first became aware of this unusual secretiveness four days ago when returning from inspection of a home that burned because the owner smoked tobacco, and after having admonished him for his sin, I happened to peer into Malama's old palace grounds, where I spotted several kahunas I knew, and they were supervising the building of a large new house.

" 'What are you building there?' I called.

" 'A small house,' they replied evasively.

" 'What for?' I inquired.

" 'The other houses have grown musty,' they lied.

" 'What other houses?' I prodded.

" 'Those over there,' they said, waving their arms in some vague direction.

" 'Exactly which ones?' I insisted.

"This question they did not answer, so I pushed my way into the compound and inspected the new house, finding it spacious, with real doors, windows and two Chinese mirrors. 'This is a very substantial house,' I said to the kahunas, but they shrugged me off by saying, 'It's a pretty small house,' so I left the deceiving rogues and went in turn to each of the other houses and smelled them, and not one was musty, so I challenged the kahunas and asked, 'Tell me what you are building,' and they replied, 'A house,' and I left the conspirators, convinced that something suspicious is afoot, but what it is I do not know."

Abner was pondering these exasperating mysteries when he saw from his Dutch door a line of seven natives coming down from the hills bearing maile branches and great bouquets of ginger flowers. Leaving his Bible-translating, he hurried to the roadway and demanded, "Why are you bearing maile and ginger?"

"We don't know," the Hawaiians replied.

"Who sent you to the hills?" Abner insisted.

"We don't know."

"Where are you taking the flowers?"

"We don't know."

"Of course you know!" he fumed. "It's ridiculous to say you don't know where you're going," and he limped after them to the waterfront, where they wandered off, each in his own accidental direction.

Infuriated, Abner stood for some minutes in the hot sun trying to piece together his various clues. Then, jamming his hands into his coat pockets, he stomped over to J & W's and said brusquely, "John, what's going on in Lahaina?"

"What do you mean?" Whipple parried.

"I just encountered seven natives bringing down maile and ginger. Why are they doing that?"

"Why didn't you ask them?"

"I did, and they'd tell me nothing."

"Probably some kind of ceremony," Whipple guessed.

Abner both despised and feared this word, for it conjured up forbidden rites and heathen sex orgies, so he asked tentatively, "You mean . . . pagan ceremonies?"

Then Whipple remembered. "Now that you bring it up, two days ago some of the whalers wanted extra supplies of tapa for calking. Usually I can find a hundred yards by snapping my fingers, but I went to a dozen homes, and they were all making tapa, but no one had any for sale."

"What were they doing with it?" Abner pressed.

"They all said the same thing. 'It's for Kelolo.' "

At this, Abner placed before the doctor the various bits of evidence he had collected, and when they had studied the facts, he asked, "John, what's going on?"

"I don't know," Whipple replied. "Have Kelolo and his children been in church recently?"

"Yes, as pious as they ever were."

"I'd keep my eye on Kelolo," Whipple laughed. "He's a wily old shark." And for the rest of that day Abner brooded over the fact that an event of obvious significance had been masked from his surveillance; but his present exasperation was nothing compared to what it became when in the late afternoon he heard as if from a distant valley the muffled, haunting throb of a pagan drum. He listened, and it stopped. Then it began again, and he cried, "The hula!"

Without even informing Jerusha of where he was going, he started out in search of the long-forbidden hula, and he followed the echoes from one area to the next, until at last he pinpointed them as coming from a house on the edge of town. Hurrying along a winding footpath, he was determined to catch the lascivious revelers and punish them, when suddenly from behind a tree a tall native casually stepped into the middle of the path, asking, "Where are you going, Makua Hale?"

"There's a hula in that house!" Abner said ominously, but the man must have been a sentry, for when Abner reached the place from which the drum had echoed, he found only a collection of sweet-faced men and women practicing hymns, with never a drum in evidence.

"Where did you hide them?" he stormed.

"Hide what, Makua Hale?"

"The drums."

"We had no drums, Makua Hale," they said with the most winning simplicity. "We were singing hymns for Sabbath."

But when he reached home again, he heard once more the sound of drums, and he told Jerusha, "Something is happening in this town, and it drives me mad that I can't find out what it is." He ate no supper, but later, as the moon was rising, he announced sternly: "I shall not go to bed till I discover what evil is afoot."

Against Jerusha's protests he donned his white shirt, best stock, claw-hammer coat and beaver hat. Then, fortifying himself with a stout cane, he went out into the warm tropical night and for the first several minutes stood silent under the stars and the sighing palms, trying desperately to detect what was occurring in his parish, but he heard nothing.

He wondered if Murphy had revived the hula in his grog shop, but when he crept past the saloon it was orderly. He then went to the pier, suspecting that whalers might have conspired with Kelolo in organizing a debauch, but the ships were silent in the ghostly moonlight.

And then, as he stood at the far end of the pier, staring at the ships, he happened to see out of the corner of his eye a flickering light along the shore some distance to the south. He dismissed it with the thought: "A night fisherman with his torch on the reef," but it did not move as a fisherman's should, and he muttered, "That's not one torch. It's several." And with this he remembered the new grass house at Malama's, and he recalled the kahunas, and like a fish drawn to the torches, he limped off the pier and started walking along the edge of the coral reef, past the fort, past the great alii homes and out toward Malama's, and as he walked silently through the sand, the torches grew brighter and it became obvious that a considerable celebration was in progress, one at which he was not welcome. He therefore moved stealthily, slipping from one coconut palm to the next until at last he came upon a hidden spot from which he could spy upon the palace grounds, and the first thing he saw was a concentration of guards at the gate that led from the public road into the compound, and he thought with satisfaction: "Those guards are there to keep me out. What evil are my people up to?"

He had not long to wait, for from a crowd of men who had been feasting on roast pig, Kelolo stepped forth in brilliant yellow robes, accompanied by six kahunas in feathered capes. Kelolo dropped his hand, and from an area near the beach a night drum began to sound, and then another, and finally a high-pitched variant which established a throbbing, disciplined rhythm. Suddenly, from the crowd, six women whom Abner had seen in the house singing hymns moved forth, naked to the waist and with red flowers in their hair, necklaces of polished black nuts about their shoulders and anklets of shark's teeth which clicked as they began an ancient hula.

Abner, who had often railed against this dance, had never seen it, and now as the swaying skirts made of ti leaves moved in the faltering shadows, he noticed how solemn and graceful the dance was, for the women seemed to be disembodied spirits, undulating in response to night winds: a movement would start in their heads, work its way along their supple arms, and pass to their hips in one unbroken symphony of motion. "This isn't what I expected," Abner muttered. "I understood that naked men and women . . ." But his fleeting concession was interrupted by what now took place, for he stood appalled as a chanter leaped before the dancers and began to cry mournfully, yet in exultation:

"Great Kane, guardian of the heavens,
Great Kane, guardian of the night,
King of the gods, ruler of all men,
Kane, Kane, Kane!
Attend our ceremony, bless our shore!"

And as Abner stared in disbelief, from the new grass house Kelolo appeared, bearing in his reverent hands the ancient stone of Kane. It should have been long since destroyed, but it had survived through Kelolo's love, and now he placed it upon the low stone altar near the shore. When it was in position he shouted, "Great Kane, your people welcome you home!" Over the crowd a deep silence settled as each Hawaiian filed past Kelolo to deck the altar with flowers, and when this was done the kahunas chanted. Then at a signal from Kelolo the drums hammered out a new and wilder rhythm; the hula dancers swayed more joyously; and the people of Lahaina welcomed back their ancient god.

In spite of Abner's hundred sermons and two hundred hymns about destroying heathen idols, this stone was the first he had seen, and he stared at it with unholy fascination, for the curious combination of reverence and ecstasy it inspired in these worshipers bespoke its real force, and through it the little missionary comprehended much of Hawaii that he had not known before: its persistent religious passions, its abiding sense of history, and its mysteriousness. With all his heart he longed to rush forth and strike down the altar that kept these un-Christian forces alive.

But his attention was diverted from the idol to the figure of a man who now appeared from the new grass house. It was Keoki Kanakoa, in a golden trance, his mechanical movements betraying the deep hypnosis into which he had fallen. He was naked to the waist, his body rubbed with oil; about his loins he wore a brown tapa and across his left arm a feathered cape. His helmet was in the old style, with an elevated comb sweeping from the base of the neck to the forehead, and he wore a necklace of human hair from which dangled a huge whale's tooth fashioned into a hook.

As he walked toward the statue of Kane, a priest chanted: "He comes, the perfect man. His hair is dark and reddish, his figure is commanding, triangular from shoulders down, with narrow hips. He bears a straight back, has no deformity, no blemish. His head is squared from molding while an infant. His nostrils flare. His neck is short and muscular, and his eyes are intoxicating like the tree that lures fish into the ponds. He is the perfect man and he comes to worship Kane!"

In a trance, the young alii moved to the altar, bowed and cried: "Great Kane, forgive your son. Accept him once more." And from the shadows Abner prayed: "Forgive him, Almighty God! He is in the possession of evil men and knows not what he does."

Abner now had to suffer a sharper blow, for from the grass house appeared Noelani wearing a golden tapa and Malama's famous whale-tooth necklace. She bore flowers in her hair and moved solemnly toward the altar, while the priest cried: "She comes, the perfect woman. Her skin is flawless, soft and melting like the waves of ocean, lustrous and smooth like the banana blossom. She is fairer than the lehua petal, lovelier than the opening buds of breadfruit. Her nostrils flare from her straight nose. Her brow is clean and low. Her lips are full and her back is straight. Her buttocks are rounded, with cheeks like the bursting moon, solid like the foundations of Maui. She is the perfect woman, and she comes to worship Kane."

Abner, stunned by this double apostasy, began to mumble: "They can't go back to Kane! They know the catechism. Keoki's been to Yale. They're Congregationalists. They're members of my church and I forbid it."

But the apostasy, complete though it was, formed merely the prelude to an event of much greater significance, for from the group of kahunas, whose night of triumph this was, a tall priest stepped forward bearing a black tapa, such as Abner had not seen before, and after a passionate prayer to Kane, this priest swirled the tapa wide in the night air, and when it was completely unfolded, brought it down about the shoulders of the brother and sister, crying: "From this moment on, you shall share forever the same tapa!" And he led the couple toward the waiting house.

The drums leaped to wild rhythms. Dancers created violent gestures which erased memories of earlier beauty, and the kahunas chanted: "Noelani and Keoki are married." Abner could tolerate no more. He leaped from his hiding place, swinging his stout club and shouting, "Abomination! Abomination!"

Before the astonished gathering could apprehend him, he leaped to the altar and with a mighty swipe of his club sent the sacred stone of Kane spinning into the dust. In fury he kicked at the maile branches and the ginger. Then, dropping his club, he marched solemnly to the married couple, ripped away the black tapa, and cried, "Abomination!"

By now the Hawaiians were recovered from their amazement, and Kelolo, aided by two kahunas, pinioned Abner, but they treated him gently, for they knew he was the priest of the other god, and what he had done was only his duty. So Kelolo pleaded softly, "Dear little friend, go home. Tonight we talk with other gods."

Abner broke loose and pointed his finger at Keoki, crying, "In God's eyes this is an outrage." Keoki looked at him glassily, and Abner cried, "Keoki, what has happened?"

The giant young alii stared at his old friend and mumbled, "I begged you, Reverend Hale, to make me a minister. If your church doesn't want me . . ."

"A minister?" Abner shouted, and suddenly the hideousness of this night—the hulas, the living stone, the drums and the kahunas—overwhelmed him and he began to laugh hysterically. "A minister?" he repeated several times, until Kelolo placed his hand gently but firmly over the missionary's mouth and had him dragged away from the ceremonies, but the God-driven little man struggled loose and rushed back almost to the bridal couple before he was apprehended.

"Keoki!" he shouted. "Are you proceeding with this marriage?"

"As my father before me," Keoki replied.

"Infamous!" Abner moaned. "It puts you outside the pale of civilized . . ."

"Hush!" an imperious voice commanded, and Abner drew back. It was Noelani who came close to him and said softly, "Beloved Makua Hale, we are not doing this to hurt you."

Abner looked at the beautiful young woman with flowers in her hair and he argued, with equal control, "Noelani, you are being tempted by these men to commit a grave sin."

The Alii Nui did not argue, but pointed instead toward the dark hills, saying, "In former days we followed our own gods, and our valleys were filled with people. We have tried following yours, and our islands are sunk in despair. Death, awful sickness, cannon and fear. That is what you have brought us, Makua Hale, although we know you did not intend it to be so. I am the Alii Nui, and if I die without child, who will keep the Hawaiian spirit alive?"

"Noelani, dear little girl of my hopes, there are dozens of men . . . right here . . . who would be proud to be your husband."

"But could their children be designated Alii Nui?" Noelani countered, and this line of pagan reasoning so infuriated Abner that he drew back and cried in dismal voice, "Abomination! Malama would curse you from her grave!"

Later, Kelolo confessed that he should have kept silent, but he could not, and asked tauntingly, "What directions do you think Malama gave me when she whispered on her deathbed?"

In horror the little missionary, his pale face and watery blond hair shining in the torchlight, stared at Kelolo. Could what the alii said be true? Had Malama commanded this obscenity? The repulsiveness of this possibility was more than he could accommodate at the moment, and he stumbled from the compound while the kahunas restored Kane, and the drums resumed their nuptial beat.

Bedazed, Abner moved along the dark and dusty road whose stones in recent years had witnessed so many changes. He saw the shadowy houses of the king and the wooden stores of the Americans who had scorned God and fought the mission. In the roads the whalers were snug-anchored, his permanent enemies, and at Murphy's grog shop somebody was playing a lonely concertina. How alien these things were to his lacerated spirit.

In the deep night he left the town and climbed a barren field strewn with rocks, and when he stumbled upon a clump of dwarfed trees he sat among their roots and looked back at his silent parish as if he were no longer responsible for it. To the south he could see the monstrous torches of the pagans. In the roads he could spot the swaying night-lights of the whalers, and between lay the grass-roofed shacks of the people. How miserable and grubby this town really was, how pitiful. What a minimum impression he had made upon Lahaina, how inconsequential his accomplishments. Malama had tricked him. Keoki had betrayed him. And Iliki was God knows where. Now even the gentlest of them all, Noelani, had turned against him and had rebuked his church.

For nearly ten years he had worn only one coat; God had not once sent him a pair of trousers that fitted; he had acquired only such learned books as he could beg from distant Boston; his wife had slaved in a wretched hut; and he had accomplished nothing. Now, as dawn began breaking over his little town, he studied in humiliation of spirit the shimmering sea, the mocking whalers and the palace grounds where the torches were slowly burning out. And he wished ardently that he could call down upon this entire congregation, saving only the mission house and its uncomplaining occupants, some awful Biblical destruction.

"Floods! Winds from the hills! Pestilence! Destroy this place!" But even as he begged God to inflict such punishment, the perverse lesser gods of the vicinity were preparing to launch what would be his crowning humiliation, for in the night that was to follow, the goddess Pele herself would visit once more her devotee Kelolo, and the upshot of this ghostly convocation would haunt Abner Hale for many months.

When John Whipple, rising early to sweep out the store, saw Abner staggering down from the hills back to town, he ran out and grabbed the little man, asking, "Abner, what has happened?"

Hale started to explain, but he could not pronounce the vile words. He hesitated dumbly for a moment, his eyes failing to focus properly, and then he pointed at a group of Hawaiians coming along the road from the palace. They wore maile in their hair, and a light step; they carried a drum and walked in triumph as they had a thousand years before, and Abner said weakly, "Ask them." And he stumbled off to bed.

Later that day he dispatched a letter to the missionaries in Honolulu reporting: "At four o'clock this morning, January 4, 1832, in the old palace of Malama the kahunas triumphed and the dreadful deed was done."

In daylight, when the auguries were studied and the kahunas were satisfied that a good marriage had been launched, they assured Keoki: "This night you have done a fine thing for Hawaii. The gods will not forget, and when your child is born you will be free to go back to your own church once more and become a minister." But Keoki, shivering from the burdens which the gods throw upon some shoulders, knew that this could not be.

At the following dusk Kelolo, gratified that he had protected the succession of his family in these heavenly islands, walked among the shadows and as he did so he met, for the last time on earth, the silent, delicate form of Pele, keeper of the volcanoes, dressed in silken robes, with strange glasslike hair standing out in the night breeze. She obstructed his pathway beneath the palms and waited for him to approach her, and Kelolo could see that her face was radiant with contentment, and when she took her place beside him, walking mysteriously through whatever trees came into her way along the narrow path, he felt tremendous consolation. And they continued thus for some miles, each happy in the other's company, but when the walk ended, Pele did what she had never done before. She paused dramatically, raised her left hand and pointed south, directly through the Keala-i-kahiki Channel and onto Keala-i-kahiki Point, and she stood thus for some minutes, as if commanding Kelolo with her fiery yet consoling eyes.

He spoke for the first time and asked, "What is it, Pele?" but she was content merely to point toward Keala-i-kahiki, and then, as if wishing to bid farewell to this great alii, her dear and personal friend, she brushed past him, kissing him with fiery lips and vanishing in a long silvery trail of smoke. He stood for a long time, engraving in his memory each incident of her visit, and that night when he returned to his solitary shack outside the palace grounds he took down his two most sacred treasures: the whitened skull of his wife Malama and a very old stone, about the size of a fist, curiously shaped and well marked. It had been given him more than forty years before by his father, who had averred that the occult powers of the Kanakoas derived from this stone, which one of their ancestors recovered on a return trip to Bora Bora. It was, his father had sworn, not merely sacred to the goddess Pele; it was the goddess; she was free to roam the islands and to warn her people of impending volcanic disasters; but her spirit resided in this rock, and it had done so for generations out of mind, long, long before even the days of Bora Bora. And through the night Kelolo sat with his treasures, trying to unravel the divine mystery of which they were the most significant parts. In the morning his confusion was clarified, for a swift ship sped into Lahaina Roads with news that a massive surge of the volcano on Hawaii was threatening the capital town of Hilo and the citizens prayed that the Alii Nui Noelani would enter upon the swift ship and return, to stop the flow of lava that must otherwise wipe out the town.

When the news was brought to Noelani, her impulse was to send Kelolo instead, for he was the friend of Pele. Furthermore, her discussions with Dr. Whipple had satisfied her that volcanoes were the result of natural forces whose eruption could almost be predicted scientifically, and she realized that the island stories of Pele were nonsense, but before she could discuss these conclusions with the messengers from Hilo, Kelolo hurried up and said, "You must go, Noelani. If Pele is destroying Hilo, it must be in punishment, and you should go where the lava is white-hot and remind her that Hilo loves her."

"You are the friend of Pele," Noelani replied. "You must go."

"But I am not the Alii Nui," Kelolo said gravely. "Here is a chance for you to win the people to you forever."

"I cannot believe that Pele has anything to do with this lava," Noelani objected.

"I saw her last night," Kelolo said simply. "I talked with her."

Noelani looked at her father in amazement. "You saw Pele?" she demanded.

"I walked with her for two miles," Kelolo replied.

"Did she give you any message?" Noelani asked incredulously.

"No," Kelolo lied. "But of course she warned me of the volcano on Hawaii. Yes, she pointed toward Hawaii." But he knew that she had not done this; she had pointed in quite a different direction.

"And you wish me to go to Hilo?" Noelani asked.

"Yes, and I will entrust to your care a stone that will enable you to halt the lava," Kelolo assured her.

And it was in this way, in the year 1832, that the Alii Nui Noelani Kanakoa left Lahaina with the curse of Abner Hale in her ears—"This is madness, an abomination"—carrying a sacred stone and traveling by ship to the port town of Hilo, where from the bay she could see the overpowering advance of glowing lava, rolling slowly upon itself and crushing in fiery embrace all it encountered. The town was obviously doomed; by the next night the lava must encompass it, and from shipboard there seemed no use for a young woman to try to stop it.

But the local kahunas breathed with relief when they saw Noelani alight, laden with the mana that heals, and start her painful climb to the lava face. Behind her streamed the entire population of the town, save only the local missionaries who were outraged by this heathenish performance. Up through the palm trees at the edge of town, through the nau brushes, and on into the scrubby brush marched the solemn, hushed procession. Now only a few yards ahead lay the crawling, crackling snout of lava: as each new flow cascaded down the mountainside it sped over former flows that in the meantime had cooled, using them as a passageway to lower ground, and as the living white-hot flow came to the dead tip of old lava, it poised a moment in the air, then rushed out in many new directions, consuming here a tree, there a house and beyond a pigpen. There would be a hissing and crackling of fire, and the doomed object would burn away in a sudden, fatal gasp. Then, as the ugly snout cooled, it formed a channel for the next burning flow.

It was to this creeping, crawling, devouring face that the young woman Noelani journeyed, and as she approached the living fire she underwent a transformation, for what she had been summoned to do was no less than to confront the fire goddess herself and to challenge her in a work that had been carried on by volcanoes since long before the coming of the Polynesians, and in the mystery of these last moments, in the awful inner fires that were burning away at her reason, Noelani lost all sense of ever having been a Christian. She was a daughter of Pele, one in whose family the very being of the goddess had resided, and now, returning to the suzerainty of the fire goddess, Noelani planted her feet before the on-surging lava and decided that here she would stand and if need be, die.

Holding the sacred rock of Pele aloft, she cried, "Pele! Great goddess! You are destroying the town of those who love you! I pray you to halt!"

And standing there with the stone aloft, she watched new fires reach the ugly snout and start to gush forward toward the town of Hilo, and as the fires trembled, she threw into them tobacco, and two bottles of brandy which flamed furiously, and four red scarves, for that was a color Pele loved, and a red rooster and finally a lock of her own hair. And the fires of Pele hung in the snout, consumed the tobacco, and slowly froze into position. The flow of lava had halted at Noelani's feet, but there were no cheers, only the soft prayers of all who had trusted that Pele would never destroy the town of Hilo. The fires went out. The probing fingers consumed no more homes, and in a daze of glory and confusion Noelani returned to her ship and went once more to Lahaina, there to await the birth of the child who, when she was gone, would take her place as intercessor with the gods.

This halting of the lava was the worst single blow Abner Hale experienced in Lahaina, for coming so quickly after the defection of Keoki and his sister, it was interpreted as confirming their marriage; while Noelani's demonstrated ability to influence the ancient gods convinced Hawaiians that they still survived, and many began drifting away from the Christian church. But what hurt Abner most was the hilarity with which Americans greeted the miracle. One profane captain kept shouting, "From here on count me a firm believer in Madame Pele!" Another promised, "Now if Noelani will only take care of the storms, I'll join her church, too."

Abner, suffering at each defection from his church and wincing at the American jibes, became obsessed with the lava incident and went about arguing with anyone who would listen: "The burning rock came so far and stopped. What's so miraculous about that?"

"Ah, but who stopped it?" his tormentors would parry.

"A woman stands before a nose of lava as it's about to die down, and that's a miracle," he snorted contemptuously.

"Ah, but what if she hadn't been there?" the logicians queried.

After some weeks Abner went at last, and grudgingly, to consult with John Whipple, and the young scientist reassured him. "When the internal pressures of a volcano become powerful enough, they erupt into violence. Depending solely upon the interior forces within the earth, and nothing more, lava is spewed forth and rolls down mountainsides. If there's enough lava, it's got to reach the ocean. If there isn't, it stops somewhere en route."

"Are these things known?" Abner asked.

"By anyone with a grain of intelligence," Whipple replied. "Look at Lanai. Anyone can see it was a volcano once. Look at our own Maui. At one time it had to be two separate volcanoes, gradually coalescing along that line. I would guess that at some time all the separate islands we see from this pier were one great island."

"How could that have been?" Abner queried.

"Either the islands sank or the sea rose. Either explanation would do."

The grandeur of this concept was too difficult for Abner to accept, and he retreated to certainty: "We know that the world was created four thousand and four years before the birth of Christ, and there is no record of islands having risen or fallen." The idea was repugnant to him.

Whipple was going to ask about the Flood, but he changed the subject and casually remarked, "Abner, why did you put yourself in such a bad light at the marriage of Keoki and Noelani? You surrendered a lot of influence that week."

"It was an abomination, unnatural, unclean!" Abner stormed.

"I've been thinking about it a great deal," Whipple reflected. "What's so dreadful about it? Now really, don't quote me incidents from the Bible. Just tell me."

"It's abhorrent and unnatural," Abner stormed, still hurting from the actions of his two preferred Hawaiians.

"What's really so abhorrent about it?" Whipple pressed.

"Every civilized society . . ." Abner began, but his companion grew impatient and snapped: "Damn it, Abner, every time you start an answer that way I know it's going to be irrelevant. Two of the most completely civilized societies we've ever had were the Egyptians and the Incas. Now, no Egyptian king was ever allowed to marry anybody but his sister, and if I can believe what I've heard, the same was true of the Incas. They prospered. As a matter of fact," Whipple continued, "it's not a bad system, scientifically. That is, if you're willing to kill off ruthlessly any children with marked defects, and apparently the Egyptians, the Incas and the

Hawaiians were willing to do so. Have you ever seen a handsomer group of people than the alii?"

Abner felt that he was going to be sick, but before he could react to Whipple's astonishing reflections, the doctor said, "Noelani has asked me to attend her at the birth of the baby."

"Of course you rebuked her," Abner said with assurance.

"Oh, no! A doctor could practice an entire lifetime and not meet such an opportunity," Whipple explained.

"You would be partner to such a crime?" Abner asked, stunned by the prospect.

"Naturally," Whipple said, and the two men walked back from the pier in silence, but when Abner reached home and sent the children out into the walled yard he confided in whispers to his wife the nauseating news that John Whipple was preparing to attend Noelani, but to his surprise Jerusha replied, "Of course. The girl deserves all consideration. This must be doubly frightening for her."

"But John Whipple, a consecrated Christian!"

"The important thing is that he's a doctor. Do you suppose I ever rested easily, knowing that a totally untrained man would be my attendant when the children were born?"

"Were you so afraid?" Abner asked in surprise.

"I began by being," Jerusha said, "but my love for you made it possible to control my fears. Even so, I'm glad that Brother John is going to tend the girl."

Abner started to rant, but Jerusha had in these months of his defeat heard enough, and now she said firmly, "My dearest husband, I am afraid you are making a fool of yourself."

"What do you mean?" he gasped, rising and walking with agitation to the door.

"You are fighting the kahunas, and Kelolo, and Keoki and Noelani, and even Dr. Whipple. In church you speak without benevolence. You act as if you hated Lahaina and all that was in it. You've even withdrawn from your children, so that Micah told me, 'Father hasn't taught me Hebrew for two months.' "

"I have been sorely tried," Abner confessed.

"I appreciate the shocks you've suffered," Jerusha said tenderly, pulling her tense little husband into one of the whaling chairs. "But if, as I think, we are here engaged in a tremendous battle between the old gods and the new . . ." She saw that this phraseology hurt Abner, so she quickly modified it. "What I mean is, between heathenish ways and the way of the Lord, then we ought to fight with our subtlest resources. When the old seems about to reconquer the islands, we ought to combat it with . . ."

"I've warned them all!" Abner shouted, rising from his chair and striding about the earthen floor. "I told Kelolo . . ."

"What I meant was," Jerusha said gently, rising to be with her agitated husband, "that in these crucial times you ought to be calmer than usual, quieter, and more forceful. You've told me how you pointed at the evil three, Keoki, Noelani and Kelolo, and told them in turn, 'God will destroy you!' But you haven't told me or shown me how with Christ's gentle love you have tried to guide the people in these confusing times. I've watched you become increasingly bitter, and, Abner, it must stop. It is you who are destroying the good you have accomplished."

"I feel as if I had achieved nothing," he said from the depths of his spiritual humiliation.

Jerusha caught her husband's passing hand and imprisoned him, turning his pinched face to hers. "My dearest husband," she said formally, "if I were to recount your accomplishments in Lahaina it would take the rest of my life. Look at that little girl in the sunlight. If you had not been here, she would have been sacrificed."

"When I see her," Abner said with racking pain in his heart, "I can see only little Iliki, that sweetest of all children, being passed from one whaling ship to another."

The words were so unexpected, for Abner had not spoken of Iliki for some time, that Jerusha, recalling her dearest pupil, felt bitter tears welling into her eyes, but she fought them back and said, "If in losing Iliki we impressed the islanders . . . and, Abner, they were impressed!" She stopped and blew her nose, concluding her remarks with a firm command: "My dearest counselor, you are to smile. You are to preach about great and lofty subjects. You are to win these people to the Lord with bonds of charity so profound that the islands will be God's forever. You . . . must . . . preach . . . love."

With this master theme drummed into his ears by Jerusha, week after week, Abner Hale launched into the series of sermons which completed the winning of Lahaina, for as he spoke of the good life and the effect of God's love upon mankind, he found that whereas he had believed that the islanders had turned away from the Lord, following the example of Kelolo and his children, exactly the contrary was the case; for the common people sensed that in Kelolo's reversion to the old ways there was no real hope for them; and Abner's thoughtful, quiet words of consolation found their way into many hearts that had rejected his earlier ranting.

He preached a doctrine which was new to him . . . "The Holy Word of God as Interpreted by Jerusha Bromley, Modified by the Mysteries Encountered in an Alien Land." He continued to hammer forcefully at man's inescapable sin, but his major emphasis was now upon the consoling intercession of Jesus Christ. And what held his listeners doubly was his return to the tactic he had used as a very young man when preaching to the whalers on the Falklands: he addressed himself exactly to those problems which were perplexing his congregation, so that when he spoke of Christ's compassion he said bluntly, "Jesus Christ will understand the confusions faced by His beloved son, Keoki Kanakoa, and Jesus will find it possible to love His erring servant, even as you and I should love him."

These words, when they reached Keoki in the grass palace, shattered him and drove him to the seashore, where he walked for hours, pondering the nature of Christ, as he recalled Him from the early, secure days in the mission school at Cornwall, in distant Connecticut. Then Jesus was perceptible reality, and the eroding loss of this concept agonized Keoki.

When it was known that Noelani was approaching her time of delivery and that her child must be born before the next Sabbath, Abner took public cognizance of this fact, and instead of ranting against the circumstances in which the child had been conceived, he spoke for more than an hour and a half on the particular love Christ has for little children, and he recalled his own emotions at the birth of his two sons and two daughters, of his love for the child Iliki, who was now lost—for as he receded from the facts of Iliki's disappearance, she became younger and younger in his memory—and of the joy that all Lahaina must feel that their beloved Alii Nui was about to have a child. Since Hawaiians loved nothing more than children, with whom they were gentle and understanding, the two thousand worshipers sniffled quietly during the last fifteen minutes of the sermon, so that without quite knowing how he had accomplished the strategy, Abner found that his words of compassion had quite won Lahaina away from Kelolo and his kahunas, whereas his earlier ranting had been driving the Hawaiians back to the old gods. It was with confusion, therefore, that Lahaina awaited the birth of its next Alii Nui: as loyal Hawaiians they rejoiced that their noble line was to be continued; as Christians they knew that an evil thing had been done by Kelolo and his children.

Noelani bore twins, and Dr. Whipple, after he left the grass palace, reported to his waiting wife, "We must prepare ourselves for an ugly moment, Amanda. The boy was a handsome child, but the girl was deformed. I suppose they will abandon her before morning." And when it was whispered through the town that Keoki Kanakoa, with his own hands, had taken his malformed daughter, and had placed her at the edge of the tide for the shark-god Mano, a wave of revulsion swept through the town.

On Sunday the Lahaina church was jammed with nearly three thousand people, as in the old days, but on the way to service Jerusha said quietly to her husband, "Remember, my beloved husband, God has spoken on this subject. You are not required to." And on the instant Abner threw away the text on which he was prepared to thunder, Luke 23, verse 34: "Father, forgive them; for they know not what they do," and spoke instead from those majestic words of Ecclesiastes which had been much in his mind of late: "One generation passeth away, and another generation cometh: but the earth abideth for ever. The sun also ariseth, and the sun goeth down. . . . All the rivers run into the sea; yet the sea is not full; unto the place from whence the rivers come, thither they return again. . . . The thing that hath been, it is that which shall be; and that which is done is that which shall be done: and there is no new thing under the sun. . . . There is no remembrance of former things; neither shall there be any remembrance of things that are to come."

He spoke of the permanence of Maui, of how the whales came back each year to play in the roads, and of how the sunset moved majestically through the months from the volcano of Lanai to the tip of Molokai. He referred to the whistling wind that could blow down churches and of the dead past when Kamehameha himself had trod these roads in mighty conquest. "The earth abideth forever," he cried in soft Hawaiian, and Jerusha, listening to the inspired flow of images, knew that the hatred he had recently held for Lahaina was now discharged, for he passed on from the physical world that endures to the human society which occupies the world. "With all its imperfections it endures," Abner confessed; but promptly he went on to his permanent vision of Geneva as it had been ruled by Calvin and Beza, and by suggesting many unspoken comparisons, he led his huge congregation to the truth he himself was seeking: some forms of human behavior are better than others; and at this point he returned to an idea which had, through the years, become a passion with him: that a society is good when it protects children. "Jesus Christ loves even children who are not perfect," he preached, and on this awful contrast he concluded.

"What did he say about the baby?" Keoki asked nervously, fingering his maile leaves in the old grass palace as his spies reported to him.

"Nothing," the men replied.

"Did he rave about our sin?" the agitated young man pressed.

"No. He spoke of how beautiful Maui is." There was a pause and the men explained, "He did not speak either of you or of Noelani. But at one point I thought he intended saying that if you ever want to return to the church, he will forgive you."

The effect of these words upon Keoki was startling, for he began to tremble as if someone were shaking him, and after a while he retired with his confusions to a corner of his room, placing himself formally upon a pile of tapa, as if he were already dead, and saying, "Go away." As his friends departed they whispered among themselves, "Do you think he has decided to die?"

The question was seriously discussed, for the Hawaiians knew that Keoki was tormented by doubts arising from two religions in conflict, and that whereas he had reverted with apparent willingness to Kelolo's native gods, he had not easily cleansed himself of Abner's God, and the incompatible deities warred in his heart. They also knew, as Hawaiians, that if Keoki ever decided to die, he would do so. They had watched their fathers and uncles announce, "I am going to die," and they had died. Therefore, when one young man repeated his question: "Do you think Keoki has decided to die?" the group pondered it seriously, and this was their consensus: "We think he knows that he cannot survive with two gods fighting for his heart."

ACTUALLY, the question was of no importance, for Lahaina was about to be visited by a pestilence known as the scourge of the Pacific. On earlier trips to Hawaii this dreadful plague had wiped out more than half the population, and now it stood poised in the fo'c's'l of a whaler resting in Lahaina Roads, prepared to strike once more with demonic force, killing, laying waste, destroying an already doomed population. It was the worst disease of the Pacific: measles.

This time it started innocently by jumping from the diseased whaler and into the mission home, where immunities built up during a hundred generations in England and Massachusetts confined the disease to a trivial childhood sickness. Jerusha, inspecting her son Micah's chest one morning, found the customary red rash. "Have you a sore throat?" she asked, and when Micah said yes, she informed Abner, "I'm afraid our son has the measles."

Abner groaned and said, "I suppose Lucy and David and Esther are bound to catch it in turn," and he took down his medical books to see what he should do for the worrisome fever. Medication was simple and the routine not burdensome, so he said, "We'll plan for three weeks of keeping the children indoors." But it occurred to him that it might be prudent to see if John Whipple had any medicine for reducing the fever more quickly, and so he stopped casually by J & W's to report, "Worse luck! Micah seems to have the measles and I suppose . . ."

Whipple dropped his pen and cried, "Did you say measles?"

"Well, spots on his chest."

"Oh, my God!" Whipple mumbled, grabbing his bag and rushing to the mission house. With trembling fingers he inspected the sick boy and Jerusha saw that the doctor was perspiring.

"Are measles so dangerous?" she asked with apprehension.

"Not for him," Whipple replied. He then led the parents into the front room and asked in a whisper, "Have you been in contact with any Hawaiians since Micah became ill?"

"No," Abner reflected. "I walked down to your store."

"Thank God," Whipple gasped, washing his hands carefully. "Abner, we have only a slight chance of keeping this dreadful disease away from the Hawaiians, but I want your entire family to stay in this house for three weeks. See nobody."

Jerusha challenged him directly: "Brother John, is it indeed the measles?"

"It is," he replied, "and I would to God it were anything else. We had better prepare ourselves, for there may be sad days ahead." Then, awed by the gravity of the threat, he asked impulsively, "Abner, would you please say a prayer for all of us . . . for Lahaina? Keep the pestilence from this town." And they knelt while Abner prayed.

But men from the infected whaler had moved freely through the community, and on the next morning Dr. Whipple happened to look out of his door to see a native man, naked, digging himself a shallow grave beside the ocean, where cool water could seep in and fill the sandy rectangle. Rushing to the reef, Whipple called, "Kekuana, what are you doing?" And the Hawaiian, shivering fearfully, replied, "I am burning to death and the water will cool me." At this Dr. Whipple said sternly. "Go back to your home, Kekuana, and wrap yourself in tapa. Sweat this illness out or you will surely die." But the man argued, "You do not know how terrible the burning fire is," and he sank himself in the salt water and within the day he died.

Now all along the beach Hawaiians, spotted with measles, dug themselves holes in the cool wet sand, and in spite of anything Dr. Whipple could tell them, crawled into the comforting waters and died. The cool irrigation ditches and taro patches were filled with corpses. Through the miserable huts of the town the pestilence swept like fire, burning its victims with racking fevers that could not be endured. Dr. Whipple organized his wife, the Hales and the Janderses into a medical team that worked for three weeks, arguing, consoling and burying. Once Abner cried in frustration, "John, why do these stubborn people insist upon plunging into the surf when they know it kills them?" And Whipple replied in exhaustion, "We are misled because we call the fever measles. In these unprotected people it is something much worse. Abner, you have never known such a fever."

Nevertheless the little missionary pleaded with his patients, "If you go into the water, you will die."

"I want to die, Makua Hale," they replied.

Jerusha and Amanda saved many lives by forcing their way into huts where they took away babies without even asking, for they knew that if the fevered infants continued their piteous moaning their parents would carry them to the sea. By wrapping the children in blankets and dosing them with syrup of squill, thus encouraging the fever to erupt through skin sores, as it should, the women rescued the children, but with adults neither logic nor force could keep them from the sea, and throughout Lahaina one Hawaiian in three perished.

In time the measles reached even Malama's walled-in compound, where it struck Keoki, who welcomed it, and his baby son Kelolo. Here the Hales found the shivering Kanakoa family, and Jerusha said promptly, "I will take the little boy home with me." And there must have been a great devil near Abner's heart, for when his wife had the dying child in her arms he stopped her and asked, "Would it not be better if that child of sin . . . ?"

Jerusha looked steadily at her husband and said, "I will take the boy. This is what we have been preaching about in the new laws— All the children." And she carried the whimpering child and placed him among her own.

When she was gone, Abner found that Keoki had escaped to the seashore where he dug a shallow grave into which salt water seeped, and before Abner could overtake him he had plunged in, finding relief at last. Abner, limping along the reef, came upon him and cried, "Keoki, if you do that you will surely die."

"I shall die," the tall alii shivered.

Compassionately, Abner pleaded, "Come back, and I will wrap you in blankets."

"I shall die," Keoki insisted.

"There is no evil that God cannot forgive," Abner assured the quaking man.

"Your God no longer exists," Keoki mumbled from his cold grave. "I shall die and renew my life in the waters of Kane."

Abner was horrified by these words, and pleaded, "Keoki, even in death do not use such blasphemy against the God who loves you."

"Your god brings us only pestilence," the shivering man replied.

"I am going to pray for you, Keoki."

"It's too late now. You never wanted me in your church," and the fever-racked alii splashed his face with water.

"Keoki!" Abner pleaded. "You are dying. Pray with me for your immortal soul."

"Kane will protect me," the stricken young man insisted.

"Oh, no! No!" Abner cried, but he felt a strong hand take his arm and pull him from the grave.

It was one-eyed Kelolo, who said, "You must leave my son alone with his god."

"No!" Abner shouted passionately. "Keoki, will you pray with me?"

"I am beginning a dark journey," the sick man replied feebly. "I have told Kane of my coming. No other prayers are necessary."

The incoming tide brought fresh and colder waters into the grave, and at that moment Abner leaped into the shallow pit and grasped his old friend by the hands. "Keoki, do not die in darkness. My dearest brother . . ." But the alii drew away from Abner and hid his parched face with his forearms.

"Take him away," the young man cried hoarsely. "I will die with my own god." And Kelolo dragged Abner from the grave.

When the pestilence was ended, Abner and Jerusha brought the baby Kelolo, now healthy and smiling, back to the palace, where Noelani took the child and studied it dispassionately. "This one will be the last of the alii," she predicted sadly. "But it may be better that way. Another pestilence and we will all be gone."

Quietly, Abner said, "Noelani, you are aware that Jerusha and I love you above all others. You are precious to God. Will you return to His church?"

The tall, gracious young woman listened attentively to these contrite words and for herself was inclined to accept them, for she had never taken the kahunas seriously, but when she thought of her dead brother her resolve was hardened, and she replied with bitterness, "If you had shown Keoki half the charity you now show me he would not be dead." And it was coldly apparent that she would never return to the church . . . at least not to Abner Hale's church.

ONE DAY in early 1833, after John Whipple had recovered from his exhaustion due to the pestilence, he was accosted by a sailor who asked, "You Doc Whipple?"

"I am," John said.

"I was directed to hand you this personally," the sailor explained.

"Where are you from?" the doctor asked.

"*Carthaginian.* We're in Honolulu."

Eagerly, yet with apprehension, Whipple opened the letter, which said simply:

"Dear Dr. Whipple. You have good sense. Can you get Abner and Jerusha Hale out of Lahaina for a week? I intend to build them a house. Your trusted friend, Rafer Hoxworth."

"Tell your captain yes," Whipple said.

"When can he arrive?" the sailor inquired.

"Next Monday."

"He will be here."

So Whipple fabricated an intricate plot, whereby Abner was called to what the missionaries called "a protracted meeting" at Wailuku, where long ago he had tended Urania Hewlett at her death. To Abner's surprise, the Whipples said, "Amanda and I need a rest. We will join you, for holiday."

"The children?" Jerusha asked, frightened, for she had never left them during a single night since Micah's birth.

"Mrs. Janders'll care for the children," John insisted, and although both Abner and Jerusha thought it perilous to risk their offspring to a woman who allowed Hawaiians to nurse her babies, they at last consented, and the four who had known one another so well aboard the *Thetis* began their pleasant hike to Wailuku, but when they reached the summit of the pass that divided the two halves of the island, John Whipple stopped and stared sadly back at the additional valleys that had been depopulated by the measles and said, "Abner, somehow we've got to get a virile new people into these islands. Because if dying Hawaiians were able to marry strong newcomers . . ."

"Whom could you get?" Abner asked, mopping his forehead.

"I used to think other Polynesians would do," Whipple replied. "But recently I've changed my mind. It'll have to be Javanese. A totally new blood stream." As he paused he idly compared the parched leeward areas he had just left with the green windward area they were approaching. "Curious," he mused.

"What is?" Abner asked.

"I was looking at the two halves of this island," Whipple replied. "The rain falls over here, where it isn't needed, but it never falls on our side, where the big fields lie barren. Abner!" he cried with positive delight. "Why couldn't a man bring the useless rain over to where it's needed?"

"Do you seek to correct God's handiwork?" Abner snorted.

"In such matters, yes," John replied.

"How could you bring rain through a mountain?" Abner challenged.

"I don't know," Whipple mused, but he kept staring at the contrast between rainy windward and parched leeward.

They were not long on their journey before the *Carthaginian* hove into Lahaina Roads and Captain Rafer Hoxworth strode ashore. One-eyed Kelolo and a band of able policemen met the fiery whaler at the pier and leveled six guns at his chest. "Dis place kapu for you, kapena! We no aloha for you, you damn hell!" the old alii warned, in his best pidgin.

Hoxworth, brushing aside the guns, announced: "I come only to build a house."

"No girls on the ship!" Kelolo said sternly.

"I want no girls," Hoxworth assured him, striding briskly up to the mission house. To his following sailors he said, "Get every movable thing out of that house. And be careful!"

The removal took only a few minutes, and when Hoxworth saw how pitifully little the Hales had—their only substantial furniture being the chairs and tables he had provided them—he held his big right hand over his mouth, for he was biting his lip with incredulity. "Cover it up," he said, and when this was carefully done, he applied a match to the old grass house, and in a moment it blazed into the air, with its burden of insects and memories. When the ground was cleared he said, "Dig."

The cellar was broad and deep. It would be cool in the blazing hot summers at Lahaina, and when it was done Captain Hoxworth lined it with building stones hewn from coral, and these he continued some distance above the earth, so that when he started to erect the house itself, it had a solid foundation. Now he ordered his sailors to bring him the corner posts, each numbered, and he began the fascinating task of reassembling the house exactly as it had been when standing on the wharf in Boston.

In three days the job was well launched and obviously on its way to success, and it was while lounging in the offices of Janders & Whipple, that Captain Hoxworth, having told Pupali and all his women to go to hell and leave him alone, heard the story of Keoki Kanakoa and his sister Noelani. "You mean that tall, handsome girl I saw skimming naked past my ship one day on a surfboard?" he asked quizzically.

"Yes. All this happened to her," Janders said gloomily.

"Why, hell!" Hoxworth growled. "She's the best-looking girl the islands ever produced. You mean she's out there in that grass shack . . . alone?"

"She has the usual women-in-waiting," Janders explained.

"I know," Hoxworth said contemptuously, making huge circles with his hands to indicate the women who usually attached themselves to the alii. "I mean . . . she's just there?"

"Yes."

"That's a hell of a way to live!" he boomed. "Just because she got mixed up with a lot of crazy nonsense. Janders, I'm going out there."

"I wouldn't," the older man said. "They don't remember you well in this town."

"To hell with memories!" Hoxworth cried, slamming his big fist onto the arm of his chair. "I'm thinking of staying in Honolulu, Janders. Sail my ship to Canton in the China trade. Maybe build a couple of ships. Could I get cargoes here?"

"If your charges are low enough," Janders replied cautiously. "I've got a lot of skins I'd like to get to China."

"I think you'll get 'em there," Hoxworth said, and he strode out of the office and along the main road to the grass palace of the alii. At his approach, guards ran to inform Kelolo, but before the old man could prevent Hoxworth from doing so, the bold captain had bowed graciously, shoved open the gate, and marched into the grass palace where he found Noelani.

"Ma'am," he said, extending his big right paw, "I've been wanting to meet you ever since I saw you riding naked past my ship. That must have been thirteen years ago. You were a dazzling beauty in those days, ma'am. You're lovelier now."

"Have you come to find someone else to sell?" Noelani asked coldly.

"No, ma'am. I've come to find me a wife. And I feel in my bones that you're the one."

Noelani started to reply to this abrupt assertion, but before she could do so, Hoxworth thrust upon her a bolt of choice Canton silk and a flood of words: "Ma'am, I suppose you know why I came back to Lahaina. My actions last time have preyed upon my conscience, and I deplored seeing an American man and woman living as those two did. If I offended you on my earlier visit, I now apologize, but with that out of the way, ma'am, I want to tell you that I propose running my ship henceforth in the China trade. I've bought a house in Honolulu, and for some time I've been looking for a wife."

"Why did you not find a wife in Boston?" Noelani asked coldly.

"Tell you the truth, ma'am," Hoxworth replied . . . But at this moment Kelolo rushed up with some guards and burst into the room to save the princess; but she, in turn, dismissed her father and said that she wished to talk with the captain.

"Truth is," he continued as if there had been no interruption, striding back and forth before the doorway leading to the garden, "I proposed once to one of those peaches-and-white-linen women of Boston, and I failed to win her. Since then I've come to prefer the lustier women of the islands."

"Where is Iliki?" the alii asked.

"I hope she's in good hands," Hoxworth said bluntly. "Where would she be if she were here?"

The question caused Noelani to reflect, and to gain time she asked, "When will the house be finished?"

"In two days, ma'am, and that's why I think it important that you dine with me tonight aboard ship. I want you to see your quarters . . . in case you should ever decide to join me on one of the trips to Canton."

The sound of this word, this distant city from which had come her clothes and her furniture and which she had never expected to see—nor had she any reason to see it—so captivated Noelani that she betrayed her excitement, whereupon Hoxworth said bluntly, "Noelani, you've had a bad time here, caught up in things of which you were no part. Why not leave it all? It's a sad, messy business that you will never conquer. I offer you a wild, exciting life."

"I have a son, you know," the proud woman said tentatively.

"Bring him with you. I've always wanted a tyke of my own aboard ship."

"He belongs to the people . . ." she hesitated.

"Then leave him with the people," he said firmly, and before she could protest, he had caught her by the hand and drawn him to her, kissing her harshly upon the mouth and pulling at her garments.

"Please," she whispered.

"Go to the door and tell the women to guard it. You're entertaining your husband-to-be."

She pushed him away, stood solemnly before him and asked, "Could you forget that I was once married to . . ."

"Noelani!" he chided. "How many of the girls of this village have I kept in my cabin? That's also past. Now I need a wife."

"I meant, that it was my brother who . . ."

He pondered this question for a moment, then laughed again and said reassuringly, "With me each day that dawns begins a new year. I have no memories."

The tall captain's words were warm in her ear, the kind of bold, sweet words an alii liked, and she thought: "This kapena is much like an alii. He is tall, eager to fight, and he is the leader of his men. He is tired of running after waterfront women. He owns an important ship and he was willing to take my son as his own. He is not pious, but I think he is honest. The day of the Hawaiian is dead, but the years of the white man are upon us." To Hoxworth she said quietly, "I will go with you to the ship."

He kissed her again and felt her wealth of hair cascading upon his hands, and it aroused him as the kisses of dark island girls had always done, and he whispered, "Tell the women to guard the door," but she refused and said, "Not in this room. It is a center of the old ways. I will go with you to your ship." And the town of Lahaina was astonished to see Captain Hoxworth and Noelani, the Alii Nui, walking down the dusty road beneath the palm trees, talking idly as if they were lovers. But they were more astonished when the tall girl, marvelously beautiful now that she was seeing daylight again, climbed into the captain's rowboat and went out to the *Carthaginian,* where she stayed till dawn, and when at parting she looked at the handsome, well-kept cabin which was to be hers, she thought: "He is a real man, and I will be faithful to him. I will eat his food to please him. I will dress as he prefers, so that other men shall look at him and say, 'Kapena is the lucky one.' I will never say no to him"—and then a soft smile came to her face, as it would later come to the thousand Hawaiian girls who would marry Americans—"for I know that with my own words I can win him to a gentler life."

Noelani saw Captain Hoxworth on each of the next two days, and on the last day of his visit to Lahaina, while his men were dragging a complete set of furniture from the *Carthaginian* to the new mission house, she was alone in the grass palace wrapping in tapa cloth two heavy thigh bones; one Keoki had given her before his death, and the other she had received directly for herself. Taking the bundles in her arms, she went out to her father's small house and said to him, "Kelolo, my beloved father, I am leaving Lahaina, and I dare not take these oppressive gifts with me. You must return them to their grave. We cannot any longer live with such memorials haunting us."

Reverently, he accepted the two great thigh bones, placing them tenderly on the earth before him. "Are you determined to go to Honolulu with the American?" he asked.

"Yes. I am seeking a new life."

"May it be a good one," he said gently through his broken and lisping lips. He did not rise to bid her good-bye, for although he understood the pressures which were forcing her to act as she did, he could not condone them; and he was certain that she was rejecting the only true vocation and happiness she would know on earth. "May the goddess Pele . . ." he began, but she hushed his wish, unable to bear any further invocations.

Yet on her part she said, "May the gods be good to you, Kelolo. May the long canoe ride swiftly until the rainbow comes for your departure." She studied his worn old figure with its circular scars about the face and its gaping eye socket, and then she left, to board the ship, but when she reached the pier the sailors told her, "The kapena is not aboard yet," and they directed her to the mission house, where, looking into the bright new room, she saw her intended husband sitting on a kitchen chair, turned backward, its arched back under his chin, and he staring moodily at the floor; and as she watched he rose and carried the chair with him, and set it down three or four times with great violence, making the entire house shudder with his fury. And for some minutes he stood there, pounding the chair into the floor and holding his head down, with his eyes closed and knots standing out on his forehead in dark passion; and she recalled his earlier words and thought: "He can boast that he has no memories, but I am pleased that he has. I thought he remembered only trivial things like selling Iliki." And after he had thrashed the chair into the floor a dozen more times, to control himself from kicking the entire house into splinters, he carefully returned it to its place, gave the small wooden room one last lingering look and came out into the bright sunlight.

"We'll go," he said, and villagers, who had heard of the impending marriage, followed them to the pier, where they watched as the big captain caught Noelani in his arms and lifted her into the longboat.

On the way home from Wailuku, John Whipple and his wife, as soon as they reached the summit of the trail, began gazing into the distance so markedly that Abner finally asked, "What are you looking for?"

"A great surprise," John explained mysteriously, but the four had reached the last small hill before he was able to spot, beneath the branching trees, the roof line of the new mission house. "I see it now!" he cried. "Can you?"

The Hales looked futilely at the outlines of Lahaina and saw nothing. There was the broad reach of sea, the hills of Lanai, the dusty trails. And then Jerusha gasped, "Abner! Is that a house?"

"Where?"

"At the mission! Abner! Abner!" And she broke into a run and dashed down off the hill, with her bonnet flying behind and her skirts causing dust, and when she reached the road she rushed on ahead, not waiting for anyone to catch her, crying all the time, "It's a house! It's a house!"

Finally, gasping with excitement, she stood beside the stream and looked across the walled-in yard to where the old grass house had stood, and there rose, as in a magic story, a New England farmhouse, snug and secure. She put her left hand to her mouth and looked dumbly first at the house and then at the approaching three, and finally she ran desperately to Abner and kissed him in public. "Thank you, my dearest friend and companion," she said weakly.

But he was more surprised than she and looked at Whipple for enlightenment, and for the time being John thought it permissible to tell only part of the truth, so he explained: "Your father sent it out from Boston, Jerusha. We wanted to surprise you." Later, when the association with Captain Hoxworth was fully developed, the two missionaries were so happy with their home that neither made complaint. They took the gift as having come from Charles Bromley, in Walpole, and they thought it proper to ignore the intermediary by whom the gift had been delivered, and who in fact had initiated the idea. Jerusha thought it a marvelous house in these respects: it did not harbor bugs; it did not have an earthen floor; it had a proper cellar for storing food; it had separate rooms for the children; it had a desk where Abner could work; and it had a kitchen. Jerusha was proud when the Hawaiians came to see it.

The first official visitor was Kelolo, bringing with him a large square of paper which he had got from J & W and on which he wanted Abner to print the name NOELANI, after which, for no apparent reason that could be ascertained at the time—although later his purpose became clear—he sat on and on until Abner felt that he might have to ask the one-eyed old man to go. He recalled how his wife Malama had always loved the church, how Keoki had wanted to become a minister, and Noelani's happy marriage in Honolulu. There seemed much more that he wished to say, but he did not say it, and at sunset when Jerusha interrupted, "Kelolo, my dear friend, we are about to have our sea biscuit and salt beef. Will you join us?" he gripped her hands passionately and wished her a world of luck. Finally, when he stood alone with Abner, he predicted, "Your church will last when you and I are both upon the rainbow, Makua Hale. It is a fine church, and through it you have done much good in Lahaina." He then inquired if he might embrace the little missionary, and in the Hawaiian manner he rubbed noses and said farewell.

It was not yet dark when he walked down the dusty road, past the taro patch and the royal grounds over the little bridge where the whaling boats came for clear water and onto the grounds that Malama had loved. As he walked he thought happily: "There is always a chance that the night marchers may come along to take me away," and he listened hopefully for the footfalls, but in vain. The walk did not tire him particularly, but he did feel himself to be an old man, and when he reached his small house he rested for a while before wrapping in the paper the three treasured objects he intended for his daughter: Malama's necklace, the whale tooth hung on the hair of his hundred friends, his feathered cape, and the ancient red stone of Pele.

When this was done, he placed the package in the middle of the room and proceeded to gather up his four remaining treasures: the skull of

Malama, her right thigh bone which he had given Keoki, and her left, which had been Noelani's heirloom now rejected; and most significant of all, the sacred stone of Kane, which he had protected from the missionaries for so many years.

He carried these objects to the altar by the sea, where a canoe waited, unmanned and with a solitary paddle. Reverently, he moved the three bones onto a low tapa-covered table perched in the prow. Then, ceremoniously, he covered them with maile leaves, whose memorable fragrance marked the night. This ritual completed, he placed the sacred stone on the platform which had so infuriated Abner, and here for the last time he spoke with his god.

"We are not wanted any longer, Kane," he reported frankly. "We have been asked to go away, for our work is done. Malama is dead with a different god. Keoki is gone, and Noelani spurns you. Now even the kahunas worship elsewhere. We must go home.

"But before we leave, great Kane," the old man pleaded quietly, "will you please lift from your children in Hawaii the burdens of the old kapus? They are heavy and the young no longer know how to live with them."

He started to carry the god to the canoe, but as he did so the awfulness of his act oppressed him and he whispered to Kane, "It was not my idea, gentle Kane, to take you from the islands you have loved. It was Pele who pointed to Keala-i-kahiki, the way that we must go. Now we shall go home."

So speaking, Kelolo gathered up the god and wrapped him in a cape of yellow feathers, placing him in a position of honor in the prow. He then turned and looked for the last time at the grass palace, where he had known Malama, greatest of women and the most complete. "I am taking your bones back to Bora Bora," he assured her, "where we shall sleep in peace beside the lagoon." Bowing to the house of love, and to the rocky altar, and to the kou trees whose shade had protected him, he climbed into the canoe and started paddling resolutely toward Keala-i-kahiki, and as he stood out into the ocean itself, he chanted a navigational song which his family claimed had been composed by some ancient ancestor on his way from Hawaii to Bora Bora:

"Sail from the Land of the Little Eyes,
Southward, southward
To the oceans of burning heat . . ."

By morning he had entered exactly those oceans, and without water or food he paddled resolutely into them, a near-blind, toothless old man, bearing his god and the relics of the woman he had loved.

JERUSHA ENJOYED for less than three years the clean wooden house her father had sent her, for perversely, although she had managed to maintain her health in the grass shack, she could not do so in her comfortable home. "She's worked herself to death," Dr. Whipple said bluntly. "If she'd allow Hawaiian women to care for her children . . ."

Abner would not hear of this, so Whipple suggested, "Why not send her back to New Hampshire? Three or four cold winters with lots of apples and fresh milk. She'd recover." This time it was Jerusha who was adamant.

"This is our island, Brother John," she insisted stubbornly. "When I first saw it from the railing of the *Thetis,* I was afraid. But through the years it has become my home. Did you know that some time ago Abner was invited to Honolulu, but it was I who refused."

"Then I can give you only one medicine," Whipple concluded. "Less work. More sleep. More food."

But with four children and a girls' school, Jerusha found little time for resting, until at last she awakened one morning with her entire chest in a viselike grip that she could not adequately describe, except that she found much difficulty in breathing. Abner placed her beside an open window and hurried to fetch the doctor, but when Whipple reached the room, Jerusha was gasping horribly.

"Put her to bed, quickly!" John cried, and when he lifted his friend's wife, he was appalled at how little she weighed. "Amanda," he thought, "weighs more than she." And he sent the children, running by themselves, to Captain Janders' home, and then he said quietly to Abner, "I am afraid she's dying."

There was no need to whisper, for Jerusha sensed that she was near death, and she asked if Amanda and Luella could come into the room, and when the women were there she sent for her children and said that she would like to hear, once more, the great mission hymn, and all in the room, including the dying woman, chanted:

"From Greenland's icy mountains,
From India's coral strand;
Where Africa's sunny fountains
Roll down their golden strand;
From many an ancient river,
From many a palmy plain,
They call us to deliver
Their land from error's chain."

"We have labored to do so," Jerusha said wanly, and seeing that death was strangling at her throat, Amanda Whipple began to whisper the hymn that had launched them on their individual adventures on the golden strands. "Blest be the tie that binds," Amanda began, but Abner could not join in the painful words, and when the wavering voices reached the poignant second verse, which seemed written particularly for those who travel in God's work to far places, he fell into a chair and held his hands before his face, unable to look at the frail figure on the bed who sang in the perfect fellowship of which she was the symbol:

"We share our mutual woes;
Our mutual burdens bear;
And often for each other flows
The sympathizing tear."

"My beloved husband," she gasped in great pain, "I am going to meet our Lord. I can see . . ." And she was dead.

She was buried in the Lahaina church cemetery, with a plain wooden cross, and with her children at the graveside, watching the white clouds sweep down from the mountains; but after the ceremony was ended, and the crowd dispersed, Amanda Whipple could not rest content with the niggardly marking of her grave, and she had carved in wood, which was later reproduced in stone, an epitaph which might have served for all missionary women: "Of her bones was Hawaii built."

In later years it would become fashionable to say of the missionaries, "They came to the islands to do good, and they did right well." Others made jest of the missionary slogan, "They came to a nation in darkness; they left it in light," by pointing out: "Of course they left Hawaii lighter. They stole every goddamned thing that wasn't nailed down."

But these comments did not apply to Jerusha Hale. From her body came a line of men and women who would civilize the islands and organize them into meaningful patterns. Her name would be on libraries, on museums, on chairs of medicine, on church scholarships. From a mean grass house, in which she worked herself to death, she brought humanity and love to an often brutal seaport, and with her needle and reading primer she taught the women of Maui more about decency and civilization than all the words of her husband accomplished. She asked for nothing, gave her love without stint, and grew to cherish the land she served: "Of her bones was Hawaii built." Whenever I think of a missionary, I think of Jerusha Hale.

In the hours following Jerusha's death, the Americans in Lahaina held long discussions as to what should be done with the four Hale children, and it was tentatively agreed that Mrs. Janders should take them until such time as a ship could be found to carry the youngsters back to the Bromleys in Walpole, but since these plans had been worked out without consulting Abner, they were obviously not binding on him, and to the general surprise he announced, when Mrs. Janders offered to take the children, that he would continue to care for them; and they stayed inside the mission wall—Micah, aged thirteen; Lucy, ten; David, six; Esther, four—while their father tended their needs. In this he was much aided by Micah, a sallow, serious child who read voraciously and who had a vocabulary even greater than his erudite father's, for often while the Whipple and Janders children were roustabouting near the mission grounds, Micah Hale, with nothing better to do, sat hunched inside the wall reading for pleasure either a Hebrew dictionary or Cornelius Schrevelius' *Greek-Latin Lexicon.* The two little girls were dressed as Abner thought appropriate, in fitted basques with full-length sleeves, plain flowing skirts, pantaloons to the ankle, and flat straw hats with ribbon streamers, all dredged up from the bottoms of the charity barrels, and they too became extremely fast readers with vocabularies that astonished their elders. Only on Sundays did the general population see the Hale children, for then their father washed and polished them, easing them one by one into their best apparel and leading them solemnly behind him to the big church. At such times many mothers in the community observed, "They are so pallid. Like their mother."

All might have gone well, however, for Abner was a father who demonstrated deep love for his children, except that in the spring of 1837 the *Carthaginian* put into Lahaina on a routine visit to pick up Janders & Whipple furs for an intended run to Canton, and while the handsome ship was loading, Captain Hoxworth idly roamed the tree-lined streets of the town; suddenly he snapped his fingers and asked a Hawaiian, "Where is Mrs. Hale buried?" Stepping briskly, the tall, powerful captain strode to the cemetery, stopping only at a wayside house to buy some flowers; and his intentions were peaceful, but when he reached the grave he had the great bad luck to find Abner Hale there, tending the grass that had grown up beside Amanda Whipple's improvised marker; and when the whaler spotted Abner, the author of his constant grief, he flew into a dark and savage rage, shouting, "You goddamned little worm! You killed this girl! You worked her like a slave in this climate!" And he dove for Abner, catching him below the knees and bearing him violently onto the grave, where he began punching him about the head. Then, struggling to his feet while Abner was still prone, he started raining kicks at the little man, crashing his heavy boots into Abner's head and chest and stomach.

Under such treatment, Abner fainted, but to lose the hateful enemy thus infuriated Captain Hoxworth additionally, and he grabbed him from the grave and began throwing him down again with tremendous force, shouting, "I should have kept you among the sharks, you dirty, dirty, dirty bastard."

How far the dreadful punishment would have continued is uncertain, for natives, hearing the fight, hurried in to rescue their beloved little minister, but when they reached him, they thought him dead. With love they carried him to the mission house, where unthinkingly they allowed the four Hale children to see their father's mutilated figure, and the three younger ones began to weep, but sallow-faced Micah kneeled over his father's battered face and began washing away the blood.

In the days that followed, it became quite apparent to Dr. Whipple that Abner had suffered severe damage in the head, Captain Hoxworth's huge boots having either displaced a piece of bone or dislodged a set of nerve ends; and for several days Abner looked blankly at his commiserating friends, who said, "We have told Hoxworth he can never again come into this port."

"Who is Hoxworth?" Abner asked dully.

But under Whipple's care, the missionary recovered, although ever afterwards the people of Lahaina would frequently see him stop on his walks, joggle himself up and down as if resetting his brain, and then continue, an uncertain man who now required a cane. There was one particularly uncomfortable moment during his recovery when he discovered that his four children were not with him, but were lost somewhere among the heathen of Maui. He began to rant, and his voice raised to a wailing lament, but Amanda produced the children, for she had been tending them in her own home, and he was pacified.

Both the Whipples and the Janderses were surprised, upon his recovery, to find that not only did he insist upon keeping the children with him; the children much preferred their life within the mission confines to the freer existence outside; and as soon as he was able, Abner reestablished the curious, walled-in household on the mission grounds.

Then, in 1840, an unexpected visitor arrived in Lahaina, and the pattern of life was permanently broken, for the arrival was a tall, emaciated, very striking-looking Congregational minister dressed in jet-black and wearing a stovepipe hat that made him seem twice his natural height. At the pier he announced, "I am Reverend Eliphalet Thorn, of the American Board of Commissioners for Foreign Missions, of Boston. Can you lead me to Reverend Hale?"

And when the gaunt old man, spare and effective as a buggy whip, strode into the mission house, he was instantly aware of all that must have transpired, and he was appalled that Abner had tried to keep his children with him. "You should either find yourself a new wife, or return to friends in America," Thorn suggested.

"My work is here," Abner replied stubbornly.

"God does not call upon his servants to abuse themselves," Thorn countered. "Brother Abner, I am making arrangements to take your children back to America with me."

Instead of arguing against this sensible decision, Abner asked carefully, "Will Micah be able to enter Yale?"

"I doubt that the boy's preparation is adequate," Thorn countered, "living so far from books."

At this, Abner summoned his scrawny, sallow-faced son and bade him stand at attention, hands at sides, before the visitor from Boston. In a steady voice Abner directed, "Micah, I want you to recite the opening chapter of Genesis in Hebrew, then in Greek, then in Latin, and finally in English. And then I want you to explain to Reverend Thorn seven or eight of the passages which cause the greatest difficulty in translation from one language to the next."

At first Reverend Thorn wanted to interrupt the exhibition as unnecessary; he would accept Abner's word that the boy could perform this feat, but when the golden words began to pour forth, the gaunt old missionary sank back and listened to their pregnant promises. He was struck by the boy's feeling for language and was unhappy when he stopped, so that he asked, "How does such a passage sound in Hawaiian?"

"I can't speak Hawaiian," Micah explained.

When the boy was gone, Thorn said, "I'd like to meet some of the Hawaiian ministers."

"We have none," Abner replied.

"Who is to carry on the work when you go?" Thorn asked, in some surprise.

"I am not going," Abner explained.

"But the vitality of the church?" Thorn pressed.

"You can't trust Hawaiians to run a church," Abner insisted. "Has anyone told you about Keoki and his sister Noelani?"

"Yes," Eliphalet Thorn said coldly. "Noelani told me . . . in Honolulu. She now has four lovely Christian children."

Abner shook his head, trying to keep all things in focus, but for a moment he could not exactly place where he had known Eliphalet Thorn before, and then it became clear to him, and he recalled the manner in which the grave, gaunt man had gone from college to college in the year 1821. "What you must do, Reverend Thorn," Abner explained eagerly, "is go back to Yale and enlist many more missionaries. We could use a dozen more here at least."

"We have never intended sending an unlimited supply of white men to rule these islands," Thorn replied severely, and his accidental use of the word *rule* reminded him of his major responsibility in visiting Hawaii, but the subject was difficult to broach, and he hesitated.

Then he coughed and said bluntly, "Brother Abner, the Board in Boston is considerably displeased over two aspects of the Hawaiian mission. First, you have set up a system of bishoprics with central control in Honolulu, and you must know that this is repugnant to Congregationalism. Second, you have refused to train up Hawaiians to take over their churches when you depart. These are serious defects, and the Board instructed me to rebuke those responsible for these errors."

Abner stared coldly at his inquisitor and thought: "Who can know Hawaii who has not lived here? Reverend Thorn can throw down rebukes, but can he justify them?"

Thorn, having met the same kind of stubborn resistance in Honolulu, thought: "He is accusing me of intemperate judgment on the grounds that I know nothing of local conditions, but every error begins with a special condition."

Eliphalet Thorn was not at ease in delivering rebukes, and having warned Abner, he turned to happier topics, saying, "In Boston the tides of God seem always to run high, and I wish you could have witnessed the phenomenal changes in our church during the past few years. Our leaders have brought to the fore God's love and have tended to diminish John Calvin's bitter rectitude. We live in a new world of the spirit, Brother Abner, and although it is not easy for us older men to accommodate ourselves to change, there is no greater exaltation than to submit to the will of God. Oh, I'm convinced that this is the way He intends us to go." Suddenly, the inspired minister stopped, for Abner was looking at him strangely, and Thorn thought: "He is a difficult, custom-ridden man and cannot possibly understand the changes that have swept Boston."

But Abner was thinking: "Jerusha instituted such changes, and greater, in Lahaina seven years ago. Without the aid of theologians or Harvard professors she found God's love. Why is this tall man so arrogant?" A single conciliatory word from Thorn would have encouraged Abner to share with him the profound changes Jerusha had initiated in his theology, but the word was not spoken, for Thorn, noticing Abner's aloofness, thought: "I remember when I interviewed him at Yale. He was excitable and opinionated then. He's no better now. Why are the missions cursed with such men?"

Then, driven by that perverse luck which often frustrates full communion, Thorn stumbled upon a vital subject, and the manner in which it developed confirmed his suspicion that in Abner Hale the Church had acquired one of those limited, stubborn men lacking in capacity for growth who are such impediments to practical religion. "Brother Abner," the questioning began, "I have come here to join you in ordaining any Hawaiians who are ready for the ministry. Will you assemble your candidates?"

"I have none," Abner confessed.

Thorn, already satisfied that he had identified Abner's character, did not raise his voice. "I'm not sure I understand, Brother Abner. When young Keoki betrayed the church, didn't you immediately recruit eight or ten better prospects?"

"What I thought was," Abner began, but his head felt out of balance, and he jogged himself from the right hip. With compassion Reverend Thorn waited, and Abner continued: "I felt that since the church had suffered such a terrible disgrace, it would be better if . . ." Then he caught a vision of Keoki standing before the altar of Kane, with the maile leaves about his shoulders and the whale's tooth. "Well," he concluded, "I thought the most important thing was to protect the church from another such debacle."

"So you conscripted no potential ministers?" Thorn asked quietly.

"Oh, no! You see, Reverend Thorn, unless you live with the Hawaiians you can't really understand . . ."

"Brother Abner," the visitor interrupted. "I have brought with me two fine young men from Honolulu."

"Missionaries?" Abner cried excitedly. "From Boston?"

"No," Thorn explained patiently, "they're Hawaiians. I'm going to ordain them in your church, and I would be particularly happy if you could nominate some young man of Lahaina who seems destined for the church . . ."

"The Hawaiians in Lahaina, Reverend Thorn . . . Well, I don't even allow my children to associate with the Hawaiians in Lahaina. There's this man Pupali, and he had four daughters, and his youngest, Iliki . . ." He stopped and his mind became brutally clear and he thought: "He would not understand about Iliki."

The ordination ceremonies impressed Lahaina more deeply than any previous church activity, for when the congregation saw two of their own people promoted to full responsibility for Christianizing the islands, they felt at last that Hawaiians had become part of the church, and when Reverend Thorn promised that within a year some young man from Lahaina itself would be ordained, there was little discussed in the next days except one question: "Do you suppose they might choose our son?" But on the next Sunday came even more welcome news, for Thorn announced that the missionary board in Honolulu had decided that one of the two ordained Hawaiians, Reverend Jonah Keeaumoku Piimalo, should remain in Lahaina to preach in the big church and assist Reverend Hale.

When Thorn sensed the joy that this announcement occasioned, he happened to be looking at John Whipple, who turned sideways to his little wife, Amanda, and shook her hand warmly as if the family had long discussed this move, and Thorn thought: "Isn't it perverse? I like Whipple, who left the church, much better than Hale, who stayed. With his doctoring the poor and building a good business, Whipple is much closer to my idea of God than the poor little fellow sitting here beside me."

On the next morning Reverend Thorn sailed back to Honolulu, en route to Boston, taking with him the four Hale children, and when they left their father at the pier Abner said solemnly to each, "When you have learned the civilized manners of New England be sure to come back, for Lahaina is your home," but to his brilliant son Micah he added, "I shall be waiting for you, and when you return a minister I shall turn my church over to you." Thorn, overhearing these words, winced and thought: "He will forever regard it as his church . . . not God's . . . and surely not the Hawaiians'."

It now came time for Thorn to bid good-bye to the missionary whom he had inducted into the service nineteen years before, and he looked compassionately at the halting little man and thought: "What a profound tragedy. Brother Hale has never even dimly perceived the true spirit of the Lord. If the score were tallied, I suspect he has done far more harm than good."

Abner, his mind now beautifully clear, looked at his imperious inquisitor and saw him once more as the black-frocked judge he had been on that visit to Yale in 1821. He thought: "Brother Eliphalet moves about the world dispensing advice and thinks that by coming to Lahaina for a few days he can detect where we have gone astray. What does he know of cannon? Has he ever faced a rioting mob of whalers?" And with a sense of deep sorrow Abner discovered: "He will never know." Then, his mind still competent, he developed an equally haunting thought: "I doubt that anyone will ever know . . . except Jerusha and Malama. They knew."

"Farewell, Brother Abner," Eliphalet Thorn called.

"Farewell, sir," Abner replied, and the packet stood out to sea.

IN THE YEARS that followed, Abner became one of the human signposts of the old capital, an increasingly befuddled man, limping about the city, stopping to adjust his brains and clicking his head sideways to relieve passing darts of pain. He no longer lived in the mission house, for others came to assume the major responsibilities of the church, but he frequently preached in flowing Hawaiian, and whenever it was known that he would occupy the pulpit, the church was crowded.

For all official duties he continued to wear the shiny old claw-hammer coat he had bought in New Haven and the black beaver hat. His shoes and other apparel he got as best he could from the charity barrels, and in time his life settled into a perfected routine, marked by three recurring highlights. Whenever a new ship anchored in the roads, he would hurry down to the pier and ask its people whether, in their travels, they had come upon the Hawaiian girl Iliki. "She was sold from here to an English captain and I thought that perhaps you might have intelligence of her." No one had.

His second calendar-marking moments came when, from the rude desk in the grass house in which he now lived, he released for printing another of his metrical renderings of the Psalms in Hawaiian, and when the printed sheets appeared, he would distribute the Psalms to his parishioners, and at the next church service would lead them in singing their praises.

The final triumph, of course, came whenever he received mail from his children in America. His sister Esther, now married to a minister in western New York, cared for the two girls, while the boys were the responsibility of the Bromleys. Each of the children's portraits had been drawn in black pencil at a studio in Boston, and they now looked down gravely from the grass wall: handsome, sensitive, alert faces.

Micah, having graduated with top honors from Yale, was already a minister, preaching in Connecticut, but the most exciting news was that Lucy had met young Abner Hewlett, studying at Yale, and had married him. It was Abner's intention to send his old friend Abraham Hewlett a brotherly letter of congratulation upon the joining of the two mission families, but he could not forget the fact that Abraham was married to a Hawaiian, nor could he forgive; and the subsidiary fact that the Hewletts were prospering exceedingly with their lands, and were now wealthy, did not alleviate Abner's distrust of anyone who would consort with the heathen.

One of the saddest aspects of these years was the fact that all who witnessed the visible impairment of Abner's faculties could at the same time observe John Whipple's cultivation of his. Always a handsome young man, he now flowered into an enviable maturity: he was tall, lean, sharp-eyed, and bronzed from surfing. His jaw was prominent, and the fact that he had a heavy beard, which he shaved twice each day, gave him a dark, manly look, which he accentuated by wearing dark suits very closely fitted with six-button waistcoats. His black hair, at forty-four, was untouched by gray, whereas Abner's was actually whitened, so that to see the two men of equal age side by side was shocking, and this was partly the reason why islanders always referred to Abner as the old man.

Whipple also prospered in trade, for whalers now jammed the roads —325 in 1844; 429 in 1845—and they had to buy from J & W. Following Captain Janders' driving precept, "Own nothing, control everything," John had become a master in manipulating the lands and wealth of others, and if an upstart attempted to open a major industry in Lahaina, it was usually Whipple who discovered the tactic whereby the man could be either bought out or squeezed out. When Valparaiso begged for more hides, it was Dr. Whipple who recalled seeing huge herds of goats on neighboring Molokai, and it was he who organized the expeditions to the windward cliffs. As honest as he was clever, he paid any man he employed a fair wage, but when his most skilled huntsman was tempted to organize a goat-shooting team of his own, selling the hides and tallow directly to an American brigantine for extra profit, the man suddenly found he could hire no boats to transport his hides, and after three months' labor had rotted away on Molokai, the venture was abandoned and he returned to work for J & W. Abner never understood how John Whipple could have learned so much about business.

Once, on a trading mission to Valparaiso, Whipple's schooner was laid over for two weeks in Tahiti, and John, as was his custom, improved the wasting hours by studying something of Tahitian ways and words, and it was out of this casual experience that he wrote the essay which dominated Polynesian research for some decades: "The Theory of Kapu," in which he made this provocative suggestion. "In our concern over why the Tahitian says *tabu* and the Hawaiian *kapu* we are apt to digress into theories which, while entrancing, are probably irrelevant. What we must remember is that a group of learned English scientists transliterated the Tahitian language and set it into western ways, while a body of not so well-trained American missionaries did the same job for Hawaiian. In each case we must suspect that the visitors crystallized what was not really there. Would it not be wiser to believe that when the English spelled their word *tabu,* what they actually heard was something quite different—somewhere between *tabu* and *kapu,* but slightly inclining toward the former—whereas when the Americans wrote their word *kapu,* what they heard was also something quite different—somewhere between *tabu* and *kapu,* but inclining slightly toward the latter? Much of the difference that we now observe between written Tahitian and written Hawaiian must be accountable for not by the actual differences between the languages but by the differences in the ears of the men who transliterated them.

"Thus we have many words for *house: whare, fale, fare, hale,* but they are all one word, and we should like to know how many of these differences can be attributed to the defective ear of the white man, whose system of spelling did much to crystallize error. I recall an educated Hawaiian who said to me one day in his native tongue, 'I am going to see Mr. Kown.' I replied, 'Kimo, you know his name is Mr. Town,' and he agreed, pointing out, 'But in Hawaiian we have no letter T, so we can't say Town.' And he pronounced the name perfectly. We had imposed limits on his speech that did not exist before we arrived on the scene.

"At the same time, however, the visitor from Hawaii to Tahiti is visibly struck by the changes that occurred when Polynesians from the latter islands journeyed north. In Hawaii their stature increased. Their skin became lighter. Their speech became sharper. Their tools underwent obvious changes, and of course their gods were transmuted. Most spectacular was the transformation of the bold, angular and oftentimes lascivious Tahitian hula into the languorous, poetic dance of Hawaii. Change occurred in all things: religion changed from wild vitality to stately formalism; government became stable and self-perpetuating; and what in Tahiti was merely ornamental featherwork became in Hawaii a subtle art of rare beauty. Thus the development of Tahiti's god of the sea, Ta'aroa, into Hawaii's god of hell, Kanaloa, becomes a change in both orthography and theology, but the latter is the greater.

"In our studies of Polynesia we should start from this premise: Nothing that came to Hawaii remained unchanged; flowers, processes, words and men there found new life and new directions. But we must not be deceived by outward appearances, and especially not by word forms, into estimating the differences to be greater than they actually are. Scratch a Hawaiian, and you find a Tahitian."

Abner's avocation was the Seamen's Chapel, where he would often sit for hours with Chaplain Cridland, the sailor whom he himself had brought to God, and he thought: "Of all things I have accomplished, that accidental conversion of Cridland has borne the most fruit." He felt that no life was more difficult or more fraught with temptation than that of sailors, and he was happy that he had been instrumental in erasing Lahaina's brothels and grog shops.

He existed on a pittance sent by the mission board, for he was no longer a full-fledged missionary, but Dr. Whipple kept close watch upon him, and if he required pocket money, either Janders or Whipple saw to it that he got a little. Once, a visitor, seeing the lonely grass shack, adorned only with the portraits of his children, asked compassionately, "Have you no friends?" And Abner replied, "I have known God, and Jerusha Bromley, and Malama Kanakoa, and beyond that a man requires no friends."

Then, in 1849, exhilarating news reached Lahaina and transformed Abner Hale into a spry, excited father, for Reverend Micah Hale wrote from Connecticut that he had decided to leave New England—it was too cold for his taste—and to live permanently in Hawaii, "for I must see once more the palm trees of my youth and the whales playing in Lahaina Roads." Many mission children, after their years at Yale, wrote the heartening news that they were coming home, for the islands generated a persuasive charm that could exert itself across thousands of miles, but what qualified Micah's letter as unusual was the fact that he was determined to cross overland to California, for he wanted to see America, and he predicted that sometime near the end of 1849, he would be boarding a ship out of San Francisco.

Consequently, Abner found a map of North America and hung it on the grass wall, marking it each day with his son's imaginary progress across the vast continent, and from deductions that were remarkably accurate, he announced one day to the crowd in the J & W store in late November of 1849, "My son, the Reverend Micah Hale, is probably arriving in San Francisco right now."

When Micah climbed down out of the Sierra Nevadas and started along the Sacramento to the booming San Francisco of the gold rush, he was a handsome, tall young man of twenty-seven, with dark eyes and brown hair like his mother and the quick intelligence of his father. The sallowness and delicate stature of his youth had been transmuted into an attractive bronze, and his chest had filled out from his long hike in the company of gold-seekers crossing the continent. He stepped forward eagerly, as if anticipating excitement at the next tree, and he had won the respect of his fellow travelers by preaching a simple Christianity characterized by God's abiding love for his children, and the respect of the muleteers by nipping straight whiskey when the nights were cold.

In wild and vigorous San Francisco he made acquaintance with many adventurers who had come from Hawaii to the gold fields and was asked to preach in one of the local churches, where after a brief reading of the Bible he captivated his audience by predicting that one day "America will sweep in a chain of settled towns from Boston to San Francisco, and will then move on to Hawaii, to which the American democracy must inevitably be extended. Then San Francisco and Honolulu will be bound together by bonds of love and self-interest, each advancing the work of the Lord."

"Do you consider the Americanization of Hawaii assured?" a San Francisco businessman probed, after the sermon.

"Absolutely inevitable," Micah Hale replied, reflecting his father's love of prophecy. Then, grasping the man's hands in his own, he said forcefully, "My friend, that a Christian America should extend its interests and protection to those heavenly islands is ordained by our destiny. We cannot escape it, even if we would."

"When you use the word *we,*" the businessman asked, "are you speaking as a citizen of Hawaii or as an American?"

"I'm an American!" Micah replied in astonishment. "What else could I be?"

"Reverend," the Californian said impulsively, "you're alone in the town and I'd esteem it a signal honor if you'd have dinner with me. I have a businessman from Honolulu visiting me, and he used to be an American. Now he's a citizen of the islands."

"I'd like to meet him," Micah agreed, and he drove with his new friend through the excitement of the city to a point overlooking the bay. There they left their team and climbed a steep hill on foot until they reached a prominence which commanded a scene of far-stretching beauty.

"My empire," the man said expansively. "It's like looking out on creation!" He led the young minister inside and introduced him to a tall, powerfully built man with eyes set wide apart and a wealth of black hair that grew long at the ears. "This is Captain Rafer Hoxworth," the Californian said.

Micah, who had never before seen his father's enemy, drew back in loathing. Hoxworth saw this and was challenged by the fact that the young man might insult him by refusing to shake hands. Accordingly, he activated his considerable charm, stepped forward and extended his huge hand, smiling compassionately as he did so. "Aren't you Reverend Hale's son?" he asked in an extra deep, friendly voice.

"I am," Micah said guardedly.

"You look very much like your mother," Hoxworth reflected, as he held onto the minister's hand. "She was a beautiful woman."

Repelled by the sea captain of whom he had heard so many ugly reports, yet fascinated by the man's calculated vitality, Micah asked, "Where did you know my mother?"

"In Walpole, New Hampshire," Hoxworth replied, releasing Micah's hand, but holding him at attention with his dynamic eyes. "Have you ever been to Walpole?" And he launched into a rhapsody on that fairest of villages, and as he spoke he could see that he was whittling away at Micah Hale's resolve, and then with a sense of animal delight he saw that the young man was not listening to him but was looking over his shoulder at someone who had entered the room, and instinctively he wanted the young man to become fascinated, involved, hurt.

In fact, Micah was staring at two people who stood inside the doorway. The first was Noelani Kanakoa Hoxworth, whom he had last seen in his father's church at Lahaina, and if she had been beautiful in those days, she was now radiant, in a dress of jet-black velvet, her hair piled high and as shimmering as a polished kukui nut, and wearing about her slim brown neck a single gold chain from which dangled a glistening whale's-tooth hook. Micah hurried over, grasped her hand and said, "Noelani, Alii Nui, I am so pleased to see you." The tall woman, who now knew Hong Kong and Singapore as well she had once known Lahaina, bowed graciously.

But it was not really Noelani that Micah had rushed to greet, for behind Mrs. Hoxworth stood the most beautiful girl Micah had ever seen. She was as tall as he, very slender, with wide shoulders and tapered hips over which a tight-waisted gown of many gores was fitted. She wore her dark hair piled on her vivacious head, and her complexion was set off thereby, for it was absolutely smooth and of a brownish-olive cast. Her eyes were unusually sparkling and her lips showed white and even teeth. At her ear she wore a large California flower, and when her father said, "Join us, Malama. This is Reverend Hale, from Lahaina," she moved gracefully into the room, bowed slightly, and extended her hand in the American manner.

"Meet my daughter, Malama," Captain Hoxworth said, and he was grimly pleased to mark her effect upon the young minister.

That dinner was the most exciting in which Micah had so far participated, surpassing even those held at Yale when the president of the college conversed brilliantly with his students, for Captain Hoxworth spoke of China; the Californian told of his trip southward to Monterey; and Mrs. Hoxworth, unlike the disciplined women who had often eaten with Reverend Hale in New England, was effusive in her recollections of storms at sea and the adventures one could experience in ports like Bangkok and Batavia.

"Do your ships go everywhere in the Pacific?" Micah asked.

"Wherever there's money," Hoxworth replied bluntly.

"Have you ever sailed with your parents?" Micah asked the girl at his side.

"This is my first trip," Malama replied. "Up to now I've been at the Oahu Charity School in Honolulu."

"Are you liking San Francisco?" Micah continued.

"It's much more vigorous than Hawaii," she replied. "But I miss the sunny rainstorms at home. A visitor from Philadelphia came to Honolulu not long ago and asked how to get to J & W's, and he was told, 'Go down to the first shower and turn left.' " The dining companions applauded the story, and young Malama blushed prettily, but what everyone waited to hear was Micah's account of crossing the prairies, and under the excitement of Malama's obvious interest in him, he expanded on his theme in a manner he had not intended.

"The land reaches for a thousand miles in all directions, a waving, wonderful sea of possibilities," he exclaimed. "I dug into it a dozen times, and it was rich, dark soil. A hundred thousand people could live there. A million, and they would be lost in its immensity."

"Tell us what you said about the movement of America to San Francisco and on to the islands," the Californian suggested, and at this, Rafer Hoxworth leaned forward and chewed on his expensive Manila cigar.

"I can see the day," Micah expounded, "when there will be wide and well-traveled roads connecting Boston and this town. People will occupy the lands I saw, and enormous wealth will be created. Schools, colleges, churches will flourish. Yale College couldn't begin to accommodate the millions . . ." He was prophesying, like Ezekiel.

"What was your idea about Hawaii?" Captain Hoxworth interrupted impatiently.

"When that takes place, Captain, there will be a natural impulse for America to leap out across the Pacific and embrace Hawaii. It will happen! It's got to happen!"

"Do you mean that America will go to war against the Hawaiian monarchy?" Hoxworth pursued, edging his hands forward on the table.

"No! Never!" Micah cried, intoxicated by his own visions. "America will never employ arms to extend its empire. If this excitement over gold continues to crowd California with people, and if Hawaii flourishes, as it must one day, the two groups of people will naturally see that their interests . . ." He stopped in some embarrassment, for he sensed that whereas Captain Hoxworth agreed with what he was expostulating, Mrs. Hoxworth did not, and he said, "I beg your pardon, ma'am. I'm afraid I presumed when I explained what the Hawaiians will think at that moment."

To his relief, Noelani replied, "There is no need to apologize, Micah." Then she added, "It is clear that Hawaii must one day fall prey to America, for we are small and weak."

"Ma'am," Micah assured her with explosive confidence, "the people of America will not tolerate bloodshed."

Quietly, Noelani reported, "We have been assured that there will shortly be bloodshed within your own country . . . over slavery."

"War? In America?" the young minister replied. "Never! And there will never be war with Hawaii, either. It is equally impossible."

"Young man," Captain Hoxworth interrupted on the spur of the moment, "my ship is departing for Honolulu in the morning. I'd be proud to have you accompany us." Then he added the explanation calculated to inspire the heart of any minister: "As my guest."

Micah, who instinctively knew that he should have no intercourse with this family enemy, hesitated, but at that moment, to Captain Hoxworth's sardonic satisfaction and to Micah's confusion, Malama placed her hand on his and cried, "Please join us!"

Micah blushed and stammered, "I had planned to visit San Francisco for some days."

"We won't wait!" Hoxworth boomed, in his calculated impression of a robust older friend. "We're making so much money running food from Lahaina to the gold fields that a day lost is a fortune foundered."

"You can see San Francisco later," Malama said winsomely, and when Micah looked into her deep Polynesian eyes he felt logic pass into confusion, so that even though he had hiked three thousand miles to see the phenomenon of the west he said weakly, "I'll move my things aboard . . . even though it is the Sabbath."

On the *Carthaginian,* Micah did not spend much time discussing America with Captain Hoxworth or Hawaii with his wife. Instead, he tagged along wherever Malama moved, and with her he watched the stars and the dolphin and the changing clouds. The first days were cold, and she wore an Oregon fur that framed her face in caressing beauty, and once when the night wind was blowing the edges of fur about her eyes, Micah felt positively impelled to raise his hand and brush the fur away, whereupon she accidentally leaned upon his fingers, and he felt how remarkably soft her skin was, and he kept his hand near her cheek and then almost unknowingly allowed it to slip around behind her neck, pulling her lips to his. It was the first time he had kissed a girl and he felt for a moment as if a family of dolphin had struck the ship, and he drew back amazed, at which the tall island girl laughed and teased: "I do believe you've never kissed a girl before, Reverend Hale."

"I haven't," he admitted.

"Did you enjoy it?" she laughed.

"It's something that should be saved for a starry night aboard ship," he said slowly, taking her properly into his arms.

Rafer Hoxworth, who had planned these events, watched with gratification as young Micah Hale became increasingly entangled with Malama. Nevertheless, he experienced contradictory emotions toward the boy: he despised him and wanted to hurt him in some tormenting way; yet at the same time he saw constantly how much the young minister resembled Jerusha Bromley, and when at meals the young fellow spoke so intelligently of America's destiny, Hoxworth was proud; so that on the seventh day he announced unexpectedly to his wife, "By God, Noelani, if the boy wants to marry Malama, I'll say, 'Go ahead.' We could use him in the family."

"Don't intrude into the Hale household again," his wife pleaded. "Besides, what would you do with a minister in the family?"

"This one won't be a minister long," Hoxworth predicted confidently. "Too much get-up-and-go."

That afternoon Captain Hoxworth called his daughter to his book-lined cabin and said, "Malama, you intending to marry young Hale?"

"I think so," she replied.

"My blessing," Hoxworth said, but when his daughter brought her suitor, trembling, into the cabin to plead for her hand, Hoxworth subjected the young man to a humiliating examination, focused primarily on money and the inevitability that a clergyman would never have enough of it to support a ship captain's daughter, particularly one who had expensive tastes, and after about fifteen minutes of this, Micah Hale, who had boxed at Yale and who had worked hard in the wagon train crossing the prairies, lost his temper and said, "Captain Hoxworth, I didn't come in here to be insulted. A minister has a fine, good life, and I will hear no more of your abuse."

He stamped out of the cabin and ate his next three meals with the crew, and when Malama, in tears, came to find him he said proudly, "I'll come back to your table when the captain of this ship personally apologizes." After another day had passed, during which Noelani and her daughter cajoled Captain Hoxworth with assurances that Micah had acted correctly, the gruff captain surrendered, rammed a cigar into his teeth, and of his own accord sought out the young minister. Thrusting forth a huge hand he said with a show of real acceptance, "Glad to have a man like you in the family, Mike. I'll perform the ceremony tomorrow morning."

He hated the young man, yet he wanted him for a son. Partly because he knew that such a marriage would infuriate old Abner Hale and partly because he sensed that a half-caste girl like Malama required a strong husband, he proceeded with the ceremony, and as the ship passed into tropical waters, he assembled all hands aft, stood Malama and her mother to starboard and young Micah Hale to port, and bellowed forth a wedding service which he had composed himself. At the conclusion he roared, "Now if the groom will kiss the bride, we'll issue a triple ration of rum for all hands. Mister Wilson will divide the crew into halves. One half can get blind-drunk now, but the other half must wait till nightfall." It was a wild, joyous ocean wedding, and when the *Carthaginian* reached Honolulu, Captain Hoxworth immediately transshipped the newly married couple to Lahaina, for he was still not allowed to visit that port.

As the island boat entered Lahaina Roads, boxed in as it was between the glorious islands, Micah caught his breath and looked alternately at the wild hills of Maui, the soft valleys of Lanai, the barren rise of Kahoolawe and the purple grandeur of Molokai. He whispered to his wife, "As a little boy I was brought to that pier to see the whales playing in these roads, and I always thought of this water as the reflection of heaven. I was correct."

Now the packet began discharging its passengers into the crowd of islanders who regularly jammed the little pier to greet any casual ship, but before Micah and his wife could disembark, some men at the rear shouted, "Let him through!" And with intense joy, Micah discovered that the newcomer was his father, whom he had not seen for nine years.

"Father!" Micah shouted, but Abner had not been told that his boy was aboard the packet, and kept moving forward in his accustomed way, limping more, cocking his white head on the right side and stopping occasionally to adjust his brains. Coming upon a sailor he grabbed him by the shirt and asked, "On your travels did you by chance come upon a little Hawaiian girl named Iliki?" When the sailor said no, Abner shrugged his shoulders and started back to his grass hut, but Micah vaulted over the railing that separated him from the crowd and rushed to overtake his father. When the white-haired clergyman—then only forty-nine years old—realized that it was his son who stood before him, he stared for a moment, approved his handsome appearance and said, "I am proud, Micah, that you performed so well at Yale."

It was a curious greeting, this reference to Yale above all other values involved at the moment, and Micah could only grasp the diminishing shoulders of the old man and embrace him warmly, whereupon Abner's mind cleared perfectly and he said, "I have waited so long for you to take over the preaching in our church." Then, behind his son's elbow, he saw a tall, lovely olive-skinned young woman approaching and instinctively he drew away.

"Who is this?" he asked suspiciously.

"This is my wife, Father."

"Who is she?" Abner asked, afraid.

"This is Malama," Micah explained with tenderness.

For a moment the beloved old name confused Abner Hale, and he tried to clarify his thoughts, and when he had done so he bellowed, "Malama! Is she Noelani Kanakoa's daughter?"

"Yes, Father. This is Malama Hoxworth."

The trembling old man retreated, dropped his cane and slowly raised his right forefinger, leveling it at his daughter-in-law. "Heathen!" he croaked. "Whore! Abomination!" Then he looked in dismay at his son and wailed, "Micah, how dare you bring such a woman to Lahaina?"

Malama hid her face and Micah tried to protect her from his raving father, but scarifying, unforgivable words poured forth: "Ezekiel said,

'Thou hast gone a whoring after the heathen!' Get out! Unclean! Abomination! Foul, foul in the eyes of God. I will never see you again. You contaminate the island."

There was no halting the fiery old man, but in time Dr. Whipple rescued the bridal couple and led them to the refuge of his home, where he bluntly explained to the weeping Malama that Reverend Hale sometimes seemed insane, probably due to the fact that her father had once kicked him in the head. "I am so ashamed," she replied. "I will go to him and assure him that I understand."

Micah could not stop her, and she hurried along the brook, past the mission house and up to the grass shack into which she saw Abner Hale disappear in tottering rage. "Reverend Hale!" she pleaded. "I am sorry that . . ."

He looked out from his shack and saw a woman who seemed much like Noelani, more like Rafer Hoxworth, and she was his son's wife. "Abomination!" he rasped. "Whore! Contaminator of the islands!" And as she gazed in horror, he limped over to the wall, reached up and ceremoniously ripped away the pencil sketch of his elder son. Tearing it into shreds, he threw them at Malama, whimpering, "Take him from Lahaina. He is unclean."

Those were the circumstances under which Micah Hale, most brilliant of the mission children, resigned from the ministry and became partner with Captain Rafer Hoxworth, a man he feared and who hated him, but they formed a brilliant pair—Hoxworth bold and daring, Hale most far-seeing of the Hawaii traders—and in time all ports in the Pacific became familiar with the trim ships which flew the blue flag of the H & H line.

IV

From the Starving Village

IN THE YEAR 817, when King Tamatoa VI of Bora Bora and his brother Teroro fled to Havaiki-of-the-North, there to establish a new society, the northern sections of China were ravaged by an invading horde of Tartars whose superior horsemanship, primitive moral courage and lack of hesitation in applying brute force quickly overwhelmed the more sophisticated Chinese, who vainly and at times only half-heartedly tried to resist them. As the difficult years passed, Peking fell, and the coastal cities, and it became apparent that the Tartars had entered China to stay.

The effect of the invasion fell most heavily upon the great Middle Kingdom, the heartland of China, for it was these lush fields and rich cities that the Tartars sought, so toward the middle of the century they dispatched an army southward to invest Honan Province, some three hundred and fifty miles below Peking and south of the Yellow River. In Honan at this time there lived a cohesive body of Chinese known by no special name, but different from their neighbors. They were taller, more conservative, spoke a pure ancient language uncontaminated by modern flourishes, and were remarkably good farmers. When the Tartar pressures fell heavily upon their immediate neighbors to the north, those neighbors supinely accepted the invaders, and this embittered the group of which I now wish to speak.

In a mountain village, in the year 856, the farmer Char Ti Chong, a tall, thin man with handsome high-boned face and a profusion of black hair which he wore in an unruly manner, swore to his wife Nyuk Moi, "We will not surrender these good lands to the barbarians."

"What can you do?" his stolid, sensible wife countered, for in her twenty-three years with Char she had heard some fairly far-reaching promises, most of which had come to nothing.

"We will resist them!" Char proposed.

"With grain stalks as an army?" Nyuk Moi asked wearily. She was a thin, angular woman who seemed always on the verge of complaining, but her life was so difficult that she rarely wasted her strength in whining. Her hopeful father had named her after the most beautiful object he had seen, a scintillating pendant resting among a rich man's jewels; unfortunately, she had not lived up to this name, Nyuk Moi, Plum Jade, but she possessed what was better than beauty: an absolutely realistic evaluation of life. "So you are determined to fight the invaders?" she asked.

"We will destroy them!" her husband repeated stoutly, certain that his boasts had already made his lands more secure.

They were not good lands, and in other parts of the world they would hardly have been deemed worthy of defense, for although the Middle Kingdom contained many rich fields, farmer Char had none of them. His three acres lay tilted skyward at the point where the rocks of the Honan mountains met what might charitably be called the arable fields. There was no running water, only sporadic rainfall, and the soil was not markedly productive. But largely because of Char's endless effort, this land did sustain a family of nine: Char, his wife Nyuk Moi, his old and battle-worn mother, and six children. The living was not good, for the Chars had no ducks or chickens, and only two pigs, but it was no worse than that enjoyed by most of the other families in the mountainous village.

What the invading Tartars would have done with this walled-in village, had they ever got to it, was a mystery, for they could scarcely have squeezed out of it a single grain of wheat more than it already yielded, and if they took much away, the village would starve, but it became a fixation with Char and his friends that the Tartars, after satiating themselves with Peking, were certain to burst into this ancient village, so that the farmers formed the habit of convening each night in the farmhouse of their wisest member, General Ching, to discuss plans for the defense of their land, for now there was no government to protect them.

This Ching was not a real general, of course, but merely a stocky, red-faced wanderer who had chanced to be near Peking one day when the emperor's henchmen required an army in a hurry. Ching had been swept up, and in a long campaign found that he liked military life, which was a disreputable fact in itself. After the war, which proved fruitless, for the Tartars quickly overran the very areas Ching had been pacifying, he returned home to the mountain and to his resolute, stubborn associates, regaling them month after month with stories of his campaigns in the north.

"We will place men here and here," stout-hearted Ching proposed. He was a courageous man of whom it was said, "He can march forty miles in a day and fight that evening." He had a broad, resolute face, and in many of the things he did in the years following his impromptu military service he displayed great fortitude, so that although he was clearly a braggart, men did not begrudge him his title of general and listened when he predicted: "The Tartars will approach our village by this route. What other way would a sensible general choose?"

But before General Ching's theories could be tested, an enemy far worse than the Tartars, and far more familiar, descended upon the village. The rains did not fall as required, and a hot sun blazed remorselessly in the copper sky. Seedlings withered before the middle of spring, and by midsummer even drinking water was at a prohibitive premium. Families with old people began to wonder when the ancient fathers and mothers would die, and babies whined.

Farmer Char and his wife Nyuk Moi had lived through four famines and they knew that if one practiced a rigid discipline and ate the roots of grass and chewy tendrils dug from the forest, there was always a chance that one's family would survive. But this year the famine struck with overpowering force, and by midsummer it became apparent that most of the village families must either take to the road or die among the parched and blazing hills. Therefore, when the sun was most intense, Char and his wife fetched mud bricks from the almost vanished village stream and walled up the entrance to their home, placing a cross of black sticks where the door had been. When the house was almost sealed, Char went inside and weighed for the last time the little bag of seed grain upon which life would depend when his family returned next spring. Hefting it in his hand, he assured his miserable group: "The seed grain is now locked inside. It will wait for us."

He then climbed out and swiftly closed the opening. When this was done, he turned his back sorrowfully upon his home and led his family out of the walled village and onto the highway. For the next seven months they would roam over the face of China, begging food, eating garbage where there was any, and trying to avoid selling their daughters to old men with food. Twice before, Char and Nyuk Moi had experienced the wandering months and had brought their brood home intact and they felt confident that they could do the same this time, for as they started on the dreadful pilgrimage Char swore hopefully, "In seven months we will be back here . . . all of us." But this time Nyuk Moi was not so hopeful, and Char noticed that his wife kept her two pretty daughters close to her, day and night.

Concerning only one thing did the Chars have no fear. During their absence their house would be inviolate. Highwaymen might murder them along the road. Slave buyers in cities might try to filch their daughters. Possibly, soldiers would wipe out all the wandering families in a general massacre. And corrupt officials might trick any family into slavery. But no one in China would break into a house that had been sealed with mud and across whose door sticks had been crossed, for even an idiot knew that unless the house was there when the travelers returned, and unless the seed grain was secure, life itself—and not only that of the family in question—would perish. So while the Chars wandered across northern China, seeking almost hopelessly for food, their house stood sacrosanct.

In the autumn of 856 in a city on the northern borders of Honan, farmer Char was bitterly tempted. There the rains had been good and the crops were fine. For several weeks Char and his family went out to the harvested fields at night and crawled across them, on hands and knees, smelling out lost grains that even the insects had missed, and in this cruel way they had uncovered just enough hidden morsels to stay alive. Nyuk Moi cooked the gleanings with a kind of aerated mud, some grass, and a bird that had not been dead too long. The resulting dish was not too bad.

But when a spell of four successive days passed with no gleanings to be found and when no birds died, at least not within reach of the starving family, the servant of a rich man came to the tree where the Chars were sleeping, and he carried in a bag a bundle of freshly baked cakes, whose aroma drove the smaller Char children mad with hunger, for they were the kind of cakes Nyuk Moi had often baked, and the servant said bluntly, "My master would consider buying your oldest daughter."

Char, at the point of starvation, found himself asking seriously, "Would he keep her for his own?"

"Perhaps for a time," the servant said, rustling his package. "But sooner or later he sends most of the girls on to the city."

"How much would he give us?" Char asked pitifully.

The servant grew expansive and said, "Cakes, enough grain to live on till the spring."

"Come back in an hour," Char said, and as the man disappeared, swinging his tempting bundle of aromatic cakes, Char assembled his family, saying frankly, "The owner of the fields has offered to buy Siu Lan."

Nyuk Moi, who had foreseen that this must soon happen, drew her quiet child to her and, placing the girl on the ground between her bony knees, asked, "Is there no other way?"

"The gleanings are no more," Char said despondently. "Winter comes soon. This time we'll be lucky if we get home with any children."

Nyuk Moi did not rail at her husband, for she knew of no alternative to propose, not even one, and the family had about agreed to sell Siu Lan, Beautiful Orchid, when they heard a whistling, and some stranger was whistling a song long familiar in their village and not known much elsewhere. "Who's out there?" Char cried.

The stranger, recognizing his village's accent, shouted, "General Ching!" And in a moment he hurried up, square-faced, sallow with hunger, but as ebullient as ever. "How goes the famine with you?" he asked boisterously. "With me not so good."

Char said sadly and without explanation, "We are meeting to decide about selling our oldest daughter, Siu Lan."

"I'd buy her!" General Ching cried, bowing gallantly to the frightened girl. "Anybody'd buy her!"

"The rich man's servant is coming back within the hour to hear our answer," Char added.

General Ching's agile mind swept into military action. "Servant? Rich man?" he snapped, his hungry eyes darting about in the darkness. And in an instant he had a complete plot. "We will tell the servant that we will sell the girl. I'm your older brother. I make the decisions. Then you and I and Nyuk Moi and your older boy will deliver her. As soon as the servant gets close enough to the house so that we know where the rich old man lives, we kill him, take everything he has and send the booty back with the boy. We then enter the house, present Siu Lan, and as the rich old man steps forward to take her, we murder him. There may be a fight, so each of you, Char, Nyuk Moi and Siu Lan must be prepared to kill. Siu Lan, do you think you could kill a man?"

"Yes," the frail girl said.

"Good," General Ching said, rubbing his fleshless hands.

"Will the plan work?" Char asked.

"If it doesn't, we will die of starvation anyway," the general replied.

"If they catch us, what will they do?" the oldest boy asked.

"They will put us in cages," General Ching explained, "and starve us to death and carry us from village to village so that other starving people will see what happens if farmers kill to get food, and at the end, when they see we are almost dead, they will take us out of the cage and cut us up into three hundred little pieces and hang our heads on the town gate. So, you understand the risks?" he asked coldly.

"Yes," the Chars replied.

"Ssssshhhh," General Ching whispered. "Here comes the servant."

The man bustled up, officious and well fed, still rustling his bundle of cakes, and said, "Have you made up your minds?"

"I am the older brother," General Ching announced. "We have discussed it and have agreed to sell." Whereupon the servant led Siu Lan and her mother Nyuk Moi and the oldest boy and Char and the general back toward his master's house, and when they had gone far enough so that everyone saw clearly how the rich man's home was laid out, and where the entrances were, the general strangled the servant and threw the cakes to the boy, who ran back with them to the starving children and the old grandmother.

"Now it takes courage," Ching said solemnly. He led the way into the rich man's house, presented Siu Lan, and said, "Master, we have produced the girl."

"Where is Ping?" the man asked suspiciously.

"He is giving the cakes to the starving children," square-faced Ching said gently. "Master, have you ever seen your own children starve?"

"No," the man swallowed hard, trying not to look at Siu Lan, who was most temptingly beautiful.

"I have," Ching said softly. "In this famine I have buried three of my children."

"Oh, no!" Nyuk Moi gasped, and something in the manner by which she betrayed the fact that she did not know of General Ching's misfortune uncovered the plot to the rich, canny old man, and he tried to pull a bell which would summon servants, but General Ching coldly intervened, grasped the man's fat arm and bent it backwards.

"Three of my children have died," Ching repeated slowly, "and now you will die." With tremendous force, he closed his bony hands about the man's throat and strangled him, but in dying the man who bought girls for the city managed to utter a cry, and a servant rushed in with a weapon, trying to slash at General Ching, but Char leaped upon the man and the weapon fell to the floor, whereupon Nyuk Moi grabbed it and killed the intruder.

When the two bodies were kicked into a corner, General Ching said, "I have buried my children, and I have lived on clay, but tonight I am going to feast." And he ransacked the house, bringing forth all the food and wine he could find. Then he sent Siu Lan to fetch the children, and the feast lasted till midnight, with the general and Char's old mother singing mountain songs. Then, almost drunk with wine, the general said, "All the time we have been drinking I have been wondering, 'How can I help Char's family escape? With six children and a grandmother?' I'm sure I could manage for myself, but with so many in your family I don't know what to suggest. Shall we scurry to the city and try to lose ourselves there? Or shall we hide in the hills?"

It was then that tough-minded Nyuk Moi proposed: "This is a time of war, and soldiers are everywhere. So I believe that when the authorities discover these deaths they will first cry, 'Soldiers did this!' So they will waste valuable time looking for soldiers, and we will march far into the hills. Later, when they change their minds and say, 'It must have been starving farmers,' we will be so far away it won't be worth their while to follow us, for some new battle will engage them. Therefore we must hurry to the hills."

"Would you feel better if I stayed with you?" General Ching asked.

"Of course," Nyuk Moi replied. "You are now our brother."

"But will our plan work," the general asked, "if we have to take along the old grandmother?"

"We will take her," Char said firmly.

The general frowned and said, "Well, anyway, I will join you, for this famine has killed my entire family."

So the little band struggled back toward the mountains, planning their route so as to arrive home in time for spring planting, but as they approached their walled-in village scarifying news awaited them, for in their absence the Tartars had come and had broken open the inviolate seals and had stolen the seed grain. When Char stood before the sanctuary he had so carefully sealed and saw its shattered door, he experienced a bitterness he had never before known, not even in those moments when he was preparing to sell his daughter. He wanted to fight and slay, and in his anger he cried, "What kind of men are they, that they would break open a sealed house?"

Futilely he looked at General Ching, then dashed about the village summoning all the outraged farmers. Pointing at his trusted friend, he cried, "General Ching has shown us how to dispose our men so that when the Tartars come back we can annihilate them. I have found that Ching is a fine military strategist, and I think we had better adopt his plan. Let us kill these damnable barbarians . . . all of them."

General Ching, quivering with excitement at the prospect of military action, made a great show of assigning his troops to strategic points, but as he did so he heard Nyuk Moi's cold rational voice asking, "What are we fighting to protect? This village? We have no seed to build this village up again."

And as the farmers considered this fact, and as they felt hunger come upon them, even in the clement spring, they began to wonder, and at this moment a solitary outpost unit of the Tartars—two brutal men in furs and on big horses—swept into the village, rode briskly about, and reined up before Char's house. The men were so obviously conquerors that General Ching's bold strategies were not even attempted, and the villagers listened as the invaders shouted in barbarous Chinese, "You have three days to abandon this village. All men above the age of fifteen will join the army. Women may go where they like." The men pulled back on their horses, wheeled madly in the dust, and rode off.

That night General Ching proposed his plan. "When I was in the army I heard of a place they call the Golden Valley. In the morning we start marching there, and everyone who can walk will accompany us. For here there is no hope."

Char asked, "What do you mean, everyone who can walk?"

And Ching replied, "The old folks will have to stay behind. They cannot encumber us on the road."

Families looked in apprehension at their older members and a mournful silence fell across the village, so that General Ching was forced to move from family to family, saying bluntly, like a soldier, "Old man, you cannot come with us. Old woman, you have seen your life."

When he reached Char's family he pointed directly at Char's mother and said harshly, "Old woman, you were brave the night we murdered the rich man, so you will understand."

Char remonstrated, "General, it is not within our religion to abandon a mother. Confucius is strict in this regard: 'Honor thy parents.' "

"We are going on a long journey, Char. Maybe a thousand miles over mountains and rivers. The old cannot come with us."

One of the frightened men of the village edged into the conversation and asked, "Have you ever been to what you call the Golden Valley?"

"No," Ching replied.

"Are you sure it is where you say?" the man continued.

"No, I have only heard tales about it . . . while I was in the army. Good land. Gentle rivers."

"Do you think we can get there from here?" the doubtful one asked.

General Ching grew impatient and pulled up his rags so that he looked more like a soldier. "I don't know the pathway, or whether we will be accepted when we get there. I don't know how long the journey will take. But by the demons of hell I know that I do not want to live any longer in a land where men break into sealed houses and where you starve three years in every ten." Suddenly sweeping his arms to include all the village, he stormed: "I don't know where we're going, but Siu Lan is going with me, and the rest of you can rot in hell."

Quickly he wheeled about and faced Siu Lan, the girl he had rescued from the old man, and he bowed before her as a proper general would, and said softly, "May the felicitations of a thousand years rest upon you." Then he turned gravely to Char and explained: "Old friend, I am not pleased to marry your beautiful daughter in this rude and uncivil way. I would like to send you a thousand cakes and a hundred pigs and barrels of wine. I would like to dress her in brocades from Peking and send a horse for her and musicians. But, Brother Char, we are starving to death and I at least am going south. Forgive me for my rudeness." He then faced Nyuk Moi and said gallantly, "Char's wife, let us make believe the famine is not upon us. I shall go to my house for the last time and wait there in the darkness. Will you consent, please, to bring your daughter to me in formal style?" He bowed low and left.

Farmer Char organized the marriage procession, and from the low stone houses streamed out the old people who had been condemned to stay behind, and they marched behind the bride, and one man played a flute, but there were no gifts and no brocades. At the door of General Ching's house, where there had once been many children, Char knocked twice and cried, "Awake! Awake! It is dawn, and we bring your bride!" It was nearly midnight, of course, and when the general appeared he was dressed in rags, but he had seen proper weddings and he bowed gravely to Siu Lan, and the flute played madly, and everyone pretended to exchange the customary gifts, and the general took his bride.

At dawn next morning, in the spring of 857, Char, then forty-four years old, assembled his family and said to them, "On our journey we must listen to General Ching, for he is a sensible man, and if we have any hopes of reaching a better land, it will be because of his genius. Therefore we must obey him."

When the rude army mustered, the Chars were first in line, followed by two hundred starving men and women ready to follow General Ching on the exodus south, but when it came time to bid farewell to this parched and inhospitable combination of rock and reluctant soil, the women in the procession could not control their tears. There was the memorable rock where the farmer Moo, a man much set upon by fate, had finally killed his wife. Here was the tree where the soldiers had hanged the bandit who had stayed hidden by the village for six weeks. There was the house where babies were born. It was a lucky house, that one, perpetually filled with children. And outside the village walls stood the fields where men and women toiled. How sweet this village had been. If there was food, all shared. If there was none, all starved together, and women wept at the memory of those days, now gone forever.

But there were certain houses at which not even the reminiscing women dared look, for they held the old people, and one house held not only two old women but also a baby that could not be expected to live; out of respect for the feelings of the departing army the old people remained hidden inside. They would stay in the village awhile. The Tartars would abuse them, and they would die.

In the entire army only one person dared look at the houses where the old people were left, and that was General Ching. He was not really a military man, in the honest sense of the word, but he had seen a great deal of fighting and much killing, and now as he stood at the village gateway, he was not ashamed to look back at the living tombs, for they held men and women who had been kind to him in days past. One old woman had given him her daughter, the mother of the three children who had starved to death, and for these patient old people he felt a compassion wider than the plains of China.

Suddenly he raised his arms to the cloudless spring heavens and shouted, "Old people inside the walls! Die in peace! Be content that your children shall find a better home! Die in peace, you fine old people!" And biting his lips he led his band down onto the plains.

But they had gone only a few miles when by prearrangement, from behind a rock on the trail, stepped forth Char's old mother, and Char announced firmly, "I have told her that she can come with us."

General Ching rushed up and thrashed his hands in the air, screaming, "This isn't military! She has got to stay with the others."

Char looked at the general coldly and said, "Who hid you in the fields after our triple murder? Who had courage that night?"

"Don't speak to me of murders!" Ching roared. "You are murdering the chances of the entire army."

"Who ever said that you were a general to lead an army?" Char shouted, and the two men, almost too weak to march, began fighting, but their blows were so weak that neither damaged the other, so that soon Nyuk Moi had pulled off her husband Char, and Siu Lan had pacified her new husband, the general.

"Brother Char," the general said patiently between gasps, "from the beginning of history there have been soldiers, and soldiers have rules."

"General Ching," Char replied, "from the beginning of history there have been mothers, and mothers have sons." These simple words were to live in Chinese history as the filial words of Char the farmer, but at the moment they did not much impress General Ching.

"She cannot come with us," he commanded icily.

"She is my mother," Char argued stubbornly. "Does not the old man Lao-tse tell us that a man must live in harmony with the universe, that he must give loyalty to his parents even before his wife?"

"Not even a mother can be allowed to imperil our march," General Ching responded. "She will stay here!" he cried dramatically, pointing to the rocks behind which she had been hidden.

"Then I shall stay with her," Char said simply, and he seated his old mother on a large rock and sat beside her. To his wife and five children he said, "You must go on," and the assembly began to disappear in the distant dust, so that Char's mother said, "Faithful son, the other old people were left behind. It is only right that I too should stay. Hurry, catch up with Nyuk Moi."

"We shall stay here and fight the Tartars," Char said stubbornly, but as he sat he saw a figure running back from the disappearing mob, and it was General Ching.

"Char," he said, in surrender, "we cannot go without you. You are a stalwart man."

"I will rejoin you, with my mother," Char replied.

"You may bring her," General Ching consented. "She will represent all of our mothers." Then he added, "But I will not accept you, Char, unless you apologize to the entire body for having made fun of me as a soldier."

"I will apologize," Char agreed. "Not from shame, but because you really are a very fine soldier."

Then General Ching said to the old woman, "Of course you know that you will not live to see the new land."

"If a journey is long enough, everyone must die along the way," the old woman replied.

AS GENERAL CHING'S resolute group moved south from Honan Province they acquired people from more than a hundred additional villages whose sturdy peasants, like Ching's, refused to accept Tartar domination. In time, what had started as a rabble became in actuality a solid army, with General Ching courageously willing to forge ahead in any risks while his lieutenant, General Char, guarded the rear and fought off bandits and stray bands of Tartars who sought to prevent the exodus.

Across great mountain ranges the travelers moved, down swollen rivers and past burned villages. Winter came and deep snows, summer and the blazing heat of central China. At times General Ching was forced to lay siege to large cities, until food was given, and had China been at peace, imperial troops would undoubtedly have cut the marauders to shreds and crucified the leaders, but China was not at peace, and the great trek continued.

Years passed, and the stolid, resolute men of Honan struggled southward, a few miles a day. Sometimes they bogged down at a river bank for two or three months. The siege of a city might delay them for a year. They ate, no one knew how. They stole from all. In the high mountain passes in winter their feet, wrapped in bags, left bloody trails, but everyone was constantly on the alert to fight. More than a thousand children were born, and even they fell under the simple rules of General Ching: "No old people can join us. You must submit to the government of Ching and Char. We never break into a sealed house."

There was only one element in the army that successfully defied General Ching, and that was Char's old mother. Like a resilient field hoe whose suppleness increases with age, the wiry old woman thrived on the long march. If there was plenty of food, she was able to gorge herself without the stomach sickness that assaulted the others at such a time; and if there was starvation ahead, she apparently had some inner source of strength that carried her along. General Ching used to look at her and swear, "By the fires of hell, old woman, I think you were sent to torment me. Aren't you ever going to die?"

"Mountains and rivers are like milk to me," she replied. And she became the symbol of the group: an indomitable old woman who had known starvation and murder and change. She refused to be carried, and often when her son, General Char, rejoined the group after some rear-guard action against local troops who were trying to disperse the army, he would throw his sword upon the ground and lie exhausted beside his mother, and she would say, "My years cannot go on forever, but I am sure that you and I will see a good land before I die."

The years passed, and this curious, undigested body of stalwart Chinese, holding to old customs and disciplined as no other that had ever wandered across China, probed constantly southward, until in the year 874 they entered upon a valley in Kwangtung Province, west of the city of Canton. It had a clear, swift-running river, fine mountains to the rear, and soil that seemed ripe for intensive cultivation. "I think this is what we have been looking for," General Ching said as his minions stared down at the rich promise below them. "This is the Golden Valley."

He held a consultation with General Char and his lieutenants, and then called in Char's fantastically old mother. "What do you think?" he asked her solemnly.

"From what I can see, it looks good," she said.

The general rose, cupped his hands, and faced north. "You old people, dead back there in the walled village!" he shouted. "Your children have found their new home." Then he glared at Char's mother and said, "You can die now. It is really outrageous how long you have lived."

The occupation of the valley was not so simple a task as General Ching and his advisers had hoped, for the river bed was occupied by a capable, fiercely compact group of southerners whom Ching and his cohorts held to be not Chinese at all, for they spoke a different language, ate different food, dressed differently, followed different customs and hated above all else the old-style Chinese from the north. At first, Ching attempted to settle the problem directly, by driving the southerners out, but their troops were as well trained as his, so his army had little success. Next, he tried negotiation, but the southerners were more clever than he and tricked him into surrendering what advantages he had already gained. Finally, when military occupation of the entire valley proved unfeasible, the general decided to leave the lowlands to the southerners and to occupy all the highlands with his people, and in time the highlanders became known as the Hakka, the Guest People, while the lowlanders were called the Punti, the Natives of the Land.

It was in this manner that one of the strangest anomalies of history developed, for during a period of almost a thousand years these two contrasting bodies of people lived side by side with practically no friendly contact. The Hakka lived in the highlands and farmed; the Punti lived in the lowlands and established an urban life. From their walled villages the Hakka went into the forests to gather wood, which their women lugged down onto the plains in bundles; the Punti sold pigs. The Hakka mixed sweet potatoes with their rice; the Punti, more affluent, ate theirs white. The Hakka built their homes in the U formation of the north; the Punti did not. The Hakka remained a proud, fierce, aloof race of people, Chinese to the core and steeped in Chinese lore; the Punti were relaxed southerners, and when the lords of China messed up the government so that no decent man could tell which end of the buffalo went forward, the Punti shrugged their shoulders and thought: "The north was always like that."

In addition to all these obvious differences, there were two of such gravity that it could honestly be said, "No Punti can ever comprehend a Hakka, and no Hakka cares whether he does or not." The upland people, the Hakka, preserved intact their ancient speech habits inherited from the purest fountain of Chinese culture, whereas the Punti had a more amiable, adjustable language developed during two thousand years spent far outside the influence of Peking. No Punti could understand what a Hakka said; no Hakka gave a damn about what a Punti said. In certain pairs of villages, they lived within three miles of each other for ten centuries, but Hakka never spoke to Punti, not only because of inherited hatreds, but because neither could converse in the other's language.

The second difference, however, was perhaps even more divisive, for when the outside conquerors of China decreed that all gentlewomen, out of respect for their exalted position, must bind their feet and hobble about like ladies on cruel and painful stumps, the Punti willingly kowtowed to the command, and Punti villages were marked by handsome, well-dressed wives who sat through long years of idleness, the throbbing pain in their feet only a distant memory. In this respect, the Punti village became a true portrait of all of China.

But the self-reliant Hakka women refused to bind the feet of their girl babies, and once when a general of the imperial army strode into the High Village and commanded that henceforth all Hakka women must have small feet, the Hakka began to laugh at his folly, and they continued to ridicule the idea until the general retreated in confusion. When he returned with a company of troops to hang everyone, the Hakka women fled to the mountains and were not caught. In their resolve to be free they were fortified by their memories of three resolute ancestors: General Char's old mother, who had lived to be eighty-two and who survived the long trek south in better shape than most of the men; her practical daughter-in-law Nyuk Moi, who had ruled the Golden Valley for a decade after her husband's death; and the gentle, iron-willed Siu Lan, the learned widow of General Ching, who ruled the area for another decade after Nyuk Moi's death. They were revered as the ideal prototypes of Hakka womanhood, and for anyone to think of them marching with bound feet was ridiculous. Furthermore, as Ching the seer prudently pointed out in 1670: "If our women bind their feet, how can they work?" So the Hakka women laughed at the government edicts and remained free. Of course, the Punti ridiculed them, and on those rare occasions when a Hakka woman wandered into Canton, the city people stared, but these resolute, difficult, obstinate guests from the north refused to be dictated to.

Of course, not all of General Ching's army settled in the Golden Valley, but all the Chars and the Chings did, and they built on the sides of the mountain a group of U-shaped low houses inside a mud wall, and this came to be known as the High Village; whereas the village along the river bank, in which the Punti lived, was always known as the Low Village; and in the two, certain sayings became common. When Punti children played, they taunted their fellows: "Quack like a duck and talk like a Hakka," but in the High Village people frequently cried, with adequate facial gestures: "I am not afraid of heaven. I'm not afraid of earth. But the thing I do fear is listening to a Punti trying to speak Mandarin." There were other folk sayings in the two villages that got closer to the fundamental differences between Hakka and Punti; for in the High Village, Hakka mothers would warn their daughters: "You continue as lazy as you are, and we'll bind your feet and make you a Punti." But in the Low Village, Punti mothers threatened their sons: "One more word out of you, and I'll marry you to a Hakka girl." This latter was held to be a rather dreadful prospect, for Hakka girls were known to make powerful, strong-willed, intelligent wives who demanded an equal voice in family matters, and no sensible man wanted a wife like that.

The High Village and the Low Village had only one thing in common. At periodic intervals, each was visited by disaster. In some ways the perils of the Low Village were the more conspicuous, for when the great river rose in flood, as it did at least once every ten years, it burst forth from its banks with a sullen violence and engulfed the farmlands. It surged across fields of rice, swept away cattle, crept high up the walls of the village houses, and left a starving people. Worse, it threw sand across the fields, so that subsequent crops were diminished, and in the two years after a flood, it was known that one lowland person in four was sure to perish either from starvation or from plague.

What the Hakka, looking down on this recurring disaster, could never understand was this. In the year 1114, with the aid of nearly sixty thousand people, Hakka and Punti alike, the government built a great spillway which started above the Low Village and which was intended to divert the flood waters away from that village and many others, and the idea was a capital one and would have saved many lives, except that greedy officials, seeing much inviting land in the bottom of the dry channel and along its sides, reasoned: "Why should we leave such fine silted soil lying idle? Let us plant crops in the channel, because in nine average years out of ten, there is no flood and we will make a lot of money. Then, in the tenth year, we lose our crops, but we will already have made a fortune and we can bear the loss." But over a period of seven hundred years the Hakka noticed that the escape channel for the river was never once used, and for this reason: "We can see there is going to be a flood," the officials argued, "and a great many people are bound to be killed. But if we open the floodgates to save the villages, our crops in the channel will be destroyed. Now let's be sensible. Why should we allow the waters to wash away our crops in the one year when we will be able to charge highest prices for them?" So the gates remained closed, and to protect one thirtieth of one per cent of the land around the villages, all the rest was laid waste. Flood after flood after flood swept down, and not once were the gates opened to save the people. The backbreaking work of sixty thousand peasants was used solely to protect the crops of a few already rich government officials, whose profits quadrupled when the countryside was starving. This the Hakka could never comprehend. "It is the way of China," Ching the seer explained, "but if it were Hakka fields being destroyed, I am sure we would kill the officials and break down the floodgates."

The Punti, on the other hand, were unable to understand Hakka behavior when drought struck the High Village. One Punti woman told her children, "There is no sensible way of explaining a people who wall up their houses with mud, place crossed sticks before the door, and then wander about the countryside for six months eating roots and clay." The Punti did learn one thing about the Hakka, however, and that was never to touch the walled-up houses or disturb the seed grain. During the great famine of 911 a body of Punti had invaded the deserted High Village and had carried away the seed grain, but there was much death when the theft was discovered, and this did not happen again.

For eight hundred years following the settlement in 874, the Hakka and the Punti lived side by side in these two starving villages—as they did throughout much of southern China—without a single man from the High Village ever marrying a woman from the Low Village. And certainly no marriage could be contracted the other way around, for no Low Village man would want to marry a woman with big feet. When it came time for a man in the High Village to marry, he faced something of a problem, for everyone in his community was named either Char or Ching, after the two famous generals who had led the Hakka south, and to contract a marriage within such close relationships would have been incestuous; the Chinese knew that to keep a village strong required the constant importation of new wives from outside. So in late autumn, when the fields were tended and time was free, missions would set out from the High Village to trek across the mountains to some neighboring Hakka village twenty miles away, and there would be a good deal of study and discussion and argument and even downright trading, but the upshot always was that the High Village committee came home with a pretty fair bundle of brides. Of course, at the same time missions from other Hakka villages were visiting the High Village to look over its women, and in this way the Hakka blood was kept strong. Two additional rules were followed: no man could marry into a family into which his ancestors had married until five generations had elapsed; and no girl was accepted as a potential bride unless her horoscope assured a bountiful relationship with her proposed husband. By these means the Hakka perfected one of the most rigid and binding family systems in China. Pestilence, war, floods and Punti threatened the group, but the family continued, and every child was proudly taught the filial words of Char the farmer: "From the beginning of history there have been mothers, and mothers have sons."

In 1693 a Punti man of no standing whatever ran away with a Hakka woman, the first such marriage ever recorded in the Golden Valley, and a brawl started which lasted more than forty years. No similar marriages were attempted, but serious fighting between the Hakka and the Punti erupted on many occasions, and during one terrible campaign which involved a good deal of southern China, more than one hundred thousand people were massacred in scenes of horror which dug one more unbridgeable gulf between the two peoples. In surliness, in misunderstanding and in fear the two groups lived side by side, and no one in the area thought their enmity strange. As Ching the seer pointed out: "From the beginning of history, people who are not alike have hated one another." In the Low Village the sages often explained the bitterness by asking, "Do the dog and the tiger mate?" Of course, when they asked this question, they threw out their chests a little at the word *tiger* so that no one could misunderstand as to who the dogs were.

IN THE YEAR 1847, when young Reverend Micah Hale was preaching in Connecticut—the same year in which Dr. John Whipple sailed to Valparaiso to study the export of hides—Char, the headman of the High Village, had a daughter to whom he gave a name of particular beauty: Char Nyuk Tsin, Char Perfect Jade, and it was this girl's destiny to grow up in the two decades when Hakka fortunes degenerated in scenes of great violence. Nyuk Tsin was not a tall child, nor was she alluring, but she had strong feet, capable hands and fine teeth. Her hair was not plentiful, and this bothered her, so that her mother had several times to reprimand her, saying, "Nyuk Tsin, it doesn't matter how you dress your hair. You haven't very much, so accept the fact." But what the little girl lacked in adornment, she made up in quick intelligence. Her father had to tell her only once the famous saying of the Char family: "From the beginning of history there have been mothers, and mothers have sons." When Char spoke of family loyalty, the conspicuous virtue of the Hakka, his daughter understood.

She was therefore distressed when many people in the High Village began to whisper that headman Char had gotten into serious trouble and had run away. She could not believe that her father had the capacity to be evil, but sure enough, in due time, soldiers invaded the High Village and announced: "We are searching for the headman Char. He has joined the Taiping Rebellion, and if he dares to come back to the village, you must kill him." The men kicked Nyuk Tsin's mother several times and one of them jabbed a gun into the girl's stomach, growling, "Your father is a murderer, and next time we come back it's you we're going to shoot."

Nyuk Tsin was six that year, 1853, and she saw her father only once thereafter. Well, that is not entirely correct, but let us grant for the present that she saw him only once, for he did return to the High Village late one night and mysteriously. The first thing he did was embrace his skinny little girl and tell her, "Ah, Jade, your father has seen things he never dreamed of before. Horses of his own! I captured an entire Punti city . . . not a village like that one down there. Jade, they all bowed as I came in. Low, girl. Like this!" Later he embraced her as if she were his beloved and not his eight-year-old daughter, and he took her with him to watch his Hakka friends enlist in his great venture. Pointing at the frightened would-be soldiers, he said, "To begin with, all soldiers are afraid, Nyuk Tsin. Me? I trembled like a bird gathering seeds. But the important thing is to have loyalty in your heart. When General Lai tells me, 'General Char, occupy that city!' do you suppose I stop to question, 'Now what is General Lai up to?' No, indeed. I occupy the city, and if I have to kill fifty thousand enemy to do it, I kill them. Jade," he cried warmly in the mountain darkness, "we are headed far north. I may never see you again." He swept the quiet girl into his arms and held her close to him. "Take care of your mother," he said, and the men dashed down the mountainside after him.

Nyuk Tsin did see her father again. In 1863, when she was a thin, extremely well-organized girl of sixteen, capable of bearing huge loads of wood and of caring for her mother and the rest of her family, General Wang of the imperial forces marched into the High Village and commanded his drummer to roll the drum a long time, so that all the villagers assembled. Then, with the aid of an interpreter, for such a general would never know how to speak Hakka, he ordered a herald bearing a black object to read an official announcement.

The man kept the black object in his left hand, stepped forward and read in a high nasal voice: "The Taiping rebel chief named Char, who was captured at Nanking and brought under guard to Peking, having confessed that he was a fellow conspirator with Lai Siu Tsuen, who himself has falsely assumed the title of General of the North, was tried and put to death last month by being slowly cut into three hundred small pieces over a period of nine hours, according to just law, and his head was exposed at the city for three days as a warning to all."

Having said this, the herald passed the decree to another, and with his free hand drew away the black covering, disclosing in a wire cage the head of General Char. Ants had gotten to it, and flies, so that the eyeballs were gone and the tongue, but the dedicated man's features were clear, and the head was fixed to a pole in the middle of the village, after which General Wang announced sternly: "This is what happens to traitors!" Then he demanded: "Where is the widow of the traitor Char?" The villagers refused to identify the wife of their great leader, but Nyuk Tsin's mother put her children aside and announced proudly, "I am his wife."

"Shoot her," General Wang said, and she fell into the village dust.

Later the High Village remembered sardonically General Wang's platitudes about traitors, for it was hardly less than two weeks after his brave appearance in their village that he studied the various opportunities confronting him and decided to become a traitor himself.

The year 1864 was therefore a truly terrible one in the Golden Valley, for half the time General Wang was rampaging through the villages seeking loot, while during the other half government troops were in pursuit of the traitor. Wang, having discovered the High Village, rarely passed it by, and in time even enlisted a good many Hakka into his band. This gave the government troops title to whatever they could find in the High Village, and they often shot Hakka farmers for the fun of it. Nyuk Tsin, by virtue of not looking too pretty and of working long hours hauling wood to the lowlands, which made her seem much older than she was, escaped rape, but many of the other Hakka girls did not.

At this time Nyuk Tsin was living meagerly in the home of her uncle, who, following the execution of her father and mother, was required by village custom to take her in. This uncle, a hard, unhappy one, reminded her constantly of two dismal facts: she was already seventeen years old and unmarried; and because she was her rebellious father's daughter the soldiers might at any time return to the High Village and shoot both her and her uncle. These two conditions were cause enough for her uncle to cut down on her food rations and increase the bundle of wood she was required to lug down onto the plain.

Nyuk Tsin was not married because of a most unfortunate event over which she had no control. Her horoscope, which had been carefully cast when envoys from a distant Hakka village came seeking wives for the Lai family, showed the thin girl to be doubly cursed: she was born under the influence of the horse and was therefore a headstrong, evil prospect as a wife; and she was clearly a husband-killer, so that only a foolish man would take her into his home. There were, of course, favorable aspects to her future, such as a promise of wealth and many descendants, and these might have encouraged an avaricious husband to discount the peril, except that her horoscope divulged an additional disgrace: she would die in a foreign land. Adding together her willfulness, her husband-killing propensity and her burial in alien soil, the Hakka of the High Village knew that in Char Nyuk Tsin they had an unmarriageable girl, and after a while they stopped proposing her to visiting envoys.

She therefore worked her life away in the near-starving village. She had two items of clothing: a dark-blue cotton smock and a pair of dirty cotton trousers to match. She also had a conical wicker hat, which she tied under her chin with a length of blue cord, and big strong feet for climbing down to the valley with huge burdens of wood; as far as she could see into the future, this was going to be her life. And then, on the festive night before the holiday of Ching Ming, when the Low Village required extra firewood for the great celebrations that were in progress, Nyuk Tsin left the High Village at dusk and started down the steep trail. She had barely reached the plain when a group of four men sprang at her from behind rocks, scattered the wood, slipped a gag into her mouth, jammed a bag over her head, and kidnaped her. When day broke, and her uncle found that she had not returned, he uttered a brief prayer that something permanent had happened to her, and it had. She was never again seen in the High Village.

It must not be assumed that during these troubled times the Punti fared any better than the Hakka. In fact, since the traitorous troops of General Wang disliked climbing mountains, there was a good deal more raping and kidnaping in the Low Village than in the High; but this was halted whenever the wild river went into its periodic flood and starvation threatened to wipe out the village completely.

These were bad years, but they were terminated in early 1865 by the arrival in the Low Village of a man reputed to be fantastically rich, and within six weeks this amazing Punti had broken open the floodgates so that the river was diverted and the village spared, had bought off the traitor General Wang and then betrayed him to government forces, and had made the village not only secure but happy. The man who accomplished these miracles was a wiry, clever Punti, Kee Chun Fat, whose name meant Spring Prosperity and who had been born fifty-two years earlier right there in the Low Village. In 1846 he had emigrated to California, where he had worked in the gold fields, acquiring the eleven thousand dollars which made him, according to Low Village standards, one of the richest men in the world.

As he moved about the village, making many decisions regarding the extensive Kee family of which he was now the effective if not titular head, he wore a long pigtail, a black skullcap edged in blue satin, a gray silken coatlike garment that fell to his ankles and was tightly buttoned at the neck and heavy brocaded shoes. His lean frame kept him from making an imposing, patriarchal figure, but his evocation of energy made him the unquestioned dictator of the village. In California he had learned to read English but not Chinese, and he could figure percentages, so that as soon as he unpacked he started lending money to his relatives at forty per cent interest per year.

When the Kee family asked admiringly, "How could a man like you, who is not a soldier at all, be so brave as to argue with General Wang?" he laughed slyly and explained, "When you've had to live by outsmarting Americans, it's very easy to manage a fool like General Wang." Of course, this answer was meaningless to the Punti, so they said, "We still don't understand how you did it."

Kee Chun Fat had an explanation for everything, so he replied, "In Peking a man is emperor, but I have found that in the world money is emperor."

"Did you give General Wang money?" the villagers pressed.

"I gave him enough to keep him hanging around," Uncle Chun Fat explained. "Then I told the government troops where he was, and promised them money if they would hang him, and they did."

There was much discussion among the Kee family as to how Uncle Chun Fat had made his great fortune in America, and one had only to pose the question for the head of the family to explain: "America has gold fields where money is easily made. There are gangs of men laying telegraph wires, and money is easy there, too. But where do you suppose the money is easiest of all? Where they're building railroads. Tell me, do you think that I brought home with me only the money you have seen here in the Low Village? Oh no, my good friends! I made that much in the gold fields in one year. Washing for the miners. Cooking food. My real money is in an English bank in Hong Kong." And he produced a book to prove it but only he could read the writing.

Uncle Chun Fat's stories of America were tantalizing. Once he said,

"The best part of California is not the money but the women. A man can have three Indian wives and any number of Mexicans. But not at the same time." Young men with their lips watering asked more about this, but Uncle Chun Fat has already passed on to other matters. "What I would like to do," he explained to his assembled family, "is to restore the ancestral hall until it is known as the finest in China. We will do honor to our great ancestor, Prince Kee Tse of the Hsiang Dynasty, from whom we are sprung." As he said these words he recalled the illustrious prince who had invaded Korea nearly three thousand years before, and he told his clan, "It is strange to live in America, where most men do not even know who their grandfathers were. We shall make the name of Prince Kee renowned once more throughout China." Chun Fat had an older brother who had never amounted to much; nevertheless this Kee Chun Kong was still nominal head of the family, and Chun Fat was careful not to usurp any of his moral prerogatives. But time was short, and in practical matters the energetic Californian had to make one swift decision after another, for which he was forgiven in view of the fact that he was paying for everything. Therefore, as the yearly festival of Ching Ming approached, when honorable men pay obeisance to their ancestors, he dispatched runners with this command: "All members of the Kee family shall return to the ancestral hall to celebrate Ching Ming." He then spent nearly a thousand dollars beautifying the low tile-roofed building which was the spiritual focus of the Kee clan.

One of his messengers traveled as far south as the evil little Portuguese city of Macao, across the bay from Hong Kong, and there in the Brothel of Spring Nights he delivered his command to a handsome, sharp-eyed young man who cooked for the brothel and helped in other ways. Kee Mun Ki was twenty-two at the time, a clever opportunist, with a brisk pigtail, quick gambler's hands and an ingratiating smile. His father, hoping that his son would mature into a solid, gifted scholar, had named him Pervading Foundation, but he had wandered from academic pursuits, finding himself skilled at luring young girls into the brothel and in gambling with European sailors who frequented Macao. When the messenger from the Low Village arrived, young Mun Ki was in the midst of an impressive winning streak and showed no intention of leaving the Portuguese city. "Tell my father," he explained, "that this year I must miss the feast of Ching Ming. Ask him to offer prayers to our ancestors on my behalf."

"It was not your father who sent for you," the runner explained.

"Is he dead?" the young gambler asked in apprehension.

"No, he's well."

Relieved, Mun Ki asked, "Then who presumes to send for me?"

"Your uncle, Chun Fat," the messenger explained.

The young brothel assistant could not remember his uncle, who had left the Punti village when Mun Ki was only three, so again he dismissed the command. "I can't return this year," he explained. "Business is good here in Macao." He pointed to the freshly painted brothel and to the red dragons on the gambling hall nearby.

Then the messenger delivered the striking news that was to modify the young pimp's life. He said, "Uncle Chun Fat has come back to our village with several million American dollars."

"He's rich?" the adroit young nephew asked.

"He's very rich!" the messenger replied in an awe-filled voice.

"We'd better leave at once," Mun Ki said forcefully. He went in to see the brothel keeper and reported, "My father summons me home to the Low Village." That sounded impressive.

"Then you must go," piously replied the Punti who ran the house. "Children must honor their parents. But if you find any extra girls in the village, bring them back. We can always use extra Punti."

As Mun Ki and the messenger hiked along the river bank to their village, the soft airs of spring brushed over them, and they were deeply moved by the sight of rice fields just bursting into a limpid green; but when they came within sight of home, they saw the bright red paint that had been lavished on the ancestral hall, and Mun Ki whistled: "Oooooh, he must be very rich," and he hurried home to report to his uncle on the Eve of Ching Ming.

Uncle Chun Fat was thoroughly impressed by his nephew, for he recognized in Mun Ki his own quick shrewdness. "How is work in the brothel?" he inquired.

"Good," his nephew dutifully replied. "You can always steal a little something from the Europeans. But I make most of my money gambling with the sailors."

Uncle Chun Fat studied the boy's hands and said, "You ought to go to America."

"Could I prosper there?"

"Prosper! My dear nephew, any Punti who cannot make his way in America must be very stupid indeed." Encouraged by the boy's attentiveness, Chun Fat expatiated upon his favorite theme: "It's ridiculously easy to make a fortune in America if you remember two things. Americans understand absolutely nothing about Chinese, yet they have remarkably firm convictions about us, and to prosper you must never disappoint them. Unfortunately, their convictions are contrary, so that it is not always easy to be a Chinese."

"I don't understand what you are saying," Kee Mun Ki interrupted.

"You will in a moment," his uncle replied. "First, the Americans are convinced that all Chinese are very stupid, so you must seem to be stupid. Second, they are also convinced that we are very clever. So you must seem to be clever."

"How can a man be stupid and clever at the same time?" the young pimp pleaded.

"I didn't say you were to *be* stupid and clever. I said you had to *seem* to be."

"How is that possible?" the handsome young gambler inquired.

"I left America with forty-one thousand dollars in gold because I discovered the answer," Uncle Chun Fat gloated.

"For example?" the student pressed.

"Take the gold fields," the Californian began. "For two years they watched me travel from camp to camp, observing everything. But they thought: 'He's a stupid Chinaman and he don't see anything.' And I will confess I did my best to look stupid. When I had learned as much as possible, I went into San Francisco . . . Mun Ki, when you do go to America, be sure to go to San Francisco. What a marvelous city! So much happening!"

"Where did the clever part come, Uncle," the young man interrupted.

Chun Fat liked the boy's attention to detail, and continued: "In San Francisco I went to all the newcomers and told them, 'I can tell you which land to buy,' and they always said to one another, 'These Chinese are very clever. If anybody knows where the good land is, they do.' And I got rich."

"Stupid and clever," the young man mused. "That's difficult."

"Not necessarily," his uncle corrected. "You see, the Americans want to believe, so you don't have to work too hard. It's difficult only when you want to convince the same man, on the same day or even at the same instant, that you are both stupid and clever. Like on the railroad gang."

"What happened there?" Mun Ki inquired.

His uncle began to laugh heartily and said, "There was this big American boss. When you go to America, Mun Ki, never try to be the boss, not even if they ask you to, which they won't, because you can always make more money by not being the boss. Well, anyway, if I wanted to run the restaurant for the gang, at my own prices, I had to get permission from this big American, and I simply could do nothing with him until on a certain day when he cried in desperation, 'You stupid goddamned Chinaman!' And then I knew things would pretty soon be going my way, because if you can get the boss to yell at you, 'You stupid goddamned Chinaman,' everything is going to be all right."

Uncle Chun Fat never finished this particular narrative because he was reminded that the household must rise next morning at cockcrow in order to pay proper respect to the dead; and as the village lay sleeping beside the river, with the ghosts of its ancestors ready to assume their positions for the day of celebration, an old watchman who had long performed this ceremony gathered his gong and beater and waited till the third hour of the night. Then, as the first cock crowed, the old man went out into the dark streets and began beating his gong.

"Ching Ming!" he called to the living and the dead alike. Walking down the winding road that led to the ancestral hall, he continued to beat his gong, and he saw with pleasure lights coming on in the low houses; a young attendant hastened to light torches at the hall, and before the first shimmering darts of sunrise began to sweep in from the east, the Low Village was awake, and Mun Ki's ineffective father took his position of superiority at the ancestral hall, but it was brash Uncle Chun Fat who hurried busily about, telling the Kees what he wanted them to do.

Kee Mun Ki, from the brothel in Macao, left his home and walked solemnly to the hall, where a flight of nine scrubbed steps led to the pavilion in which the ancestral tablets were kept. Here he deposited his gifts and made obeisance to those from whom his family honor had descended. He then left the pavilion and joined the members of his family, standing at attention while his father prayed and while his uncle began a bombastic speech: "I am going to buy land on this side, and some more on this side, and what you have seen so far is really nothing. There will be a spacious hall, and where our tablets now stand, we will have not wood but the finest stone. The Kees will be known for their magnificence." And then his crafty eyes fell upon the extensive family gathered before him and he sighed to himself: "All those poor idiots starving here year after year when they could be making their fortunes in America." But he knew from experience that the Kees were not the kind of people who would venture forth to unknown lands, and he became lost in admiration of himself for having had the courage to do so.

He was therefore in a receptive frame of mind when a surprising event occurred in the Golden Valley, one totally without precedent. It was on April 19, 1865, when the fields were beginning to recover from the flood, that a merchant from Canton appeared in the Low Village, leading an American. Normally, any stranger who wandered from the quays of Canton would have been executed, but this man was different, for as a scholar he had requested freedom to travel inland, and it had been granted, so that now he stood in the bright spring sunlight, looking with an appreciative eye upon the strange world thus uncovered to him.

It took the Cantonese merchant about four seconds to recognize that in this village Uncle Chun Fat was the man to deal with, so he said directly, "The stranger has come all the way from the Fragrant Tree Country to hire people to work in the sugar fields."

Chun Fat stood enraptured, and his mind leaped back to that memorable day when his ship had stopped in Honolulu and he had been allowed to come on deck to see the great green hills behind the city. How marvelously beautiful those few hours had been, for storms had swept down from the heights and Chun Fat had watched the copious rain spread out like a blanket of benevolence over the rich land. "The Fragrant Tree Country!" he cried. "To go there would be like going to heaven itself."

Excited with a wild joy he ran into his house and reappeared with a sandalwood box which he had purchased in Canton for the preservation of his silks, and he passed it around his family, explaining: "Smell it! In the country of which he speaks the air is like this twenty-four hours a day."

"Is it better than America?" his nephew asked.

Chun Fat hesitated. He had loved the wild cold mountains of California, and the lusty grandeur of San Francisco and the Mexican women with their songs, but he could not forget the Fragrant Tree Country. "It is a softer land," he said.

"Could a man make money there?" Mun Ki pressed.

"It's gentler," his uncle replied, and Mun Ki's mind was made up in that instant, for he thought: "If my uncle loves a land more for its beauty than for its money, it must be a wonderful land indeed."

Mun Ki was therefore the first to step forward and volunteer. "I'll go to the Fragrant Tree Land," he announced firmly, and when the American in the dark suit held out his hand, the Cantonese merchant shouted in Punti, "Take the hand, you idiot! Take it!"

This infuriated Uncle Chun Fat, who snapped: "We do not require a Cantonese fool who has shoes like rags to tell us how to act. Stand back or I'll break your head." Then, to the American, he said, in English, "Me Chun Fat, long time California. My boy, he go."

The American again extended his hand graciously and said, "I am Dr. John Whipple. I would like to hire about three hundred men for the sugar fields."

Uncle Chun Fat looked at the slim, gray-haired American in the expensive suit and instinctively recognized him as a big boss. "How much you offer to pay that one?" he asked, indicating with contempt the Cantonese.

"I'm afraid that's none of your business," Dr. Whipple replied. "But what did you have in mind?"

Chun Fat did some fast calculating. In the Kee family alone there were more than one hundred and forty able-bodied men. "Boss, I get you all men two dollars each man."

Now John Whipple did his own calculating. The Cantonese merchant whom he had brought with him could speak English, and had helped in that regard, but he had no sense of how to enlist labor. It was pretty obvious that this wily fellow from California knew what was required. But two dollars a head? "I'll give you one dollar and a half a head," he proposed.

Uncle Chun Fat studied this for some time, then replied slowly, "Who gonna argue with women? Who speak everything right?" He enumerated a long list of tasks he could be counted on to perform. "Two dollars," he said firmly.

"One-seventy-five," Whipple countered.

"Boss," Uncle Chun Fat smiled sweetly, "I top man here. Unless I speak, they no go."

"Two dollars," Dr. Whipple surrendered. Instantly Uncle Chun Fat thrust his hand out and grabbed Whipple's, shouting to his people in

Punti, "When you shake hands like this, by god, you believe what you say! I'm warning you, everyone of you!"

He was appalled, however, by Dr. Whipple's one stipulation: "Sir, I do not agree to this bargain unless half the men you send are Hakka."

Chun Fat looked at the stranger blankly. Finally, he repeated dully, "Hakka?"

"Yes, you know. Hakka. Up there."

"How in the world did he know about the Hakka?" Chun Fat thought despairingly. "Did that foul Cantonese . . ." To Dr. Whipple he said, "Why you want Hakka? No good Hakka."

Dr. Whipple looked him sternly in the eye, and his forty years of trading for J & W fortified his judgment. "We have heard," he said slowly, "that Hakka are fine workmen. We know that the Punti are clever, for we have many in Hawaii. But Hakka can work. Shall we go up to that village?"

Uncle Chun Fat faced a desperate impasse. He could see as clearly as he could see his hand those lush valleys of the Fragrant Tree Land. Good heavens, a hard-working Chinese set loose there could make a million dollars if he were clever! And think of the advantage to the Low Village to have three hundred Kees working there and sending money back home regularly. Uncle Chun Fat could be sure of getting not less than fifteen cents out of every incoming dollar. It would be a calamity, a disaster worse than a flood, for the Kees to miss such an opportunity. But this stern, straight man had mentioned the Hakka . . .

"Dr. Whipple," Uncle Chun Fat began cautiously, "maybe Hakka work well but too much fight."

"I will go to the village alone," Dr. Whipple said sternly.

"How you talk with Hakka?" Chun Fat asked slyly.

Dr. Whipple smiled superiorly at the wily negotiator and said simply, "My friend from Canton will do the translating."

"But he no speak Hakka," Uncle Chun Fat said evenly, smiling back at his visitor.

With no evidence of frustration Whipple asked, "Do you speak Hakka?"

"Only one man speak Hakka. My boy Kee Mun Ki. In army he learn few words."

"I suppose you want two dollars for each Hakka, too?" Whipple suggested hesitantly.

"Yes, because speak Hakka very difficult."

"Let's go," Whipple said with a resigned shrug of his shoulders, and then from the manner in which Chun Fat hesitated he realized with amazement that no one from the Low Village had ever climbed to the High Village. "You've never been up there?" he asked.

"Hakka up there," Chun Fat shuddered.

When Dr. Whipple saw how difficult it was proving to be to reach Hakka country, he was momentarily inclined to forget the matter and was about to surrender and allow Chun Fat to supply only Punti, but then his scientific interest asserted itself and he reflected: "I came here to initiate an experiment to see who would best satisfy our labor needs on the plantations, Punti or Hakka, and I'm not going to be bluffed out of that study now." So he said firmly, "If you can't lead the way, I will." And for all his sixty-six years he was as spry as the Chinese, and after a sturdy climb the travelers came at last to the gateway of the walled village, and as they entered and saw the frugal U-shaped homes and the brooding, worm-eaten pole in the central square, on which perched the skull of Char the rebel, Whipple looked about him as if he had come upon familiar terrain and thought: "The climb was worth it. This feels like a New England village. I'm home again, in China." The feeling was intensified when strong, sullen and suspicious Hakka began cautiously gathering about him, and he could see in their conservative faces portraits in yellow of his own ancestors. Motioning to Kee Mun Ki to interpret, he said, "I have come to take one hundred and fifty of you to the sugar fields of the Fragrant Tree Country." There was much subdued discussion of this, heightened by Uncle Chun Fat, who officiously passed among the Hakka his sandalwood box, with the assurance: "Where you're going smells like this."

In the end one hundred and thirty Hakka were conscripted for the Whipple plantations, with promises of twenty more to be gathered from other mountain villages, and as the deal was being formalized with much cautious nodding, Whipple happened to notice that these upland women did not bind their feet, and he pointed to one woman and asked Uncle Chun Fat, "Why are their feet normal?" And the Californian replied, "They Hakka. Not got good sense." And Whipple asked, "Would women be allowed to come to the Fragrant Tree Country?" And Chun Fat replied, "Maybe Hakka women. Not proper Punti women." At the moment Whipple said no more about it, but he thought to himself: "Some day we'll need many Chinese women in Hawaii. Be a good idea to bring these Hakka in. They look strong and intelligent."

WHEN DR. WHIPPLE and his Cantonese guide had returned to Hong Kong, there to wait in Whipple's ship for the arrival of the three hundred plantation hands, Uncle Chun Fat engaged in a flurry of action. He assembled his extensive family in the open area before the newly painted ancestral hall, and on its steps he had an imposing chair placed, in which he sat, wearing his satin skullcap, expensive gown and brocaded shoes. To his right, but a little behind him, sat his legal wife, a woman of fifty, while to his left and farther behind sat the two attractive unofficial wives to which he, as a wealthy man, was entitled. The meeting got right down to business, with Uncle Chun Fat informing his four hundred-odd relatives: "This is an opportunity that may never come again. Think of it!" and he leaned back so that the Kees could see him in his days of lassitude. "A young man goes to the Fragrant Tree Country, works a dozen years, sends his money home to the Low Village, where his wife is bringing up fine sons, and after a while he returns a very wealthy man and takes two or three young wives. He is happy. His wife is happy because she no longer has to work. The young wives are happy because they have a rich man. And," he said dramatically, pointing casually behind him with his thumb, "he can build a respectable ancestral hall in honor of his distinguished family."

He allowed this recipe for earthly happiness to mature in the minds of his listeners and then said, "I am distressed that Dr. Whipple would not take his entire shipload from our village, for we could have supplied him, but even so our opportunity is historic. I am going to point to the strongest young men, and you are the ones who will start for Hong Kong . . . in three weeks."

Uncle Chun Fat rose, passed through the crowd, and arbitrarily nominated eighty-six Kees to volunteer for the journey. Somc did not want to go, but they were powerless, for wasn't Chun Fat the richest man in the world? Who could argue with such a man? When this job was done their Uncle Chun Fat asked, "We now have remaining sixty-four places for the Low Village. Who should fill them?" And there was public discussion of this important point until the gambler Kee Mun Ki, who was proving to be a rather clever young man, pointed out: "Why not take the men who are about to marry girls from our family?" But Uncle Chun Fat rejected this, for it would take money from the village, and made an even wiser proposal, which the family recognized at once as a sound course of action: "We will send everyone who owes us substantial sums of money. And their wages will come to us." In this way the list was completed. Of the one hundred and fifty Punti who were sent, one hundred and ten did not want to go.

Following the nominations, there was a moment of relaxation during which Uncle Chun Fat studied his vast family with care, and when the mood was right he coughed twice, and the crowd dutifully lapsed into silence to hear what the great man had to say. Chun Fat, looking thoughtfully over the heads of the gathering, said slowly, knowing that what he was about to propose would come as a surprise to his clan, "I want everyone who, for the honor of his family, has volunteered to go to the Fragrant Tree Country to get married before he leaves this village."

A blizzard of excitement struck the Kee family, and many young men who had been forced by Uncle Chun Fat to accept exile to the sugar fields now indicated that they did not propose further to wreck their lives by hastily taking a wife. Grandly, aloofly, Uncle Chun Fat allowed the storm to rage, and when it had reached a climax, he coughed again, and somehow the quiet cough of a rich man is louder than the braying of six paupers, and the great family grew silent. "For example, in my brother's family I have decided that his son Kee Mun Ki should marry at once, and I have consequently been in contact with . . ." And here he paused dramatically to allow the family to savor his next words, and no one listened with more apprehension than the young gambler Mun Ki, for no one had told him he was about to marry. "I have been consulting with the Kung family of the next village and they have agreed to betroth their daughter Summer Bird to my nephew. Negotiations are already under way to celebrate this marriage, and, Mun Ki, I must congratulate you."

The young gambler gave a silly grin, accompanied by the required show of joy, for he recognized that Uncle Chun Fat had done a good thing for him. The Kungs of the next village, though not so rich as the Kees of this, were nevertheless a distinguished family, the principal difference being that their leader had gone not to California but only to Canton and had returned not with more than forty thousand dollars but with six. Nevertheless, it was a match that all in the Low Village approved, even though no one had yet seen the intended bride.

"So I insist that every young man marry," Chun Fat concluded. "Families can start sending out messengers at once to find likely girls, and I think it would be proper if celebrations were combined, so as to save money." Now that the marriages were agreed upon, and the families realized that they must actually set out to find wives for their departing sons, a new storm of agitation swept over the Kees, and again Uncle Chun Fat waited grandly in his satin skullcap until it had pretty well run its course. Then, with the grandeur of the ancestral hall looming behind him as if to fortify his edicts, he coughed quietly and gave the young men certain assurances. "You young travelers, like Mun Ki, must not think that because you are required to marry here in the Low Village that you may not also take wives in the new land. Oh no, indeed! There is only one reason why you must get married here, and establish your home here, with your legal wife waiting patiently for your return. If you do these things, then no matter where you go, you will always think of this village as your permanent home. You will yearn for the day when, like me, you stride up these sacred steps," and sweeping his expensive gown about him, he marched into the ancestral hall, from which he cried with real passion, "and you will bow humbly before the tablets of your ancestors. For your home is here." Gravely he bowed before the memorials of the ancients whose energies had built this village, and in deeply moving syllables he said, "When the white men abused me in California, I remembered this pavilion with my family tablets, and I gained strength to endure their abuse. When the snows were unbearable in Nevada, I remembered this ancestral hall, and they became endurable. Marry a girl from this valley, as I did thirty years ago. Leave her here with your home, and no matter where you go, you will come back." Then, adding a more immediately practical note, he reminded them: "And you will always send money back to this village."

Grandly, he left the ancestral tablets and returned to his chair, from which he reasoned directly: "But we know that it is always better when a Chinese man has some woman with him, so it would be wise if, when you get to the Fragrant Tree Country, you took a wife there too. And the reason I say this is that while I was in America I noticed again and again that the Chinese men who made the most money were those with women. You might think it ought to be the other way around, but as long as I had no woman I did rather poorly . . . gambling . . . bad houses . . . and I may as well confess it, I got drunk every night for almost a year. Well, anyway, I found this Mexican woman and pretty soon I had her washing for the miners and cooking their food. And consider this, you Kees who are departing for a strange country. Even though I had to pay much money for her food, for she ate like a pig, and even though she was always wanting a new dress, it was only because of her that I saved any money. Therefore, it seems to me that if a bright young man like my nephew Mun Ki were to marry the Kung girl here, and then also find a strong wife for himself in the Fragrant Tree Country . . . but be sure to get one who can work . . . well," and Uncle Chun Fat coughed modestly, hiding his lips with his silken-sleeved hand, "it would not surprise me at all if he were to return to this village a much richer man than I am."

With a new flush of modesty he dropped his eyes and allowed this dazzling prospect to capture his family. Not for a summer's moment did he believe that Mun Ki or anyone else would come close to his record of more than forty thousand dollars, but from the corner of his eye he saw with assurance that some of the young men were instinctively looking out across the fields and planning where, among the hills, they would build their cemeteries when they returned with staggering riches. But from the rear of the family came a nagging question: "When Mun Ki returns a wealthy man, does he bring his strange wife back to this village?"

"Certainly not," Uncle Chun Fat said evenly.

"What does he do with her?"

"He leaves her where he found her."

A buzz of admiration swept over the crowd, for the solution was both right and simple. The Low Village would be contaminated if it had to accept wives with strange customs, and while the elders were congratulating Chun Fat on his perspicacity, he quieted them and told the sprawling family: "The other wives will be able to care for themselves. When I left California I had three wives. A Mexican in San Francisco and two Indians in different parts of the mountains. They had helped me, so I helped them. I gave each one a thousand dollars." The crowd gasped at Chun Fat's compassion, and he concluded: "Because the important thing in a man's life is to return home to his village, to find his patient wife waiting, and in his old age to acquire two or three beautiful young girls of good family." Behind him his three wives smiled gently as he said, "Believe me, under those circumstances a man's joy is great."

When the young gambler Mun Ki accepted the betrothal his uncle had arranged for him, Chun Fat sent the Kungs in the next village not the customary thousand cakes—"Your daughter is worth one thousand pieces of gold, but please accept these poor cakes"—but two thousand and forty-three, the idea being that the number really could have been as large as he wished. Each cake was the size of a plate: soft sponge cakes, cakes stuffed with chopped nuts and sugar, hard flat cakes, cakes lined with rich mince, and others decorated with expensive sweetmeats. He also sent sixty-nine pigs, four chickens with red feathers, and four large baked fish. Then, to prove his munificence, he added forty-seven pieces of gold, each wrapped in red paper. The procession that carried these things to the Kungs was a quarter of a mile in length.

From two of the ceremonial pigs the bride's family cut off the heads and tails, wrapped them in silk and returned them to the Kees, indicating that the largesse had been both humbly and impressively received by the bride's family. But on her own account she sent three gifts to the groom: an embroidered red cloth which he would use as a belt, a wallet for the worldly wealth which she would help him earn, and two pairs of pants.

It was obviously going to be a tremendous wedding, and it dwarfed the thirty-one others that were proceeding at the same time. Two weeks before the Kees were scheduled to depart for the ship waiting at Hong Kong, the ceremony took place amid all the grandeur the two Lowland villages could provide, and when the days of celebration ended, young Kee Mun Ki brought his bride home and tried mightily to impregnate her before the time for sailing, but he failed.

On the morning when Uncle Chun Fat assembled his hundred and fifty Punti for the three-day hike to Canton, where they would board a river steamer for Hong Kong and the American ship, he saw before him a rather bleary-eyed, sexually exhausted group of men. "A good march along the river will toughen them up," he reassured himself, because he realized that if he could deliver his volunteers in good condition, he had a right to expect that subsequently Dr. Whipple would commission him to conscript many more, all at two dollars a head. He therefore moved among his troops encouraging them to spruce up, but when he came to his nephew Kee Mun Ki, he scarcely recognized him. The young gambler had been drunk for two weeks, hardly out of bed for ten days, and looked as if he might collapse during the first hundred yards of the march to Canton. Realizing that he had to depend upon this youth for transmitting orders to the Hakka, Uncle Chun Fat started slapping him back and forth across the cheeks, and slowly the young man's eyes began to focus. "I'll be all right," the gambler mumbled. "In

Macao once I was drunk for three weeks. But not with a fine wife like the Kung girl." And Chun Fat saw with pleasure that when his nephew's services were really required, the brash young gambler would be ready. "You'll do well in the Fragrant Tree Country," Chun Fat reassured the young man. "I expect to," the young husband replied. It was just a little insulting, the way in which he spoke to his uncle on a man-to-man basis, as if they were equals.

Now came a moment of intense excitement, for down from the hills marched the contingent of Hakka, thin men, dressed in rude, tough clothing, their pigtails long and their faces tanned. Two months before, the arrival of such a group would have signified war; now it occasioned only mutual disgust. Defiantly, the Hakka marched up to where the Punti stood, and against his own prejudices Uncle Chun Fat thought: "They'll do well in the new country." Because he was making two dollars a head on the Hakka, and hoped to make more in the future, he wanted to go up to them and bow in greeting, but he realized that this might be interpreted as Punti subservience and would never be forgiven by his family, so he glared at them as custom required. For a long moment the two groups stood staring insolently at each other. During nearly a thousand years they had lived side by side without ever speaking; they had met only in death and violence; there had been only one marriage. Now, with their inherited hatreds, they were going to travel in a small ship to a small island.

Mun Ki broke the spell. Pulling himself together, he stepped forward and said to a man named Char, leader of the Hakka, "We will start to Canton now. Some of your men look tired already."

Char studied the young Punti to see if this was intended as an insult, and replied evenly, "No wonder they look tired. They've been drunk for two weeks . . . like you."

"I got married," Mun Ki explained.

"So did they," the Hakka Char said, and the antagonists smiled.

The contingents started forward, but as they did, the Punti looked for the last time at their Low Village and its bright red ancestral hall. This was their home, the soil of their heart, the abiding place of their ancestors. Their wives were here. Many had sons whose names were already on the tablets in the pavilion. The graves where the ghosts of their forefathers walked at night were in this land, and to leave the Golden Valley even for a few years was punishment almost beyond the bearing. "I will come back soon!" Mun Ki called, not to his wife, nor to his domineering uncle, nor to any living person. "I will come back!" he called to his ancestors.

It took three days to reach Canton, the Punti moving together in one group, the Hakka in another, and during this vigorous exercise Kee Mun Ki whipped himself back into his customary lean condition. His eyes cleared and his wits sharpened, and as he entered the great city, seeking out Dr. Whipple to deliver the workers, he wondered if he could slip away for a few hours for some intense gambling with the British sailors at the quay, but unfortunately Dr. Whipple had a river boat waiting and herded his charges directly aboard. When they were assembled he spoke to them in quiet English, and his interpreter explained: "The American has discovered that if he tries to take you men out of China by way of Hong Kong, where his ship is visible in the bay, the government will execute every one of you. For daring to leave China. So we are sailing to Macao, where it will be possible to depart without being killed."

Quickly Mun Ki moved up to the interpreter and said, "In Macao I must see my old employer and bid him farewell. Please tell the American."

There was some discussion and the interpreter said, "All right. But the others must stay overnight inside a compound until the ship arrives from Hong Kong."

Mun Ki congratulated himself and began daydreaming of the great fortune he would make on his last hours at the gambling tables, when the interpreter returned and dashed his fantasies by announcing: "The American remembers that you are the only one who can speak with the Hakka, so you will not be allowed to leave the compound."

Mun Ki tried to appeal this unfair decision, but the interpreter, after discussing the protest with Whipple, said bluntly, "You will stay inside the compound."

When the coastline of Macao appeared, with its low white Portuguese buildings shining in the sunlight, and its military guard loafing about in European uniforms, the Punti and Hakka workers lined the river boat to study the strange port: a foreign city nestling on the coast of China, a city with one European for every two hundred Chinese, a curious, lawless enclave that was neither China nor Portugal but the worst of each. But to Mun Ki, well versed in the evil ways of Macao, it was a pragmatist's paradise. He saw the tiled roofs of the Brothel of Spring Nights and thought tenderly of some of the girls he had helped to bring there, strong, happy girls who enjoyed their work. Farther on he saw the gambling halls, where he had known both success and failure, and as the river boat drew closer to the shore, so his excitement mounted, until at last he moved swiftly among the Punti, whispering, "Lend me your money! I am going to the gambling halls and I will return with two for one." Some were suspicious of their brash cousin; others respected him for his daring, and in time he had a considerable number of coins. "I'll see you tomorrow," he whispered. "Say nothing to the fool from Canton."

So when the river boat touched the quay, and there was much jostling among the Chinese and calls back and forth between the Portuguese officials, Mun Ki slipped deftly away, disappeared into the piles of merchandise stacked along the quay, and hurried up a back alley to the

Brothel of Spring Nights. "You must have celebrated the festival of Ching Ming as never before," the brothel keeper observed icily.

"I got married," Mun Ki explained.

"Ah, that's very good!" the keeper expounded. "Every man should have a loyal and patient wife. I count the beginning of my happiness from the day I married and began having a large family."

"I am also leaving China for the Fragrant Tree Country," Mun Ki said honestly. "I've come to get my things."

"You're leaving me!" the proprietor stormed. "After I've spent all this time and money training . . ." Suddenly he stopped ranting and asked, "Did you say the Fragrant Tree Country?"

"Yes. Sugar fields."

"Now that's really strange!" the brothel keeper cried, tapping his knee with his forefinger. "I have some rather important work that requires doing in that country. Yes." He went to a file of papers and sorted out one from a Punti who had gone to the Fragrant Tree land some years before, and this man, remembering how well the Brothel of Spring Nights had been run in Macao, had written to the proprietor asking for certain assistance. Holding the letter between his teeth, Mun Ki's superior studied the young gambler and then asked, "Would you be willing to execute a rather difficult commission for me?"

"Do I get paid?" Uncle Chun Fat's nephew asked bluntly.

"You do."

"I'll do it."

"I thought you would."

"What's the job?"

"I've got a girl tied up in the little room. Been planning to ship her to Manila. We can't use her here, as you'll see. Will you deliver her to my friend in the Fragrant Tree Country?"

"I will. Which room?"

"The one where the Russian girl used to be."

Mun Ki forgot his gambling for a moment, walked down a narrow hall, and kicked open the familiar door. Inside, the blinds were drawn, and in the darkness, on the floor, lay a trussed-up girl, knees lashed to chin, almost unconscious from hunger and lack of water. With his foot Mun Ki rolled her over and saw that she was dressed in a cheap blue cotton smock and trousers; her big feet proved that she was a Hakka. In disgust Mun Ki slammed the door and returned to his employer.

"Who wants a Hakka?" he demanded.

"Nobody," the brothel keeper agreed. "I paid some of General Wang's soldiers to kidnap half a dozen girls, and they brought back this one. I was going to send her to Manila. Over there they don't know the difference."

"How much for me if I take her to the Fragrant Tree Country?" Mun Ki asked.

"Twenty Mexican dollars," the proprietor replied.

"Paid now? I'd like to double it in the gambling rooms."

"Half paid now," the canny brothel keeper agreed.

He gave Mun Ki the ten Mexican dollars, and the young man was about to dash over to the gambling, but the proprietor suggested, "Maybe you better feed her. She's been tied up for two days. The soldiers seem to have treated her rather badly before they turned her in, and I was afraid she might run away after I had paid for her."

"Did you give much?" Mun Ki inquired.

"For a Hakka? That I couldn't use?"

The young gambler returned to the room, yelled for a maid to bring him some hot tea and rice, and then parted the curtains. He saw at his feet a young Hakka woman of about eighteen. Even when her face healed she would probably not be a pretty woman, and the manner in which she was gagged and trussed did not permit any estimate of her general appearance. Therefore, more in a spirit of investigation than humanity Mun Ki kneeled down and started to untie the merciless ropes. As he loosened one after the other, he could hear the girl groaning with relief, but he noticed that even so her limbs did not automatically stretch out toward their normal position, for they had been constricted so long that some of their muscles had gone into spasm. Again motivated by investigation, he started gently to unfold her hands and pull her arms down along her body. He pushed her shoulders back and could hear joints creaking in protest. She groaned deeply and fainted, but then the maid brought the tray, and he applied tea to her lips and gradually she regained consciousness and began to drink. She was so desperate for liquids that even Mun Ki was impressed, and he sent for more tea. As its warmth circulated through her body, the girl began to return to an awareness of where she was, and she looked in terror at the man who held her, but the manner in which he started to feed her the rice, waiting until she had chewed each grain lovingly, lest someone steal it from her . . . this made her think that perhaps he might not be like the others who had captured her that night before the Ching Ming festival. The things they had done in the three weeks they had dragged her and their other captives through the countryside she had already forgotten, for they were too terrible to remember. Instinctively she felt that this man would not treat her so.

Char Nyuk Tsin was the first Hakka the young gambler had ever touched, and it was with instinctive loathing that he now did so, and yet it was a strange fact that her response to his kindness moved him and made him want to be kinder yet. He held her shoulders in his left arm and fed her warm rice with his right, and when the maid brought in some cabbage broth, he gave her the spoon and encouraged her to eat, but her wrists were so swollen from the ropes that she could not do so. He therefore started to massage them, and gradually blood circulated to her fingers and she could hold the spoon, but she could not operate her shoulders. So he massaged her back and neck, and instinctively his hand slipped forward over her shoulders and he felt her hard little breasts. Almost against his will there came a moment of awakening, and he felt memories of his soft young wife from the Kung village come flooding over him, and he lifted away Nyuk Tsin's smock and caressed her body, and then he slipped off her trousers, and when her knees and ankles remained in their rigid, muscle-locked condition, he gently massaged them until they relaxed, and he saw with increasing pleasure how slim and beautiful this girl's body was. Reminded of his bride, he quickly slid out of his clothes and threw them against the door, saying to the Hakka girl as he did so, "I will not hurt you."

When he had been with her for some time the proprietor came back to the little room to advise him on how to deliver the girl to the brothel keeper in Honolulu, but when he pushed open the door a little way and saw what the young people were up to, he advised in Punti, "Use her as you wish, but tie her up again when you're through."

The voice of the boss awakened Mun Ki to his responsibilities, and with real fright he grabbed at his pants to see if while he had been engaged with the girl some clever man had stolen his gambling money in the way that he, Mun Ki, had sometimes picked the pockets of preoccupied customers in the Brothel of Spring Nights. His money was secure, so he quickly dressed and said to the naked girl, "I must go to the gambling. Put your clothes on."

And as he waited for her to do so, he picked up the cords, and when she turned to face him she saw the cruel, biting cords and tears came into her eyes and she pleaded with Mun Ki and took his hands and promised, "I will not run away."

He held the ropes and studied her, and something in the manner in which she looked at him convinced him that she would not flee; so, still grasping the ropes, he led her to his room in a hovel in back of the brothel, where he sat her upon the floor. Dangling the ropes before her terrified face he seemed to ask: "Am I required to use these?" and she looked at him as if to promise: "You do not need the cords." Against his better judgment, he started to leave, but to do so with the girl unbound was obviously ridiculous, so he decided upon a sensible solution. With one end of a fairly long rope he tied the Hakka girl's left wrist; the other end he attached about his own waist, and when this was done he said, "Come."

When he passed the desk of the brothel the proprietor saw what he was doing, and said, "A good idea." Then the man asked professionally, "Will she make a good girl for my friend?"

"Yes," Mun Ki assured him, and he led his captive to his favorite gambling hall. But when they were in the street he stopped and asked her, "What is your name?" and she answered, "Char Nyuk Tsin," and he replied, "Perfect Jade! That's a good name." To himself he thought: "In a brothel it's a very good name. A man can remember it when he comes back the next time."

The gamblers were playing fan-tan, in which from a large pile of snowy-white ivory buttons the dealer withdrew a handful, whereupon the crowd bet as to whether the number to be left over at the end was one, two, three, or none. Or, if the gamblers wished, they could bet simply on whether the ivory buttons would turn out to have been odd or even. When the bets were placed, the amazingly deft dealer started to pull his buttons away from the pile in lots of four, and it was striking how skilled the players were in discerning, while the pile of buttons still contained fifty or sixty, what the number left over at the end was bound to be.

Using his own and other Punti money, Mun Ki had a satisfactory run at fan-tan, and he felt that perhaps the fact that he had been kind to the Hakka girl had brought him good luck, so he took his earnings to the mah-jongg room, where the clattering ivory tiles evoked their perpetual fascination. When at the beginning of each game the players built their wall, it was customary for them to slam the tiles down with maximum force, creating an echo that accentuated the natural excitement of the game, and likewise, when a player scored a coup and exposed his pieces he slammed them onto the noisy table. Mah-jongg as played in Macao was a wild, exhilarating game, and now Mun Ki decided to test his luck at a table where real gamblers played for high stakes. Placing Nyuk Tsin behind him, and twitching the cord now and then to be sure she was still tied, he joined three waiting men. Two had long, wispy beards and costly gowns. The other was more like Mun Ki, a young, aggressive gambler. At first one of the older men protested, "I do not wish to play in a room where there is a woman," but Mun Ki carefully explained, "I am taking her to a brothel in the Fragrant Tree Country and am responsible for her." This the men understood; in fact, the man who had protested thought: "Probably he will have his mind on the girl and will lose more quickly."

But Mun Ki had not entered the game to lose. Mah-jongg, unlike fan-tan, did not depend so much on luck as on the skill with which one played the pieces luck sent him; and the young gambler, thinking that this might be his last day in a big mah-jongg contest, breathed deeply as he used both hands to help mix the 144 tiles at the start of the game. With loud energy he banged his pieces down to make the wall and then watched carefully as he rolled his dice to help determine where that wall should be broached to begin the gambling. With intense excitement he grabbed his tiles in turn and remembered Nyuk Tsin only when he leaned forward to reach the tiles and felt her rope tugging at his waist. When his tiles were arranged—and he had long since learned to keep them in haphazard formations from which his clever opponents could deduce nothing—he was ready to play, but the bearded man who had originally protested against Nyuk Tsin, said, "She has got to sit on the floor where she can't spy." So before the game began in earnest, the Hakka girl sat on the floor, but this was not entirely satisfactory to Mun Ki, who was afraid that she might slip away, so he forced her to sit under the table, against his feet, and there she remained for the long hours during which the four players slammed down their tiles with great force.

From her position under the table Nyuk Tsin noticed that she could detect when Mun Ki was attempting some daring coup, holding back tiles in hopes of building them into some fantastic combination that would win him much money, for then his ankles became tense, the little bones stood out and his feet began to sweat. At such times she prayed for his success, and she must have been attuned to some powerful god of good fortune, for her man won. At dusk he tugged on the rope and said, "We'll go home." But as they returned to the dusty streets of Macao, hawkers swarmed about them, attracted by the rumor: "The young fellow from the brothel was a big winner." They brought flowers and bits of cloth and steaming kettles of food, and Mun Ki found real pleasure in playing the role of a generous winner. Fingering the torn cotton fabric of his girl's smock he said, "This one needs a new dress, believe me." And with grandiloquent gestures that all could admire, he announced: "We will have four lengths of that!" He was even more generous when it came to food, and hungry Nyuk Tsin had black eggs, dried fish, noodles and crystallized ginger. As they lounged beneath a dentist's sign he announced to the crowd: "I am really a very lucky gambler. I can see what's in the other man's mind."

As the night wore on, he drew the cord tighter to him, so that Nyuk Tsin could not stray, and he bought bits of food for worthless characters he had long known in the Portuguese city. When the civil guard passed by, he nodded to them, and when one asked, "Why do you have the girl tied up?" he replied in the patois of the port city, "I am delivering her to a brothel in the Fragrant Tree Country."

The police nodded approvingly, and then one stopped. "Are you sailing on that American ship in the bay?"

"I suppose so," Mun Ki replied.

Instantly the policeman grew confidential, and whispered, "I'd better warn you, then. The American who bought you in the village came to us today to have you arrested. You'd better hide."

"I'm reporting in the morning," Mun Ki assured him. "But thanks." And he gave the policeman a coin.

"Thank you, Mun Ki!" the official bowed. "That's a nice girl you're taking with you."

"She's only a Hakka, but she brings luck," Mun Ki replied.

Finally he led his captive back to the Brothel of Spring Nights, where he showed his former boss how he had multiplied the ten Mexican dollars eight times. "This girl brings luck," he said.

"Are you going to tie her up again in the little room?" the proprietor asked.

"She'll sleep with me tonight," Mun Ki explained.

"All right," the prudent businessman replied, "but remember what you learned here about breaking girls in. Feed them and beat them."

"I'll take care of her," Mun Ki assured him. "Were the police here for me?"

"Of course," his boss replied. "Your ship's sailing tomorrow."

"I'll be there."

Tugging the cord, he led Nyuk Tsin down the narrow hallway, out the back door of the brothel and on to the hovel where he slept. Locking the door, he untied the rope from his waist, but fastened it even more securely about Nyuk Tsin's wrist. She explained that she needed to attend to her bodily functions, so he opened the door and allowed her to go outside while he lounged in the doorway, testing the rope now and then to be sure that she was still secured. When she returned he said, "Now we must pack for the journey."

He had provided a wooden tub into which he jammed his accumulated treasures: a teapot, five bamboo cups, two good rice bowls, a metal pot, a porcelain tea set with a small copper strainer, a bamboo tray for steaming vegetables and a large knife. The incense burner, the kitchen god and the ancestral tablet which proved who he was were tucked into place, followed by his extra clothes and a pair of good sandals. Over this tub he now tied securely a piece of canvas stolen from a Dutch ship.

In a wicker basket Nyuk Tsin packed the food for the trip: soy vinegar, pickled cabbage, spices, dried fish, seeds to chew on and several chunks of flattened duck. The implements for cooking also went into the basket: chopsticks, a charcoal stove, one old cup and two old rice bowls.

The little room now contained only a bed and a poem. The former would be rolled up in the morning; the latter, which explained the manner in which the names of one Kee generation followed another, was contained in a red-lined book in which the genealogy was kept, and as the most precious of Kee Mun Ki's possessions, it would be the last to leave and would be carried by Mun Ki himself.

Surveying the quarters in which he had lived with reasonable happiness, and from which he had moved out to become a skilled gambler, Mun Ki sighed. Then, seeing Nyuk Tsin standing forlorn in the middle of the dimly lit room, he said, "You may undress now," and when she untied her wrist and dropped away her clothes, and when he saw that the cord marks were disappearing from her body, he smiled and indicated that she could sleep with him. Since she had expected to be tied up again and thrown onto the floor, she came to him gratefully and was not afraid when he began quietly to enjoy her. He was the first man who had ever touched her with what could even remotely be termed affection, and she found herself reciprocating. They had a vigorous passage of love and Mun Ki thought: "In some way she's better than my Kung wife." When they were through he remembered to reach for the cord to tie her to him, but when he took her wrists she pleaded: "It is not necessary." He was tempted to believe her, but he knew that if she ran away he would not only look the fool but would also be required to refund the ten Mexican dollars plus whatever his boss had paid the kidnapers, so he lashed her wrists to his; but he did allow her to sleep beside him.

In the morning, when they were dressed, he finally threw away the rope, for he thought: "If I report to Dr. Whipple leading this girl by a rope, he will hardly believe my story that I am married to her," and on his ability so to convince the American depended the success of this voyage. But when the rope fell in the dust of the little room, Nyuk Tsin stooped down and retrieved it for tying her basket of food. When they left the room, Nyuk Tsin carried the tub and the heavy basket. Mun Ki carried the feather-light bedroll and the genealogy book, but after he had stepped into the filthy yard behind the brothel, Nyuk Tsin called to him and pointed to the wall above where the bed had stood and where a sign now hung that she could not read. Mun Ki whistled at his forgetfulness and recovered the omen of special good fortune: "May This Bed Yield a Hundred Sons!" Tucking it under his arm, he led his woman to the waiting ship.

At the quay Dr. Whipple stood ready to berate the only man he had who could converse with the Hakka, and as soon as Mun Ki appeared, the Cantonese interpreter started shouting at him, but he ignored the man and marched contritely up to the American. Bowing his head in feigned apologies he said softly, "I am a thousand times humble, sir, for having run away." Then, producing the overburdened Nyuk Tsin, he said simply, "I had to find my good wife."

"Your wife!" the interpreter stormed. "No women are allowed on this . . ."

Dr. Whipple, noticing the girl's big feet, asked, "Isn't she a Hakka?"

"Yes," Mun Ki replied, and the American scientist, remembering how he had once idly considered the desirability of importing some Hakka women to Hawaii, asked, "Do you wish to take her with you?"

When this was interpreted, Mun Ki piously nodded and explained: "I could not bear to leave her behind."

"I'm willing to try it," Whipple announced. Then he warned Mun Ki: "But when she gets to Hawaii, she's got to work."

"She'll work," Mun Ki assured him.

At this moment the hundred and fifty Hakka men saw Char Nyuk Tsin for the first time since her abduction on the Eve of Ching Ming, and they began to cry to her, and Mun Ki knew that if they explained who she was, his fanciful story would be exploded, but he also realized that no one on the quay but he could understand what they were saying, so he nudged Nyuk Tsin and told her, "Speak to them." Pushing her toward the Hakka, he followed behind and cried to the men, "This girl is my wife." And the Hakka saw about his waist a red marriage belt and they began to wonder what had happened. "Are you indeed married to the Punti?" they shouted. Mun Ki jabbed his girl in the back and whispered, "Tell them you are." So Nyuk Tsin informed her countrymen, none of whom had ever befriended her after her parents' death, "He is my husband." And the Hakka looked at her in scorn and would have no more to do with her, for their parents had often warned them about what had happened to the disgraceful Hakka girl who had married a Punti man in 1693.

This problem settled, quick-thinking Mun Ki now faced one far more serious, for Dr. Whipple was calling, through his interpreter, for the married couple to join him, but when Mun Ki and Nyuk Tsin started to do so, they had to pass through the Punti contingent, and these men were even more outraged at Mun Ki than the Hakka had been. They, too, had been well drilled in the evil that had befallen the Punti man who had dared to marry a Hakka girl back in 1693, and they drew away from Mun Ki as if he were unclean, but as he passed each group he muttered to those from whom he had borrowed: "Last night. Big winnings. Lots of money for you." And this softened their anger.

When he reached Dr. Whipple, the American said, "We will have to ask the captain of the ship if he will accept another passenger. And if he says yes, you will have to pay passage money for your wife."

He therefore sent a sailor in search of the captain, and in a moment a towering American loomed among the Chinese, a man in his seventies, with stout muscles and a sea cap jammed on the back of his head. He had fierce, dynamic eyes and looked at the men about to board his ship as if he hated each one of them with deep, personal anger. Brushing them away as he strode through their groups, he came up to Whipple and asked, "What is it, John?"

"Captain Hoxworth," the trim, gray-haired scientist began, "I find one man who wants to bring his wife along."

"You willing to pay five dollars' passage money?" Hoxworth asked.

"Yes. I'll get it from the man."

"Then it's simple," the captain growled. "She can come."

Dr. Whipple conveyed this news to Mun Ki, who grinned happily, explaining to the interpreter, "A man would not like to leave his wife in Macao." Dr. Whipple was impressed by this sentiment and asked Captain Hoxworth, "Where will the couple sleep?"

"In the hold!" Hoxworth snapped with some surprise that the question should have been asked. "Where the hell do you suppose they would sleep?"

"I thought," Whipple began, "that with her the only woman, and three hundred men . . ."

"In the hold!" Hoxworth shouted. Then, addressing the Chinese, who could not possibly understand him, he roared, "Because when this ship sails I don't want to see one goddamned Chinee anywhere but locked up in the hold. I'm warning you."

"Rafer," Dr. Whipple began again. "In the case of this couple, couldn't they stay with . . ."

Captain Hoxworth turned quickly, pointed his long forefinger at his missionary friend, and snapped: "They'll stay in the hold. How do I know this rascal isn't a pirate? How do you know he's married? There'll be no pigtailed Chinee anywhere on this ship except locked up below."

Reluctantly Dr. Whipple explained to Mun Ki that if he insisted upon bringing his wife along, she would have to share the hold along with two hundred and ninety-nine other men, but to his confusion Mun Ki evidenced no surprise and Captain Hoxworth observed: "It's nothing to them. They live like animals."

The moment had now arrived when the Chinese were to board the *Carthaginian* as it lay alongside the Macao quay, and Portuguese officers, in brilliant uniforms, took their places at the gangplank, checking off numbers rather than the names. The Cantonese interpreter said farewell, and the three hundred Chinese men and their one woman were left alone in two hostile groups, Hakka and Punti, with no one who could converse with the Americans who ran the ship and with only one man, Mun Ki, who could make himself understood to both contingents. However, their thoughts were diverted from their plight by the natural excitement involved in climbing aboard the schooner from whose mast flew the blue H & H flag. When the first Chinese stood at the top of the gangplank and saw before him the great open ocean, he hesitated in natural apprehension, which was increased when a sailor grabbed his pitiful store of belongings to stow them aft. The Punti started after his precious bundle, but he was halted by Captain Hoxworth, who grabbed him by the pigtail, spun him around and with a forceful kick sent him stumbling across the deck. "Get down into the hold, you stupid Chinee!" Hoxworth roared, and when the uncomprehending Punti stood in bewilderment, the captain kicked him again. The Chinese staggered backward toward the open hold, missed the ladder and plunged headfirst fourteen feet into the dark interior of the ship.

Instantly the remaining Chinese became tense, and Captain Hoxworth sensed this, for he whipped around, grabbed a belaying pin and took three determined steps toward the men climbing up the gangplank. Cursing them in a language they could not understand, he grabbed the arm of the next Punti, swung him about, and launched him toward the ladder. When the Chinese had sense enough to climb down, the big American roared, "There's gonna be no trouble aboard this ship!" And he brandished his belaying pin as the future plantation hands disappeared into the dark hold.

As they went below, the Chinese caught a last glimpse of their homeland, and unconsolable sorrows assaulted them, for it was a miserable thing when a man left China, and some sensed that never again would they see this great land; no matter how harshly China had treated them it was still the Middle Kingdom, the heavenly land suspended between mere earth and the residence of the gods: the sweeping plains, the rice fields in the spring, the glorious mountains, and the wild, cruel rivers. It was a land men could love, and for each who now deserted it, there came a memory of the village where his ancestral pavilion waited his return.

Just before it was Nyuk Tsin's turn to enter the hold, a thoughtful Punti climbed back out to advise Captain Hoxworth that the first man who had been thrown into the ship had broken his ankle, but when the good Samaritan reached the deck Hoxworth became furious and clouted the man with his belaying pin, knocking him back into the hold, where his friends caught him. "Don't any of you goddamned Chinee pirates come up onto my deck!" the captain bellowed.

Nyuk Tsin was the last person down the ladder, and as she prepared to descend, she saw Dr. Whipple smiling at her while Captain Hoxworth monitored her with his belaying pin. Beyond them she caught a last glimpse of China, and when she thought of the brutal way in which this land had murdered her parents, and of the near starvation in which she had lived, and of the archaic terror she had known with her kidnapers, she was glad to see the end of China. Since she was only a woman, her name appeared in no ancestral hall and there were no ties binding her to the mountains other than the memory of the animal-like loads her uncle had piled upon her, so as she saw her homeland for the last time she whispered to herself, "Farewell, cursed land. I shall never see you again."

Then she saw at the bottom of the ladder the young gambler, Mun Ki, the only person in many years who had been kind to her, and gladly she climbed down to be with him, and she was gratified when he extended his hand to help her; but she did not know that he was doing so to prevent her from breaking a leg, for an accident like that would seriously diminish her value when it came time to sell her in Honolulu.

As she reached bottom, the ladder was hauled out and heavy boards were dropped across the opening. When it became apparent that the hold was to be completely closed, the Chinese began a loud wail of protest, and Captain Hoxworth shouted, "Get the muskets!" When they were produced he ordered three sailors to kneel along the edge of the hold, and then he shouted, "Fire!" Shots whistled past the pigtails and crashed into the bulkheads. The terrified Chinese fell to the floor and the last boards of the covering were hammered into place. Now only a faltering light filtered in through a narrow grating, and there was no air, but a sail was rigged on deck so that when the ship was in motion, a breeze would be trapped and funneled below. There was no regular supply of water, only one foul bucket for slops, and such bedding as each man had brought of his own, nor were there any blankets for those who tried to sleep. It was in these quarters that Nyuk Tsin started housekeeping with her gambler, Mun Ki, and his two hundred and ninety-nine companions.

One thing was settled quickly. The Punti took their position forward and the Hakka aft, for naturally neither group wished to contaminate itself with the other, and for Nyuk Tsin there was a moment of hesitation when she felt that perhaps she ought to settle down with her own people, but they showed that they wanted nothing to do with a Hakka girl who had married a Punti; and at the same time the Punti made no effort to welcome her, so she took her position in a corner of the Punti terrain, and there she was left alone with her husband. The Punti did, however, bring to her their fellow with the broken ankle and they suggested in signs that she repair the damage. She studied the man's leg and concluded that the break was not complicated, so she made a splint of chopsticks and lashed it in place with ends of cloth. Then she borrowed bedding from others and made a rude mattress on which the man rested. If there had been water, she would have washed his face, too.

Now there was a motion of the ship, a swaying in the offshore breezes and finally the slow, steady roll of the ocean itself. Before long the hold was a confused agony of seasickness, with men vomiting everywhere and then rolling indifferently in it. Nyuk Tsin became so nauseated that she hoped the ship would sink, and in this stench the first awful night passed.

At dawn a sailor opened the grating to pass down some buckets of water, shouting to his mates, "You want to smell the other side of hell?"

His friends came over and took a whiff. "How do they stand it?" they asked.

The first explained, "They're Chinee. They like it that way," and he jammed the grating back, forgetting to reset the deck sail so that fresh air could funnel in. The day grew increasingly hot and there was insufficient water to wash away the appalling smell, so that most of the three hundred got sicker than before. They sweated, retched, went to the toilet, filled the foul bucket and then used the floor. The heat grew unbearable and the man with the broken ankle started to rave about going home.

In the afternoon a little more water was passed down and the sailor shouted, "For Christ's sake, now smell it!" And his mates agreed that with a hold full of Chinee you could do nothing. This time, however, someone remembered to tip the sail into the breeze, and by evening the hold was beginning to settle into the routine that would be followed for the next forty-six days. At eight in the morning and at four in the afternoon kettles of rice were lowered into the hold, along with stray ends of salt beef. There was no point in trying to serve vegetables or fish. Water was never plentiful, but a system was devised whereby at signals the slop bucket would be hauled up on a rope and emptied. The deck sail was tended so that a minimum breeze was funneled in, but never enough to permit a man a full breath of clean, cold air. The awful smell never abated, a mixture of urine, sweat, bowel movements and seasickness, but it was surprising that even those with especially sensitive stomachs did in time grow accustomed to it, for the odor seemed to represent them, forming a vital part of their foul, cramped quarters.

Providentially Mun Ki had brought with him some playing cards, and when his seasickness abated he set up a gambling corner where each day, as long as sunlight filtered through the grating, he tried to win back the money he had paid his Punti friends. He was adept with cards and won small amounts from most of his adversaries, announcing often, as he patted the back of his pigtail: "I'm a very lucky fellow. I understand the run of cards." When an opponent lost his stake, the nimble-witted gambler suggested: "I'll lend you some so the game can continue," and strict accounts were kept of who owed whom and how much. Significantly, no Punti ever promised: "Mun Ki, when we get to the Fragrant Tree Country I will pay you what I owe you." Instead, they assured him: "When I earn some money, I will send it to Uncle Chun Fat in the Low Village." For that was home. That was where accounts were kept, the permanent address of a man, the known anchor.

One evening when the faltering light no longer permitted gambling, Mun Ki looked at the girl he was convoying to the brothel keeper in Honolulu and reflected: "Perfect Jade! Not exactly perfect with those ugly feet." In comparison he recalled his soft young wife from the Kung village, well brought up and with small feet, and he would recall the enchanting manner in which a girl with bound feet walked, not like a man at all, but swaying in the ambient light like a flower, her hips moving in a special way calculated to drive a man crazy with desire. Thinking of the subtle poetry with which his young wife moved, he next recalled his memorable days of playing with that delectable girl, and he reconstructed the things they had done together in the silken bed. He became tumescent, and before night fell with its utter darkness, he studied Nyuk Tsin and thought: "But she can be fun, in her own way, too." He drew her to him and tried to slip his hands under her clothes, but the Punti were so crowded in the filthy hold that instinctively she drew away, for many were watching her. "They are looking," she whispered.

This irritated Mun Ki, so impulsively he stood and announced: "I am a married man and it is outrageous that I cannot sleep with my wife. I am going to build a corner." He unrolled all of his bedding, and with the point of a knife began tearing slivers of wood from the bulkhead until he got two stout ones started upon which he could hang his partitions, and before night fell completely, he had cut off a private corner, and when he brought Nyuk Tsin inside he told her that now she could undress, and when they lay locked together on the rough boards of the floor he told her, "Except for your disgraceful feet, you are almost as good as my Kung wife."

Thereafter, whenever the gambling declined in interest and the long dreary days ended in shadows, Mun Ki would announce: "Well, I am building our corner again!" And the other men, Punti and Hakka alike, honored his arrangement and during the daylight hours treated Nyuk Tsin with increased respect. On the bulkhead Mun Ki hung his good-luck sign: "May This Bed Yield a Hundred Sons." And although he was unaware of the fact, the sign was effective, and in due course Nyuk Tsin would bear him a son.

AT THE BEGINNING of the second week it became obvious that the broken ankle of the Punti man was not going to heal, for some of the splintered bones had caused wounds that were now well festered, and a dangerous blue line had begun to form along the man's leg. Therefore, one morning when the grating was opened to haul up the slop bucket, one of the Punti men swung himself aloft with the intention of asking the sailors for help, but when they saw his ominous yellow face and the long pigtail appearing on deck, they panicked and began to shout, "Mutiny! Mutiny!"

The first mate came rushing forward, grabbing a pin as he ran, and Captain Hoxworth left the bridge, leaping swiftly down the ladders onto the deck. By this time one of the sailors had swung a powerful fist at the startled Punti, knocking him toward the first mate, who brought his pin down across the man's skull with full force. This knocked the Chinese unconscious and into the path of the onrushing captain, who, when he saw the fallen mutineer, began to kick him in the face, driving his heavy leather shoes into the inert man's cheekbones until there was a sickly collapse of the man's facial structure.

When the terror ended, the captain shouted to his sailors, "You, there! Throw this damned pirate back in the hold." Two sailors grabbed the inert Punti and tossed him headfirst down the opening.

"Goddamnit!" Hoxworth shouted in frustration. "We should never have sailed without someone who can speak Chinee." He stormed for a moment, then commanded: "Mister Aspinwall, fetch the guns." When they were produced, Hoxworth directed his men to fire into the bulkheads over the cowering Chinese.

"Don't ever try to mutiny my ship!" Hoxworth stormed, cursing the coolies and stalking back to his bridge.

He was met there by an ashen-faced Dr. Whipple, who demanded bitterly, "Was such brutality necessary, Captain Hoxworth?"

The tall seafarer, fleshy and prosperous, stared ahead over the prow of his ship and said, "John, you'd better keep out of this."

"I can't be partner to such brutality," the gray-haired doctor said firmly.

"You afraid of blood?" Hoxworth asked. "Or afraid of losing your investment?"

Dr. Whipple refused to acknowledge this insulting query, and continued as if he had not heard it: "As a Christian I cannot tolerate your behavior toward men I conscripted in good faith."

The older man continued conning his ship and said calmly, "Dr. Whipple, how many vessels do you think were mutinied last year by Chinee pirates who smuggled themselves aboard?"

"I don't know," Whipple replied.

"Eleven," Captain Hoxworth said evenly. "That is, eleven that we know about. We haven't the remotest knowledge of what's lurking in that hold. Pirates . . . cutthroats . . . mutineers. You guess. All I'm saying is, that a Hoxworth & Hale ship is never going to be mutinied by any Chinee. That's why I personally supervised this little adventure."

"But to kick an unconscious man!"

"Dr. Whipple, I respect your principles. I like the way you carry out your business. But in my business, the minute a captain is either afraid or unwilling to kick his enemy to a pulp, he's on the verge of losing his ship. I have nineteen ships now, and I don't propose to lose a damned one of them to a bunch of murderous Chinamen."

Dr. Whipple studied these remarks in silence, then moved to the doorway leading from the bridge. In resolute, unhurried words he said, "Captain, although I respect your fears, I must dissociate myself from your actions. They were brutal and indefensible."

The doctor considered this statement a morally crushing one and left the bridge, but big Captain Hoxworth bounded after him, caught him by the arm, swung him around, and growled, "Once a missionary, always a missionary. Doctor, you don't know a goddamned thing about running a ship, and you ought to keep your nose out of it. This is not work for a missionary. It's work for a man." Shoving Whipple away in contempt, he stalked back to the bridge, from which he ran his ship and from which, figuratively, he ran his entire line of prosperous vessels.

John Whipple did not allow his anger at such treatment to obscure his judgment. In years of trading around the Pacific he had often met obstinate men and the cruel situations which they produce, and he had learned that in such confrontations his only chance of winning lay in doing exactly what in conscience ought to be done. It was by reliance upon this conviction that he had quietly made his way in such disparate jungles as Valparaiso, Batavia, Singapore and Honolulu. Now he went calmly to his cabin, next door to the one where the captain had kept the two young Chinese girls during the Hong Kong layover, and took up his doctor's kit. Checking it as he had learned to do more than forty years before, he carried it sedately to the locked grating and said to the sailor on guard, "Open it and let me in."

"The captain would . . ."

"Open it," Whipple commanded. "There's a man dying down there." And he took a belaying pin and started knocking away the wedges that held the grating in place. When it had swung free, he saw that no ladder could be fitted into it, so he held his bag between his knees, grabbed the edge of the opening, and swung himself down into the stinking hold. "What a horrible smell!" he mumbled through clenched teeth as he joined the three hundred and one Chinese.

Compared to the brightness of the day on deck, all was gloom and shadowy darkness in the hold, and as his eyes slowly became accustomed to the tenebrous hell, and his nose to its rankness, he saw that two men lay stretched out in the middle near where he had landed, while the others stood huddled in two clearly separated groups. He thought: "They will be the Punti and the Hakka." And he could not be certain when they might leap at him, as in justice they were entitled to do. But each of three hundred had seen him before, in the villages, and therefore he seemed like an old friend, which he now proceeded to prove he was.

Ignoring both the uncertainty and the danger of his position, he knelt beside the man whose face had been kicked in, checked the extent of damage, and spread beside him objects that the Chinese could see were medicines. Carefully, by keeping one thumb pressed inside the unconscious man's mouth, first at one place and then at another, he began to mold the bones back into line, thinking: "It's merciful that he is still insensible." He next medicated the open wounds where the heavy boot had cut the skin and saw with some pleasure that the man's eyes were not badly damaged. Looking up at the circle of inquisitive faces, he communicated his real joy at this discovery, and the Chinese understood.

At this point, Nyuk Tsin came to him and directed his attention to the man with the broken ankle, and he studied with admiration the splint made of chopsticks. Again he demonstrated his approval, and again everyone understood, so that Nyuk Tsin gained even greater acceptance than she had before enjoyed. But it was also apparent to Dr. Whipple that the injured Chinese could well lose his leg unless quick remedies were effected, so he shouted through the grating, "Send me down some hot water, right away." But when the sailor opened the grating, everyone below could hear the captain's great voice shouting, "Who in the hell ordered you to touch that grating?" And the sailor replied, "Dr. Whipple is down there tending the sick Chinese." There was a moment of ominous silence, the sound of heavy feet striding across the foredeck, and an echoing slap across someone's face, followed by a deluge of scalding water down the grating.

"There's his hot water, by God! And I'll teach you to open a grating!" There were ugly sounds, such as the Chinese had heard before, but this time, looking at Whipple amongst them, they could be sure that it was an American who was receiving a beating.

Then, in the mournful semi-darkness, a face that could not be clearly discerned pressed close to the grating and bellowed, "John Whipple, are you down there with those goddamned Chinee pirates?"

"I am giving them medical care," Whipple said.

"Well, if you love the Chinee so much, you can stay down there!" and he ordered the new sailors who assumed the grating-watch: "If he makes a single move to get out, bash him in the face with a board."

In the next hour John Whipple made one of the two or three fundamental discoveries of his long and scientific life. He found that men of good will who could understand not a single word of the other's language, could nevertheless communicate with reasonable accuracy and with profound perceptions that were neither logic nor sentiment. If a man wanted strongly enough to be understood, he was, and before sixty minutes had passed, Dr. Whipple had somehow explained to both the Hakka and the Punti that the damaged ankle could be saved if he could use their sparse reserves of water, that the unconscious man need not die, that the slop bucket should have the rim washed each day with the remnants of what water was left, and that only one section of wall away from the wind should be used for urinating, whether the man was a Hakka or a Punti, and when in the late afternoon it came time for him to urinate, he used that designated spot and saw with some satisfaction that the urine ran quickly out of the hold along a break in the floor. He smelled the area closely and concluded, "With this heat it'll be horrible in two days, but better than before."

To punish the mutineers for actions which, in Hoxworth's opinion as he reported in his log, could well have led to the loss of the *Carthaginian,* no food or water was passed down through the grating that day, nor was the slop bucket hauled up, and as twilight fell and the card games ceased, John Whipple settled down for his first long night of hell in the crowded hold, but as he prepared to lie upon the bare boards, Nyuk Tsin moved among the Hakka men and found a few extra cloths. Vermin had already begun breeding in the rags, but Whipple used them and thanked their owners. But the smell of the hold nauseated him.

It was not until four o'clock the following afternoon that the grate was opened and some water sent down, and Whipple was astonished at the sensible discipline imposed at this moment by the gasping Chinese. Kee Mun Ki stood forth as the leader of the Punti, and a tall, rugged man as spokesman for the Hakka, and the water was justly divided and apportioned, after which Dr. Whipple shouted, "Will you send down four more buckets of water, please?"

There was a hushed convocation aloft to consider this request and after a moment the heavy sound of boots. Through the grating Captain Hoxworth shouted, "What is it you want?"

"We require four more buckets of water," Whipple replied evenly.

"What you require and what you get are two different matters," Hoxworth stormed. "I'm dealing with a mutiny."

"Will you have your men haul up the slops?" Whipple pleaded.

"No!" Hoxworth replied, and marched off.

During the second awful night there was both hunger and acute suffering from lack of water, but Dr. Whipple explained to the Chinese that Captain Hoxworth was mentally unbalanced and that everyone, including Whipple, must be careful not to exasperate him. The stench was worse that night, if possible, for not much breeze came through the grating, but next morning four extra buckets of water were sent down and some food. When Whipple was given his share, his stomach revolted and he thought: "Good God! Do we serve them this? To eat?" The long day passed, and Dr. Whipple, unable to occupy himself merely by tending the broken ankle and the crushed jaw, found himself thinking: "No one who journeys to a distant land ever has it easy. Things were better on the *Thetis,* but were they really much better? At least in the Pacific there isn't constant seasickness. Now if this were the Atlantic . . ."

But the Chinese, in these same empty hours, were thinking: "I'll bet a rich American like this one never knew such things before." And although Whipple and his Chinese friends could talk about many things, on this fundamental fact of emigration they could never communicate. Even when each had the full vocabulary of the other, this basic fact of brotherhood—that all have known misery—could not be shared, for just as Abner Hale had refused to believe that the Polynesians had suffered heroic privation in getting to Hawaii, so the Chinese of the *Carthaginian* would never accept the fact that the wealthy white man had known tribulation too.

The day droned on. The smells lessened when Dr. Whipple showed the men how he wanted the slop bucket washed down. It helped, too, when he sloshed a full bucket of water in the urinal corner. The man with the broken face moaned less often, and the ominous red streaks up the groin of the other sick man diminished. There were card games and some shouting among the Punti over an incident which Whipple did not understand, and suddenly Mun Ki rose and announced something, whereupon he and his wife started hanging rude blankets across a corner of the hold.

"Goodness!" Dr. Whipple said to himself when he discovered what the contrivance was for. And the meaningless day passed into meaningless night. But before the light vanished, the grating was kicked aside and Captain Hoxworth shouted abruptly, "You ready to come up, Whipple?"

"I brought these people aboard this ship," the doctor said quietly. "I'll stay with them till the sores are healed."

"As you wish. Here's some bread." And a loaf of bread banged down into the hold. The Chinese, to whom Whipple offered some, did not like it, but Whipple observed that it was mainly the Hakka who were willing to try something new.

On the third day the grating was kicked aside, some of the boards of the hatch covering were removed, and a ladder was thrust down into the hold. Armed sailors stood guard as Dr. Whipple slowly climbed up and adjusted his eyes to bright daylight. Before he departed, the Chinese signified that they were sorry to see him go, and he replied that he would send them more water and better food. Then the boards were hammered home again.

Whipple's meeting with Captain Hoxworth was a painful one. For the first two hours the captain avoided him, but at lunch they had to meet, and Whipple said flatly, "Rafer, we have got to give those people more water."

"We will," Hoxworth grunted.

"And they must have better food."

"At the price we agreed to haul them, Doctor, that's impossible."

"It isn't impossible to keep filth out of the rice."

"Our cook ain't trained in this Chinee stuff, Doctor."

"He's got to feed them better."

"Not at these prices," Hoxworth replied stubbornly.

Dr. Whipple, now sixty-six, was afraid of very little, and without throwing down a blunt challenge, observed: "Two days ago you accused me of being a missionary. It's been many years since I thought of myself as such, but as I grow older I'm increasingly proud to accept the charge. I am a missionary. I've always been one. And, Rafer, do you know the truly damnable thing about a missionary?"

Hoxworth suspected that he was being challenged by a man at least as smart as he was, and replied cautiously, "I think I know the worst about missionaries."

"No, Captain, you don't, because if you did you would never treat me as you have the past two days. You have never learned the one respect in which missionaries must be feared."

"What?" Hoxworth asked.

"They write."

"They what?"

"They write. They have an absolute mania for taking pen in hand and writing a book, or a memorial, or a series of letters to the newspapers." Icily he stared at the big sea captain and said, "Rafer, I have never written, yet, of what I think of the way you treated Abner Hale, your partner's father, because that was a personal thing and could possibly be excused. But unless you feed these Chinese better, when we get to Honolulu I am going to write. I am going to write a series of letters, Rafer, that will forever cast a stigma upon the blue flag that you love so well. Whenever an H & H ship puts into port, someone will have heard about those letters. Because missionaries have one terrible power, Rafer. They write. They are the conscience of the Pacific."

There was an ominous silence, broken finally by Hoxworth's slamming his fist onto the table till the dishes rattled. "Why, goddamn it, this is nothing but blackmail."

"Of course!" Whipple agreed. "Blackmail is the only refuge of the literate man against barbarism. And you're a barbarian, Rafer."

"What is it you want?" the captain growled.

"Twice as much rice a day. And decent meat. Water three times a day. The slop bucket to come up three times a day. And I will be free to go down into the hold once a day to check the sick."

"I will not run the risk of having this ship mutinied," Hoxworth stormed. "I will not uncover that hold till we reach Honolulu."

"I'll go down through the grating," Whipple countered.

"You'll get back as best you can," Hoxworth warned.

"The Chinese will lift me back."

"You seem very fond of . . ." Hoxworth did not finish this insult but asked confidentially, "Tell me, Doctor, what's happening with that Chinee girl? Do them men take turns?"

"She's the wife of one man," Whipple replied coldly. "They live in one corner of the hold."

"Tell me, does this man, well, does he . . ."

"Yes. Behind a sheet which he hangs from the bulkhead."

"Well, I'll be damned!" the captain mused. "You wouldn't find three hundred American sailors letting a man get away with anything like that. No, sir!"

"Maybe the Chinese are more civilized," Whipple said and left.

It was with pride that he accompanied the first additional ration of water into the hold. He was there when the improved food came down, and by this time the awful stench had abated somewhat, for he had taken upon himself the job of setting the deck sail properly so as to wash fresh air down into the noisome hold. The poison was now abated from the broken ankle, and the second man's face was healing. Some of the Punti, directed by Whipple, were fraternizing with the Hakka, and Mun Ki, on one special day toward the end of the voyage, actually wanted Nyuk Tsin for herself alone, and not because he had been daydreaming of his naked Kung wife. He was finding Nyuk Tsin a most pleasurable and hard-working woman.

On one particularly hot day the Chinese were startled to hear a terrifying sound forward, as of chains running out, and they thought some disaster had overtaken them, for they knew nothing of ships, but it immediately became apparent that the motion of the *Carthaginian* had ceased; at last the ship was home. After much coming and going on deck, the boards covering the hold were knocked away and the ladder was dropped down. One by one the Chinese climbed back into daylight, rubbed their eyes in pain, and gradually saw the white shoreline of Honolulu, the palm trees, the distant majesty of Diamond Head, and far behind the flat land the mountains rising green and blue and purple, shrouded in misty storms. As was customary on almost each day of the year, a rainbow hung in the valleys, and the Chinese thought this a particularly good omen to mark their arrival at the Fragrant Tree Country. How beautiful, how exceedingly marvelous the land seemed that day.

There were others, too, who felt that the arrival of the *Carthaginian* was a good omen, for the Honolulu *Mail* carried a report which stated: "We are told on good authority that Whipple & Janders, utilizing the H & H schooner *Carthaginian,* will shortly be depositing in Honolulu a new cargo of more than three hundred Celestials destined for the sugar fields. These able-bodied hands, for we have been assured that Dr. John Whipple went personally to China to secure only strong young males—many of them Hakka this time—will be available on five-year contracts at the rate of $3 cash a month, food and found, plus three Chinese holidays a year. At the end of ten or fifteen years of work in our fields, it is confidently expected that the Chinese will return to their homeland, especially since they have not brought their own women with them, and it can hardly be supposed that they will find any here.

"Sugar men who have already utilized Chinese on our plantations say this of them. For all kinds of work they are infinitely superior to the shiftless Hawaiians. They eat less, obey better, are not subject to illness, are more clever in mastering new jobs, make fine carpenters when trained, and have a noticeable affinity for agricultural life. The employer must be stern, not beat them too often, and above all must not show signs of vacillation, for like all Orientals, the Chinese respect and love those who exercise a firm authority and despise those who do not.

"We are fortunate in acquiring such admirable workmen for our plantations and we are sure that after these industrious Chinese have worked out their terms and have saved their wages, they will return to China, leaving in these islands an enviable reputation for industriousness while taking back to China wealth they could not otherwise have dreamed of. The sugar industry welcomes these Celestials, and we feel confident that the true prosperity of our islands will date from this day."

On such truly amicable terms the Chinese went ashore at the Fragrant Tree Country, but in their disembarkation there was this profound difference among them: the Punti thought: "This will be a good home for five years, and then I will see the Low Village again," and no Punti had this determination to a greater degree than Kee Mun Ki; but the Hakka thought: "This is a good land to make a home in, and we shall never leave," and no Hakka thought this more strongly than Char Nyuk Tsin.

If the Chinese sometimes irritated Hawaii by refusing to call the new land anything but the Fragrant Tree Country, the islands retaliated in a rather striking manner. Inside the hot customs shed an immigration official was shouting, "All right! Attention! All Pakes over here!" No one moved, so he shouted again, this time pronouncing the word slowly:

"Pa-kays, over here." Again there was no response, so he yelled, "You Chinks! Line up!"

It was said that when the first Chinese landed in Hawaii the islanders asked them, "What shall we call you?" And the most sedate of the travelers replied, "It would be proper if you called me 'Pak Yeh,' " which meant Older Uncle. And from that time on, the Chinese were called Pakes.

As it came Kee Mun Ki's turn to face the interpreters he trembled, for he knew that soon he must make a fundamental decision concerning the Hakka girl Char Nyuk Tsin, but any perplexity over her was driven from his mind when an official, a large Hawaiian with a few phrases of Chinese, scowled at the man in front of Kee Mun Ki and growled, "What's your name?"

The Punti stood silent in fear, so the huge Hawaiian shouted, "What's your name?" Still the man remained awe-struck, so that a Chinese scholar employed for the purpose hurried up and said in good Punti, "Tell the man your name."

"Leong Ah Kam," the Chinese replied.

"Which of the names is the important one," the Hawaiian asked.

"Leong," the interpreter explained.

"How'd you spell it?" the Hawaiian asked.

"Well," the scholarly interpreter hedged, "in English this name Leong is rather difficult. It could be made into Lung or Long or Ling or Liong or Lyong."

The big official studied the problem for a moment. "Lung sounds silly," he growled, not because he was angry at the Chinese standing before him but because he was bedeviled by this constant problem of finding names for immigrant Chinese. Suddenly his face brightened into a generous smile and he pointed a big, pudgy finger at the laborer Leong Ah Kam, and fastening upon the last two names, he announced: "From now on your real name is Akama. And don't you forget it."

Carefully he printed the name on a white card: "This man's official name is L. Akama." It was in this manner that the Chinese got their Hawaiian names. Ah Kong became Akona. Ah Ki became Akina, and sometimes the simple Ah Pake, The Honorable Chinese, became Apaka. As in the past, Hawaii still modified all things that came to it, and the Punti laborer Leong Ah Kam became L. Akama.

It was now Kee Mun Ki's turn, and when the interpreter asked him his name he said firmly, "Kee Mun Ki, and I want to be known as Kee."

"What did he say?" the Hawaiian asked.

"He said that he wished to be known as Kee."

"How would you spell it?" the Hawaiian asked. When he heard the reply he tested the name several times, found it satisfactory, and printed: "This man's official name is Kee Mun Ki," and the tricky little gambler felt that he had won a victory. But before he had time to savor it, he was faced by two new problems, for outside the fence of the immigration area a thin, sharp-eyed Chinese was calling in whispers to him, and the young gambler knew by instinct that this was a man he did not wish to see; but the calling continued and Mun Ki had to move toward the fence.

"Are you the one who brought the girl?" the wiry man asked in Punti.

"Yes," Mun Ki replied honestly.

"From the Brothel of Spring Nights?"

"Yes."

"Thank the gods!" the nervous visitor sighed. "I need a new girl badly. It looks like she's a Hakka."

"She is," Mun Ki replied.

"Damn!" the visitor snapped. "Did he knock off the price? Her being a Hakka?"

"There is no price," Mun Ki said carefully.

The wiry man's face grew stern. "What?" he asked.

"I am going to keep her for myself," Mun Ki replied.

"You thief! You robber!" The man outside began to make such a protest that officials came up on the inside of the fence and shouted at him. "That is my girl!" the infuriated Punti shrieked, forgetful of the fact that he was incriminating himself. One of the Punti interpreters called a Hakka clerk and together they addressed Char Nyuk Tsin.

"The man outside says that you were sold to him," the Hakka interpreter explained.

"What man?" Nyuk Tsin asked in bewilderment.

"That small, nervous man," the official replied, and from the manner of the questioning, and from the look of the excited little man, and from the great embarrassment of her husband, Nyuk Tsin slowly realized that she had been brought to Hawaii to be sold into a house no different from the Brothel of Spring Nights. She could feel once more the ropes about her wrists, and although it had been some weeks since she recalled the hideous nights with her kidnapers, she could now remember. She did not panic, but with real courage fought down the terror that welled into her throat. Brushing aside the Hakka interpreter, she went boldly to Mun Ki and stood before him so that he would have to look at her.

His downcast eyes saw her big feet, her strong body, her capable hands and finally her unpretty but appealing face. He looked directly in her eyes for some moments and thought: "She is worth whatever she may cost. This one can work."

And with a clear voice, whose words Nyuk Tsin could understand, Mun Ki said, "This girl is not for sale. She is my wife."

No Hawaiians or Americans had so far become involved in this quarrel between two Chinese men, and as always the various interpreters were determined that the misunderstanding be settled within the Chinese community. So the Punti interpreter said, "That's all very well, but the man outside says he paid fifty dollars for this girl."

"He is correct," Mun Ki said. "And I will give him my own fifty dollars." He untied his wedding belt, dipped down into a pouch that his Kung wife had embroidered for him, and produced fifty Mexican dollars. It was like giving up part of his immortal spirit for Mun Ki the gambler to surrender these dollars, for he had intended to multiply them many times, but he passed them through the fence.

"It's better to handle everything among ourselves," the Punti official whispered, but the brothel proprietor began screaming that he had been robbed of an important asset, whereupon Mun Ki leaped to the fence, thrust his right arm through and caught the nervous little man by the neck.

"I will thrash you!" he cried. "I owed you money and like an honest man I have paid it."

"What's going on over here?" Dr. Whipple called.

"Nothing," the Chinese officials blandly replied.

"You, out there? What's the fighting about?"

"Me no fight!" the brothel keeper exclaimed, looking astonished that anyone should have thought that he was involved in trouble.

"What name did they give you?" Whipple asked Mun Ki. "Let's see the paper. Yes, Mun Ki. That's a fine name. Sounds Hawaiian. Interpreter, will you tell this man that I would like to have him and his wife work for me. Ask him if he can cook."

"Can you cook?" the Punti asked Mun Ki.

"I was the best cook in the best brothel in Macao," the gambler replied.

"I don't think the American missionary would understand," the Punti thought. To Whipple he said, "The man says he can cook."

"Explain to him that if he works on the sugar plantation he earns three dollars a month, but as a cook boy only two dollars. His wife gets fifty cents a month. But there are many advantages."

"What?" Mun Ki asked.

"You learn English. You become skilled. And you live in town, so that if later you want to open a store . . ."

"I'll be your cook," Mun Ki said, for although the explanations given by Whipple were interesting, the young gambler had swiftly foreseen an additional advantage that outweighed all the rest: in the city he would be closer to the big gambling games.

It was for these reasons that Kee Mun Ki and his Hakka wife Nyuk Tsin became the household servants of the Dr. John Whipples; but as the Chinese stooped to recover their luggage, Mun Ki taking the light bedroll and Nyuk Tsin the heavy tub and basket, she saw tied to the latter the rope with which she had been lashed up in the Brothel of Spring Nights, and it reminded her that it was the quick, clever man who walked ahead who had saved her from such things and who, with his own cherished gold pieces, had purchased her freedom. So as she tagged along behind him, weighed down with burdens, she thought: "May that good man have a hundred sons."

ON CLOSER INSPECTION, Honolulu of 1865 proved far less glamorous than its physical setting. Because Hawaii could provide no lumber, nor skilled stonemasons to work the product of its quarries, the houses of the city were meanly built, each foot of timber being conserved for practical rather than aesthetic use. Buildings were therefore low, formless and hastily put together. In the central area they crowded in upon each other and were usually not painted. Streets were unpaved and very dusty, and although a few business thoroughfares had rude sidewalks made of granite ballast hauled from China, in most areas pedestrians had to use the fringes of the road. There were, however, a good police force and an active fire department, but judging from the numerous scars that showed where flames had gutted whole rows of attached buildings, the latter seemed to enjoy only a modest success.

Business establishments occupied big rambling buildings, often made of brick carried as ballast from England, and stores sprawled aimlessly over many haphazard counters. At the corner of Fort and Merchant streets in a bright new brick building distinguished by green cast-iron shutters, Janders & Whipple had the town's largest emporium, but the most impressive commercial building stood on an opposite corner: Hoxworth & Hale's huge shipping headquarters. Sharp-eyed Mun Ki, comparing Honolulu's grubby appearance with the grandeur of Canton, where impressive stone buildings lined the waterfronts, was frankly disappointed in the contrast.

Meanwhile, other Punti from the *Carthaginian* were discovering that the lush tropical growth of the island was confined to the inaccessible mountains, whereas the land on which they were to work was really more bleak and barren than that which they had fled in China. This depressed them and they thought: "Uncle Chun Fat lied to us. Not even a Chinese can make his fortune on such a barren island." Out of a hundred average fields surrounding Honolulu, not less than ninety were desert, for on them no rain fell. The vast acreages west of Honolulu, which belonged to the Hoxworth family through inheritance from the last Alii Nui, Noelani, were practically worthless, thirsting for water. But scattered across the island there were small valleys in which an occasional bubbling stream fed the fields, and here the Chinese were put to work. Some grew rice for the booming California market. Others worked on small sugar plantations. A few lucky men were taught to ride horses, and became cowboys on the parched rangelands, and many were put to work growing vegetables; but as they started their new tasks, each man carried in his memory an exciting picture of Honolulu's close-packed streets and dusty enterprise, and all thought: "I've got to get back to Honolulu. That's where the life is."

Hawaii's reception of the Chinese was somewhat dampened by Captain Rafer Hoxworth's frightening account of his heroic escape from mutiny, and the newspapers were peppered with predictions from other seafaring men that Honolulu had entered upon a period of maximum danger, when the possibility of an armed Chinese uprising, with all white men murdered in their beds by slinking Celestial fiends, was a distinct possibility. Captain Hoxworth volunteered several interviews with the press in which he contended that only his swift reaction to the first attempts at mutiny had preserved his ship, and thereafter he became known as the intrepid captain who had quelled the Chinese mutiny.

The friends of Dr. John Whipple were therefore apprehensive when the doctor took into his home the Kees to serve as cook and maid, and men stopped him several times on the street to ask, "Do you think it wise, John, to harbor in your home such criminal characters?"

"I don't find them criminal," Whipple responded.

"After the mutiny?"

"What mutiny?" he always asked dryly.

"The one that Rafer Hoxworth put down on the *Carthaginian.*"

Dr. Whipple never openly refuted the captain's story, for he knew that what is mutiny to one man is not to another and it was his nature to make generous allowances, but he often did observe sardonically: "Even very brave men sometimes see ghosts." He was content to have the Kees working for him.

On the day of their arrival Dr. Whipple piled their luggage into his dray and then led his two servants on foot leisurely up Nuuanu Street toward his home, and although he could not speak Chinese, he explained the structure of the city to the young couple. "The first street we cross is Queen, Queen, Queen." He stopped and drew a little map in the dust and made them repeat the name of the cross street. At first they failed to understand what he was doing, so deftly he drew a ship and pointed back to the *Carthaginian,* and immediately they caught on, for it was Dr. Whipple's conviction that any man not an imbecile could be taught almost anything.

"Merchant, King, Hotel," he explained. Then he left big Nuuanu Street and took a detour to the corner of Merchant and Fort to show his Chinese the J & W store. "This is where I work," he said, and his servants were impressed, the more so when he picked up several bolts of dark cloth and handed them to Nyuk Tsin.

Finally he came to the broad east-west street named in honor of Great Britain, Beretania, and when he had taught the Chinese how to say that important name, he showed them that they stood on the corner of Nuuanu and Beretania. They understood, and then he pointed to a substantial picket fence that surrounded a large property on the ocean-western corner, and when he had reviewed with them just where this stood, he opened the gate and said, "This will be your home."

They smiled, three people with three different languages, and the Chinese looked in awe at the Whipple homestead. Set amid three acres of land, it was built on coral blocks and consisted of a large one-story wooden building completely surrounded by a very wide porch. All interior rooms were thus dark and cool and were accessible to the veranda. The coral base of the house was masked by luxuriant croton plants, recently brought to Hawaii by the captain of an H & H ship, and these produced large varicolored leaves, iridescent in rain or sunlight, so that the sprawling house nestled in tropic beauty.

Dr. Whipple called, and from the front door his wife appeared, a small, white-haired New England woman wearing an apron. She hurried across the porch and onto the lawn, extending her hands to the Chinese. "This is my wife," Dr. Whipple explained formally, "and this is the cook Mun Ki and the maid Mrs. Kee." Everyone bowed and Mrs. Whipple said, "I should like to show you to your new home," and she demonstrated how the Whipple dining room stood at the rear of the big wooden house, and how there was a covered runway from it to an outside kitchen, where all the food was cooked, and another runway leading off to a small wooden house, and this was to be theirs. She pushed open the door and showed them a compact, clean room, which she herself had dusted that morning. Leading off from it was another, and while they stood there conversing they knew not how, the dray arrived with their luggage and stores of food, utensils and bedding.

"These are for you," Mrs. Whipple said warmly, taking Nyuk Tsin's hand and leading her to the boxes. That afternoon one of the Hewlett women asked, "Amanda, how will your Chinese learn to cook if they can't understand a word you say?"

"They'll learn," Amanda replied forcefully, for she shared her husband's New England conviction that human beings had brains; so for the first four weeks of their employment, the Kees went to school. Little Amanda Whipple was up at five, teaching Mun Ki how to cook American style, and she was impressed both with his clever mind and his fearful stubbornness. For example, on each Friday during the past four decades it had been Amanda's ritual to make the family yeast, and for the first two Fridays, Mun Ki studied to see how she performed this basic function in American cookery. He watched her grate the potato into a stone jar of almost sacred age and add a little salt and a lot of sugar, after which she poured in boiling water, allowing all to cool. Then, ceremoniously, she ladled in two tablespoonfuls of active yeast made the Friday before, and the strain continued. For forty-three years Amanda had kept one family of yeast alive, and to it she attributed her success as a cook. She was therefore appalled on Mun Ki's third Friday to enter the cookhouse full of ritualistic fervor, only to find the stone jar already filled with next week's yeast.

With tears in her eyes, she started to storm at Mun Ki, and he patiently listened for some minutes, then got mad. Flashing his pigtail about the kitchen he shouted that any fool could learn to make yeast in one week. He had been courteous and had studied for two weeks and now he wanted her out of the kitchen. Not understanding a word he was saying, she continued to mourn for the lost yeast, so he firmly grabbed her shoulders and ejected her onto the lawn. On Monday the new batch of yeast was as good as ever and she consoled herself philosophically: "It's the same strain, sent forward by different hands." Suddenly, she felt the elderly white-haired woman she was.

Mun Ki also had difficulty understanding why Americans ate so much, and he would consistently omit dishes to which the robust appetites of the white men had become accustomed. A typical Whipple dinner, served at high noon in the heat of the day, consisted of fish chowder, roast beef with Yorkshire pudding, creamed cabbage cooked in ham fat, delicious chewy biscuits made of taro and drenched in butter, mashed potatoes, candied yams, pickled mango, alligator pear salad with heavy dressing, French bread with guava jelly, banana pie marvelously thick and rich, followed by coffee with cream, and cigars. If guests were present, two extra vegetables were served and French brandy.

Later, the Chinese would eat steamed cabbage with no fat, a little fish cooked with soybean sauce, a bowl of rice and some unsweetened tea, and it was often remarked that Hawaii must agree with the Orientals, because even though they worked harder than the white men, they lived longer.

When she finished supervising the preparation of food, little Amanda Whipple, in her sixties, turned her attention to Nyuk Tsin and taught the hard-working Chinese girl how to care for a large house. Dusting was particularly stressed and caused some difficulty, because in China, Nyuk Tsin's mother had waited for a likely omen before bothering to dust, whereas energetic Mrs. Whipple demanded that it be done regularly every day. The floors had to be dusted, the flowered china lamps, the chandelier, the rosewood love seat with its multiple curlicues, the endless embroidered decorations, the peacock chair from Canton and the bamboo furniture that never looked clean. Nyuk Tsin's special nightmare was the great fish net on the parlor wall from which shells, leis and other keepsakes were hung. In fact, there was scarcely an inch of the Whipple house that did not contain some gimcrack whose main purpose was gathering dust.

In comparison, the Kee household contained one table bearing the genealogy book, a flint lighter, a candle and a wine bottle. There was also a rope bed above which hung the impressive sign: "May This Bed Yield a Hundred Sons."

According to the agreement reached by Whipple and his Chinese, Mun Ki received two dollars a month and his wife was to have received fifty cents, but when Mrs. Whipple saw how excellent Nyuk Tsin's work was, from five in the morning till nine at night, seven days a week, her generosity was touched, so she paid the girl a full dollar each month, and from this salary of $36 a year the two Chinese were required to clothe themselves, pay for the birth and education of their children, provide for entertainment and luxuries, and send money home to the official wife in China. They did all these things, but their problems were eased a bit by the unnecessary generosity of the Whipples. Unexpected gifts here and there added to the family treasury, and the allotment of an acre of good land which Nyuk Tsin could farm for herself allowed the couple to earn some real money, for Nyuk Tsin was a fine farmer and soon appeared on the streets of Honolulu with a bambo pole across her shoulders and two baskets of fresh vegetables slung from the ends. She hawked her wares mainly among the Chinese, accumulating from them a growing store of American dimes, Australian shillings and Spanish reals, for Hawaii had wisely decided that any of the world's money could circulate freely within the kingdom.

The Kee funds were further augmented by some shrewd enterprise on the husband's part, for each day as soon as breakfast was finished, he hurried down Nuuanu Street to Chinatown, where nondescript shacks huddled together in ugly profusion and where white men rarely went. His destination was a particularly disreputable hovel in which sat an elderly Chinese with wispy beard and a brush and book in which he entered bets as they were offered. Behind him, on the wall, hung a luridly colored sketch of a man, with twenty-eight parts of his body indicated: nose, ankle, knee, elbow . . . The game which had captured Mun Ki's whole imagination consisted of placing a bet as to which of these words would appear in the sealed capsule that stood under a glass on the table before the game's operator. Most of the Chinese in Hawaii played the game, at odds of thirty to one, which gave the player an advantage, except that if there were too many winners the prize was proportionately lowered; the bank never lost. Nevertheless, the odds were enticing, and each day upon rising, families would inquire of one another: "Did you dream of an elbow last night?" Careful attention was also paid to any sudden pain, or to an accident involving any part of the body. But mostly it was dreams that brought good fortune, and it was uncanny how the dreams of Mun Ki kept pointing the way to the lucky word.

"You here again with the winning word?" the game's manager asked sourly.

"Today it's bound to be chin," Mun Ki assured him. "I woke last night with my chin itching furiously, and I can read through the glass and see the word written on the paper."

"How much are you betting?"

"Two dimes."

The proprietor's face betrayed his displeasure as he brushed the entry into his book. "You're a clever man, Mun Ki," he grumbled. "Why don't you join me in this business?"

"I'm a cook," Mun Ki replied. "It's better to win from you than work for you."

"What I have in mind," the older gambler proposed, "is for you to collect bets at the far end of town and bring them in here by ten each morning."

"Then I couldn't bet for myself, could I?" Mun Ki asked.

"No, then you'd be part of the game."

From one of the towers along the waterfront a clock struck eleven, people crowded in from the alleys of Chinatown, the excitement grew intense, and the proprietor ceremoniously lifted away the glass to uncover the capsule. To prevent the quick substitution of a word on which no one had bet that day—a trick that had often been tried in the past—a man was selected at random, and under the most careful scrutiny he opened the capsule and shouted: "Chin!" Mun Ki leaped with joy and cried, "I had two dimes bet, because I woke with a definite itch on my chin." He explained to everyone the precise minute at which he had wakened and his thoughts at that propitious moment. With his two dimes and his dream he had won two months' normal wages.

He was about to leave the gambling shack when the old proprietor caught his arm and said, "You ought to join me. Today you made a lot of money, but I make it every day."

"You do?" Mun Ki asked.

"Every day. If too many win, I cut the prize. I send hundreds of dollars back to China."

"Could I?" the younger gambler asked.

"Easily. If you worked with me."

It was in this way that the cookhouse of the missionary home at Nuuanu and Beretania became one of the principal outposts of the chi-fa word game. Mun Ki kept on hand a supply of the gaudy posters which showed the twenty-eight parts of the human body that might be named; and for each bet he took he got six per cent from the bank and fifteen per cent of the prize money from the winner, if the ticket won; and he became one of the chi-fa's best operators, for as he had proved by paying the brothel operator full price for Nyuk Tsin, he was meticulously honest with both his employer and his customers. His chief return, however, came from his happy idea of having the chi-fa poster printed in Hawaiian and in enlisting dozens of native gamblers. They enjoyed doing business with him, and bought so many tickets that soon there were chi-fa drawings both at eleven and at four. With the money he made, Mun Ki slipped away two or three afternoons a week for the wild fan-tan and mah-jongg games that ran uninterruptedly in Chinatown. He was a fierce competitor, and his store of dimes and reals and shillings grew steadily.

The only disagreement the Kees had with the Whipples occurred when it became obvious that Nyuk Tsin was going to have a baby. For some months she had hidden the fact behind her loose smock, so that when Mrs. Whipple finally did discover it she said, "You must do no more housework, Mrs. Kee. Rest." But that same afternoon she saw Nyuk Tsin trudging down Nuuanu with two huge baskets of vegetables at the ends of her bamboo pole. Amanda stopped her carriage, climbed down, and commanded her maid to drop the burden and wait till Mun Ki could be sent to pick it up; but when the cook arrived he studied the situation in astonishment and said, "Swinging the bamboo pole is the best thing a pregnant woman can do. It gets her ready."

That night Dr. Whipple went out to the Chinese house and said, "I'll make arrangements to deliver the baby." He was disturbed when Mun Ki explained in the little English he had picked up: "No need doctor. I bring baby." It was a rather difficult point to argue, since neither man was proficient in the other's language, but Dr. Whipple got the distinct impression that Mun Ki was arguing: "In China husbands always deliver their wives' babies. Who else?"

"I think I'd better get an interpreter," the confused doctor interrupted. He went to fetch the scholarly man who served as unofficial Chinese consul, and explained: "I'm afraid my servant here is intending to deliver his wife himself."

"Why not?" the consul asked.

"It's preposterous! I'm a doctor, living right here." Then, fearing that perhaps money might be the problem, he assured the consul: "I'll do it without charge."

Patiently the consul explained this to Mun Ki, who was awed by the presence of an official and who wanted to avoid trouble. "My wife and I don't need the doctor," he said quietly.

"Explain that there will be no charge," Whipple began, but he was interrupted by the consul, who, after listening to Mun Ki, explained: "If this man were in China, and if his other wife were pregnant, he would deliver her."

"What other wife?" Whipple asked in bewilderment.

"The wife here is only his number two wife. The real wife stays at home with the ancestors in China."

"Do you mean to say . . ." Whipple spluttered, but again the consul interrupted to explain: "Mun Ki says that his Uncle Chun Fat has three wives in China, two in California and one in Nevada."

"Does he also have children?" Whipple asked.

There was some discussion of this, and Mun Ki reported: "Seven in China, four in California, two in Nevada."

"And did this uncle deliver all of his thirteen sons?" Whipple snorted. "I'm sure they must have all been sons."

"Of course," the consul replied blandly.

"Of course he delivered them, or of course they were sons?"

This confused the consul, and he suggested: "Maybe we had better start again," but Dr. Whipple had had enough. Pointing at Mun Ki he snapped: "Do it your uncle's way. He seems to have had more experience than me." And he left.

Working by himself, Mun Ki produced a fine boy, but everyone in the white community was outraged to think that the barbarous Chinese would follow such a custom. "And to think," one of the Hewlett girls cried, "all the time not fifty feet away there was one of the best doctors in Hawaii! Really, the Chinese are scarcely human." And it was generally agreed that for a stubborn man to insist upon delivering his own wife when practical, proved assistance from a real doctor was available, was proof that the Chinese were not civilized.

The Whipples got another shock when they asked what the chubby, healthy little boy was to be called. "We haven't been told yet," Mun Ki replied.

"How's that?" Whipple asked.

Mun Ki said something about not yet having taken the poem to the store to find out what the child's name would be. Dr. Whipple started to ask, "What poem?" but he felt he'd better not, and said no more about the name, but some days later Mun Ki asked Mrs. Whipple if he and his wife could be absent for a few hours, and when Amanda asked why, he explained: "We must take the poem to the store to find out what the baby's name is." Mrs. Whipple called her husband and said, "You were right, John. The Kees are taking a poem to the store so as to get a name for their baby."

"I'd like to see this," Dr. Whipple said, for such things were of concern to him, and Mun Ki said he would be honored to have such a distinguished man assisting at the naming of his first son, but before they started to the store Whipple asked, "Could I see the poem?" And from the precious genealogical book Mun Ki produced a card containing the poem from which all names in the great Kee family were derived. It was an expensive, marbled, parchment-like cardboard bearing in bold poetic script fourteen Chinese characters arranged vertically in two columns. "What is it?" Whipple asked, his scientific curiosity aroused, but Mun Ki could not explain.

The Chinese store to which the trio headed stood at the corner of Nuuanu and Merchant streets and was known simply as the Punti store, for here that language was spoken and certain delicacies favored by the Punti were kept in stock. The storekeeper, an important man in Honolulu, recognized Dr. Whipple as a fellow tradesman and ceremoniously offered him a chair. "What's this poem my cook is talking about?" Whipple asked, whereupon the Punti said, "Not speak me. Him. Him."

And he pointed to a scholar who maintained a rude office in the corner of the store, where he wrote letters in Chinese and English for his Punti clients. Gravely the letter-writer picked up the poem and said, "This belongs to the Kee family. From it they get their names."

"What's it say?"

"That's not important. This one happens to read: 'Spring pervades the continents; earth's blessings arrive at your door. The heavens increase another year; and man acquires more age.' "

"What's it got to do with names?" Whipple asked.

"The answer is very complicated, and very Chinese," the scholar replied. "But we are very proud of our system. It is probably the sanest in the world."

"Can you explain it?" Whipple asked, leaning forward in his chair.

"In China we have only a few family names. In my area less than a hundred. All one syllable. All easy to remember. Lum, Chung, Yip, Wong. But we have no given names like Tom or Bob."

"No names?" Whipple asked.

"None at all. What we do is take the family name, Kee, and add to it two ordinary words. They can be anything, but taken together they must mean something. Suppose my father were a Kee and believed that I would be the beginning of a long line of scholars. He might name me Kee Chun Fei, Kee Spring Glorious. That's the kind of name we seek for your cook's boy."

"Where does the poem come in?" Whipple pressed.

"From the poem we receive the mandatory second name. All men in the first generation had to be named Chun, Spring, from the first word in the poem. All their offspring in the second generation had to be named Mun, Pervades. And all in the third generation, like the boy we are considering today, must be named from the third word in the poem, Chow, Continent. There is no escaping this rule and the benefit is this. If your cook Kee Mun Ki meets a stranger named Kee Mun Tong, they know instantly that they are of the same generation and are probably cousins."

"Sounds sensible," Whipple admitted.

"So the naming of this man's son has got to start Kee Chow, because that's what the poem says."

"Then why doesn't he just add any third name he likes?"

"Ah!" pounced the letter-writer. "There's the problem! Only a scholar can be trusted to pick that third name, for on it depends the child's entire good fortune. I'll ask Mun Ki who gave him his third name." There was a furious exchange of Chinese, after which the letter-writer reported triumphantly: "His parents summoned a learned priest from Canton. The man spent three days pondering his name. He consulted oracles and horoscopes, and finally the right name was selected. You see, a man's name can influence his entire life."

"So the Chinese in Hawaii consult with you because you are a scholar?" Whipple asked.

"Alas, there are some who are so ignorant they do not even know their family poems, and such people don't care what they name their sons. But Mun Ki comes from a strong family. They saw to it that he carried his family poem with him."

The scholar now ignored Whipple and began a long conversation with Mun Ki, and after fifteen or twenty minutes he returned to Whipple and explained: "I have been inquiring of Mun Ki what his hopes are for his son, for this is important in choosing a name."

The discussion continued for some time, and gradually the scholar began getting some paper in place and a Chinese brush, and after about an hour of speculation on the name, he reported to Whipple: "We are beginning to narrow it down. We are trying to find a word which will harmonize with Kee and Chow but at the same time add dignity and meaning. It must be a word that sounds well, looks well when written, has its own peculiar meaning, and combines well with the second word in the name. It must also express the father's hopes for his son, so you will excuse me if I concentrate on this and propose several possibilities."

With his brush he began drafting a variety of Chinese characters, and some he rejected as too feminine for a strong son like Mun Ki's, and others because they had alternative readings that might offend. Sometimes Mun Ki refused a name, and gradually the scholar began to confine the possibilities to a few choices. At last, in triumph, he announced the boy's name: "Kee Chow Chuk, the Kee who Controls the Center of the Continent."

He asked, "Isn't that a splendid name?" and Dr. Whipple nodded, whereupon the scholar took Mun Ki's genealogical book and on the appropriate page wrote down the bright new name, filled with parental hope. The scholar studied the handsome characters with obvious pleasure and told Whipple, "There's a name that looks good from any angle. It's what we call auspicious." He then took a sheet of writing paper and asked Mun Ki, "What's your village?" and when the cook replied, the letter-writer made a few swift strokes addressing the letter to that village, advising the elders that Kee Mun Ki was dutifully reporting the fact that he had a son whose name was Kee Chow Chuk, and in the ancestral clan book that name should be recorded. The family was going on. In remote Hawaii there was now a Kee who paid respect to his ancestors, who would in due time start sending money home, and who finally would return to the village, for to live elsewhere was unthinkable.

And then, as Kee Mun Ki and Nyuk Tsin were leaving the Punti store, the scholar made a dramatic gesture which changed the entire history of the Kees in Hawaii. As if a vision had possessed him, the name-giver cried, "Halt!" And with slow, stately gestures he tore up the letter to the Low Village, scattering its shreds upon the floor. Trancelike he approached Mun Ki, took away the genealogical book and splashed black ink across the propitious name he had just composed. Then, in a low voice, he explained: "Sometimes it comes like a flash of lightning on a hot night. After you have pondered a name for many hours you catch a vision of what this child can be, and all the old names you have been considering vanish, for a new name has been written across your mind in flame."

"Have you such a name for Mun Ki's boy?" Whipple asked respectfully.

"I have!" the scholar replied, and with bold strokes of his brush he put down the fiery name: Kee Ah Chow. He repeated it aloud, awed by its splendor.

"I thought it had to be Kee Chow Ah," Dr. Whipple suggested.

"It does!" the scholar agreed. "But sometimes rules must be broken, and this child's name is surely Kee Ah Chow."

The scholar handed the new name to Mun Ki and explained in Punti: "As you were leaving the store I had a sudden vision of your life. Your family is bold and you will venture far. You will have many sons and great courage. The world is yours, Mun Ki, and your first-born must have a name that signifies that fact. So we shall call him Kee Ah Chow, the Kee who Controls the Continent of Asia. And your next sons shall be Europe and Africa and America and Australia. For you are the father of continents."

Mun Ki smiled deprecatingly, for the words were sweet. He had always imagined himself as rather special, a man nominated by the gods, and it was good to hear a scholar confirming the fact. Giving Nyuk Tsin an imperative shove, he started to leave the store, but again the scholar stopped them, pointing imperatively at Nyuk Tsin and crying, "And her name shall be Wu Chow's Mother, for she is to be the mother of continents."

This prophetic announcement caused embarrassment, and Mun Ki had to explain in Punti: "She is not my wife. My real wife is a Kung girl in China. This one is merely . . ."

The scholar folded his hands, studied Nyuk Tsin, and replied in Punti, "Well, that's the way of China. Maybe it's better, seeing that she's a Hakka." He shrugged his shoulders and turned to go, then paused and added, "Let her be known as Wu Chow's Auntie." Mun Ki nodded and told his wife her new name.

Dr. Whipple was perplexed by this exchange of words he could not understand, but he judged the matter under discussion was one of importance, and from the manner in which Nyuk Tsin stood, the blood of shame rising to her ears, he guessed that they were talking about her, but no one explained what was being said. Finally Mun Ki bowed. Wu Chow's Auntie bowed. Together they recovered the poem and the name book, and when Mun Ki handed them to Nyuk Tsin to carry he touched her hand and said proudly, "We are going to have many sons."

The scholar, for his important role in naming the Kee's first-born, received a fee of sixty cents, and Mun Ki considered the money well spent, for he was certain that his child was properly launched; but Dr. Whipple, who was then much concerned with the manner in which his own children and grandchildren were occupying themselves in Hawaii, was even more deeply impressed by the incident. He recognized it as symbolizing one of the strengths of the Chinese: "They exist within a hierarchy of generations. Their names tell where they belong, and remind them of their parents' hopes for them. A Chinese lives within a defined system, and it's a good one. No matter where he goes, his name is listed in a village, and that's home. We Americans drift where we will.

We have no name, no home, no secure address. I'd like to know more about the Chinese."

So although he was then sixty-seven years old and preoccupied with important matters, John Whipple began his last scientific work: a study of the Chinese whom he had brought to Hawaii, and much of what we know today about those early Orientals—those strange, secret people imported to work the sugar—we know from what he wrote. It was Whipple who cast a shadow of fear across the other sugar planters by publishing an article in the Honolulu *Mail:* "We are deluding ourselves if we persist in the belief that these intelligent, thrifty and hard-working people will long be content to stay upon the plantations. Their natural destiny is to work as accountants and mechanics in our cities. They will be excellent schoolteachers and I suppose some will become bankers and enterprisers of great force. As soon as their indentures are discharged, they are flocking to our cities to open stores. More and more, the commerce of our countryside will fall into their industrious hands. Therefore, it behooves us to look about and find other workmen to take care of our cane fields for us; for the Chinese are not going to persist in a condition of servitude. They will learn to read and write, and when they have done this, they will demand a share in the government of these islands.

"There may be some who decry this development, but I for one applaud it. Hawaii will be a stronger community when we use our Chinese to their fullest advantage, and just as I would never have been content to be merely a field hand, doing the same chore over and over again, so I am gratified when I see another man who, like me, is determined to better himself. At one point, when I was engaged in the business of bringing Chinese to these islands, I believed that when their indentures were discharged they would return to China. Now I am convinced that they will not do so. They have become part of Hawaii and we should encourage them to follow in our footsteps. Let them become educated. Let them initiate new industries. Let them become fellow citizens. For through them the dying Hawaiian race will be regenerated."

Honolulu's reaction was simple and dramatic: "The sonofabitch ought to be horsewhipped!"

Captain Rafer Hoxworth stormed: "We brought those damned Chinamen here under the specific understanding that after five or ten years in the sugar fields they'd go home. Good God! Whipple wants them to stay! It's by God downright indecent."

Captain Janders' son, and now Dr. Whipple's partner in J & W, said, "The old man must be out of his mind! Why, one of our biggest problems in running the plantations is that as soon as the Chinese get a chance they leave us and open a store in Honolulu. I can take you to Nuuanu Street and show you half a dozen shops started by men who ought to be working for me right now, growing cane."

But what infuriated Hawaii most was the sly manner in which the

Chinese, who had no women of their own, had been stealing Hawaiian women, and marrying them, and having babies by them. In spite of the fact that the babies were some of the most handsome ever bred in the islands, extraordinarily intelligent and healthy, the white community was outraged and passed laws to stop these criminal marriages. One edict forbade any Chinese from marrying a Hawaiian girl unless he became a member of the Christian church. The speed with which Chinese men learned the catechism was staggering, and one Chinese passed along to another the correct answers to the critical questions, so that it was not uncommon for a Chinese to utter, as his first words in broken English, the complete Nicene Creed plus explanations of the Trinity, the Virgin birth and Calvin's doctrine of predestination. One minister, after examining several such impromptu scholars, told a fellow Calvinist, "With my own ears I heard these men answer every important question correctly, and at the end I was tempted to ask one more, 'What does it all mean?' but I have never dared to ask even my Boston friends that fearful question, and I eschewed doing so here."

Actually, the Chinese made good Christians and did so without reservation. They were determined to have women, and conversion seemed a cheap price to pay. Those lucky ones who married Hawaiian girls with land and who grew to great wealth from manipulating that land, founded substantial Christian families and supported the large churches that were built by other Chinese; but when a male grandson was born, these prudent men went quietly to the Punti store and worked out a proper Chinese name for the boy, and sent that name back to the village hall, where it was written in the clan book.

As for the Hawaiian women, they preferred Chinese husbands to any other, for there were no men in the islands who loved women and children more than the pigtailed Chinese, and it was not uncommon to see a thin, bedraggled Chinese man, who had slaved all day on the docks for H & H, come home to where a hugely fat Hawaiian wife watched in idleness as he did the laundry, washed the children and cooked the evening meal. A Chinese husband brought presents and spent time educating his sons. He saw that his daughters had ribbons, and on Sunday he would take his whole brood to church. It became recognized in the islands that the very best thing that could happen to a Hawaiian girl was to catch herself a Chinese husband, for then all she had to do was laugh, wear fine brocades and rear babies.

But there was a subtler reason why the Hawaiians tolerated Chinese marriages: they saw with their own eyes that Chinese-Hawaiian children were superb human specimens. When the first such girls began to mature Honolulu was breathless at their beauty. They had long black hair with just a suggestion of a wave running through it, olive skin, a touch of mystery about their eyes and handsome teeth. They were taller than their Chinese fathers, much slimmer than their copious mothers, and they combined the practicality of the Chinese with the gay abandon of the Hawaiian. They were a special breed, the glory of the islands; and practically every writer from America or England who took part in launching the lively fable of the beautiful Hawaiian girl, had in his mind's eye one of these first Chinese-Hawaiian masterpieces; and they justified all that was written about romantic Hawaii.

The boys were promising in another way. They were quick to learn, good at games, very good at business and best of all at politics. They had a shameless charm in soliciting votes for their candidates, were gifted in repartee, and had a basic honesty which the public grew to respect. So the Hawaiians, who had been a vanishing race—400,000 in 1778, 44,000 in 1878—suddenly received a vital impetus from the Orient and began to re-establish themselves through the Chinese-Hawaiian mixture, until in later years the part-Hawaiian was to become the fastest-growing component in the islands.

Captain Rafer Hoxworth, watching the beginning of this miracle, spoke for all his Caucasian friends except Dr. Whipple when he said, "Any Chinese who leaves a plantation to become a peddler should be immediately deported, but any who touches a Hawaiian girl should be hung."

In the Honolulu *Mail* the Hewletts reported more moderate reactions: "Hawaii is ruined. The Chinese are fleeing the plantations, and who will raise our sugar?"

Dr. Whipple, having gained only contumely from his last public writing on the Chinese, confined his subsequent thoughts to his diary: "It was on the island of Oahu in 1824 that I first saw measles sweep through a Hawaiian village, leaving eighty per cent of the people dead, and it was soon after that I began considering what we could do to infuse new life into this lovable race which I had grown to cherish so dearly. I foresaw that only the introduction of some vital new blood could prevent the annihilation of these fine people. Erroneously, I thought that stronger Polynesians from the south might accomplish the reversal, but we imported such Polynesians and nothing happened. Later, I trusted that Javanese might suffice, and perhaps they would have, but we were unable to acquire them. And now the Chinese have arrived and they have served exactly as I long ago predicted they would. For my part in effecting this salvation of a race, I am humbly proud. At present the temper of the time is against me in this matter, so I keep my own counsel, but I am confident that the judgment of the future will support me. The best thing I ever did for Hawaii was to import Chinese."

As he wrote in his lamp-lit study, Mun Ki and his wife, in their small house nearby, were starting another son, the Continent of Europe.

NYUK TSIN and her husband had been in Hawaii about a year when the entire Chinese community was aroused by news filtering into Honolulu from the island of Maui, where many Chinese workers were engaged on plantations. As the Chinese got the news, this is what happened: toward dusk one hot day an elderly clergyman with a limp and carrying a cane forced his way into one of the temporary Chinese temples erected there for the use of the laborers, and disrupted worship. One woman who had been in the temple at the time reported: "The little man struck everything with his cane, knocked down the statue of Kwan Yin, tore up the golden papers and shouted words at us. When we refused to leave the temple, for it was ours and built with our effort and none of theirs, his great anger turned toward us, and he tried to strike us with his cane, shouting at us all the time. But since he was an old man, it was easy for us to avoid him."

The Chinese generally felt that this was but one more evidence of the hard life they were to have on the plantations, and much indignation resulted from the old man's unexpected attack. Asked the Chinese, Punti and Hakka alike: "Don't the white men respect gods?" And the divergence between the Chinese and the Caucasian increased.

To the white men, the incident at the Buddhist temple was deplorable, and planters both on Maui and on the other islands quickly got together small sums of money which they handed to the offended Chinese, so that some of the damage growing out of the attack was rectified. Dr. Whipple, as spokesman for the planters, went personally to Maui to mollify the laborers, and after a period of tension, reasonably good relations were restored, and all whites who employed Chinese took special pains to assure the strangers that they were free to worship as they pleased. Thus, in the mid-1860's, a true religious freedom was established in the islands: Congregationalists, Catholics, Episcopalians, Mormons, Buddhists and Confucianists worshiped side by side in relative harmony.

When peace among the Chinese had been restored, the white planters took up the problem of wizened Abner Hale, and younger offspring of the old families, men like the Hewletts, the Whipples and the Hoxworths, convened in Honolulu to see what to do about the old man. Reported one of the Hewletts, honestly: "That pitiful fanatic, bursting in that way with his cane and his shouts of 'Abomination! Corruption!' almost ruined everything we've accomplished with the Chinese. We've got to make the old fool behave."

"Years ago he did the same thing with the Hawaiians, as I understand," Bromley Hoxworth explained. "One famous night when my mother was getting married to her brother, he burst into the ceremony and lashed about with his cane, destroying idols and raising merry hell. He still thinks he's fighting the old Hawaiian gods."

"Somebody's got to advise him that things have changed," one of the Whipple boys insisted. "Knocking down Hawaiian idols when it does no harm is one thing, but destroying Buddhas when we're trying to keep our Chinese help happy is quite another."

The group turned to David Hale and suggested: "Can you talk to him, Dave?"

"I'd rather not," the alert young man evaded. "I've never been able to make much sense with Father."

"What we really ought to do is to get him off Maui altogether," Brom Hoxworth proposed. "Truly, he oughtn't to be there alone. He messes up the Seamen's Chapel and interferes with the Chinese. He's really a dreadful nuisance, and I agree with the others, Dave, that you've got to talk with him. Convince him that he ought to live in a little house here in Honolulu . . . where we could watch him."

"I've tried that. So has Micah. The old man simply won't listen to any proposal which requires his leaving Maui. If you raise the question, he says stubbornly, 'My church is here, and my graves are here.' And that's that."

"Whose graves?" Brom Hoxworth asked.

"My mother's grave, and your grandmother's," the intense younger Hale explained. "He plays gardener for them, and insists now and then upon preaching in the old stone church that he built. But I'm sure the minister would be delighted to see him get out of Maui."

One of the Whipple boys spoke: "Looking at the whole thing frankly, the fact that he's left alone on Maui reflects on all of us, really. It looks as if we had cut the old man off . . . didn't want him, because he's sort of wandering in his mind. Now, I know that's not the truth. I happen to know definitely that my father invited Reverend Hale to live with him, and your mother, Brom, did the same, and of course we all know that both Micah and David asked him to live with them. So our skirts are clean, as it were, but even so we get a good deal of opprobrium for allowing him to stay in that filthy little house of his."

"And now if he's going to start meddling with the Chinese," young Hoxworth pointed out, "he's really got to be cleaned out."

The group therefore proposed that Dr. Whipple be dispatched once more to Lahaina to reason with Abner, and with some reluctance the trim, white-haired leader of Janders & Whipple climbed aboard the *Kilauea* and ploughed his way through the rough channel to Maui. He had barely started down the pier when he saw his rickety old friend pecking his way among the crowd and accosting one of the sailors from the ferry.

"Did you happen to hear any news of a little girl named Iliki?" he asked querulously.

"No, sir," the patient sailor replied, for he was asked this question at each arrival of the *Kilauea*.

Sadly the old man shook his head, turned and started for his home, but Dr. Whipple called, "Abner!" and the lame missionary stopped, turned about in the sunlight and studied his visitor. At first he could not quite understand who the thin, erect man in the black suit was, and then his mind cleared momentarily.

"John," he said softly, still refusing to accord the apostate his former title of Brother.

"I've come over to talk with you," Whipple explained patiently.

"You've come over to reprimand me for smashing the heathen temple," Abner replied contentiously. "Don't waste your words. If the bloody sacrificial rocks of the Hawaiians were evil and worthy to be destroyed, the gaudy red and gold temples of Buddha merit the same treatment."

"Let's walk along to our offices," Whipple suggested.

"We used to talk here, John, and this is still good enough for me." He sat down on a coconut log, under the kou trees, where he could see the roads. "Not many whalers come here any more," he mused. "But do you see that skeleton of a ship on the reef over there? The *Thetis*. How long ago we shipped on that rare vessel, John! You and Amanda, I and Jerusha. Later, you know, it was Malama's ship. Now it rusts on the rocks, like you and me."

"That's what I wanted to see you about, Abner," Dr. Whipple said quietly. "All of your friends, and I in particular, want you to leave Lahaina and come over to Honolulu to live with us. You are rusting on the reef, Brother Abner, and we want to take you home."

"I could never leave Lahaina," the old man said stubbornly. "Jerusha is here, and so is Malama, and I couldn't leave them. My church is here and all of the people I have brought to God. I see the *Thetis* every day . . ." and with mention of the old ship that had brought him to his triumphs and his troubles his mind grew dim, and he added pathetically, as if he were aware that he was losing the thread of his argument, "And I expect Iliki to come back soon, and I should not like to be absent on that day." He looked up in childish victory at his old friend, as if this line of reasoning were irrefutable.

Dr. Whipple, who had seen a good deal of the death of minds and men, showed no irritation with his old friend's obstinacy. "Abner," he reasoned patiently, "the younger men who run the plantations are most determined that you not be allowed to disrupt their good relationships with the Chinese."

"Those pigtailed heathens worship idols, John. I tell you I have seen it with my own eyes!"

"The Chinese are rather difficult to handle at best, Brother Abner," John quietly agreed, "but when you smash their temples, wholly extraneous problems are introduced."

"John, you and I labored for many years to erase the evils of heathenism from these islands, and in our old age we certainly can't sit idly by and see our victory snatched from us."

"Brother Abner," the doctor rationalized, "the Chinese problem is different from what we faced with the Hawaiians."

Abner's mind cleared and he stared coldly at his old friend. "Different?" he asked.

Dr. Whipple noticed that Hale's eyes had lost their film, and he thought to make the most of these moments of lucidity, so he spoke rapidly: "The Chinese religion is an old and distinguished form of worship. Buddha and Confucius both existed long before the birth of Christ, and the systems of ethics which they evolved have dignity. They must not be confused with the raw, pagan rituals that we found here on Hawaii when we arrived. Furthermore, the Hawaiians were steeped in ignorance and required leadership to the light, but the Chinese had a flowering civilization while Massachusetts was still a wilderness, so they do not need the same kind of spiritual instruction that we had to give the Hawaiians. But what disturbs the younger men most, including your sons Micah and David, who commissioned me to come here to talk with you, is that the Hawaiians were never really a part of our society. They lived on the outskirts, as it were, but the Chinese we need. Our whole economy depends upon harmonious relations with them, and anything which runs the risk of driving them from the plantations cannot be tolerated." He had ended his comments with a threat which he had not intended when he started, but there it was.

Abner missed the threat, for halfway through his friend's monologue he had clearly caught its central theme, and now he drew back appalled at the ravages which years and success can effect in a man who had originally launched his career in honor and dignity. The lame little missionary studied his visitor with contempt, and pity, and said finally, with the sorrow of Jeremiah and Ezekiel in his voice, "Dear John, I am ashamed to see the day when wealth and concern for a sugar plantation could force you to come to Maui and tell me, 'It was all right to destroy the gods of the Hawaiians, because they didn't work in our fields, but we need the Chinese to make money for us, so their heathen gods we must honor.' I am ashamed to witness such corruption in the soul of a good man, John, and I now think you had better get back on the boat and go home."

Dr. Whipple was stunned by the turn the conversation had taken, and he again resorted to threats: "Your sons say that if you don't . . ."

With some dignity old Abner Hale rose to his unsteady feet and dismissed his visitor: "I was not afraid of the whaling captains, nor of their rioting sailors, and I am not afraid of my own sons. There is good in the world, John, and there is evil. There is God in the universe, and there are heathen idols, and I have never been confused as to whose side in the great Armageddon I fight upon. An idol is an idol, and if a Christian is tempted to make money from an idol, then that idol above all others ought to be destroyed, for as Ezekiel commanded: 'Thus saith the Lord God, Repent, and turn yourselves from your idols; and turn away your faces from all your abominations.' I wish to talk with you no further upon these matters, John, but when you have left I will pray that before you die you will recover once more the sweet, clean soul you brought to these islands . . . but lost somewhere among the sugar fields."

The little missionary turned his back on his old friend and limped off to his small and dirty shack. When Dr. Whipple tried to overtake him and reason with him, saying, "Abner, you must come to Honolulu with me," the missionary brushed him away and would not speak, and when Whipple followed him right to the door of the filthy hovel in which he was spending his last days, Abner slammed that door against him and Whipple could hear him kneeling against a chair and praying for the corrupted soul of his one-time roommate on the *Thetis*.

Dr. Whipple returned to Honolulu and issued instructions to his managers on Maui that they must assume responsibility for keeping Abner Hale away from the Buddhist temples, for it was imperative that the Chinese be protected from any additional disturbances. The Hale boys sent regular funds to Lahaina, in care of the plantation managers, so that their father could be insured good food and medical care. Twice a year they begged the weak old man to come to Honolulu and live with them, and twice a year he refused.

It was in 1868 that Nyuk Tsin and the Chinese community throughout Hawaii finally realized how strange and barbarous the white man's society really was, for word came into Honolulu that the ancient father of the Hales had died alone, ignored and untended on the island of Maui. The news was difficult to believe, and Nyuk Tsin gathered with her Hakka friends at the Hakka store, while Mun Ki sat on his haunches in the Punti store trying to get the appalling news into focus. In both stores this was the news:

"You say the father of all these famous and rich people was allowed to die in poverty?"

"Yes. I was there, and I saw them find his old worn-out body in the cemetery."

"What was he doing there, this old man?"

"He had gone to care for his wife's grave, and then he was doing the same for the grave of some Hawaiian lady. It looked as if he had died late in the afternoon, falling over the Hawaiian grave, and he was there all night."

"You say he lived in a pitiful little house?"

"So small and dirty you wouldn't believe it."

"And here his children have such big houses. Have you seen the houses of his children?"

"No. Are they good and fine?"

"Li Lum Fong works for his son Micah, and he says Micah's house is one of the best in Honolulu. The old man's first daughter is married to

Hewlett, and they have much wealth. His second daughter is wed to one of the Whipples, and they have a big house, and his second son also married a Whipple, so he is very rich."

"Have his children grandchildren among whom the old man could have lived?"

"The families have two grandchildren, and five, and five, and six."

"And he died alone?"

"He died alone, caring for the graves, but no one cared for him."

When this was said, this harsh summary of the white man's fundamental unconcern for human values and respect for one's ancestors, the Chinese in the various stores sat glum, bewildered. Some of them, reminded of their longing to see some ancestral hall in a remote Chinese village, would rock back and forth on their haunches, trying vainly to comprehend a family with four big houses and eighteen grandchildren who had allowed an old man to die alone and untended. How could the families be indifferent to the bad luck attendant upon such an untended death? In such discussions the Chinese often wanted to speak, to say, "How I long to see my father in the High Village!" but no words came, and they returned to their gloomy discussion of Abner Hale's death.

"Wasn't he the old man who knocked down the Chinese temples?"

"Yes. I saw him once running in with a club. He limped, but when he was knocking down temples he was extremely vigorous, and the plantation managers had to put a guard on him, every day, and if the little old man started for a temple the guard would shout, 'Here he comes again!' and white men would run out and capture him and take him home."

"You would think, under those circumstances, that it would be the Chinese who wanted to see him dead, and yet it is we who are mourning him, and his own family cares nothing about his death."

But in the big houses there was profound, silent grief. A Mormon missionary told Micah Hale: "On the last day your father met the ferry and inquired after the girl Iliki. He then picked some flowers and I met him on the road leading to the church graveyard. He shook his stick at me and cried, 'You are an abomination. You should be driven from the islands.' If I had had my thoughts about me, I should have followed him then, for he seemed weak and faltering, but so often we do not do that which we should, and I passed him by, keeping away from his stick. He certainly went on to the church and tried to get the pastor to allow him to preach again on Sunday, but as you know, he wandered so much that preaching was hopeless, and the minister put him off. That was the last anyone saw of him. He was found fallen across the grave of an alii nui of Maui, a woman, I believe, that he himself had brought into the church.

"That night I had a clear premonition that I had done an un-Christian thing in passing your father by, and once I started to see if he had gotten home correctly, but I failed to do so, but on my morning walk I stopped by his house to wish him well, and he was gone. I hurried out to the cemetery, expecting to find him fallen along the way, but as I explained, he had died at the grave.

"Mr. Hale, I'll not mince words. There were, as you are well aware, harsh comments made concerning your father's death alone in Lahaina, but I know and all like me know how hard you tried to make his last days easier. He was an obstinate man and would permit no kindness. I suffered from his sharp tongue, so I know. I want to reassure you that the true facts are known, and only the fools of the city condemn you."

As I have said, there was profound grief in the four Hale houses, for the children could remember how their father had cared for them, and loved them, and taught them, and changed their sheets when they had fevers and sacrificed his life for them, that they might be worthy children. They could see him, a father of terrible wrath, keeping them tightly confined to the small, walled-in garden; and they remembered his dreadful lamentations when Reverend Eliphalet Thorn took them away from his care. From that day on, each of the four Hale children had tried vainly to return to his father the love he had spent on them, but he would not accept it. He rejected his oldest son Micah for having married a part-Hawaiian. He scorned David for refusing to become a minister. He despised Lucy for having married young Hewlett, who although he was pure white was nevertheless half-brother to half-castes. And he ignored Esther, his baby, for having married a Whipple who had publicly made fun of missionaries. The sorrow of his four children was deep.

But they were also New Englanders, and when the Honolulu community whisperingly condemned them for having abandoned their poor old dim-witted father, allowing him to die in a filthy shack in distant Lahaina, the Hales felt it imperative that they appear in public. They accepted the scorn and walked proudly as if there were no whispers following them. When aggravating hostesses tempted them with invitations, to see how they were bearing up, they accepted, and they moved normally in Honolulu society, grimly bearing the charges made against them. It was their duty.

But the Chinese servants, seeing this, were more perplexed than ever, and in the stores they added to the whispers: "Li Lum Fong told me that last night Micah Hale and Mrs. Hewlett and Mrs. Whipple all went to a party. Now please tell me, please explain how a family that allows their poor old father to die in poverty, untended, can be so shameless as to appear in public, drinking alcohol and laughing? Even before the first year of mourning has ended."

"You will never understand these heartless people," the Chinese agreed.

WHEN MUN KI'S SON Asia started growing into a bow-legged, chubby-faced little toddler, he was promptly joined by the Continent of Europe and later Africa, who rioted around the kitchen floor as their parents prepared meals for the Whipples; and with the coming of these children a curious transformation occurred in the relationship between Mun Ki and his wife. Many centuries earlier Confucius had pointed out that the harmonious existence of husband and wife was most difficult to sustain: "Between the two let there be respect."

It was common, therefore, in Chinese families for a husband never to hand his wife anything, for to do so seemed to imply: "I wish to give you this. You must take it." Instead, he placed the object near his wife and she picked it up at her own time. Some ignored this particular convention, but there was another that all observed. As the scholar at the Punti store had explained to Dr. Whipple, a respectful husband never spoke his wife's name, neither in public nor at home. As soon as a girl married she became simply Mun Ki's wife; that was her profession and her personality. But when children arrived, special care was taken to hide her name from them, and there was scarcely a Chinese growing up in Hawaii who knew his mother's name. It was never spoken.

In Mun Ki's case the problem was further complicated by the fact that his Hakka girl was not properly a wife at all, but merely a concubine, and she must never be called Mother; to do so would be offensive. It is true that she had borne the three sons, but their real mother was the official Kung wife who had remained dutifully behind in the Low Village. By Chinese custom this first wife would be the legal mother of any children Mun Ki might have, anywhere in the world.

So the scrawny Hakka girl became Wu Chow's Auntie—the Auntie of the Five Continents—and by this name she was known throughout the city. She considered herself fortunate, because in many families concubines like her were known contemptuously as "That One" or more simply "She," but Mun Ki was not willing to give her those names, for he was impressed by the Punti scholar's prediction that his Hakka wife was going to bear many sons and that they would share the continents. So whenever the tricky little gambler addressed his wife as Wu Chow's Auntie, he felt a special love for her.

Not one of her children or many grandchildren would ever know her name, nor would they think of her as Mother, for as Mun Ki sternly reminded the boys: "Your mother lives in China." And the boys became convinced that in the Low Village their mother waited for them, and it was to her they owed their devotion. In time a photographer traveled out from Canton, and in some villages he was stoned as a sorcerer attempting to steal men's spirits with his magic, but in the Low Village,

Uncle Chun Fat, who had been in California, said to his nephew's pretty wife, "Get your picture taken and send it to the Fragrant Tree Country." She did, and the Kee boys grew up with this brown-tinted picture of a regal-looking, well-dressed Punti woman staring down at them from the wall; and this photograph evoked in them a sterner sense of filial responsibility than Nyuk Tsin ever did.

She was not concerned with these matters, for as a Hakka she was governed by two supreme drives: above all else she wanted an education for her sons, and to attain it she would sacrifice anything; after that she wanted to own some land. To attain either of these goals she required money, and she had been in Honolulu only a few weeks before she started hawking vegetables. Now, without telling the Whipples, she took in the laundry of unmarried Hakka men, but one day Dr. Whipple asked his wife, "Amanda, what's all that blue clothing doing on the back lawn?"

"We don't have any blue clothing," she replied, and they investigated.

"No more laundry!" Dr. Whipple ordered, but by that time she had already earned her beginning store of coins.

She then switched to serving meals on the side to bachelor Chinese, and this proved fairly profitable until Amanda Whipple grew suspicious of the many strange men who were trailing up Nuuanu and slipping through the back garden gate. "John, forgive my evil mind," she said one night, "but do you think our maid is . . . well . . . all these men?"

"After all, she is only the cook's second wife, and I suppose that if he thinks he can earn a little more money."

"John! How horrible!"

They agreed that something must be done and Dr. Whipple appointed himself detective. Some days later he staggered into the sitting room, choking with laughter. "Ah, these evil Chinese!" he chuckled. "Amanda, Captain Hoxworth should see what's going on in our back yard. It'd prove every suspicion he ever had."

"John! What is it?"

"Mrs. Kee, horrible thought, is serving hot meals. To unmarried men."

Mrs. Whipple broke into an embarrassed laugh and ending by asking, "Why do our servants try so many ways to make extra money? We pay them good wages."

"They are determined to educate their children," Dr. Whipple explained.

"Good for them, but not by running a restaurant on our property." Again Nyuk Tsin was ordered to desist, but again she wound up with more coins than when she started.

Her big venture came when she discovered that two acres of swampland on the Whipple property could be converted into money. This time she went to Dr. Whipple and in the barbarous pidgin that all Honolulu spoke, conveyed to him the following: "Could I use this swampland?"

"What for?" he asked.

"To grow taro."

"Do you Pakes eat taro?"

"No. We will make poi."

"You don't eat poi, do you?"

"No. We will sell it to the natives."

Dr. Whipple made some inquiries and found that Nyuk Tsin had a good idea. The Hawaiians were now working for wages in livery stables and mechanics' shops and no longer wanted to waste their time making poi, so that the profession had fallen into the hands of Pakes. The bizarre idea appealed to Whipple and he told Amanda, "I've owned that swampland for years but it took a Pake to show me what to do with it. The more I see these people, the better I like them."

As the days passed he became increasingly impressed by what Nyuk Tsin could accomplish with land. Whenever she found a few minutes' respite from her long hours as maid, she would hurry down to her taro patch, tie her conical hat under her chin, roll up her blue trousers and plunge barefooted into the soft mud. She built dikes better than most men and constructed ingenious waterways that drained the land so it could be tilled and later flooded for taro. Dr. Whipple, watching her beaver-like industry, thought: "She has a positive affinity for the land." He was not surprised, therefore, when she came up to him one hot day, wiping her muddy hands on a bunch of grass, to ask, "Will you sell me the swamp?"

"Where would you get the money?" he teased.

She astounded him by disclosing how much she had already saved. "The rest I will get from selling poi, and year after year I will pay you the money."

This pleased Whipple, for it was the kind of frugal bargaining his own New England ancestors had probably engaged in when they wanted to send their sons to college; but he had to disappoint her. "This land's too close to our house to sell. But there's some up the valley I might let you have."

"Can we go see it?" Nyuk Tsin asked. "Now?" Her lust for land was such that she would have walked miles to see a field. For nearly fifty generations her Hakka people had yearned for rich valley lands, and here she stood among the choicest, determined to own some. That day it wasn't convenient for Dr. Whipple to take her up the valley to see the useless swampland he had in mind and later he forgot, but Nyuk Tsin never did.

Her progress to ownership was deterred by two setbacks. First her husband vetoed the idea of buying land, explaining: "We won't be here long. It would be foolish to buy land that we would have to abandon when we sailed back to China."

"I want a field," Nyuk Tsin argued in her stubborn Hakka way.

"No," Mun Ki reasoned, "our plan must be to save every dime we can get and take our wealth back to the Low Village. When we reach there, I'll send you on up to the High Village, because you wouldn't feel at ease among the Punti and my wife wouldn't want you around."

"What will happen to the boys?" Nyuk Tsin asked.

"Well, since they're really Punti, with Punti names, they'll stay with their mother." Seeing her shock he added hastily, "Of course, I'll give you a little of the money we've saved and you can buy yourself a piece of land in the Hakka village, and probably we'll see each other from time to time along the road."

"I would rather have the land here," Nyuk Tsin pleaded.

"Wu Chow's Auntie!" Mun Ki snapped. "We're not staying here."

Her second setback involved poi, for clever as the Chinese were, they could not master the trick of making this island staple. Nyuk Tsin raised the taro beautifully, and Dr. Whipple said he had rarely seen better. She harvested it correctly, removing first the dark green leaves to sell as a spinach-like vegetable. Then she peeled the stalks for cooking like asparagus, the flowers having already been sold to be eaten like cauliflower. This left the big, dark corms for the making of poi. In the raw state they contained bitter crystals of oxide that made them inedible, but when boiled and peeled they were delicious, except that they looked like Roquefort cheese. It was these boiled corms that Nyuk Tsin hauled to her poi board, a six-foot-long trough in which she hammered the taro with a lava-rock pounder, smashing and gradually liquefying the mass until finally a glob of sticky, glutinous paste resulted. This was poi, the world's most remarkable starch: it was alkaline rather than acid; it was more easily digestible than potatoes, more nourishing than rice; an infant of two weeks could eat poi with safety, while an old man whose stomach was riddled with ulcers could enjoy it with relish. Dr. Whipple, who amused his associates by having poi at his meals instead of bread or potatoes, termed it: "The only perfect food."

Hawaiians loved poi and were relieved when the Pakes took over the grueling work of manufacturing it, but they could not learn to like poi the way Nyuk Tsin and her husband made it. On days when poi was ready to be sold, it was an island custom to hang along the street a small white flag, and when Nyuk Tsin first displayed hers she had many pleased customers, but later they complained that her product lacked quality. Her poi was not the bland, neutral food they craved, and with apologies they inquired if she had been careful to keep her utensils clean, for whereas in ordinary living the Hawaiians were fanatics about cleanliness, in the making of poi they were maniacs. If a fly lighted on a poi bowl, they would throw the contents out, and the damning word was passed along that Pake poi wasn't clean. Worse, it had lumps.

A further complication developed. The dollar that formed the basic currency of the islands was broken down into three conflicting coin systems: ten American dimes equaled a dollar; so did eight Spanish reals;

so did four English shillings. The latter could be chopped in half with a cold chisel to make eight sixpences to the dollar. Since dimes and reals were of about the same size, the Hawaiians tried to convince the Chinese that a dime worth ten cents was just as good as a real worth twelve and a half, whereas for her part Nyuk Tsin tried to collect reals and pay back dimes, so there was constant warfare.

When the Kees made up their fifth batch of poi, the white flag flapped outside for a long time before any customers appeared, but finally a big Hawaiian woman ambled in, dipped her finger into the purplish paste and tried it upon her tongue. With obvious disgust she grumbled, "I'll take three bundles, for half price, in dimes."

This was too much for Nyuk Tsin. Weighing hardly one third as much as her huge customer, she leaped forward and started shoving the woman back into the roadway, while the big Hawaiian started slapping at her as if she were an irritating fly. A considerable row ensued, which brought Dr. Whipple into the yard with an edict: "No more poi to be sold."

This embittered Mun Ki, who foresaw the loss of much money, and he condemned his wife for being so stupid as not to know how to make poi; but a worse humiliation was to follow. The Kees now had several gallons of the ugly-looking paste and frugal Nyuk Tsin ordered everyone to eat it instead of rice. As her husband bravely gulped the unpalatable starch he made wry faces and then discovered with dismay that his sons preferred it to rice.

Banging down his bowl he cried, "This settles it! We're going back to China as soon as our contract ends."

"Let's sign for five more years," Nyuk Tsin pleaded.

"No!" Mun Ki stormed. "I will not tolerate the day when my own sons prefer poi to rice. They're no longer Chinese." And he made a motion to throw out the poi, but Nyuk Tsin would not permit this. "All right, Wu Chow's Auntie," he grumbled. "I'll eat the poi, but when it's finished, I'm going back to China." Uncle Chun Fat had undoubtedly made a million dollars in California, but it was obvious that his nephew wasn't going to emulate him in Hawaii.

However, one good did come from the poi fiasco. Nyuk Tsin, always an experimenter, discovered that if she cut the stalks of her taro plants into short segments and packed them in heavy brine, with stones loaded on top of the barrel to keep the brew compressed, in time the stalks became pickled. With steamed fish or pork they were delicious, and as a result of her invention she acquired unexpected funds from her taro patch. She sold the flowers as vegetables, the leaves for spinach, and the uncooked roots to the king's poi factory on Fort Street. But the stems she kept for herself, and when they were properly pickled she loaded them into her two baskets and slung her bamboo pole across her shoulder. Barefooted, she went through the town hawking her

Chinese sauerkraut. Dr. Whipple, observing her buoyant recovery from defeat, said to her one day, "Mrs. Kee, do you remember that field that I spoke about?"

Nyuk Tsin's eyes grew bright and Whipple marked how eagerly she awaited his next words, so he said slowly, "I've looked it over, and it isn't worth much, so I'm not going to sell it to you." Nyuk Tsin's face became a study in yellow despair, and Whipple was ashamed of his trick, so he added quickly, "I'm going to give it to you, Mrs. Kee."

Nyuk Tsin was only twenty-two at the time, but she felt like a very old woman who had lived a long life, hoping for certain things that were only now coming to pass. Her almond-shaped eyes filled with tears and she kept her hands pressed closely to her sides. To herself she thought: "The land could have been mine, rich land in the Fragrant Tree Country," and at this thought a pair of tears rolled down her cheeks. Aloud, she said as a dutiful wife, "Wu Chow's Father tells me I must not bother with land in this country. Soon we shall be returning to China."

"Too bad," Whipple replied, ready to dismiss the subject as one of no importance.

But in the mind of the stubborn Hakka woman the land hunger that she had inherited from generations of her forebears welled up strongly. In a kind of dumb panic she stood on the Whipple lawn and watched Dr. Whipple walking away from her, taking with him her only chance of salvation—the promise of land—and in response to a force greater than herself she called, "Dr. Whipple!"

The elderly scientist turned and recognized the agony through which his serving girl was going. Returning to her he asked gently, "Mrs. Kee, what is it?"

For a moment she hesitated, and tears splashed down her sun-browned face. Unable to speak, she stared at him and her mouth moved noiselessly. Finally, in a ghostly voice, she whispered her decision: "When Wu Chow's Father returns to China, I shall remain here."

"Oh, no!" Dr. Whipple interrupted quickly. "A wife must stay with her husband. I wouldn't think of giving you the land on any other terms."

The shocking probability that she was going to lose her land after all emboldened the little Chinese woman, and she confessed in a whisper: "He is not my husband, Dr. Whipple."

"I know," he said.

"He brought me here to sell me to the man you saw that day outside the fence. But he grew to like me a little, so he bought me for himself."

Dr. Whipple recalled the scene at the immigration shed and he sensed that what Nyuk Tsin was saying was true. But he was a minister at heart, and he now advised his maid: "Men often take women for strange reasons, Mrs. Kee, and later they grow to love them, and have happy families. It is your duty to go back to China with your husband."

"But when I get there," Nyuk Tsin pleaded, "I will not be allowed to stay with him in the Low Village. He would be ashamed of my big feet."

"What would you do?" Whipple asked with growing interest.

"I would have to live up in the Hakka village."

Dr. Whipple's conscience had often been stung by the inequities he witnessed in life, but he was convinced that obedience to duty was man's salvation. "Then go to the High Village, Mrs. Kee," he said gently. "Take your sons with you and lead a good life. Your gods will support you."

With cold logic she explained: "But my sons will be kept in the Low Village and I will be banished from them. They would not want it known that I was their mother."

Dr. Whipple walked away from the Chinese maid, kicked at the grass for some minutes, and returned to ask her several questions: How did she meet Kee? Was it true that he had brought her to Hawaii to sell her? Was it true that if she returned to China she would be banished from both her husband and her sons? Where were her parents? When he heard of her kidnaping and of her bleak future he thought for some time, then said bluntly, "We'd better go look at the land."

He opened the wicker gate and led the barefooted woman with the basket hat about a mile up the Nuuanu Valley until they came to a low-lying field, an ancient taro patch now fallen into disuse. Much of it consisted of a swamp running down to the banks of the Nuuanu Stream, but as Whipple and his Chinese servant looked at it that day they could visualize it as it might become: the far end would raise fine taro; the dryer land would be good for vegetables; in that corner a woman could have a little house; and in years to come, the city of Honolulu would reach out to encompass the area. It was an interesting piece of land, worth little as it stood; worth a fortune when energy and planning had been applied to it.

"This is your land, Mrs. Kee." The strange-looking couple shook hands and walked back to the Whipple mansion.

Nyuk Tsin did not divulge this compact to her husband, nor did she tell him of her intentions to remain in Hawaii when he left, for Mun Ki was a good man. As long as he was with his concubine in a strange land he was both kind and considerate, but as a realist he knew she could share no part of his life when he returned to China, and it never occurred to him that this future fact would in any way influence his present relationship. He loved Nyuk Tsin and treasured her four sons. She was pregnant again and he was happy. He was doing well as a runner for the chi-fa game and had established himself as one of the principal mah-jongg gamblers in Honolulu. He particularly liked the Whipples, who were exacting but just employers, and once he observed to the doctor: "It looks as if my six-year cycle began with my arrival here."

"What's the cycle?" Whipple asked, for although he was appalled at the callousness shown by Mun Ki in his proposed treatment of Nyuk Tsin when they returned to China, he liked the brash young man and found him interesting.

"The Chinese say, 'Three years of bad luck, six years of good,' " Mun Ki explained.

After the cook had passed along to other work, Dr. Whipple stood reflecting on this chance phrase, and it explained much about the Chinese. He observed to Amanda: "We Christians focus on the Old Testament: Seven fat years have got to be followed by seven lean ones. The world balances out. Good luck and bad equate. It summarizes the Jewish-Christian sense of remorseless justice, one for one. But the Chinese envisage a happier world: 'If you can stick out three bad years, six good ones are sure to follow.' That's a much better percentage, and it's why the Chinese I meet are such indefatigable optimists. We Anglo-Saxons brood on the evil that has to follow good. The Pakes know that good always triumphs over evil, six to three."

One afternoon he entertained an insight that struck him like a vision: "In fifty years my descendants here in Hawaii will be working for the Chinese!" At the time when this thought came to him he was watching Nyuk Tsin rebuilding her waterways after a storm, patiently leading the runaway waters back home to her taro patch, and as he saw the muddy stream bringing richness to her soil, he pounded his fist into his palm and said, "I've been talking about it for nearly fifty years. Now I'm going to do it."

He drove down to the J & W offices and summoned all the young Janderses and Whipples and showed them a map of Oahu Island. "Four fifths of it's a desert," he said crisply, reminding them of something they already knew. "It grows nothing but cactus and you can't even raise decent cattle on it. The other fifth over here gets all the water it needs, but the land is so steep you can't farm it, so the water runs out to sea. Boys, I've often talked about building a ditch to trap that water over there," and he pointed to the rainy windward side, "and lead it over here." And he banged his fist down on mile after mile of barren acreage. "This week I'm going to start."

One of his own sons was first to speak, saying, "If God had wanted the water to fall on these dry lands, He would have ordered it, and any action contrary to God's wish seems to me a reflection on His infinite wisdom."

Dr. Whipple looked at his son and replied, "I can only cite you the parable of the talents. God never wants potential gifts to lie idle."

One of the Janders boys, a profound conservative, argued: "J & W is overextended. There's no money for chancy adventures."

"A good firm is always overextended," Whipple replied, but seeing that the younger men would surely vote against his using J & W funds, he quickly added, "I don't want you to put up any of your own money, but I'm surely going to gamble all of mine. All I want from you is lease rights to your worthless land on the dry side."

When he had control of six thousand acres of barren soil, he hired two hundred men and many teams of mules and with his own money launched the venture that was to transform his part of Oahu from a desert into a lush, succulent sugar plantation. With shovels and mule-drawn sledges, he dug out an irrigation ditch eleven miles long, maintaining a constant fall which swept the water down from high mountainsides and onto the arid cactus lands. When his ditch faced some deep valley that could not be avoided, he channeled his water into a narrow mouth and poured it into a large pipe which dropped down to the valley floor and climbed back up to the required elevation on the other side, where it emptied out into the continuation of the ditch. Water, seeking its former level, rushed down the pipe and surged back up the other side without requiring pumps.

When the ditch was finished and its effect upon the Whipple fortunes evident, he convened the J & W men and showed them the map of Oahu, with arable areas marked in green. "We're bringing water about as far as we can in ditches. Yet look at this map. We're using less than twenty per cent of our potential land. Ninety per cent of our rainfall still runs back into the ocean. Gentlemen, long after I'm dead somebody will think of a way to pierce these mountains and bring that water over to this side, where it's needed. I beg of you," the white-haired scientist pleaded, "when the project becomes feasible, and sooner or later it must, don't hesitate. Pool your funds. Go into debt if necessary. Because the man who controls that water will control Hawaii."

One of the more conservative Janderses, who chafed at working under Whipple, whispered, "They always get dotty in their old age." And the firm became so preoccupied with making money from John Whipple's ditches that they quite forgot his vision of a tunnel through the heart of the mountains.

WHILE NYUK TSIN and her husband were suffering reversals in the manufacture of poi, they observed that difficulties were also visiting their favorite guest. Captain Rafer Hoxworth, when he dined at the Whipples, showed in his face the strain that had overtaken him with the illness of his gracious wife, Noelani, the tall and stately Hawaiian lady whose charm was so much appreciated by the Chinese. In 1869 it became apparent to Nyuk Tsin, as she served the big dinners, that Mrs. Hoxworth needed medical care, and as the year progressed, the tall Hawaiian woman grew steadily less able to sit through a long dinner without showing signs of exhaustion, and Nyuk Tsin grieved for her.

The haoles, as Caucasians were called in the islands, were not able to understand what had brought their beloved friend so close to death, but the kanakas, as the Hawaiians were known, understood. Of their declining sister they said, "Ho'olana i ka wai ke ola.—Her life floats upon the water." But if Noelani herself was aware of this sentence, she betrayed her reactions to no one. She gave the appearance of a placid, pleased Hawaiian woman, graceful in motion and relaxed in countenance. She seemed like a secure brown rock facing the sea and richly clothed in sunlight; about her whispered the waves of her husband's affection and that of her friends.

Like a true alii, Noelani slept a good deal during the day in order to conserve her strength, but as evening approached she came alive, and when her two-horse carriage with its imported English coachman drove up to the big Hoxworth house on Beretania Street she displayed all the excitement of a child. Stepping grandly into the carriage she commanded the Englishman: "You may take me to the Whipples. But hurry." When she arrived she was a figure of striking beauty. Already tall, she accentuated the fact by wearing high tortoise-shell combs in her silvery white, piled-up hair and a dress with a train of at least three feet which trailed as she entered. In the middle of this train was sewn a loop which could be passed over the fingers of her left hand, the kanaka loop it was called, and guests enjoyed watching how deftly Noelani could kick her train with her right foot, catching the kanaka loop with her left hand. Her dresses were made of stiff brocade edged with delicate Brussels lace. She wore jade beads that blended marvelously with her dark skin, jade rings and jade bracelets, all purchased in Peking. Near her heart she wore a thin gold watch from Geneva, pinned into place by a jeweled butterfly from Paris, while in her right hand she customarily carried a Cantonese fan made of feathers and pale ivory. Over all, she wore her Shanghai stole, four feet wide, embroidered in red roses that stood off from the fabric, and edged with a two-foot fringe of Peking knots. Captain Hoxworth, who loved buying her gifts, once said, "A smaller woman would be dwarfed by such an outfit, but Noelani's always been a giant." When she entered a room, her dark eyes flashing, she was a very noble lady, the symbol of a valiant race. And she was dying.

She loved her clothes and parties and having her children about her, for if an evening passed when less than a dozen friends were in attendance, she felt lonely, as if in her last days her Hawaiian friends had deserted her. Then she would tell her husband, "Rafer, drive down to Auntie Mele's and see if there's anyone having a talk." And if there was, the entire group would be brought up to the Hoxworths' to visit with Noelani, who found breathing increasingly difficult.

Her children had married well, and she found great delight in her fourteen grandchildren. Malama, her oldest daughter, had of course married brilliant Micah Hale. Bromley and Jerusha had each married one of the Whipple children, while Iliki had married a Janders, so that when the Hoxworths were assembled, most of the great island families were represented, and there was much talk of Lahaina in the good old days. In these autumnal hours Noelani enjoyed most her discussions with Micah Hale, who now played such an important role in Hawaii, for he was not only head of H & H, he was also a nobleman with a seat in the upper house of the legislature, a member of the Privy Council, and the administrator of the Department of Interior. Often Noelani reminded him: "I was recalling our first conversation, Micah, on that Sunday in San Francisco when you and I were both so certain that America would absorb our islands. Well, it hasn't happened yet, nor will it in my lifetime. Kamehameha V will not sell one foot of land to the United States."

"We will unite," her bearded son-in-law assured her. "I am more positive than ever, Noelani, that our destiny will be achieved shortly."

"You've been telling me that for twenty years and look what's happened. Your country has been torn apart by civil war, and mine has drifted happily along, just as it always was."

"Do not believe it, Noelani," Micah reproved, stroking his copious beard as if he were addressing a legislature. "Each wave that reaches the shores of these islands brings new evidence that we will shortly be one land. I expect it to happen within ten years."

"Why are you so sure?" Noelani pressed.

"For one simple reason. America will need our sugar. In order to safeguard the supply, she will have to take over the islands."

"Are you working for that purpose, Micah?" the elderly woman asked.

"Indeed, as are all men of good sense."

"Does the king know this?"

"He appreciates the problem better than I do. He prays that Hawaii will remain independent, but if it cannot, he prefers that the United States absorb the islands."

"I'm glad I shall not live to see it," Noelani said wearily as the Chinese servants began bringing in the food.

When the Hoxworths dined with the Whipples the thing that impressed Nyuk Tsin was the extraordinary gentleness with which Captain Rafer cared for his wife. Throughout the Chinese community he was the favorite haole, for although he had abused the coolies on their voyage to Hawaii, and cursed them for leaving the plantations, in other respects he had proved a just friend. The man whose face he had kicked in got a good job, and the one whose ankle was broken when he was pitched into the hold was given money to import a wife into the islands. Whenever an H & H ship arrived with a cargo of special food for the Chinese, Captain Hoxworth was there to supervise the unloading, for he loved the smell of faraway places, and he was a familiar visitor to both the Punti and the Hakka stores. He slapped women on the backside and joked with men. If he happened to be carrying a bottle of whiskey, which he often was, he would knock off the cork, take a swig, wipe the bottle with his wrist, pass it to the Chinese, and then take another swig when it returned to him. He had a free and easy way that the Chinese appreciated and a capacity for suddenly imposing his will upon them which they respected. In private he railed against the Chinese peril; in public he treated them decently.

It was his obvious love for his Hawaiian wife which impressed them most, and the tall, rugged old captain with his white sideburns never looked more appealing than when he was gently helping Noelani into her carriage for a visit to some friend's for dinner. At such times he hurried before her to the carriage carrying her cashmere blanket, which he fixed on the rear seat. Then he waited and held out his strong right arm for her to lean on as she climbed painfully into the conveyance. Next he tucked the blanket about her feet and then adjusted her stole over her shoulders. Then he walked sedately in front of the horses—never around the rear of the carriage—and patted them on the flanks and on the noses. Then he came back to the rear door of the carriage and climbed in beside his tall Hawaiian wife. Giving his English driver a signal, he would sit back with her and nod to the evening strollers while his horses pranced through the dusty streets. Apart from the king, Captain Hoxworth was the most dignified and memorable man in Hawaii, and he knew it.

November nights can be cold in Hawaii, for then the days are short and the sun is low in the heavens, and as November, 1869, progressed, it became obvious to all that Noelani must soon be confined permanently to bed in her last lingering illness, for Dr. Whipple said, "I can't find what's wrong, but obviously she ought to stop going out so much." To this, Captain Hoxworth replied, "Noelani's not an ordinary woman. She is the Alii Nui of these islands and she will continue to ride with me as long as her strength permits, for she thinks it proper to move about among her people."

The nights grew colder and Captain Hoxworth wrapped his wife in more shawls. Once, when she seemed extremely weak and bordering on collapse, he asked her, "Would you prefer, my dear, to stay at home this night?"

"No," she said. "Why should I?"

So he helped her into the carriage and they drove not directly down Beretania but by way of King Street and Nuuanu and he pointed out various sights to her, as if she were a tourist seeing Honolulu for the first time. "That's where we're building the new H & H receiving warehouses," he explained, "and I propose buying land here for our office building. Over there's where the Chinese are opening a store for vegetables and meat."

He kept his sensitive finger on the pulse of Honolulu as it throbbed toward new life, but at the same time he kept close to his wife as she spent her last energies. At dinner that night, at the Hewletts', he altered the seating arrangements so that he could stay near her, and when she faltered he said calmly, "This may be the last time Lady Noelani will dine with friends." But she had rallied, and as December came she told her husband that she enjoyed more than anything else her evening drives with him, so on the eighth night in December he had the carriage roll up to take her to the Whipples' for dinner, but when Nyuk Tsin saw her enter the dining room, like a tall, shrunken brown ghost, she gasped.

At dinner that evening Captain Hoxworth shocked everyone but Noelani by saying a terrible thing: "When Noelani's mother, the great Alii Nui of Maui lay dying, her husband used to creep in to see her on his hands and knees, bringing her maile from the hills. I think it a shame and lacking in dignity to see a sweet Hawaiian lady with no maile chains about her, so I have asked some of my men to fetch us maile from the hills, and I should like to bring it to my Alii Nui."

He went to the door and whistled loudly for his coachman, and the Englishman ran up with maile chains and Captain Hoxworth placed the fragrant vines about his wife's shoulders. Then he took a chair far from her and said slowly, "The first time I saw Noelani must have been in 1820, when she was a girl. And I saw her on a surfboard, standing up with not a stitch of clothes on, riding toward the shore like a goddess. And do you know when I saw her next? In 1833. I walked out to her home, knocked on the door, and the first words I ever said to her were, 'Noelani, I've come to find me a wife.' And do you know what her first words to me were? 'Captain Hoxworth, I will go with you to the ship.' So we went aboard the *Carthaginian,* and she never left." He smiled at his wife and said, "Looking at the way people get engaged and married today, I'd say they had very little romance in their bones." He winked at her and then looked at the guests.

"To you young men who aren't married, I've only one bit of advice. Hang around the shore till you see a beautiful Hawaiian girl surfing in, completely naked. Marry that one, and you'll never regret it."

He took the sick woman home that night, and she never appeared on the streets of Honolulu again. Her death was a strange passing, a mysterious disappearance. No doctor could explain why she was dying, but it was obvious that she intended to do so. Like the poetic race of which she was the noblest part, she drifted casually away, and in late December she announced: "I will die in early January." The sad news spread through the Hawaiian community, so that all during the festivities of that season big women appeared at the Hoxworth door, barefooted and with flowers, explaining: "We have come to grieve with our sister." For hours they would sit about her bed, saying nothing, and at dusk, like ponderous, doomed creatures, they would slip away, leaving their flowers behind. Before Noelani died she summoned her son-in-law, dark-bearded Micah Hale of the Privy Council, and she directed him: "Look after Hawaii, Micah. Give the king good advice."

"Each time, before I counsel with him, I pray that God will direct me in the right way," he assured her.

"I don't want you merely to be pious," she said. "I want you to be right."

"It is only through prayer that I can discern the right," he countered.

"Are you as determined as ever to take Hawaii into the Union?" she asked.

"I will see it happen," he insisted.

Noelani began to weep and said, "It will be a sad day for the Hawaiians. On your day of triumph, Micah, be gentle and understanding with your wife. Malama will support you, of course, but on the day you exterminate the Hawaiian kingdom, she will also hate you."

Austere Micah Hale wanted to be lenient at this moment, the last during which he would see his powerful mother-in-law, but like a prophet from the Old Testament he was forced to add, "In the affairs of nations there is a destiny, Noelani, and it cannot be avoided."

She replied, "In the affairs of races there is a destiny, too, and ours has not been a happy one." He bowed and started to leave, but she called him to her bedside and said, "I should like to pray with you, Micah." He kneeled and she intoned: "God, survey the actions of this headstrong young man with the beard. Inspire him with gentleness as well as rectitude."

At her funeral in the old Makiki burial grounds Captain Hoxworth caused excitement by refusing to leave her grave. He remained there for several hours, not weeping or carrying on, but standing beside the grave and looking down across Honolulu toward the ships and out to Diamond Head. At Waikiki the surf was rolling in, and he could see the little figures of men riding upon the waves, and the skies were blue with cloud racks piled upon the horizon, and below lay the sea, the restless, turbulent sea upon which his life had been led.

"How wonderful it's been," he thought. "I wouldn't change a day of it. Even now, somewhere out there, the sperm whales are breeding, and I'm part of them. Go to it, whales! Soon enough somebody like me'll come along and stick a harpoon in you. Have fun while you can!"

Captain Hoxworth had never taken great pleasure in his children, allowing them to develop as they would, but now with Noelani gone he suddenly transformed himself into the benevolent old head of the family, and it became his habit to convene his son and his three daughters with their families and to sit benignly at the head of his table, dispensing charm and affection. He spoke of the old days in the South Pacific and of his adventures in China. It was his opinion that a man had to wait until he was dead to know the meaning of God, unless he happened to have known the sea in his youth.

"To sail before the mast when you're thirteen, to know the abuse of wind and foul captains, to find the spiritual solace that arises from the fo'c's'l, and then to drive yourself inch by inch to the captaincy and then the ownership of the vessel, these are the ultimate tests of a man. It's in such contests with fate that a man comes to know exactly how he stands with God. And don't you forget it, you young men who came to your positions the easy way," and he looked sharply at his son Bromley and his sons-in-law: Janders, Whipple, Hale.

He had already spotted Micah as by far the ablest of the group, and at his family dinners, to which the younger men willingly came, he talked more and more to Micah. "Any enterprise of moment is like commanding a ship, Micah. There are plots against the captain, and he's got to put them down ruthlessly. You may not like to kick a man in the face, I never did, but it may be the only way you can maintain control of your ship. And that's what's important. Control."

It was his opinion that the next decade would produce a series of fundamental crises which would determine the future of Hawaii, and, more important, the future of the powerful firms that sought to control the business enterprise of Hawaii. "Disregard the dear, fat, old kings. They are of no consequence whatever and should be kept around to amuse the people. The important thing is Hoxworth & Hale and Janders & Whipple and Hewlett's. Keep them on the right track, and the kings'll have to follow suit."

When he talked thus he was disturbed to find that Micah Hale did not agree with him. "We must settle this problem of the foolish kings," Hale insisted. "It is infuriating to see them wasting the substance of this kingdom, and I am more determined than ever to do something about it."

"Micah!" Captain Hoxworth reproved. "You be content with making H & H the most powerful company in the Pacific, and the kings'll take care of themselves. Remember what I say. Hell, son, you'll be the real king, the one that matters."

"It is not the destiny of Americans that they should live under kings," Micah repeated stubbornly.

"I'll tell you what the destiny of America is," Hoxworth boomed, thrusting his handsome, white-haired head forward among his children. "If Hawaii prospers and makes money, America will suddenly discover that we're part of its destiny. But if you allow the firms to fool around and squander our inheritance, America won't give a damn for us."

In these discussions with Micah the wiry old captain tended to ignore his ineffective son, Bromley, and when Micah argued against him on the matter of Hawaii's civil government, falsely holding it to be of more importance than the profitable governance of H & H and the other big companies, Hoxworth noticed that among his listeners one quick intelligence matched his own, and without ever directing himself purposely and obviously at this attentive listener, be began tailoring his comments so that Bromley's thirteen-year-old boy, Whip, could understand, and he was gratified to see how soon this wiry, quick boy with the sharp eyes caught on.

"I have always held," he said, speaking ostensibly to the boy's uncle, Ed Janders, who had married Iliki—it was curious the way in which Captain Hoxworth named his own children after women he had loved: Jerusha, Bromley, Iliki; but his wife had understood—"I've held that a man's life should begin at thirteen. He should go to sea, or engage in great enterprises. His mind should already have grappled with the idea of God, and he should have read half the fine books he will read in his entire lifetime. Any single minute lost after you're thirteen is an hour irretrievably gone." It was interesting to the old captain that Iliki's husband didn't understand a word he was saying, but his grandson Whip Hoxworth understood it all.

The captain therefore formed the habit of taking the high-spirited boy with him as he rode about Honolulu, and that year the community became accustomed to seeing handsome Captain Hoxworth parading the streets with his alert grandson, introducing him formally to his business associates and explaining shipping customs to the boy. One day the minister asked, "Captain, isn't the boy attending school any more?" And Hoxworth replied, "What I'm teaching him he can't get in school."

He took his grandson down to the wharves to see the H & H ships come in from Java and China, and he made the boy stay down in the fo'c's'l for entire days while he went about other work, saying, "If you've got a good imagination, and I think you have, you can construct what it must have been like to sail before the mast." He also said, "There is one thrill of the sea that every man must discover for himself, the arrival at some strange port after a long voyage. Whip, remember this. Travel about the world. See the forbidden cities and dive into them."

He said this while standing 'tween decks in a converted whaler, and in the half-darkness he added, "Whip, the two greatest things in life are sailing into a strange port and thinking, 'I can make this city mine,' and sailing into the harbor of a strange woman and saying, 'I can make this woman mine.' Whip, when I'm dead I don't want you to remember me as I was in church or as I looked sitting at the big table at night. I want you to remember me as I was."

He left his gig at the wharves and walked westward from the bustling docks until he and his grandson came to a section of evil-smelling little houses strung along a network of alleys. "This is Iwilei," Captain Hoxworth explained. "Rat Alley, Iwilei, and down here I'm king." But if his words were true, he was a king incognito, for no one in the alleys of Iwilei spoke to him. A few Chinese who had made money that week gambling, a few sailors, a few minor men from the smaller businesses of Honolulu ambled past, intent upon their business, and the first thing young Whip Hoxworth noticed was that in Iwilei even men who knew each other did not speak, as if by magic a man was invisible because he wished to be so.

"This is where I often come," the old captain explained, and he led his grandson into a dark and inconspicuous shack, the inside of which was well lighted and tastefully decorated. A Chinese who imported his girls from Macao, ran the place; he nodded deferentially to Hoxworth, who said, "I want to see all the girls."

A truly motley crew lined up in bathrobes and slips: a Spaniard from Valparaiso with no high combs in her hair; an Italian girl from Naples who had shipped into Honolulu on a whaler; an Irish girl from Dublin who knew Captain Hoxworth and who gave him a kiss—young Whip liked her and she smiled at him; two Chinese girls and one Javanese, who seemed forbidding and aloof. "Who's the youngest girl here?" Captain Hoxworth asked.

"This China girl," the curator of masterpieces replied.

"Can she speak English?"

"No. She don't have to."

"Today she have to," Hoxworth replied. "You go out and find me the youngest girl you can, but she's got to speak English. I want her to explain things to my boy here." When the proprietor left to scurry about among the sinks of Iwilei, the Chinese and Javanese girls retired, but the others who could speak English gathered about the captain and his charge, admiring the young man.

"How old is he?" the pleasant Irish girl asked.

"Thirteen," Hoxworth replied, putting his virile arm about the questioner. "And at thirteen it's high time a man gets to know what delicious things women are. How old were you, Noreen, when you discovered the fun in men?"

"I was thirteen," the happy Irish girl replied.

"And you, Constanza?"

"I was twelve, in back of the cathedral in Naples."

"I was fourteen myself," Hoxworth apologized. "And it happened in your home city, Raquella, and that's why I've always treasured Valparaiso. I had shipped on a whaler . . . well, you wouldn't be interested, but I spied on the sailors to see where they were going with such determination, and I marched in after them and said, 'Me, too!' And everybody roared with laughter as I plunked down my shillings, but thereafter they treated me with more respect. And, Whip, they'll treat you with more respect, too. Not because they'll know you were here. That's got to be kept a secret. But because you'll know something the others don't know. And this knowledge is what makes some men men, while the lack of it keeps other men boys . . . all their lives. I'm afraid that your uncles and your father are boys. Goddamnit, I want you to be a man."

The brothel keeper returned with a Chinese girl of uncertain age, but she seemed younger than the rest. She wore a black silk smock covering white pajama pants. She was barefooted and had her hair in a long braid, so that she looked completely alien to the boy who was intended to be her guest. He looked at her with frank curiosity, and when she saw his confused yet eager face, she smiled and took a step toward him. "I like to show him things," she said.

Young Whip was momentarily afraid, and although he did not draw back, neither did he step valiantly forward, so his grandfather benignly put his left arm about the little Chinese girl and his right about his grandson. "Remember what I said about ships sailing into strange ports? Anybody can be brave enough to love a girl of his own color, but to be a man, Whip, you've got to stare right into the eyes of the brown girls and yellow and whatever you meet up with, and say, 'You're a woman and you're mine.' Because what a man's got to discover is that there's no gain in loving a particular woman. It's the idea of woman that you're after. Now you be real sweet with this pretty little Chinese girl. Because she can teach you the first steps in this grand discovery."

Giving the curious pair his benediction, he pushed them gently toward the darkened hallway that led to the private rooms, and as they disappeared, hand in hand, he grabbed the Irish girl and cried, "Goddamn, Noreen, it's exciting! Imagine! The first time!"

The Chinese girl led Whip to a stall and showed him the furnishings. "Pretty, you think?"

"It's real nice," he stammered, holding tighter to her warm hand.

She pushed him away from her, turned to face him and said, "It's possible have much fun with a woman. You see?" And slowly she pulled her smock over her head, and when she had tossed the rustling silk onto a chair she smiled at Whip, placed her small brown hands under her breasts and moved her shoulders sideways in a slow rotary motion. "These made for men," she explained, and without further instruction young Whip moved forward, pulled her hands away and replaced them with his own. Instinctively he lifted the small breasts to his lips, and as he was doing so the girl slipped off her trousers. It would have pleased Captain Hoxworth could he have witnessed how little instruction his grandson really required.

But in other matters the boy needed substantial guidance. He was a wild-willed lad with only an average record at school, and his grandfather surprised him by insisting that he read long and difficult books like *Pendennis* and *Jane Eyre,* while the students at Punahou were struggling with *Oliver Twist* and *The Legend of Sleepy Hollow*. Captain Hoxworth also drilled his grandson on the necessity for showing a profit on anything one went into in the line of business, and his business principles were simple: "If you sell something, never give samples away. Make the bastards pay. And keep an eye on the help or they'll steal the company right out from under you."

There was one lesson, however, which the ramrod-straight old captain impressed upon his tough-minded grandson above all others: "Living seventy years is a tremendous adventure. You're thirteen now. You've probably only got fifty-seven Christmases left. Enjoy each one as if you would never see another, for by God the day soon comes when you won't. You've only got about two and a half thousand more Saturday nights remaining. Get yourself a girl and enjoy her. Never take a girl lightly. You may never sleep with another. Or she may be the one you'll always remember as the best of the lot. But goddamnit, Whip, don't be a weak old man before your time. Don't be like your father and your uncles. God, Whip, you can't even imagine what Hawaii's going to be like in twenty years, or fifty. Maybe nobody'll be growing sugar. Maybe they won't need ships any more. Maybe this whole city and the hills behind will be part of China. But be courageous about guessing. Be on top of the wheel as it turns, not dragging along at the bottom."

At this moment in his grandfather's harangue young Whip made the old man extremely happy. The idea that Hawaii might one day be part of China did not entirely impress young Whip, but the mention of that country reminded him of Iwilei and he said, boldly, "I'd like to see that Chinese girl again."

"So would I!" the old man roared, and he hitched his horse and led his grandson down into Rat Alley, but when they got to the Macao man's place, the Chinese girl could not be found, so Whip smiled as before at the Irish lass, who was heavier than he was, but his grandfather roared, "No, by God! Noreen's mine." And he rustled up Raquella from Valparaiso, and the Spanish girl was so pleased with the idea of being with a bright-eyed young boy that when she had him alone she tore at him like a tigress, and he fought with her, tearing a red welt across her back until with a tempestuous sigh of joy she pulled him onto the floor and taught him things no boy in Honolulu and few men knew.

And it was strange, but when he left Iwilei that day he was not thinking of women, but of strange ports, and the insatiable fighting of the world, and of ships—his ships—traveling to all parts of the globe to bring home strange people and stranger produce. "I don't want to go back to Punahou," he announced that evening at his grandfather's big table.

"What do you want to do?" asked his proper father, whose main job in life was hiding the fact that he was half-Hawaiian.

"I want to go to sea," young Whip replied.

"That you shall!" his grandfather promised, but this was a promise that was most difficult to keep, and for a while it seemed as if the stuffy uncles, who did not know the wild, free girls of Iwilei, would triumph.

"The boy has got to finish Punahou and go to Yale," Bromley Hoxworth insisted.

"To hell with Yale," Captain Hoxworth shouted. "Yale never did good for any man who wasn't already formed by his own experiences. Your son is a different breed, Bromley. He's for the sea."

"He's got to get an education to prepare him for his later responsibilities with H & H," Bromley insisted.

"Listen to me, you blind, blind men!" Hoxworth stormed. "That is exactly my purpose in sending him to sea. So that he can obtain the education in the world that he will require if he is going to run your companies well. It is for your sakes that I want him to sail before the mast. Because there has got to be somebody in this timorous outfit who has developed courage and a free new way of looking at things." He slumped back in his chair and said, "I'm growing tired of arguments."

The uncles supported Bromley, bearded Micah proving especially effective with his contention that a new day had arisen in Hawaii, one that required the exercise of prudence and conservative management. "It is our job to hold onto our position and consolidate our good fortune while we ponder what can be done about bringing these islands into the American orbit. Caution, hard work and intellectual capacity are what we require. Bromley's right. The place to acquire those virtues is at Yale."

"Colossal horse manure!" Captain Hoxworth responded from his slumped position at the head of the table. "The abilities you're referring to, Micah, can always be bought for fifteen hundred Mexican dollars a year, and do you know why they can be bought as cheaply as that? Because your goddamned Yale College can always be depended upon to turn out exactly that kind of man in bigger supply than the market can possibly absorb. But a man of daring, schooled at sea and in commerce and in knockdown fights . . ." He rose from the table and left in disgust. "Such men don't come cheap. Nobody turns them out in large quantities."

The uncles kept young Whip sequestered from his grandfather, lest the stubborn old man ship the boy on one of the many H & H cargo carriers about to sail from Honolulu. To balk what they suspected was the old captain's plan, they prepared to ship Whipple back to New England, where in rather quieter quarters he could prepare himself for Yale; but one March morning in 1870 Captain Hoxworth ferreted out where his grandson was being kept, and he drove there hurriedly in his gig and told the boy: "Hurry, Whip, we've got only a few minutes."

"For what?"

"You're shipping to Suez."

The stalwart young fellow, now almost fourteen and tall for his age, smiled at his erect old grandfather and said, "I have no clothes here."

"Come as you are. You'll appreciate clothes more if you have to work for them."

They drove rapidly to the docks, where Whip automatically headed for a large H & H ship which seemed ready to put out to sea, whereupon his grandfather caught his arm, wheeled him about in the sunlight, and asked scornfully, "Good God, Whip! Do you think I'd ship you on one of my own boats? There's what you ride in, son!" And he pointed to a three-masted weather-beaten old whaler from Salem, Massachusetts.

The years had not been good to this ship, for she had entered the whaling trade after its peak had been reached, and without ever finding her logical place among the wandering ships of the world, she had stumbled from one occupation to another. Three times she had changed her rigging and now sailed as a barkentine, bound for a speculative run to Manila for an overload of mahogany which the Khedive of Egypt required for a palace he was building. She had already waited at the pier half an hour beyond her announced time of departure, but since she had consistently missed the master schedule by which the oceans of the world operate, this was no new experience. Nevertheless, her captain chafed and he was not in a good humor when Rafer Hoxworth hurried up with his grandson.

"This is the boy I told you of," Hoxworth said.

"Looks strong," the surly captain snarled. "Get below."

"I'd like a minute with him," Hoxworth said.

"You can have six," the captain agreed.

Quickly Rafer Hoxworth swung himself down into the fo'c's'l, grabbed his grandson by the arms and said hurriedly, "Once you leave this harbor, Whipple, that evil-tempered man topside has the absolute power of life and death over you. His word is law, and he's no puny Yale professor. He's a tough, cruel man, and you'll get no sympathy from either him or me if you play the coward.

"Now, Whip, if you get into a fight, and you will, remember one thing. Fight to kill. There's no other rule. And when you've got a man fairly licked and on the deck, always kick him in the face so that when he gets up he can't contend that he almost had you down. Bruise him, scar him, mutilate him so that he can never forget who's boss. And when you've done this, help him up and be generous.

"Whip, you've tasted Chinese girls and Spaniards. There are a thousand more to sample. Try 'em all. That's the one thing you'll do in life that you'll never regret. Whip, I want you to come home a man."

As the fleeting seconds passed, the youth wished vainly that he could prolong this moment endlessly, for he felt deeply attached to this wild old grandfather of his, but the last question he asked was so surprising both to himself and to his grandfather that Rafer Hoxworth fell back a few steps: "Grandfather, if you liked the girls at Iwilei so much, how did you feel about Noelani? I can't get this straight."

There was a moment of silence, and then Rafer said, "When Noelani's mother died she weighed close to four hundred pounds. Your great-grandmother. And every day her husband crawled into her presence on his hands and knees, bringing her maile chains. That's a good thing for a man to do."

"But how can you love a lot of girls and one woman, too? At the same time?"

"You ever study the skies at night, Whip? All the lovely little stars? You could reach up and pinch each one on the points. And then in the east the moon rises, enormous and perfect. And that's something else, entirely different."

He shook his grandson's hand and scrambled topside, waved to the surly captain, and leaped down onto the dock. The old whaler creaked and groaned as her ropes were loosened. A fresh wind came down off the mountains in back of Honolulu, and a voyage was commenced.

When it was discovered what Hoxworth had done with his grandson, the entire community was outraged. Bromley Hoxworth and his brothers-in-law talked for a while of dispatching one of the H & H ships to intercept the dirty old whaler and take the boy off, but Hoxworth pointed out: "He signed papers, and if you know the captain of that ship, the only way that boy will ever get off is either to die at sea and be buried feet-first under a scrap of canvas, or serve his time properly like a man."

Later, Honolulu softened toward the resolute old captain and the citizenry began to speak of him with amused affection, recognizing him for what he was: the leading resident of the islands. If he entered a bank, he was treated with deference. In church he was bowed to by the pastors, and at the library, which he had always supported with generous gifts, he was accepted as the patron saint of learning. The Chinese of Honolulu referred to him as "that courtly, sweet old man."

He died in June, 1870, full of years and public acclaim. At his deathbed were Hales and Whipples and Janderses and Hoxworths—the leaders of Hawaii—but the surviving mortal on whom his thoughts rested was his grandson Whip, happily bedded down in a Manila brothel with an agile little Cochinese lately imported from Saigon.

ON THE AFTERNOON of Captain Rafer Hoxworth's funeral, Dr. John Whipple, then seventy-one years old but spare and well preserved, returned from the cemetery to his home, where he found the pregnant Nyuk Tsin waiting for him, and he supposed that finally she had surrendered her prejudices and had come to ask his medical advice upon her condition, but that was not the case. She said, "Mun Ki him sore leg, you help," and she requested a medicine to stop the itching that had arisen from her husband's work in the taro patch. Dr. Whipple was acquainted with this curious irritation that sometimes resulted from the immersion of one's legs in a taro bog, so he handed Nyuk Tsin a small jar of unguent, but as he did so he had the clear thought: "I'm getting careless as I grow older. I really ought to see the man's leg for myself." Months later he was to chide himself for this oversight, but in the days immediately following he did not.

Nyuk Tsin applied the unguent to her husband's itching leg, and as she had predicted, within a few days the irritation disappeared, and he proceeded with his work as cook. On the fourth day Dr. Whipple happened to remember about the salve he had prescribed, and asked casually, "Leg, how he come?" And Mun Ki assured him, "Good too much."

But some time later the cook again experienced strange sensations in his right leg and the beginnings of the same in his left, and once more it was apparent to him that American doctors understood very little about the human body, so this time he tonicked himself with Chinese herbs—at night so that none could watch except his wife, who brewed them—and this time the medicine was effective, and the irritation left for good. Mun Ki was pleased, and vowed that thereafter he would fool no more with Dr. Whipple.

But in July he noticed a new sore on the big toe of his right foot, and this one did not respond to normal Chinese medication. When he pointed this out to his wife, Nyuk Tsin argued: "Try the white doctor's unguent," and although Mun Ki knew this to be folly, he allowed his wife to smear it upon the toe, and to Mun Ki's confusion, the sore healed perfectly, and he was perplexed. "You watch!" he warned his wife. "This white man's medicine cures nothing. Next week the sore will be there again."

And to his personal gratification, he was right. The sore reappeared, and worse than before. He therefore drank more Chinese herbs and to a certain extent the sore improved, but now a dreadful itching occurred, and before long it passed over to his left foot as well. Then, to his dismay, a very small lesion opened on his left forefinger, and nothing either drove it away or subdued it, and he hid this fact from Dr. Whipple but he could not hide it from his wife.

Nyuk Tsin could never remember, in later years, just how the horrible, unspoken word first passed between herself and her husband, but she could remember the growing dread that filled their days—still with no words spoken and with life proceeding casually between them—until one morning, when she heard her husband scratching his legs, she went to him boldly, took him by the hands and said, "Wu Chow's Father, I must go to see the Chinese doctor." He dropped his eyes away from hers, sat staring at the floor and finally agreed: "You had better see him."

After the noonday meal was served, Nyuk Tsin slipped out through the garden gate and hurried downtown to the Chinese temple, where after much bowing she lighted incense before the compassionate picture of Lu Tsu, to whose wisdom she confided these facts: "Wu Chow's Father has an itching that will not go away, and his finger is sore. We are afraid, Lu Tsu, and hope that you who know all medicines will aid us." She prayed for a long time, then sought out the priest, a shaven-headed man with a kindly face and a bamboo holder containing nearly a hundred numbered slivers of wood. Carefully he moved the bamboo in an arc, repeating old prayers of proved efficiency, and gradually one of the sticks worked itself loose from the others, and it was number forty-one, a number which contained elements of hope. On a small piece of paper the priest wrote "Forty-one" and for a dime he gave it to Nyuk Tsin.

She took her prescription across the river to a dirty little drug shop in Rat Alley, and when she handed it to the herb doctor he said, "Ah, forty-one is a very good medicine. You're lucky today." Behind him he had row after row of boxes containing precious herbs, and from box forty-one he measured out a spoonful and said, "You must brew a strong tea and drink it with a prayer. Is it for pregnancy?"

"No," the honest woman replied, "it's for Wu Chow's Father."

The doctor's expression did not change, but he thought quickly: "Aha! Another one who is afraid to come in person!" To Nyuk Tsin he said casually, "This is a fine medicine for itching legs."

"I'm glad," Nyuk Tsin said, not noticing that it was not she who had introduced the subject of itching legs.

Then, as she was about to leave, the doctor said in an offhand manner, "I'm sure this will cure your man, but if it doesn't, remember! I know all the medicines. Remember." And as soon as Nyuk Tsin had gone, the doctor ran into another alley and cried, "Look Sing! Look Sing! Follow that one."

"Which one?" the loafer asked.

"The Hakka woman, with the big feet." But Nyuk Tsin was hurrying home by a different route, and that day the spy did not overtake her. When he reported his failure to the herbalist the latter shrugged his shoulders and said, "She'll be back."

Medicine forty-one was completely ineffective and the growing agony in Nyuk Tsin's mind could not be put to rest. "Wu Chow's Father," she implored, "you must come with me to the Chinese doctor."

"I am afraid," Mun Ki said.

"He told me he knew all the medicines," Nyuk Tsin assured him, so when the dishes were washed and the four babies placed in the care of another Chinese woman, Nyuk Tsin led her husband slowly, and in breathless fear, down Nuuanu Street and across the river to Rat Alley. As they approached their meeting with the doctor, they formed an unusual pair, for Nyuk Tsin in her black smock and trousers did not hobble obediently behind her pigtailed husband, as Punti custom required; she marched side by side with him in the Hakka way, for she was his wife, and if what she suspected was true, in the days to come Mun Ki was going to need her as never before; and he sensed this need and was content to have his strong wife walking beside him.

When they reached Rat Alley, and saw the row of shacks where the girls lived, Nyuk Tsin experienced an abiding gratitude toward the man who had kept her for himself instead of selling her to the brothel keepers, and in apprehension of what her life would have been like had Mun Ki not bought her, she drew closer to him, and when the alley narrowed she even took his hand, and at first he was constrained to throw it back, but he held onto it, and he could feel her fingers softly protecting the unmanageable sore on his index finger, and in that wordless moment a compact was built, and each understood it, for Nyuk Tsin was saying: "No matter what the doctor reports, I shall stay with you."

When the doctor saw them entering his shop he knew what their fears were, and he was certain that this meant money for him. He therefore held his soft, thin hands together professionally and smiled at the worried couple. "Did the medicine cure the itching?" he asked in Punti.

"No," Nyuk Tsin replied. "And now Wu Chow's Father has a sore on his toe."

"I would like to see it," the doctor replied, but when he had drawn a curtain aside so that sunlight could fall upon the floor where Mun Ki's foot stood, and when he kneeled down to inspect the unhealed lesion and the sickly white flesh around it, he instinctively recoiled in horror, even though he had known, when he knelt down, what he was going to see, and Nyuk Tsin marked his action.

"Are there other sores?" the doctor inquired in a subdued voice.

"On his other toes, and this finger, and his shins hurt," Nyuk Tsin explained in broken Punti.

Gravely the doctor examined each of these lesions. Then he rubbed his hands as if to cleanse himself of some terrible scourge. Nyuk Tsin watched this gesture, too, and asked bravely, "Is it the mai Pake, the Chinese sickness?"

"It is," the doctor whispered.

"Oh, gods of heaven, no!" Mun Ki gasped. He shivered for a moment in the gloomy office and then looked like a thrashed boy pleading with his father. "What must I do?"

Now the doctor's natural cupidity subdued any humane reactions, and he assumed his best professional manner—for he was not a doctor at all but a field hand who hated hard work—and assured Mun Ki: "There's nothing to worry about, really. For the mai Pake I have an unfailing remedy."

"You do?" Mun Ki pleaded with animal ferocity. "You can cure these sores?"

"Of course!" The doctor smiled reassuringly. "I have several patients, and not one has had to surrender himself to the white doctors." But Nyuk Tsin was studying the man carefully, and she knew that he was lying. She therefore said, openly, "Wu Chow's Father, this man has no cure. Right now we should turn ourselves in to the white doctors." Her husband caught the phrase, "turn ourselves in," and his wife's implied promise that she would share the illness with him was more than he could at that moment bear, and he began to weep.

"Come," Nyuk Tsin said bravely. "We will go now and talk with Dr. Whipple."

But the Iwilei doctor, fearing to lose a patient who seemed to have money and a good job, protested, in rapid Punti: "Are you, a respectable Punti gentleman, going to give up a chance of escape simply because a stupid Hakka wife thinks she knows more about the mai Pake than I do? Sir, have you thought of what it means if you report to the white doctors?" And he began conjuring up evil pictures: "The police coming to capture you? The little boat at the pier? The cage on deck? The journey to the island? Sir, your wife is pregnant now. Suppose it is a son. Why, you'll never see your own son. Have you thought about that? And all the time I have a certain cure right here."

Of course Mun Ki had thought of these extremities, and now to hear his fears paraded openly had an appalling effect upon him, and he collapsed against the doctor's table, mumbling, "Is it really the mai Pake?"

"It is the mai Pake," the doctor repeated coldly. "The Chinese sickness. You have it; and in another month unless you cure yourself with my herbs, your face will begin to grow big, and your eyes will have a film upon them, and your hands and feet will begin to fall away. Look even now, you poor man!" And he grabbed Mun Ki's index finger and pierced it with a dirty needle, and Mun Ki could feel no pain. "You have the mai Pake, my friend," the quack doctor repeated, and as he saw his patient quivering with fear, he added, "The disease that the white doctors call leprosy."

"You are sure?"

"Any white doctor will see that you have leprosy, and you know what they will do then? The cage on the little boat."

"But can you cure me?" Mun Ki pleaded in terror.

"I have cured many patients of the mai Pake," the herbalist replied.

"No, Wu Chow's Father," Nyuk Tsin pleaded, knowing in her heart that this doctor was a fraud, but the herbalist realized that only a little additional pressure was required to make Mun Ki one of his most profitable patients, so he interrupted forcefully: "Be silent, stupid woman. Would you deprive your husband of his only chance of salvation?"

This challenge was too reasonable for Nyuk Tsin to combat, so she retired to a corner and thought: "My poor, foolish husband. He will waste his money with this evil man, and in the end we shall have to run away to the hills anyway."

So Mun Ki, in the silence, made his decision. "I will try your cures," he said, and the quick-witted doctor replied, "It will take a little time, but trust in me and you will be cured. How much money did you bring with you?" Mun Ki, in panic, opened his purse and showed the doctor his meager store of dimes and shillings and reals, and the doctor said happily, "Well, this will more than pay for the first bundles of herbs, so you see it isn't going to cost much, after all." But when Nyuk Tsin started to draw back some of the reals, the doctor prudently slipped his hand over the coins and suggested: "I'll give you more herbs so you won't have to come all the way back to Iwilei so soon."

"The herbs will cure me?" Mun Ki pleaded.

"Without fear," the doctor reassured him, and with their cloth-wrapped bundle of herbs Mun Ki and his wife left the medical man and walked home.

But now they were a different couple, for the unspoken fears that had haunted them when they journeyed to Iwilei had become realities: Mun Ki was a leper, and the law said sternly that he must give himself up, and be exiled for the rest of his life to a dismal lepers' island. He was different from all men, for he was irretrievably doomed to die of the most horrible disease known to man: His toes would fall away and his fingers. His body would grow foul, and from long distances it would be possible to smell him, as if he were an animal. His face would grow big and thick and scaly and hairy, like a lion's; and his eyes would glass over like an owl's in daylight; and then his nose would waste away, and his lips fall off, and the suppurating sores would creep across his cheeks and eat away his chin until at last, faceless, formless, without hands or feet, he would die in agony. He was a leper. Those were the thoughts of pigtailed Mun Ki on the hot July day in 1870 when he walked bedazed and in mental anguish back from Iwilei.

His wife, walking boldly beside him and keeping his doomed fingers in her protecting hand, had a much simpler thought: "I will stay with him, and if he must hide in the hills, I will hide with him, and if he is caught and sent to the leper island, I will go with him." In these simple thoughts she found solace, and never once in the months that followed did she deviate from them.

When she led her stupefied husband back to the kitchen at Dr. Whipple's she did exactly as the quack doctor had ordered: she brewed the ugly-smelling herbs and made her husband drink the broth. Where the doctor had pierced the finger with his dirty needle, she cleaned the wound, sucking it with her lips. Then she put Mun Ki to bed and cooked the evening meal, serving it by herself.

"Mun Ki not well," she explained in the spacious dining room.

"Shall I look at him?" Dr. Whipple asked.

"No," she said. "He be good quick."

Nyuk Tsin had to keep her diseased husband—for the quack's medication did no good whatever—away from public view, for that year there had been a general roundup of lepers, and some one hundred and sixty had been shipped off to the leper island to perpetual banishment and slow death; suspicious watchers had perfected tricks whereby to trap unsuspected lepers. One man boasted: "I can look at the eye of a leper and spot the disease every time. There's a certain glassiness you just can't miss."

Another argued: "What you say's true, but that comes late in the disease. The trick is to spot it early, before others can be contaminated.

The way to do this is to look for thickening of the facial skin. That's the sure sign."

"No," the first man countered. "There's only one sure sign. When you shake a man's hand, dig your fingernail into his flesh, and if he doesn't wince, you've got a leper every time."

Nyuk Tsin, watching her husband carefully, felt relieved that neither his eyes nor his facial skin yet betrayed the secret ravages of the disease, but she also noticed that he shivered more noticeably than before and that the sores on his feet were growing. "Somebody will see them, and they will tell the police," she thought. To prevent this she went to the Chinese temple, and ignoring Lu Tsu, who had betrayed her, she knelt before the statue of Kwan Yin, the goddess of mercy, and prayed: "Help me, gentle Kwan Yin, to keep Wu Chow's Father free. Help me to hide him."

These were evil years, indeed, in Hawaii. Before the coming of the white man, leprosy had been unknown. Then, in some unfathomable way, the alii contracted it, possibly from a passing sailor who had become infected in the Philippines, and from 1835 on, the great ravager had swept through the nobles of the island, so that the disease was secretly known as the mai alii, the sickness of the nobles, but coincident with the arrival of the Chinese, the virulent killer attacked the common people, who therefore gave it a permanent name: the mai Pake. In the areas from which the Hakka and Punti had come, leprosy was rarely known and it had never been a conspicuously Chinese disease, but the unfortunate name was assigned, and it stuck, so that in 1870 if a Chinese was caught with it, the measures taken against him were apt to be more stringent than those taken against others; so spies were more active among the Chinese, since rewards were greater.

These were the years when an otherwise decent man would study his enemy's face, and when he saw a pimple or impetigo or eczema he would denounce his enemy, and the man would be hunted down, arrested and thrown into the cage. There was no appeal, no hope, never an escape. The doomed man had only one chance to enjoy even the meanest decencies during the long years of his exile: if some unafflicted person, fully aware of her actions, volunteered to accompany him to the leper settlement, she was free to go in expectation of making his inevitable death a little easier. The saintly persons who stepped forward to share the hell of leprosy became known as the kokuas, the helpers. Mostly they were Hawaiian women who thus surrendered their own lives to aid others, and sometimes they themselves contracted the awful disease and died in exile; so that from those agonizing years the word *kokua* was to gain a special meaning, and to say of a woman in Hawaii, "She was a kokua," was to accord her a special benediction unknown in the rest of the world.

Therefore, in the middle of September, when Nyuk Tsin was pregnant with her fifth child and when it became wholly apparent to her that Mun Ki would not be cured and that the quack's herbs were of no use whatever, she waited one day until the evening meal ended and then she sent the children away and knelt before her husband, sharing with him the resolve she had made more than a month before: "Wu Chow's Father, I shall be your kokua."

For some minutes he did not speak, nor did he look at the woman kneeling before him. Instead, he slowly picked up one of her needles and stuck it carefully into each finger of his left hand. When he had tested his fingers twice he said, "There is no feeling."

"Shall we hide in the hills?" she asked.

"No one has spied upon me yet," he replied. "Maybe next week the herbs will work."

"Wu Chow's Father," she reasoned, "the doctor is a quack."

He put his hand upon her lips and said, "Let's try once more."

"We have almost no money left," she pleaded. "We must save it for the children."

"Please," he whispered. "I feel sure that this time the herbs will work."

So she took the last precious dimes and reals of her family and plodded down to Iwilei in the hot September sunlight, and when she entered Rat Alley, she noticed that two men watched her carefully, and first she thought: "They think I am one of the girls," but quickly she realized that they were not looking at her in that way, and she gasped: "They're spies, watching to see who visits the doctor. If they report Mun Ki they'll get a little money." So she hurried down a different alley and then up another and finally slipped into the doctor's office.

He was happy and hopeful. "Is your Punti husband getting well?" he asked graciously. And something in the man's manner that day cautioned Nyuk Tsin, and she lied: "He's very grateful to you, Doctor. All the sores have gone and much of the itching in his legs. It's been a wonderful relief to us."

The doctor was surprised at this news and asked, "But nevertheless you wish a few more herbs?"

"Yes," Nyuk Tsin replied, sensing a great evil about her. "A little for the legs, and he'll be cured."

"He'll be cured?" the doctor repeated curiously.

"Yes," Nyuk Tsin explained, feigning happy relief. "It seems not to have been mai Pake after all. More like a sore from the taro patch."

"Where does the cured man live?" the doctor asked casually, as he filled the jar, and the manner in which he spoke convinced Nyuk Tsin that he was in league with the spies outside, and that he was turning over to them the names of his clients, so that after the afflicted Chinese had used up all their funds on herbs, he could squeeze a few more reals from the government as a reward for turning them into the leper authorities.

"We live at Malama Sugar," Nyuk Tsin said quietly.

"Nice plantation," the doctor replied casually. "Which camp?"

"Number Two Camp," Nyuk Tsin replied, but when the cautious, probing doctor handed her the herbs and started to pick up her family's last coins, she could no longer tolerate him, and she swept the coins back into her own hand and grabbed a blue jar and knocked the top off and shoved the jagged glass into the doctor's face, and when the glass cut him and his own quackery entered his eyes, causing them to pain, she threw the money in his face and whispered in a hushed, hate-choked voice: "Did you think you fooled me? I know you are reporting secretly to the police. You pig, you pig!" In uncontrollable fury she smashed half a dozen pots of herbs to the floor, kicked them about with her bare feet, and then grabbed the broken blue jar to assault the doctor again, but he fled whimpering to the rear of his office, so she hurried away down a side alley, but she paused long enough to peer back at the doctor's shack, and when that man's cries had continued for a moment, the two spies hurried up and went inside to rescue their conspirator, while Nyuk Tsin returned, by a devious path, to Dr. Whipple's. When she reached home, she did not immediately go inside the gate, but walked on, stopping now and then to see if she were being followed. Then she went empty-handed to her husband and said, "The doctor was a spy. He was going to report us tonight, because his helpers were there, waiting."

"What did you do?" Mun Ki asked.

"I hope I cut his eye out," Nyuk Tsin replied.

That night she matured her second plan, for when the evening meal was over, she left the Whipple grounds and moved quietly about the Chinese community, going to families which had come to Hawaii with her in the hold of the *Carthaginian,* for all such men were brothers, and she said to each, "Will you take into your home one of the sons of your brother Mun Ki?"

Almost invariably the Chinese would listen, say nothing, look at Nyuk Tsin, and finally ask, "Is it the mai Pake?" and without fear, for she knew that no *Carthaginian* man would betray his brother, she always replied honestly, "It is." Then the man would ask, "And are you going to be his kokua?" And when Nyuk Tsin replied, "I am," the man said either, "I will take one of your children," or, "I can't take a child myself, but let us see Ching Gar Foo, because I am sure he'll take one." But she noticed that they shuddered when they came near her.

By midnight Nyuk Tsin had disposed of her four sons and her household goods and had made arrangements with a cook for one of the Hewlett families that when her unborn child arrived, Nyuk Tsin would return it to Honolulu by ship from the leper island to be cared for by that cook. She was therefore in a relieved if not hopeful mood when she returned to tell her husband that his sons would be cared for, but when she reached the Whipple grounds she saw an unaccustomed light in her quarters, and she started running toward where Mun Ki was supposed to be sleeping, but when she burst into the little wooden shack she saw Dr. Whipple standing beside the bed with a lamp in his right hand.

The American doctor and the Chinese woman looked at each other in silent respect, and she saw that tears were running down the white-haired man's face. He lifted Mun Ki's hand and pointed to the lesions, and Nyuk Tsin, following the course that Dr. Whipple's finger took across the doomed hand, had to look away. "It's leprosy," the doctor said. Then he held the lamp before his maid's face and asked, "Did you know?"

"Yes," she said.

"I understand," he replied. Then, putting the lamp down he started to question her, but she asked, "Did bad men whisper you?"

"No," Whipple replied. "It occurred to me that I hadn't seen Mun Ki for some time and I recalled his itching legs. I was in bed, Mrs. Kee, and it suddenly came to me: 'Mun Ki has leprosy,' so I came out here, and I was right."

"Morning come next day he go away?"

"Yes," Dr. Whipple said matter-of-factly, but the terror of his words overtook him and he said in a shaking voice, "Mrs. Kee, let us all pray." And he kneeled in the little shack, and asked his maid to do the same, and he formed Mun Ki's doomed hands into a Christian temple, and prayed: "Compassionate and merciful God, look down upon Thy humble servants and bring courage to the hearts of these needful people. Help Mun Ki to face the next days with a fortitude of which his gods would be proud. Help Mrs. Kee to understand and accept the things that must be done." His voice broke and for some moments he could not speak; then, through tears that choked him he begged: "Compassionate God, forgive me for the terrible duty I must discharge. Forgive me, please, please forgive me."

When the prayer was said he slumped upon the floor and seemed not to have the strength to rise, but he did so and asked Nyuk Tsin, "Do you know what I must do?"

"Yes, Doctor. Tomorrow police."

"I must," he replied sorrowfully. "But you can stay here as long as you wish, and all your children," he assured her.

"I kokua," she said simply.

He had to look away from her face as the crushing force of this word struck him, for he knew what it meant: the banishment, the horrors of the leper settlement, the sons lost forever . . . He thought: "I would not have the courage." Then he recalled that it had been Mun Ki's plan to abandon Nyuk Tsin as soon as they got back to China, and to take her children from her, and now she was volunteering to go kokua with him. Slowly he raised his head and looked at Nyuk Tsin. She was a small Chinese woman with not much hair, slanted eyes, brown wrinkles about her mouth, but she was his sister, and he stepped forward and kissed her on each cheek, saying, "I should have known that you would go kokua." He turned away to stanch his tears and then asked brightly, like a minister, "Now, what can we do about the children?"

"Tonight I fix one boy here one boy here one boy here, all fix." She told him which families would take whom, and when this was explained she asked, "Tomorrow police?"

"Yes, I must. In God's mercy I must."

"I know, Doctor. Long time ago I speak my husband, 'Police go,' but we hope."

"God will forgive those who hope," the old man said.

As soon as he was gone, Mun Ki was out of bed, explosive with energy. "We will run to the hills!" he swore. "The police will never find us there."

"How will we eat?" Nyuk Tsin pleaded.

"We'll take food," Mun Ki explained excitedly. He had visions of a free life in the mountains. He and Nyuk Tsin would work for nobody and maybe even the sores would go away. "Hurry!" he cried. "We must be gone before the police come."

Nyuk Tsin looked at her husband with incredulity. How could he hope to lose himself in the hills back of Honolulu, when the police would be on his trail within six hours and when every Hawaiian who saw two Chinese struggling through the trails would know they were mai Pake? It was ridiculous, insane, as impractical as the reliance upon the quack doctor, and she was about to tell him so, but then she looked in a new way at her quixotic husband and saw him as a temporary assembly of earth and bone and confused desire and a pigtail and hands that would soon fall apart with leprosy. He was a man who could be very wise and the next minute quite stupid, as now; he was a human being who loved children and old people but who was often forgetful of those his own age. He was a mercurial gambler charged with hope: he had hoped that the quack doctor could cure him; now he hoped that somehow the forests would hide him. But above all he was her man: even though he was a Punti he had chosen her as his woman, and she loved him more than she loved her own sons. If he had this crazy desire to try his luck once more in the hills, she would go with him, for he was an obstinate man and sometimes a foolish one, but he was a man who deserved to be loved.

It was two o'clock in the morning when Nyuk Tsin finished hiding in high places anything that might hurt her children. Then she went to each child as he slept on the long polished board and fixed his clothes, so that in the morning when the boys were discovered, they would be presentable, and she straightened her bed. Then she took her husband's hand and led him out the Whipple gate and up toward the mountains back of Oahu. She did not depart unnoticed, for Dr. Whipple, unable to sleep, had kept watch on the Chinese quarters, suspecting an attempted flight, but when it eventuated, and he saw the thin little Chinese woman guiding her doomed husband toward the hills, he could not bring himself to stop them or to sound an alarm, and when she carefully returned to close his gate lest his dogs escape, he prayed: "May God have mercy upon those who hope." At first he was inclined to go down and bring the Chinese babies into the house, but he thought: "That might arouse somebody. Anyway, I'm sure Nyuk Tsin left them in good condition." So he sat by the window, guarding the house where the babies slept.

But after a while his New England conscience, undaunted by forty-eight years in the tropics, made him reason: "The children must not be left in that contaminated house another minute. Rescue now might save them from the disease, whereas an hour's delay might give it to them," so in the darkness before dawn he led his wife to the Chinese house, gently wakened the children so as not to frighten them, undressed them so that not a shred of their old garments came with them, and carried them into the Whipple home.

When this was done, Dr. Whipple studied his watch and thought: "Nyuk Tsin and her man have had two hours' lead. It will be all right to call the policemen," and he sent a servant after the officials. When they arrived he reported: "Mun Ki has leprosy. We must burn the house and everything in it," and with his own matches he ignited both the Chinese house and the cooking shed. Then, pointing to the Nuuanu Valley, he said, "I think they headed for those hills."

Throughout the morning he expected the police to appear with the two Chinese, but their capture was delayed. The afternoon also passed, and so did the evening, without the Whipple servants' being apprehended. This seemed strange to the doctor, and early next morning he inquired of the police what had happened.

"There's no trace of them," the officers explained.

"I'm sure they went up the Nuuanu," Dr. Whipple assured them.

"If they did, they vanished," the police replied.

An ugly thought came to the doctor and he asked, "Did you look at the foot of the Pali?"

"We thought of suicide," the police assured him, "and we studied the Pali rocks, but they didn't jump."

Day by day the mystery deepened. Nyuk Tsin and her dream-spinning husband had accomplished the miracle Mun Ki had relied upon: they had fled to the mountains and had somehow disappeared. Fortunately, the quack herbalist and his two spies had had the good luck to report Nyuk Tsin's suspicious behavior to the police before Dr. Whipple did: "We are sure she is hiding her husband, who is mai Pake." So they got their reward, and the herbalist often pointed out to his friends: "If I had waited till next morning, the leper would have been gone and I would have received nothing. This proves that it is always best to perform your duty promptly and let the sluggards lie abed lazily till the next convenient day."

At the end of a week the police came again to Dr. Whipple and confessed: "We've been to every grass house between here and the other seacoast. No Chinese. We've been wondering if your servants could have doubled back and gone into hiding somewhere right around here. You spoke of arrangements made by the woman to give her children away. Which families did she choose?"

A minute search of those premises also failed to reveal the fugitives, so the police said, "We are faced by a mystery. Somehow Nyuk Tsin and her husband have made themselves invisible." And so as far as active energy was concerned, the official search for the leper ended.

On the night that Nyuk Tsin led her husband through the Whipple gate, and then turned back to close it lest the dogs escape, she walked rapidly toward the mountains, and as she stepped boldly forth Mun Ki, trailing a few paces behind, could not help seeing her big, unbound feet and he thought: "On a night like this it's all right for a woman to have such feet." But reflection on this ancient problem that separated the Punti and the Hakka served to remind him of the mournful fact that he would never again see his village, and he grew disconsolate and lost his optimism and said, "It will soon be morning, and they will find us."

His wife, who originally had advised against this ridiculous attempt to escape, now became the one who urged her husband on, assuring him: "If we can get even to the lower hills before dawn, we will be safe," and she began to formulate stratagems, one of which she put into effect as dawn broke.

"We will hide beneath those thickets," she said, "close to the road where no one will look."

"All day?" her irresolute husband asked.

"Yes. There's a trickle of water running through and I have some balls of cold rice."

They approached the thicket from a roundabout way, so as not to leave footprints leading into it, and when daylight brought travelers to the road, none saw the leper and his kokua. Nor did the police when they hurried past. Nor did the children on their way to school. All day stout-hearted Nyuk Tsin kept her man hidden, and for long periods they slept, but when Mun Ki was sleeping and his wife was awake, she was distraught by the manner in which her man shivered, for leprosy seemed to be accompanied by a slow fever that kept an infected man forever cold and stricken with trembling.

That night Nyuk Tsin wakened her husband, counted her rice balls, and started on up the mountainside. She did not know where she was going, for she was impelled by only one driving consideration: the longer they evaded the police, the longer they were free; and such a simple doctrine anyone could understand. They grew hungry, cold and weak, but she drove them both on, and in this manner they escaped capture for three days, but they approached starvation and exhaustion.

"I have no more strength to walk," the sick man protested.

"I will lend you my shoulders," Nyuk Tsin replied, and that night, with

Mun Ki hanging on to his wife's back, but using his own sick legs to walk whenever he could, they made some progress toward their unknown goal, but it was cruelly evident that this was the last night Mun Ki could move, so when morning came his wife bedded him down in a hidden ravine, washed his face with cold water running out of the hills, and set forth to find some food.

That day it rained, and while Nyuk Tsin sloshed through the mountains gathering roots and trying vainly to trap a bird, her afflicted husband shivered on the cold ground while surface water crept in below his shoulders and hips, soon making him wet and colder still. It was a dismal, hungry night, with a handful of roots to chew and not even a remnant of hope to rely upon; and it became Mun Ki's intention, when morning came, to crawl out to the highway and wait until the searching police found him.

But Nyuk Tsin had other plans, and in the hour before dawn she told her shivering husband, "Wu Chow's Father, stay here and I promise you that I shall return with food and help." She smoothed the damp earth about him and saw with dismay that it was going to rain again that day, but she told him to be of cheer, for she would soon return. Crawling carefully among the trees parallel to the highway, she looked for narrow trails leading off into the hills, and after a while she came upon one, well trod, and this she followed for several hundred yards until she came upon a clearing in which an almost-collapsed grass shack stood, with a three-hundred-pound Hawaiian woman sitting happily in front. Cautiously, but with confidence, Nyuk Tsin walked down the path to greet the huge woman, but before the Chinese maid could speak in explanation of her unexpected appearance in the clearing, the big Hawaiian woman asked, "Are you the Chinese who is mai Pake?"

"My husband, hidden in the ravine, is the one," Nyuk Tsin replied in Hawaiian.

The big woman began to rock back and forth on her unsteady chair, lamenting, "Auwe, auwe! It is so terrible, the mai Pake." Then she looked at the Chinese and said, "For three days the police have been here every day, searching for you."

"Could you please let us have some food?" Nyuk Tsin begged.

"Of course!" the big woman cried. "We don't have much. Kimo!" she called unexpectedly, and from the lowly grass house a big, fat, lazy Hawaiian man appeared, with no shirt and a pair of almost disintegrating sailor's pants held up by a length of rope. He was not shaved or washed and apparently he had slept in his pants for several months, but he had a huge, amiable, grinning face.

"What is it, Apikela," he asked, using her Biblical name Abigail.

"The mai Pake is hiding in the ravine," Apikela explained. "He hasn't eaten for four days."

"We better get him some food!" Kimo, the Biblical James, replied. And he hurried back into the grass house and soon reappeared with a ti leaf full of poi, some baked breadfruit and a few chunks of coconut. "No rice," he joked.

"I'll take it to the sick man," Nyuk Tsin replied.

"I'll go with you," Kimo volunteered.

"It isn't necessary," Nyuk Tsin protested, for she did not want to involve these kind people with the police.

"How are you going to carry him back here?" Kimo demanded.

Nyuk Tsin could scarcely believe the words she was hearing. Without looking at Kimo she asked softly, "Then I can hide him here . . . for a few days?"

"Of course!" Apikela laughed, rocking back and forth. "Those damned police!"

"It's a terrible thing to catch sick men and send them to a lonely island," Kimo agreed. "If a man's going to die, let him die with his friends. He's soon gone, and nobody is poorer." He wrapped up the food and said, "Show me where the poor fellow is."

But now Apikela rose and said, "No, Kimo, I'll go. If police are on the road it will be better if I am the one they question. Because I can claim I'm on my way to work, and if they come here it will look less suspicious if you are asleep in the house as usual."

Kimo considered this logic for a moment and agreed with his shrewd wife that things would give a better appearance if the day's routine were not broken, so he went back to bed; fat Apikela marched slowly down the path; and Nyuk Tsin kept up with her by creeping through the rain forest, and the two women had progressed only a little way when Apikela stopped, motioned to the Chinese and said, "It would seem more reasonable if I had two chains of maile about my neck. Go back and ask Kimo for them." And when the huge woman had placed the spicy maile leaves about her shoulders, the procession resumed.

Her strategy was a good one, for when she reached the highway, with Nyuk Tsin cowering behind in the forest, police came by on horses and asked, "Have you seen the mai Pake Chinese?"

"No," she replied blandly.

"What are you doing abroad so early, Apikela?"

"Gathering maile vines, as usual," she said.

They saw the vines and believed. "If you see the Chinese in your clearing, come out to the road and report them."

"I will," the gigantic woman agreed, and slowly she moved on down the road.

Now Nyuk Tsin ran ahead, and it was fortunate that she did so, for when she reached the spot where she had left her husband, she saw that Mun Ki had disappeared, and she experienced a moment of despair, but she was soon able to pick up his tracks through the muddy leaves and she guessed that he was headed toward the highway, to give himself up. In panic Nyuk Tsin followed his trail and saw him just as he was about to climb an embankment and cry to passing strangers. Leaping ahead, she dashed up behind him and caught his legs, grappling with him and dragging him back down into the forest. "I have brought you food," she gasped.

"Where?" he asked, sure that his wife's empty hands proved the hoax.

"There!" Nyuk Tsin replied, and through the trees that edged the highway she pointed to the figure of a huge woman, rolling and wheezing along in a tentlike brown dress made of Boston fabric. She wore maile chains about her neck and an unconcerned, happy smile upon her enormous brown face.

"Who's that?" Mun Ki whispered.

"Apikela," his wife replied, and darted out to haul the Hawaiian maile-gatherer into the forest. The big woman looked at the leper's sad condition and tears came into her eyes. Handing Nyuk Tsin the bundle of food, she gathered the scrawny Chinese to her capacious bosom and whispered, "We will take care of you."

For nearly a month Apikela and her slothful husband Kimo sequestered the Chinese, sharing with them their meager supplies of food. Because there were now four to feed, Apikela had to go each day into the forest to gather maile, which her husband prepared for market by skillfully slitting the bark, cutting out the pithy core, and leaving a fragrant supple vine that could be woven into leis. Periodically he lugged the maile into Honolulu, peddling it among the flower merchants. With the money thus gained he would shoot a few games of pool, buy some breadfruit, a little pork and some rice. Since Hawaiians rarely ate rice, this purchase occasioned comment, which Kimo rebuffed by observing, "I'm switching to rice so I'll be smart, like a Pake."

Once when big, lazy Kimo ambled home with rice, Nyuk Tsin bit her lip and asked, "Why do you do this for us, Kimo?" And Apikela interrupted, saying, "When we were children going to the church we were often told of how Jesus loved the lepers, and it was a test of all good men how they treated those who were sick. And no leper ever came to Jesus without receiving aid, and no leper will come to the house of Kimo and Apikela to be turned away."

"How much longer can we hide here?" Nyuk Tsin asked.

"Until the man dies," Apikela said resolutely.

And they lived like this for another week, and then a spy in the Honolulu store put two and two together, reasoning: "Kimo never before sold such amounts of maile. And he never bought rice, either. It is Kimo who is hiding the mai Pake Chinese!" And this man hurried to the police and told them, "I am certain that Kimo and Apikela, in the clearing up toward the Pali, are hiding the mai Pake." So the spy got a good reward for his ability to think cleverly, and that afternoon the police crept in upon the clearing. When they charged out, Nyuk Tsin grabbed a frail stick and tried desperately to fight them off, and big Apikela tried to wrestle with them, and Kimo shouted, "Who was the evil man who betrayed us?" But weak and shivering Mun Ki walked out of the little near-collapsing grass shack and gave himself up. The police were so pleased with having taken the fugitives that they started immediately to hustle them away, but Nyuk Tsin cried in Hawaiian, "Let us at least thank these good people," but she was not allowed this courtesy, and as she was dragged down the path and onto the highway she looked back and saw the two enormous Hawaiians weeping as their friends were hauled into final custody.

When Dr. Whipple heard that his Chinese servants had been captured, he hurried to the leper station, where the afflicted were assembled for shipment to their outcast island, and sought out Nyuk Tsin and her husband. "I wish you had escaped," he told them in Hawaiian. "I am sorry to see you here."

"Have you taken the children to their homes?" Nyuk Tsin asked.

"Are you determined to be a kokua?" Whipple countered.

"Yes."

"You're free to leave here, if you wish. Until the boat sails." He drove her to his home and showed her the four children, fat and happy in American clothes. She started to laugh and said, "They don't look like Chinese." She gathered them up and said that she would walk with them to their new homes, but Dr. Whipple piled them into his carriage, and they started forth on their unpleasant mission. At the first house, a Punti's, she delivered a son and said, "Bring him up to be a good man." The Punti replied, "It will be difficult, but we'll try."

At the second house, a Hakka's, she said, "Teach him to speak all the languages," and the Hakka grudgingly took the child. At the third, another Punti's, she begged: "Bring him up to honor his father." And at the last house, another Hakka's, she warned again: "Teach him to speak all the languages." Then she asked the doctor to drive her to the Hewlett home, and there she found the cook and his wife and spoke of the child that was not yet born, and she said to these Punti, "You are to keep this child as your own. Give it your name. Teach it to revere you as its just parents."

"When will the child get here?" the people asked.

"As soon as a ship leaves from the leper island," Nyuk Tsin replied, and the intended parents shivered with apprehension.

On the way back to the quarantine station, Dr. Whipple drove a short distance up Nuuanu Valley to the land which he had given Nyuk Tsin. Placing stones at the corners of a seven-acre field, he assured her, "Mrs. Kee, I have entered this plot at the land court and paid taxes on it. When your husband dies, because he can't live much longer, you come back here and start a little garden and get your children back with you."

From the carriage Nyuk Tsin looked at the wet land, and it seemed impossibly beautiful to her. "I will remember this land," she said in Hawaiian.

But when Dr. Whipple started to turn the horses around, he saw coming toward him two huge Hawaiians, and when they detected Nyuk

Tsin in the carriage, they cried, "Pake, Pake! We have come for the children!"

They ran as fast as their enormous bulk permitted and caught hold of their friend's hands. "Surely you will let us keep the children for you," they pleaded.

"You have such a small house," Nyuk Tsin protested.

"It's big enough for children!" Apikela cried expansively, opening her arms like swinging gates. "Please, Pake wahine! You'll let us have the children?"

Nyuk Tsin spent some time considering this strange request, and she wished that Mun Ki were present to help her, but she was sure he would approve her conclusion: "The Punti and the Hakka families might grow weary of our children, even though we are all from the *Carthaginian.* But Apikela and Kimo will love them forever." So Nyuk Tsin spoke for her family: "We will give the children to you." And she asked Dr. Whipple to drive back to the houses where the children were and she explained to the Chinese: "It will be better this way because Apikela and Kimo will be able to keep all the children together. But I hope, for my husband's sake, that you will give them some money from time to time."

"Money? For keeping children?" fat Apikela asked in astonishment, and Nyuk Tsin thought how strange it was that Chinese families with good jobs always found it difficult to accept one strange child, but Hawaiians who had nothing could invariably find space for one child, or three, or five. She last saw her boys heading back up the Pali, one baby in Apikela's arms, one in Kimo's, and the two older boys trudging happily behind.

When the time came for the panel of doctors to certify that Mun Ki was indeed a leper, and therefore subject to banishment for life without right of appeal, they reported: "Aggravated case of leprosy. Lesions both external and internal. Banishment to Kalawao imperative." The papers were signed. The three doctors left, and Whipple said to the condemned man, "Mun Ki, wherever a human being goes, there is a challenge. Be the best man you can, and your gods will look with favor upon you. And may my God in His heaven protect you. Good-bye." Bowed with the grief that comes upon all men who watch the swinging changes of life, Dr. John Whipple went home.

Two days later forty condemned lepers were assembled and marched through the streets of Honolulu toward the pier where the leper ship, *Kilauea,* waited. As the ghostly men and women walked, the citizens of the city drew back in horror, for some hobbled along on feet that had no toes and others stared vacantly ahead from horrible faces that had no cheeks and whose lips and noses had fallen away. In silence the doomed lepers approached the *Kilauea,* a small, snout-nosed little craft of four hundred tons with a grimy smokestack and filthy decks. Forward, some cattle had been tethered for the short, rough haul to the leper colony, and as the ship rocked slowly these beasts lowed mournfully. When the lepers appeared, a gangplank was lowered and nauseated policemen herded the doomed men and women aboard; but when the final moment came when the lepers were to be cut off forever from their families, a monstrous wailing began.

"Auwe, auwe!" howled women whose husbands were being dragged away.

"Farewell, my son!" an old man shouted, his face bathed in tears.

"We shall meet in heaven, by the cool waters!" wept a sister whose brother was being shoved onto the ugly ship, this unimpressive ferry to hell.

"Auwe, auwe!" mourned the multitude of watchers as they watched the stricken ones slowly climb the gangplank, overcome by terror and shaking.

In a sense, the lamentation of those on shore was traditional and formalized; but the sounds that now emitted from the decks of the *Kilauea* were not, for the hopeless lepers lined the railings of the ship and cried back their piteous farewells. Condemned women waved with hands that bore no fingers. Men cried good-bye from faces that had no recognizable features. Some of the lepers were too far progressed in the disease to be able to stand by themselves, and they wailed without purpose, adding their cries to the general lament.

But occasionally, among the forty victims, one would appear whose countenance or character aroused in all an instinctive outburst of sorrow. The first such harrowing case was that of a bright little girl about ten years old who had left the pier with not a member of her family present to bid her farewell. On her face beginning sores were visible as she hurried up the gangplank, and it was obvious to all that she would soon be completely ravaged by the disease, but in wonder and confusion she stepped onto the gently swaying deck of the *Kilauea,* not able to comprehend the awful step she was taking. Out of compassion an older woman, also condemned to exile, leaned down to comfort the girl, but when the child saw the awful chinless face coming toward her, she screamed, not realizing that soon she would look the same.

The next case was that of a man well known for his swimming prowess, a big, handsome fellow with broad chest and strong arms. Many came to see him leave for the island from which no leper had ever returned, and as he stood at the head of the gangplank, turning back to wave his hands at his friends, showing them fingers with the first joints already eaten away, the misery of his condition infected everyone and cries of "Auwe, auwe!" sounded. This communion of sorrow affected him, and he hid his face, whereupon the weeping increased.

But the third case was entirely different, so dreadful that it occasioned no public display of sorrow. It was that of a very lovely young wife, with flowers in her hair, on whose body no one could identify the fatal marks.

Her feet were clean and her fingers, too. There was no infection on her face, but her eyes were glassy, so the well-informed crowd knew that here was one in whom the sickness lay accumulating its strength inside, ready to erupt generally in one massive sore. The death of this girl would be horrible, a total disintegration, and those who watched her walking slowly and with grace up the gangplank kept their sorrow to themselves.

But she was not to depart in peace, for her husband broke from the crowd of watchers and tried to dash up the gangplank after her, shouting, "Kinau, Kinau, I will be your kokua." Guards restrained him, and his wife Kinau, named after one of Hawaii's most able queens, looked back down the gangplank and with visible compassion cried, "You may not join me, Kealaikahiki." And with considerable dignity she stepped onto the *Kilauea* and ordered the guards to drag her husband away. Impassively, she watched him go, and if she heard his frantic cries, she did not indicate the fact, and he disappeared from the dock altogether, crying, "Kinau! Kinau! I shall be your kokua."

When the doomed Hawaiians were all aboard, the police produced the Chinese Kee Mun Ki, and since the disease from which he suffered was known as the mai Pake, the crowd somehow understood that he personally was the cause of this day's tragedy, and they mumbled strongly against him. Alone, looking neither right nor left, he passed through the hostile groups until at last he stood at the gangplank, and then two huge Hawaiians hurried forward to bid him good-bye. They were Kimo and his wife Apikela, and without fear they embraced the leper, kissed him on the cheeks, and bade him farewell. With some relief, the thin, shivering Chinese man walked up the gangplank. He had hoped, on this last journey, that Dr. Whipple would be present to bid him good-bye, but the doctor could no longer suffer the sight of people whom he had helped condemn taking their last farewells. Among the group sailing that day were more than twenty upon whose investigating boards he had sat, and he could not bear to see them go, partly at his command. On days when the *Kilauea* sailed, he stayed home and prayed.

When Mun Ki was safely aboard, the captain shouted, "Open the cage!" And two sailors went aft to a wicker cage that had been built on the deck of the leper ship, and they swung back on its hinges a latticed gate, and when it was open, other sailors, careful not to touch the lepers, growled, "All right! All right! Get in!"

The cage was not large, nor was the door high, and one by one the condemned people stooped, crawled in, and found their places. The wicker gate was lashed shut, whereupon the captain called down reassuringly, "There will be a man stationed by you at all times. If we start to sink, he'll cut open the gate."

While this encagement of the lepers was under way, two other sailors had appeared with buckets of soapy water and now proceeded to wash down the handrails of the gangplank, after which normal passengers were allowed to board, and when they had hurried below to escape the smell of the forty caged lepers the captain shouted, "All right! Kokuas board!"

From the wailing crowd some dozen Hawaiians, men and women alike, stepped forward and in a kind of spiritual daze groped for the clean handrails of the gangplank. They were the kokuas, that strange band of people who in Hawaii in the later years of the nineteenth century proved that the word love had a tangible reality, and as each kokua reached the deck of the *Kilauea* a police marshal asked carefully, "Are you sure you know what you are doing in volunteering for the lazaretto?" And one man replied, "I would rather go with my wife to the lazaretto than stay here free without her."

No one, looking at the kokuas, could have predicted that these particular people would have been so moved by love. True, there were some old women whose lives were nearly spent and it was understandable that they should join the leprous men with whom they had lived so long; and there were older men who had married young women who had fallen prey to the disease, and it was also understandable that these men might prefer to remain with their girls; but there were also men and women of the most indiscriminate sort who climbed the gangplank to embrace other women and men of no apparent attraction whatever, so that the people on the dock had to ask themselves: "Why would a man in good health volunteer for the lazaretto in order to be with such a woman?" And to this question there was no answer except the word love.

No kokua came to stand beside the little ten-year-old girl, and none came to be with the beautiful Kinau. But there was general surprise when the police dropped their arms and allowed the Chinese woman, Nyuk Tsin, to join her husband, and as she reached the gangplank, once more the two huge Hawaiians, Kimo and Apikela, stepped forward to embrace her, and Apikela placed about the sloping shoulders of her yellow-skinned friend a chain of maile, saying, "We will love your children."

The gangplank was hauled aboard. The cattle tethered forward began lowing pitifully. The crowd ashore started shouting, "Auwe, auwe!" and the *Kilauea* stood out to sea with its horrible burden. When Dr. Whipple, inland in his study, heard the whistle blow farewell, he prayed, "Oh, may God have mercy upon them." For he alone, of all who heard the whistle blowing, understood what lay ahead for Nyuk Tsin and Mun Ki. He had seen the lazaretto.

THE ISLAND of Molokai, to which the caged lepers were heading, was one of the most strangely beautiful islands in the Hawaiian group. It lay in the blue Pacific like a huge left-handed gauntlet, the open wristlet facing westward toward the island of Oahu, the cupped fingers pointing eastward toward Maui. The southern portion of Molokai consisted of rolling meadowland, often with gray and parched grasses, for rainfall was slight, while the northern portion was indented by some of the most spectacular cliffs in the islands. For mile after mile these towering structures rose from the crashing surf, sometimes reaching more than three thousand feet into the air, their faces sheer rock, their flanks marked by dozens upon dozens of shimmering waterfalls. These cliffs formed, at their bases, delectable valleys that probed inland half a mile to end in soaring walls of granite, but narrow and restricted though they were, these valleys were perhaps the finest in Hawaii. Upon the cliffs white goats ranged, so that a boat coasting the north shore of Molokai passed constantly beneath magnificent cliffs, trembling waterfalls and the antics of a thousand goats. Sailors, when the days were idle, would discharge guns aimlessly at the cliffs to make the goats scamper up walls of rock that no man could have negotiated. Thus, the uninhabitable north coast of Molokai was completely cut off from the gentle meadows of the south coast, where some two thousand normal islanders lived.

Jutting out from the isolated yet magnificent northern coast stood the thumb of the gauntlet, a small, verdant peninsula that had been formed millions of years later than the main island, for when the initial volcanoes that accounted for Molokai had long since died away, an afterthought-eruption occurred offshore. It did not rise from a major volcano, nor did it build a major island; it was content merely to add a peninsula of lovely proportions, from whose grassy shores one could look west and east toward the towering cliffs. It was a majestic spot, a poem of nature, and from the earliest memories of Hawaiian history, fortunate fishermen had lived here, building themselves a good community and calling it Kalawao.

Then in 1865, the year in which the Kees left China, the Hawaiian government tardily faced up to the fact that in the strange new disease called mai Pake it faced an epidemic of the most virulent sort. It was ironic that leprosy should have been named the Chinese sickness, for the scourge neither came from China nor did it especially affect the Chinese, but some kind of quarantine was necessary, and the heavenly peninsula of Kalawao was nominated to be the lazaretto. It was generally known that leprosy was contagious but no one knew of a cure; so in frenzied eagerness to take some kind of action, the government's medical advisers said: "At least we can isolate the afflicted." In desperation the lepers were hunted down; the Hawaiians living at Kalawao were exiled forever from their peninsula; and the *Kilauea* started its dismal voyages to the lazaretto. In the previous history of the world no such hellish spot had ever stood in such heavenly surroundings.

On the first day of November, 1870, the ferry *Kilauea* stood off the eastern edge of the peninsula, dropped anchor some hundred yards from the cliff-lined shore and rolled with the surf beneath the leaping goats. The captain ordered one section of the deck railing removed, and sailors began shoving into the sea huge casks of salt beef, cured salmon and dehydrated poi. When the cargo was thus thrown into the waves, lepers from Kalawao swam out to the ship and started guiding the stores to shore, for the colony had no pier at which supplies could be landed in an orderly way.

Now from the front of the ship cattle were led aft, and amidst great bellowing were shoved into the ocean where swimming lepers leaped upon their backs and guided them to shore. Occasionally a frightened cow would toss her rider and head for the open sea, but stout swimmers would overtake her and force her toward the land. A sailor, tiring of the sport provided by the swimmers, discharged his musket aimlessly at the cliffs, and from their cage the lepers saw wild goats leap up the cliffs like the flight of song, flying from crag to crag, and these white animals became the symbol of a freedom forever lost to them.

A longboat was lowered, with three sailors at the oars, and the police marshal who had accompanied the lepers, ordered the cage opened, and called off names, and saw each afflicted man and woman into the boat. There the government's responsibility ended, for the policeman did not enter the boat himself. He watched it move toward the shore, dump its human cargo on the beach, and return. Then he checked off another complement, and in this way the forty lepers were thrown ashore with no stores of clothing, no money, no food and no medicine.

When the condemned were all ashore, the marshal announced formally to the kokuas: "You are now free to accompany your husbands and wives, but you do so of your own free will. The government has no concern in what you are about to do. Is it your wish to go ashore and live with the lepers?"

The kokuas, staring with horrified fascination at the lazaretto, could barely scrape their tongues with words. "I am willing," an old man rasped, and he climbed down into the boat. "I am willing," a young wife reported, and with trepidation she went down. Finally the marshal asked Nyuk Tsin, "Do you do this thing of your own free will?" and she replied, "I am willing." The longboat set out for shore, and Nyuk Tsin approached the leper settlement at Kalawao.

She was surprised to see, as the green peninsula drew near, that it contained practically no houses, and she asked one of the rowers, in Hawaiian, "Where are the houses?" And he replied, unable to look her in the eyes, "There are no houses."

And there were none . . . to speak of. There were a few grass huts, a few remnants of homes left by the Hawaiians who had been expelled five years before, but there were no houses as such, nor any hospital, nor store, nor government building, nor functioning church, nor roads, nor doctors, nor nurses. In panic Nyuk Tsin stared at the inviting natural setting and looked for signs of community life. There were no police, no officials of any kind, no ministers, no mothers with families, no one selling cloth, no one making poi.

The prow of the longboat struck shore, but no one moved. The sailors waited and then one said, as if ashamed to be part of this dismal scene,

"This is Kalawao." Appalled by what faced them, the kokuas rose and left the boat. "Aloha," the sailor cried as the boat withdrew for the last time. The *Kilauea* put back out to sea, and Nyuk Tsin, trying to find Mun Ki among the stranded lepers, cried to no one: "Where is the hospital?"

Her plea was heard by a big, tall Hawaiian man known to the lepers as Kaulo Nui, Big Saul of the Bible. He had no nose and few fingers, but he was still a powerful man, and he came to Nyuk Tsin and shouted in Hawaiian, "Here there is no law. There is nothing but what I command."

The newcomers were as frightened by this state of affairs as was Nyuk Tsin, but Big Saul ignored them, and pointing his mutilated hand at the Chinese couple, said, "You brought the mai Pake! You will live apart."

"Where?" Nyuk Tsin asked boldly.

"Apart," the big man said. Then his eye fell on the young wife Kinau, who still had flowers in her hair, and he moved toward her, announcing: "This woman is for me."

Kinau drew back in horror from the huge, noseless man whose hands were so badly deformed. She shuddered, and Big Saul saw this, so to teach her the required lesson, he grabbed her by the left arm, pulled him to her, and kissed her on the mouth. "You're my woman!" he announced again.

Nyuk Tsin expected to see someone—who, she could not guess—step forward to knock the big man down, but when none did, the awful fact of Kalawao slowly dawned upon her, as it did upon all the others. Big Saul, holding onto the shuddering Kinau, glared at the newcomers and repeated the news: "Here there is no law."

Nor was there any. In all of Kalawao there was no voice of government, no voice of God, no healing medicine. In the houseless peninsula there was not even a secure supply of water, and food was available only when the *Kilauea* remembered to kick into the sea enough casks and cattle. In truth, the lepers had been thrown ashore with nothing except the sentence of certain death, and what they did until they died, no man cared.

If any of the newcomers thought differently, they were disabused by what happened next, for Kinau was an uncommonly pretty girl, and the fact that she had no open lesions made her extraordinary in the doomed community, so that Big Saul and his rowdier companions became excited by her beauty and could not wait till nightfall, when such things usually occurred, and three of them dragged her behind a wall that still stood, a remnant of a house where a family of fishermen had once lived, and the two who joined Big Saul were among the most loathsome of the group, for their bodies were falling away, but they thought: "We have been thrown away by Hawaii. No one cares and we shall soon be dead." So they dragged Kinau behind the wall and started, with their fragmentary hands, to tear away her clothes.

"Please! Please!" she begged, but nothing could be done to interrupt the three hungry men, and when she was naked they admired her, and pinched her body and explored it and laughed, and then in turn two held her down while the other mounted her, and in time she fainted.

For five days Big Saul and his cronies kept her to themselves, after which any others who thought themselves strong enough to force their way into the group were free to join, and when they saw the naked Kinau, as yet unblemished, they were hungry with old memories of the days when they were whole men, and they cared nothing about what they did.

Occasionally Big Saul left the girl, to make decisions as to how the lepers should dispose themselves, and he was adamant that the Chinese must stay apart, so Nyuk Tsin and her husband were forced to live at the outer edge of the community of six hundred dying men and women. For the first six days they slept on bare earth; and they found an abandoned wall against which they built a rough lean-to, using shrubs and leaves, for there was no lumber of any kind. For their bed they had only raw earth, and when rain came it crept under them so that Mun Ki, already shivering with ague, came close to dying of pneumonia. Then Nyuk Tsin, using her bare hands, for there were no implements, scraped together a platform of earth and covered it with twigs and leaves, and this made a bed into which the water could not creep unless the rainfall was unusually heavy.

The two outlawed Chinese were forbidden access to the food barrels until all others had partaken, and even then Big Saul decreed that they live on half-rations, and if it had not been for Nyuk Tsin's resourcefulness they would have starved. On the reef she found small edible snails, and in one of the deserted valleys she discovered dry-land taro that had gone wild. With twigs she collected from the cliffs she built a small underground oven in which she baked the taro, so that life apart from the others had minor compensations. Certainly, the Kees lived better than the pathetic lepers who could no longer walk.

In Kalawao in 1870 there were over sixty such unspeakable persons: their feet had fallen away, their hands were stumps, and they crawled about the settlement begging food which they themselves could neither obtain nor prepare. Horrifying echoes of humanity, they often had no faces whatever, excepting eyes and voices with which to haunt the memories of those who came upon them. There was no medicine for them, no bed, no care of any kind. They crawled along the beach of Kalawao and in God's due time they died. Usually they did not even find a grave, but were left aside until their bones were cleaned and could be laid in a shallow ditch.

Sometimes the authorities in Honolulu forgot to send the *Kilauea* with replenishments of food, and then the settlement degenerated into absolute terror. Big Saul and his cronies commandeered whatever supplies remained, and protected their rights with violence. The death rate soared, four or five cases each day, and a legless woman might lie in the path all day screaming for food or water, and no one would listen to her, hoping that in the cold night she would die. And usually she did, and her tormented body might lie there, just as she had left it, for a day or even three, until Big Saul commanded someone to remove it.

There was no law in Kalawao and there was almost no humanity. What made the situation doubly terrible was that regularly the ugly little ferryboat *Kilauea* appeared offshore with an additional cargo of lepers, and when they were thrown ashore with nothing, Big Saul would move among them telling them the ultimate, terrifying truth: "Here there is no law."

After six weeks of keeping the beautiful young wife Kinau a prisoner, during which time more than eighteen men enjoyed her unmarked body, she was turned loose for whoever wanted her. She was allowed one flimsy dress, but the way in which she wore it proved that she had by God's grace lost her mind. She could remember nothing of what had happened to her, and she walked in a daze, unable to focus on the present, so that for a space of three or four months whatever man wanted her simply grabbed her and took her to where he slept on the cold earth and played with her for as long as he wished. Then he shoved her along, and she moved like a ghost, her dress askew and no flowers in her matted hair, until some other man wanted her, and then she was his. The women of Kalawao felt sorry for her, but each had her own problem, so that no one tended the poor crazy girl.

In the fourth month, in February of 1871, that is, the virulent leprosy that abided in Kinau broke loose, and within the space of a few weeks she became a horribly riddled thing, a walking corpse with thick, bloated face, shivering lips about to fall away and sickening illness in her breasts. Now men left her alone, but in her dementia she took off her flimsy dress and exposed the sores of her body. She walked slowly from Big Saul to his first lieutenant and then on to his second, whimpering, "Now I should like to lie with you again." She became such a sore on the community that men could not stand seeing her approach, her body falling apart, and finally Big Saul said, "Somebody ought to knock that one on the head." So on a dark night, somebody did, and she lay dead in the path for two days before she was finally dragged away for burial.

Of course, no woman was safe on Kalawao, for Big Saul and his men were free to take whom they liked, and those who arrived on the beach with no men to protect them suffered grievously, for they were usually women not far advanced in the disease, and to be raped repeatedly by men with no faces or with hands eroded to stumps was unbearable, but there was no escape, and Kalawao was filled with women who fell into a kind of stupor, crying to themselves, "Why has God punished me?"

It must not be assumed that women were blameless for the degeneration that overtook Kalawao, for there were many presentable women who felt: "I have been abandoned by society. There is no law here and no one cares what I do." Such women helped the men brew a raw and savage liquor from roots of the ti plant, or muddy beer from stewed sweet potatoes, and for weeks at a time, whole sections of the leper population stayed madly drunk, coursing loudly through the settlement, brawling, screaming indecencies at the general population and winding up in some public place naked and lustful, there to indulge themselves with one another to the applause of cheering witnesses. Those who inflamed these orgies and who seemed to enjoy them most were women, and it was not uncommon in those days, when no priests or ministers or government officials were present to protect order, to see a half-naked woman, at the end of a nine-day drunk, stagger into a public place and cry, "I can have intercourse with any four men here, and when I'm through with them, they'll be half dead." And volunteers would leap at the offer, and there would be a wild, insane testing to see if she could make good her challenge, and when she was finished, she would fall asleep in a drunken, exhausted stupor, right on the ground where she lay, and the night rains would come and no one would cover her, and after a few years she would die, not of leprosy, but of tuberculosis.

If anyone in those years had wished to see humanity at its positive lowest, humanity wallowing in filth of its own creation, he would have had to visit Kalawao, for not only was the peninsula cursed by leprosy; it was also scarred by human stupidity. The peninsula had two sides, an eastern where cold winds blew and rain fell incessantly, and a western where the climate was both warm and congenial; but the leper colony had been started on the inclement eastern shore, and there the government insisted that it be kept while the kindly western shore remained unpopulated. The eastern location, being close to the towering cliffs, received its first sunlight late in the day and lost it early in the afternoon; but on the western slope there was adequate sun. Most ridiculous of all, even though the cliffs threw down a hundred waterfalls, none had been channeled into the leper settlement. At first a little had been brought down by an inadequate, tied-together pipe, but it had long since broken, so that all water had to be lugged by hand several miles, and often dying people with no kokuas to help them would spend their last four or five days pleading helplessly for a drink which they were never given. For six indifferent years no official in Honolulu found time to concern himself with such problems or allocate even miserly sums to their solution. In ancient times it had been said, "Out of sight, out of mind," and rarely in human history had this calloused apothegm been more concisely illustrated than at the Kalawao lazaretto. The government had decreed: "The lepers shall be banished," as if saying the words and imprisoning the leprous bodies somehow solved the problem.

IT WOULD NOT be fair, however, to say that during these appalling first years no one cared. Brave Christian ministers from other islands sometimes visited Kalawao to solemnize marriages of dying people who did not wish to live their last days in sin. Catholic priests and Mormon disciples occasionally made the rough crossing to the lazaretto, and their arrivals were remembered long after they had left. Dr. Whipple had come, at the age of seventy, to see what the settlement needed, and he reported: "Everything." At one point a group of religious lepers had actually started a church, and leafing through their treasured Bible had come upon that glowing passage of hope in which the Apostle John reported: "And as Jesus passed by, he saw a man which was blind from his birth. And his disciples asked him, saying, Master, who did sin, this man, or his parents, that he was born blind? Jesus answered, Neither hath this man sinned, nor his parents: . . . He spat on the ground, and made clay of the spittle, and he anointed the eyes of the blind man with the clay, And said unto him, Go, wash in the pool of Siloam. . . . He . . . washed, and came seeing." The lepers called their church—it had no building, for Honolulu could spare no lumber—Siloama, and it kept their hope alive, for every leper was convinced that somewhere in the world there must be a pool of Siloam, or a medicine, or an unguent that would cure him.

Because Nyuk Tsin was pregnant, she escaped the attentions of Big Saul and his ruthless gang, but as her birth time approached she forgot him and suffered apprehensions of a different nature. For one thing, the lack of water troubled her, and she wondered what her husband would do when the baby came, for he had only one small receptacle for water and no fire at which to heat it. Mun Ki promised: "I'll ask some of the Hawaiian women to help, and they'll have buckets." But Big Saul would permit no one to go near the Chinese shed, and on the final day Nyuk Tsin gave birth to her fifth son under conditions that would not have been permitted had she been an animal: no water, no clean clothes waiting for the child, no food to speed the mother's milk, no bed for the infant except the cold ground; there was not even clean straw upon which the mother could lie. Nevertheless, she produced a ruddy-faced, slant-eyed little fellow; and then her great worries began.

No one knew at that time how the contagion of leprosy operated, for it was a fact that many kokuas like Nyuk Tsin lived in the lazaretto for years in the most intimate contact with lepers without ever acquiring the mai Pake, so mere contact could not be the explanation; but she had learned that if children below the age of eight stayed very long in contact with leprosy, they were sure to catch it; so she nursed her infant as best she could and prayed for the arrival of the next *Kilauea*. While she waited, she did many things to make her son prematurely strong. She exposed him daily to the winds so that he would know them; she fed him constantly to build health; she slapped him vigorously to make him resist shock; but at night she cuddled him warmly between her sallow breasts, and she loved him desperately.

When the *Kilauea* finally arrived, she was filled with excitement and a determination to act carefully. Therefore, as soon as the first longboat arrived with its cargo of lepers she went down to the landing and called to one of the rowers, "My baby is to go back on your ship," and she made as if to enter the longboat with the child, but the sailors of the *Kilauea* were perilously afraid that some day the Kalawao lepers might try to capture their ship and escape, and Nyuk Tsin's motion seemed as if it could be the beginning of such an attempt, so the sailor swiftly knocked her down with an oar and shouted to his mates, "Push off! Push off!" But when they were safely at sea, Nyuk Tsin, protecting her son, struggled back to her feet and called again, "It is my baby who is to go back on your ship."

"We'll ask the captain," shouted back one of the sailors, and on the next trip in he yelled, "Where's the Pake with the baby?" and Nyuk Tsin almost stumbled she ran so fast to give her reply, but she was near tears when the sailor shoved the baby back and said, "Captain wants to know where the baby goes." Nyuk Tsin eagerly explained: "He goes to Dr. Whipple, in the big house."

"Doc Whipple died last month," the sailor growled, and prepared to shove off.

Nyuk Tsin was staggered by this news and sought frantically for an alternative. "Give the baby to Kimo and Apikela, the maile gatherers," she cried eagerly.

"Where in hell's that?" the sailor asked, and they rowed back to the ship. On the next trip they advised the agonized Chinese woman that they thought they'd better not take the child, because they had no idea what to do with it when they got to Honolulu, and since there was no wet nurse aboard on this trip, the baby would have no food for a full day. Nyuk Tsin tried to explain that the captain could give the child to any Chinese, and as for food, she had made little bags filled with poi which he could suck. But the longboat pulled away, and in complete panic Nyuk Tsin saw the *Kilauea* prepare to steam off, so without knowing what she was attempting she walked out into the surf, with her child in her arms, and she started vainly to attempt swimming to the departing ship, but as soon as she was in the water the fine Hawaiian swimmer who had shared the leper cage with Mun Ki saw her plight, and leaped in beside her, grasped the infant in his left arm and started swimming strongly toward the ship. The captain saw him coming and halted the engine for a moment until the powerful brown man caught hold of a rope and with a heave pulled himself up and threw the child into the arms of a waiting sailor. Then, with the same movement, he dropped back into the sea and started a long, easy stroke which carried him back to the leper settlement.

The *Kilauea* sounded its whistle. The white goats sprang higher up the cliff sides. And Nyuk Tsin stood with her husband Mun Ki as their son Australia vanished; but all who stood with them watching the ship go, knew that no matter where the child was taken, or to whom, it was better off than it would have been on Kalawao.

IN THE SEVENTH MONTH of their stay on Kalawao, the depredations of Big Saul and his cronies finally threatened the Chinese, because Nyuk Tsin was recovered from her pregnancy. Therefore, the men began to study her, saying among themselves, "A man could have a good time with her, and she's not diseased at all."

Accordingly, three of them swooped down one night on the grassy shack and grabbed for Nyuk Tsin. But she and her husband had long ago prepared themselves for this event, and the invaders were met by two fighting Chinese armed with sharply pointed sticks. It was a bitter, silent fight, with doomed Mun Ki rising from his bed of leaves to battle desperately with Big Saul, while Nyuk Tsin, with pointed sticks in her hands, slashed and jabbed at the other two.

Once she was caught around the waist by arms that had only fragmentary hands, and she could smell the foul breath of a leper dragging her to him, but she jabbed backward with her sticks, and he screamed with pain and released her. Now there were two Chinese against two invaders, and like a jungle animal she instinctively ignored her own assailant and sprang for the jugular of Big Saul, the leader, and with great force she jabbed her remaining stick at the side of his head and it must have struck either his ear and gone in there or the soft part of his temple, for it pressed inward . . . long and sharp and pleasingly. At the same time Mun Ki ripped upward with his sharp stick, and Big Saul gasped.

Clutching his two vital wounds, he staggered away into the night and began shouting, "The Pakes have killed me!" This diverted his unwounded helper, who ran to assist his chief while the third man stumbled in the darkness with three inches of stick protruding from his left eye.

"The Pakes have killed me!" Big Saul bellowed, and he awakened all the community, so that by the time he actually did stagger mortally wounded into a circle of torches, all who could walk were present to witness his gasping, clutching death. Silently they withdrew from the ugly corpse. There were few who had not suffered at the hands of Big Saul, and now that they saw his leprosy-riddled body in the dust, they were content to leave him. His blinded crony slipped away into the night, and silence fell upon the lepers of Kalawao.

For the two Chinese it was a dreadful night. They could not know that the community at large approved the death of Big Saul and the blinding of his bully companion. They could not know, huddling alone together in the dark night, that no one in Kalawao was ignorant of how the huge man had met his death: "He went to rape the Pake girl, and her husband killed him. Good for the Pake."

Toward morning it began to rain, and the mournful drops, falling upon the leafy roof and creeping across the floor, first in tiny traces and finally in a small river, added to the misery, and Nyuk Tsin whispered to her shivering companion, "We did the right thing, Wu Chow's Father. The others should have done this years ago."

"Have we any sticks left?" Mun Ki asked

"I lost both of mine," his wife confessed.

"I have one left, and there's another hidden under the leaves. I think that when they come to seize us in the morning, we should fight until we are dead."

"I think so, too," Nyuk Tsin replied, and she went to the corner of the miserable hut and from the muddy earth picked up the other weapon. In the lonely silence, not knowing when Big Saul's men would re-attack, they waited, and Nyuk Tsin said, "I am glad, Wu Chow's Father, that I came with you. I am humbly honored that tonight you fought to help me."

"I have forgotten that you are a Hakka," he replied.

The rain increased, and for a moment the couple thought they heard the noise of lepers assembling to attack them, but it was only the rustle of water down the sides of the cliff, so Nyuk Tsin asked, "Do you forgive me for my ungainly feet?" And her husband replied, "I don't see them any more."

They huddled together in the cold, dark night and Mun Ki said, "You must promise, Wu Chow's Auntie, that if you ever escape from here, you will be sure to send my real wife in China as much money as possible."

"I promise," Nyuk Tsin replied.

"And you must enter my boys' names in the village hall."

"I will do so."

"And when you send the news to the hall, you don't have to mention that you are a Hakka. It would embarrass my wife."

"I will not say anything to the letter-writer," Nyuk Tsin promised.

"And you must promise to bury me on the side of a hill."

"I shall, just as if we were in China."

"And you must promise to bring my sons to honor my grave."

"I shall do so," Nyuk Tsin agreed, and Mun Ki said, "When dawn comes we will die, Wu Chow's Auntie, and the promises you have made mean nothing, but I feel better." Through the long, rainy night they waited and when the gray, cold dawn arrived, Mun Ki the gambler said, "Let's wait for them no longer. Let's march out to meet them." And the two Chinese left the foul grass lean-to, each with a jagged, sharp piece of wood in his right hand.

It was with horror that they saw, slumped in the rain-filled path, the dead body of Big Saul, for they knew that this doomed them to retaliation from the others of the gang, but as they cautiously approached the village, their sticks ready for the final fight, they saw with amazement that the Hawaiian lepers did not draw back in enmity, but moved forward in conciliation, and slowly the deadly sticks were lowered and at last the two Chinese stood surrounded by dying men and women who said, "You did a good thing." And one woman who had been sadly abused by Big Saul and his gang, but who had stubbornly refused to go insane, said quietly, "We are determined that Kalawao shall be a place of law."

The resurrection of this dreadful lazaretto, where for six years condemned human beings had been thrown upon the beach to die without a single incident of assistance from the society that had rejected them, dated from that morning when the determined woman whose spirit had not been broken by leprosy, or rape, or indignities such as few have known said solemnly, "Kalawao shall be a place of law."

A rude organization was evolved, consisting of people responsible for parceling out the food, a team to bring water into the village, and informal policemen who were to stop the aimless rape of unprotected women. Girls who arrived on the beach unattached were ordered to pick a man quickly, and to stay with him; and when a young wife argued: "But I am married, and I love my husband," older women told her sternly, "You have left the world. You are in a waiting station for hell. Pick a man. We warn you." So some women passed in turn from one dying man to another, but in an orderly fashion and not according to the rule of rape.

Children, banished without their parents, were given to kokuas who took them as their own, and fed them. And one law was paramount: when an old man or an old woman was clearly about to die, he must no longer be left in the open fields; he must have some kind of shelter.

Even when the settlement thus disciplined itself, the government in Honolulu gave little help. Lepers were still thrown upon the beaches to die, and there was no medicine, no lumber, no consolation. But in mid-1871 a Hawaiian who had read many books arrived in the lazaretto, and he launched a more formal government, one of whose first decisions was that the two Chinese must no longer be banished to the foot of the cliff but must be allowed to live among the others. This decision was applauded among the lepers, since it was generally agreed that the coming of limited humanity to Kalawao dated from the night when Mun Ki decided to protect his wife from the rapists, or die. A rude hospital was started, with no doctors but with leper nurses; and women who could read opened a school for children born in the lazaretto. A committee begged the government to send regular supplies of food—five pounds of fresh meat a week for each inmate plus twenty pounds of vegetables or poi—and sometimes it arrived. Gardens were started and a water supply, and the women insisted: "Kalawao shall be a place of law."

There were, of course, still no organized houses in the leper settlement, and over half the afflicted people slept year after year under bushes, with no bedding and only one change of clothing. These naturally died sooner than even the ravages of leprosy would have dictated, and perhaps this was a blessing, but even the most horrible crawling corpses somehow longed for homes of their own, a shack with a grass roof where they could preserve the illusion that they were still human beings.

Therefore, in June, 1871, Nyuk Tsin, after five weeks of living inside the community, but on the bare ground, decided: "Wu Chow's Father, we are going to build ourselves a house!" Her shattered husband had already begun to lose his toes and fingers and could not be of much help, but she made believe that it was he who was doing the work, and to keep his interest focused on the future, she discussed each step of the building with him. Daily she trudged to a ruined Hawaiian house built a century before and hauled back heavy stones, standing with them in her arms while he decided exactly where they should be placed. In time a wall was built, and the two shivering Chinese had at least some protection from the winds that howled across Kalawao in the stormy season.

Next she sought the ridgepole and the few crossbeams that were essential for the roof, but this was a difficult task, for the government in Honolulu had consistently forgotten to ship the lepers expensive lumber, which had to be imported all the way from Oregon; for although the leaders of the state were practicing Christians and although their consciences bled for the lepers, they instinctively thought: "Those with mai Pake will soon be dead. Why, really, should we waste money on them?" So to get her precious timbers Nyuk Tsin stationed her husband along the shore, where he prayed both for the arrival of driftwood and for the speed to grab it before someone else did. Once he hobbled proudly home with a long piece of timber, and the ridgepole of the roof was slung into place. Now, when the two Chinese lay in their house abuilding, they could look up through the storm and see that promising ridgepole and think: "Soon the rains will be kept away."

While her husband guarded the shore, Nyuk Tsin taught herself to climb the lower cliffs that hemmed in the leper peninsula, and after a while she became as agile as a goat, leaping from one rock to another in search of small trees that could be used as crossbeams; but goats had roamed these cliffs so long that few trees survived where once forests had stood; but wherever the agile Chinese woman spotted a fugitive she climbed for it, as if she were racing the goats for treasure.

These were days of alternate exhilaration and despair. It was good to see Mun Ki taking an active interest in life, such as it was, and Nyuk Tsin often felt a surge of personal pride when she uprooted a tree high on the cliffs; but in the afternoons when the couple gathered pili grass and braided the panels for their future roof, exasperation would overcome them, and Mun Ki often cried, "We have the grass panels finished, but nowhere can we find the crossbeams on which to tie them." Those were the days when the missionary advisers to the king, in Honolulu, argued: "We must not waste money on Kalawao."

One day a whole board, long enough if carefully split to provide crossbeams for an entire roof, washed ashore from some distant wreck, and for a moment Mun Ki thought that he had secured it for himself, but a big man named Palani, whose feet were still sound, rushed down and captured it. So the Chinese continued to sleep under the open roof, with the rain upon them night after night; but they were luckier than many, and they knew it, for they had side walls to protect them from the wind; they had the solid ridgepole of their roof; and they had the pili-grass panels finished and waiting to be slung into position.

More, they had a rude kind of spiritual peace. Mun Ki, sitting on the rocks by the sea, waiting for driftwood, often looked toward the cliff where his sure-footed wife risked her life daily in search of timber, and a change came over him. He was not aware of it, but Nyuk Tsin began to sense that her husband no longer felt inwardly ashamed of her Hakka strength. Once he had even gone so far as to admit grudgingly, "I watched you climbing on the high rocks. I would be afraid to climb there." This gave her much consolation, but the spiritual repose derived principally from another development. As long as the two Chinese had been total outcasts, even among the lepers, there had been a kind of enforced loyalty between them, for if either fought with the other, there was truly no hope left, so they were bound together by bonds of ultimate despair. But now that they were accepted into the full community, and were recognized for the prudent, loyal people they were, they were free to be ordinary people, husband and wife, and they could argue about how the house should be built, and sometimes Mun Ki, his patience strained by his stubborn Hakka wife, would stomp off in anger, hobbling on his toeless feet to the beach, where he would sit with dying Hawaiian men and confess to them: "No man can understand a woman," and the suffering men would recount their defeats at the hands of women. Then, when the day was done, he would hobble back to his home and wait for Nyuk Tsin, and when he heard her coming his heart was glad. At one such conciliation he confessed: "If you were not my kokua, I should be dead by now," and with no pride of either Punti or Hakka he looked at her in the tropical dusk and said, "Dr. Whipple was right. Wherever a man goes he finds a challenge. Today the committee asked me to handle the distribution of food, because they know I am an honest man. In fact," he admitted proudly, "I am also on the committee itself."

They suffered one major worry: what had happened to their baby? In questioning the sailors from the *Kilauea* they discovered nothing. Someone vaguely remembered that the child had been handed to a man on the dock at Honolulu, a Chinese perhaps, but he was not sure. With Dr. Whipple dead there was no way for Nyuk Tsin to send an orderly inquiry, so the two Chinese spent some months of quiet anxiety, which was heightened when an incoming leper said, "I know Kimo and Apikela. They gather maile, but they have only four Pake children." The parents fretted, but Nyuk Tsin often repeated: "Wherever the boy is, he's better off than here."

Mun Ki found escape from his worry through a fortunate discovery. One day while keeping guard at the beach, hoping for another timber, he happened to notice that some of the small black volcanic pebbles that lined the shore resembled the beans used in the game of fan-tan, and he started to gather them, and when he had well over a hundred of matched size he spent a long time searching for a completely flat rock, and although he did not find one, he did stumble across a slab which could be made reasonably smooth by polishing with another stone held flat against the surface. When it was ready he spread upon it the bean-like pebbles and began picking them up in his damaged hands, slamming them back down on the flat rock, and counting them out in fours. In time he became so skilled in estimating his initial grab that he could guess with fair accuracy whether the residue would be one, two, three or four; and after he had done this for some days he called to some Hawaiians and showed them the game. For the first two days he merely tested his wits against theirs, and it was one of the Hawaiians who suggested, "We could play a game with those pebbles," and Mun Ki replied casually, "Do you think so?"

Since no one had any money, they looked along the beach to find something they could use as counters, and they came upon some hard yellow seeds dropped by a bush that grew inland, and it was obvious that these would make good substitutes for coins, and in this way the historic fan-tan game of the lepers at Kalawao began. When Mun Ki was banker it was uncanny how, using his two stumps of hands, he could grab a number of pebbles, apparently at random, and estimate whether the total was even or odd; and when bets were placed he was able to hide one of the pebbles, catching it between the base of his thumb and the heel of his damaged hand. If most of his adversaries had their yellow buttons on even, he would drop the hidden pebble, make the residue come out odd, and pocket the profits; but if the bets were concentrated on the odd, he would retain the palmed counter and win again.

The game continued for weeks, and more than a dozen men became so excited about it that as soon as the sun was up, they hurried to the beach where the sharp-eyed Pake gambler was willing to stand off their challenges. They played for nothing, only yellow seeds, but they developed agonies of hope over large bets, and in time one of their number, the big excitable man named Palani, the Biblical Paul, began to accumulate most of the buttons. When Mun Ki saw this he was pleased, and on the day when Palani finally cornered the seed-wealth of the lepers his Chinese adversary reported to Nyuk Tsin: "Palani is getting caught, just as we planned. Pray for me."

In the following days Palani began to lose. If he bet on evens, Mun Ki would drop the hidden pebble in his palm and throw down an odd number, and whenever the Hawaiian decided to risk a lot of seeds and go for a big win on a specific number, say three, it was a simple matter for Mun Ki to make the pebbles come out even, so that they couldn't possibly yield a three. The residue might be two or four, but never three.

Slowly Palani's pile diminished, but Mun Ki knew from the past that the cultivation of a sucker demanded patience and skill, so on some days Palani triumphed; but over the long haul he lost, and the afternoon came when Mun Ki ruthlessly drove him down to a mere handful of seeds. Excitement among the lepers was great as the fan-tan game progressed, and many were standing about when the Chinese finally broke his adversary completely, whereupon the Hawaiian spectators started joshing the loser, which was what Mun Ki wanted. When the joking was at its height, the Chinese said casually, "Palani, why don't we play this way. You have the ridgepole for your house, and I have one for mine. It's ridiculous for neither of us to have a complete roof, so I'll play for your ridgepole against mine."

There was an excited hush about the flat rock, and Mun Ki prayed that the Hawaiian would rise to the challenge, but when the big man did so he added a stipulation which left the Chinese stunned. To begin with, Palani said simply, "All right, I'll play for the timber . . . tomorrow," and Mun Ki tried to mask his joy, but then the big man added, "And tomorrow we won't pick up pebbles by hand. We'll scoop them up in a cup. And you won't count them, Mun Ki. Keoki over there will count them."

"Don't you trust me?" Mun Ki pleaded.

The big Hawaiian stared at the little gambler and said, "We'll scoop them up in a cup." And he marched off with his friends.

Mun Ki sat alone for a long time glumly staring at the pebbles on the fan-tan rock. Carefully he recapitulated each incident in his relationship with Palani: "It all goes back to that day when I saw the big timber first. But he had good feet, so he dashed out and got it for himself. I must have shown my temper. So all along he's known what I've been planning. Letting him win and then making him lose. That evil man! All the time I was teasing him, he was really playing with me, letting me make him win and then letting me make him lose. So that while I thought I was trapping him into gambling for his roof, he was trapping me into gambling for mine. These damned Hawaiians."

Distraught, he hobbled home, looked up at his precious ridgepole and threw himself upon his wife's mercy. "Tomorrow we may lose our roof," he said solemnly.

"We have no roof . . . yet," Nyuk Tsin replied.

"We have the ridgepole," Mun Ki replied glumly. "And we're going to lose it."

"Our ridgepole?" his wife shouted.

"Nyuk Tsin, be quiet!" he pleaded.

"What have you been doing?" she shouted again, pushing him against the wall. "Did you gamble away our timber?"

"We still have a chance," he assured her, and then he explained how while he was leading big dumb Palani into a trap, the wily Hawaiian had really been leading him into one.

"Oh, husband!" Nyuk Tsin cried, and she began to weep, but he comforted her, and all night the two Chinese tried to figure out what their chances were, now that Palani had insisted that they play the game honestly.

As dawn broke, the sleepless Mun Ki was figuring with a stick in the wet sand and suddenly he looked up toward his wife with a beatific smile upon his thick, leprous lips. "Our good luck is beginning today," he assured her, and his sweating over the ridepole ceased. "Three years ago we started the taro patch, and that was the beginning of our bad luck. We lost our money, got sick, were tricked by the Chinese doctor, and had to leave home. But the three years are over. Now our good-luck cycle is beginning, Nyuk Tsin!" he cried triumphantly. "We have six years of good luck ahead of us. Today I'll win Palani's ridgepole and tonight we'll sleep under our own roof!"

In an ecstasy of hope he led Nyuk Tsin down to the fan-tan rock, where Palani and his Hawaiians were waiting. The pebbles were on the flat surface, and beside them stood a metal cup with a handle. After some discussion it was agreed that the game should be played in this way: Palani would scoop a cupful of pebbles, and the umpire Keoki, closely watched by Nyuk Tsin, would count them out in fours until the residue was known. Mun Ki, in the meantime, would bet on odd or even and would also stipulate a specific number. Thus, if he nominated even and four, and if the pebbles left a residue of four, he would win two points for his even guess and four points for having guessed the exact number. On the other hand, if he wished to hedge his bets, he could nominate even and three, which would still yield him four points if three came up. Then he would scoop up the pebbles, and Palani would name his bets, and the first man to win one hundred points would win the other's roof.

Palani, content that he now had the Chinese in an honest game, was satisfied that he would win, but Mun Ki, joyous in the start of his six-year cycle of good luck, was positive that he would triumph. He watched the big Hawaiian scoop the pebbles, hold them aloft, and wait for his guess. "Odd and three," Mun Ki cried, and the pebbles were deposited before the umpire. Eagerly the circle of faces closed in for the count.

It was a ghoulish crowd that watched the battle for the ridgepoles. Some men had no hands and some lacked feet. The lips of some had fallen away and there were many noses missing. From the group arose the unmistakable stench of the leper, and brown skins were often marked with huge sickly-white areas. Hair had fallen out and sometimes eyes. These were the caricatures of men, those cursed by a malevolent nature so remorseless that few in the world who were not lepers could imagine. These fan-tan players were indeed the walking corpses, the crawling souls so foul that sound men, seeing them, could only shudder. They were the dead, the bodies thrown onto the beach at Kalawao, the forgotten, the abominated.

But now in the bright sunlight they laughed merrily, and if the judge had inadequate fingers with which to count in fours, he was allowed to keep his job because he was known as a trustworthy man. "Odd and one," he cried. "Two points to the Pake." The crowd cheered.

When it came time for Mun Ki to scoop the pebbles a difficulty presented itself. Although he had been able to play the game with his stumps, he did not have enough fingers to grasp the handle of the cup, so after two trial attempts he appealed to the crowd, and his request was granted: he passed the cup to Nyuk Tsin, and she scooped the pebbles. "Odd and three," Palani cried.

When the judge had counted, he announced: "Even."

"It's our lucky year!" Mun Ki shouted joyfully, and then he stopped to explain how a Chinese has three bad years followed by six good ones. "The good ones started last night!" he chuckled, and on Palani's next scoop he scored six points, for he bet on even and two, and that's how the pebbles fell.

At the midway mark Mun Ki was leading by a score of fifty to thirty-nine, and it was indeed uncanny how he picked up points. "It's our lucky year!" he exulted, and as the sun grew hot it became apparent that Palani was bound to lose his roof. Nevertheless, he played his numbers stolidly to the end, and when the Chinese gambler had fairly won, one hundred to eighty-three, the big Hawaiian jumped up, stretched and said, "I myself will carry the timber to your house!" And the Hawaiians formed a procession, those who could walk, and when they got Palani's driftwood to the stone walls which Nyuk Tsin had built, they cut it into lengths for crossbeams, and men who were agile leaped onto the top of the walls, lashed the beams in place and began tying down the pili grass that others passed to them. By midafternoon the roof was done, and Mun Ki, appraising it proudly, explained to all: "This is really my lucky year."

But Nyuk Tsin saw the disappointment in big Palani's misshapen face, and without consulting her husband she went to the man and said, "In our new house there is room for another," and she took Palani by the hand and led him inside. The crowd cheered her generosity and then watched Mun Ki to see what he would do, but he cried, "This is the beginning of my six lucky years."

Taking the dying man Palani into their home was one of the best things Nyuk Tsin ever did, for he had been a sailor and he was a great liar; during a storm he would sit in the dark hut and tell the Pakes of distant lands, and it seemed wonderful to Nyuk Tsin that one man could have had so many experiences. "Asia, Africa, America!" he cried. "They're all fine lands to see." And as he talked, Mun Ki and his wife began to visualize the distant continents and to appreciate what a surpassing treasure their sons were going to inherit. One night Mun Ki said, "When you go back to the boys, Wu Chow's Auntie, make them learn to read. They should know about the things that Palani has been telling us." Once he actually said, "I am glad I came to the Fragrant Tree Country. A man should have great adventures."

Palani's fo'c's'l yarns also awakened Nyuk Tsin's imagination, and she saw how much better it was to live closely with her neighbors rather than apart as she had had to do as a Hakka wife, and sometimes at night, when rain fell over their roof, the three strange companions found a positive joy in sitting together, and this was the beginning of Nyuk Tsin's remarkable service to Kalawao. When big Palani died she helped bury him and then brought into her roofed house a man and wife, and when they died she buried them. She became known as the "Pake Kokua," and whenever a new ferryload of lepers was dumped ashore on the terrible and inhospitable beaches of Kalawao, she went among them and showed them how to obtain at least some comfort during the first weeks when they had to sleep in the open. She taught them to build houses, as she had done, and day after day she climbed the cliffs seeking out short timbers for others. Her most particular contribution was this: when the ferry threw ashore some young girl she would keep the girl in her house for a week or so, and there the girl was safe, as if she had come upon one of the ancient and holy sanctuaries maintained by the Hawaiians before the white man came, and during these days of grace Nyuk Tsin would bring to the girl a chain of possible husbands and would say sternly, "You have come here to die, Liliha. Do so in dignity." And many marriages, if they could be called such, were both arranged and consummated in Nyuk Tsin's house, and word seeped back to Honolulu about the Pake Kokua.

For his part, Mun Ki reveled in his time of good luck. He kept his fan-tan game running and was delighted one day to find that the leper ferry had brought him a Cantonese man, near death, who had managed to hide out in Iwilei for two years before the quack herbalist turned him in, and who was as good a gambler as he. They would play fan-tan by the hour, with Mun Ki insisting, "Pick up the pebbles in the cup, please."

And then the leprosy, which had been accumulating in enormous reserves throughout his body, burst forth horribly in many places and he could not leave the stone house Nyuk Tsin had built for him. She could provide him with no medicine, neither for his awful sores nor for the pneumonia that attacked him. She could get him no choice food . . . just salt beef and poi. There were no blankets to ease the hard earthen bed. But there was Nyuk Tsin's patient care, and as the ghastly days progressed, with death extremely tardy, she sat with her husband and attended to his last instructions.

"You are obligated to send money to my wife," he reminded her.

"And when the boys are married, send word to the village. Try any ventures you wish, for these are my lucky years."

As death approached, he became unusually gentle, a poor wasted shadow of a man, a ghost, and he told the self-appointed governor of the settlement, "The fan-tan game belongs to you." At the very end he said to Nyuk Tsin, "I love you. You are my real wife." And he died.

She scratched his grave into the sandy soil, choosing the side of a hill as she had promised, where the winds did not blow and where, if there was no tree, there was at least a ledge of rock upon which his spirit could rest on its journeys from and to the grave.

Nyuk Tsin now turned her house into a hospital, and no longer were stumps of human beings seen abandoned in open fields. She cared for them until they died, and there were sometimes five or six days in a row when she never saw a whole living person. She cared for those who were beyond the memory of God, and there was no human being so foul in his final disintegration but that she could tend him. In Honolulu the government could find no way to send medicine to the abandoned, nor bandages nor even scalpels to cut away lost members, but Nyuk Tsin devised tricks of her own, and many Hawaiians blessed her as the Pake Kokua. If anyone had asked her: "Pake, why do you work so hard for the Hawaiian lepers?" she would have replied: "Because Kimo and Apikela took me in."

In these days she formed one habit. As each dusk came she sat apart and took off all her clothes. Starting with her face she would feel for signs of leprosy, and then her breasts, and then her flanks. She studied each hand with care and then inspected her legs. Finally she lifted her big feet and looked at each toe in turn, and when she was satisfied that for another day she was free of leprosy, she dressed and went to bed. She had to perform this inspection at dusk, for the government in Honolulu could not find the funds to provide the lepers with lamps and oil, so that when night fell, the utter blackness of hell descended upon the lazaretto, and ugliness rode the night. But Nyuk Tsin, even though she was now an unattached woman, was left alone, and she slept in peace, for she knew that so far she was not leprous.

In early 1873 word was sent to Nyuk Tsin that in reward for her help at Kalawao she would be permitted to return to civilization, provided that upon her arrival in Honolulu three doctors would certify that she was free of leprosy. The news excited much discussion among the lepers, but one reaction dominated: although all were sorry to see her go, none begrudged her the right. So in the period between ships this twenty-six-year-old Chinese girl moved about the peninsula of Kalawao. She climbed up to the crater where the volcano which had built the island had once flourished, and she crossed over to the westward side of the peninsula where, in her opinion, the tiny settlement at Kalaupapa offered a much better home for future lepers than the eastern side at Kalawao. But mostly she looked at the towering cliffs that hemmed in the peninsula, and she watched the wild white goats leaping in freedom. To herself she said, "I never expected to leave Kalawao. May those who are left behind find decency."

On the day of Nyuk Tsin's departure from the lazaretto the little *Kilauea* chugged into position beneath the cliffs; casks and cattle were kicked into the surf; and a longboat came in with its first load of condemned; and although Nyuk Tsin had decided to go out to the ship on the first return trip, she now changed her mind and moved among the quivering newcomers, explaining conditions to them in her broken Hawaiian; and when the last incoming boat arrived, the sailors had to warn her: "Hey, Pake! More better you come, eh?" As she went to the boat she met climbing out of it a small, white-faced man in black priest's clothing. He wore glasses and his eyes were close together. His hair was combed straight forward like a boy's; his trip among the cattle had made him dirty, and his fingernails were filthy. Now, as he stepped ashore at Kalawao he was breathing deeply, as if in a trance, and he stared in horror at what he saw. To the self-appointed governor he said in an ashen voice, "I am Father Damien. I have come to serve you. Where is a house in which I may stay?"

Nyuk Tsin was so surprised to think that a white man would volunteer to help her lepers that she did not find words to cry, "You may have my house!" By the time she thought of this, the sailors were already pulling her into the longboat, and so she left, but as she went she could see the lepers explaining to the priest that in Kalawao there were no houses and that he, like any other newcomer, would have to sleep as best he could on the bare ground under a hau tree.

WHEN NYUK TSIN RETURNED from the lazaretto she was dominated by one desire, to recover her children, and as soon as the *Kilauea* docked she hurried off, a thin, sparse-haired Chinese widow of twenty-six wearing a blue smock, blue trousers and a conical bamboo hat tied under her chin and reaching out over her closely wound bun in back. She was barefooted, and after an eventful life of eight years in Hawaii, owned exactly what she wore—not even a toothbrush or a smock more—plus seven undeveloped acres of boggy land left to her by Dr. Whipple. As she plodded up Nuuanu Valley she did not pause to study the land, but as she went past she did think: "I shall have to start spading it tonight."

She was on her way to the forest home of Kimo and Apikela, and when at last she reached the footpath leading off the highway and into the dense vegetation, she broke into a run, and the wind pulled her basket hat backward, so that it hung by the cord around her neck, and at last she burst into the clearing where her children ought to be, but the family was inside the house, and she got almost to the door before Apikela saw her. The big Hawaiian shouted, "Pake! Pake!" and hurried over to embrace her, lifting her clear off the ground, but even while huge Apikela was holding her, Nyuk Tsin was looking over the woman's shoulder and counting. There were only four boys, from seven years down to four, standing in the shadows, frightened by this intruder.

"Where's the other boy?" Nyuk Tsin finally gasped.

"There's no other boy," Apikela replied.

"Didn't you get the baby from the ship?"

"We heard of no baby."

Nyuk Tsin was tormented by the loss of her child, yet overjoyed to see her other sons, and these dual emotions immobilized her for a moment, and she stood apart in the small grass house looking first at big Apikela, then at drowsy Kimo, and finally at her four hesitant sons. Then she forgot the missing child and moved toward her boys, as if to embrace them, but the two youngest naturally drew back because they did not know her, while the two oldest withdrew because they had heard whispers that their mother was a leper. Nyuk Tsin, sensing this latter fear, hesitated, stopped completely and turned to Apikela, saying, "You have cared well for my babies."

"It was my joy to have them," the huge Hawaiian woman laughed.

"How did you feed them?" Nyuk Tsin asked, feasting her eyes on her robust sons.

"You can always feed children," Kimo assured her. "Sometimes I worked. Sometimes the Pakes gave us a little money."

"Do they have the other child?" Nyuk Tsin asked.

"They never spoke," Apikela replied. Then the big woman noticed how frightened the boys were of their mother, and with a gigantic, embracing sweep of her huge arms she gathered them up as she had often done before. When they were huddled against her warm and ample body, she gave her belly a sudden flick, opened her arms and ejected a tangle of arms and legs at Nyuk Tsin. The scrawny little Chinese woman was engulfed, and then a strange thing happened. It was she who feared the leprosy, and instead of embracing her sons, she withdrew as if she were unclean, and the boys stared silently at their mother while she drew her hands behind her, lest she touch one of them.

"I am afraid," she said humbly, and Apikela withdrew the children.

After a noisy meal during which the boys chattered with Kimo, and Apikela asked a dozen aimless questions about Kalawao, Nyuk Tsin said, "I must go down to look at my land," and she set off for the four-mile jog back down the valley to where the boggy land lay, but again she passed it without stopping, for she was on her way to see the Punti and Hakka families, but none of them knew of her son. Because they were *Carthaginian* families, they felt obligated to help Mun Ki's widow, so they scraped together a set of garden tools, some seeds, a bag of taro corns and a bamboo carrying-pole with two baskets attached. With these Nyuk Tsin returned to her land, and there she worked till nearly midnight.

The low and boggy section she enclosed in dikes, for there taro would prosper. Furthermore, building the taro bed also drained the intermediate land, uncovering good alluvial soil, which she tilled for Chinese vegetables. This left a smaller, but still adequate high area where vegetables for the haoles could be grown. Thus, from the first night, Nyuk Tsin stumbled upon the system she was to follow for many years: taro for the Hawaiians, Chinese cabbage and peas for the Orientals, lima beans, string beans and Irish potatoes for the haoles. For she knew they all had to eat.

At dawn each day she slung her bamboo pole across her shoulder, hooked on the two baskets, jammed her conical basket hat upon her head, and set out barefooted for her garden. As her vegetables ripened, she loaded her baskets and began her long treks through Honolulu, and no matter how much business she produced at any one house, she was never as concerned with the money as she was to see whether this family happened to have a Chinese boy about four years old. She didn't find her son, but she developed a vegetable business that was becoming profitable.

When night fell, Nyuk Tsin continued working, putting her field in order, and after the stars had come out she would carefully place in her baskets those vegetables which she had not sold. Swinging them onto her shoulder, she would begin her four-mile trek back up the valley to the clearing where her sons were already asleep. There were many days when she never saw them, but as she sat in the night darkness with Kimo and Apikela she talked mostly of their future, and one night, when she had trudged up the valley in a heavy rain, she arrived home cold and wet and she was driven to recall the days in the lazaretto when the leper Palani told them of the world. So she woke her sons and stood before them, muddy and wet, and they rubbed their heavy eyes, trying to understand what she was saying. They could hardly speak Chinese and she was not adept in Hawaiian, but she explained: "Somewhere in Honolulu you have a brother, and his name . . ." The boys began to fidget, and she commanded them to stand still, but they could not understand.

"Eh, you kanaka!" Apikela shouted. "Shush! Your auntie speak you! Damned Pakes!" And the boys stood silent.

Slowly Wu Chow's Auntie spoke: "Your father wanted you to share the entire world. He wanted you to study . . . to be bright boys. He said, 'Work hard and the world will belong to you.' "

She took her first son by the hand and drew him into the middle of the room, saying, "Asia, you must honor your father by working hard." The sleepy-eyed boy nodded, quite unaware of the commission he had been given.

To each of her sons she repeated this paternal command: "Work hard." And when they stood at attention, she added, "And you must help me find your brother Australia."

"Where is he?" Asia asked.

"I don't know," Wu Chow's Auntie replied, "but we must find him."

When the confused and sleepy boys returned to bed, the little Chinese woman sat for a long time with the two Hawaiians, trying to decide which of her sons promised to be the most intelligent, and this was important, for Nyuk Tsin realized that she would be able to give only one a full-scale education in America and it was essential that the right one be identified early and concentrated upon. Now she asked Kimo, "Which do you think is best?"

"I like Europe," Kimo replied.

"You like him," Nyuk Tsin agreed, "but who is cleverest?"

"America is cleverest," the big man said.

Nyuk Tsin thought so too, but she checked with Apikela. "Do you think America has courage for a fight?" she asked.

"Africa is the most stubborn fighter," Apikela replied.

"But which one would you send to the mainland?"

"America," Apikela replied without hesitation.

By 1875 Nyuk Tsin had saved nearly twenty-five dollars, and if such a rate of income were to continue, she could obviously afford to educate all of her sons, but she knew that there was heavy obligation upon this money, so when it reached the even twenty-five-dollar mark she bundled it up, took her four sons with her, and marched formally down to the Punti store. "I want you to understand what we are doing," she said several times, and when she reached the store, she lined the boys up so that even six-year-old America could follow the transaction that was about to occur.

In those years the Chinese did not use banks, for there were no Chinese establishments, and what Oriental could trust a white man in the handling of money? Wealth was kept hidden until a responsible accumulation was made, and then it was carried, as on this day, to the Punti store or to the Hakka store, and there, in complete confidence, it was handed over to the storekeeper, who, for three per cent of the total, would manage, by ways only he knew, to transmit the balance either to the Low Village, as in the present case, or to the High Village if the recipient were to be a Hakka. Wars came and revolutions. Hawaii prospered or suffered loss. Men died and ships were captured by pirates, but money sent from the Punti store in Honolulu invariably reached the Low Village.

"This money is for the wife of Kee Mun Ki," Nyuk Tsin explained to the storekeeper. When he nodded she said, "A widow in the Low Village. Tell her that as dutiful sons her four boys send the money. And they send as well their filial respect." Again the storekeeper nodded and began to write the letter.

When it was completed, in strange Chinese characters that few in Hawaii could read, Nyuk Tsin proudly handed it to each of the boys and said, "You are sending money to your mother. As long as she lives you must do this. It is the respect you owe her." Gravely the little pigtailed boys in clean suits handled the letter, and each, in his imperfect way, could visualize China, with his mother sitting in a red robe and opening the letter and finding his money inside. When the letter was handed back to the storekeeper for transmitting, Nyuk Tsin stood her boys in line and said, "Remember! As long as your mother lives, this is your duty." And the boys understood. Big Apikela was like a mother in that she sang to them and kissed them; and Wu Chow's Auntie was sometimes like a mother because she brought them food; but their real mother, the one that counted, was in China.

Since the day on which the money was taken to the Punti store was already ruined, Nyuk Tsin decided to explore something that she had heard of with great excitement. She led her four bright-faced boys back up Nuuanu Valley, taking them off into a smaller valley where in a field a large building stood. It belonged to the Church of England, for as soon as the Hawaiian alii discovered the gentle and pliant religion of Episcopalianism with its lovely ceremonies, they contrasted it to the bleak, un-Hawaiian Calvinism of the Congregationalists, and before long most of the alii were Church of England converts. They loved the rich singing, the incense and the robes. One of the first things the English missionaries did was to open the school which Nyuk Tsin now approached, and to the surprise of the islands the Englishmen announced: "In our school we will welcome Chinese boys." The idea of having Orientals in any large numbers in the big, important school at Punahou would in 1875 have been repugnant, and also prohibitively expensive to the Chinese, so the ablest flocked to Iolani, where Nyuk Tsin now brought her sons.

She was met by one of the most unlikely men ever to inhabit Hawaii, Uliassutai Karakoram Blake, a tall, reedy Englishman with fierce mustaches and a completely bald head, even though he was only twenty-eight. His adventurous Shropshire parents had been with a camel caravan heading across Outer Mongolia from the town of his first name to the town of his second when he was prematurely born, "jolted loose ere my time," he liked to explain, "by the rumbling motion of a camel which practically destroyed my sainted mother's pelvic structure." He had grown up speaking Chinese, Russian, Mongolian, French, German and English. He was now also a master of pidgin, a terrifying disciplinarian and a man who loved children. He had long ago learned not to try his Chinese on the Orientals living in Hawaii, for they spoke only Cantonese and Punti, and to him these were alien languages, but when Nyuk Tsin spoke to him in Hakka, it sounded enough like Mandarin for him to respond, and he immediately took a liking to her.

"So you want to enroll these four budding Lao-tses in our school?" he remarked in expansive Mandarin.

"They are not Lao-tses," she corrected. "They're Mun Ki's."

Uliassutai Karakoram Blake, and he demanded of his acquaintances his full name, looked down severely at Nyuk Tsin and asked, "Is there any money at all in the coffers of Mun Ki, y-clept Kee?"

"He's dead," she replied.

Blake swallowed. He liked this practical woman, but nevertheless he tried to smother her with yet a third barrage of words: "Have you any reason to believe that these four orphaned sons of Mun Ki have even the remotest capacity to learn?"

Nyuk Tsin thought a moment and replied, "America can learn. The others aren't too bright."

"Madam," Uliassutai Karakoram cried with a low bow that brought his mustaches almost to the floor, "in my three years at Iolani you are the first mother who has even come close to assessing her children as I do. Frankly, your sons don't look too bright, but with humble heart I welcome Asia, Europe, Africa and America into our school." Very formally he shook the hand of each child, then roared in pidgin, "Mo bettah you lissen me, I knock you plenty, b'lee me." And the boys did believe.

In later years, when Hawaii was civilized and lived by formal accreditations, no teacher who drifted off a whaling boat one afternoon, his head shaved bald, no credentials, with mustaches that reached out four inches, and with a name like Uliassutai Karakoram Blake could have been accepted in the schools. But in 1872, when this outlandish man did just that, Iolani needed teachers, and in Blake they found a man who was to leave on the islands an indelible imprint. When the bishop first stared at the frightening-looking young man and asked, "What are your credentials for teaching?" Blake replied, "Sir, I was bred on camel's milk," and the answer was so ridiculous that he was employed. If Blake had been employed in a first-rate school like Punahou, then one of the finest west of Illinois, it wouldn't have mattered whether he was capable or not, for after Punahou his scholars would go on to Yale, and oversights could be corrected. Or if the teachers in the school were inadequate, the parents at home were capable of repairing omissions. But at Iolani the students either got an education from the available teachers, or they got none at all, and it was Blake's unique contribution to Hawaii that with his fierce mustaches and his outrageous insistence upon the niceties of English manners, he educated the Chinese. He made them speak a polished English, cursing them in pidgin when they didn't. He converted them to the Church of England, while he himself remained a Buddhist. He taught them to sail boats in the harbor, contending that no man could be a gentleman who did not own a horse and a boat. Above all, he treated them as if they were not Chinese; he acted as if they were entitled to run banks, or to be elected to the legislature, or to own land.

In these years there were many in Hawaii who looked apprehensively into the future and were frightened by what they saw. They did not want Chinese going to college or owning big companies. They were sincerely afraid of Oriental businessmen and intellectuals. They hoped, falsely as it proved, that the Chinese would be perpetually content to work on the plantations without acquiring any higher aspirations, and when they saw their dream proving false, and the Chinese entering all aspects of public life, they sometimes grew panicky and talked of passing ridiculous laws, or of exiling all Chinese, or of preventing them from entering certain occupations. What these frightened men should have done was much simpler: they should have shot Uliassutai Karakoram Blake.

For when the first Chinese plantation worker saved, through bitter labor, the few pennies needed to send his son to Iolani, a kind of revolution was launched which nothing in world history had so far proved capable of reversing. When Blake taught the first Chinese boy the alphabet, the old system of indentured labor was doomed. Because a boy who could read would sooner or later come upon some book that would give him an idea, and a boy with an idea could accomplish almost anything. During these years in Hawaii, the Chinese were not particularly well treated. Hell-raising lunas on the plantations—gang foremen—often thought it hilarious to tie two Chinese together by their pigtails and abuse them both at the same time. Other lunas, on a drunk, found delight in tying the pigtail of a passing Oriental to the tail of a horse, and lashing the horse into a gallop. The Chinese retaliated until it became a standing rule among lunas: "Never go into a field where more than six Chinese are working with cane knives. Never." And one night an infuriated Chinese, for no reason that anyone ever developed, screamed into the bedroom of the French consul and with a long knife massacred him. These were not easy years, and the Chinese were by no means the docile Orientals that the Honolulu *Mail* had reported on their arrival. They were apt to be mean, fearfully quick to revenge insults, and positively unwilling to extend their contracts at three dollars a month for fourteen hours of hard work a day. Deep tensions were created, and the Chinese experiment might have failed, except that Uliassutai Karakoram Blake was quietly teaching his boys: "The same virtues that are extolled in China will lead to success in Hawaii. Study, listen to your parents, save your money, align yourselves with honest men." He also laid great emphasis upon the wisdom of conforming to the mores of the majority. "Cut your pigtails," he counseled, "and dress like Americans. Join their churches. Forget that you are Chinese."

A boy asked, "But if we ought to drop Buddhism, why don't you?" And Uliassutai replied, "When I leave Hawaii, I shall return to England, where freedoms of all kind are permitted. But you will not leave these islands. You will have to live among Americans, and they despise most freedoms, so conform." He was a difficult, opinionated man, and he transformed a race.

In these days, when Nyuk Tsin came to work in the early morning twilight, she led her four sons with her, and for the hours before school opened, they labored in the field with her. As schooltime approached, she dipped a rag in the muddy water of the taro patch and cleaned her sons, sending them off to their lessons. When day ended, they were back among the vegetables, and after nightfall they all reached home, where big Kimo had a hot supper waiting for them. After a year of this severe regime Kimo, exhausted by the amount of work the Chinese were doing, suggested, "Why don't we all leave this house and build a little house down the valley? We'll keep this land for a vegetable field. Then nobody will have to walk so far, and I'll be close to the poolroom."

Nyuk Tsin considered this for some time and said, "I don't like to give up even an inch of the vegetable field for a house."

"But look!" Kimo argued. "For a little corner of the vegetable field, you'll get a whole lot of land up here."

"If we do that," Nyuk Tsin countered, "Apikela will have to walk great distances for her maile. And I can walk better than Apikela."

"What I had in mind," Kimo explained, "was that Apikela should stop bothering with the maile and help you with the vegetable field down there. That way, the boys can study longer for their school."

The plan was so reasonable that next day Nyuk Tsin invited Kimo to accompany her to the vegetable field, and the huge man explained how little land would be taken off by the house, and he reminded her how much forest land she would be getting in exchange, and on the spur of the moment she said, "Good."

They took down the upland house and for several nights slept in the open while the lowland house was building, and after a while the first of the famous Kee houses stood on Nuuanu Street. This one was a ramshackle affair, neither waterproof nor tidy, but it comfortably housed five Chinese and two Hawaiians. In a way, it was also responsible for the good fortune of the Kees, for one day when Nyuk Tsin was trudging up the valley toward her new fields, which because they were so high did not produce as well as the lower, she was stopped by a handsome young man of twenty who was riding in a gig and who called, "You the Pake who has the field in there?" She said that she was, and he reined in his horse, climbed down, and extended his hand. "I'm Whip Hoxworth," he said, "and I'd like to see your field, if I may." He tied the horse to a tree and tramped in with her, kicked the soil, rubbed some through his palms, and said, "Pake, I'd like to make a deal with you. I brought back with me from Formosa, nearly lost my head doing it, about a hundred pineapple plants. I've tried growing them in low fields, and they don't work. Seems to me a field at this elevation might be nearer to what they knew in Formosa. Tell you what I'll do. I'll give you all the plants that are now living. And if you can make them grow, you can have them. All I want is some of the fruit and some of the seed."

"Can you sell pineapple?" Nyuk Tsin asked suspiciously.

Whip Hoxworth turned and pointed expansively back down the valley, and although trees cut off his view, that did not disturb him. "Every house you can see down there will want to buy your pineapples, Pake. Is it a deal?"

It was, and young Whip Hoxworth had made a shrewd guess, for Nyuk Tsin's upper field was exactly the soil needed for the Formosa pineapple, which was markedly sweeter and in all ways superior to the grubby degenerates that had been introduced into the islands half a century before. Now Nyuk Tsin hiked out of her upper Nuuanu fields day after day, her back loaded with pineapples which she hawked through the city. Her vegetables from the lower field also prospered, but best of all, her four sons were learning their necessary lessons.

In only one venture was Nyuk Tsin failing and that was, as before, her taro bed, for not satisfied with selling the brutish bulbs to the natives, and the leaves to anyone who wanted to steam them for vegetables, while keeping the stalks to herself for pickling and serving with fried mullet, thus exacting three profits from the accommodating taro, she allowed Kimo and Apikela to talk her into boiling down the roots and converting them once more into poi. This time the procedure worked exactly right, and the resulting poi was a rich, gooey, purplish color that made the mouth of any Hawaiian water when he saw it, and a considerable market developed for this Pake poi, as it was called. But very few Hawaiians were able to buy any, for big Apikela and bigger Kimo worked so hard at cultivating the taro that when mealtime came they were famished, and Nyuk Tsin, gobbling a few handfuls of cold rice with perhaps a bit of pickled taro stalk, sat by aghast at the amounts of poi her two gigantic housemates consumed. Kimo, now weighing nearly three hundred and fifty pounds, would lumber over to the poi buckets, ladle himself out a quart or more and serve Apikela an equal amount. Pecking at half a dozen fish, some cold pork, a baked breadfruit and what was left of a can of Oregon salmon, they would dip two fingers, held scooped like loose fishhooks, into the poi, twirl them around the sticky mass, and swing them deftly to their mouths. With a sweet sucking sound they inhaled the delicious paste, and looked happily at each other as they did so.

With dismay, Nyuk Tsin realized that none of her poi was getting onto the market. Yet she did not complain, for these great placid people had adopted her children when she was with the lepers. Even now Nyuk Tsin felt that she could not get along without them, for they tended the boys, did the laundry, brought the gossip home from the poolroom, and took care of the poi. But in prudence Nyuk Tsin felt she had to protect herself, so at last she said to Kimo, "I would like to buy your upper fields."

"Buy?" Kimo asked in astonishment. "You can have them."

"Maybe it's better if I buy them, properly."

"They're yours," Apikela insisted.

"Could we go to the land office and sign the papers?" Nyuk Tsin asked. "And I'll pay you."

Big Apikela lifted her Chinese friend in the air and sat her on her lap, saying, "Kimo and I have no use for the land. We have no children."

"You have the four boys," Nyuk Tsin corrected.

"Good idea!" Kimo cried. "We'll give the land to our boys." So the three of them went down to the land office and registered the sale of the upper fields to the Kee boys, and when the white man asked, through his interpreter, "And what fee changed hands?" the two huge Hawaiians looked confused, and the official explained, "There has to be a recognized fee, or the sale isn't legal."

Nyuk Tsin began to say that she had a bagful of dimes and reals and Australian gold pieces saved for her sons' education and she was willing, but Kimo interrupted, and with a grand gesture said, "We sell this Pake our land in return for all the poi we can eat." And that was what Nyuk Tsin had been thinking about in the first place, and that was how the deed was registered.

It was a strange and yet typical Hawaii-like life that Nyuk Tsin now led. Her four sons spoke mainly Hawaiian and English, and she communicated with them only in broken Hawaiian. They were carefully taught to think of the shadowy woman in China as their mother, but they considered Apikela their mamma, just as she thought of them as her sons. Nobody in the household even knew Nyuk Tsin's name, the Hawaiians always calling her merely the Pake, and her children knowing her as Auntie. In food, language and laughter the establishment was Hawaiian. In school-book learning, business and religion it was American. But in filial obedience and reverence for education it was Chinese.

Nyuk Tsin's years fell into an almost sacred routine. On the first of March she went to the land office and paid her taxes on her two properties, and her most valued physical possession became a box in which she kept her receipts. For her they were a kind of citizenship, a proof that she had a right to stay in the Fragrant Tree Country.

In September and June she washed her one suit of clothes with special care, dressed her hair with a fresh cloth, and accompanied her four sons to discuss their education with Uliassutai Karakoram Blake, who found delight in talking Chinese with her and who said that her sons were doing well. Her insistence upon this was fanatical, and whenever she talked with Blake she hammered one question: "Which of my four sons has the best mind?" And the big, fierce man would reflect and reply, "America." She was pleased to know that her brilliant son was doing well in school, for she loved to visualize the day on which he would set out to the mainland for his advanced schooling, to be supported by all the others.

In April and October, Nyuk Tsin faithfully trekked down to the Punti store with an appropriate number of dollars and sent them off to Kee Mun Ki's family in the Low Village. Always she took her four sons with her, even though it meant keeping them out of school, for she impressed them with this: "Even more important than education is filial duty, and you are four brothers who must work extra hard to pay the respect due your father and his family." She made each of the boys actually finger the money as it was turned over, and each of them touched the resulting letter. "Now you can go back to school," she said. Sometimes she thought it strange that she should be inculcating these ancient Chinese virtues not in the powerful Hakka language but in a broken Hawaiian pidgin. However, the virtues were self-evident and the boys understood.

Such was the year of Nyuk Tsin, the Pake Kokua, the Auntie. For herself she had one blouse, one pair of trousers, no shoes and one basket hat. She had a bamboo carrying-pole, two baskets, a poi factory that made no money, and two parcels of land that would one day be worth more than a million dollars. But the revolution in which this slim-hipped Chinese woman was involved stemmed mainly from the fact that she had four bright boys in Iolani, and when they were ready to move into Honolulu's economic life, fortified by Uliassutai Blake's inspired learning and their Auntie's frugal common sense, there would be little that could stop them.

And then one day in 1879, as Nyuk Tsin was leading her sons to the Episcopal church, she saw a Hawaiian family entering with seven children, and one of the boys looked Chinese. She began studying this child and concluded that he must be about eight years old, which would be the age of her missing son. She was not sure that he was Chinese, for he blended perfectly with his Hawaiian brothers and sisters, but when service ended she sent her sons home with thirteen-year-old Asia and quietly followed the Hawaiian family to their residence. She found it to be a large, rambling house on Beretania Street far out Diamond Head way, and the eight-year-old boy seemed fully at home there. She tried to ask a passer-by what the family's name was but could not make the man understand.

She now revised her peddling routes and walked miles out of her way to keep check on the big Hawaiian house, and in time she found that the Chinese boy went to school, seemed normally bright, and was known only by a Hawaiian name. Once she lugged her pineapples onto the veranda of the house itself and tried to engage the mother of the household in conversation, but the latter wanted no pineapples. When she had exhausted all her own ingenuity, she decided to discuss the matter frankly with Apikela, but as she was about to do so, her intuition warned her that the big Hawaiian woman would sympathize with her fellow Hawaiian who now had the child, rather than with its rightful mother Nyuk Tsin; furthermore, she concluded that this was the kind of adventure that would appeal to Kimo, who considered himself not exactly fitted for other kinds of work. Accordingly, she took the big, shirtless man aside and said, "Find out who those people are."

"I don't have to find out," he replied simply. "That's Governor Kelolo Kanakoa's house."

"Find out where they got the Pake child."

"Good," Kimo grunted, and he set off to the poolroom and in a short time reported: "The governor was on the docks one day when a ship came in with a little baby boy, and no one knew what to do with it, so naturally the governor said, 'I'll take him,' and he did." Kimo shrugged his shoulders as if to say, "Isn't that simple?" And then he saw what Nyuk Tsin was driving at. "The boy belongs to Kelolo!" he warned. "He fed him. He brought him up."

"But he's a Pake," Nyuk Tsin argued. "He's mine."

"Of course!" Kimo agreed. "He's your boy, but he belongs to the governor."

Patiently, but with swelling emotion, Nyuk Tsin reasoned: "I did not give the child to the governor. I sent him to you, to keep for me till I got home."

"But what did it matter who got the child?" Kimo reasoned back. "The boy has a home and parents who love him. He has others to play with and enough food. What does it matter?"

"I want him to grow up to be a Chinese," Nyuk Tsin argued, growing nervous.

"I don't understand," Kimo said blankly. "When I was young my father always had two or three sailors who had fled their ships, hiding out in our fields up there. Swedish, Americans, Spaniards, it didn't matter. Sometimes they had babies with my sisters, and where are the babies now? I don't know, neither do my sisters. And are they Spanish or Hawaiian? Who cares?"

Nyuk Tsin found herself making no headway with Kimo, so against her better judgment she enlarged the debate to include Apikela, and as she suspected, the big Hawaiian woman instinctively sided with the boy's Hawaiian mother. "You must think of how much the governor's wife has grown to love this boy," Apikela reasoned.

"But she has six children of her own!" Nyuk Tsin replied in growing despair.

"They aren't all her own!" Apikela replied triumphantly. "Some were left in the street and one I know comes from Maui."

"I am going to get my son," Nyuk Tsin said stubbornly.

"Pake!" Apikela warned. "He is no longer your son."

Nyuk Tsin spoke unwisely: "Are the other four boys no longer my sons, either?"

Softly Apikela replied, "No, Pake, they are not yours alone. They are now my sons too." She did not have the words to explain that in the Hawaiian system the filial-parent relationship was completely fluid, and son-ship derived not from blood lines but from love. No child was ever left abandoned, and some of the most touching narratives of Hawaiian history stemmed from the love of some peasant woman who heard the cries of an unwanted girl baby whom the alii had left beside the sea to perish, and the peasant woman had rescued the child and had raised it as her own until war came, or some other great event, and then the child was revealed in full beauty. It had happened again and again. Apikela was unable to explain all these things to her Pake friend, but she did add this: "In all the Hawaiian families you see, there will always be one child that was found somewhere. A friend gave the child to the family, and that was that."

Stubbornly Nyuk Tsin repeated her question: "Then my boys are not my sons?"

"Not yours alone," huge Apikela repeated. The little Chinese woman, steeled in the Hakka tradition of family, stared at her big Hawaiian friend, reared in the softer tradition of love, and each woman typified the wisdom of her race, and neither would surrender, but as always, it was the copious Hawaiian who made the overture of peace: "Surely, Pake, with four boys we have enough for two mothers." And the big woman was so persuasive that even though Nyuk Tsin despised the concept being offered, and saw in it an explanation of why the Hawaiians were dying out and the Chinese were thriving, she could not ignore the testimony of love that she saw in the happy faces of her sons. Even if they did have to live suspended between Hawaiian love and Chinese duty, they were thriving; so at last Nyuk Tsin allowed herself to be drawn into Apikela's great arms and cherished, as if she were a daughter and not an equal. Then the big woman said, "Now that our tempers are at peace, let us go see the governor's wife."

Sedately, she and Kimo and the Pake walked down Nuuanu to Beretania and then out toward Diamond Head, and when they got to the governor's big house, Apikela said softly, "I will speak," and as if she were an ambassador from the court of the Nuuanu taro patch to the high court of Beretania Street, she explained to the governor's wife: "The Pake thinks your seventh child is hers."

"Probably is," Governor Kelolo's wife agreed easily. "I think my husband found him on a boat."

"The Pake would like to take the boy home with her," Apikela said softly.

The governor's wife looked down at her hands and began to cry. Finally she said gently, "We think of the boy as our own."

"See!" Apikela said, and she withdrew from the interview, for there was obviously nothing more to say.

But Nyuk Tsin was just beginning. "I appreciate what you did for the boy. He looks very clean and intelligent. But he is my son, and I would like to . . ."

"He is very happy here," the governor's wife explained.

"He is my son," Nyuk Tsin struggled. She felt as if she were engulfed in a mass of cloud or formless foam. She could push it back, but always it returned to smother her. The three big Hawaiians were falling upon her, strangling her with love.

Again the governor's wife was speaking: "But we think of him as our son, too."

"If I went to court, what would the judge say?" Nyuk Tsin threatened.

Now both the governor's wife and Apikela began to weep, and the former said, "There is no need to involve the judges. Apikela said that you had your four sons with you. Why not leave the fifth boy with us? We love him very much."

"He is my son," Nyuk Tsin stubbornly argued, but the phrase really had little meaning to the three Hawaiians. Obviously, the attractive boy was a son in many more ways than this thin Chinese woman could understand.

At this point the governor himself entered, a tall, handsome man in his late forties. He was generous in his attitude toward everyone and listened patiently, first to Apikela, then to his wife, and finally to Nyuk Tsin. When he spoke he said, "Then you are the Pake Kokua?"

"Yes," Nyuk Tsin replied.

"Every Hawaiian owes a debt to you, Kokua." He formally extended his hand. Then he remembered: "It was about eight years ago. I was at the docks on some kind of business. I wasn't governor then, had just come over from Maui. And this ship came in with a sailor who had a screaming baby, and he said, 'What shall I do with it?' And I said, 'Feed it.' And he said, 'I got no tits.' So I took the boy and brought him home." He paused significantly, then added, "And we made him one of our sons."

"Now I want him," Nyuk Tsin said forcefully.

"And it would seem to me," the governor said, ignoring her, "that it might be a very good thing if this Chinese boy continued to grow up in this house, among the Hawaiians. We two races need to understand each other better." Then he stopped and said bluntly, "I love the boy as my own son. I don't think I could let him go."

"The judge will give him to me," Nyuk Tsin said coldly.

Tears came into the big man's eyes and he asked, "Have you no other children of your own?"

"I have four," Nyuk Tsin replied.

"Then leave the boy with us. Please don't speak of judges."

The governor's wife brought in tea, and Nyuk Tsin was invited to sit in the best brocaded chair, and Kimo asked if they happened to have any poi. The meeting lasted for four patient hours, and the little Chinese woman was positively beat down by love. When her son was summoned she saw that he was big and bright and strong. He was not told that the strange Chinese woman in the smock and trousers was his mother, for he called the governor's wife that, and after he was dismissed, many proposals were made, and Nyuk Tsin consented to this: her fifth son would continue to live with the governor, but he must be told who his real mother was . . . And here Nyuk Tsin began to get mixed up, because she also insisted that the boy be given the Chinese name Oh Chow, the Continent of Australia, and that twice each year he accompany his brothers to the Punti store when the money was sent to his real mother in China.

"His real mother?" the governor asked.

"Yes," Nyuk Tsin explained. "His real mother is in China. I am merely his auntie."

"I thought you gave birth to the boy in Kalawao," the governor checked.

"I did," Nyuk Tsin assured him. "But his mother is in China."

The governor listened patiently and asked, "Could you please explain this again?" and as Nyuk Tsin repeated the curious rigmarole he realized that he was comprehending very little of it.

So Nyuk Tsin took Australia to the Punti store, where his name was duly forwarded to the ancestral hall in the Low Village, while he continued to be known in Hawaii as Keoki Kanakoa, the son of the last governor of Honolulu. He met his brothers, Asia, Europe, Africa and America, and then returned to the big rambling house. He called Nyuk Tsin, whose name he never knew, Auntie, and he vaguely understood that in China he had a real mother, to whom it was his duty to send money twice a year.

There was one other thing that Nyuk Tsin insisted upon. Four acres of Governor Kanakoa's choicest upland in Manoa Valley, then a wet, forested wilderness, were officially deeded over to the boy Australia Kee, otherwise known as Keoki Kanakoa, and after these were cleared, Nyuk Tsin grew pineapples on them. She was now thirty-two years old, and except for a really gaunt thinness and a lack of hair she was what one might call an attractive woman; but even though there was an appalling lack of women for Chinese men—246 women; 22,000 men—none of the latter ever considered Nyuk Tsin as a wife. She had proved herself to be a husband-killer and she was probably also a leper.

So she lived spiritually apart from her sons and her community. Each night after the others were in bed, she stripped herself naked and with a small lamp inspected each area of her body, and when she had finally cleared even her big feet of suspicion she sighed and said to herself, "Still no leprosy." And if she avoided this, nothing else mattered.

WHEN WHIPPLE HOXWORTH RETURNED to Hawaii in 1877 he had brought with him only a hundred pineapple plants and a bag of miscellaneous seeds to show for his seven years abroad, but he had already become the man who was destined to rebuild the structure of the islands. He was tall, wiry-thin, quick both in muscle and wit and unusually well trained in the use of his fists. He had the insolent assurance of his paternal grandfather, Captain Rafer Hoxworth, plus the distinguished bearing that had characterized his maternal grandfather, Dr. John Whipple. He also exhibited certain other behavior patterns of those two men.

Like Captain Rafer, young Whip had an insatiable desire for women, and following quickly upon the Chinese girl who had taught him lessons at the age of thirteen, he had enjoyed the wild companionship of strange women in most of the world's major ports. His entire earnings for seven years had been spent freely on these women, and he regretted not a penny of his loss, for he had made an essential discovery: he had it within his power to make women happy. Sometimes at a formal party, when as a budding second mate he was invited to a home of distinction in Perth or Colombo or Bangkok, he would enter the room and physically feel the lines of communication establishing themselves between him and certain women, and as the night wore on he would stare quietly, yet with insolent power, at the most likely of these companions, and he would seek her out for a dance and say certain modest yet fire-filled things to her, and the atmosphere often became so charged with passion that when he had maneuvered to find himself alone with the woman, she would thrust herself into his arms and encourage him to do with her as he wished, even though a few hours before they had not known of each other's existence. Whenever he entered a party he hesitated a moment at the doorway and thought: "Who will be in there tonight?" For he had found that there was always someone.

In his reflections during long days at sea young Whip never thought in polished terms of "milady's glove" or "my dear Miss Henderson." He thought of girls as strong young animals, naked and stretched out on a bed. That's how he liked women and that's how they liked to be when they were with him. They were utterly enjoyable playmates, and to think of them otherwise was a waste of energy. He made no distinctions as between married or unmarried women; he derived no special pleasure from cuckolding a married man; nor did he find women of any particular nationality or color especially desirable. If he could not gain entrance in Suez to the soiree of a French nobleman, he was quite content to pay down his livres at an established house and take his pick of the professional companions, but even though he often preferred this simple and direct method of acquiring a partner, he had also learned to be a professional gallant, and if he came upon some shy young lady who seemed worth the effort, he stood willing to humble himself before her as a traditional suitor out of a book, sending her flowers and candy, writing her short notes in his vigorous style, and dancing a rather impressive attendance upon her; for he always remembered his grandfather's advice: "When your great-grandmother Malama lay dying, she weighed over four hundred pounds, and her husband crawled in to see her every morning on his hands and knees, bringing her maile. That's not a bad thing for a man to do." Young Whip loved women passionately. He knew that they complemented his life and he was willing to do almost anything to make them happy.

As might be expected, his behavior when he returned from his seven years' cruise took Honolulu rather by surprise. He completely terrified the Hale and Hewlett girls by professing to each in turn his Persian-Egyptian type of love, acquired, as he intimated, by long travels in a camel caravan toward ruined cities of antiquity. The poor girls never really understood what the dashing young man was talking about, but they did discover that he had a great determination to get their underwear off as quickly as possible, so that pretty soon it was agreed among the missionary daughters that they would prefer not to be escorted by their Cousin Whip. He discovered early that one of his full cousins, Nancy Janders, was amenable to his attentions, and they entered into a disgraceful series of performances that ended with Whip being caught in her bedroom completely stripped at five o'clock one morning. Nancy was not to be bullied by her parents and cried that a girl had a right to get to know young men, but that very night young Whip's gig was left stranded at the entrance to Rat Lane down at the Iwilei brothels because a violent fight had broken out over an Arabian girl, and Whip had got cut across his left cheek with a sailor's knife. The next day Nancy Janders' father packed her off to the mainland and young Whip started fooling around with a Portuguese-Hawaiian girl, a great beauty whose grandfather had reached the islands via the Azores. She and Whip engaged in a brilliant courtship, marked by her riding openly with him through the gayer streets of the city and then hustling secretly off to California to have a baby.

By this time some of the younger men of town had given the young seafarer his permanent name. It was bestowed following a brawl in which Whip fought three English sailors outside the impressive H & H building on Fort Street. His austere father rushed down from his offices above the street in time to see his lithe son stretched out cold from a combination of a British blow to the side of the head and a stiff British kick to the groin. While the handsome boy lay in the dusty street, a nearby bartender doused him with a bucket of cold water, but as the fallen fighter gradually began to feel the throbbing pain in his crotch, he bellowed, "Somebody hit me again!" He looked up to see his father's beard staring down at him and he wanted to faint from humiliation and pain, but he scrambled to his feet and hobbled off.

From then on they called him "Wild Whip," and he seemed dedicated to the principle that every man must prove his right to whatever nickname has been bestowed upon him. He did not drink much, nor did he engage in fist fights willingly. In many respects he was a clean, handsome young man. But if he did not seek trouble, neither did he avoid it, and he developed a characteristic gesture, when a fight loomed, of shrugging his shoulders and ambling a few lazy steps forward before exploding into furious action. Normally he would have lost his nickname as he grew older, for he became content to by-pass general brawls, and that aspect of his wildness diminished; but as it regressed, his passion for women increased, and it was his adventures in this field that contantly lured him back into trouble. He often recalled his grandfather's apt simile: "Girls are like lovely little stars. You could reach up and pinch each one on the points." Wild Whip's capacity for reaching and pinching was insatiable, and in this he was a true grandson of Rafer Hoxworth.

But he also resembled in many ways his maternal grandfather, Dr. John Whipple, for in addition to that gallant man's physical handsomeness young Whip had inherited his abiding interest in science. Wherever he had gone during his seven years at sea, Whip had studied plants, grown to love local flowers, and collected specimens of trees and fruits that looked as if they might do well in Hawaii. But three particular discoveries had given him almost as much pleasure as leaping stalwartly into bed with a new girl. He had found the jungle orchids of Malaya positively enchanting, and he had gathered several dozen prime specimens of purple and crimson and burnt-gold beauties which he had shipped home by way of an H & H freighter out of Singapore. They now flourished in a lath house which he had constructed in back of the Hoxworth home on Beretania Street, and it was a major characteristic of their owner that as soon as they established themselves in Hawaii, they were given freely to others who might fancy them. Young Whip made his money running ships and working plantations; the rare plants he brought into the islands were free to anyone who would care for them as diligently as he, so that in later years when Hawaii became famous for its orchids, that fame was but an extension of Whip Hoxworth's personal concern with beauty. He also brought in ginger flowers, and two varieties of bird-of-paradise, that strange, almost unbelievable exotic which produced a burnished blue and red canoe out of which sprang a fantastic flower construction in purple and gold. All these Whip gave away.

He was also responsible for both the Formosa and the New Guinea pineapple, establishing the former through the help of the Chinese vegetable huckster, Mrs. Kee. The latter, which was more acid and therefore much tastier, he failed to perpetuate. Twice in later years he endeavored to make this contrary pineapple grow, but with no success. He had his agents looking for a new strain which would combine the virtues of the Formosa and New Guinea types, but he did not find any.

But his major contribution at this period was a tree which later came to bear his name. He found it growing near Bombay, and when he first tasted its fruit he cried, "This tree we've got to have in Hawaii." Accordingly, he shipped four saplings home, but they died. He ordered four more and directed them to be planted in Kona on the big island, but they also died. He got four more, each in its own washtub of Bombay soil, and it was these that grew. When they produced their first fruit—a handsome hard rind that turned gold and red and speckled green, inside of which rested a big flat seed surrounded by delicious yellow meat—his neighbors asked what strange thing he had this time.

"Watch!" he said crisply. "You're about to taste the king of fruits." He gripped one, took out his knife and gashed a complete circle around the long axis. Then he spun the knife, point-over-end, into the tree and with two hands gripped the halves of the fruit, twisting them in opposite directions. The fruit tore apart and for the first time the people of Hawaii tasted Whip's luscious discovery.

"Like baked nuts with a touch of apple," one man judged.

"Something like a peach with a trace of turpentine," another said.

"What is it, Whip?"

"A Bombay mango," Hoxworth replied.

"We used to have mangoes around here years ago," the man replied. "But as I recall they were stringy. Couldn't hardly eat 'em."

"There are mangoes and mangoes," Whip agreed. "Trick is, to find the good ones. Then take care of them."

In later years many people grew to despise Wild Whip Hoxworth, for he developed into the ruthless operator his grandfather had been. The extension of H & H from merely a strong shipping line into the dictator-company of the islands was not accomplished easily, and if men hated Wild Whip they had a right to, but no one ever failed to remember with keen appreciation his first major gift to Hawaii. Whenever a hungry man reached up, knocked down a Hoxworth mango, circled it with his knife and sucked in the aromatic fruit, he instinctively paid tribute to Wild Whip. Other varieties came later, but the Hoxworth remained what its discoverer had once claimed it to be: "the king of fruits."

When Whip saw his mangoes established and had given several hundred saplings away to his friends, he turned his attention to the affairs of H & H, whereupon he ran headfirst into his bearded uncle, stern Micah Hale, a symbol of rectitude and a man determined not to have the H & H empire sullied by the escapades of his wild young nephew. Consequently, there was no opening for Whip. When he applied for a job, his grim-faced uncle stared at him over his copious beard and said, "You've outraged all the girls in our family, young man, and we have no place for you."

"I'm not applying for a wife," Whip snapped. "I'm applying for a job."

"A man who isn't appropriate for a husband, isn't appropriate for a job . . . not with H & H," Uncle Micah replied, enunciating one of the firmest rocks of his company's policies, for like most of the great emperors of history, the Hales and Whipples and Janderses realized that an institution had to go forward on two levels: it produced intelligent sons to carry on when the old men died, and it produced beautiful daughters to lure able young husbands into the enterprise. It was an open question as to whether the great families of Hawaii prospered most from selling sugar at a good price or their daughters to good husbands. "There's no place for you in H & H," Uncle Micah said with finality.

When Whip appealed to his father, he found that sensitive and confused weakling quite unwilling to fight with Micah, who now controlled the family ventures. "Your behavior has been such . . ." Whip's father began plaintively, whereupon his son said, "Stow it."

There was a good deal of argument within the family, but Uncle Micah said firmly, "Our success in Hawaii depends upon our presenting to the public an attitude of the most strict rectitude. There has never been a scandal in the big firms, and there won't be as long as I control them. I think that Whipple ought to go back to sea. We'll reward him justly for his part ownership of the business, but he must stay out of Hawaii."

And then clever Micah thought of a happy solution. Recalling his nephew's interest in growing things, he suggested a compromise: Wild Whip would divorce himself completely from all H & H enterprises, and an announcement of this fact would be made public so as to absolve men like Micah Hale and Bromley Hoxworth from responsibility for his future actions, and in return Whip would be given four thousand acres of the family's land to do with as he wished. When the assembled Hoxworths and Hales delivered this ultimatum to their errant son, Wild Whip smiled graciously, accepted the four thousand acres, and said evenly, "Jesus, are you goddamned missionaries going to regret this day!"

He harnessed up two good horses and started westward to survey the lands he had been given. He drove some distance out of town, shaking the dust from his nose and staring at the bleak, grassless hills that rose to his right. Above them stood the barren mountains of the Koolau Range, and as far as he could see nothing grew. He drove past Pearl Harbor and out to where the land began to level off between the Koolau Mountains to the right and the Waianae Range to the left. Ahead lay his land. It was bleak, barren, profitless. Looking at it he recalled his Uncle Micah's description of the deserts of western America when that young minister traversed them in 1849: "They were lands where nothing grew, not even grass."

Grimly amused, Wild Whip tied his horses to a rock, for there were no trees, and got out to study his inheritance at closer quarters. When he kicked away the surface growth of lichen and dried scrub grass, he found that the soil was a rich reddish color that his Grandfather Whipple had once explained as the result of the gradual breaking down of volcanic rocks. "It's rich in iron," Whip mused. "Probably grow things like mad if it could get water."

He looked back at Pearl Harbor and saw the wide expanse of salt sea water, useless to a farmer. He looked up at the sky and saw no clouds, for few arrived here with rain, and then he happened to look toward the Koolau Range to his right, and above its peaks he saw many dark clouds, riding in upon the trade winds that bore down constantly from the northeast, and he could almost smell the water falling out of those clouds. It fell, of course, on the other side of the mountains and gushed furiously down steep valleys and back out to sea. His Grandfather Whipple had trapped a little in his ditches, but the bulk was as useless as the salt water of Pearl Harbor.

It was then that his great design came to him. "Why not build a tunnel right through the mountains and bring that water over here?" He visualized a system of ditches and dikes, all serving to bring the rich waters of the other side down to his parched lands. "I'll build that tunnel!" he swore. "I'll make this land so rich that by comparison Uncle Micah's boats will be worth nothing." He pointed his lone right forefinger at the Koolau Range and announced to those impassive giants: "Some day I'm going to walk right through your bowels. Be ready."

Curiously, Whip's great fortune was built in quite a different manner. When he saw that he was not wanted in his family's business, and when he had finished inspecting his imperial and useless acres, he decided to leave Hawaii, and he did so in memorable fashion. He had never forgotten how relatively pleasant it had been sleeping surreptitiously with his responsive cousin, Nancy Janders, still banished to the mainland, and now as he was about to leave he began paying deadly court to her saucy younger sister Iliki. It was a whirlwind affair, interspersed with wild nights in Rat Alley with a little French girl, and it culminated in pretty Iliki's slipping into men's clothes as a passenger aboard a British freighter whose captain married her to Whip on the journey to San Francisco. When the joint families heard of the scandal, they prayed that young Iliki would find a happiness which they felt sure would escape her; but when, in America, Iliki's older sister Nancy heard of the marriage she cried, "Damn them, damn them! I hope they both live in hell."

Wild Whip didn't, because he found considerable joy in his lively cousin, but Iliki did, for she discovered to her consternation and embarrassment that her husband had no intention of being loyal to her or of giving up his customary visits to local brothels. In San Francisco he had dashing affairs with several married women of otherwise good repute, and a running relationship with two popular Spanish courtesans from a waterfront institution of ill fame. In other ways he was a good husband, and when his son was born in 1880, he insisted that the boy be named Janders Hoxworth after his wife's father. He proved himself to be a doting husband and was obviously pleased to parade on Sunday after church with his wife on his arm and his son surrounded by lace in the perambulator which he proudly pushed.

But in late 1880 Iliki's sister visited them on her way back to Honolulu, and Nancy was now a striking New York beauty, and it was not long before Nancy's hatred of Wild Whip became once more the passionate love she had earlier known for this gallant gentleman. At first Whip sneaked away to Nancy's hotel, where they fell into wild, tormenting embraces. All the longing of three years rushed back upon poor Nancy Janders, and she abandoned restraint. She would lie in bed completely undressed, waiting for Whip to bound up the hotel stairs, and as soon as he burst into the room and locked the door, she would spring upon him and kiss him madly, throwing him onto the bed with laughter that welled up from her entire being. Sometimes she kept him imprisoned for a whole day, and it became obvious to her sister Iliki what was going on.

At first the gay little wife could not imagine what she ought to do; she wondered whether she was supposed to break into the hotel room and confront the guilty pair or whether custom required her to weep silently, but her problems were resolved when on a day which took her shopping she returned unexpectedly to find that bold Nancy had trailed Whip to his own home, had undressed in Iliki's room, and had pulled Whip into bed with her. When Iliki arrived, they stared up at her from her own sheets. Nobody made a scene. Nancy pouted: "I had him first. He's decided to stay with me."

"Put some clothes on," Iliki said, amazed at her restraint. When they were dressed Nancy announced defiantly, "Whip and I are going to live together."

Iliki did not bother to argue with her husband, for she knew that no matter what he promised, it was of no consequence. He was not like other men, and with deep sorrow—for she loved him very much—she saw that he was destined to bounce from one woman to another without ever resting with one, and she thought: "He'll have a very lonely life."

She left San Francisco with her son Janders and returned on an H & H liner to Honolulu, where she lived a long, full life as a divorcee, doing much good in the community. The natural history museum flourished largely because of her energies.

Her husband Whip and her sister Nancy enjoyed a wild time in San Francisco. Whip got a formal divorce but did not bother to marry Nancy, because, as he pointed out, "I'll never make a good husband." Nancy, finding in sex a complete gratification, was content to tag along on whatever terms he proposed, nor was she distressed when she uncovered suspicious circumstances that seemed to prove that her companion was also the consort of several well-known waterfront girls. What she liked best, however, apart from the passionate moments when he came home after a long absence, were the intense days when he took her with him to talk with men who had built tunnels. They were an odd, dedicated group of experts, willing to tackle nature on any terms, and they convinced Whip that if he could scrape together enough money, they could penetrate the Koolau Mountains and bring water to his dusty lands. Surreptitiously, he sent one of the engineer geologists to Hawaii, and in the guise of bird-collecting this keen fellow tramped the Koolaus and satisfied himself that tunneling them would present no unusual problems. "As a matter of fact," he reported, "it looks to me as if the mountains were built in layers tilted on end. If that's true, when you drill your tunnel you'll not only collect all the water you trap in outside ditches to lead into your tunnel, but the porous rock above the tunnel will probably deliver an equal amount of its own. This could be a profitable undertaking, so far as water's concerned."

"How long would the tunnel have to be?"

"Eight, ten miles," the engineer replied.

"Can you build a tunnel that long?" Whip asked.

"Any tunnel is simply a function of money," the engineer replied. "If you've got the money, I can get the dynamite."

"In this case, how much?"

"Four million."

"Don't forget my name," Whip said.

This report seemed to be the final answer to Whip's land problem. He didn't have the four million dollars then, but there was always a chance he might one day have it. He therefore decided to return to Hawaii, but Nancy Janders said, "I wouldn't, Whip."

"Why not?"

"Well, Iliki's there. That'll be embarrassing for you. And I certainly can't go back with you."

"I don't think you should," Whip said coldly, and a few days later he added, "You ought to be looking for a man for yourself, Nance."

"You through with me?" Nancy asked.

"No place for you in Hawaii," he said truthfully. "How you fixed for money?"

"The family sends me my share," she assured him.

"Nance," he said in his most friendly manner, "I sure hope you have a wonderful life from here on out. Now you better get some clothes on."

She had been gone only a few hours when there was a knock at his hotel-room door, and a little man in an overcoat that reached down to his ankles entered. "My name's Overpeck, Milton Overpeck, and I hear you're interested in drilling a tunnel."

"That's right," Whip said. "Sit down, Mr. Overpeck. You like whiskey?"

"I like anything," Overpeck said.

"You a tunnel man?"

"Well, yes and no," the little man replied, gulping a huge draft of whiskey. Coughing slightly he asked, "I understand you're drilling your tunnel in order to get water."

"You've followed me around pretty well, Mr. Overpeck. Another whiskey?"

"Look, son, if you calculate on getting me drunk and outsmarting me, quit now, because you simply can't do it."

"I'm offering it in hospitality," Whip assured him.

"I never accept hospitality unless the host joins me. Now you gulp one down and catch up, and we can have a fine talk."

The two men, Whip Hoxworth twenty-four years old and Milton Overpeck in his early fifties, guzzled straight whiskey for several hours, during which the little engineer fascinated the Hawaiian landowner with a completely new theory about water. The doughty drinker, whose eyes were bright and clear after three quarters of a bottle, apparently knew more about Hawaii than Whip did, at least about the island of Oahu.

"My theory is this," he explained, using pillows, books and newspapers to build his island. "This volcano here and this one here built Oahu. That's perfectly obvious. Now, as they built, one surely must have overflowed the rightful terrain of the other. I judge all volcanic rock to be porous, so in Oahu it seems to me you have got to have a complex substructure, the bulk of it porous. All the fine water that falls on your island doesn't run immediately out to sea."

"Well, the engineer I sent out there did say that he thought the mountains were probably porous," Whip remembered.

"I'm not interested in the mountains you see above land," Overpeck snapped. "I'm interested in the subterranean ones. Because if, as I suspect, there was a rising and a falling of the entire mountain mass . . ." He stopped, studied his friend and said, "Sorry, you're drunk. I'll be back in the morning." But as he was about to leave he said, "Don't sleep on a pillow tonight. Leave everything just as it is."

Whip, through bleary eyes, tried to focus on the turmoil in his room and asked, "What's all this got to do with tunnels?"

"I wouldn't know," Overpeck replied. "I'm a well man meself."

He appeared at seven next morning, chipper as a woodchuck, his long overcoat flapping about his ankles in the cold San Francisco weather. He surprised Whip by completely dismissing the intricate construction of pillows, books and newspapers. "Best thing is to show you," he said cheerily. "Wells'll be the making of Hawaii." And he led Whip down to the foot of Market Street, where grimy ferries left for the other side of the bay, and when after a long walk through Oakland they stood before a well he had recently dug he pointed with unconcealed admiration at a pipe protruding from the ground, from which gushed a steady volume of water that rose fourteen feet into the air.

"Does it run like this all the time?" Whip asked.

"Day and night," Overpeck replied.

"What does it?"

"Artesian, that's what it is. Artesian."

"How many gallons a day?"

"A million four."

"How long will it last?"

"Forever."

This was what Wild Whip had been dreaming of, a steady source of fresh water, but he had imagined that the only way to get it was to drive a tunnel through the mountains. If Overpeck were correct, where the water really lay was at his feet, but in business Whip was both daring and cautious. He was willing to take almost any gamble to obtain water, but he wanted assurance that he had at least a fair chance of winning. Carefully he asked, "Why did you have to bring me all the way over here to show me this well? Why didn't you show me one in San Francisco?"

"Artesian water don't happen everywhere," Overpeck replied.

"Suppose there isn't any on my land in Hawaii?"

"My job is to guess where it is," Overpeck answered. "And I guess it's under your land."

"Why?"

"That's what I was explaining with the pillows and the newspapers," he said.

"I think we better go back to the hotel," Whip said. "But wait a minute. How did you get the well down there?"

"A special rig I invented."

"How far down did you go?"

"Hundred and eighty feet."

"You want to sell the rig?"

"Nope."

"I didn't think so." The two men returned to the ferry, and as Whip studied the cold and windy hills of San Francisco, imagining them to be Hawaii, he became increasingly excited, but when little Mr. Overpeck assured him that a layer of cap rock must have imprisoned enormous stores of sweet water under the sloping flatlands of Oahu, Whip could feel actual perspiration break out on his forehead.

"What kind of deal can we make, Overpeck?" he asked bluntly.

"You're sweating, son. If I find water, I'm handing you millions of dollars, ain't I?"

"You are."

"I'm a gambler, Mr. Hoxworth. What I want is the land next to yours."

"How much?"

"You pay for getting the rig over there. You give me three dollars a day. And you buy, before we start, one thousand acres of land. If we get water, I buy it from you for what you paid. If we don't, you keep it."

"Are the chances good?"

"There's one way we can test my theory without spending a cent."

"How?"

"Think a minute. If there really is a pool of inexhaustible water hiding under your land, the overflow has got to be escaping somewhere. Logically, it's running away under the sea level, but some of it must be seeping out over the upmost edge of the cap rock. Go out to your land. Tell people you're going to raise cattle. Walk along the upper areas until you find a spring. Calculate how high above sea level you are, and then walk back and forth along that elevation. If you find half a dozen more springs, it's not even a gamble, Mr. Hoxworth. Because then you know the water's hiding down below you."

"You come out and check," Whip suggested.

"People might guess. Then land values go up."

Whip reflected on this shrewd observation and made a quick decision. "Buy yourself a good bull. Bring him to the islands with you and we'll announce that you're going to help me raise cattle. Then everybody'll feel sorry for me, because lots of people have gone bust trying that on the barren lands. Takes twenty of our acres to support one cow, and nobody makes money."

Three weeks later little Mr. Overpeck arrived in Honolulu with a bull and announced to the Honolulu *Mail* that he was going to advise Mr. Whipple Hoxworth in the raising of cattle on the latter's big ranch west of the city. He led his bull out to the vast, arid, useless acres, and as soon as he got there he told Whip, "Buy that land over there for me." And Whip did, for practically nothing, and the next day he concluded that he had been victimized by the shrewd little man, for they tramped both Whip's acres and Overpeck's, and there were no springs.

"Why the hell did you bother me with your nonsense?" the young man railed.

"I didn't expect any springs today," Overpeck said calmly. "But I know where they'll crop out after the next big storm up in the mountains," and sure enough, three days after the rain clouds left, along the line that Overpeck had predicted, he and Whip discovered sure evidences of seepage. They stood on the hillside looking down over the bleak and barren acres, Whip's four thousand and Overpeck's one, and the little man said, "We're standing on a gold mine, Mr. Hoxworth. I'm mortally certain there's water below. Buy up all the land you can afford."

Eight weeks later the little man reappeared in Hawaii without any cattle, but with nine large boxes of gear. This time he informed the *Mail:* "It looks as if Mr. Hoxworth's investment in cattle is going to be lost unless somehow we can find water on those acres."

He set up a pyramidal wooden derrick about twelve feet high, at the bottom of which were slung two large iron wheels connected by an axle upon which rope could be wound when the wheels were turned by hand. This rope went from the axle and up to the top of the derrick, where it crossed on a pulley and dropped down to be lashed to the end of a heavy iron drill. Laboriously Overpeck cranked the heavy wheels until the iron drill was hauled to the top of the derrick. Then he tripped a catch and jumped back as the drill plunged downward, biting its way through sand and rock. Laboriously he turned the wheels and lifted the drill back into position; then a swift whirrrrr, and the next bite was taken.

"How long will this take?" Hoxworth asked, amazed at the effort required.

"A long time."

"Have you the strength?"

"I'm boring for a million dollars," the wiry little man replied. "I got the strength."

Days passed and weeks, and the determined engineer kept hoisting his drills, breaking their points on almost impenetrable hard pan, sharpening them by hand, and hoisting them once more. "You ought to have an engine," Whip growled as the work made slow progress.

"When I get some money, I'll get an engine," Overpeck snapped.

Now Whip saw the little fighter in a new light. "All your life you've been broke, haven't you?"

"Yep. All my life I was waiting for a man like you."

"Are we going to hit water?"

"Yep."

At two hundred feet the drills were hammering their way through cap rock, once soft ocean mud but now, millions of years later, rock as hard as diamonds. Whip grew despondent and was afraid to pass through the streets of Honolulu, where people already hated him for the way he had treated his former wife, Iliki Janders, and where they now laughed at him for his folly in trying to raise cattle on his barren acres. At first, when those who had sold additional land saw Overpeck's drilling rig, there had been consternation: "Has Whip bamboozled us? Did he know there was water below that rubble?" Such fears relaxed when it was apparent that no water existed. "He's down to two hundred and fifty feet and is running out of rope," spies reported.

And then on the fourteenth of September, 1881, Milton Overpeck's plunging drill crashed through the last two inches of cap rock, and up past the iron, past the rope, gushed cold sweet water at the rate of one million three hundred thousand gallons a day. When it gurgled to the top of the well it kept rising until it reached the apex of the twelve-foot derrick and stood a steady fourteen feet in the air, hour after hour, month after month.

When Whip saw the glorious sight he became agitated and cried, "We must save that water!" But little Mr. Overpeck assured him, "Son, it'll run forever." They scooped out a large depression in which the water was impounded and then pumped to wherever it was needed. They drilled additional wells, all by hand, and Whip said, "Overpeck, it's ridiculous for you to do so much work. Let's buy an engine that'll do it for you," but the determined little man replied, "I finish these wells, I'm never going to work again. I'm going to get a hotel room, lease my land to you, and live easy."

He did all these things, but he had failed to anticipate the natural future of a man like Overpeck in Hawaii. One of the unmarried Janders girls smelled him out, checked the land records to be sure he owned the land he said he did, and married him. Thus his thousand acres was brought safely back into the grand alliance of Hoxworth-Whipple-Hale-Janders-Hewlett.

Whip worked like a maniac organizing his own acres, now six thousand, plus the thousand he leased from Overpeck, and by means of pumps and ditches brought water to all of it. He bought out the old Malama Sugar Plantation and transferred its name and operation to his new lands. Then, with the touch of genius that characterized his business dealings, at the age of twenty-six he turned the entire management of his sugar lands over to Janders & Whipple, and he set out to see more of the world.

In late 1883 he returned to Honolulu with a cargo of new orange trees from Malaya; some excellent coffee beans from Brazil; the amazing torch ginger flower, a red slashing thing; and a tall, dark Spanish wife Aloma Duarte Hoxworth, who quickly bore him a son whom she insisted upon calling Jesus Duarte Hoxworth and whom Honolulu called Jadey, derived from his initials. Aloma Hoxworth was a sensation in the islands, for she was by nature an exotic creature and she quickly announced to her husband that his days of roistering on Rat Alley were ended. But it was easier for her to issue such instructions than to enforce them, so one night when Whip came home from delightful hours with a Chinese prostitute, Aloma Duarte tried to carve him up with a long knife. She gashed him badly across the scar in his left cheek, but before she could strike again he kicked her in the stomach, knocked her breathless against the wall, and proceeded to break her jaw and wrist.

"No one comes at me with a knife," he explained publicly, and when the once-beautiful woman was mended she decided to bring brutality charges against him in the Honolulu courts, but against her stood the mute testimony of the jagged gash in Wild Whip's cheeks, and her lawyers advised her to drop charges. When she did so, Micah Hale, Bromley Hewlett and Mark Whipple visited her and advised her that they were ready to provide her with a small but adequate annuity if she would agree to leave the islands.

"There's no place for you here," Micah explained.

"I'm taking Jadey with me," she threatened.

"Whip won't allow that," her father-in-law warned.

"Jadey is for me!" Aloma Duarte stormed.

"He belongs in the islands," Micah reasoned with her, and in the end she left exactly as the family had originally planned, with exactly the annuity they had suggested. In New York she told a friend, "I was more afraid of the three bearded ones than I was of my husband. He comes at you with his fists, but they soft-talk you to death. In Hawaii they run things pretty much their own way. But they were generous."

And west of Honolulu, the once barren lowlands that had formerly required twenty acres to nourish a cow, blossomed into the lushest, most profitable agricultural lands in the world. When the sugar cane stood eight feet tall, bursting with juice, for mile after mile you could not see the red volcanic soil, nor could you see the water that Wild Whip had brought to it. All you could see was money.

IN 1885 Nyuk Tsin could no longer postpone decision about her sons, and as she studied Ah Chow, Au Chow, Fei Chow, Mei Chow and Oh Chow she realized both how difficult her job was going to be and how important. At Iolani, the Church of England school, she was giving the boys the best education available to them on the islands. Had they been able to get into Punahou, they would have learned more and would have associated with the missionary children who were destined to rule Hawaii, but for both financial and social reasons, entry there was forbidden, and they had done well at the second-rate school.

But now the older boys were ready for advanced education, and it was clear that each merited college and university. They were bright boys, well behaved, industrious and alert. Their pigtails were well tended and they had learned to keep their nails clean. They had good teeth and clear skins. They were reasonably good at games and spoke four languages with skill: Punti, Hakka, Hawaiian and English. Each was above high-school ability in mathematics and abstract reasoning, and to choose among them the boy on whose shoulders the entire burden of the family should fall was difficult indeed.

Nyuk Tsin was confused as to which of her boys ought to go to America, nor could she decide what he ought to study when he got there. In early 1885, therefore, she began her long inquiry, starting with Uliassutai Karakoram Blake, and he wasn't of much help because he vigorously espoused two directly conflicting criteria. As an Englishman he swore: "No boy is worth educating unless he's proved himself good at games. Europe is the one. He has spirit and quickness of hand. He looks you in the eye when he gives you an answer. Fine, clean-cut lad to be trusted. Grow up to be a substantial man." That much was easy to understand, but when Uliassutai had said that—sort of in deference to British tradition—he promptly added, "But of course England's the only place in the world where a man can get ahead simply because he has good character and the brain of an ass. Everywhere else you have to have intelligence, and let's face up to it, Wu Chow's Auntie, your son Europe is an ass, and I'm afraid that's done it. The only one who shows the quick intelligence required in a scholar is America. But he's so appalling at games I can never take him seriously. Probably turn out to be a pretty poor sort in the end, a thinker and all that. I'd never waste me money on him, but in France he'd likely end up in the cabinet."

Nyuk Tsin pretty well agreed with Uliassutai in his analysis of the two boys. Europe was going to make friends wherever he went and was a fine, congenial boy, not too good at books, but an admirable son. America was clearly the ablest but he had a shy, withdrawing quality that sometimes frightened her. She concluded that what Blake was saying, in his cryptic way, was that he could not make the final choice.

Apikela and Kimo were certainly not obscure. "The only one is Australia," they said firmly. "He speaks such good Hawaiian he sounds educated already." When Nyuk Tsin tried to press them on things like character, ability to work, or insight in business they gave a quick, easy answer: "Only one's Australia. When he sings a song, you can hear the words so beautifully." Nyuk Tsin pointed out: "You two are with the boys more than I am. What do you see in them?" And again the answer was direct: "Australia is the one who will lead a happy life, because he has such a handsome smile and he knows how to laugh." Whenever the boy visited the Kee house, slipping away from his Hawaiian parents, Nyuk Tsin would hear him joking with Kimo and Apikela, and once when she said to him, "Maybe you will go to America for your education," he had replied, "I like it here." His friends were divided into four almost equal groups: Punti, Hakka, Hawaiians and haoles. At Iolani he was elected president of his class and sang in the glee club. "Then you would send Australia to college?" Nyuk Tsin pressed, and big Apikela replied, "Oh, yes! He'd have a lot of fun at college." Nyuk Tsin pointed out: "But we're sending him to study," and the Hawaiians laughed, "Give him just as much as his tired little head will take, and forget the rest."

The Chinese community was again fairly clear in its recommendation. Partly because Asia was the oldest son and therefore to be respected unless he proved himself inadequate, but mainly because he had already opened a restaurant on Hotel Street that did a good business, he was their overwhelming choice. The Punti said, "This boy can be trusted. He buys wisely and sells with intelligence. At nineteen he's already a better businessman than my son at twenty-five. I wish he were my boy." The Hakka told Nyuk Tsin: "We have watched your boys for some years, and the others sometimes seem more Hawaiian than Chinese, but Asia is different. He has a real Chinese understanding, and he will do well." Few Chinese deviated from this strong recommendation, and when Nyuk

Tsin arranged a marriage for him with a Punti wife whose father owned land, he built himself even more solidly into the Chinese community. Asia Kee was bound to become a powerful man.

That left Africa, the middle son. He excelled neither in games nor in books, nor was he inclined toward business or singing. His face was rather squarish and unlike his brothers he wore his pigtail tied at the end in a blunt knot. He would fight anyone who got in his way, but he was not offensively aggressive. His principal characteristic was hesitancy in making up his mind, accompanied by a bulldog tenacity when he had done so. His personal affections were kept well masked: he had no special regard for either Uliassutai Blake, Apikela or Wu Chow's Auntie. He studied each of them and knew their strengths but not their love. His brothers rarely shouted to him to join them in a game, but they often asked him the schedule for the next day's lesson. His mother studied him with a good deal of care and concluded: "In his stubborn, square-faced way, Africa is deeper than the others."

She had almost as much trouble trying to decide what the chosen son should study if he got to America. Here Uliassutai Blake was clear-cut in his advice: "The world is run by those who can manipulate, Wu Chow's Auntie. There are only two decent vocations open to a man of talent. He should become a messiah and lead us into eternal darkness, or he should study to be a lawyer, and then God alone knows what he may accomplish. If I were a lawyer I would run for Parliament. If your son becomes a lawyer he will coach you in how to cheat the government, and heaven knows, that's to be learned by all of us. Lawyer, Wu Chow's Auntie, nothing less." When she asked him, "Who would make the best lawyer?" he replied without equivocation, "America." She thought the same.

Kimo and Apikela were of no help. They pondered the problem for a long time, their great brown bodies wrestling with strange ideas, and finally Kimo asked, "Why should fine boys like this be anything? Asia has a restaurant. Europe has a store. Australia has more friends than anyone in school. They like Hawaii. They fit in. Why bother them with all these big ideas?" Nyuk Tsin, who appreciated the insight of these huge friends, asked, "But which do you like better, a lawyer or a doctor or a dentist?" The two Hawaiians studied this for some time and replied, "For a Hawaiian a lawyer is better because he makes such wonderful speeches, but for a Pake maybe a doctor is better because he makes so much money."

The Chinese community was more practical. The Punti almost to a man advised medicine: "A doctor is always respected. He gets paid. He becomes a leading man in the city, and we need Chinese doctors." The Hakka pointed out: "It takes two more years to become a doctor. Leave that to the haoles. Your boy should be a dentist. Quicker and in the long run just as much money."

One hot July day in 1885 Nyuk Tsin was hurrying down Nuuanu, her two baskets of pineapples balancing on her carrying-pole the way conflicting advice balanced in her mind, and she was thinking of lawyer versus doctor and Asia versus America when two horses pulling a J & W dray reared in the air, dashed down Hotel Street, and threw their wagon against one of the poles that held up the roof of Asia Kee's Chinese restaurant. The first pole snapped off and the sudden weight thrown upon the second caused it to collapse, allowing the roof to fall into Hotel Street. No one was hurt and a Hawaiian caught the reins of the runaway horses and easily brought them to rest.

Asia, who was inside the restaurant, exploded onto the street shouting curses at the horses who had so unexpectedly plunged his dining room into chaos. Nyuk Tsin hurried up, adding to the confusion by shouting, "I saw them! I saw them!" And the Hawaiian policemen agitated everyone by roaring, "Don't bring those horses back this way! Turn them around and get them out of here!" When the beasts reared he bellowed, "Turn them around!" A man from J & W hurried up to assure everyone that the driver was at fault because he had stopped to watch a pool game, and was going to be fired; and then amidst the confusion Nyuk Tsin, herself in great agitation, saw her son Africa, who had been helping wash dishes at his brother's restaurant, moving among the crowd and quietening the Chinese. "All right, Wu Chow's Auntie!" he said forcefully. "No more shouting. Nobody's hurt. Did you see what happened? Where were you standing?" And while the policeman fought with the man who had caught the horses, making him turn them around lest they stampede again, Africa Kee quietly got the names of all who had witnessed the accident. "The driver was nowhere to be seen?" he asked repeatedly. "You saw the wagon hit the pole?" By the time Africa reached the J & W man, the latter's story about the driver's having been in a poolroom had been changed. It was now quite a different story, but Africa had the names of everyone who had heard the first version. The extent of the damage was not great, and the cash award grudgingly given by J & W did not amount to much, but restitution was made and the money went into the fund that would send Africa Kee to Michigan . . . to become a lawyer.

He was seventeen years old when Wu Chow's Auntie made her decision, and the family had practically no spare cash to spend on their living in Hawaii, let alone to send a boy to America. Yet in those important days Nyuk Tsin started many ventures. She made Asia and Europe, who were already in business, borrow money to pay Africa's ship passage. She sold pineapples and vegetables six hours a day, tilled her fields eight hours and kept two for scouting around. Finally, one evening when the scholar at the Punti store assured her that the time was auspicious, she washed her muddy feet, brushed her one blue uniform, tied a widow's cloth about her sparsely haired head and topped it with her wicker hat. Brushing her cheeks with her hands so that she might look as presentable as possible, she left home without speaking to anyone, and walked resolutely down Nuuanu, where she purchased a bag of brown, chewy candies covered with poppy seed.

Clutching the candy in her hand, she entered busy Hotel Street, in the heart of Chinatown, and turned right, walking past Asia's restaurant and Europe's vegetable stand, while she looked for a narrow alley that cut back among a maze of Chinese shacks. At last she found it, and with a prayer to Kwan Yin for mercy on her mission, she ducked beneath the bamboo poles that suspended drying laundry completely across the alley. Finally she reached a kitchen door which belonged to a house somewhat more pretentious than the rest, yet one of which few haoles could have known the existence, for it was well hidden by hovels. This was the home of Ching, Honolulu's wealthiest Hakka, and it was presumptuous of Nyuk Tsin to be calling there. She knocked and waited obediently until the tall, well-fed mistress of the house appeared and looked out in the darkness to identify her impecunious visitor. The taller woman did not speak, and Nyuk Tsin said deferentially, "May a thousand benedictions fall upon you on this auspicious night, my dear mother-in-law." The phrase was an honorary one and implied no relationship, so the wealthy woman accepted it imperiously and said, "Come in, my dear sister-in-law. Have you had your meal?"

This again was a formality, so Nyuk Tsin replied, as custom required, "I have eaten, but how about you?"

She was impressed by the munificence of the kitchen and its close attention to detail. The two windows were sufficiently high so that the Ching money could not leak out; the doors were not in a straight line, which kept the dragon of happiness from escaping; and the land leading up to the doors did not slope away from the house, so that good fortune did not drift away. The kitchen had a brick stove on which a permanent teapot rested, and now the Ching woman poured Nyuk Tsin a cup of the stale stuff, not too big a cup, which would have accorded Nyuk Tsin an esteem she did not merit, nor too small, which would have brought reflections of niggardliness upon the Chings.

"Be seated, my dear sister-in-law," the wealthy woman said. In her outward appearance, nothing betrayed the fact that she controlled a good deal of money. She wore no jewelry, no paint, no combs in her hair. Her simple dress was the same as Nyuk Tsin's and she also was barefooted; but to her visitor's calculating eye Mrs. Ching was obviously a person of wealth: her kitchen was crowded with food! Three hams hung from bamboo poles, and five glistening dried ducks, their bills hanging downward with drops of redolent oil gathering at the tips. There were bunches of white cabbage, baskets of vegetables and bags of nuts. Throughout the kitchen there was the grand confusion loved by people who have money, and Mrs. Ching grandly swept aside some of the clutter that hid her table, making a small space on which Nyuk Tsin placed her bag of candies. Neither woman spoke of the bag, but each was painfully aware of its presence, and as the conversation developed, they stared at the candies with positive fascination.

"Why do you come to my poor house on such an auspicious night, my dear sister-in-law?" the older woman asked with studied sweetness.

Nyuk Tsin sat with her stubborn, hard-working hands folded in her lap and her brown feet flat on the floor. Bluntly she said, "Since I am not as wealthy as my honored mother-in-law, I cannot afford to hire a go-between, so I have been shameful and have broken the rules of decent behavior. I have come to ask for your daughter, Siu Kim."

Mrs. Ching showed no surprise, but unconsciously she drew back and took her hands far from the candies. Nyuk Tsin detected this and was hurt, but she continued to smile frankly at her hostess. Finally, after an awkward moment, Mrs. Ching said in a silken voice, "I thought your son Ah Chow already had a wife."

"He does, my dear mother-in-law," Nyuk Tsin replied evenly, launching her first barb of the evening. "I arranged a very fine marriage for him with the Lam girl."

Mrs. Ching said, "A Punti, I believe?"

Nyuk Tsin dropped her eyes modestly and confessed: "A Punti, yes, but she brought a good deal of gold with her and now my son owns his restaurant."

"He owns the building?" Mrs. Ching inquired in surprise.

"Completely," Nyuk Tsin said with firmness, "but of course our family controls it."

"It was my understanding that your second son was intending to marry a Hawaiian."

"He is," Nyuk Tsin confessed. She waited so that Mrs. Ching could react with distaste, then added quietly, "I was able to find him a Hawaiian girl with several large pieces of land."

"Indeed! And does the land now belong to your family?"

"It does."

"Mmmmmm," Mrs. Ching mused. She leaned forward ever so slightly and the talk resumed. She said, "I observe that your youngest son plays mainly with Hawaiians. I suppose that one day he will marry one."

"There are many Hawaiian girls who seem to like my son, and fortunately they all have large land holdings," Nyuk Tsin said. Then, to establish herself on an equal footing with Mrs. Ching, she added boldly, "Since my family will not return to China, I think it best that the boys find wives here."

"So that you were even willing to allow your oldest son to marry a Punti?"

Nyuk Tsin was not going to be stampeded by this woman. With a good deal of self-possession she said, "I want my family to live in the new style. Not as in the High Village that you and I knew as girls."

Mrs. Ching sensed a rebuke in these words and said bluntly, "What you mean is that you are building a family into which a decent Hakka girl, like my daughter Siu Kim, would hardly want to marry and into which I would not permit her to marry."

This was an important speech, for although it was harsh, Nyuk Tsin did not know whether Mrs. Ching was formally ending negotiations or whether she was trying legitimately to undermine Nyuk Tsin's bargaining position so that when final discussions of money came up, the girl's side could drive a harder bargain. At any rate, Nyuk Tsin felt that the time had come for her to detonate her first bomb, so she dropped it gently, letting it explode among the hams and glistening dried ducks. "I realize, my dearest mother-in-law, that a wealthy woman like you would have objections to marrying a fine girl like Siu Kim into a poor family like ours, but there is one thing you have overlooked. Yesterday the scholar at the Punti store cast my son Africa's horoscope," and she placed on the crowded table, beside the bag of candy, a slip of paper, "and when it was done, the scholar gasped for sheer pleasure, for he said, 'I have never seen a finer horoscope for a young man in my entire life.' That's what he said."

The two women, neither of whom could read, studied the precious slip of paper, and Mrs. Ching asked cautiously, "Are you sure this is your son's?"

"It is."

"And it speaks well?"

Modestly Nyuk Tsin looked down at her feet. In a soft voice she said, "Money, knowledge, a position even better than a scholar in China, a long prosperous life with many children—those were the words for my son."

The two women sat in silence, for each knew what a rare thing was before them. They stared at the premonitory paper and slowly Mrs. Ching rose. "My dear sister-in-law, I think I had better make some more tea." With bounding joy Nyuk Tsin heard these words, for they erased any that had been said earlier, but modestly she kept her eyes down and did not watch Mrs. Ching as she brewed fresh tea—not the old stuff waiting on the back of the stove—and poured it into a fine China cup. This was, up to then, the moment of greatest triumph in Nyuk Tsin's life, and she tasted the fine fresh tea.

"Siu Kim," Mrs. Ching began on a fresh tack, "is an unusual girl and she has been asked for by more than a dozen men, some of them with considerable wealth." Nyuk Tsin sipped her tea and courteously allowed Mrs. Ching to run up the bargaining price for her daughter. Over the edge of her cup, the ruder-mannered younger woman studied the bag of candies and thought: "I will let her talk about her daughter for five minutes, and then I'll explode my next cannon."

When Mrs. Ching finished explaining why, in common decency, she had to save Siu Kim for a wealthier man than Africa Kee was apt to be, Nyuk Tsin said bluntly, "It is not every day that an average Hakka girl like Siu Kim has a chance to marry a man who is going to graduate from a fine college in America and become a lawyer. I should think, as her mother, that you would jump at this opportunity and throw in a good dowry as well."

Mrs. Ching was stunned by this news, but she was no mean negotiator. She did not raise an eyebrow but asked in a silky voice, "How can a vegetable woman possibly send her son to America?"

Meticulously Nyuk Tsin counted off: "We own the land up Nuuanu. We own the land in the forest. We own very fine fields in Manoa. Asia owns his restaurant and Europe has paid large sums toward the building where his vegetable store is. Each of my sons works, as do I, and I am sure that right now we have enough money to send Africa to Michigan."

Mrs. Ching was visibly jolted by this narration and she now wheeled into position her heaviest ammunition: "Your son's prospects sound . . . well, interesting. But of course his father was a leper."

Nyuk Tsin did not flinch: "The main reason why I was able to make such a favorable marriage with the Hawaiian girl, who brought us so much land, was that the Hawaiians know me as the Pake Kokua, and they have said that if Africa does become a lawyer, they will send all their business to the son of the Pake Kokua."

The two tough-minded Hakka women glared at each other in mutual respect, and as they did so, Mrs. Ching made her decision. Imperceptibly, she allowed her right hand to steal across the table. She extended two fingers and slowly encircled the bag of brown candy dusted with poppy seeds. Noiselessly she pulled it toward her, and Nyuk Tsin, witnessing these climactic gestures, thought: "I must not cry." And she fought back her tears, lest they spill out of her sloping eyes and betray to the Ching woman her great joy. With this acceptance of the candy, the marriage was agreed upon.

Up to this time Nyuk Tsin had not yet seen Siu Kim, and of course Africa Kee was not even aware that his auntie was planning his marriage. Neither he nor Siu Kim was told anything, especially since the basic financial negotiations were to consume the better part of a year, but one day Nyuk Tsin saw the attractive girl for whom she had been bargaining, and she admitted to Mrs. Ching: "Your daughter, Beautiful Gold, is even more desirable than you told me." But as she said these words, she happened to look past Siu Kim, who was then thirteen, and in the doorway behind, wearing a blue and gold Chinese dress, stood Siu Kim's eleven-year-old sister, Siu Han, and Nyuk Tsin sucked in her breath with pleasure. "What is that one's name?" she asked, and Mrs. Ching replied simply, "Siu Han, Beautiful Girl, but she will be saved for a very wealthy man." Nyuk Tsin smiled at the little girl and remembered her name.

These were exciting years in the Kee house. The original grass shack had been replaced by one of the ugliest buildings in Honolulu: an unadorned two-story bleak wooden house, to which had been appended as afterthoughts a collection of lean-to sheds. A mango tree and a coconut palm gave some shade, but there was no lawn nor any flowers. Pigs were kept in the yard and chickens in the kitchen, but the dominant occupants were enormous Kimo, who did all the cooking for the family, and sprawling Apikela, who did the washing and made the poi. There was a running battle between Nyuk Tsin on the one hand and everyone else on the other: she liked rice and Chinese food; they insisted upon poi and American-style food. When, at the end of a long day's work she begged for rice, big Kimo at the stove shrugged his shoulders and the boys yelled, "Oh, Auntie! Who wants rice?" If she did, she had to cook it herself because Kimo refused to bother.

Her two married sons lived with her, of course, one family to a room, and Apikela took care of the babies that began to arrive regularly. What with the pigs and the chickens and the babies it was a noisy, happy island home. There were many like it, for Chinese and Hawaiians lived together easily. At the poolroom one day Kimo came upon a new importation from Portugal, a ukulele, and like a boy he badgered Nyuk Tsin until she bought him one. Then Apikela demanded one, and Europe's wife, and songs from the Chinese house filled the valley.

In the middle of 1886, when Africa Kee was eighteen, it was announced that early next year he would marry the wealthy Hakka girl, Ching Siu Kim. He started looking about the city to see who she was, and one day he saw her walking in Aala Park, but he could not be sure that she was the girl picked out for him, and he thought: "It would be pleasant if she were a girl like that one."

The wedding was an impressive affair, with many guests, for the Chings were important, and before Africa Kee finally climbed aboard the ship to go to Michigan, he was already the father of three children. Dutifully he took the family genealogical book and the poem to the scholar in the Punti store, and there the man gave his sons their names. The poem showed that the name of this fourth generation must be Koon, Earth, and accordingly the two boys' names were Koon Chuk, the Center of the Earth, and Koon Yuen, the Essence of the Earth Which Produces All, but their parents called them simply Sam and Harvey. The Chinese names were duly forwarded to the Low Village, so that when twenty-one-year-old Africa finally enrolled at Michigan he was not only head of a burgeoning family left behind in Honolulu, but also the member of a powerful clan whose existence had continued in the Low Village for thousands of years, but the memory which recurred most often to Africa as he studied law in Michigan concerned an event which took place on his last morning in Honolulu.

Nyuk Tsin assembled her five sons and led them to the letter-writer at the Punti store. There she delivered fifty dollars that the family in Honolulu desperately needed for its various ventures. Asia and Europe gasped to see this amount of money being stolen from the Kees, and certainly Africa could have used it in Michigan, but Nyuk Tsin said, "Your mother in China may need this money. It may be a bad year for the crops. It is your duty above everything else to pay respect to your mother." If, at Michigan, Africa Kee excelled at law it was partly because he understood the fundamental fact that law directs the ongoing of society. It is rooted in the past, determines the present, and protects the future. Better than any other student in the law school, Africa appreciated these conservative principles.

On the day he sailed to America on the H & H liner *Molokai,* Nyuk Tsin climbed aboard a little island steamer and made her first pilgrimage to her husband's grave at the leper settlement of Kalawao, for she, too, was imbued with this sense of continuity, and if her ablest son was that day setting forth for a new world, it was only because the dead gambler Kee Mun Ki had been good to her. This time the island steamer did not swing around the peninsula and throw its passengers brutally ashore into the cold and unprotected hell of Kalawao. The vessel sailed directly to the pier at Kalaupapa, on the kindly side of the peninsula, and discharged its cargo decently. Doctors and nurses were on hand to assist the new lepers, and the big white Missionary Home for Lepers provided them a place to sleep. At the Missionary Hospital they still found no medicine that combated the disease itself, but they found charitable care that protected them from pneumonia and tuberculosis, which had once been so prevalent.

Nyuk Tsin walked through the clean new settlement and up past the volcano crater. Then she stopped and an ache past understanding assailed her, for she looked down upon the most beautiful sight she had ever seen. It was more dramatic than the hills of China, lovelier than the valleys of Honolulu. In the distance rose the soaring cliffs of Molokai, with white spray beating upon their rock bases and gossamer waterfalls leaping from their summits to fall three thousand silvery feet. The ocean was blue and the small islands that clustered offshore formed handsome patterns. The fields of Kalawao, now empty of lepers, were soft and green as they had been a thousand years before that horrible disease was known in the islands. Two vacant churches, one Protestant and one Catholic, stood where once there had been terror. The house she had built with her own hands no longer had a roof. "How sweet," she thought, "were the days Mun Ki and Palani and I spent there. Oh, how I wish I could see those two good men once more." In her mind's eye she saw them not with noses and lips falling away and with stumps of hands, but as men. "How I would like to see them once more playing fan-tan on the shore."

That night she spent at Kalawao in the home of a kokua she had known years before, and on the next morning at cockcrow, in the third hour, she left the house and went to her husband's grave, so that she would be there when his spirit rose to walk about the valley. In the moonlight she carefully replaced any rocks that had fallen away.

She brushed the earth and pulled weeds. Carefully she erected a slab on which his name, Kee Mun Ki, had been printed in gold letters. Then she undid a bundle and ceremoniously placed a fine set of new dishes about the grave, putting into them the three required delicacies: roast pig, chicken and fish. On saucers she placed oranges, boiled rice, little cakes with caraway, and brown candies with poppy seed. Then she lit a small candle, so that its incense would infuse the atmosphere and make it congenial to the ghost, and when these preparations were completed, she waited for the dawn.

When her husband's ghost appeared he found no tree to roost in, as he would have expected in China, where trees were plentiful and where they were kept near graves for just that purpose, but he did find a perching place on the rocky cliffs that rose behind his grave, and there in the warm sunlight, away from the cold ocean breezes, he sat with his dutiful wife.

She explained in a quiet voice: "Three of the boys are married, Wu Chow's Father, and although I was not able to arrange perfect marriages with huge dowries, I did as well as could be expected. Mrs. Ching, as you would expect, argued very strongly against me, and at the last she even brought up an unpleasant fact. 'Your husband died of leprosy,' she said, but I didn't lose my temper, for there was more important business at hand, and at last she gave in.

"Ah Chow has four children, Au Chow has three and Fei Chow three. I am going to try very hard to get Mrs. Ching's youngest daughter to marry Oh Chow, but I may have a good deal of trouble there, for the girl is a beauty and will be able to command a high price.

"At the house things go well. Kimo and Apikela look after things for us all, and they are precious people. The fields yield as before, and pineapples continue to sell well. Ah Chow has a fine restaurant that is always busy and Au Chow has a good vegetable business.

"But the good news, Wu Chow's Father, is that your son Fei Chow is already on a ship going to Michigan to study to be a lawyer. When I put him aboard the vessel I could see you and Palani in our little house down there, dreaming of going around the world and seeing strange places.

"Think! Think! Our son, our own child, is going to be a scholar!"

In gratitude for this great boon Nyuk Tsin fell silent and tears trembled on her lids, and the sun rose higher in the heavens, and she stayed by the grave. At eleven she asked, "Is it not hot on those rocks? You really ought to have a tree, Wu Chow's Father." And in the later afternoon she left the grave and the meal she had set for the ghost.

On her walk back toward Kalaupapa she passed the old graveyard and saw a new stone, larger than the others, and she wondered who of her friends lay buried there, so she waited until a Hawaiian leper came by with hardly any face, and she asked him, "Who lies in that grave?" And the man said, "Father Damien. He died one of us."

When she reached Kalaupapa she found that while she was talking with her husband the settlement had discovered who she was, and she returned to see many people waiting for her. "Pake Kokua!" they called, and many came to greet her who had known her in the evil days. Some she recognized, for the disease had been kind to them, but others no eyes but God's could see as human beings. "Pake Kokua!" they all cried. "It's good to have you back."

She sat down on a rock, a little Chinese woman with a sunburned face, and they gathered around. A priest came up and asked in Hawaiian, "Are you the one they call the Pake Kokua?" She said that she was, and he said, "You are remembered in this place." She asked if it was true that Father Damien had died of leprosy, and the priest said, "Only last spring." "Did he suffer?" Nyuk Tsin asked, and the priest replied, "Here everyone suffers." She said, "Kalaupapa is better than Kalawao used to be," and the young man said, "When the people in Honolulu wakened to their responsibility, it had to become better." She asked, "Have you found any drug that cures?" And he replied, "The infinite mercy of God has not yet shown us the way, but He will not permit a thing like leprosy to continue without a cure. Meanwhile, we pray."

In late 1889 Nyuk Tsin spent most of her spare time arguing with the Ching family about terms on which their youngest daughter, Ching Siu Han, might be given to her youngest son Australia. She told Mrs. Ching frankly, "The boy is very good at school, and I don't worry about him in that regard, but having grown up with Hawaiians he is more like them than a Chinese. He's got to marry a Chinese girl. Otherwise he will be lost to us."

Mrs. Ching pointed out: "You allowed Au Chow and Mei Chow to marry Hawaiian girls."

Nyuk Tsin argued: "Those girls brought much land with them, and the marriages were good for the boys. But Oh Chow's problem is different. He doesn't require land. He requires a strong-minded Chinese wife." But her antagonist felt that Siu Han, being rather prettier than average, ought to be saved for a better prospect than Australia.

At this time Siu Han, who was now a sparkling Chinese girl of fifteen, had begun to show her headstrong nature and had broken away from the severe old Chinese custom which required girls to hide at home. While her sister, Africa's wife, tended her three babies, Siu Han liked to walk up and down Hotel Street, and because she was unusually attractive this caused much comment in the Chinese community. On one such trip she met Nyuk Tsin, who said to her, "Have you ever seen my son Australia?"

"No," the girl said.

"He's in his brother's restaurant. Let's have a bowl of noodles together."

So Nyuk Tsin and the pretty young girl went into Asia's place and sat down, and in a moment Australia appeared and was astonished to see them, for Wu Chow's Auntie had never before entered the place. He sat down with them, and Nyuk Tsin asked bluntly, "Don't you think your brother's wife's sister is attractive?" Obviously, Australia did, and after a few minutes Nyuk Tsin found occasion to leave the table and talk with her son Asia, who said, "It's disgraceful to bring a girl like that in here."

In the weeks that followed, Nyuk Tsin often asked Australia, "Why don't you help your brother at the restaurant?" And whenever her only unmarried son did so, Nyuk Tsin managed to find Siu Han somewhere in Chinatown, and she would bring the two together, so that before the year was out it was not Wu Chow's Auntie who was arguing with the wealthy Chings that they permit their only remaining daughter to marry Australia; it was the daughter herself who did all the talking. "My rascal girl," Mrs. Ching called her. Nyuk Tsin prudently dropped out of the picture, and in early 1890 a marriage was announced.

At the wedding Nyuk Tsin, then forty-three years old but looking closer to sixty, sat silent and thanked the Hakka gods that they had been so good to her; then her attention was attracted to a Hakka woman who had brought as a gift a small sandalwood box, carried from Canton, and as Nyuk Tsin smelled that aromatic present she thought: "This is indeed the Fragrant Tree Country."

BY THE TIME the last decade of the nineteenth century opened, Wild Whip Hoxworth was concentrating his considerable energy on two projects: women and making Hawaii part of the United States. For a while his performance in the former field was the more spectacular, for after his divorce from the Spanish woman Aloma Duarte he spent his free time with a strange assortment of creatures who could be counted upon to drift ashore from passing ships. They were women without faces, but with memorable bodies, and it was uncanny how as soon as they touched shore they made a direct line to Wild Whip, as if he had the capacity to send out messages that he could be found lolling on the porch of the Hawaiian Hotel. Quickly, these drifting women moved their luggage—they never had much—into the rooms Whip occupied and after a while each moved along to Manila or Hong Kong. Many would have enjoyed staying, but Whip was too smart to allow that.

From time to time he spent his weekends in Rat Alley, across the river in Iwilei, and one of the most common sights at the Hawaiian Hotel, built by the king for the entertainment of important guests, was the deferential appearance of some Chinese brothel keeper with news for Whip that a new girl had come in or that an old one wished particularly to see him. It was understandable that women liked Whip, for at thirty-three he was tall and lean, with knife scars across his left cheek and black hair that rumpled in the wind. He had flashing white teeth and slow, penetrating eyes. He was careful of his appearance, and when he rode horseback along the dusty roads of his sugar plantations, he could speak to his hands in masterful pidgin, with appropriate touches of Chinese, Japanese, Hawaiian or Portuguese to fit the individual workman with whom he talked, but for all sentences, regardless of language, he adopted the lilting accent brought to the islands by Mexican cowboys, so that each statement ended with an upward song: "Eh, you Joe! What you theenk? You holo holo watah?" The words *think* and *water* were heavily accented and given an ingratiating melody. While his men were in the fields, tending the cane, Wild Whip often stopped by their homes to talk with their women, and it naturally happened that occasionally these women would appreciate his courtly manners and he found great pleasure in suddenly leaping into bed with them and having a wild few minutes, after which he called, as he rode off, "Eh, you Rosie, ne? Take care you boy he come home, he one fine man I theenk." Twice he had been slashed at with machetes, and when he reflected upon that occupational hazard he supposed that some day he would die in a scene of wild brutality and the sanctimonious newspapers of the islands would scream the scandal, and at the prospect he laughed, thinking: "What a great way to die!"

Then, in late 1892, Wild Whip became galvanized into even wilder action in a completely different arena, for the United States was beginning to show signs of once more discriminating against the importation of Hawaiian sugar. The great planters of cane in Louisiana were determined to end the reciprocity arrangements whereby Hawaii sent sugar to the mainland tax-free while the United States was allowed to send certain goods into Hawaii and also to use Pearl Harbor as a naval base. Cried the Louisiana sugar men: "We don't need their sugar and we don't need Pearl Harbor."

For thirty years the New Orleans sugar tycoons had been waging war against Hawaii, and they had managed to hold the profits of Hawaiian planters like Wild Whip Hoxworth to reasonable limits, but they had failed to kill off the industry. Now a new factor had entered the battle against Hawaii: the huge western states of Colorado and Nebraska were beginning to grow beets and to grind them into sugar, and they, too, wanted to destroy Hawaiian competition. Within a few years it was likely that a coalition of Louisiana, Alabama, Mississippi, Colorado and Nebraska, plus such new states as Wyoming and Utah, would form to drive Hawaiian sugar forever out of the market, and when this happened sugar planters like Wild Whip would see their massive fortunes begin to vanish.

"In sugar, there's only one rule," Whip told the sugar planters he had assembled. "Either we sell to the United States, or we don't sell. Our sole aim must be to protect that market."

"We're losing it," John Janders pointed out. "Right now I represent eleven of your major sugar plantations, and with the way those bastards from Louisiana and Colorado are trying to strangle us, I can see nine of your eleven outfits going into bankruptcy. One more serious cut in our American market, and I don't know what we'll do."

"Excuse me, John," Whip interrupted. "You're right in what you say, but I'm afraid you're mincing words. I happen to have the figures, and by God, nobody can listen to these without panic. Since the McKinley Tariff every damned sugar man in Louisiana and Colorado has been getting a subsidy of two cents a pound, whereas sugar imported from Hawaii has been penalized. What's it all mean? During the first twelve months of this McKinley abortion our profits have dropped five million dollars. I don't mean the profits of Hawaii. I mean the profits of the nine men sitting in this room. Now as to the actual invested value of our plantations, they've lost twelve million dollars. And it's going to get worse and worse."

He paused to allow discussion of the peril in which the Hawaiian sugar men found themselves, for up to the moment of this meeting, the great planters had known they were in danger but no one had had the courage to accumulate the depressing figures; now under Whip's lashing they had to face facts. Companies were going to go bankrupt and men were going to lose plantations their fathers had built.

"What do you think we should do?" John Janders asked. He was a year older than Whip and eight centuries more conservative.

Whip parried the question and observed, "Obviously, John, unless we do something we're going to lose Hawaii. It's going to subside into the barren, useless batch of islands it was in 1840." There was a hush, and Whip continued: "Those aren't just words, either. Two more bad years, John, and you'll be bankrupt. Absolutely pau. Dave Hale may be able to hold out a little longer, but Harry Hewlett can't." Then he thumped himself in the chest and added, "I'm good for eighteen months, and then I'm bankrupt. Gentlemen, I don't propose to go bankrupt."

It was a sober group of Hales, Hewletts and Janderses who listened to these gloomy but accurate words. Finally Dave Hale asked, "How you going to escape, Whip?"

With carefully studied words Whip replied, "I've asked that the doors be closed, gentlemen, because what you and I are about to do is ugly work, so if any of you have weak kidneys I'll give you time to go out and take a piss right now. And don't bother to come back." He waited in silence and could see that the sugar men were breathing hard. "I'll give you two more minutes," he said, "and after that, there's no turning back." He put his watch on the table, and when the seconds had passed he said simply, "Gentlemen, we are now duly constituted as the Committee of Nine and no one here must have any illusions. This afternoon I want you quietly to buy up all the available guns in Honolulu." He put his left hand to his chin and with his thumb rubbed the scar that crossed his face like jagged lightning. When the shock of his first command had been absorbed he added, "Yes, we're going to launch a revolution, win control of these islands, and turn them over to the United States. Once we've done that, Louisiana and Colorado can go to hell. They'll be powerless to destroy us."

"Do you think the United States will accept us?" Dave Hale asked timorously.

Wild Whip dropped both hands on the table and said harshly, "Gentlemen, the days ahead are going to be damned difficult. But there is one thing we must never doubt. The United States is going to accept Hawaii." He thundered his fists on the table and repeated, "We are going to be part of America."

"How . . ." Dave Hale began.

"I don't know how!" Whip interrupted. "But we're going to join America and we're going to make all the goddamned money growing sugar that we want to."

John Janders spoke quickly: "Whip, you know I'm even stronger for sugar than you are, because I've got more to lose. But take my advice on one thing. Don't organize this revolution around sugar. Among ourselves, here in the committee, all right. But don't let the outside world know. For them you've got to have an idea bigger than sugar."

Young Hale added, "John's right. The big American newspapers will never support us if our revolution is built on sugar."

One of the Hewlett boys, who owned the biggest sugar plantation of all, suggested: "Somehow we've got to work in the word democracy. Red-blooded Americans on these islands are sick of living under a corrupt monarchy."

"That's it!" John Janders cried. "Something the American Congress can get hold of. American citizens yearning to be free."

Wild Whip smiled at his associates. "You fellows have a lot of sense. I agree with you that if we stand forth as a sugar revolution, the bastards in Louisiana and Colorado would crucify us. I can hear them now, bleeding for the monarchy. But I have a better idea, gentlemen. You and I are going to start this revolution, and we're going to direct it, and when everyone else gets scared, we're going to fire the guns. But," and he paused for effect, "not one of us is going to appear before the public."

"Who will?" Dave Hale asked.

"We'll get the lawyers who handle our plantation affairs, and the newspaper people and some schoolteachers and a couple of ministers,"

Whip snapped. "This is going to be the most respectable revolution in history. You're going to hear more high-flown sentiments than you thought existed, because I've decided on the ideal man to stand before the public."

"Who you thinking of?" Hale probed.

Whip looked directly at the young man and said, "Your Uncle Micah."

David Hale gasped and said, "He'll never revolt against the monarchy. He's a citizen of Hawaii and takes it very seriously."

"We're all citizens of Hawaii," Whip replied, "and we all take it seriously. That's why we're going to save these islands."

"But Uncle Micah's been an adviser to the crown, a personal friend of all the kings. He's an ordained minister . . ."

"For those very reasons we've got to have him," Whip interrupted. "He won't support us willingly. He'll preach against us, and he'll despise our revolution, but the force of circumstance will make him our leader. Believe me, it'll be Uncle Micah Hale with his long white beard who will send the final letter to President Harrison: 'Hawaii is yours.' "

At this point John Janders threw some very cold water upon the revolution: "I got a letter from Washington which said that everyone there thinks Grover Cleveland will be elected again this year."

At the mention of this portly, strong-willed Democrat, the Committee of Nine grew glum, for in his previous administration Cleveland had delivered several staggering blows against Hawaiian sugar and it was likely that he would do so again; but more important, the idealistic reformer had come out strongly against the spirit of manifest destiny then popular in America. "The United States wants no empire," Cleveland had proclaimed, and it was the shadow of this great bulk that fell across the incipient revolution. But not even Grover Cleveland frightened Wild Whip Hoxworth: "To hell with his mealy-mouthed nonsense about international morality. We'll start the revolution right away. Wind it up fast. And have Uncle Micah throw the islands to Harrison before the next election is held. By the time Cleveland's President, we'll be part of America."

"Can we do it in the time available?" one of the Hewlett boys asked.

"If we work," Whip replied. The Committee of Nine broke up their first meeting and each man took upon himself three jobs: buy all available guns; find respectable citizens to stand before the public as front men of the revolution; and test every friend to see who could be depended upon to help overthrow the Hawaiian monarchy. When the frightened, but determined, sugar planters were gone, Whip Hoxworth was left with the most difficult job of all. He had to find some way of making white-bearded, righteous old Micah Hale assume leadership of the revolt.

It was not a strong monarchy to begin with. In 1872 the great Kamehameha line had ended in sickness and frustration, to be followed by a succession of amiable but incompetent alii. One had sought to revive paganism as the consolidating force of Hawaiian life; another had tried to abrogate the constitution and take Hawaii back to an absolute monarchy unrestrained by any middle-class legislature; there had been palace revolutions, the election of kings according to their personal popularity, and a shocking scandal in which one king was caught trying to peddle an opium concession twice over to two different Chinese gamblers. This sad decline of the Hawaiian state had caused deep concern among the missionary families, and although some men of rectitude like Micah Hale loyally supported the royal line, they were grieved when attempts were made to legalize opium and lotteries.

Even so, had the customary succession of amiable and handsome kings continued and had they allowed their iron-willed New England advisers to run the kingdom, Micah Hale and his responsible associates would probably have been able to keep the tottering monarchy viable; but on January 29, 1891, royalty of a far different sort ascended the throne and trouble was inescapable. Queen Liliuokalani was a short, moderately stout woman of regal bearing. She had large, determined lips, a high pile of graying hair, and wrists laden with jewels. In black satin fringed with ostrich feathers and bearing a feathered ivory fan, she was an imposing woman with a stubborn will. It was her custom to deliver important messages seated in front of a golden-yellow cape of feathers, both because this was an antique royal custom which set off her dignity and because she was slightly crippled and did not move with grace. For many years she had been plain Lydia Dominis, strong-minded wife of a slim haole of Italian descent, with whom she lived in a large white mansion called Washington Place. Upon the death of her brother, the king, she ascended the throne, bringing with her a desire to reverse the trend toward haole domination and a determination to cast aside New England influences like Micah Hale.

She was a highly intelligent woman and had traveled to the courts of Europe, where the role played by Queen Victoria impressed her, and she had a love of political power. Had she acquired the throne immediately after the passing of the Kamehameha, she might have made Hawaii a strong and secure monarchy, for she had a lively imagination and much skill in manipulating people; but she attained ultimate power too late; republicanism had infected her people; sugar had captured her islands. And although she did not know it, her enemy was no longer the stately political leader Micah Hale; it was the gun-running, determined plantation owner Wild Whip Hoxworth. Against the former she might have had a chance; against the latter she was powerless.

Without ever identifying her enemies, this headstrong, imaginative woman tried to combat republicanism, Congregationalism and sugar, but she succeeded only in driving those disparate forces together in a coalition. Hawaiians who were tired of the monarchy and its silly pretensions conspired against the queen, although most who joined the coalition did so in hope of currying favor with the Americans. Missionary families came out boldly against the corruption, absolutism and paganism of the monarchy, but many who cried loudest in public against these evils also owned businesses that would prosper under American rule. And lawyers were forceful in their arguments against the excesses of the monarchy and in defense of human rights, but mostly they fought to protect sugar. As the queen's obstinate reign continued, the coalition against her became more powerful.

In early 1893 the headstrong woman determined to eliminate the influence of men like the statesman Micah Hale and his insolent nephew Whip Hoxworth. Accordingly, she let it be known that she intended to abrogate the present constitution, which hampered her absolute power, to put the legislature under royal control, and to revoke the voting rights of many citizens and generally restore the ancient prerogatives of the monarchy. She was a notable figure when she made this disclosure: queenly, posed against yellow feathers dating back two hundred years, a lei of plumeria about her shoulders and a train of satin four feet long piled about her crippled foot. As she spoke she did not make it clear, but it was her intention to take Hawaii back to the good old days that France had enjoyed in 1620.

That afternoon Wild Whip Hoxworth summoned the Committee of Nine, and his conspirators convened in an upper room of Janders & Whipple on Merchant Street, an earlier proposal that the members meet at Hoxworth & Hale having been vetoed because of the fear that Micah Hale, still stoutly attached to the monarchy, might hear of the plot. Wild Whip was concise in his opening statement: "Our headstrong queen is to be congratulated. Her silly acts have made revolution obligatory."

The Hewlett boys were fearful of overt action and counseled caution, but straightforward John Janders said gruffly, "We've got to overthrow the monarchy in the next two days or lose our last opportunity to capture the government."

"Do you mean to incite a bloody revolution?" David Hale asked.

"If necessary," Janders replied, and no further vote was taken.

"Then it's revolution!" Whip Hoxworth announced, issuing a statement rather than a question. The committee cheered, and Whip said, "Our plan must be to strike quickly and to gain control of all the main points in the city."

"What about the other islands?" one of the Hales asked.

"To hell with the other islands," Hoxworth snapped. "The post office, the banks, the palace, the armory. We win them and we control Honolulu. Win Honolulu and we have Hawaii. Janders, tell the committee what you learned today."

John Janders rose, coughed, and spoke formally: "This morning I had a two-hour talk with the American Minister, and we studied the law with great care. It is quite clear, he advised me, that if the revolution quickly acquires control of the major points in Honolulu, so that an observer could logically say, 'the committee controls the city,' the United States will have sufficient cause to contend that we are the *de facto* government. The Minister will promptly recognize us. The monarchy will be at an end. And we will be on our way to incorporation within the United States."

"But what about the American troops in the harbor?" one of the Hewlett boys asked. "Will the ship captains send their troops ashore to fight against us?"

A broad smile came over the scarred face of Wild Whip as he lounged at the head of the table. The committee looked at him, satisfied that he had uncovered some trick for neutralizing the American forces, but he did not divulge the plan. "Tell them what we arranged, John," he said.

Burly John Janders explained: "We have entered into a solemn agreement with the American Minister and with the ship captains that as soon as we start the revolution, they will send ashore the maximum number of troops. Their orders will be simple: 'Protect American lives.' "

"But we're Hawaiian citizens," David Hale protested.

"We're also Americans," Janders replied blandly, "and we're the Americans who are going to be protected."

Fighting back a sardonic smile, Whip leaned forward across the table and said, "It's a plan that can't fail. We launch our drive against the ten key targets. Immediately fighting begins, American troops storm ashore. What can the Hawaiians think? They'll reason, 'The American troops have come to fight against the queen!' So they'll throw down their arms and we'll capture the ten key spots. And as soon as we control them the American Minister will announce: 'The United States formally recognizes the *de facto* government.' At that moment what in hell can the queen do?"

John Janders cried, "How can we lose?"

Soberly David Hale pointed out, "We can lose easily . . . if Uncle Micah appeals to the world powers against our revolution."

"He will not do so," Whip promised.

"He's a man of great honor," Hale insisted. "And he's sworn allegiance to Hawaii."

"It's my job to get Uncle Micah on our side," Whip said flatly. "He'll be there."

The Hewlett boys consulted, and one said, "We'll leave the revolution unless we can depend on Micah Hale to represent us before the world."

"He will be with us," Whip promised. "Not in the fighting. He's too old a man for that. But when it's over, he'll step forth as our leader."

"Can we depend on this?" the Hewlett boys asked.

Whip leaped up and crashed his chair aside. "Goddamn it!" he yelled.

"If our whole success depends on Micah Hale, do you suppose I'm going to let him escape? Of course you can depend upon it. He'll be with us."

Then Janders spoke: "Whip's got to take care of that. We've got to stir up public enthusiasm for the revolution. What we need is a big mass meeting on Monday. Lots of speeches about human decency and men's inalienable rights."

"But I don't want to see any of this committee making speeches," Whip warned. "Get some of the lawyers and men like Cousin Ed Hewlett. He's part-Hawaiian and rants well."

Things seemed to be going so well that the Committee of Nine—that is, eight of them—began to relax: the revolution was at hand; the ten key spots were invested; the American Minister had recognized the new government; President Harrison had accepted it as part of the Union; and sugar was more profitable than ever. But Wild Whip brought the conspirators back to reality, pointing out in icy tones: "At the mass meeting on Monday I want everyone to be within quick reach of his guns."

"Will there be trouble?" one of the Hewletts asked.

"Not if we're ready for it," Whip replied.

As the others quietly left the cellar and circulated through the agitated city, dropping ideas here and there, Wild Whip walked eastward on King Street toward the Hale mansion across from the palace, and when he reached the white picket fence and the wide green lawns in which Malama Hale took such pride, he nodded graciously to that stately half-Hawaiian lady and asked, "Is Uncle Micah in?"

"He's in his study," Malama said gently.

Whip entered without knocking, and before he spoke he closed the door. His uncle was surrounded by his father's missionary books, brought over from Lahaina, and by a substantial theological and legal library. As principal adviser to four kings he had been required to give many legal opinions, and his fine mind found pleasure in doing so. From the 1870's on he had paid little attention to the ventures of H & H, leaving that to the Hoxworths and his nephews; he had gladly accepted his proper share of the firm's enormous profits and had applied his income to the betterment of Hawaii. The Missionary Home for Lepers at Kalaupapa, the library, Punahou and the church had benefited from his charities, but mainly he had spent his income on helping to run the government efficiently. When one of the kings took a grand tour around the world, stopping off in most of the major capitals, it was Micah Hale who accompanied him at his own expense and who paid for many of the essentials. Most of the legal books owned by the cabinet were also purchased by Micah, for he constantly harangued his contemporaries: "We are all of mission extraction, and until Hawaii is completely stable, the job of our fathers is not completed." No island throughout the Pacific ever had a better public servant than Micah Hale, for if he was liberal with his money, he was thrice generous with his energy. Of the fine laws that were often cited in Europe to prove that Hawaii was civilized, an astonishing proportion had sprung from his energetic mind; and what was remarkable in that period was his capacity to rise above personal interest: any laws passed in his regime that favored either sugar planters or shippers were proposed not by him but by the Janderses, the Whipples and the Hewletts who proliferated in the government. Four kings had thought of Micah Hale as their one trustworthy American adviser, yet each had known that he favored the ultimate submission of Hawaii to the United States. The present queen knew of his stand, and it had irritated her and she had dismissed him from all of his offices. He was seventy years old, of better than medium height, stately in bearing and with a long, spadelike white beard. He dressed only in white, including white-powdered shoes, and in public refused to wear glasses. This was the man that faced Whip Hoxworth on the night of Saturday, January 14, 1893.

"Uncle Micah," Whip began forthrightly, refusing the chair offered him, "there's bound to be a revolution within the next two days."

"Have you fomented it?" the spare old man asked.

"Yes, sir, I have. And the Hale boys and the Hewletts and Janderses. The Whipples have also joined us and my brother. There can be no retreat."

Micah leaned back in his office chair and studied his nephew. "So there's going to be a revolution?"

"Yes, sir." Whip was accustomed to addressing older people in the style he had been taught aboard the whaler.

"How old are you, Whip?"

"Thirty-six."

"How many wives have you had?"

"Two."

"How many knife battles in Iwilei?"

"Twenty, thirty."

"How many illegitimate children?"

"I'm supporting half a dozen or more."

"Do you know what they call you around town, Whip?"

"Wild Whip. They call me that to my face. I don't care."

"I wasn't thinking about what they call you to your face. I was thinking of the other name."

"What other name?"

"The Golden Stud. That's how you're known, Whip. And you consider yourself qualified to step forth as the leader of a commune dedicated to the overthrow of a duly constituted government?"

"No, sir, Uncle Micah, I don't."

"I thought you said your group was plotting the revolution."

"We are. And I'm directing it. And when I say, 'Fire,' by God, sir, we'll fire. So don't be in the way. And I'm well qualified to direct a revolution, Uncle Micah, because there's nothing on this earth I fear, and within two days I'll have a new government in Hawaii. But I am not qualified to step forth as the public leader of the revolution. You're right on that, and I know it."

"Who is to be the leader?"

"You are." As Micah gasped at this suggestion, Whip sat down.

The two men, so unalike, stared at each other, and each sensed the tremendous New England force of the other. Micah Hale lived by a code of fierce rectitude and he persuaded those who associated with him to do the same, while Whip Hoxworth had never outgrown the brawling fo'c's'ls of the Pacific. He knew that all men were swine and that they enjoyed being kicked into line; yet on the eve of the revolution he also knew that certain focal points of history required a man better than himself to stand forth as leader. There were limits to what even Whipple Hoxworth could attain without the assistance of decency.

"This is pretty much a sugar revolution, isn't it, Whipple?" Micah asked.

"From my point of view, yes, sir. From yours, no, sir."

"How can there be two interpretations of an evil act, Whipple?"

"If there weren't two interpretations of our necessary act, Uncle Micah, I wouldn't be here pleading with you. I want a revolution so that sugar will be forever made safe in these islands. You want it so that the islands can join the United States in accordance with a destiny that you foresaw fifty years ago. Uncle Micah, you've always been right, and you are tonight. Hawaii is doomed unless it contrives some trick to make America accept these islands. And I control that trick. Sir, the only way your dream will ever be realized is through me."

"Not so, Whipple. The day will come when Washington will see the inevitability of annexation."

"Never! Only actions make things inevitable."

"Justice and dawning conscience produce inevitability. Slowly, Washington will see what the right step is. And we must rely upon Washington to take it."

"No! If you live to be a hundred, you'll die talking about the slow inevitability of justice. There's going to be a revolution, my revolution, and you're going to lead it so that your dream of justice can come true."

Micah Hale rose slowly and stared down at his vigorous young nephew. "I am appalled, Whipple, that you so misjudged me as to think that I would be partner to such an evil action. I will not divulge your plans, although I should. But now you had better go."

To his surprise, his scar-faced nephew did not rise. Insolently he kept his position, raised one foot to kick his uncle's chair into place, and said, "Now we understand each other. Sit down, Uncle Micah, and let's talk about revolution. Let's forget everything we've said so far. And you might as well forget about threatening to divulge our plans to the government. Charley Wilson knows about them and wanted to arrest us all, but the cabinet didn't have the guts to back him up. So let's see what you and I can do for one another. You despise my position and I think yours is pathetic. Okay, let's not revert to that again. Uncle Micah, there's going to be a revolution in two days. You can't possibly stop it. We've got the American Minister waiting on the edge of his chair to recognize our *de facto* government. We've got American troops out there in the harbor just itching to swarm ashore and protect decent Americans against Hawaiian savages. We've got our targets pinpointed and our schedules laid. Even if you were to inform the queen herself, you'd only move up the timetable by the hours you stole from us." He leaned forward and looked hard into his uncle's eyes. "It's a revolution, Uncle Micah."

Micah Hale was not the kind of man to find his lips going dry at moments of crisis. He had weathered too many abortive revolutions when only his courage had saved the government from irresponsible outrage, and he did not sense any unusual quickening of his pulse now. With eyes as hard as his nephew's, but from a different cause, he said, "You've thought of everything."

"Let's accept the revolution as accomplished," the young sugar planter proposed. "I'm not the man who ought to stand before the bar of world opinion and explain why it was necessary. My record wouldn't read very well in London or Berlin. So let's say my part of the revolution has been successful, and that all it represents is my personal greediness . . . sugar . . . land. What happens then? America won't accept us. Maybe Japan would."

The idea that Wild Whip was developing had several other subsidiary clauses, but bearded old Micah Hale did not hear them, for with the mention of the word Japan he was suddenly transported to the mysterious city of Tokyo in the year 1881, when he served as privy councilor to the last king of Hawaii on the latter's triumphal journey around the world. The royal party was stopping in a Japanese mansion that contained no chairs; the floors were of the most exquisite wood polished by centuries of use and the sliding doors were joyous to behold. It was March and a horde of busy gardeners scurried about pruning pine trees with gnarled red branches. A row of plum trees showed white blossoms, cherries were eager to burst into bloom, and as the first warm days of the year approached, the Hawaiian party relaxed to enjoy the gracious scenery.

Suddenly Micah had looked up and asked, "Where's the king?" No one knew. At first there was excitement; then, as the hours passed, there was panic, on the part of both the Americans and the Japanese, for the King of Hawaii was clearly missing. No one had seen him leave the spacious grounds of the mansion and a frantic search revealed no betraying signs of foul play. He had vanished, a great hulk of a man dressed in conspicuous western clothes and a long black London-tailored coat. It was one of the few times that Micah Hale had experienced real dread, for he was aware that in relatively recent years Japanese samurai, outraged at the invasion of foreigners, had sliced off the heads of several. Consequently he knelt in the chairless room and prayed: "God, save the king! Please!"

In the third hour of panic, the king appeared, in jovial mood, holding his shoes. He had obviously been crawling through the stream that separated the mansion from the Imperial Palace, and he had obviously been having a rare time. He refused to explain where he had spent the missing three hours and he went to bed that night highly pleased with himself. In the morning the emperor's chamberlain waited until the king was occupied with other matters and then quietly slipped in to see Micah.

"Utterly extraordinary," the little man in the shiny black London morning coat said in good English. "Yesterday afternoon we heard this strange noise at the Imperial Palace, and the guards were about to shoot an intruder when I saw that it was your king. He was barefooted, muddy, laughing. His great brown face was wet with perspiration when he pushed aside the shoji, walked with his dirty feet over the tatami and said, 'I'd like to talk with the emperor.' We were appalled, because nothing like this had ever happened before, but Mutsuhito is a superb man and he said, 'I'd like to talk with you.' And they went into Mutsuhito's private audience chamber. And what is astonishing, they stayed there for nearly three hours."

Micah Hale wiped his forehead and straightened out his beard. "Believe me, Excellency, it was not I who sent the king."

"Hardly," the chamberlain replied. "In view of what he talked about."

"What did he speak of?" Micah probed.

"Don't you know?" the Japanese asked.

"No."

"The king said, 'Hawaii is tired of being pushed this way and that by America and England and Russia. It is a Pacific power and must remain so.' " The chamberlain paused for effect and it became apparent that Micah was expected to pursue the inquiry.

Instead he relaxed, bowed to the chamberlain and said, "I am grateful to you for having looked after my king."

"Are you a subject of his Majesty?" the Japanese asked.

"Yes. When I took service with the government, I swore allegiance to Hawaii."

"How interesting. Would you care to join me in a cup of English tea?"

"I'd be delighted," Micah said. They walked through lovely pine-laden gardens and came to a small rustic house, where a serving-maid waited.

"What your king proposed," the Japanese said, afraid that Micah was not going to ask, "was that the heir to his throne, the Princess Kaiulani, be given in marriage to the son of the emperor, so as to bind Japan and Hawaii closer together."

Micah lost his aplomb. He choked on his tea, spilled it, slammed the cup down, and gasped, "What did you say?"

"He proposed an alliance of mutual interest, to be sealed by the marriage of the princess to one of our princes. When I heard the facts, Mr. Hale, I choked, too."

The two diplomats stared at each other, aghast. Finally Micah stammered, "What had I better do?"

"You'd better get the king out of Japan immediately."

"Of course, of course. But I mean . . . with the emperor?"

"A formal offer of marriage has been extended. It's got to be considered by the Imperial family . . . and the staff. In a year or so we'll send an answer."

"Excellency, please take pains to insure that the answer is no."

"It is now beyond my control. How old is your princess?"

"Let me see, she's six."

"We have time."

That night Micah completed plans to whisk his unpredictable king out of Japan, but as they sat at supper, the king still having said nothing concerning his impromptu visit with the emperor, Micah studied his fat, jolly face and thought: "I wonder what transpires in that surprising brain? How did he think up a state marriage with the Japanese royal family? Where did he get the idea for an alliance with Japan? Such a thing would destroy all hope of eventual union with America! My goodness, what can we expect him to do when he gets to Europe!" From that prophetic day, Micah Hale had appreciated the inherent danger that Hawaii might one day associate itself with Japan. He had therefore fought against the importation of Japanese farmers onto the sugar plantations, but greedy men like John Janders and the Hewlett boys had insisted upon it. He was frightened by the adroit manner in which the little Japanese, who had begun arriving in the 1880's, accommodated themselves to Hawaiian life, and he had tried to pass laws forbidding them to leave the plantations and open stores. When alone with friends he often referred to the "Yellow Menace," and he foresaw that the Japanese would multiply and grasp for political power in a way that the more easygoing Chinese never would. Therefore he had constructed an international-relations platform that had only two planks: "Make Hawaii American. Keep the Japanese away."

Consequently, when Wild Whip uttered the phrase, "It begins to look as if Japan might . . ." vibrant chords were struck in Micah Hale's memory. "What was that last point, Whip?" he asked his nephew.

"I was saying that if you want to see your basic dream come to pass, you can do it only through me."

"I mean about Japan," Micah explained, and suddenly Whip realized that his uncle had heard nothing of his last statements. He had been daydreaming about some forgotten incident that Whip didn't know about, but with sure instinct, Whip knew that his uncle's reverie concerned Japan and that it had produced fear. He therefore decided to play upon that fear.

"I was saying about Japan, that there is a good deal of evidence that the Yellow Menace would be glad to take Hawaii if the United States doesn't."

"Do you think so?" Micah asked fearfully.

"What more natural?" Whip asked, shrugging his shoulders.

"Do you think Japan would extend herself so far from her own islands?"

"Not by design, but if we don't get Hawaii into the United States, she'll have to."

"I am terribly afraid of that," Micah admitted. "And if not Japan, then England or Germany."

"Obviously, if we allow the islands to lie around unwanted, someone will surely grab them."

"But suppose the monarchy cleansed itself," Micah temporized. "Suppose we got rid of Liliuokalani and put somebody else on the throne?"

Wild Whip saw that his uncle was clutching at straws, so he hammered home his points: "The revolutionists will tolerate no Hawaiian monarch. None that you could propose, Uncle Micah, would be acceptable."

His nephew's position startled the white-bearded old man and he said, "Then even though you are uncertain of what comes next, you're determined to overthrow the monarchy?"

Whip was not to be trapped into such an admission of irresponsibility. Suavely he replied, "But we are certain of what comes next, Uncle Micah. You come next. You justify us before world opinion and lead us into the United States. It's what you've always wanted. It's what you know is right."

The two men fell into silence, as Micah, a leader on whom all the glories and perquisites available to the kings of Hawaii had been visited, considered what he must do. He was caught in wild currents of confusion, and any antagonist other than Wild Whip Hoxworth would have retired at this moment and allowed his uncle to study the matter through the remainder of the night, but now the mark of Whip's character stood out. He rose from his chair, went to the door, stretched as if he were leaving, looked out at the stars dancing over Diamond Head and turned back toward his uncle. Lifting a chair and placing it so that its back faced Micah, he sat with his arms folded across the top of the back and his legs straddling the seat. This brought his scarred face close to his uncle's, and he said coldly, "Uncle Micah, so far we've been sparring. Now we've got to get down to the bedrock base of this revolution. There's no escape. You've got to stand before the public."

Micah replied: "I cannot betray the Hawaiians who have befriended me."

Whip said: "But you're ready to betray the Americans who own these islands."

Micah replied: "When I took my oath of allegiance to Hawaii, I believed what I was doing. I became a Hawaiian."

Whip said: "I didn't. I remained an American. I'm going to call on American warships to protect my property for me."

Micah replied: "You can act that way. I can't."

Whip said: "That is not the action we're talking about, Uncle Micah. I'm saying that I am determined to lead a revolution against a weak and corrupt form of government. I'm going to win my part of the revolution. But only you can carry it to its logical conclusion: union with America."

Micah replied: "And that I refuse to do."

Whip said: "If you shared your stubborn conclusion with the silly queen, she'd applaud. But if you told Aunt Malama how you were wasting the tides of history and allowing them to slip away from you, even though she's a Hawaiian she'd say you were stupid."

Micah replied: "I cannot betray these good people."

Whip said: "Then you will allow the forces of history to betray them to Japan."

Micah replied: "That's a risk we'll have to take."

Whip said: "It's not a risk, Uncle Micah. It's a certainty. These islands are doomed. There is only one way to save them. Pick up our revolution and lead it to a good end."

Micah replied: "I will not prostitute myself to protect a gang of sugar robbers."

Whip said: "Unless you protect us, every good thing you have ever wanted for Hawaii will be lost."

Micah replied: "I would relinquish even union with America rather than attain it as a result of unchristian acts."

Whip said: "I am surprised you speak of Christianity. Are you willing to abandon these islands to opium, lotteries, debauchery, with streets unsafe for women?"

Micah replied: "These are problems we must solve within the framework of established government, not by revolution."

Whip said: "Where was the framework of your established government when the late king used to convene his Ball of String Society?"

Micah replied: "That was an aberration. God has surely punished him for that."

Whip said: "It was the mark of the monarchy. The old fool stood facing a crowd of beautiful women and threw a ball of string at them. He held one end and the girl who caught the ball followed him obediently to bed."

Micah replied: "I hardly expected you to preach morality."

Whip said: "I'll preach anything that will end the monarchy."

Micah replied: "The one evil thing I did in my life was to ally myself with your grandfather against my own father. God has never forgiven me for this, and I often wake at night in dreadful sweat and lie there for hours reflecting upon the devilish compact I made with Captain Hoxworth. Now you ask me to make a worse with his grandson. I can't risk any more sleepless nights, Whipple."

Whip said: "The alliance between you and old Rafer Hoxworth may have been unholy in its inception. But look at the good it's done Hawaii. The building, the jobs, the ships, the fields. Somebody had to accomplish those things, Uncle Micah. Your influence in doing them the right way was fundamental. Now you have got to ally yourself with me to insure a proper culmination to our revolt."

Micah replied: "Must a good man always use such evil instruments as you and your grandfather?"

Whip said: "Yes. Because good men never have the courage to act. You can only direct and safeguard movements already set into motion by men like me."

Micah replied: "I will not compound the evil I did once. I will not help you, Whip."

Whip said: "You do not hurt me, Uncle Micah, but you destroy the future of these islands."

He bowed and left his austere uncle. It was nearly three in the morning when he walked down the path to King Street, and his last view of Micah was of the white-bearded old man sitting erect at his desk, staring at his books.

At the secret meeting of the committee held the next day, Sunday, January 15, Wild Whip reported frankly to his conspirators: "Uncle Micah will not join us."

"Then I can't either," said David Hale. Two of the Hewletts also withdrew.

John Janders suggested: "We'd better not try to force the revolution. If Micah Hale's against it, he might inflame public opinion against us. Then we'd be lost. I'm going to call off tomorrow's mass meeting."

There was a buzz of excitement and Wild Whip could feel the resolve of the would-be revolutionists ebbing away like the surf after a high tide. Men in groups were discussing how, having just coached Ed Hewlett in what to tell the mob tomorrow, they must now cancel his oratory.

"You may have misunderstood me," Whip said quietly. The revolutionists stopped retreating, eager to hear any words of direction. "I meant to say that Uncle Micah will not join us willingly. What I didn't say was that I shall force his hand, and make him join. Everything goes ahead as planned. In two days, gentlemen, Hawaii will be a republic, and the men in this room will govern it. With Micah Hale as our face to the world."

"How do you propose accomplishing that?" one of the Hales asked. "If Uncle Micah makes up his mind . . ."

"Your uncle is a patriot," Whip replied. "He loves Hawaii and is loyal to it. He will never see these islands disintegrate into formless revolution. He'll be with us."

"How will you force his hand?"

"I think we can get the American troops to march ashore tomorrow night . . . just after the mass meeting. This will accomplish two ends. It will encourage our side and scare hell out of the monarchists. We occupy the government buildings, throw the queen out, and on Monday morning Micah Hale will have to join us."

"Are you certain of this?" one of the trembling Hales asked.

"I am going to begin drafting the proclamations now," Whip replied, "for him to sign, and I want David Hale and Micah Whipple to help me."

The revolution that overthrew the Hawaiian monarchy and passed the government into the hands of the sugar planters was under way. In her palace, the wild-willed queen shuddered as she saw American troops file ashore to invade her territory. She was disposed to fight them, for she knew that this was a cruel perversion of the ordinary relationships between sovereign nations, but the sugar planters quickly immobilized her loyal troops, and she was left defenseless, a stubborn, anachronistic woman in her mid-fifties, regal in appearance but totally unaware that the nineteenth century was ebbing to a close and taking with it the concepts of government to which she adhered.

However, in the dying moments of her reign she was not completely without support, for after her troops were disbanded without firing a shot, a squad of volunteer loyalists materialized from the alleys of Honolulu and marched out to defend their queen. In their ranks, and typical of their quality, waddled the old kanaka maile gatherer, Kimo. He had a musket that he had grabbed from a man in a pool hall and he held his uniform—a pair of sagging pants and that was all—about his waist with a length of red rope. His hair had not been combed for some days, he needed a shave and he was barefooted, but like his companions he gave every evidence of being willing to die for his queen. The sparkling American troops with new rifles watched in amazement as the volunteers marched up to give them battle, but a courageous officer in whites ran unarmed to the leader of the irregulars and said, "There's no war. The queen has abdicated."

"She's what?" the leader of the loyalists asked.

"She's abdicated," the young American said. Then he shouted, "Anybody here speak Hawaiian?"

A haole bystander idled up and asked, "What you want, General?"

"Tell these men that there is to be no war. The queen has abdicated."

"Sure," the haole agreed. Turning to Kimo and his men he said, "Eh, you kanaka! Liliuokalani pau. She go home. You pau too. You go home."

And so far as the actual fighting was concerned, in this manner the revolution ended. Kimo trundled his unused musket back to the poolroom and listened to the gibes of his friends. Then in great disturbance of spirit, for he knew that he had participated in the death of a world he had loved—the horses prancing in gold tassels, the royal guard marching in bright uniforms, the queen going forth in a gilt carriage—he walked slowly down Beretania Street and up Nuuanu to the small house where he lived with his wife Apikela and his Chinese family. He went directly to bed and lay there without talking or laughing until he died.

The provisional government, with Micah Hale as ostensible head and the sugar planters directing from behind, swept away the seventeenth-century anachronisms proposed by Queen Liliuokalani. Each act of the efficient new government was directed toward one clear goal: union with America. David Hale and Micah Whipple were rushed to Washington to force a Treaty of Annexation through the Senate before congenial President Harrison and his Republicans left office on March 4, because it was known that the newly elected President, Grover Cleveland, opposed what had been happening in Hawaii; and soon frantic appeals for moral support were speeding back to Honolulu, for the treaty commissioners Hale and Whipple reported: "There is considerable opposition to the manner in which the revolution was carried out. Cannot Micah Hale make a strong statement, relying upon his faultless reputation to give it force? Else we are lost."

It was under these circumstances, in February, 1893, that Micah Hale retired to his study on King Street and wrote for a New York journal: "Any sane man looking at these islands today has got to admit that they require supervision by the United States of America. The indigenous citizens are for the most part illiterate, steeped in idolatry, committed to vain shows of monarchical display and totally unsuited to govern themselves." In these harsh but true words, the son of a missionary, in his seventy-first year, summarized what his group had accomplished; but since he wrote as a profound patriot and as one who loved Hawaii above all else, he did not understand what he was saying. Furthermore, he went on to point out a great truth that others both in Hawaii and America were overlooking: "Hawaii cannot lie idle and unwanted in the middle of the Pacific. The islands seem to lie close to America, but they also lie close to Canada and on the route from that great land to Australia and New Zealand. There is every reason for Hawaii to become Canadian. They also lie close to Russia-in-Asia and except for an accident of history might even now belong to that great power. And to anyone who has sailed from Honolulu to Yokohama or to Shanghai, these islands lie perilously close to Japan and China. For more than half a century I have believed that their destiny lies with America, but it is not as I once thought an inevitable destiny. If at this crucial moment of history, our logical destiny is frustrated, an illogical one will triumph and Hawaii, the gem of the Pacific, will belong to Canada or to Russia or to Japan. It is to prevent such a catastrophe that we pray for the United States to accept us now." This widely reprinted article was taken from the Hale mansion on King Street by Wild Whip Hoxworth and delivered to one of his ships waiting in the harbor, but as old Micah Hale handed it to his nephew, he was freshly appalled that he should be using such an evil agent to accomplish so good a purpose.

Micah's plea achieved nothing, for Louisiana and Colorado sugar interests prevented the lame-duck Senate of February, 1893, from jamming the Treaty of Annexation through, and five days after Grover Cleveland assumed the Presidency he sternly withdrew the treaty and rebuked those who had sought to foist it upon the American public. Now doleful news reached Hawaii. The Secretary of State wrote: "The United States will not accept the Hawaiian Islands on the terms under which they have been offered. It would lower our national standard to endorse a selfish and dishonorable scheme of a lot of adventurers. I oppose taking these islands by force and fraud, for there is such a thing as international morality."

President Cleveland was of a similar opinion and personally dispatched an investigator to Honolulu to inquire into America's role in the unsavory revolution, and by one of the tricks of history the investigator turned out to be a Democrat from Georgia and a member of a family that had once held slaves. When preliminary news of his appointment reached Hawaii, the Committee of Nine were apprehensive lest he report against them, but when his slave-holding status was revealed, they sighed with visible relief. "As a good Southerner he'll understand our problems," John Janders told the conspirators, and they all agreed.

But Whip Hoxworth, considering the matter carefully, judged: "We may be in for deep trouble. Since Cleveland's investigator comes from Georgia, he probably despises niggers."

"Of course he does," Janders agreed. "He'll see through these Hawaiians right away."

"I doubt it," Whip cautioned. "Granted that he hates niggers. As a sensible human being he'll try to compensate and prove that he doesn't hate other people with dark skins."

"Why would he do that?" Janders demanded.

"Don't ask me why!" Whip replied. "Just watch."

And when the investigator arrived he did exactly as Whip had predicted. Hating Negroes at home, he had to like Hawaiians abroad. It was a profound compulsion and it permitted him, a Georgia man, to understand the revolution better than any other American understood it at the time. He talked principally with Hawaiians, was bedazzled by the idea of speaking directly with a queen, became an ardent royalist, and suppressed evidence given by white men. His report to President Cleveland was a crushing rebuke to the sugar men; they had, he discovered, conspired with the American Minister to overthrow a duly constituted government; they had worked in league with the captain of an American vessel; they had deposed the queen against the will of the Hawaiian people; they had done all this for personal gain; and it was his opinion that Queen Liliuokalani, a virtuous woman, should be restored to her throne.

His report aroused such a storm in Washington that David Hale and Micah Whipple saw there was no hope of forcing the United States to accept Hawaii, and they returned to Honolulu with the glum prediction: "We will never become part of America while Grover Cleveland is President. His Secretary of State is already asking, 'Should not the great wrong done to a feeble state by an abuse of the authority of the United States be undone by restoring the legitimate government?' There's even talk of restoring the queen by force of American arms."

"What would happen to us?" members of the Committee asked.

"Since you're American subjects," a consular official explained, "you'd be arrested, hauled off to Washington, and tried for conspiring to overthrow a friendly power."

"Oh, no!" the conspirators protested. "We're Hawaiian subjects. Our citizenship is here."

September and October, 1893, were uneasy months in Hawaii, and Wild Whip's gang maintained power by only a nervous margin. Each arriving ship brought ominous news from Washington, where sentiment had swung strongly in favor of Queen Liliuokalani, and it was generally assumed that she would shortly be restored to power; but just before this was about to occur the obstinate woman committed an act so appalling to the Americans that she forever discredited the monarchy. What Wild Whip had been unable to gain for himself, the queen won for him.

Late in the year President Cleveland dispatched a second investigator to check upon the specific terms under which Liliuokalani should be returned to her throne, for as Cleveland pointed out, America never wished to profit from the misfortunes of her neighbors. The new investigator plunged the Committee of Nine into despair by announcing that the annexation of Hawaii by America was no longer even under discussion, whereupon he entered into formal discussions with the queen as to what steps she wanted America to take in restoring her crown.

No difficulties were encountered, and the investigator had to smile when the queen pointed out, "One of the charges made against us most often, sir, was that we were a small kingdom overly given to a love of luxurious display. To this charge I must plead guilty, because from the first our kings selected as their advisers men of the missionary group, and we found that no men on earth love panoply and richly caparisoned horses and bright uniforms and medals more than men who have long been dressed in New England homespun. I have four pictures here of state occasions. You see the men loaded with gold and medals. They aren't Hawaiians. They're Americans. They demanded the pomp of royalty, and we pampered them."

"Speaking of the Americans," the investigator asked, "what kind of amnesty will you provide for the revolutionists?"

"Amnesty?" Queen Liliuokalani asked, inclining her large and expressive head toward the American. "I don't understand."

"Amnesty," the investigator explained condescendingly. "It means . . ."

"I know what the word means," Liliuokalani interrupted. "But what does it mean in this circumstance?"

"Hawaii's undergone some unfortunate trouble. It's over. You're restored to your throne. President Cleveland assumes that you'll issue a proclamation of general amnesty. It's usually done."

"Amnesty!" the powerful queen repeated incredulously.

"If not amnesty, what did you have in mind?"

"Beheading, of course," the queen replied.

"What was that?"

"The rebels will have to be beheaded. It's the custom of the islands. He who acts against the throne is beheaded."

The American investigator gasped, then swallowed hard. "Your Excellency," he said, "are you aware that there are over sixty American citizens involved?"

"I did not know the number of traitors, and I do not think of them as Americans. They have always claimed to be Hawaiians, and they shall be beheaded."

"All sixty?" the investigator asked.

"Why not?" Liliuokalani asked.

"I think I had better report to President Cleveland," the perspiring investigator gulped, excusing himself from the august presence; and that night he wrote: "There are factors here which we may not have considered adequately in the past." After that there was no more talk of restoring the monarchy.

Thus, in late 1893, it became apparent that the United States would neither accept Hawaii in view of the besmirched character of the men who had led the revolution nor restore a monarchy that threatened to behead more than sixty American citizens. So the islands drifted year by year, ships without moorings. Hawaiians grew to hate the haoles who had defrauded them of their monarchy, and haoles despised the weak-kneed American senators who refused to accept their responsibilities and annex the islands. Sugar planters suffered, and it looked as if Colorado and Louisiana would keep Hawaiian sugar out of the mainland permanently. The great ships of the H & H carried less cargo, and both the British and the Japanese began wondering what, in decency, they ought to do about this rudderless ship drifting across the dangerous Pacific. In desperation the sugar men proposed a treaty which would allow them to peddle their accumulating sugar to Australia, and it was predicted that Hawaii would soon have to join the British Empire.

At this juncture Micah Hale saved Hawaii, and he was well prepared for his role. Years before in Lahaina his missionary father had kept him penned up in a walled garden where he had done nothing but study history, the Bible and his father's fierce sense of rectitude. Particularly, he had served two apprenticeships which now fortified him in the job of building a new government: he had watched his father translate the book of Ezekiel, so that the stern phrases of that obdurate prophet lived in his mind; and he had listened when his lame little father explained how John Calvin and Theodore Beza had governed Geneva in accordance with the will of God.

The first thing Micah Hale did was to deprive Wild Whip Hoxworth of any connection with the government. Next he insisted upon moral laws and fiscal responsibility. But above all, like a true missionary, he wrote. For the newspapers he wrote justifications of his government. For magazines he explained why the Hawaii revolution, which he had not wanted, was similar to the uprisings that had brought William and Mary to the English throne. To Republican senators he wrote voluminously, providing them with ammunition to be fired against the Democrats, and to long-forgotten friends across America he wrote inspired letters, begging them to accept Hawaii. He lived solely for the purpose of making his islands part of the United States, and his pen, as it pushed across paper in the quiet hours after midnight, was the only real weapon the islanders had left.

It was not a liberal government that Micah founded. When the wealthy men who were to draw up a new constitution met, he lectured: "Your job is to build a Christian state in which only responsible men of good reputation and solid ownership of property are allowed to govern." Explicit property qualifications were set for all who served and all who voted to have them serve. No man could be a member of the senate who did not own $3,000 worth of property untouched by mortgages, or who did not possess a yearly income of $1,200. In order to vote for a senator, a man was required to own $3,000 worth of property or to have an income of $600. Explained Micah: "In other parts of the world the uneducated workingman raises his voice in anger against his superiors, but not in Hawaii." Wherever possible, advantages were given to plantation owners, for upon them rested the welfare of the islands.

On one point Micah was adamant: no Oriental must be allowed to vote or to participate in the government in any way. "They were brought to these islands to labor in the cane fields, and when their work was done they were supposed to go back home. There was no intention that they stay here, and if they do so, there is no place in our public life for them." Therefore, at Micah's suggestion, cleverly worded literacy tests were required for suffrage, and no Chinese or Japanese, even if he were wealthy and a citizen, could possibly pass them.

In many respects Micah's government was too liberal for the sugar men who had thrown it into power, and there were many Hales and Whipples and Hewletts among the missionary group who opposed his radical liberalism, while the Janderses and Hoxworths considered him insane with French republican principles; for once the electorate had been restricted to the well-to-do, Micah was lenient and just in all other matters. He insisted upon trial by jury, the rights of habeas corpus, freedom of religion and all the appurtenances of an Anglo-Saxon democracy. But when in the later stages of the constitutional convention he was asked, "What kind of government are you building here?" he replied quickly, "One that will mark time decently until the United States accepts us."

From this great basic principle he never wavered. A lesser man than Micah might have been tempted by his power, but this austere New Englander was not. He awarded himself no medals, erected no fanciful structures of power about his erect white-suited figure. In the five years following the revolution of 1893 this ordained minister never once let a day pass without getting down on his knees and praying, "Almighty God, bring our plan to fruition. Make us part of America."

Micah's training as a Calvinist enabled him to face many crises with an absolute conviction that he was right, and when ugly decisions had to be made, he was willing to make them. In 1895 an armed revolution broke out against his government, and with unequivocating force he put it down, then arrested Queen Liliuokalani for her supposed complicity in it. When weak-livered men counseled caution in dealing with the fiery queen, Micah said, "She will be tried on charges of treason against this republic." And he stood firm when a jury subservient to the sugar men brought in a verdict of guilty. Of course, any other jury would have had to do the same, for the queen, refusing to honor the usurpers from America who had stolen her throne, naturally worked against them and, although there were conflicting reports on the matter, probably also encouraged her followers to open rebellion; the new nation had no recourse but to try her for treason, and when the sugar men found her guilty, it was Micah's responsibility to imprison her.

The powerful, headstrong woman was incarcerated in an upper room of the palace, and while her imprisonment was rigorously policed, it was never physically unpleasant, and before long her adherents were circulating the greatest state paper ever produced by a sovereign of the islands. It was a song transcribed by Liliuokalani while in prison, and although she had composed it some years before, it had gained little notice; now its lament swept the island and the world, "Aloha Oe": "Gently sweeps the rain cloud o'er the cliff, borne swiftly by the western gale." One of the missionary men said of this song: "While she was free Queen Liliuokalani never did a thing for her people, but when she was in jail she expressed their soul." Micah Hale, hearing the melody, said, "Let her go free," and she left for Washington, there to fight against him bitterly.

When the revolution was put down and the new government stabilized, it seemed for a brief interval as if President Cleveland and the Democrats might accept Hawaii. Mainland newspapers were beginning to write: "The moral stature of Micah Hale has gone far to correct the evils perpetrated by younger Americans during the revolution." At last Micah reported to his cabinet: "I am beginning to see hope."

And then Wild Whip Hoxworth exploded across the front pages of America, and editors wrote: "This violent young man has served to remind us of the viciousness whereby men like himself stole Hawaii from Queen Liliuokalani." And hope of annexation evaporated.

The trouble started during a three-day orgy at a Chinese brothel on Rat Alley in Iwilei. Whip had driven down to see a Spanish girl picked off a ship just in from Valparaiso, and he was enjoying himself when one of the sailors from the ship appeared with a claim that the girl belonged to him by right of purchase. A dreadful brawl ensued in which the intruding sailor was well whipped and kicked about the face. When he recovered, he stormed back into the brothel with two friends armed with knives, and they started to carve pieces out of Whip's face, but the Valparaiso girl sided with Whip and crashed a stool into the face of the leader, who, already weak from the beating Whip had earlier administered, collapsed, whereupon Whip kicked him about the head so furiously that the man nearly died.

Wild Whip was not arrested, of course, not only because the affair had happened in Iwilei, which was more or less outside police jurisdiction, but also because there were many witnesses to the fact that three men had come at him with knives, and he had two scars to prove that they had cut him before he had manhandled them. This affair might have passed without more than local notice except that the wounded sailor was a man of obstinate character, and as soon as he was discharged from the hospital he bought himself a gun, waited for Whip in a Hotel Street bar, and shot him through the left shoulder as he walked by.

It was news of this shooting that reached America, where it vitiated much that Micah Hale had been accomplishing, but insofar as Hawaii was concerned, the worst was yet to come, for at the height of the scandal, Wild Whip got married, and this was almost insupportable, for the girl he married—with his left arm in a sling—was Mae Forbes. She was a beautiful girl of twenty, with long black hair, sinewy charm and perfect complexion. She had a soft low voice and was known to be of impeccable reputation, for her father, recognizing her beauty, had brought her up with extra care. Normally, the marriage of a vigorous young man like Wild Whip to a beautiful girl like Mae Forbes would have been acclaimed, especially as it was a love match and there was some hope that Mae might tame the fiery Hoxworth.

Instead, the marriage was so offensive to Hawaii that it overshadowed all of Wild Whip's former behavior, because Mae Forbes sprang from a rather curious parentage. Her grandmother was the daughter of one of the lesser alii families from Maui, and her grandfather, Josiah Forbes, was a strong-minded, able Englishman from Bristol, who had jumped ship on the Big Island to make a small fortune pressing sugar. Later he married his Maui sweetheart, a fine Hawaiian woman, and they had a pert daughter, but she was a headstrong girl who liked to do as she wished, and at the age of nineteen she married a Chinese farmer named Ching, so that her daughter who went by the name of Mae Forbes was really Ching Lan Tsin, Perfect Flower Ching, and her marriage to Whipple Hoxworth was the first example of an Oriental, or part-Oriental, in her case, marrying into a major island family. It was a terrifying foretaste of the future, and Wild Whip was ostracized.

Even though his behavior had damaged Hawaii he would probably have been allowed to remain in the islands except for a public brawl he engaged in with the Hewlett boys. It arose when he found that some of the Committee of Nine had developed second thoughts about the revolution and were now preaching against union with America: "Somebody pointed out that as soon as we come under American law, our contracts for forced labor will be declared void, and we won't be free to import any more Japanese."

"Anything wrong with that?" Whip asked scornfully.

"How can we grow sugar without contract labor?"

"Frankly, and all sentiment aside, what good does contract labor do you?"

"Well, they've got to work where we say, at a fixed wage, and if they don't we can depend on our judges to make them."

"Well, I'll be goddamned!" Whip snorted. "Don't you men ever read the papers? Of course our labor laws will be rejected by America."

"Then we don't want to join America," one of the Hewlett boys said.

"What do you propose?" Whip asked politely.

"Join England. She allows contract labor. Or go it alone."

Whip was stunned. The revolution was slipping away from him. First Cleveland frustrated it and now the original conspirators were talking of union with England. "Look," he said carefully, "you don't need the old labor contracts. For the last eleven years I've not dragged one of my men into court. If they want to leave, okay. I give them good food, a fair deal, a little humor, and they make more sugar for me than they do for all of you put together. Believe me, that's the pattern of the future."

One of the Hewlett boys was offended by this vision and added, unwisely, "There's one more thing you do for the men, Whip."

"What?"

"You also sleep with their wives."

Like a volcano about to build a new island, Wild Whip erupted from his chair, lunged at the Hewletts and would have maimed the man who had insulted him had not other committee members pinioned him.

That night Micah Hale summoned Whip to his study on King Street. "You must leave the islands, Whipple."

"But the revolution's falling apart!" Whip protested

"Revolutions always do," Micah replied.

"These poor bastards are talking of joining England, or going it alone. Just to make a few more dollars on their labor contracts."

"That's all beside the point, Whipple. You're contaminating the new nation, and for the good of all, you've got to go."

"But I'm determined to fight this insidious idea of surrender. I'll not let this revolution . . ."

"Get out!" Micah thundered. "I'm trying to save Hawaii, and I can't do it if you're here. You're an evil, corrupt bully, and these islands have no place for you. Go!"

The old man shoved Whipple from the door, so in the vital years that followed, Wild Whip traveled abroad with his Chinese-Hawaiian wife, his two facial scars offsetting her crystalline beauty; and from a distance he followed the affairs of home. He was in Rio when word arrived of McKinley's election to the Presidency, and he paused in his work long enough to tell Ching-ching, as he called his wife, "In two years the islands'll join America. Thank God it's over."

"Shall we return for the celebrations?" Ching-ching asked.

"No," Whip scowled. "It's Uncle Micah's show. All I did was get him started." He said no more about annexation, for he was on the trail of something that was to have almost as profound an effect upon Hawaii as her union with the United States. One morning he burst into his wife's room in their hotel in Rio de Janeiro, crying, "Ching-ching! I want you to taste something."

"What are you doing?" she laughed, for she was not yet out of bed and he was wheeling in a small table bearing one dish, a knife and a fork.

"I'm bringing you one of the most delicious things yet invented. Tuck a towel under your chin." He threw her one of his shirts and tied the sleeves about her pretty olive throat. Then from a paper sack he produced a large, golden, barrel-shaped pineapple. Holding it aloft by its spiny leaves, he asked, "You ever see a more perfect fruit than this?"

"Very large for a pineapple," Ching-ching remarked. "Where'd you get it?"

"More than six pounds. They tell me ships bring them down here regularly from French Guiana. They're called Cayennes, but wait till you taste one." With a large, sharp knife Wild Whip proceeded to slice away the hard outer skin and the series of eyes. Soon a most delicious aroma filled the room and a golden juice ran down off the tip of the knife, staining the tablecover.

"Watch out, Whip!" his wife cautioned. "It's dripping."

"That's what makes it smell so good," he explained. With a sturdy cut across the middle of the pineapple he laid it in half, then sliced off a perfect circle of heavy, golden, aromatic fruit. He slapped it onto the plate, handed Ching-ching a fork and invited her to taste her first Cayenne.

"That's heavenly!" she cried as the slightly acid juice stained her chin. "Where did you say they grow?"

"Up north."

"We ought to plant these in Hawaii," she suggested.

"I propose to," he replied.

When Micah Hale was approaching seventy-six and was more tired than he dared admit, word reached Honolulu that in Washington the House of Representatives had finally approved annexation by a vote of 209 to 91. That night Micah's vigil began, for at dinner he said to his wife Malama, "We have two more weeks to wait, and then we'll know what the Senate is going to do."

"Are you confident?" his gracious Hawaiian wife inquired.

"If prayer to an understanding God is efficacious, then I am confident."

The Hales ate in candlelight and sat across from each other so that verbal communication was quick and direct. Malama, in her sixty-fifth year, was stately rather than vivacious. She had not gone to flesh as had so many of her Hawaiian sisters, and her silvery gray hair was complemented by the pale light. She retained her saucy manner of tilting her head quizzically when an idea amused her, and now she said softly, "It will be proper for Hawaii to submerge itself in America. We're a poor, weak group of islands, and anyone who had really wanted us in the last fifty years could have snatched us. It's better this way."

Micah, momentarily relaxed by the good news from Congress, asked, "Do you know, Malama, how sorry I am that it had to be your husband who did the things of the last five years?"

"It had to be somebody," she said to the erect, austere missionary.

"Of all the Hawaiians, you understood most clearly," he said. "But I suppose that's to be expected. Noelani's daughter and Malama's granddaughter." At the mention of these distinguished names he unexpectedly found tears in his eyes, and he wanted to hide his face in his hands, but Malama saw them, and if she had been sitting beside her husband, she would, Hawaiian-fashion, have comforted him, but on this important night they sat apart and only ideas sped between them, not love. Micah said, "It would have been so much better if you had been queen and not Liliuokalani. You would have understood, but she never could."

"No," Malama said slowly, "it was better that we had a headstrong, volatile Hawaiian. Let the world see us dying as we actually were."

"Dying?" Micah repeated in surprise.

"Yes, dying," Malama said with subtle firmness. "Soon our islands will be Oriental and there will be no place for Hawaiians."

His wife's comments were strange, and Micah pointed out: "But in the constitution we were careful to put up safeguards against the Japanese."

"That's only a paper, Micah," she pointed out. "We Hawaiians know that we're being pushed over in the canoe."

"You'll be protected!" Micah cried.

"We had an earlier constitution that was supposed to protect us," Malama said, "but it didn't prevent the sugar robbers from stealing our lands . . . and then our country."

"Malama!" Micah gasped. "Are you contending that only cupidity directed this revolution? Do you refuse to see the forces of American democracy at work here?"

"All I can see is that when our fields were barren no one wanted us, but when they were rich with sugar, everyone wanted us. What else can I conclude?"

Micah was disturbed by the turn this conversation was taking and he went far back into memory: "Do you recall the first time I ever saw you? In San Francisco? And I said then, before I ever saw a sugar field, 'Hawaii must become a part of the United States?' I thought so for moral reasons, and my motivations have never changed."

"Not yours, Micah. But others' changed. And in the end you were pitifully used by a gang of robbers."

"Oh, no, Malama! As it worked out, it was I who used them. Hawaii's going to be annexed, on my terms."

"It was stolen by fraud," Malama said coldly. "We poor, generous Hawaiians were abused, lied about, debased in public and defrauded of our nation."

"No!" Micah protested, rising and walking around the table to be with his wife.

"I would rather you did not touch me now, Micah," she said without bitterness. "What do you think I have felt, when I met with my Hawaiian friends, and they asked me, 'How could Micah Hale write the things he did about us?' "

"What things?" Micah cried, returning disconsolately to his chair. "I never wrote anything about you."

To his surprise, Malama took from her pocket, where in bitterness she had kept it until this moment should arise, a clipping from one of his major articles, and in sorrow she read it: " 'The indigenous citizens are for the most part illiterate, steeped in idolatry, committed to vain shows of monarchical display and totally unsuited to govern themselves.' What abominable words."

"But I wasn't writing about you," he protested. "I was writing to help make these islands a part of America."

"You were writing about Hawaiians," Malama said quietly.

Micah, in his white suit, sat staring at the tablecover brought years ago from China. He was astonished at his wife's position in this matter and he thought of several lines of explanation that might be helpful in describing the choices he had faced, but when he looked up at her grave, accusing face, he realized that none would be of use. Therefore he said, "I am sorry if I have offended you, Malama." And she replied, "I am sorry, Micah, if I have brought up unpleasant subjects on your night of triumph. But we must not fool ourselves by words. Hawaii was stolen. Its liberties were raped." In stately manner this daughter of the alii rose, kicked her train behind her, and left the dining room. Micah, disconsolate, watched her depart, then dropped his head on the table for some minutes, after which he rose and walked to his study, where he composed a long and passionate letter of instructions to his representatives in Washington, telling them: "You must see every senator at least once a day. Tell him that the manifest destiny of America consists of an extension of God's grace to these islands. We cannot delay much longer, for the Japanese and English are beginning to make unpleasant moves and tardiness is suicide. Plead with them. Leave no argument to chance, and if the senators from Louisiana and Colorado fight with dirty weapons, fight back. We have got to make these islands American in this session. To your hands I commit the fate of Hawaii."

During the days that followed, Micah and Malama Hale avoided each other as much as possible. With each elating letter from Washington, for chances in the Senate looked increasingly good, the distance between the American missionary and the Hawaiian alii grew greater, and it was borne home to Micah a thousand times how sorrowful a thing it is to destroy a sovereignty. It was right that Hawaii become American. It was inevitable, and he was increasingly proud of his role in accomplishing this benediction; but it was also tragic, and in these last days the tragedy was greater than the joy.

On July 6, 1898, the American Senate finally accepted Hawaii by a vote of 42 to 21. In thc Senate gallery David Hale, Micah's personal emissary to Congress, wept, and his assistant Micah Whipple said, "This is the beginning of America's greatness in world politics." One week later, on July 13, the news reached Honolulu, and an excited sailor discharged a gun. Nerves were on edge and some thought this might be the beginning of a counter-revolution, but soon the electrifying word swept through the city and men ran out into the streets and embraced one another. It was wild, joyous day, with enough noise to be heard around the globe, but Wild Whip Hoxworth, in the jungles of French Guiana, did not hear the news for almost two months. When he did he said to Ching-ching, "Well, we're Americans at last. You feel any different?"

"You may be an American," Ching-ching replied. "I'm still a Chinese. I don't think your country will ever want me."

On August 12, 1898, by proclamation of President McKinley, Hawaii joined the United States, but in the islands this happy event seemed more like a funeral than a birth. No Hawaiians appeared that day, for they mourned in secret, but a good many Americans in tight coats, brown plug hats and patent-leather shoes roamed the streets wearing gaudy badges that showed Uncle Sam entering into matrimony with a Negro woman—the mainland manufacturers having been unable to visualize a Hawaiian—accompanied by the rubric: "This is our wedding day."

Out of deference to the Hawaiians, the day's ceremonies were kept brief. Soldiers marched and sailors came ashore from an American warship. At eleven forty-five a distinguished group of men responsible for the revolution appeared on the grandstand, led by Micah Hale. As he took his place, he looked out upon the gathering and saw Americans, Chinese, Portuguese and Japanese, but never a Hawaiian. When the once-impressive band began the Hawaiian anthem, the gasps that came from the horns would not have done justice to a group of beginners, for one by one the weeping Hawaiian members of the band had crept away, refusing to play the final dirge of their nation. The anthem ended in a sob and Micah began reading: "With full confidence in the honor, justice and friendship of the American people . . ." He had first dreamed of this day while crossing the Nebraska prairies in 1849. Now, almost half a century later, he had made it come to pass.

On the platform that day there was one Hawaiian, Malama Kanakoa Hale, for Micah had pleaded with her: "It is your duty," and as an alii she had understood these words. Dressed in regal black and purple, with a flowery hat and an ivory fan, she was an imposing figure, the final symbol of her defeated race. Even when the warships boomed their salute of twenty-one guns and when the flag she had loved so well came down, she had the fortitude to stare ahead. "I will not let them see me weep," she muttered to herself.

But when the ceremonies were ended, a most shameful thing occurred, and to Malama it would always epitomize the indecency by which her nation had been destroyed. As the Hawaiian flag fell, an American caught it and, before he could be stopped, whisked it away to the palace cellar where, with a pair of long shears, he cut the emblem into strips and began passing them out as souvenirs of the day.

One was jammed into Micah's hand and he looked down to see what it was, but his eyes were so strained from writing letters on behalf of Hawaii that he could not easily discern what he held, and imprudently he raised it aloft. Then he saw that it contained fragments of the eight stripes symbolizing the islands of Hawaii and a corner of the field, and he realized what a disgraceful thing had been done to this proud flag. Hastily he crumpled it lest his wife see and be further offended, but as he pushed the torn cloth into his pocket he heard from behind a cry of pain, and he turned to see that his wife had at last been forced to cover her face in shame.

AS THE NINETEENTH CENTURY drew to a close, and as Hawaii accustomed itself to being a part of the United States, it gradually became apparent to the residents of Honolulu that in the Kee family Hawaii had another of those great, intricate Chinese units which were destined, by force of numbers alone, to play an important role in the community. There was old Mrs. Kee—known to the family simply as Wu Chow's Auntie—now fifty-two years of age and bent from arduous work. There were her five clever sons, Asia, Europe, Africa, America and Australia, and their five wives, a prolific brood with a total of thirty-eight children and a promise of more to come. Thus, as the century ended, there were already forty-nine Kees in the family, many of them approaching marriageable age. In two more decades the Kees would probably number more than two hundred.

To Nyuk Tsin, who still sold pineapples and taro-stem pickles through the town barefooted, her two baskets hanging down from her bamboo carrying-stick and her conical woven hat darting along the alleys of Chinatown, the multiplication of her offspring was gratifying indeed, and whenever on her daily huckstering trips she reached the point where Hotel Street crossed Maunakea, in the heart of Chinatown, she felt a glow of satisfaction. Years ago she had made a cold calculation that of her five sons—who shared the world among them—it would be Africa who would grow into the ablest. He had been given the education, and now at the age of thirty-one he was a leader in the Chinese community: Africa Kee, Lawyer. The sign in gold letters said so, but what it did not say was that the building in which his office stood was also his and that several of the stores in Chinatown belonged either to him or to his brothers.

Actually, the specific title to these buildings was of little consequence, for although to outward appearances it was Asia Kee who owned the profitable restaurant on Hotel Street, it was really owned by the Kees as a family. Under Nyuk Tsin's guidance, the five brothers had formed a combination known in Hawaii by the expressive term hui, pronounced hooey—"Them Kees got a hui workin' "—and it was this informal corporation, the great Kee hui, that effectively controlled the family income. If Australia's lovely wife, the Ching girl, acquired from her family a small inheritance, it did not go to Australia or to his children. It went into the hui, for no member of the Kee family could begin to identify the benefits he himself had already drawn from the hui. His clothes, his education, the education of his sons, his home, his start in business: all these things had been paid for by the hui; and if he were willing to hand over everything he was to earn for the rest of his life, he still could never discharge his debt to the hui.

No one felt this obligation more than Africa. It was through the energies of his four brothers that he had received his legal education at Michigan. To maintain him in law school they had deprived themselves; yet they never complained, for they agreed with Nyuk Tsin that the ablest of their group must be educated, to help protect the rest. And Africa Kee did just that. At present the Kee hui controlled seven businesses, and Africa guided each along the narrow path between conservative prudence and radical recklessness. He financed every new venture and advised when earlier ones should be liquidated. He selected which real estate to buy, what corner to lease for a store, and which mainland college the Kee grandsons should be sent to. For the present he was the central brain power of a trivial Chinese empire of dirty little shops, grubby efforts to make money and small landholdings. But it was not his intention that the Kee empire should remain small, and whenever he met with his brothers—they in pigtails and Chinese dress; he shorn and in the clothes he had learned to wear at Michigan—he preached one doctrine: "This hui has got to grow." To make it do so, Africa gambled in a manner that would have pleased his father, and the Kees rarely held property for even a week before borrowing heavily on it to buy more property, on which they also borrowed as soon as possible. All the Kee stores bought on credit, but obligations were carefully met as such came due. The hui never had any cash; it always owed debts that would have staggered a haole; and under Africa's calculating guidance it was beginning to prosper.

Nyuk Tsin, pleased with the manner in which he was taking hold of business problems, did not dominate her family, except in three particulars. Every Kee child had to be educated, and during the year 1900 this apparently impecunious Chinese family was preparing to send three grandsons to college in America—doctor, dentist, lawyer—and within the next decade fourteen more Kees would be ready to go. Nyuk Tsin herself went barefooted in order to save money to pay mainland tuitions, and it did not matter to her if her sons' wives were forced to do the same. The sprawling family lived with terrifying frugality in order to pinch off each fugitive penny that might be saved to provide some sparkling grandson with an education.

In this profound resolve Nyuk Tsin was constantly abetted by the wild-eyed Englishman, Uliassutai Karakoram Blake, who enjoyed walking down from the Church of England school to visit with her in Chinese. He said, "I used to curse the Yankee threat to Hawaii, and at one time I wanted to take arms against America, but when annexation took place I shrugged my shoulders and said, 'America's no worse than England. They're both bloody robbers, and if I can stand one I suppose I can stand the other.' "

He encouraged Nyuk Tsin to educate her grandchildren to their maximum capacity. "Have you ever stopped to figure, Wu Chow's Auntie, what it cost you to make Africa a lawyer? And how much you've already got back in return? Well, be assured that in the future the rate of return will be even greater." He was a flamboyant man and his ferocious mustaches flourished in the little Nuuanu room as he spoke of the future: "Science, mathematics, speculation! Who knows where they will lead? But wherever they take us, Wu Chow's Auntie, only the educated man will be able to follow." She always felt better after a talk with Uliassutai Blake; she wished she had gone to school to such a teacher. For his part, the eccentric Englishman found real joy in talking with one of the two people who understood his dynamic interpretation of the world. The other was a thin, hawk-eyed young revolutionary then seeking refuge in Hawaii: Sun Yat Sen. Even better than Nyuk Tsin, he comprehended what his teacher Blake was talking about.

The second particular in which Nyuk Tsin dictated to her family was the matter of houses; she considered it a waste of money to build pretentious homes, especially since reliable people spent their time working outside. Therefore she kept as many of her sons jammed into the bleak clapboard house and its sprawling sheds as possible. Obviously, not all forty-nine Kees could crowd into even that commodious shack, but an astonishing number did. Asia and his family were excused to live in back of the restaurant; Europe and his brood were permitted to live over the vegetable store, but all the others crowded somehow into the Nuuanu residence. There the Hawaiian wives cooked fairly regular meals and the grandchildren learned to talk pidgin and eat poi. By 1899 Africa could well have afforded a home of his own, but even though Nyuk Tsin allowed him to juggle every cent the hui commanded, she did not consider him capable of deciding where he wanted to live, so at thirty-one with a wife and five children, he stayed on at the old house. "It saves money," she said. The bulging house now owned four ukuleles, and fat Apikela, white-haired and benevolent, taught all her grandchildren how to strum the little instrument. It was a noisy house, with a Hawaiian mother and a hard-working, silent Chinese auntie.

The third particular in which Nyuk Tsin dominated her family was in the purchase of land. Her Hakka hunger for this greatest of the world's commodities would never be satiated, and she was haunted by a recurring nightmare: she saw her constantly increasing brood and there was never enough land for each Kee to stand upon and to raise his arms and move about. So whenever the Kee hui had a few dollars left over after paying education bills, she insisted that they acquire more land. To do so in Honolulu was not easy, for generally speaking, land, Hawaii's most precious resource, was not sold; it was leased. Nor was it parceled into acres or lots; it was leased by the square foot. The Hoxworths owned tremendous areas of land, inherited from the Alii Nui Noelani, and so did the Hewletts, inherited through the old missionary's second wife. The Kanakoa family had huge estates; and the Janderses and the Whipples, although they owned little, controlled enormous areas through leases. Whoever owned land grew wealthy, and it was the ironclad law of the great haole families never to sell. Hawaiians were willing to sell, but their land was usually in the country. Therefore, when the bent little Chinese woman Nyuk Tsin decided to get enough Honolulu land for her multiplying family her interests threw her directly athwart the established wealth of the island.

I remarked some time back that if the haoles in Hawaii had wanted to protect themselves from the Chinese they should have shot Uliassutai Karakoram Blake. That chance passed, and the Chinese got their education. In 1900, if the haoles had still wanted to maintain their prerogatives, and apparently they did, they should have shot Nyuk Tsin; but none had ever heard of her. They thought that the guiding force behind the Kee family was the lawyer, Africa, and they kept a close watch on him.

In late 1899 Africa found himself hemmed in, unable to make a move, and he had to report to his auntie: "It's getting almost impossible to buy land. The haoles simply won't sell."

"How much money does the hui have?" Nyuk Tsin asked.

"Four thousand dollars in cash, and we could convert more."

"Have you tried to buy business land toward Queen Street?"

"No luck."

"Leases?"

"No luck."

The Kee empire, almost before it got started, was stalemated, and it might have remained so had it not received dramatic assistance from a rat.

On Thanksgiving day in 1899 the blue-funneled H & H steamer *Maui* put into harbor after an uneventful trip from Bangkok, Singapore, Hong Kong and Yokohama. As its seamen curled their landing lines artfully through the air and then sent heavy hawsers after them, this brown rat that was to salvage the fortunes of the Kee hui scuttled down from ship to shore, carrying a hideful of fleas. It ran through some alleys and wound up in the grimy kitchen of a family named Chang.

On December 12, 1899, as the old century lay dying, an old man named Chang also lay dying with a dreadful fever that seemed to spring from large, purplish nodules in his armpits and groin. When young Dr. Hewlett Whipple from the Department of Health picked his way through the alleys to certify that the man had died of natural causes, he studied the corpse with apprehension.

"Don't bury this man," he ordered, and within ten minutes he had returned, breathless, with two other young doctors, each of whom carried a medical book. In silence the three men studied the corpse and looked at one another in horror.

"Is it what I think it is?" Dr. Whipple asked.

"The plague," his associate replied.

"May God have mercy on us!" Whipple prayed.

The three doctors walked soberly back to their Department of Health, trying to mask from the general public the terror they felt, for they knew that in Calcutta the plague had once killed thousands in a few weeks; there was no known remedy, and when this dreadful disease struck a community, the epidemic had to burn itself out in frightful death and terror. When they reached their Department office, the three doctors closed the doors and sat silent for a moment, as if trying to muster courage for the things they must now do. Then Dr. Whipple, who had inherited his great-grandfather's force of character, said simply, "We must burn that house immediately. We must set aside a special burying ground. And we must inspect every house in Honolulu. It is absolutely essential that not a single sick person be hidden from us. Are you agreed?"

"There will be protests against the burning," one of the other doctors argued.

"We burn, or we face a calamity of such size that I cannot imagine it," Dr. Whipple replied.

"I'd rather we talked with the older doctors."

They did, summoning them in fearful haste, and the older men were sure that their junior colleagues must have been panicked by some ordinary disease with extraordinary developments. "It's unlikely that we have the plague in Honolulu. We've kept it out of here for seventy years."

Another argued: "I think we ought to see the body," and four of the established physicians started to leave for the grimy little shack in Chinatown, but Dr. Whipple protested.

"You'll create consternation among the Chinese," he warned. "I went and hurried away for my associates. Now if you appear, they'll know something is wrong."

"I'm not going to announce that we have the plague in this city until I see for myself," a big, solidly built doctor said, "and I want two experienced men to come along with me."

"Before you go," Whipple asked, seeing that they were leaving without medical books, "what symptoms would convince you that it is truly the plague?"

"I saw the plague in China," the older doctor evaded haughtily.

"But what symptoms?"

"Purplish nodules in the groin. Smaller ones in the armpits. Marked fever accompanied by hallucinations. And a characteristic smell from the punctured nodules."

Dr. Whipple licked his lips, for they were achingly dry, and said, "Dr. Harvey, when you go, take a policeman along to guard the house. We must burn it tonight."

An ominous hush fell upon the room, and Dr. Harvey finally asked, "Then it is the plague?"

"Yes."

There was an apprehensive silence, a moment of hesitation, followed by Dr. Harvey's stubborn insistence: "I cannot authorize the required steps until I see for myself."

"But you will take a policeman?"

"Of course. And you can be talking about what we must do next . . . in the unlikely event that it is indeed the plague." He hurried off, taking two frightened companions with him, and it was a long time before he returned; and during this interval the three younger doctors on whom the burden of a quarantine would fall were afraid that their older confreres would refuse to sanction emergency measures until the plague had established itself, but in this uncharitable supposition they quite underestimated Dr. Harvey.

After an hour he rushed into the Department of Health, ashen-faced and with the news that it was the bubonic plague. He had searched all houses in the immediate vicinity and had uncovered another dead body and three cases near death, so on his own recognizance he had alerted the Fire Department to stand by for immediate action of the gravest importance. "Gentlemen," he puffed, "Honolulu is already in the toils of the bubonic plague. May God give us the strength to fight it."

That night the terror began. The determined doctors summoned government officials and told them coldly: "The only way to combat this scourge is to burn every house where the plague has struck. Burn it, burn it, burn it!"

A timorous official protested: "How can we burn a house without permission of the owner? In Chinatown it'll take us weeks to find out who owns what. And even if we don't make mistakes we'll be subject to lawsuits."

"Good God!" Dr. Harvey shouted, banging the table with his fist. "You speak of lawsuits. How many people do you think may be dead by Christmas? I'll tell you. We'll be lucky if our losses are less than two thousand. Whipple here may be dead, because he touched the body. I may be dead, because I did, too. And you may be dead, because you associated with us. Now burn those goddamned buildings immediately."

The government summoned the Fire Department and asked if they had perfected any way to burn one building and not the one standing beside it. "There's always a risk," the fire fighters replied. "But it's been done."

"Is there wind tonight?"

"Nothing unusual."

"Could you burn four houses? Completely?"

"Yes, sir."

"Don't do anything. Don't say anything." Nothing happened that night.

For three agonizing days the debate continued, with the doctors appalled by the delay. In the unspeakable warrens of Chinatown they uncovered three dozen new cases and eleven deaths. Old men would suddenly complain of fevers and pains in their groin. Their faces would become blanched with pain, then fiery red with burning temperatures. Their desire for water was extraordinary, and they died trembling, a hideous smell enveloping them whenever one of their nodules broke. It was the raging, tempestuous plague, but still the finicky debate continued.

At last Drs. Harvey and Whipple announced the facts to the general public: "Honolulu is in the grip of an epidemic of bubonic plague. The death toll cannot at this time be predicted, and the most severe measures must be taken to combat the menace."

Now general panic swept the city. A cordon was thrown around Chinatown and no one inside the area was allowed to move out. Churches and schools were suspended and no groups assembled. Ships were asked to move to other harbors and life in the city ground to a slow, painful halt. It was a terrible Christmas, that last one of the nineteenth century, and there was no celebration when the new year and the new century dawned.

During Christmas week the fires started. Dr. Whipple and his team showed the firemen where deaths had occurred, and after precautions were taken, those houses were burned. Chinatown was divided roughly into the business area toward the ocean and the crowded living areas toward the mountains, and although the plague had started in the former area, it now seemed concentrated in the closely packed homes. Therefore the doctors recommended that an entire section be eliminated, and the government agreed, for by burning this swath across the city, a barrier would be cut between the two areas. The condemned area happened to include Dr. John Whipple's original mansion, now crowded by slums, and his great-grandson felt tears coming to his eyes when he saw the old family home go up in flames that he himself had set. It was a ghastly business to burn down a city that one had worked so hard to build, but the fires continued, and patrols kept back the Chinese who sought to escape the doomed areas and circulate generally throughout the city. Refugee camps were established in church grounds, with tents for those whose houses had been burned and sheds for cooking food. Mrs. Henry Hewlett supervised one camp, Mrs. Rudolph Hale another, and Mrs. John Janders a third on the slopes of Punchbowl, the volcanic crater that rose on the edge of the city. Blankets were supplied by teams that searched the city, Mrs. Malama Hoxworth having taken charge of that effort. David Hale, Jr., and his uncle Tom Whipple set up the field kitchens and ran them, riding from one camp to the other on horseback.

Inspection teams were organized and every room in Honolulu was visually checked twice each day, to be sure that no new cases of the plague went unreported, and consonant with the missionary tradition from which they had sprung, it was the Hales and the Hewletts and the Whipples who volunteered for the particularly dangerous work of crawling through the Chinatown warrens to be sure no dead bodies lay hiding. It was a dreadful sight they saw, a fearful condemnation of their rule in Hawaii.

The streets of Chinatown were unpaved, filthy alleys that wound haphazardly past open cesspools. The houses were collapsing shacks that had been propped up by poles in hopes of squeezing out one more year's rent. Inside, the homes were an abomination of windowless rooms, waterless kitchens, toiletless blocks. Stairwells had no illumination and what cellars there were stood crowded with inflammable junk. No air circulated that was not filthy. After only two generations of use, Chinatown was overcrowded to the point of suffocation, all made worse by the fact that those whose homes had already been burned had managed, by one trick or another, to slip through quarantine cordons so as to remain with their friends rather than suffer banishment to the refugee camps, and with them they brought the plague. If one had searched the world, seeking an area where a rat bearing the fleas which bred bubonic plague could most easily infect the greatest number of unprotected people, Honolulu's Chinatown would have stood high on the list. The police had known of the pitiful overcrowding; the Department of Health had known of the unsanitary conditions; and the landlords had known best of all the menace they were perpetuating; but nobody had spoken in protest because the area was owned principally by those who were now inspecting it: the Hales, the Hewletts and the Whipples; and they had found that Chinese did pay their rents promptly. Now from this open sore the plague threatened to engulf the island, and as the inspectors bravely toured the infected areas day after day, exposing themselves to death and sleeping at nights in restricted tents lest they contaminate their own families, they often thought: "Why didn't we do something about this sooner?"

By January 15, 1900, eight substantial areas had been completely razed and innumerable rats that might have carried their infected fleas to uncontaminated sections of the city were destroyed; and it seemed as if a general eruption of the plague had been mercifully prevented. Three thousand Chinese were already in refugee camps from which they could not spread contagion, but unknown thousands were hiding out in the narrow warrens to which they had fled and they now began to accomplish what the rats could not. As the reports came into headquarters that night, each with tales of fresh death and new infection, it became hideously apparent to Dr. Whipple that the epidemic was not halted and that the fate of Honolulu hung in a precarious balance.

On the sixteenth he convened his doctors again, a group of exhausted men who understood how fearful the next week could be, for by their own inspection they had proved that the plague stood poised in upper Chinatown, ready to explode across the entire city, and they knew that on this day they must either take final steps to drive it back or surrender the general community to its ravages; and the only cure they knew was fire. Dr. Whipple was first to speak: "Our teams found twenty-nine new cases yesterday."

"Oh, hell!" Dr. Harvey cried in acute frustration. He folded his arms on the table and bowed his head upon them, retiring from this part of the discussion.

"All the cases this week, and most of the deaths, have been concentrated toward the mountains," Whipple explained, pointing to a map, "and we can thank God that they seem to be leading out of the city rather than in toward the heart."

"That's the only good news we've had," snapped an older doctor who had found seven cases in the mountain area.

Dr. Whipple hesitated, then said, "Our obligation is clear."

"You mean to burn that entire outlying area?"

"I do."

"Jesus, they'll explode. They just won't permit it, Whipple."

Dr. Whipple pressed his hands to his forehead and pleaded: "Have you an alternative?"

"Look, I'm not arguing one way or another," the older man explained. "I'm just saying . . . Hell, Whipple, there must be five hundred homes in that area!"

"And every one infected with the bubonic plague."

"I want no part of this decision!" the older doctor protested.

"Nor me!" another cried. "Christ, Whipple, that's half the city!"

From his position with his head on his arms, Dr. Harvey asked harshly, "If your arm is infected with blood poisoning that is certain to destroy your entire body, what do you do?"

There was no answer, so after a moment he slammed his fist onto the table and shouted, "Well, what in hell do you do? You cut it off! Burn those areas. Now!"

"Only the government can make this decision," Whipple said in slow, terrified tones. "But it's got to make it."

"We are withdrawing from this meeting," two of the doctors warned. "Let it be recorded."

Dr. Harvey shouted, "And let it be recorded that I did not withdraw. Burn the goddamned city or perish."

On the eighteenth of January, 1900, the emergency committee decided to burn a very substantial area of Honolulu in a last prayerful attempt to save the general population, and when the doomed areas were marked in red two facts became apparent: they were not in the center of town but in the residential district; and almost everyone who lived in the area was Chinese. Two members of the cabinet, as they faced the map, were in tears, and a man named Hewlett, who had a good deal of Hawaiian blood, asked, "Why does misery always fall on those least able to bear it?"

"You burn where the plague has fallen," a cabinet member named Hale replied. "And it's fallen on the Chinese."

"Stop this talk!" the chairman cried. "There's already an ugly rumor that we're burning Chinatown as punishment because the Pakes left the sugar fields. I don't want to hear any of that libel in this room. We're burning Chinatown because that's where the plague is."

Hewlett, part-Hawaiian, felt that he was being unduly hectored, so he asked, "Would you burn here," and he banged the haole areas of the map, "if that's where the plague was? Would you burn your own houses?"

"The plague didn't come to our houses," the chairman replied. "It came to the Chinese."

On the nineteenth of January the Fire Department gave all its men the day off and advised them to sleep as much as possible in preparation for a hard day's work on the twentieth. The Honolulu *Mail* in its edition that day reported: "We beg all citizens of our city to be especially alert tomorrow and to watch for flying sparks, because although the able laddies of our Fire Department have proved over and over again that they know how to set fire to one house and save the next, the very magnitude of the job they now face increases the ever-present danger of a general conflagration. Brooms and buckets of water should be at hand throughout the city."

When word of the proposed burning reached Chinatown, it created panic and many tried vainly to force their way through the cordons that kept everyone within the plague area. Those whose homes were to be razed were rounded up and solemnly marched away to a refugee camp on the slopes of Punchbowl, where they could look down at their doomed homes, and this last view of buildings which they had worked so hard to acquire inspired them with a dumb rage, and that night there were many unpleasant scenes. One Chinese who knew a little English rushed up to Mrs. John Janders, the supervisor of the Punchbowl camp, and screamed, "You doing this on purpose!"

"No," she said quietly, "it is the plague."

"No plague!" the furious Chinese cried. "Your husband own my store. He say all time, 'More rent! More rent!' I not pay so he decide to burn."

"No," Mrs. Janders argued reasonably. "Mr. Apaka, it is the plague. Believe me, it would not otherwise be done." But the Chinese knew better, and through the long night of January 19 they watched the mysterious lights of the city and waited in bitterness for the fires to begin.

Fortunately, the twentieth was a calm day with no wind that might have agitated the planned blaze. At eight in the morning the firemen, according to a schedule worked out to provide maximum protection for the rest of the city, poured liberal amounts of kerosene over a small shack diagonally across from where the Whipple mansion, burned earlier, had stood. The shack certainly merited destruction, for it had already caused the deaths of five plague victims and the illness of three others. At eight-ten a match was applied to the kerosene, and the filthy hovel exploded in flame.

As it blazed, a slight breeze started blowing from the northeast. It crept down from the mountains and as it funneled into the valleys that led into Honolulu it increased in speed, so that by the time it reached the flaming shack it was prepared to blow the sparks in exactly the opposite direction from that intended by the Fire Department. Within three minutes half a dozen shacks not on the list were ablaze, but they were easily evacuated and were of little value, so the fire fighters simply surrounded them and beat out any sparks that might escape toward the center of the city where property was of real value.

Then at eight-thirty the capricious wind blowing down from the hills arrived in an unpredicted gust and whipped a flurry of sparks high into the air. Fortunately, the land across from the fire had already been razed, so there was no danger of spreading the flames in that direction, but the wind seemed sent from hell, for it suddenly veered and deposited many active sparks on the large Congregational church that had been completed in 1884 directly across from where the old Whipple mansion had stood. The church had two soaring steeples, for the king had reasoned: "A man has two eyes so he can see better and two ears so he can hear better. My church has got to have two steeples so it can find God better." Now the steeples were in peril, and firemen noted that if any of the embers flamed to life on those tall spires, the rising wind would surely whip sparks clear across the areas previously burned and throw them down into the valuable center of the city, so two brave Hawaiians scrambled up the sides of the church seeking to reach the steeples, and one man arrived in time to stamp out the fires beginning on his, but the other did not, and when he pulled himself onto the upper ledge of his steeple, he found it already ablaze and he barely escaped.

In a few minutes the great tall church became a torch. Its bell plunged to the basement, clanging through the flames. The famous pipe organ, imported from London, melted into lumps of useless metal, and stained-glass windows crashed into the fire. As the church burned furiously in the morning wind, many who had helped build it with their dimes and personal labor gathered to weep. But what was most important was not the loss of the church, but the fact that its unusual height made it a target for every gust that blew down the valley, and even as the people gathered at its foot to mourn, far over their heads the wind was scattering a multitude of sparks. Had the fire occurred at night, the sight would have been one of fairylike splendor, with stars of fire darting across the dark sky; but in an ominous daylight the passage of the flames occasioned no beauty and only dread. For they sped high in the air across the already burned-out areas, a few falling harmlessly on charred land but most flying on into the very heart of the city, where they descended upon dried-wood roofs, there to ignite the fires that were to destroy almost all of Chinatown. With Old Testament accuracy the embers which flew out from the Christian church fell only upon heathen homes. If the Christians of Honolulu had righteously planned to destroy every Chinese building in the city, they could have accomplished the fact no more skillfully than did the sparks erupting from their doomed church.

The first blaze in downtown Chinatown occurred at nine-forty, when a sizable ember fell upon a closely packed area of houses and ignited a central one. Gangs of firemen quickly surrounded the house to extinguish the fire, and after considerable effort succeeded in doing so; but while they were at that job, another ember struck a house of somewhat special nature. On the outside it looked like an ordinary home, but when it started to burn, all the Chinese nearby fled, and Hawaiian firemen alone were left to fight its flames.

"Come back!" an old Chinese man kept wailing in a language the firemen could not understand. Grabbing a young Chinese he shouted, "Tell them to come back!"

A group of daring Chinese hurried forward toward the burning house, grabbed the firemen by the hands and pulled them away. "Mo bettah you come back!" they yelled.

The firemen, who were terribly afraid of the Chinese after the troubles of the night before and who had been cautioned that the Orientals might attempt a riot when the burnings started, interpreted this strange behavior as the start of communal rioting, and stopped fighting the fire in order to protect themselves from the Chinese, and it was fortunate that they did so, for as they left, the house exploded. In a golden, smoky gasp of flame, the little house simply disintegrated, and then the firemen understood: it was one of the closed sheds in which some trivial Chinese merchant had kept his kerosene. But what the firemen did not understand was that the explosion, frightful though it had been, was merely the beginning of something worse; for now from the ruins a series of fantastic fiery rockets exploded through the city. Some threw stars into the air. Others pinwheeled through streets, and still others went up with a crazy, violent zigzag through the morning sky, falling at last on the roof of some new house, there to burn with vigor until its shingles too were ablaze; for the shed had harbored not only kerosene but also a store of fireworks for the Chinese New Year.

With the explosion of the shed, any hope of saving downtown Chinatown was lost, and for the next seven hours the anguished Chinese on the Punchbowl hillside, huddling behind the barbed wire of their refugee camp, could spot the progress of the huge blaze from one of these kerosene dumps to the next. All day the little sheds exploded with violence, throwing their flames into new areas, and wherever the fire went, sooner or later it found out a horde of fireworks, and when they soared into the air with their burdens of flame they seemed invariably to fall back onto areas that were not yet ablaze. And to make the destruction of Chinatown certain, the vagrant wind kept blowing from its unusual quarter in the hills. By midafternoon, it was apparent that hardly a Chinese house in mid-city would be spared.

When it became obvious that all was doomed, the Chinese fell into panic. Old men who could barely walk after forty-five years of work in the cane fields began running into burning houses to salvage some item of family life which they prized above any other, and they soon appeared in the crowded streets hauling carts, or running with bamboo carrying-poles, each with some useless treasure. No one thought to bring blankets or food, both needed in the refugee camps, and soon the streets leading out from Chinatown were jammed with a miscellaneous horde: barefoot old women in blue smocks, men in laboring shirts, pretty young girls, their hair in braids, and round-faced babies. From a Japanese tea house two geisha girls, their faces ashen with talcum powder, hurried nervously in pin-toed, mincing steps that kept their brightly colored kimonos swaying in the smoke, while old Punti women hobbled behind on stubby feet. The pigtailed men tried to lug burdens which would have staggered horses and which soon staggered them. The escape routes became a litter of lost wealth and it was pitiful to see families who had never owned much, stooping as they ran, picking up valuables they had always coveted, only to abandon them later in the same breathless way as their owners had had to do.

Now the major tragedy of the day approached, for as the fleeing Chinese, with flame and firecracker at their back, sought to break out from Chinatown they ran into solid rows of impassive policemen whose merciless job it was to hold them back within the plague-ridden area. There was no intention whatever—absolutely none, the police commissioner later swore—to trap the Chinese within the fiery area, but there was an ironclad insistence that they move out by established routes that would take them not into the uninfected parts of Honolulu but into the barbed-wire refugee camps, where doctors could watch them for new outbreaks of the plague.

"They won't let us out!" a poor, dimwitted Chinese woman began screaming. "They want us to burn, in the houses they set afire."

She made a futile attempt to dash past a policeman, but his orders required him to push her back toward the burning area, from which there was an orderly escape route, could she but find it.

"He's pushing me into the fire!" the woman screamed, and men who had been free from panic suddenly realized that they were not going to be allowed out of the doomed area, and they began a concentrated rush toward the policemen.

"They're breaking out!" the officers called, and behind them, from the parts of the city where there was no plague, white volunteers rushed up bearing clubs and crowbars and guns.

"Get back!" they shouted. "There's a safe way out!"

At this point, when a deadly general riot seemed inevitable, the United States army marched onto the scene with several hundred trained soldiers, guns at the ready, and they were moved into position along all the main exit routes from Chinatown. "Under no circumstances are you to fire unless I give the order," their captains said, and they marched stolidly on until they stood shoulder to shoulder with the police.

To the distraught Chinese, bombarded by their own fireworks, the arrival of the soldiers was intolerable. To them it meant that any who tried to escape the burning area were to be shot, and because language between the groups was such a difficult barrier, no one could explain that the soldiers were there merely to halt the spread of infection. There was a way out of Chinatown, and it led to safety, but tempers were growing so violent that it seemed unlikely that this way would ever be found.

"They're coming at us again!" a corporal cried, as sixteen Chinese prepared for a mass dash through the lines.

"Don't fire!" the captain of that sector shouted. "Don't you dare fire."

"What am I supposed to . . ." There was a wild crush. Policemen beat at the pigtailed bodies while soldiers jammed at their bellies with the butts of their guns. The defense line sagged for a moment until volunteer reserves rushed up with boards torn hastily from picket fences. Lustily they clubbed the panicky Chinese over the head, driving them back toward the fire.

"We can't hold next time!" the corporal warned, and as if to accent the peril of the moment, a large store of fireworks exploded, adding to the frenzy of all.

"Don't you fire!" the captain warned each of his men.

"By God, if I go down beneath a bunch of damned Chinks I'm gonna fire!" the corporal shouted, disregarding the cautions of his superior, and it was then apparent that on the next charge from the Chinese a general massacre must surely begin.

At this moment, when the frightened captains were licking their lips and preparing to give the only sensible order they could: "Fire to repel rioters," Dr. Hewlett Whipple rushed up and shouted, "Let me through! And for Christ's sake, don't fire!"

He forced his way through the police lines and ran into the middle of the central group of terrified Chinese. Putting his arms about the shoulders of the ringleaders he pleaded: "Don't try to break out of here! Don't run toward the lines again. Please, please!"

"You want us die?" a laundryman screamed at him.

"We won't die," Whipple said as calmly as he could, and something in the unexpected manner in which he said "we" disarmed the Chinese and they listened. "We're going to run up Nuuanu," he explained. "We can all get out there." And pushing the principal rioters before him, he started running up Nuuanu, and the plague-ridden Chinese ran behind him, and in time the riot abated and the trembling young soldiers, wiping their ashen foreheads, returned their guns to safety and marched away.

Of the Chinese families that were stricken on that awful day of January 20, 1900, when Chinatown was burned—by the will of God, the haoles said; by plan, the Chinese claimed—none was struck so hard as the Kees. When the first kerosene depot exploded, its flames burned down Africa Kee's office and destroyed his records. A whole barrage of firecrackers ripped through Asia Kee's restaurant and the resulting fires leveled it. Europe's Punti store was completely lost and so was America's dry-goods emporium. Every business building owned by the Kees was burned, including the homes of two of the brothers. Their families escaped with what they wore and little else. Only the cluttered house up Nuuanu was saved, but even its occupants—except Nyuk Tsin, who was working in the forest fields—had been herded into the concentration camps.

When Nyuk Tsin came barefooted out of the hills, with her two swaying baskets filled with pineapples, and found that much of Honolulu had been destroyed, including all the possessions of the Kee hui, and when she found that her family was dispersed—many of them dead, she supposed—she experienced a sullen terror, but she fought against it and said, as she stared at her empty home, "I must find my sons."

Fortunately, by force of habit she kept with her the swaying baskets of pineapples, so that when she had climbed the steep sides of Punchbowl and had come to the refugee camp the guards were pleased to see her and shouted, "Thank God, at last a Pake with food!" They let her pass, and after an hour of milling through the crowd she succeeded in collecting four of her five sons. No one had seen Asia leave his restaurant after the firecrackers had ripped it apart and it was reported that he was dead.

On the hillside overlooking Pearl Harbor, where the night lights of distant ships could be seen coming on, Nyuk Tsin convened her dazed family. They sat on rocks and looked down upon the desolate ruins of Chinatown, and in the silence of their crushing defeat Nyuk Tsin's Hakka instinct warned her that now was the time for her clan to pull courage out of its spasmed belly. As a woman she knew that on such nights of despair men were apt to surrender to the fate that had overtaken them, but it was a woman's job to prevent them from doing so. In the fading twilight she could see in the sensitive, shocked faces of Europe and America a willingness to declare the Kee empire ended. Blunt-faced Africa showed some of the fighting spirit to be expected in an educated man, but not much, while young Australia was burning with outrage because a soldier had struck him in the gut with a rifle. It was not much of a family that Nyuk Tsin had that night, nor was she herself in condition to inspirit her sons, for inwardly she was grieving for Asia, lost in the fire.

But she said quietly, so that no one else could hear, "It is unthinkable that the government will ignore what has happened."

"They destroyed all of Chinatown," America said with anguish in his voice. "They burned our stores on purpose because we wouldn't work on their sugar plantations."

"No," Nyuk Tsin reasoned, "the wind came by accident."

"That isn't so, Wu Chow's Auntie!" Europe cried, ugly with despair. "The merchants wanted this done. Last week they threw all the food I had ordered from China into the bay. They were determined to wipe us out."

"No, Europe," Nyuk Tsin calmly argued, "they were afraid your shipments might bring more of the plague."

"But they didn't throw the haole shipments overboard!" Europe shouted, with tears in his voice. "They came from China, too."

"They're afraid," Nyuk Tsin explained. "Men do strange things when they're afraid."

"I never want to see Honolulu again," America groaned. "They burned our stores on purpose."

"No," Nyuk Tsin patiently reasoned, "they were afraid that . . ."

"Wu Chow's Auntie!" America cried. "Don't be a fool!"

There was a harsh slap in the night and Nyuk Tsin said, "Behave yourself." Then she drew her sons closer about her and began again: "It is inconceivable that we will be left without compensation. Surely, surely we must believe that the government will pay us for what has happened."

For the first time Africa spoke. Cautiously and with the slow accent of a lawyer he asked, "Why do you think so?"

"I knew Dr. Whipple," Nyuk Tsin replied. "The old one. And men like him, Africa, simply do not allow injustice to stand."

"It was men like him who burned our stores on purpose," America whined. There was another harsh slap and Nyuk Tsin cried furiously, "No more words about the past! There was fire. We have lost everything. Now we are going to gain everything."

Africa's studious voice asked, "Wu Chow's Auntie, do you think that men like old Dr. Whipple will be listened to in the days to come?"

"Perhaps they won't be," Nyuk Tsin admitted, "but there is something new in Hawaii. The United States cannot afford to see us treated badly. Out of pride . . . or to show the world that they look after their people . . ." Her voice trailed off and she reflected for a moment. Then she said vigorously, "Sons, I am absolutely convinced that either our own government or the United States will pay us back for this fire. Let's not argue about it another minute."

"What you are thinking of," Africa said slowly, thinking aloud, "is that we must protect ourselves and see to it that we get our share of whatever money is distributed to those who have lost, regardless of where the money comes from."

Nyuk Tsin thought: "No matter how much we paid for his education, it was worth it." And she was also pleased at the way in which Africa's sensible statement of the problem awakened in her sons their old hui spirit; the Kee hui was again in operation. "I think," she said, "that Africa must devote his whole time to organizing a committee right away for just payment to all of us who have lost in the fire. Make the world realize that there is no question of whether claims will be paid. It is only a question of how much. Africa, you must appear on every platform. Whenever there is a meeting, you must speak. You must become the voice of all the Chinese. You will represent everybody and you will let it be known that you refuse to accept any fees. Work, work, work. Give statements to the paper and let them print your picture. But always speak as if you were positive that the money will be paid. Soon you will have others saying it, and in time they too will believe it." She paused, then added, "The money is absolutely going to come."

Europe broke in to ask, "How much can we claim for?"

"How many buildings did we have?" America asked.

The hui waited while Africa counted up in his mind. "We would have a very substantial claim," he said finally. "The restaurant, the stores, the houses, my office. The Kee claim could be one of the biggest."

"Oh, no!" Nyuk Tsin interrupted. "Because if that were the case, you could never stand forth as the leader of the claims committee. We will put in some of our claims as Wu Chow's Auntie. And wherever possible we will claim in the names of your Hawaiian wives. The Kee claim itself must not be large. Africa, it's your job to see that it isn't. Use the Chings, anybody, if you have to."

At this point Australia made one of the most pregnant observations of the night: "I don't think I ever want to see Chinatown again. After what they did to it today."

Coldly, yet with compassion for those with less courage than herself, Nyuk Tsin remarked, "There will be many in the next weeks who feel as you do, Australia. Today will be a memory too terrible to accept. They will decide to surrender their land in Chinatown. And if they do, we will buy it."

There was a long silence as the brothers looked down at the scarred city, visible now and then through the low clouds of smoke that hung in the valleys. On the ocean beyond, the long surf came rolling in, impartially as it had for millions of years, and the Kee boys somehow understood what their mother was urging them to do. From despair hope rises; from defeat victory. There are only three bad years, followed by six wonderfully rich ones. The city is burned, but it must be rebuilt. The family is nearly destroyed, but if there is one man left alive, or one woman, it must go on. Night falls with the smell of destruction, but day rises with the smell of wet mortar . . . and building resumes.

Nyuk Tsin added: "We must never try to convince any man that he wants to leave Chinatown. We must be careful to drive no unfair bargains. And although we can't pay much now, we can promise to pay a great deal in the future. Our credit is good. They know a Kee will pay."

Nyuk Tsin added: "If two pieces of land are for sale, try to buy the one nearest the ones we already own, because stores in the future will be bigger, and we can put our parcels of land together and make each one more valuable than it was before."

Nyuk Tsin added: "Africa, in the last stages of the committee you must insist that you cannot serve on the board that will actually distribute the money. Because if you are on that board, you could not rightfully give substantial amounts to the Kees, but if you are not on it, everyone who is will say, 'If it hadn't been for Africa, we wouldn't be here today.' And they will be generous on our behalf."

Nyuk Tsin added: "As I came through the burned areas I saw that the only thing that was left standing anywhere was the iron safes. The haoles will think them no longer of use. Australia, it will be a good job for you to buy them all. Then figure out some way to make them work again." When her youngest son protested: "Wu Chow's Auntie, I've never worked on safes," she replied sharply, "Learn."

Toward daybreak Nyuk Tsin added: "If we succeed, people will hate us for owning so much land and they will say we stole it from people after the fire. Ignore them. A city belongs to those who are willing to fight for it."

Finally, Nyuk Tsin added: "I have a little money saved and many vegetables. All of our women and girls must work as servants with haole families, for that will feed the women and also give us money. Europe and America must start to visit every haole store tomorrow, begging for supplies on easy credit so that they can open new stores. Do it tomorrow, while the haoles are sorry for what happened today, for they will give you terms tomorrow that you will not be able to get next week." She smiled at her four sons and said, "We must work."

But at dawn Uliassutai Karakoram Blake puffed up the hillside with a list of names of men who were safe at another camp on the other side of Nuuanu River, and when he read in loud Chinese syllables: "Asia Kee, who runs the restaurant," then Nyuk Tsin dropped her head in her hands.

V

From the Inland Sea

IN THE YEAR 1902, when the reconstruction of Honolulu's Chinatown was completed, one of the isolated farm villages of Hiroshima-ken, at the southern end of Japan's main island, stubbornly maintained an ancient courtship custom which everyone knew to be ridiculous but which, perhaps for that very reason, produced good results.

When some lusty youth spotted a marriageable girl he did not speak directly to her, nor did he invite any of his friends to do so. Instead, he artfully contrived to present himself before this girl a dozen times a week. She might be coming home from the Shinto shrine under the cryptomeria trees, and suddenly he would appear, silent, moody, tense, like a man who has just seen a ghost. Or, when she returned from the store with a fish, she would unexpectedly see this agitated yet controlled young man staring at her.

His part of this strange game required that he never speak, that he share his secret with nobody. Her rules were that not once, by even so much as a flicker of an eye, must she indicate that she knew what he was doing. He loomed silently before her, and she passed uncomprehendingly on. Yet obviously, if she was a prudent girl, she had to find some way to encourage his courtship so that ultimately he might send his parents to the matchmakers, who would launch formal conversations with her parents; for a girl in this village could never tell which of the gloomy, intense young men might develop into a serious suitor; so in some mysterious manner wholly understood by nobody she indicated, without seeing him or without ever having spoken to him, that she was ready.

Apart from certain species of the bird kingdom, where courtship was conducted with much the same ritual, this sexual parading was one of the strangest on earth, but in this village of Hiroshima-ken it worked, because it involved one additional step of which I have not yet spoken, and it was this next step that young Sakagawa Kamejiro found himself engaged in.

In 1902 he was twenty years old, a rugged, barrel-chested, bowlegged little bulldog of a man with dark, unblemished skin and jet-black hair. He had powerful arms which hung out from his body, as if their musculature was too great to be compressed, and he gave the appearance of a five-foot, one-inch accumulation of raw power, bursting with vital drives yet confused because he knew no specific target upon which to discharge them. In other words, Kamejiro was in love.

He had fallen in love on the very day that the Sakagawa family council had decided that he should be the one to go on the ship to Hawaii, where jobs in the sugar fields were plentiful. It was not the prospect of leaving home that had aroused his inchoate passions, for he knew that his parents, responsible for eight children and one old woman, could not find enough rice to feed the family. He had observed how infrequently fish got to the Sakagawa table—and meat not at all—so he was prepared to leave.

It happened late one afternoon when he stood in the tiny Sakagawa paddy field and looked out at the shimmering islands of the Inland Sea, and he understood in that brilliant moment, with the westering sun playing upon the most beautiful of all waters, that he might be leaving Hiroshima-ken forever. "I said I would go for only five years," he muttered stubbornly to himself, "but things can happen. I might never see these islands again. Maybe I won't plough this field . . . ever again." And a consuming sorrow possessed him, for of all the lands he could imagine, there could be no other on the face of the earth more exciting than these fields along the coastline of Hiroshima-ken.

Kamejiro was by no charitable interpretation of the word a poet. He was not even literate, nor had he ever looked at picture books. He had never talked much at home, and among the boys of the village he was known to be a stolid fighter rather than a talker. He had always ignored girls and, although he followed his father's advice on most things, had stubbornly refused to think of marriage. But now, as he stood in the faltering twilight and saw the land of his ancestors for the first time—in history and in passion and in love, as men occasionally perceive the land upon which they have been bred—he wanted brutishly to reach out his hand and halt the descending sun. He wanted to continue his spiritual embrace of the niggardly little field of which he was so much a part. "I may never come back!" he thought. "Look at the sun burning its way into the sea. You would think . . ." He did not put his thoughts into words, but stood in the paddy field, mud about ankles, entertaining tremendous surges of longing. How magnificent his land was!

It was in this mood that he started homeward, for in the Japanese custom all rice fields were gathered together while the houses to which they pertained clustered in small villages. Thus arable land was not wasted on housing, but the system did require farmers to walk substantial distances from their fields to their homes, and on this night little bulldog Sakagawa Kamejiro, his arms hanging out with their powerful muscles, walked home. Had he met some man who had earlier insulted him, as often happened in village life, he would surely have thrashed him then and there, for he thought that he wanted to fight; but as he walked he happened to see, at the edge of the village, the girl Yoko, and although he had seen her often before, it was not until then—when she walked with a slight wind at her dress and with a white workingwoman's towel about her head—that he realized how much like the spirit of the land she was, and he experienced an almost uncontrollable desire to pull her off the footpath and into the rice field and have it over with on the spot.

Instead, he stood dumb as she approached. His eyes followed her and his big arms quivered, and as she passed she knew that this Kamejiro who was earmarked for Hawaii would watch her constantly throughout the following days, and she began to look for him at strange locations, and he would be there, stolid, staring, his arms hanging awkwardly down. Without ever acknowledging by a single motion of her own that she had even seen him, she conveyed the timeless message of the village: "It would not be unreasonable if you were to do so."

Therefore, on a soft spring night when the rice fields were beginning to turn delicate green, the sweet promise of food to come, Sakagawa Kamejiro secretly dressed in the traditional garb of the Hiroshima-ken night lover. He wore his best pair of trousers, his clean straw zori and a shirt that did not smell. The most conspicuous part of his costume, however, was a white cloth mask which wound about his head and covered his nose and mouth. Thus properly attired, he slipped out of the Sakagawa home, down a back path to Yoko's and waited several hours as her family closed up the day's business, blew out the lights and threw no more shadows on the shoji. When he was satisfied that Yoko had retired, with a reasonable chance that her parents might be sleeping, he crept toward the room which from long study he had spotted as hers, and in some mysterious way known only in the villages, she had anticipated that this was the night he would visit her, so the shoji had been left unlocked, and in a moment he slipped bemasked into the room.

Yoko saw him in the faint moonlight, but said nothing. Without removing his mask, for that was essential to the custom, he crept to her bed and placed his left hand upon her cheek. Then he took her right hand in his and held her fingers in a certain way, which from the beginning of Japan had meant, "I want to sleep with you," and of her own accord she changed the position of his fingers, which timelessly had signified, "You may."

With never a word spoken, with never a mask removed, Kamejiro silently slipped into bed with the intoxicating girl. She would not allow him to remove her clothing, for she knew that later she might have to do many things in a hurry, but that did not inconvenience Kamejiro, and in a few stolid, fumbling moments he made her ready to accept him. Not even at the height of their passion did Yoko utter a word, and when they collapsed mutually in blazing gratification and he fell asleep like an animal, she did not touch the mask, for it was there to protect her. At any moment in the love-making she could have pushed him away, and he would have had to go. The next day they could have met on the village street—as they would tomorrow—and neither would have been embarrassed, for so long as the mask was in place, Yoko did not know who was in her room. So long as the mask protected him, Kamejiro could not suffer personal humiliation or loss of face, for no matter what Yoko said or did, it could not embarrass him, for officially he was not there. It was a silly system, this Hiroshima courtship routine, but it worked.

When Kamejiro wakened, there was a moment when he could not recall where he was, and then he felt Yoko's body near his and this time they began to caress each other as proper lovers do, and the long night passed, but on the third sweet love-making, when the joy of possession completely captured them, they grew bolder and unwittingly made a good deal of noise, so that Yoko's father was awakened, and he shouted, "Who's in the house?"

And instantly Yoko was required to scream, "Oh, how horrible! A man is trying to get into my room!" And she continued to wail pitifully as lights flashed on throughout the village.

"Some beast is trying to rape Yoko-san!" an old woman screamed.

"We must kill him!" Yoko's father shouted, pulling on his pants.

"The family is forever disgraced!" Yoko's mother moaned, but since each of these phrases had been shouted into the night in precisely these intonations for many centuries, everyone knew exactly how to interpret them. But it was essential for the preservation of family dignity that the entire village combine to seek out the rapist, and now, led by Yoko's outraged father, the night procession formed.

"I saw a man running down this way!" the old woman bellowed.

"The ugly fiend!" another shouted. "Trying to rape a young girl!"

The villagers coursed this way and that, seeking the rapist, but prudently they avoided doing two things: they never took a census of the young men of the village, for by deduction that would have shown who was missing and would have indicated the rapist; nor did they look into the little barn where rice hay was kept, for they knew that the night fiend was certain to be hiding there, and it would be rather embarrassing if he were discovered, for then everyone would have to go through the motions of pretending to beat him.

In the hay barn, with chickens cackling, Kamejiro put on his pants, knocked the mud off his zori, and tucked away his white mask. When this was done, he had time to think: "She is sweeter than a breeze off the sea." But when he saw her later that day, coming from the fish stall, he looked past her and she ignored him, and this was a good thing, for as yet it was not agreed that Yoko would marry him, and if she elected not to do so, it was better if neither of them officially knew who had attempted to rape her. In fact, during that entire day and for some days thereafter Yoko was the acknowledged heroine of the village, for as one old woman pointed out: "I cannot remember a girl who screamed more loudly than Yoko-san while she was defending herself against that awful man . . . whoever he was." Yoko's father also came in for considerable praise in that he had dashed through every alley in the village, shouting at the top of his voice, "I'll kill him!" And farmers said approvingly to their wives, "It was lucky for whoever tried to get into that house that Yoko's father didn't catch him."

So the last days before the ship's departure were spent in this make-believe manner. Kamejiro, the object of much admiration because of his willingness to go to Hawaii, worked hard in the family rice field, not because his labor was required, but because he loved the feel of growing rice. Neighbors, whose ancestors had farmed nearby fields for thousands of years, came by to say farewell, and to each he said, "I'll be back." And the more he said these words the more he believed that only death would prevent him from returning to the tiny, mountain-shaded, sea-swept fields of Hiroshima-ken.

Three or four nights a week he donned his magic mask and climbed more or less surreptitiously into bed with Yoko, and they found each other so completely enjoyable, and so mysterious in the unknowing night, that without ever facing up to the problem, they drifted into a mute understanding that one day they would marry. Kamejiro, finding endless delight in the girl's soft body, prayed that she might become pregnant, so that he would be forced to marry her before he left for Hawaii, but this was not to be, and as the final week began, he spoke haltingly with his mother.

"When I have been in Hawaii for a little while, and after I have sent you a lot of money, I think I may get married." He blushed a deep red under his dark skin and prepared to confide: "At such time, will you speak to Yoko-chan for me?" But his mother had long waited for this opportunity to advise her favorite son, and now she poured forth her fund of Hiroshima wisdom.

"Kamejiro, I have heard that it is a terrible thing for a man to travel overseas the way you are doing. Not that you will be robbed, because you are a strong man and able to handle such things as well as any." She was in her fifties, a small, stoop-shouldered woman with deep wrinkles from endless hours in the sun. She loved rice and could eat four bowls at any meal, but she could never afford to do that, so she remained as skinny as she had been in her youth, when Kamejiro's father had crept into her sleeping room.

"What mothers worry about, Kamejiro," she explained, "is that their sons will marry poorly. Every day that you are gone I shall be anxious, because I shall see you in the arms of some unworthy woman. Kamejiro, you must guard against this. You must not marry carelessly. When it comes time to take a wife, appoint prudent friends to study her history. Now these are the things I want you to bear in mind.

"The best thing in the world is to be a Japanese. What wonderful people the Japanese are. Hard-working, honest, clean people. Kamejiro, your father and I have heard that in Hawaii the people are careless and very dark. If you were to marry one of them . . ." She started to weep, real, mournful tears, so after a while she went to the hanging bucket at the fire and took herself a little rice in a bowl. Thus fortified, she continued. "If you were to marry such a woman, Kamejiro, we would not want you back in this village. You would have disgraced your family, your village, and all Japan."

Kamejiro listened carefully, for in these matters his mother was wise. She always collected gossip and in the last three weeks had walked fifteen miles to talk with people who had heard various bits of news about Hawaii. "Never marry a Chinese," she said firmly. "They are clever people and there are many of them in Hawaii, I am told, but they don't wash themselves as often as we do and no matter how rich they get, they remain Chinese. Under no circumstances can you return to this village if you have a Chinese wife.

"Kamejiro, many men from Hiroshima-ken are tempted to marry girls from the north. You've seen some of those pitiful women down here. They can't talk decently, and say zu-zu all the time, until you feel ashamed for them. I have no respect at all for girls from the north, and I have never seen one who made a good wife. I will admit that they're a little better than Chinese, but not much. If you are ever tempted to marry a northern girl, think of Masaru's wife. Zu-zu, zu-zu! Do you want a girl like that?" she asked contemptuously.

Using chopsticks to flick the rice grains into her wrinkled but vigorous mouth she proceeded. "A good many men try wives from the south, too, but what respectable man really wants a Yamaguchi-no-anta? Do you, in your heart, really respect Takeshi-san's wife. Do you want a woman like that in your home? Would you want to present such a girl to me some day and say, 'Mother, here is my wife.' And when I asked where she was from, would you feel satisfied if you had to confess, 'She's a Yamaguchi-no-anta?' "

Now the wise old woman came to the most difficult part of her sermon, so once more she fortified herself with a little rice, filling up the bowl with tea and a garnish of dried seaweed. "I would be heartbroken," she began, "if you married a northern girl or a southern girl, but to tell you the truth I would try to be a very good mother to them, and you would not curse me for my actions. But there are two marriages you may not make, Kamejiro. If you do, don't bother to come home. You will not be welcome either in the village or in this house or in any part of Hiroshima-ken." Solemnly she paused, looked out the door to be sure no one was listening, and proceeded.

"If you marry when I am not at hand, Kamejiro, ask your two closest friends to seek out the girl's history. You know the obvious problems. No disease, no insanity, nobody in jail, all ancestors good, strong Japanese. But then ask your advisers this: 'Are you sure she is not an Okinawan?' " Dramatically she stopped. Putting down her rice bowl she pointed at her son and said, "Don't bring an Okinawa girl to this house. If you marry such a girl, you are dead."

She waited for this ominous statement to wind its way through her son's mind, then added, "The danger is this, Kamejiro. In Hiroshima-ken we can spot an Okinawan instantly. I can tell when a girl comes from Okinawa if I see even two inches of her wrist. But in Hawaii I am told people forget how to do this. There are many Okinawans there, and their women set traps to catch decent Japanese. I wish I could go with you to Hawaii, for I can uncover these sly Okinawans. I am afraid you won't be able to, Kamejiro, and you will bring disgrace upon us."

She started to cry again, but rice stanched the tears, and she came to the climax of her warning: "There is of course one problem that every devoted son looks into before he marries, because he owes it not only to his parents but also to his brothers and sisters. Kamejiro, I said that if you married an Okinawa girl you were dead. But if you marry an Eta, you are worse than dead."

The wave of disgust that swept over Kamejiro's face proved that he despised the Eta as much as his mother did, for they were the untouchables of Japan, the unthinkables. In past ages they had dealt in the bodies of dead animals, serving as butchers and leather tanners. Completely outside the scope of Japanese civilization, they scratched out horrible lives in misery and wherever possible fled to distant refuges like Hawaii. A single trace of Eta blood could contaminate an entire family, even to remote unattached cousins, and Kamejiro shuddered.

His mother continued dolefully: "I said I could spot an Okinawan, and I could protect you there. But with an Eta . . . I don't know. They're clever! Crawling with evil, they try to make you think they're normal people. They hide under different names. They take new occupations. I am sure that some of them must have slipped into Hawaii, and how will you know, Kamejiro? What would you do if word sneaked back to Hiroshima-ken that you had been captured by an Eta?"

Mother and son contemplated this horror for some minutes, and she concluded: "So when it comes time to marry, Kamejiro, I think it best if you marry a Hiroshima girl. Now I don't like girls from Hiroshima City, itself, for they are too fancy. They cost a man money and want their photographs taken all the time. I've seen a lot of girls from Hiroshima City, and although I'm ashamed to say so, some of them don't seem much better than an ordinary Yamaguchi-no-anta. And from what I have seen, a lot of the girls from the other end of Hiroshima-ken aren't too reliable, either. So don't be taken in just because a strange girl tells you she's a Hiroshima-gansu. It may mean nothing.

"And be careful not to marry into any family that has ever had an undertaker. Avoid city families if you can. To tell you the truth, Kamejiro, it would be best if you married a girl from right around here. Of course, I don't think much of the families in Atazuki Village, for they are spendthrift, but I can say there are no finer girls in all Japan than those in our village. So when the time comes to marry, go to a letter-writer and have him send me a message and when it is read to me, I'll find you a good local girl, and trust me, Kamejiro, that will be best." She paused dramatically, then added in an offhand manner, "Say, a fine strong girl like Yoko-chan." Kamejiro looked at his mother and said nothing, so she finished her rice.

When it came time for him to bid his parents farewell he assured them that he would never do anything to bring disgrace upon them, or upon Japan. His gruff father warned, "Don't bring home an Okinawan or an Eta." His mother summarized a larger body of Hiroshima morality by reminding him, "No matter where you go, Kamejiro, remember that you are a Japanese. Put strength in your stomach and be a good Japanese. Never forget that some day you will return to Hiroshima-ken, the proudest and greatest in all Japan. Come home with honor, or don't come home."

Then his father led him to one side and said quietly, "Be proud. Be Japanese. Put power in your stomach."

As he set forth from the village he saw by the shrine the flowering girl Yoko-san and he wanted to leave his weeping parents and rush over to her, shouting, "Yoko-chan! When I have made money I will send for you!" But his stocky legs were powerless to move him in that direction, and had he gone his voice would have been unable to speak, for officially they did not know each other, and all the exciting things that had transpired behind the darkened shoji had not really happened, for he had never removed his mask.

So he departed, a tough, stalwart little man with arms hanging down like loaded buckets, yet as he passed the shrine, looking straight ahead, he somehow received Yoko's assurance that if he cared to write for her, she would come; and a considerable happiness accompanied him on his journey.

For the first two miles his path lay along the Inland Sea, and he saw before him the shifting panorama of that wonderland of islands. Green and blue and rocky brown they rose from the cool waters, lifting their pine trees to the heavens. On one a bold crimson torii rose like a bird of god, marking some ancient Shinto shrine. On others Kamejiro saw the stained stone outlines of Buddhist temples, perched above the sea. How marvelous that footpath was! How the earth sang, while the rice fields swept their ripening grain back and forth in the winds creeping inland from the sea.

With every step Kamejiro encountered some unexpected beauty, for he was traversing one of the most glorious paths in the world, and the singing of that day would never leave his ears. Once he stopped to stare in wonder at the multitude of islands and at the magnificence of their position within the sea, and he swore, "A little time will pass and I will return to the Inland Sea."

When the *Kyoto-maru* landed him in Honolulu he advised the immigration interpreter: "Stamp my paper for five years." Fortunately, he could not understand the official when the latter muttered to his assistant, "I wish I believed these little yellow bastards were gonna stay only five years."

There were others in Hawaii, however, who welcomed the Japanese ungrudgingly, for that day the Honolulu *Mail* editorialized: "Janders & Whipple are to be congratulated on having completed plans for the importation of 1,850 strong and healthy Japanese peasant farmers to work our sugar fields, with prospects for as many more at later intervals as may be required. We journeyed to the *Kyoto-maru* yesterday to inspect the new arrivals and can report that they seemed a sturdy lot. Lunas who have worked earlier crews of Japanese state unanimously that they are much superior to the unfortunate Chinese whom they are replacing. They are obedient, extraordinarily clean, law-abiding, not given to gambling and eager to accomplish at least eighty per cent more honest labor than the lazy Chinese ever did.

"Japanese avoid the Chinaman's tendency to combine into small and vicious groups. Themselves an agrarian people, they love plantation work and will stay in the fields, so that the trickery whereby in recent years crafty Orientals fled from honest work in the cane fields, so as to monopolize our city shops, can be expected to end. Japanese are notoriously averse to running stores, but J & W have taken the added precaution of importing only strong young men from rural areas. There are no wily Tokyo dwellers lurking ominously in their gangs. Plantation owners can expect a rapid improvement in the appearance of their camps, too, for Japanese love to garden and will soon have their buildings looking attractive.

"In two respects we are particularly fortunate in getting these Japanese. First, we have been assured that their men do not contract alliances with women of any other race but their own, and we can look forward confidently to a cessation of the disgraceful scenes of aging Oriental men marrying the best young Hawaiian girls of our islands. Secondly, because of the feudal structure of Japanese society, in which every Japanese is loyal unto the death to his master, firms like J & W are going to find that their new laborers will probably be the most loyal available on earth. Lunas who have worked them say they love authority, expect to be told what to do, respond promptly to crisp if not abusive treatment, and are accustomed to smart blows from time to time when their work is not up to par. Unlike their Chinese cousins, they neither resent honest correction nor combine secretly against those who administer it.

"All in all, we think that future history will show that the true prosperity of Hawaii began with the importation of these sturdy workmen, and when, at the end of their employment, they return to Japan, each with his pocketful of honestly earned gold, they will go with our warm aloha. Today we welcome them as fortunate replacements for the Chinese who have turned out so badly. Aloha nui nui!"

OF THE 1,850 Japanese laborers who debarked that September day in 1902, most were assigned to plantations on Oahu, the island that contained Honolulu, and they were depressed by the barren ugliness of the inland areas. They had not seen cactus before, but as farmers they could guess that it spoke ill of the land upon which it grew, and the dull red dust appalled them. They judged that no water came to these parts, and although they had not themselves grown cattle, they could see that the spavined beasts which roamed these desolate acres suffered from both thirst and hunger. They were disappointed in the parched land which showed so little promise, and one farmer whispered to his friends, "America is much different from what they said."

But Kamejiro Sakagawa was not to be disappointed, for he was among a batch of workers dispatched to another area, and when he reached it he saw immediately that his new land was among the fairest on earth. Even the glorious fields along the Inland Sea of Japan were no finer than the area which he was expected to till. To reach this veritable paradise young Kamejiro was not marched along the dusty roads of Oahu; he was led onto a small inter-island boat which at other times was used for the transport of lepers, and after a long, seasick night, he was marched ashore on the island of Kauai. At the pier a tall, scar-faced man waited impatiently on a horse, and when the captain of the boat was inept at docking, he shouted orders of his own, as if he were in command. At his side ran a little Japanese, and as his countrymen finally climbed down out of the boat, this interpreter told them, "The man on the horse is called Wild Whip Hoxworth. If you work good, he is good. If not, he will beat you over the head. So work good."

As he spoke, Wild Whip wheeled his horse among the men, reached down with his riding crop and tilted upward the face of Kamejiro Sakagawa. "You understand?" he growled. The little interpreter asked, "Ano hito ga yutta koto wakari mashita ka?" When stocky Kamejiro nodded, Whip lowered the riding crop, reached down and patted the new laborer on the shoulder.

Now he wheeled his horse about and moved into position at the head of the line. "We march!" he shouted, leading them off the pier onto a red-baked road where a group of sugar-cane wagons, hitched to horses, waited. "Climb in!" he yelled, and as the Japanese crawled into the low wagons whose sides were formed of high stakes bound together by lengths of rope, he moved to the head of the train and shouted, "On to Hanakai!" And the procession left the port town and moved slowly northward along the eastern coast of the island.

As the men rode they saw for the first time the full grandeur of Hawaii, for they were to work on one of the fairest islands in the Pacific. To the left rose jagged and soaring mountains, clothed in perpetual green. Born millions of years before the other mountains of Hawaii, these had eroded first and now possessed unique forms that pleased the eye. At one point the wind had cut a complete tunnel through the highest mountain; at others the erosion of softer rock had left isolated spires of basalt standing like monitors. To the right unfolded a majestic shore, cut by deep bays and highlighted by a rolling surf that broke endlessly upon dark rocks and brilliant white sand. Each mile disclosed to Kamejiro and his companions some striking new scene.

But most memorable of all he saw that day was the red earth. Down millions of years the volcanic eruptions of Kauai had spewed forth layers of iron-rich rocks, and for subsequent millions of years this iron had slowly, imperceptibly disintegrated until it now stood like gigantic piles of scintillating rust, the famous red earth of Kauai. Sometimes a green-clad mountain would show a gaping scar where the side of a cliff had fallen away, disclosing earth as red as new blood. At other times the fields along which the men rode would be an unblemished furnace-red, as if flame had just left it. Again in some deep valley where small amounts of black earth had intruded, the resulting red nearly resembled a brick color. But always the soil was red. It shone in a hundred different hues, but it was loveliest when it stood out against the rich green verdure of the island, for then the two colors complemented each other, and Kauai seemed to merit the name by which it was affectionately known: the Garden Island.

For out of its lush red soil, teeming with iron, grew a multitude of trees: palms that clung to the shore; pandanus that twisted itself into dense jungle; banyans with their thousand aerial roots; hau and kou, the excellent trees of the islands; swift-growing wild plum that had been imported from Japan to provide burning fagots for the laborers; and here and there a royal palm, its moss-pocked trunk rising majestically toward the heavens. But there was one tree specially dedicated to Kauai, and it made both life and agriculture on the island possible. Wherever the powerful northeast trades whipped sea and salt air inland, killing everything that grew, men had planted the strange, silky, gray-green casuarina tree, known sometimes as the ironwood. Groves of this curious tree, covered with ten-inch needles and seed cones that resembled round buttons, stood along the shore and protected the island. The foliage of the casuarina was not copious and to the stranger each tree looked so frail that it seemed about to die, but it possessed incredible powers of recuperation, and what it thrived on most was a harsh, salty trade wind that whipped its fragile needles into a frenzy and tore at its cherry-bark trunk; for then the casuarina dug in and saved the island. The sea winds howled through its branches; its frail needles caught the salt; the force of the storm was broken; and all who lived in the shadow of the casuarina tree lived securely.

As the Japanese rode through this verdant wonderland, a storm flashed in from the sea, throwing tubs of water over the land, but Wild

Whip, holding his prancing horse under control, shouted to his interpreter, "Ishii-san, tell the men that on Kauai we don't run from storms!" The frail little interpreter ran from wagon to wagon, shouting, "On this island it rains a dozen times a day. Soon the sun comes out. We never bother." And as he predicted, after a few minutes the wild storm moved on to sulk in a valley until a rainbow was flung across it, and it was toward this rainbow that Kamejiro and his companions rode.

They had come to the valley of Hanakai, the Valley of the Sea, but they were not yet aware of that fact, for the highway upon which they rode was at this point more than a mile inland; but leading off from it, to the right and toward the sea, appeared a spectacular lane. It was marked by twenty pairs of royal palms, gray-trunked and erect, that Whip had sent home from Madagascar on one of the H & H ships, and these magnificent sentinels guarded the road as stone lions had once stood watch for the Assyrians. Entering the deep shade of the lane, the workmen sensed that they were approaching something special, and after a while they came upon twenty pairs of Norfolk pine, those exalted sculptural trees that had originally grown on only one South Pacific island, from which Whip had some years ago recovered two hundred young trees which he had scattered throughout Hawaii. Beyond them came the beauty of the Hoxworth lane: to the left and north stood an unbroken line of croton bushes imported by Whip from Guadalcanar in the Solomons, and of all that grew on his plantations, these were his favorites, these low sparkling bushes whose iridescent green and red and purple and gold and blue leaves were a constant source of wonder; but to the right ran a long row of hibiscus trees, low shrublike plants that produced a dozen varieties of fragile, crepelike flowers, each with its own dazzling color; Whip's favorite was the bright yellow hibiscus, bigger than a large plate and golden in the sunlight.

The lane now turned sharply south and entered upon a huge grassy area. As was the custom in Hawaii at that time, no specific roadway led up to the Hoxworth mansion. Over the spacious lawn, guests drove as they wished, for no matter how badly the grass was scarred by such usage, the next day's inevitable rain and sunlight cured it. On the lawn there were only two trees. To the right stood an African tulip tree with dark green leaves and brilliant red flowers scattered prodigally upon it, while to the left rose one of the strangest trees in nature, the golden tree which Whip had found in South America. Each year it produced a myriad of brilliant yellow flowers, and since it stood some fifty feet high, it was a spectacular exhibit.

The house was long and low, built originally in China of the best wood, then taken apart and shipped in an H & H cargo ship to Hanakai. It ran from northeast to southwest, and its southern exposure consisted of eight tall Greek pillars supporting a porch upon which the life of the mansion took place. For at Hanakai the view from the lanai—the open porch—commanded attention. A soft green grassy lawn fell away to the edge of a steep cliff some three hundred feet above the surface of the sea, which here cut deeply inland forming the bay of Hanakai. When a storm of major proportions fell upon Kauai, the wild ocean would sweep its penetrating arm into the bay and find itself impounded. Then it would leap like a caged animal high up the sides of the red cliff. Its topmost spray would poise there for a moment, then fall screaming down the sheer sides. To see such a storm at Hanakai was to see the ocean at its best. But to the north and east, from where the storms blew, there was a row of trees, not visible from the mansion, and it was upon these that the life of Hanakai depended, for they were the casuarina trees, and it was their needles that sifted out the salt and broke the back of the wild storm; they were the speechless, sighing workmen, and if the golden tree was the marvel of that part of Kauai, it existed solely because the casuarinas fought the storms on its behalf.

Within the protection of the casuarinas Wild Whip paused to review the beauty of his favorite spot in the islands. It had been given him by his doting grandfather, Captain Rafer Hoxworth, who had got it from the Alii Nui Noelani, and here Whip had brought his treasures from around the world. Hawaii's best mangoes grew at Hanakai, its most brilliant hibiscus and its best horses. As Whip now studied the red earth and heard the ocean growling at the cliffs he muttered, "Lucky Japanese who came here to work."

Kamejiro and his fellow laborers did not, of course, accompany Whip to the mansion. At the end of the lane Mr. Ishii, the interpreter, took them off in quite the opposite direction, toward the casuarina trees, and after half a mile he brought them to a long low wooden building consisting of a single room. It contained three doors, a few windows, half a dozen tables and some sagging wooden beds. Outside were two unspeakably foul toilets with a well between. There were no trees, no flowers, no amenities of any kind, but there was a copious amount of red mud, a thicket of wild plum from which firewood could be cut, and in all directions the green wilderness of growing sugar canes. This was the Ishii Camp, so known because of the interpreter who ran it.

In this particular camp, there were no women, no facilities for recreation, no doctor, and no church. There was lots of rice, for Wild Whip insisted that his men be fed well, and in each camp—for this was merely one of seven on Hanakai Plantation—one man was appointed fisherman, bringing to the table whatever he caught on the fruitful reefs of Kauai. It was Whip Hoxworth's full intention that any laborer whom he imported should work for him five or ten years, save his money, and return to Japan. There was thus no need for women or churches, and little need for doctors, since he hired only the ablest-bodied.

At Hanakai the Hoxworth laborers rose at four in the morning, ate a hot breakfast, hiked to the fields so as to be there at six and worked till six at night, hiking back to the Ishii Camp on their own time. For this they were paid sixty-seven cents a day, but they did get their food and a sagging bed. During harvest, of course, they worked nineteen hours a day for no extra money.

On the first workday Kamejiro Sakagawa marched home at dusk, feeling great strength in his bones, and looked about for some place in which to bathe, for like all Japanese he was fanatic in his attention to cleanliness, and he was dismayed to find that no provisions had been made. Water could be pumped from the well, but who could bathe properly in cold water? On this first night he had to make do, protestingly, and he listened to his mates growling as they recalled the sweet, hot baths of Hiroshima, and that night he went to see Ishii-san and said, "I think I will build a hot bath for the camp."

"There's no lumber," Ishii-san said. It was his job to protect the interests of Mr. Hoxworth and he did so.

"I saw some old boards at the edge of the sugar field," Kamejiro replied.

"You can have them, but there are no nails," Ishii-san warned.

"I saw some nails where the irrigation ditch was mended."

"Were they rusted?"

"Yes."

"You can have them."

On his second full day ashore in Hawaii, Kamejiro began building his hot bath. It was most tedious work, for he could not find lumber that fitted nor could he get hold of a piece of galvanized iron for the bottom, where the fire was to be built. At last he grabbed Ishii-san, who was skittish about the whole affair, and made the interpreter speak to Mr. Hoxworth—Hoxuwurtu, the Japanese men called him—and the tall boss growled, "What do you want galvanized iron for?"

"To take a bath," Kamejiro said.

"Use cold water. I do," Hoxworth snapped.

"I don't!" Kamejiro snapped back, and Hoxworth turned in his saddle to study the runty little man with the long arms that hung out from his body.

"Don't speak to me that way," Hoxworth said ominously, pointing his riding crop at him.

"We have to be clean," Kamejiro insisted, not drawing away from the crop.

"You have to work," Hoxworth said slowly.

"But after work we want to be clean," Kamejiro said forcefully.

"Are you looking for a fight?" Hoxworth cried, dropping from his horse and throwing the reins to an attendant. Ishii-san, the interpreter, began to sweat and mumbled his words, replying on behalf of Kamejiro, "Oh, no, sir! This man is a fine workman!"

"Shut up!" Hoxworth snapped, pushing his little assistant aside. Striding up to Kamejiro he started to grab him by the shoulders, but as he did so he saw the enormous musculature of the stubborn workman, and he saw also that Kamejiro had no intention of allowing even the boss to touch him, and the two men stood in the cane field staring at each other. The other Japanese were terrified lest trouble start, but Kamejiro, to his surprise, was unconcerned, for he was studying the big American and thinking: "If he comes one step closer I will ram my head into his soft belly."

In mutual respect the tension dissolved, and Wild Whip asked Ishii-san, "What is it he wants?"

"He's building a bath for the camp," Ishii repeated.

"That's what I don't understand," Hoxworth replied.

"Japanese cannot live unless they have a bath each day," Kamejiro explained.

"Pump the water and take a bath," Whip said.

"A hot bath," Kamejiro replied.

For a long moment the two men stared at each other, after which Whip laughed easily and asked, "So you've got to have some corrugated iron?"

"Yes," Kamejiro said.

"You'll get it," Hoxworth replied. As if they were boys playing, Whip winked at Kamejiro, and chucked him under the chin with the whip. With one finger the Japanese laborer slowly moved the crop away, and the two men understood each other.

When the bath was built, a square tub four feet deep on stilts, Kamejiro rigged a triple length of bamboo which delivered water from the pump. Beneath the galvanized iron he built a fire with wild plum branches, and when the water was hot he clanged a piece of iron to summon the camp. Each man stripped, hung his clothes on a pole spiked with nails, and was allowed one panful of hot water with which to soap down outside the tub and rinse off. Then, mounting three wooden steps, he climbed into the steaming water and luxuriated for four minutes. While he was doing this, the next man was cleansing himself, and as the first crawled out reluctantly, the second climbed in eagerly. Kamejiro tended the fire and added new water as it was needed.

The first ten men to use the water paid a penny each, and cast lots to determine who had the right to climb in first. After the first ten, each man paid half a cent, and as many as wished used the water. Long after night had fallen, when the pennies were safely stowed away and the other men were eating their evening meal, Kamejiro himself would undress, place one more stick under the iron—for he liked his bath hotter than most—and after carefully soaping himself outside and washing off, he would climb into the remnants of the water. Its heat would encompass him and make him forget Hiroshima and the difficulties of the day. To the east the casuarina trees kept away the storm, and in the hot bath all was well.

When he returned to his bunk he invariably looked with deep respect at his only significant possession, the black-framed portrait of the Japanese emperor. Before this grim and bearded leader the little workman bowed; the one reality in his life was that the emperor personally knew of his daily behavior and was grieved when things went poorly. Each night before he went to sleep he weighed his day's actions and hoped that the emperor would approve.

In order to collect the firewood needed for the hot bath, Kamejiro rose at three-thirty each morning and worked while the others were eating. When the wood was safely stored, he grabbed two rice balls, a bit of pickle and part of a fish, munching them as he ran to the fields. At six, when the day's work ended, he dashed home ahead of the rest to get the fire started, and was not free to eat until the last bath had been taken. Then he accepted what was left and in this way he saved the money for the important step he was to take thirteen years later in 1915.

It was not easy to accumulate money, not even when one worked as hard as Kamejiro did. For example, in 1904 events transpired in Asia which were to eat up his savings, but no man worthy of the name would have done less than he did under the circumstances. For some months Japan had been having trouble with Russia, and the emperor's divine word to his people had reached even remote Kauai, where with trembling voice Ishii-san had read the rescript to all the assembled Japanese: "As it is Our heartfelt desire to maintain the peace of the East, We have caused Our government to negotiate with Russia, but We are now compelled to conclude that the Russian government has no sincere desire to maintain the peace of the East. We have therefore ordered Our government to break off negotiations with Russia and have decided to take free action for the maintenance of Our independence and self-protection."

"What does it mean?" Kamejiro asked.

"War," an older man explained.

Now Ishii-san's voice rose to an awed climax as he delivered the distant emperor's specific message to all loyal Japanese: "We rely upon your loyalty and valor to carry out Our object and thereby keep unsullied the honor of our Empire."

"Banzai!" a former soldier shouted.

"Japan must win!" the workmen began to cry.

Ishii-san waited for the tumult to die down, then announced: "On Friday an officer of the emperor himself will come to Hanakai to collect money for the Imperial army. Let us show the world what loyal Japanese we are!" He hesitated a moment, then announced: "I will give eleven dollars."

A gasp went up from the crowd as men realized how much of his meager salary this represented, and another was inspired to cry, "I will give nineteen dollars." The crowd applauded, and as the ante rose, Kamejiro was swept up by the fervor of the moment. Japan was in danger. He could see his parents' fields overrun by Russian barbarians, and he thought how insignificant were his savings from the hot bath. In an ecstasy of emotion, seeing the grave, bearded emperor before him, he rose and cried in a roaring voice, "I will give all my bath money! Seventy-seven dollars."

A mighty cheer went up, and a Buddhist priest said, "Let us in our hearts resolve to protect the honor of Japan as Sakagawa Kamejiro has done this day." Men wept and songs were sung and Ishii-san shouted in his high, weak voice, "Let every man march by and swear allegiance to the emperor." Instinctively the workmen formed in orderly ranks and fell into martial rhythms as they marched past the place where the Buddhist priest stood. Pressing their hands rigidly to their knees, they bowed as if to the august presence itself and said, "Banzai! Banzai!"

When the excitement was over, and the emperor's emissary had left with the money, the camp settled down to the agony of waiting for war news. It was rumored that Russian troops had landed on the island of Kyushu, and Kamejiro whispered to Ishii-san at night, "Should we return to Honolulu and try to find a boat back to Japan?"

"No," Ishii said gravely. "After all, what we have heard is only a rumor."

"But Japan is in danger!" Kamejiro muttered.

"We must wait for more substantial news," Ishii-san insisted, and because he could read and write, people listened to him. And the year 1904 ended in apprehension.

But in January, 1905, his prudence was rewarded when word reached Kauai that the great Russian bastion at Port Arthur had surrendered to a Japanese siege. Kauai—that is, the Japanese living there—went wild with joy and a torchlight procession was held through the plantation town of Kapaa; and the celebrations had hardly ended when word came of an even more astonishing victory at Mukden, followed quickly by the climactic news from the Strait of Tsushima. A Russian fleet of thirty-eight major vessels had engaged the Japanese under Admiral Togo; nineteen were immediately sunk, five were captured, and of the remaining fourteen, only three got back to Russia. More than 10,000 of the enemy were drowned and 6,000 taken prisoner. For their part, the Japanese lost only three minor torpedo boats and less than 700 men. The Honolulu *Mail* called Tsushima "one of the most complete victories any nation has ever enjoyed at the expense of a major rival."

Kamejiro, listening to the stunning news, burst into tears and told his friend Ishii-san, "I feel as if my hot-bath money had personally sunk the Russian ships."

"It did," Ishii-san assured him. "Because it represented the undying spirit of the Japanese. Look at the poor Americans! Their president speaks to them, and nothing happens. No one pays attention. But when the emperor speaks to us, we hear even though we are lost at the end of the world."

Kamejiro contemplated this for a moment, then asked, "Ishii-san, do you feel proud today?"

"I feel as if my heart were a balloon carrying me above the trees," Ishii-san replied.

"I can feel guns going off in my chest every minute," Kamejiro confided. "They are the guns of Admiral Togo." Again tears came into his eyes and he asked, "Ishii-san, do you think it would be proper for us to say a prayer for that great admiral who saved Japan?"

"It would be better if the priest were here. That's his job."

"But wouldn't it be all right if we ourselves faced Japan and said a prayer?"

"I would like to do so," Ishii-san admitted, and the two laborers knelt in the red dust of Kauai and each thought of Hiroshima, and the rice fields, and the red torii looking out over the Japan Sea, and they prayed that their courageous country might always know victory.

By this time Kamejiro had saved, from his wages and the hot bath, an additional thirty-eight dollars, and the camp suspected this, so when word reached Kauai that a splendid victory celebration was to be held right in the heart of Honolulu, for all Hawaii to see, and that the island of Kauai was invited to send two men to march in Japanese uniforms and play the roles of immortal military leaders like Admiral Togo, everyone agreed that Kamejiro should be one of the men, because he could pay his own way, and a man named Hashimoto was the other, because he also had some savings, and in late May, 1905, the two stocky laborers set out on the inter-island boat *Kilauea* for Honolulu. There the committee provided them with handsome uniforms which local Japanese wives had copied from magazine pictures, and Kamejiro found himself a full colonel in memory of a leader who had personally thrown himself upon the Russian guns at the siege of Port Arthur. This Colonel Ito had been blown to pieces and into national immortality. It was with bursting pride that Colonel Sakagawa lined up on the afternoon of June 2, 1905, to march boldly through the streets of Honolulu and across the Nuuanu to Aala Park, where thousands of Japanese formed a procession that proceeded solemnly to the Japanese consulate, where a dignified man in frock coat and black tie nodded gravely. A workman from one of the Janders & Whipple plantations on Oahu was dressed in Admiral Togo's uniform, and from the steps of the consulate he led the Banzai and the formal marching broke up. Kamejiro and his fellow Kauai man, Hashimoto, walked back to Aala Park, where exhibitions of Japanese wrestling and fencing were offered to an appreciative crowd; but the victory celebration was to have overtones of another kind which Kamejiro would never forget, for at ten o'clock, when the crowd was greatest, a pathway was formed and eight professional geisha girls from one of the tea houses passed through the confusion to take their places on the dancing platform, and as they went one walked in her gently swaying manner quite close to Kamejiro and the powder in her hair brushed into his nostrils and he admitted, for the first time in three years, how desperately hungry he was for that girl Yoko back in Hiroshima.

A haze came over his eyes and he imagined that the mask was once more upon his face while he prepared to slip into her sleeping room. He could feel her arms about him and hear her voice in his ear. The crowd pressed in upon him but he was not part of it; he was in Hiroshima in the spring when the rice fields were a soft green, and a horrible thought took possession of him: "I shall never leave Kauai! I shall die here and never see Japan again! I shall live all my life without a woman!"

And he began, in his agony, to walk among the crowd and place himself so that he might touch this Japanese wife or that. He did not grab at them or embarrass them; he wanted merely to see them and to feel their reality; and his glazed eyes stared at them. "I am so hungry," he muttered to himself as he moved so as to intercept a woman at least twenty years older than he. She shuffled along with her feet never leaving the ground, Japanese style, and the soft rustle of her passing seemed to him one of the sweetest sounds he had ever heard. Instinctively he reached out his hand and clutched at her arm, and the shuffling stopped. The housewife looked at him in amazement, pushed his hand down, and muttered, "You are a Japanese! Behave yourself! Especially when you wear such a uniform!"

Mortified, he fled the crowd and found Hashimoto, who said abruptly, "Those damned geisha girls are driving me loony. Let's find a good whorehouse."

The two Kauai laborers started probing the Aala region, but a stranger told them, "The houses you want are all in Iwilei," so they hurried to that quarter of the city, but the houses were filled with richer patrons and the two could gain no entrance.

"I'm going to grab any woman I see," Hashimoto said.

"No!" Kamejiro warned, remembering the admonition of the woman he had touched.

"To hell with you!" the other shouted. "Girl! Girls!" he shouted in Japanese. "Here I come to find you!" And he dashed down one of the Iwilei alleys. Kamejiro, now ashamed to be in such a place while dressed as Colonel Ito, who had sacrificed his life at Port Arthur, fled the area and returned to the park, where he sat for hours staring at the dancers. This time he kept away from women, and after a long time an old Japanese man came up to him with a bottle of sake and said, "Oh, Colonel! What a glorious war this was! And did you notice one thing tonight? Not one damned Chinese had the courage to appear on the streets while our army was marching! I tell you, Colonel! In 1895 we defeated the Chinese. And in 1905 we defeated the Russians. Two of the finest nations on earth. Who will we fight ten years from now? England? Germany?"

"All the world can be proud of Japan," Kamejiro agreed.

"What is more important, Colonel," the drunk continued, "is that here in Hawaii people have now got to respect us. The German lunas who beat us with whips. The Norwegian lunas who treat us with contempt. They have got to respect us Japanese! We are a great people! Therefore, Colonel, promise me one thing, and I will give you more sake. The next time a European luna dares to strike you in the cane fields, kill him! We Japanese will show the world."

It was a tremendous celebration, worthy of the impressive victory gained by the homeland, and even though it used up much of Kamejiro's savings and reminded him of how lonely he was, he felt it had been worth while; but it had one unfortunate repercussion which no one could have foreseen, and long after the celebration itself had faded into memory, this one dreadful result lived on in Kamejiro's mind.

It started in the whorehouses of Iwilei, after Kamejiro had abandoned his lusty friend Hashimoto to the alleys, for that young man had forced his way into one of the houses and had been soundly thrashed by half a dozen Germans who resented his intrusion. Thrown into one of the gutters, he had been found by a Hawaiian boy who did pimping for a group of girls, and this boy, in the custom of the islands, had lugged the bewildered Japanese home, where his sister had washed his bruises. They had been able to converse only in pidgin, but apparently enough had been said, for when Hashimoto returned to the Kauai ship, he had the sister in tow. She was a big, amiable, wide-eyed Hawaiian who carried with her only one bundle tied with string, but she seemed to like wiry, tough-minded Hashimoto and apparently intended to stay with him.

"I am going to marry her," Hashimoto stoutly informed Kamejiro, who still wore his colonel's uniform, and something about either the victory celebration or the uniform made Kamejiro especially patriotic that day, for as soon as his friend said the fatal words, "I am going to marry her," he sprang into action as if he were in charge of troops. Grabbing Hashimoto by the arm he warned, "If you do such a thing, all Japan will be ashamed."

"I may not ever go back to Japan," Hashimoto said.

Impulsively, like a true colonel, Kamejiro struck Hashimoto across the face, shouting, "Don't ever speak like that! Japan is your home!"

Hashimoto was astonished at Colonel Sakagawa's unexpected behavior but he recognized that he deserved the rebuke, so he mumbled, "I'm tired of living without a woman."

This introduced a less military note into the discussion, and Kamejiro quit being an Imperial colonel and became once more a friend. "Hashimoto-san, it was bad enough to go to such a house, but to bring home one of the girls, and to marry her! You must put strength in your stomach and be a decent Japanese."

"She isn't from one of the houses," Hashimoto explained. "She's a good girl from a good hard-working family."

"But she's not Japanese!" Kamejiro argued.

He made no progress with Hashimoto, who was determined not to live alone any longer. Since there were no Japanese girls available on Kauai, he would live with his Hawaiian and marry her. But in his ardor for feminine companionship he had failed to consider the even greater ardor of the Japanese community, and when it was noised abroad what he had done, he experienced the full, terrible power of the sacred Japanese spirit.

"You have sullied the name of Japan," warned the older men, who had learned to live without women.

"You have disgraced the blood of Japan," others mourned.

"Have you no pride, no Yamato spirit?" younger men asked.

"Don't you realize that you bring disgrace upon us all?" his friends pleaded.

Hashimoto proved himself to be a man of fortitude. "I will not live alone any longer," he repeated stubbornly. "I am going to live with my wife, the way a man should."

"Then you will live forever apart from the Japanese community," a stern old man cried. He had been in Kauai for many years, also longing for a woman, but he had behaved himself as a decent Japanese should, and now on behalf of all the emperor's subjects he pronounced the ostracism: "Because you have been shameless, and because you have not protected the sacred blood of Japan, you must live apart. We don't want a man like you to work with us or to eat with us or to live with us. Get out."

Hashimoto began to feel the awful force of this sentence, and pleaded, "But a man needs a woman! What do you expect me to do?"

A fiery younger man replaced the one who had delivered the ostracism, and this one shouted belligerently, "We don't expect you to marry other women! You're no Chinese who is willing to marry anybody he can get his hands on. You're a Japanese!"

"What am I to do?" Hashimoto screamed. "Live alone all my life?"

"Use the prostitutes each month, like we do," the fiery young man cried, referring to the girls which the plantation bosses provided on paydays, moving them from camp to camp according to schedule.

"But the time comes when a man doesn't want prostitutes any longer," Hashimoto pleaded.

"Then live without them," an older man snapped. "Like Akagi-san. Eh, you Akagi-san? How many years you live without a woman?"

"Nineteen," a wiry veteran of the cane fields replied.

"And you, Yamasaki-san?"

"Seventeen," a sunburned Hiroshima man replied.

"They're decent, honest Japanese!" the younger man shouted. "They will wait here till they die, hoping for a Japanese wife, but if none arrives they would not think of marrying anyone else. In them the Japanese spirit is high. In you, Hashimoto, there is no honor. Now get out!"

So Hashimoto left Ishii Camp and lived with his Hawaiian wife in the town of Kapaa. He had to be fired by Hanakai Plantation, for other Japanese refused to work with an outcast who had sullied the blood of Japan. Sometimes when men from the camp went into Kapaa to play a little pool or get drunk on okolehau, a potent illegal brew made from the root of the ti plant, they would meet their former friend Hashimoto, but they never spoke. He could not attend the Japanese church, nor any of the socials, nor play in Japanese games, nor listen to the heroic reciters who came from time to time from Tokyo, spending days among the camps, reciting the glories of Japanese history.

From all such normal intercourse Hashimoto was excluded, and although the dreadful example of his banishment was frequently recalled by other young men who may have wanted women and who were certainly tempted to marry Hawaiian or Chinese or drifting white girls, his proscribed name was never mentioned. Men hungry for girls did not warn each other: "Remember what happened to Hashimoto!" Instinctively they remembered, for of him it had once been said: "All Japan will be ashamed of what you have done." And the young men were convinced that throughout every village of Japan the evil word had been passed: "Hashimoto Sutekichi married a Hawaiian woman and all Japan is ashamed of him." What Honolulu thought of the marriage was unimportant, for Honolulu did not matter, but what Japan thought was of towering concern, for every man in Ishii Camp intended one day to return to Japan; and to take back with him any wife other than a decent Japanese was unthinkable.

THE YEARS following annexation had not been kind to Wild Whip Hoxworth. In business the more stodgy members of Hoxworth & Hale had kept him from assuming any position of leadership within the company, so that even though his sugar lands irrigated by artesian wells flourished and made him a millionaire several times over, he was denied for moral reasons the command of H & H to which his talents entitled him. So he had come to Kauai.

With driving energy he had imported hundreds of Japanese laborers and had built irrigation ditches, cleared land, and shown Kauai how to grow sugar by the most improved methods. He had erected his own mill and ground his own cane, filling the stubby cargo ships of the H & H line with his product.

With equal energy he had built the mansion at Hanakai, personally placing the croton bushes and the hibiscus. When the cut timbers arrived from China he supervised their erection, and it was he who added the idea of a broad area covered by flagstone through whose chinks grass grew, so that one walked both on the firmness of stone and the softness of grass. When he finished he had a magnificent house, perched on the edge of a precipice at whose feet the ocean thundered, but it was a house that knew no happiness, for shortly after Whip had moved in with his third wife, the Hawaiian-Chinese beauty Ching-ching, who was pregnant at the time, she had caught him fooling around with the brothel girls that flourished in the town of Kapaa. Without even a scene of recrimination, Ching-ching had simply ordered a carriage and driven back to the capital town of Lihue, where she boarded an H & H steamer for Honolulu. She divorced Whip but kept both his daughter Iliki and his yet-unborn son John. Now there were two Mrs. Whipple Hoxworths in Honolulu and they caused some embarrassment to the more staid community. There was his first wife, Iliki Janders Hoxworth, who moved in only the best missionary circles, and there was Ching-ching Hoxworth, who lived within the Chinese community. The two never met, but Hoxworth & Hale saw to it that each received a monthly allowance. The sums were generous, but not so much so as those sent periodically to Wild Whip's second wife, the fiery Spanish girl Aloma Duarte Hoxworth, whose name frequently appeared in New York and London newspapers.

During these early years of the twentieth century, Wild Whip lived alone at Hanakai, a driven, miserable man. Periodically he spent lost days in some back room of the Kapaa brothels, competing with his field hands for the favors of Oriental prostitutes. At other times he would pull himself together and organize the dreamlike sporting events that were a feature of Kauai. For example, he kept a large stable of quarter horses and a fine grassy oval on which to race them at meetings where Chinese and Hawaiian betters went wild and lost a year's wages on one race. Part of Whip's distrust of the Japanese stemmed from the fact that they did not bet madly on his horse races, for he said, "A man who can't get excited about a horse race is really no man at all, and you can have the little yellow bastards." But when it was pointed out that the Japanese enabled him to grow more cane than any other plantation in the islands, he always acknowledged that fact: "Work is their god and I respect them for it. But my love I reserve for men who like horses."

The highlight of any season came when Wild Whip organized one of his polo tournaments, for this was the conspicuous game of the islands, and he maintained a line of thirty-seven choice ponies. The games took place on a lovely grassy field edging the wild cliffs of Hanakai, but the high moment of any game occurred when a sudden shower would toss a rainbow above the players so that two riders fighting for the ball could pass mysteriously from shower into sunlight and back into the soft, misty rain. A polo game at Hanakai was one of the most beautiful sports a man could witness, and islanders often walked for miles to sit along the croton bushes.

Wild Whip played a fine game, and in order to maintain the quality of his team, always hired his lunas personally. Sitting carelessly in a deep chair, he watched the man approach down the long lanai and studied his gait. "Limber, supple, nice walk that one," he would muse. His first question was invariable: "Young man, have you a good seat?" If the man stuttered or failed to understand what a good seat implied, Whip courteously excused him from further consideration. But if the man said, "I've been riding since I was three," Whip proceeded with the interview. Traditionally, on Kauai, lunas were either German immigrants or Norwegians, and among themselves they circulated the warning: "Don't apply at Hanakai unless you're good at polo."

When he hired a man Whip laid down three requirements: "Polished boots that come to the knee, and I want them polished till they gleam. White riding breeches, and I want them white. And finally, lunas on Hanakai never strike the workmen."

Actually, few of the Germans and Norwegians were good at polo when they first started work, but Whip gave lessons every afternoon at four, and in time even the Japanese became proud when their boss and their lunas defended Hanakai's championship against all comers from Kauai.

But major excitement occurred periodically when a picked team from Honolulu, consisting mostly of Janderses and Whipples and Hewletts who had perfected their game at Yale—for many years in a row the stars of the Yale four came from Hawaii—chartered a boat to bring their ponies and their cheering section on an invasion of Kauai. Then haoles from all the local plantations moved out to Hanakai; enormous beds ten feet square were thrown along the lanai, with eight or ten haphazard people to the bed, and kitchens were set up behind the casuarina trees. In the evenings gala dances were held with men in formal dress and women brilliant in gowns from Paris and Canton. Frequently, tournaments were staged with four or five competing teams, and all lived at Hanakai for a week. Then life was glorious, with champagne and flirtations, and often Wild Whip succeeded in sequestering one of the visitors' wives in some darkened bedroom, so that over the polo games at Hanakai there hung always the ominous shadow of potential scandal.

There was another shadow, too, for if the polo field and the croton bushes were made possible only by the protecting rim of silent casuarina trees which kept away the storms and the killing salt, so the life of the haoles was protected by the rim of silent Japanese laborers who lived in the womanless huts and who kept away the sweat, the toil and the work of building the future.

It was curious that when the men of Hawaii returned to Yale for alumni celebrations, and when their former classmates who now lived in respectable centers like Boston and Philadelphia asked, "What holds a brilliant man like you in Hawaii?" the Janderses and the Hales and the Whipples usually replied longingly, "Have you ever seen a polo game at Hanakai? The ocean at your feet. The storms sweeping in with rainbows. When your pony slips, he leaves a bright red scar across the turf. You could live a hundred years in Philadelphia and never see anything like the polo season at Hanakai." The Yale men who had gone to live in Philadelphia never understood, but their former classmates who had played polo along the Hawaii circuit never forgot that Hawaii in those years provided one of the best societies on earth.

When the polo players had departed, when the field kitchens were taken down, and when the patient little Japanese gardeners were tending each cut in the polo turf as if it were a personal wound, Wild Whip would retire to his sprawling mansion overlooking the sea and get drunk. He was never offensive and never beat anyone while intoxicated. At such times he stayed away from the brothels in Kapaa and away from the broad lanai from which he could see the ocean. In a small, darkened room he drank, and as he did so he often recalled his grandfather's words: "Girls are like stars, and you could reach up and pinch each one on the points. And then in the east the moon rises, enormous and perfect. And that's something else, entirely different." It was now apparent to Whip, in his forty-fifth year, that for him the moon did not intend to rise. Somehow he had missed encountering the woman whom he could love as his grandfather had loved the Hawaiian princess Noelani. He had known hundreds of women, but he had found none that a man could permanently want or respect. Those who were desirable were mean in spirit and those who were loyal were sure to be tedious. It was probably best, he thought at such times, to do as he did: know a couple of the better girls at Kapaa, wait for some friend's wife who was bored with her husband, or trust that a casual trip through the more settled camps might turn up some workman's wife who wanted a little excitement. It wasn't a bad life and was certainly less expensive in the long run than trying to marry and divorce a succession of giddy women; but often when he had reached this conclusion, through the bamboo shades of the darkened room in which he huddled a light would penetrate, and it would be the great moon risen from the waters to the east and now passing majestically high above the Pacific. It was an all-seeing beacon, brilliant enough to make the grassy lawns of Hanakai a sheet of silver, probing enough to find any mansion tucked away beneath the casuarina trees. When this moon sought out Wild Whip he would first draw in his feet, trying like a child to evade it, but when it persisted he often rose, threw open the lanai screens, and went forth to meet it. He would stand in the shimmering brilliance for a long time, listening to the surf pound in below, and in its appointed course the moon would disappear behind the jagged hills to the west.

It was uncanny, at such moments, how the Hawaiian men who worked for Whip would sense his mood. In twos and threes, they would appear mysteriously with ukuleles, strumming them idly in subtle island harmonies, and Whip would hear them and would cry, "Eh, you! Pupule, you come!" And the men would unostentatiously gather about him, and he would grab a ukulele and begin to chant some long-forgotten song his grandmother had taught him. He became a Hawaiian, moody, distant, hungry for the message of the night; and for hours he would sing with his men, one song after another. A field hand would grunt, "Eh, boss? You got some okolehau?" And Whip would open some whiskey, and the bottle would pass reflectively from mouth to mouth, and the old laments of Hawaii would continue. At dawn the men would inconspicuously shuffle away, one or two at a time, but the man whose ukulele Wild Whip had borrowed would linger on until at last he would have to say, "Mo bettah I go now, boss," and the long night would end.

After such interludes Wild Whip always turned to his pineapples. On a well-protected plateau about the size of two tennis courts, perched at the head of the Hanakai valley and about two hundred yards from the African tulip tree, he had constructed a special field and fertilized it for the propagation of pineapples, for it was Whip's belief that ultimately the growing of this fruit on high fields and sugar on low was the destiny of Hawaii. To anyone who would listen, he was eager to explain his theories.

"Look! The two things are natural partners. Sugar needs water, a ton of water for each pound of sugar. Pineapple doesn't. Sugar thrives on low fields, pineapples on high. At the very point on a hillside where it's no longer profitable to irrigate for sugar, that's where pineapple grows best. And if you have sugar growing down here and pineapple up there, when the fruit gets ripe you drench it in sugar, can it, and sell both at a huge profit.

"Why in hell do you suppose I came to Kauai? Because it offers an ideal combination of sugar lands and pineapple lands. Before I leave, I'll have the secret that'll make Hanakai the richest plantation in the world."

Whenever Whip looked at the land of Hawaii, with its fortunate combination of high dry fields and low wet ones, he became excited; but when he looked at his experimental pineapple beds, he became furious. For he had in his trial fields more than nineteen different kinds of pineapple, "and not one of them worth a goddamn." He showed his visitors all that he had found so far: "That one with the savage hooks along its leaves—they'd cut you into pieces trying to harvest in a field full of them—they're the Pernambuco and you can have every damned Pernambuco ever grown. The striped one is the Zebrina, looks good but the fruit's foul. That interesting one in three colors is the Bracteatus, and for a time I had hopes for it, but the fruit's too small. I have plants that look like rat tails, others that look like whips, some with teeth like sickles. The only two possibly worth bothering with are the Guatemala and the New Guinea, but they don't prosper here."

"That means you have nothing really worth working on?" agriculturists asked.

"Yep. Wouldn't try to grow any of 'em commercially."

"Then you conclude that pineapples aren't suited to Hawaii?"

"Well . . . I wouldn't admit that."

"You got something else in mind? Some new breed?"

"Maybe . . . maybe some day we'll find exactly the right fruit for these islands."

At such times Hoxworth became hard and secretive, for if he was no longer obsessed by any one woman, and if he had reached a reluctant truce with the standard patterns of love, he did entertain a positive lust for something he had once seen. In 1896 a Rio de Janeiro hotel had served him a Cayenne pineapple, and the instant he had seen that barrel-shaped, sweet and heavy fruit he had known that this was the pineapple for Hawaii. He had expected that it would be simple to go to some agriculturist and say, "I'd like five thousand Cayenne plants," and he had tried to do so; but he quickly found that the French who controlled that part of the Guiana coast where this fortunate mutation of the pineapple family had developed were as excited about its prospects as he. No Cayenne plants were allowed outside the colony. At the seaport of Cayenne, outgoing luggage was minutely inspected, so that when Whipple Hoxworth and wife Ching-ching, from Rio, arrived in French Guiana, the government knew before they landed that he was the big planter from Hawaii and that he was going to try to steal some Cayenne plants. Consequently, with Gallic perfidy they served Whip an endless succession of perfect Cayenne pineapples, heavy, succulent and aromatic. But no Cayenne plant did he see. When he casually suggested a visit to one of the plantations, it rained. When he tried to bribe a scurrilous type to bring him some roots, the man was a government spy placed outside the hotel for that special purpose. And when in frustration he decided to go home empty-handed, the customs officials searched every cubic inch of his luggage with the smiling assurance that "we suspect attempts are being made to smuggle guns to the prisoners on Devil's Island." Whip smiled back and said, "I agree, you must be very careful." So he got no pineapple plants.

He bought substitutes and cared for them tenderly, for he realized that the Cayenne itself must have sprung from some chance cross-fertilization of two types which of themselves were nothing. Therefore, the meanest rat-tailed, scrawny plant in Whip's experimental field received the same care as the best Guatemala; but the fruit that resulted fell so far short of a Cayenne that Whip became increasingly morbid on the subject. From Australia he imported plants that were supposed to be Cayennes, but they did not produce the smooth-skinned fruits he had known in South America. He could taste them now, and he imagined them being forced into cans cut to their size. He was haunted by this perfect pineapple, which he knew existed but which lay beyond his reach, and he became obsessed with the idea of acquiring a bundle of mother plants. For a time he considered a secret overland expedition from Paramaribo in Dutch Guiana, but discussions with geographers who knew the area convinced him that the intervening jungle was impenetrable. He tried suborning French colonial officials, but the government trusted its own subordinates no more than it trusted Whipple Hoxworth and checked them constantly, so that even though he poured some twenty thousand dollars' worth of bribes into Guiana, he got no pineapple plants in return.

And then one day a lanky Englishman named Schilling rode up to Hanakai on a wobbly horse, dismounted and asked for a whiskey soda. "I believe I am the man you are looking for," Schilling said in clipped accents.

"I don't need any more lunas," Whip replied, "and besides, you aren't husky enough."

"I have no intention of working for a living," the lanky Englishman replied. "I have come to sell you something."

"I can think of nothing that I require," Whip snapped.

"I can think of something that you will want to pay a great deal of money for, Mr. Hoxworth."

"What?"

"Two thousand prime Cayenne crowns."

As if his hand had frozen, Whip stopped pouring the whiskey. He made no pretense of not being interested, and his Adam's apple moved up and down in his dry throat. He put the whiskey bottle down, turned, and looked steadily at his visitor. "Cayenne?" he asked.

"Prime crowns."

"How?"

"My father was a Dutchman before he became a British subject. He knows people in the Guianas."

"Are the crowns vital?"

"They're already growing in a hothouse in England."

Wildly Hoxworth grabbed the tall man's arm. "You're sure they're growing?"

"I've brought a photograph," Schilling replied, and he produced a snapshot of himself standing inside a greenhouse with pineapples growing about his feet, and from the hearts of several of the plants rose incontestably the distinctive Cayenne fruit.

"Mr. Schilling . . ." Whip began nervously.

"Dr. Schilling, botanist. I'll sell you the Cayennes, Mr. Hoxworth, but I want the job of raising them here in Hawaii."

"A deal!" Wild Whip agreed. "I'll send a special ship to pick them up. Can you keep them alive across the Atlantic and around the Horn?"

"I'm a botanist," Dr. Schilling replied.

While he waited for the Englishman's return, Wild Whip directed his feverish energy into laying out a special field to accommodate the two thousand crowns that Schilling had contracted to deliver, and as he worked he thought: "I'd like to find a man I could trust to care for these pineapples the way I'd do it." And he remembered the stocky Japanese field hand who had been willing to fight him over the matter of galvanized iron for the hot bath. "That's the kind of man I want," he mused. "Someone with guts."

He saddled his horse and rode out to the sugar fields until he spotted Kamejiro. "Eh, you one fella!" he shouted.

"You speak me?" the rugged little Japanese asked with a friendly grin.

"How you like work boss-man one field?" And the compact was sealed. Now Kamejiro ran each morning from the camp to till the pineapple field, pulverizing the earth with his hands. And each night he ran back to tend his hot bath. Wild Whip, seeing him always in a hurry, thought: "That one does the work of three men," and he raised his pay to seventy-five cents a day.

Under Whip's direction, Kamejiro plowed the land to a depth of two feet, and when its rich redness lay in the sunlight, Whip was pleased, for books had told him that above all else the pineapple required iron, and Kauai was practically solid iron. Every three months the field was turned again and special guano fertilizers were introduced to make it productive. Ditches were dug completely around the area to draw off unnecessary water, and a windbreak of wild plum and casuarina was planted to ward off any chance salt spray. Few brides have ever had homes arranged for them with the meticulous care that Wild Whip exercised in building this all-important seed bed. When it was done, he stood in the middle of its finely aerated soil and shouted to Kamejiro, "Bimeby all fields up there pineapple, eh?" And he pointed in all the upland directions as far as he could see, for he intended them all to be crowded with Cayenne plants, four thousand to the acre, and the money that he had so far made growing sugar would turn out to have been children's coins for playing store.

The first crop of Cayennes surpassed Whip's hopes. Dr. Schilling proved himself both a botanist and a dipsomaniac, and from the front room of the Hanakai mansion, which he obviously intended never to leave, the tall Englishman directed the successful propagation of the plants that were to revolutionize the Hawaiian economy. Of the first two thousand Cayennes which had been abducted from the fields of French Guiana, nearly nineteen hundred grew to luscious maturity, and these first pineapples were an astonishment to the citizens of Hawaii. Whip, as was his custom, gave the fruit away and told everyone, "Start tilling your upland fields now. Gold is about to drip out of them in a fragrant flow."

A pineapple plant produces slowly, only one fruit at the end of two years—technically it is a sorosis or bundle of fruits, each of the composite squares being the result of a separate flower—but when the fruit has matured, the plant offers four separate ways of propagating new plants: the crown of the pineapple fruit can be carefully torn off and planted; slips that have started growing from the base of the fruit can be lifted off and planted; suckers that have begun to spring out from the base of the plant can be used in the same way; or the stump itself can be cut up into chunks and planted like potatoes. From each surviving plant Dr. Schilling was thus able to recover one crown, three or four slips, two or three suckers, and two or three stump sections. By 1910 the pineapple industry was established in Hawaii.

But in 1911 it was overtaken by disaster, for the fields which Wild Whip had so carefully prepared stopped nourishing the plants, and they began to turn a sickly yellow. In panic Whip commanded Dr. Schilling to sober up and find out what was happening, but the drunken Englishman could not focus on the problem, so Whip stormed through the mansion which he now shared with Schilling and smashed all bottles containing alcohol. Then Dr. Schilling pulled himself together and spent some time in the fields. "I must make some experiments," he reported, and a corner of the mansion was given over to test tubes and beakers, but all Schilling was doing was using fresh pineapples for the distillation of a super-fine grade of alcohol which he liked better than whiskey, and he was soon incommunicado.

Wild Whip solved this impasse by beating the Englishman into insensibility, then throwing him into a cold bath. Apparently others had treated Schilling in this manner, for he took no great offense, shivering in the tub and whimpering like a child. "By God," Hoxworth shouted, "you brought these plants here and you'll find out what's wrong with them."

He dressed the gawky scientist, put his shoes on, and personally led the shaky man into the fields. "What's wrong with those plants?" he stormed.

"Look, Brother Hoxworth! You can't stand there and command me to find out what's happened. The human mind doesn't work that way."

"Yours will!" Hoxworth roared.

"Suppose I start to walk down that path and down that road and never look at these plants again. Then what?"

"Then by the time you get to the road, Dr. Schilling, you can't walk. Because both your legs are broken."

"I believe you would," the shaken Englishman said.

"You bet I would," Whip growled. "Now get to work." He stood back, stared in shock, and yelled, "Now what in hell are you doing?"

"I'm tasting the soil," Dr. Schilling replied.

"Oh, for Christ's sake," Whip snorted and left.

It took Dr. Schilling four weeks to make up his mind about the pineapple plants, and when he reported to his employer it was obvious that he himself scarcely believed his own conclusions. "This is extraordinary, Brother Hoxworth, and you won't believe it, but those plants are starved for iron."

"Ridiculous!" Hoxworth stormed. He was sick and tired of this infuriating Englishman and was at last ready to throw him off the plantation.

"No," Dr. Schilling replied soberly. "I'm convinced that they are about to die for lack of iron."

"That's preposterous!" Hoxworth stormed. "This goddamned island is practically solid iron. Look at the soil, man!"

"It's iron, that's true," Schilling agreed. "But I'm afraid it must be iron in some form that the plants cannot use."

"How can they stand in solid iron and not be able to use it?"

"That," Schilling said, "is why the universe will always be a mystery."

"Are you fooling with me?" Hoxworth asked ominously.

"Who would dare?" Schilling replied.

"What do you want us to do?" Hoxworth asked quietly.

"I want to sprinkle iron, in a different kind of solution, over these plants."

"No! It's totally preposterous. You get back out there and find out what's really wrong."

"It's iron," Schilling said stubbornly.

"How can you be sure?"

"I can taste it."

"Have you run any tests on it?"

"No. I don't have to."

"Well, run some tests. No! Don't! You'd just distill yourself some more alcohol. What kind of iron do you want?"

"Iron sulfate."

As a result of this decision, in late 1911 Kamejiro Sakagawa marched through the experimental fields of the Hanakai Pineapple Plantation lugging a bucket of spray, which he directed onto the yellow leaves of the perishing plants, and as he passed, the solution of sulfate of iron ran down the narrow leaves and penetrated to the red soil about the roots. As if by magic the sickly plants began to revive, and within four days the yellow leaves were returning to their natural color. The Cayennes were saved, and when it was proved, as Dr. Schilling suspected, that they had been standing in iron yet starving for iron, Wild Whip joyously gathered up an armful of ripe fruit and tossed it onto the mansion floor.

"Brew yourself some alcohol and stay drunk as long as you like," he commanded.

Sometimes Kamejiro, running to work and running back to tend his hot bath, would not see the tall Englishman for weeks at a time, and then as he cut the lawn he would find Schilling in a basket chair by the side of the cliff, staring down at the play of surf as it struck the opposite rocks.

Schilling was a surprising man, a drunken, besotted individual who could think. One day when he was driving into Kapaa with Whip in one of the first cars on Kauai, he spotted a junk yard and said, "You ought to buy that, Brother Hoxworth."

"That junk? Why?"

"You're paying a lot of money for iron sulfate, and that's what it is. Rusty junk to which sulphuric acid has been applied."

So Whip bought the junk yard and launched an iron sulfate factory, and in later years, when automobiles had become numerous, he bought all the old wrecks on Kauai for four dollars each, piled them up, drenched them with gasoline and burned away the rubber and the horse hair. When what was left had rusted he treated the junk with sulphuric acid and remarked, "Everyone who eats pineapple is eating the handiwork of Henry Ford, God bless him."

But in the growing of pineapple, which brought hundreds of millions of dollars into the territory, when one problem was licked, the next arose, for apparently the Cayenne did not enjoy growing in Hawaii and fell prey to one disaster after another. When the iron problem was solved, the mealy-bug arose, and once more the industry seemed doomed.

The ugly, louselike little bugs were moved from place to place by ants, who tended them like milch cows, living off their sweet, nutritious exudations. Particularly, the mealy-bugs loved pineapple, whose growth they destroyed, and it seemed an act of conscious malevolence when millions of ants hiked several miles to deposit their cows upon the precious pineapples. Dr. Schilling studied the problem for several months, while field after field of Wild Whip's choicest Cayennes wilted and died from the infestation. Then he hit upon a dual solution which halted the mealy-bugs: around each field he planted decoy rows of pineapple, and these intercepted the mealy-bugs and kept them from invading the productive areas; and around the entire field he laid long boards soaked repeatedly in creosote, and these fended off the ants and their ugly cows. After this victory over the little lice he subsided into a year-long lethargy of drunkenness, awaiting the next disaster.

It came when Whip's canning manager reported: "Because the Cayennes are so big we can't fit them into the cans, and waste forty per cent of the fruit trimming them down to can size."

"What in hell do you want me to do?" Whip snarled, wearied by the constant battle to keep his fields productive.

"What we've got to have is smaller Cayennes," the manager explained.

So Wild Whip stormed back to Hanakai, shook his English expert into reasonable sobriety, and said, "Dr. Schilling, you've got to make the pineapples smaller."

Through a golden haze that had been accumulating for thirteen months the scraggly Englishman said, "The mind of man can accomplish anything. Draw me the pineapple you want."

Whip went back to the canning manager, and together they drew on paper the specifications of the perfect pineapple. It had to be sufficiently barrel-shaped to leave a good rim of fruit when the core was cut out. It had to be juicy, acid, sweet, small, without barbs on the leaves, solid and golden in color. With a ruler and French curves the two men constructed the desired fruit, and when Whip thrust the paper at Schilling he said, "That's what we want."

Schilling, glad to have an alternative to drunkenness, replied, "That's what you'll get." He inspected every pineapple field on Kauai, comparing the available fruit against the ideal image, and whenever he found something close to the printed specifications, he marked that plant with a flag, and after four years of this infinitely patient work he announced, "We have built the perfect pineapple." When he delivered the first truckload to the cannery, the manager was ecstatic. "Our problems are over," he said.

"Until the next one," Schilling replied.

In 1911 a woman writer from New York, who had once stayed in Honolulu four weeks, wrote a rather scurrilous book about Hawaii in which she lamented three things: the influence of the missionaries who had maliciously killed off the Hawaiians by dressing them in Mother Hubbards; the criminality of companies like Janders & Whipple who had imported Orientals; and the avarice of missionary descendants like those in Hoxworth & Hale who had stolen the lush lands of Hawaii. After her book had created something of a sensation throughout America she returned to the islands and in triumph came to Kauai, where at a splendid polo tournament she was presented to Wild Whip Hoxworth. His team had just defeated Honolulu, and he was flushed with victory and should have been in a gracious mood, but as he was introduced to the lady author he thought he understood who she was and asked coldly, "Are you the good lady who wrote *Hawaii's Shame?*"

"Yes," she replied proudly, "I am," for she was accustomed to being fawned over. "What did you think of it?"

"Ma'am," Whip said, carefully placing his polo mallet on a rack lest he be tempted to use it in an unorthodox manner, "I thought your book was complete bullshit."

The polo players and their ladies recoiled from Whip's savage comment, and some began to offer the startled lady their apologies, but

Whip interrupted. "No, there will be no apologies. Stand where you are, ma'am, and look in every direction. Whatever you see was brought into these islands by men like me. The sugar upon which our economy rests? My Grandfather Whipple, a missionary, brought that in. The pineapples? I'm the grandson of missionaries and I brought them in. The pine trees, the royal palms, the tulip trees, the avocados, the wild plum, the crotons, the house and the horses. We brought them all in. The Hoxworth mango, best fruit in the world, is named after me. And as for the Orientals. Heh, Kamejiro, you come, eh? This bandy-legged little man has done more work in Hawaii . . . he's built more and he will continue to build more than a dozen of the people you were wailing about. I brought him in here and I'm proud of it. I'm only sorry he doesn't intend to stay. Now, ma'am, if you have any more questions about Hawaii, I'd be glad to answer 'em. Because I hope you'll go home and write another book, and this time not be such a horse's ass."

He bowed and left her gagging. In Honolulu, of course, his polo-field speech, as it was termed, was a momentary sensation, since, as one of the Hale women explained, "If one were picking a man to defend the missionaries, he would hardly pick Wild Whip."

He and his drunken English friend lived on at Hanakai, with fairly frequent visits to the brothels at Kapaa. At the cliffside mansion he entertained a good deal, and in his leisurely talks over brandy he began to expound the first coherent theory of Hawaii: "What I visualize is an island community that treasures above all else its agricultural lands. On them it grows bulk crops of sugar and pineapple and ships them to the mainland in H & H ships. With the money we get we buy the manufactured goods our people need, things like iceboxes, automobiles, finished lumber, hardware and food. Thus the ships go one way loaded and come back loaded. That's the destiny of Hawaii, and anyone who disturbs that fine balance is an enemy of the islands."

He was willing to identify the enemies of Hawaii: "Anyone who tampers with our shipping ought to be shot. Anyone who tries to talk radical ideas to our field hands ought to be run off the islands. Anyone who interferes with our assured supply of cheap labor from Asia strikes a blow at sugar and pineapple."

Once he confided: "H & H have run the ships cheaply and faithfully. I see no reason why any radical changes are required. And I think you must admit that J & W have run the plantations well. Nobody can lodge a complaint against them. As long as these two firms continue to serve the islands justly, it seems to me the welfare of Hawaii is assured, and for outsiders like that goddamned woman author to go around raising a lot of questions is downright ingratitude."

In 1912 the campaign for President on the mainland grew rather warm, and for the first time in some years Democrats felt that they had a good chance of sending their man, Woodrow Wilson, to the White

House. Of course, citizens of Hawaii could not vote for the national offices, but in the island elections a few pathetic Democrats began to parrot the optimism existing on the mainland, and one misguided liberal even went so far as to appear before a mass meeting of six in the nearby town of Kapaa. Out of sheer curiosity over a human being who dared to be a Democrat in Hawaii, Wild Whip insinuated himself as the seventh listener and stood appalled as the man actually sought votes for his party: "There is a new spirit abroad in America, a clean, sharp wind from the prairies, an insistent voice from the great cities. Therefore I propose to do something that has never before been done in these islands. I, a Democrat and proud of the fact, am going to visit each of the sugar and pineapple plantations to explain in my words what the ideas of Woodrow Wilson and his adherents mean. Tell your friends that I'll be there."

In some agitation Wild Whip rode home and carefully took down all the firearms he kept at Hanakai. Inspecting each, he summoned his lunas and said, "I just heard a Democrat say he was coming here to address our workmen. If he steps six inches onto Hanakai, shoot him."

One of the lunas who had been through high school asked deferentially, "But doesn't he have the right to speak?"

"Right?" Whip thundered. "A Democrat have the right to step onto my plantation and spread his poison? My God! I say who shall come here and who shall not. This is my land and I'll have no alien ideas parading across it."

Lunas in 1912 were not apt to be easily frightened, and this one stuck to his guns. "But if this man is a spokesman for one of the political parties . . ."

"Von Schlemm!" Whip roared in profound amazement. "I'm astonished at such talk from you. Can't you remember what that filthy Democrat, Grover Cleveland, did to Hawaii? Are you old enough to recall how those corrupted Democratic senators voted against us time and again? What surprises me is that somebody hasn't already shot this dirty little bastard. No Democrat has a place in Hawaii, and if one tries to walk onto my plantation he'll crawl home with broken legs."

The aspiring politician did try to invade Hanakai, and Wild Whip, backed up by four heavily armed lunas, met him at the edge of the red-dust road. "You can't come in here, mister," Whip warned.

"I'm a citizen in pursuit of my political rights."

"You're a Democrat, and there's no place for you in these islands."

"Mr. Hoxworth, I'm coming to your plantation to speak to your men about the issues in the election."

"My men don't want to hear the nonsense you talk."

"Mr. Hoxworth, there's a new wind blowing across America. Woodrow Wilson is going to be elected President. And he promises a fair deal for all men. Even your workmen."

"I tell my workmen how to vote," Whip explained. "And they vote for the welfare of these islands. Now you go back to Honolulu and don't give me any more trouble." The four lunas moved in upon the visitor.

"How is it going to sound," the politician asked, "if I report to the press that I was forcibly thrown off Hanakai Plantation?"

Wild Whip, still lean and hard at fifty-five, reached forward, grabbed the offensive radical by the shoulders, and shook him as if he were a child. "No paper would publish such rubbish. Christ, if a rattlesnake tried to crawl onto my plantation and I shot it, I'd be a hero. I feel obligated to treat a Democrat the same way. Get out."

The visitor calmly smoothed his shirt, straightened his sleeves, and announced: "In pursuit of man's inalienable rights, I am going to come into your plantation."

"If you try it," Whip said, "you'll be thrown out on your inalienable ass."

The politician walked boldly onto the red soil of Hanakai and started for the lane of royal palms and Norfolk pines. He had gone only a few steps when the four lunas grabbed him, lifted him in the air, and threw him roughly back onto the road, where he fell heavily upon the inalienable portion of his anatomy, as Whip had predicted. While the surprised visitor sat in the red dust Whip advised him: "Go back to Honolulu. No Democrat will ever be allowed on this plantation."

But when the man had gone, Whip began to appreciate the real danger involved, so he summoned his lunas. "You are to tell every man on this plantation entitled to a vote that he is not to bother voting for this man or that. He's to vote the straight Republican ticket. One cross mark is all he needs."

"We can warn them," one luna pointed out, "but can we enforce it?"

"There's a way," Whip replied cryptically, and when the local elections came that year he stationed himself six feet from the Hanakai voting booth and as each of his qualified laborers approached he looked the man in the eye and said, "You know how to vote, don't you, Jackson?"

"Yes, sir, Mr. Hoxworth."

"See that you do it," Whip replied ominously, but he left nothing to chance. When Jackson was in the booth, with the protecting canvas about him so that no one could spy upon his ballot or the way he marked it, he reached for the voting pencil. It was tied to the end of a piece of string which led aloft, passing through an eyelet screwed into the ceiling of the booth, so that if he was about to mark his ballot Democratic, the string was ready to form a clear angle to the far right and thus betray his perfidy. But to make doubly sure, Whip had previously ordered that all pencils used for voting be of maximum hardness, and that the paper on the shelf in the voting booth be soft, so that when Jackson voted he was forced to punch his pencil strongly onto the ballot, leaving on the back side an easily read indication of how he had voted. Jackson folded his ballot and handed it to the Portuguese clerk, but that official paused before placing it in the ballot box, and in that moment Wild Whip was free to inspect the back.

"All right, Jackson," Whip muttered as the man left.

As soon as the voting was over, Whip assembled his lunas and reported: "Jackson, Allingham and Cates voted Democratic. Get them out of here before midnight."

"What shall we tell them?"

"Nothing. They know the evil they've done."

And he stood in the shadows of the royal palms as the three traitors were thrown onto the public road, their bundles of goods under their arms.

It was as a result of this election, and the dangers represented by it —Wilson ruling in Washington, men like Jackson beginning to vote Democratic on Kauai—that Wild Whip made his decision. "I'm going back to Honolulu," he told Dr. Schilling. "You're welcome to live here and take care of the pineapples."

"What are you intending to do?" Schilling asked.

"There's a spirit of rebellion in the world. Crazy liberal thinking. Probably infected my own company. I'm going back to take over control of H & H."

"I thought they threw you out? Exiled you?"

"They did," Wild Whip confessed. "But in those days I didn't own the company."

"Do you now?"

"Yes, but the Yale men running it don't know it."

"You going to chop off a lot of heads?" Schilling asked with the fiendish joy of childhood.

"Not if they're good men," Whip replied, disappointing his permanent guest. And by Christmas Eve, 1912, he was in sole, dictatorial control of the great H & H empire, and although heads did not roll in the Schilling sense of the word, every man who was suspected of having voted Democratic was fired. "In Hawaii and in H & H," Whip explained without rancor, "there is simply no place for such men."

ANY GENERAL CONCLAVE of the great Kee hui was apt to be impressive. The older sons, like Asia, who ran the restaurant, retained their Chinese names—Kee Ah Chow—and wore pigtails and black sateen suits; but the younger sons cut their pigtails and wore contemporary American dress. They also preferred the English translations of their names, such as Australia Kee instead of Kee Oh Chow.

When the hui converged upon the ugly house up Nuuanu, they formed colorful processions. Some brought their wives and by 1908 were able to bring grown grandsons along with their pretty Chinese and Hawaiian wives. On festive occasions great-grandchildren appeared in number, tumbling about the grounds on which the family still grew taro and pineapples. The Kees, counting their wives and husbands, now numbered ninety-seven, but of course they were never able to convene at one time, because a dozen or so were apt to be at school on the mainland. Neither Yale nor Harvard had yet known a Kee, but Michigan, Chicago, Columbia and Pennsylvania did, and it was possible for a Chinese in Hawaii to be born, financed, protected at law, married, tended medically and buried—all at the hands of Kees. In addition, he could rent his land from them, and buy his vegetables, his meat and his clothes.

The most conspicuous member was still Nyuk Tsin. In 1908 she was sixty-one years old, and although she no longer lugged pineapples through the streets in her famous twin baskets, she still grew them and supervised others in the peddling. Year by year she grew shorter, thinner, balder, and although her face showed the wrinkling of age, her mind retained the resilience of youth. Her life consisted of purposeful ritual. Each year, with solemn dignity, she accompanied her brilliant son Africa to the tax office to pay her taxes. Twice a year she took eight or ten members of her family to the Punti store where they sent money to her husband's real wife in China. She had died in 1881, but the family in the Low Village continued to write letters of grateful acknowledgment on her behalf. Every two or three years Nyuk Tsin assembled as many of her family as possible for the trip to the leper colony at Kalawao, where they reported to their ancestor. And each fall, as if she were sending sacrifices to the gods, she took six or eight of her ablest grandsons down to the Hoxworth & Hale docks and bought them tickets for the mainland. The old woman conserved human resources just as carefully as she had the irrigated land of her first taro patch.

Therefore, it was she who now called the great hui into formal meeting, for two matters of prime importance, and far beyond the capacity of lawyer Africa to solve, had been brought to her attention; and while her great-grandchildren played in the dusty yard she talked to the thirty-odd elders who met with her.

The children of Africa Kee needed guidance, and Nyuk Tsin said, "Africa's oldest daughter, Sheong Mun, whom you prefer to call Ellen, is in deep perplexity, and I am not wise enough to counsel her."

"What has she done?" Asia's wife asked.

"She has fallen in love with a haole," Nyuk Tsin replied. A hush fell over the assembly, for although the Kees, under Nyuk Tsin's approval if not her outright urging, had always felt free to marry Hawaiians, none had yet made any signs of wanting to marry white Americans, and Ellen's bold proposal represented a jolt in family procedures. The clan turned to look at Africa's daughter, a bright-eyed, quick, handsome girl of twenty, and she looked back.

"Who is the white man?" Asia asked, exercising his prerogative as oldest son.

"Tell him, Sheong Mun," the old woman said.

In a soft voice taught her by the women teachers at the Episcopalian school, Ellen said, "He is a junior officer on one of the navy ships at Pearl Harbor."

A chorus of gasps came from the hui. A white man and a military man, too! This was indeed, as Wu Chow's Auntie had warned, a major problem, and Europe, who had married a Hawaiian girl, said, "It's bad enough to want to marry a white man, because they don't make good husbands and they take money out of the family. But to marry a military man is really indecent. No self-respecting girl . . ."

Australia interrupted: "We're not in China. I know some fine navy men."

Europe replied stiffly: "I don't."

Asia observed: "I had hoped never to see one of my family want to marry a soldier."

Australia snapped: "He's a sailor, and there's a big difference."

Europe said: "Military men are military men, and they make miserable husbands."

Australia cried: "Why don't you take those ideas back to China? That's where they came from."

At this, Nyuk Tsin intervened and said in her low, imperative voice, "It would be much better if Sheong Mun had fallen in love with a Chinese boy, or if she had come to me as a dutiful girl and said, 'Wu Chow's Auntie, find me a husband.' But she has done neither of these things."

"The worse for her," Asia said sadly. "In my restaurant I see many girls who stray from the old patterns, and they all suffer for it."

"Ridiculous!" Australia's wife snapped. "Asia! You know very well that when I was a girl I used to hide in your restaurant and kiss Australia behind the dried ducks. And nothing bad came of it except that I married your lazy brother."

"That was the beginning of what I'm talking about," Asia warned.

"Ridiculous!" Australia's wife, a high-spirited Ching beauty, laughed. "Because do you know who used to whistle at me to let me know your brother was waiting?" The Kees looked at the bright-eyed young wife, and with a dramatic gesture she pointed directly at Nyuk Tsin, sitting gray-haired and solemn at the head of the family. "That one did it! She's worse than any of us!"

The family roared at the old woman's embarrassment, and finally Nyuk Tsin wiped her blushing face and said softly, "I must admit I arranged it. But remember that Ching Siu Han was a Chinese girl. And a Hakka. And could be trusted. Today we are talking about something much different. A white man. And a soldier."

"Wu Chow's Auntie!" Ellen interrupted. "He's not a soldier. You must forget your old prejudices."

Asia asked, "Will he bring any land into our hui? Any money?"

"No," Ellen said resolutely. "In fact, he'll take money out. Because I have got to have two hundred dollars for clothes and more later for other things."

Together the Kees sucked in their breath and faced the day they had long feared. Sooner or later, some member of the family would want to marry a white man. Now it had come and those who dreaded the event suspected that Africa with the radical new ideas he had acquired at Michigan must somehow be at fault. Therefore, the older members of the family began staring at the lawyer, and he suffered from their harsh gaze. Finally Europe asked brusquely, "Tell us, Africa. What do you think of this?"

There was a long hush in the hot room, and voices of children could be heard. Finally Africa spoke. "I am humiliated," he said. "I am ashamed that it is my daughter who wants to marry outside our circle of acquaintance. I have given her a good education and her mother has tried to teach her to be a decent Hakka. I am humiliated and I do not know what to do." Suddenly the pressure upon him became great and he hid his face in his hands, sobbing quietly. The disgrace he had brought upon the family immobilized his speech, so his wife added, "He feels that he must accept the shame for what his daughter has done."

At this solemn moment Australia interjected a happier note. "Of course it's his responsibility. If a man goes to Michigan, he picks up foreign ways. I suppose that's why we sent him to Michigan. Remember, Asia, it was your sons who went to Pennsylvania. It was your sons who brought American friends into our homes, and it was one of those friends who met Sheong Mun. Bang! They're in love! Ellen, if your stingy father won't give you the two hundred dollars I will."

"It isn't the money that I want so much, Uncle Australia, as your blessing."

"You have mine!"

"And mine!" Australia's wife chimed.

"Have I yours, Wu Chow's Auntie?"

The family turned to look at Nyuk Tsin, sitting with her worn hands in her lap. "I am concerned with only one problem, Sheong Mun," the old woman said. "When your children are born they will be the children of a white man, and they will be lost to our family. Promise me that you will send me a letter each time you have a child, and I will go to the Punti scholar and find his true name, and we will write it in our book and send the name back to China, as we have always done."

"My sons will not want Chinese names," hard-headed Ellen countered.

"Later they will," the old woman said. "They will want to know who they are, and in the book the information will be waiting for them."

As the Kees dispersed over the face of the world, marrying with men who worked in strange lands, letters arrived constantly for Nyuk Tsin. Her sons would read them to her, and she would note the births of all children. For each son she got a proper name, and registered it in China, and as she predicted this day in 1908, the time did come when the boy so named would want to know what the Chinese half of his ancestry signified, and men would arrive in Honolulu whom you would not recognize as Chinese, and they would meet old Nyuk Tsin, and she would take down a book she could not read, and the interpreter would pick out the information and the Chinese-German-Irish-English boy would understand a little better who he was.

But on this particular day the old woman was concerned with Africa's children, and after it had been grudgingly agreed that the lawyer's daughter, Kee Sheong Mun, known locally as Ellen Kee, could marry her sailor, Nyuk Tsin coughed and said, "It is time we think again about getting Hong Kong into Punahou."

Asia groaned, America rose and left the room in disgust, and the rest of the family turned to stare at Africa's youngest son, a square-headed, wrinkle-eyed boy of fifteen. Among the family it was believed that young Koon Kong, who was known as Hong Kong, had inherited his father's intellectual brilliance. He was most able at figures, knew Punti, Hakka, English and Hawaiian well, and seemed unusually gifted at managing money, for he augmented whatever he got hold of by lending it out to his numerous cousins. His rate of interest was a standard, inflexible ten per cent a week which he enforced by meticulous collections on Friday after school. As his name Koon indicated, he was of the fourth generation—Koon Kong, Earth's Atmosphere—and he was of the earth. In his generation of Kees there were twenty-seven boys carrying the name Koon, one brother and twenty-six cousins, and he was the cleverest of them all. If any Kee was ever going to elbow his way into Punahou, Hong Kong was the one, and as the problem opened for discussion, the family grew tense.

"Will Hong Kong's mother tell us how her son is doing in school?" the matriarch began.

Mrs. Africa Kee, the older of the striking Ching girls, said, "His marks have been excellent. His behavior has been spirited but has brought no reprimand. I am proud of my son's accomplishment and feel that he merits the interest the family is taking in him."

"Does Hong Kong think he can do the work at Punahou . . . if he is accepted?" Nyuk Tsin asked.

The boy was embarrassed by the attention focused on him, but he yearned to get into Punahou, so he bore the indignity. Hunching up one shoulder he said, "If the Lum boy can do the work, I can do the work."

At the mention of the Lum boy, the Kees grew bitter. For a dozen years they had been trying to get one of their sons into Punahou, Hawaii's source of excellence, but for one reason or another they had never succeeded, even though they were a fairly wealthy family and could boast of Africa as a leading professional man. Yet the Lums, who really did not amount to much except that their father was a dentist and a man who loved to speak in public, had maneuvered one of their boys into the cherished haven.

Nyuk Tsin said, "I think that this time we really have a good chance. I have asked a dear old friend to counsel with us as to what we must do to get Hong Kong accepted." She gave a signal and a grandson ran out to bring back a tall, bald Englishman with outrageous white mustaches and a flamboyant energy that projected him into the hot room, where he kissed Nyuk Tsin and cried in flowery Chinese: "Ah ha! We plot against the white people! Strike the tocsin! China shall rise!"

It was Uliassutai Karakoram Blake, the mad schoolteacher and the trusted friend of all Chinese. He was older and stouter but no more subdued, and now he locked his hands behind his neck, rocking to and fro as if he were going to fall over. "Beloved and prolific Kees," he said, "let us face the truth. There are good schools and there are great schools, and every family is entitled to send his ablest sons to the greatest. Iolani, where I slave for a pittance, is a good school. Punahou is a great school. It lends authority and glamour and caste. England is built on such foundations and so is Hawaii. Let a man use a wrong knife, and he is condemned to the Liberal Party for life."

"What's he talking about?" one of Australia's boys whispered.

"I'm talking about you!" Uliassutai Karakoram Blake shouted in English, flailing his arms out and thrusting his head a few inches from the face of the startled young Chinese. "Stand up!" Awkwardly the boy rose and Blake pointed at him as if he were an exhibit.

"Behold the scion of the Kee hui," he said in erudite Chinese. "He has done well at Iolani School, but he has not yet been accepted at Punahou. He is therefore limited to a perpetual secondary acceptance in Honolulu. He cannot associate with the men who rule the city. He cannot learn to speak with their inflections. He lacks their peculiar polish. And he must remain the rest of his life a Chinese peasant. Sit down!"

Blake turned his back on the boy and said to the elders, "The compassionate Buddha knows that at Iolani I have given you Chinese the salt of my blood and the convolutions of my brain, and I have raised you from ignorance into light, and the compassionate Buddha also knows that I wish I had done half as well with my light as you wonderful people have done with yours. If I had, I wouldn't now be toiling out the evening years of my life as an underpaid schoolmaster. Africa, how much did you earn last year?"

The Chinese loved this ridiculous man and his circumlocutions. With his British regard for proprieties and his Oriental love of bombast, he seemed Chinese, and now he got to the meat of his visit: "You might think that I, as an Iolani teacher who had brought Hong Kong to this point of his education, would object to the proposal that you now transfer him to Punahou. Not at all. A family like yours is entitled to have a son at the best school Hawaii can provide. There he will rub elbows with future lawyers, business giants, community leaders. If I were a Kee, I would suffer any humiliation to get my son into Punahou. Hong Kong, stand up. I tell you, Kees, there is as fine a boy as Hawaii has ever produced. He merits the best. Hong Kong, depart."

When the embarrassed boy had gone, Uliassutai Karakoram said, "Wu Chow's Auntie, it will be very difficult indeed for you to get that boy into Punahou. He's too intelligent, and your family is too able. The white people want to have one or two Chinese in their school, but not the best. They prefer slow, stolid boys of no great imagination. The Lum boy is ideal. Hong Kong is not, because even Buddha himself would refuse to prophesy what Hong Kong may one day accomplish. Africa, are you aware that you have sired a revolutionary genius?"

"Hong Kong has far more power than I ever had, Mr. Blake," Africa confessed to his old teacher.

"Wu Chow's Auntie!" Uliassutai Karakoram pleaded suddenly. "Would you not consider trying to get some other grandson into Punahou?"

"No," Nyuk Tsin replied evenly. "He is a brilliant boy. He deserves the best."

The big Englishman shrugged his shoulders and said, "If you're determined to go against my advice, let's see what evil tricks you ought to attempt this time. Who visited Punahou last time?"

Mrs. Africa Kee, a handsome, modern Chinese wife, raised her hand. "Stand up!" Blake snapped. He studied her carefully, dressed as she was in western style, and said, "Couldn't we send someone a little less . . . modern? White people feel safer when an Oriental looks more like a coolie."

There were some things the Kees would not tolerate, which was what made them a significant family, and now Africa said simply, "If my son applies to Punahou, his mother goes with him."

"May Buddha bless all stubborn people," Blake said magniloquently, "for without them this would be a most miserable world. But could not your wife dress a little more inconspicuously? She must look prosperous enough to pay the tuition, yet not so self-assured that she would ever say anything in a meeting of the children's parents. We want her to look unalterably Chinese, yet aspiring to become a decent American. We want her to look proud enough to clean her fingernails, yet humble enough to remain slightly stooped over as if she lugged baskets of pineapples about the town." He bowed grandly to Nyuk

Tsin and said, "Do you think your son's wife can acquire the proper look of a Chinese appealing to white people for help?"

"No," Nyuk Tsin said coldly.

"I thought not," Blake said sadly. "Then you are prepared for Hong Kong to be rejected again?"

At this point America, whose two sons had tried in vain to enter Punahou, returned to the meeting and growled, "We are prepared to be rejected forever, Mr. Blake."

"I am sorry that you were not all born a little more stupid," the flamboyant Englishman said, "because then, with your money, you'd be accepted gracefully. But of course, if you had been more stupid . . . that one in particular," and he pointed at Nyuk Tsin, "why you wouldn't have the money you now have, and you would be kept out of Punahou on grounds of poverty."

"Do you think Hong Kong has a chance this time?" Nyuk Tsin pleaded.

"No," Blake said. "If I were a white man in Honolulu, I would never allow one of you damned Kees anywhere. You're smart. You work. You gang together. You're ambitious. First thing you know you'll be teaching your daughters to lure white men into marriage."

"Sheong Mun is going to marry a naval officer," Nyuk Tsin said softly.

In the hot room Uliassutai Karakoram Blake stopped ranting. He looked at the fresh, handsome child he had once taught. Little Ellen Kee, who could sing so charmingly. Gravely he went up to her, kissed her on the cheeks and said, quietly, "May the compassionate Buddha have mercy upon us all. The years of our lives are so short and the currents of the world are so strong. Good-bye, dear Kees. You will not get into Punahou . . . not this time."

When he was gone the elders of the family considered the many ideas he had proposed, and Nyuk Tsin said, "That strange man is right. Hong Kong's mother does look too modern, as if she were forcing her way upon the haoles. It will be too easy to reject her. This time we really must send someone else. How about Europe's wife? She's Hawaiian."

"No!" Africa cried. "He is my son, and he will report to Punahou with his own mother, and if they reject us again, let it be so."

"This time, then, I will go along," Nyuk Tsin announced. "I will be barefooted and I will represent the old ways."

"No!" Africa protested again. "My wife, who will dress as she pleases, will take my son to Punahou and seek admission. I will tolerate no subterfuges."

"Africa," the old matriarch said softly, "the school has shown that it will accept one or two Chinese. Now it is terribly important that one of our boys be chosen. Please, this time allow me to arrange things."

"I have business on the Big Island," Africa said solemnly. "I shall go there and bear no part of this humiliation." He left the room and the clan breathed more easily, for he was a stubborn man.

"Now, when the Lums got their son into Punahou," Nyuk Tsin counseled, "the boy's mother wore a very plain dress, and her hair straight back, and she kept her eyes on the floor. I am therefore going to say flatly that Hong Kong's mother cannot go this time."

"I will go with my husband to the Big Island," Africa's wife announced, and she too left the plotters.

After much discussion, and after carefully studying the devices by which earlier Chinese families had managed to get sons into Punahou, the Kees hit upon an involved strategy. Barefoot Nyuk Tsin would go in smock and pants to give the proper coolie touch. Europe's wife would go as a pure-blooded Hawaiian to show that the Kees respected local traditions. And Australia's wife, the pretty Ching girl, would go in a very modest western-style dress to prove that the family knew how to eat with a knife and fork. The boy Hong Kong, who had an intellectual ability four levels higher than anyone then studying at Punahou, would tag along in a carefully selected suit that bespoke both the ability to pay tuition and a quiet gentility not common among newly rich Chinese families.

It was a hot day when the four Kees drove up to Punahou in a rented carriage, it having been decided that this was slightly more propitious than walking, and in the interview the three women played their roles to perfection, but Hong Kong squinted slightly and thought just a little too long before answering questions, brilliant though his replies were, and in due time the family got the news: "We regret that this year, due to overcrowded conditions, we can find no place for your son, whose marks and general deportment seemed otherwise acceptable."

The letter was delivered to Africa in his law offices, and he sat for a long time pondering it. At first he was consumed with rage at the humiliation his family had willingly undergone, and then he spent about an hour shoving the formal letter about his desk into this position and that. Finally he summoned his son and waited until the boy came in breathless from play along the river. In even, unimpassioned tones he said, "Hong Kong, you will not go back to school any more."

"I thought you said I was to go to Michigan."

"No. What you require to learn, son, you can learn right here. Tonight you will start reading this book on Hawaiian land systems. When you're through I'll give you your examination . . . sitting in that chair. Are those your schoolbooks?"

"Yes."

"You'll never need them again." Slowly Africa Kee, who loved education, took the books and tore them apart. Throwing them into the wastebasket he said, "When you study your new book you are to memorize the end of every chapter. Hong Kong, you're going to get an education that no man in Hawaii has ever had before."

Ultimately, of course, the Kees did squeeze a boy into Punahou. It happened in a most peculiar way. In 1910 the Republican Party had difficulty finding the right man to run for the legislature from Chinatown and somebody made the radical proposal, "Why don't we run a Chinaman?"

"Oh, no!" one of the Hewlett boys protested. "I don't want that radical Africa Kee in government."

"I wasn't thinking of him. I was thinking of his brother Australia."

A hush fell over the caucus and smiles began to play upon the faces of the white men who ran the islands, for Australia was a man whom men could like. He wasn't too bright, played a good ukulele, was honest, didn't have too much education but did have a host of friends among both the Chinese and the Hawaiians, with whom he had been reared. Furthermore, he had an appealing nickname, Kangaroo Kee, and without even taking a vote the caucus decided that he was their man.

Kangaroo Kee was elected by a huge majority and kept on getting elected, and in time he became the leading Chinese in the Republican Party, a man everyone loved and trusted. Fortunately, he had a son who like himself was gloriously average, and in 1912 Punahou felt that at last it had found a Kee who could be safely admitted to the school.

On the day this boy enrolled, Nyuk Tsin walked secretly to the entrance of the school and hid behind one of the palms to watch one of her grandsons at last enter the great school. As she saw the bright faces of the haole children gathering for the beginning of the new term, chatting of vacation experiences, she recognized here a Hale and there a Whipple, and thought: "The white people are crazy to allow Chinese in this school. This is the secret of how they rule the islands and they have a right to protect their interests."

Then, coming up the street, she saw her grandson walking with his father, the politician Kangaroo Kee, and she withdrew into the shadows, mumbling to herself, "This boy knows nothing. He is not worthy of this great school. But he is our beginning."

FOR THIRTEEN YEARS Kamejiro Sakagawa rose every morning at three-thirty to cut wild plum, storing it for his hot bath. He then ran to work, labored till sunset, ran home and lighted his fire. He now charged two cents for the first ten men to enjoy the clean hot water, a penny each for all who cared to follow. Over the course of a year he obviously earned quite a few dollars, and like all the Japanese laboring on Hanakai he watched with excitement as his hidden funds reached toward the mystic number: $400.

From the arrival of the first Japanese back in the 1880's, it had been agreed that a man who could return to Hiroshima with $400 in cash could thenceforth live like a samurai. "With four hundred dollars," the workmen assured one another, "a man could buy three good rice fields, build a large house, get all the kimonos you would ever need, and live in splendor." Every plantation laborer was determined that he would be the man to accumulate the $400, and almost none did.

It was appalling how the money slipped through the fingers of a well-intentioned man. In Kamejiro's case his weaknesses were neither gambling nor women nor alcohol; no, his were far more expensive—friendship and patriotism—and they kept depleting his funds. If a workman faced what appeared to be an insoluble crisis, he went at last to Kamejiro and said bluntly, "I have got to have eighty-one cents."

"Why don't you borrow from the Japanese money lender in Kapaa?" Kamejiro asked.

"In Kapaa if you borrow eighty-one cents, next payday you have to pay back the loan and eighty-one cents more," the workman explained, and he was correct. No white man in Hawaii ever abused Oriental labor as viciously as the Orientals themselves did. Men close to the Japanese consulate had organized a racket whereby incoming workmen were required to pay a deposit to safeguard their papers for eventual return to Japan, and the substantial sums of money were kept year after year with no interest, and when the time came to leave, the deposit often could not be found, and some Japanese became very rich. At every point, vicious practices gnawed away the financial security of the workmen, and interest rates of one hundred per cent a month were common. So usually, rugged little Kamejiro had to cough up the money for his friends.

Some of the Japanese men had begun to bring brides in from Japan, and this was always costly, throwing unusual burdens upon the whole community. There were photographs to be taken in Kapaa, fares to be paid, travel to Honolulu to complete the paper work, and store-bought black suits in which to be married. The amount of connubial bliss underwritten by stalwart Kamejiro was considerable; and this was a self-defeating game, because he found that as soon as a man and woman got together, there were apt to be babies which caused further financial crises. There was thus a constant drain upon his resources and at times it seemed as if he were paying for the family happiness of everyone but himself.

His biggest expenditures, however, arose from patriotism. If a priest came through Kauai telling of a new war memorial, Kamejiro was the man who contributed most heavily. When consular officials from Honolulu appeared to explain the great events transpiring in the homeland, Kamejiro paid their hotel bills. He contributed to the Japanese school, to the Japanese church, and above all to the Japanese reciters who passed through the islands periodically.

These men were the joy of Kamejiro's life, and whenever one was announced he worked with greater speed, impatient for the Sunday afternoon when the entire Japanese community would gather in some park of casuarina trees, sitting on beds of dried needles to wait for the appearance of the reciter. At one-thirty, after the Japanese had enjoyed their lunch of sushi and sashimi, a movable platform of boards, covered by a traditional cloth, was put into position, with a low lectern bearing a closed fan. A hush fell over the crowd, and the visitor from Japan, usually an elderly man with bald head and wide-shouldered starched uniform whose points swept out like butterfly wings, stepped onto the platform in white tabi, bowed many times, and sat on his haunches before the lectern. For some moments he seemed to pray that his voice would be strong, and then, as his audience waited breathless in the sunlight, he picked up the folded fan and began chanting.

"I . . . shall . . . speak . . . of . . . the . . . Battle . . . of . . . Ichi-no-tani," he cried in mournful voice, singing each pregnant word and holding onto it. In those first moments he seemed like an imprisoned volcano, about to burst into wild fury, and as the events of that battle, which had taken place more than seven hundred years before, began to unfold, the man's voice began to acquire new force. He projected himself into each of the characters in turn; he was the brave warrior Kumagai; he was the handsome youth Atsumori; he was the horse, the cliff, the flute; he was the brilliant hero Yoshitsune; and all the women. As his excitement grew, the veins of his head stood out as if they might burst and his neck muscles could be seen like pencils under the skin. At the various crises of the ancient battle, he roared and whispered, sobbed and screamed with joy; but when it came time for Atsumori to die—this bewitching young warrior playing a flute—the man reported grief as if it were a tangible thing, and the entire audience wept.

How terribly real was the heroism of Japan, there under the casuarina trees. How fair and loyal the women were, how brave the men. And as the battle drew to its tragic conclusion, with the plantation hands sobbing for the lost dead, the reciter added lines that were not originally part of the epic, but which he had been told were especially appropriate for distant colonies like this one on Kauai: "And . . . as . . . the . . . ghost . . . of . . . Atsumori . . . left . . . the . . . plain . . . of . . . Ichi-no-tani," the reciter cried mournfully, "he looked back upon the gallant warriors who had slain him and thought: 'These are the brave soldiers of Japan, and while they live there is no danger to the homeland. They can march for miles through hardship. They can live on nothing to support their emperor. They fear no enemy and withdraw from no storm. They are the bravest men on earth, fighting for just causes and the glory of Japan. How strong they are, how noble, how fine it is to see them on the battlefield. Oh, how I long to be with them again, the brave warriors of Japan.' "

A program consisted of four recitations, and since each lasted more than an hour, with famous ones like *Ichi-no-tani* requiring nearly two, the afternoon usually crept on toward darkness before the recital ended. How one man, taking so many varied parts and throwing his voice up and down the scale as if by magic, could last five hours was always a mystery, but in time a convention grew up at the Hanakai readings which made the last item on the program the best of all. It was initiated when a reciter announced: "Today I have a special reward! The story of Colonel Ito, who threw himself upon the Russian guns at Port Arthur." And someone remembered that their own Sakagawa Kamejiro had once played the role of Colonel Ito in the victory procession in Honolulu, and he was sent to fetch his uniform; so while the reciter told the impassioned story of Colonel Ito and the Russian guns, Kamejiro, five-feet-one-inch tall and with arms like hoops, stood rigidly at attention beside the platform, wearing the Imperial uniform which had been sewed up by the women of Honolulu. At such moments a strange thing occurred; he became Colonel Ito. He could see the Russian guns and smell their powder. When the emperor spoke as the troops were leaving Tokyo, Kamejiro could hear the august words, and when the colonel died, defending Japan against the barbarians, Kamejiro died, too, and entered the pantheon of heroes. Spiritually he was part of Japan, a warrior who had never yet borne arms, but who stood ready to die for his emperor. It was after such moments of exaltation that he contributed most heavily to war funds and military hospitals and all such good works.

The constant pull of Japan and its emotional history was so great that Kamejiro did not know one Japanese who intended remaining in Hawaii. All labored twelve hours a day for seventy-three cents, the pay having been raised, in hopes of returning to Hiroshima with $400 and a bright future, and although from the presence of an increasing number of white-haired men and women it was obvious that the majority never saved enough money to get home, not even the most despairing ever admitted that they had given up hope.

One night at the conclusion of a Japanese movie the Buddhist priest called for attention, and a spotlight was thrown upon him by the projectionist. "I want Sakagawa Kamejiro to step forth," the priest said, and the stocky little workman moved into the lights, blinking and keeping his left fist to his mouth. "His Imperial Majesty's consulate in Honolulu has directed me," the priest said, "to award this scroll to Sakagawa Kamejiro in recognition of his contributions on behalf of the brave sailors who lost their lives at the Fukushima catastrophe. All Japan is proud of this man."

To Kamejiro the last words were not an empty phrase. He believed that every village in Japan knew of his loyal behavior and he could visualize word of his deportment creeping to his parents' home, and he could see how happy they were that their son was a decent Japanese. All Japan was proud of him, and for Kamejiro that was sufficient.

For thirteen years he lived in this manner, excited by his recurring contacts with Japan and hopeful that one day soon he would accumulate the $400 plus the boat fare home; but one spring day in 1915, when the casuarina trees were throwing bright nodules at the tips of their needles, ready for the year's growth, and when blossoms were coming onto the pineapples nestling in the red earth, Kamejiro heard a bird cry. It was not a sea bird, for he knew their voices as they swept aloft on the spume thrown up by the cliffs. Perhaps it was from Tahiti, where it had been wintering; possibly it was merely crossing Kauai on its way to Alaska for the rich, insect-laden summer months; and Kamejiro never actually saw the bird, but he heard it winging past him and he stopped dead in the middle of the pineapple field and thought: "I am thirty-three years old and the years are flying past me."

He entered into a period of terrible depression, and a vision came to him which he could not expel: he saw Yoko waiting in Hiroshima, beside the rice fields, and birds were flying past her, too, and she held out her hands, and mists came from the Inland Sea and obliterated her pleading. For the first time he did not rise at three-thirty, and he failed to tend his hot baths, throwing the job onto a friend. He wandered about, gnawed at by an insatiable hunger, and he contemplated going to Kapaa and the brothels, but he rejected the idea, and at last he worked himself toward the decision that hundreds had made before him: "For a little while I shall forget about returning to Japan, but I will use my money to send for Yoko."

He was hoeing pineapple when he made this decision, and it was only two o'clock in the afternoon, but he dropped his hoe and walked in a kind of glorious daze out to the main highway and on into Kapaa, where the ostracized Hashimoto had a photograph shop and an agency for ships traveling to Japan. Smothering his pride and approaching the renegade, Kamejiro said, "I want to get my picture taken to send to Japan."

"Go home and shave," Hashimoto said bluntly. "And wear the dark suit."

"I have no suit."

"Ishii Camp has one. All the men use it."

"I don't want to wear a borrowed suit."

"What girl will want to marry you if you send a photograph without a dark suit?"

"Who said anything about girls?"

"Obviously, you want to get married. I'm glad for you and will take a fine picture. But shave first and wear the dark suit."

"How much will it all cost?" Kamejiro asked.

"Photograph three dollars. Boat fare for the girl seventy. Her train expenses and dresses and the feast back home, maybe seventy. Total one hundred forty-three dollars."

Such an amount would delay the accumulation of $400 by another three or four years at least, and Kamejiro hesitated. "I don't know about that," he said. "Please don't tell anybody."

"I take pictures. I talk to nobody."

"I may be back," Kamejiro said.

"You will be," Hashimoto predicted. Then, as he did with all the Japanese who had ostracized him, he added brutally, "You will marry the girl and you will never return to Japan. Make up your mind about that."

Kamejiro swallowed hard and avoided looking at the photographer. "I am going back to Japan," he said. "You have done me a favor, Hashimoto-san. For a moment I was hungry for a wife and thought: 'I will spend my money that way.' But you have shown me what that means. Good night. I won't be back."

But as he left the photographer's store, a brood of children, half-Japanese, half-Hawaiian, swept past him shouting in a language that no man living could understand—the wild, sweet pidgin of childhood, composed of all languages—and they bumped into him, and a little girl, her hair cut square in the Japanese fashion, cried, "Gomennasai!" and on the impulse of the moment Kamejiro stooped and caught the child, bringing her face to his, and for an instant she remained limp in his arms. Then she kicked free and cried in Hawaiian and Portuguese, "I must go with the others!" And from the doorway, Hashimoto, still hating the men who had driven him out, laughed and said, "It was my daughter you were holding. I have six children, four of them boys."

In great agitation Kamejiro walked home, and the smell of the little girl's hair burned his nostrils so that when he reached the camp and saw the long, bleak, womanless barracks in which he had been living for thirteen years, he rushed directly to Ishii-san and said, "You must write a letter home."

"Are you thinking of getting married?" the scribe asked, for he recognized the symptoms.

"Yes."

Unexpectedly, the thin little letter-writer grasped Kamejiro's hand and confided: "I have been thinking the same thing. What would it cost?"

"Not much!" Kamejiro cried excitedly. "Photograph three dollars. Fare seventy. Maybe a hundred and forty-three altogether."

"I am going to do it!" Ishii-san announced. "I've been thinking about it all this year."

"So have I," Kamejiro confessed, and he sat upon the floor as Ishii-san got out his brushes: "Dear Mother, I have decided to take a wife and later I will send you my photograph so that you can show it to Yoko-chan and she can see how I look now. When you tell me that she is willing to come to Hawaii, I will send the money. This does not mean that I am not going to come back home. It only means that I shall stay here a little longer. Your faithful son, Kamejiro."

It took nine weeks to receive an answer to this letter, and when it arrived Kamejiro was stunned by its contents, for his mother wrote: "You must be a stupid boy to think that Yoko-chan would still be waiting. She got married twelve years ago and already has five children, three of them sons. What made you suppose that a self-respecting girl would wait? But that is no loss, for as you can see I am sending you the photograph of a very fine young lady named Sumiko who has said that she would marry you. She is from this village and will make a lovely wife. Please send the money."

A photograph four inches by three fluttered to the bed, face down. For several moments Kamejiro allowed it to lie there, unable to comprehend that when he turned it over it would show not Yoko, whom he had kept enshrined in his memory, but some girl he had never known. Gingerly, and with two fingers, he lifted the edge of the picture and dropped his head sideways to peer at it. Suddenly he flipped it over and shouted, "Oh! Look at this beautiful girl! Look at her!"

A crowd gathered to study the photograph, and some protested: "That girl will never marry a clod like you, Kamejiro!"

"Tell them what the letter says!" Kamejiro instructed Ishii-san, and the scribe read aloud the facts of the case. The girl's name was Sumiko, and she was willing to marry Kamejiro.

"Is she a Hiroshima girl?" a suspicious man inquired.

"She's from Hiroshima-ken," Kamejiro replied proudly, and a sign of contentment rose from the long bunkhouse.

On one person the photograph of Kamejiro's good luck had a depressing effect, for in an earlier mail Ishii-san had received a picture of the bride his parents had picked for him. She was a girl called Mori Yoriko, which was a pleasing name, but her photograph showed her to be one of those square-faced, stolid, pinch-eyed peasant girls that Japan seemed to produce in unlimited numbers. Ishii-san's mother assured him that Mori Yoriko could work better than a man and saved money, but the scribe felt that there was more to marriage than that, especially when, as in his case, the husband could read and write. He was patently disappointed and asked to see Kamejiro's picture again. Sumiko, as he studied her, appeared to have the classic type of beauty: gently slanted eyes, fine cheekbones, low forehead, pear-shaped face and delicate features. She looked like the girls whose pictures were painted on the sheets advertising Japanese historical movies, and Ishii-san said, "She's very pretty for a Hiroshima girl. Maybe she's from the city."

"No," Kamejiro assured him. "My mother would never send a city girl."

The next day the two would-be husbands borrowed Ishii Camp's publicly owned black suit, the tie that went with it, and the white shirt; they wrapped their treasure in a sheet, hired a taxi and drove into Kapaa, where Hashimoto the photographer told them, "Take turns with the suit, and be sure to comb your hair."

When Kamejiro climbed into the strange clothes, Hashimoto had to show him how to tie the tie, after which the stocky field hand plastered his hair down with a special grease Hashimoto provided for that purpose. Kamejiro then moved into range of the camera, posing rigidly and refusing to smile. The finished picture, even though it was properly styled and mounted, would have excited few prospective brides, and Hashimoto did not consider it one of his best. Nevertheless, Kamejiro mailed it with a fully paid ticket from Tokyo to Honolulu. Then he waited.

In late 1915 Ishii-san and Kamejiro received notice that their brides were arriving at Honolulu on the old Japanese freighter *Kyoto-maru*. The news did not occasion the joy that might have been expected, because it had been hoped at the camp that the two girls might arrive by separate ships, for then each husband, when he went to get his wife, could have worn the black suit, thus corresponding to the photographs sent to Japan. As things now stood, one man would wear the suit and not disappoint his bride, but the other would clearly have to wear his laboring clothes and stand before his bride as he really was. It was the character of Kamejiro to say quickly to his friend, "Since you can read and write, it is proper for you to wear the suit." And the camp agreed that this was the only logical solution.

The lovers, alternately ardent and afraid, left Lihue by the small ship *Kilauea* and went to Honolulu, where they took one room in a dingy Japanese inn on Hotel Street. Since they arrived on the evening before the *Kyoto-maru* was expected, they ate a meager supper of rice and fish, then hiked up Nuuanu and bowed low before the symbol of their emperor. As they were doing so an official in black cutaway hustled out on some important meeting and snapped: "Don't stand around here like peasants. Go about your work." Obediently the men left.

They were impressed by the big homes on Beretania Street but were shocked by the dirty alleys of Chinatown, where one miserable hovel leaned against the next. Ishii-san said, "They told me that fifteen years ago this whole neighborhood was burned down and the Chinese wanted to rebuild it like a proper city without alleys and mean houses, but the white people wanted it the way it was before, so it was built that way again." The two men, recalling the clean roads and immaculate homes of their childhood, shook their heads at the white man's ways.

Before they went to sleep that night Ishii-san spread before him the two photographs, and he spent a long time comparing them, and his disappointment at the tricks of fate became apparent in his features.

"My mother didn't choose very well, I'm afraid," he said. "Isn't it strange, Kamejiro, to think that a great ship out there is bringing a woman with whom you will spend the rest of your life?"

"I'm nervous," Kamejiro confessed, but his nervousness that night was nothing to what he would experience during the next days; for when the *Kyoto-maru* docked, the seven Japanese men who had come to meet their picture brides were told, "We never let the women out of quarantine for three days."

"Can't we even see them?" Ishii-san implored.

"No contact of any kind," the immigration man warned.

Later, the ardent grooms found that if they bribed one of the attendants, they could press their faces against a hole the size of a half-dollar that had been bored into the door behind which the incoming brides were imprisoned, and the third man in line was Kamejiro. Squinting so as to make his eye smaller, he peered through the miserable peephole and saw seven women idly sitting and standing in groups. He looked from one to the other and was unable to detect which was Sumiko, and he looked back beseechingly at the guard who spoke no Japanese. Applying his eye once more to the circle, he looked avidly at the seven women, but again he could not isolate his intended wife, and in some confusion he turned the peephole over to his successor.

"Is she beautiful?" Ishii-san asked.

"Very," Kamejiro assured him.

"Did you see Yoriko?"

"I think so."

"Does she look pretty good?"

"She looks very healthy," Kamejiro said.

When Ishii-san left the peephole he was trembling. "She's a lot bigger than I am," he mumbled. "Damn my mother!"

"Oh, Ishii-san!" Kamejiro protested. "She's a Hiroshima girl. She's bound to make a good wife."

On the second and third days the men returned to spy upon their wives, and by a process of elimination Kamejiro discovered whom he was to marry. He had failed at first to find her because she was by all odds the loveliest of the girls and he had not been able to believe that she was intended for him. Commiserating with his friend Ishii-san's disappointment, he had the delicacy not to revel in the beauty of his own wife; but as the hours passed, leading up to the moment when the doors would be thrown open, he became frightfully nervous and excited.

"I am beginning to feel sick!" he told Ishii-san.

"I already am," the letter-writer confided.

"I think I may go away and come back later," Kamejiro whispered.

"Wait a minute!" one of the husbands snapped. "Look at the poor women!"

Kamejiro felt himself shoved to the peephole and for the last time he saw the seven brides. They knew that the hour of meeting was at hand, and the bravery that had marked their earlier behavior now fled. Without adequate water or combs, they made pathetic attempts to pretty themselves. They smoothed down one another's rumpled, sea-worn dresses, and tucked in ends of hair. One woman applied her fingertips to her forehead, as if she considered it ugly, and tried to spread its skin more smoothly over the heavy bones. In the corner one girl wept, and after a brief attempt at trying to console her, the others left her alone with her misery. But there was one thing that each girl in her final moments of panic did: she studied the photograph clutched in her hand and desperately tried to memorize the features of the man she was about to meet. She was determined that she would know him and that she would walk up to him unerringly and bow before him. But now all were weeping and the photographs were blurred.

A gong rang and Kamejiro jumped back from the door. Slowly the hinges swung open and the brides came forth. No tears were visible. The placid faces under the mounds of black hair looked steadily, inquiringly forward, and the first sound heard was a muffled gasp of pain. "Oh!" one of the brides sighed. "You are so much older than the picture."

"It was taken a long time ago," the man explained. "But I will be a good husband." He held out his hand, and the girl, controlling herself, bowed until her head almost touched his knees. They formed the first pair.

The next girl, the one who had been weeping alone in the corner, walked straight to her man, smiled and bowed low. "I am Fumiko," she said. "Your mother sends a thousand blessings." And she formed up the second pair.

The third girl was Mori Yoriko, Ishii-san's bride, and as he had feared, she was much more robust than he. She was a true Hiroshima country girl, red-cheeked, square-faced, squint-eyed. Knowing that she was less beautiful than any of the others, she made up for her deficiencies in stalwart courage and a burning desire to make herself into a good wife. She found Ishii-san and bowed low, her big hands held close to her knees. "Mr. Ishii," she whispered, "I bring you the love of your mother." Then, as if she knew reassurance was necessary, she quickly added in a halting whisper, "I will be a good wife."

The last girl to find her husband was Sumiko, the prettiest of the lot, and her recalcitrance sprang not from any lack of wit but from the shock she had received when she first saw Kamejiro. He did not wear the black suit in which he had been photographed, nor was his hair pasted down. His clothes were those of a mean peasant and his arms were brutally awkward. He was grim-faced, like an angry, stupid man, and he was twice as old as she had expected. Last in line, and with only one man unattached, Sumiko obviously knew who her husband was, but she refused to accept the fact.

"No!" she cried imperiously. "That one is not my man!"

"Oh!" Kamejiro gasped. "I am Sakagawa Kamejiro. I have your picture."

She slapped it from his hand and then threw hers upon it, stamping upon them. "I will not marry this man. I have been deceived."

At this outburst the first bride, who had also found a husband she did not want, shook Sumiko and cried in rapid Japanese, "Control yourself, you selfish little fool! In such an affair who expects to find a champion?"

"I will not marry this animal!" Sumiko wailed, whereupon the first bride, who had gracefully accepted her disappointment, delivered a solid slap across the girl's face.

"On the entire trip you were a mean, nasty child. You ought to be ashamed. Go to that good man and humble yourself before him." The first bride placed her hand in the middle of Sumiko's back and projected her across the hushed immigration room.

Sumiko would have stumbled except that from the astonished couples Ishii-san sprang forth to rescue her. He caught her by the waist and held her for a moment. Then, looking at Kamejiro and his own intended bride, he said with a frankness that startled even himself, "Kamejiro, you and Yoriko make a better pair. Give me Sumiko." And the beautiful girl, finding herself in the presence of a cultured man who wore a black suit, suddenly cried, "Yes, Kamejiro, you are too old for me. Please, please!"

In stolid bewilderment, Kamejiro looked down at the picture and recalled how deeply over the past months he had grown to love it. Then he looked up at square-faced, chapped-cheeked Mori Yoriko and thought: "She is not the girl in the picture. What are they doing to me?"

He hesitated, the room whirling about him, and then he felt on his arm the hand of the first bride, who had slapped Sumiko, and this quiet-voiced girl was saying, "I do not know your name, but I have lived with Yoriko for three weeks, and of all the brides here, I assure you that she will make the best wife. Take her."

The humiliated country girl, who had been so painfully rejected by her intended husband, found tears welling into her unpretty eyes, and she wanted to run to some corner, but she stood firm like the rock from which she had been hewn and bowed low before the stranger. "I will be a good wife," she mumbled, fighting to control her voice.

Kamejiro looked for the last time at the well-remembered picture on the floor, then picked it up and handed it to his friend Ishii-san. "It will be better this way," he said. Returning to the girl who still bowed, he said gently, "My name is Sakagawa Kamejiro. I am from Hiroshima-ken."

"My name is Mori Yoriko," the peasant girl answered. "I also am from Hiroshima."

"Then we will get married," he said, and the seven couples were completed.

DURING THE YEARS when Kamejiro Sakagawa and his bride Yoriko were discovering how lucky they were to have stumbled into their improvised marriage, the missionary families in Honolulu were experiencing a major shock, for one of their sons was proving to be a fiery radical, and reports of his behavior startled all Hawaii.

In these years Hawaii seemed filled with Hales and Whipples and Hewletts and Janderses and Hoxworths. In some classes at Punahou sixteen out of twenty-four students would bear these or related names. Only skilled genealogists tried to keep the blood lines straight, for Hales were Hoxworths and Hoxworths were Whipples, and fairly frequently a Hale would marry a Hale and thus intensify the complications, so that in time no child really understood who his various cousins were, and an island euphemism gained popularity: "He is my calabash cousin," which meant that if one went back far enough, some kind of blood relationship could be established.

Hawaii came to consider this Hale-Whipple-Hewlett-Janders-Hoxworth ménage simply as "the family" and to recognize its four salient characteristics: its children went to Punahou; its boys went to Yale; invariably it found some kind of good-paying job for every son and for the husband of every daughter; and members of the family tried to avoid scandal. Therefore, when one of the boys became a radical, the family was deeply jolted.

As long as he had stayed at Punahou, this renegade had done well, but this was not unusual, for the family expected its sons to prosper there. Take the case of Hoxworth Whipple, who gained international honors for his work on Polynesian history. He started his scholarly investigation while still at Punahou, although later he took his B.A. at Yale, his M.A. at Harvard, his Ph.D. from Oxford and his D.Litt. from the Sorbonne. He received honorary degrees from eleven major universities, but when he died in 1914 the Honolulu *Mail* announced simply: "The great scholar was educated at Punahou." None of the rest really mattered.

In the year that the great scholar died, crowded with honors, the young member of the family who was to become the radical was graduating from Punahou. He was Hoxworth Hale, in all outward respects a typical sixteen-year-old boy. He was neither tall nor short, fat nor thin. His hair was not black nor was it blond, and his eyes displayed no single prominent color. He was not at the top of his class nor yet at the bottom, and he was outstanding in no one scholastic accomplishment.

He had played games moderately well but had never won fist fights against boys larger than himself.

Young Hoxworth Hale, named after the noted scholar, was most noted for the fact that he had uncommonly pretty sisters, Henrietta and Jerusha, and they lent him a spurious popularity which he would not otherwise have enjoyed. There was a good deal of chivvying to see which of his friends would win the favors of the charming sisters, and of course in later years his younger sister became engaged to one of her calabash cousins, a Whipple, whereupon Hoxworth's father told the family, "I think it's high time somebody married a stranger. Get some new blood into this tired old tree." His words were not taken in good grace, because he had married his cousin, a Hoxworth girl, and it was felt that he was casting aspersions upon her; nevertheless, when his oldest daughter began displaying outward tendencies and actually became engaged to a man named Gage from Philadelphia, he expressed his pleasure. But later Henrietta met a boy from New Hampshire named Bromley and the two discovered that way, way back her great-great-great-great-grandfather Charles Bromley and his great-great-great . . . well, anyway, she felt a lot more congenial with Bromley than she ever had with her fiancé Gage, so she married the former because, as she pointed out, "he seems more like one of the family."

When young Hoxworth Hale left Punahou it was understood that he would go on to Yale, and in New Haven this undistinguished youth was to explode into a prominence no one had anticipated. Not having wasted his limited intellectual reserves in preparatory school, he was ready to blossom in college and gradually became both a scholar and a polished gentleman. In his grades he did markedly better than boys who had surpassed him at Punahou, while in sports he captained the polo team and served as assistant manager of the basketball team. He acquired the lesser amenities and in politics ran successfully for president of his class.

It was this unlikely youth who became the radical. His commitment began one day in his junior year when a Professor Albers from Leipzig was ending a lecture on the theory of imperialism with this shrewd observation: "The Congregational-Church-cum-Boston-merchant invasion and capture of Hawaii is the exact counterpart of the Catholic-Church-cum-Paris-entrepreneur rape of Tahiti. The proof of this analogy lies, I think, in the demonstrated manner whereby the missionaries who went to Hawaii, though they did not call in the American gunboats as did their French cousins in Tahiti, nevertheless, by revolutionary means, stole the land from the Hawaiians and wound up possessors of the islands."

Professor Albers' class contained, in addition to young Hoxworth Hale, his calabash cousin Hewlett Janders, two Whipples and a Hewlett, but these other descendants of the missionaries were content to stare in embarrassment at their arm rests. Not so Hoxworth; he coughed once, coughed twice, then boldly interrupted: "Professor Albers, I'm sorry but I'm afraid you have your facts wrong."

"I beg your pardon," the German professor spluttered.

"I mean that whereas your facts on Tahiti may be correct, those on Hawaii are definitely in error."

"Don't you stand when you address remarks to your professor?" the Leipzig-trained scholar demanded, growing red. When Hoxworth got to his feet, Albers referred to his notes and began quoting an impressive list of sources: "The journals of Ellis, Jarves, Bird, the researches of Amsterfield, de Golier, Whipple. They all tell the same story."

"If they do," Hoxworth said, "they're all wrong."

Professor Albers flushed and asked, "What is your name, young man?"

"Hoxworth Hale, sir."

"Well!" Albers laughed. "Your testimony on this matter is hardly unimpeachable."

This contempt goaded Hale into making a reply that infuriated the professor: "You cited Jarves. Have you ever read Jarves?"

"I do not cite sources I have not read," Albers fumed.

"Jarves happened to be a friend of some of my ancestors, and they held him in keen regard because he was the first impartial observer to defend the missionaries, and I've read what he wrote, in the original papers in which he wrote it, and what he wrote, sir, simply doesn't support your thesis."

The class broke up in something of a scandal and for some weeks the word *missionary* had a curious force of its own at Yale. Professor Albers, goaded by his young tormentor, marshaled an impressive battery of anti-clerical critics whose gibes at all churches and their nefarious skill in capturing the land of backward countries pleased the young iconoclasts of that day, and for several biting weeks the professor carried the day, and the dormitories rang with the famous gibes against the Hawaiian missionaries: "They came to the island to do good, and they did right well." "No wonder the islands were lighter when they left; they stole everything in sight." "They taught the natives to wear dresses and sign leases." And most cutting of all: "Before the missionaries came to Hawaii, there were four hundred thousand happy, naked natives in the mountains killing each other, practicing incest, and eating well. After the missionaries had been there awhile, there were thirty thousand fully clothed, miserable natives, huddled along the shore, paying lip service to Christianity and owning nothing." In Professor Albers' classes such lines of reasoning became increasingly popular, and for the first time Yale, the source of missionaries, took a serious look at what they had really accomplished. In those exciting days it was downright unpleasant to be a Whipple or a Hewlett, for the fact was often cited that Dr. John Whipple had abandoned the church to become a millionaire, and that Hewlett had left to steal land from the defenseless natives.

In the fifth week of the intellectual investigation, Hoxworth Hale, then a junior, nineteen years old, asked for time to read to the class the results of some work he had been doing on his account, and in cold, dispassionate phrases he developed this thesis: "In the third decade of the last century a series of little ships brought missionaries to Hawaii. There were twelve ships in all, bearing a total of fifty-two ordained missionaries, brought to the islands at a cost of $1,220,000. At the end of nearly thirty years of religious and social service in the islands, the missionaries controlled practically no land, except in the case of one Abraham Hewlett who had married a Hawaiian lady and whose family lands have always been kept in her name for the welfare of her people. The Whipples owned no land whatever. Nor did the Hales except, in later days, a few building lots on which their homes have been built. In fact, in 1854 the Hawaiian government took cognizance of the unfortunate position of the mission families and passed a special law allowing those who had served the islands well to buy small parcels of land at favorable prices. And the government did this, Professor Albers, because they were afraid not that the missionaries would take over the islands, but that they would go back to America and take their children with them. The minutes of the government on this matter are explicit: 'June, 1851, the missionaries who have received and applied for lands have neither received nor applied for them without offering what they considered a fair compensation for them. So far as their applications have been granted, your Majesty's government have dealt with them precisely as they have dealt with other applications for land. It will not be contended that missionaries, because they are missionaries, have not the same right to buy land in the same quantities and at the same prices as those who are not missionaries. But, besides what is strictly due to them, in justice and in gratitude for large benefits conferred by them on your people, every consideration of sound policy, under the rapid decrease of the native population, is in favor of holding out inducements for them not to withdraw their children from these islands. We propose a formal resolution declaring the gratitude of this nation to the missionaries for the services they have performed, and making some provision to insure that their children remain in these islands.' "

At this point Hoxworth looked directly at his professor and continued: "Dr. Albers, the provisions of this resolution were carried out, and the investigating committee found that the missionaries who had worked so long in Hawaii had acquired so little that the community as a whole applauded when the government provided that any missionary who had served in the islands for eight years be allowed to buy 560 acres of government lands at a price of fifty cents an acre lower than what the average white newcomer would have to pay. Since the average price at that time was $1.45 an acre, this represents a reduction of exactly 34.5 per cent, or one percent per year for arduous and faithful service. So far as I can find, the missionaries acquired land in absolutely no other way, and even so, most of them were then too poor to take advantage of the government's offer.

"Hawaii desperately wanted the mission families to stay in the islands, and it has been justly said that the most significant crop grown by the missionaries was not sugar, but their sons. Now, if you want to argue that the brilliant young mission sons who left Hawaii, studied here at Yale and then returned to the islands, usurped a disproportionate number of important jobs in medicine, law, government and management, you would be on good grounds, but if you do so argue, don't blame the missionaries. Blame Yale.

"I conclude that it is neither fair nor accurate to accuse these families of stealing land which they never came into possession of. It was the non-mission families, the New England sea rovers, who got the land. Then, the land having been obtained by these men, it is true that mission sons managed it, for a fee, but would you have had it lie fallow? The facts you cite apply to Tahiti. They simply do not apply to Hawaii."

He sat down, flushed with excitement, and expected the applause of his classmates for having dared argue with the arrogant professor, but what Hoxworth had said was not popular. It ran against the grain of the age and was not believed. Jokes about missionaries continued, and Hale saw that whereas he had gained nothing with his contemporaries he had placed himself at a serious disadvantage with the faculty. But what grieved him most was that his Punahou associates, Hewlett Janders and the others, felt rather ashamed that a subject which would have died with only momentary embarrassment had now been so thoroughly ventilated as to force all members of the class to be either anti-missionary or pro, and nearly everyone fell into the first category, and the Punahou men were infuriated that one of their own number had stirred up the mess.

So Hoxworth Hale's first venture into public argument backfired rather badly, but his studies had disclosed to him his ancestors, so that no matter how witty the gibes against missionaries became, he knew what the facts were, and this knowledge, in the subtle way that knowledge has, fortified him in many ways and made him a stronger man.

His preoccupation with researches into Hawaiian history developed an accidental concomitant which outraged all of Yale and led to his temporary withdrawal from the university. He was in the library one day, reading files of an early Honolulu newspaper, the *Polynesian,* for he wished to refresh his mind as to what that journal's excitable editor, James Jackson Jarves, had actually said about missionaries, and for a while he got bogged down in the story of how Jarves had protested when a French warship roared into Honolulu, insisting that French wines be imported in unlimited amounts, and of how the French authorities threatened to lash him through the streets with a cat-o'-nine-tails. Next he turned the yellowed pages to read of the time when the British consul actually did horsewhip poor Jarves for defending Hawaii against British intrusions into local affairs, and he began to laugh to himself: "Jarves must have been a wild-eyed young man . . . like me." And the conceit pleased him, and he felt sympathy for the strange, will-o'-the-wisp editor who had so befriended Hawaii and the missionaries, until he suddenly looked at the name again: James Jackson Jarves! Hadn't he heard that name in another context?

He hurried from the library and went to the exhibition hall where one of the glories of Yale University stood: the collection of early Italian masterpieces gathered together by a curious man named James Jackson Jarves, who had lived in Florence in the 1850's. Hoxworth hurried into the gallery and walked among the strange, faraway, gold and blue painting of an age he could not even begin to comprehend. He was unprepared to like the art he saw in the Jarves collection, and he did not try to do so, for it was in no way similar to the work of Raphael and Rembrandt, which he had been taught was true art; but as he gazed at the affectionate little paintings—more than a hundred of them—he sensed that they had been collected by someone who had loved them, and he asked an attendant, "Who was this man Jarves?" The man didn't know, so Hale sought out another, and finally the curator: "Who was Jarves?"

The curator had a brief memorandum on the forgotten donor and said, "An American writer on art who lived in Florence in the middle years of the last century. A close friend of Elizabeth and Robert Browning and John Ruskin. In his own way, an eminent man, and America's first writer on art."

"Did he ever live in Hawaii?"

"No. But late in life he did write the first book in English on Japanese art. He discovered prints as art forms, so he must have lived in the Orient, although I have no knowledge of the fact."

"Hawaii isn't in the Orient," Hale explained.

"Isn't it considered part of Asia?"

"No," Hale replied sharply and left. In those days he did not think much of faculty members.

He was puzzled. It seemed most unlikely that two men of such dissimilar natures as the rambunctious Hawaiian editor and the polished Italian art connoisseur could have been the same man, and yet there was the name: James Jackson Jarves; so he continued his researches and discovered at last that his Hawaiian Jarves had failed to make a living with his *Polynesian* and had fled in disgust to Florence, where he became the first great American collector of paintings, the first

American art philosopher, and the first writer on Japanese aesthetics. He felt a proprietary interest in the strange man and thought: "That's not bad for a Hawaii boy!"

And then, as he looked into the peculiar circumstances whereby Yale acquired the Jarves paintings, he became appalled at the unsavory tricks the college had used to steal them, and he forgot all about missionaries and began digging into the events of 1871, when the former editor of the *Polynesian* was fifty-three years old and in sore need of money. Yale had loaned him $20,000 on his paintings, and he had been unable to repay the debt, so the college put the entire collection up for public auction, 119 masterpieces in all, worth $70,000 or $80,000 then . . . over a million dollars in 1917. But college authorities had quietly forewarned potential bidders that any buyer must take the entire collection in one lump, and the rumor had circulated that even if this were done, the college would not yield clear title to the pictures, so that any prospective buyer must beware of lawsuits; and on the day of the sale there were no bidders, and Yale acquired the collection for what Jarves owed the college.

"This is a scandal!" Hoxworth cried, and to his amazement he found himself deeply involved in art problems, and now when he passed through the Jarves collection, he thought: "These marvelous masterworks!" He wrote a long letter to the college paper, asking why a college with Yale's background should have conspired at such a nasty business, and hell broke loose.

Hoxworth was defamed on the Yale campus as a radical who had raped the reputation of his own college; but a Boston art critic wrote: "The general outline of the facts so patiently developed by young Mr. Hale have long been known in art circles but hitherto they have not been publicly aired, out of courtesy to a revered institution whose deportment otherwise has been above reproach." So once more one of the most essentially conservative young men Hawaii ever sent to Yale found himself the center of controversy, and this one far exceeded in general interest his spirited defense of the missionaries, for it involved the honor of the university itself.

At the height of the controversy the campus newspaper evolved a logical way for Hoxworth to apologize, but just as he had refused to accommodate himself to Professor Albers' erroneous data on Hawaii, so he now refused to condone what Yale had done to his favorite Hawaiian editor, James Jackson Jarves. Yale had stolen the pictures, and Hoxworth bluntly reiterated his charges. And then late one afternoon as he walked disconsolately through the collection a completely new thought came to him: "It really doesn't matter to Jarves now whether Yale stole the pictures or not, just as it doesn't matter whether the missionaries stole the land or not. What counts, and the only thing that counts is this: What good did the institution accomplish? If Yale had not picked up the pictures, forcibly perhaps, where would they be now? Could they possibly have served the wonderful purposes they serve here in New Haven? If the missionaries had stepped aside and allowed Hawaii to drift from one degeneracy to another, what good would have been accomplished? Yale is better by far for having had such a solid beginning for its art school, and Hawaii is better for having had the missionaries. The minor blemishes on the record are unimportant. It doesn't matter what an arrogant fool like Albers says. Janders and the rest were right to ignore him. The fact is that in Hawaii today there are sugar plantations, and pineapple, and deep reservoirs and a lot of different people living together reasonably well. If Yale stole the pictures, they're entitled to them because of the good use to which they put them. And I'm not going to argue with anyone any more about the missionaries stealing Hawaii. If they did, which I don't admit, they certainly put what they stole to good purposes." He saw then, that gloomy afternoon when he was being hammered by his friends, that there were many ways to judge the acts of an institution, and the pragmatic way was not the worst, by any means.

Thus he started his education, that marvelous, growing, aching process whereby a mind develops into a usable instrument with a collection of proved experience from which to function, and he was suddenly tired of Yale, and Punahou men, and professors trained at Leipzig, and problems relating to James Jackson Jarves. Consequently, he walked casually out of the gallery, nodded a grave farewell to the pictures he would never bother to see again, and reported to the New Haven post office where, on April 28, 1917, he enlisted in the army and went to France.

ON AUGUST 19, 1916, an event occurred which was to change the history of Hawaii, but as in the case of most such events, it was not so recognized at the time. It happened because one of the German lunas was both drunk and suffering from a toothache, the latter condition having occasioned the former.

Normally, the plantation lunas were a tough, cynical, reasonably well-behaved lot. Imported mostly from Germany and Norway—with one man sending for his brother and both calling upon a cousin, so that luna families were constantly being refreshed from the old country—they were employed by firms like Janders & Whipple to supervise field hands for two reasons. It was unthinkable that an Oriental could rise above minor roles, partly because few ever learned to speak English and partly because none intended to remain in Hawaii, but mostly because haoles could not visualize Chinese or Japanese in positions of authority. And from sad experience, the great plantation owners had discovered that the Americans they could get to serve as lunas were positively no good. Capable Americans expected office jobs and incapable ones were unable to control the Oriental field hands.

Therefore Hawaii was forced to import Europeans to run the plantations, and if the upper crust of Hawaiian society consisted of New England families like the Hales and the Whipples, the second and operating layer was built of Europeans who had once been lunas but who had now left the plantations for businesses of their own. Of the Europeans, the Germans were the greatest successes, both as lunas and as subsequent citizens, and it was ironic that the historical event of which I speak should have been precipitated by a German, but his toothache can probably be blamed.

He was on his way through Ishii Camp at six o'clock one morning, his boots polished and his white ducks freshly pressed. Of late he had been pestered by Japanese laborers in the long bunkhouses who had taken to guzzling large amounts of soy sauce in order to induce temporary fevers, which excused them from work that day, and he was determined to end this farce. If a man claimed a fever, he personally had to breathe in the face of the German luna, and God help him if he smelled of soy sauce.

In the nineteenth century, lunas had had a fairly free hand in abusing Oriental labor, and there were instances in which sadistic foremen lashed the pigtails of two Chinese together and tied the knot to a horse's tail, whipping the beast as he dragged the terrified Orientals through the red dust. Other lunas had formed a habit of beating either Chinese or Japanese as one would thrash a recalcitrant child, and by such methods the Europeans had maintained a ruthless dictatorship of the cane fields, but with the coming of pineapple, where an abused man seeking revenge could easily pass down a row of flowering plants and knock off hundreds of the tiny individual flowers, so that the resulting fruit would lack some of the small squares of which it should have been built, the lunas by and large surrendered their old prerogatives of lash and fist, and life in the plantations was not too bad.

But on August 19, 1916, this German luna found two of his Japanese suffering from "soy-sauce fever," and he cuffed them out to the fields, temperature or no. He then left the long barracks where bachelors stayed and entered the minute wooden house where Kamejiro Sakagawa and his wife Yoriko lived, and to his disgust he found the former in bed. The luna did not stop to recall that for fourteen years Kamejiro had never once requested a day off for illness, so that malingering was not likely. All the German saw was another Japanese in bed, claiming a fever.

"You breathe my face," he growled in thick pidgin.

Kamejiro, who did not even know of the soy-sauce trick, failed to grasp the instructions, which convinced the luna of his perfidy. Shaking the little laborer, he shouted again, "You breathe my face!" He leaned over the bed, and since the wife Yoriko had felt sorry for her stricken husband and had both bathed him and fed him some rice and soy sauce, the unmistakable odor of the strong black sauce struck the luna's nose, and something in what he interpreted as the mock-bewilderment of the little Japanese infuriated him, and with a judgment clouded by alcohol and his own substantial pain, he dragged the sick man from his bed and began thrashing him with the whip most lunas carried.

He had struck Kamejiro some dozen blows, none of them very effective because of the crowded nature of the cabin, when he realized from Mrs. Sakagawa's behavior and the flushed appearance of her husband that perhaps the man really was sick. But he had launched a specific course of action and found himself incapable of turning back. "Get dressed," he growled, and as bewildered Kamejiro, sick for the first time in Hawaii, climbed into his clothes, the luna stood over him, flexing the whip. He drove Kamejiro out of the cabin and into the pineapple fields, announcing to the others: "Soy-sauce pilikia pau! Plenty pau!"

Kamejiro, with a high fever, worked till noon and then staggered to one knee. "He's fainting!" the Japanese cried, and work stopped while they hauled him back to his cabin. The German luna, frightened by this twist of events, hurried for the plantation doctor and said, "You've got to say it was soy-sauce fever. We've got to stick together."

The doctor, an old hack who had proved himself unable to hold down any other job, understood, but he was nevertheless appalled at the high fever in the Japanese, and before he publicly announced that the man had been malingering, he dosed him well. Then he supported the luna and gave a stormy lecture in pidgin against the evils of drinking soy sauce. But when he rode back with the luna he warned: "The little bastard won't die this time, but sometimes they really are sick."

"How can you tell?" the German asked, and so far as he was concerned the incident was closed.

But not for Kamejiro Sakagawa. For fourteen years he had given his employer the kind of loyalty that all Japanese are expected to give their superiors. Every monologue delivered by the frenetic, bald-headed reciter dealt with the loyalty that an inferior owed his master. The suicides, the immolations and the feat of Colonel Ito at Port Arthur had all stemmed from this sense of obedience, and the reason that reciters came from Tokyo to such remote areas as Kauai was that the Imperial government wanted to remind all Japanese of their undying loyalty to superiors, in this case the emperor and his army. None had mastered the lesson more firmly than Kamejiro; to him loyalty and rectitude were inborn nature, and the high point of his life continued to be the moment when he dressed in Colonel Ito's uniform to stand at attention while the chanters screamed the story: "Colonel Ito and the

Russian Guns at Port Arthur." In his dream life, Kamejiro was that colonel.

But what had happened to him now? When the fever abated he mumbled to his closest friends, "The worst part was not the whip, although it stung. But when I had fallen on the floor, he kicked me! With his shoe!"

If the German luna had been asked by a judge if this had truly happened, he would not have known, for to him the kick was of no significance. But to a Japanese it was an insult past enduring. It was no use to argue with Kamejiro that a kick was no worse than a thrashing from a whip. He knew that in Japanese recitations the most terrifying scene came when the villain, having knocked the hero down, takes off his zori and ceremoniously strikes the fallen hero, for then men like Kamejiro gasped, knowing that only death could avenge this ultimate insult.

"He kicked you?" one of the older men asked in a whisper.

"Yes."

"An ignorant, uneducated German kicked a Japanese?"

"Yes."

"All Japan will be ashamed of this day," the visitor mumbled and sharing this shame, departed.

When the Sakagawas were left alone, Kamejiro turned his face to the wall and began to sob. He could not understand what had happened, but he knew that revenge of some kind was imperative. As his visitor had clearly said, "All Japan will be ashamed."

His lumpy, square-faced wife understood the agony he felt and tried by various gentle means to placate him and poultice with kindness his festering sores, but she accomplished nothing, and at sunset her husband announced his plan: "I will borrow Ishii-san's sword, and after the darkness has fallen I will creep to the luna's house and on his front steps I will cut out my bowels. This will bring him great shame and the honor of Japan will be restored."

"No!" Yoriko pleaded. "This stupid German would not understand."

"When he stumbles upon my body in the morning, he will understand," Kamejiro replied.

"Oh, no!" Yoriko wept. She had not yet lived with her husband for a year, but she had found him to be one of the finest men she had ever known or heard of. He was kind and jovial. He saved his money and was generous with friends. He got drunk sometimes but fell into laughing fits when he did and had to lean on her to get home. And at all public gatherings of the Japanese, he represented the honor of the homeland. In his uniform of Colonel Ito he was as handsome a man as she had seen, and she did not want him, not even for the honor of his country, to commit hara-kiri before the house of a clod like the German luna.

"Kamejiro," she whispered. "Forget the sword. There is a better way. Wait till you are stronger. I will feed you rice and fish and you will become powerful as before. Then hide along the path, and when the luna comes along, leap at him and knock him down and then kick him with your zori."

"Germans are big men," Kamejiro reflected.

"Then get some of the others to help you," Yoriko plotted.

"I would not hide," Kamejiro replied. "That would offend the honor of Japan."

"Then walk up to him," Yoriko counseled, "and knock him down."

The German luna seemed rather bigger to Kamejiro than he did to Yoriko, so on his feverish bed the little laborer worked out an alternative plot that would both humiliate the luna and restore his own besmirched honor. He waited until his strength returned, bided his time while he spied on the luna, and then laid his trap. Planting himself along a road which the German had to traverse on his way to the overseers' quarters, he trembled with excitement as he saw the towering luna approach. When the German was almost abreast of him, he called sharply, "Mr. Von Schlemm!"

Startled, the luna stopped and drew his fists into a protective position. Then he saw that his accoster was the model workman Kamejiro, and he forgot that he had recently whipped the man. He dropped his guard slightly and asked, "What fo' you call?"

To his amazement, the little Japanese bent down, carefully took off his zori, stood erect like a major in a German play, and tapped the man facing him on the shoulder with the dusty Japanese shoe. At this moment Kamejiro expected to be knocked down by the luna, whereupon his friends hiding in the bushes were supposed to leap out and thrash the luna roundly.

But nothing happened. The big, bewildered German stared at his strange assailant, looked down at the one bare foot, and shrugged his shoulders. "You speak, Kamejiro?" he asked, unable to comprehend what was happening.

In disgust with a man so lacking in honor, Kamejiro turned his back and started hobbling with one shoe and one bare foot back to his quarters. The big luna, more perplexed than ever, watched him disappear, then shrugged his shoulders again and went along to his quarters, but as he walked he thought he heard in the sugar cane beside the road the muffled and derisive laughter of men, but when he turned suddenly to find them, he saw nothing but the waving cane.

That night Sakagawa Kamejiro was a hero among the Japanese of Ishii Camp. "Tell us again how you humiliated the luna!" his admirers begged.

"I went up to him just as I told my wife I would and I called, 'Eh, you, Mr. Von Schlemm!' Then I took off my zori and struck him on the head with it."

"On the head?" asked the Japanese who had not been in the cane. "And he did nothing?"

One of the men who had been hiding in the cane explained: "He was astonished! He was afraid! I could see him tremble! What a sorry man he was that moment!"

"I think we had better celebrate with some sake," an older man suggested, proud of the manner in which Kamejiro had recovered the honor of Ishii Camp, but before the celebration could be properly launched, Ishii-san himself ran breathlessly in from Kapaa with shocking news. At first he could not speak, but then, with tears bursting from his bloodshot eyes, he blurted out: "My wife has run away!"

"Sumiko-san?" everyone cried.

"She has run away to Honolulu," the stricken man wailed. "She said she could not live in Kauai any longer."

"What was the matter?" one of the older men asked. "Weren't you able to pin her down in bed?"

"We had a good time in bed," Ishii-san explained, "but she laughed at me for having no suit. I pleaded with her . . . Maybe some of you heard the fights in our house."

He stood, a dejected man, ashamed of his fiasco and humiliated, and some of the men of Ishii Camp felt exceedingly sorry for him, for he could read and write and he had spent a good deal of money bringing a wife from Japan, and the one he finally got turned out to be the most beautiful Japanese girl in Hawaii, but he had not been able to hold her. There was a silence in the camp, and then Mrs. Sakagawa, the stocky, square-faced woman he had rejected, went up to him and said, "Forget this ill-mannered girl, Ishii-san. On the boat we grew to despise her and we knew she would never make a good wife. The blame is not yours. I announce to everyone here that the blame is not Ishii-san's."

The little scribe looked into the face of the rugged woman he had imported from Hiroshima, and in great dejection mumbled, "Then you forgive me, Yoriko-chan?"

"I forgave you long ago," the stocky peasant girl replied, "for you enabled me to find my true husband." She used the Japanese word Danna-san, Sir Master, and although she had never yet allowed Kamejiro to master her at anything, she sang the word in a lilting, wifelike manner and dropped her eyes, and all the men there thought: "How lucky Kamejiro was to make that swap."

In their own little house Kamejiro whispered to his wife, "Tonight I shivered to think that Sumiko might have been my wife."

"She would have run away from you, too."

"I was lucky! I was lucky!" Kamejiro chanted. "The four hundred thousand gods of Japan were looking out for me that day."

Yoriko looked down at her man and asked, "Did you truly strike Von Schlemm-san on the head with your zori?"

"I did."

"All Japan is proud of you, danna-san."

They fell together on the bed, and Kamejiro said, "It's very funny to me, but I knew little about girls and I thought that when a man and woman got married and slept together, babies always came along pretty quickly."

"Sometimes they do," Yoriko assured him.

"But not for us . . . it seems."

"We must work harder," Yoriko explained, and they blew out the oil lamp.

She also worked hard at other tasks. When the pineapples ripened, she helped harvest them at fifty-four cents a day. Later she would get a few days' employment stripping the crowns of unnecessary leaves so that when planted they would germinate faster. For this difficult and tedious work she got seventy-five cents a thousand crowns, and by applying a dogged concentration to the job, she learned to strip upwards of four thousand a day, so that she became the marvel of the plantation, and husbands in other camps asked their wives, "Why can't you strip crowns the way Kamejiro's wife does?" and the wives snapped, "Because we are human beings and not machines, that's why."

Yoriko also took over the cooking of meals for bachelors in the long house. They provided the food and she did the work. Now both she and her husband rose at three-thirty each day, he to gather wood both for his bath and for her stove, she to prepare the men's breakfasts, and together they earned substantial wages, but their goal of $400 clear in cash continued to slip away from them. There were military events in Japan to be underwritten, and various Imperial requests forwarded by the consulate in Honolulu. There were priests to support and schoolteachers who educated the young, for who would want to take children back to Hiroshima if they knew no Japanese? And although the Sakagawas had no children of their own, they helped those who did.

But most often the flight of dollars was accounted for by some personal tragedy within the camp community, as on the evening when Ishii-san burst into their home with a plea for thirty dollars. "I've got to go to Honolulu, right away," he mumbled, trying to keep back his tears.

"Sumiko?" Mrs. Sakagawa asked.

"Yes. Hashimoto-san, the photographer at Kapaa, was in Honolulu to buy another camera and he discovered that the man who took Sumiko away left her in the city and she . . ." He could not finish.

"And she's working in one of the brothels?" Yoriko asked coldly.

"Mmmmmmm," Ishii-san nodded, his face buried in his hands from humiliation.

"That is her destiny, Ishii-san," the Hiroshima woman assured him. "Leave her there. You can do nothing."

"Leave her there?" Ishii-san screamed. "She's my wife!"

"Believe me, Ishii-san," Mrs. Sakagawa asserted, "that one will be no wife, never."

"Then you won't let me have thirty dollars?" the little scribe pleaded.

"Of course we will," Kamejiro said, and although his wife protested at the waste, for she knew the trip to be useless, the passage money was delivered.

Five days later little Mr. Ishii, his eyes ashamed to meet those of his friends, returned alone to Kauai. For a long time no one questioned him about his wife and he went about his work with his head down, until finally at breakfast one morning in the long room Kamejiro banged the table and asked in a loud voice, "Ishii-san, is your wife still working in the brothel?"

"Yes," Ishii-san replied, happy that someone had openly asked the question.

"Then in due time you will divorce the no-good whore?"

"Yes," the scribe replied.

"You're better off that way," Kamejiro said, "but remember that you owe me thirty dollars." The men laughed and that was the last Ishii Camp heard of beautiful Sumiko, but sometimes at the dock Kamejiro, fascinated by the peril he had so narrowly escaped, inquired of sailors from Honolulu, "Whatever happened to that girl Sumiko?" and finally he learned, "She went back to Japan."

That night when he started to tell his wife Yoriko the news, he was interrupted by her own startling intelligence: "We are going to have a baby!"

Kamejiro dropped his hands and all thoughts of Sumiko vanished. "A baby!" he cried with explosive joy. "We'll name him Goro."

"Why Goro?" Yoriko asked in her practical way. "That's no name for a first son."

"I know," Kamejiro admitted. "But years ago I decided that my first son should be Goro. The name sounds good." And it was agreed.

I HAVE SAID that the heroic encounter between Kamejiro Sakagawa and the German luna Von Schlemm was one with historic consequences, and that is true, but they did not become apparent until forty years later. What followed immediately was that as soon as word of the affair reached Honolulu, Kamejiro's revenge was inflated into an incipient riot, and plantation managers whispered apprehensively about "that Japanese who kicked the bejeezus out of the German luna." Fortunately, Wild Whip was absent at the time, on vacation in Spain, but as soon as he climbed down off the H & H liner he was told about it.

His neck muscles tensed and blood rushed to the ugly scars across his cheek. "Who was the Jap?" he asked.

"Man named Kamejiro Sakagawa," an H & H official replied, and for several moments Wild Whip remained stationary on the dock, repeating the name "Kamejiro!" and looking off toward the Koolau Range. His tension increased, and on what seemed like an impulse he grabbed the reporting official by the collar.

"How soon can I get a boat to Kauai?" he rasped, and as the little inter-island craft left for the Garden Island, the H & H official mumbled, "God help that poor Jap when Whip gets hold of him."

When the ferry reached Lihue, Wild Whip in great agitation leaped onto the dock, hired a taxi and went roaring out to Hanakai, where as soon as he reached his plantation he bellowed, "Bring me that goddamned Kamejiro who thinks he can kick my lunas around."

When Kamejiro approached, holding his cap in his hands, as was the custom when speaking to a white man, Whip rushed up to him and yelled, "I hear you smashed up my luna?"

Kamejiro did not understand what was happening, and thought: "I'm going to be fired. And with a baby girl to feed, what shall I do?"

"Well?" Whip growled. "Were you the one who did it?"

The little Japanese fumbled with his cap and said weakly, "I not hit the luna like you say . . . hontoni . . . Hoxuwortu. You b'lee me. I speak truth."

Suddenly Wild Whip grabbed Kamejiro by the shoulders and stuck his face close to his workman's. "Little man," he asked, "are you as tough as they say?"

"What is tough?" Kamejiro countered suspiciously.

"That day when we argued about the iron for your hot bath? Would you really have fought with me?"

Now Kamejiro understood, and since he was about to be fired anyway, he felt no caution. "Yes," he said, jabbing Whip in the stomach with his finger. "I going to smash you here . . . with my head."

"I figured that was your plan," Whip laughed evenly. "Do you know what my plan was? When you ducked your head, I was going to . . ." With a brutal uppercut of his right fist he swung at Kamejiro's head, stopping his knuckles an inch from the workman's nose. "I'd have killed you!"

Kamejiro glared back at his boss and replied, "Maybe I too quick for you. Maybe your fist never hit." He brought his own around with dreadful force, arresting it just short of Wild Whip's belly.

To his surprise, the boss exploded in gales of nervous laughter, embracing his gardener as if he had found a great treasure. "That settles it!" he shouted. "Kamejiro, you're a man I can respect." Jamming his strong hands under the little man's armpits, he danced the astonished Japanese up and down, crying, "Start to pack, you tough little bastard, because you and I have a date with a mountain."

Kamejiro broke free and studied Whip suspiciously. He had seen his boss before in these wild, fantastic moods and he assumed that Whip was either drunk or morbid over some pineapple problem. "Bimeby you be mo bettah," he assured him.

Whip laughed, grabbed his workman again, and dragged him onto the lawn, where he could point to the sweet, green mountains of Kauai. Gently he explained, "You and I are going over to Oahu, Kamejiro. And we're going to blast a puka right through the mountains. We'll get more water . . ."

"What you speak, Hoxuwortu?" the little Japanese asked.

"We're going to dynamite a tunnel right through the mountains, and you're going to do the dynamiting."

Kamejiro looked at his boss suspiciously. "Boom-boom?" he asked.

"Takusan boom-boom!" Whip replied.

"Sometime boom-boom kill," Sakagawa countered.

"That's why I wanted a man with guts," Whip shouted. "Good pay. One day one dollar."

"Mo bettah one dollar half," Kamejiro proposed.

Whip studied the tough little workman and laughed. "For you, Kamejiro, one dollar half."

He extended his hand to the stocky workman, but Kamejiro held back. "And one piece iron for hot bath?"

"All the iron you want. I hear you have a baby."

"One wahine," Kamejiro confessed with shame.

"Bring her along . . . and your wife," Whip cried, and the contract was confirmed.

The camp to which Kamejiro moved his family was high on the rainy side of the Koolau Range on Oahu, and to operate his hot bath for the Japanese workmen Kamejiro required a waterproof shed which he and Yoriko built at night. Yoriko also managed the commissary and by dint of literally endless work the two thrifty Japanese managed to acquire a considerable nest egg, but its size was due not primarily to their hard work but rather to the fact that in these inaccessible mountains the representatives of the consulate could not reach them, and so Kamejiro passed two full years without discovering how badly his homeland needed money.

He was occupied in the thrilling business of hauling great loads of dynamite deep into the tunnel, boring holes into which it was tamped, and then exploding it with dramatic effect. Technically, the job should have been simple and, if time-proved precautions were observed, free from real danger; but the Koolau Range presented perplexing features which made the job not only unpleasant but downright dangerous.

Millions of years before, the rocks of which the mountains were constructed had been laid down on a flat shoreline, with alternate layers of impermeable cap rock and easily permeable conglomerate. Later, a general uptilting had occurred, standing these alternate layers upright, with their ends exposed to the ceaseless rains. For millions of years torrential cascades had seeped down through the permeable layers and deep into the recesses of the island, thus feeding the underground reservoirs which Wild Whip and his driller, Mr. Overpeck, had tapped some thirty-five years before. Now, when inquisitive Kamejiro drove his drill into the impermeable cap rock all was well; but when he got to the permeable conglomerate it was as if he had pushed his drill into solid water, and often the drill would be washed from his hands as the impounded torrents gushed out. Eight million gallons of unexpected water a day flooded the tunnel, and Kamejiro, working in the middle of it, was constantly soaked; and since the water was a uniform sixty-six degrees, he was frequently threatened with pneumonia.

Wild Whip, watching him work, often thought: "He's the kind of man you could wish was an American."

Of course, the phrase was meaningless, for both the Americans and the Japanese clearly understood that none of the latter could become citizens. The law forbade it, and one of the reasons why the Japanese consulate kept such close check on its nationals was that America had said plainly: "They are your people, not ours." For example, when Japanese working on the tunnel found their food inedible they trudged in to their consulate, as was proper, and made their protest directly to the Japanese government. This accomplished nothing, for the consulate officials came from a class in Japan that exploited workers far worse than anyone in Hawaii would dare to; therefore the officials never presented protests to men like Wild Whip Hoxworth. Indeed, they marveled that he treated his Japanese as well as he did. When the tunnel workers had made their speeches, the consulate men replied abruptly: "Get back to work and don't cause trouble."

"But the food . . ."

"Back to work!" the Japanese officials roared, and the men went back. Of course, when in desperation they went to Wild Whip himself, he took one taste of the food and bellowed, "Who in hell calls this suitable for human beings?" And the diet was improved . . . just enough to forestall open rebellion.

But there was one aspect of dynamiting in the Koolau Range that involved real danger, and that was when an apparently normal charge hung fire. For some such failures there were detectable reasons: a fuse might be faulty; or the exploding charger had not delivered a proper spark; or a connection had torn loose. It might seem that these defects should have been easy to correct, but there was always an outside chance that a true hang-fire existed: the fuse had been well lit and had started burning, but for some mysterious reason it had hesitated en route. At any moment it could resume its journey to the massive charge and any who happened to be investigating its momentary suspension would be killed.

Whenever a hang-fire occurred, anywhere in the tunnel, men shouted, "Eh, Kamejiro! What you think?" And he hurried up to take charge.

He had a feeling about dynamite. Men claimed he could think like a stick of TNT, and he seemed to know when to wait and when to go forward. So far he had seen four men killed as a result of ignoring his judgment, and in the later stages of drilling his word became final. If he said, "I'll look at the connection," men watched admiringly as he did so; but if he said, "Too much pilikia," everyone waited. Once he had held up operations for two hours, and in the end a thousand tons of basalt had suddenly been torn loose by a true hangfire. Thanks to Kamejiro, no one was killed and that night one of the shaken workmen called from his hot bath: "Today, Mrs. Sakagawa, all Japan was proud of your husband!"

When the last remaining fragment of basalt was pierced, blown apart by Kamejiro's final concentration of dynamite, Hawaii began to appreciate what Wild Whip had accomplished. Twenty-seven million gallons of water a day poured down to join the artesian supplies developed earlier, and it became possible to bring into cultivation thousands of acres that had long lain arid and beyond hope. In the traditional pattern of Hawaii, the intelligence and dedication of one man had transformed a potential good into a realized one.

At the final celebration of the first great tunnel through the mountains, a speakers' platform was erected on which the governor sat, and three judges, and military leaders, and Wild Whip Hoxworth. Florid speeches were made congratulating the wise engineers who had laid out the plans, and the brave bankers who had financed it, and the sturdy lunas who had supervised the gangs; but there were no Japanese to be seen. It was as if, when the plans were formulated and the money provided, the puka had dug itself. But late that afternoon Wild Whip, who had a feeling for these things, sought out stocky little Kamejiro Sakagawa as he was tearing down the hot bath on the rainy side, and he said to the dynamiter, "Kamejiro, what you do now?"

"Maybe get one job dynamiter."

"They're hard to get." Whip kicked at the muddy earth and asked, "You like to work for me again, Hanakai?"

"Maybe stop Honolulu, maybe mo bettah."

"I think so, too," Whip agreed. "Tell you what, Kamejiro. I could never have built this tunnel without you. If I'd thought about it, I'd a had you on the platform today. But I didn't and that's that. Now I have a little plot of land in Honolulu, big enough for a garden. I'm going to give it to you."

"I don't want land," the little dynamiter said. "Pretty soon go back to Japan."

"Maybe that's best," Whip agreed. "I'll do this. Instead of the land, I'll give you two hundred dollars. And if you ever want to go back to Hanakai, let me know."

So Kamejiro turned down land, which if he had taken it, would one day have been worth $200,000. In its place he accepted $200, but this transaction was not so silly as it sounds, for this $200 plus what he and his wife had saved gave them at last the full funds they needed for a return to Japan.

They left the rainy hillside where they had worked so long and so miserably and turned joyously toward Honolulu and the offices of the *Kyoto-maru,* but when they got to the city they were immediately visited by officials from the consulate who were taking up a collection for the brave Imperial navy that had been fighting the Germans and a collection for the brave settlers who were going to the new colonies of Saipan and Yap. They were pounced on by Buddhist priests who were going to build a fine temple up Nuuanu. And Mr. Ishii had come over from Kauai to try his luck in Honolulu and needed a hundred and fifty dollars.

"Kamejiro!" his wife pleaded. "Don't give that man any more money. He never pays it back."

"Whenever I look at poor Ishii-san, I am reminded that I stole his legitimate wife, and all my happiness is founded on his misfortune," Kamejiro said softly. "If he needs the money, he must have it."

So the return to Japan was momentarily delayed, and then Yoriko announced: "We are going to have another baby," and this time it was a boy, to be named Goro as planned. He was quickly followed by three brothers—Tadao in 1921, Minoru in 1922, and Shigeo in 1923—and the subtle bonds that tied the Sakagawas to Hawaii were more and more firmly tied, for the children, growing up in Hawaii, would speak English and laugh like Americans, and grow to prefer not rice but foods that came out of cans.

WHEN Kamejiro Sakagawa finished his work in the tunnel, and when the money he had saved dribbled through his hard hands in one way or another, he hoped, vainly as it proved, that he might find a similar job as dynamiter, but none developed. He therefore took his wife and two children to the artesian plantation west of Honolulu, the original Malama Sugar, and there he went to work, twelve hours a day for seventy-seven cents a day.

He was also given an old clapboard house twenty feet wide and fourteen feet deep, from which six square feet were cut for a porch. There was a sagging lean-to shed in which Yoriko did the cooking over an iron pan. The house stood on poles one foot high, providing an under space into which children could crawl on hot days. It was a dirty, cramped, unlovely living area, but fortunately it contained at the rear just enough space for Kamejiro to erect a hot bath, so that in spite of the meager income the family was somewhat better off than the neighbors, who had to pay to use the Sakagawa bath.

Furthermore, the family income was augmented by Mrs. Sakagawa, who worked in the sugar fields for sixty-one cents a day, leaving her children with neighbors. Each dusk there came a moment of pure joy when the family reconvened and the lively youngsters, their jet-black hair bobbed straight across their eyes, rushed out to meet their parents. But these moments of reunion were also apt to have overtones of confusion, for grudgingly the Sakagawas had to confess that they could not always understand what their children were saying. For example, one night when they asked in Japanese where a neighbor was, little Reiko-chan, a brilliant, limpid-eyed beauty, explained: "Him fadder pauhana konai," and her parents had to study the sentence, for *him fadder* was corrupted English, *pauhana* was Hawaiian for the end of work, and *konai* was good Japanese for has not come.

It therefore became apparent to Kamejiro that if he intended returning his daughter to Japan, and he did, he was going to have a hard time finding her a decent Japanese husband if she could not speak the language any better than that, so he enrolled her in the Japanese school, where a teacher from Tokyo kept strict order. Over his head loomed a great sign, with characters which Kamejiro could not read but which the teacher, a frail young man, explained: "Loyalty to the emperor." Added the instructor: "Here we teach as in Japan. If your child does not learn, she will suffer the consequences."

"You will teach her about the emperor and the greatness of Japan?" Kamejiro asked.

"As if she were back in Hiroshima-ken," the teacher promised, and from the manner in which he banged his knuckles against the heads of misbehaving boys, Kamejiro felt assured that he had put his child into good hands.

Actually, Reiko-chan required no discipline, for she learned both quickly and with joy. She was then the youngest child in school but also one of the ablest, and when she ran barefooted home at night, babbling in fine Japanese, Kamejiro felt proud, for she was learning to read and he could not.

There were other aspects of his life at Malama Sugar about which he was not happy, and these centered upon money. It was more expensive to live on Oahu than it had been on Kauai, yet his wages were lower. Rice, fish, seaweed and pickles had all gone up in price, yet there were now five children to feed, and the boys ate like pigs. Clothes too were more expensive, and although Yoriko was frugal, she did need a new visiting dress now and then. One morning, as the sun was beginning to rise, Kamejiro watched his hard-working wife setting out with her hoe and it occurred to him: "She's been wearing the same skirt, the same dotted blouse, the same white cloth about her face and the same straw hat for five years. And they're all in rags."

But when it came time for him to buy her a new outfit, he found that he did not have the money, and he realized that even with two adults working, the Sakagawa family was existing perilously close to the starvation level. He was therefore in a receptive frame of mind when an unusual visitor arrived at Malama Sugar. It was Mr. Ishii, who was now acting as traveling agent for the Japanese Federation of Labor, and his information was that after a series of talks with the big planters like Whipple Hoxworth, his organization was going to win decent wages for the Japanese.

"Listen to this!" he whispered to a group of workmen with whom he met secretly. "We are asking for one dollar and twenty-five cents a day for men, ninety-five cents for wahines. Can you imagine how that will improve your living? The workday will be cut back to eight hours, and there will be bonuses in December if the year has been a good one. If you have to work on Sundays, overtime. And for the wahines, they'll be allowed to quit work two weeks before the baby is born."

The men listened in awe as this vision of a new life dawned in the little hut, but before they had a chance to ascertain when all this was going to take place, a sentinel outside whistled, then ran up with frightening news: "Lunas! Lunas!"

Four big Germans burst into the meeting place, grabbed little Mr. Ishii before he could escape, and hauled him out into the dusty yard. They manhandled him no more than necessary, being content to give him a scare with three or four good knocks, then kicked him onto the road leading back toward Honolulu. "Don't you come onto Malama Sugar with your radical ideas," they warned him. "Next time, plenty pilikia!"

While two of the lunas made sure that the little agitator left the plantation, the other two returned to the room where the clandestine meeting had been held. "Nishimura, Sakagawa, Ito, Sakai, Suzuki," one of the lunas recited while the other wrote. "A fine way to treat Mr. Janders and Mr. Whipple. Whose house is this? Yours, Inoguchi?" The biggest luna grabbed Inoguchi by the shirt and held him up. "I'll remember who the traitor was," the luna said, staring at the workmen. With a snort of disgust he threw the man back among his fellows, and the two Germans stamped out. But at the gate they stopped and said ominously, "You men go to your homes. No more meetings, understand?"

As Kamejiro left he whispered to Inoguchi, "Maybe a long time before we get what Ishii-san promised?"

"I think so, too," Inoguchi agreed.

From that night on, conditions at Malama Sugar grew increasingly tense. To everyone's surprise, little Mr. Ishii exhibited unforeseen reservoirs of heroism, for against really considerable odds, and in direct opposition to seven lunas, he managed time and again to slip back into the plantation to advise the men of how the negotiations were going. When he was caught, he was beat up, as he expected to be, and he lost one of his front teeth; but after twenty-two years of relative ineffectiveness in everything he attempted, he had at last stumbled upon an activity for which he was pre-eminently suited. He loved intrigue and rumor; he cherished the portrait of himself as a worker for the common good; so he came back again and again, until at last the lunas assembled all the field hands and said, "Anyone caught talking with the Bolshevik Ishii is going to be thrown out of his house and off the plantation. Is that clear?"

But the Japanese had caught a vision of what Mr. Ishii was trying to do, and at great danger to themselves they continued to meet with him, and one day in January he told them gravely, and with the sadness that comes from seeing fine plans destroyed, "The managers will not listen to our demands. We shall have to strike."

The next day Honolulu was marked by many pamphlets bearing the unmistakable touch of Mr. Ishii, his florid manner of expression and his hope: "Good men and ladies of Hawaii. We, the laborers who grow the sugar upon which you live, address you with humility and hope. Did you know, as you drive past our waving fields of cane, that the men who grow it receive only seventy-seven cents a day? On this money we raise our children and teach them good manners and teach them to be decent citizens. But on this money we also starve.

"We love Hawaii and consider it a great privilege and pride to live under the Stars and Stripes, which stands for freedom and justice. We are happy to be part of the great sugar industry and to keep the plantations running profitably.

"We love work. Thirty-five years ago when we first came to Hawaii the lands where we now work were covered with ohia and guava and wild grass. Day and night have we worked, cutting those parasites and burning the grass. Our work has made the plantations, but of course it is indisputable that we could not have succeeded were it not for the investments made by wealthy capitalists and the untiring efforts of the lunas and administrators. But Hawaii must not magnify the contributions of the capitalists and forget the equal contributions of the laborers who have served faithfully with sweat on their brows.

"Look at the silent tombstones in every locality. They are the last emblems of Hawaii's pioneers in labor. Why should they die in poverty while others get rich from their labors? Why should hard-working men continue to get seventy-seven cents a day? The other day a plantation manager said, 'I think of field hands as I do jute bags. Buy them, use them, buy others.' We think of ourselves as human beings and as members of the great human family. We want $1.25 a day for an eight-hour day. And in the interests of common humanity we deserve it."

This extraordinary preamble to the workers' demands was received differently in four different quarters. When Kamejiro Sakagawa and his co-workers heard the flowery words read to them in Japanese, with lunas at hand to take down the names of everyone attending the meeting, Kamejiro listened with amazement that his friend Mr. Ishii should have caught so exactly the emotions that motivated the workers. With tears in his eyes he said, "Inoguchi-san? Have you ever heard a better piece of paper? He says that we are part of the great human family. Did you ever think of yourself that way before?"

"All I think," Inoguchi-san replied, "is that there's going to be trouble."

To his wife Yoriko, Kamejiro said, "When I heard Ishii-san's statement, I was glad for every dollar I ever loaned him. It looks as if we will get all we have asked for, because that is a very powerful bit of reasoning."

His stolid wife was more of Inoguchi's turn of mind. "We had better get ready to go hungry," she warned. And that day the strike began.

When the manifesto reached Wild Whip Hoxworth, the head of the planters' association gagged before he got to the end of it. "Mad Russian Bolshevism!" he bellowed. "Get the planters together!" When the leaders of the sugar industry were assembled, he went over the statement line by line. " 'We, the laborers,' " he read scornfully. "As if they had convened themselves into some kind of revolutionary tribunal. 'On this money we starve.' What a degrading, horrible play to the emotions. 'Good men and ladies of Hawaii!' As if by appealing to them they could by-pass those of us responsible for wages. By God, gentlemen, this document strikes at the very roots of society. It's rampant, red, pillaging Russianism, and if there is any man in this room who breaks ranks to give those little yellow bastards an inch, I'll personally knock him down and kick his weak-livered guts in. Is that understood?"

The other planters, who were perhaps more appalled by the Bolshevik-inspired manifesto than Wild Whip, for they had studied it in a calmer light and understood its implications better than he, showed no signs of disagreeing with their leader, and when he was satisfied on that point he passed to additional matters. "Now who in hell among you made that stupid statement about workmen and jute bags?" There was silence, and after a moment he slammed the paper on the table and growled, "It's true, and everyone here knows it's true. But don't say such things. Shut up. It's nobody's business what you and I do or think. Shut up. There's a dreadful spirit abroad in the world today, and I blame it all on Woodrow Wilson. Appealing to the people over the heads of their government. Just like this dirty sheet. From now on, I'll do the talking."

He summoned a secretary and dictated, while his astonished compatriots listened: "We have studied the statement of the Federation of Japanese Labor in Hawaii and are pleased to note its temperate tenor, its cautious manner of argument, and its refusal to stoop to violent or ill-founded reasoning. The men who wrote it are to be congratulated upon their restraint, which in previous similar disputes was not conspicuous.

"We regret, naturally, that a group of alien workmen, not citizens of this territory, should feel constrained to tell us how to manage the greatest industry in the islands, and it is our duty as loyal Americans to point out that in these years following a great war in which the principles of democracy were once more sustained against alien and unnatural enemies, the state of our economy, strained as it was by the war effort, simply cannot undertake any further aggravated expenses. A moment's analysis of what is requested in these demands will satisfy any impartial . . ."

He went on and on in a tone of sweet reasonableness, and when the secretary had left he said to the sugar men, "That's how we'll handle the little bastards. This is a strike of alien Japanese Bolsheviks against the bulwarks of American freedom, and by God don't let anybody forget . . . not for a minute. That's the ground we'll lick them on."

At the offices of the Honolulu *Mail* the workers' document had a staggering effect, for it was the first one in a long series of complaints to show any signs of mature composition. "Some fiendishly clever man wrote this!" the editor stormed. "Hell, if you didn't know what it was all about you might think Thomas Jefferson or Tom Paine had done it. In my opinion, this is the most dangerous document ever to have appeared in Hawaii, and it's got to be fought on that basis."

The entire staff was summoned to analyze the inflammatory document, after which the editor retired to his sanctum. Carefully, and with much polishing, he wrote: "This morning the citizens of Hawaii were at last able to comprehend what has been going on in the Japanese-language schools, in the Buddhist temples, and in the murky confines of the Imperial consulate. The manifesto of the Bolshevik Japanese labor union at last drew the gauze from before our eyes. Citizens of Hawaii, we are faced by no less than an organized attempt to make these islands a subsidiary part of the Japanese empire. Already the first loops of the tentacles have been swept about Kauai and Maui and Oahu. There is afoot an evil design to remove from positions of leadership those noble and hard-working sons of American pioneers who made these islands great and to supplant them with crafty Orientals whose sole purpose is not the betterment of their people but the aggrandizement of a distant and alien empire.

"The Japanese plotters appeal to the people of Hawaii to support their cause. This newspaper appeals to the people of Hawaii to consider what it will mean to each and every one of us if the present strike should be successful. In place of far-seeing men like the Whipples, the Janderses, the Hales and the Hoxworths who have built these islands to their present position of magnificence, we would have aliens attempting to run our industries. Sugar and pineapple would languish. No cargoes would move to the mainland. Our schools would wither and our churches would be closed.

"We must fight this strike to the end. Not a single concession must be granted. The entire citizenship of Hawaii must unite against this alien threat. For the issue at stake is brutally clear: Do we wish Hawaii to be part of America or part of Japan? There is no point in expressing the question in any other terms, and every American who has a streak of decency in him will know how to answer the terrible challenge that has been thrown down before him. This strike must fail! There must be no wavering, for any who do waver are traitors to their nation, their homes and their God.

"Lest there be any misunderstanding as to the position of this newspaper at this time of grave crisis we wish to say this: If at any time in the process of this strike there is a choice between the total economic ruination of these islands and the turning of them over to the evil designs of the Japanese labor leaders, we unflinchingly declare that we will not only prefer but will encourage the former."

The fourth place in Honolulu where the manifesto occasioned an unexpectedly violent reaction was in the Japanese consulate, on Nuuanu. There the second secretary got a copy at about eight o'clock, read it, felt the blood leave his face, and rushed in to see his superior, who studied it with quivering hands. "Those fools! Those fools!" the consul cried. He had not yet seen the editorial in the Honolulu *Mail,* but he could visualize what was going to be said. Throwing the document down, he strode back and forth in his carpeted room, then shouted at his assistant, "Why don't those damned Japanese laborers learn to be content with what they have? The fools! Their wages here are twice what they'd be in Japan. And they get good treatment." He continued fuming, then assembled his entire staff.

"You have severe orders," he said coldly. "This consulate will do absolutely nothing to support the strikers. If a deputation marches on this consulate, as it has always done in the past, they are to be received with no warmth whatever. It is imperative that this strike be broken quickly."

"Suppose the strikers seek repatriation?" an underling asked.

"Their job is to stay here, work here, and send their money back home," the consul snapped.

"What shall we do if they appeal against police brutality?" the same underling pressed.

"Summon me. I'll make the usual formal protests, but we must avoid seeming to be on the side of the workmen. Remember, workmen do not govern Hawaii, and our responsibility is to people like Whipple Hoxworth who do."

"One more question, sir. Suppose the strikers ask for food?"

"Not to be granted. Gentlemen, this strike is a dangerous manifestation. If the phrases appearing in this document were to be used in Japan, those responsible would be jailed for life . . . or would be executed. I am appalled that decent Japanese field hands would dare to use such language. Our job is to force these men back to work. The strike must be broken, because if it isn't, the newspapers will begin to accuse the emperor of having fomented it."

The strike was broken, of course, but mainly by a series of adventitious developments, for on the day in February when the plantations evicted the Japanese laborers, telling them to live in the fields if necessary, by purest chance an influenza epidemic of the most virulent dimensions erupted, and in one crowded rural area where the strikers were living ten to a room or under trees, more than fifty of the workmen died. In all some five thousand strikers collapsed, many of them with no beds to sleep in and without hot food, and the subsequent death toll was interpreted by the superstitious as proof that the strike was against the will of God.

The Sakagawa family trudged twenty-six miles into Honolulu, hoping that Mr. Ishii could find them some place to stay, but he could not, and they at last took up residence with more than four hundred others in an abandoned sake brewery, where rats crawled over the children at night. There Reiko-chan caught the flu and it seemed that she was going to die. At first her mother was tempted to rail at Kamejiro for having supported the strike and having brought such misery upon his family, but when she saw with what passionate care he tended Reiko, even though she was a girl, the stolid woman forgave her husband and said, "Danna-san, we will win the strike this time, I am sure."

But next day the Board of Health met and listened to Wild Whip Hoxworth as he pointed out: "We're engaged in war, gentlemen, and in war you use every weapon you have. Every one. I passed by the old sake brewery last night, and it's a health menace. I want the people in there evicted, and I want it closed."

"Sir, there's a lot of children in there with the flu," a doctor protested.

"That's why it's got to be closed," Hoxworth replied.

"But these people will have no place to go," the doctor argued.

"I know. I want them to learn what it means to strike against the elements of law and order in a community."

"But, sir, we've got to think . . ."

"Close that goddamned brewery!" Hoxworth bellowed, and it was closed.

The temperature in Hawaii never indulges in extremes, except on the tops of the volcanic mountains, where snows persist through much of the year, but February nights can be miserably chilling, and for two influenza-ridden nights the Sakagawas slept on the ground near Iwilei. Kamejiro held the sick girl Reiko in his arms and his wife cradled Shigeo, the baby, and the nights were bad, but on the third day Mr. Ishii found them and said, "I have found a hut where an old woman died," and they wolfed down the food that she would have eaten had she lived.

For three weeks the epidemic raged and the deaths of exposed workmen reached toward the hundred mark. At the end of this time, Mr. Ishii, Kamejiro and Inoguchi-san organized a committee of sixteen who marched lawfully up Nuuanu to the Japanese consulate, seeking help in that quarter. They were met by an official in black-rimmed glasses, cutaway coat and nervous grin. Allowing Mr. Ishii to do their speaking, the men said, "We are being very poorly treated by the Americans, and we must come to the Imperial government for help."

"The Imperial government is protecting Japanese interests with studious care," the official assured the deputation. "Only yesterday His Excellency protested to the Chief of Police against keeping the Japanese from holding legal meetings."

"But they are throwing us out of our homes, and our men are dying in the fields," Mr. Ishii said quietly.

With equal calmness the spokesman explained, "His Excellency only last week looked into the law and found that the plantations have the right to expel you . . . if you strike."

"But there is a great sickness in these islands," Mr. Ishii protested.

"Then perhaps the strike ought to terminate," the spokesman suggested.

"But we can't live on seventy-seven cents a day."

"In Japan your brothers surely live on much less," the official assured the strikers, and the fruitless interview was concluded.

Another accident which worked against the strikers was the discovery, in early May, of a schoolbook used in the Japanese schools which had a long passage explaining what was meant by the phrase used by Japan's first emperor, "All the world under a roof of eight poles." Quite obviously, the book explained to the children of Japan—and it was never intended for use in Hawaii but had somehow got into the islands by mistake—it was the Emperor Jimmu Tenno's idea that all the world must some day be united into one great family paying homage to the sun goddess and obedience to the emperor, her lineal descendant. Cried the Honolulu *Mail:* "If anyone has wanted proof of the contentions of this newspaper that Japan intends one day to conquer the world, with Hawaii as the first step in the conquest, this evil little book proves the fact beyond contention. All the world under one roof! The local Japanese Bolsheviks have already taken the first step in that domination, and unless we remain steadfast and defeat their foul aspirations, we shall be the first foreign territory to be submerged beneath the Japanese roof." If sugar men were growing faint-hearted as the long strike headed for its sixth harrowing month, this timely discovery of what was being taught in Japan fortified them.

Finally, there was the disgraceful affair of dynamiting the home in which Inoguchi-san of Malama Sugar was living. No one was killed, fortunately, but when the Honolulu *Mail* disclosed that Inoguchi had been dynamited because he had been in secret negotiations with the sugar planters, telling them nightly what Mr. Ishii and the committee were planning next, the community had to acknowledge that the Japanese labor leaders really were a group of determined Bolsheviks. Swift police raids swept up nineteen of the leaders, including Mr. Ishii, and threw them into jail on charges of criminal conspiracy. Wild Whip Hoxworth visited the judges involved and pointed out that the charges might better be criminal syndicalism, and they thanked him for his interest in the case.

But now the question arose as to who had taught the committee how to handle dynamite, and a reporter remembered that Kamejiro Sakagawa, who had not yet been arrested, had learned the trade while working on the tunnel. He was known to be a friend of Mr. Ishii's, and so the police arrested him. He was thrown into jail, even though he had had nothing to do with the dynamiting, whereupon his wife Yoriko proved to the police that he had been at home caring for his sick children. The sugar committee, who were advising the district attorney as to how he should handle the case, refused to accept this alibi, pointing out: "A clever man like Sakagawa didn't have to be actually at the scene of the crime. He could well have prepared the sticks in advance and shown his fellow conspirators how to explode them. He is obviously guilty." And he was kept in jail.

Then the strike ended, with the workmen having gained little, and sugar was once more produced by some of the cheapest labor in America. H & H made millions carrying fresh cargoes to California, and J & W made more millions managing the plantations in the good old way. The conspirators were brought to trial and Mr. Ishii was sentenced to ten years in jail. He sagged when the words were thrown at him, falling backwards as if they had actually struck him, and from that day on he was never much of a man again. He grew to mumble and imagine things, and no one took much account of him.

Surprisingly, Kamejiro, the dynamiter by trade, was not convicted, for one day before the trial began he had a visitor in his cell. It was Wild Whip Hoxworth, lean and tall and handsome, flushed with victory. "Eh, you, Kamejiro. Boys say you plant dynamite. That true?"

"No, Mr. Hoxuwortu. No."

"Me, I think no too." And Wild Whip told the district attorney, "You better drop charges against Sakagawa. He wasn't involved."

"How do you know?" the young lawyer asked, nervous with excitement over the trial that was going to make his reputation.

"Because he told me so," Whip explained.

"And you're going to take his word?"

"He's the most honest man I know. Besides, his alibi is a good one."

"But I think we've got to convict the actual dynamiter, whether his alibi is good or not."

"Turn him loose!" Whip thundered. He was sixty-six years old and tired of arguing with fools.

So on the morning that the trial convened, Kamejiro was quietly set free. Of course, he was never again able to get a job at Malama Sugar, for the great plantations prudently maintained blacklists in order to keep out troublemakers, and he had now proved himself one who fought with lunas and supported Bolsheviks like Ishii. He found a small, rat-infested shack in the Kakaako area of Honolulu, from which he did odd jobs, principally the cleaning out of privies after midnight. Children whose fathers had better jobs called him "King of the Night Brigade," and indeed the name King was fitting, for whatever he was required to do, he did with the most earnest skill, so that in spite of the fact that he was surreptitiously known as Sakagawa the Dynamiter, the man who had tried to kill Inoguchi, people nevertheless continued to seek him out when their privies needed unloading, for he merited the title, "King of the Night Brigade."

IN 1926 the disreputable old English botanist Dr. Schilling developed another striking idea about the growing of pineapple. Recovering from a four-month drunk, he turned fresh, if bloodshot, eyes upon the great fields of Kauai, and as he studied the swarms of Japanese women hoeing out the weeds from the red soil, he thought: "Why don't we spread paper over the whole damned field, punch holes in it where we plant the baby pineapple, and make it impossible for weeds to grow?"

He got some asphalt paper, rolled it across a trial field, and planted a crop of pineapple in the small holes he had punched in the black covering. To his surprise, the simple trick not only killed off all the weeds, saving hundreds of dollars in labor charges, but also provided two unforeseen advantages which proved to be more profitable than even the extermination of weeds: the paper trapped moisture and held it about the roots of the plants, and on sunny days it accumulated heat which was later dissipated exactly when the plants required it.

When Wild Whip saw the results of the experiment he gave an instant and dramatic order: "Hereafter all pineapple on our plantations will be grown under paper," and he worked diligently with Dr. Schilling and the California wood-pulp people in devising a special paper that resisted water for the first seven months of its life, then slowly disintegrated so that by the tenth month the field was clean. When the project was completed, Wild Whip reminded the pineapple men: "You can always find somebody from Yale who can accomplish anything you want. Treat them well, pay them a little, and call them Doctor. That's all they expect. But somebody with brains has got to set the problem for them."

And then, in 1927, this nonpareil of planters died at the brawling, bruising age of seventy. He died, as he had often predicted, of no ordinary disease but from an aggravated cancer of the prostate occasioned, the islands felt sure, by his numerous cases of gonorrhea and syphilis, plus cirrhosis of the liver brought on by endless overdoses of alcohol, all aggravated by the fact that the small airplane in which he was flying back from Hanakai Plantation to Honolulu flew into the mountain that he had pierced with his great tunnel. He had lain exposed in cold rain for nearly twenty-four hours, but even under those conditions the vital old man fought a fairly even contest with death for a period of three weeks, during which he summoned to his hospital bed the leading members of H & H and J & W, including all who might logically aspire to his chairmanship.

Raising himself in pain to a sitting position, which appalled the nurses, he grunted, "We're entering a difficult period, and our job is to make half a dozen right decisions." He spoke as if he were to be with the managers for many years to come, and possibly forever. "I'm sure our present prosperity can't continue forever, and when there's a leveling off, sugar and pineapple will be hard hit. Thank God, it doesn't seem likely the Democrats will ever return to Washington, so we don't have to worry about radical communism. But we do have to worry about keeping our share of the market.

"We've got to have somebody heading up our enterprises who is clever enough to anticipate the future and bold enough to fight what's wrong. I've given a good deal of thought as to who that should be, and I've come up with only one solid conclusion. Don't ever, under any conceivable circumstances, allow either of my sons, Jesus Duarte or John, to meddle in this business. Pay them well, pay them regularly, and keep them to hell out of Hawaii. If my other son, Janders, had lived . . . well, that might have been a different story.

"Naturally I've thought a great deal about Mark Whipple. He has his father's brains and would have been my first choice, except that being a West Point man, he thinks he ought to stay with the army, and maybe he's right. But if he ever decides to resign his commission, get him back into the company quick.

"I've also given a good deal of consideration to Hewie Janders," and here the big, rugged, florid man who had starred as guard at Yale blushed, but Wild Whip continued, "and I fear that Hewie's attributes do not include intellectual force, which is what we need now.

"I've passed over, as you can see, all the older fellows, because we need somebody who's going to give our firms a long, continued and strong leadership. So I've chosen as my executor, and the man to vote my shares as long as he remains intellectually and morally capable, this fellow." And he reached out and took the hand of Hoxworth Hale, then twenty-nine years old and aching for authority. The other directors could not protest the decision, nor had they any cause to do so, for Hale was obviously the man to take over at this juncture.

"Three rules, Hoxworth, and the rest of you listen. Don't ever sell sugar short. I went into pineapple, that's true, but only when I had a solid, secure base in sugar. You do the same. Protect sugar by research, protect your quotas by legislation, protect the plantations, protect your labor supply. Stay with sugar. It's better than money, more dependable than blood.

"Second, never allow labor to rear its head an inch. Study what's happened on the mainland. If a labor leader tries to get onto these islands, throw him back into the ocean and tell him to swim, but don't even show him which way California is. Be careful of the Japanese. They're making sounds like they wanted a union. Trust only the Filipinos, because nobody else can be trusted. But if the bolo-boys attempt any foolishness, bat them down.

"Third, you've got to keep mainland firms from forcing their way into our economy. Don't let the chain stores in. Don't let outfits like Gregory's and California Fruit onto these shores. We have a good system here, one that we've worked damned hard to perfect, and we don't want a lot of radical new ideas polluting it. If such gangsters try to invade, sell them no land, refuse to handle their shipping, tie them up on credit, strangle the bastards."

He had spoken rather forcefully and now fell back on his pillow, aching in the cancered prostate, in his failing kidneys and in each of his four broken bones. The nurses dragooned a passing doctor, who cried, "Good God, gentlemen, you're most inconsiderate! Now you get out of here!"

Whip fell into a little sleep, and when in the late afternoon he woke, it was with considerable elation of spirit, for he was reviewing in imagination a series of pictures he had first invented with his wonderful old grandmother, Noelani, the Alii Nui from Lahaina. On her last trip to the Orient, Noelani had acquired a set of Japanese color prints showing what were called the eight loveliest scenes on earth. It contained a mountain in snow, boats returning to shore, wild geese descending, and sunset. "It is things like these," gracious old Noelani had told her grandchildren, "that are the real beauty of life." They had played a game: "Let's decide what the eight loveliest scenes of Hawaii are." And now Wild Whip, himself older than Noelani when she had umpired the contest, reviewed the permanent grandeurs of his islands.

For the mountain in the snow, they had chosen the great volcanoes of the big island, mysteriously clothed in white, yet standing within the tropics. Geologists considered them the highest single mountains in the world—19,000 feet below the ocean, almost 14,000 above. Nowhere in the world could boats returning to shore be lovelier than at Lahaina, where the roads were caught between islands. The wild geese descending were, of course, the single most glorious sight in Hawaii: the myriad waterfalls at the leper settlement of Kalawao. "How beautiful they were," Whip thought. "How beautiful."

The evening glow, which the men who designated the eight supreme views liked especially, could be seen nowhere with finer effect than at the deep red canyon of Kauai, an incredible gash through fifty million years of scintillating rock; at dusk it seemed filled with demonic force. And as for night rain, much loved by the Japanese, where could it be seen to more poetic effect than on the gloomy lava beds of the big island, those convoluted and tormented beds which had overrun the first settlers from Bora Bora?

The next two scenes were from Oahu, queen of the islands. Once Wild Whip had seen an autumn moon, gray and silver in radiance, shining on the plains that lay at the foot of the Pali, and he had been captivated by the subtle interplay of dark forms and moonlit shadows. The evening bell, which Chinese loved for its memories of home, Whip and his grandmother had assigned to Honolulu, for it was indeed memorable to sit on some broad lanai on a Honolulu hillside, listening to the evening bells of the churches and watching the lights of the city come on.

There was an eighth view, the sunset sky, the end of the day, the last glimpse of earth, and Whip could never recall where Noelani had placed this concluding view; but for himself, as he thought of his islands now, he could place it only at Hanakai. He saw the Norfolk pines and the royal palms, the trees and flowers he had brought in from all over the world. He saw the wild cliffs and the storms of winter leaping upon them, but most of all he saw beyond the grassy polo field the light green of sugar and higher up the dark blue-green of pineapple. How beautiful Hawaii was, how cherished by the ancient deities.

He died a Hawaiian, leaving his wild spirit to haunt the places he had loved. He was attended only by a pretty little Filipino girl he had picked up on Kauai. In his last minutes he tried to dictate a note to his seductive, brown-skinned playmate, but to his distress found she could not write, so he bellowed for a nurse, for he wanted to warn his successor: "Hoxworth, best way to keep labor controlled is to keep hand in legislature at all times." But when the nurse arrived to take this message, Wild Whip was dead, the builder of the islands who had been unable to build his own life, and the authorities spirited his little Filipino girl back to Kauai. The glowing sums of money old Whip had promised her she never got.

At twenty-nine Hoxworth Hale assumed control of the vast holdings, and when he first took the chair that Wild Whip had occupied for fifteen years, he realized that he must seem like a boy presuming to do a man's work, but at least he was dressed correctly for his new role: a dark-blue four-button suit with tight vest, an Egyptian-cotton shirt with detachable stiff collar and a heavy blue and red tie. His cuff links were of gold and pearl, and his hair was parted severely on the right-hand side. He was clean-shaven and steady of mind, and he was determined to send forward the fortunes of the family.

He was not unaccustomed to command, for quick upon the heels of his impulsive enlistment in the American Expeditionary Force in 1917, he had become a sergeant, and in France had won a battlefield commission, demobilizing as a captain. His troops had great regard for him; he tried to be a brave, self-contained young leader, willing to assault any objective. His men also found him fun to be with, for he posed as having the insouciance that all young men in uniform like to think they have, and his company was one of the best.

After the war he completed his education at Yale, a quiet young man of twenty-two whose early radicalism had been abandoned somewhere in France, and he never once wandered back to see the notorious Jarves paintings. When he graduated he was already a conservative businessman, eager to make his contribution to Hoxworth & Hale, but in California on his way back to Hawaii he met a lovely girl whose father was a rancher with large land holdings. For a while it looked as if they were going to marry, but one night she spoke disparagingly of Honolulu and suggested that Hoxworth remain in California: "Hoxy! You could have your father assign you to the San Francisco office!"

His reply had been both cold and distant: "We send only nephews who aren't too bright to California." The courtship ended and after that no one ever again called him Hoxy.

When he had been at work for some time in the head office in Honolulu he married his third cousin, Malama Janders, who was Hewie Janders' sister, and within a year he had a son Bromley, whom he prudently registered for both Punahou and Yale. It was true that whenever business took him to San Francisco, he experienced a sense of deep excitement when he first saw the California coastline, and he often wondered what had become of the pretty rancher's daughter; but that was about as errant a thought as he ever had.

Now, in 1927, Hoxworth Hale was these things, and in each he was an almost perfect exemplification of the archetype: he was a Hale, a Punahou graduate, a Yale man, the head of a great island firm, and a man married to his cousin. Therefore, when he spoke at his first meeting of the H & H board, his colleagues listened: "There is an unfortunate spirit of agitation in the world today, and I believe our first concern must be the protection of our position by exercising some kind of logical control over the legislature."

He outlined a sensible plan whereby his impressive cousin, big Hewie Janders, got himself elected president of the senate, while half a dozen assorted lawyers, treasurers and accountants who worked for the big firms ran for lesser seats. For speaker of the house Hoxworth shrewdly selected the jovial, relaxed Chinese politician Kangaroo Kee, to whom he offered several lucrative contracts; and so carefully did the new young leader plan that before long Hawaii passed into that secure and reasonable period when most of its legislation was decided upon first at quiet meetings held in the board room of H & H, whence it was sent to trusted representatives who could be depended upon to enact laws pretty much as proposed by Hoxworth Hale and his close associates.

The board room of H & H was on the second floor of a large, fortlike building that stood at the corner of Fort and Merchant, and from this combination of facts the powerful clique that ran Hawaii came to be known simply as The Fort. It included, of course, H & H and also J & W. The Hewletts were members, as were some of the lesser planters from the big island. Banks, railways, trust companies and large estate owners were represented, but exactly what The Fort consisted of no man could properly say; it was simply the group who by common consent were entitled to meet on the second floor of H & H, a close-knit, cohesive body of men who were determined to give Hawaii a responsible form of government.

The Fort rarely abused its power. If some crackpot legislator not subservient to it wanted to curry favor with his constituents by shouting, "I promised you I'd get a playground for Kakaako, and I'll get you a playground for Kakaako," they let him yell, and at one of their meetings Hoxworth Hale would ask, "Is there any reason why there shouldn't be a playground at Kakaako?" and if such a project did not imperil any fundamental interest of The Fort—and if its cost could be passed on to the general public without raising real estate taxes—the playground was allowed to go through. But if this same legislator subsequently shouted, "Last year plantation trains running without lights killed four people, so I insist upon lights where plantation trains cross public roads," then The Fort moved quietly but massively into action. "We've looked into costs of such lights," Hoxworth Hale would tell his directors, "and they would cut our sugar profits to the bone." Somehow such bills were iceboxed in committee, and no amount of yelling by infuriated legislators could get them unfrozen.

Any major bill affecting either sugar, pineapple or land had to be actually drafted by The Fort itself; such bills were too important to be left to the whims of a legislature. But it was to Hoxworth Hale's credit that he did not allow grossly abusive bills to be proposed: "My interpretation of democracy is that business must never intrude into ordinary legislative processes, except where matters of vital importance are at stake and then never for selfish motives." At some sessions of the legislature forty-nine out of fifty bills were not interfered with in any way; but this was partly because the legislators had learned to ask, before proposing a bill, "Will The Fort go for this?" It was common prudence not to propose something that The Fort would automatically have to fight.

A fine example of Hoxworth Hale's statesmanship came one January when his wife, a Janders girl with a warm concern for human rights, said at breakfast, "Hoxworth, have you seen the casualty lists that resulted from the New Year's fireworks?"

"Were they bad, Malama?" he asked. One of the annual highlights in Hawaii was the Chinese New Year, when the Chinese practically blew the city apart with detonations of the most spectacular sort.

"This year one boy was killed and fourteen were seriously maimed," Malama reported. "Really, these fireworks must be outlawed."

Hoxworth, who agreed that the practice of blowing off arms and legs was ridiculous, told his wife, "If you can outlaw them by legal means, go ahead."

Consequently, Mrs. Hale enlisted a committee of fifty public-spirited ladies—all of them haole, unfortunately—who descended upon the legislature with a bill to halt the crippling of children. The first legislators approached thought: "Mrs. Hale! Probably got The Fort behind her. Better pass this bill." So the famous anti-fireworks bill was introduced.

And then all hell broke loose! By comparison, the New Year's pyrotechnic display was a subdued affair, for Chinese legislators shouted on the floor, "This is discrimination! We have always blown up fireworks on New Year's."

To everyone's surprise, the Chinese quickly gained support from the Hawaiians. "We love fireworks!" they protested.

A bombastic Portuguese legislator gave an impassioned plea for the right of little people to have their fun just one night a year, and a huge lobby of storekeepers, who made more than seventy per cent profit selling firecrackers, began to disrupt all customary legislative procedures.

At this point jovial Kangaroo Kee, speaker of the house and supposed to be a creature of The Fort, displayed leadership of an unexpected sort. Handing the gavel over to a friend, he descended to the floor of the house and delivered one of the most impassioned bits of oratory heard in Hawaii for many years. He shouted: "This evil bill is an attempt to deprive the Chinese of Hawaii of an inalienable right! It is religious persecution of the most abominable sort! Do the haole women who brought in this bill need fireworks for their religious ceremonies? No! But do Chinese need them for their ceremonies?"

He paused, and from the entire Chinese-Portuguese-Hawaiian contingent of the house went up a great, throbbing cry in defense of religious freedom. So Kangaroo Kee continued: "I warn the people who have dared to bring this bill onto the floor of this house that if it is voted into law, I will instantly resign! I can stand political domination. I can stand economic retaliation. But I cannot stand religious persecution!" Men wept and the hall echoed with cheers.

That afternoon Hoxworth Hale summoned The Fort and asked

glumly, "What in hell has happened around here? Why do we suddenly wind up as religious persecutors?"

"Your wife started it all by wanting to save children from fireworks," big Hewie Janders reminded him. "And my wife, damn her bleeding heart, gave your wife support."

"All I know," Hoxworth growled, "is that the Chinese are threatening to start a new political party. The Hawaiians are charging religious persecution. The Portuguese have enlisted both of them behind that grade-crossing bill. And Kangaroo Kee submitted his resignation this morning. Says he'll suffer no more dictation from tyrants. Gentlemen, we better do something."

Hewie Janders suggested: "Could you make a formal statement. In defense of religious freedom and firecrackers?"

"Get a secretary," Hoxworth snapped, and when the young man arrived, the head of The Fort dictated his memorable announcement beginning: "The Islands of Hawaii have always known religious freedom, and among those who have defended this basic concern of all men none have excelled the Chinese. To think that unfeeling persons should have seen fit to trample upon one of the most cherished rituals of Chinese religion, namely, the explosion of fireworks at festive seasons, is repugnant."

At this point Hewie Janders pointed out: "But it was your wife and mine who did it, Hoxworth! If you release such a statement, they're going to boil."

To this Hale replied, "When the structure of society is endangered, I don't care whose feelings get hurt."

The upshot of his retreat was that Mrs. Hale and Mrs. Janders considered their husbands contemptible cowards, and said so; Kangaroo Kee, breaking down into a copious flow of tears, announced to the house that he had reconsidered his resignation because the leaders of Hawaii had magnanimously reaffirmed their belief in religious freedom; the dangerous Chinese-Hawaiian-Portuguese coalition was broken up; and merchants sold more fireworks than ever before. On the next Chinese New Year two children were blinded, a girl had three fingers blown off and there were sixteen cases of disfiguring burns; but the islands were happy. The Honolulu *Mail,* summarizing the wild night, called it a splendid manifestation of island charm. But Hoxworth Hale, whose wife pointed out that the blindings and maimings were exactly what her bill had been intended to prevent, remarked glumly to The Fort: "We must never again outrage the firecracker vote."

It was under Hale's direction that The Fort insinuated its men onto the public boards that controlled things like the university and the parks, and once when an outside writer took pains to cross-reference the 181 most influential board members in Hawaii, he found that only thirty-one men in all were involved, and that of them twenty-eight were Hales, Whipples, Hoxworths, Hewletts and Janderses . . . or their sons-in-law. "A very public-spirited group of people," the writer concluded, "but it is often difficult to tell one board from the other or any from the board of H & H."

The Honolulu *Mail* was owned by The Fort, but its function in the community was never blatantly abused. It was a good paper, Republican of course, and it frequently supported positions which The Fort could not have approved but which the general public did; but when an issue involved land, sugar or labor, the *Mail* wrote forceful editorials explaining how the public good was involved and how government ought to respond. Once when a *Mail* reporter was sent to fifteen different sugar-growing areas to write a series of articles proving how much better off the people of Hawaii were than laborers in Jamaica, Fiji and Queensland, his returning letters were first studied in The Fort, "to be sure he maintains the proper historical perspective." The *Mail* was scrupulously fair in reporting activities of the underground Democratic Party, but the articles were written as if a benevolent old man was chuckling over the actions of imbecile and delinquent children.

The endless chain of appointed office holders sent out from Washington—too often incompetent and gregarious politicians—was quickly absorbed into The Fort's genial social life: hunting trips to the big island, boating parties, picnics by the sea. Sometimes a newcomer could sit on the bench for six months without ever meeting a Chinese other than a defendant in a court case or a Japanese who was not dressed in white and serving sandwiches. Such officials could be forgiven if they came to think of Hawaii as The Fort and vice versa and to hand down their decisions accordingly.

But Hoxworth Hale's greatest contribution lay in a general principle which he propounded early in his regime, and it is to his credit that he perceived this problem long before any of his contemporaries, and his adroit handling of it earned The Fort millions upon millions of dollars. He announced his policy flatly: "No military man stationed in Hawaii above the rank of captain in the army or lieutenant in the navy is to leave these islands without having been entertained by at least three families in this room." Then he added, "And if you can include the lower ranks, so much the better!" As a result of this rule, the constant flow of military people who passed through Hawaii came to think of big Hewlett Janders and gracious Hoxworth Hale as the two commanders of the islands, men who could be trusted, men who were sound; and in the years that were about to explode, making Hawaii a bastion of the Pacific, it was very difficult for Washington to send any senior admiral or general to Honolulu who did not already know The Fort intimately. Therefore, when a contract was to be let, bids weren't really necessary: "Hewlett Janders, the fellow I went hunting with ten years ago, he can build it for us." More important, when the procurement and engineering offices in Washington began to assume major importance in America's rush program of military expansion, the rising young men who crowded those offices almost had to be the ones that Hoxworth Hale and Hewie Janders had entertained so lavishly in the previous decade.

Nothing Hoxworth accomplished was more important than this establishment of a personal pipeline direct to the sources of power in Washington. Again, he never abused his prerogatives. He never called generals on the phone, shouting, as did some, "Goddam it, Shelly, they're talking about eminent domain on three thousand acres of my choicest sugar fields." Usually this made Washington determined to go ahead with condemnation proceedings. Hoxworth Hale acted differently: "This you, Shelly? How's Bernice? We're fine out here. Say, Shelly, what I called about was the proposed air strip out Waipahu way. That's a good site, Shelly, but have your men studied what the landing pattern would be with those tall mountains at the end . . . Yes, Shelly, the ones we went hunting on that weekend . . . Yes, I just want to be sure your men have thought about that, because there's another strip of land a little farther makai . . . Yes, that means toward the sea in Hawaiian, and I was wondering . . . Yes, it's our land, too, so there's no advantage to me one way or the other . . . Be sure to give Bernice our best."

Hawaii in these years of benevolent domination by The Fort was one of the finest areas of the world. The sun shone, the trade winds blew, and when tourists arrived on the luxury H & H liners the police band played hulas and girls in grass skirts danced. Labor relations were reasonably good, and any luna who dared strike a worker would have been instantly whisked out of the islands. The legislature was honest, the judges sent out from the mainland handed down strict but impartial decisions, except in certain unimportant cases involving land, and the economy flourished. It is true that mainland firms like Gregory's and California Fruit protested: "My God, the place is a feudal barony! We tried to buy land for a store and they said, 'You can't buy any land in Hawaii. We don't want your kind of store in the islands.' "

It was also true that Chinese or Japanese who wanted to leave the islands to travel on the mainland had to get written permission to do so, and if The Fort felt that a given Oriental was not the kind of man who should represent the islands in America, because he tended toward communist ideas, speaking of labor unions and such, the authorities would not let him leave, and there was nothing he could do about it. Hewlett Janders in particular objected to the large number of young Chinese and Japanese who wanted to go to the mainland to become doctors and lawyers, and he personally saw to it that a good many of them did not get away, for, as he pointed out: "We've got fine doctors right here that we can trust, and if we keep on allowing Orientals to become lawyers, we merely create problems for ourselves. Educating such people above their station has got to stop."

Once in 1934, after Hoxworth and his team had performed miracles in protecting Hawaii from the fury of the depression—it fell less heavily on the islands than anywhere else on earth—he was embittered when a group of Japanese workers connived to have a labor man from Washington visit the islands, and Hale refused to see the visitor. "You'd think they'd have respect for what I've done keeping Hawaii safe from the depression. Every Japanese who got his regular pay check, got it thanks to me, and now they want me to talk with labor-union men!"

He refused three times to permit an interview, but one day the man from Washington caught him on the sidewalk and said hurriedly, "Mr. Hale, I respect your position, but I've got to tell you that under the new laws you are required to let labor-union organizers talk to your men on the plantations."

"What's that?" Hoxworth asked in astonishment. "Did you say . . ."

"I said," the visitor, an unpleasant foreign type, repeated slowly, "that under the law you are required to permit labor-union organizers access to your men on the plantations."

"I thought that's what you said," Hale replied. "Good heavens, man!" Then, taking refuge in a phrase he had often heard Wild Whip declaim, he said, "If I saw a rattlesnake crawling onto one of my plantations and I shot him, I'd be a hero. Yet you want me voluntarily to open my lands to labor organizers. Truly, you must be out of your mind." He turned abruptly and left.

"Mr. Hale!" the labor man called, catching up with him and grabbing his coat.

"Don't you ever touch me!" Hale stormed.

"I apologize," the man said contritely. "I just wanted to warn you that Hawaii's no different from the rest of America."

"Apparently you don't know Hawaii," Hale said, and left.

In his cold, efficient governance of The Fort he manifested only two peculiarities which could be construed as weaknesses. Whenever he had a major decision to make he spent some time alone in his office, pushing back and forth across his polished desk a reddish rock about the size of a large fist, and in the contemplation of its mysterious form he found intellectual reassurance. "The rock came from his great-great-grandmother on Maui," his secretary explained. "It's sort of a good-luck omen," she said, but what the good luck derived from she did not know and Hale never told her. Also, whenever The Fort started a new building Hale insisted that local kahunas be brought in to orient it. Once a mainland architect asked, "What's a man with a Yale degree doing with kahunas?" and Hale replied, "You'd be surprised. In our courts it's illegal to force a Hawaiian to testify if a known kahuna is watching in the courtroom." The architect asked, "You certainly don't believe such nonsense, do you?" and Hale replied evasively, "Well, if I were the judge, I would certainly insist that any known kahunas be barred from my courtroom. Their power is peculiar."

One unspoken rule regarding The Fort was observed by all: The Fort did not exist; it was a phrase never mentioned in public; Hale himself never spoke it; and it was banned from both newspaper and radio. The building in which the men met remained as it was during Wild Whip's tenancy: a rugged red-stone commercial headquarters built like a fort and bearing a simple brass plate that read: Hoxworth & Hale, Shipmasters and Factors.

BACK IN THE 1880's, when the Chinese vegetable peddler Nyuk Tsin decided to educate her five sons and to send one of them all the way to Michigan for a law degree, Honolulu had been amazed at her tenacity and instructed by the manner in which she forced four of her sons to support the fifth on the mainland. But what Hawaii was now about to witness in the case of Japanese families and their dedication to learning made anything that the Chinese had accomplished look both dilatory and lacking in conviction. Specifically, the penniless night-soil collector Kamejiro Sakagawa was determined that each of his five children must have nothing less than a full education: twelve years of public school, four years at the local university, followed by three at graduate school on the mainland. In any other nation in the world, such an ambition would have been insane; it was to the glory of America, and especially that part known as Hawaii, that such a dream on the part of a privy-cleaner was entirely practical, if only the family had the courage to pursue it.

From the Kakaako home each morning the five Sakagawa children set forth to school. They were clean. Their black hair was bobbed straight across their eyes and their teeth had no cavities. They walked with an eager bounce, their bright scrubbed faces shining in sunlight, for to them school was the world's great adventure. Their education did not come easily, for it was conducted in a foreign language: English. At home their mother spoke almost none and their father knew only pidgin.

But in spite of language difficulties, the five Sakagawas performed brilliantly and even teachers who might have begun with an animus against Japanese grew to love these particular children. Reiko-chan set the pattern for her brothers. In her first six grades she usually led her class, and when teachers had to leave the room to see the principal, they felt no compunction about turning their classes over to this adorable little girl with the delicately slanted eyes and the flawless skin. Reiko-chan was destined to be a teacher's pet, and early in life she decided that when she graduated from the university, she would be a teacher too.

The boys were a more rowdy lot, and no teacher in her right mind would have turned her class over to them. They specialized in the rougher games, for in accordance with the ancient rule that all who came to Hawaii were modified, the four Sakagawa boys were obviously going to be taller than their father, with better teeth, wider shoulders and straighter legs. It was noticeable that they threw like Americans and could knock bottles off fences with surprising accuracy, but their mastery of English fell markedly below their sister's, a fact of which they were proud, for in the Honolulu public schools anyone who spoke too well was censured and even tormented by his classmates. To be accepted, one had to speak pidgin like a moron, and above everything else, the Sakagawa boys wanted to be accepted.

The success of this family in the American school was the more noteworthy because when classes were over, and when haole children ran home to play, the five Sakagawas lined up and marched over to the Shinto temple, where the man who was a priest on Sundays appeared in a schoolteacher's black kimono to conduct a Japanese school. He was a severe man, much given to beating children, and since he was proud of the fact that he spoke no corrupting English and had only recently come from Tokyo, he tyrannized the children growing up in an alien land. "How can you ever become decent, self-respecting Japanese," he stormed, "if you do not learn to sit properly upon your ankles. Sakagawa Goro!" and the heavy rod fell harshly across the boy's back. "Do not fidget. Will you feel no shame when you return home and visit friends and fidget?" Bang, went the rod. Bang and bang again.

The priest was contemptuous of everything American and impressed upon his charges that they were in this alien land for only a few years until they took up their proper life, and when he described Japan, his eyes grew misty and a poetry came into his voice. "A land created by the immortal gods themselves!" he assured them. "In Japan there is no rowdyism like here. In Japan children are respectful to their parents. In Japan every man knows his place and all do reverence to the emperor. No man can predict what impossible things Japan will some day accomplish." He taught from the same books that were used in Tokyo, using the same inflections and the same stern discipline. For three hours each day, when other children were rollicking in the sun, the Sakagawas sat painfully on their ankles before the priest and received what he called their true education.

There was much agitation against the Japanese-language schools, as they were called, and there was no doubt that the priests taught an un-American, Shintoistic, nationalistic body of material, but in those years not a single child who attended the schools got into trouble with the police. Among the Japanese there was no delinquency. Parents were obeyed and teachers were respected. In the Japanese schools a severe rectitude was taught and enforced, and much of the civic responsibility that marked the adult Japanese community derived from these austere late-afternoon sessions; and it was a strange thing, but not a single child in later years ever remembered much of the jingoistic nonsense taught by the priests; few ever wanted to go back to Japan; but all learned respect for an established order of life. It was as if the great freedoms enjoyed in the American school in the first part of the day insulated the child against the nationalistic farrago of the afternoon, so that most Japanese children, like the Sakagawas, assimilated the best from both schools and were not marred by the worst of either.

Actually, their true education in these years took place at home. In their tiny Kakaako shack, which would have been cramped even for a family of three, their mother enforced the rigid rules of cleanliness that she had learned as a child. Nothing was left on the floor. No dish went unwashed. Chopsticks were handled so that no food dropped. Clothes were put away neatly, and the child who did not bathe completely at least once each day was a hopeless barbarian, no better than a Chinese. Their father's influence was more subtly felt. He saw the world as divided sharply into the good and the bad and he never hesitated long in defining where any given action fell. It was good to honor one's country, it was good to die heroically, it was good to attend to what one's superiors said, it was good to have education. He lived a life of the most fierce propriety in which stealing was bad, and gambling, and speaking back, and tearing one's clothes. He was a harsh disciplinarian, but he rarely struck his children, relying instead upon the force of his character. He loved his children as if they were mysterious angels that had been allowed to live with him for a little while, and if the mean little shack was sometimes barren of food, it was never lacking in love.

The children engaged in nonsensical jokes which their parents could not understand. Reiko-chan had a series of remarks which her brothers greeted with shouts no matter how often she recited them: "What did the hat say to the hatrack? You stay here and I'll go on a head." Six times a week the boys could scream with delight over that one. "What did the carpet say to the floor? Don't make a move, I got you covered!" And "What did the big toe say to the little toe? Don't look back, but we're being followed by a heel."

The boys had rougher games, including one in which Goro would grab a brother's ear and ask sweetly, "Do you want your ear any longer?" If the brother said no, Goro would pretend to twist it off. If the answer was yes, Goro would jerk vigorously on the ear and shout, "Then I'll make it longer!" This usually led to a fight, which was what Goro had intended.

But on two basic principles the Sakagawa children would permit no joking. No one was allowed to call them Japs. This was a word so offensive to the Japanese that it simply could not be tolerated, for throughout America it was being used in headlines and cartoons to depict sneaking, evil little men with buckteeth. No haole could appreciate the fervor with which Japanese combated the use of this word.

Nor were they to be called slant-eyes. They argued: "Our eyes are not slanted! It's only because we have no fold in our eyelids that they look slanted." But of course in this they were wrong. Reiko-chan's little eyes were delightfully slanted, low near the nose and tilting upward in saucy angles. It was she who came home with one of their best games. Putting her two fingers at the corners of her lovely eyes, she pulled them way up and chanted, "My mother's a Japanese." Then she pulled them far down and sang, "And my father's a Chinese." Then, moving her forefingers to the middle of her eyebrows and her thumbs below, she spread her eyes wide apart and shouted, "But I'm a hundred per cent American."

When Kamejiro first saw this trick, he rebuked his daughter and reminded her: "The proudest thing in your life is that you're a Japanese. Don't ever laugh about it." But at the same time he became vaguely aware that with the arrival of children his family had become entangled in values that were contradictory and mutually exclusive: he sent his offspring to American schools so that they would succeed in American life; but at the same time he kept them in Japanese school so that they would be prepared for their eventual return to Japan. The children felt this schizophrenia and one day at the close of the American school Goro went not to the Japanese teacher but directly home, where Kamejiro met him with the question, "Why are you home?"

"I'm not going to the Japanese school any longer."

Kamejiro held his temper and asked patiently, "Why not?"

"I don't want to be a Japanese. I want to be an American."

For several moments Kamejiro held his hands to his side, in self-discipline, but he could not do so for long. Suddenly he grabbed his oldest son, lifted him in the air, tucked him under one arm and ran with him furiously to the temple, where after bowing ceremoniously to the priest, his son still under his arm, he threw the boy into the midst of the scholars. "He said he didn't want to be a Japanese!" he stammered in rage, then bowed and left.

Slowly the tall priest rose and reached for his rod. Moving silently in his bare feet to where Goro lay on the tatami, he began to flail the boy unmercifully. When he had finished he returned solemnly to his rostrum, sat meticulously upon the floor and cried in a quivering voice, "Sakagawa Goro, what are the first laws of life?"

"Love of country. Love of emperor. Respect for parents."

Even in their names, the Japanese children experienced this constant hauling in two directions. At the American school it was Goro Sakagawa;

at the Japanese, Sakagawa Goro. And when the beating was over, Goro waited for an opportunity and whispered to his brother Tadao, "I will never go back to Japan."

"Who spoke?" the priest cried sharply.

"I did," Goro replied. For him to lie would have been unthinkable.

"What did you say?"

"I said that when I grow up I will never go back to Japan."

Ominously the priest reached for the rod once more, and this time the beating he delivered was both longer and more severe. At the end he asked, "Now will you go back to Japan?"

"No," Goro stubbornly replied.

That night the priest told Kamejiro, "We can have no boy like this in the Japanese school. He lacks the proper sincerity."

"He will be back on Monday," Kamejiro said dutifully, bowing before his intellectual superior. "Believe me, Sensei, he will be back."

That was Wednesday evening, and when bruised Goro started to go to bed his father caught his hand and said quietly, "Oh, no! You will not sleep tonight."

"But I must go to school tomorrow," Goro pleaded.

"No. For you there is no more school. Tonight you start to work with me." And Kamejiro made the boy dress in warm clothes and that night he took him on his rounds to clean out privies. Goro was appalled at the work his father did, at the humiliation of it, at the way late strolling drunks ridiculed him, at the stench. But bow-legged little Kamejiro said nothing. Hauling his son with him, he did his work, and at dawn the two night prowlers took their hot bath and breakfasted as the other children went to school.

On Thursday, Friday and Saturday nights young Goro continued to clean out privies, until he felt so sick that he was afraid even to walk beside his resolute father. At dawn on Sunday, as the brilliant tropical sun came over Diamond Head, Kamejiro said to his son, "This is the way men have to work when they do not have an education. Are you ready to apologize to the priest?"

"Yes."

"And you're ready to apply yourself . . . in both schools?"

"Yes."

On Monday afternoon Kamejiro took Goro back to the temple and stood in the doorway while his son announced to the entire class: "I apologize to all of Japan for what I said last Wednesday. I apologize to you, Sensei, for my evil behavior. I apologize to you, Father, for having been such an ungrateful son."

"Are you now willing to go back to Japan?" the priest asked.

"Yes, Sensei."

"Then sit down and we will resume our studies." After that experience, there were no more disturbances among the Sakagawa children.

There was one item of education which Kamejiro could delegate to no one. Whenever he took his family for a stroll through Kakaako he kept on the alert, and from time to time would grasp his left wrist with his right hand, and then his children knew. "Is that one?" the boys whispered.

"That's one," Kamejiro replied in hoarse, awe-struck tones, and in this way the Sakagawas learned to spot the Etas, those untouchables who had filtered into Hawaii. Mrs. Sakagawa lectured Reiko-chan concerning the worst fate that could befall any girl: "There was a girl in Kakaako named Itagaki, and without knowing it she married an Eta. Her family had to go to another island in disgrace."

There were ways a self-respecting family could protect itself from Etas, and Kamejiro often told his children, "When the time comes for you to marry, I'll go to the detective and he will tell me whether the other party is an Eta or an Okinawan." There were two such detectives in Hawaii, and since they kept dossiers on every Japanese family, few Etas or Okinawans were unknown to them. Their services were costly, but since they enabled prospective brides and grooms to avoid the shame of mismating, the general community was willing to pay their fee.

Then, as Reiko-chan approached the age when she must move on to a more advanced school, her father's attention was diverted from Etas and directed to a matter of more immediate importance. The haole citizens of Hawaii, properly disturbed by the abominable English spoken in the schools, united to demand at least one school on each island where all children would speak acceptable English, and out of this agitation the so-called English-standard school developed. To attain entrance a child had to undergo a verbal examination to prove that he was not corrupted by pidgin and would thus not contaminate his classmates, who were usually trying to gain entrance to some mainland college.

The basic concept of the English-standard school was meritorious, for in other schools there often appeared to be no standards at all and even teachers sometimes taught in pidgin; but the manner in which students were selected for these superior schools was one of the most shameful subterfuges ever permitted in the islands. Plantation managers soon let it be known that they would look with disfavor upon teachers who admitted to the preferred schools too many children of Oriental ancestry; so automatically the schools became costly private schools with superior facilities paid for out of general taxation but largely restricted to haole children. This discrimination was easy to enforce, for teachers who interviewed prospective enrollees were encouraged to disbar any child who evidenced even the slightest accent or the misuse of a single word; and a miserable mockery developed whereby teachers, who knew they were under the surveillance of plantation managers, conducted tests of Japanese and Filipino children, whose failures were ordained before they spoke a word. Of course, a few sons of Oriental doctors and lawyers were admitted, lest the abuse of tax dollars become too odious, but for the most part the English-standard school became another device to keep Orientals on the plantations, where they were supposed to belong. As Hoxworth Hale pointed out, when as a member of the Board of Education he encouraged the establishment of the schools: "We mustn't educate field hands beyond their capacity."

In Honolulu the English-standard school was Jefferson, a superb institution with superior playing fields, laboratories and teachers. With real anxiety Japanese fathers like Kamejiro Sakagawa watched the results of the first entrance tests at Jefferson. Almost no Japanese children gained admittance, and Kamejiro warned: "See! You lazy children who will not study. None of your friends got into the fine school! But you will get in, because from now on you will study twice as much as before." He launched an ingenious program whereby his five children attended two different Christian churches each Sunday, listening to the preacher use good English. At any free public lecture, there would be Kamejiro and his five children. He could not understand what was being said, but when he got the young students home he would seat them in a circle and make them repeat again and again what the speaker had said, and in the speaker's intonation. Before long, Reiko-chan and Goro were adept in English.

The Sakagawa children had now reached the apex of their educational schizophrenia. In their American school they learned that all people were created equal, but their father kept teaching them who the Etas were, and the Okinawans. In their Japanese school they learned formal Japanese and were beaten if they made mistakes, but at night they drilled one another in proper English. Their parents spoke little of the language, but they insisted that their children converse with each other in English. It was a crazy, conflicting world, but there was this refuge of assurance: when they were with other children like themselves they spoke only a wild, free pidgin whose syllables sang on the ear like the breaking of waves along the beach.

When Reiko-chan was a long-legged, flashing-eyed girl of twelve she was ready to take her all-important verbal examination for admission into the privileges of Jefferson. Her parents washed her with unusual care, dressed her in a white smock with ruffles, and polished her shoes. Kamejiro wanted to accompany her, but she begged him not to do so, only to find when she got to Jefferson that he was required to be with her. She ran back to get him, and when her mother saw how heated up she had become in doing so, she was given another bath, and with her father's apprehensive hand in hers she returned to Jefferson, where a teacher picked up the report from Reiko's elementary school and read silently: "Reiko Sakagawa. Grades A. Behavior A. Knowledge of American customs A. English A." The investigating teacher smiled and passed the report approvingly along to the other two members of the board, but one of these had at her elbow an additional report on the Sakagawa girl, and this said simply, "Father, privy cleaner."

"How do you spend your days this summer?" the first teacher asked.

In a sweet, clear voice Reiko-chan replied, with careful attention to each syllable, "I help my mother with the washing. And on Sundays I go to church. And when we have a picnic I help my brothers get dressed."

The three teachers were impressed with the precision of the little girl's speech. Obviously she was a girl who belonged in whatever excellent schools a community could provide, and the first teacher was about to mark the official ballot "Passed," when the third teacher whispered, "Did you see this? Her father?"

The damning paper was passed from hand to hand and the teachers nodded. "Failed," wrote the first. Then, smiling sweetly at Reiko-chan, she explained: "We are not going to accept you at Jefferson, my dear. We feel that you speak a little too deliberately . . . as if you had memorized."

There was no appeal. Kamejiro and his brilliant daughter were led away and in the summer sunlight the father asked in Japanese, "Did you get in?"

"No," she said, trying desperately not to cry.

"Why not?" her father asked in dumb pain.

"They said I spoke too slowly," she explained.

It was Kamejiro, and not Reiko-chan, who began to weep. He looked at the fine school, at the lovely grounds, and realized what a great boon his family had lost. "Why, why?" he pleaded. "At home you talk like a fire machine! Why do you talk slow today?"

"I wanted to be so careful," Reiko-chan explained.

Kamejiro felt that his daughter had failed the family through some conscious error, and his rage overcame him. Raising his arm, he was about to punish her when he saw that tears were hanging in her eyes, so instead of thrashing her as he intended, he dropped on one knee and embraced her. "Don't worry," he said. "Goro will get in. Maybe it's even better that way, because he's a boy."

Then he grabbed his daughter lovingly by the hand and said, "We must hurry," and the event toward which he hurried proved how deeply confused he was, for after having tried with all his prayers to get Reiko-chan into Jefferson so that she could be even more American, he now rushed her back home and into a kimono so that she could join her brothers in demonstrating that she was perpetually a Japanese. For this was the emperor's birthday, and the community was assembling at the Japanese school. As each family entered, the parents bowed almost to the floor before the portrait of the august emperor, then led their children to an allotted place on the tatami, where they sat on their ankles. At eleven the teacher appeared, ashen-faced, so grave was his responsibility that day. A former army officer rose and explained, "In Japan today, if the teacher who reads the Imperial Rescript mispronounces even one word or stumbles once, he is required to commit hara-kiri. Let us pay attention as we hear the immortal words of the Emperor Meiji as to what makes a good Japanese."

Slowly, painfully, the teacher began reading. In Japanese life the Imperial Rescript was unlike anything that western nations knew. It had started out in 1890 as a simple announcement of what Japan's educational policy should be, but the nation had found its clear statement of citizenship so appealing that the Rescript had been made immortal. Children and soldiers had to memorize it and lead their lives according to its precepts. It taught love of country, complete subjugation to the divine will of the emperor, and obedience to all authority. In beautiful language it taught a staggering theory of life, and in humble attention to it, Japan had grown strong. When the teacher ended his reading of the terrifying words, huge drops of perspiration stood out on his forehead, and each member of his audience was freshly dedicated to Japan and willing to sacrifice his life at the command of the emperor.

The army officer rose and said, "Let us remember Japan!" And all bowed, thinking of that distant, sweet and lovely land.

The crowd now went outside, where an arena had been set up, and two enormous men visiting from Japan waited, stripped down to the merest loincloths, and after a priest had prayed over them, they went to their respective corners of the arena and grabbed handfuls of salt, which they scattered about the mat upon which they were to wrestle. Kamejiro whispered to his attentive boys, "Haoles who say Japanese are runty should see these men!" The preparations continued with painful deliberateness for forty minutes, then in a flash of speed, the two giants crashed into one another, groaned and hefted until one pushed the other across the boundary. The Japanese cheered, then burst into hilarious laughter as two of their own fatties, men from the plantations, appeared nearly naked to conduct their own wrestling match.

In the afternoon, officials from the consulate drove up in a black car and told the listeners, "Grave events are shaping up in Asia. The perpetual evil of China once more threatens us, and we cannot say what fearful measures our august emperor may be required to take. On this solemn day, may we rededicate our lives to the land we love." There was a great deal more about the ominous events that imperiled the homeland, but nobody was very clear as to what they were. However, a collection was taken to aid the emperor in this hour of need, and the Sakagawas contributed money that had been intended for a new dress for Reiko-chan. She was allowed to place the coins in the box, and she quivered with love of Japan as she did so.

Now the celebrants moved to the public square in Kakaako, where under a banyan tree they performed the ancient, ritualistic bon dances of Japan. The children were an important part of this dance, weaving in slow measures in and out, their colorful kimonos swaying in the soft night breezes, and one group of elderly ladies, who had learned their bon dances in villages thousands of miles from Hawaii, found tears in their eyes as they watched delicate Reiko-chan moving through the graceful figures. One old woman asked, "I wonder if she knows how beautiful she is? Such a flawless skin and her eyes so Japanese!"

Kamejiro, who overheard these words of praise, blushed and told the women, "We are training Reiko-chan so that when she returns to Japan she will be recognized as a fine Japanese."

"She is one now," the women said approvingly.

When the emperor's birthday celebration ended, the old confusions returned, and Kamejiro warned his sons, in one breath, "This sacred day should remind you of how important it is that we get our family back to Japan," and, "You boys saw that Reiko-chan missed getting into Jefferson. You are not to miss." So the tiny Sakagawa shack became a drill hall with all the children speaking English.

Even in its first year Jefferson demonstrated its success. With better teachers and better facilities it promised to turn out graduates who were proficient in English and who were sure to make good records at mainland colleges. Some of the plantation owners began to wonder if perhaps the English-standard schools weren't too good. Hoxworth Hale observed: "Why you get almost as fine an education at Jefferson as you do at Punahou. No tax-supported school has to be that good." But there were other protests of a more serious nature, for it had become apparent to laboring groups that their children were not going to be admitted to the superior schools, no matter how proficient their English, and some radical labor men began to argue: "We pay taxes to support these fine schools to educate those who don't need them. It is our own children who ought to be going to those schools, for then the differences between groups in the community would be diminished."

Sometimes at night, as Kamejiro listened to Reiko-chan drilling her brothers in English, he thought: "Everybody in Hawaii has it better than the Japanese. Look at those damned Kees! They have big stores and their sons go to Punahou. When the Chinese came to Hawaii, things were easy."

Now it was Goro's turn to try his luck at Jefferson, and like his sister he reported to the jury of three teachers. Like her he brought with him a rather striking report: "Grades A. Behavior B. Knowledge of American customs A. English A. This boy has unusual capacities in history." The test began, and he spoke with delightful fluency, explaining the Civil War to the teachers.

It looked as if they would have to accept him, when one teacher used a device that had been found effective in testing a child's real knowledge of English. She slowly lifted a piece of paper and tore it in half. "What did I do to the paper?" she asked.

"You broke it," Goro said promptly.

Again the teacher tore the paper and asked, "What did I do to it this time?"

"You broke it again," Goro said.

"We're sorry," the chairman announced. "She tore the paper. The word is tore." And Goro was rejected.

When his father heard the news he asked dumbly, "What was the word again?"

Goro explained, "I said broke when I should have said tore."

"Broke!" Kamejiro cried in anguish. "Broke!" He did not know the word himself, but he was outraged that his son should have misused it. He began beating him about the shoulders, crying, "How many times have I told you not to say broke? You stupid, stupid boy!" And he continued hammering his son, not realizing that if it had not been the word *broke* it would have been some other, for the children of Japanese men who dug out privies were not intended to enter Jefferson.

IN 1936 Kamejiro Sakagawa faced a most difficult decision, for it became apparent that his grand design of educating five children from kindergarten through graduate school could not be attained. The hard-working family simply did not have the money to keep going. It was therefore necessary that some, at least, of the children quit school and go to work, and discussions as to the various courses open to the Sakagawas kept the family awake many nights.

The fault was not Kamejiro's. He would have been able to maintain the four boys in school and at the same time permit Reiko-chan to begin her university course except that news from China was increasingly bad. Time after time either the priest at the language school or the consular officials reported to the Japanese community that the emperor was facing the gravest crisis in Japanese history. "This sacred man," the priest intoned, "tries to sleep at night with the burden of all Japan on his shoulders. The very least you can do is to support our armies in their victorious march across China." The armies were always on the verge of victory, and certainly the Japanese newsreels showed the capture of one new province each week, but the Japanese forces never seemed to get anywhere, and in August of that year the consular official made a very blunt statement: "I want fifty thousand dollars sent from these islands to help save the Japanese army."

The Sakagawas contributed seventy of those dollars and that night assembled the family. "Reiko-chan cannot go to college," Kamejiro said bluntly. The brilliant little girl, president of the girls' club at McKinley and an honor student, sat primly with her hands in her lap. As a good Japanese daughter she said nothing, but Goro did. "She knows more than any of us. She's got to go to college. Then she can become a teacher and help pay our way."

"Girls get married," Kamejiro rationalized quietly. "Pretty girls get married right away, and the education and income are lost."

"She could promise not to get married," Goro suggested.

"It is boys who must be educated," Kamejiro pointed out, "though why both you and Tadao failed to get yourselves into Jefferson I cannot understand. Are you stupid? Why don't you learn to speak English right?" he fumed in Japanese.

"Please," the gentle girl begged, "you've seen that only the sons of people the plantation leaders like get into the good schools."

Kamejiro turned to look at his daughter. The idea she had suggested was startling to him and repugnant. "Is that right?" he asked.

"Of course it's right," Reiko-chan replied. "And Minoru and Shigeo won't get in, either."

"Nothing wrong with McKinley," Goro snapped, defending the wonderful rabbit-warren of a school where Orientals and Portuguese and indigent haoles went. It was a comfortable, congenial school, arrogant in its use of pidgin even in classrooms, and many of the islands' political leaders graduated from it, even if none of the business tycoons did. A boy could get his jaw broken at McKinley for speaking good English, but he could also get a good education, for the school always contained dedicated teachers who loved to see brilliant boys like Goro prosper.

"Forget McKinley," Kamejiro told his children. "What kind of job can Reiko-chan get that will bring in the most money?"

"Let her work for three years, then Tadao and I can get jobs," Goro suggested, "and she can go on to the university."

"No," Kamejiro corrected. "I have noticed that if boys stop, they never go back. Reiko-chan must work from now on."

It was at this point that the quiet girl almost sobbed, and her brothers saw the involuntary contraction of her shoulders. Goro, a big husky boy, larger than his father, went to his sister's chair and put his hand on her arm. "Pop's right," he said in English. "You'll get married. Pretty girl like you."

"We speak in Japanese!" Kamejiro rebuked. "Sit down. Now what kind of job?"

"I could be a typist," Reiko suggested.

"They pay nothing for Japanese typists," Kamejiro replied.

"Could she work for a doctor?" Tadao asked. He was a slim, wiry boy, taller than Goro but not nearly so rugged. "That's good pay."

"She's got to have training, and we have no money," Kamejiro replied. He waited for a moment, almost afraid to discuss openly what was in his mind. Then he swallowed and said, "I was talking with Ishii-san and he said . . ."

"Please, Father!" the boys interrupted. "Not Ishii-san! If you listen to what he says . . ."

"Ishii-san's a fool," Reiko laughed. "Everyone knows that."

"This family is indebted to Ishii-san," Kamejiro said forcefully. He often used this phrase, but he never explained to the children why they were indebted to the curious little man whose ideas got stranger each year. "And Ishii-san pointed out that the easiest way for a Japanese to make lots of money is . . ." He paused dramatically.

"Stealing!" Goro joked in English. His father knew something irreverent had been said, but not what, so he ignored his son.

"Ishii-san is going to lend me the money," Kamejiro explained with nervous excitement, "and I am going to open a small barbershop on Hotel Street where the sailors are. And all the chairs will have girl barbers."

Slowly, as if gripped by a nameless horror, the four boys turned to look at their pretty sister. She sat apart, watching her mother, who was washing rice, but in her silence the color left her cheeks, for she understood that her immediate destiny was not the university or nursing or stenography; she was going to be a lady barber. She knew that there was already one shop of lady barbers on Hotel Street, and men flocked in and whoever owned the shop was making a lot of money, and the girls were getting tips. "But who are the girls?" Reiko thought mutely. "They have hardly been through grammar school."

"So I have asked Sakai-san if he would allow his daughter Chizuko to work for me," Kamejiro reported, exuding hope, "and he said yes, if I watch her closely and prevent her from becoming familiar with strange men. And Rumiko Hasegawa will work with us too, so that with three chairs and with me to sweep up and shine shoes, we ought to do very well."

Unexpectedly, Goro threw his arms on the table and began to weep. When his father asked, "Now what's wrong?" the sixteen-year-old boy mumbled, "Reiko-chan is the best one of us all."

"Then she will be willing to help her brothers get their education," Kamejiro said quietly.

Now the mother, from her corner where she was preparing food, spoke, and she observed: "It is the duty of a Japanese girl to help her family. I helped mine when I was young, and it made me a better wife. If Reiko-chan works hard and earns her own money, she will appreciate it more when her husband gives her some to spend on her children. It is her duty."

"But a lady barber!" Goro cried through his sobs.

"As a barber she will earn more money," his mother replied.

Goro rushed to his sister and embraced her. "When I become a lawyer and make a million dollars," he said in rapid English, "it will all be yours." The tears coursed down his face. Then Tadao, who was doing exceptionally well in school, but not so well as his sister had done in the same classes, began to weep, and the two younger boys, who knew how their sister had dreamed of becoming a teacher, sobbed. This was too much for Kamejiro, whose cruel duty it had been to make this decision, and he began to find tears splashing down his cheeks.

Only Mrs. Sakagawa did not cry. "It is her duty," she assured her trembling menfolk, but then she saw the tears in her lovely daughter's eyes, and she could no longer hide the fact that duty is often too terrible to bear. Gathering her child to her bosom, she wept.

Kamejiro Sakagawa's barbershop was an immense success. It opened just as American military installations in Hawaii were beginning to boom, so that navy men from Pearl Harbor and army boys from Schofield Barracks crowded into Hotel Street to get tattooed by local artists and shaved by lady barbers. But the principal reason for Kamejiro's prosperity was the crystal-like beauty of the three Japanese girls who staffed his chairs. They were olive-skinned, dark-haired, soft-eyed young ladies who looked especially appealing in crisp white uniforms which they delighted in keeping clean. Men often dropped by just for an extra trim to watch the girls, for there was the double excitement of a lady barber who was also a Japanese. Before long, regular customers were begging the pretty girls for dates.

That was where Kamejiro came in. Early in the life of his barbershop he had taught his girls how to stab with their scissors fresh customers who were trying to feel their legs. He also showed them that one of the best ways to handle difficult suitors was to push a hot towel in the man's face just as he was making his proposal. He encouraged his girls to discourage persistent Lotharios by nicking them slightly with the razor, especially on the ear lobe where one bled freely, but this gambit sometimes had reverse results, for the girls usually felt repentance for this act and made over the wounded customer so prettily, daubing him with styptic and asking in a sweet voice, "Does it hurt?" that the men came back stronger than before.

At closing time each night there were loungers outside in Hotel Street waiting for the girls, but Kamejiro formed his barbers into a squad, marched them to the Sakai girl's home, and cried proudly, "Sakai-san! Here's your daughter safe and sound." He then marched to the Hasegawas' and cried, "Here's Rumiko, safe and sound." At the doorway to his own home he invariably informed his wife, "Here's our girl, safe at home." The Japanese community marveled at how well Kamejiro was doing, and all agreed that his Reiko-chan was a most excellent barber.

Then in 1938, during Goro's last year at McKinley High, a real bombshell struck the Sakagawa family, an event so unanticipated that it left the household breathless. One afternoon in late July three men in blue suits came to the house in Kakaako and asked, "Mrs. Sakagawa, where's Tadao?"

Yoriko could speak little English, so she said, "Tadao, he not here."

"When he come home?" one of the men in a stiff white collar asked.

"Me not know."

"Tonight?"

"Hontoni, hontoni!" she nodded. "For sure."

"You tell him to wait here," the men said, and if they had smiled, as they should have done, they would have eased the apprehensions of the Sakagawa household enormously, but they did not, for Mrs. Sakagawa, hunched up from great work and somewhat wrinkled, scared them, and they stared at her as she stared at them.

When the family convened that night, Mrs. Sakagawa was the center of attraction. Four times she acted her role in the afternoon's ominous encounter, and everyone began pressing seventeen-year-old Tadao for the details of what offense he had committed, for the family assumed that the men were detectives. No other haoles in blue suits and white collars ever visited Japanese homes, and slowly the unincriminated members of the Sakagawa family began to coalesce against the first Sakagawa boy to have gotten into trouble. The awful, terrifying rectitude of the Japanese family asserted itself, and Reiko-chan cried, "You, Tadao. What did you do? All day I work and see no-goods on Hotel Street. Is my brother to be one of these?"

"Tadao!" Kamejiro cried, banging the table. "What wrong thing have you done?"

The tall, quiet boy could not answer, so his stockier brother Goro shouted, "You and your damned foolishness! Suppose the police take you, no more teams at McKinley for you. And I'll be ashamed to go on the field. Tell us! What have you done?"

The guiltless and bewildered boy shivered before the anger of his family. So far as he knew he had done nothing, yet the men had been there. Kamejiro, who had worked desperately hard to keep his family decent Japanese of whom Hiroshima would be proud, saw that his efforts had come to naught, and began mumbling in his hands. "No man can bring children up right," he swore, his chin trembling with shame and sorrow.

There was a knock at the door, and the Sakagawas looked at each other with last-minute dismay. "You stand there!" Kamejiro whispered to his son, placing him where the men could reach him. There would be no running away in his family. Then, biting his lip to hide his disgrace, he opened the door.

"Mr. Sakagawa?" the leader asked. "I'm Hewlett Janders, and this is John Whipple Hoxworth, and this gentlemen in back," and he laughed easily, "this is Hoxworth Hale. Good evening." The three business leaders of Hawaii entered the small room, stood awkwardly for a moment, then laughed when Reiko called in English, "Boys, get them some chairs!".

"We could use some," big Hewlett Janders laughed. "Mighty fine house you have here, Mr. Sakagawa. Rarely see such beautiful flowers any more. You must have a green thumb."

Goro translated rapidly and Kamejiro bowed. "Tell them I love flowers," he said. Goro translated this and apologized: "Father is ashamed of his English."

"You certainly handle the language well," Hewlett replied. "You're Goro, I take it?"

"Yes, sir."

The three men looked at him approvingly, and finally Hewlett said, jokingly, "You're the young fellow we hate."

Goro blushed, and Reiko-chan interrupted, asking, "We thought it was Tadao you wanted to see. This is Tadao."

"We know, Miss Sakagawa. But this is the young rascal we worry about."

There was a moment's suspense. No one quite knew what was happening, nor what odd turn this strange meeting was going to take next. It was Hoxworth Hale, oldest and most prim of the visitors who spoke, and as always he tried to speak to the heart of the matter. "We are an informal alumni committee from Punahou School. We're sick and tired of seeing our team run over by first-class athletes like this Goro over here. Young man, you have a marvelous future. Basketball, baseball and most of all football. If you ever need any help, come see me."

"Then you didn't come to arrest one of us?" Reiko-chan asked.

"Good heavens no!" Hale replied. "Did we give that impression this afternoon?"

"My mother doesn't understand . . ." Reiko began, but the relief she felt was so great that she could not speak. She put her hand to her mouth to stop its quivering, then put her arm about Tadao.

"Good gracious no!" Hale continued. "Quite the contrary, Miss Sakagawa. In fact, we're so impressed by your family that we've come here tonight to offer your brother Tadao a full scholarship at Punahou, because we need a running halfback like him."

No one spoke. The older Sakagawas, not comprehending what was happening, looked at Goro for translation, but before he could begin, big Hewlett Janders clapped his arm about the boy's shoulder and said, "We wanted you, too, Goro, but we felt that since you're a senior, you probably ought to finish at McKinley. Besides, we have fairly good tackles at school. But you've got to promise one thing. In the Punahou game, don't tackle your brother."

"I'll tear him to shreds if he's Punahou," Goro laughed.

"You wrecked us for the past two years," Janders acknowledged, punching the boy in a friendly manner.

Now Tadao spoke. "How could I pay my way at Punahou?" he asked. "Besides the tuition, that is?"

"You'll be there two years," Hale explained. "No charges at all for tuition or books. You can have a job right now at H & H taking care of forms. And completely off the record, we would like to give you one hundred dollars, twenty now, the rest later, for some clothes and things like that."

John Whipple Hoxworth, a sharp-eyed, quick-minded man added, "Tell your father that we are doing this not only because you have great promise as a football player, but because we know you are a fine boy. If you were otherwise, we wouldn't want you at Punahou."

Hoxworth Hale said, "It won't be too easy for you, son. There aren't many Japanese at Punahou. You'll be alone and lonely."

Reiko-chan answered for her brother: "It's the best school in the islands. To go there would be worth anything."

"We think so," Hale replied. And the three men shook hands with Tadao, the new boy at Punahou.

When the men were gone, Kamejiro exploded. "What happened?" he shouted at Goro.

"Tadao has been accepted at Punahou," the interpreter replied.

"Punahou!" The name had rarely been mentioned in the Sakagawa household. It was a school that had no reality to the Japanese, a haole heaven, a forbidden land. A Japanese boy could logically aspire to Jefferson, and in recent years some were making it, but Punahou! Kamejiro sat down, bewildered. "Who applied to Punahou?" he mumbled.

"Nobody. The school came to him because he has good grades and can play football."

"How will he pay?"

"They have already paid him," Goro explained, pointing to Tadao's money.

It was at this point, as Kamejiro studied the twenty dollars, that the Sakagawa family as a whole acknowledged for the first time, openly and honestly, that the boys would probably not return to Japan; for they could see Tadao at Punahou, one of America's greatest schools, working with the finest people in the islands, and graduating and going on to college and university. He would become a doctor or a lawyer, and his life would be spent here in America; and the family looked at him in this moment of realization and they saw him as forever lost to Japan; for this was the power of education.

The three blue-suited alumni who visited that night had warned Tadao that life at Punahou would be difficult, but the source of the difficulty they failed to identify. It came not from Punahou, where

Tadao's football prowess won respect, but from Kakaako, where the submerged people had long ago suspected Tadao because of his mastery of English. Now he was openly stigmatized as a haole-lover, and six times in September, Kakaako gangs waylaid him as he came home from football practice and beat him thoroughly. "We'll teach you to be better than we are!" they warned him. When he made three touchdowns against a team mainly of Japanese and other pidgin-speakers, they hammered him desperately, shouting, "You goddamned traitor! Who do you think you are, playing for Punahou?"

Tadao never tried to enlist Goro's aid. This punishment from Kakaako was something he had to absorb. He learned to keep his hands over his face so that his teeth would not be broken, and he quickly mastered the art of using his feet and knees as lethal weapons. By mid-October the assaults ended, especially since McKinley was having a good year with Goro as one of its brightest stars.

This football business in Honolulu was one of the strangest aberrations in the Pacific. Because Chinese, Japanese and Filipinos were mad about games, and because haoles like Janders, Hoxworth and Hale constantly recalled their days of glory at Punahou, the islands were sports-crazy and the easiest way to sell a newspaper was to work up a frenzy over football or basketball. Having no college league to focus on, the entire community bore down on the high schools. Radio commentators reported breathlessly that Akaiamu Kalanianaole had damaged a tendon in his right foot and would not be able to play Saturday for Hewlett Hall. Newspapers carried enormous photographs of fifteen-year-old boys, growling ferociously under captions like "Tiger Chung About to Tear into Punahou." Youths who should have been thinking of themselves as unshaven adolescents having trouble with the square roots of decimals, were forced to believe that they were minor Red Granges, and all the publicity that on the mainland was thrown at mature professional athletes, was in Hawaii directed at callow youths in high school. Consequently, from one year to the next, disgraceful scandals erupted in which adult gamblers bribed these boys to throw games. Then headlines moralized over the lack of character-training in the schools and occasionally some bewildered lad was actually thrown into jail for "corrupting the fabric of our sports world," while the adult gamblers who framed him went free.

At no time did this great Hawaiian nonsense flourish with more abandon than in the fall of 1938 when Goro Sakagawa was playing his last year at McKinley and his brother Tadao his first at Punahou. As the Thanksgiving Day classic between the two schools approached, all the local newspapers carried flamboyant stories about the two dramatic young men. The *Mail* got a fine shot of their father Kamejiro standing before his barbershop with a Punahou pennant in one hand, a McKinley banner in the other. "Impartial!" the caption read. It was one of the first pictures of a Japanese other than a criminal or an embassy official to appear outside the sports pages of a Honolulu newspaper.

On the day of the game there were two half-page spreads, one of Goro looking like an insane bulldog about to tear a squirrel apart and one of Tadao straight-arming an imaginary tackler. "Brother against Brother" read the headlines, two inches tall. It was a great game, and except for an extraordinary play by Goro in the last fifteen seconds, Tadao's three flaming touchdowns would have led Punahou to victory. That night, as he walked home through Kakaako, confused by the plaudits of the huge crowd who had eulogized him as the star of the Punahou team, he got his worst beating from the toughs. When they left him they warned: "Don't you never play like that against McKinley again!"

He stumbled home, his face bleeding from three different cuts, and Goro had had enough. "You know who did it?" he asked.

"Yes."

"Let's go!" They took sixteen-year-old Minoru and fifteen-year-old Shigeo along. Goro gave each a baseball bat or a railing from a picket fence, and they cruised Kakaako until they came upon seven members of the gang. "No mercy!" Goro whispered, and with deadly efficiency the four brothers moved in. Next morning the newspapers, writing of the game, called it, "Triumph of the Sakagawa Brothers," and when Goro saw the headline he told Tadao, "We didn't do so bad last night, either."

While the Sakagawa boys were thus clawing their way up the ladder of island life, boys of Hawaiian ancestry were enjoying quite a different experience. When old Abraham Hewlett on the island of Maui took as his second wife a handsome Hawaiian girl, he found that her family owned about half of what was to become the hotel area of Waikiki. Eventually the Hewlett lands were valued at over one million dollars an acre, and because of the far-sighted missionary generosity of old Abraham, the entire income was applied to Hewlett Hall, where boys and girls of Hawaiian blood were entitled to a free education. Under the guidance of a board usually composed exclusively of Hales, Hewletts and Whipples, the famous Hawaiian school developed into a marvelous institution. It had a sparkling band, one of the finest choruses in the islands, loving teachers and handsome dormitories. All was free, and an outsider looking casually at the school could have been forgiven if he had concluded: "Hewlett Hall has been the salvation of the Hawaiian race."

Actually, the facts were somewhat contrary. Physically, Hewlett Hall was about perfect, but intellectually it was limited by the vision of the great families who dominated its board. They sent their sons to Punahou and Yale. It never seriously occurred to them that Hawaiian boys had exactly the same capacities as haoles; consequently, they consciously forced Hewlett Hall into a trade-school mold; its directors, with the greatest love in the world, rationalized: "The Hawaiians are a delightful, relaxed race. They love to sing and play games. They make wonderful mechanics and chauffeurs. Their girls are excellent teachers. Let us encourage them to do these things even better." And the Hawaiians, by their own friends, were so encouraged.

Now in the old days when a brilliant Chinese boy had fallen under the wing of preposterous Uliassutai Karakoram Blake, he was told daily: "You are as great a human being as I have ever known. There is nothing of which you are not capable." And these boys grew into doctors, political leaders and bankers. When outstanding Japanese boys like Goro Sakagawa crammed themselves into McKinley High—called locally Mikado Prep—they invariably found some inspired woman teacher imported from Kansas or Minnesota who told them: "You have a mind that can accomplish anything. You could write great books or become a fine research doctor. You can do anything." So the Chinese boys and the Japanese battled their way to proficiency, but the Hawaiians were not so goaded. They were given everything free and were encouraged to become trustworthy mechanics, and no society has ever been ruled by trustworthy mechanics and loyal schoolteachers.

Back in 1907 when Dr. Hewlett Whipple was made a member of the board for Hewlett Hall, he had tried manfully to revitalize the curriculum and to find dynamic teachers like old Uliassutai Karakoram Blake, but the Hales and Hewletts stopped him: "We must not try to educate these fine Hawaiian children above their natural capacity." After three years of futile struggling, Dr. Whipple resigned, and on the night he quit he told his wife, "With love and money we have condemned these people to perpetual mediocrity. Hewlett Hall is the worst thing that has happened to the Hawaiians since the arrival of measles and the white man." So while the Chinese and Japanese learned to manipulate their society, the Hawaiians did not.

IN THE FALL of 1941 Honolulu was presented with evidence that Punahou, at least, was capable of producing young scholars who could turn out historical research of high literary merit. Proof appeared in the form of a mimeographed pamphlet late one Friday afternoon as school was dismissing, and by Friday night the entire haole community had heard of it, with widely varying reactions; even some of the Orientals, by habit indifferent to literary accomplishment, were chuckling.

No one reacted more violently than Hoxworth Hale, a sedate man, for by the time he had finished reading the fourth line of the manifesto he was apoplectic and felt, with reason, that a scandal had occurred which required action, a conclusion which the officials at Punahou had acted upon an hour earlier. Later, when he reviewed the matter, Hoxworth realized that he should have anticipated trouble, for he recalled that for some time his son Bromley had been behaving mysteriously.

With the aid of a professional carpenter, whom he paid out of his own funds, young Brom had erected a curious structure on the back lot, and when asked what it was, had repeatedly insisted: "A play pen for adults." It stood unrelated to anything else, a half-room, with no ceiling and only two wooden walls, into which were cut four small openings, in back of which were built little boxes. The ridiculous structure did have a wooden floor, five feet ten inches long by five feet one inch wide. Two-by-fours propped up the walls, and Hoxworth noted that several of his son's friends were working on the project. One day, for example, crew-cut young Whipple Janders, with a new Leica picked up on his family's last trip to Germany, had called, "Hey, Mr. Hale. Would you help us a minute?"

"What can I do, Whip?"

"I want you to model this contraption."

"Only if you tell me what it is."

"Brom calls it a play pen for adults," Whipple had explained. "Some crazy idea of his."

"How do you want me to model it?" Hoxworth had asked.

"I want to see if a grown man could fit into one of our little boxes."

"You mean in there?"

"Yes. It's well braced."

"You want me to climb in?"

"Sure. Use the ladder."

Hoxworth was perpetually unprepared for the blasé manner in which modern children ordered their parents around, and with some misgivings he climbed into the bizarre box, stretched his legs out as far as they would reach, and laughed pleasantly at young Whipple Janders.

"I should have an Arrow collar on," he said.

"You're in sharp focus just as you are, sir," Whip replied, snapping several shots with his Leica. "Thank you very much, Mr. Hale."

Hoxworth, reading the inflammatory publication, thought back on those scenes and acknowledged that he had been tipped off. Whatever happened now was in part his fault. "But how can you anticipate children?" he groaned. The publication bore this title:

SEX ABOARD THE BRIGANTINE
or
They Couldn't Have Been Seasick All the Time
or
THERE WAS FRIGGIN' IN THE RIGGIN'
A speculative essay on missionaries by Bromley Whipple Hale

"It is acknowledged by my many and devoted friends at Punahou that I yield to no man in my respect for the missionary stock from which I, and many of my most intimate friends, derive. I count among my dearest possessions the time-worn memorials that have come down in my family, those treasured reminders of the hardships which my forebears suffered in Rounding the Horn in their thirst for salvation through good deeds. But more precious I count the blood of those stalwart souls as it courses through my veins and makes me the young man I am today. Therefore, when I speak of certain inquiries of a scientific nature which I have been conducting as an outgrowth of my studies in a revered school which itself has certain mission overtones, and where I have imbibed only the purest instruction, I speak as a Hale, a Whipple, a Bromley and a Hewlett. In fact, I may ask in all modesty, a trait for which I have been noted by my friends: Who of my generation, the sixth, could speak with greater propriety of mission matters? In equal modesty I would have to reply: No one.

"Bred as I was on missionary mythologies, I have always been profoundly impressed by several aspects of the long journey from Boston to Hawaii as undertaken by my ancestors. There was dreadful seasickness, from which almost all suffered constantly. There was binding biliousness which yellowed the eye and slowed the step, much as constipation does in our less euphemistic age. There were cramped quarters shared by eight where common decency required that there should have been only two. And there were the inconveniences of no fresh laundry, the same stinking clothes used week after week, and the uncontrollable boredom of life in unaccustomed quarters.

"No mission child has suffered more from a vicarious contemplation of these hardships than I. In fact, I have recently gone so far as to reconstruct the actual conditions under which my forebears struggled against the sea, and for several nights I have tried to live as they must have lived, endeavoring by these means to project myself into their reactions. In the first pictures that accompany this essay will be found my responses to the hardships borne by my ancestors."

Hoxworth Hale turned the page gingerly and found that Whipple Janders' Leica had been used to excellent effect. From the bunk leered Bromley Hale, his body contorted by the narrow quarters and . . .

"Good God!" Hoxworth gasped. "Isn't that Mandy Janders?" He studied the next photograph, which showed how husband and wife slept in the narrow bunks, and sure enough, there was his son Bromley Hale snoring while pretty, long-legged Amanda Janders, in a poke bonnet, lay beside him, staring in disgust. "Oh, my God! I'd better call Mandy's father right away," he said weakly, but the essay held him captive, just as it was imprisoning everyone in Honolulu lucky enough to possess one of the three hundred mimeographed copies accompanied by Whip Janders' glossy photos.

"As can be clearly seen," Bromley Hale's essay continued, "life aboard the brigantines must have been exactly as bad as our forebears have reported. But it has always seemed to me that our good ancestors were strangely silent on one important matter. Life on the brigantines was unadulterated hell, granted. But life went on. Oh, yes indeed, it went on. In fact, aided by the superb libraries resident in Honolulu, I have assembled certain statistics about just how fast life did go on. Take, for example, the brig *Thetis,* on which some of my ancestors, both on my father's side and on my mother's, reached these hospitable shores. The *Thetis* departed Boston on September 1, 1821 and reached Lahaina on March 26, 1822, after a passage of 207 storm-ridden days.

"Applying to these data certain facts which have been established beyond chance of successful contradiction in Botany 2, any child born to the eleven mission couples prior to May 27, 1822, must have been conceived—in holy wedlock to be sure—on land in New England, and any infant born after December 21, 1822 must by the same reasoning have been conceived on land in Hawaii. But surely, any child born to these particular mission families between May 27 and December 21, 1822, could have been conceived nowhere else but aboard the bouncing brig *Thetis.* Let us look at what happened to the occupants of one stateroom:

Parents	*Offspring*	*Born*
Abner and Jerusha Hale	son Micah	October 1, 1822
John and Amanda Whipple	son James	June 2, 1822
Abraham and Urania Hewlett	son Abner	August 13, 1822
Immanuel and Jeptha Quigley	daughter Lucy	July 9, 1822."

Relying upon old records, Bromley Hale proved that of the eleven mission couples aboard the *Thetis,* nine had produced offspring within the critical period. In turn, he moved to each of the other revered missionary companies, establishing departure and arrival dates, against which he compared the birth records until at last he was able to present a fairly staggering array of statistical evidence. "Good God," Hoxworth groaned, "if a boy spent half as much ingenuity on something important . . ." But like the rest of Honolulu, he read eagerly on.

"Does not this amazing fecundity aboard the brigantines suggest rather directly that in the crowded staterooms there must have been one additional occupation whereby the idle time was whiled away, an occupation which our forefathers, through considerations of modesty, did not report to us? I think so.

"In what I am now about to discuss, I consider myself far from an expert, but from having hung around poolrooms and from arguments with my betters during football rallies, I think it fairly well established that for a human male to impregnate a human female—and God forbid that he try his tricks on any other—requires on the average not one act of intercourse but at least four. As I understand it, that is the normal experience of the human race, popular novels and sentimental movies that rely upon lucky coincidence notwithstanding. Therefore, it can be seen that for the nine pregnancies achieved aboard the *Thetis* . . ."

Hoxworth slumped in his chair. "This boy has a diseased mind," he groaned. "Now he's getting clinical!" Hoxworth was right: young Bromley had produced all sorts of hilarious statistical tables and at one point had fortified them with resounding rhetoric: "I think I may be allowed the privilege of at least taking into consideration the theories lately advanced by His Holiness in the Vatican, which theories establish beyond much doubt the fact that for the human female there is a period which the ecclesiastics designate as 'safe,' and although it is naturally repugnant for me, a Congregationalist, to rely upon the word of a Catholic dignitary in discussing the secret lives of a gang of Calvinists, and although the nicety of the situation is not lost upon me, nevertheless . . ."

The phone rang, the first of many calls that were to be made that night. It was Hewlett Janders and he was screaming, "Did you see that goddamned photograph that your goddamned son had of my daughter . . ."

"Don't roar, Hewlett! I just got the wretched thing."

"Have you finished it yet, Hoxworth?"

"No, I'm only on page five."

"Then you haven't got to the part yet where he says, and listen, Hoxworth, I'm quoting your son. He adds up the total number of acts of sexual intercourse . . . Goddamn it, Hoxworth, what kind of monster have you reared?"

Later, after a dozen similar interruptions, Hoxworth reached his son's first conclusion: "So if we consider all these facts, which I hold to be statistically incontrovertible, we find that the brig *Thetis,* for sure, and all the other missionary ships probably, were not the angelic torture barges we have been taught, but—and I use the phrase literally—floating hells of concupiscence."

"No wonder they've been phoning," Hoxworth moaned. But his cup was far from running over, it had, in fact, reached not much over the sugar line in the bottom, for in succeeding pages Bromley discussed the heart of his investigations and shared his findings.

"What has always intrigued the scientific mind regarding the mission ships is the cramped nature of the staterooms. Again and again we have evidence that four men and four women, most of them married less than a week before entering the ship, and all of them total strangers, lived together in what could best be termed a rabbit warren. We know from incontrovertible testimony that months went by without either husband or wife ever removing his long red-flannel underwear, and we know that the heads of one couple had to be less than two feet from the heads of three other couples, with only a flimsy cloth barrier separating one family from another. Furthermore, as the following picture amply proves, an average-sized man could not stretch out full length . . ."

In anguish Hoxworth Hale turned to the picture, and his suspicion was correct. The average man whose knees were plainly doubled up was he, caught with a silly look on his face by young Whip Janders and his Leica.

Mercifully, the phone rang before he could digest the full ridiculousness of his situation. It was the headmaster at Punahou: "I suppose you've seen it, Hoxworth."

"How could such a thing have happened, Larry?" Hale groaned.

"We can never probe the minds of adolescents," the headmaster confessed.

"Does it seem as bad to you as it does to me?" Hoxworth asked.

"I haven't the time to judge degrees, Hoxworth. You realize, I'm sure, that this means . . ."

"He's got to go, Larry. I realize that."

"Thank you, Hoxworth. The important thing is, he's got to get into Yale. I've taken the liberty of dispatching a cable to my old friend Callinson at The Hill. There's a chance they'll take him. I've helped Callinson in the past."

"You think he can still make Yale?"

"We won't condemn the boy in our report, Hoxworth. Of that you can be sure."

"I appreciate this, Larry. But tell me, does this essay indicate a diseased mind?"

There was a pause, and the headmaster said reflectively, "I think we'd better leave it the way I said first. About adolescents, we can never know."

"Do you know where Bromley is?"

"No, Hoxworth, I don't."

The call ended and Hale sat in the lowering darkness. The phone immediately resumed jangling but Hoxworth let it ring. It would be some parent raising hell about what Bromley had said regarding their ancestors. "Damn them all!" Hoxworth cried in real confusion as he watched the lights of Honolulu come on, that nightly miracle that pleased him so much. His family had brought electricity to the city, just as they had brought so much more, but now that a Hale was in trouble, the vultures would want to rip him apart. Therefore, when the front doorbell rang insistently, Hoxworth was inclined to let it ring; he would not parade his hurt to the vultures. Let them pick the bones to their own ghoulish cackling.

The door opened and a cheery male voice cried, "Hey! Anybody in?" Hoxworth could hear footsteps crossing the first big room and he had a panicky thought: "It's some cheeky reporter!" And he started to run for it, when the voice called, "Hey, Mr. Hale. You're the one . . ."

"Who are you?" Hoxworth asked stiffly, turning unwillingly to see a brash-looking young man in flannel trousers and white linen coat. He carried three books under his arm, and looked disarmingly at ease.

"I'm Red Kenderdine. Brom's English teacher." He looked at a chair, and when Hale failed to respond, asked, "Mind if I sit down?"

"I don't want to talk about this thing, Mr. Kenderdine."

"Have you seen Brom yet?"

"No!" Hale snapped. "Where is he?"

"Good. I wanted very much to be the first to talk with you, Mr Hale."

"Why?"

"I don't want you to make a serious mistake, Mr. Hale."

"What do you mean?"

"First, will you agree to honor what I'm about to say as coming from a personal friend . . . and not from a Punahou master?"

"I don't even know you," Hale replied stuffily. He had never liked educators. To him they were a mealy lot.

"But Bromley does."

Hale looked at the young man suspiciously. "Are you in any way involved . . ."

"Mr. Hale, I come here as a friend, not as a conspirator."

"Excuse me, Kenderdine. Bromley has spoken well of you."

"I'm glad," the young instructor said coldly. "I'm here to speak well of him."

"You're about the only one in Honolulu . . ."

"Exactly. Mr. Hale, have you read Brom's essay?"

"All I could stomach."

"Apart from the photograph of you, which is unforgivable, did you recognize your son's essay as a marvelous piece of irony?"

"Irony! It was plain unadulterated filth. Sewer stuff."

"No, Mr. Hale, it was first-rate compassionate irony. I wish I had the talent your son has."

"You wish . . ." Hoxworth sputtered and stared incredulously at his visitor. "You sound like one of the elements we're trying to control in this community."

Kenderdine blew air from his lower lip into his nose and took a patient respite before daring to answer. Then he handed Mr. Hale three books. "These are for you, sir."

"What do I want with them?" Hoxworth growled.

"They will help you understand the extraordinarily gifted young man who happens to be your son," Kenderdine explained.

"Never heard of them," Hale snorted, at which the young master lost his temper slightly and said something he immediately wished he could recall.

"I suppose you haven't, sir. They happen to be three of the greatest novels of our time."

"Oh," Hale grunted, missing the sarcasm. "Well, I still never heard of them. What're they about?"

"Family histories, Mr. Hale. *A Lost Lady* is a great masterpiece. I wish everyone in Hawaii could read *The Grandmothers* by Glenway Wescott. It would explain so much about Honolulu and Punahou. And this last one should be read by everyone who comes from a large family with many mixed-up ramifications. Kate O'Brien's *Without My Cloak.* It's laid in Ireland, but it's about you and Bromley, Mr. Hale."

"You know, Kenderdine, I don't like you. I don't like your manner, and I think if the truth were known, Bromley probably got off on the wrong foot largely because of your bad influence. I don't know what Punahou's . . ."

"Mr. Hale, I don't like you either," the young instructor said evenly. "I don't like a man who can read one of the wittiest, most promising bits of writing I've ever known a schoolboy to write and not even recognize what his son has accomplished. Mr. Hale, do you know why Hawaii is so dreadfully dull, why it's such a wasteland of the human intellect? Because nobody speculates about these islands. Nobody ever writes about them. Aren't you ever perplexed over the fact Nebraskans write fine novels about Nebraska, and people in Mississippi write wonderful things about Mississippi? Why doesn't anybody ever write about Hawaii?"

"There was Stevenson," Hale protested, adding brightly, "and Jack London!"

"Complete junk," Kenderdine snapped disdainfully.

"Do you mean to sit there and tell me that you teach our children that Jack London . . ."

"What he wrote about Hawaii? Complete junk. What anybody else has written about Hawaii? Complete junk, Mr. Hale."

"Who are you to judge your betters?"

"I'm stating facts. And the biggest fact is that nobody writes about Hawaii because the great families, like yours, don't encourage their sons and daughters to think . . . to feel . . . and certainly not to report. You've got a good thing here, and you don't want any questions asked."

"Young man, I've heard enough from you," Hoxworth said stiffly. "I recognize you as a type too dangerous to work with young people. So, as a member of the board at Punahou . . ."

"You're going to fire me?"

"I would be derelict to my duty if I did otherwise, Mr. Kenderdine."

The young man relaxed insolently in the chair and stared at the lights of Pearl Harbor. "And I would be derelict to my duty as a human being who loves these islands, Mr. Hale, if I failed to tell you that I for one don't give a good goddamn what you do or when you do it.

I've watched you try to hold education back. I've watched you try to hold labor back. I've watched you try to hold the legislature back. There was nothing I could do about those crimes against the larger community. But when you try to hold back a proven talent, your own son, who if he were encouraged could write the book that would illuminate these islands, then I object. I didn't know anything about your son's rare and wonderful essay until I saw it. I got my copy late, but I will always treasure it. When he becomes a great man, I'll treasure it doubly. I detect in it certain of my phrases, and I'm glad he learned at least something from me."

"You're through, Kenderdine! You're out!" Hale paced back and forth before the big windows, waiting for the insolent young man to leave, but the English teacher lit a cigarette, puffed twice, and slowly rose.

"I am through, Mr. Hale. But not because of your action. I was through when I came here. Because I won't tolerate your kind of crap a day longer. I've joined the navy."

"God help America if the navy takes men like you," Hale snorted.

"And when this war comes to Hawaii, Mr. Hale, as it inevitably must, not only will I be gone, but you will be, too. Everything you stand for. The labor you hate is going to organize. The Japanese you despise will begin to vote. And who knows, perhaps even your cozy little deal with the military, whereby you and they run the islands, will be blasted. I'm through for the time being, Mr. Hale. You're through forever."

He bowed gravely, jabbed his forefinger three times at the books and winked. But as he left the room he said gently, "I've allowed you to fire me, Mr. Hale. Now you do one thing for me. Read the essay again and discover the love your son holds for the missionaries. Only a mind steeped in true love can write irony. The others write satire." And he was gone.

Alone, Hoxworth decided to call the police to find where his son was, but he reconsidered. Then Hewlett Janders stormed over, big, robust, full of action and profanity. Hoxworth found the interview rather confusing because Hewlett on reconsideration didn't want to horsewhip Bromley at all. He thought the essay a damned good bit of skylarking and said it would probably do the mission families as much good as anything that had happened in years.

"Whole town's laughing their belly off," he roared. "I thought that picture of you in the bunk was downright killing, Hoxworth. And what about that paragraph where he sums up: 'So by projection we can assume . . .' Where's your copy, Hoxworth?" He glimpsed the mimeographed publication under a davenport pillow, picked it up and thumbed through it. "By God, Hoxworth, that picture of you in the bunk is worth ten thousand votes if you ever decide to run for office. Only thing you've ever done proves you're human. Here's the part I wanted. 'So by projection we can estimate that within an area less than six feet by five, during a voyage of 207 days, no less than 197 separate acts of sexual intercourse must have taken place under conditions which prevented any of the female participants from taking off their long flannel underwear or any of the men from stretching out full length in the bunks.' Now here's the part I like," Janders laughed robustly. " 'Against its will the mind is driven to haunting suspicions: What actually went on in those crowded staterooms? What orgies must have transpired? Out of delicate regard for the proprieties I shall not pursue the probabilities, for they are too harrowing to discuss in public, but I recommend that each reader develop this matter logically to its inevitable conclusions: What did go on?' " Big Hewlett Janders slammed the essay against his leg and shouted, "Y'know, Hoxworth, I often used to ask myself that very question. How the hell do you think the old folks did it?"

"How should I know?" Hoxworth pleaded.

"Damn it all, man, it was you they photographed hunched up in one of the bunks!" Janders roared.

"Does anyone know where Bromley is?" Hale asked stiffly.

"Sure," Janders laughed. "But don't change the subject. Don't you agree that the bit I just read is hilarious? By God, I can see prim Lucinda Whipple turning cartwheels when she reads that. One fellow at the club said your boy Brom must be a genius."

"Where is he?" Hale insisted.

"Whole gang of them are having chop suey at Asia Kee's. Every fifteen minutes somebody yells, 'Author! Author!' and Brom takes a bow. Then they all sing a dirge somebody made up, 'Farewell, Punahou!' I suppose you heard that my boy Whip also got expelled. For taking the pictures. Damned glad Mandy didn't, too. Posing like that with your boy." But his raucous laughter proved that he wasn't too concerned.

"Did you see them . . . at the chop suey place?" Hoxworth asked.

"Yeah, I stopped by . . . Well, hell, I figured, it's their big night, so I dropped off a couple bottles of Scotch."

"You gave these outrageous children . . ."

"What I stopped by to see you about, Hoxworth, is that I just called that tutoring school near Lawrenceville, and they've agreed to take Whip and Brom . . . if you want to send him . . . and guarantee to get them into Yale. That's the only problem, really, Hoxworth. Get the boys into Yale."

"What school are you talking about?"

"What's the name? It's right near Lawrenceville. Mark Hewlett sent his boy there when he got busted out of Punahou. They got him into

Yale." Seeing the three novels on the low table, Janders picked one up in the way men do who never read books, and asked, "You drowning your sorrows in a good book?"

"Do you know an English master at Punahou named Kenderdine?"

"Yes. Crew-cut job."

"I had a fearful scene with him. He's at the root of this business, I'm convinced."

"He's a troublemaker. Some jerkwater college like Wisconsin or Wesleyan. I keep telling Larry, 'Get Yale men. They may not be so smart but in the long run they give you less trouble.' But Larry always drags in some genius . . . Yes, Kenderdine's Wisconsin."

"He's no longer Punahou."

"You fire him?"

"I certainly did. But you know, Hewlett, he said about the same thing you did. Said Bromley's essay would do us all a lot of good. Get people laughing. He said it was crystal-clear that Brom wrote the essay with love and affection . . . that he wasn't lampooning the missionaries."

"That's what one of the judges at the club thought," Janders recalled. "But I'll tell you what, Hoxworth. Seems it was my son who took the photo of you in the bunk, proving that sex was impossible. Well, if you can handle him, you're welcome to thrash hell out of him. I won't try because he can lick me."

The door banged and Hoxworth Hale was left alone in the big room overlooking Honolulu. For a while he studied the never tedious pattern of lights, as they came and went along the foreshores of the bay, and the bustling activity at Pearl Harbor, and the starry sky to the south: his city, the city of his people, the fruit of his family's energy. He leafed his son's startling essay and saw again the provocative last sentence: "We can therefore conclude, I think, that whereas our fathers often paced the deck of the *Thetis,* wrestling with their consciences, they usually wound up by hustling below to the cramped bunks, where they wrestled with their wives."

Idly he picked up the three books Kenderdine had left. Hefting the Irish novel, he found it too heavy and put it aside. He looked at Willa Cather's slim book, *A Lost Lady,* but its title seemed much too close to his own case, and he did not want to read about lovely ladies who become lost, for it seemed to be happening throughout his group. That left *The Grandmothers,* which was neither too heavy in bulk nor too close to home, although had he known when he started reading, it was really the most dangerous of the three, for it was a barbed shaft directed right at the heart of Honolulu and its wonderful matriarchies.

To his surprise, he was still reading the story of Wisconsin's rare old women, when the lights of Honolulu sadly surrendered their battle against the rising dawn. The door creaked open gingerly, and Bromley

Whipple Hale, flushed with pride of authorship and Uncle Hewlett's good whiskey, stumbled into the room.

"Hi, Dad."

"Hello, Bromley."

The handsome young fellow, with indelible Whipple charm stamped on his bright features, slumped into a chair and groaned. "It's been quite a day, Dad."

Grudgingly, Hoxworth observed: "You seem to have cut quite a niche for yourself in the local mausoleum."

"Dad, I got thrown out of school."

"I know. Uncle Hewlett's already made plans for you and Whipple to get into one of the good cram schools. The one thing you have to safeguard is your Yale entrance."

"Dad, I was going to speak about this later, but I guess now's . . . I don't believe I want to go to Yale. Now wait a minute! I'd like to try either Alabama or Cornell."

"Alabama! Cornell!" Hoxworth exploded. "Those jerkwater . . . Good heavens, you might just as well go to the University of Hawaii."

"That's what I wanted to do . . . seeing as how I want to write about Hawaii. But Mr. Kenderdine says that Alabama and Cornell have fine classes in creative writing."

"Bromley, where did you ever get the idea that you want to be a writer? This isn't a job for a man. I've been relying on you to . . ."

"You'll have to rely upon somebody else, Dad. There's lots of good bright young men from Harvard and Penn business schools who'd be glad . . ."

"What do you know about Harvard and Penn?"

"Mr. Kenderdine told us they were the best in the country . . . in business."

Hoxworth stiffened and growled, "I suppose your Mr. Kenderdine said that anyone who bothered to go into business . . ."

"Oh, no! He thinks business is the modern ocean for contemporary Francis Drakes and Jean Lafittes."

"Weren't they pirates?" Hoxworth asked suspiciously.

"They were adventurers. Mr. Kenderdine told Whip Janders he ought to try like the devil to get into Harvard Business School."

"But he didn't tell you that, did he?"

"No, Dad. He thinks I can write." There was a long pause in the big room as the pastel lights of morning spread across the city below, and one of those rare moments developed in which a son can talk to his father, and if Hoxworth Hale had growled in his customary manner, the moment would have passed, like the ghost of Pele ignoring one whom she considered not worth a warning, but Hoxworth's personal god sat heavily on his shoulder, and he said nothing, so that his son continued: "You and your father and all your generations used to sit up here, Dad, and look down at Honolulu and dream of controlling it. Every streetcar that ran, every boat that came to port did so at your command. I appreciate that. It's a noble drive, a civilizing one. Sometimes I've caught a glimpse of such a life for myself. But it's always passed, Dad. I just don't have that vision, and you've got to find someone who has, or you and I will both go broke."

"Don't you have any vision at all?" Hoxworth asked quietly, back in the shadows.

"Oh, yes!" The handsome young fellow pointed to Honolulu, lying tribute beneath them, and confided for the first time to anyone: "I want to control this city too, Dad. But I want to bore into its heart to see what makes it run. Why the Chinese buy land and the Japanese don't. Why the old families like ours intermarry and intermarry until damned near half of them have somebody locked away in upstairs rooms. I want to know who really owns the waterfront, and what indignities a man must suffer before he can become an admiral at Pearl Harbor. And when I know all these things, I'm going to write a book . . . maybe lots of them . . . and they won't be books like the ones you read. They'll be like *The Grandmothers* and *Without My Cloak,* books you never heard of. And when I know, and when I have written what I know, then I'll control Honolulu in a manner you never dreamed of. Because I'll control its imagination."

He was slightly drunk and fell back in his chair. His father watched him for some minutes, during which fragments of *The Grandmothers* repeated themselves in Hoxworth's agitated mind. Finally the father said, "I suppose you don't want to bundle off to the cram school?"

"No, Dad."

"What will you do?"

"There's no sweat getting into either Cornell or Alabama. I'll register Monday at McKinley High."

Hoxworth winced and asked, "Why McKinley?"

"The kids call it Manila Prep and I'd sort of like to know some Filipinos."

"You already know . . . Doesn't Consul Adujo's son go to Punahou?"

"I want to know real Filipinos, Dad."

Hoxworth Hale started to rear back, as if he were about to tell his son that he would tolerate no nonsense about McKinley High School, but as words began to formulate he saw his son etched against the pale morning light, and the silhouette was not of Bromley Hoxworth, the radical essayist who had outraged Hawaii, but of Hoxworth Hale, the radical art critic who had charged Yale University with thievery; and a bond of identity was established, and the father swallowed his words of reprimand.

"Tell me one thing, Bromley. This Mr. Kenderdine? Can his ideas be trusted?"

"The best, Dad. Unemotional, yet loaded with fire. You heard, I suppose, that we're losing him. Joining the navy. Says there's bound to be war."

There was a painful silence and the boy concluded: "Maybe that's why I want to go to McKinley now, Dad. There mayn't be too much time." He started to bed but realized that he owed his father some kind of apology, for the mimeographed essay had created a storm which he, the author, had not anticipated. "About that photograph of you, Dad . . . What I mean is, if I do become a writer, I'll be a good one." And he stumbled off to bed.

IN 1941 the Thanksgiving Day football game was largely a replay of the 1938 classic, with Punahou pitted against McKinley, but this time two Sakagawa boys played for Punahou; for Hoxworth Hale and his committee of alumni had been so pleased with Tadao's performance that they had automatically extended scholarships to the younger boys, Minoru the tackle and Shigeo the halfback. Thus it was that the former privy cleaner Kamejiro sat in the stadium along with his wife and his two older boys—Goro was in army uniform—cheering for Punahou. A newspaperman remarked: "It's a revolution in Hawaii when Sakagawa the barber and Hoxworth Hale support the same team."

Throughout Hawaii these minor miracles of accommodation were taking place. When a child felt pain he said, "Itai, itai!" which was Japanese. When he finished work it was pauhana. He had aloha for his friends. He tried to avoid pilikia and when he flattered girls it was hoomalimali, all Hawaiian words. He rarely ate candy, but kept his pockets filled with seed, a delicious Chinese confection tasting like licorice, sugar and salt all at once and made of dried cherries or plums. After a dance he did not eat hot dogs; he ate a bowl of saimin, Japanese noodles, with teriyaki barbecue. Or he had chop suey. For dessert he had a Portuguese malasada, a sweet, sticky fried doughnut, crackling with sugar. It was an island community and it had absorbed the best from many cultures. On this day, as Punahou battled McKinley in a game that was more thrilling to Honolulu than the Rose Bowl game was to California, Punahou, the haole heaven, fielded a team containing two Sakagawas, a Kee, two Kalanianaoles, a Rodriques and assorted Hales, Hewletts, Janderses and Hoxworths. That year Punahou won, 27-6, and Shigeo Sakagawa scored two of the touchdowns, so that as he went home through the streets of Kakaako the perpetual toughs taunted him contemptuously with being a haole-lover, but they no longer tried to assault the Sakagawa boys. They knew better.

Logically, the Sakagawas should have been able—what with the aid of scholarships for three of the boys—to retire Reiko-chan from the barbershop, allowing her to enroll in the university, but just as the family had enough money saved ahead for this, the consulate on Nuuanu Street convened the Japanese community and told them gravely, "The war in China grows more costly than ever. We have got to assist our homeland now. Please, please remember your vows to the emperor." And the fund had gone to help Japan resist the evil of China's aggression, though Goro asked his friends, "How can China be the aggressor when it's Japan that's done the invading?" He wanted to ask his father about this, but Kamejiro, in these trying days of late 1941, had pressing problems which he could not share with his children, nor with anyone else for that matter, except Mr. Ishii.

They began when Hawaii established a committee of American citizens whose job it was to visit all Japanese homes, beseeching the parents to write to Japan to have the names of their children removed from village registers, thus canceling their Japanese citizenship. Hoxworth Hale was the committee member who visited the Sakagawas, and with Reiko as interpreter he explained on the day after Thanksgiving: "Mr. Sakagawa, Japan is a nation that insists upon dual citizenship. But since your five fine children were born here, legally they're Americans. Emotionally they're Americans too. But because you registered their names in your Hiroshima village years ago they are also Japanese citizens. Suppose the war in Europe spreads. What if Japan and America get into it on opposite sides? Your sons might face serious difficulties if you allow them to retain two citizenships. To protect them, get it cleaned up."

The five children added their pleas. "Look, Pop," they argued. "We respect Japan, but we're going to be Americans." Their father agreed with them. He nodded. He told Mr. Hale that it ought to be done, but as always before, he refused to sign any papers. This the children could not understand and they sided with Mr. Hale when he said, "It really isn't right, Mr. Sakagawa, for you to penalize your sons, especially with three of them being Punahou boys."

But Sakagawa-san was adamant, and after Mr. Hale had left, and his family began hammering him with their arguments, he felt caged and finally kicked a chair and shouted, "I'm going away where a man can get some peace." He sought out Mr. Ishii and sat glumly with him.

"Our evil has caught up with us, old friend," he said.

"It was bound to, sooner or later," Mr. Ishii reflected sadly.

"The children are insisting that I write to Hiroshima and take their names off the village registry."

"You aren't going to do it, are you?" Mr. Ishii asked hopefully.

"How can I? And bring disgrace upon us all?"

The two men, now gray in their late fifties, sat moodily and thought of the shame in which they were involved. In their village Kamejiro had been legally married by proxy to the pretty girl Sumiko, by whom he had had five children, all duly reported; and Mr. Ishii had been legally married to Mori Yoriko, no children reported. Yet by convenient switching, Kamejiro had married Yoriko, American style, and she was the mother of the children; Mr. Ishii had likewise married Sumiko, and she had turned out to be a prostitute. How could they explain these things to the Japanese consulate on Nuuanu Street? How could they explain this accidental bigamy to the five children? Above all, how could they explain it to the village authorities in Hiroshima? "All Japan would be ashamed," Mr. Ishii said gloomily. "Kamejiro, we better leave things just as they are."

"But the children are fighting with me. Today even Mr. Hale came to the house. He had the papers in his hands."

"Of course he had the papers!" Mr. Ishii agreed. "But you watch his face when you try to explain who your wife is. Kamejiro, friend, let the matter drop."

But on Saturday, December 6, Mr. Hale returned to the shack and said, "You are the last holdout on my list, Mr. Sakagawa. Please end your sons' dual citizenship. With Goro here in the army, and Tadao and Minoru in the R.O.T.C., it's something you've got to do."

"I can't," Kamejiro said through his interpreter, Goro, who had a weekend pass from Schofield Barracks.

"I don't understand the old man," Goro said, smoothing out his army uniform, of which he was obviously proud. "He's loyal to Japan, but he's no great flag waver. I'll argue with him again when you're gone, Mr. Hale."

"His obstinacy looks very bad," Mr. Hale warned. "Especially with you in the army. I've got to report it, of course."

Goro shrugged his shoulders. "Have you ever tried to argue with a Japanese papa-san? My pop has some crazy fixed idea. But I'll see what I can do."

That Saturday night the entire Sakagawa family battled out this problem of dual citizenship, in Japanese. "I respect your country, Pop," Goro said. "I remember when I had the fight with the priest about going back to Japan. When I finally surrendered, I really intended to go. But you know what's happened, Pop. Football . . . now the army. Let's face it, Pop. I'm an American."

"Me too," Tadao agreed.

The sons hammered at him, and finally he said, "I want you to be Americans. When I put a newspaper picture like that over the sink, 'Four Sakagawa Stars,' don't you think I'm proud? Long ago I admitted you'd never again be Japanese."

"Then take our names off the citizenship registry in Japan."

"I can't," he repeated for the fiftieth time.

"Damn it, Pop, sometimes you make me mad!" Goro cried.

Kamejiro stood up. He stared at his sons and said, "There will be no shouting. Remember that you are decent Japanese sons." They came to attention, and he added sorrowfully, "There is a good reason why I cannot change the register."

"But why?" the boys insisted.

Through the long night the argument lasted, and stubborn Kamejiro was unable to explain why he was powerless to act; for even though his sons were American, he was forever Japanese, and he expected one day to return to Hiroshima; when he got there he could quietly tell his friends about the mix-up in Hawaii, but he could not do so by letter. He himself could not write, and he could not trust others to write for him. It was two o'clock in the morning when he went to bed, and as he pulled the covers up about his shoulders, on a group of aircraft carriers six hundred miles away, a task force of Japanese airmen, many of them from Hiroshima, prepared to bomb Pearl Harbor.

Shigeo, the youngest of the Sakagawas, rose early next morning and pedaled his bicycle down to Cable Wireless, where he worked on Sundays delivering cables that had accumulated during the night and those which would come in throughout the day. His first handful he got at seven-thirty and they were all addressed to people in the Diamond Head area like the Hales and the Whipples, who lived in big houses overlooking the city.

He had reached Waikiki when he heard from the vicinity of Pearl Harbor a series of dull explosions and he thought: "More fleet exercises. Wonder what it means?"

He turned his back on Pearl Harbor and pedaled up an impressive lane leading to the estate of Hoxworth Hale, and while waiting in the porte-cochere he looked back toward the naval base and saw columns of dense black smoke curling up into the morning sunlight. More explosions followed and he saw a series of planes darting and zigzagging through the bright blue overhead. "Pretty impressive," he thought.

He rang the Hale bell again, and in a moment Hoxworth Hale appeared in a dark business suit, wearing collar and tie, as if such a leader of the community were not allowed to relax. Shig noticed that the man's face was colorless and his hands trembling. The radio was making noises from a room Shig could not see, but what it was saying he could not determine. Gulping in a manner not common to the Hales, Hoxworth pushed open the screen door and said to the star of the Punahou eleven, "My God, Shig. Your country has declared war on mine."

For a moment Shig could not comprehend what had been said. Pointing back to Pearl Harbor he asked, "They having a make-believe invasion?"

"No," Hoxworth Hale replied in a hollow, terrified voice. "Japan is bombing Honolulu."

"Japan?" Shig looked up at the darting planes and saw that where they passed, explosions followed and that as the planes sped toward the mountains, puffs of gunfire traced them through the sky. "Oh, my God!" the boy gasped. "What's happened?"

Hoxworth held the door open, ignoring the cable, and indicated that Shig should come inside, and they went to the radio, whose announcer was repeating frantically, yet with a voice that tried to avoid the creation of panic: "I repeat. This is not a military exercise. Japanese planes are bombing Honolulu. I repeat. This is not a joke. This is war."

Hoxworth Hale covered his face with his hands and muttered, "How awful this is going to be." Looking at bright-eyed Shig, who was only a year older than his own son, he said, "You'll need all the courage you have, son."

Shig replied, "Outside you said, 'Your country has declared war on my country.' Yours and mine are both the same, Mr. Hale. I'm an American."

"I'm sorry, Shig. That's a mistake many of us will make in the next few days. God, look at that explosion!" The two watchers winced as an enormous thunder filled the air, accompanied by a slowly rising pillar of jet-black smoke that billowed and twisted upward from the ruins at Pearl Harbor. "Something terrible is taking place," Hale mumbled.

Then from a stairway behind him came a haunted voice, weak and piping like a child's, and he made as if to push Shigeo out the door, but before he could do so the person on the stairs had come down into the room and stood facing her husband and his visitor. It was Mrs. Hale, a frail and very beautiful woman of thirty-eight. She had light auburn hair and wide, level eyes that found difficulty in focusing. She wore a wispy dressing gown such as Shig had never seen before outside the movies, and she walked haltingly. "What is the great noise I hear, Hoxworth?" she asked.

"Malama, you shouldn't have come down here," her husband admonished.

"But I heard a shooting," she explained softly, "and I wondered if you were in trouble."

At this moment one of the bombing planes was driven off course by a burst of unexpected anti-aircraft fire, and it swerved from its planned escape route, winging swiftly over the Diamond Head area, and as it passed, Shig and Mr. Hale could see on its underbelly the red circle of Japan. "You'd better go now," Mr. Hale said.

"You haven't signed for the cable," Shig pointed out, and as Hoxworth took the cable and signed the receipt, his wife walked ghostlike to the door and looked toward Pearl Harbor, where the bombs were still exploding.

"Ahhhhhh!" she shrieked in a weird guttural cry. "It's war and my son will be killed." Throwing her filmy sleeves over her face, she ran to her husband, sobbing, "It's war, and Bromley will not come back alive."

Hale, holding his wife in his right arm, returned the receipt with his left hand and gripped Shigeo by the shoulder. "You must not speak of this," he said.

"I won't," Shigeo promised, not understanding exactly what it was that he was expected to keep secret.

Kamejiro had risen at six that morning and had gone down to the barbershop to sterilize everything again, for part of the success of his shop stemmed from his mania for cleanliness. Now he was back home waiting for his breakfast. His wife Yoriko, who never did her customers' laundry on Sunday, was leisurely preparing a meal, having already fed Shigeo. Goro, enjoying his pass, was sleeping late, but Tadao, who was in the R.O.T.C. at the university, had already risen. Reiko-chan was dressed and ready to go to an early service at the Community Church in Moiliili. Minoru, nineteen and already in training for basketball at Punahou, was also sleeping.

The first to comprehend what was happening was Goro, for when the bombs struck he thundered out of bed, ran in his shorts into the yard and shouted, "This is no game. Somebody's declared war!" He ran to the radio he had built for the family and heard official confirmation of his suspicions: "Enemy planes of unknown origin are bombing Pearl Harbor and Hickam Field." Turning to his family he announced in Japanese: "I think Japan has declared war against us."

The escape route used by those bombers who attacked the eastern segment of Pearl Harbor carried them across Kakaako, and now as they flashed by in triumph the Sakagawa family gathered on their minute lawn surrounded by flowers and watched the bright red rising sun of Japan dart by. As soon as the enemy was identified Goro shouted, "Tad! We better report right away!" Accordingly, he hurried into his army uniform and hitchhiked a ride out to Schofield Barracks, while Tadao and Minoru climbed into their R.O.T.C. uniforms, Tadao reporting to the university and Minoru to Punahou. But before the boys left, they bowed ceremoniously to their bewildered father.

The impact of these sudden happenings on Kamejiro staggered him. In an uncomprehending daze he sat down on the steps of his shack and stared at the sky, where puffs of ack-ack traced the departure of the Japanese planes. Three times he saw the red sun of his homeland flash past, and once he saw the evil snout of a low-flying Japanese fighter spewing machine-gun bullets ineffectively into the bay. He tried to focus his thoughts on what was happening and upon his sons' prompt departure for the American army; but the inchoate thoughts that were rising in his mind were not allowed to become words. Japan must have been in great trouble to have done such a thing. The boys must have been in great trouble if they left so promptly to defend America. That was as far as he could go.

At eleven o'clock that Sunday morning a group of four secret police, armed and with a black hearse waiting on Kakaako Street, rushed into the Sakagawa home and arrested Kamejiro. "Sakagawa," said one who spoke Japanese. "We've been watching you for a long time. You're a dynamiter, and you're to go into a concentration camp."

"Wait!" Reiko protested. "You know who the Sakagawa boys are. At Punahou. What's this about concentration camp?"

"He's a dynamiter, Miss Sakagawa. He gave money to Japan. And he refused to denationalize you. It's the pokey for him." The efficient team whisked bewildered Kamejiro into the hearse and it drove on, picking up other suspected seditionists.

At eleven-thirty Shigeo pedaled by on his Cable Wireless bicycle to share with the family the frightening things he had been seeing, but he said nothing of them, for Reiko's announcement that their father had been hauled away to concentration camp stunned him. This was really war, and he and all other Japanese were instantly involved. "Pop couldn't have been doing anything wrong, could he?"

The brother and sister looked at each other and it was Shigeo who formulated their doubt: "On the other hand, Pop used to prowl around every night."

"Shigeo!" Reiko-chan cried. "That's unworthy!"

"I'm only trying to think like the F.B.I.," Shig explained in justification.

They were further disturbed when Mr. Ishii, in a state of maximum excitement, ran up with this startling news: "The Japanese army is making a landing at the other end of the island. They've already captured Maui and Kauai."

"That's impossible!" Shigeo cried. "I've been all over Honolulu this morning, and I heard nothing like that."

"You'll see!" the quick little man assured them. "By tomorrow night Japan will be in complete control." To the amazement of the Sakagawa children, Mr. Ishii seemed positively exhilarated by the prospect, and Shigeo caught him by the arm.

"You be careful what you're saying, Mr. Ishii! The F.B.I. just arrested Pop."

"When the Japanese win he'll be a hero," the little man exulted. "Now everyone who laughs at Japanese will behave themselves. You watch what happens when the troops march into Honolulu." He waved a warning finger at them and dashed on down the street.

"I think he's out of his mind," Shigeo said sadly as he watched the community gossip disappear. As Mr. Ishii turned the corner, a patrol came through Kakaako, announcing with a loud-speaker: "All Japanese are under house arrest. Do not leave your homes. I repeat. Do not leave your homes."

Shigeo went up to them and said, "I'm the Sunday delivery boy for Cable Wireless."

There was a moment of hesitation, after which the patrol made the type of decision that was going to be made many times that day throughout Hawaii: the Japanese are all spies and they are all disloyal; they must be clamped into house arrest; but we know this particular Japanese and the work he is doing is essential, therefore he is excused. The patrol looked at Shig's bicycle with its clear marking, and one man asked, "Aren't you the kid who plays for Punahou?"

"Yes," Shig replied.

"You're all right. You go ahead."

"You got a pass I could use?" Shig asked. "I don't want to get shot at."

"Sure. Use this."

At two o'clock that afternoon Shig reported to his main office for his fourth batch of telegrams and he was handed one addressed to General Lansing Hommer, but since Shig knew that the general lived at the extreme end of his route, he tucked that particular message into the bottom of his pile, and as he pedaled through the western part of Honolulu toward Pearl Harbor and saw the devastation he understood better than most what had happened and what was about to happen. From the porch of one house where he delivered a cable, he could see the anchorage at Pearl Harbor itself, and alongside the piers he saw the stricken ships, lying on their sides and belching flames.

The man to whom he had given the telegram said, "Well, the goddamned Japs hit everything they aimed at. Papers said Japs couldn't fly planes because they were cross-eyed. You ask me, we better get some cross-eyed pilots. And some gunners, too. I stood on this porch for three hours and I didn't see our men hit one goddamned Jap plane. What do you think of that?"

"You mean they all got away?"

"Every one of the bastards."

"Some monkey was telling me the Japanese have already landed," Shig said.

"They'll never make it," the man replied. "So far the Japs have hit only the navy, which is a bunch of do-nothings anyway. When they try to land they run up against the dogfaces. That'll be different. I got two sons in the infantry. Plenty tough. You got anyone in uniform?"

"Two brothers."

"Infantry, I hope?"

"Yep. They're plenty tough, too."

"I don't think the yellow bastards'll make it," the man said as he ripped open his telegram.

At four thirty-one that hot, terrifying afternoon Shigeo Sakagawa reached the end of his route, and he pedaled his Cable Wireless bicycle up the long drive leading to the residence of General Hommer, where the ashen-faced military leader took the cable and scribbled his name in pencil across the receipt. His command had been virtually destroyed. The islands he was supposed to protect were at the mercy of the enemy.

Even his own headquarters had been strafed with impunity. At the end of this debacle he was forced to receive cables from Washington, but this particular one was more than he could stomach. He read it, swore, crumpled it up, and threw it on the floor. As it slowly unfolded itself, Shig could read that it came from the War Department. It warned General Hommer that from secret sources Washington had concluded that Japan might attempt to attack Pearl Harbor. With all the instantaneous systems of communications available to the government, Washington could have rushed the message through in time to prevent the holocaust, but it had transmitted this most urgent of contemporary cables by ordinary commercial wireless. It arrived ten hours late, delivered on bicycle by a Japanese messenger boy.

The speed with which Goro and Tadao rushed to offer their services to America was not matched by America in accepting those services. The 298th Infantry Regiment, which Goro joined at Schofield Barracks, was composed mostly of Japanese enlisted men commanded by non-Japanese officers, and it was this unit which was dispatched to clean up the bomb damage at Hickam Field, where dozens of American aircraft had been destroyed by Japanese bombers. When the air corps men saw the truckload of local Japanese boys invading the wrecked air strip they yelled, "They're invading!" And some frightened guards started shooting.

"Knock it off!" the 298th shouted. "We're Americans!" and in the next three days of crisis the outfit put forth a remarkable effort, working eighteen and twenty hours a day to make the airfield operable. "Best crew on the island," one haole superior reported admiringly. "Not much question as to where their loyalty rests."

But on the night of December 10 somebody in Honolulu headquarters received a message from California pointing out how energetic California was in rounding up its criminal Japanese, and some senior officer pushed the panic button. So in the silent hours before dawn three companies of trustworthy haole soldiers were sent with an extra complement of machine guns to perform one of the war's most curious tasks, and when dawn broke, Goro Sakagawa was the first Japanese boy in the 298th to look out of his tent and cry, "Christ! We're surrounded!"

His mates tumbled out of their sacks and started to rush onto the parade ground when a stern voice, coming over an impersonal metallic loud-speaker commanded: "You Japanese soldiers! Listen to me. Stay right where you are. Don't make one false move. You're surrounded by guns. Stay where you are!"

Then a different voice cried: "You Japanese soldiers. I want you to nominate one man from each tent to step outside. Quick!"

From his tent Goro stepped into the gathering light, wearing shorts and nothing more. Then the voice continued: "You Japanese soldiers inside the tents. Pass out your rifles, your revolvers, your grenades. Quick! You men outside, stack them."

When this was done the voice commanded: "If there are any non-Japanese soldiers in this encampment, they are to leave now. You have five minutes. Quick."

Friends, unable to look their Japanese partners in the eye, shuffled away, and when the five minutes were gone, only Japanese boys stood bewildered in the tents. "Does this mean prison camp?" one whispered.

"Who knows?" his mate shrugged.

What it meant the Japanese boys were now to discover. "Muster out here!" the tinny voice commanded. "As you are! As you are!" And when the bewildered troops were in line, the colonel who had spoken first advised them: "You have been disarmed as a precautionary measure. We cannot tell when your countrymen will try to attack us again and we cannot endanger our rear by having you carrying weapons among us. You will stay within this barbed-wire enclosure until you get further orders. My men have been given one simple command: If any Jap steps outside this compound, shoot!"

For three humiliating days, burdened with rumor and fear, the Japanese boys of the 298th looked out into machine-gun muzzles. Then their guard was relaxed and they were told, "You will be free to work on latrine duty, or paring potatoes, or picking up. But you'll never touch guns again. Now snap to." That took care of Goro, who went into permanent latrine duty.

When Tadao left home on December 7 he ran all the way to the university, where his unit of the R.O.T.C. had already formed up with men who lived in the dormitories, and he arrived breathless just in time to march with his outfit to repel a Japanese parachute landing that was reported to have taken place north of Diamond Head. Of course, no enemy had landed, but headquarters forgot to inform the R.O.T.C. of this, and the Japanese boys patrolled their areas for four days without relief. Japanese families in the area supplied them with rice balls into which salty pickled plums had been inserted, and the college boys kept to their lonely posts.

It was on this silent duty that Tadao Sakagawa thought out explicitly what he would do if Japanese Imperial soldiers came over the rise at him. "I'd shoot," he said simply. "They'd be the enemy and I'd shoot." At the water reservoir, Minoru Sakagawa, of the Punahou R.O.T.C., reached the same conclusion: "I'd shoot." Across Hawaii in those angry, aching days some fourteen thousand young Japanese Americans of military age fought out with themselves this same difficult question, and all came up with the same answer: "They're obviously the enemy, so obviously I'd shoot."

Then, after several weeks of distinguished duty, all Japanese boys in the R.O.T.C. were quietly told, "We no longer have any place for you in the outfit. Turn in your uniforms." They were given no reason, no alternative, so Tadao and Minoru turned in their hard-earned American uniforms and appeared next day in mufti. A haole soldier from Arkansas saw them walking along the street and jeered: "Why ain't you yellow-bellied bastards in uniform same as me? Why should I fight to protect you slant-eyes?"

Minoru, being a rather beefy tackle at Punahou, was always ready for a brawl, and he turned toward the Arkansas boy, but Tadao, a quieter type, caught his arm and dragged him along. "If you hit a soldier, they'd lynch you."

"I'll take so much," Minoru muttered, "and then somebody's going to get it."

But they were to find out that day just how much they would be required to take, for as they came down from the R.OT.C. headquarters, where their pleas for reinstatement were rejected, they saw their mother in her customary black kimono and straw geta walking pin-toed along Kakaako, shuffling in her peasant style and bent forward from the hips. She looked, Minoru had to admit, extremely foreign, and he was not surprised therefore when a crowd gathered and began to shout at her, telling her in words which she couldn't understand that no slant-eyed Japanese were wanted in the streets of Honolulu with their filthy kimonos. And before the boys could get to their mother, rowdies were actually beginning to tear off her kimono.

"Why don't you wear shoes, like decent Americans?" the rowdies cried. They hectored her into a corner, without her understanding at all what was happening, and a big man kept kicking at the offensive zori. "Take 'em off, goddamn it. Take 'em off!"

Swiftly Minoru and Tadao leaped among the crowd to protect their mother, and some sports fan recognized them and shouted, "It's the Sakagawa boys." The incident ended without further embarrassment, but Tadao, who was a diplomat, whispered to his terrified mother, "Kick off your zori. That's what made them mad." Deftly she kicked away the Japanese shoes, and the crowd cheered. On the way home Tadao warned her, "You've got to stop coming out in public wearing your kimono."

"And buy some shoes!" Minoru snapped, for like all the boys of his age, he could not understand why his parents kept to their old ways.

In the following days Minoru and Tadao were to be repeatedly tested. Having been born in America, they were technically citizens and even eligible to become President; but they were also Japanese, and were thus subjected to humiliations worse than those suffered by aliens. Several times they were threatened by drunken soldiers, and prudence told them to keep off the streets.

Nevertheless, animosity against all Japanese increased when Hawaii, staggered by the completeness with which Japan had defeated the local troops, understandably turned to any logical rationalization at hand. "You can't tell me the Japs could have bombed our ships unless the local slant-eyes were feeding them spy information," one man shouted in a bar.

"I know for a fact that plantation workers at Malama Sugar cut arrows across the cane fields, showing Nip fliers the way to Pearl Harbor," a luna reported.

"The F.B.I. has proved that almost every Jap maid working for the military was a paid agent of the Mikado," an official announced.

And the Secretary of the Navy himself, after inspecting the disaster, told the press frankly, "Hawaii was the victim of the most effective fifth-column work that has come out of this war, except in Norway."

It was therefore no wonder that many Japanese were arrested and thrown into hastily improvised jails, whereupon those not yet picked up were ready to believe the rumor that all Japanese in Hawaii were to be evacuated to tents on Molokai. But when the jails were jammed and ships actually appeared in the harbor to haul those already arrested to concentration camps in Nevada, an unusual thing happened, one which more than any other served to bind up the wounds caused by the attack on Pearl Harbor. Hoxworth Hale and Mrs. Hewlett Janders and Mrs. John Whipple Hoxworth and a maiden librarian named Lucinda Whipple went singly, and not as a result of concerted action, to the jails where the Japanese were being held. Being the leading citizens of the community, they were admitted, and as they walked through the corridors they said to the jailers, "I know that man well. He can't possibly be a spy. Let him go."

Mrs. Hewlett Janders even went so far as to bring her husband, big Hewie, to the jail in his naval uniform, and he identified half a dozen excellent citizens whom he had known for years. "It's ridiculous to keep those men in a concentration camp. They're as good Americans as I am."

"Will you vouch for them if we let them go?" the F.B.I. man asked.

"Me vouch for Ichiro Ogawa? I'd be proud to vouch for him. You come on out of there, Ichiro. Go back to work."

Some three hundred leading Japanese citizens were removed from jail by these voluntary efforts of the missionary descendants. It wasn't that they liked Japanese, or that they feared Imperial Japan less than their neighbors. It was just that as Christians they could not sit idly by and watch innocent people maltreated. In California, where the imaginary danger of trouble from potential fifth columnists was not a fraction of the real danger that could have existed in Hawaii, cruel and senseless measures were taken that would be forever an embarrassment to America: families of the greatest rectitude and patriotism were uprooted; their personal goods were stolen; their privacy was abused; and their pride as full-fledged American citizens outraged. Such things did not happen in Hawaii. Men like Hoxworth Hale and Hewlett Janders wouldn't allow them to happen; women like Miss Whipple and Mrs. Hoxworth personally went through the jails to protect the innocent.

But when Hoxworth Hale came to the cell in which Kamejiro

Sakagawa sat, a more intricate moral problem presented itself, for at first Hale was not ready to swear to the F.B.I. men, "This fellow I know to be innocent." What Hale did know was this: Kamejiro was a known dynamiter who had been in trouble during the strike at Malama Sugar; he had obstinately refused to terminate the Japanese nationality of his children; he had been prowling about all of Honolulu at night some years before Pearl Harbor; and now he was running a barbershop with his own daughter as a lure to bring in sailors and soldiers. That was the debit side. But Hale also knew one other fact: of all the young Japanese boys in Honolulu, none were finer Americans than Kamejiro's sons. Therefore, instead of passing by the cell, Hale stopped and asked to be allowed to talk with this man Sakagawa. When the cell door was opened and he sat inside with Kamejiro he told the interpreter to ask: "Mr. Sakagawa, why did you refuse to allow me to end your sons' dual citizenship?"

The old stubborn light came into Kamejiro's eyes, but when he realized that if he did not speak the truth he might never again see his sons, he softened and said, "Will you promise never to tell my boys?"

"Yes," Hale said, for he had family problems of his own. He directed the interpreter to promise likewise.

"My wife and I are not married," Kamejiro began.

"But I saw the marriage certificate!" Hale interrupted.

"American yes, but it doesn't count," Kamejiro explained. "When I sent for a picture bride to Hiroshima-ken, a girl was picked out and she was married to me there, in proper Japanese style, and her name was put in the village book as my wife."

"Then what's the problem?" Hale asked.

Kamejiro blushed at his ancient indiscretion and explained, "So when she got here I didn't like her, and there was another man who didn't like his wife, either."

"So you swapped?" Hale asked. A smile came across his lips. It seemed rather simple.

"Yes. In each country I am married to a different woman."

"But of course this is your real country and this is what counts," Hale said.

"No," Kamejiro patiently corrected. "Japan is my real home, and I would be ashamed for my village to know the wrong thing I have done."

Hale was impressed by the man's forthright defense of Japan, even in such trying circumstances, and he said condescendingly, "I don't think it would really matter, at this distance of time."

"Ah, but it would!" Kamejiro warned. And what he said struck a vibrant chord in Hale's own memories. "Because the wife I got in the exchange turned out to be the best wife a man ever found. But the wife I gave my friend turned out to be a very bad woman indeed, and his life has been ruined and I have had to sit and watch it happen. My happiness came at his expense, and I will do nothing now to hurt him any further.

At least in our village they think he is an honorable man, and I will leave it that way."

Hale clenched his hands and thought of his own reactions to just such problems and of his insistence, against the pressure of friends, that his wife Malama stay with him, even though her mind had wandered past the limits usually required for commitment to an asylum, and in that moment of loving a woman, and knowing apprehension about the fate of one's son in a time of war, Hale felt a close kinship to the little bow-legged Japanese sitting before him. To the F.B.I. man he said, "This one can surely go free." And Kamejiro returned to his family.

Of course, when the gardener Ichiro Ogawa, who had been saved from internment by Hewlett Janders, later insisted that he ought to get a raise from the $1.40 a day that Janders was paying him, big Hewie hit the roof and accused the little Japanese of being unpatriotic by demanding a raise at such a critical time in America's history. "I think of your welfare all the time, Ichiro," Hewie explained. "You must leave these things to me."

"But I can't live on $1.40 a day any more. War expense."

"Are you threatening me?" Janders boomed.

"I got to have more money," Ichiro insisted.

As soon as the Japanese had left, Janders called security at Pearl Harbor. "Lemuel," he spluttered, "I've got a workman out here whose loyalty I'm damned suspicious of. I think he ought to be carted off right now."

"What's his name?"

"Ichiro Ogawa, a real troublemaker."

And that night Ogawa was spirited away and committed to a concentration camp on the mainland, after which there was less agitation for increased wages.

NO ONE living in Hawaii escaped the effect of Pearl Harbor, and on the morning of December 8 practically no one could have even dimly foreseen the changes he would undergo. For example, gruff Hewlett Janders became to his surprise a full captain in the navy with control over harbor facilities. He wore an expensive khaki, some of the finest braid in the Pacific and ultimately a presidential citation for having kept the port cleared for war materiel.

John Whipple Hewlett's wife was caught on the mainland and had to stay there for three years. Nineteen descendants of the old New Bedford sea captain, Rafer Hoxworth, saw service in uniform, including two girls who went into the WAVES. On the other hand, a total of nine female descendants of old Dr. John Whipple married military officers whom they happened to meet in Honolulu.

Of course, the most dramatic impact fell upon the Sakagawas, but I will save discussion of that till later, for it is important that everyone understand how this large family of Japanese aliens became, by virtue of the war, full-fledged Americans. It was ironic that years of pleading for citizenship had got the Japanese nowhere—good behavior availed them nothing—but as soon as the Japanese government destroyed Pearl Harbor and killed more than 4,000 men, everything the local Japanese had wanted was promptly given them; but as I said, I should like to postpone that ironic story for a while.

Apart from the Sakagawas, the impact of that dreadful day of bombing and defeat fell heaviest upon the sprawling Kee hui. Two days after the bombing had ended, Nyuk Tsin, then ninety-four, was taken on a tour of the city by her grandson, Hong Kong, and as she saw the confusion into which the white citizens of Honolulu had fallen, she perceived that the next half year was going to provide the Kee hui with a vital opportunity for material growth, and that if it failed this rare chance, the hui would have no further claim to consideration.

That night Nyuk Tsin summoned her sons and abler grandsons, and when her little house in Nuuanu was jammed, and the blackout curtains were in place, she said, "All over Honolulu the haoles are preparing to run away. Asia, do you think the Japanese are going to invade Hawaii?"

"No."

"Then why are the haoles running away?"

"They may have better information than I do," careful Asia replied.

"Will the Japanese airplanes come back?" Nyuk Tsin pressed.

"I hear our airfields at Wheeler and Hickam were destroyed," Asia reported, "but a navy officer at the restaurant said that even so, next time we would drive the enemy planes away."

Nyuk Tsin thought about this for some time and pressed her wrinkled old hands against her sunken cheeks, then passed them back along her almost vanished hair. "Hong Kong, do you think the Japanese will be back?"

"They may try, but I don't think they'll succeed."

"Do you think Honolulu is a safe place for us to gamble in?" Nyuk Tsin asked. "I mean, will the Japanese be kept out?"

"Yes," Asia said.

"Does it matter?" Hong Kong asked. He was forty-eight, a hard, honest man who had been taught by his father, Africa Kee the lawyer, all the tricks of survival. Having been refused a standard education at Punahou, which would have softened his attitudes, he had acquired from his father a sure instinct for the jugular. As yet he was not well known in Hawaii, having been content to allow his popular uncles to stand before the community as ostensible leaders of the great Kee hui, but Nyuk Tsin, who ran the hui, knew that in Hong Kong she had a successor just as smart and diligent as herself. Therefore, when he asked, "Does it matter?" she listened.

"If Japan conquers Hawaii," Hong Kong pointed out, "we will all be executed as leading Chinese. So we don't have to worry about that. The F.B.I. won't allow us to escape to the mainland, so we don't have to worry about that, either. We've got to stay where we are, pray that the Japanese don't win, and work harder than ever before."

Nyuk Tsin listened, then dropped her thin hands into her lap. "Our adversity is our fortune," she whispered. "We can't run away, but the haoles can. Like frightened rabbits they will be leaving on every ship. And when they go, soldiers and sailors with lots of money will come in. When they arrive, we'll be here. This war will last a long time, and if we work hard, our hui can become stronger than ever before."

"What should we work at?" Asia asked.

"Land," Nyuk Tsin replied with the terrible tenacity of a Hakka peasant who had never known enough land. "As the frightened haoles run away, we must buy all the land they leave behind."

"We don't have enough money to do that," Hong Kong protested.

"I'm sorry," Nyuk Tsin apologized. "I didn't explain myself correctly. Of course we can't afford to buy. But we can put down small deposits and promise to pay later. Then we can work the land and earn the money to pay off the debts."

"But how can we get hold of enough money to start?" Hong Kong asked.

"We must spend every cent of cash we have," Nyuk Tsin replied. "Asia, you take charge of that. Turn everything into cash. Let us run the stores on Hotel Street, because that's where the soldiers will come. Put all our girls to work. Australia, could your granddaughters start a hot-dog stand in Waikiki?"

The hui laid plans to lure every stray nickel from passing military men, but the most important tactic was still to be discussed. "Tomorrow morning, every man who is able must report to Pearl Harbor," Nyuk Tsin directed. "If the shipyard was as badly damaged as they say, lots of men will be needed. They'll be afraid to employ Japanese, and our men will get good jobs. But every penny earned must be given to Asia."

The family agreed that this was the right procedure, so Nyuk Tsin turned next to Hong Kong: "Your job will be the most difficult. You are to take the money that Asia provides, and you are to buy land. That is, pay just enough to get control. And remember, when people are running away in fear, they'll accept almost any cash offer and trust in faith to get the balance."

Hong Kong listened, then asked, "Should I buy business land or private homes?"

There was some discussion of this, but Nyuk Tsin finally directed:

"Later, when the war is over, the big money will be in industrial land. But right now, when the island fills with people, everybody'll want homes."

"So what should I do?" Hong Kong asked.

"Buy homes now, and as their rents come in, apply the money to business property," Nyuk Tsin advised. Then she looked at the senior members of the hui and said, "The next years will require courage. When the war ends, people will hurry back to Hawaii and say, 'Those damned Chinese stole our land from us.' They'll forget that they ran away in fear, and we didn't. But then what they say won't matter." She laughed tremulously and chided her men: "I've never seen grown men so afraid as you are tonight. If you could run away, too, you'd do so, everyone of you. But fortunately the F.B.I. won't let you. So we must all stay here and work."

From this night meeting behind bomb-proofed windows, three changes occurred in Honolulu. First, a good many of the small stores that catered to servicemen, selling them greasy food, soft drinks and candy bars, came to be operated by members of the Kee hui. Prices were kept reasonable, the stores were kept clean, and every establishment made money. Second, at Pearl Harbor, when the accelerated rebuilding of that damaged base began, a surprising number of the auditors, senior bookkeepers, expediters and managerial assistants were named Kee. Their wages were good, their work impeccable, and their behavior inconspicuous. When draft boards asked the navy, "Are you fellows out at Pearl hoarding manpower?" the navy apologetically released Mendoncas and Guerreros, but never a Kee, for the latter were essential to the war. Third, when the military began to fly in hundreds of civilian advisers, and in the case of senior officials, their families too, these men found that if they wanted to rent quarters they had to see Hong Kong Kee; even generals and admirals were told, "Better check with Hong Kong." As the war progressed and Hawaii became horribly overcrowded, with every house renting at triple premium and every store jammed with customers, only Nyuk Tsin and Hong Kong realized how inconspicuously the Kees were converting their rent money into commercial land sites.

THE MOST subtle effect of the war fell upon Hoxworth Hale, who was only forty-three when it began. Of course he volunteered immediately, reminding the local generals of his World War I experience, but they replied that he was essential to H & H, many of whose activities tied in with military requirements. He was therefore not allowed to rejoin the army. Later, when he heard that a group of Yale men were organizing a submarine outfit, he fought to get into that, feeling that he was well fitted for submarine duty, but the navy rather stiffly pointed out that the Yale men involved were more nearly his son's age than his. He therefore had to stay in Honolulu, where he worked closely with Admiral Nimitz and General Richardson, making a substantial contribution to the war effort. Along with his other duties he served as head of the draft board and chairman of the Office of Civilian Defense.

In the former capacity he was pleased at the forthright manner in which young Japanese in Hawaii volunteered for military duty, and thought that the Army's arbitrary rejection of the boys was unwarranted, and he wrote to President Roosevelt to tell him so: "I can speak of first-hand knowledge, sir, and these Japanese boys are among the most loyal citizens you will find in the nation. Why can't you order your people to form a combat team composed of Japanese intended for use in Europe only?"

On the other hand, he was distressed that so few Chinese stepped forward to bear arms in defense of America. "If they don't volunteer," he stormed one day, "I shall direct our draft boards to flush them out with cyanide of potassium. Where are they all?" When he had civil authorities look into the matter, he found that most of them were out at Pearl Harbor, and he asked Admiral Nimitz, "Do you mean to tell me that all those Chinese boys are essential to the war effort?" He was surprised when Nimitz looked into the matter and reported curtly: "Yes. We've got to have somebody out there who can use slide rules."

In early 1942 the air corps asked Hoxworth to join a group of senior officers who were flying to various South Pacific islands to study the possibilities for new airstrips, and he of course quickly consented, for with his wife in a depressed spell during which she could not converse intelligently, with his daughter in a mainland school, and his son in the air corps, he had no reason to stay at home, and the pleasure he got from climbing into uniform, with the simulated rank of colonel, was great.

His military contribution to the journey of inspection was not significant, but his sociological observations were of real import, and whenever the PBY started to descend at bases like Johnston Island, or Canton, or Nukufetau, and he saw from the cramped windows the crystal lagoons and the wide sweep of sand upon reef, he recalled all that one of his ancestors, Dr. John Whipple, had written about the tropics, and he was able to instruct the air corps men on many points. When he first stepped upon an atoll reef he had the peculiar sensation that he had come home, and although for years he had forgotten the fact that he was part-Polynesian, that ancient ancestry came flooding back upon him, and often while the officers were inspecting possible landing areas, he would remain upon the reef, looking out to sea, and long-submerged components of his blood came surging before his eyes, and he could see canoes and voyagers.

But these were not the subtle influences of which I spoke. They began when the PBY landed on Suva Bay, in the Fiji Islands. Hoxworth climbed into a small British boat and went ashore to meet the governor, a proper Englishman with an American wife, and the visit started out like any normal wartime trip to an island that might soon be invaded by the enemy; but as the group started looking into Fiji affairs, Hoxworth Hale began building up impressions that disturbed him deeply.

"Why are the Indians here kept apart?" he inquired.

"Oh, you can't do anything with an Indian!" the British secretary to the governor replied.

"Why not?" Hoxworth asked.

"Have you ever tried working with an Oriental?" the Englishman countered. Hale made no reply, but as he studied the sugar fields in Fiji, he found them exactly like the sugar fields in Hawaii, and he had certainly worked with Japanese in precisely such surroundings, and without too much trouble. He reflected: "Indians were imported into Fiji and Japanese were imported into Hawaii, for the same purposes at about the same time. But with what different results! In Hawaii the Japanese are reasonably good Amcricans. Here the Indians are totally undigested. What went wrong down here?"

"One good thing about it, though," the Englishman pointed out. "If you Johnnies want to pre-empt land for your airstrips, you don't have to worry about the bloody Indians. They're not allowed to own any."

"Why not?" Hoxworth asked.

"Orientals? Owning land?" the smart young man asked rhetorically, but to himself Hoxworth replied: "Bloody well why not? If I understand correctly, the Kees now own half the homes in Hawaii. Best thing ever happens to a Japanese is when he gets a little piece of land and starts to tidy it up. Makes him less radical and woos him away from labor unions."

"So the Indians own none of the land?" Hoxworth asked aloud.

"No, we restrict that very severely," the young man assured him. "Nor can they vote, so we won't have any trouble there, either."

"You mean, the ones born in India can't vote," Hoxworth queried.

"Nor the ones born here," the aide explained, and Hoxworth thought: "How differently we've done things in Hawaii." And the more he saw of Fiji, the happier he was with the manner in which Hawaii's Orientals had been brought into full citizenship, with no real barriers hindering them. Did the Indians go to college? There were no colleges; but in Hawaii there were and God knows the Japanese went. Did the Indians own the land on which their crowded stores perched? No, but in Hawaii the Chinese and Japanese owned whatever they liked. Did the Indians participate in civil government? Heavens no, but in Hawaii their Oriental cousins were beginning to take over some branches. Did Indians serve as government clerks? No, but in Hawaii Chinese were sought after as government employees.

And so throughout his entire comparison of Fiji and Hawaii, Hoxworth Hale saw that what had been done to build the Orientals into Hawaiian life had been the right thing, and what the British in Fiji had done to keep the Indians a sullen, hateful half of the population was wrong; and it was from Fiji that Hale acquired his first insight into how fundamentally just the missionary descendants had been, for he concluded: "In Hawaii we have a sound base from which our islands can move into a constructive future: Japanese, Chinese, Filipinos, Caucasians and Hawaiians working together. But in Fiji, with the hatred I see between the races, I don't see how a logical solution will ever be worked out." Then he added grimly, but with humor, "By God, the next time I hear a Japanese sugar worker raising hell about a union, I'm going to say, 'Watanabe-san, maybe you better go down to Fiji for a while and see how the Indians are doing.' He'd come back to Honolulu and cry at the wharf, 'Please, Mr. Hale, let me back on shore. I want to work in Hawaii, where things are good.' "

And then, when he was congratulating himself on the superior system evolved by his missionary ancestors, he attended a banquet given by Sir Ratu Salaka, a majestic black Fijian chief with degrees from Cambridge and Munich, and when this scion of a great Fijian family appeared dressed in a native lava-lava, with western shirt and jacket, enormous brown leather shoes, and medals of valor gained in World War I, Hale intuitively felt: "In Hawaii we have no natives like this man."

Sir Ratu Salaka was a powerfully oriented man. He spoke English faultlessly, knew of the progress of the war, and stood ready, although now well along in his fifties, to lead a Fijian expeditionary force against the Japanese.

"Remember, my good friends of the air corps," he said prophetically, "when you invade such islands as Guadalcanar and Bougainville, where I have been on ethnological expeditions, you will require as scouts men like myself. Our dark skins will be an asset in scouting, our knowledge of the jungle will enable us to go where your men could never penetrate, and our habit of secrecy in movement will allow us to creep up upon our opponents and kill them silently, while their companions sit ten yards away. When you need us, call, for we are ready."

"Will you have Indian troops with you?" Hale asked.

At this question the dark-skinned host exploded with laughter. "Indians?" he snorted contemptuously. "We put out a call for volunteers and out of our population of more than a hundred thousand Indians, do you know how many stepped forward? Two, and they did so with the firm stipulation that they never be required to leave Fiji. In fact, if I remember, they weren't even willing to go to the other islands of this group. No, Mr. Hale, we wouldn't use any Indians. They didn't volunteer, and we didn't expect them to."

Hale thought: "In Hawaii, from the same number of Japanese we could have got fifteen thousand volunteers . . . . even to fight Japan. But here the Indians won't offer to fight an enemy with whom they have no ties of emotion whatever." And again he felt superior.

But when Sir Ratu Salaka finished his brandy, like the crusty English squire he was, he observed: "In Fiji, I assure you, we are not proud of the way in which we have failed to assimilate our Indian sugar workers. Some day we shall have to pay a terrible price for our neglect—civil disturbance, perhaps even bloodshed—and I as a Fijian leader am particularly aware of this tragedy. But when I visit Hawaii, and see how dismally the Polynesians have been treated there, how their lands have been stolen from them, how Japanese fill all the good governmental jobs, and how the total culture of a great people has been destroyed, I have got to say that even though our Indians are not so well situated as your Japanese, we Fijians are infinitely better off than your Hawaiians. We own our own land. I suppose that nine-tenths of the farm land you saw today belongs to Fijians. We also control the part of the government not held by Englishmen. Today our old patterns of life are stronger than they were fifty years ago. In all things we prosper, and I can think of no self-respecting Fijian who, aware of the paradise we enjoy here, would consent to trade places with a pitiful Hawaiian who had nothing left of his own. You Americans have treated the Hawaiians horribly."

A silence fell over the group, and finally Hoxworth said, "You may be surprised, Sir Ratu, and I suppose these officers will be too, but I am part-Hawaiian, and I do not feel as you suggest."

Sir Ratu was a tough old parliamentarian who rarely retreated, so he studied his guest carefully and said bluntly, "From appearances I should judge that the American half of you had prospered a good deal more than the Hawaiian half." Then he laughed gallantly and offered another round of brandy, saying to Hale, "We are talking of rather serious things, Mr. Hale, but I do think this question is sometimes worth considering: For whom do invaders hold an island in trust? Here the British have said, 'We hold these islands in trust for the Fijians,' and in doing so, they have done a great disservice, if not actual injustice, to the Indians whom they imported to work the sugar fields. But in Hawaii your missionaries apparently said, 'We hold these islands in trust for whomever we import to work our sugar fields,' and in saving them for the Chinese, they did a grave injustice to all Hawaiians. I suppose if our ancestors had been all-wise, they would have devised a midway solution that would have pleased everybody. But you gentlemen are heading east to Tahiti. Study the problem there. You'll find the French did not do one damn bit better than the English here or the Americans in Hawaii."

To this Hale added, "At least, in Hawaii, we will never have civil war. We will never have bloodshed."

Sir Ratu, a giant of a man in all ways, could not let this pass, so he added, "And in a few years you'll have no bloody Hawaiians, either." And the party broke up.

It was with badly mixed emotions that Hoxworth Hale left Fiji, but when his PBY deposited the inspecting team in American Samoa he was propelled into an even more perplexing speculation. He arrived at Pago Pago the day before the islanders were scheduled to celebrate their annexation to America, which had occurred in 1900, and he was told that since a Japanese submarine had recently bombarded Samoa, the islanders this year wished to demonstrate in special ceremonies their loyalty to America. But when Hale rose next morning he saw that the forbidding peaks which surrounded Pago Pago had trapped a convoy of rain clouds, which were in the process of drenching the islands, and he assumed that the ceremonies would be cancelled.

But he did not know Samoans! At dawn the native marines stood in the rain and fired salutes. At eight the Fita Fita band, in splendid uniforms, marched to the "Stars and Stripes Forever," and by ten all citizens who could walk lined the soggy parade ground while Samoan troops executed festive maneuvers. Then a huge, golden-brown chief with a face like a rising sun and enough flesh for two men, moved to the foot of the flag pole and made an impassioned speech in Samoan, proclaiming his devotion to America. Others followed, and as they spoke, Hoxworth Hale began to catch words and finally whole phrases which he understood, and with these Polynesian tones reverberating in his memory he experienced a profound mental confusion, so that when the Fita Fita band played the "Star Spangled Banner" and the cannon roared, he did not hear the wild cheering of the crowd.

He was comparing what he had seen in Samoa with what he remembered of the way Hawaii celebrated its Annexation Day, and he was struck by the difference. In Samoa guns boomed; in Hawaii decent people maintained silence. In Samoa people cheered; in Hawaii many wept. In Samoa not even storms could daunt the islanders who wanted to watch once more their beloved new flag rising to the symbolic tip of the island; but in Hawaii the new flag was not even raised, for Hawaiians remembered that when their islands were joined to America, the act had been accomplished by trickery and injustice. In the inevitable triumph of progress, a people had been raped, a lesser society had been crushed into oblivion. It was understandable that in Samoa, Polynesians cheered Annexation Day, but in Hawaii they did not.

To Hoxworth Hale these reflections were particularly gloomy, for it had been his great-grandfather Micah who had engineered the annexation of Hawaii, and Hoxworth was always reminded by his family that the event had coincided with his own birth, so that friends said, "Hawaii is the same age as Hoxworth," thus making a family joke of what many considered a crime. But he could also remember his great-grandmother, the Hawaiian lady Malama, as she told him before she died: "My husband made me attend the ceremonies when the Hawaiian flag was torn down, and do you know what the haoles did with that flag, Hoxy? They cut it into little pieces and passed them around the crowd."

"What for?" he had asked.

"So they could remember the day," the old lady had replied. "But why they would want to remember it I never understood."

There were many Hawaiians, even in 1942, who preferred not to speak with a Hale and who refused to eat at the same table with one. But others remembered not stern Micah who had stolen their islands but his mother Jerusha who had loved the Hawaiians, and those who remembered her would eat with the Hales while the others would not. Now, in Samoa where the rains fell, Hoxworth Hale, the descendant of both Micah and Jerusha, felt their two natures warring in his sympathies, and he wished that something could be done to rectify the injustices of Hawaiian annexation so that his Polynesians would take as much pride in their new flag as the Samoans did in theirs; but he knew that this was not possible, and the old sorrow that had attacked him at Yale when he contemplated the stolen Jarves paintings returned and he thought: "Who can assess the results of an action?" And he found no joy in Samoa.

But when he reached Tahiti, that Mecca of the South Seas, and his seaplane landed in the small bay that lies off Papeete, between the island of Moorea and the Diademe of Tahiti, making it surely the loveliest seaplane base in the world, his spirits were again excited, for these were the islands from which his people had come. This was the storied capital of the seas, and it was more beautiful than he had imagined. He felt proud to be of a blood that had started from Tahiti.

He was disappointed in the legendary girls of the island, however, for few of them had teeth. Australian canned foods and a departure from the traditional fish diet had conspired to rob girls in their teens of their teeth, but, as one of the air corps majors said, "If a man goes for beautiful gums, he can have a hell of a time in Tahiti."

What interested Hoxworth most, however, was not the girls but the Chinese. The French governor pointed out that the Americans would find a secure base in Tahiti, because the Chinese were well in hand. They were allowed to own no land, were forbidden to enter many kinds of business, were severely spied on by currency control, and were in general so held down that the Americans could rest assured there would be no problems. Hoxworth started to say, "In Hawaii our island wealth is multiplied several times each year by the Chinese, who do own land and who do go into business. The only currency control we have is that all our banks would like to get hold of what the Chinese keep in their own banks." But as a visitor he kept his mouth shut and looked.

It seemed to him that Tahiti would be approximately ten times better off in all respects if the Chinese were not only allowed but encouraged to prosper. "You hear so much about Tahiti," he said in some disappointment to the general leading his party, "but compare their roads to Hawaii's."

"Shocking," the general agreed.

"Or their health services, or their stores, or their churches."

"Pretty grubby in comparison with what you fellows have done in Hawaii," the general agreed.

"Where are the Tahiti schools? Where is the university? Or the airport or the clean hospitals? You know, General, the more I see of the rest of Polynesia, the more impressed I am with Hawaii."

The general was concerned with other matters, and on the third day he announced to his team: "It's incredible, but there simply isn't any place here in Tahiti to put an airstrip. But there seems to be an island farther north where we could probably flatten out one of the reefs and find ourselves with a pretty fine landing strip."

"What island?" Hale asked.

"It's called Bora Bora," the general said, and early next morning he flew the PBY up there, and Hoxworth Hale thus became the first part-Hawaiian ever to see his ancestral island of Bora Bora from the air. He saw it on a bright sunny day, when a running sea was breaking on the outer reef, while the lagoon was a placid blue surrounding the dark island from which rose the tall mountains and the solid, brutal block of basalt in the middle. He gasped at the sheer physical delight of this fabled island, its deep-cut bays, its thundering surf, its outrigger canoes converging near the landing area, and he thought: "No wonder we still remember poems about this island," and he began to chant fragments of a passage his great-great-grandfather Abner Hale had transcribed about Bora Bora:

> "Under the bright red stars hides the land,
> Cut by the perfect bays, marked by the mountains,
> Rimmed by the reef of flying spume,
> Bora Bora of the muffled paddles!
> Bora Bora of the great navigators."

The other occupants of the PBY were equally impressed by the island, but for other reasons. It possessed an enormous anchorage, and if necessary an entire invasion fleet could find refuge within the lagoon; but more important, the little islands along the outer reef were long, smooth and flat. "Throw a couple of bulldozers there for three days, and a plane could land right now," an engineer volunteered.

"We'll fly around once more," the general announced, "and see if we can agree on which of the outer islands looks best." So while the military people looked outward, to study the fringing reef, Hoxworth Hale looked inward, to see the spires of rock and the scintillating bays that cut far inland, so that every home on Bora Bora that he could spot lay near the sea. How marvelous that island was, how like a sacred home in a turbulent sea.

Now the PBY leveled off and started descending toward the lagoon, and Hoxworth thought how exciting it was to be within an airplane that had the capacity to land on water, for this must have been the characteristic of the first great beasts on earth who mastered flight. They must have risen from the sea and landed on it, as the PBY now prepared to do. When it was near the water, speeding along at more than a hundred miles an hour, Hoxworth realized for the first time how swiftly this bird was flying, and as it reached down with its underbelly step to find the waves, he caught himself straining with his buttocks, adjusting them to insure level flight, and then seeking to let them down into the waves, and he flew his bottom so well that soon the plane was rushing along the tiptop particles of the sea, half bird, half fish, and then it lost its flight and subsided into the primordial element, a plane that had conquered the Pacific and come at last to rest upon it.

"Halloo, Joe!" a native cried at the door, and in a moment the plane was surrounded by Bora Borans in their swift, small canoes.

Among the first to go ashore was Hale, because he knew a few words of Polynesian and many of French, and as he sat precariously on the thwarts of one of the canoes, and felt himself speeding across the limpid waters of the lagoon toward a sprawling, coconut-fringed village whose roofs were made of grass, he thought: "Hawaii has nothing to compare with this."

In a way he was right, for after the general and his staff had been fed with good sweet fish from the lagoon and red wine from Paris, the headman of the village approached with some embarrassment and said in French, which Hale had to interpret: "General, we people of Bora Bora know that you have come here to save us. God himself knows the French would do nothing to rescue us, because they hate Bora Borans, and do you know why? Because in all history we have never been conquered, not even by the French, and officially we are a voluntary part of their empire. They have never forgiven us for not surrendering peacefully like the others, but we say to hell with the French."

"Shut him up!" the general commanded. "The French have been damned good to us, Hale, and I want to hear no more of this sedition."

But the headman was already past his preamble and into more serious business: "So we Bora Borans want to help you in every way we can. You say you want to build an airstrip. Good! We'll help. You say you'll need water and food. Good! We'll help there too. But there is one matter you seem not to have thought about, and on this we will help too.

"While your flying boat sleeps in the lagoon, you will have to have some place to sleep on shore. We will put aside seven houses for you."

"Tell him we need only two," the general interrupted. "We don't want to disrupt native life."

The proud headman, dressed in a brown lava-lava and flowered wreath about his temples, did not allow the interruption to divert him: "The biggest house will be for the general, and the rest are about the same size. Now, because it is not comfortable for a man to sleep alone in such a house, we have asked seven of our young girls if they will take care of everything."

It was here that Hoxworth Hale, son of missionaries, began to blush, and when the maidens were brought forth, clean, shapely, dark-haired, barefoot girls in sarongs and flowers, he began to protest, but when the headman actually started apportioning the girls, the tallest and prettiest to the general, and a shy, slim creature of fifteen to him, Hale quite broke up and the translation stopped.

"What the hell is this?" the general asked, but then the tall, beautiful girl of seventeen who had been assigned to him, took him gently by the hand and started leading him toward his appointed house.

"My God!" the irreverent major cried. "In Bora Bora they got teeth!" And one of the girls must have known some English, for she laughed happily, and because these islanders were more primitive and ate more fish, their teeth were strong and white, and the major accepted his girl's hand and without even so much as looking at the general, disappeared.

"We can't allow this!" the general protested. "Tell them so."

But when Hale explained this decision the headman said, "We are not afraid of white babies. The island likes them." And after a while only Hoxworth Hale stood in the meeting shed, looking at his long-tressed, fifteen-year-old Polynesian guide. She was a year older than his own daughter, not quite so tall, but equally beautiful, and he was a totally confused man, and then she took his hand and said in French, "Monsieur le Colonel, your house is waiting. We had better go."

She led him along dark-graveled paths beneath breadfruit trees whose wide leaves hid the hot sun. They went along a row of coconut palms, bending toward the lagoon as they had done a thousand years before, and in time she came to a small house withdrawn from the others, and here she stopped at the trivial lintel that kept out the wandering pigs and chickens, and said, "This house is mine." She waited until he had entered, and then she joined him and untied a length of sennit that held up the woven door, and when it fell they were alone.

He stood rigid in acute embarrassment, holding onto a bundle of papers, as if he were a schoolboy, and these she took from him and then pushed him backwards slowly, until he sat on a bed with a wooden frame and a woven rope mattress, and he was as frightened as he had ever been in his life. But when she had thrown the papers into a corner she said, "My name is Tehani. And this is the house my father built me when I became fifteen. I plaited the roof of pandanus, but he built the rest."

Hoxworth Hale, then forty-four, was ashamed to be with a girl fifteen, but once when she passed where he was sitting on the bed, her long black hair moved past his face, and he smelled the fragrance of that sweetest of all flowers, the taire Tahiti, and he had never encountered that odor before, and automatically he reached up and caught at her hand, but she was moving rather swiftly, and he missed, but he did catch her right leg above the knee, and he felt her whole body stop at this command, and start to move willingly toward him. He kept hold of her leg and pulled her onto the bed, and she fell back happily and smiled up at him, with the taire flowers about her temples, and he took away the sarong and when she was naked she whispered, "I asked my father for you, for you were quieter than the others."

When the inspecting team convened late that afternoon around an improvised table under the breadfruit trees, by common but unspoken agreement, no one mentioned what had happened, and they proceeded to discuss where the airstrip should be, just as if nothing unusual had occurred, but as night fell and girls appeared with an evening meal, each officer instinctively brought his girl to the table beside him, and there was unprecedented tenderness in the way the older men saw to it that their young companions got a fair division of the food.

They had not finished eating when a group of young men with long hair in their eyes and pareus about their hips, appeared with guitars and drums, and soon the Bora Bora night was filled with echoes. The audience waited until the general's tall, slim beauty leaped into the dancing ring and executed the wild, passionate dance of that island. This was a signal which permitted the other girls to do the same, and soon one had the cocky major in the ring with her, attempting a version of the dance, and he was followed by a colonel and then by the general himself. It became a wild, frenzied, delightful dance under the stars, and all the older people who were watching applauded.

Hoxworth Hale's girl, Tehani, did not ask him to dance, knowing from what had transpired in the grass house that he was a shy man, so finally an old woman with no teeth muscled her way through the crowd, stood before Hale and did a few lascivious steps. To the surprise of everyone, Hale leaped to his feet and swung into the Hawaiian hula, at which, like most of his Honolulu contemporaries, he was skilled. The audience stopped making noise and the military visitors sat down, tired as they were from their own exertions, while Hale and the old woman performed an admirable dance. Finally, when the astonishment was becoming vocal, the major shouted, "Hale for President!" and Hoxworth broke into a much swifter version while the old woman executed a downright lewd movement, to the howls of the crowd.

At this Tehani stepped forward, firmly pushed the old beldame away and took her place, and for a few minutes Hale and the delicately formed young girl with streams of flowers in her hair, brought an ancient grace to the sands of Bora Bora. He felt himself caught up in passions he had thought long dead, while the girl smiled softly to herself and, knowing that she was the envy of all the others for her man could dance, thought: "I got the best one of the group, and I was smart enough to ask for him."

The inspecting team lingered at Bora Bora for nine days, and every night during that time the entire community held an all-night celebration. From the nearby island of Raiatea, which in the old days had been known as Havaiki, the holy island of the Polynesians, a young French government official came over with a barrel of red wine which the general insisted on buying, although the gracious young man had intended it as a gift, and at dusk each day this barrel was cocked, and anyone who wished a drink could have one. The orchestra never stopped playing. In exhaustion men would drop their drums and others would pick them up. The seven girls who were tending the guests of honor rarely left them, so that in the end even at formal meetings of the inspection staff, the Polynesian girls would be there, not understanding a word that was being spoken, but each one proud whenever her man spoke forcefully on some point or other.

During the nine days no mention was made of sex, except once when the general remarked thoughtfully, "I am amazed at what a man of forty-nine can do." But he was taking a two-hour nap morning, afternoon, and evening.

Hoxworth preferred not even to think of Tehani as a real person. She was something that happened, a dream whose confines would never be appropriately known. Having experienced a normal Punahou and Yale education, he had been roughly aware of what sex was, but never accurately, and his marriage had been a family affair, which for a while had been formally proper, like going on an endless picnic with one's fully clothed sister, but soon even that had ended, and when at odd moments in the last few years he had thought about sex he had supposed that for him, at least, it had ended in his mid-thirties. Tehani Vahine, for that was her whole name, Miss Tehani of Bora Bora, had quite other intentions. She had been taught that men of Colonel Hale's age were those who enjoyed sex most, and who were often most proficient in it; and whereas she had been wrong in both guesses about Hale, for he was both afraid and unskilled, she had never known a man who could learn so fast.

They were days of listless, idle joy. He loved her best when she wore her sarong draped carelessly about her hips, her breasts bare and her long hair sparkling with flowers. He would lie endlessly upon the rope bed and watch her movements, as if he had never seen a girl before, and sometimes with a cry of joy he would leap up, catch her in his arms and carry her to the bed in a blizzard of kisses. Once he asked her, "Is it always like this in Bora Bora?" and she replied, "Usually we don't have so much good wine." And he thought: "In other parts of the world there is a war, and in Hawaii nervous men are arguing with each other, and in New York girls are calculating, 'Should I let him tonight?' But in Bora Bora there's Tehani." Like the general, he was amazed at what a man of forty-four could do . . . if he had the right encouragement.

On the next-to-the-last day Tehani whispered, "Tell the others you won't be there tomorrow," and at dawn she sprinkled water on his face and cried, "You must get up and see the fish!"

She led him sleepily to a spot away from her house where she had a fresh tuna staked out and cleaned. "This is going to be the best dish you ever ate in your life," she assured him, "because it will be Bora Bora poisson cru. Watch me how I do it, so that when you are far away and want to remember me, you can make some and taste me in it."

She cut the fresh tuna into small fillets of about two inches in length and a quarter inch thick. These she placed in a large calabash, which she carried to the lagoon where no people came, and from the cold waters she dipped a few coconut shells full of fresh salt water which she tossed on the fillets. Then she took a club and knocked down three limes, which she cut in half and squeezed into the calabash. Carefully seeking a place where the sun shone brightest, she put the fish there to steam through the long, hot morning, cooking itself in the lime juice and sea water.

"Now comes the part where you must help me!" she cried merrily as she pointed to a sloping palm that bent over the water, holding in its crest a bundle of ripe nuts. "I shall climb up there, but you must catch the nuts for me," and before he could stop her, she had tied her sarong about her hips, had caught hold of the tree with her hands and feet, and had bent-walked right up the tree to where the nuts clustered. Holding on with her left hand, she used her right to twist free a choice nut. Then, with a wide side-arm movement, she tossed it inland, where Hoxworth caught it. "Hooray!" she cried in glee and pitched another.

When she returned to earth she found a stout stick, jammed it in the earth, and showed her partner how to husk a coconut, and when he had done so, she knocked the two nuts together until they cracked open and their juices ran into a second calabash. Then she jammed into the ground a second stick, this time at an angle, and against its blunt edge she began scraping the coconut slowly and rhythmically, until white meat, dripping with nectar, began shredding down onto taro leaves placed on the ground. As her golden shoulders swayed back and forth in the sunlight, she sang:

> "Grating the coconut for my beloved,
> Shredding the sweet meat for him,
> Salting the fish,

Under the swaying breadfruit tree,
Under the rainless sky,
I shred the sweet meat for my beloved."

When she finished grating she ignored Hoxworth, as if he were not there, and carefully gathered the shredded coconut, placing half in the calabash to join the captured coconut water, half in a tangle of brown fiber from the coconut husks, which she now caught in her slim hands and squeezed over a third calabash. As she twisted the coarse fibers, a fine rich liquor was forced out, and this was the sweet coconut milk that would complete the dish she was preparing.

Again and again Tehani squeezed the grated coconut, softly chanting her song, though now she spoke of twisting the meat for her beloved instead of grating it, and as the palms along the shore dipped toward the lagoon, Hoxworth Hale had a strikingly clear intuition: "From now on whenever I think of a woman, in the abstract . . . of womanliness, that is . . . I'll see this brown-skinned Bora Bora girl, her sarong loosely about her hips, working coconut and humming softly in the shadowy sunlight. Has she been here, under these breadfruit trees, all these last empty years?" And he had a second intuition: that during the forthcoming even emptier years, she would still be there, a haunting vision of the other half of life, the womanliness, the caretaking symbol, the majestic, lovely, receptive other half.

Overcome by his vision of past and future, he desired to revel in the accidental now, and reached out from the shaded area where she had placed him, trying to catch her leg again, but she deftly evaded him and went to a pit where yams and taro had been baking, and she now proceeded to break the latter into small purplish pieces, rich in starch, while the yams she held in her hands for a moment, showing them to her lover. "These are what our sailors call the Little Eyes of Heaven," she laughed, pointing to the eyes of the yam, which clustered like the constellation whose rising in the east heralds the Polynesian New Year.

Finally, Tehani chopped the onions and then mixed all the vegetables in with the thick, rich coconut milk, and after she had washed her hands in the lagoon, she came back and sat cross-legged before Hale, her sarong pulled far up to expose soft brown thighs, and her breasts free in the sunlight. "It's a game we play," she explained, and with him in the shadows and she in the sunlight, she started slapping his shoulders, and as she hummed her coconut song, she indicated that he was to slap hers, and in this way she passed from his shoulders to his forearms, to his flanks, to his hips and finally to his thighs, and as the game grew more intense the slaps grew gentler and her song slower, until with a culminating gesture that started out to be a slap but which ended as an embrace, Hale caught her sarong and started pulling it away, but she cried softly in her own language, "Not in the sunlight, Hale-tane," and he understood, and swept her up in his arms and carried her into the grass house, where the game reached its intended conclusion.

Toward noon she asked him in French, "Do you like the way we make our poisson cru in Bora Bora?" And she brought in the fish, well saturated in sun and lime juice, and Hale saw that the tuna was no longer red but an inviting gray-white. Into it she mixed the prepared coconut milk with its burden of taro and onions and yams. Next she tossed in a few shellfish for flavor, and over the whole she sprinkled the freshly grated, juicy coconut. With her bare right hand she stirred the ingredients and finally offered her guest three fingers full of Bora Bora raw fish.

"This is how we feed our men on this island," she teased. "Can your girls do as well?" When Hale laughed, she pushed the dripping fish into his mouth and chuckled when the white milk ran down his chin and across his naked chest. "You are so sloppy!" she chided. "But you are such an adorable man, Hale-tane. You can laugh. You are tender. You dance like an angel. And you are strong in bed. You are a man any girl could love. Tell me," she begged, "do your girls at home love you?"

"Yes," he said truthfully, "they do."

"Do they sometimes play games like the slapping game with you, and then chase you around the house just for the fun of being with you?"

"No," he replied.

"I am sorry, Hale-tane," she said. "The years go by very fast and soon . . ." She pointed to an old woman searching for shellfish along the shore: "Then we play no more games." It was with the sadness of the world turning in space, or of the universe drifting madly through the darkness, that she said these words in island French: "Et bientôt c'est tout fini et nous ne jouons plus."

"Is that why your father builds you a house of your own when you're fifteen?" Hale asked. "So you can learn the proper games?"

"Yes," she explained. "No sensible man would want to marry me unless he knew that I understood how to make love properly. Men are happiest when a girl has proved she can have a baby, and do you know what I hope, Hale-tane? I hope that when you fly away tomorrow you leave in here a baby for me." She patted her flat brown stomach which looked as if it could never contain a child. "That is my wish."

And so they lazed the day away, and ate poisson cru, the best dish that any island ever invented, and played the silly games of love that Bora Borans had been teaching their daughters for nearly two thousand years, and in due time shadows crept across the lagoon, and night fell, and after the drums had been beating at the village dancing ground for some hours, Tehani wrapped herself in a sarong and said, "Come, Hale-tane, I should like the people of Bora Bora to see me dancing with you one more time. Then, if I do have your baby, they will remember that among all the Americans, you were the best dancer."

In the morning, as the inspection team piled into the PBY for takeoff and the return to Hawaii, no one spoke of the long-haired girls of Bora Bora, or of their flashing teeth, or of the games they knew how to play, for if anyone had spoken, all would have wanted to remain on the island for another day, another week; but when the plane had torn its bulk free from the waters of the lagoon and stood perched on what the aviators called "the step," the small after-portion on which the huge boat rode on the waves until it finally soared into the air, Hale again felt the aesthetic moment when men are half of the ocean and half of the air, and in this attitude the speeding PBY whipped across the lagoon until it finally soared aloft, and all were wholly of the sky.

It was then, as Bora Bora disappeared in the brilliance of morning sunlight, that the major observed bitterly, "To think! We're going to draft decent young American boys, tear them from their mothers' arms, slam them into uniform and send them down to Bora Bora. God, it's inhuman." And for the rest of the war, and for many years thereafter, there would be a confraternity of men who met casually in bars, or at cocktail parties, or at business luncheons, and one would say to the other, "They write mostly crap about the Pacific, but there's one island . . ."

"Are you speaking of Bora Bora?" the other would interrupt.

"Yes. Did you serve there?"

"Yep." Usually, nothing more was said, because if a man had served his hitch on Bora Bora nothing more was required to be said, but whenever Hoxworth Hale met such men he invariably went one step further: "Did you ever know a slim, long-haired girl of fifteen or sixteen? Lived by the mountain. Named Tehani."

Once he met a lieutenant-commander from a destroyer-escort who had known Tehani, and the destroyer man said, "Wonderful girl. Danced like an angel. She was the first one on the island to have an American baby."

"Was it a boy?" Hale asked.

"Yes, but she gave it to a family on Maupiti. Girls there had no chance to produce American babies, and the island wanted one."

And suddenly, in the smoke-filled bar, Hoxworth Hale saw a young girl dancing beside a lagoon, and he saw on the blue waters an ancient double-hulled canoe and he thought: "I am forever a part of Bora Bora, and my son lives on in the islands." Then the memory vanished and he heard a girl's voice lamenting: "The years go by very fast, and soon we play no more games."

In time, Hale's visit to the South Seas produced other fruit than his memory of Tehani Vahine, for in addition to her lilting song of the coconut-grater, he constantly recalled his conversation with Sir Ratu Salaka in Fiji, and he began to compare all aspects of Hawaii with similar conditions in Fiji and Tahiti, and he came to this unshakable conclusion: "In every respect but one we Americans have done a better job in Hawaii than the English have in Fiji or the French in Tahiti. Health, education, building and the creation of new wealth . . . we are really far ahead. And in the way we've integrated our Orientals into the very heart of our society, we're so far ahead that no comparisons are even permissible. But in the way we have allowed our Hawaiians to lose their land, their language, and their culture, we have been terribly remiss. We could have accomplished all our good and at the same time protected the Hawaiians." But whenever he reached this conclusion he would think of Joe Tom Char, who now presided as president of the senate, and he was half-Hawaiian, half-Chinese; or of the year's beauty queen, Helen Fukuda, half-Hawaiian, half-Japanese; or of the innumerable Kees who seemed to be running Pearl Harbor, many of whom were half-Hawaiian, half-Chinese. "Perhaps we're building something in Hawaii that will be infinitely better than anything Fiji or Tahiti ever produces." At any rate, Hale returned from his trip no longer apologetic for what the missionaries had accomplished.

WHEN in the early days of the war Japanese boys in Hawaii were removed from combat units and expelled from R.O.T.C., the islands supposed that this was the end of the matter. "No Jap can be trusted, so we kicked them all out," a general explained.

But to everyone's surprise, the Japanese boys stubbornly refused to accept this verdict. Humbly, quietly, but with an almost terrifying moral force, these boys began to press for their full rights as American citizens. "We demand the inalienable privilege of dying for the nation we love," they argued, and if anyone had asked the Sakagawa boys why they said this, they would have replied,"We were treated decently at McKinley and at Punahou. We were taught what democracy means, and we insist upon our right to defend it."

Committees of Japanese boys began hammering officials with petitions. One drawn up by Goro Sakagawa read: "We are loyal American citizens and humbly request the right to serve our nation in its time of crisis. If you think you cannot trust us to fight against Japan, at least send us to Europe where this problem does not arise." The committees went to see generals and admirals, governors and judges: "We will do any national work you assign us. We will ask for no wages. We must be allowed to prove that we are Americans."

For eleven painful weeks the Japanese boys got nowhere, and then, because the three younger Sakagawas were Punahou boys, they were able to meet one of the most extraordinary men Hawaii was to produce in the twentieth century. His name was Mark Whipple, born in 1900, the son of the medical doctor who had ordered Chinatown burned, great-great-grandson of John Whipple who had helped Christianize Hawaii. This

Mark Whipple was a West Point man and a colonel in the United States army. Most of his duty had been spent outside Hawaii, but recently he had been assigned to help the high command deal with the Japanese question; and in Washington it had been assumed that when he got to Hawaii he would quickly order the evacuation of all Japanese—none of whom could be trusted—to some concentration camp either in Nevada or on the island of Molokai: "This will include, of course, all the little yellow bastards who have infiltrated themselves into such units as the 298th Infantry and the local R.O.T.C. outfits."

Colonel Mark Whipple disappointed just about everybody, for when he reached Hawaii bearing very powerful directives specifically handed him by President Roosevelt, who knew his family, he gave no quick orders, paraded no insolence, but went swiftly to work. The first man he called in for a conference was the Honolulu head of the F.B.I., who reported, as Whipple had anticipated: "So far as we have presently ascertained, there was not a single case of espionage by any Japanese other than the registered and duly appointed agents of the Japanese consulate, all of whom were citizens of Japan."

"Then the Secretary of Navy's hasty report that Pearl Harbor was betrayed by local Japanese was all hogwash?" Whipple asked.

"Yes. But he can be forgiven. Excited admirals fed him the line. Now they know better."

"Any disloyalty now?" Whipple asked.

"Quite the contrary. The young Japanese seem to be burning to get into uniform. Had two of them in here the other day. Fine boys. Got kicked out of R.O.T.C. and now want us to use them as labor battalions, anything. They offer to serve with no pay."

"You got their names?"

"Right here."

Colonel Whipple hesitated before taking the paper. "I promise you that I will not write down what you reply to my next question. But I need guidance. Will you state categorically that the local Japanese have not engaged in sabotage of any kind?"

"I will state categorically that there has not been a single case of sabotage," the F.B.I. man said.

Whipple drummed his fingers. "I'd like to see those names. Can you get the boys in here?"

As a result of that meeting the Varsity Victory Volunteers were formed, with Tadao and Minoru Sakagawa as first members. The V.V.V. were all Japanese, all boys of the highest intelligence and patriotism. They foresaw that the entire future of their people in America depended upon what they did in this war against Japan, and they decided that if they were prevented by hysteria from bearing arms, they would bear shovels. They would dig out latrines, and pick up after white soldiers, and build bridges. There would be no work too menial for them, and they would do it all for $90 a month while their haole and Chinese schoolmates earned ten times that much working for the government in civilian jobs at Pearl Harbor. As Tadao told Colonel Whipple, "We will do anything to prove that we are Americans."

Colonel Whipple, when he recommended that the V.V.V. be established, drew a good deal of criticism from his fellow officers, but he pointed out that he carried a special command from Roosevelt to see exactly what could be done with the Japanese, and he was going to explore all possibilities; but when he next proposed that no Japanese be evacuated to prison camps, neither on Molokai nor anywhere else, the roof fell in.

"Do you mean to say . . ." a South Carolina admiral bellowed.

"I mean to say, sir, that these people are loyal Americans and no purpose would be served by placing them in prison camps."

"Why, goddamn it, California has shown us the way to handle these traitors."

"What California has done is its own affair. Here in Hawaii we won't do it that way."

"By God, Whipple! You're subversive!"

But Mark Whipple was not deviated one degree from the true course he had set himself. When a convocation of his own family warned him, "There's a good deal of apprehension about you, Mark. Military people say you're imperiling your whole career," he replied, "In this matter, I have a special burden to bear which only I can bear, and I would prefer to hear no more gossip of any kind. Because what I am about to propose next is going to tear this entire military community apart. Maybe you'd better fortify your tired nerves."

What he proposed was this: "I think we had better form, right now —this week—a special unit of the United States army composed solely of Japanese boys from Hawaii. Use them in Europe. Throw them against the Germans, and when they perform as I know they will, they'll not only re-establish their credentials here but in America. They will give all free men a propaganda victory over Naziism that will reverberate around the world. With their courage, they will prove Hitler wrong on every single count of his philosophy."

A gasp went up, which was duly reported by cable to Washington, where it was augmented: "Japanese troops in the American army? And a special unit at that? Ridiculous."

But one man did not think it ridiculous, the President of the United States, and when he had studied Colonel Whipple's report he issued a statement which read: "Patriotism is not a matter of the skin's color. It is a matter of the heart."

In Hawaii there was still vigorous opposition to the formation of such a unit, but when the President's order reached Honolulu in mid-May of 1942 grudging compliance was obligatory, and one gruff general asked, "Who'd want to march into battle with a regiment of Japs behind him?"

"I would," Colonel Whipple replied.

"You mean . . . you're volunteering for the job?"

"I am, sir."

"You've got it, and I hope you don't get shot in the back."

Colonel Whipple saluted and took prompt steps to assemble into one unit all the Japanese boys already in the army—men like Goro Sakagawa of the 298th Infantry—and to pave the way for later acceptance of others like those now in the V.V.V. or those like young Shigeo who were about ready for the draft. The Whipple family was distressed that their most brilliant son was imperiling his career by such imprudent action, but as he had told them earlier, in this matter he bore a special burden.

It arose from the fact that when he was a boy in Honolulu no Chinese would speak to him, for he was the son of the man who had burned Chinatown at the instigation of the haole merchants. He could never bring himself to believe that his gentle, courageous father, Dr. Whipple, had done such a thing, but the Chinese were certain that he had. To them the name of Whipple was ugly, and they were not reluctant to demonstrate this fact to young Mark. Finally, when his own haole playmates began to tease him, he accosted his father and had asked him point-blank: "Dad, did you burn Chinatown?"

"Well, in a manner of speaking, I did."

"In order to put the Chinese merchants out of business?"

His father had stopped and bowed his head. "So now you've heard that? What did they say?"

"They say there was a little sickness, and the haole storekeepers talked you into burning Chinatown and putting all the Chinese out of business."

"Now exactly who said this, son?"

"The haoles. The Chinese didn't say it because they won't even speak to me. But I know they think it."

Dr. Hewlett Whipple was then a man of forty, and about as successful a medical practitioner as one could hope to be in Honolulu, but the weight of his son's charge was very heavy indeed upon his soul. He led his twelve-year-old son to a grassy spot under a tree on the lawn of his Punchbowl home and said, "Now you ask me all the questions that worry you, Mark. And never forget what I reply."

"Did you burn Chinatown?"

"Yes."

"And did the Chinese lose all their stores?"

"Yes."

Mark had no further questions, so he shrugged his shoulders. His father laughed and said, "You aren't going to stop there, are you?"

"You've told me what I wanted to know," the boy replied.

"But aren't you concerned about the real truth? What really happened?"

"Well, like the boys said, you admitted burning the place."

"Mark, this is what truth is. Going behind what you hear first. Asking a hundred questions until you can make up your own mind on the basis of real evidence. Now let me ask the questions that you should have. All right?"

"Okay."

"Dr. Whipple, why did you burn Chinatown? Because a dreadful plague threatened the city.

"Did burning Chinatown help save the city? It saved ten thousand lives.

"Did you intend to burn the Chinese stores? No, the fire got out of hand. It ran away from us.

"Did you do anything to help the Chinese? I ran into the middle of the fire myself and helped them to safety.

"Were you sorry that the fire got out of hand? When I got home and looked back upon the destruction I sat down and wept.

"Would you burn it again under the same circumstances? I would."

A silence fell over the Whipples and they looked down at their city. Young Mark, in those moments, caught a glimmer of what truth was, but what his father said next exploded truth from a shimmering substance playing upon the edges of the mind into a radiant reality, for he said, "There are two other questions which have to be asked, and these require longer answers. Are you ready?"

"Yes."

"Dr. Whipple, tell me honestly, were there not some haoles who were glad to see Chinatown burned? Of course there were. And some Chinese, too. Any good action in the world will be used by some to their own economic advantage. Any misfortune will be used the same way. Therefore, you would expect some to profit from the burning and to be glad that it happened. When the fire was over, these same men rebuilt Chinatown exactly as it was before, so as to keep on making a little money from the hovels. So if your Chinese friends say there were some who were glad to see the Chinese stores destroyed, they are correct. But I was not one of them.

"Dr. Whipple, can you not, even so, understand why the Chinese hate you? Of course I understand. They believe falsehood, and it's always easier to accept a lie than to find out the truth. When I move through Honolulu, this is one of the burdens I am forced to bear. The Chinese hate me. But if they knew the truth, they would not."

As a colonel in the United States army, Mark Whipple often remembered that discussion with his father, and sometimes when he was required to make his men do brutal or unpleasant work, he knew that in ignorance they would hate him, whereas if they knew the truth they would not. So when he returned to Hawaii to deal with the Japanese problem, he was motivated by an acute desire that he, Mark Whipple, should, by dealing with the Japanese honestly, erase the stigma that his father Hewlett Whipple had suffered at the hands of the Chinese. In a sense, therefore, he did not volunteer to lead the Japanese troops; he was impelled by the entire history of his family to do so; for the Whipples of Hawaii were people who tried always to keep history straight.

His all-Japanese outfit, commanded by a cadre of haole officers, was known as the 222nd Combat Team, and it became a running joke in the unit for older men to ask newcomers, "What's your outfit, son?" And when the private replied, "The Two-Two-Two," the old-timers would shout, "Listen! He's playing train!" Later they would bellow, "What's your unit?" and when the private replied, "The Two-Two-Two," they would growl, "Speak up, son! Don't stutter."

The arm patch of the Two-Two-Two consisted of a blue sky against which rose a brown Diamond Head, at whose feet rested one palm tree and three white lines of rolling surf. Below in block letters stood the pidgin motto: "Mo Bettah." It was a handsome patch, and spoke of Hawaii, but the outfit did not appreciate how much Mo Bettah home was than some other places until they set up their basic training camp at Camp Bulwer in the boondocks of Mississippi.

On the first day in town Goro Sakagawa had to go to the toilet, and through ignorance stumbled into the "White" toilet. "Get out of here, you goddamned yellow-belly!" a native growled, and Goro backed out. Others had similar experiences, so that trouble threatened, but that night Colonel Mark Whipple showed the kind of man he was. Assembling the entire unit he shouted, "You men have only one job. Allow nothing whatever, neither death nor humiliation nor fear nor hunger, to deviate you from that job. You are here to prove to America that you are loyal citizens. You can do this only by becoming the finest soldiers in the American army and the most efficient fighters.

"If the people of Mississippi want to abuse you, they are free to do so. And you will keep your big mouths shut and take it. Because if any man in this outfit causes even one shred of trouble, I will personally ride him right to the gates of hell. Are there any questions?"

"Am I supposed to take it if some local yokel calls me a slant-eyed yellow-belly?"

"Yes!" Whipple stormed. "By God yes! Because if you're so sensitive that you are willing to imperil the future of all the Japanese in America for such a cause, then by God, Hashimoto, you are a slant-eyed yellow-belly. You're a creep. You're a damned Jap. You're what everybody accuses you of being, and in my eyes you're no man."

"Then we take it?" Goro asked in deep, stomach-churning fury. "Whatever they want to call us?"

"You take it," Whipple snarled. "Can't you add, you damned, stubborn buddha-heads?" As he said this he laughed, and the tension was broken. "For the insults that one accidental man throws at you, are you willing to put into jeopardy the future of three hundred thousand Japanese? Don't be idiots. For the love of Christ, don't be idiots."

From the rear ranks a sergeant grumbled, "I guess we can take it."

Then Colonel Whipple said, "Keep this vision in mind, men. As a unit you're going to strike the German army some day. And when you do, you're going to win. Of that there can be no doubt, for I have never led finer men. And when you win, you will triumph over bigotry at home, over Hitlerism abroad, over any insult you have ever borne. Your mothers and fathers and your children after you will lead better lives because of what you do. Aren't these stakes worth fighting for?"

Colonel Whipple laid down the most rigid rules and enforced them brutally: "Not a word of Japanese will be spoken in this outfit. You're Americans. Under no circumstances are you to ask a white girl for a date. It makes local people mad. You are absolutely forbidden to date a colored girl. That makes them even madder. And they have four long trains that haul beer into this state every week. You can't possibly drink it all."

Remorselessly Colonel Whipple drove his men according to West Point traditions of military behavior and his own family traditions of civil decency. In all America no unit in training suffered more disciplinary action than the Two-Two-Two, for their colonel held them responsible both on the post and off, and at the slightest infraction, he punished them. There was only one flare-up. After a great deal of heart-probing consultation the good people of Mississippi decided that so far as public toilets and buses were concerned, the Japanese soldiers were to be considered white men and were thus obligated to use white facilities; but where socializing with the community was concerned, it was better if they considered themselves halfway between the white and the Negro and off-limits to each.

This was too much, and Goro went to see Colonel Whipple. "I appreciate what you said, Colonel, and we've been abiding by your rules. But this directive on toilets is just too much. I can urinate like a white man but I've got to socialize like a Negro. The basic thing we're fighting for is human decency. Our men don't want the kind of concessions Mississippi is willing to make. We want to be treated like Negroes."

Colonel Whipple did not rant. He said quietly, "I agree with you, Sakagawa. Decency is one unbroken fabric without beginning or end. No man can logically fight for Japanese rights and at the same time ignore Negro rights. Logically he can't do it, but sometimes he's got to. And right now is one of those times."

"You mean we're to accept what Mississippi says, even though we know that given a chance they'd treat us worse than they do the Negroes?"

"That's the tactical situation you find yourself in."

"It's so illogical our men may not be able to take it."

Again Colonel Whipple failed to bellow. Instead he picked up an order and waved it at Goro, saying, "And the reason you'll take it is this paper. The army has agreed to accept all Japanese boys who want to volunteer. Your two brothers in the V.V.V. will be transferred to the outfit tonight. Now if trouble were to start in Mississippi, all that I've managed to acquire for you fellows would be lost. So, Goro, you urinate where the haoles tell you to."

In accordance with the new directive, the army announced that it would beef up the Two-Two-Two by adding 1,500 volunteers from Hawaii and 1,500 from the mainland, but the plan didn't work because in Honolulu 11,800 rushed forward to serve, stampeding the registration booths. Seven out of eight had to be turned down, including Shigeo Sakagawa, who wept. But on the mainland only 500 volunteered, leaving a thousand empty spaces. Quickly the army returned to Hawaii and filled the gaps left by the poor response of the mainland Japanese, and in this second draft, young Shig was accepted.

When President Roosevelt compared the contrasting reactions of the two groups, he ordered Colonel Whipple to submit an explanation of what had happened, and Whipple wrote: "Far from being a cause for concern, the differential should encourage us in our devotion to the perpetual effectiveness of democracy. If the result had been any different, I should have been worried. That the Hawaii Japanese behaved well and that the mainland boys did not is to me, and I think to America, reassuring.

"In Hawaii, Japanese were free to own land. In California they were not. In Hawaii they could become schoolteachers and government employees. In California they could not. In Hawaii they were accepted into our best schools, but not in California. In Hawaii they were built into our society and became a part of us, but in California they were rejected.

"More important, when war came the Japanese on the mainland were herded into concentration camps and their belongings were ruthlessly stripped from them at five cents on the dollar. In Hawaii there was some talk of this, but it was never permitted to go very far. Right after Pearl Harbor a good many Japanese in Hawaii were rounded up for concentration camps, but my aunt tells me that she personally, along with other Caucasian leaders of the community, went to the jail and effected the release of those she knew to be loyal. In short, the Japanese in Hawaii had every reason to fight for America; those on the mainland had none; and the basic difference lay not in the Japanese but in the way they were treated by their fellow citizens.

"So is it not logical that if you tell a group of Hawaiian Japanese who have not been thrown into camps or robbed of their belongings, 'You can volunteer to help us fight oppression,' that 11,800 should leap forward? And is it not logical that if you go through concentration camps and tell the brothers of these same men, 'We have abused you, imprisoned you, humiliated you, and stolen your belongings, but now we want you to volunteer to fight for us,' is it not logical that they should reply, 'Go to hell'? I am astonished that so many of the mainland Japanese volunteered. They must be very brave men, and I shall welcome them in my unit."

When President Roosevelt read the report he asked his aide, "Who is this Mark Whipple again?"

"You knew his father, Dr. Hewlett Whipple."

"The boy sounds intelligent. Is he the one who's leading the Japanese?"

"Yes. They're on their way to Italy now."

"We should expect some good news from that outfit," the President said.

One night in September, 1943, Nyuk Tsin asked her grandson Hong Kong, "Are we overextended?"

"Yes."

"If war ended tomorrow, would we be able to hold onto our properties?"

"No."

"What do you think we should do?" the old lady asked.

"I seem to have acquired your courage," Hong Kong replied. "I say, 'Hold onto our lands.' We'll pay off as much debt as we can, and when the war ends we'll tighten our belts and live on rice until the boom starts."

"How many bad years must we look forward to?" the old matriarch asked.

"Two very difficult years. Two reasonably dangerous. If we can get through them, the hui will be prosperous."

"I'm worried," the old woman confessed, "but I agree with you that we must fight to a finish. However, I've been thinking that we might start to sell off a few of the houses, to relieve the pressure."

"The pressure is only on you and me," Hong Kong pointed out. "The others don't know about it. If you're not afraid, I'm not."

It was a curious thing for an old woman of ninety-six to be worrying about the future, but she was, and it was not her future that concerned her, but that of her great family, the on-going thing that she had started but which was now more powerful than she. Therefore she said, "It is not only our money we are gambling with, Hong Kong, but that of all the Kees, those who are working and the girls in the stores and the old people. Thinking of them, are you still willing to hold onto everything?"

"It is for them that I'm doing it," Hong Kong replied. "I know the delicate structure we've built. A house on top of a store on top of a job at Pearl Harbor on top of a little piece of land on top of an old man's savings. Maybe it's all going to crumble, but I'm willing to gamble that when it starts to totter, you and I will be smart enough to catch the falling pieces."

"I think it's beginning to totter now, Hong Kong," the old woman warned.

"I don't think it is," her grandson replied, and for once he ignored his grandmother's advice, and she said, "This is your decision, Hong Kong," and he replied, "We started our adventure when the haoles ran away from the war, and I'm not going to run away now," and she promised, "At least I won't tell the others of my fears."

He therefore held onto the fantastic, teetering structure—depending solely upon his own courage—and as Honolulu rents rose, and wages at Pearl Harbor, and profits from the stores, he applied the money Asia provided to further gambles, and the structure grew higher and more precarious, but he was never afraid of his perilous construction, and his old grandmother grew increasingly to realize that in Hong Kong she had developed a grandson she could truly admire. "In many ways," she reflected, thinking back to the High Village and the warm days of her youth, "he is like my father. He is bold, and willing to engage in great battles, and he will probably wind up with his head in a cage in the center of Honolulu." Then she thought of her father's grisly visage, staring, neckless, down upon the years, and she concluded: "Was it a bad way to die?" And the perilous gamble of the Kee hui continued.

WHILE the four Sakagawa boys were in uniform, fighting for an unqualified citizenship, their parents and their sister Reiko were experiencing grave contradictions and confusions. On the one hand, the older Sakagawas prayed for the safe return of their sons, and this implied an American victory, at least over the Germans, and accordingly they listened with gratification when Reiko-chan read them the local Japanese newspaper, the *Nippu Jiji,* which told of victory in Europe. But on the other hand, they continued to pray for Japanese victory in Asia, for their homeland was in trouble and they hoped that it would triumph, never admitting to themselves that American victory in Europe and Japanese victory in Asia were incompatible.

Then one day Mr. Ishii appeared furtively at the barbershop, whispering, "Tremendous news! I must stop by to see you tonight." And before Sakagawa-san could halt the little man, the latter had vanished into another Japanese store.

That evening, after Sakagawa had closed the barbershop and walked the girl barbers safely home, ignoring the whistles of American sailors who loafed on Hotel Street, Kamejiro said to Reiko, "You can be sure that Mr. Ishii has something very important for us," and the two hurried through the dark streets to the little cottage in Kakaako. There Mr. Ishii waited, and after the household was settled and the blinds drawn, he strode dramatically to the table where the day's issue of the *Nippu Jiji* lay and with fury tore it to bits, threw it on the floor, and spat on it.

"Thus I treat the enemies of Japan!" he cried.

"I haven't read it . . . ." Reiko pleaded, trying to halt him.

"Never again will you read that filthy propaganda!" Mr. Ishii announced grandly. "I told you, didn't I, that it was all American lies? You laughed at me and said, 'What does Mr. Ishii know about war?' My friends, I will tell you what I know. I know what is really happening in the world. And in America all good Japanese know. It is only you fools who have to read the Hawaii newspapers who do not know."

Flamboyantly, he whipped out from his coat pocket a Japanese newspaper printed in Wyoming, the *Prairie Shinbun,* and there for Reiko to see were the exciting headlines: "Imperial Forces Defeat Americans in Bougainville." "Great Japanese Victory at Guadalcanal." "President Roosevelt Admits Japan Will Win the War." Most of the stories appearing on the front pages had been picked up from Japanese shortwave broadcasts emanating from military headquarters in Tokyo, and all purveyed the straight Japanese propaganda line. One story in particular infuriated the hushed group in the Sakagawa living room: "American Marines Confess Stabbing Helpless Japanese Soldiers with Bayonets." The story came from Tokyo and could not be doubted.

When the horror at American brutality subsided, Mr. Ishii proceeded with the important news, a story in which the Wyoming editors summarized, by means of Imperial releases, the progress of the war, and it was apparent to all in the little room that Japan was not only triumphing throughout the Pacific but that she must soon invade Hawaii. "And then, Sakagawa-san, what are you going to tell the emperor's general when he strides ashore at Honolulu and asks, 'Sakagawa, were you a good Japanese?' You, with four sons fighting against the emperor. And do you know what the general is going to say when he hears your reply? He's going to say, 'Sakagawa, bend down.' And when you have bent down, the general himself is going to unscabbard his sword and cut off your head."

None of the Sakagawas spoke. They looked at the newspaper dumbly, and Reiko picked out the headlines. It was a paper published openly in Wyoming, it had passed the United States censor, and what Mr. Ishii had read from it was true. Japan was winning the war and would soon invade Hawaii. In great pain of conscience Sakagawa-san looked at the paper which he could not read and asked Reiko-chan, "Is it true?" And his daughter said, "Yes."

It was one of the most exasperating anomalies of the war that whereas the F.B.I. and naval security kept very close watch on the Japanese newspapers in Hawaii, and saw that they printed only the strictest truth, with no stories at all datelined Tokyo, the Japanese-language newspapers in the states of Utah and Wyoming were free to print whatever they wished, it having been decided by the local military that the official Japanese communiqués were so ridiculous that they would in time defeat themselves, as indeed they did. So the mainland Japanese press, often edited by die-hard samurai types, kept pouring out an incredible mess of propaganda, rumor, anti-American sentiment and downright subversive lies, and when copies of the papers reached Hawaii, where rumors were apt to be virulent, their effect was shocking.

"I will tell the emperor's general," Sakagawa-san finally explained, "that my sons fought only in Europe. Never against Japan."

"It will do no good!" Mr. Ishii said sadly. "The emperor will never forgive you for what you have done."

Sakagawa-san felt weak. He had always had doubts about sending his sons to war, and now the Wyoming paper had fortified those doubts. Dumbly he looked at his old guide, and Mr. Ishii, after enjoying the moment of humiliation, finally said, "I will put in a good word for you with the general. I will tell him you have always been a good Japanese."

"Thank you, Mr. Ishii!" the dynamiter cried. "You are the only friend I can trust."

The Sakagawas went to bed that night in considerable torment, so the next day at her barber chair Reiko waited until an intelligent-looking young naval officer sat down, and when he had done so, she asked quietly, "Could you help me, please."

"Sure," the officer said. "Name's Jackson, from Seattle."

"A man told me last night that Japan might invade Hawaii at any moment. Is that true?"

The navy man's jaw dropped; he pulled the towel away from his neck and turned to look at Reiko, who was then twenty-six and at her prettiest. He smiled at her and asked, "Good God, woman! What have you been hearing?"

"I was told on good authority that Japanese ships might attack at any time."

"Look, lady!" the officer chided. "If you're a spy trying to get secrets . . ."

"Oh, no!" Reiko blushed. Then she saw her father approaching to enforce the rule against any conversation with customers. She retied the towel, jerking it back to muzzle the navy man, and started clipping. "We're not allowed to talk," she whispered.

"Where do you have lunch?" the officer asked.

"Senaga's," she whispered.

"I'll see you there, and tell you about the war."

"Oh, I couldn't!" Reiko blushed.

"Look, I'm from Seattle. I used to know lots of Japanese girls. Senaga's."

At the counter of the restaurant, run by the Okinawa pig-grower Senaga, Lieutenant Jackson surprised Reiko by ordering sushi and sashimi, which he attacked with chopsticks. "I served in Japan," he said. "If my skipper caught me eating with chopsticks I'd be court-martialed. Unpatriotic."

"We all try to eat with forks," Reiko said.

"Now about this Jap invasion," Jackson said.

"Would you please not call us Japs?" Reiko asked.

"You're Japanese," Jackson laughed easily. "The enemy are Japs. What's your first name? Reiko, that's nice. Well, Reiko-chan . . ."

"Where did you learn Reiko-chan?"

"In Japan," he replied casually.

"Did you ever know a Reiko-chan?"

"I knew a Kioko-chan."

There was a long silence as they ate sushi, and Reiko wanted to ask many questions and Lieutenant Jackson wanted to make many comments, but neither spoke, until at the same moment Reiko pushed her fork toward the sashimi and the officer shoved his chopsticks at the raw fish. There was a clatter and laughter and Jackson said, "I was deeply in love with Kioko-chan, and she taught me some Japanese, and that's why I have my present job."

"What is it?" Reiko asked solemnly, her face flushed.

"Because I speak a little of your language . . . Well, you understand, I'm not really a navy officer. I'm a Seattle lawyer. I'm with the Adjutant General and my job is to visit Japanese families and tell them that their daughters should not marry American G.I.'s. I see about twenty families a week . . . You know how American men are, they see pretty girls and they want to marry 'em. My job is to see that they don't."

Suddenly he broke his chopsticks in half and his knuckles grew white with bitterness. "Each week, Reiko-chan, I see about twenty Japanese girls and argue with them, and every goddamned one of them reminds me of Kioko-chan, and pretty soon I'm going to go nuts."

He looked straight ahead, a man squeezed in a great vise, and he had no more appetite. Reiko, being a practical girl, finished the sashimi and said, "I must go back to work."

"Will you have lunch with me tomorrow?" the officer said.

"Yes," she said, but when he started to accompany her to the street, she gasped and said, "My father would die."

"Does he believe the Japanese fleet is coming soon?"

"Not he," she lied, "but his friend. What is the truth?"

"In one year or two we will destroy Japan."

That night Reiko-chan advised her father that there must be something wrong with the Wyoming newspaper, because Japan was not winning the war, but this infuriated Sakagawa-san, who had brought home a second copy of the *Prairie Shinbun,* more inflammatory than the first, and as Reiko patiently read it to him she herself began to wonder: "Who is telling the truth?"

Then proof came. President Roosevelt arrived in Honolulu aboard a naval ship, and the Sakagawas saw him with their own eyes and marked the way in which he rode through Honolulu, protected by dozens of secret-service men. To Sakagawa-san, this proved that America was strong, but he had not reckoned with Mr. Ishii's superior intellect, for scarcely had the long black automobiles sped by when the excited little man rushed into the barbershop with staggering news.

"Didn't I tell you?" he whispered. "Oh, tremendous! Come to Sakai's immediately."

Sakagawa turned the barbershop over to his daughter and slipped down a side street to Sakai's store, entering by a back door so as not to attract attention, for groups of Japanese were still prevented from assembling. In the back room Sakai, Mr. Ishii and several agitated older men stood discussing the exciting news. For a moment Sakagawa could not comprehend what it was all about, but soon Mr. Ishii explained everything.

"President Roosevelt has come to Hawaii on his way to Tokyo. He's going to surrender peacefully, be executed at the Yasukuni Shrine as a common war criminal, and the Japanese navy will be here in three days."

Mr. Ishii's stories always featured specific details and dates, and one would have thought that after a while his listeners would recall that for three years not one of his predictions had come to pass; but the hope of victory was so strong in the hearts of some of his audience that he was never called to task for his errors. "In three days!" he said. "Ships of the Imperial navy steaming into Pearl Harbor. But I will protect you, Sakagawa-san, and I will ask the emperor to forgive you for sending your sons to war."

When President Roosevelt left Honolulu for his execution in Tokyo, Mr. Ishii waited in a state of near-collapse for the battleships of his homeland to come steaming in from the west. For three nights he slept on his roof, waiting, waiting, and in the little house in Kakaako, his friend Sakagawa also waited, in trepidation.

On the fourth day, when it was apparent that the Imperial navy was going to be temporarily delayed, Mr. Ishii dropped the whole subject and took up instead the rumor printed in the *Prairie Shinbun* that the Japanese had captured both Australia and New Zealand. He felt, he told the Sakagawas, that it might be a good idea to emigrate to Australia, for under Japanese control there would be good lands for all.

Reiko-chan discussed each of these rumors with Lieutenant Jackson, who listened patiently as the wide-eyed barber disclosed her apprehensions. Always he laughed, and once observed: "This Mr. Ishii must be quite a jerk," but Reiko apologized for the little man: "He came from Hiroshima long ago and has lived in darkness," whereupon the naval officer said, "He better watch out what he says. He could get into trouble." At this Reiko-chan laughed and said, "Nobody ever takes Mr. Ishii seriously. He's such a sweet, inoffensive little man."

It would be difficult to characterize as a love affair a series of meetings conducted in a barbershop under the hawklike eye of Kamejiro Sakagawa and in a crowded Okinawan restaurant run by the Senaga family, for between Reiko-chan and Lieutenant Jackson there were no crushing kisses or lingering farewells, but it was a love affair nevertheless, and on one bold Tuesday, Reiko extended her lunch hour till four in the afternoon, and that sunny day there were both kisses and enraptured embraces. One Wednesday night she slipped away from home and waited for Lieutenant Jackson's Chevrolet, and they drove out to Diamond Head and parked in a lovers' lane. Local people called this, "The midnight athletes watching the under-water submarine races under a full moon." But a shore patrol, inspecting the cars, called it country necking, and when they got to the Chevvy they were astounded.

"What you doin' with a Jap, Lieutenant?"

"Talking."

"With a Jap?"

"Yes, with a Japanese."

"Let's see your papers."

"You didn't ask to see their papers."

"They're with white girls."

With a show of irritation Lieutenant Jackson produced his papers and the shore patrol shook their heads. "This beats anything," one of the sailors said. "She a local girl?"

"Of course."

"Can you speak English, lady?"

"Yes."

"Well, I guess it's all right, if a naval officer don't care whether he necks with a Jap or not."

"Look here, buddy . . ."

"You want to start something, sir?"

Lieutenant Jackson looked up at the two towering sailors and said, "No."

"We didn't think so. Good night, Jap-lover."

Lieutenant Jackson sat silent for some minutes, then said, "War is unbelievable. If those two boys live till we get to Tokyo, they'll probably fall in love with Japanese girls and marry them. With what confusion they will remember this night."

"Will our men get to Tokyo soon?" Reiko-chan asked.

The lieutenant was impressed by the manner in which she said "our men," and he asked, "Why did you say it that way?"

She replied, "I have four brothers fighting in Europe."

"You have . . ." He stopped, and on an uncontrollable impulse jumped out of the car and shouted, "Hey, shore patrol! Shore patrol!"

The two young policemen hurried back and asked, "What's the matter, Lieutenant? She turn out to be a spy?"

"Fellows, I want you to meet Miss Reiko Sakagawa. She has four brothers fighting in the American army in Italy. While you and I sit on our fat asses here in Hawaii. When you were here before, I didn't know."

"You got four men in the war?"

"Yes," she replied quietly.

"All army?"

"Yes. Japanese aren't allowed in the navy."

"Ma'am," one of the shore patrol said, a boy from Georgia, "I sure hope your brothers get home safe."

"Good night, miss," the other boy said.

"Night, fellows," Jackson muttered, and when the patrol wheeled down the road he stammered, "Reiko-chan, I think we ought to get married."

She sighed, clasped her hands very tightly, and said, "I thought your job was to keep men like you from marrying girls like me."

"It is, but have you ever noticed the way in which people in such jobs always fall prey to the very thing they are fighting against? It's uncanny. I've intervened in some three hundred cases like this, and almost every time the man has been from the Deep South."

"What has that to do with us?" Reiko-chan asked.

"You see, at home these Southern boys have been taught from birth that anyone with a different color is evil and to be despised. In their hearts they know this can't be true, so as soon as they get a fair chance to investigate a girl with a different color, they find her a human being and they suffer a compulsion to fall in love and marry her."

"Are you from the South, Lieutenant? Do you act from such a compulsion?"

"I'm from Seattle, but I have a compulsion greater than any of them. After Pearl Harbor my father, a pretty good man by and large, was the one who spearheaded the drive to throw all Japanese into concentration camps. He knew he was doing an evil thing. He knew he was giving false testimony and acting for his own economic advantage. But nevertheless, he went ahead. On the night he made his inflammatory speech over the radio I told him, 'Pop, you know what you said isn't true,' and he replied, 'This is war, son.' "

"So you want to marry me to get even with him?" Reiko asked. "I couldn't marry you on those terms."

"The compulsion is much deeper, Reiko-chan. Remember that I lived in Japan. No matter how old we both get, Reiko, never forget that at the height of the war I told you, 'When peace comes, Japan and America will be compatible friends.' I am positive of it. I am positive that my father, since he is essentially a good man, will welcome you graciously as his daughter. Because people have got to forget past errors. They have got to bind separated units together."

"You talk as if your father were the problem," Reiko said quietly.

"You mean yours is?"

"We will never get married," Reiko said sorrowfully. "My father would never permit it."

"Tell your father to go to hell. I told mine."

"But I am a Japanese," she said, kissing him on the lips.

Kamejiro Sakagawa first discovered his daughter's love affair with a haole when his good friend Sakai appeared at the barbershop one morning to say, "I am sorry, Kamejiro, but my daughter cannot work here any more."

Sakagawa gasped and asked, "Why not? I pay her well."

"Yes, and we need the money, but I can't risk having her work here another day. It might happen to her too. So many haoles coming in here."

"What might happen?" Sakagawa stammered.

"More better we go outside," Sakai said. There, along a gutter on Hotel Street, he said sorrowfully, "You have been a good friend, Kamejiro, and you have paid our girl well, but we cannot run the risk of her falling in love with a haole man, the way your Reiko has."

Little bulldog Kamejiro, his neck muscles standing out, grabbed his friend by the shoulders, rising on his toes to accomplish the feat. "What are you saying?" he roared.

"Kamejiro!" his friend protested, trying vainly to break loose from the frightening grip. "Ask anyone. Your daughter has lunch every day with the American . . . at Senaga's."

In a state of shock, little Kamejiro Sakagawa thrust his friend away and stared down Hotel Street at the Okinawa restaurant run by the pig-farmer, Senaga, and as he watched, that crafty Senaga entered the shop, taking with him a haole friend, and in this simple omen Sakagawa saw the truth of what his compatriot Sakai had charged. Reiko-chan, as good a daughter as a man ever had, strong and dutiful, had been visiting with a haole in an Okinawan restaurant. Shattered, the stocky little man, then sixty-one, leaned against a post, oblivious of the flow of sailors and soldiers about him.

It was ironic, he thought, that war should have catapulted two of the groups he hated most into such postures of success. The damned Chinese had all the good jobs at Pearl Harbor, and with the income they got, were buying up most of Honolulu. Their sons were not at war, and their arrogance was high. As allies, followers of the damnable Chiang Kai-shek, who had resisted decent Japanese overtures in China, they appeared in all the parades and made speeches over the radio. The Chinese, Sakagawa reflected that ugly morning, were doing very well.

But what was particularly galling was that the Okinawans were doing even better. Now, an Okinawan, Sakagawa mused in sullen anger as he studied Senaga's restaurant, is a very poor man to begin with, neither wholly Japanese nor wholly Chinese but making believe to be the former. An Okinawan cannot be trusted, must be watched every minute lest he set his daughters to trick a man's sons, and is a man who lacks the true Japanese spirit. There were few men in the world, Sakagawa felt, lower than an Okinawan, yet look at what had happened to them during the war!

Because in the years before 1941 they had not been accepted into Japanese society, they had banded together. Most of the garbage in Honolulu was collected by Okinawans. To get rid of the garbage they kept pigs, hundreds upon hundreds of pigs. So when the war came, and freighters were no longer available to carry fresh beef from California to Hawaii, where did everyone have to go for meat? To the Okinawans! Who opened up one restaurant after another, because they had the meat? The Okinawans! Who was going to come out of the war richer than even the white people? The Okinawans! It was a cruel jest, that an Okinawan should wind up rich and powerful and respected, just because he happened to own all the pigs.

It was with these thoughts that the little dynamiter, Kamejiro Sakagawa, hid among the crowd on Hotel Street and waited to spy upon his daughter Reiko, and as he waited he muttered to himself, "With a haole, in an Okinawan restaurant!" It was really more than he could comprehend.

At five minutes after twelve Lieutenant Jackson entered the restaurant and took a table which smiling Senaga-san had been reserving for him. The officer ordered a little plate of pickled radishes, which he ate deftly with chopsticks, and Sakagawa thought: "What's he doing eating tsukemono? With hashi?"

At ten minutes after twelve Reiko Sakagawa hurried into the restaurant, and even a blind man could have seen from the manner in which she smiled and the way in which her whole eager body bent forward that she was in love. She did not touch the naval officer, but her radiant face and glowing eyes came peacefully to rest a few inches from his. With a fork she began picking up a few pieces of radish, and her father, watching from the street, thought: "It's all very confusing. What is she doing with a fork?"

During the entire meal the little Japanese watched the miserable spectacle of his daughter having a date with a haole, and long before she was ready to leave, Kamejiro had hastened back down Hotel Street to his friend Sakai's store, asking, "Sakai, what shall I do?"

"Did you see for yourself?"

"Yes. What you said is true."

"Hasegawa is taking his daughter out of the barbershop, too."

"To hell with the barbershop! What shall I do about Reiko?"

"What you must do, Kamejiro, is find out who this haole is. Then go to the navy and ask that he be transferred."

"Would the navy listen to me?" Kamejiro pleaded.

"On such a matter, yes," Sakai said with finality. Then he added, "But your most important job, Kamejiro, is to find a husband for your daughter."

"For years I have been looking," the little dynamiter said.

"I will act as the go-between," Sakai promised. "But it will not be easy. Now that she has ruined herself with a haole."

"No! Don't say that. Reiko-chan is a good girl."

"But already everyone knows she has been going with a haole. What self-respecting Japanese family will accept her now, Kamejiro?"

"Will you work hard as the go-between, Sakai?"

"I will find a husband for your daughter. A decent Japanese man."

"You are my friend," Sakagawa said tearfully, but before he left he added prudently, "Sakai, could you please try to find a Hiroshima man? That would be better."

Mrs. Sakagawa had spent the morning at home making pickled cabbage and the afternoon at Mrs. Mark Whipple's rolling Red Cross bandages. The latter experience had been a trying one, for every woman in the room had at least one son in the Two-Two-Two except Mrs. Whipple, and her husband commanded it. Therefore, the conversation, which most of the Japanese women could not participate in, had to be about the war in Italy and the heavy casualties which the Japanese boys were suffering, but whenever grief began to stalk the room, Mrs. Whipple, one of the Hale girls, invariably brought up some new and cheering fact. Once she said, "President Roosevelt himself has announced that our boys are among the bravest that have fought under the Stars and Stripes." Later she said, "*Time* magazine this week reports that when our boys reached Salerno on leave, the other troops at the railway station cheered them as they disembarked." Mrs. Whipple always referred to the Japanese soldiers as "our boys," and other haoles in Hawaii were beginning to do the same.

So the afternoon had been an emotional one, regardless of whether the talk was of casualties or of triumphs, and Mrs. Sakagawa, whose feet were sore from the American shoes she felt obligated to wear, reached home eager for rest. Instead, she found her husband at home rather than in the barbershop, and she knew that something dire had happened. Before she could ask, Kamejiro shouted, "A fine daughter you raised! She's in love with a haole!"

The words were the harshest that Mrs. Sakagawa could have heard. There were some Japanese girls, she had to admit, who went openly with haoles, but they were not from self-respecting families, and there were a few who under the pressure of war had become prostitutes, but she suspected that these were really either Etas or Okinawans. It was unlikely that any Japanese girl, mindful of the proud blood that flowed in her veins . . .

"And Sakai took his daughter out of the barbershop lest she become contaminated too, and Hasegawa is removing his daughter tomorrow." He was about to cry, "We are ruined," but an even deeper concern overcame him, and he fell into a chair, sinking his head on his forearms and sobbing, "Our family has never known shame before."

Mrs. Sakagawa, who refused to believe that her daughter could have brought disgrace upon the family, kicked off her American shoes, wriggled her toes in comfort, and kneeled beside her distraught husband. "Kamejiro," she whispered, "we taught Reiko how to be a good Japanese. I am sure she will not disgrace us. Somebody has told you a great lie."

Violently the little dynamiter thrust his wife aside and strode across the room. "I saw them! She was almost kissing him in public. And I've been thinking. Where was she that afternoon she said she didn't feel well? Out with a haole. And where was she when she said she was going to a cinema? Riding in a dark car with a haole. I heard a car stop that night, but I was too stupid to put two and two together."

At this moment Reiko-chan, flushed with love and the brisk walk home, entered and saw immediately from her parents' faces that her secret had been discovered. Her father said simply, with a heartbreaking gasp, "My own daughter! With a haole!" Her mother was still ready to dismiss the whole scandal and asked, "It isn't true, is it?"

Reiko-chan, her dark eyes warm with the inner conviction that was to sustain her through the impending argument, replied, "I am in love, and I want to get married."

No one spoke. Kamejiro fell back into a chair and buried his face. Mrs. Sakagawa stared at her daughter in disbelief and then began to treat her with exaggerated solicitude, as if she were already illegally pregnant. Reiko smiled in quiet amusement, but then her stricken father gave an appalling gasp, and she knelt beside him, saying quickly, "Lieutenant Jackson is a wonderful man, Father. He's understanding, and he's lived in Japan. He has a good job in Seattle, but he thinks he may settle here after the war." She hesitated, for her words were not being heard, and then added, "Wherever he goes, I want to go with him."

Slowly her father pushed himself back from the table, withdrew from his daughter, and looked at her in shocked disbelief. "But you are a Japanese!" he cried in his misery.

"I am going to marry him, Father," his daughter repeated forcefully.

"But you're a Japanese," he reiterated. Taking her hand he said, "You have the blood of Japan, the strength of a great nation, everything . . ." He tried to explain how unthinkable her suggestion was, but could come back to only one paramount fact. "You're a Japanese!"

Reiko explained patiently, "Lieutenant Jackson is a respectable man. He has a much better job than any man here that I might possibly marry. He's a college graduate and has a good deal of money in the bank. His family is well known in Seattle. These things aren't of major importance, but I tell you so that you will realize what an unusual man he is."

Kamejiro listened in disgust at the rigmarole, and when it seemed likely that Reiko was going to add more, he slapped her sharply across the cheek. "It would be humiliating," he cried. "A permanent disgrace. Already even the rumor of your behavior has ruined the barbershop. The Sakai girl has quit. So has the Hasegawa. No self-respecting Japanese family will want to associate with us after what you have done."

Reiko pressed her hand to her burning cheek and said quietly, "Father, hundreds of decent Japanese girls have fallen in love with Americans."

"Whores, all of them!" Kamejiro stormed.

Ignoring him Reiko said, "I know, because that's Lieutenant Jackson's job. To talk with parents like you. And the girls are not . . ."

"Aha!" Kamejiro cried. "So that's what he does! Tomorrow I go see Admiral Nimitz."

"Father, I warn you that if you . . ."

"Admiral Nimitz will hear of this!"

The little dynamiter did not actually get to Nimitz. He was stopped first by an ensign, who was so enthralled by the stalwart, bow-armed Japanese that he passed him along to a full lieutenant who sent him on to a commodore who burst into the office of a rear admiral, with the cry: "Jesus, Jack! There's a little Japanese out here with the goddamnedest story you ever heard. You gotta listen."

So a circle of captains, commodores and admirals interrupted their work to listen to Kamejiro's hilarious pidgin as he protested to the navy that one of their officers had wrecked his barbershop and had ruined his daughter.

"Is she pregnant?" one of the rear admirals asked.

"You watch out!" Kamejiro cried. "Mo bettah you know Reiko a good wahine!"

"I'm sorry, Mr. Sakanawa. In our language *ruined* means, well, *ruined.*"

When the officers heard who it was that ruined, or whatever, the girl Reiko, they almost exploded. "That goddamned Jackson!" one of them sputtered. "His job is to break up this sort of thing."

"I've told you a dozen times," another said. "Putting a civilian into uniform doesn't make him an officer."

"That's beside the point," the senior admiral said. "What I'd like to know, Mr. Sakanawa, is this. If the boy has a good reputation, a good job, a good income, and a good family back in Seattle . . . Well, what

I'm driving at is this. Your daughter is a lady barber. It would seem to me that you would jump at the chance for such a marriage."

Little Kamejiro, who was shorter by nine inches than any man in the room, stared at them in amazement. "She's a Japanese!" he said to the interpreter. "It would be disgraceful if she married a haole."

"How's that?" the commodore asked.

"It would bring such shame on our family . . ."

"What the hell do you mean?" the commodore bellowed. "Since when is a Jap marrying a decent American a matter of shame . . . to the Jap?"

"Her brothers in Italy would be humiliated before all their companions," Kamejiro doggedly explained.

"What's that again?" the senior officer asked. "She got brothers in Italy?"

"My four boys are fighting in Italy," Kamejiro said humbly.

One of the rear admirals rose and came over to the little dynamiter. "You have four sons in the Two-Two-Two?"

"Yes."

"They all in Italy?"

"Yes."

There was a long silence, broken by the admiral, who said, "I got one son there. I worry about him all the time."

"I am worried about my daughter," the stubborn little man replied.

"And if she marries a white man, her four brothers won't be able to live down the disgrace?"

"Never."

"What do you want Admiral Nimitz to do?"

"Send Lieutenant Jackson away."

"He will go away this afternoon," the admiral said.

"May God bless Admiral Nimitz," Kamejiro said.

"That's an odd phrase," the admiral said. "You a Christian?"

"I'm Buddhist. But my children are all Christian."

When Kamejiro had been led outside, happy at the ease with which he had found a solution to his grave problem, the admiral shrugged his shoulders and said, "We'll beat the little bastards, but we'll never understand them."

Reiko-chan never saw Lieutenant Jackson again. In conformance with secret and high-priority orders he flew out of Hawaii that night, exiled to Bougainville, where, less than a week later, a body of Japanese infiltrators slipped through the jungle, attacked the headquarters in which he was serving, and lunged at him with bayonets. Knowing nothing of guns, the young lawyer tried to fight them off with a chair, but one Japanese soldier parried the chair, drove his bayonet through the lieutenant's chest, and left him strangling to death in the mud.

No one told Reiko that her lawyer was dead—there was no reason why anyone should—and she assumed that he had been fooling with her as men will, and that he had gone to other duties. When her father's barbershop had to close, because cautious Japanese families would not allow their daughters to work under a man who did not even protect his own daughter from the disgrace of a haole love affair, Reiko went to work in another barbershop, and sometimes when a naval officer came in for a haircut, and she placed the towel about his neck and saw the railroad-track insignia on his shirt, she would for a moment feel dizzy. At other times, when brash enlisted men tried to feel her legs as she cut their hair, she would jab their hands with her scissors, as her father had taught her to do, but even as she did so, she felt confused by the great passion that can exist between men and women.

The forced closing of Kamejiro Sakagawa's barbershop was actually a considerable blessing to the family, although at the time it was not so recognized, for in the first weeks the stalwart little dynamiter could find no work other than caring for lawns, a job he did not like. Then the Okinawan restaurant keeper Senaga sent a messenger saying that he needed a busboy at a new restaurant he was opening in Waikiki, where a great many soldiers and sailors went, and he would like Sakagawa-san to take the job. Kamejiro's eyes blazed as he stared at the messenger. "If Senaga had been a friend, he would never have allowed a Japanese girl to talk with a haole in his restaurant. Tell him no." But to his wife, Kamejiro swore, "I would rather die of starvation than work for an Okinawan." Then, from a totally unexpected source, the Sakagawas received the financial aid which established them as one of the stronger and more prosperous Japanese families in Hawaii. It all happened because early in 1943 Hong Kong Kee had made a speech.

The inflamed oratory which provoked the loan took place before the Japanese boys of the Two-Two-Two had become the popular heroes they were later to be. When Hong Kong spoke, Japanese were still suspect, and a haole committee, seeking to whip up patriotism for war bonds, prevailed upon him to give a short speech explaining why the Chinese could be trusted and the Japanese could not. Since the committee of patriots contained many of the leaders of Honolulu, Hong Kong was naturally flattered by the invitation and spent some time in working out a rather fiery comparison of Chinese virtues as opposed to Japanese duplicity. Then, when he got on the speakers' platform, he became intoxicated by the crowd and deviated from his script, making his remarks rather more inclusive than he had planned. "The Japanese war lords have oppressed China for many years," he cried, "and it is with joy in our hearts that we watch the great American forces driving the evil Japanese from places where they have no right to be." He was astonished at the constant applause which the mass meeting threw back at him, and thus emboldened, he extended his remarks to include the Japanese in Hawaii. It was a very popular speech, sold a lot of war bonds, and got Hong Kong's picture in the papers under the caption "Patriotic Chinese Leader Flays Japs."

The affair was a big success except in one house. In her small, ugly clapboard shack up the Nuuanu, Hong Kong's grandmother, then ninety-six years old, listened appalled as one of her great-granddaughters read aloud the account of Hong Kong's oratory. "Bring him here at once!" she stormed, and when the powerful banker stood in her room she sent the others away, and when the door was closed she rose, stalked over to her grandson and slapped him four times in the face. "You fool!" she cried. "You fool! You damned, damned fool!"

Hong Kong fell back from the assault and covered his face to prevent further slappings. When he did this his fiery little grandmother began pushing him in the chest, calling him all the while "You fool" until he stumbled backward against a chair and fell into it. Then she stopped, waited for him to drop his hands, and stared at him sorrowfully. "Hong Kong," she said, "yesterday you were a great fool."

"Why?" he asked weakly.

She showed him the paper, with his picture grinning out from a semicircle of haole faces, and although she could not read, she could remember what her great-granddaughter had reported, and now she repeated the phrases with icy sarcasm: "We cannot trust the Japanese!" She spat onto her own floor. "They are deceitful and criminal men." Again she spat. Then she threw the paper onto the floor and kicked it, for her fury was great, and when this was done she shouted at her grandson, "What glory did you get from standing for a few minutes among the haoles?"

"I was asked to represent the Chinese community," Hong Kong fumbled.

"Who appointed you our representative, you stupid man?"

"I thought that since we are fighting Japan, somebody ought to . . ."

"You didn't think!" Nyuk Tsin stormed. "You have no brains to think. For a minute's glory, standing among the haoles, you have destroyed every good chance the Chinese have built up for themselves in Honolulu."

"Wait a minute, Auntie!" Hong Kong protested. "That's exactly what I was thinking about when I agreed to make the speech. It was a chance to make the Chinese look better among the haoles who run the islands."

Nyuk Tsin looked at her grandson in amazement. "Hong Kong?" she gasped. "Do you think that when the war is over, the haoles will continue to run Hawaii?"

"They have the banks, the newspapers . . ."

"Hong Kong! Who is doing the fighting? What men are in uniform? Who is going to come back to the islands ready to take over the political control? Tell me, Hong Kong."

"You mean the Japanese?" he asked weakly.

"Yes!" she shouted, her Hakka anger at its peak. "That's exactly who I mean. They are the ones who will win this war, and believe me, Hong Kong, when they take control they will remember the evil things you said yesterday, and every Kee in Honolulu will find life a little more difficult because of your stupidity."

"I didn't mean that . . ."

"Be still, you stupid man. After the war when Sam wants to build a store, who will sign the papers giving him the permit? Some Japanese. If Ruth's husband wants to run a bus line, who will give the permit? Some Japanese. And they will hate you for what you said yesterday. Already your words have been filed in their minds."

The shadow of a government building where all the permit signers were Japanese fell heavily upon Hong Kong, and he asked, "What ought we to do?" It was symptomatic of the Kees that when one of them took a bold step, he said of himself, "I did this," but when corrective measures had to be taken, he always consulted Wu Chow's Auntie and asked, "What must we do?"

The old woman said, "You must go through Honolulu and apologize to every Japanese you have ever known. Humble yourself, as you should. Then find at least twenty men who need money, and lend it to them. Help them start new businesses." She stopped, then added prudently, "It would be better if you lent the money to those who have a lot of sons in the war, for they will be the ones who are going to run Hawaii."

In the course of his apologies to the Japanese community, Hong Kong came in time to Sakai, the storekeeper, and Sakai said in English, "No, I don't need any money, but my good friend Sakagawa the dynamiter has lost his barbershop, and he needs money to start a store of some kind."

"Where can I find him?" Hong Kong asked.

"He lives in Kakaako."

"By the way, any of his boys in the Two-Two-Two?"

"Four," Sakai replied.

"I will look him up," Hong Kong replied, and that afternoon he told Kamejiro, "I have come to apologize for what I said at the meeting."

"Mo bettah you be ashamed," Kamejiro said bluntly.

"Yes, with you having four sons in the battles."

"And all other Japanese, too."

"Kamejiro, I'm sorry."

"I sorry for you," the stocky little Japanese said, for he did not like Chinese.

"And I have come to lend you the money to start a store here in Kakaako."

Kamejiro drew back, for he had learned that anything either a Chinese or an Okinawan did was sure to be tricky. Surveying Hong Kong, he asked, "What for you lend me money?"

Humbly Hong Kong replied, "Because I've got to prove I am really sorry."

It was in this way that Kamejiro Sakagawa opened his grocery store, and because he was a frugal man and worked incredibly hard, and because his wife had a knack of waiting on Japanese customers and his barber daughter a skill in keeping accounts, the store flourished. Then, as if good fortune had piled up a warehouse full of beneficences, on New Year's Day, 1944, Sakai-san came running with breathless news.

"Pssst!" he called to Sakagawa as the latter sprayed his vegetables. "Come here."

"What?" the grocer shouted.

"Out here!"

Sakagawa left the store and allowed Sakai-san to lead him to an alley, where the latter said in awed tones, "I have found a husband for your daughter!"

"You have?" Sakagawa cried.

"Yes! A wonderful match!"

"A Japanese, of course?"

Sakai looked at his old friend with contempt. "What kind of baishakunin would I be if I even thought of proposing anyone but a Japanese?"

"Forgive me!" Sakagawa said. "You can understand, after the narrow escape we had."

"This man is perfect. A little house. More than a little money. Fine Japanese. And what else do you think!"

"Is he . . ." Sakagawa would not form the words, for this was too much to hope for.

"Yes! He's also a Hiroshima man!"

A thick blanket of positive euphoria settled over the two whispering men, for the go-between Sakai was just as pleased as Sakagawa that a fine Japanese girl had at last found a good husband, and a Hiroshima man at that. Finally Sakagawa got round to a question of lesser importance: "Who is he?"

"Mr. Ishii!" Sakai cried rapturously.

"Has he agreed to marry my daughter?" Kamejiro asked incredulously.

"Yes!" Sakai the baishakunin cried.

"Does he know about her . . . the haole?"

"Of course. I was honor-bound to tell him."

"And still he is willing to accept her?" Kamejiro asked in disbelief.

"Yes, he says it is his duty to save her."

"That good man," Sakagawa cried. He called his wife and told her, "Sakai has done it! He has found a husband for Reiko-chan."

"Who?" his practical-minded wife asked.

"Mr. Ishii!"

"A Hiroshima man!" And before Reiko-chan knew anything of her impending marriage, word that she had found a Hiroshima man flashed through the Japanese community and almost everybody was truly delighted with the girl's good fortune, especially since she had been mixed up with a haole man, but one girl, who had been through high school, reflected: "Mr. Ishii must be thirty-five years older than Reiko."

"What does it matter?" her mother snapped. "She's getting a Hiroshima man."

Reiko was in the barbershop on Hotel Street cutting the hair of a sailor when the news reached her. The girl at the next chair whispered in Japanese, "Congratulations, dear Reiko-chan."

"About what?" Reiko asked.

"Sakai-san has found you a husband."

The Japanese phrase fell strangely on Reiko's ears, for although she had long suspected that her parents had employed a baishakunin to find her a husband, she had never supposed that any solid arrangement would come to pass. Steadying herself against her chair, she asked casually, "Who did they say the man was?"

"Mr. Ishii! I think it's wonderful."

Reiko-chan kept mechanically moving her fingers, and the man in the chair warned: "Not too much off the sides, ma'am."

"I'm sorry," Reiko said. She wanted to run out of the barbershop, far from everyone, but she kept to her job. Patiently she trimmed the sailor's head just right, then lathered his neck and sideburns and asked, "You like them straight or on a little slant?"

"Any way looks best," the young man said. "You speak good English. Better'n me."

"I went to school," Rciko said quietly.

"Ma'am, do you feel well?" the sailor asked.

"Yes."

"You don't look so good. Look, ma'am . . . ."

Reiko was about to faint, but with a tremendous effort she controlled herself and finished the lathering; but when she tried to grasp the razor she could not command it, and with great dismay she looked at the frightened sailor and asked softly, "Would you mind if I did not shave your neck this time? I feel dizzy."

"Ma'am, you ought to lie down," the sailor said, wiping the soap from his sideburns.

When he left, Reiko hung up her apron and announced, "I am going home," and on the long walk to Kakaako she tried not to compare Mr. Ishii with Lieutenant Jackson, but she could not keep her mind from doing so; then as she approached the family store she fortified herself with this consoling thought: "He's a crazy little man, and more like my father than a husband, but he is a proper Japanese and my father will be happy." Thinking no more of her absent Seattle lawyer, who had never even written to her, she went into the Sakagawa store, walked up to her father, and bowed. "I am grateful to you, Father."

"He is a Hiroshima man!" Sakagawa pointed out.

At the wedding, which was a highlight of the Japanese community in February of 1944, the baishakunin Sakai commanded everything. He told the family where to stand and the priest what to do and the groom how to behave. Mr. Ishii had spent the first part of the afternoon showing the assembly the latest copy of the *Prairie Shinbun,* which proved that valiant Imperial troops had finally driven all American marines off Guadalcanal and were about to launch a major invasion of Hawaii. One guest, who had two sons in Italy, whispered to his wife, "I think the old man's crazy!"

"Ssssh!" his wife said. "He's getting married."

When the crush was greatest, Reiko-chan, in old-style Japanese dress, happened to look at her bridegroom for the first time since her engagement had been announced, and she could not hide from herself the fact that he was a pathetic, cramped-up old man; and all her American education inspired her to flee from this insane ceremony, and great dizziness came upon her and she said to one of the girls near her, "This obi is too tight, I must get some air," and she was about to run away when the baishakunin Sakai cried, "We begin!" and the intricate, lovely Japanese wedding ceremony proceeded.

When it ended, women clustered about Reiko-chan and told her, "You were beautiful in your kimono. A true bride, with flushed cheeks and downcast eyes." Others said, "It's so wonderful to think that he is also a Hiroshima man." And the crush became so oppressive that she said, "This obi is really too tight. I must get some air," and she left the wedding feast and went alone to the porch, where she began to breathe deeply and where she arrived just in time to greet a messenger boy riding up on a bicycle.

At the next moment the guests inside heard a series of screams emanating from the porch, as if an animal had been mortally wounded, and they rushed out to find Reiko-chan screaming and screaming, and they could not stop her, for in her hand she held a message from the War Department advising the Sakagawa family of certain events that had recently transpired on a river bank in Italy.

ON SEPTEMBER 22, 1943, the Triple Two looked forward across the bow of their transport and saw rising in the misty dawn the hills of Italy, and Sergeant Goro Sakagawa thought: "I'll bet there's a German division hiding in there, waiting for us to step ashore."

He was right, and as the Japanese boys climbed down out of their transport to invade the beaches of Salerno, German planes and heavy artillery tried to harass them, but their aim was wild and all the units made it without casualty except one crop-headed private named Tashimoto, who sprained his ankle. The gang passed the word along with the acid comment, "Wouldn't you know it would be a guy from Molokai?"

Salerno lay southeast of Naples and had been chosen because it provided a logical stepping-off place for an encircling movement on Rome, some hundred and fifty miles distant, and on the day of landing, the Two-Two-Two started the long march north. The Germans, knowing both of their coming and of their composition, were determined to halt them. A specific order had been issued by Hitler: "To defeat the little yellow men who are traitors to our ally Japan and who are being cruelly used as propaganda by their Jewish masters in America, is obligatory. If these criminal little men should win a victory, it would be strongly used against us. They must be stopped and wiped out."

The Japanese boys from Hawaii did not know of this order, and after they had met one line of massive German resistance after another, they concluded: "These krauts must be the best fighters in the world. This is a lot tougher than they told us it was going to be." If the Two-Two-Two gained three miles, they did so against the most formidable German resistance: mines killed boys from Maui, tanks overran fighters from Molokai; gigantic shells exploded among troops from Kauai; and dogged, powerful ground forces contested every hill. Casualties were heavy, and the Honolulu *Mail* began carrying death lists with names like Kubokawa, Higa, and Moriguchi.

The furious efforts of the Germans to halt and humiliate the Japanese boys had an opposite effect to the one Hitler wanted; Allied war correspondents, both European and American, quickly discovered that whereas other fronts might not produce good stories, one could always get something exciting with the Two-Two-Two because they were the ones that were encountering the best the enemy could provide. Ernie Pyle, among others, marched for some days with the Hawaii troops, and wrote: "I have come to expect our American boys to continue fighting in the face of great odds, but these short, black-eyed little fighters are setting a new record. They continue slugging it out when even the bravest men would consolidate or withdraw. They form a terrific addition to our team, and dozens of boys from Texas and Massachusetts have told me, 'I'm glad they're on our side.' " So Hitler's determination to hit the Japanese so hard that they would be forced to collapse in shame, backfired because they fought on in glory.

Once Ernie Pyle asked Goro Sakagawa, "Sergeant, why did you push on against that cluster of houses? You knew it was crowded with Germans."

Goro replied in words that became famous both in Italy and

America: "We had to. We fight double. Against the Germans and for every Japanese in America." Reported Pyle: "And they're winning both their wars."

September, October, November, December: the beautiful months, the months of poetry and rhythm, with nights growing colder and the soft mists of Italy turning to frost. How beautiful those months were when the boys from Hawaii first realized that they were as good fighting men as any in the world. "We fight double," they told themselves, and when they came to some Italian town, bathed in cloudless sunlight, standing forth against the hills like an etching, each tower clear in the bright glare, they attacked with fury and calculation, and bit by bit they drove the Germans back toward Rome. Colonel Whipple, delighted by the showing of his troops and pleased with the good reports they were getting in the American press, nevertheless warned his men: "It can't go on being as easy as this. Somewhere, the Germans are going to dig in real solid. Then we'll see if we're as good as they say."

In early December Hitler sent to the Italian front a fanatical Prussian colonel named Sep Seigl, unusual in that he combined a heritage of Prussian tradition and a loyalty to Naziism. Hitler told him simply, "Destroy the Japanese." And when he studied his maps he decided, "I shall do it at Monte Cassino." Colonel Seigl was a bullet-headed young man of thirty-seven whose promotion had been speeded because of his dedication to Hitler, and on three different battlefronts he had proved his capacities. At Monte Cassino he was determined to repeat his earlier performances. The Japanese would be humiliated.

So as December waned and as the Two-Two-Two slogged steadfastly up the leg of Italy toward Rome, they picked up many signs that their critical battle was going to be engaged somewhere near the old monastery of Monte Cassino, and belts tightened as they approached it. At the same time, from the north Colonel Sep Seigl was moving down to Cassino some of the ablest German units in Italy, but he did not intend to engage the Japanese on the slopes of the mountain. His troops were not permitted to construct their forward positions on that formidable pile of rock; they were kept down below along the banks of the Rapido River that here ran in a north-south direction, with the Japanese approaching from the east and the Germans dug in along the west. Surveying the German might he now had lined up along the Rapido, Colonel Seigl said, "We'll stop them at the river."

On January 22, 1944, Colonel Mark Whipple halted his Japanese troops along a line one mile east of the Rapido and told them, "Our orders are clear and simple. Cross the river . . . so that troops behind us can assault that pile of rocks up there. The Germans claim a rabbit can't get across the approaches without being shot at from six angles. But we're going across."

He dispatched a scouting party consisting of Sergeant Goro Sakagawa, his brother Tadao, who was good at sketching, and four riflemen, and at dusk on the twenty-second of January they crawled out of their hiding places and started on their bellies across the most difficult single battle terrain the Americans were to face in World War II. With meticulous care, Tadao Sakagawa drew maps of the route. Two hundred yards west of their present positions the Two-Two-Two would come upon an irrigation ditch three feet wide and four feet deep. As they crawled out of it, they would be facing German machine guns and a marsh some thirty yards wide, beyond which lay another ditch. Thirty yards beyond hid a third ditch, twice as deep, twice as wide. As the men climbed out of this one, they would face a solid wall of machine-gun fire.

When they got this far in the darkness Goro Sakagawa licked his dry lips and asked his men, "What's that ahead?"

"Looks like a stone wall."

"Jesus," Goro whispered. "You can't expect our boys to negotiate those three ditches and then climb a wall. How high is it?"

"Looks about twelve feet high."

"This is impossible," Goro replied. "You fellows, split up. You go that way, we'll go this. Let's see if there's a break in the wall."

In the darkness they found none, only a stout, murderous stone wall, twelve feet high and with a jagged top. When they reassembled, Goro said in a rasping whisper, "Christ, how can anybody get over that damned thing? With machine guns everywhere. Sssssh."

There was a sudden chatter of German guns, but the men firing them must have heard a sound in some other direction, for the firing did not come close to Goro and his men. "Well," he said when it ceased, "over we go."

Patiently and with skill, in the darkness of night, the six Japanese boys helped one another over the terrifying wall, and from it they dropped into the eastern half of the dry river bed of the Rapido. It was about seventy-five feet across, about fifteen feet deep, and every spot of its entire cross section was monitored by German machine guns. On their bellies, the six soldiers crept across the dry river and trusted that no searchlights would be turned on. In the cold night they were perspiring with fear.

But when they got to the other side of the Rapido they discovered what fear really was, for both machine guns and searchlights opened up, but the young Japanese managed to secrete themselves in crevices at the foot of the western bank; but what terrified them was not the imperative staccato of the guns or the probing fingers of light, but the monstrous nature of the river's west bank. It rose fairly straight up from the river bed, sixteen feet high, and was topped by a stout double fence of barbed wire which could be expected to contain mines at two-foot intervals.

"Are you getting this on paper?" Goro whispered to Tadao. "Cause when they see this, no general living would dare send men across this river." A passing light illuminated the wild and terrible tangles of barbed wire and then passed on. "You got it?" Goro asked. "Good. Hoist me up. I'm going through it."

Tadao grabbed his older brother's hand. "I have enough maps," he cautioned.

"Somebody's got to see what's over there."

His men hoisted him onto the top of the west bank of the river, where he spent fifteen perilous minutes picking his way inch by inch through the tangled barbed wire. He knew that at any moment he might explode a mine and not only kill himself but doom his five companions as well. He was no longer sweating. He was no longer afraid. He had passed into some extraordinary state known only by soldiers at night or in the heat of unbearable battle. He was a crop-headed, tense-bellied Japanese boy from Kakaako in Honolulu, and the courage he was displaying in those fateful minutes no one in Hawaii would have believed.

He penetrated the wire, leaving on the barbs tiny shreds of cloth which would guide him safely back, and in the darkness he found himself on the eastern edge of a dusty road that led past the foot of Monte Cassino. Hiding himself in the ditch that ran alongside the road, he breathed deeply, trying to become a man again and not a nerveless automaton, and as he lay there, face up, a searchlight played across the countryside, hunting for him perhaps, and it passed on and suddenly illuminated the terrain that rose above him, and although he had seen it from a distance and knew its proportions, he now cried with pain: "Oh, Jesus Christ, no!"

For above him rose an unassailable rocky height, far, far into the sky, and at its crest clung an ancient monastery, and from where he lay Goro realized that he and his men were expected to cross all that he had seen tonight, and that when they got to this road in which he now huddled, other fellows from Hawaii were expected to forge ahead and climb those overpowering rocks that hung above him. In the lonely darkness he shivered with fright; then, as men do at such times, he effectively blocked out of his mind the realization of what Monte Cassino was like. It was not an unscalable height. It was not mined and interlaced with machine guns. It was not protected by the Rapido River defenses, and a gang of Japanese boys were not required to assault it, with casualties that would have to mount toward the fifty-per-cent mark, or even the eighty. Goro Sakagawa, a tough-minded soldier, cleansed himself of this knowledge and crept back to his men, then back to his commanding officer.

"It'll be tough," he reported. "But it can be done."

As he spoke, Colonel Sep Seigl was reviewing the same terrain and he knew far more about it than Goro Sakagawa, for he had maps prepared by the famous Todt Labor Corps, which had built this ultimate defense of Rome. He could see that the first three ditches which the Japanese would have to cross were covered in every detail by mines and machine-gun fire, and he told his men, "I suppose scouting parties are out there right now, but if they miss the mines, they'll be lucky." He saw the plans for defending the river itself, which presented one of the most formidable obstacles any army could encounter, and whereas Goro a few minutes before had been guessing as to where the mines and machine guns were, Seigl knew, and he knew that even his own soldiers, the finest in the world, could not penetrate that defense. And west of the river, of course, lay the exposed road which could be cut to shreds with mortar fire, and beyond that the cliffs of Monte Cassino up which no troops could move. At midnight Colonel Seigl concluded: "They'll try, but they'll never make it. Here is where we bloody the nose of the traitor Japanese. Tomorrow we'll watch them wilt under fire."

January 24, 1944, began with a cold, clear midnight and it was greeted with a thundering barrage of American gunfire which illuminated the bleak river but which did not dislodge the Germans. For forty minutes the barrage continued, and a beginner at warfare might have taken heart, thinking: "No man can live through that." But the dark-skinned men of the Two-Two-Two knew better; they knew the Germans would be dug in and waiting.

At 0040 the barrage stopped and the whistles blew for advance. Goro clutched his brother by the arm and whispered, "This is the big one, kid. Take care of yourself." Progress to the first ditch was painful, for the Germans launched a counter-barrage and the first deaths at Monte Cassino occurred, but Goro and Tadao pushed stolidly ahead in the darkness, and when they had led their unit across the dangerous ditch and onto the edge of the marsh, they told their captain, "We'll take care of the mines," and they set out on their bellies, two brothers who could have been engaged in a tricky football play, and they crawled across the marsh, adroitly cutting the trip wires that would otherwise have detonated mines and killed their companions, and when they reached the second ditch Goro stood up in the night and yelled, "Mo bettah you come. All mines pau!" But as he sent the news his younger brother Tadao, one of the finest boys ever to graduate from Punahou, stepped upon a magnesium mine which exploded with a terrible light, blowing him into a thousand shreds of bone and flesh.

"Oh, Jesus!" Goro cried, burying his face in his hands. No action was required. None was possible. Tadao Sakagawa no longer existed in any conceivable form. Not even his shoes were recoverable, but where he had stood other Japanese boys swept over the marshy land and with battle cries leaped into the next ditch, and then into the next.

It took five hours of the most brutal fighting imaginable for the Japanese troops to reach the near bank of the Rapido, and when dawn broke, Colonel Sep Seigl was slightly disturbed. "They should not have been able to cross those fields. They seem rather capable, but now the fight begins."

Against the troops for which he had a special hatred he threw a wall of bombardment that was almost unbelievable, and to his relief, the advance was halted. No human being could have penetrated that first awful curtain of shrapnel which greeted the Two-Two-Two at the Rapido itself. "Well," Colonel Seigl sighed, "at least they're human. They can be stopped. Now to keep them pinned down. The Japanese cannot absorb casualties. Kill half of them, and the other half will run."

But here Colonel Seigl was wrong. Half of Goro Sakagawa had already been killed; he had loved his clever brother Tadao as only boys who have lived in the close intimacy of poverty and community rejection can love, and now Tadao was dead. Therefore, when the German shelling was at its most intense, Goro said to his captain, "Let's move across that river. I know how."

"We'll dig in," the captain countermanded.

But when Colonel Whipple arrived to inspect the battered condition of his men, Goro insisted that the river could be crossed, and Whipple said, "Go ahead and try." At this point one of the lieutenants from Baker Company, Goro's commanding officer, and a fine young officer from Kansas, said, "If my men go, I go."

"All right, Lieutenant Shelly," Whipple said. "We've got to cross the river."

So Lieutenant Shelly led forty men, with Sergeant Sakagawa as guide, down into the bed of the Rapido, at nine o'clock on a crystal-clear morning, and they came within six yards of crossing the river, when a titanic German concentration of fire killed half the unit, including Lieutenant Shelly. The twenty who were left began to panic, but Goro commanded sternly, "Up onto that bank and through that barbed wire."

It was a completely insane thing to attempt. The Rapido River did not propose to allow any troops, led by Goro Sakagawa or otherwise, to violate it that day, and when his stubborn muddy fingers reached the barbed-wire embankment, such a furious load of fire bore down upon him that he had to drop back into the river. Three more times he endeavored vainly to penetrate the barbed wire, and each time Colonel Seigl screamed at his men, "Kill him! Kill him! Don't let them get started!" But although tons of ammunition were discharged in the general direction of Sakagawa and his determined men, somehow they were not killed. Huddling in the protection of the far bank of the river, the gallant twenty waited for their companions to catch up with them, when all together they might have a chance of crashing the barbed wire.

But the firepower of the Germans was so intense that the Japanese boys who were still on the eastern bank could not possibly advance. At times the wall of shrapnel seemed almost solid and it would have been complete suicide to move a man into it. "We've got to hold where we are," Colonel Whipple regretfully ordered.

"What about those twenty out there in the river?"

"Who's in charge? Lieutenant Shelly?"

"He was killed. Sergeant Sakagawa."

"Goro?"

"Yes, sir."

"He'll get his men out," Whipple said confidently, and at dusk, after a day of hell, Goro Sakagawa did just that. He brought all of his twenty men back across the river, up the dangerous eastern bank, back through the minefields and safely to headquarters.

"Colonel wants to see you," a major said.

"We couldn't make it," Goro reported grimly.

"No man ever tried harder, Lieutenant Sakagawa."

Goro showed no surprise at his battlefield commission. He was past fear, past sorrow, and certainly past jubilation. But when the bars were pinned to his tunic by the colonel himself, the rugged sergeant broke into tears, and they splashed out of his dark eyes onto his leathery yellow-brown skin. "Tomorrow we'll cross the river," he swore.

"We'll certainly try," Colonel Whipple said.

On January 26 the Japanese troops did try, but once more Colonel Sep Seigl's able gunners turned them back with dreadful casualties. On January 27 the Japanese tried for the third time, and although Lieutenant Goro Sakagawa got his men onto the road on the other side of the river, they were hit with such pulverizing fire that after forty-five minutes they had to withdraw. That night an Associated Press man wrote one of the great dispatches of the war: "If tears could be transmitted by cable, and printed by linotype, this story would be splashed with tears, for I have at last seen what they call courage beyond the call of duty. I saw a bunch of bandy-legged Japanese kids from Hawaii cross the Rapido River, and hold the opposite bank for more than forty minutes. Then they retreated in utter defeat, driven back by the full might of the German army. Never in victory have I seen any troops in the world achieve a greater glory, and if hereafter any American ever questions the loyalty of our Japanese, I am not going to argue with him. I am going to kick his teeth in."

On January 28, Lieutenant Sakagawa tried for the fourth time to cross the Rapido, and for the fourth time Colonel Sep Seigl's men mowed the Japanese down. Of the 1,300 troops with which Colonel Whipple had started four days earlier, 779 were now casualties. Dead Japanese bodies lined the fatal river, and men with arms and legs torn off were being moved to the rear. At last it became apparent that the Germans had effectively stopped the advance of the hated Two-Two-Two. That night Colonel Seigl's intelligence reported: "Victory! The Japanese have been driven back. They're in retreat and seem to be leaving the line."

The report was partially correct. Lieutenant Goro Sakagawa's company, and the unit of which it was a part, was being withdrawn. The boys were willing to try again, but they no longer had enough men to maintain a cohesive company and they had to retreat to repair their wounds. As they passed back through a unit from Minnesota coming in to replace them, the Swedes, having heard of their tremendous effort, cheered them and saluted and one man from St. Paul yelled, "We hope we can do as good as you did."

"You will," a boy from Lahaina mumbled.

So the Germans stopped the Two-Two-Two . . . for a few hours, because in another part of the line other units from Hawaii were accumulating a mighty force, and on February 8 Colonel Sep Seigl's intelligence officer reported breathlessly, "The damned Japanese have crossed the river and are attacking the mountain itself!"

With a powerful surge the Japanese boys drove spearheads almost to the top of the mountain. They scaled heights that even their own officers believed impregnable, and they routed out more than two hundred separate machine-gun emplacements. Their heroism in this incredible drive was unsurpassed in World War II, and for a few breathless hours they caught a toehold on the summit of the mountain itself.

"Send us reinforcements!" they radioed frantically. "We've got them licked."

But reinforcements could not negotiate the cliffs, and one by one the Japanese victors were driven back from their dizzy pinnacles. As they stumbled down the steep flanks of Monte Cassino the Germans gunned them unmercifully, but at last the fragments of the force staggered back to camp and announced: "The Germans cannot be driven out." But one fact of triumph remained: the headquarters camp was now on the west bank of the Rapido. The river had been crossed. The way to Rome lay open.

It was in their bruising defeat at Monte Cassino that the Two-Two-Two became one of the most famous units of the war. "The Purple Heart Battalion" it was called, for it had suffered more casualties than any other similar-sized unit in the war. The Mo Bettahs won more honors, more decorations, more laudatory messages from the President and the generals than any other. But most of all they won throughout America a humble respect. Caucasians who fought alongside them reported back home: "They're better Americans than I am. I wouldn't have the guts to do what they do." And in Hawaii, those golden islands that the Japanese boys loved so deeply as they died in Italy, people no longer even discussed the tormenting old question: "Are the Japanese loyal?" Now men of other races wondered: "Would I be as brave?" So although the Prussian Nazi, Colonel Sep Seigl, did exactly what he had promised Hitler he would do—he crushed the Japanese at Monte Cassino—neither he nor Hitler accomplished what they had initially intended: for it was in defeat that the Japanese boys exhibited their greatest bravery and won the applause of the world.

Therefore it is strange to report that it was not at Monte Cassino that the Two-Two-Two won its greatest laurels. This happened by accident, in a remote corner of France.

After the Triple Two's had retired to a rear area in Italy, there to lick their considerable wounds and to re-form with fresh replacements from the States—including First Lieutenant Goro Sakagawa's younger brothers Minoru and Shigeo—the Mo Bettah Battalion was shipped out of Italy and into Southern France, where it was allowed to march in a leisurely manner up the Rhone Valley. It met little German opposition, nor was it intended to, for the generals felt that after the heroic performance at Monte Cassino the Japanese boys merited something of a respite, and for once things went as planned. Then, accompanied by a Texas outfit that had also built a name for itself in aggressive fighting, the Two-Two-Two's swung away from the Rhone and entered upon routine mopping-up exercises in the Vosges Mountains, where the easternmost part of France touched the southernmost part of Germany.

The Triple Two's and the Texans moved forward with calculating efficiency until they had the Germans in what appeared to be a final rout. Lieutenant Sakagawa kept urging his men to rip the straggling German units with one effective spur: "Remember what they did to us at Cassino." Hundreds of bewildered Germans surrendered to him, asking pitifully, "Have the Japanese finally turned against us too? Like the Italians?" To such questions Goro replied without emotion: "We're Americans. Move through and back." But if he kept his hard face a mask of indifference, secretly he trembled with joy whenever he accepted the surrender of units from Hitler's master race.

It was understandable, therefore, that Goro Sakagawa, like his superiors, interpreted the Vosges campaign as the beginning of the end for Hitler. But this was a sad miscalculation, for if the young, untrained Nazi troops sometimes faltered, their clever Prussian generals did not. They were now charged with defending the German homeland, and from his epic success at Monte Cassino, Colonel Sep Seigl, now General Seigl, had arrived at the Vosges to organize resistance at that natural bastion. Therefore, if he allowed his rag-tag troops to surrender in panic to the Triple Two's, it was for a reason; and in late October of 1944 this reason became apparent, for on the twenty-fourth of that month General Seigl's troops appeared to collapse in a general rout, retreating helter-skelter through the difficult Vosges terrain; and in so doing they enticed the battle-hungry Texans to rush after them, moving far ahead of American tanks and into the neatest trap of the war.

General Seigl announced the springing of his trap with a gigantic barrage of fire that sealed the bewildered Texans into a pocket of mountains. "We will shoot them off one by one," Seigl ordered, moving his troops forward. "We'll show the Americans what it means to invade German soil." And he swung his prearranged guns into position and began pumping high explosives at the Texan camp. There without food or water or adequate ammunition, the gallant Texans dug in and watched the rim of fire creep constantly closer.

At this point an American journalist coined the phrase the "Lost Battalion," and in Texas radios were kept tuned around the clock. Whole villages listened to agonizing details as the sons of that proud state prepared to die as bravely as their circumstances would permit. A sob echoed across the prairies, and Texans began to shout, "Get our boys out of there! For Christsake, do something!"

Thus what had been intended as respite for the Triple Two suddenly became the dramatic high point of the war. A personal messenger from the Senate warned the Pentagon: "Get those Texans out of there or else." The Pentagon radioed SHAEF: "Effect rescue immediately. Top priority white." SHAEF advised headquarters in Paris, and they wirelessed General McLarney, at the edge of the Vosges. It was he who told Colonel Mark Whipple, "You will penetrate the German ring of firepower and rescue those men from Texas." Lest there be any misunderstanding, another general flew in from Paris, red-faced and bitter, and he said, "We're going to be crucified if we let those boys die. Get them, goddamn it, get them."

Colonel Whipple summoned Lieutenant Goro Sakagawa and said, "You've got to go up that ridge, Goro. You mustn't come back without them."

"We'll bring 'em out," Goro replied.

As he was about to depart, Mark Whipple took his hand and shook it with that quiet passion that soldiers know on the eve of battle. "This is the end of our road, Goro. The President himself has ordered this one. Win this time, and you win your war."

It was a murderous, hellish mission. A heavy fog enveloped the freezing Vosges Mountains, and no man could look ahead more than fifteen feet. As Baker Company filed into the pre-dawn gloom, each Japanese had to hold onto the field pack of the boy in front, for only in this manner could the unit be kept together. From the big, moss-covered trees of the forest, German snipers cut down one Hawaiian boy after another, until occasionally some Japanese in despairing frustration would stand stubbornly with his feet apart, firing madly into the meaningless fog. At other times German machine guns stuttered murderously from a distance of twenty feet. But Goro became aware of one thing: firepower that an hour before had been pouring in upon the doomed Texans was now diverted.

To rescue the Lost Battalion, the Two-Two-Two had to march only one mile, but it was the worst mile in the world, and to negotiate it was going to require four brutal days without adequate water or food or support. The casualties suffered by the Japanese were staggering, and Goro sensed that if he brought his two younger brothers through this assault, it would be a miracle. He therefore cautioned them: "Kids, keep close to the trees. When we move from one to the other, run like hell across the open space. And when you hit your tree, whirl about instantly to shoot any Germans that might have infiltrated behind you."

At the end of the first day the Triple Twos had gained only nine hundred feet, and within the circle of steel wounded Texans were beginning to die from gangrene. Next morning the Japanese boys pushed on, a yard at a time, lost in cold fog, great mossy trees and pinnacles of rock. Almost every foot of the way provided General Seigl's riflemen with ideal cover, and they used it to advantage. With methodical care, they fired only when some Japanese ran directly into their guns, and they killed the Triple Two's with deadly accuracy. On that cold, rainy second day the Japanese troops gained six hundred feet, and nearly a hundred of the trapped Texans died from wounds and fresh barrages.

A curious factor of the battle was that all the world could watch. It was known that the Texans were trapped; it was known that the Two-Two-Two's were headed toward their rescue, and the deadly game fascinated the press. A Minnesota corporal who had fought with the Triple Two's in Italy told a newspaperman, "If anybody can get 'em, the slant-eyes will." In Honolulu newspapers that phrase was killed, but the entire community, sensing the awful odds against which their sons were fighting, prayed.

On the third day of this insane attempt to force the ring of fire, Baker Company was astonished to see trudging up the hill they had just traversed the familiar figure of Colonel Mark Whipple. The men well knew the basic rule of war: "Lieutenants lead platoons against the enemy. Captains stay back and encourage the entire company. Majors and light colonels move between headquarters and the companies. But chicken colonels stay put." Yet here was Colonel Whipple, a West Point chicken colonel, breaking the rule and moving into the front lines. Instinctively the Japanese boys saluted as he passed. When he reached Goro he said simply, "We're going to march up that ridge and rescue the Texans today."

This was a suicidal approach and no one knew it better than Whipple, but it had been commanded by headquarters. "I can't order my boys into another Cassino," he had protested. "This is worse than Cassino," headquarters had admitted, "but it's got to be done." Whipple had saluted and said, "Then I must lead the boys myself." And there he was.

His inspiration gave the Japanese the final burst of courage they needed. With terrifying intensity of spirit the Two-Two-Two moved up the ridge. The fighting was murderous, with Germans firing point-blank at the rescuers. Barrages from hidden guns, planted weeks before at specific spots by General Seigl, cut down the Triple Two's with fearful effect, and at one faltering point Goro thought: "Why should we have to penetrate such firepower? We're losing more than we're trying to save."

As if he sensed that some such question might be tormenting his troops and halting their flow of courage, Colonel Whipple moved among them, calling, "Sometimes you do things for a gesture. This is the ultimate gesture. They're waiting for us, over that ridge." But the men of the Triple Two could not banish the ugly thought that haunted them: "Texans are important and have to be saved. Japanese are expendable." But no one spoke these words, for all knew that the Texas fighters didn't have to prove anything; the Japanese did.

When night fell on the twenty-ninth of October the Japanese troops were still four hundred yards short of their goal. They slept standing up, or leaning against frozen trees. There was no water, no food, no warmth. Outpost sentries, when relieved, muttered, "I might as well stay here with you." There was no bed. Men ached and those with minor wounds felt the blood throbbing in their veins. Hundreds were already dead.

At dawn a German sniper, hidden with Teutonic thoroughness, fired into the grim encampment and killed Private Minoru Sakagawa. For some minutes his brother Goro was not aware of what had happened, but then young Shigeo cried, "Jesus! They killed Minoru!"

Goro, hearing his brother's agonized cry, ran up and saw Minoru dead upon the frozen ground. This was too much to bear, and he began to lose his reason. "Achhhh!" he cried with a great rasping noise in his throat. Two of his brothers had now died while under his command, and the rest of his troops seemed doomed. His right hand began trembling while his voice continued to cry a meaningless "Achhhh."

Colonel Whipple, who knew what was happening, rushed up and clouted the young lieutenant brutally across the face. "Not now, Goro!" he commanded, using a strange phrase: *Not now,* as if later it would be permissible to go out of one's mind, as if at some later time all men might do so, including Whipple himself.

Goro fell back and his hand stopped trembling. Staring in dull panic at his colonel, he tried vainly to focus on the problems at hand, but failed. He could see only his brother, fallen on the pine needles of the Vosges. Then his cold reason returned, and he drew his revolver. Grabbing Shigeo by the shoulder he said, "You walk here." Then to his men he roared, in Japanese, "We won't stop!" And with appalling force he and his team marched in among the great trees.

It was a desperate, horrible hand-to-hand fight up the last thousand feet of the ridge. Shigeo, following the almost paralyzed fury of his brother, exhibited a courage he did not know he had. He moved directly onto German positions and grenaded them to shreds. He ducked behind trees like a veteran, and when the last roadblock stood ahead, ominous and spewing death, it was mild-mannered Shigeo, the quiet one of the Sakagawa boys—though there were now only two left—who with demonic craftiness went against it, drew its fire so that he could spot its composition, and then leaped inside with grenades and a

Tommy gun. He killed eleven Germans, and when his companions moved past him to the ultimate rescue of the Texans he leaned out of the Nazi position and cheered like a schoolboy.

"You're a lieutenant!" Colonel Whipple snapped as he went forward to join the Texans, and a boy from Maui looked at Shig and said in pidgin, "Jeez, krauts all pau!"

In rough formation, with Lieutenant Goro Sakagawa at their head, the Japanese boys marched in to greet the Texans, and a tall Major Burns from Houston stumbled forward, his ankle in bad shape, and tried to salute, but the emotion of the moment was too great. He was famished and burning with thirst, and before he got to Goro he fell in the dust. Then he rose to his knees and said from that position, "Thank God. You fellows from the Jap outfit?"

"Japanese," Goro replied evenly. He stooped to help the Texan to his feet and saw that the man was at least a foot taller than he was. All the Texans, starving and parched though they were, were enormous men, and it seemed indecent that a bunch of runty little rice-eaters should have rescued them.

Against his will, for Major Burns was a very brave man and had kept his troops alive mainly through the force of his extraordinary character, the tall Texan began to weep. Then he was ashamed of himself, bit his lip till it nearly bled and asked, "Could my men have some water?" He turned to his troops and shouted, "Give these Japs a big welcome."

Goro grabbed the major as if they were two toughs back in Kakaako and said in sudden, surging anger, "Don't you call us Japs!"

"Goro!" Colonel Whipple shouted.

"What, sir?" He didn't remember what he had just said.

"All right," Whipple snapped. "Let's start down the hill."

The Japanese troops formed two lines at the entrance to the pocket in which the Texans had been trapped, and as the giant men passed to freedom between the pairs of stubby Triple Two's some of the Texans began to laugh, and soon the pocket was choked with merriment, in which big Texans began to embrace their rescuers and kiss them and jump them up into the air. "You little guys got guts," a huge fellow from Abilene shouted. "I thought we was done for."

Lieutenant Sakagawa did not join the celebration. He was watching his men, and estimated dully that of the original 1,200 Japanese boys that had set out to storm the ridge, fully two-thirds were now either dead or severely wounded. This terrible toll, including his brother Minoru, was almost more than he could tolerate, and he began mumbling, "Why did we have to lose so many little guys to save so few big ones?" It had cost 800 Japanese to rescue 341 Texans. Then his mind began to harden and to come back under control, and to discipline it he began checking off Baker Company, and he found that of the 183 men who had waded ashore with him at Salerno in September of 1943 only seven had managed to stick with the outfit through October of 1944. The rest—all 176 of them—were either dead or wounded.

Now Shigeo rushed up to advise his brother that Colonel Whipple had promoted him on the field of battle, a soldier's sweetest triumph, and the brilliant-eyed youth shouted, "Goro, I guess this time we really showed the world!" But Goro, counting the dead, wondered: "How much more do we have to prove?" And from the manner in which his mind jerked from one image to the next, he realized that he was close to mental collapse, but he was saved by a curious experience. From among the Texans a hysterical medic, his mind deranged by three shells that had exploded while he was trying to cut off a shattered leg, began moving from one Japanese to another, mumbling, "Greater love hath no man than this, that he lay down his life for his brother."

Major Burns heard the speech and yelled, "There goes that goddamned odd-ball again. Please, please, shut him up!"

But the medic had reached Goro, to whom he mumbled, "Lieutenant, indeed it is true. No man hath greater love than this, that he would march up such a fucking ridge to save a complete crock of shit like Major Burns." In his wildness the medic turned to face Burns, screaming hysterically, "I hate you! I hate you! You led us into this death trap, you crazy, crazy beast!"

Almost sadly, Major Burns, pivoting on his good leg, swung on the medic and knocked him out. "He was more trouble than the Germans," he apologized. "Somebody haul the poor bastard out."

Before any of the Texans could get to the capsized medic, Goro had compassionately pulled the unconscious fellow into his arms. A gigantic Texan came along to help, and the odd trio started down the bloody ridge, but when they had returned halfway to safety, General Seigl's last furious barrage enveloped them, and two shells bracketed Colonel Mark Whipple, killing him instantly. Goro, who witnessed the death, dropped his hold on the medic and started toward the man who had done so much for the Japanese, but at long last his nervous system gave way.

The awful "Achhhh" filled his throat, and his hands began trembling. His head jerked furiously as if he were an epileptic and his eyes went vacant like those of an imbecile. "Achhhh! Achhhh!" he began to shout hysterically, and he started falling to his right, but caught himself by clutching air. His voice cleared and he began screaming, "Don't you call me a Jap! Goddamn you big blond Texans, don't you call me a yellow-belly!"

In wild fury he began lashing out at his tormentors, stupidly, ineffectively. He kept shouting irrelevant threats at the Texans whom he had just saved, and was ready to fight even the biggest. One man from Dallas gently held him off as an adult would a child, and it was pathetic to see the stocky Japanese swinging wildly at the air, unable to reach his giant adversary. Finally he returned to the horrible achhhh sound, and at this point his brother Shigeo ran up to take command. He pinioned Goro's arms, and when the latter seemed about to break out once more, Shigeo smashed a hard right-cut to the jaw and slowed him down.

Now Goro began to whimper like a child, and two men from his outfit had the decency to cover him with a blanket, so that his disintegration would not be visible to his own troops, and in this condition they patiently led him, shivering and shuddering, out of the Vosges Mountains where the Texans had been trapped.

Toward the foothills they passed through a guard unit from their own battalion, and a young lieutenant from Able Company, a haole boy from Princeton asked, "Who you got under the blanket?" and Shigeo replied, "Lieutenant Sakagawa."

"Was he the one who got through to the Texans?"

"Who else?" Shig replied, and as the cortege of wounded and near-mad and starved and war-torn passed, the Princeton man looked at Goro Sakagawa's mechanically shuffling feet and muttered, "There goes an American."

VI

The Golden Men

IN 1946, when Nyuk Tsin was ninety-nine years old, a group of sociologists in Hawaii were perfecting a concept whose vague outlines had occupied them for some years, and quietly among themselves they suggested that in Hawaii a new type of man was being developed. He was a man influenced by both the west and the east, a man at home in either the business councils of New York or the philosophical retreats of Kyoto, a man wholly modern and American yet in tune with the ancient and the Oriental. The name they invented for him was the Golden Man.

At first I erroneously thought that both the concept and the name were derived from the fact that when races intermingled sexually, the result was apt to be a man neither all white nor all brown nor all yellow, but somewhere in between; and I thought that the Golden Man concept referred to the coloring of the new man—a blend of Chinese, Polynesian and Caucasian, for at this time Japanese rarely intermarried—and I went about the streets of Hawaii looking for the golden man of whom the sociologists spoke.

But in time I realized that this bright, hopeful man of the future, this unique contribution of Hawaii to the rest of the world, did not depend for his genesis upon racial intermarriage at all. He was a product of the mind. His was a way of thought, and not of birth, and one day I discovered, with some joy I may add, that for several years I had known the archetypes of the Golden Man, and if the reader has followed my story so far, he also knows three of them well and is about to meet the fourth, and it is interesting that none of these, in a direct sense, owed his golden quality to racial intermixtures. His awareness of the future and his rare ability to stand at the conflux of the world he owed to his understanding of the movements around him. I have known a good many golden men in the secondary, or unimportant, sense: fine Chinese-Hawaiians, excellent Portuguese-Chinese and able Caucasian-Hawaiians; but most of them had little concept of what was happening either in Hawaii or in the world. But the four men of whom I now wish to speak did know, and it is in reference to their knowledge that I wish to end my story of Hawaii, for they are indeed the Golden Men.

In 1946, when the war had ended and Hawaii was about to explode belatedly into the twentieth century, Hoxworth Hale was forty-eight years old; and one morning, when the trade winds had died away and the weather was unbearably sticky, he happened to look into his mirror while shaving, and the thought came to him: "This year I am as good a man as I shall ever be in this life. I have most of my teeth, a good deal of my hair, I'm not too much overweight, and my eyes are good enough to see distances without glasses, though close up I have a little trouble, and I suppose I'll have to see an oculist. I can still concentrate on a problem, and I derive pleasure from control of business. I like to go to work, even on mornings like this." He pummeled his midriff to start perspiration before entering the shower, and as the hot, muggy day closed in upon him he was forced to inspect the two areas in which he was no longer so good a man as he once had been.

First, there was the gnawing, never-ending pain that started when his son Bromley was shot down during the great fire of Tokyo in 1945, when the air corps practically destroyed the city. More than 70,000 Japanese had died in the great raids, and a city too, so that in one sense Bromley's death had contributed positive results, and after his raids victory for our side was assured. But Bromley Hale was a special young man. Everyone said so, and his departure left a gap both in the Hale family and in Hawaii that would never be filled, for in his last letters home, when capricious death had become so routine in his B-29 squadron as to depress all the fliers, he had spoken intimately of what he hoped to accomplish when the war ended, as soon it must.

He had written, from a hut on Iwo Jima: "We had to ditch our monstrous plane in the waters near here, and by the grace of God we were all saved, but in the going down, as I worked with the wheel I was not so much concerned about a perfect water landing as I was with my determination to do what years ago I had sworn to do while a senior at Punahou. I am determined to write a novel about—and this may stagger you, but bear with me—Aunt Lucinda Whipple. I shall have her sitting in the late afternoons in her house in Nuuanu Valley, and each day as the afternoon rains sweep down from the Pali and the white mildew grows on all things, she entertains the straggling members of our family. It has always seemed to me that Aunt Lucinda was everybody's aunt, and everybody comes to her and listens to her monotonous chatter about the old days, and nothing I write will make any sense at all—only an old woman's ceaseless vanity—until it begins to weave a spell, the kind of spell in which you and I have always lived. I shall show Aunt Lucinda exactly as she is, religious, family-proud, unseeing, unknowing, garrulous and unbelievably kind. She has become to me a web, a fatal emanation, an encroaching dream, and as our plane struck the water, I was listening not to my co-pilot, who was frantic as hell, but to dear old Aunt Lucinda. How she hated airplanes and fast automobiles and Japanese. As a matter of fact, if you took time to analyze it carefully, I guess she hated everybody but the Whipples, and the Janderses, and the Hales, and the Hewletts, and the Hoxworths. But even they gave her a lot of trouble, for she always took great pains to explain to visitors that she came from the branch of the Whipple family that had never had even a drop of Hawaiian blood, and she kept segregated in her mind those of her great family of whom this could not be said. She was suspicious of you and me, because we were not pure English stock; and of course all the Hoxworths and half the Hewletts were contaminated, and often when I spoke with her she would hesitate, and I knew she was thinking: 'I'd better not tell him that, because after all, he is one of the contaminated.'

"And from Aunt Lucinda's endless vagaries I want to construct an image of all Hawaii and the peoples who came to build it. I want to deal with the first volcano and the last sugar strike. You may not like my novel, but it will be accurate, and I think that counts for something. It is strange, I have been writing about Aunt Lucinda as if she were dead, but she is living and it may be I who shall be dead."

This dreadful hurt never left Hoxworth Hale's heart, and he started listening to Aunt Lucinda's meanderings, and he picked up the thoughts that his son had laid down: "We live in a web. Sugar cane, Hawaiian ghosts, pineapple, ships, streetcar lines, Japanese labor leaders, Aunt Lucinda's memories." The web became most tenuous, and at the same time most cruelly oppressive, when it involved the upstairs rooms where several of the great families kept the delicate women whose minds had begun to wander past even the accepted norm, and in one such room Hoxworth's own wife passed her days. In the 1920's, at Punahou, Malama Janders, as she was then, had been a laughing, poetic young lady, interested in music and boys, but as the years passed, and especially since the 1940's, her mind lost its focus and she preferred not to try understanding what had happened to her son Bromley or what her dashing daughter Noelani was doing. Her only joy came when someone drove her up Nuuanu Valley to Aunt Lucinda's, and there the two women would sit in the rainy afternoons talking of things that never quite got into sequence . . . and neither cared.

For generations the missionaries had railed against Hawaiians for having allowed brothers to marry sisters, and on no aspect of Hawaiian life was New England moral judgment sterner than on this. "It puts the Hawaiian outside the pale of civilized society," Lucinda Whipple's ancestors had stormed, particularly her great-grandfather Abner Hale, and yet the same curse had now overtaken her own great interlocking family. Whipples married Janderses, and Janderses married Hewletts, and if full brothers and sisters did not physically wed, intellectually and emotionally they did, so that a girl named Jerusha Hewlett Hoxworth was practically indistinguishable either in genes or ideas from a Malama Janders Hale, and each stayed mostly in an upstairs room.

In 1946, therefore, except for the death of his son, and the slow decline of his adored wife, Hoxworth Hale was truly as good a man as he would ever be, but those two bereavements oppressed him and prevented his enjoyment of the last powerful flowering of his talents. He therefore turned his whole attention to the government of the Hoxworth & Hale empire, and as the critical year started he relied more and more upon two stalwart resolves: "I will not give labor an inch, not another inch, especially when it's led by Japanese who don't really understand American ways. And we have got to keep Hawaii as it is. I will not have mainland firms like Gregory's elbowing their way in here and disrupting our Hawaiian economy." Behind him, to back up these two mighty resolves, he had the entire resources of H & H, totaling some $260,000,000 and all the managerial strength of J & W, now worth more than $185,000,000. Lesser outfits like Hewlett and Son had to string along, for all saw in Hoxworth Hale the cool and able man, one above the passions of the moment, who could be depended upon to preserve their way of life.

Only in his understanding of what was happening should Hoxworth Hale be considered a Golden Man. Racially he was mostly haole. Emotionally he was all haole, and he thought of himself in that way. Actually, of course, he was one-sixteenth Hawaiian, inherited through the Alii Nui Noelani, who was his great-great-grandmother. He was also part-Arabian, for one of his European ancestors had married during the Crusades, part-African through an earlier Roman ancestor, part-Central Asian from an Austrian woman who had married a Hungarian in 1603, and part-American Indian through a cute trick that an early Hale's wife had pulled on him in remote Massachusetts. But he was known as pure haole, whatever that means.

In 1946 Hong Kong Kee was five years older than Hoxworth Hale, which made him exactly fifty-three, whereas his grandmother Nyuk Tsin was ninety-nine. This was not a particularly good year for Hong Kong, because in following his grandmother's urgent advice—"Buy every piece of land that frightened haoles want to sell"—he had somewhat overextended himself and frankly did not know where he was going to find tax money to protect the large parcels of land on which he was sitting. Real estate had not been doing well; the anticipated boom in tourists had not yet materialized; and there was a prospect of long strikes in both sugar and pineapple. He had seven children in school, five in mainland colleges and two at Punahou, and for a while he considered abruptly cutting off their allowances and telling the boys to get to work and help pay taxes, but Nyuk Tsin would not hear of this. Her counsel was simple: "Every child must have the very best education possible. Every piece of land must be held as long as possible. If this means no automobiles and no expensive food, good! We won't ride and we won't eat!" The Kee hui was therefore on very short rations, and Hong Kong sent a form letter to all the Kees studying on the mainland—his own and others: "I will be able to pay only your tuition and books. If you are running an automobile, sell it and go to work. If you are faced by the prospect of spending two or even three more years in college under this plan, spend it, but for the time being there can be no more money from Hawaii!" The decision that hurt him most involved his youngest daughter, Judy. "You have to cut out private singing lessons," he told her, and it was sad to see her obey.

And then, when things were already difficult, Hong Kong surreptitiously heard that a well-known firm of mainland private detectives was investigating him. He picked up a rumor of this from one of the Ching clan who had been asked a good many questions about real-estate deals, and the interrogation had made no sense until a few days later when Lew Ching suddenly thought: "My God! Every one of those deals involved Hong Kong Kee!" And he felt obligated to lay this circumstantial evidence before his friend.

Hong Kong's first reaction was, "The income tax people are after me!" But reflection assured him that this was ridiculous, for certainly the government never used private detective agencies when they had such good ones of their own. This conclusion, however, left him more bewildered than ever, and gradually he came to suspect that The Fort had deduced that he might be overextended and was collecting evidence which would enable them to squeeze him out, once and for all. He judged that the mastermind was probably Hoxworth Hale.

His first substantial bit of evidence came, curiously, not from the Chinese, who were adroit in piecing together fragments of puzzles, but from his friend Kamejiro Sakagawa, whom he had helped establish in the supermarket business. Squat little Kamejiro bustled in one afternoon to announce bluntly: "Hong Kong, you bettah watch out, I t'ink you in big trouble. Dick from da mainland come to dis rock, ast me about you, how I git my land. Bimeby latah he go into da building H & H."

"This detective, he has no reason to bother you, Kamejiro," Hong Kong assured him. "Our deal is perfectly good."

"Whassamatta, dey ketch you from taxes?"

"Mine are okay. How about yours?"

"Mine okay too," Kamejiro assured him.

"Then don't you worry, Kamejiro. Let me worry. This has to do only with me."

"You in special trouble?" the Japanese asked.

"Everybody's always in trouble," Hong Kong assured him.

But what precise trouble he himself was in, Hong Kong could not discover. In succeeding days he caught various reports of the detectives and their work; all aspects of his varied business life were under surveillance. He never spotted any of the detectives himself, and then suddenly they vanished, and he heard no more about them. All he knew was: "Somebody knows almost as much about my business as I do. And they're reporting to Hoxworth Hale." He did not sleep easily.

In another sense, these were exciting times, for unless everything that Hong Kong and his grandmother had concluded from their studies was false, Hawaii had to be on the verge of startling expansion. Airplanes, no longer required for warfare, were going to ferry thousands of tourists to Hawaii, and many new hotels would be required. On the day that the boom started, the builders would have to come to Hong Kong, for he had the land, and he felt like a superb runner on the eve of an Olympics which would test him against athletes whom he had not previously encountered: he was a good runner, he was in tense condition, and he was willing to trust the morrow's luck. Even so, he took the precaution of discussing the detective mystery with his grandmother, and she pointed out to Hong Kong: "These are the years when we must sit tight. Wait, wait. That's always very difficult to do. Any fool can engage in action, but only the wise man can wait. It seems to me that if someone is spending so much money to investigate you, either he fears you very much, which is good, or he is weighing the prospects of joining you, which could be better. Therefore what you must do is wait, wait. Let him make the first move. If he is going to fight you, each day that passes makes you stronger. If he is going to join you, each day that you survive makes the cost to him a little greater. Wait."

So through most of 1946 Hong Kong waited, but without the confidence his grandmother commanded. Each day's mail tortured him, for he would sit staring at the long envelopes, wondering what bad news they brought; and he dreaded cables. But as he waited, he gathered strength, and as the year ended and his mind grew clearer and his financial position stronger, he began to resemble the Golden Man of whom the sociologists had spoken.

Hong Kong thought of himself as pure Chinese, for his branch of the family had married only Hakka girls, and whereas there were a good many Kees with Hawaiian and Portuguese and Filipino blood, he had none, a fact of which he was quietly proud. Of course, from past adventures of the Kee hui Hong Kong's ancestors had picked up a good deal of Mongolian blood, and Manchurian, and Tartar, plus a little Japanese during the wars of the early 1600's, plus some Korean via an ancestor who had traveled in that peninsula in 814, augmented by a good deal of nondescript inheritance from tribes who had wandered about southern China from the year 4000 B.C. on, but nevertheless he thought of himself as pure Chinese, whatever that means.

In 1946 young Shigeo Sakagawa was twenty-three years old, and now a full captain in the United States army. He was five feet six inches tall and weighed a lean 152 pounds. He did not wear glasses and was considerably better co-ordinated than his stocky and somewhat awkward peasant father. He had a handsome face with strong, clear complexion and very good teeth, but his most conspicuous characteristic was a quick intellect which had marked him in whatever military duties he had been required to perform. The three citations that accompanied his army medals spoke of courage beyond the call of duty, but they were really awards for extraordinary ability to anticipate what was about to happen.

In the memorable victory parade down Kapiolani Boulevard, Captain Shigeo Sakagawa marched in the third file, behind the flag bearers and the colonel. His feet, hardened from military life, strode over the asphalt briskly, while his shoulders, accustomed to heavy burdens, were pulled back. This brought his chin up, so that his slanted Japanese eyes were forced to look out upon the community in which they had not previously been welcome. But when he heard the thundering applause, and saw from the corner of his eye his bent mother and his stocky, honest little father, accepted at last, he felt that the struggle had been a good one. Tadao was dead in Italy, and Minoru the stalwart tackle was buried in France. Goro was absent in Japan helping direct the occupation, and the family would never be together again. The Sakagawas had paid a terrible price to prove their loyalty, but it had been worth it. When the marchers were well past the spot where the elder Sakagawas and other Japanese were weeping with joy, the parade reached the old Iolani Palace, seat of Hawaii's government, and for the first time it looked to Shig Sakagawa like a building which a Japanese might enter, just like anyone else. "This is my town," he thought as he marched.

But when he reached home after the parade and saw the photographs of dead Tad and Minoru on the wall, he covered his face with his hands and muttered, "If we Japanese are at last free, it was you fellows who did it. Jesus, what a price!"

He was therefore embarrassed when his father, still fascinated by military life, fingered his medals and said in English, "Like I tell b'fore, dey got no soldiers mo bettah Japanese."

"I wasn't brave, Pop. I just happened to see what was going to happen."

"S'pose you saw, how come you not run away?" Kamejiro asked.

"I was Japanese, so I had to stay," Shig explained. "Too much at stake. I swallowed my fear and for this they gave me medals."

"All Japan is proud of you," Kamejiro said in Japanese.

"I'm glad the emperor feels that way," Shig laughed, "because I'm on my way to help him govern Japan."

Shigeo's mother screamed in Japanese, "You're not going away to war again, are you? Goro's already in Japan, and I pray every night."

"There's no war!" her son explained warmly, clutching her affectionately by the arm. "I'll be in no danger. Neither will Goro."

"No war?" Mrs. Sakagawa asked, startled. "Oh, Shigeo! Haven't you heard? Mr. Ishii says . . ."

"Mother, don't bother me with what that crazy Mr. Ishii dreams up."

Nevertheless, Mrs. Sakagawa summoned her daughter and Mr. Ishii, and after the wiry little labor leader had carefully inspected all the doors to be sure no haoles were spying, he pulled down the shades and whispered in Japanese, "What I told you last week is true, Kamejiro-san. Under no circumstances should you allow a second son to go to Japan. He will be killed, just like Goro. For everything we have heard is a lie. Japan is winning the war and may invade Hawaii at any moment."

Shigeo thought his brain had become unhinged, and he caught Reiko's hand, asking, "Sister, do you believe your husband's nonsense?"

"Don't call it nonsense!" Mr. Ishii stormed in Japanese. "You have been fed a great collection of lies. Japan is winning the war and is accumulating strength."

"Reiko!" her brother insisted. "Do you believe this nonsense?"

"You'll have to forgive my husband," the dutiful wife explained. "He hears such strange reports at the meetings . . ."

"What meetings?" Shigeo demanded.

That night Mr. Ishii and his sister showed him. They took him to a small building west of Nuuanu where a meeting was in progress, attended by elderly Japanese. A fanatical religious leader, recently out of a concentration camp, was shouting in Japanese, "What they tell you about Hiroshima is all lies. The city was not touched. Tokyo was not burned. Our troops are in Singapore and Australia. Japan is more powerful than ever before!"

The audience listened intently, and Shigeo saw his brother-in-law, Mr. Ishii, nodding profoundly. At this moment Shigeo unfortunately tugged at his sister's sleeve, and the speaker saw him. "Ah!" he shouted. "I see we have a spy in our midst. A dirty dog of the enemy. You, Mrs. Ishii? Is he trying to tell you that Japan lost the war? Don't you believe him! He has been bought by the Americans! I tell you, he is a liar and a spy. Japan won the war!"

Against his own intelligence, Shigeo had to admit that many of the audience not only believed this crazy religious maniac, but they wanted to believe. When the meeting ended, many of the old people smiled sadly at Shigeo, who had criminally fought against Japan, and they hoped that when the emperor's troops landed they would deal kindly with him, for he had probably been seduced into his traitorous action. Many boys in Hawaii had been so tricked.

In a daze Shigeo started homeward. He wanted no more to do with Mr. Ishii and the pathetic old fools, but when he had walked some distance, he changed his mind and caught a bus that carried him down into the heart of Honolulu, and after some speculation as to what he should do, he marched into the police station and asked to see one of the detectives. The haole knew him and congratulated him on his medals, but Shig laughed and said, "What I'm going to tell you, you may take them away."

"What's up?"

"You ever hear of the Katta Gumi Society? The Ever-Victorious Group?"

"You mean the Japan-Won screwballs? Yeah, we keep a fairly close watch on them."

"I just attended a meeting. Captain, I'm shook."

"The little hut back of the old mission school?"

"Yes."

"We check that regularly. Tony, did we have a man at the mission hut tonight?"

"We didn't bother tonight," the assistant replied.

"These people are out of their minds," Shig protested.

"It's pathetic," the detective agreed. "Poor old bastards, they were so sure Japan couldn't be licked that they believe whatever these agitators tell 'em. But they don't do any harm."

"Aren't you going to arrest them?" Shig asked.

"Hell no," the detective laughed. "We got six groups in Honolulu we check on regularly, and the Japan-Won's give us the least trouble. One group wants to murder Syngman Rhee. One wants to murder Chiang Kai-shek. One dupes old women out of all their money by predicting the end of the world on the first of each month. Last year we had one couple that prepared for the second coming of Christ on the first day of eleven succeeding months. They finally came to us and said that maybe something was wrong. So your crazy Japanese are only part of a pattern."

"But how can they believe . . . All the newspaper stories and newsreels? The men who were there?"

"Shig," the detective said, plopping his hands upright on the desk. "How can you believe for eleven successive months that Jesus Christ is coming down the Nuuanu Pali? You can be fooled once, I grant, but not eleven times."

When the time came for Shigeo to sail to his new job with General MacArthur in Japan, his mother wept and said, "If there is fighting when you get to Tokyo, don't get off the ship, Shigeo." Then, recalling more important matters, she told him, "Don't marry a northern girl, Shigeo. We don't want any zu-zu-ben in our family. And I'd be careful of Tokyo girls, too. They're expensive. Your father and I would be very unhappy if you married a Kyushu girl, because they don't fit in with Hiroshima people. And under no circumstances marry an Okinawan, or anyone who might be an Eta. What would be best would be for you to marry a Hiroshima girl. Such girls you can trust. But don't take one from Hiroshima City."

"I don't think Americans will be welcomed in Hiroshima," Shigeo said quietly.

"Why not?" his mother protested.

"After the bomb?" Shigeo asked.

"Shigeo!" his mother replied in amazement. "Nothing happened to Hiroshima! Mr. Ishii assured me . . ."

When Shig Sakagawa assembled with his Tokyo-bound outfit and marched through the streets of downtown Honolulu on his way to the transport that would take them to Yokohama, he was, without knowing it, a striking young man. He possessed a mind of steel, hardened in battle against both the Germans and the prejudices of his homeland. By personal will power he had triumphed against each adversary and had proved his courage as few men are required to do. No one recognized the fact that day, for then Shig was only twenty-three and had not yet acquired his lawyer's degree from Harvard, but he was the forward cutting edge of a revolution that was about to break over Hawaii. He was stern, incorruptible, physically hard and fearless. More important, so far as revolutions go, he was well organized and alert.

As he marched he passed, without either man's knowing it, Hoxworth Hale, who was walking up Bishop Street on his way to The Fort, and if in that moment Hale had had the foresight to stop the parade and to enlist Shig Sakagawa on his side, The Fort would surely have been able to preserve its prerogatives. Furthermore, if Hale, as an official of the Republican Party, had conscripted Shig and half a hundred other young Japanese like him, Republicanism in Hawaii would have been perpetually insured, for by their traditional and conservative nature the Japanese would have made ideal Republicans, and a combination of haole business acumen and Japanese industry would have constituted a strength that no adversary could have broken. But it was then totally impossible for Hoxworth Hale even to imagine such a union, and as he walked past the parade he had the ungracious thought: "If I hear any more about the brave Japanese boys who won the war for us, I'll vomit. Where's my son Bromley? Where's Harry Janders and Jimmy Whipple? They won the war, too, and they're dead." The crowd along Bishop Street cheered the Japanese boys, and the pregnant moment of history was lost. Hoxworth Hale went to The Fort and Shig Sakagawa went to Japan.

But if Hoxworth Hale failed to grasp the nettles of history, there was another who did, for as Hong Kong Kee walked down Bishop Street in the other direction he met Kamejiro Sakagawa proudly waving to his son, and Hong Kong asked, "Which one is your boy, Kamejiro?"

"Dat one ovah dere wid de medals," Kamejiro beamed.

Since most of the Japanese were wearing medals won in Europe, Hong Kong could not determine which one was Kamejiro's son. "Is he the one who has the red patch on his arm?" Hong Kong asked.

"Hai!" old Sakagawa agreed.

"I'd like to meet your boy," Hong Kong said, and when the troops broke ranks on the dock Kamejiro said to his son, "Dis Hong Kong Kee, berry good frien'. He give me da money fo' da stoah'."

With obvious gratitude, Captain Sakagawa thrust out his hand and said, "You had a lot of courage, Mr. Kee, to gamble that way on my father. Especially during the war."

Hong Kong was tempted to bask in glory, but prudence had taught him always to anticipate trouble and to quash it in advance, so he said forthrightly, "Probably you didn't hear, but during the war I was stupid enough to make a very bad speech against the Japanese. Later, I was ashamed of myself and tried to make up."

"I know," Shig said. "My sister wrote me about your speech. But war's war."

"Things are much better now," Hong Kong said. "What I wanted to see you about, Shigeo. When you come home you ought to go to college. Maybe law school. You do well, maybe I'll have a job for you."

"You have a lot of sons of your own, Hong Kong."

"None of them is Japanese," Hong Kong laughed.

"You want a Japanese?" Shig asked, astounded.

"Of course," Hong Kong grunted. "You boys are going to run the islands."

Shig grew extraordinarily attentive. Standing directly in front of Hong Kong's metallic eyes, he studied the Chinese carefully and asked, "Do you really think there'll be changes?"

"Fantastic," Hong Kong replied. "I'd like to have a smart boy like you working for me."

"I may not work for anybody," Shig said slowly.

"That's good too," Hong Kong said evenly. "But everybody's got to have friends."

When Captain Sakagawa climbed aboard the transport he felt completely American. He had proved his courage, had been accepted by Honolulu, and now he was wanted by someone. In a sense, he was already a Golden Man, knowledgeable both in western and eastern values, for although he reveled in his newly won Americanism, he also took pride in being a pure-blooded Japanese. Of course this latter was ridiculous, for he contained inheritances from all those nameless predecessors who had once inhabited Japan: some of his genes came from the hairy Ainu to the north, from Siberian invaders, from the Chinese, from the Koreans amongst whom his ancestors had lived, and more particularly from that venturesome Indo-Malayan stock, half of whom had journeyed eastward to become Hawaiians while their brothers had moved northward along different islands to merge with the Japanese. Thus, of two ancient Malayan brothers starting from a point near Singapore, the northern traveler had become the ancestor of Shigeo Sakagawa, while the other had served as the progenitor of Kelly Kanakoa, the Hawaiian beachboy who now stood with a pretty girl watching the end of the parade.

Or, if one preferred looking north, of three ancient Siberian brothers, one bravely crossed the sea to Japan, where his genes found ultimate refuge in the body of Shigeo Sakagawa. Another crept along the Aleutian bridge toward Massachusetts, where his descendants wound up as Indian progenitors of Hoxworth Hale; while a third, less venturesome than his brothers, drifted southward along established land routes to central China, where he helped form the Hakka, thus serving as an ancestor to Hong Kong Kee. In truth, all men are brothers, but as generations pass, it is differences that matter and not similarities.

IN THE irrelevant sense of the word, this Kelly Kanakoa of whom I just spoke was already a Golden Man, for at twenty-one he was slightly over six feet tall, weighed a trim 180, and had a powerful body whose muscles rippled in sunlight as if smeared with coconut oil. He was very straight and had unusually handsome features, marked by deep-set dark eyes, a gamin laugh, and a head of jet-black hair in which he liked to wear a flower. His manner was a mixture of relaxation and insolence, and although it was more than two years since he had knocked out two sailors on Hotel Street for calling him a nigger, he seemed always half ready for a brawl, but whenever one seemed about to explode, he tried to evade it: "Why you like beef wid me? I no want trobble. Let's shake and be blalahs again."

Now, as Kelly stood watching the departing parade, he held in his right hand the slim, well-manicured fingers of a Tulsa divorcee who had come to Honolulu from Reno, seeking emotional reorientation after her difficult divorce. At the ranch where she had stayed in Nevada a fellow divorcee had told her, "Rennie! If you go to Hawaii be sure to look up Kelly Kanakoa. He's adorable." So as soon as Rennie had disembarked from the H & H flagship, *Mauna Loa,* she had called the number her friend had given her, announcing: "Hello, Kelly? Maud Clemmens told me to look you up."

He had come sauntering around to the luxurious H & H hotel, the Lagoon, wearing very tight blue pants, a white busboy's jacket with only one button closed, sandals, a yachting cap, and a flower behind his ear. When she came down into the grandiose lobby, crisp and white in a new bathing suit edged in lace, he appraised her insolently and calculated: "This wahine's gonna screw the first night."

In his job as beachboy, which he had acquired by accident because he liked to surf and had a pleasant joking way with rich women customers, he had become expert in estimating how long it would take him to get into bed with any newcomer. Divorcees, he had found, were easiest because they had undergone great shock to their womanliness and were determined to prove that they, at least, had not been at fault in the breakup of their marriages. It rarely took Kelly more than two nights. Of course when they first met him they certainly had no intention of sleeping with him, but as he explained to the other fellows hanging around the beach, "S'pose da wahine not ride a surfboard yet, how she know what she really wanna do?" It was his job, and he got paid for it, to take divorcees and young widows on surfboards.

Ten minutes after Rennie met Kelly she was on her first surfing expedition, far out on the reef where the big waves were forming. She was excited by the exhilarating motion of the sea and felt that she would never be able to rise and stand on the board as it swept her toward shore, but when she felt Kelly's strong arms enveloping her from the rear she felt assured, and as the board gathered momentum she allowed herself to be pulled upright, always in Kelly's stout arms, until she stood daringly on the flying board. For a moment the spray blinded her, but she soon learned to tilt her chin high into the wind and break its force, so that soon she was roaring across the reef, with a thundering surf at her feet and the powerful shape of Diamond Head dominating the shore.

"How marvelous!" she cried as the comber maintained its rush toward the shore. Instinctively she drew Kelly's arm closer about her, pressed backward against him and reveled in his manliness. Then, when the crashing surf broke at last, she felt the board collapse into the dying waves, and she with it, until she was underwater with Kelly's arms still about her, and of her own accord she turned her face to his, and they kissed for a long time under the sea, then idly rose to the surface.

Now she climbed back upon the surfboard, and with Kelly instructing, started the long paddle out to catch the next wave, but when their board was well separated from the others, she relaxed backwards until she felt herself against the beachboy once more, and there she rested in his secure arms, paddling idly as his adept hands began their explorations beneath her new bathing suit. Sighing, she whispered, "Is this part of the standard instruction?"

"Not many wahine cute like you," Kelly replied gallantly, whereupon she shivered with joy and brought her body closer to his, where she could feel the muscles of his chest against her neck.

It was a long, exciting trip out to where the waves formed, and as they waited for the right one, Kelly asked, "You scared stand up dis time?"

"I'm game to try anything with you," Rennie said, and she showed remarkable aptitude on the long surge in, and when the surfboard finally subsided into the broken wave, and when they were underseas for a kiss, she found to her surprise that her hands were now inside his swimming suit, clutching passionately, hungrily. When they surfaced, his black hair in his eyes like a satyr's, he laughed and said approvingly, "Bimeby you numbah one surfer, get da trophy, Rennie."

"Do I do things right?" she asked modestly.

"You very right," he assured her.

"Shall we catch another wave?" she suggested.

"Why we not go on up your room?" he asked evenly, keeping his dark eyes directly on her.

"I think we'd better," she agreed, adding cautiously, "Are you allowed upstairs?"

"S'pose you forget your lauhala hat on de beach, somebody surely gotta bring it to you," he explained.

"Is that standard procedure?" Rennie asked coyly.

"Like mos' stuff," Kelly explained, "surfin's gotta have its own rules."

"We'll play by the rules," she agreed, squeezing his hand. And when he got to her room, holding the sun hat in his powerful hands, he found that she had already climbed into one of the skimpiest playsuits he had ever seen, and in his years on the beach he had seen quite a few.

"Hey, seestah! Wedder you wear muumuu or sundress or nuttin', you look beautiful," he said approvingly, and in her natural confusion over her divorce, this was exactly what she wanted to hear, and she dispensed with the customary formalities of such moments and held out her arms to the handsome beachboy.

"Normally I'd order a Scotch and soda, and we'd talk a while . . . Let's take up where we left off under water."

Kelly studied her for a long, delicious moment and suggested, "Alla time, dese badin' suit get wet too much." And he slipped his off, and when he stood before her in rugged, dark-skinned power she thought: "If I had married a man like this there'd have been no trouble."

Now, as the parade passed down Bishop Street, she was about to leave Hawaii, and she held his hand tightly in the last minutes before boarding the *Mauna Loa*. For nine days she had lived with Kelly passionately and in complete surrender to his amazing manliness. Once she told him, "Kelly, you should have seen the pathetic little jerk I was married to. God, what a waste of years." Now she whispered, in the bright sunlight, "If we hurried to the ship, would we have time for one more?"

"Whassamatta why not?" he asked, and they clambered aboard the big ship and sought out her stateroom, but her intended roommate was already unpacking, a tall, rather good-looking girl in her late twenties. There were several embarrassed moments, after which Rennie whispered to Kelly, "What have I got to lose?"

She addressed the girl directly and said, "I'm sorry we haven't met, but would you think me an awful stinker if I borrowed the room for a little while?"

The tall girl slowly studied Rennie and then Kelly. They were an attractive couple, and she laughed, "A vacation's a vacation. How long you need?"

"About half an hour," Rennie replied. "They have a band upstairs."

"And a full orchestra right here," the girl laughed, and before she had climbed to the next deck, Rennie was undressed and in bed.

Later she confided, "For five days I've been imagining what it would be like to have you back in New York. How old are you, Kelly?"

"Twenty-one."

"Damn. I'm twenty-seven."

"You no seem twenty-seven yet, not in bed," the beachboy assured her.

"Am I good in bed?" she pleaded. "Really good."

"You numbah one wahine."

"Have you known many girls?"

"Surfin' is surfin'," he replied.

"For example, Maud Clemmens? Did you sleep with her?"

"How you like s'pose nex' week somebody ast me, 'How about Rennie? Dat wahine screw?' "

"Kelly! Such words!"

"Da whistle gonna blow, Rennie seestah," he warned her, climbing into his own clothes.

"I went down to the library, Kelly," she said softly. "And there it was, like you said. This big long book with the names written down by the missionary. It says that your family can be traced back for one hundred and thirty-four generations. It must make you feel proud."

"Don't make me feel notting," Kelly grunted.

"Why does a Hawaiian have the name Kelly?" she asked, slipping on her stockings.

"My kanaka name Kelolo, but nobody like say 'em."

"Kelly's a sweet name," she said approvingly. Then she kissed him and asked, "Why wouldn't you take me to your home?"

"It's notting," he shrugged.

"You mean, your ancestors were kings and you have nothing for yourself?"

"I get guitar, I get surfboard, I get cute wahine like you."

"It's too damned bad," she said bitterly, kissing him again. "Kelly, you're the best thing in Hawaii." They went on deck and she made a quick sign to her roommate, thanking her. The tall girl laughed and winked. When the whistle blew for the last time, warning the various beachboys who had come down to see their haole wahines off, Rennie asked hesitantly, "If some of my friends decide to come to Hawaii . . . girl friends that is . . ." She paused.

"Sure, I look out for dem," Kelly agreed.

"You're a darling!" she laughed, kissing him ardently as he pulled away to run down the gangplank. In the departure shed the beachboy Florsheim—they called him that because sometimes he wore shoes—sidled up and asked, "Kelly blalah, da kine wahine da kine blonde, she good screwin'?"

"Da bes'," Kelly said firmly, and the two beachboys went amiably back to the Lagoon.

Once or twice as the year 1946 skipped away, Kelly had fleeting doubts which he shared with Florsheim: "Whassamatta me? Takin' care lotsa wahine, all mixed up. Where it gonna get me?" But such speculation was always stilled by the arrival of some new divorcee or widow, and the fun of working it around so that he got into bed with them, while they paid the hotel and restaurant bills, was so great that he invariably came around to Florsheim's philosophy: "Mo bettah we get fun now, while we young." So he maintained the routine: meet the ship, find the girl that someone had cabled about, take her surfing, live with her for eight days, kiss her good-bye on the *Moana Loa,* get some rest, and then meet the next ship. Sometimes he looked with admiration at Johnny Pupali, forty-nine years old and still giving the wahines what he called "Dr. Pupali's surfboard cure for misery."

One afternoon he asked Pupali about his surprising energy, and the dean of beachboys explained: "A man got energy for do four t'ings. Eat, work, surf, or make love. But at one time got stuff for only two. For me, surfin' and makin' love."

"You ever get tired?" Kelly asked.

"Surfin'? No. I gonna die on an incomin' wave. Wahines? Tell you da trufe, Kelly, sometime for about ten minutes after *Moana Loa* sail, I don' nevah wanna see da kine wahine no mo', but nex' day wen anudder ship blow anudder whistle, man, I'm strip for action."

In the lazy weeks between girls, Kelly found real joy in loafing on the beach with Florsheim, a big, sprawling man who wore his own kind of costume: enormous baggy shorts of silk and cotton that looked like underwear and fell two inches below his knees, a tentlike aloha shirt whose ends he tied about his middle, leaving a four-inch expanse of belly, Japanese slippers with a thong between his toes, and a coconut hat with a narrow brim and two long fibers reaching eight inches in the air and flopping over on one side. Florsheim always looked sloppy until he kicked off his clothes and stood forth in skin-tight bathing trunks, and then he looked like a pagan deity, huge, brown, long hair about his ears and a wreath of fragrant maile encircling his brow. Even the most fastidious mainland women reveled in this transformation and loved to lie on the sand beside him, tracing his rippling muscles with their red fingernails.

Kelly preferred Florsheim as a companion because the huge beachboy could sing the strange falsetto of the islands, and together they made a gifted pair, for Kelly had a fine baritone voice. He was also skilled at slack-key, a system of guitar playing peculiar to Hawaii, in which the strings were specially tuned to produce both plucked melody and strummed chords. Many people thought of Kelly's slack-key as the voice of the islands, for when he was in good form he gave his music an urgent sweetness that no other possessed. The melodies were swift and tremulous like an island bird, but the chords were slow and sure like the thundering of the surf. When the beachboys had nothing to do, they often called, "Kelly blalah. Play da kine sleck-key like dat." He was their troubadour, but he rarely played for visitors. "I doan' like waste time haole," he growled. "Dey doan' know sleck-key."

The other pastime that he and Florsheim loved was sakura, a crazy Japanese card game played with little black cards that came in a wooden box with a picture of cherry blossoms on the cover. Any beachboy was hailed as the day's hero who could scrape together enough money to buy a fresh box of sakura cards, and through the long hot days the gang would sit beneath coconut umbrellas, playing the silly game. No other was allowed, and if a man couldn't play sakura, he couldn't be a beachboy. Of course he must also speak degenerate pidgin, as on the afternoon when Kelly was protesting the price of cube steak at the corner drug store.

"Me t'ink high too much, da kine pipty cent," he mused.

"Kelly blalah, wha' da kine da kine you speak?" Florsheim asked idly.

"Whassamatta you, stoopid? You akamai good too much da kine da kine," Kelly growled, adding with a chopping motion of his right hand, "Da kine chop chop."

"Oh!" Florsheim sang in a high, descending wail of recognition. "You speak *da kine* da kine? Right, blalah, price too moch. Pipty cent too bloody takai." And they passed to other equally important topics.

As Kelly became better acquainted with American girls, he felt sorry for them. Invariably they confided how wretched their lives had been with their haole husbands, how the men were not interested in them and how unsatisfactory sex had been. This latter knowledge always astonished Kelly, for while the girls were with him they could think of little else, and if the world had women who were better at sex than the wahines who came over to Hawaii on the *Moana Loa,* he concluded they must be real tigers. One day he told Florsheim, "How some wahine gonna be any bettah than da kine wahine we get over heah? What you s'pose da mattah wid dese haole men?"

In 1947 he got a partial answer, because Florsheim married one of his young divorcees, a girl who had a lot of money and who gave him a Chevrolet convertible, and as long as they stayed in Hawaii things went rather well, but after three months in New York they broke all to hell, and Florsheim came back alone to resume his job on the beach. On a day when there was little doing he explained to his companions, "Dese wahine da kine, seem like dey two people. Over here on a surfboard dey relax, dey screw like mad, dey don't gi'e a damn. Ova' heah I t'row my wahine in da jalopy and we go okolehau." He steered the imaginary car with his hands. "We have bes' time."

"Wha' hoppen?" Kelly asked.

"I tell you, Kelly blalah," Florsheim drawled. "She take me New York, she no like da way I dress. She no like da kine talk, and. She doan' like one goddam t'ing, I t'ink. Allatime give me hell. No more time to go bed in de apternoon, when it's de bes'. So bimeby she tell me, 'Florsheim, you gotta go night school learn speak haole no kanaka,' and I tellem, 'Go to hell. I ketchem airplane Hawaii,' and she speak me, 'Wha' you gonna use money da kine?' and I tellem, 'Seven hunnerd dollars I scoop f'um you,' and she speak, 'You dirty boa', you filthy mountain pig!' and what I tellem den, I ain't gonna repeat."

"Da kine wahine turn out like dat?" Johnny Pupali mused. "Well, da's why I tell you boys, 'Screw 'em but doan' marry 'em.' "

Florsheim reflected: "Seem like dey good wahine ova' heah, but anudder kine back home."

"You gonna keep da kine Chevvy?" Kelly asked.

"Yeah," Florsheim said, adding, "I not halp so sorry for dem wahine like I was b'fore."

The sweet days rolled on and Kelly discovered what the older beachboys already knew: that the best wahines of all were those from the Deep South. They were gentler, kinder, and in memorable ways much more loving. They seemed fascinated by Kelly's dark-brown body, and on three different occasions Kelly stayed for days at a time in one suite or another with some adorable girl from the South, without ever leaving the room and often without dressing from one day to the next. At mealtime he would throw a small towel about his waist, tucking in the ends as if it were a sarong, and the wahine from Montgomery or Atlanta or Birmingham would admire him as he lolled about the davenport. Once such a girl said, "You're awfully close to a nigra, Kelly, and yet you aren't. It's fascinating."

"Hawaiians hate niggers," Kelly assured her, and she felt better.

"How do you make your living?" she asked softly, coming to lie beside him after the food had been pushed away.

"S'pose I learn you surfin', I get paid."

"You get paid for what you did on that surfboard?" she gasped.

"Whassamatta, you no look you bill? Clerk put 'im on dere."

"Do you get paid . . . for days like this?"

"Clerk put 'im on. Rules say I'm s'pose teachin' you somethin'."

"That you are," she said softly as they lapsed off into another nap.

In time the girls he slept with became fused in his memory, for one sent another who sent another, but they always seemed to be the same girl, someone he had first met during the war. But there were a few whom he remembered forever. Once a young widow from Baton Rouge flew into the islands, and when he met her he calculated: "Dis wahine t'ree nights da kine, maybe four." He had underestimated, for in her sorrow the young woman would accept no man, yet when they stood in her cabin aboard the departing *Moana Loa* she said in a soft southern drawl, "The world is such a goddamned lonely place, Kelly."

"S'pose you lose da kine man you love, I t'ink maybe so," he said.

"I never loved Charley," she confessed, blowing her nose. "But he was a decent man, a good human being, and the world is worse off now that he's gone."

"What you gonna do bimeby?" he asked her, lolling with one arm about the end of the bed.

"I don't know," she said. "How old are you, Kelly?"

"I twenty-two, las' week."

"You have your life ahead of you, Kelly. It should be so exciting. But never kid yourself, Kelly. The world is a very lonely place."

"People come, dey go," he said philosophically.

"But when a good one comes, hold onto the memory. It's almost time for the whistle, and I wonder if I might do one thing before you go?"

"Wha' dat?" Kelly asked suspiciously.

"Could I kiss you good-bye? You've been so kind and understanding." She started to say something more, but broke into tears and pressed her beautiful white face to his. "You are such a goddamned decent human being," she whispered. "More than anything in the world I needed to meet someone like you."

Biting her lip and sniffling away her tears, she pushed him back toward the door and said, "Kelly, do you understand even remotely how deeply a woman like me prays for the success of a strong young man like you? I wish the heavens could open and give you their glory. Kelly, make a good life for yourself. Don't be a bum. For you are one of the men whom Jesus loves." And she sent him away.

Often when the surf was breaking he contemplated her words and wondered how a man went about building a good life for himself. He suspected that it consisted neither in being an old stud horse like Johnny Pupali, fun though that was, nor in wasting one's energies on a haole wife the way Florsheim had done. Yet all he knew how to do was lie in the sun, play slack-key and sakura, and teach wahines how to surf. So for the time being that had to be good enough.

In late 1947 however a night-club singer from New York arrived in the islands—a two-night wahine, she turned out to be—and she took such a boisterous joy in Kelly that one night she cried, "God, they ought to build a monument to you, Beachboy!"

She was outraged when she learned that the current popular song, "The Rolling Surf," was something that Kelly had composed on the beach and had given away to whoever wanted it. A mainland musician had glommed onto it, added a few professional twists, and made a pile of money from it.

"You ought to sue the dirty bastard!" she yelled. Later she tested Kelly's voice and found it good. "Tomorrow night, Kelly Kanakoa, you're going to sing with me. In the dining room of the Lagoon."

"I no like singin'," Kelly protested, but she asked, "What's that lovely thing you and the falsetto boy were doing with your ukuleles?"

"You speak da kine 'Hawaiian Wedding Song'?" he asked.

"The one where you start low, and he comes in high?"

Casually, Kelly started singing "Ke Kali Ne Au," the greatest of all Hawaiian songs, a glorious, haunting evocation of the islands. At the moment he was wearing a Lagoon towel as a sarong, with a hibiscus flower in his hair, and as he sang, the night-club girl sensed his full power and cried, "Kelly, nothing can stop you."

After one day's rehearsal, for the girl was a real professional and learned quickly, Kelly Kanakoa, dressed in a red and white sarong, with one of his mother's whale-tooth hooks dangling from a silver chain about his neck, and with a flower in his hair, came onto the floor of the Lagoon and started singing with the voice that was to become famous throughout the islands. "The Wedding Song" was unusual in that it provided a powerful solo for a baritone voice and a high, soaring dreamlike melody for a soprano. It was a true art song, worthy of Schubert or Hugo Wolf, and although that night's audience had heard it often before, sung by blowzy baritones and worse sopranos, they had not really heard the full majesty of the lyric outcry. Kelly was a man in love, a muscular, bronzed god, and the slim blond girl from New York was in all ways his counterfoil. It was a memorable evening, and as it ended, the singer called to Kelly while he washed down in her shower, "How'd you like to come to New York with me?"

"I doan' leave da rock," he called back.

"You don't have to marry me," she assured him, aware before he was of his apprehensions. "Just sing."

"Me 'n' da beach, we akamai," he said, and although she begged him several more times while they were in bed, he insisted that his place was in Hawaii. "See da kine wha' hoppen Florsheim!" he repeated.

"Well, anyway," she said as she dressed for the plane. "We taught one another a lot in a few days."

"You speak da trufe," Kelly agreed.

"You gonna keep on singing?" she asked.

"Skoshi singin', skoshi surfin'."

"Don't give up the surfing," she said sardonically. "You got a real good thing working for you there."

"Seestah, dis kanaka doan' aim to lose it," Kelly laughed.

"I'm sure you don't," she cracked. She was brassy, and her hair was dark at the roots, but she was a good clean companion, and Kelly appreciated her.

"I ain't able come out to da airport," he said apologetically.

"You took care of things here," she assured him, patting the bed, "and that's where it counts."

Then, in early 1948, when the tourist business was beginning to boom, he received a cable from some wahine in Boston named Rennie, but he couldn't remember who she was, but anyway she said, "MEET MOANA LOA MRS. DALE HENDERSON." And when the ship came in, Florsheim, barefooted and staring up at the railing asked, "Which one you wahine, Kelly blalah?"

"Maybe da kine," he indicated with a shrug of his shoulder.

"You s'pose she gonna lay?" Florsheim asked, appraising the slim, handsomely groomed girl who appeared to be in her early thirties.

"She look maybe two nights, maybe four," Kelly calculated, for he had found that women who spent unusual care on their appearance were often more tardy in climbing into bed than their sisters who called to the world, "Here I am, wind-blown and happy!"

Kelly, who like the other beachboys was privileged to climb aboard the *Moana Loa* before disembarkation started, elbowed his way along the crowded deck and touched Mrs. Henderson on the arm. She turned and smiled at him, a clean, unconfused greeting. When he shook hands with her he asked, "You name Dale or somethin' else? Seem like nobody can't speak man's name, woman's name no more."

"My name is Mrs. Henderson. Elinor Henderson," she replied in the crisp and self-possessed voice of a New Englander. "I'm from Boston."

Kelly very much wanted to ask, "Who dis Rennie wahine cable me? I no remember nobody in Boston." But he didn't speak. One rule he had learned in his beachboy business: never mention one woman to another, so that even though most of the customers he met had been referred to him by others, often intimate friends, he never mentioned that fact. Culling his brain furiously, he still failed to recall who Rennie was and he did not refer to her cable. But Mrs. Henderson did.

"A college classmate of mine at Smith . . ."

"Dat doan' sound like no wahine college, Smith."

"Rennie Blackwell, she told me to be sure to look you up."

Quickly Kelly composed his face as if he knew well who Rennie Blackwell was, and just as quickly Mrs. Henderson thought: "After all she told me, and he doesn't even remember her name." Wanting perversely to explore the situation further she added, "Rennie was the girl from Tulsa." Still Kelly could not place her among the nameless girls that populated his life, and now he was aware that Mrs. Henderson was playing a game with him, so he lapsed into his most barbarous pidgin and banged his head with his fist. "Sometime I no akamai da kine. Dis wahine Rennie I not collect."

Mrs. Henderson smiled and said, "She collects you, Kelly."

He was irritated with this secure woman and said, "S'pose one year pass, bimeby I say Florsheim, 'Cable here speak Elinor Henderson. Who dat one wahine?' Florsheim he doan' collect. I doan' collect."

"Who's Florsheim?" Elinor asked.

"Da kine beachboy yonder 'longside tall wahine," Kelly explained.

Mrs. Henderson laughed merrily and said, "Rennie told me you were the best beachboy in the business, but you must promise me one thing."

"Wha' dat?"

"You aren't required to talk pidgin to me any longer. I'll bet you graduated with honors from Hewlett Hall. You can probably speak English better than I can." She smiled warmly and asked, "Aren't you going to give me the lei?"

"I'm afraid to kiss you, Mrs. Henderson," he laughed, and handed her the flowers, but Florsheim saw this and rushed up, protesting, "Jeezus Crisss! Kanaka handin' wahine flowers like New York?" He grabbed the lei, plopped it around Elinor's head and kissed her powerfully.

"Florsheim's been in New York," Kelly joked. "He knows how to act like a Hawaiian."

"Florsheim? In New York?" Mrs. Henderson reflected, studying the huge beachboy with the long hair and the wreath of maile leaves. "I'll bet the city'll never be the same."

"He married a society girl," Kelly explained. "Stayed with her three months and came back. He got a Chevvy convertible out of it. In fact, we're riding back to the hotel in it."

At this point Florsheim's girl from Kansas City hustled up, heavy with leis and mascara, and giggled: "My God! Aren't these men positively divine?" She grabbed Florsheim's dark-brown arm, felt the muscles admiringly and asked, "You ever hit a man with that fist, Florsheim?"

"Nevah," the beachboy replied. "Only wimmin."

His girl laughed outrageously, and when the various bits of luggage were piled into the Chevvy, the two couples headed for the Lagoon, but when Florsheim drove up King Street and past the old mission houses, Elinor Henderson abruptly asked him to stop, and she studied the historic buildings carefully, explaining at last, "My great-great-grandmother was born in that house. Originally I was a Quigley."

"Never heard of them," Kelly said honestly.

"They didn't stay long. But I'm doing a biography of them . . . for my thesis. I teach at Smith, you know."

"You da kine wahine bimeby gonna write a book?" Florsheim asked, as he resumed the trip.

"Tell him he doesn't have to talk pidgin," Elinor suggested.

"He can't talk anything else," Kelly laughed.

"I think pidgin's just adorable," the girl in front said, and Kelly thought: "Looks like I've got a four-nighter at best, and maybe not at all, but good old Florsheim better watch out or he's going to be layin' that babe in the lobby."

Kelly's suspicion about Elinor Henderson proved correct, for she was not a four-nighter or even a six. She loved surfing and felt secure in Kelly's arms, but that was all. Yet one night when Kelly borrowed Florsheim's convertible—for the Kansas City girl had said flatly, "Why go riding in a Chevvy when you can have so much fun in bed?"—he drove Elinor out to Koko Head, where they sat in darkness talking.

"In the islands we call this kind of date, 'Watching the midnight submarine races,' " he explained.

"Very witty," she laughed.

"How's the biography coming along?" he asked.

"I'm quite perplexed," she confessed.

"No good, eh?"

"I have been sorely tempted to put it aside, Kelly."

"Why?"

There was a long pause in the darkness as the late moon climbed out of the sea in the perpetual mystery of the tropics. Along the shore a coconut palm dipped out to meet it, and the night was heavy, bearing down on the world. Suddenly Elinor turned to Kelly and took his hands. "I have been driven mad by the desire to write about you, Kelly," she said.

The beachboy was astonished. "Me!" he cried. "What's there to write about me?"

She explained in clear, swift sentences, without allowing him to interrupt: "I have been haunted by Hawaii ever since I read my great-great-great-grandfather's secret journal. He stayed here only seven years. Couldn't take any more. And when he got back to Boston he wrote a completely frank account of his apprehensions. I can see his dear old handwriting still: 'I shall write as if God were looking over my shoulder, for since He ordained these things He must understand them.' "

"What did he write?" Kelly inquired.

"He said that we Christians had invaded the islands with the proper God but with an improper set of supporting values. It was his conviction that our God saved the islands, but our ideas killed them. Particularly the Hawaiians. And at one point, Kelly, he wrote a prophetic passage about the Hawaiian of the future. I copied it down, and last night I read it again, and he was describing you."

"Gloomy prophecy?" Kelly asked.

" 'The Hawaiian is destined to diminish year by year, dispossessed, distraught and confused.' That's what the old man wrote. He must have had you in mind, Kelly."

Kelly was twenty-three years old that night, and he realized that in Elinor Henderson he was mixed up with an entirely different kind of woman. She was thirty-one, he guessed, clean, honest and very appealing. Her hair was crisply drawn back, and her white chin was both determined and inviting. He put his left hand under it and slowly brought it up to his. There was enough moonlight for him to see the visitor's eyes, and he was captivated by their calm assurance, so that for some moments the missionaries' descendant and the dispossessed Hawaiian studied each other, and finally his hand relaxed and her chin was released, whereupon she took his powerful face in her soft white hands and brought it to hers, kissing him and confessing, "I have forgotten old missionaries, Kelly. When I start to write I see only you. Do you know what I wish to call my new biography? *The Dispossessed.*"

They talked for a long time, while other cars came to observe the midnight submarine races and depart. Elinor asked directly, "Do you call this a life, Kelly? Making love to one neurotic divorcee after another?"

"Who told you?"

"I can see Florsheim, can't I?"

"Florsheim's not me."

"That isn't what Rennie Blackwell told me."

"What did she tell you?" Kelly asked.

"She said it was the one good week of her life."

"Which one was she?" he asked directly.

"I knew you didn't remember. She was the one who told her roommate on the *Moana Loa* . . ."

"Of course! Look, I don't need to be ashamed of loving a girl like that," Kelly insisted.

"Do you suppose Florsheim's going to marry the Kansas City girl?" Elinor asked.

"She's doing her damnedest to make him," Kelly laughed. "He'll stay with her four or five months and come home with a Buick."

"Why haven't you ever tried it?" Elinor probed.

"I don't need the money. I sing a little, play a little slack-key, get a little money teaching girls like you. And if I need a convertible, somebody always has one."

"Is it a life?" Elinor asked.

Kelly thought a long time, then asked, "What makes you think you can write a book?"

"I can do anything I set my mind on," Elinor replied.

"How come you're divorced?"

"I'm not."

"Your husband dead?"

"One of the best, Kelly. One of the men God puts his special finger on."

"He die in the war?"

"Covered with medals. Jack would have liked you, Kelly. You'd have understood each other. He had a thing about happiness. God, if the world knew what that man knew about being happy."

They sat in silence for some time, and Kelly asked, "Why would you call your book *The Dispossessed?* I got everything I want."

"You don't have your islands. The Japanese have them. You don't have the money. The Chinese have that. You don't have the land. The Fort has that. And you don't have your gods. My ancestors took care of that. What do you have?"

Kelly laughed nervously and began to say something but fought back the impulse, for he knew it would lead to peril. Instead he wagged his finger in Elinor's face and said, "You'd be surprised at what we Hawaiians have. Truly, you'd be astounded."

"All right. Take the four pretty girls who do the hula at the Lagoon . . . in those fake cellophane skirts. What are their names? Tell me the truth."

"Well, the one with the beautiful legs is Gloria Ching."

"Chinese?"

"Plus maybe a little Hawaiian. The girl with the real big bosom, that's Rachel Fernandez. And the real beauty there . . . I sort of like her, except she's Japanese . . . that's Helen Fukuda, and the one on the end is Norma Swenson."

"Swedish?"

"Plus maybe a little Hawaiian."

"So what we call Hawaiian culture is really a girl from the Philippines, wearing a cellophane skirt from Tahiti, playing a ukulele from Portugal, backed up by a loud-speaker guitar from New York, singing a phony ballad from Hollywood."

"I'm not a phony Hawaiian," he said carefully. "In the library there's a book about me. More than a hundred generations, and when I sing a Hawaiian song it comes right up from my toes. There's lots you don't know, Elinor."

"Tell me," she persisted.

"No," he refused. Then abruptly he made the surrender which only a few minutes earlier he had recognized as perilous. "I'll do better . . . something I've never done before.'

"What?" she asked.

"You'll see. Wear something cool and I'll pick you up about three tomorrow."

"Will it be exciting?"

"Something you'll never forget."

At three next day he drove a borrowed car up to the Lagoon and waited idly in the driveway till she appeared. When she got into the Pontiac, crisp and cool in a white dress, he turned toward the mountains and drove inland from the reef until he came to a high board fence, behind which coconut palms rose in awkward majesty. He continued around the fence until he came to a battered gate which he opened by nosing the car against it. When he had entered the grounds, he adroitly backed the car into the gate and closed it. Then he raced the engine, spun the tires in gravel, and brought the car up to a shadowy, palm-protected, weather-stained old wooden house built in three stories, with gables, wide verandas, fretwork and stained-glass windows.

"This is my home," he said simply. "No girl's ever been here before." He banged the horn, and at the rickety screen door appeared a marvelous woman, six feet two inches tall, almost as wide as the door itself, silver-haired and stately, and with a great brown smile that filled her plastic face. "Is that you, Kelolo?" she asked in a perfectly modulated voice that contained a touch of New England accent.

"Hi, Mom. Prepare for a shock! I'm bringin' home a haole wahine." Lest his mother be aware of the changes he had undergone for this girl, Kelly lapsed into his worst pidgin.

His mother left the doorway, walked in stately fashion to the edge of the porch, and extended her hand: "We are truly delighted to welcome you to the Swamp."

"Muddah, dis wahine Elinor Henderson, Smith. Muddah's Vassar." The trim Bostonian and the huge Hawaiian shook hands, each respectful of the other, and the latter said in her soft voice, "I am Malama Kanakoa, and you are the first of Kelolo's haole friends he has ever brought here. You must be special."

"Eh, Muddah, watch out!" Kelly warned. "We not in love. Dis wahine mo eight years older dan me. She all fixed mo bettah in Boston."

"But she is special," Malama insisted.

"Special too much! She gotta brain da kine, akamai too good."

The trio laughed and each instinctively felt at ease with the other. Kelly helped by explaining, "Muddah, dis wahine she come from longtime mission pamily Quigley. I not speak dis pamily, but maybe you do."

"Immanuel Quigley!" Malama cried, taking her visitor's two hands. "He was the best of the missionaries. Only one who loved the Hawaiians. But he stayed only a short time."

"I think he transmuted all his love for Hawaii into his children, and I inherited it," Elinor said. She saw that she had entered a nineteenth-century drawing room, complete with chandelier, tiered crystal cases, an organ, a Steinway piano and a brown mezzotint of Raphael's "Ascent of the Virgin" in a massive carved frame. The ceiling was enormously high, which made the room unexpectedly cool, but Elinor was distracted from this fact by an object which hung inside an inverted glass bowl set in a mahogany base. "Whatever is it?" she cried.

"It's a whale's tooth," Malama explained. "Formed into a hook."

"But what's it hung on?" she asked.

"Human hair," Kelly assured her.

Malama interrupted, removing the glass cover and handing her visitor the precious relic. "My ancestor, the King of Kona, wore this when he fought as Kamehameha's general. Later he wore it when the first mission ship touched at Lahaina. I suppose that every hair in this enormous chain came from the head of someone my family cherished." She replaced the glass cover. Then she said, "Kelly, while you show Mrs. Henderson why we call this the Swamp, I'll be getting tea. Some of the ladies are coming in."

So Kelly took Elinor to the rear of the house, through a kitchen that had once prepared two hundred dinners for King Kalakaua, and soon they were in a fairyland of trees and flowers bordering a rush-lined swamp whose surface was covered with lilies. With some irony Kelly said, dropping his pidgin now that he was again alone with Elinor, "This was the only land the haoles didn't take. Now it's worth two million dollars. But of course Mom takes care of a hundred poor Hawaiians, and she's in hock up to her neck."

To Elinor, the scene of old decay was poignant, and as red-tufted birds darted through the swamp and perched on the tips of dancing reeds, she saw the complete motif for her biography. "You really are *The Dispossessed,*" she mused, fusing reality with her vision of it.

"No, I think you have it wrong," Kelly protested. "This is the walled-in garden that every Hawaiian knows, for he tends one in his own heart. Here no one intrudes."

"Then you're contemptuous of the haole girls you sleep with?" she asked.

"Oh, no! Sleeping is fun, Elinor. That's outside what we're talking about."

"You're right, and I apologize. What I meant was, insofar as they're haoles, you're contemptuous of them?"

Kelly thought about this for a long time, tossed a pebble at a swaying bird, and said, "I don't believe I would admit that. I'm not as intolerant as the missionaries were."

"Immanuel Quigley said almost the same thing."

"I think I would have liked old Quigley," Kelly admitted.

"He was young when he served here. He became old in Ohio. What a profound man he was."

"Mom's probably ready," Kelly suggested, and he led Elinor away from the swamp and back into the spacious drawing room, where four gigantic Hawaiian women, gray-haired and gracious, waited.

"This is Mrs. Leon Choy," Malama said softly. "And this is Mrs. Hideo Fukuda."

"Did I see your very pretty daughter dancing at the Lagoon?" Elinor inquired.

"Yes," the huge woman replied, bowing slightly and beaming with pleasure. "Helen loves to dance, as I did when I was younger."

"And this is Mrs. Liliha Mendonca," Malama continued. "Her husband owned the taxi company. And this poor little dwarf over here is Mrs. Jesus Rodriques," Malama laughed. Mrs. Rodriques was only five feet nine and weighed less than 190. "I've told the ladies that Mrs. Henderson is a descendant of dear old Immanuel Quigley. We hold him very warmly in our hearts, Elinor."

"I'm surprised you're not staying with the Hales or the Whipples," Mrs. Mendonca said. "They came over on the same ship with your grandfather, or whatever he was."

"Our families were never close," Elinor explained. Each of the five Hawaiian women wanted desperately to explore this admission, but they were too well-bred to do so, and after a while Malama suggested, "I'm sure Mrs. Henderson would like to hear some of the old songs," and soon she had scraped together a couple of ukuleles and two guitars. The stately Hawaiian women preferred standing while they sang, and now along one edge of the room they formed a frieze of giants, and after a few preliminary plunks on their instruments, launched into a series of the most cherished Hawaiian melodies. They seemed like a professional chorus, so easily did their voices blend. Mrs. Choy, with marvelous darting eyes and gamin manner, sang the high parts, while Mrs. Rodriques and Mrs. Mendonca boomed massive chords that paved the musical structure. Each song contained dozens of verses, and as the last chords of one verse lingered in the air, Mrs. Fukuda in a sing-song falsetto enunciated the first words of the next. She owned a prodigious memory, and the other ladies did not enjoy singing unless she was along, for her monotonous setting of the next theme gave them much pleasure.

Dusk came over the Swamp and lamps were lit. The huge women, reminiscent of bygone splendors, stayed on, and Elinor listened enraptured to their soft conversation until Kelly interrupted brusquely and said, "I speak one kanaka play a little sleck-key tinnight. Da wahine 'n' me be goin'."

But when the women saw him about to leave, Mrs. Choy began casually humming the first bars of the "Hawaiian Wedding Song," so that Kelly stopped in the shadows by the door, and while light from the chandelier reflected upon him in variegated colors, he started softly into the great flowing passage of love. His voice was in excellent form, and he allowed it to expand to its fullest. When the time came for him to halt, Elinor wondered which of the five women would pick up the girl's part, and it was Malama. Standing vast like a monument with silvery hair, she soared into the sweeping lyric portion of the song, and after a while mother and son combined in the final haunting duet. It was an unusually fortunate rendition, and as the lingering chords died away, Mrs. Choy banged her ukulele several times and cried, "I could sing this way all night."

When Kelly and Elinor were back in the borrowed car he said, "They will, too."

Elinor asked, "When your mother came back from Vassar, what did she do?"

"In the hot afternoons she sang, and was good to the Hawaiians, and wasted her money. What else?"

Elinor began sniffling, and after a while said, "I'm bitterly tangled up, Kelly. I can't go back to the hotel."

"I have to sing," he said stubbornly.

"Do you get paid for it?" she asked between sniffles.

"Not tonight. For a friend."

"You lousy, defeated, wonderful people," she said. "Okay, take me back. For a friend you must do everything." She slumped against the door, then quickly jumped back beside Kelly. "Tell me, has this friend, as you call him, ever done anything for you?"

"Mmmmmm, well, no."

"So you sing your life away? For nothing?"

"Who's happier?" he countered. "Mom or the women you know back home?"

Early next morning Elinor Henderson reported at the library and asked Miss Lucinda Whipple for "that book which gives the genealogy of the Kanakoas." At this request Miss Whipple masked her contempt and studied Kelly's latest sleeping partner, for she had found that over the course of a year at least half a dozen awe-struck haole women, who by their ignorance of card catalogues proved they rarely saw a library, could be counted upon to ask for "that book about Kelly Kanakoa." Miss Whipple guessed that one girl probably told the next, for they appeared at regular intervals, and when they reverently returned the book, some gasped, "Gosh, his grandfather was a real king!" Miss Whipple never commented, but she did observe that with such women apparently the farthest back they could imagine was grandfather. Beyond that all was obscurity.

But this girl proved to be different. When she completed studying the long tables in the Missionary Museum publication, she asked Miss Whipple, "What authority substantiates this?"

Miss Whipple replied, "My great-grandfather, Abner Hale, transcribed this remarkable document from verbal traditions recited by a kahuna nui on Maui. A great deal of research has been done in both Tahiti and Hawaii, and the account seems to check out at most points."

"How many years do you accord each generation?" Mrs. Henderson asked.

"I suppose we ought to follow the dictionary and allot each one thirty years, but we feel that in a tropical climate, and judging from what we know to be true, twenty-two years is a safer estimate. Then, too, you will detect that what the genealogy calls two successive generations is often really one, for it was a case of brother succeeding brother rather than son succeeding father. By the way, you seem to have a substantial knowledge of Hawaii. May I ask what your interest is?"

"I am the great-great-great-granddaughter of Immanuel Quigley," Elinor explained.

"Oh, my goodness!" Miss Whipple said in a flurry. "We've never had a Quigley here before."

"No," Elinor said evenly. "As you know, my father had difficulties."

Recollection of old and bitter events did not diminish Lucinda Whipple's ardor, for her genealogical interests transcended unpleasantness, and she asked excitedly, "Shall you be in Honolulu on Saturday?"

"Yes," Elinor replied.

"Goodness, how wonderful!" Miss Whipple said. "It's the yearly anniversary of the missionaries' arrival, and I would be truly honored if you would accompany me. Imagine! A Quigley!" She went on to explain that each spring throughout her life she had attended the yearly meeting of the Mission Children's Society, and as the roll was called she had dutifully, and proudly, stood up for John Whipple, Abner Hale and Abraham Hewlett, each of whom had figured in her ancestry, as well as for the collateral line of Retire Janders, who, while not a missionary, had served with them.

"But we have never had anyone rise to honor the name of Quigley. Please, do come!"

So on a hot Saturday in April, Elinor Henderson sat among the mission offspring and sang the opening hymn, "From Greenland's icy mountains." When the exciting moment came to call the roll of those long-dead and honorable men and women who had served God in the islands, she felt a mounting excitement as the descendants of each couple rose. "Abner Hale and his wife Jerusha, brig *Thetis,* 1822," read the clerk, and there was a flurry of chairs pushing back, after which a varied crew of Hales stood at attention while the rest applauded.

"Dr. John Whipple and his wife Amanda, brig *Thetis,* 1822," the clerk intoned, and from the scraping, Elinor concluded that Dr. John must have been an unusually potent young medico, for many rose to honor him.

"Immanuel Quigley and his wife Jeptha, brig *Thetis,* 1822," called the clerk, and with a heart bursting with passion and history and the confused love of God, Elinor Henderson rose, the first Quigley ever to have done so in that society. Her rising must have inflamed bitter memories in the hearts of the Hales and the Hewletts and the Whipples, for although intractable Immanuel Quigley had suppressed his secret memoirs, which Elinor had found so damning, he had allowed enough of his ideas to escape so that his name was not a happy one among the mission families. Defiantly, his great-great-great-granddaughter stared ahead, and then she heard from the assembly a hammering of palms and wild applause. Continuing to stare ahead, for she was no more forgiving than her difficult ancestor had been, she resumed her seat as the clerk cried mournfully, "Abraham and Urania Hewlett, brig *Thetis,* 1822." Again there was a loud scraping of chairs, with many Hawaiians standing, for Abraham's offspring by Malia, his second wife, were numerous. Many of the missionary descendants considered it inappropriate for such people to rise as if they were the true descendants of blessed Urania Hewlett, but the Hawaiians got up anyway and nothing could be done about it.

That night Elinor Henderson told Kelly, "A visitor touches Hawaii at great risk. He never knows when the passions of the islands will engulf him."

"You think you know enough now to write the biography?" Kelly asked idly.

"Yes."

"You determined to call it *The Dispossessed?"*

"More than ever."

"Who do you think the dispossessed are?" Kelly taunted.

"You. Who else?"

"I thought maybe at the mission society you discovered that they were the real dispossessed," he argued.

"How do you mean?"

"They came here to bring Congregationalism, but we despised their brand of Christianity. Now most of us are Catholics or Mormons. Today we have nearly as many Buddhists in the islands as Congregationalists. Likewise, they came with a God they believed in. How many of them still have that God? And they had big ideas. Now all they have is money."

"You sound very bitter, Kelly. And in a way I'm glad."

"Do you know why the Mormons had so much success in these islands? They admit frankly. 'In heaven there are only white people.' I suppose you know that a nigger can't get a place to sleep in Salt Lake. So they tell us that if we are real good on earth and we love God, when we die God's going to make us white, and then we'll go to heaven and all will be hunky-dory."

"I don't believe Mormons think that, Kelly," she protested.

"It squares with the facts," he said carefully, but his anger was rising furiously and he was afraid of what he might say next. He tried to halt his words, but in spite of himself they rushed out: "Of course, the other Christians tell us that God loves all men, but we know that's bullshit."

"Kelly!"

"We know it! We know it!" he stormed. "It's as clear as the mountains at dawn. God loves first white men, then Chinese, then Japanese, and after a long pause He accepts Hawaiians."

"Kelly, my darling boy, please!"

"But do you know the one consolation we got? Can you guess? We know for goddamn certain that He loves us better than He loves niggers. God, I'd hate to be a nigger."

Since Elinor Henderson had greater capacity for emotion than for logical control she was, of course, unable to write her book; in fact, she was prevented from even trying by one of those strange, wild occurrences that mark the tropics. At six-eighteen on the morning following her visit to the mission society she was still asleep, but in the deep waters of the Pacific, nearly three thousand miles to the north, an event of tremendous magnitude was taking place. The great shelf that lies off the Aleutian Chain was racked by a massive submarine earthquake, which in the space of a few minutes tumbled millions of tons of submerged ocean cliff down hidden mountainsides to a new resting place on the ocean floor. It was a titanic redisposal of the earth's crust, and the ocean in whose depths it occurred was shaken so violently that a mighty rhythmic wave was launched southward at an incomprehensible speed; but even though something like seven per cent of the entire ocean was affected, the resulting wave was physically inconspicuous, never more than four or five inches high.

Actually, one shipload of sailors passed right over it without knowing, for at seven-eighteen that morning a slight swell lifted a Japanese tanker some three inches higher than it had been a moment before, but no one noticed the event and it was not recorded in the log. But if the captain had been alert, and if he had known where the wave had originated only an hour before, he could have written: "Tsunami caused by an Alaskan submarine earthquake passed under our ship. Speed southward, 512 miles an hour." And if he had thought to flash a radio warning throughout the Pacific many lives would have been saved, but he neither saw nor thought, so the epic tsunami sped on unheralded at a speed approaching that of sound. If it encountered no stationary objects like islands, it would ultimately dissipate itself in the far Antarctic, but if it did come upon an island, its kinetic energy might pile waters more than seventy feet deep upon the land and then suck them back out to sea with demonic force. The coming in of the waters would destroy little, but their awful retreat would carry away all things.

While the tsunami was passing unnoticed under the Japanese tanker, Elinor Henderson was just rising to enjoy the last effects of dawn over the Pacific, and at nine she went down to the beach to watch the beachboys playing sakura. She was amused to hear them swearing in pidgin when the run of the black cards went against them, but this morning had a special attraction in that Florsheim appeared among the boys dressed in store clothes: polished tan shoes, a suit that was not quite big enough for his huge frame, a shirt that bound a little at the collar, a knitted tie that hung awry and a tropical straw hat. Beside him stood the rich girl from Kansas City, hardly able to keep her hands off him and crying to one group after another, "God, ain't he a hunk of man? We're gettin' married in St. Louis."

Florsheim grinned and handed his Chevvy keys to Elinor: "You, seestah, tell blalah Kelly take care my jalopy." She said she would, and when she saw Kelly she asked, "How long do you think Florsheim'll stay married this time?"

"Seem like blalah Florsheim gonna look funny Kansas City da kine. So bimeby dis wahine gonna find he doan' talk so good and she gonna gi'e him lotta wahine pilikia. So come late October you gonna see blalah Florsheim back on de beach wid a Buick convertible."

"This time it'll be a Cadillac! Want to bet?" She laughed and then an idea came to her: "Kelly! As long as we have the car, why don't we go on a picnic?" She insisted upon buying all the food, and at ten o'clock, when the tsunami was less than six hundred miles from Oahu, she pointed to a snug little valley on the north shore of the island and cried, "They saved this sandy beach for us!" And Kelly spread their blankets under a palm tree.

They went swimming, and when they were drying in the sun, Elinor said, "I'm going to leave Hawaii, Kelly. Don't speak. I'm falling in love with you, and I'm not the kind of woman who goes around robbing cradles."

"I'm old enough to teach you a lot," Kelly protested.

"I would never marry you, Kelly . . . eight years younger than I am. And I will not contribute to your delinquency."

"We could have a wonderful time," he insisted, pulling her toward him.

"I think it's immoral when a girl gets involved with a man she has no possibility of marrying. It's disgraceful, the way girls use you, Kelly."

He fell silent, then started pitching pebbles at a nearby rock. Finally he said, "If you ever go to another island, Mrs. Henderson, don't ask so many deep questions. Take it as it is."

"I'll stay away from islands," she promised. "I wanted to see why my ancestors couldn't stomach this one."

"Did you find out?" he asked.

"Yes, and I can't stand it either."

"Why not?" he asked drowsily.

"I always side with the dispossessed. You know, Immanuel Quigley got into great trouble in Ohio, aiding the Indians."

"I'm sorry I wrecked your book about Quigley. Will they be angry . . . at Smith?"

"The biography of one man is the biography of all men," she said. "In the passage of time, Kelly, we all become one person."

"Do you honestly think a kanaka like me is as good as a haole like you?" he asked.

"I was once taught that if a pebble falls in the Arabian desert, it affects me in Massachusetts. I believe that, Kelly. We are forever interlocked with the rest of the world."

She saw that he was sleepy, so she cradled his sun-browned shoulders in her lap, and he asked for his guitar so that he might play a little slack-key, and he picked out melodies that spoke of the sunswept seashores that he loved. After a while the guitar fell from his hands, and he dozed.

Elinor, watching the panorama of sandy beach and palm trees, studied with interest what she thought was the changing of the tide, for the ocean waters seemed to be leaving the shore, until at last they stood far out to sea disclosing an emptier reef than any she had seen before, and she watched certain prominent puddles in which large fish, suddenly stranded, were whipping their tails in an attempt to escape. She began to laugh, and Kelly, forgetting where he was, asked drowsily, "Whassamatta you laff?" And she explained, "There's a fish trapped in a pool?" And he asked, "How da heck he stuck in dis . . ."

In horror he leaped up, saw the barren reef and the withdrawn waters. "Oh, Christ!" he cried in terror. "This is a big one!" He grabbed her in his strong arms and started dashing across the sand, past the useless Chevvy convertible and on toward higher land, but his effort was useless, for from the tormented sea the great tsunami that had sucked away the waters to feed its insatiable wave, now rushed forward at more than five hundred miles an hour.

It was not a towering wave but its oncoming force was incredible. It filled the reef. It kept coming relentlessly, across the sand, across the roads, across the fields. In low areas it submerged whole villages, but if it was not constricted and could spread out evenly, its destruction was moderate. However, when it was compressed into a narrowing wedge, as at the mouth of a valley, it roared in with accumulating fury until at last it stood more than seventy feet higher than along its accustomed shore.

In its first tremendous surge inward it trapped Kelly Kanakoa and Mrs. Henderson in their snug valley. It did not whip them about, like an ordinary breaker, for it was not that kind of wave; it merely came on and on and on, bearing them swiftly inland until Kelly, who knew how awful the outgoing rush would be, shouted, "Elinor! Grab hold of something!"

Vainly she grabbed at bushes, at trees, at corners of houses, but the implacable wave swept her along, and she could hold nothing. "Grab something!" he pleaded. "When the wave sucks back out . . ."

He was struck in the neck by a piece of wood and started to sink, but she caught him and kept his head above the rushing waters. How terrifying they were, as they came on with endless force. She was swept past the last house in the village and on up into the valley's tight confines, the most dangerous spot in the entire island from which to fight a retreating tsunami, for now the waters began to recede, slowly at first, then with speed and finally with uncontrollable fury.

She last saw Kelly almost unconscious, hanging instinctively to a kou tree upon whose branches she had placed his hands. She had tried to catch something for herself, too, but the waters were too powerful. At increasing speed she was sucked back over the route she had come, past the broken houses and the crushed Chevvy and the reef she had seen so strangely bare. As the last stones whipped past she thought: "This cursed island!" And she thought no more.

Now the drowsy life of the beachboy drifted from day to day, from week into week, and then into sleepy sun-swept months; the years of sand and sea crept on. In late November, when Florsheim drove his new Pontiac convertible off the *Moana Loa* and up to his old stand at the Lagoon, Kelly thought: "I wish I could tell Mrs. Henderson that it was neither a Buick nor a Cadillac," and the old hurt returned.

At the Swamp his mother Malama sang in the late afternoons with her Hawaiian friends: Mrs. Choy, Mrs. Fukuda, Mrs. Mendonca and Mrs. Rodriques, and they were never again bothered by Kelolo and his haole girls. For the most part he kept strictly to the Lagoon, where he sang a little, played some slack-key, and got a lot of cables. In time he found great consolation in Johnny Pupali's summary of sex: "It's the greatest thing in the world. You never get enough until you've just had some."

Once Florsheim remarked: "Kelly blalah, I t'ink dis one t'ing berry punny."

"Wha' dat?" Kelly asked.

"Allatime New York dey got pitchas wid' colors 'Come to Hawaii!' An' dey show dis rock wid wahines, grass skirts, flowahs in de hair, wigglin' de hips like to speak, 'You come to Hawaii, mister, we gonna screw till you dizzy.' "

"Ain' nuttin' wrong wid dat," Kelly reflected.

"But de punny t'ing, Kelly blalah, it ain' so easy to ketch a wahine on dis rock. It ain' dem mainland kanakas has de good time ovah heah, it's de wahines. You know what I t'ink, blalah?"

"You speak."

"I t'ink mo bettah dey get you 'n' me on de pitchas." And he fell into an exaggerated pose, his muscles flexed, his dark eyes staring out to sea past Diamond Head, and he made an ideal travel poster. Relaxing with laughter he yelled, "Kelly blalah, we de real attraction."

Later when Kelly was locked in a room with a red-hot divorcee from Los Angeles her father arrived unexpectedly and banged on the door, shouting, "Betty! I don't want you wrecking your life with any beachboy bum." But Kelly slipped out through a side hallway, so no real damage was done.

WHEN Shig Sakagawa landed at Yokohama in early 1946, he studied his ancestral homeland with care, and when he saw the starving people, the bombed-out cities and the pathetic material base from which the Japanese had aspired to conquer the world, he thought: "Maybe Pop's right, and this is the greatest country on earth, but it sure don't look it." In his first letter home he tried to report faithfully what he was seeing, but when Kamejiro heard it read, he sent his son a stern reply which said: "Remember that you are a good Japanese, Shigeo, and do not say such things about your homeland." After that Shig wrote mostly generalities.

His first days in Japan were tremendously exciting, for the bustle of Tokyo was reviving, and hordes of little workmen, each of whom looked like his father, scrambled over the bombed ruins, cleaning up as they went. Shig had never before seen such national vitality, and in time he became impressed with Japan's unconquerable resilience. Along the streets he saw innumerable elderly women like his own mother, wearing baggy canvas pants, and they worked harder than the men, lugging away big baskets of rubble. Almost while he watched, Tokyo was cleaned up and prepared for a new cycle of life. "I have to admire such people," he wrote to his father, and old Kamejiro liked this letter better than the disloyal one that had reflected upon Japan's defeat.

Shig took great interest in his work as translator for the Harvard professor whom General MacArthur had brought over to advise the Occupation on land reform. Dr. Abernethy was a curious, lanky man of most acute insights, and although he had to depend upon Captain Sakagawa for actual translations of what the Japanese farmers told him, he relied ultimately upon his own perceptions, and for the first time in his life Shig was able to study at close hand a refined human mind at work. A rice farmer would tell Shig, "I have two hundred and forty tsubo for paddy," and Shig would translate this for Dr. Abernethy, but the latter seemed hardly to be listening, for he was surveying the land himself and judging its productive quotient; so that almost before either Shig or the farmer spoke, Dr. Abernethy knew what the land was worth, and if Shig's translated evidence contradicted his, Shig had to reconcile the facts, and usually Abernethy was right.

On long jeep trips through the countryside, while Shig drove, Abernethy expounded his theories of land reform. "What General MacArthur's up against here, Shig, is a classic medieval concept of land ownership. In each area half a dozen wealthy men control the land and parcel out portions of it according to their own economic interests. That's not a bad system, really. Certainly it's a lot better than communism. But where the trouble comes is when personal economic interests, usually of an arbitrary nature, override national survival interest."

"Like what?" Shig asked, finding deep pleasure in Abernethy's willingness to talk to him on a mature, adult level. It was hell when well-meaning colonels insisted upon speaking pidgin.

"Well, like when a landowner in an area that needs more food holds back his land for other speculation, or doesn't use it at all."

"Does this happen?"

"Look around you! It's obvious that even during Japan's war for survival this landowner held his lands back. When such a thing occurs, to save your nation you ought to have a revolution. Throughout history that's been the inevitable concomitant of abusive land ownership. Fortunately, a land revolution can develop in either of two ways. In France the land was held so irrationally that the French Revolution was required before the whole rotten system could be swept away . . . with great loss of life. That's the poorest kind of revolution. In England, the same result was accomplished by taxation. In time the huge landholders simply couldn't hang onto their land any longer. Taxes were too high. So they were forced to sell, and so far as I know not a single human life was lost. That's the logical way to accomplish land reform."

"You think Japan faces the same problem as France and England?"

"All nations do," Abernethy said as they bounced along a rocky road in Shiba Prefecture. "The relationship of man to his land is simple and universal. Every nation began with land evenly distributed among producers. As a result of superior mentality or manipulative skill, able landlords begin to acquire large holdings, in which society confirms them. As long as there is no great pressure of population, these great holders are allowed to do pretty much as they wish. But when families multiply, their marriageable sons begin to look longingly at the expanse of idle land. For the moment all the conventions of society, religion, politics and custom support the large landholders, and in most nations those peasants who make the first protests are hanged. Here in Japan, when the first agitators asked for land, they were crucified, upside down. Later the pressures become greater, and you have a bloody revolution . . . unless you're smart, like the English, and then you accomplish the same end by adroitly applied taxes."

"And you think this cycle operates in all nations?" Shig pressed.

"I myself have witnessed five such revolutions at close hand. In Mexico the offenses against common sense were unbelievable, and so were the bloody reprisals. In England a smart bunch of legislators effected the change-over with marvelous simplicity. In Rumania the blood was ugly to see. Also Spain. In the western United States the cattlemen started to protect their immoral holdings with gunfire, but in time the common sense of the townspeople, applied through taxation, defeated them. No nation can avoid land reform. All it can do is determine the course it will take: bloody revolution or taxation."

"It seems to me that here in Japan we have a third choice. Land reform by fiat."

"Of course," Abernethy quickly agreed. "What you and I finally decide to order done, General MacArthur will do, and it'll turn out to be his greatest accomplishment in Japan. For it will distribute land equitably and at the same time prevent a bloody revolution."

"Then there really is a third alternative?" Shig pressed.

"Yes," Abernethy replied, "but few nations are lucky enough to lose a war to the United States."

They drove in silence for more than two miles, looking for a country lane that led to the headquarters of one of the most illogical of the large land holdings that had imperiled Japan, and when they spotted the turning, Shig studied the relatively small area involved—small, that is, as compared with Hawaii—and he began to laugh. "What's the joke?" his lanky, dour companion asked.

"I was thinking how ironic it is!"

"What?" Abernethy asked, for he loved the ironies of history.

"Here we are, you and I, doing all this work in redistributing farm lands in defeated Japan, while, actually, the situation in my own home, Hawaii, is far worse."

Dr. Abernethy sat with his knees hunched up toward his chin and waited silently till Shig looked at him. Then he smiled slyly and asked, "What do you suppose I've been talking to you about?"

Shig was so startled that he slowed down the jeep, brought it to a complete halt, and turned formally to look at his commander. "You mean you've been talking to me about Hawaii?"

"Of course. I want you to appreciate what the alternatives are."

"How do you know anything about Hawaii?"

"Anyone interested in land reform knows Hawaii. Now that Hungary and Japan have faced their revolutions, Hawaii and China remain the most notorious remnants of medievalism in the world."

"Will both have to undergo revolutions?" Shig asked.

"Of course," Abernethy replied simply. "The hardest lesson in all history to learn is that no nation is exempt from history. China's revolution will probably end in bloody confiscation. Hawaii's will probably be accomplished by peaceful taxation." He paused and asked, "That is, if smart young fellows like you have any sense."

"I still think it's sardonic that I should be over here helping to save Japan," Shig reflected. "I should be doing this same job at home." He shifted gears and headed for the small house where the nervous Japanese landlords waited.

"As I said," Dr. Abernethy repeated dourly, "few nations are lucky enough to lose wars at the right time. Lucky Japan."

This fact was hammered home when Shig finally overtook his older brother Goro, who served as translator in General MacArthur's labor division. He had been in Nagoya when Shig landed, working on a long-range program for the unionization of Japanese industry, but instead of serving a quiet intellectual theorist like Dr. Abernethy of Harvard he was with a team of red-hot American labor organizers from the A.F. of L. "This job is driving me crazy!" stocky Goro cried, rubbing his crew-cut stubble.

"Are the people you work for stupid?" Shig asked.

"Stupid! They're the smartest characters I ever met. What drives me nuts is that I work fifteen hours a day forcing Japanese into labor unions. I read them General MacArthur's statement that one of the strongest foundations of democracy is an organized laboring class, secure in its rights. And you know, I think MacArthur is right. It's the only way Japan will ever be able to combat the zaibatsu. Strong, determined unions. But by God it's maddening to be forcing onto the Japanese in Japan what the Japanese in Hawaii are forbidden to have."

"You mean unions?" Shig asked, as they drank Japanese beer in the Dai Ichi Hotel, where they were bunked.

"You're damned right I mean unions!" Goro fumed. "Let's be honest,

Shig. We practically fought a war to eliminate the zaibatsu in Japan. But you know the big firms here never controlled half as much as they do in Hawaii. You know, Shig, it's a crazy world when you fight a war to give the conquered what you refuse to give your own people back home."

Shig took refuge in a trick he often used when trying to think straight. He stopped talking and held his beer stein to his lips for a long time, but Goro used this interval to comment: "If unions are good in Japan, they're good in Hawaii. If the zaibatsu are bad in Japan, they're bad in Hawaii. Yet I'm forced to make the Japanese join unions here, and if I tried to do the identical thing in Hawaii I'd be arrested, beaten up, and thrown into jail. How bloody crazy can you get?"

"What you say is fascinating," Shig volunteered slowly. "The man I'm working for, this Dr. Abernethy, says exactly the same thing about the land problems. Only he always adds, 'A nation is lucky when it loses a war at the right time.' The more I look at what we're doing for Japan, the more I believe him."

Goro put down his beer and said solemnly, "When I get back to Honolulu, I'm going to introduce a new motto."

"What do you mean?"

" 'What's good enough for the vanquished, is good enough for the victor.' I'm going to see to it that a man in Hawaii has a right to join a union, too. Just like a man in Tokyo. And when I start, Hoxworth Hale better stand back. He won last time because labor was stupid. Next time I'll win because of what I'm learning in Japan."

"Don't commit yourself to trouble," Shig warned.

"If you don't do the same," Goro countered, "I'll be ashamed of you. You'll have wasted your war."

This was the first time Shig had heard the phrase that was to determine his behavior in the next few years. "Don't waste your war!" On this first enunciation of the basic law he said to his brother, "I've been wondering what I ought to do, Goro. Talking so much with Dr. Abernethy has convinced me of one thing. There isn't a single Japanese on Hawaii that's educated. Oh, there are smart men like Pop and medical doctors like Dr. Takanaga, but they don't really know anything."

"You're so right," Goro agreed sadly, slumping over his beer. "Have you ever talked to a real smart labor leader from New York?"

"So I thought maybe I'd go to Harvard Law School."

"What a marvelous idea!" Goro cried. "But look, kid, I don't want you to go there and just learn law."

"I have no intention of doing that," Shig replied carefully. "Dr. Abernethy suggested that maybe I'd like to live with him. His wife's a lawyer."

Goro became positively excited. "And you'd talk at night, and get a little polish and argue about world history. Shig! Take it. Look, I'd even help you with the money."

"Aren't you going on to graduate school?" Shig asked.

Goro blushed, toyed with his beer, then looked at his watch. "I think I have other plans," he confessed. "I want you to meet her."

The Dai Ichi Hotel in Tokyo stood near the elevated loop that circled the city, and not far from the Shimbashi Station. In 1946 this area was filled each night with pathetic and undernourished Japanese girls, some of the most appealing prostitutes Asia had ever produced, and the tragedy of their near-starvation was that when they began to recover their health, and their cheeks filled out, they were so confirmed in streetwalking that they could not easily convert into any other occupation, and they continued at their old trade, mastering a few English words and sometimes moving into surreptitious army quarters with their G.I. lovers.

Now, as Shig and Goro walked through the bitter cold of a Tokyo January night, the horde of girls called to them in Japanese, "Nice Nisei G.I. Would you like to sleep with a real warm girl tonight?" Shig felt sick and tried not to look at the haunting, starved faces, but they pressed near him, begging, "Please, Nisei, I make you very happy for one night. I am a good girl."

They looked exactly like the prettier Japanese girls he had known in Hawaii, and as they tugged hungrily at his arms, he thought: "Maybe there's something about losing a war that Dr. Abernethy doesn't appreciate. Maybe it isn't so good."

In time the brothers broke away from the Shimbashi girls and turned left toward the Ginza, but they kept away from that broad street which M.P.'s patrolled and headed instead for the Nishi, or west, Ginza, where they entered into an exciting maze of alleys, one of which contained a very tiny bar, not much bigger than a bedroom, called Le Jazz Bleu. Ducking swiftly inside, they found the little room thick with smoke, bar fumes and the sound of an expensive gramophone playing Louis Armstrong. Three customers sat on minute barstools, while from the rear an extremely handsome girl in western clothes approached. She was no more than twenty, tall, thin from undereating, and with an unforgettably alert face. Extending a slim hand to Goro she cried in Japanese, "Welcome to our center of culture and sedition!" And with these words she introduced Shig into one of the most fascinating aspects of postwar Japan: the intellectual revolution.

With bad luck Akemi could have become, and she knew it, a Hershey-bar girl, cadging nylons and canned beef from G.I.'s at Shimbashi Station, but in the earliest days of the Occupation she had been lucky enough to meet Goro Sakagawa, and he was not a Hershey-bar boy. It is true that he gave her whatever food and money he could afford, but she gave him little in return except exciting talk, a knowledge of Japan and more spiritual love than he knew existed in the world. It took Shig about two minutes to see that this pair was going to get married.

'Why does she work in a bar?" he asked Goro when Akemi disappeared to serve some customers.

"She wants to work, and she likes the music," Goro explained.

"Is she an Edokko?" Shig inquired, referring to the old name for Tokyo.

"The purest modenne," Goro laughed. Postwar Japanese youth prided themselves on their use of French, and to be modenne—moderne—was their highest ambition. "This girl is a terrific brain," Goro confided.

"I'll bet she's not Hiroshima-ken?" Shig teased.

"Have you seen Hiroshima?" Goro asked. "Pppssskkk!" he went, leveling his hand over the floor. "I don't want anything to do with Hiroshima."

"Mom's going to be very unhappy," Shig warned. "You come all the way to Japan and don't have sense enough to get yourself a Hiroshima girl."

"This is the girl for me," Goro said as Akemi rejoined them, and when she came to a table, his or anyone's, she added a new dimension to it, for she contained within her slim body an electric vitality which marked many people in the new Japan.

At midnight she whispered, "Soon the customers will go, and then we have real fun." Patiently she waited for the wandering drinkers to empty their glasses, and to each straggler she said a warm good night, thus insuring their subsequent return, but when the last had gone and the proprietor was turning out the lights, she sighed and said, "I wish drinks cost less. Then men would guzzle them faster."

Opening the darkened door a crack she whispered, "No M.P.'s," and the trio ducked down a series of the smallest alleys in the world, barely wide enough for two to pass if one stood sideways, and finally they came to a darkened door which Akemi-san pushed slowly open, revealing a rather large room in which more than a dozen young men and women sat in the most rigid silence, for an imported gramophone was playing music that neither Shig nor Goro could recognize, but its name was obvious, for on a music stand, with a single shaft of light playing upon it, rested the album from which the records had been taken: Mahler's *Kindertotenlied* sung by a German group. Quietly the newcomers sank to the floor, and when the music ended and more lights were lit, they saw that they were among an intense Japanese group composed of handsome young men and pretty girls. When talk began, it was all about Paris and André Gide and Dostoevski. Much of it was in French, and since Shig had acquired a smattering of that language, he was well received.

Then talk turned to the new Japan: freedom for women, the breaking up of large estates, the new role of labor, and both Shig and Goro were able to contribute much, but just as it seemed as if the old Japan were forever dead, Akemi appeared in a frail, tattered kimono which she kept by the gramophone, and the room grew deathly silent, with all assuming old, formal poses as Akemi began the tea ceremony, and as she moved through the curious and ancient ritual of making tea in a set way, and serving it just so, Shig sensed that these young Japanese were no different than he: they were caught in the changing of history, so that with part of their minds they embraced French words and everything modenne, while with the great anchors of the soul they held fast to the most inexplicable secrets of Japan. "Hawaii and Japan face the same problems," Shig mused, but when frail Akemi nodded that it was his turn, and another girl came creeping toward him on her knees, presenting him with the cup of bitter tea, he took it in both hands as he had been taught, turned the old cup until its most treasured edge was away from his unworthy lips, and drank.

When the ceremony ended, talk resumed and the girl who had brought him his bitter tea said, "American M.P.'s can destroy anything but the tea ceremony. No matter how hard you strike at our souls, you always seem to miss."

The statement irritated Shig and he said, "Not being an M.P., I wouldn't know. For myself, I bring freedom."

"What freedom?" the girl asked angrily.

"Land for the peasants," Shig said, and for a few minutes he was a hero, but then the lights lowered, the single shaft struck the music stand and Shig read: Bruckner, *The First Symphony*. This was a London recording, and he liked the music.

That night, as they made their way back through the remnant of Shimbashi girls that had caught no men for the evening, but who still hoped, not knowing what might turn up following a late brawl, Shig said, "I'd marry her, Goro. She's marvelous."

"I'm going to," his brother replied.

And in these strange ways the brothers Sakagawa discovered their ancestral homeland and saw how different it was from what their parents remembered, but they also discovered Hawaii, so that one night Goro slammed down his beer at the Dai Ichi Hotel and fumed: "It's insane that we should be here, Shig. We ought to be doing the same jobs at home." And as they worked in Japan, they thought of Hawaii.

IN 1947 the great Kee hui faced memorable excitements, for Nyuk Tsin was one hundred years old and her family initiated a round of entertainments celebrating that fact, climaxed by a massive fourteen-course dinner at Asia's brassy restaurant. The little old matriarch, who now weighed ninety-one pounds, appeared at each celebration dressed in black, her sparse gray hair pulled severely back from her temples. She chatted with her huge family and felt proud of their accomplishments, being particularly pleased when Hong Kong's youngest daughter, Judy, brought a pianist from the university, where she was studying, to sing a series of songs in Chinese. Nyuk Tsin, watching Judy's animated face, thought: "She could be a girl from the High Village. I wonder what's happening there now?"

One hundred and forty-one great-great-grandchildren attended the festivities, and upon them Nyuk Tsin poured her special love. Whenever one was presented she would ask the child in Hakka, "And what is your name, my dear?" The child's mother would poke her offspring and say in English, "Tell Auntie your name." But if the child replied, "Harry Rodriques," Nyuk Tsin would correct him and insist upon his real name, and the child would reply, "Kee Doh Kong," and by decoding this according to the family poem, Nyuk Tsin understood who was standing before her.

With her own name she also had trouble, for now there was no one alive in the world who knew what it was. Even her remaining sons, now in their agile seventies and eighties, had never known her name, for she had submerged her own personality in this powerful hui of which she was now the head. She was content to rule as Wu Chow's Auntie, the concubine without a name, but when she thought of herself it was invariably as Char Nyuk Tsin, the daughter of a brave peasant who had risen to be a general. She was deeply moved, therefore, when the celebrations were ended and her sons Asia and Europe said to her, "Wu Chow's Auntie, I see no further reason why we should continue to send money to our mother in the Low Village. She must surely be dead by now, and her family has never done anything for us."

"On the other hand," Nyuk Tsin reasoned, "she may still be alive, just as I am, and if so she would need the money more than ever. After all, she is your mother and you owe her that respect."

Only one misfortune clouded her hundredth birthday: her principal grandson Hong Kong was obviously in trouble, for he was ill at ease, nervous and irritable. Nyuk Tsin guessed that he was having difficulty meeting payments on the various ventures into which she had goaded him, and she was sorry that it was he who had to bear the burden of these trying days and not she. Therefore, when the mammoth dinner at Asia's ended, the little old lady told the women about her that she wanted to talk with Hong Kong, and after she was taken home and had examined her body for leprosy, and had inspected her big disgraceful feet, she appeared in a black gown with buttons down the right side and asked in Hakka, "Hong Kong, are things so very bad?"

"Wu Chow's Auntie, the detectives are back again," he explained.

"But you don't know whether that means good or bad," she observed.

"Detectives are never good," he assured her.

"How do you know they're back?"

"Kamejiro Sakagawa said they were digging into his land deal again. They were also asking sly questions at Australia's."

"How are we fixed for taxes and mortgage payments?" she asked.

This was the one bright spot, and he said with some relief, "Not too bad. With the money we saved last year we're out of trouble."

"Then we'll be prudent and wait," she advised. "If someone wants to hurt you, Hong Kong, keep him off balance. Make him take the first step toward you, for then you can watch him coming and take precautions."

Four days later the first step came, in the person of a husky, quiet-spoken Irishman from Boston with huge, bushy-black eyebrows, who said that his name was McLafferty and who appeared in Hong Kong's office asking idle questions about real estate, and from the assured manner in which the visitor behaved, Hong Kong deduced: "This one has the detective reports in his pocket. He knows."

Not much happened that first day. Hong Kong probed: "You looking for a hotel site? You got something else in mind?"

"What hotel sites have you?" Mr. McLafferty parried, but it was obvious that he wasn't interested. "I'll be back," he said.

As soon as he was gone, Hong Kong started half a dozen Kees on his trail, but all they turned up was that he really was Mr. McLafferty and he was a lawyer from Boston, stopping at the Lagoon. Hong Kong took this information to his grandmother, and they carefully weighed the various possibilities that might bring a Boston lawyer to Hawaii, and Hong Kong was all for dispatching a cable to a Kee who was studying at Harvard asking for detailed information on McLafferty, but his grandmother told him to wait. "Don't get excited until he makes some specific move," she cautioned him.

Two days later Mr. McLafferty returned and said casually, "If my syndicate decided on one of the big hotel sites . . . at your price? Could you deliver title to the land?"

Hong Kong realized that considering the intricate Hawaiian system of land ownership, this apparently trivial question was a trap, so he answered slowly and cautiously, "Well, I'd better explain, Mr. McLafferty, that out here we don't sell land fee simple. What I'd be willing to do is guarantee you a fifty-year lease."

"You can't sell us any land outright?" McLafferty probed cautiously.

"My hui—are you familiar with the word hui?—well my hui has a little fee simple, but not choice hotel sites. What we do have is control of some the best leases in Honolulu."

"Why don't you people sell fee simple?" McLafferty asked directly, but not bluntly. He was a careful operator.

Hong Kong decided not to waste time. "Mr. McLafferty, I don't think you're paying attention to land problems here. If you're far enough along to talk seriously about a hotel site you're bound to know that our estates never sell land. They lease it."

Mr. McLafferty liked this blunt answer, liked all he knew about Hong Kong, which was considerable, and felt that the propitious moment had come. "Could we send your secretary out? For maybe an hour?"

"Certainly," Hong Kong replied, his pulse hammering. He had learned that when this happened he must slow down . . . instantly. So he took some minutes giving his girl exaggerated instructions which Mr. McLafferty recognized as stalling. Then the wiry Chinese banker closed the door carefully, locked it, and returned to his desk, his pulse back to normal. In order to make his visitor think that he had been taken in by the hotel talk he said, "Now we have three wonderful hotel sites . . ."

"I'm not interested in hotels," the visitor said.

"What are you interested in?" Hong Kong asked evenly.

"I represent Gregory's."

The name literally exploded in the quiet office, ricocheted around Hong Kong's ears and left him stunned. Finally he asked, "You going to bull your way into the islands?"

"You have used exactly the right word," McLafferty said coldly. "Six months from now, Mr. Kee, we will have bulled our way into the biggest goddamned store right," and he whipped out a secret map of downtown Honolulu, "here." Forcefully he jabbed his finger at a prime intersection.

When Hong Kong saw the location he gasped. "The Fort will break you, Mr. McLafferty," he warned.

"Nope. We're too strong. We're ready to lose five million dollars the first three years. We have resources of nearly half a billion behind that. The Fort is not going to break us."

"But it won't let you buy that land, or lease it either. You simply aren't going to get in there."

"You're going to buy it for us, Mr. Kee."

"It's not for sale," Hong Kong protested.

"I mean, you're going to get the leases. You'll use an assumed name . . . a dozen assumed names. After today I won't see you again, but we'll arrange some system of keeping in contact. Gregory's is breaking into Honolulu, and don't you ever doubt it."

"If The Fort doesn't break you, it'll break whoever buys the land for you. It has great power to retaliate."

"We've thought about that . . . a lot, Mr. Kee."

"Why don't you call me Hong Kong?"

"And we spent more than a year analyzing your position out here. If you keep in a solvent position, Hong Kong, nobody can hurt you. And if they try, we stand ready to spend a good deal of the five million we know we'll lose, shoring you up."

Hong Kong liked this daring, cold-blooded Boston Irishman, and after a moment's reflection asked, "You have to have that specific corner."

"No other," the lawyer said.

"How long do I have?"

"Six months."

"You agree to pay fifty per cent above going rates?"

"We'll do better. You give us a strict accounting of actual costs, and we'll give you a hundred per cent commission."

"You know that if The Fort hears about this . . ."

"We know. That's why we chose you to negotiate the leases."

Hong Kong leaned back. "You're certainly aware, Mr. McLafferty, that the profit to me is not very substantial. But nevertheless you're asking me to risk my business life in a head-on tangle with The Fort. How do you reason?"

"We say this. O. C. Clemmons wants to come into these islands, but The Fort won't let them. Won't sell them land. Won't provide shipping. Won't do anything. Same with Shea and Horner, same with California Fruit. The Fort has cold-bloodedly decided that no mainland firm will be allowed in Hawaii. They are determined to set their own prices, keep competition out, garner all profits to The Fort."

"I know all that," Hong Kong said evenly. "Maybe better than you. But why should I fight your battle?"

"For two simple reasons," the lawyer said. "You're right that we can't begin to pay you for the risks you'll be taking if The Fort decides to eliminate you, as they may. But remember this, Hong Kong. Here is the real estate you control." And on his map Mr. McLafferty pointed to almost every parcel Hong Kong then held. It was remarkable that the man knew so much. "Now if Gregory's comes in, and O. C. Clemmons, and Shea and Horner, the entire economic life of Hawaii gets a boost. Land is scarce. They have got to buy from you, and every inch you have will double and treble in value. Hong Kong, you've got to believe that an expanding economy is good for everyone, a stagnant economy is bad for us all. Your profits will come indirectly. And the irony of it is, if The Fort had let us in ten years ago when we first tried, for every dollar of profit we made, they would have made six, because we would have stirred up their whole economy for them."

"The Fort has no intention of allowing things to be stirred up," Hong Kong pointed out.

"And that's my second reason, Hong Kong. Anything that helps Gregory's or California Fruit helps you people, and by you people I mean the Japanese and the Chinese. Did your spies find out who my old man was? Look, I know you sent cables to Boston to check on me. Well, my old man was Black Jim McLafferty, a bull-necked Irishman from downtown Boston with ferocious eyebrows like mine, and every fight you Chinese have had in Hawaii, we Irishmen had twice as bad in Boston. But my old man . . . Hong Kong, he was a terror. Wound up governor till the local Fort put him in jail. Then he became mayor on a vindication ticket. I'm Black Jim's son, and I don't scare easy. Believe me when I tell you that you've got to do to The Fort what my old man did to the stiff-necked Protestants in Boston."

Hong Kong did not like the way the conversation was going, so he took it onto a higher level by observing, "Seems to me what you have to do sooner or later is get a bigger piece of land on the edge of the city where you can have lots of parking."

"We plan to, after we get our first operation working."

"What you ought to do, if you're smart, is buy the second piece of land right now before prices go up."

"Exactly what I wanted to discuss next. We've already settled on the location, and we expect you to buy it for us at the same time you get the downtown leases."

"Where?" Hong Kong asked.

"At the other end of town there's a fine piece of land inside a big fence. It's called the Swamp . . ."

"Oh, no!" Hong Kong laughed. "Can't be touched."

"We'd give two million for it."

"You'd give two million . . . I'd give two million . . . anybody would, but it can't be sold."

"It's owned by an elderly Hawaiian lady called . . ." He took out a piece of paper. "Malama Kanakoa, and she has one boy they call Kelly. He's a beachboy."

"Mr. McLafferty, you have remarkable judgment where land is concerned, but this parcel is tied up in a trust. To get it you've got to buck three trustees, appointed by the court. You know who they are in this case? First comes Hewlett Janders, from The Fort. Second, John Whipple Hoxworth, from The Fort. And third, Harry Helmore, married to Abigail Hewlett, from The Fort. You think they're going to let you pick up that land?"

"We'll take it to court!" McLafferty stormed, and Hong Kong was pleased to see that the Irishman was in this fight to the finish.

"Good idea!" the Chinese agreed warmly. "And who do you suppose the judges will be who hear your appeal? Same ones who appointed the trustees. And what are the names of these judges? There's Judge Clements, married to a Whipple. There's Judge Harper, from Texas, came out a widower and married a Hoxworth. And there's Judge McClendin from Tennessee. He's not married to anybody, but his son is, to a Hale. How do you think they will hand down their decision in a case affecting The Fort?"

"Are they all crooks?" McLafferty asked bluntly.

"Not a one of them," Hong Kong replied. "In fifty years of pretty close watching The Fort I've never caught them in one crooked deal. They're very honest men, upright, trustworthy. They just happen to believe with all their hearts that only they know what is best for Hawaii. No judge ever hands down a dishonest decision. Never. They just study who's involved in the case, and if it's Hong Kong Kee versus Hoxworth Hale, why, on the face of it I've got to be wrong, because Hale is a man known to be honest, and whatever he wants to do is unquestionably for the welfare of Hawaii."

"They got it real sewed up, don't they?" McLafferty growled.

"But the best they've got is this trustee racket," Hong Kong continued. "You take this Malama Kanakoa. She has parcels of land worth ten million . . . at least. The judges say, 'Malama, you're a dear Hawaiian woman with no sense at all. We're going to put you on a spendthrift trust. Three fine haoles will look after your interests, protect you. All we're going to charge you for this service is fifty thousand dollars a year. You can have what's left.' And then the trustees, appointed by the courts, reason: 'Best way to keep a Hawaiian in line is keep 'em in debt.' So within a year poor Malama is so deep in debt to stores run by The Fort, and she owes the government so many back taxes she never can get her head above water. But year after year the trustees get their fees, before the stores, before the government, before Malama. They filter down a little money to her, and things go on and on."

"So by the trick of doing nothing and waiting, they steal the islands blind . . . but in an honest way."

Hong Kong studied this summary for some time, then cautiously observed: "I suppose so far The Fort has held us back two full generations. If we had paid labor a good wage twenty years ago, I suppose our gross island product would have increased maybe half a billion dollars each year."

"You don't call that stealing?" McLafferty asked.

"Technically you can't, if their intentions are honest. They may be dumb but they're not crooks."

"Then you'll get the land for us?" McLafferty asked.

"I have to consult my hui," Hong Kong countered, taking refuge in that word, for he knew that McLafferty would not understand if he said, "I must talk this over with my hundred-year-old grandmother."

"I needn't warn you," the Bostonian said, "that if any of your hui breathes a word of this . . ."

"My hui has been keeping secrets for almost a century," Hong Kong replied cryptically, and next day he reported: "My hui says that now's the time to strike. I have four Japanese, two Chinese and a Filipino starting to get your land. In six months you'll have it. How do I slip messages to you in Boston?"

McLafferty looked astonished. "Boston?" he repeated. "Didn't I tell you? I'm living here from now on. I'm part of the revolution that's about to hit these islands. Since I got my old man's eyebrows, I suppose that in the elections I'll be called Black Jim McLafferty. You see, I'm a working Democrat."

WHEN Hoxworth Hale, back in 1946, succeeded in frustrating the attempt of California Fruit to open a string of supermarkets in Hawaii, he reported to The Fort: "Within the past year we have been faced by formidable challenges from the mainland. This was to have been expected after the dislocations of war, and for a while it looked as if the dangerous radical movements we have detected in the population might lead to California Fruit's success, for these outsiders came very close to snapping up several leases, and at one point I was afraid they might succeed in buying out Kamejiro Sakagawa, but we applied certain pressures on the little Japanese and forestalled that. So for the time being, at least, we have turned back a very dangerous enemy. But in a larger sense it seems to me that our real danger is going to come from Gregory's. They have tried twice now to penetrate our market, and only by the most resolute action have we forestalled them. We must remain extremely alert to keep them out of Hawaii, and I shall consider any member of our group derelict to his duty who does not keep us informed of Gregory's next move.

"As for O. C. Clemmons and Shea and Horner, I feel certain we have scared them off, so that unless something unforeseen happens, we need expect no more challenges from them." Hoxworth looked steadily at his colleagues, as if to instill into each the courage to keep Hawaii free of alien influences, and the members left that meeting with added resolution, but in 1947 Hale had to summon his confreres again, and this time he reported: "Something is happening around here that I neither like nor understand. I was alerted some time ago by the clerk at the Lagoon to the fact that a Boston lawyer named James McLafferty was in our city and acting rather suspiciously. For example, he was caught talking a long time with the beachboy Kelly Kanakoa—that's Malama's rather worthless son. We put some people on Kelly and found out that this McLafferty had brought up the subject," and here Hoxworth paused for dramatic effect, "the subject of the Swamp."

A white-capped wave of excitement, marked by widely opened eyes, sped about the room, like a breaker heading for shore, and Hale continued: "So far as we can deduce from what Kelly was able to tell us, McLafferty had in mind the possibility of," again he dropped his voice to underline the enormity of what was going on, "a hotel." Once more the wave of opened eyes flashed about the room, for the owners of almost every important hotel sat that day in The Fort. "I've put tracers on this McLafferty and haven't come up with much. Hewlett, will you read us what we've found so far?"

Hewlett Janders coughed, picked up a sheet of paper, and read: "James McLafferty, B.A. Holy Cross 1921, Harvard Law School 1926. Practices law in Boston. Served as colonel in the Army Air Corps 1941-

45 in charge of land procurement for airstrips in Africa, Italy and England. Author with Professor Harold Abernethy of Harvard *Land Procurement Policies of the U. S. Army Air Corps.* Son of the infamous Black Jim McLafferty, long-time Democratic politician who served a term in jail for malfeasance while governor. Roman Catholic and visited Rome twice while on duty overseas, which endeared him to his father's constituents. He himself has never run for office." Big Hewlett Janders stopped, then added, "No clue as to who is employing him for whatever he's doing in Hawaii." Hewlett threw the paper on the table as if to say, "If you think you can make anything out of this, you're welcome to try."

Hoxworth Hale said, "Well, what does it add up to? We find that a stranger who knows a lot about land procurement, who is obviously a radical of some sort from Harvard, is interested in the Swamp . . . for a hotel. It certainly looks to me as if he were the kind of man we've been trying to keep out of our city." The men about the table nodded, so Hale continued: "Do we have any of the Kanakoa Trust men among us?"

Hewlett Janders replied, "I'm on the board, so is John Whipple Hoxworth. The third member is Harry Helmore and he can certainly be trusted."

"Will you speak for Harry?" Hale asked.

"Well, he's married to my cousin Abigail," Hewlett pointed out. "I guess I can speak for him."

"Is it agreed then that under no circumstances will Malama Kanakoa be allowed to sell the Swamp to McLafferty?"

"So far as I'm concerned," Hewlett replied. "How about you, John Hoxworth?"

"It would be criminal to admit a man like that into our city."

"Then it's agreed," Hoxworth announced, but his natural caution in these matters was not yet satisfied, so he asked, "Let's suppose for a minute that this talk about a hotel was a blind. Let's suppose that McLafferty was acting as front man for someone entirely different. Gentlemen, I think that's a fair supposition. Whom does this man really represent?"

The wily, practiced men of The Fort turned their whole attention to this problem. Slowly John Whipple Hoxworth, a thin, clever man with a typical Whipple intellect, reasoned: "The group that was most furious when we turned them back was California Fruit, but I think that out of natural vanity they would refuse to recruit an agent from Boston. It just wouldn't seem palatable to a Californian. I don't think O. C. Clemmons is going to fight again, and after two bad whippings I doubt that Gregory's will be back. Therefore I have to conclude that it's Shea and Horner. It's the kind of trick they'd pull, and after all, remember that Shea is a prominent Catholic."

"I wonder if it could be Gregory's after all?" Hoxworth mused. "Has anybody met this McLafferty yet?"

No one had, and the meeting ended with Hale's final warning: "I suppose you've all read that California Fruit has signed a contract with their labor unions? Gregory's entered into one three years ago, and you know the Shea and Horner stand. If you require any encouragement in this fight to keep men like McLafferty out of our city, keep the labor union angle in mind."

When the others had left The Fort, Hoxworth Hale sat brooding upon the things they had been discussing, and he could not comprehend how any sensible man who loved Hawaii would even consider allowing an outfit like Gregory's entrance to the islands. "Why, damn it all!" he growled. "They're outsiders. They undercut established principles, and if they made a little money, what would they do with it? Siphon it off to New York. Does it ever do Hawaii any good? Not a penny of it." He looked out his window toward the Missionary Public Library, built with family funds, then toward the Missionary Art Museum, which his Grandfather Ezra had endowed with half a million dollars and a Rembrandt. In the distance lay the Missionary Natural History Museum, housing an unmatched collection of Hawaiian artifacts, and beyond it stood the rugged, magnificent memorial to old Abraham Hewlett's love of the Hawaiian people, Hewlett Hall, where Hawaiian boys and girls were given free a first-rate education. More important were the things that could not be seen: the family professorships at the university, the Missionary Foundation for Oceanic Research, the Missionary Fund for Retired Ministers. You could scarcely touch an aspect of Hawaii which had not been improved and nourished by some member of The Fort.

"Suppose we allowed Gregory's to come in and operate as they wished," Hoxworth mused. "Let's look at Honolulu fifty years from now. Is there going to be a Gregory's Museum, or a Gregory's School for Hawaiians? They will steal our money and give us nothing in return except lower prices for a little while. Will their executives raise large families here and put their children to work in the islands? They will not. We will have soulless absentee landlordism of the worse sort. If Gregory's ever do wedge their way into the islands . . . after my death I hope . . . they will bring us nothing . . . nothing."

He walked back and forth in real perplexity and came at last to the nexus of his thinking: "No, I'm wrong. They'll bring two things. They'll bring political unrest, because half of their people will be New Deal Democrats with radical ideas. And they'll bring labor unions." These two potentialities were so abhorrent that he paused to look out over the Honolulu he loved so well. "Why don't the people down there trust us to know what's best for these islands?" he asked in some bewilderment. "You'd think they'd bear in mind all we've done for Hawaii. Why, they ought to rise up as one man and kick outfits like Gregory's or California Fruit right into the ocean. But they never seem to appreciate what's best for them."

His secretary interrupted to say, "That young Japanese is trying to see you again," and Hale shook his head furiously.

"Not me! Negotiating with labor is Hewie's problem," and he ducked out a back door, calling for Hewlett Janders. When the big man appeared, Hale commissioned him: "See if you can handle this young troublemaker once and for all," and he felt some assurance as big Hewie hitched up his belt and went forth to battle.

When Janders entered the board room he found there a confident, crop-haired, smiling young man who extended his right hand across the table and said, "I'm Goro Sakagawa, sir. I remember how good you were to my brothers."

The gesture caught big Hewie Janders off guard, and for a fleeting instant he thought: "This is the brother we didn't take into Punahou. If we had, he'd never have grown up to be a labor leader." Then he dismissed the thought and said sternly, "What is it you wish to see me about, young man?" Pointedly, he did not ask Goro to sit down.

Displaying some of the polish he had acquired while serving with General MacArthur in Japan, Goro ignored the fact that he had to remain standing and said, "They tell me your son Harry was killed on Bougainville."

"He was," Janders replied, and that made it necessary for him to ask, "Wasn't one of your brothers killed in Italy?"

"Two," Goro replied, and somehow each of the negotiators realized that Hewlett Janders of The Fort had been subtly brought down to Goro Sakagawa's level. They were equal, and Goro said, "You asked why I wanted to see you. I've been nominated by the men at Malama Sugar . . ."

"I won't discuss a labor union."

"I haven't said anything about a labor union," Goro pointed out, shifting from one foot to the other while Hewlett slumped back in his chair.

"What else would you want to talk about?" Janders snapped.

"All right, since you bring the matter up, Mr. Janders. Malama Sugar is going to organize . . ."

"Get out!" Janders said abruptly, his voice rising even though he remained seated.

Quietly Goro replied, "Malama Sugar is going to be organized, Mr. Janders. Under federal law we are entitled . . ."

"Out!" Janders shouted. Leaping to the door he called for his assistants, and when they had piled into the room he commanded: "Throw this communist out."

Goro, even stockier than he had been in high school, braced himself against the table and spoke quickly: "Mr. Janders, I'm not a communist and I'm not going to let your people throw me out, because if they did I'd have a court case against you. Then your position on the union would harden, and we'd have even more trouble discussing things intelligently. So call the dogs off."

"I will never accept a union," Janders cried. "And don't you ever come stomping back into this office."

"Mr. Janders, I promise you that the first plantation we organize will be Malama Sugar, and when we reach the final negotiations I will sit in this chair . . ." Goro reached for a chair, lifted it carefully and set it down in position. "This chair. Save it for me, Mr. Janders. The next time we meet here will be to sign papers. The name's Goro Sakagawa."

He left the room quietly and Janders dismissed his aides. Slumping into his chair he tried to understand what had happened: "A Japanese field hand stomped into my office and told me . . ." He collapsed in incredulity and called for Hoxworth Hale.

"How'd it go?" Hale asked.

"A Japanese field hand stomped into my office and told me . . ."

"Quit the dramatics, Hewie. What happened?"

"They're going to organize Malama Sugar."

"They'll never make it," Hale said firmly. He summoned The Fort and told his men, "Hewie's had a bad ten minutes. Young Sakagawa tipped his hand . . ."

"He stomped in here and tried to tell me . . ."

"Hewie!" Hale interrupted. "He didn't try to tell you. Damn it all, he told you."

"They're going to organize Malama Sugar," Janders repeated. "And if they succeed there . . . then they'll try the rest."

"This has come sooner than I expected," Hale observed. "When we beat back our Russian communists in the strikes of 1939 and 1946, I figured we had them licked. But apparently the dreadful Roosevelt virus has infected our entire society."

"But I never expected to see the day," Janders mumbled, "when a Japanese field hand could stomp into my office . . ."

Hard, competent Hoxworth Hale, who from behind the scenes had masterminded the two preceding fights against the union, now began marshaling his forces. Rapping on the table he said, "We shall present a unified force against them, and if anyone of you in this room wavers, we will show no mercy. On the one hand, the Japanese radicals will overwhelm you. And on the other, we'll ruin you. No credit. No common merchandising. No legal support. Gentlemen, you stick with us or you perish." He stopped, glared at the men, and asked, "Is that agreed?"

"Agreed," the plantation men muttered, and the strike was on.

When policies had been set and the meeting adjourned, the plantation owners stood nervously about the room, unwilling to leave, and Hale asked, "How did a decent young man like Goro Sakagawa, with three brothers in Punahou, become a communist?"

Janders replied, "I think he was assigned to the A.F. of L. in Japan."

A pall settled over The Fort. John Whipple Hoxworth mused: "To think that our government took a decent Japanese boy and instructed him in labor tactics!" Something of the world's maniacal contradiction seeped into the room and mocked the managers, and Hoxworth Hale asked sadly, "You mean that a boy who might have gone to Punahou was perverted by our own government?" On this gloomy note the first meeting of The Fort's strike committee ended.

Actually, when Hewlett Janders accused Goro Sakagawa of being a communist he was not far from the truth. When The Fort, in 1916, 1923, 1928, 1936, 1939 and 1946, refused point-blank even to discuss unionism and used every known device including force and subversion to block labor from attaining any of its legitimate ends, it made normal unionization of the islands impossible. The hard-hitting but completely American union organizers sent out from the mainland found that in Hawaii customary procedures got nowhere. Not even the vocabulary of unionism was understood, or acknowledged where it was understood, so that both The Fort and the Honolulu *Mail* invariably referred to any union activity as communism; as a result, over the course of years Hawaii developed its own rather strange definition for terms which on the mainland were understood and accepted as logical parts of modern industrial life. In brief, unionism was subversion.

There were also physical difficulties. Oftentimes mainland men whom the course of history proved to have been rather moderate labor organizers were refused entrance to the islands. If they tried to talk to plantation hands they were bodily thrown off the premises. If they tried to hire a headquarters hall, none was allowed them. They were intimidated, vilified, abused and harassed by charges of communism.

In obedience to Gresham's Law of social change, when the moderates were driven out, the radicals moved in, and from 1944 on, a group of ultra-tough labor men quietly penetrated the islands and among them were many communists, for they had seen from afar that the situation in Hawaii made it a likely spot for the flowering of the communist creed. Among the leaders was a hefty, ugly Irish Catholic from New York named Rod Burke, who had joined the Party in 1927 and who had steadily risen in its ranks until he had reached a position of eminence from which he could be trusted to lead a serious attack upon Hawaii. His first step was to marry a Baltimore Nisei, and this Japanese girl, already a communist, was to prove of great assistance to him in his grand design for capturing the islands.

For example, when Rod Burke met Goro Sakagawa, returning to Hawaii after his instructive labor experiences in Japan, Burke instantly spotted the capable young army captain as the kind of person he required for the unionization and subsequently the communization of Hawaii. So Burke said to his Japanese wife, "Get young Sakagawa lined up," and the dedicated Nisei girl succeeded in enlisting Goro not as a communist but as a labor organizer, and through him Burke conscripted other Japanese and Filipinos without confiding to them his membership in the Communist Party. In this way a solid-core labor movement was founded which in 1947 stood ready to confront The Fort and fight to the rugged, island-breaking end.

In later years Goro Sakagawa often discussed these beginnings with his lawyer brother Shigeo, back from an honors degree at Harvard, and he allowed Shig to probe his motives and understandings as they existed in early 1947. "Did you know then that Rod Burke was a communist?" Shig asked.

"Well, I never knew for sure, but I guessed he was," Goro explained. "He never gave me any proof. But I recognized him as a tough-minded operator."

"If you had these suspicions, Goro, why were you willing to hook up with him?"

"I realized from experience that old-style methods would never break The Fort. We tried reasonable unionism and got nowhere. Burke knew how to apply power. That's the only thing The Fort understood."

"Did Burke ever try to sign you up in the Party?"

"No, he figured he could use me and then dump me in favor of the dumber Japanese and Filipinos he did sign up in the Party," Goro explained.

"How did he select his men?"

"Well, he picked them up where he could. Started enlisting Japanese who didn't know too much . . . Filipinos too. But they were just for support. The real guts of the Party was Rod Burke and his wife."

"Where did that leave you?" Shig explored.

"I figured just like Burke," Goro explained. "I figured I was smart enough to use him and then dump him."

"Must have been a very interesting period," Shig said wryly.

"There were no illusions on either side," Goro confessed. "Funny thing is that my wife, Akemi, figured the Burkes out the first time she saw them. She'd come up against a lot of communists in Japan, and she spotted Mrs. Burke instantly. And I think Mrs. Burke spotted her, so nobody was fooled," Goro assured his brother.

"Did Burke sign up any really good men?" Shig asked.

"Well, most of the Japanese were dopes, pure and simple, but Harry Azechi was as able a man as we ever produced in the islands."

"Looking back on it, Goro, do you think the alliance was necessary?"

Goro had often thought about this, especially since he had known so intimately the moderate A.F. of L. men on General MacArthur's team, and he concluded: "If you remember the position taken by The Fort . . . that even a discussion of labor was communism . . . Hell,

Shig, I've told you about the time I went in to see Hewlett Janders. He made me stand like a peasant with my cap in my hands. Abused me, ridiculed me. Shig, there was no alternative."

"None?" his brother asked.

"None. Hawaii could never have moved into the twentieth century until the power of The Fort was broken. I alone couldn't have done it. The A.F. of L. men I knew in Japan couldn't have done it. Only a gutter fighter like Rod Burke could have accomplished it."

So when Hewlett Janders announced to the Honolulu *Mail* that mainland communists were endeavoring to capture the islands, he was right. And when he charged that Japanese had joined the Party under Rod Burke's leadership, he was also correct. But when he said that the leader of the plantation part of the strike, Goro Sakagawa, was also a communist, he was not right, but in those tense years the hatred of labor was so great that a relatively minor error like that didn't really matter.

The strike was a brutal, senseless, tearing affair, and it frightened Hawaii as nothing previous had ever done, not even the bombing of Pearl Harbor. Rod Burke moved swiftly to tie up the waterfront so that not a single H & H ship entered Hawaii for five and one half starving, agonized months. The Fort retaliated by cutting credit, so that everyone in the islands felt the pinch.

Goro Sakagawa led his sugar-plantation workers out on strike. The Fort retaliated by suspending all sorts of benefits, so that soon it was not the workers who felt the cruelty of social warfare, but their families.

Rod Burke allowed no cargoes of either sugar or pineapple to leave the islands and no tourists to come in. The Fort retaliated by closing two of its hotels, and the maids and waiters thus thrown out of work were less able to weather the strike than were the hotel owners.

Goro Sakagawa got the pineapple workers to join the strike. The Fort coldly announced that its food-supply warehouses were nearly empty and it could no longer distribute to stores like Kamejiro Sakagawa's, so one shopkeeper after another faced bankruptcy.

No man can understand Hawaii who does not understand the great strike. It crippled the islands to the point of despair. Newsprint ran low and the existence of the papers was threatened. Food diminished to the one-week mark, and many families went hungry. Sugar plantations saw their crops rotting in the parching sunlight. Pineapple fields went untended, and millions upon millions of unrecoverable dollars were lost. Banks watched their normal flow of business halted. Big stores had neither new stocks nor old customers. Doctors went unpaid and dentists saw no patients. The major hotels could serve only inadequate foods, and the very life of the islands ground slowly to a halt.

For a strike in Hawaii was not like a strike in Florida. It was like nothing the mainland ever knew, for in Florida if the waterfront was tied up, food could be imported by train, and if the trains were closed down, men could use trucks, and if they were struck, hungry families could organize car caravans, and if they failed, a desperate man could walk. But in Hawaii when the docks were tied up, there were no alternatives, and the islands came close to prostration. Reasonable industrial relations having proved impractical, stupidity on the part of both capital and labor nearly destroyed the islands.

At the beginning of the sixth month Goro Sakagawa, attended by four assistants, marched into the board room of The Fort, waited for the directors of the great plantations to assemble, and then sat in precisely the chair he had promised Hewlett Janders he would one day occupy, and in that symbolic moment some of the intractable fight went out of him. It was curious that seating oneself in a chair that had been insolently forbidden should affect a man, as if there were hidden emotional channels that ran from his bottom to his brain, but that is what happened. Secure in his chair, Goro said in conciliatory manner, "We think the strike has progressed long enough. We are sure you think the same. Is there not some way to end it?"

"I will not have a Japanese field hand stomp into my office . . ." Hewlett Janders began, but Hoxworth Hale looked at him in pity, as if the horrors of six months had been useless, in that Janders was using the same words he had used when the strike began.

Quietly Goro ignored him and addressed Hale, a tough negotiator: "Mr. Hale, my committee is not going to take cognizance of the fact that your negotiator, Mr. Hewlett Janders, has attacked us for being Japanese, because we know that your cousin, Colonel Mark Whipple, laid down his life that we might be free citizens. We're acting as free citizens, and I think you appreciate that fact."

The gracious tribute to Colonel Whipple softened the meeting, and all remembered what this same Goro Sakagawa, an army captain in those days, had said when it was proposed to bring Mark Whipple's body home from the Vosges Mountains: "Let them bring my brothers home, but Colonel Whipple should sleep in the heart-land of the world, where he died. No island is big enough to hold his spirit."

"What new terms have you in mind, Mr. Sakagawa?" Hale asked.

"We will never end the strike unless we get full union recognition," Goro replied, and Hewlett Janders slumped in his chair. He could see it coming: the others were willing to surrender. The communists were about to triumph. But before Hewie could speak, Goro quickly added, "Then, to match your concession, we'll accept ten cents an hour less."

"Gentlemen," Hoxworth Hale said with fresh hope, "I think Mr. Sakagawa's proposal gives us something to talk about." Subtly the spirit of Colonel Mark Whipple, who had died for these Japanese boys, invaded the room, and Hale asked quietly, "Goro, will you bring your men back in about three hours?"

"I will, Mr. Hale," the union leader assured him, but as the group started to leave, Hewie Janders asked sharply, "How do we know that communist Rod Burke'll allow us to open the piers?"

"That's what we've been negotiating about, Mr. Janders," Goro replied. "When I reach an agreement with you men, the piers are open. That's what negotiation means."

When the delegation left—three Japanese, a haole and two Filipinos—Hewlett Janders left his seat at the head of the table and said, "I cannot participate in what you men are about to do."

"I appreciate your position," Hale said coldly. "But will you bind yourself to accept what we decide?" At this question everyone turned to stare at Janders. If he refused to accept, in the name of J & W, the principal plantation operators, no one knew what the eventuality might be, and it was just possible that he might be big enough to resist both the unions and his own associates. Desperately he was tempted to fight this out to a Götterdämmerung conclusion, but he was prevented from doing so by cautious words from the man who twenty years before had taken the leadership of The Fort from him. Hoxworth Hale said slowly, "Hewie, your family and mine have always loved these islands. We cannot stand by and see them suffer any further."

The big man looked in dismay at his leader and was about to reject the proposals, but Hale reasoned: "If we must live with labor, and that seems to be the spirit of the times, let's do so with a certain grace. I'm going to call Sakagawa back and make the best . . ."

"I do not wish to be present," Janders said abruptly. He started to leave the room by the back door, but paused to warn his associates: "You're turning these islands over to the communists. I refuse to watch a Japanese field hand come stomping into my office to lay down . . ."

"But you will consider yourself bound by our decision?" Hale interrupted.

"Yes," Janders snapped grudgingly, and when Goro returned to ratify the mutual surrender, Hewlett Janders was not there.

When the great strike ended, three of Hale's plantation managers, men senior to himself, quit with these words: "We been doin' things our own way too long to be told by a bunch of slant-eyed Japs how to raise sugar." Younger men stepped forward to take their places—and it was a rueful moment when Hale discovered that he did not even know two of the replacements—and before the year ended, the new overseers were reporting: "We can work with the new system. Looks like we'll make more sugar than before." Hewie Janders snorted: "Something is eroding the character of America when young men are so eager to compromise with evil."

And then Hewie made his point. At a meeting of The Fort he rushed in with the news that one of the lesser communists had broken with Rod Burke and had signified his willingness to identify both Burke and his wife as card-carrying members of the Communist Party. This caused a flurry of excitement, which a series of substantiating phone calls raised to fever pitch. "I knew the whole lot of them were communists!" Hewie cried triumphantly. "To think that we allowed Goro Sakagawa to come stomping into this office . . ."

"I don't believe he's charged," Hale cautioned. "At least when I called Jasper he didn't . . ."

"They're all communists," Hewie warned. "I told you a year ago that Rod Burke was a red. And he was. I tell you now that Goro Sakagawa is a red. And he is."

John Whipple Hoxworth said icily, "Let's wait till they're indicted, then apply all our strength until they're convicted."

"Has anybody called the governor?" Janders asked.

"Not yet," John Whipple replied.

"I'd love to!" Janders gloated. "Last time I saw him about communism he said . . ."

"Nobody will call anybody," Hale interrupted. "A great thing has happened in our favor. Nobody must spoil it." And The Fort studied carefully how the new developments could be used to its advantage.

But the day's triumph was somewhat dampened by an assistant's report that while everyone's attention had been focused on the strike, something curious seemed to have been happening, something which he was unable to explain. Producing a map of downtown Honolulu, he pointed to certain areas hatched in red and explained: "This is the Rafer Hoxworth building, and the ground floor has been leased to a Japanese named Fujimoto. Nothing suspicious about that. He has the big dry-goods store in Kaimuki. Now this area is the restaurant whose building is owned by Ed Hewlett's widow. It's been leased to a Filipino who runs a restaurant in Wahiawa."

"What are you driving at, Charley?" Hoxworth asked impatiently.

"Look!" the assistant cried. "Within the past six months, every store in this block has been leased, except the big Joe Janders holding. Do you see what that means?"

Quiet descended over The Fort as the managers studied the map. Finally Hoxworth said, "If somebody has been leasing these sites under an assumed name . . ."

This ugly suspicion circulated, but it was soon stopped by robust Hewlett Janders, who said gruffly, "Hell, what are you worrying about? I've warned Cousin Joe a hundred times never to lease his building without clearing things with me. As long as he holds fast, there's not going to be any trouble. What could a person do, with just these little . . ."

"Call Joe," Hoxworth said imperatively.

An ominous silence surrounded bluff Hewlett as he cried warmly, "Hell-lo, Joe! This is Hewie. Joe, you haven't leased your big store site, have you?"

There was a ghastly silence, and Hewlett Janders, completely shaken, put down the phone. There was no cause to ask him what had happened; the news stood out from his sagging round face. "God damn!" Hoxworth Hale shouted, banging the table. "We've been outsmarted. Who did this?" he raged. "Hewlett, who leased that store?"

Big Hewlett Janders kept his head down, staring at the table. "I'm ashamed to say. Kamejiro Sakagawa."

"We'll break him!" Hoxworth stormed. "We'll not bring a single cargo of his into Honolulu. That man will starve on . . ."

Icy John Whipple Hoxworth was speaking: "The problem is twofold. Who engineered this damnable thing? And for whom?"

There was long discussion as to who could have accumulated enough capital and wisdom to have effected such a coup, and by a slow process of elimination all came to agree that only Hong Kong Kee could have swung it. "I'll challenge him right now," Hoxworth cried, and in a forthright manner he phoned Hong Kong and asked, "Did you buy up all the leases?" When the Chinese banker replied, Hoxworth nodded his head to his associates. "Whom were you representing, Hong Kong?" This time Hoxworth did not move his head, but listened in stunned silence. "Thank you, Hong Kong," he said, and put down the phone.

"California Fruit?" Janders asked.

"Gregory's," Hale replied.

There was an aching, dumb silence as an era came to an end. Finally one of the Hoxworths asked, "Can't we fight this in the courts?"

"I don't think so," Hale answered.

"Surely we could get Judge Harper to issue an injunction on one of these leases. He's married to my cousin and I could explain . . ."

"If Hong Kong Kee arranged those leases . . ." Hale could not go on. He dropped his head into his hands, thought for a long time and then asked his associates, "How could these people do this to us? Your family, Whipple, why they looked after the Kees. Damn it, the whole Kee hui got its start with that land Old Doc gave them. And those damned Sakagawas. Imagine Kamejiro showing such ingratitude! Buying leases behind our backs. How do you explain it? You'd think they'd feel some kind of loyalty to us. We brought them here, gave them land, looked after them when they were so damned poor they couldn't read or write. What's happening in the world when such people turn against you?"

"That's what McLafferty's been doing!" Janders shouted. "He threw us off the track, talking about that hotel."

Hale now had control of himself and said, "Gentlemen, this is the beginning of an endless fight. I personally am going to obstruct Gregory's and McLafferty at every turn. Not to keep them out of the islands, because if Hong Kong arranged the leases, they'll stand up in court . . ."

One of the Hoxworths interrupted: "You'd think that in view of all we've done for Judge Harper, we could at least rely on him to void one of the leases."

Hale ignored this stupid and unworthy observation, continuing: "We must fight for time. We'll establish branches of our own stores in Waikiki, in Waialae and across the Pali. Every one of you who controls a going concern, move a branch out into the suburbs. Multiply and tie everything up. By the time Gregory's get here, we'll have our stores so prosperous they'll die on the vine."

So, in the curious way by which a deadly catfish, when thrown into a pool of trout, eats a few of the lazy fish but inspires the others to greater exertion, so that in the end there are more trout, and better, and all because of the evil catfish, the arrival of Gregory's into Hawaii, followed by California Fruit and Shea and Horner, drove the Hawaiian economy ahead by such spurts that soon The Fort was much better off than it had been before. In the same obtuse way, the increased wages that Goro Sakagawa's union had chiseled out of The Fort really made that establishment richer than ever, because much of the money filtered back into its enterprises, and the general prosperity of the islands multiplied.

Hale's determination to fight the mainland intruders with increased economic energy of his own had one unforeseen effect upon Hawaii, and in subsequent years this was often cited as the real revolution of that trying age: if The Fort was going to compete on an equal footing with outfits like Gregory's, it could no longer afford to promote into top positions inadequate nephews and cousins and gutless second sons. So under Hoxworth Hale's sharp eye, a good many Hales and Hoxworths and Janderses and Hewletts were weeded out. His policy was forthright: "Either give them minor jobs where they can't wreck the system, or give them substantial shares of stock on which they can live while real men run the companies." As a result, what crude Hewlett Janders called "the chinless wonders" found themselves with a lot of stock, a good yearly income and freedom to live either in France or Havana; while in their places appeared a flood of smart young graduates of the Wharton School, Stanford and Harvard Business. Some, out of sheer prudence, married Whipple girls or Hales or Hewletts, but most brought their own wives in from the mainland. And all Hawaii prospered.

But of the men who dominated The Fort, only shrewd, confused Hoxworth Hale, alternately fighting and surrendering, saw what the real menace of those days was. It was not the arrival of Gregory's, nauseating though that was, nor the triumph of the unions, seditious as that was: it lay in the fact that Black Jim McLafferty was a Democrat. His legal residence was now Hawaii. He no longer worked for Gregory's but had a small law practice of his own, which he combined with politicking, and whenever Hoxworth Hale passed McLafferty's office he studied the door with foreboding, for he knew that in the long run Democrats were worse than Gregory's or unions or communists.

He was therefore appalled one morning when he saw that McLafferty's door carried a new sign: McLafferty and Sakagawa. Shigeo was back from Harvard, an expert on land reform, a brilliant legalist, and thanks to Black Jim McLafferty's foresight, an official Democrat.

FOLLOWING THE STRIKE, two of the main protagonists were taken out of circulation by family problems, and for some time not much was heard of either Goro Sakagawa or Hoxworth Hale. At first it looked as if the former's troubles were the greater, for from that day in late 1945 when Goro had first met the slim and intense young Tokyo modenne, Akemi-san, their lives had been continuously complicated. First had come harassment by M.P.'s who had tried to enforce the no-fraternization edict of the occupation, and it had been unpleasant to be dating a girl you loved when the M.P.'s had the right to intrude at any moment. Next had been the ridiculous difficulty faced by any American soldier who wanted to marry a Japanese girl, so that once Goro had remarked bitterly, "When good things are being passed out they never consider me an American, but when they're dishing out the misery I'm one of the finest Americans on record." The young lovers had evaded the anti-marriage edict by engineering a Shinto wedding at a shrine near the edge of Tokyo, and had later discovered that Goro couldn't bring a Shinto bride back to America, so there had been renewed humiliation at the consul's office, but in those trying periods Akemi-san had proved herself a stalwart girl with a saving sense of humor, and largely because she was so sweet to officialdom, her paper work was ultimately completed and by special connivance she found herself free to enter Hawaii.

In 1946, when the troop transport neared Honolulu, Akemi-san had been one of the most practical-minded brides aboard, suffering from few of the illusions whose shattering would mar the first days in America for many of the other girls. She had not been bedazzled by her young American, Goro Sakagawa. She had recognized that he was what modennes called a peasant type, stubborn, imperfectly educated and boorish; and even in the starving days when he had had access to the mammoth P.X.'s that blossomed across Japan, where his military pay had made him a millionaire compared to the Japanese, she had known that he was not a rich man. Furthermore, she had been specifically warned by friends who knew others who had lived in Hawaii that the islands were populated mostly by Hiroshima-ken people, who were clannish to a fault and not altogether contemporary. One lively Tokyo girl had whispered to her: "I've been to Hawaii. In the entire area, not one modenne." Akemi had no illusions about her new home, but even so she was not prepared for what faced her.

At the dock she was met by Mr. Sakagawa and his son-in-law Mr. Ishii, with their wives standing stolidly behind the stocky little men, and she thought: "This is the way families used to look in Japan thirty years ago." However, she took an instant liking to bulldog little Sakagawa-san, with his arms hanging out from knees, and thought, as she looked down at him: "He is like my father." But then she saw grim-faced Mrs. Sakagawa, iron-willed and conservative, and she shivered, thinking to herself: "She's the one to fear. She's the kind we had to fight against in Tokyo."

She was right. Mrs. Sakagawa never eased up. Gentle with her husband, she was a terror to her daughter-in-law. Long ago in Hiroshima, when a son brought home a wife to work the rice fields, it was his mother's responsibility to see that the girl was soon and ably whipped into the habits of a good farm wife, and Mrs. Sakagawa proposed to perform this task for Goro. In fact, as soon as she saw Akemi at the railing of the ship she realized that Goro had made a sad choice, for she whispered contemptuously to her daughter Reiko, "She looks like a city girl, and you know what expensive habits they have."

If Goro had had a well-paying job which permitted him to live away from home, things might have settled down to a mutual and smoldering disapproval in which the two women saw each other as little as possible and were then studiously polite for the sake of Goro, but this could not be, for Goro's salary at the union did not permit him to have his own home, so he stayed with his parents. Early in her battle to subdue Akemi, Mrs. Sakagawa established her theme: "When I came to Hawaii life was very difficult, and there is no reason why you should be pampered."

"Does she expect me to go out and chop a few fields of sugar each afternoon?" Akemi asked Goro one night, and in time he began to hate coming home, for each of his women would in turn try to grab him off to some corner to explain the faults of the other and the turmoil of that day.

What angered Akemi most was a little thing, yet so recurrent that it began eroding her happiness with Goro. The Sakagawas had not spoken the best Japanese even while growing up in Hiroshima, and their long imprisonment in Hawaii had positively corrupted their speech, so that they now used many Hawaiian, Chinese, haole and Filipino words, with a lilting melody to their speech borrowed from the Mexican. Much of their phraseology was incomprehensible to Akemi, but she said nothing and would have been polite enough never to have commented on this to the Sakagawas, for as she told another war bride whom she met at the store, "I find their horrible speech rather amusing," and the two girls had laughed pleasantly together.

The Sakagawas were not so considerate. They found Akemi's precise Japanese, with its careful inflections and pronunciations, infuriating. "She thinks she's better than we are," Mrs. Sakagawa stormed one night at Goro. "Always talking as if her mouth were full of beans which she didn't want to bite." Often when the family was gathered for evening meal, Akemi would make some casual observation and Mrs. Sakagawa would repeat one or two words, pronouncing them in the barbarous Hawaiian manner. Then everyone would laugh at Akemi, and she would blush.

She fell into the habit of waiting at the market till one or another of the war brides came in, and hungrily, like refugees in an alien land, they would talk with each other in fine Japanese without fear of being ridiculed. "It's like living in Japan a hundred years ago," Akemi said angrily one day. Then she broke into tears, and when the other girl handed her a mirror, so that she could make up her face and be presentable, she looked at herself a long time and said, "Fumiko, would you think that I had once been the leader of the modennes? I love Bruckner and Brahms. I was fighting to set the Japanese girl free. Now I'm in a worse prison than any of them, and do you know why it's worse? Because it's all so horribly ugly. Ugly houses, ugly speech, ugly thoughts. Fumiko, I haven't been to a concert or a play in over a year. Nobody I know, except you, has ever even heard of André Gide. I think we've made a terrible mistake." Later, when alone at the Sakagawas, she thought: "I live for the few minutes I can talk with a sensible human being, but every time I do, I feel worse than before."

One night she said forcefully, "Goro, there's an orchestra concert tonight, and I think we should go." Awkwardly they went, but she did not enjoy it because Goro felt ill at ease, and the entire audience, except for a few students, were haoles. "Don't the Japanese ever go to plays or music?" she asked, but he interpreted this as the beginning edge of a complaint, so he mumbled, "We're busy working." "For what?" she snapped, and he said nothing.

When Akemi next met Fumiko at the market she asked, "What is it they're working for? In Japan, a man and woman will work like idiots to get tickets for the theater or to buy a beautiful ceramic. What do they work for here? I'll tell you what for. So that they can buy a big black automobile, and put the old mama-san in the back, and drive around Honolulu and say, 'Now I am as good as a haole.' I'm ashamed whenever I see Japanese doctors and lawyers in their big black automobiles."

"I am too," Fumiko confessed. "To think that they surrendered everything Japanese for such a set of values."

Things got a little better when Shigeo returned from Harvard with his honors degree in law, for then Akemi had an intelligent person with whom she could talk, and they had long discussions on politics and art. Akemi was astonished to find that Shig had been to visit the museums in Boston, but he explained: "I'd never have gone on my own account, but I was living with Dr. Abernethy and his wife, and they said that any Sunday on which you didn't do something to improve your mind was a Sunday wasted, and I had a great time with them."

"Tell me about the Boston Symphony," Akemi pleaded. "In Japan we think it's one of the best."

At this point shrewd Mrs. Sakagawa took Shigeo aside and said, "You must not talk any more with Akemi-san. She is your brother's wife, and not a good girl at all, and she will try to make you fall in love with her, and then we will have a tragedy in the family. I told both you and Goro that you ought to avoid city girls, but neither of you would listen, and now see what's happened."

"What has happened?" Shigeo asked.

"Goro has been trapped by a vain and silly girl," his mother explained. "Music, books, plays all day long. She wants to talk about politics. She is no good, that one."

The reasons his mother gave did not impress Shigeo, but the fact that Akemi was temptingly beautiful in her soft Japanese way did, and he stopped being alone with her, so that her life became even more desperate than before. It was rescued by the arrival one day of a young sociologist from the University of Hawaii, a Dr. Sumi Yamazaki, whose parents were also from Hiroshima. Dr. Yamazaki was a brilliant girl who was conducting three hundred interviews with Japanese girls married to G.I.'s, and she got to Akemi late in her study, when her findings had begun to crystallize.

Akemi, hoping that her intended visitor might be a woman of sophisticated intelligence, had first dressed in her most modenne Tokyo style, so that she looked almost as if she had come from Paris; but when she saw herself in the mirror she said, "Today I want to be very Japanese," and she had changed into a languorous pale blue and white shantung kimono with silver zori, and when she met Dr. Yamazaki, she found that it was the attractive young sociologist who was dressed like a real modenne, with bright eyes and quick intelligence to match. The two women liked each other immediately, and Dr. Yamazaki made a brief mental note that she would transcribe later: "Akemi Sakagawa appeared in formal kimono, therefore probably very homesick." And after two exploratory questions the sociologist was able to categorize her hostess with precision.

"Your kimono has told me all about you, Mrs. Sakagawa," she joked, in excellent Japanese.

"Call me Akemi, please."

"These are your complaints," the clever young sociologist said. "In Tokyo you were a modenne, fighting for women's rights. Here you find yourself in an ancient Japan that even your parents never knew. You find the local speech barbarous, the intellectual outlook bleak, and the aesthetic view of life nonexistent." Dr. Yamazaki hesitated, then added, "You feel that if this is America, you had better go back to something better."

Akemi-san gulped, for she had not yet formulated that bitter conclusion, though for some time she had suspected its inevitability. Now, through the soft speech of another, the frightening words had been spoken. "Do many feel as I do, Yamazaki-sensei?"

"Would it help you to know?" the young woman asked.

"Indeed it would!" Akemi cried eagerly.

"You understand that my figures are only tentative . . ."

Akemi laughed nervously and said, "It's so good to hear a person use a word like *tentative*."

"I'm afraid you're bitter," Dr. Yamazaki said reprovingly.

"Any more than the others?" Akemi asked.

"No."

"I think you reached me just at the right time," Akemi said eagerly.

"The general pattern is this," Dr. Yamazaki said, but before she could continue, Akemi interrupted and asked, "Would you think me a very silly girl, Yamazaki-sensei, if I said that I wanted to serve you tea? I am most terribly homesick."

The two women sat in silence as Akemi prepared tea in the ceremonial manner, and when the ritual was ended, Dr. Yamazaki continued: "Suppose that a hundred local soldiers married Japanese girls. Sixty of the husbands were Japanese. Thirty were Caucasians. Ten were Chinese."

"How have the marriages worked out?" Akemi-san asked.

"Well, if you take the thirty lucky girls who married Caucasians, about twenty-eight of them are quite happy. Some of the girls say they're deliriously happy. They say they wouldn't go back to Japan even if I gave them all of Hibiya Park."

"They wouldn't go back to Japan?" Akemi gasped. "Were they girls who were interested in books or plays or music?"

"Much like you. But you see, when a haole man marries a Japanese girl, his parents are so shocked that they make a true spiritual effort to like the girl. And when they meet someone like you, gentle, well-bred, sweet to their son, they overcompensate. They love her more than is required. They make her life a heaven on earth."

"Do such people listen to music?" Akemi asked.

"Usually a haole man hasn't the nerve to marry a Japanese girl unless he's rather sophisticated culturally. Such couples experience a very full spectrum."

Akemi looked glumly at the bleak walls of the Sakagawa home, with a four-tube radio invariably tuned to a station that alternated American jazz with Japanese hillbilly songs. Whenever she and Goro went to a movie it was invariably a chanbara, a Japanese western in which the samurai hero fought sixty armed villains without suffering a wound.

"The Japanese girls who marry Chinese soldiers," Dr. Yamazaki continued, "face a different problem. The Chinese parents are totally disgusted and convinced that there is no possibility of their liking the unseen daughter-in-law, so they spend the time till she arrives hating her so much that when she finally gets here, they find she isn't anywhere near as bad as they had feared. When she demonstrates that she really loves their son, everyone reaches a plateau of mutual respect, and things go reasonably well."

"But the Japanese marriages?" Akemi asked. "You won't dare say they go well."

"Some do," Dr. Yamazaki assured her. "Where farm boys here have married farm girls from Hiroshima-ken, things work out rather well. But in a surprising number of cases, the Japanese-Japanese marriage does not do well. I think our figures are going to show that over fifty-five per cent of such marriages have run into trouble."

"Why?" Akemi pleaded.

"I was born in Hawaii myself," Dr. Yamazaki said. "From the very kind of family you married into. Stout Hiroshima peasants—and remember that even in modern Hiroshima our Hawaii people would seem very old-fashioned. Anyhow, I'm partial to the local people. But the curious fact is this. The Caucasian mothers-in-law and the Chinese realize that they have to make a special effort to understand and love their strange new daughters. So they do so, and find happiness. The stolid Japanese mothers-in-law, and God help the Japanese girl who marries my brother and who has to put up with my mother . . . Well, it's obvious. They all think they're getting the kind of Japanese bride that used to flourish in southern Japan forty years ago. They make no effort to understand, so they haven't the slightest chance of finding happiness with their new daughters."

"Do you know what's killing my marriage?" Akemi asked bluntly. Dr. Yamazaki was not surprised at the forthrightness of the question, for she had watched the dissolution of several such marriages, but now Akemi paused, and it was apparent to Dr. Yamazaki that she was supposed to guess, so she volunteered: "In Japan young men are learning to accept new ways, but in Hawaii they have learned nothing."

"Yes," Akemi confessed. "Is that what the other girls say?"

"They all say the same thing," Dr. Yamazaki assured her. "But many of them outgrow their distaste, or somehow learn to modify their husbands."

"But do you know what will keep me from doing that?" Akemi asked. "What cuts me to the heart day after day?"

"What?" the sociologist asked professionally.

"The way they laugh at my correct speech. This I will not bear much longer."

Dr. Yamazaki thought of her own family and smiled bitterly. "I have the same problem," she laughed. "I have a Ph.D. degree." Then, imitating her mother, she asked, " 'Do you think you're better than we are, using such language?' So at home, in self-defense, I talk pidgin."

"I will not," Akemi said. "I am an educated Japanese who has fought a long time for certain things."

"If you love your husband," Dr. Yamazaki said, "you will learn to accommodate yourself."

"To certain things, never," Akemi said. Then she asked abruptly, "Have you ever been married, Yamazaki-sensei?"

"I'm engaged," the sociologist replied.

"To a local boy?"

"No, to a haole at the University of Chicago."

"I see. You wouldn't dare marry a local boy, would you?"

"No," Dr. Yamazaki replied carefully.

Akemi tapped the sociologist's notebook and laughed. "Now I'm embalmed in there."

"One of many," Dr. Yamazaki said.

"But can you guess where I'd like to be?"

"In a small coffee shop in the Nishi-Ginza, surrounded by exciting conversation on books and politics and music."

"How could you guess so accurately?" Akemi asked.

"Because I'd like to be there, too," Dr. Yamazaki confessed. "That's where I met my fiancé, so I know how lovely Japan can be. But I would say this, too. Hawaii can be just as exciting. To be a young Japanese here is possibly one of the most exhilarating experiences in the world."

"But you said you wouldn't marry one of them," Akemi-san reminded her.

"As a woman, seeking happiness in a relaxed home, I'll stick with my haole from Chicago. But as a pure intellect, if I were not involved as a woman, I would much prefer to remain in Hawaii."

"Tell me truthfully, Yamazaki-sensei, do you think that any society which has as its ideal a long, black automobile can ever be a good place to live?"

Dr. Yamazaki considered the question for some moments and replied: "You must understand that the visible symbols of success which our Japanese here in Hawaii are following are those laid down by the established haole society. A big home, a powerful car, a boy going to Yale whether he learns anything or not . . . these are the symbols people living in Hawaii must accept. You can't suddenly require the Japanese to prove themselves superior to the symbols upon which they've been raised."

"For three years I've hoped my husband would," Akemi said bitterly.

"Be patient," Dr. Yamazaki pleaded, "and you'll find Hawaii improving."

"I think not," Akemi said slowly. "It's a barren, stupid place and nothing will ever change it."

The two young women parted, and that night Dr. Yamazaki called Shig Sakagawa, whom she had known at Punahou, and said, "Shig, it's none of my business, but your brother Goro is going to lose his wife."

"You think so?"

"I know so. She used every phrase the girls use before they catch the boat back to Japan. I've watched nineteen of them go back so far."

"What could he do?" Shig asked.

"Buy her three Beethoven symphonies," Dr. Yamazaki said, knowing that to blunt Goro such a step would be beyond the outer limits of imagination. Besides, Mrs. Sakagawa Senior would never allow such music in her house.

WHILE the labor leader Goro Sakagawa faced these problems—or rather did not face them—Hoxworth Hale was concerned principally with the forthcoming marriage of his daughter Noelani to her cousin twice removed, Whipple Janders, the son of bold, straightforward Hewlett Janders, on whom Hoxworth had grown to depend so much in recent years. At one time, when Noelani was younger, Hoxworth had rather hoped that she might go outside The Fort and find herself a completely new kind of husband . . . somebody from Yale, of course, but perhaps an easterner who had never seen Hawaii. For a while when Noelani was a senior at Wellesley she dated an Amherst boy, which was almost as good as Yale, but nothing had come of it, and when young Whip Janders, who was belatedly completing his Yale education, asked her to a spring dance at New Haven, each of them instinctively knew that they ought to marry. After all, they had known each other at Punahou; they were from families who understood each other; and Whip had been the closest friend of Noelani's brother, who had been killed over Tokyo.

However, at one point in their engagement Noelani had experienced haunting doubts as to the propriety of their marriage, for Whipple had returned from the war somewhat changed. He was thinner, and his fashionable crew-cut did not entirely hide a tendency toward strongly individualistic behavior. Once at a Vassar dance he had appeared in formal dress but with a garish vest made of Hong Kong silk embroidered in purple dragons. He had been a sensation, but he had also been disturbing, for he had told one of the professors' wives, "Thorstein Veblen would have loved this vest," and she had stammered, "What?" and he had given his imitation of a dying tubercular patient, adding, "If you're going to have consumption, it ought to be conspicuous." It had been gruesomely funny, but unfortunately the professor's wife didn't catch on.

Now Whip and his crew-cut were back in Honolulu, dressed in

Brooks Brothers' most austere fashion, and the wedding was about to take place. Shortly before the event, Noelani asked her father, for her mother was in one of her spells and could not comprehend questions, "Do you think it's proper for kids like us to go on intermarrying, Dad? I mean, frankly, what are the chances that our children will be more like Mother than like you?"

In considerable embarrassment, for this was the nagging fear that had made him hope that Noelani would marry some easterner, Hoxworth dodged the question and suggested: "Why don't we look into this with Aunt Lucinda. We always ask her about the family."

"Which family?" Noelani asked.

"The family . . . all of it," Hoxworth replied, and he drove his daughter up to see Aunt Lucinda in the mist-haunted house in Nuuanu Valley. When they arrived, they found that she was entertaining half a dozen ladies of nearly her own age, and most of them were drinking gin, so that the conversation wasn't exactly on focus, but there was a sweet, relaxed gentility about it.

"This is my great-niece, on my grandmother's side, Noelani Hale," Lucinda explained graciously, whisking her pale-blue lace handkerchief toward the girl. "She's Malama Janders Hale's daughter, and on Saturday she's going to marry that fine young Whipple Janders, who is the great-grandson of Clement and Jerusha Hewlett."

At once, Noelani's place in the great succession was established, and the women smiled at her admiringly, one saying, "I knew your husband's great-grandmother Jerusha very well, Noelani. She was a marvelous woman and could play polo better than the men. If young Whipple has her blood, he'll be a stalwart man, I can assure you."

"What Noelani came to ask about," Aunt Lucinda explained, "is the extent to which she is related to Whip, and I would like to say right now that in my opinion it's a good deal safer to marry into a substantial island family, whose blood lines are known, than into some purely speculative mainland family whose backgrounds could have originated God knows where." The women all agreed to this, and a Japanese maid in crisp white took their cups for more tea or their glasses for more gin.

"The only possible question about the marriage of Noelani and Whip," Aunt Lucinda began, "is that each of them," and she lowered her voice, "does have a strain of Hawaiian blood. If you go back to her great-great-grandmother on her father's side, you find Malama Hoxworth, who was the daughter of Captain Rafer Hoxworth, who was not a missionary but who was a most marvelous and courtly gentleman of the finest character and breeding. Of course, he married Noelani Kanakoa, the last Alii Nui, but I think it safe to say that the Malama of whom we are speaking . . . the one that married the great Micah Hale, that is . . . well anyway . . ." and with an airy gesture she dismissed the whole matter. One of the most gratifying aspects of talking with Aunt Lucinda was that she threw out so many names that you didn't really have to listen, for when she found herself hopelessly involved in family lines she stopped and started over again. Now she switched abruptly and said, with no one able to guess how she had arrived at the conclusion, "Anyway, no finer gentleman ever lived in Hawaii than Captain Rafer Hoxworth."

The Japanese maid brought back the drinks, and Aunt Lucinda asked, "Where was I? Oh, yes. So from that unfortunate marriage of Micah to the half-caste girl Malama . . . You know, I often wondered where Micah got the courage to appear in public so much when he was saddled with such a marriage. Well, anyway, our little Noelani here does have that strain of Hawaiian blood, but it's more than overcome, I should think, by the Hale and Whipple strains, except that the Whipple girl her great-grandfather married was not from what I like to call the uncontaminated Whipples, to which I belong, but from the branch that married into the Hewletts, which as you know were also half-castes, except for the first boy who married Lucy Hale, from whom I am descended."

The mists from the Pali began to fill the valley, and a waterfall echoed mournfully as Aunt Lucinda continued her analysis of the family lines. Most of the meandering comments she made were meaningless to her listeners, but since all were descended from these early ancestors who had done so much to build Hawaii, each kept in the back of her mind some three or four specially prized progenitors to whom she attributed her character, and whenever Aunt Lucinda mentioned one of those names, that listener snapped to attention through the gin and nodded with special approval. Through the years Lucinda had noticed that three names in particular evoked veneration: it was best to be descended from Jerusha Bromley Hale, the great missionary mother; or from Rafer Hoxworth, the courtly and gracious sea captain; or from Dr. John Whipple, the patrician intellect. Aunt Lucinda, with modesty, could point out that she was descended from two of the three, and in a way she was happy that she was not related to Captain Hoxworth, for of course all of his offspring were part Hawaiian.

"It's not that I'm against Hawaiians," she assured her visitors. "It's just that I get frightfully irritated at the hero-worship that goes on around here over the so-called Hawaiian royalty. I sit in the library and I can spot every malihini girl who is going to ask me, 'Do you have that book on Kelly Kanakoa?' I have to stop myself from warning them, 'You'll have to put your chewing gum away while you look at the pictures.' And when she hands the book back reverently she always says, 'Gee, his grandfather was a king!' As if that meant anything. I've always thought it was one of the most ridiculous aspects of Hawaiian life, the way they memorize these pathetic old lists of kings, as if a litany of imaginary names meant anything. You remember what Abner Hale, he was my great-grandfather, wrote about such ancestor worship: 'I think it impedes Hawaii as much as any other one thing, for the poor fools are so attentive to their past that they have no time to contemplate eternity.' And nothing makes me more irritated than the way a Hawaiian will point to some pathetic dregs of humanity and say accusingly, 'If the missionaries hadn't interfered, he would now be our king,' as if we had halted something fine and good. Do you know who the present king of Hawaii would be if the missionaries hadn't put a stop to such nonsense? The beachboy Kelly Kanakoa! Have you ever heard him speak? He insists on using a vocabulary of about ninety words, half of them *blalah*. Everybody Kelly likes is *blalah* except that he calls me his seestah."

Hoxworth coughed and his aunt collected her thoughts. "Oh yes, now about Whipple Janders. He went to Punahou and Yale, as you know, and had a very good record in the war. Handsome boy, but not so fleshy as his father, which is understandable, because Hewlett takes after the Hewlett side of the family, and they were always unprepossessing types, if you'll allow me to say so, Abigail, because as you know Abraham married a Hawaiian . . . well, he picked up a Hawaiian wahine after Urania died, but that's neither here nor there.

"I suppose what you're really interested in is how the intended bridegroom Whipple relates to the Hales. If you'll go back to Micah, who married the half-caste girl Malama Hoxworth, you'll remember that he had two children, Ezra and Mary, and Ezra of course was your great-grandfather, Noelani, and that takes care of that." The Japanese maid returned to pass coconut chips, toasted a delicious salty brown. "You may fill the glasses, too, Kimiko," Aunt Lucinda reminded her.

She never got back to Mary Hale, Micah's daughter, but the group understood that somehow Mary was related to Whipple Janders, but what Aunt Lucinda did say was perhaps of greater importance: "So you can see that Whipple comes from some of the finest stock in the islands. For three generations, Whipples have married Janderses, which accounts in part, I suppose, for the way in which their family fortunes have been conserved."

Turning directly to Noelani, the beautiful girl who was soon to be married, Lucinda said, "I can think of no one you could have chosen finer than Whipple Janders, and I am extremely happy for you, Noelani. When I look at your marvelous face I see your great-great-grandfather Micah Hale, the savior of these islands. You have his high forehead, his courage and his force of character. But your beauty comes from the Whipples. Isn't it strange," she asked the hushed group, "how the seed of one handsome man could have produced so much beauty in these islands? I know it's fashionable to laugh at old maids who haven't married, and I'm sure you'll think me vain if I claim that when I was young I too was a typical Whipple beauty. Kimiko, fetch me that portrait in the bedroom!" And the Japanese maid silently brought in one of the last great portraits completed by Sargent, and it showed a glowing young beauty in white, with lace and combs, and Lucinda said, "That's what I mean by the Whipple complexion. You have it, Noelani, and it's a great consolation to me to think that it will be reunited with the male side of the Whipple family. What handsome children you are bound to have!"

The maid stood awkwardly with the heavy picture, and Miss Lucinda said, "You may take it back, Kimiko." And when the maid was gone she confided: "Sargent did that of me when I was engaged to an Englishman, but Father felt that it would be better if I found a young man closer to home, and as you know I became engaged to my cousin Horace Whipple, but he . . ." She hesitated; then realizing that all of her listeners except perhaps Noelani knew the story anyway, she concluded: "Before the wedding Horace shot himself. At first it was suspected that he might have stolen money from J & W, but of course that was quickly disproved, for there has never been a case of theft in the family."

"Which family?" Noelani asked.

"The family. All of us," Aunt Lucinda replied, and when her nephew Hoxworth had departed with his attractive daughter, she summoned Kimiko to refill the glasses, remarking, "That Noelani is one of the loveliest these islands have ever produced. She did marvelously well at Wellesley, and I think we're lucky that she's come home to marry with her proper kind. After all, she comes from excellent stock."

It was a major characteristic of Hawaii that everyone claimed distinguished ancestors. In 1949 there were no Hawaiians who were not descended from kings. The Hales had constructed the myth that cantankerous old Abner from the miserable farm near Marlboro had been, were the truth known, of knightly ancestry dating far back in English history. The Kees never mentioned the fact that their progenitor was a shifty little gambler who had bought his concubine from a Macao whorehouse; he was, if you listened closely, something of a Confucian scholar. And even Mrs. Yoriko Sakagawa always loved to tell her children, "Remember that on your mother's side you come from samurai stock." Of all these gentle fables, only Mrs. Sakagawa's was true. In 1703 the great Lord of Hiroshima had had as one of his flunkies a stocky, stupid oaf whose principal job it was to stand with a feathered staff warning away chance intruders when his lord was going to the toilet. Technically, this male chambermaid was a samurai, but he had been too stupid even to hold the toilet signal well, and after a while had been discharged and sent back to his home village, where he married a local girl and became the ancestor of Yoriko Sakagawa; and if she, like the others in Hawaii, derived consolation from her supposed illustrious heritage, no harm was done.

The Hale-Janders wedding was a splendid affair, held in the flower-decked old missionary church, with Reverend Timothy Hewlett officiating; but as I said earlier, it only seemed that Goro Sakagawa was having more domestic trouble than his adversary, Hoxworth Hale, for Noelani and Whipple had been married only four months when Whipple suddenly announced, out of a clear blue sky if ever an announcement were so made: "I just don't love you, Noelani."

"What?" she asked in heartbroken astonishment.

"I'm going to live in San Francisco," he said simply.

"Is there some other girl?" Noelani pleaded, without shame.

"No. I guess I just don't like girls," he explained.

"Whip!"

"There's nothing wrong with you, Noe, but Eddie Shane and I are taking an apartment. He's the fellow I was with in the air corps."

"Oh, my God, Whip! Have you talked with anyone about this?"

"Look, Noe! Don't make a federal case of it, please. Marriage isn't for me, that's all."

"But you're willing to marry Eddie Shane, is that it?"

"If you want to put it that way, all right. I am."

He left Hawaii, and word filtered back that he and Eddie Shane had a large apartment in the North Beach area of San Fancisco, where Eddie made ceramics which were featured in *Life* magazine, in color.

Aunt Lucinda loved to explain what had happened. She said, as Kimiko passed the gin, "Go back to Micah Hale's daughter, Mary. This girl was one-eighth Hawaiian, through her mother Malama Hoxworth, who was the daughter of Noelani Kanakoa, the last Alii Nui. Now that's bad enough, but as you know, Mary Hale married a Janders, and you'd expect that rugged stock to have counterbalanced the weak Hawaiian strain, but unfortunately she married into the Janders' line that had married one of the Hewlett girls, and as you know, they were Hawaiian. So poor Whipple Janders, when he ran off with the air corps man, was only doing what could be expected, because he had Hawaiian blood from both sides of his family."

But Hoxworth Hale, seeing the effect of this pathetic marriage on his high-strung daughter Noelani, thought: "Unless I can help her, there's going to be another woman sitting upstairs in the late afternoons." But what help he should offer, he did not know.

IN 1951 Nyuk Tsin engineered her last big coup for the Kee hui, and in many ways it was her most typical accomplishment, for it derived from intelligence and was attained through courage. She was a hundred and four years old, sitting in her ugly house up Nuuanu listening to her grandson Harvey read the paper to her, when, in a shaky old voice, she interrupted: "What's that again?" Since Harvey was reading in English and speaking in Hakka, he could not be certain that he himself understood the confusing story, so phrase by phrase he repeated: "In American business today it is possible for a company which is losing money to be more valuable than it was a few years ago when it was making money."

Impetuously the old matriarch forced her grandson to read the strange concept three times, and when she had comprehended it she said in her piping voice, "That's exactly the kind of trick smart haoles think up for themselves and which we stupid Chinese never catch on to until it's too late." Accordingly, she summoned her great-grandson Eddie, Hong Kong's boy, whom she had sent to Harvard Law School, and told him: "I want a complete report on how this works."

At that time not much was known in Hawaii relating to this marriage of losing companies to those that were prosperous, but Eddie Kee applied himself to the task of assembling opinions from mainland tax courts, and within two months he was an expert in the field. Then with several tax reports airmailed in from New York he reported back to his great-grandmother in her little house, and when he came upon her she was picking lint from a shawl, and he thought: "How can she be so old and yet so interested?"

"Can you explain it now?" she asked in a high, cackling voice.

"Fundamentally," Eddie began in his best professional style, "it's an old law and a good one."

"I don't care whether it's good or bad," Nyuk Tsin interrupted, her voice suddenly lower. "What I want to know is how it works."

"Take the Janders Brewery. For years it's been losing money. Now suppose next year it makes money. It won't have to pay any taxes because recent years' losses can be used to offset next year's gains."

"Makes sense," Nyuk Tsin nodded.

"But look at what else we can do," Eddie lectured stolidly, as if addressing a class of legal students. "If the Kee hui buys the brewery, we can then add to its assets all of our old pineapple land. Then if the brewery sells the land, the profits will be offset by the past losses of the brewery. Do you see what that means, Wu Chow's Auntie?"

Little Nyuk Tsin did not reply. She sat in the late afternoon sun like a winsome old lady embroidered on a Chinese silk. She was smiling, and if an outsider had seen her beatific, wrinkled face he might have thought: "She's dreaming of an old love." But he would have been wrong. She was dreaming of the Janders Brewery, and she said, "How heavenly! We can use the Janders' losses to balance the Kee profits!"

"Wu Chow's Auntie!" Eddie cried. "You see exactly what I'm talking about."

"But I'm afraid you don't see what I've been talking about," Nyuk Tsin replied.

"What do you mean?" Eddie asked.

"Suppose that we do buy the Janders Brewery and do hide our pineapple lands inside it . . ." she began.

"That's what I've been explaining," Eddie said gently. It was the first sign that day that Wu Chow's Auntie was losing her acuity.

"But what I'm explaining," Nyuk Tsin said firmly, "is that after we have done this clever thing we will put some member of our family in charge of the brewery, and he will give it good management and he will turn what has been a loss into a profit."

Now the beatific smile passed over to Eddie's face and he said, "If you could arrange that, Wu Chow's Auntie, we'd make a fortune."

"That's what I had in mind," the old woman replied. "This law seems to have been expressly written for the Kee hui. It is our duty to use it sagaciously."

She summoned Hong Kong, and after discussing the theory of the law, told him abruptly, "Make us up a list of all the companies in Honolulu that are losing big money. Then write alongside each one the name of someone in our hui who could turn that loss into a profit."

"Where will we get the money to buy the sick companies?" Hong Kong parried.

"We don't have to buy them for cash," Nyuk Tsin replied, "but we'll need money for down payments. So we have to sell some of our holdings now and pay the taxes on our profits, but if the plan works we'll more than make up for those taxes in the end."

"Are you determined to go ahead on such a wild scheme?" Hong Kong asked. "Getting rid of profitable businesses in order to take a big gamble?"

Nyuk Tsin reflected a moment, then asked Eddie, "Does anyone else in Honolulu understand how this law works?"

"They must know," the Harvard man replied, "but they aren't doing anything about it."

Nyuk Tsin made up her mind. Clapping her hands sharply she said, "We'll go ahead. In six months everyone will know what we're doing, but by then there'll be nothing left to buy." And as Hong Kong and his son departed, old Nyuk Tsin looked at the back of the latter and thought: "I wonder what his education at Harvard cost us? It's been worth rubies and jade."

The next day Hong Kong returned to the weather-beaten old house up Nuuanu with his homework well done. Spreading papers which Nyuk Tsin could not read, he indicated all the businesses that had accumulated large losses: the brewery, a taxicab company, a chain of bakeries, some old office buildings, some stores. But now the perpetual drive of Nyuk Tsin manifested itself with unbroken force, and as each item was listed she asked simply, "How much fee-simple land does it have?" And if Hong Kong said that it owned no land of its own, she snorted: "Strike it off. Even better than accumulated back losses is land." So the final list that the Kees were going to buy contained only companies with big losses and bigger parcels of land.

But when Nyuk Tsin heard Hong Kong's second list—the Kee holdings that were to be liquidated to cover the new purchases—she perceived with displeasure that the biggest project of all was missing, and she wondered why. Beginning querulously and with a piping voice she said, "This is a good list, Hong Kong."

Hong Kong smiled and observed expansively: "Well, I thought we might as well get rid of the old projects."

"But if I heard your list correctly," Nyuk Tsin continued softly, "there was no suggestion that we sell the land upon which we are now sitting."

Hong Kong looked with some embarrassment at his son Eddie, but neither spoke, so Nyuk Tsin continued: "Surely, if we need money for new ventures, we ought to sell first of all this old taro patch. And everything on it. Didn't you think of that?"

In a burst of confidence Hong Kong said, "Of course we thought of it, Wu Chow's Auntie. But we considered this land too precious to you. We cannot sell it during your lifetime."

"Thank you, Hong Kong," the old woman replied, bowing her thin gray head. "But one of the reasons why this idea of selling old businesses to go into new is appealing to me is that we will not only make money but we will also be forced into many new operations. We will have to work and will not be allowed to grow lazy and fat." She folded her hands, smiled at her clever men and added, "Have you noticed, Hong Kong, how every Chinese family that tries to hold on to old businesses loses everything in the end?"

"But you always preached to us, 'Hold on to the land!' " Hong Kong protested.

"Ah, yes!" Nyuk Tsin agreed. "But not always the same land." Then she added, "Old land and old ideas must be constantly surrendered."

A new concept had come into the room, a concept of change and going-forwardness, and for some moments Hong Kong and his son contemplated the old woman's vision of a great family always in flux and always working hard to profit from it. The silence was broken by Nyuk Tsin, who said, "So we must sell this precious old land, Hong Kong, and in our liquidation, let it be the first to go."

"The land we will sell," Hong Kong said quietly, "but we will keep the old house for a little while longer. I could not imagine you living anywhere else."

"Thank you, my dutiful grandson," Nyuk Tsin replied. Then, briskly, she added, "So we must start this day teaching Bill how to run a brewery. Sam must study how to make money from bakeries, and I want Tom to begin reading about new ideas in architecture for old buildings." She proposed ways by which every losing venture they were about to buy could be transformed into a money-maker, and she warned: "Hong Kong, you must study carefully to see that we acquire only the best land. Eddie, organize everything in the best business procedure. I must depend upon you two to keep your eyes on everything."

As the meeting was about to break up, the old matriarch said, "It's very exciting to see a family launching out into bold new projects. You'll be proud of this day, but remember, Hong Kong, as you buy, be very secret, and do it all at once. And when you buy, always allow yourself to be forced into paying a little more than the seller has a right to hope for. When your plan is understood by all, nobody must feel he's been cheated." She paused, then added, "But don't pay too much more."

Three weeks later, at a meeting of The Fort, bluff Hewlett Janders laughed and said, "If we didn't follow the old missionary law about no alcohol here, I'd send out and buy drinks all around."

"Good news?" John Whipple Hoxworth asked.

"The best. Just managed to unload the brewery. What a millstone it's been. My sainted grandmother told me once, if she told me a hundred times, 'No good will come of a Hale going into the brewery business.' And she was so right."

"Get a good price for it?" Hoxworth Hale asked.

"I got thirty-five thousand more than I ever hoped to," Janders replied. "I've been wanting to stick Hong Kong Kee ever since he pulled that fast one in buying the Gregory's leases."

"Did you say Hong Kong?" Hoxworth asked.

"Yes. He slipped this time. Nobody can make money from that brewery."

"That's odd," Hale said. "I just sold Hong Kong the old Bromley Block. It's been losing money for years."

At this point one of the Hewletts arrived with the good news that he had unloaded the taxicab company. "To Hong Kong Kee?" a chorus asked.

"Yes, and at a good price," young Hewlett replied.

A gray silence fell over the board room while Hale looked at Janders and Janders at Hewlett. "Have we been made fools of?" Hoxworth asked slowly.

Finally dour John Whipple Hoxworth said, glumly, "I guess it's my turn to confess. I just sold Hong Kong that chain of bakeries we started before the war. Big losers."

"What's he up to?" Hewlett Janders cried. "What's that tricky Chinaman up to?"

"It must be real estate. He's buying property just to get real estate."

"No," one of the young Hewletts interrupted. "Because he just sold the old Kee taro patch. For a million five."

"My God!" Janders choked. "He's selling, he's buying. What's that wily sonofabitch up to?" The men looked at one another in exasperation, not so much because they were angry at Hong Kong, as because they suspected that he had some clever deal cooking, one which they ought to have anticipated for themselves.

The deal was clever; in truth it was, but only the first half. Anyone, if he had had the advice of a hard-working lawyer like Eddie Kee, could have bought losing firms and sold prosperous ones, making a nice profit on the transaction. That was clever. But what really counted was the fact that Bill Kee, backstopped by his father Hong Kong and his smart brother Eddie, was learning how to brew fairly good beer.

It wasn't easy, and some of the first batches, introduced by a florid advertising hullabaloo featuring the slogan "Kee Beer, Your Key to Happiness," was dreadful stuff which the local population christened "Chinese arsenic." But soon, with the aid of a Swiss-German whom the hui flew in from St. Louis, the beer began to taste reasonably palatable, and since it sold for a nickel a can less than others, workingmen began acquiring a taste for it. So without even considering the $1,800,000 worth of real estate on which the old Janders Brewery had sat, the Kee hui made a very strong profit out of that particular tax purchase.

But the big money-maker, to everyone's surprise, turned out to be the bakeries. Each store brought with it enough real estate so that of itself the deal was favorable, but Sam Kee, at the age of sixty-four, discovered a real affinity for selling cakes, and he showed substantial profits on each unit in the chain.

Not all the projects turned out so well. For example, the taxicab company resisted every attempt to make it pay, and finally Hong Kong reported to his grandmother: "This one is no good."

"Give it away," Nyuk Tsin replied.

"I hate to surrender so easily," Hong Kong protested. "There ought to be some way to make money out of taxicabs."

"Somebody else probably can," Nyuk Tsin agreed. "But not the Kees. Anyway, I don't like taxis. They seem to aim at me whenever I go out. By the way, I saw what Tom is doing to the old Bromley Block, and he's making it into quite a handsome building. If we had traded even, giving away the taro patch for the Bromley Block, we'd still have been ahead. I like to see the family working," she said.

And as the year ended, her hundred and fourth, she sat in her little house at midnight, and with a flickering oil lamp she undressed, until she stood completely naked, a tremendously frail old woman made up mostly of bones, and with the lamp moving cautiously near her body she inspected herself for leprosy. There were no spots on her hands, none on her torso, none on her legs. Now she sat down and lifted in turn each of her ungainly big feet. There were no spots on the toes, none on the heel, none at the ankles. At peace for another night, she slipped into a flannel nightgown, blew out the lamp, and went to sleep.

The coup which Nyuk Tsin had engineered had one unexpected result. The Fort, after it had an opportunity to study exactly what Hong Kong Kee had accomplished by his revolutionary manipulations, concluded, in the words of Hoxworth Hale: "We could use a man like that on some of our boards," and everyone agreed that the man had a master intellect.

After one of the meetings of Whipple Oil Imports, Incorporated, Hoxworth asked his fellow board member, jokingly, "Hong Kong, now that the Gregory's deal is over, and nobody got too badly hurt, are you happy that you sneaked the outfit into Hawaii?"

"What do you mean?" Hong Kong asked.

"Well," Hoxworth pointed out amiably, for he was growing to like the clever Chinese whose business judgments usually proved sound, "Gregory's has been here for nearly five years. They've taken enormous sums out of the Territory, but what have they done for Hawaii?"

"Like what?" Hong Kong asked.

"Like museums, schools, libraries, medical foundations."

Hong Kong thought a while and said in apparent seriousness, "Every year the manager of Gregory's has his picture in the paper handing the community drive a check for three hundred dollars." Hale looked at his new friend in astonishment, and saw that Hong Kong was laughing. "They don't do very much for Hawaii," the Chinese admitted.

"And as the years go by, Hong Kong, you'll see that they do even less. You have a lot of Kees in Hawaii, Hong Kong. How many?"

"We figure that the old grandmother has over two hundred great-great-grandchildren, but not all of them are in Hawaii."

"Have you ever thought that each one of them will be cheated just a little bit if there are no new museums or orchestras? Put it the other way, doesn't everyone of your family who grows up here go to college on the mainland a little bit stronger because of what the old families did for the islands?"

"You're right!" Hong Kong agreed hastily. "And nobody expects Gregory's to copy you. But it looks to me, Hoxworth, as if we're entering a new age. We don't have to have handouts from above any longer. We pay good wages. We tax. We get the economy moving real fast. Everybody is better off. Even you."

"Have you ever heard of an art museum financed by taxation? Do you think the smart young Japanese who are coming up so fast will put aside one penny for a good university or an orchestra? Will a dozen Gregory's ever make a decent society?"

"Hoxworth, you're going to be surprised," Hong Kong assured him. "When we get a functioning democracy here, our boys are going to vote for museums, universities, medical clinics. And they'll tax their own people like hell to pay for them. Hawaii will be the paradise people used to talk about."

"I can't believe it," Hoxworth argued. "The good society is always the reflection of a few men who had the courage to do the right thing. It is never voted into being. It is never accomplished if it's left to the Gregory's of the world." But when they parted he said something that would have been totally unthinkable two years earlier: "By the way, Hong Kong, if you spot any smart young Japanese who are as intelligent as you are, let me know."

"What do you have in mind?" Hong Kong asked.

"You're doing so well on our boards we thought it might be a good idea . . ."

"It would be," Hong Kong said quickly. "If you pick up young Shigeo Sakagawa, you'll be getting a winner."

"Isn't he running for senator . . . on the Democratic ticket?"

"Yes."

"How could I take such a man onto our boards?" Hoxworth asked.

"You won't find any good young Japanese running on the Republican ticket," Hong Kong said flatly.

"What are you, Hong Kong?" Hale asked.

"When I was poor, I was a Democrat. Now that I have responsibilities, I'm a Republican. But I make my campaign contributions only to smart young men like Shigeo . . . and they always seem to be Democrats."

"Let's talk about this again, after the election," Hoxworth said, and for the first time he started listening to Shigeo Sakagawa's campaign speeches. But as the campaign grew hotter, he heard Shig saying one night: "All over the world nations have had to fight for land reform. In England they accomplished it by the vote, and things went well. In France they had to have a bloody revolution, and all went badly. I have worked in Japan for General MacArthur, giving great landed estates to the peasants, and all the time I worked there I said to myself, 'I ought to be home in Hawaii, doing the same thing.' Because I knew what you know. Hawaii is generations behind the times. Our land is held by a few big families, and they lease it out to us in niggardly amounts as they see fit . . ."

"The young fool's a communist," Hale snorted as he turned off the radio, and there was no more talk about inviting Shigeo Sakagawa to join The Fort.

AFTER the presidential elections in 1952, Congressman Clyde V. Carter of the Thirty-ninth District in Texas appointed himself a committee of one to investigate—for the fourteenth time—Hawaii's fitness for statehood. He reached Honolulu in mid-December bearing with him only three minor prejudices: he hated to the point of nausea anyone who wasn't a white man; he knew from experience that rich men were the saviors of the republic; and he loathed Republicans. Thus he was not completely happy in Hawaii, where rich men were invariably Republicans, and where sixty per cent of the people he met were obviously not Caucasian. In the first five minutes he decided: "This place must never be a state."

He was therefore surprised when the welcoming committee, consisting of Hoxworth Hale, Whipple Janders and Black Jim McLafferty, head of the Democratic Party in the islands, gave florid but hard-hitting defenses of statehood. He was particularly impressed by what Hoxworth Hale cried over the loud-speaker: "We are an American community here, with American ideals, American standards of public behavior and a truly American system of education. Congressman Carter, we citizens of Hawaii want you to move among us as a brother. Stop anyone you see. Ask us any questions you please. We are here to be inspected. We have no secrets." The crowd applauded.

Black Jim McLafferty was also impressive. He said in a flowing brogue, "Today we citizens of God's fairest group of islands welcome a distinguished congressman from the great State of Texas. We know, Congressman Carter, that our terrain, magnificent though it is, would be lost in the confines of your vast kingdom of Texas. I am reminded, sir, of a story I heard while serving with the air corps in England, when a loyal son of Texas, somewhat under the influence of Scotch, that wonderful beverage, shouted in a local pub, 'Why, Texas is so big, you can get on a train at El Paso and travel all day and all night and all the next day and all the next night, and when you wake up the next morning, where are you? You're still in Texas!' And the Englishman replied, 'I know how it is, Jack. We got trains like that in England, too.' "

When the crowd chuckled, the congressman bowed graciously and raised his hand to Black Jim, whereupon the Democrat continued: "But what may surprise you about Hawaii, sir, is that although you have always heard that these islands are rock-ribbed Republican, which is probably why you voted against statehood at the last two sessions, I want to tell you here and now that the islands are going to be Democratic, and even though my good friend Hoxworth Hale is doing his very damnedest to keep them Republican, I'm doing just the opposite to make them Democratic, so that when you finally admit us to the Union, sir, you will be able to boast to your constituents, 'I'm responsible for bringin' Hawaii into the Union, yassuh. Best Democratic state in America, after Texas.' "

This prospect so intrigued the congressman that he asked if he could meet with McLafferty, so the Irishman, never one to miss the pregnant moment, volunteered: "Ride into town with me, and we can talk." To the dismay of the welcoming committee, who had planned things rather differently, big, comfortable Congressman Carter settled down beside Black Jim as the latter steered his 1949 Pontiac—"Never drive a better car than fifty per cent of the people who have to vote for you," his father had decreed, and Black Jim had found it a good rule.

"Do the islands really want statehood?" Carter asked, glad to be in private with a practicing politician.

"Sir, you can believe this one fact. The islands want to be a state."

"Why?" Carter asked. "We treat them real well in Congress."

"I'm sure that's what George the Third said about the colonies. 'Parliament treats them decently. Why do they want self-government?' That's why we fought the Revolution."

This marvelous bit of sophistry was quite lost on Carter, for as a boy he had lived along the Mexican border and the word *revolution* had no appeal to him whatever; were he able to repeal American history he would have done so, and the Thirteen Colonies would have gained their independence by the efforts of gentlemen in powdered wigs who made polite speeches. "What would you have under statehood that you now don't have?" he asked coldly.

"People usually answer that with some statement about taxation without representation, or the fact that under statehood we'd elect our own governor. But I have only one explanation, sir. If we were a state, we'd either elect or appoint our own judges."

"Don't you do so now?" Carter asked, for like most visitors to the islands, he knew nothing about them.

"Indeed we don't," Black Jim said with feeling. "They're appointed from Washington, and even when we have Democratic presidents, they usually appoint worn-out mainland Republicans."

"How does that hurt you?" asked Carter, who had once been a judge himself.

"We're a feudal society here . . ." McLafferty began, but again he used the wrong word, for the South Texas which Carter represented was also feudal, and as he recalled his happy youth, he rather felt that this was one of the better patterns of life. As McLafferty droned on, the congressman reflected: "By God, under a benevolent feudalism you didn't have Mexicans trying to tell decent men . . ."

"So the one vital thing," McLafferty concluded, "is to have judges from the islands. Because in our peculiar society here in Hawaii, the judges decide all the things that really matter."

"What's so wrong about that?" Carter asked.

"Congressman!" Black Jim cried, as he dodged a truck. "Hey, you! Manuelo!" he shouted at the Filipino. "You look good next time, maybe, eh?" And the little brown man yelled something back, happily, for that evening he would be able to tell his friends at the sugar plantation: "This afternoon I had a talk with Black Jim McLafferty." All the plantations hands knew him.

"What I was saying," the Irishman continued, "was that as long as judges from the mainland control the great trusts and the land laws, it's easy for the rich local Republicans to control the judges. Well, not control them, because our judges have been reasonably honest men, legally speaking, but the rich Republicans get next to them, and court decisions usually follow their interests." The more Carter heard about Hawaii, the less need he saw for change. In Texas, too, society was subtly rigged so that rich Democrats stayed fairly close to judges and legislators and got things their way. "Frankly," Carter thought, "what's wrong with that?"

He was therefore not too pleased with McLafferty—had him tagged as one of those radical northerners who call themselves Democrats—when the biggest blow of the day came. Black Jim had his offices on the ground floor of a building on Hotel Street, at the grubby edge of Chinatown, where Japanese and Filipino workmen were not afraid to visit him, and as he brought his car to the curb, Carter gasped: "Why these people are all slant-eyes."

"Almost half of the people in the islands are," McLafferty said offhandedly. "Some of the best citizens you ever saw. Only trouble I find is that most of the damned Chinese are Republicans. But I'm trying to change that."

"Can they be trusted?" Carter asked in honest fear.

"Maybe you better meet one of them," McLafferty laughed. "And there's no better one to meet than my partner . . ."

But Carter did not hear the words, for he saw to his astonishment that McLafferty, the head of the Democratic Party in Hawaii, had as his partner a Japanese: McLafferty and Sakagawa. And when Black Jim kicked open the door, the congressman saw, from the big poster inside, that this Japanese was running for office: "Sakagawa for Senator." And finally, beneath the poster he saw the Japanese himself, a crisp, crew-cut young man with polished manners and quiet deportment. Shigeo Sakagawa stuck out his hand and said, with a slight Boston accent, "Congressman Carter, we are proud indeed to welcome you to Hawaii."

The next moment was an agonizing one, for Shig's hand stayed out; the congressman, who had never before seen a Japanese face-to-face, simply could not take it. His jaw dropped as if he had been hit over the head by a falling oil derrick, and he stared at the fearsome, curious man before him. The expression on Shig's handsome face did not change as he lowered his hand. Belatedly Carter started to accept the greeting, moving his right hand slightly, but by then he saw that Shig had dropped his. Black-browed McLafferty, whom nothing fazed, said brightly, "Young Shig's going to be our first Democratic senator. He's going to win the unexpired term in the Nineteenth District."

"Good luck," Carter said awkwardly. "We need Democrats." He backed out of the office into the street, where the passing Orientals frightened him as he had rarely been scared in his life. Then, with a sigh of profound relief, he saw the big black automobiles of Hoxworth Hale and Hewlett Janders swing into view on Hotel Street, and he ran up to the cars as if their occupants were his brothers.

"We'll go now," he gasped with relief. Quickly jumping in beside Hale, and feeling himself secure at last in the Cadillac, he waved professionally at McLafferty and called, "Best of luck in the campaign."

When the big black cars had moved away, Black Jim started laughing. Slapping his leg, he returned to his office and continued laughing. "Shig," he cried, "hold out your hand!" And as Shig did so, his partner gave a hilarious burlesque of an American congressman, the friend of the people, desperately afraid to touch one of the people. "Shig," he laughed, "there's one vote for statehood we better not count on. But don't you worry about it, son. Do you know why I hauled that fat-ass sonofabitch down here to our offices? Not to give him a pitch about statehood, because what he thinks concerns me not at all. Look at the crowds outside! They're impressed that a United States congressman came down to Hotel Street to see you. Now get out there and walk over to the mailbox, casually, and post something."

"What?" Shig asked.

"I don't give a damn what. Fold up a piece of paper and stick it in the mailbox, as if you had congressmen visiting you all the time. And speak pleasantly to everybody." So Shig walked out among his constituents and acquired great face.

In the meantime, one of the recurring miracles of Hawaii was taking place. In the Roosevelt-Truman years, from 1932 to 1952, thousands of important Democratic politicians and officials passed through the islands, but they rarely saw any Democrats. At the airport or the dock they were met by either Hoxworth Hale or Hewlett Janders or by trim little John Whipple Hoxworth, and they were whisked away to the big houses of The Fort. They were fed well, wined to perfection, and told what to believe. Sometimes when the Japanese maids, in crisp white uniforms, had withdrawn, a Roosevelt appointee would ask timorously, "These Japanese, can they be trusted?" And The Fort invariably replied, "We've had Sumiko for eighteen years, and we've never known a better or more loyal maid."

At such parties the Roosevelt appointees met military leaders and stout island judges and cool, sharp Hoxworth Hale. Together these people created the impression of a solid citizenry, one that avoided scandal, one that honestly intended doing well, and one that was certainly content with things as they were. At public meetings the two men who could always be counted upon to give rousing speeches on behalf of statehood for Hawaii were Hoxworth Hale and John Whipple Hoxworth, and visiting statesmen were impressed by the arguments marshaled by these advocates, but in the privacy of The Fort these very men, without saying anything, always managed to convey an impression exactly the opposite of their speeches.

Hale always found occasion to comment: "There is one thing about our islands that you must not overlook. We have the finest judges in America." He would pause and then add, "We would truly deplore the day when Oriental lawyers, untrained in American values, took over the judgeships. We fear that the American way of life would be terminated at that instant."

"Not that the Orientals aren't brilliant," John Whipple Hoxworth usually interposed. "Perhaps clever's the word I'm looking for. They're able men, clever, but they aren't schooled in American values."

For nine languorous, pleasant days Congressman Clyde V. Carter of Texas got the standard Fort treatment, not knowing that every incident in his entertainment was leading up to the two climactic experiences reserved for visiting dignitaries. On the morning of the last day Hoxworth Hale observed brightly: "Congressman, we've been monopolizing you for more than a week, and you haven't really seen the islands for yourself. So we've arranged to drop out of the picture today. We've got a tour car for you, and we want you to go exploring." A long black car was waiting in the driveway, and Hoxworth introduced the driver. "This is Tom Kahuikahela, and he knows more about Hawaii than anyone you've met so far. Tom, this is a very important visitor, Congressman Carter. Take mighty good care of him."

Later, as Carter climbed out of the car to enjoy the glorious Pali, he found Tom Kahuikahela at his elbow, whispering, "It's to men like you, Congressman, that all of us look for the salvation of Hawaii."

"What do you mean?" Carter asked.

"Don't give us statehood, Congressman. Please." The robust Hawaiian begged.

"I thought everybody was for statehood," Carter gasped.

"Oh, no! The Hawaiians tremble for fear you'll give us statehood."

"Why?" Carter asked.

"The day we become a state, the Japanese will capture the islands."

For the rest of that day an appalled Congressman Carter listened as his driver told him the truth about Hawaii: how the local Japanese had plotted to destroy Pearl Harbor; how they were trying to marry all the Hawaiian girls so as to destroy the race; how they craftily bought all the land; how they controlled the stores and refused to extend credit to Hawaiians; how the young Japanese lawyers were planning to steal control of the islands; how truly desperate things were. "The only thing that saves us, sir, are the appointed governor and the judges."

Several times Carter interrupted. "I thought it was the Chinese who owned the land," he suggested.

"They buy it only for the sly Japanese," the driver assured him.

"It looked to me as if Black Jim McLafferty was the head of the Democratic Party here, but you say the Japanese . . ."

"They're using him for a front man . . . just for a while . . . then they take over."

"But why doesn't a man like Hoxworth Hale . . . Now surely, he must know everything you've told me. Why hasn't he told me these things?"

"He's scared to," the driver whispered ominously. "Everybody's scared of what's happening, and that's why we have to depend on good men like you to save us."

"Do all Hawaiians feel this way?" Carter asked.

"Every one," Tom Kahuikahela replied. "We dread statehood."

But Congressman Carter had not stayed on top of Texas politics for twenty-four years by being a fool, and he knew that you often found out what a man was really talking about only when he was done with his main pitch and had relaxed. Then you could sometimes slip in a fast question and dislodge the truth, so that it came tumbling out, and now Carter probed: "Just what kind of government would you like to see in the islands, Tom?"

"Well I'll tell you, sir!" the big man replied, adding a dimension beyond what his employers, Janders and Hale, had paid for. "What I'm working for is the return of the monarchy."

"What did you have in mind?" Carter asked in a confidential manner.

"Well, I'd like to see a king back on the throne, with a Hawaiian senate and the old nobles sort of running things. The big laws could be made in Washington, because we don't really need a legislature with a lot of lawyers arguing all the time. And the king would give big parties and the palace would be restored."

"Where would the United States come in?" Carter asked, and to his surprise Tom had a good answer.

"Well, like I said, we'd want you to pass the big laws, and coin our money for us, and you'd control all of our foreign policy. Our secretary of state would be appointed by your President, with approval of your Senate."

"You say my President. Isn't he yours, too?"

"To tell you the truth, sir, he isn't. My family boycotted the annexation. We keep a Hawaiian flag at home. We pray for the day when the alii come back."

"Were your family alii?" Carter asked.

"Yes, sir," Tom replied.

And Carter muttered, "I think I'm beginning to understand Hawaii."

The average people of the islands had a pretty shrewd idea of what occurred when congressmen were driven around Oahu, and they called this gambit "government by taxi driver," but they respected the device as the most effective lobby in Hawaii. But on this day a Democratic spy at a filling station phoned Black Jim McLafferty and reported: "They've got Congressman Carter going around the island today. Giving him the taxi-driver needle."

McLafferty slammed down the phone and stared at his partner. "Shig," he confided, "they're giving our boy the old 'government by taxi driver' routine. And that can hurt."

"What can we do?" Shig asked.

The two tacticians studied the problem for a long time, and finally the Irishman snapped: "Shig, one way or another I'm going to get hold of our congressman. I'm going to bring him down here, and you're going to take him home with you. Show him an average Japanese family. But, Shig, you run over there right now and see that your dad's service flag is hanging on the wall in the front room. The one with two gold stars. And you get your mother's box, the one with the glass cover and all the medals, and you see that every goddamned medal is polished and lying flat so our boy can read them. Now get going, and be back here, waiting, in half an hour. Because I'm coming back with Congressman Carter, dead or alive."

It was in this way that Congressman Clyde V. Carter, of Texas, became one of the few Democrats ever to meet a Democratic family during a visit to Hawaii. Black Jim spotted the tour car returning to Honolulu along Nimitz Highway, and he elbowed it over to the shoulder, explaining, "Congressman, I've just got a damned interesting cable from Democratic Headquarters in Washington. I thought you ought to advise me as to how I should answer it." McLafferty had peeled off the date line, trusting that Carter would fail to notice this, and his luck held, so while Carter was reading the complex message, Black Jim politely eased him out of the taxi and into the old Pontiac. "We'd better answer it at the office," he said.

When Carter entered the door of McLafferty and Sakagawa, there stood Shigeo waiting, and the young man said bluntly, "While Mr. McLafferty's answering the cable, I thought you might like to see a Japanese home. Just an average place." And although this was the last wish in Carter's mind, he could find no graceful escape, and a few minutes later he was being hauled into the Sakagawa cottage. "This whole thing's a transparent trick," he decided.

At the front door he met old and bent Mrs. Sakagawa, who knew little English and who wore funny Japanese sandals with things between the toes. Shig did the interpreting and said, "Mom, this is a famous United States congressman." Mrs. Sakagawa sucked in her breath audibly, and bowed. "And this," Shig said proudly, "is my bowlegged, tough-minded little father, Kamejiro Sakagawa." The old man sucked in his breath and bowed.

"Is he an American citizen?" Carter asked.

"Not allowed become citizen," Kamejiro said belligerently.

"That's right," Shigeo explained. "I am, because I was born here. But people like my father and mother, they were born in Japan."

"And they can't become citizens?" Carter asked in surprise. "Mexicans can."

Little Kamejiro stuck out his jaw and wagged his finger at the congressman: "Mexicans okay. Colored people okay. Anybody okay but not Japanese. How do you like dat?"

Congressman Carter, looking away from the argumentative little man, saw the service flag, with two blue stars and two gold. As a professional politician he automatically grew reverent and asked quietly, "Were you in service Mr. —" He couldn't recall the name.

"I and my three brothers," Shig said.

"And two gave their lives for America?" Carter asked.

In Japanese Shigeo asked, "Mom, where's that picture of the four of us in football uniforms?" His mother, who prized this picture above all others, found it and jabbed it into Carter's hands.

"This one is Tadao," Shigeo said of the fleet young halfback. "He died in Italy. This one is Minoru," he added. "He died in France. This is my brother Goro, a labor-union man . . ." And the spell was broken. That was all Congressman Carter required to hear, and he drew away from the picture of four average American boys. He had voted against the Norris-La Guardia Act and all of its successors, and he felt that to be a labor-union man was worse, in many respects, than being a Russian communist, because the Russians, God forgive them, didn't know any better, whereas a decent, God-fearing American who . . . The speech was running in his mind, and Shigeo knew it. The two men drew apart.

And then, by one of those lucky flukes that save some meetings and wreck others, Mrs. Sakagawa thrust into the congressman's hand her glass box of medals, and in Japanese said, "These are Minoru's. These are Tadao's. These are Goro's. And these five are Shigeo's." As she said the latter, she patted her son on his arm, and communion was reestablished.

Carter studied the medals and said, "Your family accomplished a great deal."

"Congressman," Shig began quietly, "each of us boys had to fight his way to get into uniform. We had to be better soldiers than anyone else in the world." He felt words coming into his mouth that he would be ashamed of later, but he could no longer hold them back. "We performed as perhaps no other family of boys did in the last war. We accumulated wounds and glory, and by God, sir, when you refused to shake my hand the other day I almost wept. Because whether you know it or not, Congressman, I'm one of your constituents, and by God I will never again accept such treatment from you."

"Constituent?" Carter gasped.

"Yes, sir. Congressman, have you heard of the Lost Battalion?"

Carter had not only heard of it, he had orated about it; and in relief the words came back to him: "It was one of the highwater marks of Texas bravery, sir."

"How many of your men died there, Congressman?" Shigeo pressed.

"Too many," Carter replied sorrowfully. "The scars upon Texas are great."

"Do you know why any escaped?" There was a pause, and Shig asked harshly, "Well, do you?"

"I supposed that the gallant fighters of Texas . . ."

"Horse manure!" Shig snapped. "Your men of Texas live today, sir, because my dead brother Minoru, one of the finest men who ever touched earth, and Goro and I led a gang of Japanese boys to their rescue. We lost eight hundred men rescuing three hundred Texans!" He cried bitterly, "I want you to read this." And from his wallet he produced a treasured card, and Carter took it and read it, and he saw that it had been signed by a friend of his, a governor of Texas, and it stated that in gratitude for heroism beyond the call of duty, Shigeo Sakagawa was forever an honorary citizen of the State of Texas. Said the card: "On our day of desperate need, you succored us."

Gravely Carter handed back the card, but as he did so, he kept his hand extended, saying, "In all humility, Mr. Sakanawa, I should like to shake your hand."

"I should like to shake yours," Shig said, and the moment could have been extremely fruitful for Hawaii statehood, except that Mr. Ishii chose this instant to break into his father-in-law's house with momentous news.

The skinny little man with eyes like bowls of frightened tapioca saw the tall stranger, hesitated and started to back out, but his wife Reiko-chan blocked the doorway, and Carter, always careful to catch the eye of a pretty girl, bowed in a courtly manner and said, "Have you come with your father?"

"He is my husband," Reiko-chan said in perfect English.

"This is a congressman, from Texas!" Shig announced proudly, and at this news Reiko-chan, who knew what her husband was up to, tried to edge him out of the house, but he had heard the word *congressman,* and now asked with compassion, "You come to arrange the surrender?"

"What surrender?" Carter asked.

In desperate embarrassment, Reiko-chan tugged at Mr. Ishii's sleeve, but she could not silence him. "The surrender of Hawaii to Japan," Mr. Ishii explained.

"How's that?" Carter asked.

"See what the paper says!" Mr. Ishii cried joyously, flashing the Honolulu *Mail,* which headlined: "Japanese Fleet to Make Courtesy Visit to Islands." When the paper had passed from hand to hand the excited little man cackled, "Long time, sir, I tell them, 'Japan won the war.' But nobody listen, so I ask you. 'If Japan lose, how their fleet come to Hawaii?' "

"Is he saying what I think he's saying?" Carter asked.

"He is a poor old man," Reiko-chan said softly. "Don't listen to him, Congressman."

But now Mr. Ishii produced a worn photograph of the Japanese surrendering on board the *Missouri.* "You can see who won," he explained. "The Americans had to go to Tokyo. And see how all the

American admirals are without neckties, while the Japanese have their swords. Of course Japan won."

"And what will happen when your fleet gets here?" Carter asked.

"Japanese very honorable men, sir. You see tonight when they come ashore. They behave good." He went to the door, threw it open and pointed down to the blue waters of the Pacific, where a squadron of five warships steamed under the bold red flag of the new Japan. Mr. Ishii's heart expanded, and he forgave his wife for her years of arguing against him. From his coat he whipped out a Japanese flag, long hidden, and waved encouragement to the conquerors as they came to take control of Pearl Harbor.

"I guess we'd better be going," Carter said. "I have to catch the plane." But he was not fooled by crazy old Mr. Ishii; he knew that in the Sakanawas, as he called them, he had seen a tremendous American family, and he was impressed, so that when he got McLafferty's message that the Hales would pick him up at the corner of Fort and Hotel on the way to the airport, he said, "I'd just like to stand outside and watch the people for a few minutes."

And as he stood there in the late afternoon, in the heart of Honolulu, watching the varied people of the island go past, he had a faint glimmer of the ultimate brotherhood in which the world must one day live: Koreans went by in amity with Japanese whom in their homeland they hated, while Japanese accepted Chinese, and Filipinos accepted both, a thing unheard of in the Philippines. A Negro passed by, and many handsome Hawaiians whose blood was mixed with that of China or Portugal or Puerto Rico. It was a strange, new breed of men Congressman Carter saw, and grudgingly an idea came to him: "Maybe they've got something. Maybe I wasted my time here in Hawaii, living in the big houses of the white people. Maybe this is the pattern of the future. That Japanese boy today, he's as good . . . Look at that couple. I wonder who they are. I wonder if they would mind . . ." But before he could speak to them, a long black car driven not by a chauffeur but Hewlett Janders drove up, and Hoxworth Hale jumped out to whisk the congressman back into reality. Icy John Whipple Hoxworth shared the front seat, and as the car slowly crept away from the turmoil of Hotel Street, the three senior citizens of Hawaii provided their guest with the second climax of any official visit to the islands.

Coldly, and with no inflection in his voice, Hoxworth Hale laid it on the line. He spoke rapidly and looked the congressman right in the eye. "Carter," he said, "you've seen the islands, and you've heard each man in this car make public speeches in favor of statehood. Now we've got to get down to cases. If you're insane enough to give us statehood, you'll wreck Hawaii and do irreparable damage to the United States. Save us from ourselves, sir."

Carter gasped. "Is that your honest opinion, Hale?"

"It's the opinion of almost every person you met in Hawaii."

"But why don't you . . ."

"We're afraid to. Reprisals . . . I don't know."

"Give me the facts straight," Carter said. "What's wrong with statehood?"

"This is in confidence?" Hale asked.

"You understand," Janders threw back over his shoulder, "that if you were to betray us, we'd suffer."

"I understand," Carter said. "That's often the case in governing a democracy."

"Here are the facts," Hale said simply. "The white man in Hawaii is being submerged. He has some financial power left, a good deal, I suppose. He has the courts to defend him, and an appointed governor upon whom he can rely. Sir, if you change any one of those factors, Hawaii will become a toy in the hands of Japanese. They'll control the courts and start bringing in decisions against us. They'll upset our system of land holding. They'll elect their own governor and send Japanese to Congress. Do you want to serve with a Jap?"

There was a long silence in the car, and more in the way of eliciting further information than in disclosing his own conclusions Carter replied, "This afternoon I met a Japanese, a young man named Shig Sakanawa, and for a while I thought that maybe . . ."

Janders spoke. "Did he tell you that his brother, Goro, was the leading communist in Hawaii? A proved, card-carrying, subversive, filthy communist. That's the brother of the man who's running for senator from this district. That's a picture of Hawaii under Japanese rule."

"I must admit," Carter said, "that nobody told me about this brother."

"The leader of the communist movement in Hawaii," Janders reiterated.

Carter was somewhat shaken to think how nearly he had been taken in by the plausible young Japanese lawyer, so he decided to check additional items of information. "By the way," he asked casually, "what's the sentiment out here for a return of monarchy?"

Up front Hewie Janders and John Whipple Hoxworth stared at each other in amazement and muttered, "Monarchy?" while in the back Hoxworth Hale gasped. Then he said forcefully, "Congressman . . ." but Hewie was now recovered and blurted out, "Jesus Christ, nobody in his right mind pays any attention to those monarchy crackpots."

"What were you about to say, Hale?" Carter pressed.

"As you may know, I'm descended from the royal alii of Hawaii, and my great-great-great-grandmother was one of the noblest women I've ever heard of. Her daughter was quite a girl, too. Magnificent. But if one of those pathetic, incompetent alii ever tried to get back on the throne of Hawaii, I personally would take down my musket and shoot him through the head."

"I'd do it first," Hewie Janders interrupted. "You know, sir, that Hale's great-grandfather brought Hawaii into the Union?"

"He did?" Carter asked.

"Yes," Hale said simply. "Practically by force of his own character. But I'd like to add this, sir. I'm also descended from the missionaries. And if one of them tried to come back and govern in the harsh, bigoted old way, I'd shoot him through the head, too."

"Let me get it straight then, what is it you want?"

"We don't want royalty, we don't want missionaries, and we don't want Japanese," Hale summarized. "We want things to go along just as they are."

It was a very somber carload of men that finally pulled up at the airport, and Black Jim McLafferty, as he watched them disembark, thought: "I'll bet they've been pumping that one with a load of poison." He started to join the congressman, but when Carter saw him coming, he retreated to the safety of Hewlett Janders, for he did not want to be photographed with a man, even though he was leader of the Democratic Party, who had as his partner a Japanese whose brother headed the Communist Party in the islands. "In fact," he mused as he checked his tickets, "Hawaii's a lot like most parts of the north. You can travel from state to state and never find a Democrat you really like. They're all either tarred with labor or communism or atheism or Catholicism. I'll be glad to get back to Texas."

And as he climbed aboard the Stratoclipper and sank into his comfortable seat he thought: "Basically, it's the same everywhere. A handful of substantial, honest men govern and try to hold back the mobs. If you can get along with those men, you can usually find out what the facts of the case are." He stared out the window glumly as Japanese airport mechanics wheeled away the steps while other Japanese waved wands directing the big airplane on its way. He closed his eyes and thought: "Well, I found out what I wanted. These islands won't be ready for statehood in another hundred years." And that took care of Hawaii for the eighty-third session of Congress.

IN 1952, passage of the McCarran-Walter Immigration Act was greeted with joy in Hawaii, for the new law permitted persons born in the Orient to become American citizens. Schools were promptly opened in which elderly Chinese and Japanese were drilled in the facts of American government, and it was not uncommon in those days to see old men who had worked all their lives as field hands reciting stubbornly: "Legislative, executive, judicial."

By early 1953 hundreds of Orientals were applying for the citizenship that had so long been denied them, and as Black Jim McLafferty watched this impressive stream of potential Democratic voters entering political life he made a speech in which he cried: "They built the islands, but they were kept outside."

It is true that many of the applicants did not really appreciate what citizenship meant, but on the other hand it was impressive to see old, weather-stained faces light up when the solemn words were pronounced by the federal judge: "You are now a citizen of the United States of America." And it was not uncommon to see a sedate businessman suddenly grab his old Japanese mother and swing her into the air with a joyous cry of, "I knew you could make it, Mom!"

The real heroes of these exciting days were the old people who had refused to learn English, but who now had to learn or forgo American citizenship. Their children screamed at them: "Pop, I told you for twenty years, learn to speak English. But no, you were too smart! Now you can't become a citizen."

"But why should I become a citizen now?" these old people asked. "Only a few more years."

Often the children broke into tears and sniffled: "You must learn English, Pop, because I have always wanted you to be an American."

"For me it is nothing," the old people said, "but if it will make you happy."

"It will, Pop! It'll remove the last stigma. Please learn English."

With a fortitude that is difficult to believe, these stubborn old Orientals went to the language schools. All afternoon they practiced: "I see the man," and most of the night they recited: "Legislative, executive, judicial." That so many mastered the two difficult subjects was a credit to their persistence, and when they finally received certificates they understood their value. In succeeding years, at mainland elections only about sixty per cent of the eligible voters bothered to vote; in Hawaii more than ninety per cent voted. They knew what democracy was.

In two Honolulu families the McCarran-Walter Act struck with contrasting effect. When Goro and Shigeo Sakagawa proposed to their tough old father that he enroll in the English school and get a book which explained the legislative, executive and judicial functions he surprised them by saying in unusually formal Japanese, "I do not wish to become a citizen."

Goro protested: "It's the opportunity of a lifetime!"

Continuing with his precise Japanese, Kamejiro said, "They should have made this offer fifty years ago, when I arrived."

"Pop!" Shigeo reasoned. "It's a new world today. Don't hark back to fifty years ago."

"For fifty years we were told, 'You dirty Japs can never become Americans.' For fifty years we were told, 'Go back to Japan.' Now they come to me and say, 'You're a fine old man, Kamejiro, and at last we are willing to let you become an American.' Do you know what I say to them? 'You are fifty years too late.' "

His sons were astonished to discover the depth of their father's feeling, so they turned to their mother and endeavored to persuade her, but before she could react to their pressures, old Kamejiro said flatly, "Yoriko, you will not take the examination. All our lives we were good citizens and we don't need a piece of paper to prove it now."

Then Shigeo produced two reasons which threw quite a different light on the matter. First he said, "Pop, last time I almost lost the election because people brought up that nonsense about Mr. Ishii and his crazy Japanese flag when the fleet visited here. They pointed out that he was my brother-in-law and that I probably felt the same way too. Now if you turn down citizenship they're going to shout, 'That proves it! The whole damned family is pro-Japanese!' "

Old Kamejiro reflected on this, and Shig could see that his father was disturbed, for none of the old Japanese had been more delighted during the last election than Kamejiro. He had stood for hours in his store, staring at the big poster of his son. "There our boy was," he proudly told his wife, "asking people to vote for him." When Shig won, the old man had paraded up and down Kakaako announcing the fact to all Japanese families, assuring them that at last they had a personal protector in Iolani Palace.

While Kamejiro twisted this first bait about in his mouth, Shig dangled another, more tempting than the first: "Pop, if you and Mom become citizens, in 1954 you can march up to the election booth, say, 'Give us our ballots,' and march inside to give me two more votes." Now Shig could see his father imagining election day, with himself striding to the polls, his wife trailing four feet behind. The old man loved nothing more than the panoply and ritual of life, and Shig could remember from his earliest days the pride with which his father dressed in Colonel Ito's uniform to stand beside the reciter. This had been the highlight of Kamejiro's life, matched only by the days in World War II when he saw his four sons march off to their own war. Therefore Shig was not prepared for what happened next.

"I will not take citizenship," the old man said resolutely. "If this hurts you, Shigeo, I am sorry. If my vote and Mother's cause you to lose the election, I am sorry. But there is a right time to eat a pineapple, and if that time passes, the pineapple is bitter in the mouth. For fifty years I have been one of the best citizens in Hawaii. No boys in trouble. No back taxes. So for America to tell me now that I can have citizenship, at the end of my life, is insulting. America can go to hell."

He would not discuss the question again. Once Shig and Goro approached him with the news that Immigration had a new rule: "People who have lived in the islands for a long time don't have to take their examinations in English. What that means, Pop, is that you and Mom can now become citizens without bothering with the language school."

"It would be insulting," Kamejiro said, and the boys withdrew.

Shig talked the problem over with McLafferty, and his partner said,

"Hell, your old man's right. It's as if they had told our people in Massachusetts, 'We kicked you Catholics around for two generations. Now you can all become Protestants and run for office.' Like he says, it would have been insulting."

"I don't think there's any analogy," Shig said coldly.

"Probably you're right," the Irishman agreed. "But it sounds good if the other guy doesn't listen too close."

"This may hurt me in the next election," Shig said carefully.

McLafferty boomed: "Shig, if your old man hadn't always been the way he is now, you wouldn't be the kind of guy you are. And if you weren't that kind of person, I wouldn't want you for a partner. What he's given you, nobody can take away."

"Yes, but he's become so provoked about this he says he's going back to Japan to live."

"He won't like it," McLafferty predicted.

"Wouldn't that hurt me in the election?" Shig pressed.

"My father found," McLafferty said, "that just a little scandal helped rather than hurt. It made the electorate feel that the candidate was human. That's why I warned you about never disclosing in a lawsuit that a witness kept a mistress. For sure, somebody on the jury has either had a mistress—or if she's a woman, has been one—and your evidence is bound to backfire, because the juror says, 'Hell, I had a mistress, and I'm no scoundrel.' So if your old man acts up, Shig, it won't hurt you . . . not with the people whose votes we want . . . because their old folks act up too." And that was the end of Kamejiro Sakagawa's citizenship.

With Nyuk Tsin the case was quite different. From the day she had landed in Honolulu eighty-eight years before, she had forsworn forever the starving villages of China and had determined to become a permanent resident of Hawaii. When the United States annexed the islands, she desperately sought American citizenship, but to no avail. From her frail body had descended some seven hundred American citizens, and not one had so far been in jail. In a lockbox she still kept her tax receipts covering nearly a century, and when she heard that there was a chance that she might become an American citizen, truly and without limitation, she felt that she could know no greater joy.

She therefore had her Harvard-trained great-grandson, Eddie Kee, study the new law and heckle the Immigration authorities until she understood every nuance. When the first language class convened, she was present, and although she was well over a hundred years old at the time, she drove her eager brain to its extent, and in the evenings sat listening to the English-language radio. But she was so ingrained in Chinese thought that English escaped her, and one night she faced up to her failure. She told Hong Kong, "I can't learn the language now.

Why didn't somebody force me to learn it years ago? Now I shall never become a citizen." And she looked disconsolately at her grandson.

But then Eddie arrived with the exciting news that certain elderly Orientals would be allowed to take the examinations in their own tongue, provided they were literate in it, and at this news Nyuk Tsin covered her old eyes for a moment, then looked up brightly and said, "I shall learn to write."

Hong Kong therefore hired a learned Chinese to teach the old woman what was undoubtedly the most difficult language in the world, but after a while it became apparent that she was simply too old to learn, so Eddie went to the Immigration authorities and said honestly, "My great-grandmother is a hundred and six, and she wants more than anything else in the world to become an American citizen. But she can't speak English . . . ."

"No trouble!" the examiner explained. "Now she can be examined in Chinese."

"But she can't read and write Chinese," Eddie continued.

"Well!" The examiner studied this for a while, then went into the back office, and in a moment Mr. Brimstead, an official from Washington, appeared with one question: "You say this old woman is a hundred and six?"

"Yes, sir."

"She got a family?"

"Probably the biggest in Hawaii."

"Good! We've been looking for something dramatic. Pictures we could use for publicity in Asia. You get the family together. I'll give her the exam myself and we'll waive the literacy. But wait a minute. Is she able to answer questions. I mean, is she competent?"

"Wu Chow's Auntie is competent," her great-grandson assured him.

"Because on the questions I can't fudge. You know: legislative, executive, judicial."

"Can I accompany her, to give her moral support?"

"Sure, but our interpreters will report her answers, and they have to be right."

"She will be right," the young lawyer guaranteed.

He therefore entered upon a long series of cramming sessions with his great-grandmother, teaching her in the Hakka tongue the many intricacies of American government, and this time, with citizenship hanging like a silver lichee nut before her, she summoned her remarkable energies and memorized the entire booklet.

"The father of our country?" Eddie shouted at her.

"George Washington."

"Who freed the slaves?" Hong Kong drilled.

"Abraham Lincoln," the little old woman replied, and Eddie reflected: "It's difficult to believe, but she came to Hawaii in the year that Lincoln died."

On the day of her examination, the Immigration Department assembled several newsreel cameras, officials in white coats, and about two hundred members of the Kee hui, who were told to cheer when the old lady arrived in Hong Kong's Buick. When she stepped down, brushing aside Eddie's arm, she was very short, weighed less than ninety pounds, and was dressed in an old-style black Chinese dress above which her nearly bald head rose with its deep-set eyes, legendary wrinkles and anxious smile. She did not speak to her accumulated family, for she was repeating in her mind many litanies alien to ancient China: "The capital of Alabama is Montgomery; Arizona, Phoenix; Arkansas, Little Rock; California, Sacramento."

The cameras were moved into the examination room, and an announcer said in a hushed voice, "We are now going to listen in upon a scene that is taking place daily throughout the United States. A distinguished elderly Chinese woman, Mrs. Kee, after nearly ninety years of life in America, is going to try to pass her examination for citizenship. Mrs. Kee, good luck!"

At the mention of her name, which in that form she did not recognize, Nyuk Tsin looked at the cameras, but her great-grandson said hurriedly, "Look over here. This is the examiner, Mr. Brimstead," and the announcer explained who the distinguished visitor from Washington was. The lights were adjusted; Nyuk Tsin began to sweat in nervous apprehension; and Mr. Brimstead, who was proving to be quite a ham on his first appearance before a camera, asked in a sweetly condescending voice, "Now tell us, Mrs. Kee, who was the father of our country?"

The official interpreter shot the question at the old lady in Hakka, and both Hong Kong and Eddie smiled superiorly, because they knew that Wu Chow's Auntie knew that one.

But there was silence. The cameras ground. Mr. Brimstead looked foolish and the Hakka interpreter shrugged his shoulders. "Wu Chow's Auntie!" Eddie whispered hoarsely. "You know. The father of our country!"

"Now, no coaching!" Mr. Brimstead rebuked. "This has got to be an honest examination."

"I wasn't coaching," Eddie pleaded.

"He didn't say nothing," the interpreter said in English.

"All right!" Mr. Brimstead snapped. "No coaching. Now, Mrs. Kee," and his voice was all honey again, "who was the father of our country?" Again the interpreter droned in Hakka and again there was silence. In agony Hong Kong stared at his grandmother and opened and shut his fingers by his mouth, signifying, "For God's sake, say something."

But the scene was too vital for old Nyuk Tsin to absorb. All her life she had wanted to belong: first to her brave and gallant father, whose head had perched in the village square; then to her Punti husband, who had scorned her big feet; then to her children, who were afraid of her possible leprosy; then to America, which had repulsed her as it did all Orientals. Now, when all that she hoped for was attainable, she fell mute. She heard no questions, saw no men, felt nothing. But she sensed inwardly that some golden moment, some crystal opportunity that would never come again was slipping by, and she looked up with mute anguish at the people about her.

She saw kindly Mr. Brimstead, almost wetting his pants in his eagerness for her to say something so that he could appear in the moving pictures. She saw bright young Eddie, who had coached her. She saw resolute Hong Kong, who must be praying for her to save the family reputation. And then over Hong Kong's shoulder she saw an official government etching of a long-dead hero with a determined chin and a three-cornered hat, and she heard as from a great distance the Hakka interpreter begging for the last time, "Mrs. Kee, tell the man, who was the founder of our country?" And with the floodgates of passion breaking over her, she rose, pointed at the etching of George Washington, and screamed, "That one!"

Then she started: "The capital of Alabama is Montgomery; Arizona, Phoenix; Arkansas, Little Rock; California, Sacramento . . ."

"Tell her that's enough!" Mr. Brimstead shouted. "I didn't ask that question yet."

"Keep those cameras grinding," the director shouted.

"You!" Hong Kong shouted at the interpreter. "Keep interpreting."

"The legislative passes the laws," Nyuk Tsin cried, "and the executive administers them and the judicial judges them against the Constitution."

"It's enough!" Mr. Brimstead shouted. "Tell her it's all right."

"And the Bill of Rights says that there shall be freedom of worship, and freedom of speech," Nyuk Tsin continued. "And no troops may search my house. And I may not be punished in cruel ways." She was determined to omit nothing that might swing the decision in her favor. "There are two houses in Congress," she insisted, "the Senate and the House . . ."

When she left the Immigration building, with her citizenship proved and in her hand, the Kees who had been waiting outside cheered, and she passed happily among them, speaking to each and asking, "What is your name?" and when they told her, she was able to place each one. And as she ticked off her great family she realized for the first time that they were neither Hakka nor Punti, for in Hawaii those old enmities had dissipated and all who had arrived in the *Carthaginian* had been transmuted into something new. In truth, the Kees were not even Chinese; they were Americans, and now Nyuk Tsin was an American too. Standing by Hong Kong's car she whispered, "When you are a citizen, the earth feels different."

But these fine words did not erase from Hong Kong's memory the anxiety he had suffered when in the examination room his auntie had sat in stolid silence like a Chinese peasant and now when he looked down at her citizenship paper, his former irritation returned and he protested with some petulance: "Oh, Wu Chow's Auntie! You didn't even pick up the right paper." He took the document from her and showed her where the strange name was written: Char Nyuk Tsin. But when he had read this name aloud to her, she said quietly and yet with great stubbornness, "I told the helpful man, 'Now that I am an American you must write on this paper my real name.' " And she climbed purposefully into the car, a small old woman who had made a great journey.

That night, terribly tired from the ordeal of citizenship, she lit her oil lamp, undressed, and inspected herself for leprosy. There were no lumps on her arms; her fingers were still good; her face was not deformed; and her legs were clean. Greatly relieved, she put the lamp on the floor so that she could examine her big feet, and in the morning Hong Kong found her there, a frail, naked, old dead body of bones, beside a sputtering lamp.

AS THOUSANDS of once-proscribed Orientals gained citizenship and the vote, and as labor attained fresh power, haoles gloomily predicted that their day in Hawaii was ended, and no one felt this more strongly than Hoxworth Hale, for he was passing through a period of mist and fog, and his bearings were insecure: he was unable to understand his mercurial daughter or to communicate with his elfin-minded wife, who flitted from one inconsequential subject to the next. He tried diligently to maintain control of both H & H and of Hawaii, but he suspected that each was slipping away from him. Finally, the great pineapple crisis of 1953 struck and it looked as if Hawaii itself were crumbling.

The disaster first became known when a luna on Kauai inspected one of the far fields and discovered that all the plants which should have been a rich bluish green were now a sickly yellow. He immediately thought: "Some damn fool forgot to spray for nematodes." But when he consulted the records, he found that the field had been sprayed to control the tiny worms, so one of the pineapple botanists employed by The Fort flew over to inspect the dying plants and said, "This isn't nematodes. As a matter of fact, I don't know what it is."

In the second week of the blight, the once-sturdy plants fell over on their sides, as if some interior enemy had sapped their vitality, but there were no scars, no boring insects, nothing. The botanist became frightened and phoned Honolulu to discover that plants on scattered fields throughout the islands were beginning to show similar symptoms.

It would be an understatement to say that panic struck the pineapple industry. A raging fear swept the red fields and echoed in the Fort Street offices. Hoxworth Hale bore the brunt of the anxiety, because H & H had a good deal of its wealth in pineapples, while outfits like Hewlett's and J & W, who looked to him for leadership, were even more vulnerable. The loss in one year alone threatened to exceed $150,-000,000, and still the botanists had no clue as to what was happening to their precious charges.

The famous Englishman, Schilling, who had licked mealy-bugs and nematodes, was now dead, but research scholars went through his papers to see if he had left any clues as to further apprehensions. But that was only a figure of speech, for the drunken expert had left no orderly papers and no suggestions. He had died one night in a fit of delirium tremens in a poverty ward on the island of Kauai, the nurses not recognizing who he was until after his death. Nevertheless, the botanists repeated all of Schilling's work on the pineapple and assured themselves that the fault lay not with iron, nor bugs, nor nematodes. They discovered nothing about the current disease except that hundreds of thousands of plants seemed determined to die.

In desperation, Hoxworth Hale suggested: "We know we're being attacked either by some invisible virus or by some chemical deficiency. It doesn't seem to be the former. Therefore, it's got to be the latter. I am willing to spray-feed every plant in the islands. But what with?"

A young chemist from Yale suggested: "We know the complete chemical component of the pineapple plant. Let's mix a spray which contains everything that might possibly be lacking. We'll shoot blind. At the same time, you fellows compare by analysis a hundred dead plants with a hundred unaffected ones. Maybe you can spot the deficiency."

The young man mixed a fantastic brew, a little of everything, and sprayed one of the dying fields. Almost as if by magic the hungry plants absorbed some tiny, unspecified element in the concoction, and within two days were both upright and back to proper color. It was one of the most dramatic recoveries in the history of pineapple culture, and that night for the first time in several months, Hoxworth Hale slept peacefully. In the morning his board asked him, "What was it that saved the crop?"

"Nobody knows. Now we're going to find out."

He encouraged the scientists, who withheld from the magic brew one component after another, but the fields responded dramatically no matter what was sprayed on them; and then one day zinc was omitted, and that day the plants continued to die.

"Zinc!" Hale shouted. "Who the hell ever heard of adding zinc to pineapple soils?"

Nobody had, but over the years the constant leaching of the soil and the introduction of chemical fertilizers had minutely depleted the zinc, whose presence to begin with no one was aware of, and when the critical moment was reached, the zinc-starved plants collapsed. "What other chemicals may be approaching the danger line?" Hale asked.

"We don't know," the scientists replied, but prudence warned him that if zinc had imperceptibly fled from the fields, other trace minerals must be doing so too, and he launched what became perhaps the most sophisticated development in the entire history of agriculture: "We are going to consider our famous red soil of Hawaii as a bank. From it we draw enormous supplies of things like calcium and nitrate and iron, and those are easy to replace. But we also seem to draw constant if minute supplies of things like zinc, and we haven't been putting them back. Starting today, I want the chemical components of every scrap of material harvested from our pineapple fields analyzed and their total weight calculated. If we take out a ton of nitrate, we'll put a ton back. And if we withdraw one-millionth of a gram of zinc, we're going to put the same amount back. This marvelous soil is our bank. Never again will we overdraw our account."

It was strange what depletions the scientists found: zinc, titanium, boron, cobalt, and many others. They were present in the soil only in traces, but if one vanished, the pineapple plants perished; and one night when balance had been restored to the vast plantations, and the economy of Hawaii saved, Hoxworth Hale, who had refused to surrender either to nematodes or to the depletion of trace minerals, suddenly had a vision of Hawaii as a great pineapple field: no man could say out of hand what contribution the Filipino or the Korean or the Norwegian had made, but if anyone stole from Hawaii those things which the tiniest component added to the society, perhaps the human pineapples would begin to perish, too. For a long time Hale stood at the edge of his fields, contemplating this new concept, and after that he viewed people like Filipinos and Portuguese in an entirely different light. "What vital thing do they add that keeps our society healthy?" he often wondered.

When Hong Kong Kee had served on various boards of The Fort for a testing period the unbelievable happened. He was summoned to the chambers of Judge Harper, who had married one of the Hoxworth girls, and was advised by that careful Texan: "Hong Kong, the judges have decided to appoint you one of the trustees of the Malama Kanakoa Estate."

Hong Kong stepped back as if the good judge had belted him across the face with a raw whip. "You mean that without applying, I've been appointed?"

"Yes. We felt that with Hawaii's commerce and politics falling more and more into the hands of our Oriental brothers, certain steps ought to be taken to recognize that fact."

In spite of his cynical knowledge of how The Fort and its ramifications operated, Hong Kong was visibly moved by the appointment, for he knew that when the evening papers revealed this story the extent of the Hawaii revolution could no longer be ignored. With bright young Japanese politicians taking over the legislature, the only remaining bulwark of the old order was the great trusteeships, and for The Fort voluntarily to relinquish one was an event of magnitude. Hong Kong was therefore inspired to complete frankness, for he wanted to be sure that Judge Harper knew what he was doing.

"I am deeply touched by this gesture, Judge Harper," he said with real humility. "I guess you know what it means to be the first Chinese on such a board. You judges are giving me an accolade I'll never forget. But do you know how I stand on land tenure? Leasehold? Breaking up the big estates that don't use their land creatively? You understand all those things, Judge?"

Big Judge Harper laughed and pointed to a paper on his desk. "Hong Kong, you apparently forget who your brother trustees will be. Hewlett Janders and John Whipple Hoxworth. You think they're going to let you run wild with any crazy idea?"

"But even with such men, Judge, ideas repeated often enough sometimes catch on . . . where you least expect them."

"We judges think you're the kind of man who will bring good new ideas, but we certainly aren't going to back you against your two fellow trustees."

"I'm not looking for a fight, Judge."

"We know. That's why we've appointed you. But before you take the job, Hong Kong—and I appreciate even better than you how signal an honor this is, because we have been petitioned for years to appoint some Oriental—I want you to understand with crystal clarity the nature of the task you're undertaking." The big man adjusted his considerable bulk in his judge's chair and told his secretary he didn't want to be interrupted.

"The very existence of Hawaii, Hong Kong, depends not upon what cynical outsiders like to term The Fort. The outsiders are wrong. It's not The Fort that controls Hawaii. It's the sanctity of the great trusts. They form the solid backbone of our society. The Fort is only the ribs and the people are the flesh. But the backbone has to be kept strong, and it is up to us judges to be its guardians.

"The trusts control the land and establish the systems of tenure. They control the sugar and the pineapple fields. They continue, where companies rise and fall. They remain productive while the families who profit from them subside into decay. Look at the one you're entering. It controls millions of dollars in the vital heart of Hawaii, for whom? For a dear old Hawaiian lady and her no-good beachboy son. We judges don't spend our time worrying about that trust because we're interested in those two poor Hawaiians. They aren't worth it. But the idea that Malama Kanakoa and her son Kelly are assured of a square deal from the courts is terribly important.

"What I have to say next, Hong Kong, I don't want to say sitting down." The big man rose, adjusted his dark brown suit, and pointed directly at his Chinese visitor. "In the history of our great trusts, there has never been a scandal because some trustee stole money. There have been no defalcations, no illegal conversions, no overtrading for personal commissions, no theft. The trustees have often been accused of being too conservative, but in a trustee that's not a weakness. It's a virtue. Hong Kong, so long as we were satisfied to choose our trustees from the missionary families we enjoyed a spotlessly clean record. We're now branching out, and in a sense we're taking a risk. If you make one error, I personally will hound you out of the islands. The courts will never rest till you're behind bars. If you want to do one thing which will set the Orientals in Hawaii back three generations, abuse the Malama Kanakoa Trust." He sat down, smiled at Hong Kong, and added, "Of course, if you want to prove to our entire society that Orientals are as responsible as the missionaries ever were, you have that opportunity, too."

Hong Kong wished that his grandmother were alive to guide him at this moment, but he felt that she would have counseled courage, so he said bluntly, "What will you judges say when I recommend that Malama Kanakoa go mostly into some pretty radical investments?"

Judge Harper thought this one over a long time and finally said, "One of the reasons why we judges decided to appoint you to Malama's trust is that Hoxworth Hale told us about your investing ideas. He said they ought to be looked into, that maybe they were the answer to some of these trusts with vast back-tax structures."

"Then Hoxworth Hale got me this job?" Hong Kong asked.

"You misunderstand, Hong Kong. I appointed you."

The Chinese bowed slightly, but could not keep from smiling, and soon Judge Harper joined him. Rising from his desk and putting his arm about Hong Kong's shoulders, he said, "Let's put it this way. If you turn out badly, Hoxworth doesn't suffer the opprobrium. I do. Hong Kong, you are really going to be watched. By me."

"What do they call these Negroes who are the first to move into a white neighborhood?" Hong Kong laughed. "The blockbusters? Looks as if I'm the trustbuster."

"The word has an entirely different meaning," Judge Harper pointed out amiably, but when the able Chinese had gone he had a moment of nostalgic reflection, saying to himself, "He's probably right. Appointing him was probably the beginning of the end . . . at least of the safe, comfortable, honest old system we knew."

Hong Kong drove immediately home and asked the cook, "Where is Judy?" and when he found that she was teaching at the conservatory, he drove there and went in to fetch her. Since the death of Nyuk

Tsin, the oldest woman of his family, he had found himself drawing markedly closer to Judy, his youngest girl. He liked women's habits of thought, and he particularly appreciated Judy's cool, clean reasoning.

After a few minutes she joined him, a sparkling, winsome Chinese girl of twenty-six, with two braids down her back, a starched pink dress and wide, clever eyes. She bounced into the Buick and asked, "What's up, Dad?"

"I want you to accompany me to a very important meeting. I've just been appointed a trustee for the Malama Kanakoa Trust."

"Are the judges out of their minds?" Judy chortled.

"The Fort has the ability to see the inevitable," her father said.

"Where are we going?" Judy asked.

"I want to see Malama. I'd like to find out what her ambitions are, her hopes for the land she owns, and at the same time doesn't own."

"Dad! You know Malama won't have any ideas."

"That's what everybody has said for years. But I suppose she's as bright as you or I, and I'd like to find out."

He drove toward Diamond Head until he crossed the Ala Wai canal, then turned into the gate at the board fence that surrounded the Swamp. When he drew up to the shingled house, with its spacious porch, Malama thrust open the screen door and appeared with a gigantic smile, her silver hair disheveled and her dress askew. "Hong Kong, the defender of my interests, come in! The judges told me last night!" With widespread arms she welcomed him, and Judy saw with some surprise that her father had had foresight enough to purchase a flower lei for his first visit. Graciously he bestowed it upon the woman who towered over him, then leaned up to give her two kisses while she beamed.

"Come in, my good friends!" she said expansively, adding, with the instinct that marked Hawaiians, "I never thought I should see the day when a distinguished Chinese banker was appointed one of my guardians. It is a happy day for me, Hong Kong. Your people and mine have blended well in the past, and I hope this is a good augury for the future."

"It's a new day in Hawaii, Malama," he replied.

"And is this your lovely daughter?" Malama asked, and when Hong Kong said that it was, she laughed and said, "In the old days I could never tell, when I saw a rich Chinese with a young girl, whether she was his daughter or his number four wife."

"I feel the same way when I go to a night club in New York," Hong Kong replied happily, "and see the haole bankers and their companions. We poor Chinese aren't allowed to get away with plural marriages any longer . . . only the haoles."

"I want you to meet my friends," Malama chuckled. "We gather now and then for some Hawaiian music. This is Mrs. Choy, Mrs. Fukuda, Mrs. Mendonca and Mrs. Rodriques."

Hong Kong bowed to each of the huge ladies and then returned to Mrs. Choy. "You the pretty girl named after the race horse?"

"Yes," Mrs. Choy laughed gaily. "My name is Carry-the-Mail. You see, Father won a lot of money on that horse."

"I know! My grandmother found out that my father had bet a lot of money on Carry-the-Mail, and she gave him hell, but the horse won. So my father and your father probably got drunk together, Mrs. Choy," Hong Kong said easily, and the women laughed.

"This is my daughter Judy, the musician. She has a job at the conservatory."

"How wonderful!" Malama cried, shoving a ukulele at the lovely Chinese girl, who slipped easily and without embarrassment into the great frieze of Hawaiian ladies who lined the wall of the chandeliered room. "You won't know the words, but you can hum." And the six women began an old Hawaiian song from the days when royalty lived at Lahaina, on Maui. It was true that Judy Kee knew none of the words, but she harmonized well, and once the others stopped singing while she vocalized a verse, and Mrs. Choy cried, "If we could do something about those slant-eyes, we could make her into a good Hawaiian."

The crowd laughed and Hong Kong asked easily, "What I'd like to find out, Malama, is what are the opinions of a Hawaiian who is placed on a spendthrift trust?" It was like asking the Pope his impressions of Martin Luther, but Hong Kong's blunt approach often proved best, and this was an occasion when it did, for all the Hawaiian ladies were interested in this question, which affected many of their friends.

"I'll tell you, Hong Kong," Malama confessed, as she asked Judy to help her serve tea. "I graduated from Vassar with very good grades, and I was shocked when the court said, 'You are not competent to handle your own affairs. We will pay three white men huge salaries to do it for you.' This was insulting, and I tried to fight back, but then I remembered what the sweet haole teachers had taught us at Hewlett Hall. I was Hawaiian. I was different. I was supposed to be incompetent, so I relaxed and found no shame in being judged a spendthrift. I love my friends, I love a guitar well played, I love the Swamp, so I have rather succumbed to the passing of the days. A little friendship, the birds in the Swamp . . . until I die. I am a spendthrift, so I suppose I deserve to be disciplined by a spendthrift trust."

Mrs. Fukuda said, "What always infuriates white men, and frugal Japanese like my husband, is the way a woman like Malama gives things to her friends. This they cannot understand. In their pinched and miserable hearts they can't understand it."

"What's money?" Malama asked.

"How much does the spendthrift trust allow you?" Hong Kong asked.

"I don't blame the trustees," Malama evaded. "When the courts stepped in I'd worked things around so that I owed the federal government $350,000 in back taxes. Somebody had to do something. So now all I get is $22,000 a year for myself."

"And all her friends," Mrs. Mendonca said. "After all, she is an alii nui and she does have some obligations."

"How do you like the system?" Hong Kong repeated.

"I neither understand it nor like it," Malama replied.

"Malama," Hong Kong said bluntly. "I'm going to make some radical investments for you. You'll have two very lean years, and you're going to make some kind of deal with the federal government, but if you behave, in three years you'll be off the spendthrift trust."

The faces of the five Hawaiian women bloomed like flowers after a providential rain, and Hong Kong could see them envisaging endless parties, good food, new automobiles and trips to Europe, like in the old days, but Hong Kong warned bleakly, "And when you're off the spendthrift trust, you'll be under my supervision, and you know a Chinese is ten times tougher than a haole judge."

The Hawaiians laughed, for this was the truth, and Malama cried, "I hope we can do it, Hong Kong." She kissed him on both cheeks as she placed over his head the lei he had previously given her. "I am not joking when I say that Hawaiians and Chinese have always been good for one another."

She was about to cite examples when she was interrupted by the screen door's banging open suddenly, then slamming shut as someone retreated down the porch. "Kelly!" Malama cried. "Come on in. It's only Hong Kong."

The tall beachboy shuffled into the room, barefoot, in his tight knee-length pants and waiter's jacket that failed to cover his rugged chest. He wore a yachting cap far back on his head, and his black hair was uncombed. "Apternoon, Hong Kong," he grunted.

"We've been talking about plans for the trust," Malama said graciously as she handed her son a cup of tea. He brushed it aside and plucked a few notes on his mother's ukulele.

"You da new trustee da kine?" Kelly said.

"Yes," Hong Kong said with obvious distaste for the pidgin.

"I speak true. You akamai dis trust, you fix heem up, you one damn good pella." He banged the ukulele and pointed at his mother, adding, "Because dis wahine spend, spend." He motioned with his uke to Mrs. Fukuda, who began strumming hers, and soon the women were singing, but as they entered into one of their most loved songs Kelly was aware of a Chinese voice, high and lyrical, and while he continued plunking his ukulele, he studied with approval the relaxed manner in which Hong Kong's daughter sang. Then he paid no more attention to her, but at the end of the song he grabbed a guitar and began a throbbing slack-key solo, to which the other instruments gradually joined in subdued harmonies. Finally, when the slack-key had ended, with its intricate fingerings echoing in the air, Kelly plucked the first few chords of the "Hawaiian Wedding Song," then threw the guitar to Mrs. Fukuda and rose to begin the majestic male solo. When it came time for the soprano to enter, he pushed his mother into the background, and with his right hand imperiously grabbed Judy and brought her to her feet. At the appropriate moment, he pointed at her, and for the first time in Hawaii an impressed audience heard the Chinese girl soar into the upper reaches of this passionate evocation of the islands. Her voice was like a clear bell in some island church where a true wedding was being performed, and when it came time for Kelly to join her, he did not fool around with falsettos or effects; he projected his handsome baritone until it filled the old room and caused the chandelier to sway. In the final passages Malama and the four big Hawaiian women hummed softly, so that Hong Kong remained the only listener. Against his will, for he did not like his daughter singing Hawaiian songs, he had to applaud, and the four visiting women cheered and Kelly leaped into the other room and returned with a length of tapa, which he twisted about Judy's waist. He stuck three flowers into her braids and used his right forefinger as if it were a make-up pencil, dabbing it about her eyes.

"She gonna look more Hawaiian than I do," he cried. Then he pointed in turn at each of his mother's guests. "Choy!" he cried. "Fukuda, Mendonca, Rodriques, and you, Malama!" He stood back to survey them. "Tomorrow night. Your hair long. Old muumuus. Flowers. Three ukuleles, two guitars. Da Lagoon gonna hear Hawaiian music like nevah bifore." He bowed to Judy and asked, "Seestah, you sing wit' me?"

"I will," she said simply.

Malama was an unusually outspoken woman, for a Hawaiian, and she asked, "Will it be taken with grace if a Chinese girl sings that particular song? It's so especially Hawaiian."

"Da kine people better get accustomed," Kelly snapped, "because dis wahine . . . a true meadowlark."

"What do you think, Hong Kong?" Malama asked.

It was apparent from his scowl that he was going to reserve his negative judgment until he got Judy alone, but his daughter said for him, "He'll be there, and so will I."

Back in the Buick, Hong Kong stormed: "I don't want my daughter singing in a night club!"

"But I want to sing," Judy said firmly.

"People will laugh, Judy. My daughter, singing in a club. You, a Chinese making believe you're Hawaiian."

"Dad, for a long time I've wanted to sing . . ."

"But Kelly Kanakoa! A no-good, broken-down Hawaiian!"

"What's wrong with a Hawaiian?" Judy snapped.

"I didn't raise a respectable Chinese girl to be messing around with a Hawaiian!"

"You're messing around, as you call it, with Malama."

"That's business, Judy. You're asking for trouble, girl."

"You be there tomorrow night, Dad. I want to see at least one friendly face."

The team of Kelly and Judy created a sensation in more ways than one. To the mainland tourists they were the first pair in the islands who showed any real sense of professional savoir-faire, and the five powerful gray-haired women who accompanied them on that first night were remarkable, for they set off the frail beauty of the girl and the lithe young masculinity of the baritone, so that if only the tourists had to be considered, the team was both an artistic and a financial success. But to the residents of Hawaii it was shocking on two counts. To the Chinese community it was inconceivable that on the very day that Hong Kong's appointment to the Malama Kanakoa Trust was announced, confirming as it were his respectability in the community, his well-trained daughter should appear in a public night club, her navel showing, singing and doing the hula with a man like Kelly Kanakoa. At least four major Chinese families whose sons had been thinking of marrying the delectable music teacher said flatly, "We will never accept her as a daughter-in-law." But to the Hawaiian community it was an affront past understanding that an alii family like the Kanakoas would choose as Kelly's singing partner a pure Chinese girl, and for her to presume to dress like an honest Hawaiian and thus palm herself off to the public was morally outrageous.

So the Chinese boycotted Judy and the Hawaiians boycotted Kelly, but Manny Fineberg of Clarity Records heard them on the second night and signed them up to a profitable contract, but he did stipulate, "On the cover of the album, we got to have a pure Hawaiian girl. Judy can sing like an angel, but she can't get over them slant-eyes." As the young singers were driving home that night Judy said, "Kelly, I think that for our next album we ought to form our own company, right here in Hawaii." And that was the start of Island Records, which Judy Kee ran with an iron hand, seeking out fresh talent to sing famous old songs, so that before long, half the Hawaiian melodies played in America were produced by this clever Chinese girl.

She also devised the costume by which Kelly became famous in the island night clubs. She had a tailor make him skin-tight pants, one leg blue, the other red, with frayed ends reaching below the knee. For a top she found a subdued tapalike fabric from Java and had it made into a tight jacket with long ends that tied at the waist. His hat continued to be a yachting cap, worn on the back of his head, but his shoes were heavy leather sandals which she designed and which he could kick off when he wished to dance. "You must become a visual symbol," she insisted, and she did the same, with her exotic face framed in flowers and her two braids showing over an island sarong. But the thing that tourists remembered longest was the curious whale's tooth that Kelly wore on a silver chain about his neck. It became his trademark.

Judy made other changes in Kelly. When he spoke to her, he had to speak English, but when he was on stage she encouraged him to use a wild pidgin, as when in the middle of a performance he would suddenly halt Florsheim's guitar solo and cry, "Eh you, Florsheim blalah. Las' night I t'ink. More'n hunnerd years ago de missionary come dis rock and find my gradfadder you gradfadder wearin' nuttin', doin' nuttin', sleepin' under de palm tree, drinkin' okolehau, dey raise hell. Bimeby hunnerd years later you me kanaka we doin' all de work while de missionary kids sleepin' under de palm tree, drinkin' gin, wearin' almos' nuttin', and doin' nuttin'. Florsheim blalah, wha' in hell hoppen?"

It was Judy who insisted that Florsheim learn to play the steel guitar with an electronic booster, and she also encouraged the big slob to dress in disreputable costumes so as to set off Kelly's grandeur, but there were two problems concerning the huge Hawaiian that not even Judy could solve. If he was a member of a group, everyone unconsciously spoke pidgin, even Judy; and no one could keep the big man's girls straightened out. After a while Judy stopped trying, but one change she did make. She insisted that when Kelly got cables from divorcees on the mainland, he ignore them.

"You're an important artist, Kelly!" she hammered day after day. "You don't have to peddle yourself to every neurotic dame who sends you a distress signal."

"They're friends of my friends," he explained.

"Were they good for you, Kelly?" she asked bluntly.

"No," he said.

"Then cut it out," she said simply, and in time she even got Florsheim to stop running in breathlessly with the news: "Kelly blalah, I got dem two da kine wahine, one got convertible. Kelly blalah, you help me out, huh?"

There was one point on which Judy Kee never deceived herself. It was true that the financial success of her trio stemmed from her managerial ability, but its artistic reception derived solely from the infectious Polynesian charm of her two companions. When tourists saw handsome Kelly and ponderous Florsheim, they instinctively loved them, for the Hawaiians reminded them of an age when life was simpler, when laughter was easier, and when there was music in the air. No stranger to Hawaii ever loved the islands because Judy Kee and her astute father Hong Kong were making profound changes in the social structure; people loved Hawaii because of the Polynesians. All Judy did was make it possible for her two beachboys to live, for under her guidance they earned about $70,000 a year, with time off to go swimming almost every afternoon.

Two older people followed the regeneration of Kelly and Florsheim with interest. To Malama the arrival of the strong-minded Chinese girl was a blessing from the old gods who had looked after Hawaiians. She told her tea-party friends, "I tried to make him grow up and failed. But this little Pake says jump, and he jumps. Always in the right direction."

"I hear she has the recording company in her name," Mrs. Rodriques probed.

"She does," Malama admitted. "But I suggested it. I didn't want Kelly free to shuffle out of his arrangements."

"Then if he wants to get his fair share of the company, he'll have to marry her, won't he?"

"Nothing could please me more," Malama said frankly. Then, looking sadly out over the swamp where the alii of a past age had boated, she said softly, "By ourselves, we Hawaiians cannot maintain our position in the new world that surrounds us. I was staggering under frightful burdens till Hong Kong came along. He has such a peasant, earthy power that the boards of the porch seem a little firmer when he passes."

Mrs. Mendonca said, "I never thought to witness the day when you would approve the marriage of your son to a Chinese."

Malama continued looking out the window and said gravely, "You forget, Liliha, that she is not just a Chinese girl. She is the great-granddaughter of the Pake Kokua. When nobody else on this earth dared to help the Hawaiian lepers, that woman did. Any member of her family merits our special affection." Then she looked back into the room and asked, "Where would Kelly be today if it were not for the Pake girl? Do you think I was happy, the way he used to live? One divorced woman after another? I wish the world could somehow maintain just a little corner where Hawaiians could live as they liked and prosper, but since that is not the way of the world, the next best thing is to have a Chinese helping us. They can't hurt us any worse than the haoles did."

"Do you think they'll get married?" Mrs. Mendonca asked.

Malama evaded this question by volunteering a short speech: "I remember, Carry-the-Mail, when you married Leon Choy, and all the alii wept because a fine Hawaiian girl was marrying a Chinese, and I wept too, but as I recall, my father assured your father that it was all right, and that sometimes the Chinese were good people. How different things are now, because it is no longer a question of what we five elderly Hawaiian ladies think of such a marriage. The problem is: 'Will a leading Chinese family like Hong Kong Kee's allow their daughter to marry a

Hawaiian?' We have fallen so swiftly on the slide of history." She strummed idly on her ukulele while her guests picked up an old song that had come down from better days.

The other older person who watched Kelly's new position with meticulous care was Hong Kong Kee, and one night he waited up till three in the morning to greet his beautiful, competent daughter. "Were you out there kissing him in the car?" he stormed.

"Yes."

"This is what the haoles call necking?"

"Yes."

"Well, don't let me catch you again."

"Then don't peek!" And she flounced up the stairs, but he trailed after her, protesting that the entire Chinese community was worried about her. Singing in a hotel was bad enough, but now it began to look as if . . .

"As if what?" she asked sternly, whirling about to face her anguished father.

"It begins to look as if you were thinking of marrying him," Hong Kong stammered.

"I am," Judy said.

"Oh, Judy!" her father gasped, and to her surprise the tough old warrior burst into tears. "You mustn't do this!" he pleaded. "You're a fine Chinese girl. You've got to think of your position in the community."

"Father!" Judy cried, pulling his hands down from his red eyes. "Kelly's a good boy. I love him and I think I'm going to marry him."

"Judy!" her father wept. "Don't do it." The noise awakened the rest of the family, and soon the hallway was filled with Kees, and when they heard Hong Kong's ominous warning that "Judy insists she's going to marry the Hawaiian," her brothers began to weep, too, and one said, "Judy, you can't bring this disgrace upon us."

For some time Judy had been aware of her family's apprehension about her growing friendship with Kelly, but she had considered it merely a normal expression of family concern. Now, as the weeping male members of her family stood about her, she realized that it was something much deeper. "You're a Chinese girl!" Brother Eddie stammered. "Don't you think that when I was at Harvard Law I met a lot of attractive haole girls? Even some I wanted to marry? But I didn't do it because I thought of the family here in Hawaii. And you can't do it, either."

"But Kelly's a settled-down citizen," Judy stubbornly repeated. "He makes more money than any of you, and if Dad can get the trust straightened out . . ."

"He's a Hawaiian," Mike said.

"You think I want my lovely daughter to marry a man with a vocabulary of seven hundred words, most of them *seestah* and *blalah?*" Hong Kong demanded.

"Kelly is an educated young man," Judy insisted.

"Very well," Hong Kong snapped. "If you marry him . . ."

"Don't say it, Father," Judy begged.

"If you insist upon bringing disgrace upon the whole Chinese community," Hong Kong said ominously, "we want nothing more to do with you. You're a lost girl."

The Kees went officially to bed, but through the night one after another crept to Judy's room to explain how deeply they opposed such a marriage. "It isn't that Kelly has a vocabulary of seven hundred words," one sister whispered. "It's that you're a fine Chinese girl, and he's a Hawaiian."

"Many Chinese married Hawaiians," Judy argued. "Look at Leon Choy."

"And whenever one did," the sister explained, "we all felt sorrowful. You're a Chinese, Judy. You can't do this."

"Would you feel the same way if Kelly were a haole?" Judy asked.

"Identically," the sister assured her. "You're a Chinese. Marry a Chinese."

But Judy Kee was a very tough-minded girl, and in spite of constantly renewed pressures from her entire family she came home one night at four and announced loudly: "Now hear this! Now hear this! Everybody wake up. The most precious flower of the Celestial Kingdom is going to marry Kelly Kanakoa. And what are you going to do about it?" She stomped off to bed and waited as one by one the family came to see if she were sober and in her right mind.

At first Hong Kong flatly refused to attend the wedding, as did many of the leading Chinese and some of the remaining Hawaiian alii, but Judy said bravely, "Tonight at the Lagoon, Kelly, we'll announce our engagement, and then we'll sing 'The Wedding Song' in our own honor." And they did, and among the tourists it was a very popular wedding, but among the affected citizens of Hawaii it was a catastrophe. At the last moment Hong Kong thought of his obligations to Malama Kanakoa, and out of respect for her, he attended the ceremony, but he would not walk down the aisle with his daughter.

But at The Fort, Hong Kong found that the disgrace he was suffering through his daughter's headstrong marriage brought him closer to his colleagues. Hewlett Janders, whose son Whip was still living with the air force man in San Francisco, said simply, "You can never tell about kids, Hong Kong." And Hoxworth Hale, whose daughter Noelani was still brooding about the house and trying to sneak in a divorce without publicity, clapped his Chinese friend on the shoulder and confided: "We all go through it, but by God I wish we didn't have to."

"You think I did right?" Hong Kong asked in a sudden longing to talk.

"I'd attend my daughter's wedding, no matter whom she married," Hoxworth said flatly.

"I'm glad I did," Hong Kong confessed. "But I can't bring myself to visit them."

"Wait till the first baby's born," Hoxworth wisely counseled. "It'll give you an excuse to retreat gracefully." And Hong Kong agreed, but he felt that he might not want to look at a grandchild that was only half Chinese.

TO THE SAKAGAWA FAMILY 1954 was a year that brought dislocation and frustration. It started in January when iron-willed Kamejiro, whose threats about leaving America no one had taken seriously, announced unexpectedly that he was sailing on Friday to spend the rest of his life in Hiroshima-ken. Consequently, on Friday he and his bent wife boarded a Japanese freighter and without even a round of farewell dinners departed for Japan. He told the boys, "The store will pay enough to feed me in Hiroshima. I worked hard in America, and Japan can be proud of the manner in which I conducted myself. I hope that when you're old you'll be able to say the same." Never a particularly sentimental man, he did not linger on deck gawking at the mountains he had pierced nor at the fields he had helped create. He led his wife below decks, where they had a sturdy meal of cold rice and fish, which they enjoyed.

It was usually overlooked in both Hawaii and the mainland that of the many Orientals brought to America, a substantial number preferred returning to their homelands, and in the years after World War II there was a heavy flow from America to Japan, of which the Sakagawas formed only an inconspicuous part. With their dollar savings such emigrants were able to buy, in the forgotten rural areas of Japan, fairly substantial positions in a poverty-stricken economy, and this Kamejiro intended doing. He would buy his Japanese relatives a little more land beside the Inland Sea and there it would wait, the family homestead in Hiroshima-ken, in case his boys Goro and Shigeo ever decided to return to their homeland.

The old folks' departure grieved Shigeo, because the more solidly American he became, with a seat in the senate and a canny man like Black Jim McLafferty as his partner, the more he appreciated the virtues old Kamejiro had inculcated in his sons; but Goro felt otherwise, for although he too treasured his father's moral teachings, he was glad to see his stern, unyielding mother go back to Japan, for he felt that this would give him a chance to keep his own wife, Akemi-san, in America. Accordingly, he and Shigeo gave Akemi a comfortable allowance, command of the Sakagawa house, and freedom from the old woman's tyranny. The brothers never laughed at Akemi's precise speech, and they showed her that they wanted her to stay.

But it was too late. One morning, as they were breakfasting, she said, "I am going back to Japan."

"Why?" Goro gasped.

"Where will you get the money?" Shigeo said.

"I've saved it. For a year I've bought nothing for myself and eaten mainly rice. I haven't cheated you," she insisted.

"No one's speaking of cheating, Akemi dear," Goro assured her. "But why are you leaving?"

"Because Hawaii is too dreadfully dull to live in," she replied.

"Akemi!" Goro pleaded.

She pushed back from the table and looked at the hard-working brothers. "In Hawaii I'm intellectually dead . . . decomposing."

"How can you say that?" Shig interrupted.

"Because it's true . . . and pitifully obvious to anyone from Japan."

"But don't you sense the excitement here?" Shig pleaded. "We Japanese are just breaking through to power."

"Do you know what real excitement is?" she asked sorrowfully. "The excitement of ideas? Quests? I'm afraid Hawaii will never begin to understand true intellectual excitement, and I refuse to waste my life here."

"But don't you find our arrival as a group of people exciting?" Shig pressed.

"Yes," she granted, "if you were going to arrive some place important it would be exciting. But do you know what your goal is? A big shiny black automobile. You'll never arrive at music or plays or reading books. You have a cheap scale of values, and I refuse to abide them any longer."

"Akemi!" Goro pleaded in real anguish. "Don't leave. Please."

"What will you do?" Shig asked.

"I'll get a job in a Nishi-Ginza bar where people talk about ideas," she said flatly, and that day she started to pack.

When it became obvious that she was determined to leave Hawaii, Goro disappeared from his labor office for several days, and Shigeo found him sitting dully at home, waiting for Akemi-san to return from the market, where she was informing her envious war-bride friends that she was sailing back to Japan. Goro's eyes were red, and his hands trembled. "Do you think that all we've been working at is useless, Shig?" he pleaded.

"Don't believe what this girl says," Shig replied, sitting with his brother.

"But I love her. I can't let her go!"

"Goro," Shigeo said quietly, "I love Akemi-san almost as much as you do, and if she walks out, I'm broken up, too. But I'm sure of one thing. You and I are working on something so big that she can't even dimly understand it. Give us another twenty years and we'll build here in Hawaii a wonderland."

Goro knew what his brother was speaking of, but he asked, "In the meantime, do you think we're as dull as she says?"

Shig thought several minutes, recalling Boston on a Friday night, and Harvard Law with its vital discussions, and Sundays at the great museums. "Hawaii's pretty bad," he confessed.

"Then you think Akemi-chan's justified?" Goro asked with a dull ache in his voice.

"She's not big enough to overlook the fact that we're essentially peasants," Shig replied.

"What do you mean?" Goro argued contentiously. "We got good educations."

"But fundamentally we're peasants," Shig reasoned. "Everybody who came to these islands came as illiterate peasants. The Chinese, the Portuguese, the Koreans, and now the Filipinos. We were all honest and hard-working, but, by God, we were a bunch of Hiroshima yokels."

Goro, lacerated by his wife's threatened desertion, would not accept this further castigation and cried, "Yokels or not, our people now get a decent wage in the sugar fields and our lawyers get elected to the legislature. I call that something."

"It's everything," Shig agreed, pressing his arm about his brother's shoulder. "The other things that Akemi-chan misses . . . they'll come later. It's our children who'll read books and listen to music. They won't be peasants."

Goro now changed from misery to belligerency and cried, "Hell, fifty years from now they'll put up statues to guys like you and me!" And he thought of many things he was going to tell his wife when she returned, but when he saw her come into the room, after carefully removing her geta at the door and walking pin-toed like a delicate Japanese gentlewoman, his courage collapsed and he pleaded, "Akemi-chan, please, please don't go."

She walked past him and into her room, where she completed her final packing and when she was ready to go to the boat she said softly, "I'm not running away from you, Goro-san. You were good to me and tender. But a girl has only one life and I will not spend mine in Hawaii."

"It'll grow better!" he assured her.

In precise Japanese the determined girl replied, "I would perish here." And that afternoon she sailed for Japan.

Mr. Ishii, of course, wrote a long letter in Japanese script to the Sakagawas in Hiroshima-ken, and when the local letter reader had advised Mrs. Sakagawa of its contents, Goro began getting a series of delighted letters from his mother, which Ishii-san read to the boys, for although they could speak Japanese they could not read it: "I am so glad to hear that the superior-thinking young lady from Tokyo has gone back home. It's best for all concerned, Goro, and I have been asking through the village about suitable girls, and I have found several who would be willing to come to America, but you must send me a later picture of yourself, because the one I have makes you look too young, and the better girls are afraid that you are not well established in business. I am sending you in this letter pictures of three very fine girls. Fumiko-san is very strong and comes from a family I have known all my life. Chieko-san is from a very dependable family and when made-up looks rather sweet. Yuri-san is too short, but she has a heart which I know is considerate, for her mother, whom I knew as a girl, tells me that Yuri is the best girl in the village where taking care of a home is concerned. Also, since Shigeo now has a good job and ought to be looking for a wife, I am sending him two pictures of the schoolteacher in the village. She is well educated and would make a fine wife for a lawyer, because even though she went away to college, she is originally from this village. After the grave mistake Goro made with the girl from Tokyo, I am sure it would be better if you boys both found your wives at home."

The brothers spread the five photographs on the table and studied them gloomily. "It's too bad we're not raising sugar cane," Goro growled. "That quartet could hoe all the fields between here and Waipahu."

The next mail brought three more applicants, stalwart little girls with broad bottoms, gold teeth and backs of steel. Mr. Ishii, after reading the letters to the brothers, got great pleasure from studying the photographs and making therefrom his own recommendations. "Of all the things I have done in my life," he explained, "I am happiest that I married a Hiroshima girl. If you boys were wise, you would do the same thing."

Then came the letter that contained two better-than-average pictures, and as they fluttered out, Mr. Ishii studied the portraits with care and said, "I think these may be the ones," but his spirits were soon dampened by a passage from Mrs. Sakagawa which he could not find the courage to finish reading to the boys. It began, "Last week donna-san and I went to see Hiroshima City, a place we had not visited before, and I am ashamed to have to say that what the Americans reported is true. The city was bombed. It was mostly destroyed and you can still see the big black scars. Ishii-san, who will be reading this letter to you, ought to know that the damage was very bad and from looking at this city I don't see how anyone could believe any longer that Japan won the . . ."

Mr. Ishii's voice trailed off. For a long time he sat looking at the fatal pages. Coming as they did, from his own mother-in-law, and a

Hiroshima woman too, he could not doubt their veracity; but accepting her statement meant that all his visions for the past thirteen years since Pearl Harbor were fallacious, his life a mockery. The boys were considerate enough not to mention the facts which their mother had hammered home, and when the time came for them to go to work, they said goodbye to the little old man, their brother-in-law, and left him staring at the letter.

At about eleven that morning a Japanese man came running into the law offices of McLafferty and Sakagawa, shouting in English, "Jesus Christ! He did it on the steps of the Japanese Consulate."

Shig experienced a sinking feeling in his throat and mumbled, "Ishii-san?" and the informant yelled, "Yes. Cut his belly right open."

"I'll go with you," McLafferty called, and the two partners roared up Nuuanu to where, from the days of the first Japanese in Hawaii, the little bow-legged laborers had taken their troubles. At the consulate a group of police waited for an ambulance, which in due time screamed up, and Shig said, "I'm a relative. I'll go with him." But the little old labor leader was dead. He had felt that if his fatherland had indeed lost the war, the only honorable thing he could do was to inform the emperor of his grief, so he had gone to the emperor's building, and with the emperor's flag in his left hand, had behaved as his institutions directed. With his death, the Ever-Victorious Group died also, and the sadness of national defeat was at last brought home even to the farthest remnants of the Japanese community.

After the funeral Shigeo faced his first difficult decision of the year, for Goro hurried home late one afternoon with this dismaying news: "The communist trials begin next month, and Rod Burke wants you to defend him."

Shig dropped his head. "I knew it would come . . . sooner or later," he said. "But why does he have to ask me just as I'm getting ready to run for a full term as senator?"

Goro replied, "That's when the case was called. Will you take the job?"

Shig had anticipated that the communists would seek him as their counsel, and he had tried to formulate a satisfactory reply to the invitation; but whereas it is easy to prefabricate an answer to an expected question like "Shall we go to Lahaina next week?" it is not so easy to anticipate the moral and emotional entanglements involved in a more complex question like, "Am I, as a lawyer, obligated to provide legal aid to a communist?"

"I wish you hadn't asked me," Shig stalled.

"I wish Rod hadn't asked me," Goro countered.

"Are you determined to help him?" Shig asked.

"Yes, I'd have accomplished nothing without him."

"But you're sure he's guilty?"

"I suppose so," Goro granted. "But even a communist is entitled to a fair trial . . . and a defending lawyer."

"Why me?"

"Because you're my brother."

"I can't answer this one so fast, Goro."

"Neither could I at first," Goro said. "Take your time."

So Shigeo spent long hours walking the streets of Kakaako, wondering what he ought to do. He reasoned: "In Hawaii I have one overriding responsibility—the land laws. To do anything about these, I've got to keep getting re-elected. If I defend Rod Burke, I'll surely lose all the haole votes I apparently picked up last time, and that would mean I'd be licked in November. So from that point of view I ought to say no.

"But Rod Burke isn't the only defendant. There's his Japanese wife and two other Japanese. And if I go into court and give those people a stirring defense, I'll bind the Japanese vote to me forever, simply because I have dared to defend the underdog. So although I might lose this election, I'd probably be in stronger position next time, and the time after that.

"But are my personal interests the ones that ought to determine this decision? A man charged with a crime has a right to a lawyer, and when the community is most strongly against him, his right is morally greatest. Somebody has got to defend Rod Burke, and I suppose it ought to be me.

"But I am not just the average, non-attached lawyer of the case books. I'm the first Japanese to get into the senate from the Nineteenth. I'm the one who has a chance of getting in again. If my brother Goro has come to represent labor, then I represent a cross-section of all the Japanese. That's a major responsibility which I ought not destroy carelessly.

"But there are others in our family than Goro and me. There are Tadao and Minoru, and they gave their lives defending an ideal America. They never found it for themselves . . . certainly not here in Hawaii. But in Italy and France, fighting to defend America, they did find it. So did Goro and I. And what we found is definitely threatened by a communist conspiracy. How then can I go into court and defend identified communists?"

And then came the question of the age. It struck Shigeo as he was walking past a sashimi parlor on Kakaako Street, as it was striking hundreds of similar Americans in garages or at the movies or in church: "But if I turn my back on a supposed communist, how do I know that I am not turning my back on the very concept of liberty that I am seeking to protect? Honest men can always get someone to defend them. But what does justice mean if apparently dishonest men can find no one?"

So through this precise waltz the mind of Shigeo Sakagawa swayed, day after day. Finally he took his confusion to Black Jim McLafferty, asking, "How are you going to feel, Jim, first, as head of the Democratic Party, and second, as head of McLafferty and Sakagawa, if your partner defends the communists?"

Now it was Black Jim's turn to follow the devious paths of logic, emotion, politics, patriotism and self-interest. His two most interesting comments were stolen right from his father's Boston experiences: "It never hurts a Democratic lawyer to defend the underdog," and "As long as my half of our partnership is known to be Catholic, you're fairly free to defend whom you want to." Then, drawing from his Hawaiian experience, he added, "It would be a damned shame for the first Japanese elected from the Nineteenth to be thrown out of office on an irrelevancy." But prudently he refused to give a concrete recommendation.

With McLafferty's concepts adding to his confusion, Shigeo walked more miles, and the consideration which finally made up his mind for him was one that seemed at first wholly irrelevant. He recalled Akemi-san, his former sister-in-law, saying, on the day she left Hawaii, "In the entire Japanese community of Hawaii I have never encountered one idea." And Shig thought: "I have an idea. I have a concept that will move the entire community ahead," and he decided not to imperil his land-reform movement, so he refused his brother's request. "I won't defend the communists," he said, "and may God forgive me if it is cowardice."

"At least I do," Goro said.

This long travail explained why, when the electioneering season finally opened, Senator Shigeo Sakagawa spoke with unusual force and seriousness on the problem of land reform. He drew up charts showing how The Fort, and its members through their directorships on the great trusts, controlled the land of Hawaii. He pointed out how they released this land in niggardly amounts, not for social purposes, but to keep up values, "the way the diamond merchants of South Africa release an agreed-upon number of diamonds each year, to keep up prices. It's legitimate to do that with diamonds, which a man can buy or not, as he pleases, but is it right to do it with land, upon which we all exist or perish?"

His most damning chart was one which showed that certain families contrived to have their land, which they held back for speculation, assessed by a compliant government at two per cent of its real value, whereas three hundred typical shopkeepers with small holdings from which they lived had theirs assessed at fifty-one per cent of its real value. "You and I," Shig cried to his audiences, "are subsidizing the big estates. We allow them to pay no taxes. We encourage them to hold their land off the market. We permit them a tax refuge under which they can speculate. I am not angry at these families. I wish I were as smart as they appear to be. Because you and I know that when they sold their last piece of land to Gregory's for the big new store, they sold it for $3,000,000. What value had they been paying taxes on? $71,000. Because you and I have been careless, we have allowed the Hewletts to keep valuable land off the market and pay taxes on it at one-fortieth of its real value."

In public parks, on the radio and on television Shigeo Sakagawa hammered home his dominant theme, and when citizens asked him if he was a radical, advocating the breaking up of landed estates the way they did in Russia, he kept his temper and replied, "No, I am a conservative English parliamentarian, trying to do in Hawaii what men like me accomplished in England one hundred years ago. Remember this. I am the conservative. It is the people who think that this problem can be endlessly postponed who are the radicals. Because their course leads to tragedy, mine to democracy."

But at every rally somebody sooner or later heckled: "Aren't you a communist, too, like your brother Goro?"

Shigeo had worked out a good answer to this question. He dropped his arms, looked off into space, and said quietly, "In any American election that's a fair question, and the voters have a right to an honest answer. I wonder in what form I can best give you my answer?" He seemed to be thinking, and after a moment, in a very relaxed voice he started speaking.

"Is the man who asked that question old enough to remember the McKinley-Punahou game of 1938? It was in the last fifteen seconds of the game, if you'll remember, and Punahou was trailing by four points, 18–14. Then, from a rather rough scrimmage, Punahou's star back broke loose, and I can see him now dashing down the sideline . . . ten yards, twenty, forty. He was going to score a magnificent touchdown and win the game, and I can remember even to this day how thrilled I was to see that run, because that runner was my brother Tadao Sakagawa, the first ordinary Japanese ever to get into Punahou and one of the greatest stars they ever had.

"But can you recall what happened next? From the McKinley players a tackle got up from one knee and started out like a fire engine after my brother, and although Tad could run fast, this McKinley man ran like the wind, and on the five-yard line, that close mind you, this McKinley man brought my brother down and saved the game. You all know who he was. He was my other brother, Goro, the one who had wanted to get into Jefferson and couldn't.

"Now the point of my story is this. Goro could have held back and let his brother Tad score the winning touchdown and be the biggest hero of the year, but he never wavered in his duty. He tackled his own brother on the five-yard line and saved the day. That's the way we Sakagawas were brought up by our parents. Duty, duty, duty.

"But the more important point of my story is this. Do you know where the great halfback Tadao Sakagawa is now? Buried beneath a military cross in the Punchbowl. He gave his life for America. And where is his brother, Minoru Sakagawa? Buried beneath a military cross in the Punchbowl. He also gave his life for his country. That is also the kind of boys we Sakagawas are. Tough, resolute, uncompromising fighters.

"I will tell you this. If my brother Goro Sakagawa was, as you charge, a communist, I would personally hound him out of the islands. I would never cease fighting him. I would tackle him down the way he tackled down Tadao, for I will make no compromise with communism."

Then his voice would take on a harder tone as he continued: "But Goro Sakagawa is not a communist. He is a very fine labor leader, and the good he has done for the working people of Hawaii is beyond calculation. I am for such labor leaders, and I want that fact to be widely known. Goro and I are two edges of the same sword, he in labor, I in politics. We are cutting away old and unfair practices. We are slashing at the relics of feudalism."

In conclusion his voice changed to one of exhortation: "And neither Goro nor I will stop, because we can remember the day our father took us to the old plantation camp on Kauai and showed us the barracks where the lunas used to tramp through with whips and lash the field hands, and we swore that that would stop. Now, sir, you who asked the question about communism, I want to ask you two questions in return: where were you when my brothers Minoru and Tadao were giving their lives for American democracy? What have you done comparable to what Goro and I have done to clean up the democracy they saved? Won't you please come up to see me after the rally, and if you have done half as much as we have done, I want to embrace you as a damned good American, because, brother, you are certainly not a communist, nor am I."

The audience always applauded madly at this point, and when Black Jim McLafferty first heard the reply he cried, "My God, we've got to plant somebody in the audience to ask that question every night. I never heard a better answer. Demagoguery at its best, and of course you know what they call demagoguery at its best? Oratory." But Shig refused to have anybody planted, because he was afraid that that might cut the edge of his conviction, because his answer had this merit: on more than half the occasions at which he used it, the questioner did come up afterwards to talk about old army days or the unhappy plantation experiences of his family, so that Shig's reply actually converted hecklers into supporters, which, as McLafferty pointed out, "is about the best you can expect of any answer."

But one thing that McLafferty said rankled in Shig's memory: the word *demagoguery*. "Am I guilty of that?" he asked himself, and as he analyzed each portion of his well-known reply, he could explain everything until he got to the part about the lunas, and then he always stumbled. "What actually happened?" he asked himself. "One day, one luna hit my father one time. The first time Pop told about it, he told the truth. 'Here is where the luna hit me that day.' Then our family constructed the legend: 'Here is where the lunas used to beat us.' And finally it comes out: 'Here is where the lunas used to beat all the Japanese.' " And he saw clearly that this conversion of the truth was indeed demagoguery of the worst sort, because it kept alive community hatreds, which, even if they had been legitimately founded were better dead in the graves of memory; but the speech did get votes, and one night after a particularly heated rally he put the problem frankly to Black Jim. "That part about the lunas beating the Japanese? Do you think I ought to keep saying that?"

Black Jim was tooling his old Pontiac down Kapiolani Boulevard and for some time said nothing. Then grudgingly he admitted, "It gets votes."

"What I asked was, 'What do you think of it?' " Shig pressed.

"Well, when I hear it coming, I usually go out in the alley," Black Jim confessed. "Just in case I have to vomit." So Shig dropped that part of his demagoguery, but he noticed that when Goro unveiled the murals at his new labor headquarters, there was the plantation camp with lunas slashing their way through the laborers with bull whips, and Shigeo thought: "This is the greatest evil that grows out of a wrong act. Somebody always remembers it . . . in an evil way."

When the campaign reached its height, complicated by the trial of the communists, Shigeo received in his office a visitor he had never heard of and whose existence surprised him. It was a young haole woman, twenty-six years old and marked by a pallid beauty. She said nervously, "My name is Noelani Hale Janders. I'm divorced but I haven't taken back my maiden name. I like what you've been saying on the radio, and I wish to work in your campaign."

"What was the name again?" Shig asked.

"Noelani Hale is my real name," she explained.

"What Hale is that?" Shig asked.

"Hoxworth Hale is my father."

"Sit down," Shig said weakly. When he had caught control of himself he pointed out, "Are you sure you've heard what I've been saying, Mrs. Hale?"

"It's Mrs. Janders," Noelani said. "Didn't you read about my divorce? It was rather messy?"

"I didn't," Shig apologized.

"I understand very well what you're saying, Senator Sakagawa, and your views coincide with my own."

"But have you heard what I said about land reform?" he pressed.

"That's what we're talking about," Noelani said in her precise Bostonian accent.

"You would hurt your father very much if you were active in my campaign," Shigeo warned. "As a matter of fact, you would probably hurt me, too."

"I studied politics at Wellesley," she replied firmly.

"Were you at Wellesley?" he asked.

"While you were at Harvard," she said. "Amy Fukugawa pointed you out one day, at the symphony."

"What's Amy doing?" he asked.

"She married a Chinese boy. Both their parents disowned them, so they're very happy in New York. He's a lawyer."

"Do you understand what I'm saying about land reform, Mrs. Janders? How what I say will affect your father, and his friends?"

"I want to know just one thing," Noelani said. "When you speak of breaking up the big estates . . ."

"I'm not sure I've ever used that phraseology," he corrected. "I say that the big estates must not be allowed to hold out of productive use the land they are not using for constructive agriculture."

Noelani sighed with relief and said, "But under your system would you permit lands that are being used legitimately for sugar and pineapple some kind of preferential treatment?"

"Look, Mrs. Janders," Shig cried. "Apparently I haven't made myself clear on this point."

"You haven't," she said, "and that's why I wanted to help, because I knew you were too smart not to have thought about the fundamental problem of land in Hawaii."

"What problem do you mean?" the expert asked.

She picked up two books and placed them on the desk. "Let's call this book Hawaii," she said, "and this one California. Now our problem is to get all the things we need, like food and building materials and luxuries, from California out here to Hawaii, and also to pay for them after we get them here. Let's call this inkwell our ship. We can fill it up in California every day of the year and haul to Hawaii the things we need. But how are we going to pay for them? And what is the ship going to carry back from Hawaii to California, so that it won't have to go back empty, which would double the freight costs on everything?"

She paused, and Shigeo plopped the inkwell down on the Hawaii book, saying, "I know very well that the ship has got to take back some bulk crop like sugar or pineapple. The sale of agricultural products provides the money on which we live. And the freight that sugar and pineapple pay going to the mainland helps pay the freight of food and lumber coming this way. I know that."

"You certainly haven't explained it to the people," Noelani said critically. "Because the important point is this. You fighting young Japanese have got to reassure Hawaii that legitimate farm lands will be protected for the welfare of everybody. As to the lands that have been hiding along the edges of the legitimate farms, held there for tax-free speculation, I think even my father knows they must be sold off to the people."

"You spoke of helping," Shig said. "What did you have in mind?"

"I'd like to help you put into words, for the radio and television, just what we've been talking about. It will insure your election."

"But why should Hoxworth Hale's daughter want to help a Japanese get elected?" Shig asked suspiciously.

"Because I love these islands, Senator. My people were here long before yours arrived, so I am naturally concerned about what happens to Hawaii."

"You ought to be a Republican," Shig said.

"For the time being, they're worn out," Noelani replied. "I've been living a long time with worn-out people, so I'm ready to accept new ideas."

Shig felt certain that when Hoxworth Hale saw his daughter's car with its bright-red bumper-banner, "Please Re-elect Senator Shigeo Sakagawa" the commander of The Fort would explode, but instead a most unexpected event transpired, for one afternoon Hong Kong Kee strolled into the McLafferty and Sakagawa offices and sat down with Shig. "I am in lots of trouble if my Republican friends see me down here," the Chinese said.

"What's up?" Shig inquired.

"I have a big surprise for you, Shigeo," Hong Kong confided.

"Trouble?" Shig asked, for in an election period every visitor brings anxiety.

"In a way," Hong Kong confessed. "Hoxworth Hale and his boys commissioned me to ask you how about coming on the board of Whipple Oil Imports, Incorporated. They figure a smart young Japanese on the board will help them sell more to Japanese customers."

Shig was quite unprepared for such a suggestion and studied Hong Kong carefully. He liked the shrewd Chinese, and appreciated what he had done for the Sakagawas, never mind the motives. But he was appalled that Hong Kong had consented to be used so crudely by The Fort in an attempt at political blackmail, and it was with difficulty that he restrained himself when he replied, coldly, "The Fort cannot buy me off on this land-reform business, and you can tell them so."

Hong Kong instantly realized the unfavorable position he appeared to be in, but instead of showing his embarrassment he said quietly, "Nobody at The Fort wants you, Shigeo, if your price is no higher than that. They know you're going to fight this land deal through to a conclusion. But what you don't know is, they're not too worried. They know it's inevitable."

"So they offer me a trivial directorship at such a time! It's contemptible."

"No, Shigeo, it's sensible. Two years ago they asked me to nominate some promising young Japanese. I said Shigeo. Last year they asked again. I said Shigeo. This is not a hasty idea. The Fort has had you in mind for a long time."

"I'd be false to my people if I joined up with their principal enemy," Shig said stubbornly.

"Maybe when you get elected one more time, Shigeo, you will stop talking about 'my people.' All the people in Hawaii are your people, and you better start thinking that way."

"If I took a job from The Fort, every Japanese in Hawaii would say I had turned traitor," Shig replied truthfully.

"I'll tell you this, Shigeo," the quick-minded Chinese corrected. "Until the time comes when you accept a job with The Fort, on your own terms, you are a traitor to your people. The whole purpose of you young Japanese getting elected to office, and you know how strong I work for you, is to bring you into the full society of Hawaii. You've got to get on the boards. You've got to get appointed trustees for the big estates."

"Trustees?" Shig laughed. "After what I've been shouting about the estates?"

"Exactly," Hong Kong replied. "Because if you show yourself interested, before the year ends you'll be suggested as a trustee."

"By whom?" the young senator asked contemptuously.

"By Hoxworth Hale and me," Hong Kong snapped. And as the young Japanese fell silent, the Chinese banker explained his view of Hawaii. He said: "The haoles are smarter than I used to think, Shigeo. First they worked the Hawaiians, and threw them out. Then they brought in my grandmother, and threw her out. Then they got your father, and dropped him when the Filipinos looked better. They always pick the winner, these haoles, and I respect them for it.

"So I work hard and show them I can run real estate better than they can, and they make me a partner. Other educated Chinese are breaking in, too. If you smart young Japanese don't pretty soon start joining up in the real running of Hawaii, it only means you aren't clever enough for anybody to want you. Getting elected is the easy part, Shigeo, because you can rely upon stupid people to do that for you, but getting onto the boards, and running the schools, and directing the trusts is the real test. Because there you have to be selected by the smartest people in Hawaii. Shigeo, I want you to join this board."

The young Japanese thought for a long time. If he were to join, he would be a spiritual traitor to his family and to his class. He could no longer say to his Japanese friends, "It was in the fields on Kauai that the lunas used to horsewhip our fathers. Well, those days are past." He would lose the sweet solidarity that he felt when he and Goro and the other young Japanese swore: "We are as good as the haoles." He would lose so much that had kept him fighting.

He temporized: "Hong Kong, you must know that no matter what The Fort offers me, I'm still going to fight for this land reform."

"Damn it!" Hong Kong cried. "It's because you're going to fight for it that they want you. They know you're right, Shigeo."

"All right!" the young senator snapped. "Tell them that after the election I'll join."

"After the election it will have no moral force," Hong Kong pleaded.

"After the election," Shigeo repeated, and he applied himself with greater dedication to the campaign that was to alter life in Hawaii, for he and Black Jim McLafferty had whipped together a sterling slate of young Japanese veterans. All the boys were mainland-educated. Some appeared on the hustings lacking arms that had been lost in Italy or legs shot off in France, and if they had so desired, they could have appeared with their chests covered with medals. In contrast to former elections, the serious young men spoke on issues, and pressed home Senator Shigeo Sakagawa's figures on land reform. There was great excitement in the air, as if this October were an intellectual April with ideas germinating.

One night Noelani Janders said, as she drove Shigeo home from four outdoor rallies, "For a moment tonight, Shig, I had the fleeting sensation that we were going to win control of both the house and the senate. There's a real chance that a hell of a lot of you Japanese are going to be elected. It's terribly exciting."

Then the campaign, at least so far as Shigeo Sakagawa was concerned, fell completely apart, because one day without any previous announcement, old Kamejiro and his stooped wife climbed down off a Japanese freighter, took a bus out to Kakaako, and announced: "We have decided to live in America."

Goro and Shig embraced them as warmly as their stubborn, rocklike father would allow and tried to uncover the reasons for this sudden change of plans. All they could get from Kamejiro was this: "I'm too old to learn to use those goddamned Japanese toilets. I can't stay bent down that long." He would say no more.

Mrs. Sakagawa allowed several hints to fall. Once she observed: "The old man said he had grown so soft in America that he was no longer fit to be a real Japanese." At another time she said sorrowfully, "If you have been away from a farm for fifty-two years, when you go back the fields look smaller." As for herself, she said simply, "The Inland Sea is so terribly cold in winter."

Once, in late October when Shigeo was particularly nervous over the election, he snapped at his father: "I've seen a hundred of you people leave Hawaii, saying, 'I'm going back to the greatest land on earth!' But when you get there, you don't like it so much, do you?"

To his surprise old Kamejiro strode up to him, drew back and belted him severely across the face. "You're a Japanese!" he said fiercely. "Be proud of it!"

Mrs. Sakagawa had come home with several new photographs of Hiroshima-ken girls, and she arranged them on the kitchen table, admiringly, but when her boys showed no interest she sadly put them away. One night when she could not sleep she saw her youngest son come driving home with a haole girl, and it looked to her as if he had kissed the girl, and she called her husband and they confronted Shigeo, fearfully, and said, "Did you come home with a haole girl?"

"Yes," the young senator replied.

"Oh, no!" his mother groaned. "Kamejiro, speak to him."

The embittered session lasted for some hours, with old Kamejiro shouting, "If you get mixed up with a haole woman, all Japan will be ashamed!"

Mrs. Sakagawa held that it was the gods themselves who had inspired her return to America in time to save her son from such an irrevocable disgrace. She wept, "With all the fine girls I told you about from Hiroshima, why do you ride home with a haole?"

Strong threats were made, in the course of which Shigeo's mother cried, "It's almost as bad as if you married a Korean," at which Goro, who was now awake, pointed out, "Who said anything about getting married?" and Mrs. Sakagawa replied, "It's the same everywhere. Haole girls, Korean girls, Okinawa girls, Eta girls, all trying to trap decent Japanese boys."

This was too much for Goro, who suggested, "Mom, go to bed," but when she saw in Goro visible proof of the wreck her older son had made of his life she wept again and mourned, "You wouldn't listen to me. You went ahead and married a Tokyo girl, and see what happened. Let me warn you, Shigeo, haole girls are even worse than Tokyo girls. Much worse."

Goro pleaded ineffectively, "Shig, tell her that you're not marrying the girl."

"I saw him kissing her!" his mother cried.

"Mom," Goro cried. "I kissed a Filipino girl the other night. But I'm not marrying her."

Mrs. Sakagawa stopped her ranting. Dropping her arms she stared at her son and repeated dully, "A Filipino girl?" The idea was so completely repugnant that she could find no words with which to castigate it, so she turned abruptly on her heel and went to bed. Chinese girls, Okinawans, even Koreans you could fight. But a Filipino!

When the old people were gone, Goro asked quietly, "There's nothing between you and the haole, is there?"

"I don't think so," Shig replied.

"Look, blalah," Goro said, reverting to an old and dear phrase of their pidgin childhood, "she's a Hale, a Janders, a haole, a divorcee, all in one. Don't try it. You're strong, but you're not that strong."

Election Day, 1954, was one that will never be forgotten in Hawaii. Hula teams surrounded voting places. Candidates wearing mountainous flowered leis passed out sandwiches to haole voters and sushi to Japanese. Bands blared all day long, and trucks with long streamers ploughed through the streets. It was a noisy, gala, wonderful day, and that night when the votes were tallied, Hawaii realized with astonished pain that for the first time since the islands had joined America, Democrats were going to control both houses. The days were forever past when Republicans dominated by The Fort could rule the islands with impunity.

Then, toward midnight, when each specific contest approached final settlement, a second discovery was made, even more sobering than the first. Of the Democratic victors, the majority were going to be young Japanese. In the senate, out of fifteen seats, Japanese won seven. In the house, out of thirty seats, Japanese won fourteen. On the board that ran Honolulu, out of seven vacancies, Japanese won four, and at midnight Hewie Janders, sitting glumly with John Whipple Hoxworth and the Hewlett boys, faced the unpalatable facts: "Gentlemen, we are now to be governed from Tokyo. And may God help us."

Black Jim McLafferty's team of brilliant young Japanese war veterans had swept into commanding power. Their average age was thirty-one. The average number of major wounds they had received in battle was two. Their average number of medals was four. They were honor graduates, of great mainland universities like Harvard, Columbia, Michigan and Stanford, and together they would compose the best-educated, most-decorated group of legislators elected that day in any of the forty-eight American states; there would be no finer legislature than that put together by the serious young Japanese lawyers of Hawaii.

Some pages back in this memoir I predicted that when, in 1916, the drunken luna Von Schlemm unfairly thrashed the sick Japanese field hand Kamejiro Sakagawa, the act was bound to have historic consequences which would not appear obvious for nearly forty years. Now, on Election Day of 1954, this old and almost forgotten event came home to roost. The Japanese, convinced that their laboring parents had been abused by the lunas, voted against the Republicans who had supervised that abuse. Von Schlemm's single blow had been transmuted by oratory into daily thrashings. In the early part of the campaign Senator Sakagawa, who should have known better, used this incident to lure the Japanese vote, but later he had the decency to drop such inflammatory rabble-rousing. In the labor troubles that haunted our islands, Goro Sakagawa originally used this same incident to inflame his workers, but later he also reconsidered and abandoned his irresponsible harangues. Nevertheless, for a few months in 1954 it looked as if a deep schism had been driven down the middle of our community, pitting Japanese against haole, but the Sakagawa boys had the courage to back away from that tempting, perilous course. They reconciled haole and Japanese, and it is to their credit that they did so. If there was one man in the history of Hawaii that I should have liked to strangle, it was that accidental, unthinking luna Von Schlemm. By the grace of God, our islands finally exorcised the evil that he so unwittingly initiated.

When the election returns were all in, toward two in the morning, and the Democratic victors were flushed with congratulations, Black Jim McLafferty leaned back in his chair at headquarters and warned Senator Sakagawa: "This victory is going to delay statehood. Last year our enemies rejected us on the grounds that Hawaii wasn't ready because the Japanese weren't Americanized. When they hear these returns, they'll reject us again because you Orientals are too damned well Americanized. But whether we ever become a state or not, we're going to build a great Hawaii."

His reflections were interrupted by the entrance into headquarters of a man whom no one expected to see there, for stern, black-coated Hoxworth Hale appeared bearing a maile lei whose fragrance was apparent even above the tobacco smoke and the shouting. The commander of The Fort looked gloomily about the unfamiliar terrain, then saw Shigeo Sakagawa among a group of cheering friends and noticed the bright-red lipstick on his yellow cheek, as if strangers had been kissing him. Moving toward the most important victor in the senatorial contests, Hoxworth extended his hand and said, "Congratulations." Then he placed the maile chain about the young Japanese boy's shoulders and said, "You'll forgive me if I don't kiss you."

"I'll do that for you, Dad," Noelani said, adding her lipstick to the collection.

Hoxworth studied the victorious senator for a moment and asked wryly, "How is it none of you smart young fellows are Republicans?"

"You never invited us," Shig replied with a nervous laugh.

In distinct tones that many could overhear, Hoxworth said, "Well, I want it on record this time, Senator Sakagawa. I'm inviting you to join the board of Whipple Oil. I would be proud to work with a man like you."

The crowd gasped, and Shigeo replied, "On the morning after I introduce my land-reform bill, I'll join you. That is, supposing you still want me."

"You'd be foolish to accept before," Hoxworth said, and with this the proud, lonely man, descendant of the missionaries and owner of the islands, excused himself from a celebration where he was not wholly at ease. When he was gone, Shig's friends cried, "My God! He asked a Japanese to join his board," but Noelani said, "That's not important. Look! He gave Shig a maile lei. Coming from my father that's better than a crown."

I can speak with a certain authority about these matters, because I participated in them. I knew these Golden Men: the lyric beachboy Kelly Kanakoa; the crafty Chinese banker Hong Kong Kee; and the dedicated Japanese politician Shigeo Sakagawa. I was there when they became vital parts of the new Hawaii.

It was I who engineered the coalition that defeated Senator Sakagawa's radical land reform. It was I who warned Noelani Janders against the needless folly of falling in love with a Japanese boy, and I told Shigeo Sakagawa frankly that he would damage his career if he allowed it; for in an age of Golden Men it is not required that their bloodstreams mingle, but only that their ideas clash on equal footing and remain free to cross-fertilize and bear new fruit.

So at the age of fifty-six I, Hoxworth Hale, have discovered that I, too, am one of those Golden Men who see both the West and the East, who cherish the glowing past and who apprehend the obscure future; and the things I have written of in this memoir are very close to my heart.

GENEALOGICAL CHARTS

Principal

(whose names appear in bold type on the following charts)

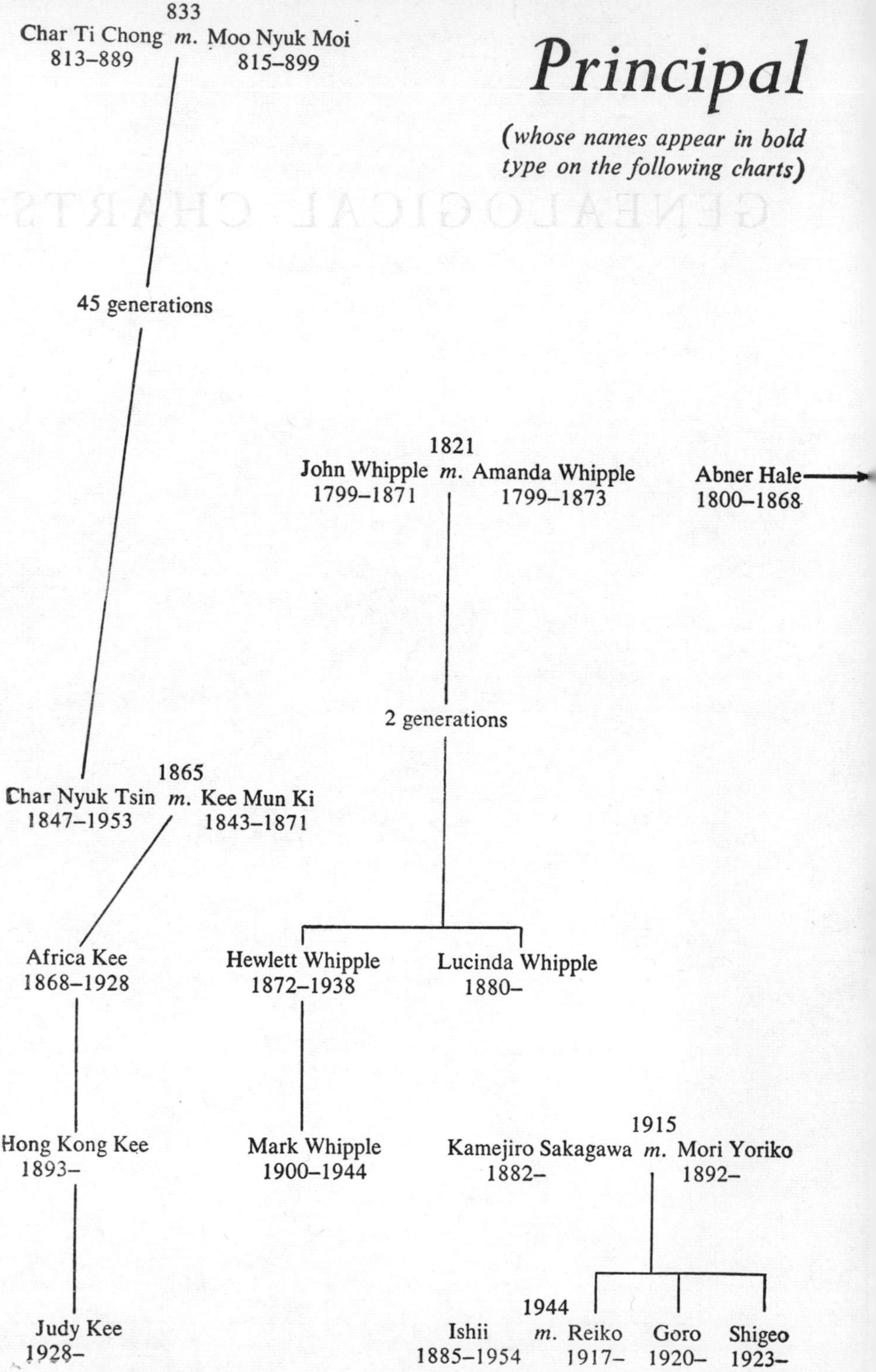

Characters

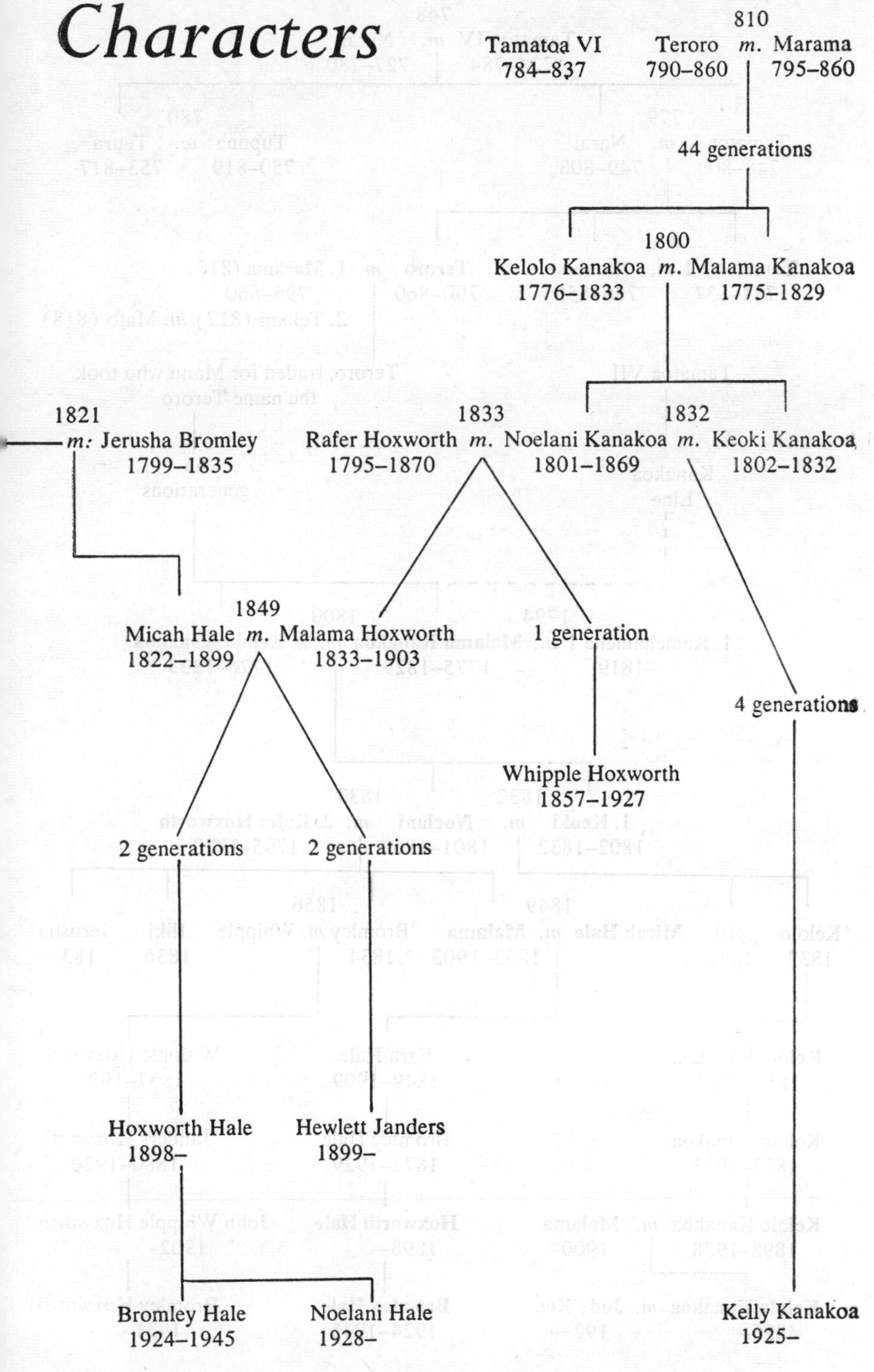
Tamatoa VI
784–837
810
Teroro m. Marama
790–860 795–860
44 generations
1800
Kelolo Kanakoa m. Malama Kanakoa
1776–1833 1775–1829
1821
m. Jerusha Bromley
1799–1835
1833
Rafer Hoxworth m. Noelani Kanakoa
1795–1870 1801–1869
1832
m. Keoki Kanakoa
1802–1832
1849
Micah Hale m. Malama Hoxworth
1822–1899 1833–1903
1 generation
4 generations
Whipple Hoxworth
1857–1927
2 generations
2 generations
Hoxworth Hale
1898–
Hewlett Janders
1899–
Bromley Hale
1924–1945
Noelani Hale
1928–
Kelly Kanakoa
1925–

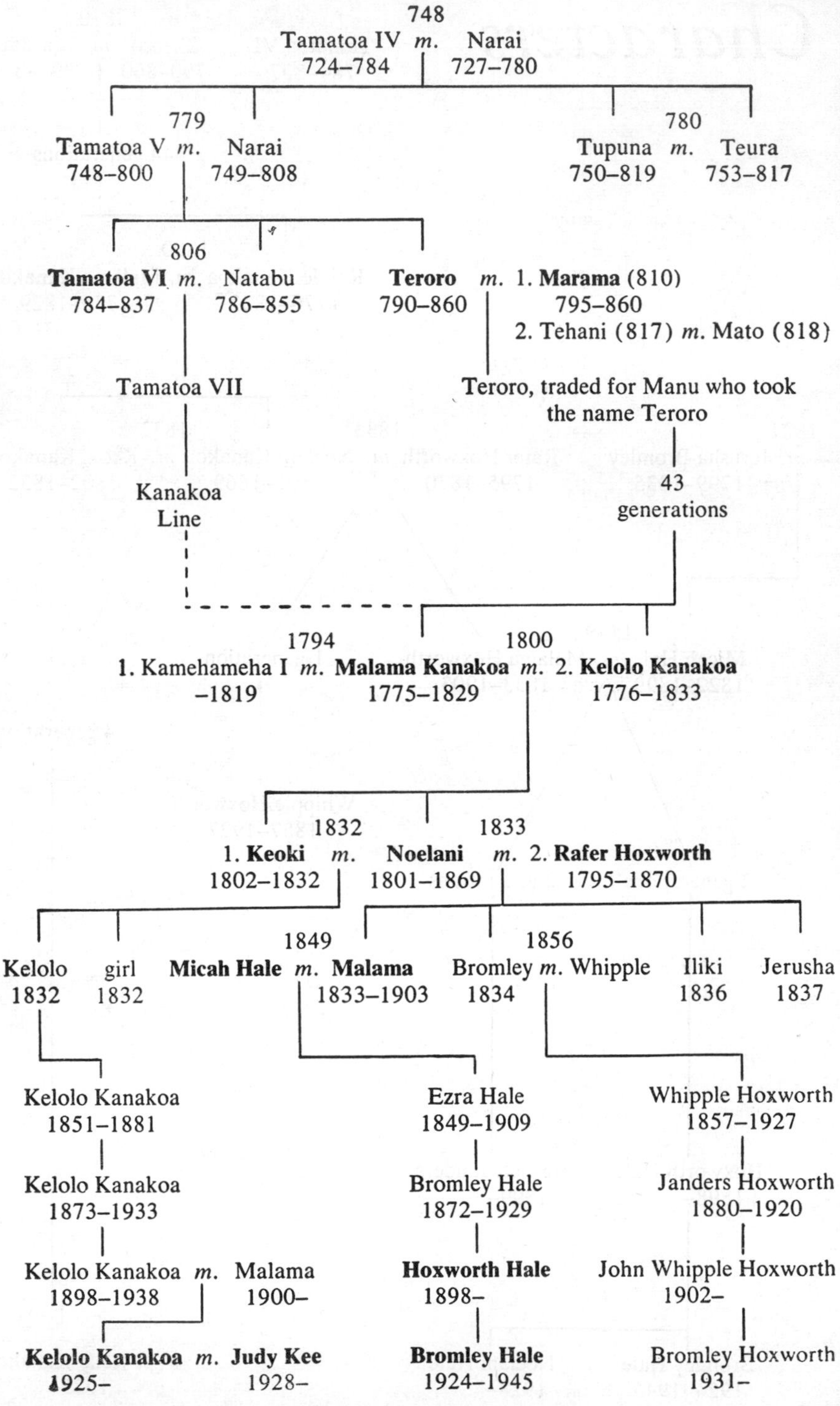

748
Tamatoa IV m. Narai
724–784 727–780
779
Tamatoa V m. Narai
748–800 749–808
780
Tupuna m. Teura
750–819 753–817
806
Tamatoa VI m. Natabu
784–837 786–855
Teroro m. 1. Marama (810)
790–860 795–860
2. Tehani (817) m. Mato (818)
Tamatoa VII
Teroro, traded for Manu who took the name Teroro
Kanakoa Line
43 generations
1794
1. Kamehameha I m. Malama Kanakoa m. 2. Kelolo Kanakoa
–1819 1775–1829 1776–1833
1800
1832
1. Keoki m. Noelani m. 2. Rafer Hoxworth
1802–1832 1801–1869 1795–1870
1833
Kelolo 1832
girl 1832
1849
Micah Hale m. Malama
1833–1903
1856
Bromley m. Whipple
1834
Iliki 1836
Jerusha 1837
Kelolo Kanakoa 1851–1881
Kelolo Kanakoa 1873–1933
Kelolo Kanakoa m. Malama
1898–1938 1900–
Kelolo Kanakoa m. Judy Kee
1925– 1928–
Ezra Hale 1849–1909
Bromley Hale 1872–1929
Hoxworth Hale 1898–
Bromley Hale 1924–1945
Whipple Hoxworth 1857–1927
Janders Hoxworth 1880–1920
John Whipple Hoxworth 1902–
Bromley Hoxworth 1931–

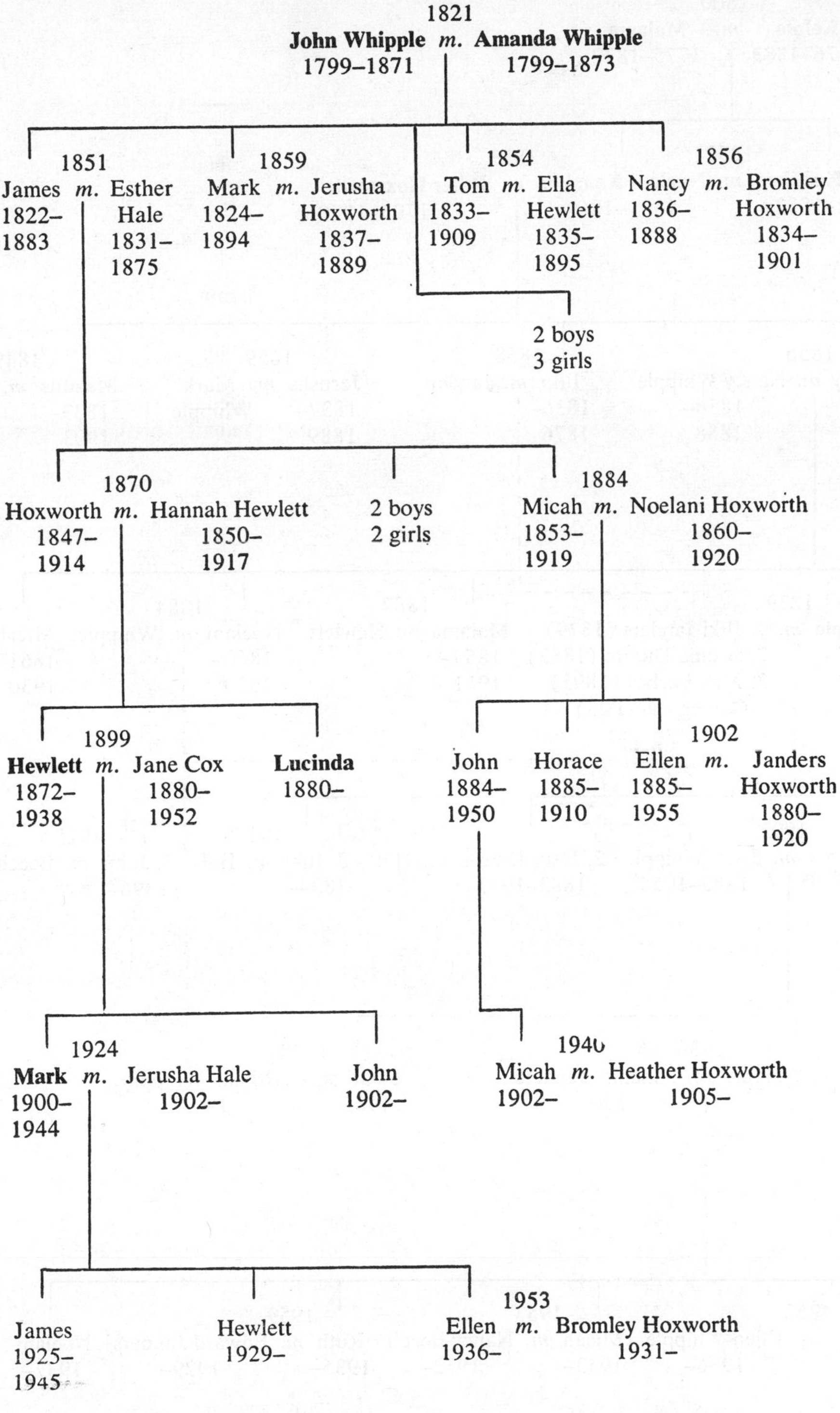
1821
John Whipple m. Amanda Whipple
1799–1871
1799–1873
1851
James m. Esther Hale
1822–1883
1831–1875
1859
Mark m. Jerusha Hoxworth
1824–1894
1837–1889
1854
Tom m. Ella Hewlett
1833–1909
1835–1895
1856
Nancy m. Bromley Hoxworth
1836–1888
1834–1901
2 boys
3 girls
1870
Hoxworth m. Hannah Hewlett
1847–1914
1850–1917
2 boys
2 girls
1884
Micah m. Noelani Hoxworth
1853–1919
1860–1920
1899
Hewlett m. Jane Cox
1872–1938
1880–1952
Lucinda
1880–
John
1884–1950
Horace
1885–1910
1902
Ellen m. Janders Hoxworth
1885–1955
1880–1920
1924
Mark m. Jerusha Hale
1900–1944
1902–
John
1902–
1940
Micah m. Heather Hoxworth
1902–
1905–
James
1925–1945
Hewlett
1929–
1953
Ellen m. Bromley Hoxworth
1936–
1931–

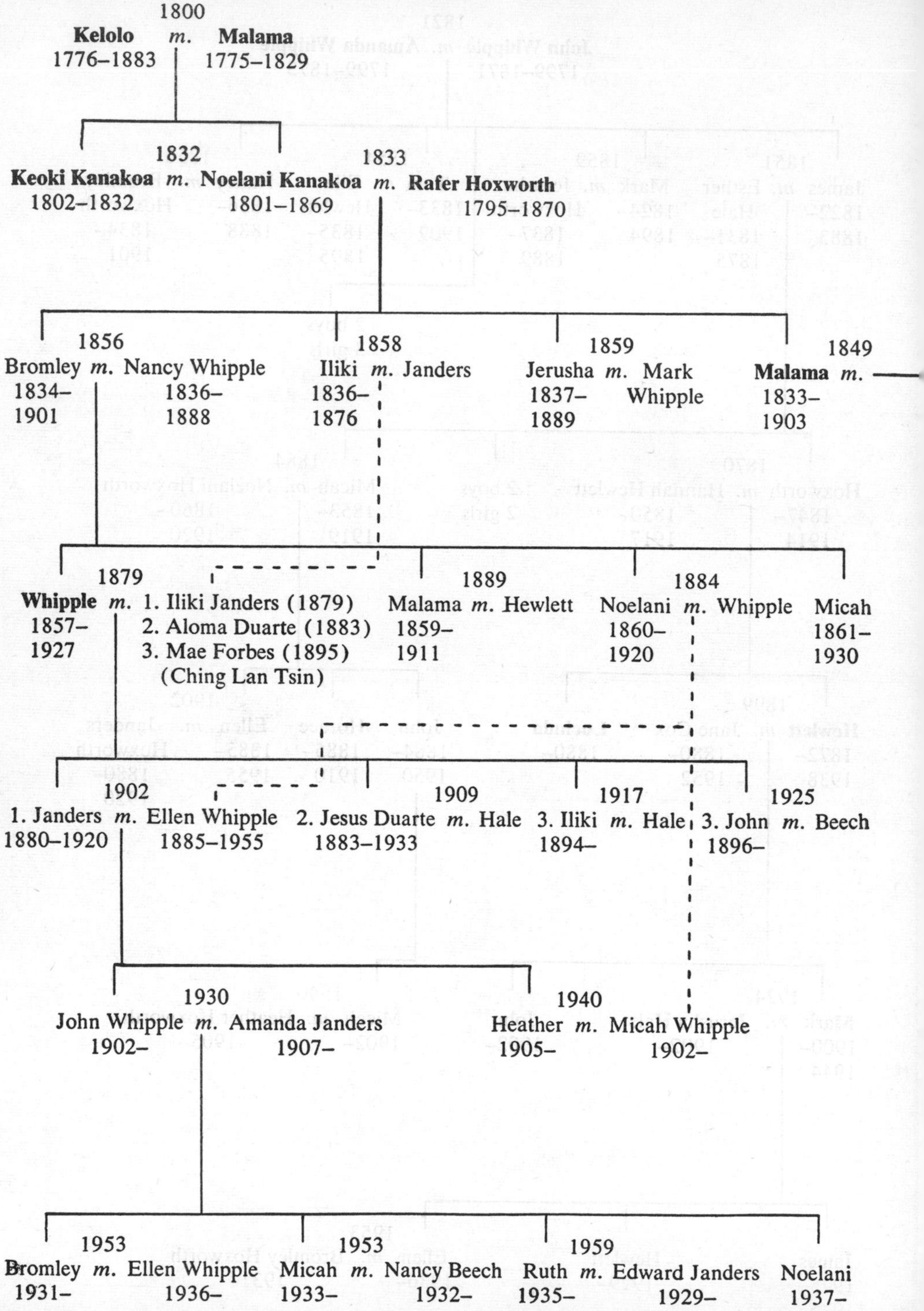

1800
Kelolo m. Malama
1776–1883
1775–1829
1832
Keoki Kanakoa m. Noelani Kanakoa
1802–1832
1801–1869
1833
m. Rafer Hoxworth
1795–1870
1856
Bromley m. Nancy Whipple
1834–1901
1836–1888
1858
Iliki m. Janders
1836–1876
1859
Jerusha m. Mark Whipple
1837–1889
1849
Malama m.
1833–1903
1879
Whipple m. 1. Iliki Janders (1879)
2. Aloma Duarte (1883)
3. Mae Forbes (1895)
(Ching Lan Tsin)
1857–1927
1889
Malama m. Hewlett
1859–1911
1884
Noelani m. Whipple
1860–1920
Micah
1861–1930
1902
1. Janders m. Ellen Whipple
1880–1920
1885–1955
1909
2. Jesus Duarte m. Hale
1883–1933
1917
3. Iliki m. Hale
1894–
1925
3. John m. Beech
1896–
1930
John Whipple m. Amanda Janders
1902–
1907–
1940
Heather m. Micah Whipple
1905–
1902–
1953
Bromley m. Ellen Whipple
1931–
1936–
1953
Micah m. Nancy Beech
1933–
1932–
1959
Ruth m. Edward Janders
1935–
1929–
Noelani
1937–

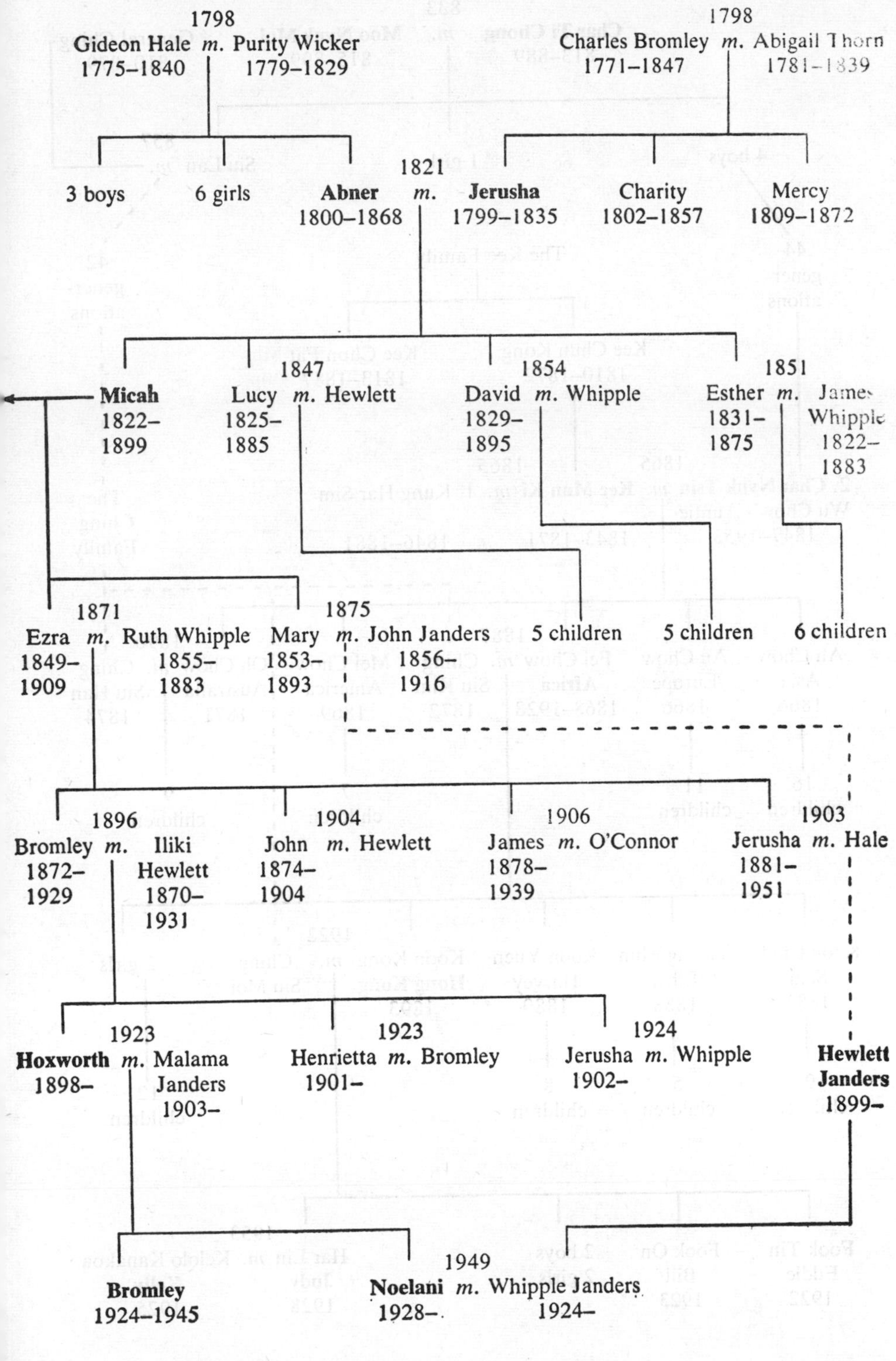
1798
Gideon Hale m. Purity Wicker
1775–1840
1779–1829
1798
Charles Bromley m. Abigail Thorn
1771–1847
1781–1839
3 boys
6 girls
1821
Abner m. **Jerusha**
1800–1868
1799–1835
Charity
1802–1857
Mercy
1809–1872
Micah
1822–1899
1847
Lucy m. Hewlett
1825–1885
1854
David m. Whipple
1829–1895
1851
Esther m. James Whipple
1831–1875
1822–1883
1871
Ezra m. Ruth Whipple
1849–1909
1855–1883
1875
Mary m. John Janders
1853–1893
1856–1916
5 children
5 children
6 children
1896
Bromley m. Iliki Hewlett
1872–1929
1870–1931
1904
John m. Hewlett
1874–1904
1906
James m. O'Connor
1878–1939
1903
Jerusha m. Hale
1881–1951
1923
Hoxworth m. Malama Janders
1898–
1903–
1923
Henrietta m. Bromley
1901–
1924
Jerusha m. Whipple
1902–
Hewlett Janders
1899–
Bromley
1924–1945
1949
Noelani m. Whipple Janders
1928–
1924–

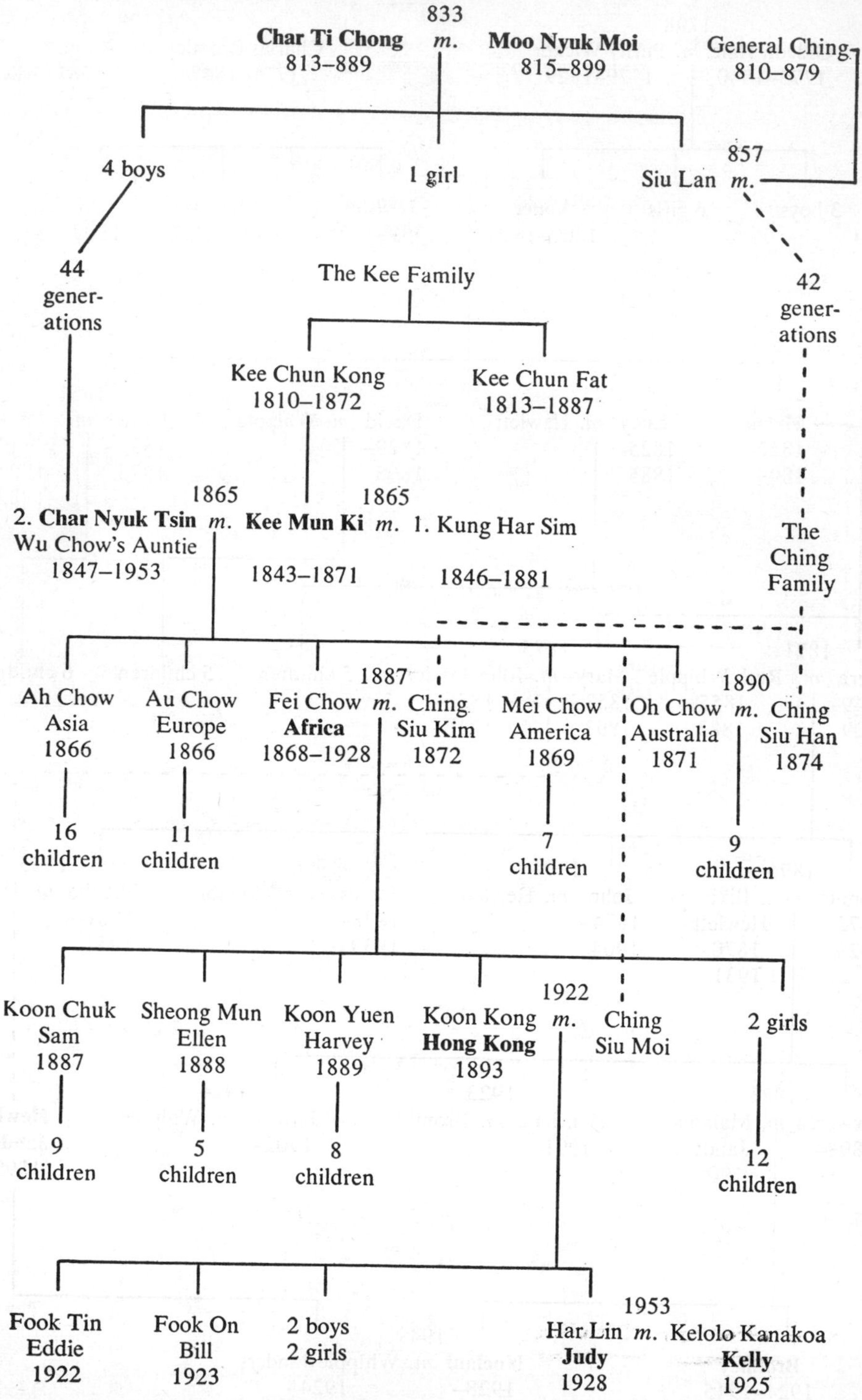
833
Char Ti Chong m. Moo Nyuk Moi
813–889
815–899
General Ching
810–879
4 boys
1 girl
857
Siu Lan m.
44 generations
42 generations
The Kee Family
Kee Chun Kong
1810–1872
Kee Chun Fat
1813–1887
1865
1865
2. Char Nyuk Tsin m. Kee Mun Ki m. 1. Kung Har Sim
Wu Chow's Auntie
1847–1953
1843–1871
1846–1881
The Ching Family
Ah Chow
Asia
1866
Au Chow
Europe
1866
1887
Fei Chow m. Ching Siu Kim
Africa
1868–1928
1872
Mei Chow
America
1869
1890
Oh Chow m. Ching Siu Han
Australia
1871
1874
16 children
11 children
7 children
9 children
Koon Chuk
Sam
1887
Sheong Mun
Ellen
1888
Koon Yuen
Harvey
1889
1922
Koon Kong m. Ching Siu Moi
Hong Kong
1893
2 girls
9 children
5 children
8 children
12 children
Fook Tin
Eddie
1922
Fook On
Bill
1923
2 boys
2 girls
1953
Har Lin m. Kelolo Kanakoa
Judy
1928
Kelly
1925

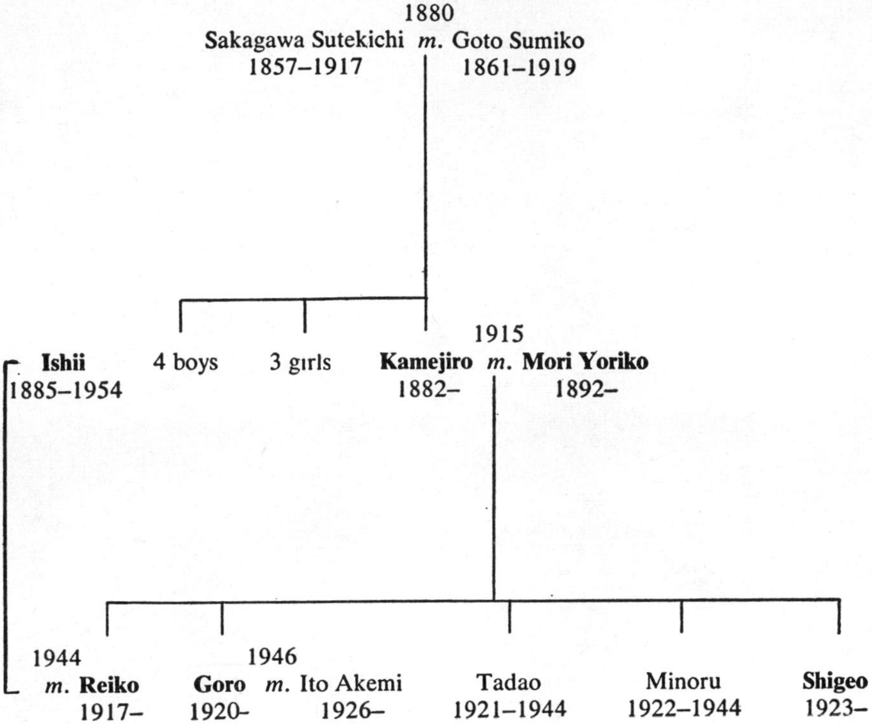
1880
Sakagawa Sutekichi m. Goto Sumiko
1857–1917
1861–1919
Ishii
1885–1954
4 boys
3 girls
Kamejiro
1882–
1915
m. Mori Yoriko
1892–
1944
m. Reiko
1917–
Goro
1920–
1946
m. Ito Akemi
1926–
Tadao
1921–1944
Minoru
1922–1944
Shigeo
1923–

ABOUT THE AUTHOR

JAMES A. MICHENER was born in New York City in 1907 and grew up in Doylestown, Pennsylvania, which he left at fourteen to bum his way cross-country. The years that followed, with their great variety of odd jobs and experience, were an important part of his early education. Feeling the need for some more formal training, he entered Swarthmore College and studied in the honors course. After some post-graduate years of "teaching others how to teach" he became an associate editor in the textbook department of a publishing firm, where his stay was interrupted by World War II.

Out of his wartime experience with the Navy in the Solomon Islands came *Tales of the South Pacific* (Pulitzer Prize, 1947), which was adapted into the musical *South Pacific* by Rodgers, Logan and Hammerstein. There followed *The Fires of Spring*, an autobiographical novel; *Return to Paradise; The Voice of Asia; The Bridges at Toko-ri; Sayonara; The Floating World:* The Story of Japanese Prints; *The Bridge at Andau;* and (with A. Grove Day) *Rascals in Paradise.*

KAUAI
HANAKAI
KAPAA
LIHUE
OAHU
KOOLAU RANGE
NUUANU PALI
HONOLULU
WAIKIKI
PEARL HARBOR
DIAMOND HEAD
The Islands
KREDEL
MILES
0 5 10 15 20 25 30
159
158